The Tale of
Genji

THE TALE OF GENJI

The Arthur Waley Translation of Lady Murasaki's Masterpiece
with a new foreword by Dennis Washburn

TUTTLE Publishing
Tokyo | Rutland, Vermont | Singapore

"Books to Span the East and West"

Tuttle Publishing was founded in 1832 in the small New England town of Rutland, Vermont [USA]. Our core values remain as strong today as they were then—to publish best-in-class books which bring people together one page at a time. In 1948, we established a publishing outpost in Japan—and Tuttle is now a leader in publishing English-language books about the arts, languages and cultures of Asia. The world has become a much smaller place today and Asia's economic and cultural influence has grown. Yet the need for meaningful dialogue and information about this diverse region has never been greater. Over the past seven decades, Tuttle has published thousands of books on subjects ranging from martial arts and paper crafts to language learning and literature—and our talented authors, illustrators, designers and photographers have won many prestigious awards. We welcome you to explore the wealth of information available on Asia at www.tuttlepublishing.com.

Published by Tuttle Publishing, an imprint of Periplus Editions (HK) Ltd.

Copyright © 2010 Periplus Editions (HK) Ltd.
Cover image by Christie's, London

All rights reserved. No part of this publication may be reproduced or utilized in any form or by any means, electronic or mechanical, including photocopying, recording, or by any information storage and retrieval system, without prior written permission from the publisher.

Library of Congress Cataloging-in-Publication Data
Murasaki Shikibu, b. 978?
 [Genji monogatari. English]
 The tale of Genji : a novel in six parts / by Lady Murasaki ; translated from the Japanese by Arthur Waley ; with a new foreword by Dennis Washburn.
  xxvii, 1155 p. ; 21 cm.
 ISBN 978-4-8053-1081-6 (pbk.)
 I. Waley, Arthur. II. Title.
 PL788.4.G4E5 2010
 895.6'314--dc22

2009036277

ISBN 978-4-8053-1081-6
ISBN 978-4-8053-1900-0 (for sale in Japan only)

Distributed by

North America, Latin America & Europe
Tuttle Publishing
364 Innovation Drive
North Clarendon, VT 05759-9436 U.S.A.
Tel: 1 (802) 773-8930; Fax: 1 (802) 773-6993
info@tuttlepublishing.com
www.tuttlepublishing.com

Japan
Tuttle Publishing
Yaekari Building 3rd Floor
5-4-12 Osaki Shinagawa-ku
Tokyo 141 0032
Tel: (81) 3 5437-0171; Fax: (81) 3 5437-0755
sales@tuttle.co.jp; www.tuttle.co.jp

Asia Pacific
Berkeley Books Pte. Ltd.
3 Kallang Sector #04-01/02
Singapore 349278
Tel: (65) 6280-1330; Fax: (65) 6280-6290
inquiries@periplus.com.sg
www.tuttlepublishing.com

27 26 25 24   8 7 6 5   2406CM
Printed in China

TUTTLE PUBLISHING® is a registered trademark of Tuttle Publishing, a division of Periplus Editions (HK) Ltd

Contents

Foreword ix
Introduction xviii

PART ONE
THE TALE OF GENJI

List of Most Important Persons 2
Genealogical Tables 3
   Kiritsubo 4
   The Broom-Tree 18
   Utsusemi 45
   Yugao 52
   Murasaki 80
   The Saffron-Flower 109
   The Festival of Red Leaves 129
   The Flower Feast 147
   Aoi 154

PART TWO
THE SACRED TREE

List of Most Important Persons 186
Genealogical Tables 187
   The Sacred Tree 188
   The Village of Falling Flowers 223
   Exile at Suma 226
   Akashi 253
   Tie Flood Gauge 283
   The Palace in the Tangled Woods 306
   A Meeting at the Frontier 323
   The Picture Competition 327
   The Wind in the Pine-Trees 343

PART THREE
A WREATH OF CLOUD

List of Most Important Persons 360
   A Wreath of Cloud...................................... 362
   Asagao 383
   The Maiden 398
   Tamakatsura... 434
   The First Song of the Year 468
   The Butterflies 480
   The Glow-Worm 494
   A Bed of Carnations.................................. 509
   The Flares... 527
   The Typhoon 530

PART FOUR
BLUE TROUSERS

List of Most Important Persons 542
   The Royal Visit 544
   Blue Trousers 562
   Makibashira... 567
   The Spray of Plum-Blossom........................ 594
   Fuji No Uraba 604
   Wakana, Part I 619
   Wakana, Part II 654
   Kashiwagi... 685
   The Flute 699
   Yugiri 709
   The Law 736
   Mirage 744

PART FIVE
THE LADY OF THE BOAT

List of Most Important Persons	754
Niou	756
Kobai	766
"Bamboo River"	774
The Bridge Maiden	800
At the Foot of the Oak-Tree	824
Agemaki	850
Fern-Shoots	905
The Mistletoe	917

PART SIX
THE BRIDGE OF DREAMS

List of Most Important Persons	952
The Mistletoe (continued)	954
The Eastern House	973
Ukifune	1010
The Gossamer-Fly	1059
Writing-Practice	1100
The Bridge of Dreams	1145

Foreword

The translation of *The Tale of Genji* by Arthur Waley (1889-1966) in six parts between 1921 and 1933 was a seminal achievement. Widely praised at the time of its publication for its stylistic beauty and its masterly rendering of characters and setting, the work showed that literary translation, especially from Asian languages, was not merely a narrow scholarly or instrumental pursuit, but a task that could be considered an art form in itself. Its success directly inspired the generation of scholars and translators that was responsible for the subsequent development of Japanese Studies as an academic institution in both Europe and the Americas, and, most important, it represented a milestone in the transmission of knowledge about Japanese culture, making it accessible to a global readership.

The impact of Waley's translation is in part a reflection of the canonical status of *The Tale of Genji*, which has occupied a central position in Japan's cultural history over the past millennium. Like other classics of world literature, it possesses a depth and complexity capable of sustaining multiple interpretations. Murasaki Shikibu's narrative has served as a source work for countless other artists. It has also inspired readers from different eras and cultures, who have discovered in its fictional representation of courtly Heian society ethical concerns and aesthetic values that resonate with their own understanding of the meaning and significance of human experience.

Over the centuries *The Tale of Genji* has been interpreted variously as an idealization of the beauty of evanescence, as a romance centered on the role sexual relationships played in political intrigue at the court, or as a tale that exemplifies the truth of fundamental Buddhist concepts such as the mutability of life and the need to cultivate detachment from the world. By the eighteenth century the work's importance as a key cultural text was widely accepted, and Nativist (*kokugaku*) scholars such as Motoori Norinaga (1730-1801) pursued sophisticated linguistic research that further promoted the idea that Murasaki Shikibu's literary art exhibited the essence of Japanese ethics and identity. The canonical status conferred on *The Tale of Genji* took on even greater significance during the latter half of the nineteenth century when Japan, having opened up to the Western world and embarked on the project of remaking itself as a modern imperial power in Asia, felt compelled to claim a special place in the geopolitical order it was reengaging. This claim was largely justified by looking back to Japan's past, especially its great literary and artistic traditions, and finding there evidence of a superior civilization.

Prompted by this form of aesthetic nationalism, Suematsu Kenchō (1855-1920), a leading Meiji Period (1868-1912) politician and author, composed the first English translation of *The Tale of Genji*, which was published in London in 1882. This was a heavily abridged version, and Suematsu's decision to write a loose adaptation rather than a rigorously literal translation reflected his own conflicted opinion about the intrinsic literary value of the narrative. On the one hand, he was convinced of the importance of making the work available to an international readership as a way to display the native genius of Japan. On the other hand, he believed that Murasaki Shikibu's literary techniques were relatively primitive when compared to what he believed were the more sophisticated modern techniques employed by Western novelists.[*] This combination of parochial pride and a sense of cultural inferiority was not uncommon among Meiji intellectuals and public figures, and explains Suematsu's decision to adapt the text both structurally and stylistically in a manner that, in his view, would better accord with the expectations of an English-speaking readership.

Suematsu's conflicted feelings are the product of attitudes specific to Meiji Japan and of a more general ambivalence that all literary translators experience. Because Suematsu thought it inappropriate to even attempt to reproduce in English the rich ambiguities of Murasaki Shikibu's language, he subjected himself to the criticism that he was not being true to the original. His defense was that classical Japanese language and the culture of the court were so alien to modern sensibilities that treating such a difficult text in a literal way would have made it incomprehensible to Victorian-era readers. It may seem easy now to dismiss this defense, but moving across the border between languages and cultures inevitably demands concessions and compromises, even for translators whose sole aim is to create a literal version that strictly follows the rhetorical logic of the original. Since something is always gained and lost in a translation, the only way to gauge its achievement rigorously and fairly is to be mindful of the particular standards, operating at any given historical moment, by which readers determine what constitutes successful.

Suematsu's experience illustrates the special challenges that await the translator who seeks to bring a classical work into the present, and thus sets the context for a brief consideration of the conditions that made

---

[*] For a more complete account of the assumptions that guided Suematsu and the criticisms of his translation see Patrick Caddeau, *Appraising Genji: Literary Criticism and Cultural Anxiety in the Age of the Last Samurai*, Albany, NY: State University of New York Press, 2006, pp. 148-154.

Waley's translation possible. The task that confronted Waley in the 1920s was monumental, and his training for it was rather unusual. He had been born into comfortable circumstances in Tunbridge Wells, Kent in 1889. His father, David Frederick Schloss, was an economist whose family was Anglo-Jewish. The difficulties posed by his ethnic heritage (or at least his consciousness of those difficulties) are evident in Waley's decision to change his surname in 1914, adopting his paternal grandmother's maiden name. He attended Cambridge University, where he took a degree in Classics in 1910, and in 1913 he was appointed to a post in the British Museum overseeing the collection of Oriental Prints and Manuscripts. In order to catalogue items he had to learn to read Chinese and Japanese, and it was from these beginnings that he began to work on literary translations, starting with poetry in Chinese, which led to a brief professional association with Ezra Pound. After achieving success as a translator, he quit his job at the British Museum in 1929, maintaining his scholarly credentials by lecturing at the University of London's School of Oriental and African Studies. During the period of his life when he translated *The Tale of Genji* he resided in Bloomsbury, and was friends with members of the Bloomsbury Group, some of whom he had met during his college years.*

In spite of his enormous linguistic talents, Waley had to work on *The Tale of Genji* largely in isolation (it is well known that he never visited Japan), and he did not have at his disposal the quality or volume of postwar commentaries and editions that from the 1950s on helped make the original text more accessible to specialists and non-specialists alike. Moreover, he did not have a model to follow (Suematsu's translation notwithstanding) for developing a literary style in English that would create an appropriate analogue for Heian Period court vernacular.

Waley's early personal and professional background helped shape his conception of literature and of translation as an art in a number of key ways. Whatever anxieties his family background may have provoked, he was a member of an elite group of scholars and intellectuals; and the simple fact that he took on *The Tale of Genji* in the manner he did suggests that he shared, or at least was never bothered enough to question, his generation's confidence, born of imperialist assumptions, in its cultural superiority and the universality of its standards of aesthetic tastes.

The elite world Waley inhabited may well have been insular and self-absorbed—Pound, for example, derided some of Waley's early translations of Chinese poetry as being fussy and too academic—but it was not the

---

* For a full account of Waley's life, his works, and his literary connections, see John Walter de Gruchy's fascinating study *Orienting Arthur Waley: Japonism, Orientalism, and the Creation of Japanese Literature in English*, Honolulu: University of Hawai'i Press, 2003.

only world he inhabited. His literary connections, especially with the Bloomsbury Group, put him in contact with a circle of writers who were on the cutting edge of literary Modernism. These interactions undoubtedly reinforced his already strong propensity to privilege a belief in the priority of genius and the individual talent (to borrow Eliot's phrase) in the creation of new art. However, in occupying these two worlds Waley had to reconcile the perceived divide between the work of the scholar and that of the poet in order to treat translation as a form of art that attempts not only to capture, through careful attention to historical and linguistic research, the parochial qualities of the original text that make it worthy of translation, but also to conform to broad contemporary literary standards.

It is not clear if Waley was ever seriously bothered by his lack of direct connection with modern Japan, but it is likely that he was not. The isolation in which he worked and the palpable need for control that his approach implied may have originated in his personal circumstances, since he viewed his own ethnicity as a potential hindrance to full assimilation into the institutional elites of imperial Britain. However, it seems equally plausible to view his approach to the task of translation in more narrowly artistic terms as a means for self-expression. After all, his fascination for Heian culture was of a piece with the *Japonism* that had such a profound effect on European art in the late nineteenth and early twentieth centuries. It was a kind of exoticism that further emphasized the universalized aesthetic superiority of the West over the particularized local cultures of the East.

The assumptions that guided Waley's conception of translation as a form of literary art found explicit expression in his views about the fundamental nature of Heian court culture. In discussing some of the literary techniques in *The Tale of Genji* that appeared modern to him, he once compared Murasaki Shikibu's use of foreshadowing with that of Proust. He later regretted the comparison, insisting that the great cultural divide between Murasaki's epoch and twentieth-century Britain made any such general resemblances purely accidental.* For example, he argued that a preoccupation with the present moment pervaded Heian aesthetics, but was careful to stress that there was a difference between that preoccupation and Modernist obsessions with making art new for the present. He described tenth-century court society in Japan as "a purely aesthetic and, above all, a literary civilization. Never, among people of exquisite cultivation and lively intelligence, have purely intellectual pursuits played so small a part. What strikes us most is that the past was almost a blank....

---

* Arthur Waley, "Introduction," *The Bridge of Dreams*, Boston: Houghton Mifflin, 1933, pp. 22-23.

It is indeed our intense curiosity about the past that most sharply distinguishes us from the ancient Japanese.... Their absorption in the present, the fact that with them 'modern' was invariably a term of praise, differentiates them from us in a way that is immediately obvious."*

Waley is struck by the Heian court conception of the "modern" (*imamekashi*), which he sees as remarkably lacking in historical consciousness. At the same time, Heian aesthetics, grounded on the value of experiencing the present moment, was surely a source of the almost primitivist appeal of Murasaki Shikibu's work to Waley's generation, which was so acutely preoccupied with the ironies of its own historical position that it was possible to conceive, in the manner of Virginia Woolf, that "on or about December, 1910 human character changed."†

Waley's characterization of Heian court culture as lacking historical consciousness is a debatable proposition, but it provides an example of how the tensions created by his efforts to reconcile his scholarly work with his artistic aims shaped his reading of classical Japanese literature. He may have viewed the ancient Japanese with some slight condescension, and yet his admiration for the aestheticism of the Heian court, its tendency to value the lyrical beauty to be found in the experience of the present moment, grew out of the Modernist sensibility he shared with his literary peers. His translation thus conveys the tone and manner of a romance while at the same time emphasizing certain rhetorical elements in the original that would have been familiar and appealing to his readership: the use of multiple narrative perspectives, the complex play of poetic language, the creation of an illusion of psychological interiority, and the broadly realistic mode of representation.

Pointing out that Waley's approach placed relatively more stress on those aspects of the work that make it 'modern' in no way suggests that his assumptions led to a misreading of the original. Indeed, his observation that Heian court culture was largely defined by an aesthetic sensibility that valued the 'modern' highlights one of the most important narrative elements of *The Tale of Genji*. Genji, for example, is driven by what might be quite properly termed a modernist impulse. He strives to be original, to embrace discontinuity from the past and champion the new as a means to establish the standards for conduct and taste and thereby achieve political and cultural empowerment. He embodies a subversive tendency to undo cultural norms and replace them with those of his own creation. In striving to remake his world and gain priority, he effectively desires to become the embodiment of the tradition itself.

---

* Arthur Waley, *The Pillow Book of Sei Shōnagon*, London: George Allen and Unwin, 1957, pp. 9-11.

† Virginia Woolf, "Mr. Bennett and Mrs. Brown," in *Collected Essays*, vol. 1, London: Hogarth, 1966, p. 320.

The problem confronting an ideal hero such as Genji is that the creative process cannot be allowed to stop. It must be continuous, for when it ceases the hero becomes conventional and, paradoxically, can no longer embody the tradition of an aesthetic of the present moment. This paradox largely determines the structure of the work as a whole. The sense of time lost, of the evanescence of human life, is palpable, and it is only by the process of constant renewal, which places supreme value on the experience of the present moment, that the loss of time can somehow be recovered—if not literally, then as an aesthetic value that is universal and timeless.

The spiraling structure of *The Tale of Genji* is the most fundamental expression of Murasaki Shikibu's aesthetic. The characters constantly give voice to their belief that the past and future are woven together in the present by the bonds of karmic destiny. Yet narrative time moves inexorably forward, and the impossibility of sustaining the world in the present moment by arresting the flow of time haunts Genji and leads him to act out his longings through his search for an ideal woman, who can serve as a substitute for his dead mother, and through the ebb and flow of his political defeats and triumphs.

The desire to assert the significance of the present is central to the original conception of *The Tale of Genji*. Extreme sensitivity to change and loss is the fundamental ethical value in the text and the primary trait of the hero. Though ever mindful of the religious teaching that all is mutable, Genji refuses ultimately to withdraw from the evanescent world and repeatedly seeks to re-affirm the present and his own ideal qualities. The repetitive pattern of the narrative, the spiral structure created by the constant effort to halt the flow of time and make the present new again, renders impossible any type of formal closure. The only possible ending for such a character is to write him out of the story, without actually depicting his death, when repetitiveness and conventionality threaten to close off the very process of storytelling itself.

As noted above, Waley looked at *The Tale of Genji* through the lens of a reader whose tastes were shaped by the great European novels of the nineteenth and twentieth centuries, and thus he read the work as the product of a society interested in aesthetic rather than intellectual pursuits. However, the scholarly and cultural assumptions behind that mildly condescending judgment were tempered by the rhetorical similarities between Murasaki Shikibu's narrative and the modern novel and by the sense that Genji's consciousness of time lost spoke to Modernist sensibilities. In trying to capture both the strangeness and the familiarity (or perhaps the universality) of *The Tale of Genji*, Waley produced a translation that often sacrificed literalness and precision in the name of literary art. For readers of his generation the distortion produced by this particular emphasis was not an especially urgent problem. The notion that a translation could actually improve on the original was not uncommon, if the reception of the work of other important translators during the period—the Russian novels rendered into English by Constance Garnett or C. K. Scott Moncrieff's version of *A la recherche du temps perdu*—is any indication. Assuming that the literary value of a translation may be judged on its own merits apart from the original, it follows that—in the manner of Augustan Period revisions of Shakespeare—a translation may potentially be the superior work of art.

The reputation of Waley's translation since its publication remains high, but now the praise is more often qualified. It continues to be admired as a work of art that in some ways improves on the original, and is thus original itself, but it is also draws certain complaints that it is rather anachronistic, plays too fast and loose with the original, and shows a cavalier attitude toward historical accuracy. Waley continues to be revered with considerable justification as one of the greatest translators of Japanese literature, but his most important work is viewed by some as a bit of a historical curiosity that has been superseded by subsequent, more accurate versions.

In a sense, the opinions about Waley's version of *The Tale of Genji* parallel the ambivalent status that haunts all literary translation. Translating is a humbling task because it heightens our awareness of the parochial nature of particular languages, and thus unavoidably raises issues of faithfulness, originality, and influence. A translation is a kind of virtual palimpsest, a writing over of one language by another that acts as a mediating barrier to the very text it makes intelligible. As a mediation of something assumed to be authentic, translation can be justified only if it maintains the pretense that it is accurate and sincere in its attitude toward the original.

Of course, translation is so fundamental to cultural exchange that its contradictory nature can seem like an analytical illusion, something that is there only when one thinks about it. That may help explain why the dominant ideal of translation is transparency, for the belief that the presence of a translator should not be detectable helps sustain the illusion that the reader is experiencing the words of the original in an unmediated way. Of course, the preference for invisibility comes with its own costs, since it ignores the fact that literary translation is a special type of reading in which the sensibility of the translator merges with that of the original text. Recent concerns that the ideal of transparency may foreclose artistic possibilities may account for the gradual shift in the reputation of translators like Waley, Garnett, and Moncrieff.

The concern with accuracy and sensitivity to cultural difference has been a guiding motivation for all subsequent English-language versions of *The Tale of Genji*. Edward Seidensticker produced a more literal translation that emphasized a cleaner, simpler diction. His terse, clipped style creates a fine sense of narrative movement, but it also runs counter to the more fluid effects created by Murasaki Shikibu's language. Moreover, Seidensticker shared with Waley a strong editorial consciousness, one that tries to shape the translation to fit the expectations of mid-twentieth century American literary tastes. As a result, Seidensticker occasionally elides difficult passages (a tendency that appears in his translations of modern novels as well) or even omits materials that seem too culturally specific.

Helen McCullough, who was a preeminent scholar of classical Japanese literature, produced a partial translation, but it is worth considering her work here in part because of her enormous expertise. She strives for an even more literal rendering than Seidensticker, and succeeds in creating a neutral, transparent style. Precise and careful almost to a fault, her version is in some ways the antithesis of Waley's in that it is far more accurate, but also flatter in tone and affect.

The most recent version, by Royall Tyler, strives to be faithful to the original in different ways. It attempts to replicate the flow of the original by maintaining some of the quirkier characteristics of the language—for example, the different titles by which characters are identified from chapter to chapter, the elliptical style of the poetry, or the sliding, unstable shifts in narrative perspective in certain scenes. While trying to be stylistically faithful, Tyler also strives to be more scholarly than Seidensticker or Waley by the liberal use of footnotes to help contextualize cultural practices or identify poetic allusions. The result is a denser text, more accurate than Waley's version perhaps, but also more difficult to follow and lacking the pleasing rhythms and sense of narrative drive that Waley achieved.

Each of these more recent versions contributes in their own way to helping the English-speaking reader better understand *The Tale of Genji*. In doing so, they also pose an obvious and inescapable question. Why, if they are all more accurate, should we bother reading Waley's translation anymore? The reason lies in the ambivalent nature of the process of translation.

The value of a literary translation is not the instrumental function of conveying knowledge about another culture, but the way it fosters habits of critical thinking through the act of negotiating linguistic difference. A literary translation brings into play the practice of both poetics and criticism in an effort to harmonize languages and thereby make other cultures accessible. But in the act of harmonizing languages and cultures, a translation forces the reader to acknowledge, even if only for a moment, the limits of his or her own assumptions about art and ethics. In this regard Waley's version, perhaps more than any other, succeeds in challenging the reader to come to terms with the fundamental aesthetic that defined the culture of the Heian court. It continues to command respect and admiration, for like any great work of literary art it makes its readers self-reflective, a necessary condition for both intellectual and emotional understanding.

It is in no way a negative judgment, then, to conclude that Arthur Waley did not produce the impossible, that is, he did not produce *the* definitive translation of *The Tale of Genji*. What Waley did create is literary art of extraordinary beauty that brings to life in English the world Murasaki Shikibu imagined. The beauty of his art has not dimmed, but like the original text itself, retains the power to move and enlighten.

Dennis Washburn
Dartmouth College

Introduction

MURASAKI SHIKIBU was born about A.D. 978. Her father, Tametoki, belonged to a minor branch of the powerful Fujiwara clan. After holding various appointments in the Capital he became Governor first of Echizen (probably in 1004); then of a more northerly province, Echigo. In 1016 he retired and took his vows as a Buddhist priest.

Of her childhood Murasaki tells us the following anecdote:* "When my brother Nobunori† (the one who is now in the Board of Rites) was a boy my father was very anxious to make a good Chinese scholar of him, and often came himself to hear Nobunori read his lessons. On these occasions I was always present, and so quick was I at picking up the language that I was soon able to prompt my brother whenever he got stuck. At this my father used to sigh and say to me: "If only you were a boy how proud and happy I should be." But it was not long before I repented of having thus distinguished myself; for person after person assured me that even boys generally become very unpopular if it is discovered that they are fond of their books. For a girl, of course, it would be even worse; and after this I was careful to conceal the fact that I could write a single Chinese character. This meant that I got very little practice; with the result that to this day I am shockingly clumsy with my brush."

Between 994 and 998 Murasaki married her kinsman Fujiwara no Nobutaka, a lieutenant in the Imperial Guard. By him she had two daughters, one of whom married the Lord Lieutenant of Tsukushi and is reputed (very doubtfully) to be the authoress of an uninteresting novel, *The Tale of Sagoromo*. Nobutaka died in 1001, and it was probably three years later that Murasaki's father was promised the governorship of Echizen. Owing to the machinations of an enemy the appointment was, at the last minute, almost given to someone else. Tametoki appealed to his kinsman the Prime Minister Fujiwara no Michinaga, and was eventually nominated for the post.

Murasaki was now about twenty-six. To have taken her to Echizen would have ended all hope of a respectable second marriage. Instead Tametoki arranged that she should enter the service of Michinaga's daughter, the very serious-minded Empress Akiko, then a girl of about sixteen.

---

* *Diary*, Hakubunkwan text, p. 51.
† Died young, perhaps about 1012, while serving on his father's staff in Echigo.

Part of Murasaki's time was henceforth spent at the Emperor's Palace. But, as was customary, Akiko frequently returned for considerable periods to her father's house. Of her young mistress Murasaki writes as follows:*
"The Empress, as is well known to those about her, is strongly opposed to anything savoring of flirtation; indeed, when there are men about, it is as well for anyone who wants to keep on good terms with her not to show herself outside her own room... I can well imagine, that some of our senior ladies, with their air of almost ecclesiastical severity, must make a rather forbidding impression upon the world at large. In dress and matters of that kind we certainly cut a wretched figure, for it is well known that to show the slightest sign of caring for such things ranks with our mistress as an unpardonable fault. But I can see no reason why, even in a society where young girls are expected to keep their heads and behave sensibly, appearances should be neglected to the point of comicality; and I cannot help thinking that Her Majesty's outlook is far too narrow and uncompromising. But it is easy enough to see how this state of affairs arose. Her Majesty's mind was, at the time when she first came to Court, so entirely innocent and her own conduct so completely impeccable that, quite apart from the extreme reserve which is natural to her, she could never herself conceivably have occasion to make even the most trifling confession. Consequently, whenever she heard one of us admit to some slight shortcoming, whether of conduct or character, she henceforward regarded this person as a monster of iniquity.

"True, at that period certain incidents occurred which proved that some of her attendants were, to say the least of it, not very well suited to occupy so responsible a position. But she would never have discovered this had not the offenders been incautious enough actually to boast in her hearing about their trivial irregularities. Being young and inexperienced she had no notion that such things were of everyday occurrence, brooded incessantly upon the wickedness of those about her, and finally consorted only with persons so staid that they could be relied upon not to cause her a moment's anxiety.

"Thus she has gathered round her a number of very worthy young ladies. They have the merit of sharing all her opinions, but seem in some curious way like children who have never grown up.

"As the years go by Her Majesty is beginning to acquire more experience of life, and no longer judges others by the same rigid standards as before; but meanwhile her Court has gained a reputation for extreme dullness, and is shunned by all who can manage to avoid it.

"Her Majesty does indeed still constantly warn us that it is a great mistake to go too far, 'for a single slip may bring very unpleasant con-

---

* *Diary*, p. 51.

sequences,' and so on, in the old style; but she now also begs us not to reject advances in such a way as to hurt people's feelings. Unfortunately, habits of long standing are not so easily changed; moreover, now that the Empress's exceedingly stylish brothers bring so many of their young courtier-friends to amuse themselves at her house, we have in self-defense been obliged to become more virtuous than ever."

There is a type of disappointed undergraduate, who believes that all his social and academic failures are due to his being, let us say, at Magdalene instead of at St. John's. Murasaki, in like manner, had persuaded herself that all would have been well if her father had placed her in the highly cultivated and easy-mannered entourage of the Emperor's aunt, Princess Senshi.*

"Princess Senshi and her ladies," Murasaki writes, "are always going off to see the sunset or the fading of the moon at dawn, or pursuing some truant nightingale amid the flowering trees. The Princess herself is a woman of marked character, who is determined to follow her own tastes, and would contrive to lead at Court a life as detached as her present existence at the Kamo Shrine. How different from this place, with its perpetual: "The Empress has been summoned into the Presence and commands you to attend her," or "Prepare to receive His Excellency the Prime Minister, who may arrive at any moment." Princess Senshi's apartments are not subject to the sudden alarms and incursions from which we suffer. There one could apply oneself in earnest to anything one cared for and was good at; there, occupied perhaps in making something really beautiful, one would have no time for those indiscreet conversations which at our own Court are the cause of so much trouble. There I should be allowed to live buried in my own thoughts like a tree-stump in the earth; at the same time, they would not expect me to hide from every man with whom I was not already acquainted; and even if I addressed a few remarks to such a person, I should not be thought lost to all sense of shame. Indeed, I can imagine myself under such circumstances becoming, after a certain amount of practice, quite lively and amusing!"

While pining for the elegance and freedom of Princess Senshi's Court, Murasaki was employed by her earnest young mistress for a purpose that the world would have considered far more improper than the philandering of which Akiko so sternly disapproved. The Empress had a secret desire to learn Chinese. The study of this language was considered at the time far too rough and strenuous an occupation for women. There were no grammars or dictionaries, and each horny sentence had to be grappled and mastered like an untamed steer. That Akiko should wish to learn

---

* 966-1035. Vestal at Kamo during five successive reigns. One of the most important figures of her day; known to history as the Great Vestal.

Chinese must have been as shocking to Michinaga as it would have been to Gladstone if one of his daughters had wanted to learn boxing. Murasaki had, as we have seen, picked up something of the language by overhearing her brother's lessons. She did everything in her power to conceal this knowledge, even pretending (as she tells us in the *Diary*) that she could not read the Chinese characters on her mistress's screen; but somehow or other it leaked out: "Since the summer before last, very secretly, in odd moments when there happened to be no one about, I have been reading with Her Majesty the two books of 'Songs.'* There has of course been no question of formal lessons; Her Majesty has merely picked up a little here and there, as she felt inclined. All the same, I have thought it best to say nothing about the matter to anybody…"

We gather, however, that what in the long run made Akiko's Court distasteful to Murasaki was not the seriousness of the women so much as the coarseness and stupidity of the men. Michinaga, Akiko's father, was now forty-two. He had already been Prime Minister for some fourteen years, and had carried the fortunes of the Fujiwara family to their apogee. It is evident that he made love to Murasaki, though possibly in a more or less bantering way. In 1008 she writes: "From my room beside the entrance to the gallery I can see into the garden. The dew still lies heavy and a faint mist rises from it. His Excellency† is walking in the garden. Now he has summoned one of his attendants and is giving directions to him about having the moat cleared. In front of the orange trees there is a bed of lady-flowers (*ominabeshi*) in full bloom. He plucks a spray and returning to the house hands it to me over the top of my screen. He looks very magnificent. I remember that I have not yet powdered my face and feel terribly embarrassed. 'Come now,' he cries, 'be quick with your poem, or I shall lose my temper.' This at any rate gives me a chance to retire from his scrutiny; I go over to the writing-box and produce the following: 'If these beyond other flowers are fair, 'tis but because the dew hath picked them out and by its power made them sweeter than the rest.' 'That's right,' he said, taking the poem. 'It did not take you long in the end.' And sending for his own ink-stone he wrote the answer: 'Dew favors not; it is the flower's thoughts that flush its cheeks and make it fairer than the rest.'"

The next reference to Michinaga's relations with Murasaki is as follows: "His Excellency the Prime Minister caught sight of *The Tale of Genji* in Her Majesty's room, and after making the usual senseless jokes about it, he handed me the following poem, written on a strip of paper against which a

---

* The third and fourth body of Po Chü-i's poetical works, including *Magic, The Old Man with the Broken Arm, The Prisoner, The Two Red Towers,* and *The Dragon of the Pool,* all of which are translated in my "170 Chinese Poems."

† Michinaga.

spray of plum-blossom had been pressed: 'How comes it that, sour as the plum-tree's fruit, you have contrived to blossom forth in tale so amorous?' To this I answered: 'Who has told you that the fruit belies the flower? For the fruit you have not tasted, and the flower you know but by report.'*

"One night when I was sleeping in a room which opens onto the corridor, I heard someone tapping. So frightened was I that for the whole of the rest of the night I lay dead still on my bed, scarcely daring to breathe. Next morning came the following poem from His Excellency: 'More patient than the water-rail that taps upon the tree-root all night long, in vain I loitered on the threshold of your inhospitable room.' To this I answered: 'So great was your persistence that for a water-rail I did indeed mistake you; and lucky am I to have made this merciful mistake.'"†

Again, in 1010: "Today His Excellency had an audience with the Emperor; when it was over they came out of the Audience Chamber together, and banqueted. As usual, His Excellency became very drunk and, fearing trouble, I tried to keep out of his way. But he noticed my absence and sent for me, crying out: 'Here's your mistress's papa taking dinner with the Emperor; it is not everyone who gets the chance of being present on an occasion like this. You ought to be uncommonly grateful. Instead of which your one idea seems to be how to escape at the earliest possible moment. I can't make you out at all!'

"He went on scolding me for some time, and then said: 'Well, now you are here, you must make a poem. It is one of the days when the parent's‡ poem is always made by a substitute. You will do as well as anybody; so be quick about it...' I was afraid at first that if I showed myself he would behave in such a way as to make me feel very uncomfortable. But it turned out that he was not so extraordinarily drunk after all; indeed, he was in a very charming mood and, in the light of the great lamp, looked particularly handsome."

It has often been observed that whereas in her commonplace book (the *Makura no Soshi*) Sei Shonagon§ scarcely so much as mentions the existence of the other ladies-in-waiting, Murasaki refers constantly to her companions, and to one of them at least she was evidently very strongly attached. Her great friend was Lady Saisho. "On my way back from the Empress's rooms I peeped in at Saisho's door. I had forgotten that she had been on duty at night and would now be having her morning sleep. She had thrown over her couch various dresses with bright-colored linings, and on top of them had spread a covering of beaten silk, lustrous

---

* "You have neither read my book nor won my love." Both poems contain a number of double meanings which it would be tedious to unravel.

† *Kui-na* means "water-rail" and "regret not."

‡ The parent of the Empress.

§ Lady-in-waiting to the Empress Sadako, Akiko's predecessor.

and heavily scented with perfume. Her face was hidden under the clothes; but as she lay there, her head resting on a box-shaped writing-case, she looked so pretty that I could not help thinking of the little princesses in picture books. I raised the clothes from her face and said to her: 'You are like a girl in a story.' She turned her head and said sharply: 'You lunatic! Could you not see I was asleep? You are too inconsiderate...' While she was saying this she half raised herself from her couch and looked up at me. Her face was flushed. I have never seen her so handsome. So it often is; even those whom we at all times admire will, upon some occasion, suddenly seem to us ten times more lovely than ever before."

Saisho is her constant companion and her fellow victim during the drunken festivities which they both detested. The following is from a description of an entertainment given on the fiftieth day after the birth of the Empress Akiko's first child: "The old Minister of the Right, Lord Akimitsu, came staggering along and banged into the screen behind which we sat, making a hole in it. What really struck us was that he is getting far too old* for this kind of thing. But I am sure he did not at all know that this was the impression he was making. Next followed matching of fans, and noisy jokes, many of which were in very bad taste.

"Presently the General of the Right came and stood near the pillar on our left. He was looking at us and seemed to be examining our dresses, but with a very different expression from the rest. He cannot bear these drunken revels. If only there were more like him! And I say this despite the fact that his conversation is often very indecent; for he manages to give a lively and amusing turn to whatever he says. I noticed that when the great tankard came his way he did not drink out of it, but passed it on, merely saying the usual words of good omen. At this Lord Kinto† shouted: 'The General is on his best behavior. I expect little Murasaki is somewhere not far off!' 'You're none of you in the least like Genji,' I thought to myself, 'so what should Murasaki be doing here?'... Then the Vice-Councilor began pulling about poor Lady Hyobu, and the Prime Minister made comic noises which I found very disagreeable. It was still quite early, and knowing well what would be the latter stages of an entertainment which had begun in this way, I waited till things seemed to have come to a momentary pause and then plotted with Lady Saisho to slip away and hide. Presently however the Prime Minister's sons and other young Courtiers burst into the room; a fresh hubbub began, and when they heard that two ladies were in hiding they tracked us down and flung back the screen behind which we had ensconced ourselves. We were now prisoners..."

---

* He was now sixty-four.
† Fujiwara no Kinto (966-1041), famous poet; cousin of Michinaga.

The *Diary* contains a series of notes chiefly upon the appearance but also in a few cases upon the character of other ladies at Court. Her remarks on Lady Izumi Shikibu, one of the greatest poets whom Japan has produced, are of interest: "Izumi Shikibu is an amusing letter-writer; but there is something not very satisfactory about her. She has a gift for dashing off informal compositions in a careless running hand; but in poetry she needs either an interesting subject or some classic model to imitate. Indeed it does not seem to me that in herself she is really a poet at all.

"However, in the impromptus which she recites there is always something beautiful or striking. But I doubt if she is capable of saying anything interesting about other people's verses. She is not intelligent enough. It is odd; to hear her talk you would certainly think that she had a touch of the poet in her. Yet she does not seem to produce anything that one can call serious poetry..."

Here, too, is the note on Sei Shonagon,[*] author of the famous *Makura no Sosbi:* "Sei Shonagon's most marked characteristic is her extraordinary self-satisfaction. But examine the pretentious compositions in Chinese script which she scatters so liberally over the Court, and you will find them to be a mere patchwork of blunders. Her chief pleasure consists in shocking people; and as each new eccentricity becomes only too painfully familiar, she gets driven on to more and more outrageous methods of attracting notice. She was once a person of great taste and refinement; but now she can no longer restrain herself from indulging, even under the most inappropriate circumstances, in any outburst that the fancy of the moment suggests. She will soon have forfeited all claim to be regarded as a serious character, and what will become of her[†] when she is too old for her present duties I really cannot imagine."

It was not likely that Murasaki, who passed such biting judgments on her companions, would herself escape criticism. In her diary she tells us the following anecdote: "There is a certain lady here called Sayemon no Naishi who has evidently taken a great dislike to me, though I have only just become aware of it. It seems that behind my back she is always saying the most unpleasant things. One day when someone had been reading *The Tale of Genji* out loud to the Emperor, His Majesty said: "This lady has certainly been reading the Annals of Japan. She must be terribly learned."

---

[*] See p. xxii. Shonagon was about ten years senior to Murasaki. She was lady-in-waiting first to the Empress Sadako (died, A.D. 1000); then to Sadako's sister Princess Shigesa (died, A.D. 100a); finally to the Empress Akiko.

[†] Murasaki suggests that Shonagon will lose Akiko's confidence and be dismissed. There is indeed a tradition (*Kojidan,* Vol. II) that when some courtiers were out walking one day they passed a dilapidated hovel. One of them mentioned a rumor that Sei Shonagon, a wit and beauty of the last reign, was now living in this place. Whereupon an incredibly lean hag shot her head out at the door, crying "Won't you buy old bones, old rags and bones?" and immediately disappeared again.

Upon the strength of this casual remark Naishi spread a report all over the Court that I prided myself on my enormous learning, and henceforth I was known as 'Dame Annals' wherever I went."

The most interesting parts of the *Diary* are those in which Murasaki describes her own feelings. The following passage refers to the winter, of A.D. 1008: "I love to see the snow here,* and was hoping from day to day that it would begin before Her Majesty went back to Court, when I was suddenly obliged to go home.† Two days after I arrived, the snow did indeed begin to fall. But here, where everything is so sordid, it gives me very little pleasure. As, seated once more at the familiar window, I watch it settling on the copses in front of the house, how vividly I recall those years‡ of misery and perplexity! Then I used to sit hour after hour at this same window, and each day was like the last, save that since yesterday some flower had opened or fallen, some fresh songbird arrived or flown away. So I watched the springs and autumns in their procession, saw the skies change, the moon rise; saw those same branches white with frost or laden with snow. And all the while I was asking myself over and over again: 'What has the future in store for me? How will this end?' However, sometimes I used to read, for in those days I got a certain amount of pleasure out of quite ordinary romances; I had one or two intimate friends with whom I used to correspond, and there were several other people, not much more than acquaintances, with whom I kept up a casual intercourse. So that, looking back on it now, it seems to me that, one way and another, I had a good many minor distractions.

"Even then I realized that my branch of the family was a very humble one; but the thought seldom troubled me, and I was in those days far indeed from the painful consciousness of inferiority which makes life at Court a continual torment to me.

"Today I picked up a romance which I used to think quite entertaining, and found to my astonishment that it no longer amused me at all. And it is the same with my friends. I have a feeling that those with whom I used to be most intimate would now consider me worldly and flippant, and I have not even told them that I am here. Others, on whose discretion I completely relied, I now have reason to suspect of showing my letters to all and sundry. If they think that I write to them with that intention they cannot know very much of my character! It is surely natural under such circumstances that a correspondence should either cease altogether or become formal and infrequent. Moreover, I now come here so seldom that in many cases it seems hardly worthwhile to renew former friend-

---

* At the Prime Minister's.
† Her parents' house.
‡ After the death of her husband.

ships, and many of those who wanted to call I have put off with excuses... The truth is I now find that I have not the slightest pleasure in the society of any but a few indispensable friends. They must be people who really interest me, with whom I can talk seriously on serious subjects, and with whom I am brought into contact without effort on my side in the natural course of everyday existence. I am afraid this sounds very exacting! But stay, there is Lady Dainagon. She and I used to sleep very close together every night at the Palace and talk for hours. I see her now as she used to look during those conversations, and very much wish that she were here. So I have a little human feeling, after all!"

A little later in the same winter Murasaki sees the Gosechi dancers* at the Palace, and wonders how they have reached their present pitch of forwardness and self-possession: "Seeing several officers of the Sixth Rank coming towards them to take away their fans, the dancers threw the fans across to them in a manner which was adroit enough, but which somehow made it difficult to remember that they were women at all. If I were suddenly called upon to expose myself in that fashion I should completely lose my head. But already I do a hundred things which a few years ago I should never have dreamed myself capable of doing. So strange indeed are the hidden processes which go on in the heart of man that I shall no doubt continue to part with one scruple after another till in the end what now appears to me as the most abandoned shamelessness will seem perfectly proper and natural. Thus I reflected upon the unreality of all our attitudes and opinions, and began sketching out to myself the probable course of my development. So extraordinary were the situations in which I pictured myself that I became quite confused, and saw very little of the show."

The most direct discussion of her own character comes in a passage towards the end of the diary: "That I am very vain, reserved, unsociable, wanting always to keep people at a distance—that I am wrapped up in the study of ancient stories, conceited, living all the time in a poetical world of my own and scarcely realizing the existence of other people, save occasionally to make spiteful and depreciatory comments upon them— such is the opinion of me that most strangers hold, and they are prepared to dislike me accordingly. But when they get to know me, they find to their extreme surprise that I am kind and gentle—in fact, quite a different person from the monster they had imagined; as indeed many have afterwards confessed. Nevertheless, I know that I have been definitely set down at Court as an ill-natured censorious prig. Not that I mind very much, for I am used to it and see that it is due to things in my nature which I cannot possibly change. The Empress has often told me that,

---

* See below, p. 421.

though I seemed always bent upon not giving myself away in the royal presence, yet she felt after a time as if she knew me mote intimately than any of the rest."

The *Diary* closes in 1010. After this we do not know one solitary fact concerning Murasaki's life or death; save that in 1025 she was still in Akiko's service and in that year took part in the ceremonies connected with the birth of the future Emperor Go-Ryozen.

The Composition of Genji

It is generally assumed that the book was written during the three or at the most four years which elapsed between the death of Murasaki's husband and her arrival at Court. Others suggest that it was begun then, and finished sometime before the winter of 1008. This assumption is based on the three references to *The Tale of Genji* which occur in the *Diary*. But none of these allusions seem to me to imply that the *Tale* was already complete. From the first reference it is evident that the book was already so far advanced as to show that Murasaki was its heroine; the part of the *Tale* which was read to the Emperor* was obviously the first chapter, which ends with a formula derived directly from the early annals: "Some say that it was the Korean fortune-teller who gave him the name of Genji the Shining One." Such "alternative explanations" are a feature of early annals in most countries and occur frequently in those of Japan. Lastly, Michinaga's joke about the discrepancy between the prudishness of Murasaki's conduct and the erotic character of her book implies no more than that half a dozen chapters were in existence. It may be thought odd that she should have shown it to anyone before it was finished. But the alternative is to believe that it was completed in seven years, half of which were spent at Court under circumstances which could have given her very little leisure. It is much more probable, I think, that *The Tale of Genji,* having been begun in 1001, was carried on slowly after Murasaki's arrival at Court, during her holidays and in spare time at the Palace, and not completed till, say, 1015 or even 1020. The middle and latter parts certainly give the impression of having been written by someone of comparatively mature age. In 1022 the book was undoubtedly complete, for the *Sarashina Diary* refers to the "fifty-odd chapters of *The Tale of Genji.*" In 1031 Murasaki's name is absent from a list where one might expect to find it, and it is possible that she was then no longer alive.†

The Empress Akiko lived on till 1074, reaching an even riper age than Queen Victoria, whom in certain ways she so much resembled.

---

* For the Emperor's remark, see above, p. xxiv.
† Murasaki was outlived by her father, so that it is improbable that she reached any great age.

PART ONE
THE TALE OF GENJI

LIST OF MOST IMPORTANT PERSONS (alphabetical)

Aoi, Princess............ Genji's wife.
Asagao, Princess .... Daughter of Prince Momozono. Courted in vain by Genji from his 17th year onward.
Emperor, The........... Genji's father.
Fujitsubo............... The Emperor's consort. Loved by Genji. Sister of Prince Hyobukyo; aunt of Murasaki.
Genji, Prince............ Son of the Emperor and his concubine Kiritsubo.
Hyobukyo, Prince........ Brother of Fujitsubo; father of Murasaki.
Iyo no Suke .... Husband of Utsusemi.
Ki no Kami .... Son of Iyo no Kami, also called Iyo no Suke.
Kiritsubo............... Concubine of the Emperor; Genji's mother.
Kokiden .... The Emperor's original consort; later supplanted by Kiritsubo and Fujitsubo successively.
Koremitsu.............. Genji's retainer.
Left, Minister of the...... Father of Aoi.
Momozono, Prince....... Father of Princess Asagao.
Murasaki............... Child of Prince Hyobukyo. Adopted by Genji. Becomes his second wife.
Myobu .... A young court lady who introduces Genji to Princess Suyetsumuhana.
Nokiba no Ogi.......... Ki no Kami's sister.
Oborozukiyo, Princess .... Sister of Kokiden.
Omyobu............... Fujitsubo's maid.
Right, Minister of the .... Father of Kokiden.
Rokujo, Princess......... Widow of the Emperor's brother, Prince Zembo. Genji's mistress from his 17th year onward.
Shonagon .... Murasaki's nurse.
Suyetsumuhana, Princess .. Daughter of Prince Hitachi. A timid and eccentric lady.
To no Chujo .... Genji's brother-in-law and great friend.
Ukon.................. Yugao's maid.
Utsusemi............... Wife of the provincial governor, Iyo no Suke. Courted by Genji.
Yugao .... Mistress first of To no Chujo then of Genji. Dies bewitched.

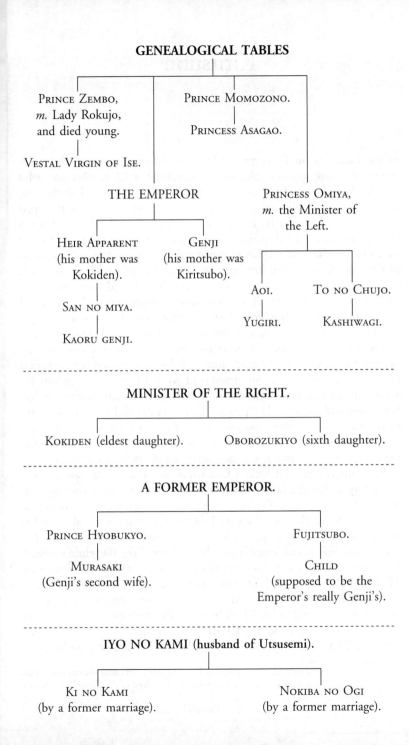

Kiritsubo*

At the Court of an Emperor (he lived it matters not when) there was among the many gentlewomen of the Wardrobe and Chamber one, who though she was not of very high rank was favored far beyond all the rest; so that the great ladies of the Palace, each of whom had secretly hoped that she herself would be chosen, looked with scorn and hatred upon the upstart who had dispelled their dreams. Still less were her former companions, the minor ladies of the Wardrobe, content to see her raised so far above them. Thus her position at Court, preponderant though it was, exposed her to constant jealousy and ill will; and soon, worn out with petty vexations, she fell into a decline, growing very melancholy and retiring frequently to her home. But the Emperor, so far from wearying of her now that she was no longer well or gay, grew every day more tender, and paid not the smallest heed to those who reproved him, till his conduct became the talk of all the land; and even his own barons and courtiers began to look askance at an attachment so ill-advised. They whispered among themselves that in the Land Beyond the Sea such happenings had led to riot and disaster. The people of the country did indeed soon have many grievances to show: and some likened her to Yang Kueifei, the mistress of Ming Huang.† Yet, for all this discontent, so great was the sheltering power of her master's love that none dared openly molest her.

Her father, who had been a Councilor, was dead. Her mother, who never forgot that the father was in his day a man of some consequence, managed despite all difficulties to give her as good an upbringing as generally falls to the lot of young ladies whose parents are alive and at the height of fortune. It would have helped matters greatly if there had been some influential guardian to busy himself on the child's behalf. Unfortunately, the mother was entirely alone in the world and sometimes, when troubles came, she felt very bitterly the lack of anyone to whom she could turn for comfort and advice. But to return to the daughter: In due time she bore him a little Prince who, perhaps because in some previous life a close bond had joined them, turned out as fine and likely a man-child as well might be in all the land. The Emperor could hardly

---

* This chapter should be read with indulgence. In it Murasaki, still under the influence of her somewhat childish predecessors, writes in a manner which is a blend of the Court chronicle with the conventional fairy-tale.

† Famous Emperor of the T'ang dynasty in China; lived A.D. 685-762.

contain himself during the days of waiting.* But when, at the earliest possible moment, the child was presented at Court, he saw that rumor had not exaggerated its beauty. His eldest born prince was the son of Lady Kokiden, the daughter of the Minister of the Right, and this child was treated by all with the respect due to an undoubted Heir Apparent. But he was not so fine a child as the new prince; moreover the Emperor's great affection for the new child's mother made him feel the boy to be in a peculiar sense his own possession. Unfortunately she was not of the same rank as the courtiers who waited upon him in the Upper Palace, so that despite his love for her, and though she wore all the airs of a great lady, it was not without considerable qualms that he now made it his practice to have her by him not only when there was to be some entertainment, but even when any business of importance was afoot. Sometimes indeed he would keep her when he woke in the morning, not letting her go back to her lodging, so that willy-nilly she acted the part of a Lady-in-Perpetual-Attendance.

Seeing all this, Lady Kokiden began to fear that the new prince, for whom the Emperor seemed to have so marked a preference, would, if she did not take care, soon be promoted to the Eastern Palace.† But she had, after all, priority over her rival; the Emperor had loved her devotedly and she had borne him princes. It was even now chiefly the fear of her reproaches that made him uneasy about his new way of life. Thus, though his mistress could be sure of his protection, there were many who sought to humiliate her, and she felt so weak in herself that it seemed to her at last as though all the honors heaped upon her had brought with them terror rather than joy.

Her lodging was in the wing called Kiritsubo. It was but natural that the many ladies whose doors she had to pass on her repeated journeys to the Emperor's room should have grown exasperated; and sometimes, when these comings and goings became frequent beyond measure, it would happen that on bridges and in corridors, here or there along the way that she must go, strange tricks were played to frighten her or unpleasant things were left lying about which spoiled the dresses of the ladies who accompanied her.‡ Once indeed someone locked the door of a portico, so that the poor thing wandered this way and that for a great while in sore distress. So many were the miseries into which this state of affairs now daily brought her that the Emperor could no longer endure to witness her vexations and moved her to the Koroden. In order to make room for her he was obliged to shift the Chief Lady of the Wardrobe to

---

* The child of an Emperor could not be shown to him for several weeks after its birth.
† I.e. be made Heir Apparent.
‡ She herself was of course carried in a litter.

lodgings outside. So far from improving matters he had merely procured her a new and most embittered enemy!

The young prince was now three years old. The Putting on of the Trousers was performed with as much ceremony as in the case of the Heir Apparent. Marvelous gifts flowed from the Imperial Treasury and Tribute House. This too incurred the censure of many, but brought no enmity to the child himself; for his growing beauty and the charm of his disposition were a wonder and delight to all who met him. Indeed many persons of ripe experience confessed themselves astounded that such a creature should actually have been born in these latter and degenerate days.

In the summer of that year the lady became very downcast. She repeatedly asked for leave to go to her home, but it was not granted. For a year she continued in the same state. The Emperor to all her entreaties answered only "Try for a little while longer." But she was getting worse every day, and when for five or six days she had been growing steadily weaker her mother sent to the Palace a tearful plea for her release. Fearing even now that her enemies might contrive to put some unimaginable shame upon her, the sick lady left her son behind and prepared to quit the Palace in secret. The Emperor knew that the time had come when, little as he liked it, he must let her go. But that she should slip away without a word of farewell was more than he could bear, and he hastened to her side. He found her still charming and beautiful, but her face very thin and wan. She looked at him tenderly, saying nothing. Was she alive? So faint, was the dwindling spark that she scarcely seemed so. Suddenly forgetting all that had happened and all that was to come, he called her by a hundred pretty names and weeping showered upon her a thousand caresses; but she made no answer. For sounds and sights reached her but faintly, and she seemed dazed, as one that scarcely remembered she lay upon a bed. Seeing her thus he knew not what to do. In great trouble and perplexity he sent for a hand litter. But when they would have laid her in it, he forbad them, saying "There was an oath between us that neither should go alone upon the road that all at last must tread. How can I now let her go from me?" The lady heard him and "At last!" she said; "Though that desired *at last* be come, because I go alone how gladly would I live!"

Thus with faint voice and failing breath she whispered. But though she had found strength to speak, each word was uttered with great toil and pain. Come what might, the Emperor would have watched by her till the end, but that the priests who were to read the Intercession had already been dispatched to her home. She must be brought there before nightfall, and at last he forced himself to let the bearers carry her away. He tried to sleep but felt stifled and could not close his eyes. All night long messengers were coming and going between her home and the Palace.

From the first they brought no good news, and soon after midnight announced that this time on arriving at the house they had heard a noise of wailing and lamentation, and learned from those within that the lady had just breathed her last. The Emperor lay motionless as though he had not understood.

Though his father was so fond of his company, it was thought better after this event that the Prince should go away from the Palace. He did not understand what had happened, but seeing the servants all wringing their hands and the Emperor himself continually weeping, he felt that it must have been something very terrible. He knew that even quite ordinary separations made people unhappy; but here was such a dismal wailing and lamenting as he had never seen before, and he concluded that this must be some very extraordinary kind of parting.

When the time came for the funeral to begin, the girl's mother cried out that the smoke of her own body would be seen rising beside the smoke of her child's bier. She rode in the same coach with the Court ladies who had come to the funeral. The ceremony took place at Atago and was celebrated with great splendor. So overpowering was the mother's affection that so long as she looked on the body she still thought of her child as alive. It was only when they lighted the pyre she suddenly realized that what lay upon it was a corpse. Then, though she tried to speak sensibly, she reeled and almost fell from the coach, and those with her turned to one another and said, "At last she knows."

A herald came from the palace and read a proclamation which promoted the dead lady to the Third Rank. The reading of this long proclamation by the bier was a sad business. The Emperor repented bitterly that he had not long ago made her a Lady-in-Waiting, and that was why he now raised her rank by one degree. There were many who grudged her even this honor; but some less stubborn began now to recall that she had indeed been a lady of uncommon beauty; and others, that she had very gentle and pleasing manners; while some went so far as to say it was a shame that anybody should have disliked so sweet a lady, and that if she had not been singled out unfairly from the rest, no one would have said a word against her.

The seven weeks of mourning were, by the Emperor's order, minutely observed. Time passed, but he still lived in rigid seclusion from the ladies of the Court. The servants who waited upon him had a sad life, for he wept almost without ceasing both day and night.

Kokiden and the other great ladies were still relentless, and went about saying "it looked as though the Emperor would be no less foolishly obsessed by her memory than he had been by her person." He did indeed sometimes see Kokiden's son, the first-born prince. But this only made him long the more to see the dead lady's child, and he was always sending trusted servants, such as his own old nurse, to report to him upon the boy's progress. The time of the autumn equinox had come. Already the touch of the evening air was cold upon the skin. So many memories crowded upon him that he sent a girl, the daughter of his quiver-bearer, with a letter to the dead lady's house. It was beautiful moonlit weather, and after he had dispatched the messenger he lingered for a while gazing out into the night. It was at such times as this that he had been wont to call for music. He remembered how her words, lightly whispered, had blended with those strangely fashioned harmonies, remembered how all was strange, her face, her air, her form. He thought of the poem which says that "real things in the darkness seem no realer than dreams," and he longed for even so dim a substance as the dream-life of those nights.

The messenger had reached the gates of the house. She pushed them back and a strange sight met her eyes. The old lady had for long been a widow and the whole charge of keeping the domain in repair had fallen upon her daughter. But since her death the mother, sunk in age and despair, had done nothing to the place, and everywhere the weeds grew high; and to all this desolation was added the wildness of the autumn gale. Great clumps of mugwort grew so thick that only the moonlight could penetrate them. The messenger alighted at the entrance of the house. At first the mother could find no words with which to greet her, but soon she said: "Alas, I have lingered too long in the world! I cannot bear to think that so fine a messenger as you have pressed your way through the dewy thickets that bar the road to my house," and she burst into uncontrollable weeping. Then the quiver-bearer's daughter said, "One of the Palace maids who came here, told his Majesty that her heart had been torn with pity at what she saw. And I, Madam, am in like case." Then after a little hesitation she repeated the Emperor's message: "'For a while I searched in the darkness of my mind, groping for an exit from my dream; but after long pondering I can find no way to wake. There is none here to counsel me. Will you not come to me secretly? It is not well that the young prince should spend his days in so desolate and sad a place. Let him come too!' This he said and much else, but confusedly and with many sighs; and I, seeing that the struggle to hide his grief from me was costing him dear, hurried away from the Palace without hearing all. But here is a letter that he sent."

"My sight is dim," said the mother. "Let me hold His letter to the light." The letter said:

"I had thought that after a while there might be some blurring, some slight effacement. But no. As days and months go by, the more senseless, the more unendurable becomes my life. I am continually thinking of the child, wondering how he fares. I had hoped that his mother and I together would watch over his upbringing. Will you not take her place in this, and bring him to me as a memory of the past?" Such was the letter, and many instructions were added to it together with a poem which said "*At the sound of the wind that binds the cold dew on Takagi moor, my heart goes out to the tender lilac stems.*"

It was of the young prince that he spoke in symbol; but she did not read the letter to the end. At last the mother said "Though I know that long life means only bitterness, I have stayed so long in the world that even before the Pine Tree of Takasago I should hide my head in shame. How then should I find courage to go hither and thither in the great Palace of a Hundred Towers? Though the august summons should call me time and again, myself I could not obey. But the young prince (whether he may have heard the august wish I know not) is impatient to return, and, what is small wonder, seems very downcast in this place. Tell his, Majesty this, and whatever else of my thoughts you have here learnt from me. For a little child this house is indeed a sorry place..." "They say that the child is asleep," the quiver-bearer's daughter answered. "I should like to have seen him and told the Emperor how he looks; but I am awaited at the Palace and it must be late."

She was hastening away, but the mother: "Since even those who wander in the darkness of their own black thoughts can gain by converse a momentary beam to guide their steps, I pray you sometimes to visit me of your own accord and when you are at leisure. In years past it was at times of joy and triumph that you came to this house, and now this is the news you bring! Foolish are they indeed who trust to fortune! From the time she was born until his death, her father, who knew his own mind, would have it that she must go to Court and charged me again and again not to disappoint his wishes if he were to die. And so, though I thought that the lack of a guardian would bring her into many difficulties, I was determined to carry out his desire. At Court she found that favors only too great were to be hers, and all the while must needs endure in secrecy the tokens of inhuman malice; till hatred had heaped upon her so heavy a load of cares that she died as it were murdered. Indeed, the love that in His wisdom He deigned to show her (or so sometimes it seems to me in the uncomprehending darkness of my heart) was crueler than indifference."

So she spoke, till tears would let her speak no more; and now the night had come.

"All this," the girl answered, "He himself has said, and further: 'That thus against My will and judgment I yielded helplessly to a passion so reckless that it caused men's eyes to blink was perhaps decreed for the very reason that our time was fated to be so short; it was the wild and vehement passion of those who are marked down for instant separation. And though I had vowed that none should suffer because of my love, yet in the end she bore upon her shoulders the heavy hatred of many who thought that for her sake they had been wronged.'

"So again and again have I heard the Emperor speak with tears. But now the night is far spent and I must carry my message to the Palace before day comes."

So she, weeping too, spoke as she hurried away. But the sinking moon was shining in a cloudless sky, and in the grass-clumps that shivered in the cold wind, bell-crickets tinkled their compelling cry. It was hard to leave these grass-clumps, and the quiver-bearer's daughter, loath to ride away, recited the poem which says "Ceaseless as the interminable voices of the bell-cricket, all night till dawn my tears flow." The mother answered "Upon the thickets that teem with myriad insect voices falls the dew of a Cloud Dweller's tears"; for the people of the Court are called *dwellers above the clouds*. Then she gave the messenger a sash, a comb and other things that the dead lady had left in her keeping—gifts from the Emperor which now, since their use was gone, she sent back to him as mementoes of the past. The nursemaids who had come with the boy were depressed not so much at their mistress's death as at being suddenly deprived of the daily sights and sensations of the Palace. They begged to go back at once. But the mother was determined not to go herself, knowing that she would cut too forlorn a figure. On the other hand, if she parted with the boy, she would be daily in great anxiety about him. That was why she did not immediately either go with him herself or send him to the Palace.

The quiver-bearer's daughter found the Emperor still awake. He was, upon pretext of visiting the flower-pots in front of the Palace which were then in full bloom, waiting for her out of doors, while four or five trusted ladies conversed with him.

At this time it was his wont to examine morning and evening a picture of The Everlasting Wrong,[*] the text written by Teiji no In,[†] with poems by Ise[‡] and Tsurayuki,[§] both in Yamato speech, and in that of the men beyond the sea, and the story of this poem was the common matter of his talk.

Now he turned to the messenger and asked eagerly for all her news. And when she had given him a secret and faithful account of the sad place whence she had come, she handed him the mother's letter: "His Majesty's gracious commands I read with reverence deeper than I can express, but their purport has brought great darkness and confusion to my mind." All this, together with a poem in which she compared her grandchild to a

---

[*] A poem by the Chinese writer Po Chü-i about the death of Yang Kuei-fei, favorite of the Emperor Ming Huang. *See* Giles, *Chinese Literature,* p. 169.
[†] Name of the Emperor Uda after his retirement in A.D. 897.
[‡] Poetess, 9th century.
[§] Famous poet, 883-946 A.D.

flower which has lost the tree that sheltered it from the great winds, was so wild and so ill-writ as only to be suffered from the hand of one whose sorrow was as yet unhealed.

Again the Emperor strove for self-possession in the presence of his messenger. But as he pictured to himself the time when the dead lady first came to him, a thousand memories pressed thick about him, and recollection linked to recollection carried him onward, till he shuddered to think how utterly unmarked, unheeded all these hours and days had fled.

At last he said "I too thought much and with delight how with most profit might be fulfilled the wish that her father the Councilor left behind him; but of that no more. If the young Prince lives, occasion may yet be found... It is for his long life that we must pray."

He looked at the presents she had brought back and "Would that like the wizard you had brought a kingfisher-hairpin as token of your visit to the place where her spirit dwells," he cried, and recited the poem: *Oh for a master of magic who might go and seek her, and by a message teach me where her spirit dwells.*

For the picture of Kuei-fei, skilful though the painter might be, was but the work of a brush, and had no living fragrance. And though the poet tells us that Kuei-fei's grace was as that of "the hibiscus of the Royal Lake or the willows of the Wei-yang Palace," the lady in the picture was all paint and powder and had a simpering Chinesified air.

But when he thought of the lost lady's voice and form, he could find neither in the beauty of flowers nor in the song of birds any fit comparison. Continually he pined that fate should not have allowed them to fulfill the vow which morning and evening was ever talked of between them—the vow that their lives should be as the twin birds that share a wing, the twin trees that share a bough. The rustling of the wind, the chirping of an insect would cast him into the deepest melancholy; and now Kokiden, who for a long while had not been admitted to his chamber, must needs sit in the moonlight making music far on into the night! This evidently distressed him in the highest degree and those ladies and courtiers who were with him were equally shocked and distressed on his behalf. But the offending lady was one who stood much upon her dignity and she was determined to behave as though nothing of any consequence had taken place in the Palace.

And now the moon had set. The Emperor thought of the girl's mother in the house amid the thickets and wondered, making a poem of the thought, with what feelings she had watched the sinking of the autumn moon: "for even we Men above the Clouds were weeping when it sank."

He raised the torches high in their sockets and still sat up. But at last he heard voices coming from the Watch House of the Right and knew that the hour of the Bull* had struck. Then, lest he should be seen, he went into his chamber. He found he could not sleep and was up before daybreak. But, as though he remembered the words "he knew not the dawn was at his window" of Ise's poem,† he showed little attention to the affairs of his Morning Audience, scarcely touched his dried rice and seemed but dimly aware of the viands on the great Table, so that the carvers and waiting-men groaned to see their Master's plight; and all his servants, both men and women kept on whispering to one another "What a senseless occupation has ours become!" and supposed that he was obeying some extravagant vow.

Regardless of his subjects' murmurings, he continually allowed his mind to wander from their affairs to his own, so that the scandal of his negligence was now as dangerous to the State as it had been before, and again there began to be whispered references to a certain Emperor of another land. Thus the months and days passed, and in the end the young prince arrived at Court. He had grown up to be a child of unrivalled beauty and the Emperor was delighted with him. In the spring an heir to the Throne was to be proclaimed and the Emperor was sorely tempted to pass over the first-born prince in favor of the young child. But there was no one at Court to support such a choice and it was unlikely that it would be tolerated by the people; it would indeed bring danger rather than glory to the child. So he carefully concealed from the world that he had any such design, and gained great credit, men saying "Though he dotes on the boy, there is at least some limit to his folly. And even the great ladies of the Palace became a little easier in their minds."

The grandmother remained inconsolable, and impatient to set out upon her search for the place where the dead lady's spirit dwelt, she soon expired. Again the Emperor was in great distress; and this time the boy, being now six years old, understood what had happened and wept bitterly. And often he spoke sadly of what he had seen when he was brought to visit the poor dead lady who had for many years been so kind to him. Henceforward he lived always at the Palace. When he became seven he began to learn his letters, and his quickness was so unusual that his father was amazed. Thinking that now no one would have the heart to be unkind to the child, the Emperor began to take him to the apartments of Kokiden and the rest, saying to them "Now that his mother is dead I know that you will be nice to him." Thus the boy began to penetrate the Royal Curtain. The roughest soldier, the bitterest foeman could not have looked on such a child without a smile, and Kokiden did not send him away. She had two daughters who were indeed not such fine children as

---

* One A.M.
† A poem by Lady Ise written on a picture illustrating Po Chü-i's *Everlasting Wrong*.

the little prince. He also played with the Court Ladies, who, because he was now very pretty and bashful in his ways, found endless amusement, as indeed did everyone else, in sharing his games. As for his serious studies, he soon learnt to send the sounds of zithern and flute flying gaily to the clouds. But if I were to tell you of all his accomplishments, you would think that he was soon going to become a bore.

At this time some Koreans came to Court and among them a fortune-teller. Hearing this, the Emperor did not send for them to come to the Palace, because of the law against the admission of foreigners which was made by the Emperor Uda.* But in strict secrecy he sent the Prince to the Strangers' quarters. He went under the escort of the Secretary of the Right, who was to introduce him as his own son. The fortune-teller was astonished by the boy's lineaments and expressed his surprise by continually nodding his head: "He has the marks of one who might become a Father of the State, and if this were his fate, he would not stop short at any lesser degree than that of Mighty King and Emperor of all the land. But when I look again—I see that confusion and sorrow would attend his reign. But should he become a great Officer of State and Councilor of the Realm I see no happy issue, for he would be defying those kingly signs of which I spoke before."

The Secretary was a most talented, wise and learned scholar, and now began to conduct an interesting conversation with the fortune-teller. They exchanged essays and poems, and the fortune-teller made a little speech, saying "It has been a great pleasure to me on the eve of my departure to meet with a man of capacities so unusual; and though I regret my departure I shall now take away most agreeable impressions of my visit." The little prince presented him with a very nice verse of poetry, at which he expressed boundless admiration and offered the boy a number of handsome presents. In return the Emperor sent him a large reward from the Imperial Treasury. This was all kept strictly secret. But somehow or other the Heir Apparent's grandfather, the Minister of the Right, and others of his party got wind of it and became very suspicious. The Emperor then sent for native fortune-tellers and made trial of them, explaining that because of certain signs which he had himself observed he had hitherto refrained from making the boy a prince. With one accord I they agreed that he had acted with great prudence and the Emperor determined not to set the child adrift upon the world as a prince without royal standing or influence upon the mother's side. For he thought "My own power is very insecure. I had best set him to watch on my behalf over the great Officers of State." Thinking that he had thus agreeably settled the child's future, he set seriously to work upon his education, and saw to it that he

---

* Reigned 889-897. The law in question was made in 894.

should be made perfect in every branch of art and knowledge. He showed such aptitude in all his studies that it seemed a pity he should remain a commoner and as it had been decided that it would arouse suspicion if he were made a prince, the Emperor consulted with certain doctors wise in the lore of the planets and phases of the moon. And they with one accord recommended that he should be made a Member of the Minamoto (or Gen) Clan. So this was done. As the years went by the Emperor did not forget his lost lady; and though many women were brought to the Palace in the hope that he might take pleasure in them, he turned from them all, believing that there was not in the world anyone like her whom he had lost. There was at that time a lady whose beauty was of great repute. She was the fourth daughter of the previous Emperor, and it was said that her mother, the Dowager Empress, had brought her up with unrivalled care. A certain Dame of the Household, who had served the former Emperor, was intimately acquainted with the young Princess, having known her since childhood and still having occasion to observe her from without. "I have served in three courts," said the Dame, "and in all that time have seen none who could be likened to the departed lady, save the daughter of the Empress Mother. She indeed is a lady of rare beauty." So she spoke to the Emperor, and he, much wondering what truth there was in it, listened with great attention. The Empress Mother heard of this with great alarm, for she remembered with what open cruelty the sinister Lady Kokiden had treated her former rival, and though she did not dare speak openly of her fears, she was managing to delay the girl's presentation, when suddenly she died.

 The Emperor, hearing that the bereaved Princess was in a very desolate condition, sent word gently telling her that he should henceforward look upon her as though she were one of the Lady Princesses, his daughters. Her servants and guardians and her brother, Prince Hyobukyo, thought that life in the Palace might distract her and would at least be better than the gloomy desolation of her home, and so they sent her to the Court. She lived in apartments called Fujitsubo (Wisteria Tub) and was known by this name. The Emperor could not deny that she bore an astonishing resemblance to his beloved. She was however of much higher rank, so that everyone was anxious to please her, and, whatever happened, they were prepared to grant her the utmost license: whereas the dead lady had been imperiled by the Emperor's favor only because the Court was not willing to accept her.

 His old love did not now grow dimmer, and though he sometimes found solace and distraction in shifting his thoughts from the lady who had died to the lady who was so much like her, *yet* life remained for him a sad business.

Genji ("he of the Minamoto clan"), as he was now called, was constantly at the Emperor's side. He was soon quite at his ease with the common run of Ladies in Waiting and Ladies of the Wardrobe, so it was not likely he would be shy with one who was daily summoned to the Emperor's apartments. It was but natural that all these ladies should vie eagerly with one another for the first place in Genji's affections, and there were many whom in various ways he admired very much. But most of them behaved in too grown-up a fashion; only one, the new princess, was pretty and quite young as well, and though she tried to hide from him, it was inevitable that they should often meet. He could not remember his mother, but the Dame of the Household had told him how very like to her the girl was, and this interested his childish fancy, and he would like to have been her great friend and lived with her always. One day the Emperor said to her, "Do not be unkind to him. He is interested because he has heard that you are so like his mother. Do not think him impertinent, but behave nicely to him. You are indeed so like him in look and features that you might well be his mother."

And so, young though he was, fleeting beauty took its hold upon his thoughts; he felt his first clear predilection.

Kokiden had never loved this lady too well, and now her old enmity to Genji sprang up again; her own children were reckoned to be of quite uncommon beauty, but in this they were no match for Genji, who was so lovely a boy that people called him Hikaru Genji or Genji the Shining One; and Princess Fujitsubo, who also had many admirers, was called Princess Glittering Sunshine.

Though it seemed a shame to put so lovely a child into man's dress he was now twelve years old and the time for his Initiation was come. The Emperor directed the preparations with tireless zeal and insisted upon a magnificence beyond what was prescribed. The Initiation of the Heir Apparent, which had last year been celebrated in the Southern Hall, was not a whit more splendid in its preparations. The ordering of the banquets that were to be given in various quarters, and the work of the Treasurer and Grain Intendant he supervised in person, fearing lest the officials should be remiss; and in the end all was perfection. The ceremony took place in the eastern wing of the Emperor's own apartments, and the Throne was placed facing towards the east, with the seats of the Initiate-to-be and his Sponsor (the Minister of the Left) in front.

Genji arrived at the hour of the Monkey.* He looked very handsome with his long childish locks, and the Sponsor, whose duty it had just been to bind them with the purple filet, was sorry to think that all this would soon be changed and even the Clerk of the Treasury seemed loath to sever

---

* Three P.M.

those lovely tresses with the ritual knife. The Emperor, as he watched, remembered for a moment what pride the mother would have taken in the ceremony, but soon drove the weak thought from his mind.

Duly crowned, Genji went to his chamber and changing into man's dress went down into the courtyard and performed the Dance of Homage, which he did with such grace that tears stood in every eye. And now the Emperor, whose grief had of late grown somewhat less insistent, was again overwhelmed by memories of the past.

It had been feared that his delicate features would show to less advantage when he had put aside his childish dress; but on the contrary he looked handsomer than ever.

His sponsor, the Minister of the Left, had an only daughter whose beauty the Heir Apparent had noticed. But now the father began to think he would not encourage that match, but would offer her to Genji. He sounded the Emperor upon this, and found that he would be very glad to obtain for the boy the advantage of so powerful a connection.

When the courtiers assembled to drink the Love Cup, Genji came and took his place among the other princes. The Minister of the Left came up and whispered something in his ear; but the boy blushed and could think of no reply. A chamberlain now came over to the Minister and brought him a summons to wait upon His Majesty immediately. When he arrived before the Throne, a Lady of the Wardrobe handed to him the Great White Inner Garment and the Maid's Skirt,* which were his ritual due as Sponsor to the Prince. Then, when he had made him drink out of the Royal Cup, the Emperor recited a poem in which he prayed that the binding of the purple filet might symbolize the union of their two houses; and the Minister answered him that nothing should sever this union save the fading of the purple band. Then he descended the long stairs and from the courtyard performed the Grand Obeisance.† Here too were shown the horses from the Royal Stables and the hawks from the Royal Falconry, that had been decreed as presents for Genji. At the foot of the stairs the Princes and Courtiers were lined up to receive their bounties, and gifts of every kind were showered upon them. That day the hampers and fruit baskets were distributed in accordance with the Emperor's directions by the learned Secretary of the Right, and boxes of cake and presents lay about so thick that one could scarcely move. Such profusion had not been seen even at the Heir Apparent's Initiation.

That night Genji went to the Minister's house, where his betrothal was celebrated with great splendor. It was thought that the little Prince looked somewhat childish and delicate, but his beauty astonished everyone.

---

* These symbolized the unmanly life of childhood which Genji had now put behind him.

† The *buto*, a form of kowtow so elaborate as to be practically a dance.

Only the bride, who was four years older, regarded him as a mere baby and was rather ashamed of him.

The Emperor still demanded Genji's attendance at the Palace, so he did not set up a house of his own. In his inmost heart he was always thinking how much nicer *she** was than anyone else, and only wanted to be with people who were like her, but alas no one was the least like her. Everyone seemed to make a great deal of fuss about Princess Aoi, his betrothed; but he could see nothing nice about her. The girl at the Palace now filled all his childish thoughts and this obsession became a misery to him.

Now that he was a "man" he could no longer frequent the women's quarters as he had been wont to do. But sometimes when an entertainment was afoot he found comfort in hearing her voice dimly blending with the sound of zithern or flute and felt his grown-up existence to be unendurable. After an absence of five or six days he would occasionally spend two or three at his betrothed's house. His father-in-law attributing this negligence to his extreme youth was not at all perturbed and always received him warmly. Whenever he came the most interesting and agreeable of the young people of the day were asked to meet him and endless trouble was taken in arranging games to amuse him.

The Shigeisa, one of the rooms which had belonged to his mother, was allotted to him as his official quarters in the Palace, and the servants who had waited on her were now gathered together again and formed his suite. His grandmother's house was falling into decay. The Imperial Office of Works was ordered to repair it. The grouping of the trees and disposition of the surrounding hills had always made the place delightful. Now the basin of the lake was widened and many other improvements were carried but "If only I were going to live here with someone whom I liked," thought Genji sadly.

Some say that the name of Hikaru the Shining One was given to him in admiration by the Korean fortune-teller.†

---

* Fujitsubo.

† This touch is reminiscent of early chronicles such as the *Nihongi,* which delight in alternative explanations. In the subsequent chapters such archaisms entirely disappear.

The Broom-Tree

Genji the Shining One... He knew that the bearer of such a name could not escape much scrutiny and jealous censure and that his lightest dallyings would be proclaimed to posterity. Fearing then lest he should appear to after ages as a mere good-for-nothing and trifler, and knowing that (so accursed is the blabbing of gossips' tongues) his most secret acts might come to light, he was obliged always to act with great prudence and to preserve at least the outward appearance of respectability. Thus nothing really romantic ever happened to him and Katano no Shosho[*] would have scoffed at his story.

While he was still a Captain of the Guard and was spending most of his time at the Palace, his infrequent visits to the Great Hall[†] were taken as a sign that some secret passion had made its imprint on his heart. But in reality the frivolous, commonplace, straight-ahead amours of his companions did not in the least interest him, and it was a curious trait in his character that when on rare occasions, despite all resistance, love did gain a hold upon him, it was always in the most improbable and hopeless entanglement that he became involved.

It was the season of the long rains. For many days there had not been a fine moment and the Court was keeping a strict fast. The people at the Great Hall were becoming very impatient of Genji's long residence at the Palace, but the young lords, who were Court pages, liked waiting upon Genji better than upon anyone else, always managing to put out his clothes and decorations in some marvelous new way. Among these brothers his greatest friend was the Equerry, To no Chujo, with whom above all other companions of his playtime he found himself familiar and at ease. This lord too found the house which his father-in-law, the Minister of the Right, had been at pains to build for him, somewhat oppressive, while at his father's house he, like Genji, found the splendors somewhat dazzling, so that he ended by becoming Genji's constant companion at Court. They shared both studies and play and were inseparable companions on every sort of occasion, so that soon all formalities were dispensed with between them and the inmost secrets of their hearts freely exchanged.

---

[*] The hero of a lost popular romance. It is also referred to by Murasaki's contemporary Sei Shonagon in Chapter 145 of her *Makura no Soshi*.

[†] His father-in-law's house, where his wife Princess Aoi still continued to live.

It was on a night when the rain never ceased its dismal downpour. There were not many people about in the palace and Genji's rooms seemed even quieter than usual. He was sitting by the lamp, looking at various books and papers. Suddenly he began pulling some letters out of the drawers of a desk which stood near by. This aroused To no Chujo's curiosity. "Some of them I can show to you," said Genji, "but there are others which I had rather..." "It is just those which I want to see. Ordinary, commonplace letters are very much alike and I do not suppose that yours differ much from mine. What I want to see are passionate letters written in moments of resentment, letters hinting consent, letters written at dusk..."

He begged so eagerly that Genji let him examine the drawers. It was not indeed likely that he had put any very important or secret documents in the ordinary desk; he would have hidden them away much further from sight. So he felt sure that the letters in these drawers would be nothing to worry about. After turning over a few of them, "What an astonishing variety!" To no Chujo exclaimed and began guessing at the writers' names, and made one or two good hits. More often he was wrong and Genji, amused by his puzzled air, said very little but generally managed to lead him astray. At last he took the letters back, saying, "But you too must have a large collection. Show me some of yours, and my desk will open to you with better will." "I have none that you would care to see," said To no Chujo, and he continued: "I have at last discovered that there exists no woman of whom one can say 'Here is perfection. This is indeed she.'" There are many who have the superficial art of writing a good running hand, or if occasion requires of making a quick repartee. But there are few who will stand the ordeal of any further test. Usually their minds are entirely occupied by admiration for their own accomplishments, and their abuse of all rivals creates a most unpleasant impression. Some again are adored by over-fond parents. These have been since childhood guarded behind lattice windows[*] and no knowledge of them is allowed to reach the outer-world, save that of their excellence in some accomplishment or art; and this may indeed sometimes arouse our interest. She is pretty and graceful and has not yet mixed at all with the world. Such a girl by closely copying some model and applying herself with great industry will often succeed in really mastering one of the minor and ephemeral arts. Her friends are careful to say nothing of her defects and to exaggerate her accomplishments, and while we cannot altogether trust their praise we cannot believe that their judgment

---

[*] Japanese houses were arranged somewhat differently from ours and for many of the terms which constantly recur in this book *(kicho, sudare, sunoko,* etc.) no exact English equivalents can be found. In such cases I have tried to use expressions which without being too awkward or unfamiliar will give an adequate general idea of what is meant.

is entirely astray. But when we take steps to test their statements we are invariably disappointed."

He paused, seeming to be slightly ashamed of the cynical tone which he had adopted, and added, "I know my experience is not large, but that is the conclusion I have come to so far." Then Genji, smiling: "And are there any who lack even one accomplishment?" "No doubt, but in such a case it is unlikely that anyone would be successfully decoyed. The number of those who have nothing to recommend them and of those in whom nothing but good can be found is probably equal. I divide women into three classes. Those of high rank and birth are made such a fuss of and their weak points are so completely concealed that we are certain to be told that they are paragons. About those of the middle class everyone is allowed to express his own opinion, and we shall have much conflicting evidence to sift. As for the lower classes, they do not concern us."

The completeness with which To no Chujo disposed of the question amused Genji, who said "It will not always be so easy to know into which of the three classes a woman ought to be put. For sometimes people of high rank sink to the most abject positions; while others of common birth rise to be high officers, wear self-important faces, redecorate the inside of their houses and think themselves as good as anyone. How are we to deal with such cases?"

At this moment they were joined by Hidari no Uma no Kami and To Shikibu no Jo, who said they had also come to the Palace to keep the fast. As both of them were great lovers and good talkers, To no Chujo handed over to them the decision of Genji's question, and in the discussion which followed many unflattering things were said. Uma no Kami spoke first. "However high a lady may rise, if she docs not come of an adequate stock, the world will think very differently of her from what it would of one born to such honors; but if through adverse fortune a lady of highest rank finds herself in friendless misery, the noble breeding of her mind is soon forgotten and she becomes an object of contempt. I think then that taking all things into account, we must put such ladies too into the "middle class." But when we come to classify the daughters of Zuryo,* who are sent to labor at the affairs of distant provinces—they have such ups and downs that we may reasonably put them too into the middle class.

"Then there are Ministers of the third and fourth classes without Cabinet rank. These are generally thought less of even than the humdrum, ordinary officials. They are usually of quite good birth, but have much less responsibility than Ministers of State and consequently much greater peace of mind. Girls born into such households are brought up in

---

* Provincial officials. Murasaki herself came of this class.

complete security from want or deprivation of any kind, and, indeed often amid surroundings of the utmost luxury and splendor. Many of them grow up into women whom it would be folly to despise; some have been admitted at Court, where they have enjoyed a quite unexpected success. And of this I could cite many, many instances."

"Their success has generally been due to their having a lot of money," said Genji smiling. "You should have known better than to say that," said To no Chujo, reproving him, and Uma no Kami went on: "There are some whose lineage and reputation are so high that it never occurs to one that their education could possibly be at fault; yet when we meet them, we find ourselves exclaiming in despair "How can they have contrived to grow up like this?"

"No doubt the perfect woman in whom none of those essentials is lacking must somewhere exist and it would not startle me to find her. But she would certainly be beyond the reach of a humble person like myself, and for that reason I should like to put her in a category of her own and not to count her in our present classification.

"But suppose that behind some gateway overgrown with vine-weed, in a place where no one knows there is a house at all, there should be locked away some creature of unimagined beauty—with what excitement should we discover her! The complete surprise of it, the upsetting of all our wise theories and classifications, would be likely, I think, to lay a strange and sudden enchantment upon us. I imagine her father rather large and gruff; her brother, a surly, ill-looking fellow. Locked away in an utterly blank and uninteresting bedroom, she will be subject to odd flights of fancy, so that in her hands the arts that others learn as trivial accomplishments will seem strangely full of meaning and importance; or perhaps in some particular art she will thrill us by her delightful and unexpected mastery. Such a one may perhaps be beneath the attention of those of you who are of flawless lineage. But for my part I find it hard to banish her..." and here he looked at Shikibu no Jo, who wondered whether the description had been meant to apply to his own sisters, but said nothing. "If it is difficult to choose even out of the top class..." thought Genji, and began to doze.

He was dressed in a suit of soft white silk, with a rough cloak carelessly slung over his shoulders, with belt and fastenings untied. In the light of the lamp against which he was leaning he looked so lovely that one might have wished he were a girl; and they thought that even Uma no Kami's "perfect woman," whom he had placed in a category of her own, would not be worthy of such a prince as Genji.

The conversation went on. Many persons and things were discussed. Uma no Kami contended that perfection is equally difficult to find in other spheres. The sovereign is hard put to it to choose his ministers.

But he at least has an easier task than the husband, for he does not entrust the affairs of his kingdom to one, two or three persons alone, but sets up a whole system of superiors and subordinates.

But when the mistress of a house is to be selected, a single individual must be found who will combine in her person many diverse qualities. It will not do to be too exacting. Let us be sure that the lady of our choice possesses certain tangible qualities which we admire; and if in other ways she falls short of our ideal, we must be patient and call to mind those qualities which first induced us to begin our courting.

But even here we must beware; for there are some who in the selfishness of youth and flawless beauty are determined that not a dust-flick shall fall upon them. In their letters they choose the most harmless topics, but yet contrive to color the very texture of the written signs with a tenderness that vaguely disquiets us. But such a one, when we have at last secured a meeting, will speak so low that she can scarcely be heard, and the few faint sentences that she murmurs beneath her breath serve only to make her more mysterious than before. All this may seem to be the pretty shrinking of girlish modesty; but we may later find that what held her back was the very violence of her passions.

Or again, where all seems plain sailing, the perfect companion will turn out to be too impressionable and will upon the most inappropriate occasions display her affections in so ludicrous a way that we begin to wish ourselves rid of her.

Then there is the zealous housewife, who regardless of her appearance twists her hair behind her ears and devotes herself entirely to the details of our domestic welfare. The husband, in his comings and goings about the world, is certain to see and hear many things which he cannot discuss with strangers, but would gladly talk over with an intimate who could listen with sympathy and understanding, someone who could laugh with him or weep if need be. It often happens too that some political event will greatly perturb or amuse him, and he sits apart longing to tell someone about it. He suddenly laughs at some secret recollection or sighs audibly. But the wife only says lightly "What is the matter?" and shows no interest.

This is apt to be very trying.

Uma no Kami considered several other cases. But he reached no definite conclusion and sighing deeply he continued: "We will then, as I have suggested, let birth and beauty go by the board. Let her be the simplest and most guileless of creatures so long as she is honest and of a peaceable disposition, that in the end we may not lack a place of trust. And if some other virtue chances to be hers we shall treasure it as a godsend. But if we discover in her some small defect, it shall not be too closely scrutinized. And we may be sure that if she is strong in the virtues of tolerance and amiability her outward appearance will not be beyond measure harsh.

"There are those who carry forbearance too far, and affecting not to notice wrongs which cry out for redress seem to be paragons of misused fidelity. But suddenly a time comes when such a one can restrain herself no longer, and leaving behind her a poem couched in pitiful language and calculated to rouse the most painful sentiments of remorse, she flies to some remote village in the mountains or some desolate seashore, and for a long while all trace of her is lost.

"When I was a boy the ladies-in-waiting used to tell me sad tales of this kind. I never doubted that the sentiments expressed in them were real, and I wept profusely. But now I am beginning to suspect that such sorrows are for the most part affectation. She has left behind her (this lady whom we are imagining) a husband who is probably still fond of her; she is making herself very unhappy, and by disappearing in this way is causing him unspeakable anxiety, perhaps only for the ridiculous purpose of putting his affection to the test. Then comes along some admiring friend crying "What a heart! What depth of feeling!" She becomes more lugubrious than ever, and finally enters a nunnery. When she decided on this step she was perfectly sincere and had not the slightest intention of ever returning to the world. Then some female friend hears of it and "Poor thing," she cries; "in what an agony of mind must she have been to do this!" and visits her in her cell. When the husband, who has never ceased to mourn for her, hears what she has become, he bursts into tears, and some servant or old nurse, seeing this, bustles off to the nunnery with tales of the husband's despair, and "Oh Madam, what a shame, what a shame!" Then the nun, forgetting where and what she is, raises her hand to her head to straighten her hair, and finds that it has been shorn away. In helpless misery she sinks to the floor, and do what she will, the tears begin to flow. Now all is lost; for since she cannot at every moment be praying for strength, there creeps into her mind the sinful thought that she did ill to become a nun and so often does she commit this sin that even Buddha must think her wickeder now than she was before she took her vows; and she feels certain that these terrible thoughts are leading her soul to the blackest Hell. But if the *karma* of their past lives should chance to be strongly weighted against a parting, she will be found and captured before she has taken her final vows. In such a case their life will be beyond endurance unless she be fully determined, come good or ill, this time to close her eyes to all that goes amiss.

"Again there are others who must needs be forever mounting guard over their own and their husband's affections. Such a one, if she sees in him not a fault indeed but even the slightest inclination to stray, makes a foolish scene, declaring with indignation that she will have no more to do with him.

"But even if a man's fancy should chance indeed to have gone somewhat astray, yet his earlier affection may still be strong and in the end will return to its old haunts. Now by her tantrums she has made a rift that cannot be joined. Whereas she who when some small wrong calls for silent rebuke, shows by a glance that she is not unaware; but when some large offence demands admonishment knows how to hint without severity, will end by standing in her master's affections better than ever she stood before. For often the sight of our own forbearance will give our neighbor strength to rule his mutinous affections.

"But she whose tolerance and forgiveness know no bounds, though this may seem to proceed from the beauty and amiability of her disposition, is in fact displaying the shallowness of her feeling: 'The unmoored boat must needs drift with the stream.' Are you not of this mind?"

To no Chujo nodded. "Some," he said, "have imagined that by arousing a baseless suspicion in the mind of the beloved we can revive a waning devotion. But this experiment is very dangerous. Those who recommend it are confident that so long as resentment is groundless one need only suffer it in silence and all will soon be well. I have observed however that this is by no means the case.

"But when all is said and done, there can be no greater virtue in woman than this: that she should with gentleness and forbearance meet every wrong whatsoever that falls to her share." He thought as he said this of his own sister, Princess Aoi; but was disappointed and piqued to discover that Genji, whose comments he awaited, was fast asleep.

Uma no Kami was an expert in such discussions and now stood preening his feathers. To no Chujo was disposed to hear what more he had to say and was now at pains to humor and encourage him.

"It is with women" said Uma no Kami, "as it is with the works of craftsmen. The wood-carver can fashion whatever he will. Yet his products are but toys of the moment, to be glanced at in jest, not fashioned according to any precept or law. When times change, the carver too will change his style and make new trifles to hit the fancy of the passing day. But there is another kind of artist, who sets more soberly about his work, striving to give real beauty to the things which men actually use and to give to them the shapes which tradition has ordained. This maker of real things must not for a moment be confused with the carver of idle toys.

"In the Painters' Workshop too there are many excellent artists chosen for their proficiency in ink drawing; and indeed they are all so clever it is hard to set one above the other. Bur all of them are at work on subjects intended to impress and surprise. One paints the Mountain of Horai; another a raging sea-monster riding a storm; another, ferocious animals from the Land beyond the sea, or faces of imaginary demons. Letting their fancy run wildly riot they have no thought of beauty, but only of how best they may astonish the beholder's eye. And though nothing in their pictures is real, all is probable. But ordinary hills and rivers, just as they are, houses such as you may see anywhere, with all their real beauty and harmony of form—quietly to draw such scenes as this, or to show what lies behind some intimate hedge that is folded away far from the world, and thick trees upon some unheroic hill, and all this with befitting care for composition, proportion, and the like—such works demand the highest master's utmost skill and must needs draw the common craftsman into a thousand blunders. So too in handwriting, we see some who aimlessly prolong their cursive strokes this way or that, and hope their flourishes will be mistaken for genius. But true penmanship preserves in every letter its balance and form, and though at first some letters may seem but half-formed, yet when we compare them with the copybooks we find that there is nothing at all amiss.

"So it is in these trifling matters. And how much the more in judging of the human heart should we distrust all fashionable airs and graces, all tricks and smartness, learnt only to please the outward gaze! This I first understood some while ago, and if you will have patience with me I will tell you the story."

So saying, he came and sat a little closer to them, and Genji woke up. To no Chujo, in rapt attention, was sitting with his cheek propped upon his hand. Uma no Kami's whole speech that night was indeed very much like a chaplain's sermon about the ways of the world, and was rather absurd. But upon such occasions as this we are easily led on into discussing our own ideas and most private secrets without the least reserve.

"It happened when I was young, and in an even more humble position than I am today," Uma no Kami continued. "I was in love with a girl who (like the drudging, faithful wife of whom I spoke a little while ago) was not a full-sail beauty; and I in my youthful vanity thought she was all very well for the moment, but would never do for the wife of so fine a fellow as I. She made an excellent companion in times when I was at a loose end; but she was of a disposition so violently jealous, that I could have put up with a little less devotion if only she had been somewhat less fiercely ardent and exacting.

"Thus I kept thinking, vexed by her unrelenting suspicions. But then I would remember her ceaseless devotion to the interests of one who was after all a person of no account, and full of remorse I made sure that with a little patience on my part she would one day learn to school her jealousy.

"It was her habit to minister to my smallest wants even before I was myself aware of them; whatever she felt was lacking in her she strove to acquire, and where she knew that in some quality of mind she still fell behind my desires, she was at pains never to show her deficiency in such a way as might vex me. Thus in one way or another she was always busy in forwarding my affairs, and she hoped that if all down to the last dew-drop (as they say) were conducted as I should wish, this would be set down to her credit and help to balance the defects in her person which meek and obliging as she might be could not (she fondly imagined) fail to offend me; and at this time she even hid herself from strangers lest their poor opinion of her looks should put me out of countenance.

"I meanwhile, becoming used to her homely looks, was well content with her character, save for this one article of jealousy; and here she showed no amendment. Then I began to think to myself 'surely, since she seems so anxious to please, so timid, there must be some way of giving her a fright which will teach her a lesson, so that for a while at least we may have a respite from this accursed business.' And though I knew it would cost me dear, I determined to make a pretence of giving her up, thinking that since she was so fond of me this would be the best way to teach her a lesson. Accordingly I behaved with the greatest coldness to her, and she as usual began her jealous fit and behaved with such folly that in the end I said to her, 'If you want to be rid forever of one who loves you dearly, you are going the right way about it by all these endless poutings over nothing at all. But if you want to go on with me, you must give up suspecting some deep intrigue each time you fancy that I am treating you unkindly. Do this, and you may be sure I shall continue to love you dearly. It may well be that as time goes on, I shall rise a little higher in the world and then…'

"I thought I had managed matters very cleverly, though perhaps in the heat of the moment I might have spoken somewhat too roughly. She smiled faintly and answered that if it were only a matter of bearing for a while with my failures and disappointments, that did not trouble her at all, and she would gladly wait till I became a person of consequence. 'But it is a hard task,' she said, 'to go on year after year enduring your coldness and waiting the time when you will at last learn to behave to me with some decency; and therefore I agree with you that the time has come when we had better go each his own way.' Then in a fit of wild and uncontrollable jealousy she began to pour upon me a torrent of bitter reproaches, and with a woman's savagery she suddenly seized my little finger and bit deep into it. The unexpected pain was difficult to bear, but composing myself I said tragically, 'Now you have put this mark upon me I shall get on worse than ever in polite society; as for promotion, I shall be considered a disgrace to the meanest public office and unable to cut a genteel figure in any capacity, I shall be obliged to withdraw myself completely from the world. You and I at any rate shall certainly not meet again,' and bending my injured finger as I turned to go, I recited the verse 'As on bent hand I count the times that we have met, it is not one finger only that bears witness to my pain.' And she, all of a sudden bursting into tears... 'If still in your heart only you look for pains to count, then were our hands best employed in parting.' After a few more words I left her, not for a moment thinking that all was over.

"Days went by, and no news. I began to be restless. One night when I had been at the Palace for the rehearsal of the Festival music, heavy sleet was falling; and I stood at the spot where those of us who came from the Palace had dispersed, unable to make up my mind which way to go. For in no direction had I anything which could properly be called a home. I might of course take a room in the Palace precincts; but I shivered to think of the cheerless grandeur that would surround me. Suddenly I began to wonder what she was thinking, how she was looking; and brushing the snow off my shoulders, I set out for her house. I own I felt uneasy; but I thought that after so long a time her anger must surely have somewhat abated. Inside the room a lamp showed dimly, turned to the wall. Some undergarments were hung out upon a large, warmly-quilted couch the bed-hangings were drawn up, and I made sure that she was for some reason actually expecting me. I was priding myself on having made so lucky a hit, when suddenly, 'Not at home!' and on questioning the maid I learnt that she had but that very night gone to her parents' home leaving only a few necessary servants behind. The fact that she had till now sent no poem or conciliatory message seemed to show some hardening of heart, and had already disquieted me. Now I began to fear that her accursed suspiciousness and jealousy had but been a stratagem to make me grow weary of her, and though I could recall no further proof of this I fell into great despair. And to show her that, though we no longer met, I still thought of her and planned for her, I got her some stuff for a dress, choosing a most delightful and unusual shade of color, and a material that I knew she would be glad to have. 'For after all,' I thought, 'she cannot want to put me altogether out of her head.' When I informed her of this purchase she did not rebuff me nor make any attempt to hide from me, but to all my questions she answered quietly and composedly, without any sign that she was ashamed of herself.

"At last she told me that if I went on as before, she could never forgive me; but if I would promise to live more quietly she would take me back again. Seeing that she still hankered after me I determined to school her a little further yet, and said that I could make no conditions and must be free to live as I chose. So the tug of war went on; but it seems that it hurt her far more than I knew, for in a little while she fell into a decline and died, leaving me aghast at the upshot of my wanton game. And now I felt that, whatever faults she might have had, her devotion alone would have made her a fit wife for me. I remembered how both in trivial talk and in consideration of important matters she had never once shown herself at a loss, how in the dyeing of brocades she rivaled the Goddess of Tatsuta who tints the autumn leaves, and how in needlework and the like she was not less skilful than Tanabata, the Weaving-lady of the sky."

Here he stopped, greatly distressed at the recollection of the lady's many talents and virtues.

"The Weaving-lady and the Herd boy," said To no Chujo, "enjoy a love that is eternal. Had she but resembled the Divine Seamstress in this, you would not, I think, have minded her being a little less skilful with her needle. I wonder that with this rare creature in mind you pronounce the world to be so blank a place."

"Listen," replied Uma no Kami. "About the same time there was another lady whom I used to visit. She was of higher birth than the first; her skill in poetry, cursive writing, and lute-playing, her readiness of hand and tongue were all marked enough to show that she was not a woman of trivial nature; and this indeed was allowed by those who knew her. To add to this she was not ill looking and sometimes, when I needed a rest from my unhappy persecutress, I used to visit her secretly. In the end I found that I had fallen completely in love with her. After the death of the other I was in great distress. But it was no use brooding over the past and I began to visit my new lady more and more often. I soon came to the conclusion that she was frivolous and I had no confidence that I should have liked what went on when I was not there to see. I now visited her only at long intervals and at last decided that she had another lover.

"It was during the Godless Month,* on a beautiful moonlight night. As I was leaving the Palace I met a certain young courtier, who, when I told him that I was driving out to spend the night at the Dainagon's; said that my way was his and joined me. The road passed my lady's house and here it was that he alighted, saying that he had an engagement which he should have been very sorry not to fulfill. The wall was half in ruins and through its gaps I saw the shadowy waters of the lake. It would not have been easy (for even the moonbeams seemed to loiter here!) to hasten past so lovely a place, and when he left his coach I too left mine.

"At once this man (whom I now knew to be that other lover whose existence I had guessed) went and sat unconcernedly on the bamboo skirting of the portico and began to gaze at the moon. The chrysanthemums were just in full bloom, the bright fallen leaves were tumbling and tussling in the wind. It was indeed a scene of wonderful beauty that met our eyes. Presently he took a flute out of the folds of his dress and began to play upon it. Then putting the flute aside, he began to murmur 'sweet is the

---

* The tenth month.

shade"* and other catches. Soon a pleasant-sounding native zithern† began to tune up somewhere within the house and an ingenious accompaniment was fitted to his careless warblings. Her zithern was tuned to the autumn-mode, and she played with so much tenderness and feeling that though the music came from behind closed shutters it sounded quite modern and passionate,‡ and well accorded with the soft beauty of the moonlight. The courtier was ravished, and as he stepped forward to place himself right under her window he turned to me and remarked in a self-satisfied way that among the fallen leaves no other footstep had left its mark. Then plucking a chrysanthemum, he sang:

> Strange that the music of your lute,
> These matchless flowers and all the beauty of the night,
> Have lured no other feet to linger at your door!

and then, beseeching her pardon for his halting verses, he begged her to play again while one was still near who longed so passionately to hear her. When he had paid her many other compliments, the lady answered in an affected voice with the verse:

> Would that I had some song that might detain
> The flute that blends its note
> With the low rustling of the autumn leaves.

and after these blandishments, still unsuspecting, she took up the thirteen-stringed lute, and tuning it to the *Banjiki* mode§ she clattered at the strings with all the frenzy that fashion now demands. It was a fine performance no doubt; but I cannot say that it made a very agreeable impression upon me.

"A man may amuse himself well enough by trifling from time to time with some lady at the Court; will get what pleasure he can out of it while he is with her and not trouble his head about what goes on when he is not there. This lady too I only saw from time to time, but such was her situation that I had once fondly imagined myself the only occupant of her thoughts. However that night's work dissolved the last shred of my confidence, and I never saw her again.

---

* From the *saibara* ballad, *The Will of Asuka:* "Sweet is the shade, the lapping water cool, and good the pasture for our weary steeds. By the Well of Asuka, here let us stay."

† The "Japanese zithern"; also called *wagon*. A species of *koto*.

‡ As opposed to the formal and traditional music imported from China.

§ See *Encyclopédie de la Musique,* p. 247. Under the name Nan-lü this mode was frequently used in the Chinese love-dramas of the fourteenth century. It was considered very wild and moving.

"These two experiences, falling to my lot while I was still so young, early deprived me of any hope from women. And since that time my view of them has but grown the blacker. No doubt to you at your age they seem very entrancing, these 'dewdrops on the grass that fall if they are touched,' these 'glittering hailstones that melt if gathered in the hand.' But when you are a little older you will think as I do. Take my advice in this at least: beware of caressing manners and soft, entangling ways. For if you are so rash as to let them lead you astray, you will soon find yourselves cutting a very silly figure in the world."

To no Chujo as usual nodded his assent, and Genji's smile seemed such as to show that he too accepted Uma no Kami's advice. "Your two stories were certainly very dismal," he said, laughing. And here To no Chujo interposed: "I will tell you a story about myself. There was a lady whose acquaintance I was obliged to make with great secrecy. But her beauty well rewarded my pains, and though I had no thought of making her my wife, I grew so fond of her that I soon found I could not put her out of my head and she seemed to have complete confidence in me. Such confidence indeed that when from time to time I was obliged to behave in such a way as might well have aroused her resentment, she seemed not to notice that anything was amiss, and even when I neglected her for many weeks, she treated me as though I were still coming every day. In the end indeed I found this readiness to receive me whenever and however I came very painful, and determined for the future to merit her strange confidence.

"Her parents were dead and this was perhaps why, since I was all she had in the world, she treated me with such loving meekness, despite the many wrongs I did her. I must own that my resolution did not last long, and I was soon neglecting her worse than before. During this time (I did not hear of it till afterwards) someone who had discovered our friendship began to send her veiled messages which cruelly frightened and distressed her. Knowing nothing of the trouble she was in, although I often thought of her I neither came nor wrote to her for a long while. Just when she was in her worst despair a child was born, and at last in her distress she plucked a blossom of the flower that is called 'Child of my Heart' and sent it to me."

And here To no Chujo's eyes filled with tears.

"Well," said Genji, "and did she write a message to go with it?" "Oh nothing very out-of-the-ordinary," said To no Chujo. "She wrote: 'Though tattered be the hillman's hedge, deign sometimes to look with kindness upon the Child-flower that grows so sweetly there.' This brought me to her side. As usual she did not reproach me, but she looked sad enough, and when I considered the dreary desolation of this home where every object wore an aspect no less depressing than the wailing voices of the crickets in the grass, she seemed to me like some unhappy princess in an ancient story, and wishing her to feel that it was for the mother's sake and not the child's that I had come, I answered with a poem in which I called the Child-flower by its other name 'Bed-flower,' and she replied with a poem that darkly hinted at the cruel tempest which had attended this Bed-flower's birth. She spoke lightly and did not seem to be downright angry with me; and when a few tears fell she was at great pains to hide them, and seemed more distressed at the thought that I might imagine her to be unhappy than actually resentful of my conduct towards her. So I went away with an easy mind and it was some while before I came again. When at last I returned she had utterly disappeared, and if she is alive she must be living a wretched vagrant life. If while I still loved her she had but shown some outward sign of her resentment, she would not have ended thus as an outcast and wanderer; for I should never have dared to leave her so long neglected, and might in the end have acknowledged her and made her mine forever. The child too was a sweet creature, and I have spent much time in searching for them, but still without success.

"It is, I fear, as sorrowful a tale as that which Uma no Kami has told you. I, unfaithful, thought that I was not missed; and she, still loved, was in no better case than one whose love is not returned. I indeed am fast forgetting her; but she, it may be, cannot put me out of her mind and I fear there may be nights when thoughts that she would gladly banish burn fiercely in her breast; for now I fancy she must be living a comfortless and unprotected life."

"When all is said and done," said Uma no Kami, "my friend, though, pine for her now that she is gone, was a sad plague to me while I had her and we must own that such a one will in the end be sure to make us wish ourselves well rid of her. The zithern-player had much talent to her credit, but was a great deal too light-headed. And your diffident lady To no Chujo, seems to me to be a very suspicious case. The world appears to be so constructed that we shall in the end be always at a loss to make reasoned choice; despite all our picking, sifting and comparing we shall never succeed in finding this in all ways and to all lengths adorable and impeccable female."

"I can only suggest the Goddess Kichijo"* said To no Chujo "and I fear that intimacy with so holy and majestic a being might prove to be impracticable."

At this they all laughed and To no Chujo continued: "But now it is Shikibu's turn and he is sure to give us something entertaining. Come Shikibu, keep the ball rolling!" "Nothing of interest ever happens to humble folk like myself," said Shikibu; but To no Chujo scolded him for keeping them waiting and after reflecting for a while which anecdote

---

* Goddess of Beauty.

would best suit the company, he began: "While I was still a student at the University, I came across a woman who was truly a prodigy of intelligence. One of Uma no Kami's demands she certainly fulfilled, for it was possible to discuss with her to advantage both public matters and the proper handling of one's private affairs. But not only was her mind capable of grappling with any problems of this kind; she was also so learned that ordinary scholars found themselves, to their humiliation, quite unable to hold their own against her.

"I was taking lessons from her father, who was a Professor. I had heard that he had several daughters, and some accidental circumstance made it necessary for me to exchange a word or two with one of them who turned out to be the learned prodigy of whom I have spoken. The father hearing that we had been seen together, came up to me with a wine-cup in his hand and made an allusion to the poem of The Two Wives.* Unfortunately I did not feel the least inclination towards the lady. However I was very civil to her; upon which she began to take an affectionate interest in me and lost no opportunity of displaying her talents by giving me the most elaborate advice how best I might advance my position in the world. She sent me marvelous letters written in a very far-fetched epistolary style and entirely in Chinese characters; in return for which I felt bound to visit her, and by making her my teacher I managed to learn how to write Chinese poems. They were wretched, knock-kneed affairs, but I am still grateful to her for it. She was not however at all the sort of woman whom I should have cared to have as a wife, for though there may be certain disadvantages in marrying a complete dolt, it is even worse to marry a bluestocking. Still less do princes like you and Genji require so huge a stock of intellect and erudition for your support! Let her but be one to whom the *karma* of our past lives draws us in natural sympathy, what matter if now and again her ignorance distresses us? Come to that, even men seem to me to get along very well without much learning."

Here he stopped, but Genji and the rest, wishing to hear the end of the story, cried out that for their part they found her a most interesting woman. Shikibu protested that he did not wish to go on with the story, but at last after much coaxing, pulling a comical wry face he continued: "I had not seen her for a long time. When at last some accident took me to the house, she did not receive me with her usual informality but spoke to me from behind a tiresome screen. Ha, Ha, thought I foolishly, she is sulking; now is the time to have a scene and break with her. I might have known that she was not so little of a philosopher as to sulk about trifles; she prided herself on knowing the ways of the world and my inconstancy did not in the least disturb her.

---

* A poem by Po Chü-i pointing out the advantages of marrying a poor wife.

"She told me (speaking without the slightest tremor) that having had a bad cold for some weeks she had taken a strong garlic-cordial, which had made her breath smell rather unpleasant and that for this reason she could not come very close to me. But if I had any matter of special importance to discuss with her she was quite prepared to give me her attention. All this she had expressed with solemn literary perfection. I could think of no suitable reply, and with an 'at your service' I rose to go. Then, feeling that the interview had not been quite a success, she added, raising her voice, 'Please come again when my breath has lost its smell.' I could not pretend I had not heard. I had however no intention of prolonging my visit, particularly as the odor was now becoming definitely unpleasant, and looking cross I recited the acrostic 'On this night marked by the strange behavior of the spider, how foolish to bid me come back tomorrow'* and calling over my shoulder 'There is no excuse for you!' I ran out of the room. But she, following me, 'If night by night and every night we met, in daytime too I should grow bold to meet you face to face.' Here in the second sentence she had cleverly concealed the meaning, 'If I had had any reason to expect you, I should not have eaten garlic.'"

"What a revolting story!" cried the young princes, and then, laughing, "He must have invented it." "Such a woman is quite incredible; it must have been some sort of ogress. You have shocked us, Shikibu!" and they looked at him with disapproval. "You must try to tell us a better story than that." "I do not see how any story could be better," said Shikibu, and left the room.

"There is a tendency among men as well as women" said Uma no Kami, "so soon as they have acquired a little knowledge of some kind, to want to display it to the best advantage. To have mastered all the difficulties in the Three Histories and Five Classics is no road to amiability. But even a woman cannot afford to lack all knowledge of public and private affairs. Her best way will be without regular study to pick up a little here and a little there, merely by keeping her eyes and ears open. Then, if she has her wits at all about her, she will soon find that she has amassed a surprising store of information. Let her be content with this and not insist upon cramming her letters with Chinese characters which do not at all accord with her feminine style of composition, and will make the recipient exclaim in despair "If only she could contrive to be a little less mannish!" And many of these characters, to which she intended the colloquial pronunciation to be given, are certain to be read as Chinese, and this will give the whole composition an even more pedantic sound than it deserves. Even among

---

* There is a reference to an old poem which says: "I know that tonight my lover will come to me. The spider's antics prove it clearly." Omens were drawn from the behavior of spiders. There is also a pun on *hiru* "day" and *hiru* "garlic," so that an ordinary person would require a few moments' reflection before understanding the poem.

our ladies of rank and fashion there are many of this sort, and there are others who, wishing to master the art of verse making, in the end allow it to master them, and, slaves to poetry, cannot resist the temptation, however urgent the business they are about or however inappropriate the time, to make use of some happy allusion which has occurred to them, but must needs fly to their desks and work it up into a poem. On festival days such a woman is very troublesome. For example on the morning of the Iris Festival, when everyone is busy making ready to go to the temple, she will worry them by stringing together all the old tags about the 'matchless root';* or on the 9th day of the 9th month, when everyone is busy thinking out some difficult Chinese poem to fit the rhymes which have been prescribed, she begins making metaphors about the 'dew on the chrysanthemums,' thus diverting our attention from the far more important business which is in hand. At another time we might have found these compositions quite delightful; but by thrusting them upon our notice at inconvenient moments, when we cannot give them proper attention, she makes them seem worse than they really are. For in all matters we shall best commend ourselves if we study men's faces to read in them the "Why so?" or the "As you will," and do not, regardless of times and circumstances, demand an interest and sympathy that they have not leisure to give.

"Sometimes indeed a woman should even pretend to know less than she knows, or say only a part of what she would like to say..."

All this while Genji, though he had sometimes joined in the conversation, had in his heart of hearts been thinking of one person only, and the more he thought the less could he find a single trace of those shortcomings and excesses which, so his friends had declared, were common to all women. "There is no one like her" he thought, and his heart was very full. The conversation indeed had not brought them to a definite conclusion, but it had led to many curious anecdotes and reflections. So they passed the night, and at last, for a wonder, the weather had improved. After this long residence at the Palace Genji knew he would be expected at the Great Hall and set out at once. There was in Princess Aoi's air and dress a dignified precision which had something in it even of stiffness; and in the very act of reflecting that she, above all women, was the type of that single-hearted and devoted wife whom (as his friends had said last night) no sensible man would lightly offend, he found himself oppressed by the very perfection of her beauty, which seemed only to make all intimacy with her the more impossible.

He turned to Lady Chunagon, to Nakatsukasa and other attendants of the common sort who were standing near and began to jest with them.

---

* The irises used for the Tango festival (5th day of 5th month) had to have nine flowers growing on a root.

The day was now very hot, but they thought that flushed cheeks became Prince Genji very well. Aoi's father came, and standing behind the curtain, began to converse very amiably. Genji, who considered the weather too hot for visits, frowned, at which the ladies-in-waiting tittered. Genji, making furious signs at them to be quiet, flung himself on to a divan. In fact, he behaved far from well.

It was now growing dark. Someone said that the position of the Earth Star[*] would make it unlucky for the Prince to go back to the Palace that night; and another: "You are right. It is now set dead against him." "But my own palace is in the same direction!" cried Genji. "How vexing! where then shall I go?" and promptly fell asleep. The ladies-in-waiting, however, agreed that it was a very serious matter and began discussing what could be done. "There is Ki no Kami's house" said one. This Ki no Kami was one of Genji's gentlemen-in-waiting. "It is in the Middle River," she went on; "and delightfully cool and shady, for they have lately dammed the river and made it flow right through the garden." "That sounds very pleasant," said Genji, waking up, "besides they are the sort of people who would not mind one's driving right in at the front gate, if one had a mind to."[†]

He had many friends whose houses lay out of the unlucky direction. But he feared that if he went to one of them, Aoi would think that, after absenting himself so long, he was now merely using the Earth Star as an excuse for returning to more congenial company. He therefore broached the matter to Ki no Kami, who accepted the proposal, but stepping aside whispered to his companions that his father Iyo no Kami, who was absent on service, had asked him to look after his young wife.[‡] "I am afraid we have not sufficient room in the house to entertain him as I could wish." Genji overhearing this, strove to reassure him, saying "It will be a pleasure to me to be near the lady. A visit is much more agreeable when there is a hostess to welcome us. Find me some corner behind her partition...!" "Even then, I fear you may not find..." but breaking off Ki no Kami sent runner to his house, with orders to make ready an apartment for the Prince. Treating a visit to so humble a house as a matter of no importance, he started at once, without even informing the Minister, and taking with him only a few trusted body-servants. Ki no Kami protested against the precipitation, but in vain.

The servants dusted and aired the eastern side-chamber of the Central Hall and here made temporary quarters for the Prince. They were at pains to improve the view from his windows, for example by altering the

---

[*] The "Lord of the Center," i.e. the planet Saturn.

[†] I.e. people with whom one can be quite at ease. It was usual to unharness one's bulls at the gate.

[‡] Ki no Kami's stepmother.

course of certain rivulets. They set up a rustic wattled hedge and filled the borders with the choicest plants. The low humming of insects floated on the cool breeze; numberless fireflies wove inextricable mazes in the air The whole party settled down near where the moat flowed under the covered bridge and began to drink wine.

Ki no Kami went off in a great bustle, saying that he must find them something to eat. Genji, quietly surveying the scene, decided this was one of those middle-class families which in last night's conversation had been so highly commended. He remembered that he had heard the lady who was staying in the house well spoken of and was curious to see her. He listened and thought that there seemed to be people in the western wing. There was a soft rustling of skirts, and from time to time the sound of young and by no means disagreeable voices. They did not seem to be much in earnest in their efforts to make their whispering and laughter unheard, for soon one of them opened the sliding window. But Ki no Kami; crying "What are you thinking of?" crossly closed it again. The light of a candle in the room filtered through a crack in the paper-window. Genji edged slightly closer to the window in the hope of being able to see through the crack, but found that he could see nothing. He listened for a while, and came to the conclusion that they were sitting in the main women's apartments, out of which the little front room opened. They were speaking very low, but he could catch enough of it to make out that they were talking about him.

"What a shame that a fine young Prince should be taken so young and settled down forever with a lady that was none of his choosing!"

"I understand that marriage does not weigh very heavily upon him," said another. This probably meant nothing in particular, but Genji, who imagined they were talking about what was uppermost in his own mind, was appalled at the idea that his relations with Lady Fujitsubo were about to be discussed. How could they have found out? But the subsequent conversation of the ladies soon showed that they knew nothing of the matter at all, and Genji stopped listening. Presently he heard them trying to repeat the poem which he had sent with a nosegay of morning-glory to Princess Asagao, daughter of Prince Momozono."* But they got the lines rather mixed up, and Genji began to wonder whether the lady's appearance would turn out to be on a level with her knowledge of prosody.

At this moment Ki no Kami came in with a lamp which he hung on the wall. Having carefully trimmed it, he offered Genji a tray of fruit. This was all rather dull and Genji by a quotation from an old folk-song hinted

---

* We learn later that Genji courted this lady in vain from his seventeenth year onward. Though she has never been mentioned before, Murasaki speaks of her as though the reader already knew all about her. This device is also employed by Marcel Proust.

that he would like to meet Ki no Kami's other guests. The hint was not taken. Genji began to doze, and his attendants sat silent and motionless.

There were in the room several charming boys, sons of Ki no Kami, some of whom Genji already knew as pages at the Palace. There were also numerous sons of Iyo no Kami; with them was a boy of twelve or thirteen who particularly caught Genji's fancy. He began asking whose sons the boys were, and when he came to this one Ki no Kami replied, "he is the youngest son of the late Chunagon, who loved him dearly, but died while this boy was still a child. His sister married my father and that is why he is living here. He is quick at his books, and we hope one day to send him to Court, but I fear that his lack of influence..."

"Poor child!" said Genji. "His sister, then, is your stepmother, is that not so? How strange that you should stand in this relationship with so young a girl! And now I come to think of it there was some talk once of her being presented at Court, and I once heard the Emperor asking what had become of her. How changeable are the fortunes of the world." He was trying to talk in a very grown-up way.

"Indeed, Sir," answered Ki no Kami; "her subsequent state was humbler than she had reason to expect. But such is our mortal life. Yes, yes, and such has it always been. We have our ups and downs—and the women even more than the men."

Genji: "But your father no doubt makes much of her?"

Ki no Kami: "Makes much of her indeed! You may well say so. She rules his house, and he dotes on her in so wholesale and extravagant a fashion that all of us (and I among the foremost) have had occasion before now to call him to order, but he does not listen."

Genji: "How comes it then that he has left her behind in the house of a fashionable young Courtier? For he looks like a man of prudence and good sense. But pray, where is she now?"

Ki no Kami: "The ladies have been ordered to retire to the common room, but they have not yet finished all their preparations."

Genji's followers, who had drunk heavily, were now all lying fast asleep on the verandah. He was alone in his room, but could not get to sleep. Having at last dozed for a moment, he woke suddenly and noticed that someone was moving behind the paper-window of the back wall. This, he thought, must be where she is hiding, and faintly curious he sauntered in that direction and stood listening. "Where are you? I say. Where are you?" whispered someone in a quaint, hoarse voice, which seemed to be that of the boy whom Genji had noticed earlier in the evening. "I am lying over here," another voice answered. "Has the stranger gone to sleep yet? His room must be quite close to this; but all the same how far off he seems!" Her sleepy voice was so like the boy's that Genji concluded this must be his sister.

"He is sleeping in the wing, I saw him tonight. All that we have heard of him is true enough. He is as handsome as can be," whispered the boy. "I wish it were tomorrow; I want to see him properly," she answered drowsily, her voice seeming to come from under the bedclothes. Genji was rather disappointed that she did not ask more questions about him. Presently he heard the boy saying, "I am going to sleep over in the corner-room. How bad the light is," and he seemed to be trimming the lamp. His sister's bed appeared to be in the corner opposite the paper-window. "Where is Chujo?" she called. "I am frightened, I like to have someone close to me." "Madam," answered several voices from the servants' room, "she is taking her bath in the lower house. She will be back presently." When all was quiet again, Genji slipped back the bolt and tried the door. It was not fastened on the other side. He found himself in an anteroom with a screen at the end, beyond which a light glimmered. In the half-darkness he could see clothes boxes and trunks strewn about in great disorder. Quietly threading his way among them, he entered the inner room from which the voices had proceeded. One very minute figure was couched there who, to Genji's slight embarrassment, on hearing his approach pushed aside the cloak which covered her, thinking that he was the maid for whom she had sent. "Madam, hearing you call for Chujo* I thought that I might now put at your service the esteem in which I have long secretly held you." The lady could make nothing of all this, and terrified out of her wits tried hard to scream. But no sound came, for she had buried her face in the bedclothes.

"Please listen" said Genji. "This sudden intrusion must of course seem to you very impertinent. You do not know that for years I have waited for an occasion to tell you how much I like and admire you, and if tonight I could not resist the temptation of paying this secret visit, pray take the strangeness of my behavior as proof of my impatience to pay a homage that has long been due." He spoke so courteously and gently and looked so kind that not the devil himself would have taken umbrage at his presence. But feeling that the situation was not at all a proper one for a married lady she said (without much conviction), "I think you have made a mistake." She spoke very low. Her bewildered air made her all the more attractive, and Genji, enchanted by her appearance, hastened to answer: "Indeed I have made no mistake; rather, with no guide but a long-felt deference and esteem, I have found my way unerringly to your side. But I see that the suddenness of my visit has made you distrust my purpose. Let me tell you then that I have no evil intentions and seek only for someone to talk with me for a while about a matter which perplexes me." So saying he took her up in his arms (for she was very small) and was carrying

---

* Chujo means "Captain," which was Genji's rank at the time.

her through the anteroom when suddenly Chujo, the servant for whom she had sent before, entered the bedroom. Genji gave an astonished cry and the maid, wondering who could have entered the anteroom, began groping her way towards them. But coming closer she recognized by the rich perfume of his dress that this could be none other than the Prince. And though she was sorely puzzled to know what was afoot, she dared not say a word. Had he been an ordinary person, she would soon have had him by the ears. "Nay," she thought, "even if he were not a Prince I should do best to keep my hands off him; for the more stir one makes, the more tongues wag. But if I should touch this fine gentleman..." and all in a flutter she found herself obediently following Genji to his room. Here he calmly closed the door upon her, saying as he did so, "You will come back to fetch your mistress in the morning." Utsusemi herself was vexed beyond measure at being thus disposed of in the presence of her own waiting-maid, who could indeed draw but one conclusion from what she had seen. But to all her misgivings and anxieties Genji, who had the art of improvising a convincing reply to almost any question, answered with such a wealth of ingenuity and tender concern, that for a while she was content. But soon becoming again uneasy, "This must all be a dream—that you, so great a Prince, should stoop to consider so humble a creature as I, and I am overwhelmed by so much kindness. But I think you have forgotten what I am. A Zuryo's wife! There is no altering that, and you...!" Genji now began to realize how deeply he had distressed and disquieted her by his wild behavior, and feeling thoroughly ashamed of himself he answered: "I am afraid I know very little about these questions of rank and precedence. Such things are too confusing to carry in one's head. And whatever you may have heard of me I want to tell you for some reason or other I have till this day cared nothing for gallantry nor ever practiced it, and that even you cannot be more astonished at what I have done tonight than I myself am." With this and a score of other speeches he sought to win her confidence. But she, knowing that if once their talk became a jot less formal, she would be hard put to it to withstand his singular charm, was determined, even at the risk of seeming stiff and awkward, to show him that in trying so hard to put her at her ease he was only wasting his time, with the result that she behaved very boorishly indeed. She was by nature singularly gentle and yielding, so that the effort of steeling her heart and despite her feelings, playing all the while the part of the young bamboo-shoot which though so green and tender cannot be broken, was very painful to her; and finding that she could not longer think of arguments with which to withstand his importunity, she burst into tears; and though he was very sorry for her, it occurred to him that he would not gladly have missed that sight. He longed however to console her, but could not think of a way to do so, and said at last, "Why do you treat me so unkindly? It is true that the manner of our meeting was strange, yet I think that Fate meant us to meet. It is harsh that you should shrink from me as though the World and you had never met." So he chided her, and she: "If this had happened long ago before my troubles, before my lot was cast, perhaps I should have been glad to take your kindness while it lasted, knowing that you would soon think better of your strange condescension. But now that my course is fixed, what can such meetings bring me save misery and regret? *Tell none that you have seen my home*" she ended, quoting the old song.* "Small wonder that she is sad" thought Genji, and he found many a tender way to comfort her. And now the cock began to crow. Out in the courtyard Genji's men were staggering to their feet, one crying drowsily, "How I should like to go to sleep again," and another "Make haste there, bring out his Honor's coach." Ki no Kami came out into the yard, "What's all this hurry? It is only when there are women in his party that a man need hasten from a refuge to which the Earth Star has sent him. Why is his Highness setting off in the middle of the night?"

Genji was wondering whether such an opportunity would ever occur again. How would he be able even to send her letters? And thinking of all the difficulties that awaited him, he became very despondent. Chujo arrived to fetch her mistress. For a long while he would not let her go, and when at last he handed her over, he drew her back to him saying "How can I send news to you? For, Madam," he said, raising his voice that the maid Chujo might hear, "such love as mine, and such pitiless cruelty as yours have never been seen in the world before." Already the birds were singing in good earnest. She could not forget that she was no one and he a Prince. And even now, while he was tenderly entreating her, there came unbidden to her mind the image of her husband Iyo no Suke, about whom she generally thought either not at all or with disdain. To think that even in a dream he might see her now, filled her with shame and terror.

It was daylight. Genji went with her to the partition door. Indoors and out there was a bustle of feet. As he closed the door upon her, it seemed to him a barrier that shut him out from all happiness. He dressed, and went out on to the balcony. A blind in the western wing was hastily raised. There seemed to be people behind who were looking at him. They could only see him indistinctly across the top of a partition in the verandah. Among them was one, perhaps, whose heart beat wildly as she looked...?

The moon had not set, and though with dwindled light still shone crisp and clear in the dawn. It was a daybreak of marvelous beauty. But in

---

* *Kokinshu* 811, an anonymous love-poem.

the passionless visage of the sky men read only their own comfort or despair; and Genji, as with many backward glances he went upon his way, paid little heed to the beauty of the dawn. He would send her a message? No, even that was utterly impossible. And so, in great unhappiness he returned to his wife's house.

He would gladly have slept a little, but could not stop trying to invent some way of seeing her again; or when that seemed hopeless, imagining to himself all that must now be going on in her mind. She was no great beauty, Genji reflected, and yet one could not say that she was ugly. Yes, she was in every sense a member of that Middle Class upon which Uma no Kami had given them so complete a dissertation.

He stayed for some while at the Great Hall, and finding that, try as he might, he could not stop thinking about her and longing for her, at last in despair he sent for Ki no Kami and said to him "Why do you not let me have that boy in my service—the Chunagon's son, whom I saw at your house? He is a likely looking boy, and I might make him my body-servant, or even recommend him to the Emperor." "I am sensible of your kindness," said Ki no Kami. "I will mention what you have said to the boy's sister." This answer irritated Genji, but he continued: "And has this lady given you stepbrothers my lord?" "Sir, she has been married these two years, but has had no child. It seems that in making this marriage she disobeyed her father's last injunctions, and this has set her against her husband."

Genji: "That is sad indeed. I am told that she is not ill looking. Is that so?"

Ki no Kami: "I believe she is considered quite passable. But I have had very little to do with her. Intimacy between stepchildren and stepparents is indeed proverbially difficult."

Five or six days afterwards Ki no Kami brought the boy. He was not exactly handsome, but he had great charm and (thought Genji) an air of distinction. The Prince spoke very kindly to him and soon completely won his heart. To Genji's many questions about his sister he made such answers as he could, and when he seemed embarrassed or tongue-tied Genji found some less direct way of finding out what he wanted to know, and soon put the boy at his ease. For though he vaguely realized what was going on and thought it rather odd, he was so young that he made no effort to understand it, and without further question carried back a letter from Genji to his sister.

She was so much agitated by the sight of it that she burst into tears and, lest her brother should perceive them, held the letter in front of her face while she read it. It was very long. Among much else it contained the verse "Would that I might dream that dream again! Alas, since first this wish was mine, not once have my eyelids closed in sleep."

She had never seen such beautiful writing, and as she read, a haze clouded her eyes. What incomprehensible fate had first dragged her down to be the wife of a Zuryo, and then for a moment raised her so high? Still pondering, she went to her room.

Next day, Genji again sent for the boy, who went to his sister saying "I am going to Prince Genji. Where is your answer to his letter?" "Tell him," she answered, "that there is no one here who reads such letters." The boy burst out laughing. "Why, you silly, how could I say such a thing to him. He told me himself to be sure to bring an answer." It infuriated her to think that Genji should have thus taken the boy into his confidence and she answered angrily, "He has no business to talk to you about such things at your age. If that is what you talk about you had better not go to him any more." "But he sent for me," said the boy, and started off.

"I was waiting for you all yesterday," said Genji when the boy returned. "Did you forget to bring the answer? Did you forget to come?" The child blushed and made no reply. "And now?" "She said there is no one at home who reads such letters." "How silly, what can be the use of saying such things?" and he wrote another letter and gave it to the boy, saying: "I expect you do not know that I used to meet your sister before her marriage. She treats me in this scornful fashion because she looks upon me as a poor-spirited, defenseless creature. Whereas she has now a mighty Deputy Governor to look after her. But I hope that you will promise to be my child, not his. For he is very old, and will not be able to take care of you for long."

The boy was quite content with this explanation, and admired Genji more than ever. The prince kept him always at his side, even taking him to the Palace. And he ordered his Chamberlain to see to it that he was provided with a little Court suit. Indeed he treated him just as though he were his own child.

Genji continued to send letters; but she, thinking that the boy, young as he was, might easily allow a message to fall into the wrong hands and that then she would lose her fair name to no purpose, feeling too (that however much he desired it) between persons so far removed in rank there could be no lasting union, she answered his letters only in the most formal terms.

Dark though it had been during most of the time they were together, she yet had a clear recollection of his appearance, and could not deny to herself that she thought him uncommonly handsome. But she very much doubted if he on his side really knew what she was like; indeed she felt sure that the next time they met he would think her very plain and all would be over.

Genji meanwhile thought about her continually. He was for ever calling back to memory each incident of that one meeting, and every recollection filled him with longing and despair. He remembered how sad she had looked when she spoke to him of herself, and he longed to make her happier. He thought of visiting her in secret. But the risk of discovery was too great, and the consequences likely to be more fatal to her even than to himself.

He had been many days at the Palace, when at last the Earth Star again barred the road to his home. He set out at once, but on the way pretended that he had just remembered the unfavorable posture of the stars. There was nothing to do but seek shelter again in the house on the Middle River. Ki no Kami was surprised but by no means ill pleased, for he attributed Genji's visit to the amenity of the little pools and fountains which he had constructed in his garden.

Genji had told the boy in the morning that he intended to visit the Middle River, and since he had now become the Prince's constant companion, he was sent for at once to wait upon him in his room. He had already given a message to his sister, in which Genji told her of his plan. She could not but feel flattered at the knowledge that it was on her account he had contrived this ingenious excuse for coming to the house. Yet she had, as we have seen, for some reason got it into her head that at a leisurely meeting she would not please him as she had done at that first fleeting and dreamlike encounter, and she dreaded adding a new sorrow to the burden of her thwarted and unhappy existence. Too proud to let him think that she had posted herself in waiting for him, she said to her servants (while the boy was busy in Genji's room), "I do not care to be at such close quarters with our guest, besides I am stiff, and would like to be massaged; I must go where there is more room," and so saying she made them carry her things to the maid Chujo's bedroom in the cross-wing.

Genji had purposely sent his attendants early to bed, and now that all was quiet, he hastened to send her a message. But the boy could not find her. At last when he had looked in every corner of the house, he tried the cross-wing, and succeeded in tracking her down to Chujo's room. It was too bad of her to hide like this, and half in tears he gasped out, "Oh how can you be so horrid? What will he think of you?" "You have no business to run after me like this," she answered angrily. "It is very wicked for children to carry such messages. But," she added, "you may tell him I am not well, that my ladies are with me, and I am going to be massaged…" So she dismissed him; but in her heart of hearts she was thinking that if such an adventure had happened to her while she was still a person of consequence, before her father died and left her to shift for herself in the world, she would have known how to enjoy it. But now she must force herself to look askance at all his kindness. How tiresome he must think her! And she fretted so much at not being free to fall in love with him, that in the end she was more in love than ever. But then she remembered suddenly that her lot had long ago been cast. She was a wife. There was no sense in thinking of such things, and she made up her mind once and for all never again to let foolish ideas enter her head.

Genji lay on his bed, anxiously waiting to see with what success so young a messenger would execute his delicate mission. When at last the answer came, astonished at this sudden exhibition of coldness, he exclaimed in deep mortification, "This is a disgrace, a hideous disgrace," and he looked very rueful indeed. For a while he said no more, but lay sighing deeply, in great distress. At last he recited the poem "I knew not the nature of the strange tree* that stands on Sono plain, and when I sought the comfort of its shade, I did but lose my road," and sent it to her. She was still awake, and answered with the poem "Too like am I in these my outcast years to the dim tree that dwindles from the traveler's approaching gaze." The boy was terribly sorry for Genji and did not feel sleepy at all, but he was afraid people would think his continual excursions very strange. By this time, however, everyone else in the house was sound asleep. Genji alone lay plunged in the blackest melancholy. But even while he was raging at the inhuman stubbornness of her newfound and incomprehensible resolve, he found that he could not but admire her the more for this invincible tenacity. At last he grew tired of lying awake; there was no more to be done. A moment later he had changed his mind again, and suddenly whispered to the boy, "Take me to where she is hiding!" "It is too difficult," he said, "she is locked in and there are so many people there. I am afraid to go with you." "So be it," said Genji, "but you at least must not abandon me," and he laid the boy beside him on his bed. He was well content to find himself lying by this handsome young Prince's side, and Genji, we must record, found the boy no bad substitute for his ungracious sister.

---

* The *hahakigi* or "broom-tree" when seen in the distance appears to offer ample shade; but when approached turns out to be a skimpy bush.

Utsusemi

Genji was still sleepless. "No one has ever disliked me before," he whispered to the boy. "It is more than I can bear. I am sick of myself and of the world, and do not want to go on living any more." This sounded so tragic that the boy began to weep. The smallness and delicacy of his build, even the way in which his hair was cropped, gave him an astonishing resemblance to his sister, thought Genji, who found his sympathy very endearing. At times he had half thought of creeping away from the boy's side and searching on his own account for the lady's hiding-place but soon abandoned a project which would only have involved him in the most appalling scandal. So he lay, waiting for the dawn. At last, while it was still dark, so full of his own thoughts that he quite forgot to make his usual parting speech to his young page, he left the house. The boy's feelings were very much hurt, and all that day he felt lonely and injured. The lady, when no answer came from Genji, thought that he had changed his mind, and though she would have been very angry if he had persisted in his suit, she was not quite prepared to lose him with so little ado.

But this was a good opportunity once and for all to lock up her heart against him. She thought that she had done so successfully, but found to her surprise that he still occupied an uncommonly large share of her thoughts.

Genji, though he felt it would have been much better to put the whole business out of his head, knew that he had not the strength of mind to do so and at last, unable to bear his wretchedness any longer he said to the boy, "I am feeling very unhappy. I keep on trying to think of other things, but my thoughts will not obey me. I can struggle no longer. You must watch for a suitable occasion, and then contrive some way of bringing me into the presence of your sister." This worried the boy, but he was inwardly flattered at the confidence which Genji placed in him. And an opportunity soon presented itself.

Ki no Kami had been called away to the provinces, and there were only women in the house. One evening when dusk had settled upon the quiet streets the boy brought a carriage to fetch him. He knew that the lad would do his best, but not feeling quite safe in the hands of so young an accomplice, he put on a disguise, and then in his impatience, not waiting even to see the gates closed behind him, he drove off at top speed. They entered unobserved at a side-gate, and here he bade, Genji descend.

The brother knew that as he was only a boy, the watchman and gardeners would not pay any particular attention to his movements, and so he was not at all uneasy. Hiding Genji in the porch of the double-door of the eastern wing, he purposely banged against the sliding partition which separated this wing from the main part of the house, and that the maids might have the impression he did not mind who heard him enter he called out crossly, "Why is the door shut on a hot night like this?" "My lady of the West"* has been here since this morning, and she is playing go with my other lady." Longing to catch sight of her, even though she were with a companion, Genji stole from his hiding-place, and crept through a gap in the curtains. The partition door through which the boy had passed was still open, and he could see through it, right along the corridor into the room on the other side. The screen which protected the entrance of this room was partly folded, and the curtains which usually concealed the divan had, owing to the great heat, been hooked up out of the way, so that he had an excellent view.

The lady sitting near the lamp, half-leaning against the middle pillar must, he supposed, be his beloved. He looked closely at her. She seemed to be wearing an unlined, dark purple dress, with some kind of scarf thrown over her shoulders. The poise of her head was graceful, but her extreme smallness had the effect of making her seem somewhat insignificant. She seemed to be trying all the while to hide her face from her companion, and there was something furtive about the movements of her slender hands, which she seemed never to show for more than a moment.

Her companion was sitting right opposite him, and he could see her perfectly. She wore an under dress of thin white stuff, and thrown carelessly over it a cloak embroidered with red and blue flowers. The dress was not fastened in front, showing a bare neck and breast, showing even the little red sash which held up her drawers. She had indeed an engagingly free and easy air. Her skin was very white and delicate, she was rather plump, but tall and well built. The poise of her head and angle of her brow were faultless, the expression of her mouth and eyes was very pleasing and her appearance altogether most delightful. Her hair grew very thick, but was cut short so as to hang on a level with her shoulders. It was very fine and smooth. How exciting it must be to have such a girl for one's daughter! Small wonder if Iyo no Kami was proud of her. If she was a little less restless, he thought, she would be quite perfect.

The game was nearly over, she was clearing away the unwanted pieces. She seemed to be very excitable and was making a quite unnecessary commotion about the business. "Wait a little," said her companion very quietly, "here there is a stalemate. My only move is to counter-attack over

---

* Ki no Kami's sister, referred to later in the story as Nokiba no Ogi.

there..." "It is all over," said the other impatiently. "I am beaten, let us count the score" and she began counting, "ten, twenty, thirty, forty" on her fingers. Genji could not help remembering the old song about the wash-house at Iyo ("eight tubs to the left, nine tubs to the right") and as this lady of Iyo determined that nothing should be left unsettled, went on stolidly counting her losses and gains, he thought her for the moment slightly common. It was strange to contrast her with Utsusemi,* who sat silent, her face half-covered, so that he could scarcely discern her features. But when he looked at her fixedly, she, as though uneasy under this gaze of which she was not actually aware, shifted in her seat, and showed him her full profile. Her eyelids gave the impression of being a little swollen, and there was at places a certain lack of delicacy in the lines of her features, while her good points were not visible. But when she began to speak, it was as though she were determined to make amends for the deficiencies of her appearance and show that she had, if not so much beauty, at any rate more sense than her companion.

The latter was now flaunting her charms with more and more careless abandonment. Her continual laughter and high spirits were certainly rather engaging, and she seemed in her way to be a most entertaining person. He did not imagine that she was very virtuous, but that was far from being altogether a disadvantage.

It amused him very much to see people behaving quite naturally together. He had lived in an atmosphere of ceremony and reserve. This peep at everyday life was a most exciting novelty, and though he felt slightly uneasy at spying in this deliberate way upon two persons who had no notion that they were observed, he would gladly have gone on looking, when suddenly the boy, who had been sitting by his sister's side, got up, and Genji slipped back again into his proper hiding-place. The boy was full of apologies at having left him waiting for so long: "But I am afraid nothing can be done today; there is still a visitor in her room." "And am I now to go home again?" said Genji; "that is really too much to ask." "No, no, stay here, I will try what can be done, when the visitor has gone." Genji felt quite sure that the boy would manage to find some way of cajoling his sister, for he had noticed that though a mere child, he had a way of quietly observing situations and characters, and making use of his knowledge.

The game of go must now be over. A rustling of skirts and pattering of feet showed that the household was now retiring to rest. "Where is the young master?" Genji heard a servant saying, "I am going to fasten this

---

* This name means "cicada" and is given to her later in the story in reference to the scarf which she "discarded as a cicada sheds its husk." But at this point it becomes grammatically important that she should have a name and I therefore anticipate.

partition door," and there was the sound of bolts being slipped. "They have all gone to bed," said Genji; "now is the time to think of a plan." The boy knew that it would be no use arguing with his sister or trying beforehand in any way to bend her obstinate resolution. The best thing to be done under the circumstances was to wait till no one was about, and then lead Genji straight to her. "Is Ki no Kami's sister still here?" asked Genji. "I should like just to catch a glimpse of her." "But that is impossible," said the boy, "she is in my sister's room." Indeed," said Genji, affecting surprise. For though he knew very well where she was he did not wish to show that he had already seen her. Becoming very impatient of all these delays, he pointed out that it was growing very late, and there was no time to be lost.

The boy nodded, and tapping on the main door of the women's quarters, he entered. Everyone was sound asleep. "I am going to sleep in the anteroom," the boy said out loud; "I shall leave the door open so as to make a draught" and so saying he spread his mattress on the ground, and for a while pretended to be asleep. Soon however, he got up and spread the screen as though to protect him from the light, and under its shadow Genji slipped softly into the room.

Not knowing what was to happen next, and much doubting whether any good would come of the venture, with great trepidation he followed the boy to the curtain that screened the main bedroom, and pulling it aside entered on tiptoe. But even in the drab garments which he had chosen for his disguise, he seemed to the boy to cut a terribly conspicuous figure as he passed through the midnight quietness of the house.

Utsusemi meanwhile had persuaded herself that she was very glad Genji had forgotten to pay his threatened visit. But she was still haunted by the memory of their one strange and dreamlike meeting, and was in no mood for sleep. But near her, as she lay tossing, the lady of the go party, delighted by her visit and all the opportunities it had afforded for chattering to her heart's content, was already asleep. And as she was young and had no troubles she slept very soundly. The princely scent which still clung to Genji's person reached the bed. Utsusemi raised her head, and fancied that she saw something move behind a part of the curtain that was only of one thickness. Though it was very dark she recognized Genji's figure. Filled with a sudden terror and utter bewilderment she sprang from the bed, threw a fragile gauze mantle over her shoulders and fled silently from the room.

A moment later Genji entered. He saw with delight that there was only one person in the room, and that the bed was arranged for two. He threw off his cloak, and advanced towards the sleeping figure. She seemed a more imposing figure than he had expected, but this did not trouble him. It did indeed seem rather strange that she should be so sound asleep.

Gradually he realized with horror that it was not she at all. "It is no use," thought Genji, "saying that I have come to the wrong room, for I have no business anywhere here. Nor is it worth while pursuing my real lady, for she would not have vanished like this if she cared a straw about me." What if it were the lady he had seen by the lamplight? She might not after all prove a bad exchange! But no sooner had he thought this than he was horrified at his own frivolity.

She opened her eyes. She was naturally somewhat startled, but did not seem to be at all seriously put out. She was a thoughtless creature in whose life no very strong emotion had ever played a part. Hers was the flippancy that goes with inexperience, and even this sudden visitation did not seem very much to perturb her.

He meant at first to explain that it was not to see her that he had come. But to do so would have been to give away the secret which Utsusemi so jealously guarded from the world. There was nothing for it, but to pretend that his repeated visits to the house, of which the lady was well aware, had been made in the hope of meeting her. This was a story which would not have withstood the most cursory examination, but, outrageous as it was, the girl accepted it without hesitation.

He did not by any means dislike her, but at that moment all his thoughts were busy with the lady who had so mysteriously vanished. No doubt she was congratulating herself in some safe hiding-place upon the absurd situation in which she had left him. Really, she was the most obstinate creature in the world! What was the use of running after her? But all the same she continued to obsess him.

But the girl in front of him was young and gay and charming. They were soon getting on very well together.

"Is not this kind of thing much more amusing than what happens with people whom one knows?" asked Genji a little later. "Do not think unkindly of me. Our meeting must for the present remain a secret. I am in a position which does not always allow me to act as I please. Your people too would no doubt interfere if they should hear of it, which would be very tiresome. Wait patiently, and do not forget me." These rather tepid injunctions did not strike her as at all unsatisfactory, and she answered very seriously "I am afraid it will not be very easy for me even to write to you. People would think it very odd." "Of course we must not let ordinary people into our secret," he answered, "but there is no reason why this little page should not sometimes carry a message. Meanwhile not a word to anyone!" And with that he left her, taking as he did so Utsusemi's thin scarf which had slipped from her shoulders when she fled from the room.

He went to wake his page who was lying not far away. The boy sprang instantly to his feet, for he was sleeping very lightly, not knowing when his help might be required. He opened the door as quietly as he could. "Who is that?" someone called out in great alarm. It was the voice of an old woman who worked in the house. "It is I," answered the boy uneasily. "What are you walking about here for at this time of night?" and scolding as she came, she began to advance towards the door. "Bother her," thought the boy, but he answered hastily, "It's all right, I am only going outside for a minute," but just as Genji passed through the door, the moon of dawn suddenly emerged in all her brightness. Seeing a grown man's figure appear in the doorway, "Whom have you got with you?" the old lady asked, and then answering her own question, "Why it is Mimbu! what an outrageous height that girl has grown to!" and continuing to imagine that the boy was walking with Mimbu, a maid-servant whose lankiness was a standing joke in the house, "and you will soon be as big as she is, little Master!" she cried, and so saying came out through the door that they had just passed through. Genji felt very uncomfortable, and making no answer on the supposed Mimbu's behalf, he stood in the shadow at the end of the corridor, hiding himself as best he could. "You have been on duty, haven't you dear?" said the old lady as she came towards them. "I have been terribly bad with the colic sine yesterday and was lying up, but they were shorthanded last night, and I had to go and help, though I did feel very queer all the while." And then without waiting for them to answer, "Oh, my pain, my poor pain," she muttered, "I can't stop here talking like this," and she hobbled past them without looking up.

So narrow an escape made Genji wonder more than ever whether the whole thing was worthwhile. He drove back to his house, with the boy riding as his postillion.

Here he told him the story of his evening's adventure. "A pretty mess you made of it!" And when he had finished scolding the boy for his incompetence, he began to rail at the sister's irritating prudishness. The poor child felt very unhappy, but could think of nothing to say in his own or his sister's defense.

"I am utterly wretched," said Genji. "It is obvious that she would not have behaved as she did last night unless she absolutely detested me. But she might at least have the decency to send civil answers to my letters. Oh, well, I suppose Iyo no Kami is the better man..." So he spoke, thinking that she desired only to be rid of him. Yet when at last he lay down to rest, he was wearing her scarf hidden under his dress. He had put the boy by his side, and after giving much vent to his exasperation, he said at last, "I am very fond of you, but I am afraid in future I shall always think of you in connection with this hateful business, and that will put an end to our friendship." He said it with such conviction that the boy felt quite forlorn.

For a while they rested, but Genji could not sleep, and at dawn he sent in haste for his ink-stone. He did not write a proper letter, but scribbled on a piece of folded paper, in the manner of a writing exercise, a poem in which he compared the scarf which she had dropped in her flight to the dainty husk which the cicada sheds on some bank beneath a tree.

The boy picked the paper up, and thrust it into the folds of his dress. Genji was very much distressed at the thought of what the other lady's feelings must be; but after some reflection he decided that it would be better not to send any message.

The scarf, to which still clung the delicate perfume of its owner, he wore for long afterwards beneath his dress.

When the boy got home he found his sister waiting for him in very ill humor. "It was not your doing that I escaped from the odious quandary in which you landed me! And even so pray what explanation can I offer to my friend?" A fine little clown the Prince must think you now. I hope you are ashamed of yourself."

Despite the fact that both parties were using him so ill, the boy drew the rescued verses from out the folds of his dress and handed them to her. She could not forbear to read them. What of this discarded mantle? Why should he speak of it? *The coat that the fishers of Ise left lying upon the shore...** those were the words that came into her mind, but they were not the clue. She was sorely puzzled.

Meanwhile the Lady of the West† was feeling very ill at ease. She was longing to talk about what had happened, but must not do so, and had to bear the burden of her impatience all alone. The arrival of Utsusemi's brother put her into a great state of excitement. No letter for her? She could not understand it at all, and for the first time a cloud settled upon her gay confiding heart.

Utsusemi, though she had so fiercely steeled herself against his love, seeing such tenderness hidden under the words of his message, again fell to longing that she were free, and though there was no undoing what was done she found it so hard to go without him that she took up the folded paper and wrote in the margin a poem in which she said that her sleeve, so often wet with tears, was like the cicada's dew-drenched wing.

---

* Allusion to the old poem, "Does he know that since he left me my eyes are wet as the coat that the fishers... left lying upon the shore?"
† The visitor.

Yugao

It was at the time when he was secretly visiting the lady of the Sixth Ward.* One day on his way back from the Palace he thought that he would call upon his foster-mother who, having for a long while been very ill, had become a nun. She lived in the Fifth Ward. After many enquiries he managed to find the house; but the front gate was locked and he could not drive in. He sent one of his servants for Koremitsu, his foster-nurse's son, and while he was waiting began to examine the rather wretched-looking by street. The house next door was fenced with a new paling, above which at one place were four or five panels of open trellis work, screened by blinds which were very white and bare. Through chinks in these blinds a number of foreheads could be seen. They seemed to belong to a group of ladies who must be peeping with interest into the street below.

At first he thought they had merely peeped out as they passed; but he soon realized that if they were standing on the floor they must be giants. No, evidently they had taken the trouble to climb on to some table or bed which was surely rather odd!

He had come in a plain coach with no outriders. No one could possibly guess who he was, and feeling quite at his ease he leant forward and deliberately examined the house. The gate, also made of a kind of trelliswork, stood ajar, and he could see enough of the interior to realize that it was a very humble and poorly furnished dwelling. For a moment he pitied those who lived in such a place, but then he remembered the song "Seek not in the wide world to find a home; but where you chance to rest, call that your house," and again, "Monarchs may keep their palaces of jade, for in a leafy cottage two can sleep."

There was a wattled fence over which some ivy-like creeper spread its cool green leaves, and among the leaves were white flowers with petals half-unfolded like the lips of people smiling at their own thoughts. "They are called Yugao, 'Evening Faces,'" one of his servants told him; "how strange to find so lovely a crowd clustering on this deserted wall!" And indeed it was a most strange and delightful thing to see how on the narrow tenement in a poor quarter of the town they had clambered over rickety eaves and gables and spread wherever there was room for them

---

* Lady Rokujo. Who she was gradually becomes apparent in the course of the story.

to grow. He sent one of his servants to pick some. The man entered at the half-opened door, and had begun to pluck the flowers, when a little girl in a long yellow tunic came through a quite genteel sliding door, and holding out towards Genji's servant a white fan heavily perfumed with incense, she said to him, "Would you like something to put them on? I am afraid you have chosen a wretched-looking bunch," and she handed him the fan. Just as he was opening the gate on his way back, the old nurse's son Koremitsu came out of the other house full of apologies for having kept Genji waiting so long—"I could not find the key of the gate," he said. "Fortunately the people of this humble quarter were not likely to recognize you and press or stare; but I am afraid you must have been very much bored waiting in this hugger-mugger back street," and he conducted Genji into the house. Koremitsu's brother, the deacon, his brother-in-law Mikawa no Kami and his sister all assembled to greet the Prince, delighted by a visit with which they had not thought he was ever likely to honor them again.

The nun too rose from her couch: "For a long time I had been waiting to give up the world, but one thing held me back: I wanted you to see your old nurse just once again as you used to know her. You never came to see me, and at last I gave up waiting and took my vows. Now, in reward for the penances which my Order enjoins, I have got back a little of my health, and having seen my dear young master again, I can wait with a quiet mind for the Lord Amida's Light," and in her weakness she shed a few tears.

"I heard some days ago," said Genji, "that you were very dangerously ill, and was in great anxiety. It is sad now to find you in this penitential garb. You must live longer yet, and see me rise in the world, that you may be born again high in the ninth sphere of Amida's Paradise. For they say that those who died with longings unfulfilled are 'burdened with an evil Karma in their life to come.'"

People such as old nurses regard even the most blackguardly and ill-favored foster-children as prodigies of beauty and virtue. Small wonder then if Genji's nurse, who had played so great a part in his early life, always regarded her office as immensely honorable and important, and tears of pride came into her eyes while he spoke to her.

The old lady's children thought it very improper that their mother, having taken holy orders, should show so lively an interest in a human career. Certain that Genji himself would be very much shocked, they exchanged uneasy glances. He was on the contrary deeply touched. "When I was a child," he said, "those who were dearest to me were early taken away, and although there were many who gave a hand to my upbringing, it was to you only, dear nurse, that I was deeply and tenderly attached. When I grew up I could not any longer be often in your company. I have not even been able to come here and see you as often as I wanted to. But in all the long time which has passed since I was last here, I have thought a great deal about you and wished that life did not force so many bitter partings upon us."

So he spoke tenderly. The princely scent of the sleeve which he had raised to brush away his tears filled the low and narrow room, and even the young people, who had till now been irritated by their mother's obvious pride at having been the nurse of so splendid a prince, found themselves in tears.

Having arranged for continual masses to be said on the sick woman's behalf, he took his leave, ordering Koremitsu to light him with a candle. As they left the house he looked at the fan upon which the white flowers had been laid. He now saw that there was writing on it, a poem carelessly but elegantly scribbled: "The flower that puzzled you was but the *Yugao*, strange beyond knowing in its dress of shining dew." It was written with a deliberate negligence which seemed to aim at concealing the writer's status and identity. But for all that the hand showed a breeding and distinction which agreeably surprised him. "Who lives in the house on the left?" he asked. Koremitsu, who did not at all want to act as a go-between, replied that he had only been at his mother's for five or six days and had been so much occupied by her illness that he had not asked any questions about the neighbors. "I want to know for a quite harmless reason," said Genji. "There is something about this fan which raises a rather important point. I positively must settle it. You would oblige me by making enquiries from someone who knows the neighborhood. Koremitsu went at once to the house next door and sent for the steward "This house," the man said," belongs to a certain Titular-Prefect. He is living in the country, but my lady is still here; and as she is young and love company, her brothers who are in service at the Court often come here to visit her." "And that is about all one can expect a servant to know," said Koremitsu when he repeated this information. It occurred at once to Genji that it was one of these Courtiers who had written the poem. Yes, there was certainly a self-confident air in the writing. It was by someone whose rank entitled him to have a good opinion of himself. But he was romantically disposed; it was too painful to dismiss altogether the idea that, after all, the verses might really have been meant for him, and on a folded paper he wrote: "Could I but get a closer view, no longer would they puzzle me—the flowers that all too dimly in the gathering dusk I saw." This he wrote in a disguised hand and gave to his servant. The man reflected that though the senders of the fan had never seen Genji before, yet so well known were his features, that even the glimpse they had got from the window might easily have revealed to them his identity. He could imagine the excitement with which the fan had been dispatched and the disappointment when for so long a time no answer came. His somewhat rudely belated arrival would seem to them to have been purposely contrived. They would all be agog to know what was in the reply and he felt very nervous as he approached the house.

Meanwhile, lighted only by a dim torch, Genji quietly left his nurse's home. The blinds of the other house were now drawn and only the firefly glimmer of a candle shone through the gap between them.

When he reached his destination* a very different scene met his eyes. A handsome park, a well-kept garden; how spacious and comfortable it all was! And soon the magnificent owner of these splendors had driven from his head all thought of the wooden paling, the shutters and the flowers.

He stayed longer than he intended, and the sun was already up when he set out for home. Again he passed the house with the shutters. He had driven through the quarter countless times without taking the slightest interest in it; but that one small episode of the fan had suddenly made his daily passage through these streets an event of great importance. He looked about him eagerly, and would have liked to know who lived in all the houses.

For several days Koremitsu did not present himself at Genji's palace. When at last he came, he explained that his mother was growing much weaker and it was very difficult for him to get away. Then drawing nearer, he said in a low voice, "I made some further enquiries, but could not find out much. It seems that someone came very secretly in June and has been living there ever since; but who she really is not even her own servants know. I have once or twice peeped through a hole in the hedge and caught a glimpse of some young women; but their skirts were rolled back and tucked in at their belts, so I think they must have been waiting-maids. Yesterday some while after sunset I saw a lady writing a letter. Her face was calm, but she looked very unhappy, and I noticed that some of her women were secretly weeping." Genji was more curious than ever.

Though his master was of a rank which brought with it great responsibilities, Koremitsu knew that in view of his youth and popularity the young prince would be thought to be positively neglecting his duty if he did not indulge in a few escapades, and that everyone would regard his conduct as perfectly natural and proper even when it was such as they would not have dreamed of permitting to ordinary people.

"Hoping to get a little further information," he said, "I found an excuse for communicating with her, and received in reply a very well-worded answer in a cultivated hand. She must be a girl of quite good position." "You must find out more," said Genji; "I shall not be happy till I know all about her."

---

* Lady Rokujo's house.

Here perhaps was just such a case as they had imagined on that rainy night: a lady whose outward circumstances seemed to place her in that "Lowest Class" which they had agreed to dismiss as of no interest; but who in her own person showed qualities by no means despicable.

But to return for a moment to Utsusemi. Her unkindness had not affected him as it would have affected most people. If she had encouraged him he would soon have regarded the affair as an appalling indiscretion which he must put an end to at all costs; whereas now he brooded continually upon his defeat and was forever plotting new ways to shake her resolution.

He had never, till the day of his visit to the foster-nurse, been interested in anyone of quite the common classes. But now, since that rainy night's conversation, he had explored (so it seemed to him) every corner of society, including in his survey even those categories which his friends had passed over as utterly remote and improbable. He thought of the lady who had, so to speak, been thrown into his life as an extra. With how confiding an air she had promised that she would wait! He was very sorry about her but he was afraid that if he wrote to her Utsusemi might find out and that would prejudice his chances. He would write to her afterwards…

Suddenly at this point Iyo no Suke himself was announced. He had just returned from his province, and had lost no time in paying his respects to the Prince. The long journey by boat had made him look rather swarthy and haggard. "Really," thought Genji, "he is not at all an attractive man!" Still it was possible to talk to him; for if a man is of decent birth and breeding, however broken he may be by age or misfortune, he will always retain a certain refinement of mind and manners which prevent him from becoming merely repulsive. They were beginning to discuss the affairs of Iyo's province and Genji was even joking with him, when a sudden feeling of embarrassment came over him. Why should those recollections make him feel so awkward? Iyo no Suke was quite an old man, it had done him no harm. "These scruples are absurd," thought Genji. However, she was right in thinking it was too queer, too ill assorted a match; and remembering Uma no Kami's warnings, he felt that he had behaved badly. Though her unkindness still deeply wounded him, he was almost glad for Iyo's sake that she had not relented.

"My daughter is to be married," Iyo was saying, "and I am going to take my wife back with me to my province." Here was a double surprise. At all costs he must see Utsusemi once again. He spoke with her brother and the boy discussed the matter with her. It would have been difficult enough for anyone to have carried on an intrigue with the Prince under such circumstances as these. But for her, so far below him in rank and beset by new restrictions, it had now become unthinkable. She could not however bear to lose all contact with him, and not only did she answer his letters much more kindly than before, but took pains, though they were written with apparent negligence, to add little touches that would give him pleasure and make him see that she still cared for him. All this he noticed, and though he was vexed that she would not relent towards him, he found it impossible to put her out of his mind.

As for the other girl, he did not think that she was at all the kind of person to go on pining for him once she was properly settled with a husband; and he now felt quite happy about her.

It was autumn. Genji had brought so many complications into his life that he had for some while been very irregular in his visits to the Great Hall, and was in great disgrace there. The lady[*] in the grand mansion was very difficult to get on with; but he had surmounted so many obstacles in his courtship of her that to give her up the moment he had won her seemed absurd. Yet he could not deny that the blind intoxicating passion which possessed him while she was still unattainable, had almost disappeared. To begin with, she was far too sensitive; then there was the disparity of their ages,[†] and the constant dread of discovery which haunted him during those painful partings at small hours of the morning. In fact, there were too many disadvantages.

It was a morning when mist lay heavy over the garden. After being many times roused Genji at last came out of Rokujo's room, looking very cross and sleepy. One of the maids lifted part of the folding-shutter, seeming to invite her mistress to watch the Prince's departure. Rokujo pulled aside the bed-curtains and tossing her hair back over her shoulders looked out into the garden. So many lovely flowers were growing in the borders that Genji halted for a while to enjoy them. How beautiful he looked standing there, she thought. As he was nearing the portico the maid who had opened the shutters came and walked by his side. She wore a light green skirt exquisitely matched to the season and place; it was so hung as to show to great advantage the grace and suppleness of her stride. Genji looked round at her. "Let us sit down for a minute on the railing here in the corner," he said. "'She seems very shy," he thought, "but how charmingly her hair falls about her shoulders," and he recited the poem: "Though I would not be thought to wander heedlessly from flower to flower, yet this morning's pale convolvulus I fain would pluck!" As he said the lines he took her hand and she answered with practiced care: "You hasten, I observe, to admire the morning flowers while the mist still lies about them," thus parrying the compliment by a verse which might be understood either in a personal or general sense. At this moment a very

---

[*] Rokujo.

[†] Genji was now seventeen; Rokujo twenty-four.

elegant page wearing the most bewitching baggy trousers came among the flowers brushing the dew as he walked, and began to pick a bunch of the convovuli. Genji longed to paint the scene.

No one could see him without pleasure. He was like the flowering tree under whose shade even the rude mountain peasant delights to rest. And so great was the fascination he exercised that those who knew him longed to offer him whatever was dearest to them. One who had a favorite daughter would ask for nothing better than to make her Genji's handmaiden. Another who had an exquisite sister was ready for her to serve in his household, though it were at the most menial tasks. Still less could these ladies who on such occasions as this were privileged to converse with him and stare at him as much as they pleased, and were moreover young people of much sensibility—how could they fail to delight in his company and note with much uneasiness that his visits were becoming far less frequent than before?

But where have I got to? Ah, yes. Koremitsu had patiently continued the enquiry with which Genji entrusted him. "Who the mistress is," he said, "I have not been able to discover; and for the most part she is at great pains not to show herself. But more than once in the general confusion, when there was the sound of a carriage coming along past that great row of tenement houses, and all the maid-servants were peering out into the road, the young lady whom I suppose to be the mistress of the house slipped out along with them. I could not see her clearly, but she seemed to be very pretty.

"One day, seeing a carriage with outriders coming towards the house, one of the maids rushed off calling out 'Ukon, Ukon, come quickly and look. The Captain's carriage is coming this way.' At once a pleasant-faced lady no longer young, came bustling out. 'Quietly, quietly,' she said holding up a warning finger; 'how do you know it is the Captain? I shall have to go and look,' and she slipped out. A sort of rough drawbridge leads from the garden into the lane. In her excitement the good-lady caught her skirt in it and falling flat on her face almost tumbled into the ditch: 'A bad piece of work His Holiness of Katsuragi* made here!' she grumbled; but her curiosity did not seem to be at all damped and she stared harder than ever at the approaching carriage. The visitor was dressed in a plain, wide cloak. He had attendants with him, whose names the excited servant-girls called out as one after another they came near enough to be recognized; and the odd thing is that the names were certainly those of To no Chujo's† grooms and pages."

---

* The god of bridges. He built in a single night the stone causeway which joins Mount Katsuragi and Mount Kombu.
† Genji's brother-in-law.

"I must see that carriage for myself," said Genji. What if this should be the very lady whom Chujo, at the time of that rainy night's conversation, despaired of rediscovering? Koremitsu, noting that Genji was listening with particular attention continued: "I must tell you that I too have reason to be interested in this house, and while making enquiries on my own account I discovered that the young lady always addresses the other girls in the house as though they were her equals. But when, pretending to be taken in by this comedy, I began visiting there, I noticed that though the older ladies played their part very well, the young girls would every now and then curtsey or slip in a 'My Lady' without thinking; whereupon the others would hasten to cover up the mistake as best they might, saying anything they could think of to make it appear that there was no mistress among them," and Koremitsu laughed as he recollected it.

"Next time I come to visit your mother," said Genji, "you must let me have a chance of peeping at them." He pictured to himself the queer, tumbled-down house. She was only living there for the time being; but all the same she must surely belong to that "bottom-class" which they had dismissed as having no possible bearing on the discussion. How amusing it would be to show that they were wrong and that after all something of interest might be discovered in such a place!

Koremitsu, anxious to carry out his master's every wish and intent also on his own intrigue, contrived at last by a series of ingenious stratagems to effect a secret meeting between Genji and the mysterious lady. The details of the plan by which he brought this about would make a tedious story, and as is my rule in such cases I have thought it better to omit them.

Genji never asked her by what name he was to call her, nor did he reveal his own identity. He came very poorly dressed and—what was most unusual for him—on foot. But Koremitsu regarded this as too great a tribute to so unimportant a lady, and insisted upon Genji riding his horse, while he walked by his side. In doing so he sacrificed his own feelings; for he too had reasons for wishing to create a good impression in the house, and he knew that by arriving in this rather undignified way he would sink in the estimation of the inhabitants. Fortunately his discomfiture was almost unwitnessed, for Genji took with him only the one attendant who had on the first occasion plucked the flowers—a boy whom no one was likely to recognize; and lest suspicions should be aroused, he did not even take advantage of his presence in the neighborhood to call at his foster-nurse's house.

The lady was very much mystified by all these precautions and made great efforts to discover something more about him. She even sent someone after him to see where he went to when he left her at daybreak; but be succeeded in throwing his pursuer off the scent and she was no wiser than before. He was now growing far too fond of her. He was miserable if anything interfered with his visits; and though he utterly disapproved of his own conduct and worried a great deal about it, he soon found that he was spending most of his time at her house.

He knew that at some time or another in their lives even the soberest people lose their heads in this way; but hitherto he had never really lost his, or done anything which could possibly have been considered very wrong. Now to his astonishment and dismay he discovered that even the few morning hours during which he was separated from her were becoming unendurable. "What is it in her that makes me behave like a madman?" he kept on asking himself. She was astonishingly gentle and unassuming, to the point even of seeming rather apathetic, rather deficient perhaps in depth of character and emotion; and though she had a certain air of girlish inexperience, it was clear that he was not by any means her first lover; and certainly she was rather plebeian. What was it exactly that so fascinated him? He asked himself the question again and again, but found no answer.

She for her part was very uneasy to see him come to her thus in shabby old hunting-clothes, trying always to hide his face, leaving while it was still dark and everyone was asleep. He seemed like some demon-lover in an old ghost-tale, and she was half-afraid. But his smallest gesture showed that he was someone out of the ordinary, and she began to suspect that he was a person of high rank, who had used Koremitsu as his go-between. But Koremitsu obstinately pretended to know nothing at all about his companion, and continued to amuse himself by frequenting the house on his own account.

What could it mean? She was dismayed at this strange lovemaking with—she knew not whom. But about her too there was something fugitive, insubstantial. Genji was obsessed by the idea that, just as she had hidden herself in this place, so one day she would once more vanish and hide, and he would never be able to find her again. There was every sign that her residence here was quite temporary. He was sure that when the time came to move she would not tell him where she was going. Of course her running away would be proof that she was not worth bothering about any more, and he ought, thankful for the pleasure they had had together, simply to leave the matter at that. But he knew that this was the last thing he would be likely to do.

People were already beginning to be suspicious, and often for several nights running he was unable to visit her. This became so intolerable that in his impatience he determined to bring her secretly to the Nijo-in.* There would be an appalling outcry if she were discovered; but that must be risked.

---

* His own palace.

"I am going to take you somewhere very nice where no one will disturb us," he said at last. "No, no," she cried; "your ways are so strange, I should be frightened to go with you." She spoke in a tone of childish terror, and Genji answered smiling: "One or the other of us must be a fox-in-disguise.* Here is a chance to find out which it is!" He spoke very kindly, and suddenly, in a tone of absolute submission, she consented to do whatever he thought best. He could not but be touched at her willingness to follow him in what must appear to her to be the most hazardous and bizarre adventure. Again he thought of To no Chujo's story on that rainy night and could not doubt that this must indeed be Chujo's fugitive lady. But he saw that she had some reason for wishing to avoid all questions about her past, and he restrained his curiosity. So far as he could see she showed no signs of running away; nor did he believe that she would do so as long as he was faithful. To no Chujo, after all, had for months on end left her to her own devices. But he felt that if for an instant she suspected him of the slightest leaning in any other direction it would be a bad business.

It was the fifteenth night of the eighth month. The light of an unclouded full moon shone between the ill-fitting planks of the roof and flooded the room. What a queer place to be lying in thought Genji, as he gazed round the garret, so different from any room he had ever known before. It must be almost day. In the neighboring houses people were beginning to stir, and there was an uncouth sound of peasant voices: "Eh! how cold it is! I can't believe we shall do much with the crops this year." "I don't know what's going to happen about my carrying-trade," said another, "things look very bad." Then (banging on the wall of another house), "Wake up, neighbor. Time to start. Did he hear, d' you think?" and they rose and went off each to the wretched task by which he earned his bread.

All this clatter and bustle going on so near her made the lady very uncomfortable, and indeed so dainty and fastidious a person must often in this miserable lodging have suffered things which would make her long to sink through the floor. But however painful, disagreeable or provoking were the things that happened, she gave no sign of noticing them. That, being herself so shrinking and delicate in her ways, she could yet endure without a murmur the exasperating banging and bumping that was going on in every direction, aroused his admiration, and he felt that this was much nicer of her than if she had shuddered with horror at each sound. But now, louder than thunder, came the noise of the threshing-mills, seeming so near that they could hardly believe it did not come from out of the pillow itself. Genji thought that his ears would burst. What many of

---

* Foxes, dressed up as men, were believed to be in the habit of seducing and bewitching human beings.

the noises were he could not at all make out; but they were very peculiar and startling. The whole air seemed to be full of crashings and bangings. Now from one side, now from another, came too the faint thud of the bleacher's mallet, and the scream of wild geese passing overhead. It was all too distracting.

Their room was in the front of the house. Genji got up and opened the long, sliding shutters. They stood together looking out. In the courtyard near them was a clump of fine Chinese bamboos; dew lay thick on the borders, glittering here no less brightly than in the great gardens to which Genji was better accustomed. There was a confused buzzing of insects. Crickets were chirping in the wall. He had often listened to them, but always at a distance; now, singing so close to him, they made a music which was unfamiliar and indeed seemed far lovelier than that with which he was acquainted. But then, everything in this place where one thing was so much to his liking seemed despite all drawbacks to take on a new tinge of interest and beauty. She was wearing a white bodice with a soft, grey cloak over it. It was a poor dress, but she looked charming and almost distinguished; even so, there was nothing very striking in her appearance—only a certain fragile grace and elegance. It was when she was speaking that she looked really beautiful, there was such pathos, such earnestness in her manner. If only she had a little more spirit. But ever as she was he found her irresistible and longed to take her to some place where no one could disturb them: "I am going to take you somewhere not at all far away where we shall be able to pass the rest of the night in peace. We cannot go on like this, parting always at break of day." "Why have you suddenly come to that conclusion?" she asked, but she spoke submissively. He vowed to her that she should be his love in this and in all future lives and she answered so passionately that she seemed utterly transformed from the listless creature he had known, and it was hard to believe that such vows were no novelty to her.

Discarding all prudence he sent for the maid Ukon and bade her order his servants to fetch a coach. The affair was soon known to all the household, and the ladies were at first somewhat uneasy at seeing their mistress carried off in this fashion; but on the whole they did not think he looked the sort of person who would do her any harm. It was now almost daylight. The cocks had stopped crowing. The voice of an old man (a pilgrim preparing for the ascent of the Holy Mountain) sounded somewhere not far away; and, as at each prayer he bent forward to touch the ground with his head, they could hear with what pain and difficulty he moved. What could he be asking for in his prayers, this old man whose life seemed fragile as the morning dew? Namu torai no doshi, "Glory be to the Savior that shall come": now they could hear the words. "Listen," said Genji tenderly, "is not that an omen that our love shall last through many lives to come?" And he recited the poem: "Do not prove false this omen of the pilgrim's chant: that even in lives to come our love shall last unchanged."

Then unlike the lovers in the "Everlasting Wrong" who prayed that they might be as the "twin birds that share a wing" (for they remembered that this story had ended very sadly) they prayed, "May our love last till Maitreya comes as a Buddha into the World." But she, still distrustful, answered his poem with the verse: "Such sorrow have I known in this world that I have small hope of worlds to come." Her versification was still a little tentative.*

She was thinking with pleasure that the setting moon would light them on their way, and Genji was just saying so when suddenly the moon disappeared behind a bank of clouds. But there was still great beauty in the dawning sky. Anxious to be gone before it was quite light, he hurried her away to the coach and put Ukon by her side.

They drove to an untenanted mansion which was not far off. While he waited for the steward to come out Genji noticed that the gates were crumbling away; dense shinobu-grass grew around them. So somber an entrance he had never seen. There was a thick mist and the dew was so heavy that when he raised the carriage-blind his sleeve was drenched. "Never yet has such an adventure as this befallen me," said Genji, "so I am, as you may imagine, rather excited," and he made a poem in which he said that though love's folly had existed since the beginning of the world, never could man have set out more rashly at the break of day into a land unknown. "But to you this is no great novelty?" She blushed and in her turn made a poem: "I am as the moon that walks the sky not knowing what menace the cruel hills may hold in store; high though she sweeps, her light may suddenly be blotted out."

She seemed very depressed and nervous. But this he attributed to the fact that she had probably always lived in small houses where everything was huddled together, and he was amused at the idea that this large mansion should overawe her. They drove in, and while a room was being got ready, they remained in the carriage which had been drawn up alongside of the balustrade. Ukon, looking very innocent all the while, was inwardly comparing this excursion with her mistress's previous adventures. She had noticed the tone of extreme deference with which this latest lover had been received by the steward, and had begun to draw her own conclusions.

The mist was gradually clearing away. They left the coach and went into the room which had been prepared for them. Though so quickly improvised, their quarters were admirably clean and well provided, for the steward's son had previously been a trusted house-servant of Genji's and

---

* We gather later that she was only nineteen.

had also worked at the Great Hall. Coming now to their room he offered to send for some of Genji's gentlemen. "For," he said, "I cannot bear to see you going unattended." "Do nothing of the kind," said Genji; "I have come here because I do not wish to be disturbed. No one but yourself is to know that I have used this house," and he exacted a promise of absolute secrecy. No regular meal had been prepared, but the steward I brought them a little rice porridge. Then they lay down again to sleep together for the first time in this unfamiliar and so strangely different place.

The sun was high when they woke. Genji went and opened the shutters himself. How deserted the garden looked! Certainly here there was no one to spy upon them. He looked out into the distance: dense woods fast turning to jungle. And nearer the house not a flower or bush, but only un-kept, autumn grasslands, and a pond choked with weeds. It was a wild and desolate place. It seemed that the steward and his men must live in some outbuilding or lodge at a distance from the house; for here there was no sign or sound of life. "It is, I must own, a strange and forsaken place to which we have come. But no ghost or evil fairy will dare molest you while I am here."

It pained her very much that he still was masked;* and indeed such a precaution was quite out of keeping with the stage at which they had now arrived. So at last, reciting a poem in which he reminded her that all their love down to this moment when "The flower opened its petal to the evening dew" had come from a chance vision seen casually from the street, half-turning his face away, for a moment he let her see him unmasked. "What of the 'shining dew?'" he asked, using the words that she had written on the fan. "How little knew I of its beauty who had but in the twilight doubted and guessed..."—so she answered his poem in a low and halting voice. She need not have feared, for to him, poor as the verses were, they seemed delightful. And indeed the beauty of his uncovered face, suddenly revealed to her in this black wilderness of dereliction and decay, surpassed all loveliness that she had ever dreamed of or imagined. "I cannot wonder that while I still set this barrier between us you did not choose to tell me all that I longed to know. But now it would be very unkind of you not to tell me your name." "I am like the fisherman's daughter in the song,"† she said, "'I have no name or home.'" But for all that she would not tell him who she was, she seemed much comforted that he had let her see him. "Do as you please about it," said Genji at last; but for a while he was out of temper. Soon they had made it up again; and so the day passed. Presently Koremitsu came to their

---

* I.e. covered part of his face with a scarf or the like, a practice usual with illicit lovers in mediaeval Japan.

† *Shin Kokinshu,* 1701.

quarters, bringing fruit and other viands. He would not come in, for he was frightened that Ukon would rate him mercilessly for the part he had played in arranging the abduction of her mistress. He had now come to the conclusion that the lady must possess charms which he had wholly overlooked, or Genji would certainly never have taken all this trouble about her, and he was touched at his own magnanimity in surrendering to his master a prize which he might well have kept for himself. It was an evening of marvelous stillness. Genji sat watching the sky. The lady found the inner room where she was sitting depressingly dark and gloomy. He raised the blinds of the front room, and came to sit with her. They watched the light of the sunset glowing in each other's eyes, and in her wonder at his adorable beauty and tenderness she forgot all her fears. At last she was shy with him no longer, and he thought that the newfound boldness and merriment became her very well. She lay by his side till night. He saw that she was again wearing the plaintive expression of a frightened child; so quickly closing the partition-door he brought in the great lamp, saying: "Outwardly you are no longer shy with me; but I can see that deep down in your heart there is still some sediment of rancor and distrust. It is not kind to use me so," and again he was cross with her.

What were the people at the Palace thinking? Would he have been sent for? How far would the messengers pursue their search? He became quite agitated. Then there was the great lady in the Sixth Ward.* What a frenzy she must be in! This time, however, she really had good cause to be jealous. These and other unpleasant considerations were crowding into his head, when looking at the girl who lay beside him so trustfully, unconscious of all that was going on in his mind, he was suddenly filled with an overwhelming tenderness towards her. How tiresome the other was, with her eternal susceptibilities, jealousies and suspicions! For a while at any rate he would stop seeing her. As the night wore on they began sometimes to doze. Suddenly Genji saw standing over him the figure of a woman, tall and majestic: "You who think yourself so fine, how comes it that you have brought to toy with you here this worthless common creature, picked up at random in the streets? I am astonished and displeased," and with this she made as though to drag the lady from his side. Thinking that this was some nightmare or hallucination, he roused himself and sat up. The lamp had gone out. Somewhat agitated he drew his sword and laid it beside him, calling as he did so for Ukon. She came at once, looking a good deal scared herself. "Please wake the watchman in the cross-wing," he said," and tell him to bring a candle." "All in the dark like this? How can I?" she answered. "Don't be childish," said Genji,

---

* Lady Rokujo.

laughing and clapped his hands.* The sound echoed desolately through the empty house. He could not make anyone hear; and meanwhile he noticed that his mistress was trembling from head to foot. What should he do? He was still undecided, when suddenly she burst out into a cold sweat. She seemed to be losing consciousness. "Do not fear, Sir," said Ukon, "all her life she has been subject to these nightmare fits." He remembered now how tired she had seemed in the morning and how she had lain with her eyes turned upwards as though in pain. "I will go myself and wake someone," he said; "I am tired of clapping with only echoes to answer me. Do not leave her!" and drawing Ukon towards the bed he went in the direction of the main western door. But when he opened it, he found that the lamp in the cross-wing had also gone out. A wind had risen. The few attendants he had brought with him were already in bed. There was indeed only the steward's son (the young man who had once been Genji's body-servant), and the one young courtier who had attended him on all his visits. They answered when he called and sprang to their feet. "Come with a candle," he said to the steward's son," and tell my man to get his bow and keep on twanging the string as loud as he can. I wonder anyone should sleep so soundly in such a deserted place. What has happened to Koremitsu?" "He waited for some time, but as you seemed to have no need of him, he went home, saying he would be back at daybreak."

Genji's man had been an Imperial Bowman, and making a tremendous din with his bow he strode towards the steward's lodge crying "Fire, Fire," at the top of his voice. The twanging of the bow reminded Genji of the Palace. The roll call of night courtiers must be over; the Bowman's roll call must be actually going on. It was not so very late.

He groped his way back into the room. She was lying just as he had left her, with Ukon face downwards beside her. "What are you doing there?" he cried. "Have you gone mad with fright? You have heard no doubt that in such lonely places as this fox-spirits sometimes try to cast spell upon men. But, dear people, you need not fear. I have come back, and will not let such creatures harm you." And so saying he dragged Ukon from the bed. "Oh, Sir," she said, "I felt so queer and frightened that I fell flat down upon my face; and what my poor lady must be going through I dare not think." "Then try not to add to her fright," said Genji, and pushing her aside, bent over the prostrate form. The girl was scarcely breathing. He touched her; she was quite limp. She did not know him.

Perhaps some accursed thing, some demon had tried to snatch her spirit away; she was so timid, so childishly helpless. The man came with the candle. Ukon was still too frightened to move. Genji placed a screen

---

* To summon a servant.

so as to hide the bed and called the man to him. It was of course contrary to etiquette that he should serve Genji himself and he hesitated in embarrassment, not venturing even to ascend the dais. "Come here," said Genji impatiently; "use your common-sense." Reluctantly the man gave him the light, and as he held it towards the bed, he saw for a moment the figure which had stood there in his dream still hovering beside the pillow; suddenly it vanished. He had read in old tales of such apparitions and of their power, and was in great alarm. But for the moment he was so full of concern for the lady who now lay motionless on the bed that he gave no thought to that menacing vision, and lying down beside her, began gently to move her limbs. Already they were growing cold. Her breathing had quite stopped. What could he do? To whom could he turn for help? He ought to send for a priest. He tried to control himself, but he was very young, and seeing her lying there all still and pale, he could contain himself no longer and crying "Come back to me, my own darling; come back to life. Do not look at me so strangely!" he flung his arms about her. But now she was quite cold. Her face was set in a dull, senseless stare.

Suddenly Ukon, who had been so busy with her own fears, came to herself again, and set up the most dismal weeping. He disregarded her. Something had occurred to him. There was a story of how a certain minister was waylaid by a demon as he passed through the Southern Hall. The man, Genji remembered, had been prostrate with fear; but in the end he revived and escaped. No, she could not really be dead, and turning to Ukon he said firmly: "Come now we cannot have you making such a hideous noise in the middle of the night." But he himself was stunned with grief, and though he gave Ukon distracted orders, scarce knew what he was doing. Presently he sent for the steward's son and said to him: "Someone here has had a fright and is in a very bad way. I want you to go to Koremitsu's house and tell him to come as quickly as he can. If his brother the priest is there too, take him aside and tell him quietly that I should like to see him at once. But do not speak loud enough for the nun, their mother, to hear; for I would not have her know of this excursion." But though he managed to say the words, his brain was all the while in a hideous turmoil. For added to the ghastly thought that he himself had caused her death there was the dread and horror with which the whole place now inspired him.

It was past midnight. A violent storm began to rise, sighing dismally as it swept the pine-trees that clustered round the house. And all the while some strange bird—an owl, he supposed—kept screeching hoarsely. Utter desolation on all sides. No human voice; no friendly sound. Why, why had he chosen this hideous place?

Ukon had fainted and was lying by her mistress's side. Was she too going to die of fright? No, no. He must not give way to such thoughts.

He was now the only person left who was capable of action. Was there nothing he could do? The candle was burning badly. He lit it again. Over by the screen in the corner of the main room something was moving. There it was again, but in another corner now. There was a sound of footsteps treading cautiously. It still went on. Now they were coming up behind him...

If only Koremitsu would return! But Koremitsu was a rover and a long time was wasted in looking for him. Would it never be day? It seemed to him that this night was lasting a thousand years. But now, somewhere a long way off, a cock crowed.

Why had fate seen fit to treat him thus? He felt that it must be as a punishment for all the strange and forbidden amours into which in these last years he had despite himself been drawn, that now this unheard of horror had befallen him. And such things, though one may keep them secret for a time, always come out in the end. He minded most that the Emperor would be certain to discover sooner or later about this and all his other affairs. Then there was the general scandal. Everyone would know. The very gutter boys would make merry over him. Never, never must he do such things again, or his reputation would utterly collapse...

At last Koremitsu arrived. He prided himself on being always ready to carry out his master's wishes immediately at whatever hour of the night or day, and he thought it very provoking of Genji to have sent for him just on the one occasion when he was not to hand. And now that he had come, his master did not seem able to give him any orders, but stood speechless in front of him.

Ukon, hearing Koremitsu's voice, suddenly came to herself and remembering what had happened, burst into tears. And now Genji, who while he alone was there had supported and encouraged the weeping maidservant, relieved at last by Koremitsu, could contain himself no longer, and suddenly realizing again the terrible thing that had befallen him, he burst into uncontrollable weeping. "Something horrible has happened here," he managed to say at last, "too dreadful to explain. I have heard that when such things as this suddenly befall, certain scriptures should be read. I would have this done, and prayers said. That is why I asked you to bring your brother..."

"He went up to the mountain yesterday," said Koremitsu. "But I see that there has been terrible work here afoot. Was it in some sudden fit of madness that you did this thing?" Genji shook his head. So moved was Koremitsu at the sight of his master weeping that he too began to sob. Had he been an older man, versed in the ways of the world, he might have been of some use in such a crisis, but both of them were young and both were equally perplexed. At last Koremitsu said: "One thing at least is clear. The steward's son must not know. For though he himself can be depended upon, he is the sort of person who is sure to tell all his relatives, and they might meddle disastrously in the affair. We had best get clear of this house as quietly as we can." "Perhaps," said Genji; "but it would be hard to find a less frequented place than this." "At any rate," Koremitsu continued, "we cannot take her to her own house; for there her gentlewomen, who loved her dearly, would raise such a weeping and wailing as would soon bring a pack of neighbors swarming around, and all would quickly be known. If only I knew of some mountain-temple—for there such things are customary* and pass almost unnoticed." He paused and reflected. "There is a lady I once knew who has become a nun and now lives on the Higashi Yama. She was my father's wet-nurse and is now very old and bent. She does not of course live alone; but no outside people come there." A faint light was already showing in the sky when Koremitsu brought the carriage in. Thinking that Genji would not wish to move the body himself, he wrapped it in a rush-mat and carried it towards the carriage. How small she was to hold! Her face was calm and beautiful. He felt no repulsion. He could find no way to secure her hair, and when he began to carry her it overflowed and hung towards the ground. Genji saw, and his eyes darkened. A hideous anguish possessed him.

He tried to follow the body, but Koremitsu dissuaded him, saying, "You must ride back to your palace as quickly as you can; you have just time to get there before the stir begins," and putting Ukon into the carriage, he gave Genji his horse. Then pulling up his silk trousers to the knee, he accompanied the carriage on foot. It was a very singular procession; but Koremitsu, seeing his master's terrible distress, forgot for the moment his own dignity and walked stolidly on. Genji, hardly conscious of what went on around him, arrived at last in ghostly pallor at his house. "Where do you come from, my Lord?" "How ill you look."... Questions assailed him, but he hurried to his room and lay behind his curtain. He tried to calm himself, but hideous thoughts tormented him. Why had he not insisted upon going with her? What if after all she were not dead and waking up should find that he had thus abandoned her? While these wild thoughts chased through his brain, a terrible sensation of choking began to torment him. His head ached, his body seemed to be on fire. Indeed he felt so strange that he thought he too was about to die suddenly and inexplicably as she had done. The sun was now high, but he did not get up. His gentlemen, with murmurs of astonishment, tried every means to rouse him. He sent away the dainties they brought, and lay hour after hour plunged in the darkest thoughts. A messenger arrived from the Emperor: "His Majesty has been uneasy since yesterday when his envoys sought everywhere for your Highness in vain."

---

* The bringing of a corpse. Temples were used as mortuaries.

The young lords too came from the Great Hall. He would see none of them but To no Chujo, and even him he made stand outside his curtain while he spoke to him: "My foster-mother has been very ill since the fifth month. She shaved her head and performed other penances, in consequence of which (or so it seems) she recovered a little and got up, but is very much enfeebled. She sent word that she desired to see me once more before she died, and as I was very fond of her when I was a child, I could not refuse. While I was there a servant in the house fell ill and died quite suddenly. Out of consideration for me they removed the body at nightfall. But as soon as I was told of what had happened I remembered that the Fast of the Ninth Month was at hand and for this reason I have not thought it right to present myself to the Emperor my father. Moreover, since early morning I have had a cough and very bad headache, so you will forgive me for treating you in this way."

"I will give the Emperor your message. But I must tell you that last night when you were out he sent messengers to look for you and seemed, if I may venture to say so, to be in a very ill humor." To no Chujo turned to go, but pausing a moment came back to Genji's couch and said quietly: "What really happened to you last night? What you told me just now cannot possibly be true." "You need not go into details," answered Genji impatiently. "Simply tell him that unintentionally I became exposed to a pollution, and apologize to him for me as best you can." He spoke sharply, but in his heart there was only an unspeakable sadness; and he was very tired.

All day he lay hidden from sight. Once he sent for To no Chujo's brother Kurodo no Ben and gave him a formal message for the Emperor. The same excuse would serve for the Great Hall, and he sent a similar message there and to other houses where he might be expected.

At dusk Koremitsu came. The story of Genji's pollution had turned all visitors from the door, and Koremitsu found his palace utterly deserted. "What happened?" said Genji, summoning him, "you are sure that she is dead?" and holding his sleeve before his face he wept. "All is over; of that there is no doubt," said Koremitsu, also in tears; "and since it is not possible for them to keep the body long, I have arranged with a very respectable aged priest who is my friend that the ceremony shall take place tomorrow, since tomorrow chances to be a good calendar day." "And what of her gentlewoman?" asked Genji. "I fear she will not live," said Koremitsu. "She cries out that she must follow her mistress and this morning, had I not held her, she would have cast herself from a high rock. She threatened to tell the servants at my lady's house, but I prevailed upon her to think the matter over quietly before she did this. "Poor thing," said Genji, "small wonder that she should be thus distracted. I too am feeling strangely disordered and do not know what will become of me."

"Torment yourself no more," said Koremitsu. "All things happen as they must. Here is one who will handle this matter very prudently for you, and none shall be the wiser." "Happen as they must. You are right," said Genji, and so I try to persuade myself. But in the pursuit of one's own wanton pleasures to have done harm and to have caused someone's death—that is a hideous crime; a terrible load of sin to bear with me through the world. Do not tell even your sister; much less your mother the nun, for I am ashamed that she should even know I have ever done that kind of thing."* "Do not fear," answered Koremitsu. "Even to the priests, who must to a certain extent be let into the secret, I have told a long made-up tale," and Genji felt a little easier in his mind.

The waiting-women of his palace were sorely puzzled: "First he says he has been defiled and cannot go to Court, and now he sits whispering and sighing." What could it all mean? "Again I beg you," said Genji at last, "to see that everything is done as it should be." He was thinking all the time of the elaborate Court funerals which he had witnessed (he had, indeed, seen no others) and imagined Koremitsu directing a complicated succession of rituals. "I will do what I can; it will be no such great matter," he answered and turned to go. Suddenly Genji could bear no longer the thought that he should never see her again. "You will think it very foolish of me," he said, "but I am coming with you. I shall ride on horseback." "If your heart is set upon it," said Koremitsu, "it is not for me to reason with you. Let us start soon, so that we may be back before the night is over." So putting on the hunting-dress and ocher garments in which he had disguised himself before, he left his room.

Already the most hideous anguish possessed him, and now, as he set out upon this strange journey, to the dark thoughts that filled his mind was added a dread lest his visit might rouse to some fresh fury the mysterious power which had destroyed her. Should he go? He hesitated; but though he knew that this way lay no cure for his sadness, yet if he did not see her now, never again perhaps in any life to come would he meet the face and form that he had loved so well. So with Koremitsu and the one same groom to bear him company he set out upon the road.

The way seemed endless. The moon of the seventeenth night had risen and lit up the whole space of the Kamo plain, and in the light of the out runners' torches the countryside towards Toribeno now came dimly into sight. But Genji in his sickness and despair saw none of this, and suddenly waking from the stupor into which he had fallen found that they had arrived.

The nun's cell was in a chapel built against the wall of a wooden house. It was a desolate spot, but the chapel itself was very beautiful. The

---

* I.e. pursued illicit amours.

light of the visitor's torches flickered through the open door. In the inner room there was no sound but that of a woman weeping by herself; in the outer room were several priests talking together (or was it praying?) in hushed voices. In the neighboring temples vespers were over and there was absolute stillness; only towards the Kiyomizu were lights visible and many figures seemed to throng the hillside.*

A senior priest, son of the aged nun, now began to recite the Scriptures in an impressive voice, and Genji as he listened felt the tears come into his eyes. He went in. Ukon was lying behind a screen; when she heard him enter, she turned the lamp to the wall. What terrible thing was she trying to hide from him? But when he came nearer he saw to his joy that the dead lady was not changed in any way whatsoever, but lay there very calm and beautiful; and feeling no horror or fear at all he took her hand and said, "speak to me once again; tell me why for so short a while you came to me and filled my heart with gladness, and then so soon forsook me, who loved you so well?" and he wept long and bitterly by her side.

The priests did not know who he was, but they were touched by his evident misery and themselves shed tears. He asked Ukon to come back with him, but she answered: "I have served this lady since she was a little child and never once for so much as an hour have I left her. How can I suddenly part from one who was so dear to me and serve in another's house? And I must now go and tell her people what has become of her; for (such is the manner of her death) if I do not speak soon, there will be an outcry that it was I who was to blame, and that would be a terrible thing for me, Sir," and she burst into tears, wailing, "I will lie with her upon the pyre; my smoke shall mingle with hers!"

"Poor soul," said Genji," I do not wonder at your despair. But this is the way of the world. Late or soon we must all go where she has gone. Take comfort and trust in me." So he sought to console her, but in a moment he added: "Those, I know, are but hollow words. I too care no longer for life and would gladly follow her." So he spoke, giving her in the end but little comfort.

"The night is far spent," said Koremitsu; "we must now be on our way." And so with many backward looks and a heart full to bursting he left the house. A heavy dew had fallen and the mist was so thick that it was hard to see the road. On the way it occurred to him that she was still wearing his scarlet cloak, which he had lent her when they lay down together on the last evening. How closely their lives had been entwined!

Noting that he sat very unsteadily in his saddle, Koremitsu walked beside him and gave him a hand. But when they came to a dyke, he lost

---

* Pilgrimages to Kiyomizu Temple are made on the seventeenth day.

hold and his master fell to the ground. Here he lay in great pain and bewilderment. "I shall not live to finish the journey," he said; "I have not strength to go so far." Koremitsu too was sorely troubled, for he felt that despite all Genji's insistence, he ought never to have allowed him, fever-stricken as he was, to embark upon this disastrous journey. In great agitation he plunged his hands in the river and prayed to Our Lady Kwannon of Kiyomizu. Genji too roused himself at last and forced himself to pray inwardly to the Buddha. And so they managed to start upon their journey again and in the end with Koremitsu's help he reached his palace.

This sudden journey undertaken so late at night had seemed to all his household the height of imprudence. They had noted for some while past his nightly wanderings grow more and more frequent; but though often agitated and preoccupied, never had he returned so haggard as that morning. What could be the object of these continual excursions? And they shook their heads in great concern. Genji flung himself upon his bed and lay there in fever and pain for several days. He was growing very weak. The news was brought to the Emperor who was greatly distressed and ordered continual prayers to be said for him in all the great temples and indeed there were more special services and purification-ceremonies and incantations than I have room to rehearse. When it became known that this prince, so famous for his great charm and beauty, was likely soon to die, there was a great stir in all the kingdom.

Sick though he was he did not forget to send for Ukon and have her enrolled among his gentlewomen. Koremitsu, who was beside himself, with anxiety concerning his master, yet managed on her arrival to calm himself and give to Ukon friendly instruction in her new duties; for he was touched by the helpless plight in which she had been left. And Genji whenever he felt a little better, would use her to carry messages and letters, so that she soon grew used to waiting upon him. She was dressed in deep black and though not at all handsome was a pleasant enough looking woman.

"It seems that the same fate which so early stayed your lady's course has willed that I too should be but little longer for this world. I know in what sore distress you are left by the loss of one who was for so many years you mistress and friend; and it was my purpose to have comforted you in your bereavement by every care and kindness I could devise. For this reason, indeed, it grieves me that I shall survive her for so short a time." So, somewhat stiltedly, he whispered to Ukon, and being now very weak he could not refrain from tears. Apart from the fact that his death would leave her utterly without resource, she had now quite taken to him and would have been very sorry indeed if he had died.

His gentlemen ran hither and thither, distracted; the Emperor's envoys thronged thick as the feet of the raindrops. Hearing of his father's distress and anxiety, Genji strove hard to reassure him by pretending to some slight respite or improvement. His father-in-law too showed great concern, calling every day for news and ordering the performance of various rites and potent liturgies; and it was perhaps as a result of this, that having been dangerously ill for more than twenty days, he took a turn for the better, and soon all his symptoms began to disappear. On the night of his recovery the term of his defilement also ended and hearing that the Emperor was still extremely uneasy about him, he determined to reassure the Court by returning to his official residence at the Palace. His father-in-law came to fetch him in his own carriage and rather irritatingly urged upon him all sorts of remedies and precautions.

For some while everything in the world to which he had now returned seemed strange to him and he indeed scarce knew himself; but by the twentieth day of the ninth month his recovery was complete, nor did the pallor and thinness of his face become him by any means ill.

At times he would stare vacantly before him and burst into loud weeping, and seeing this there were not wanting those who said that he was surely possessed.

Often he would send for Ukon, and once when they had been talking in the still of the evening he said to her, "There is one thing which still puzzles me. Why would she never tell me who she was? For even if she was indeed, as she once said, 'a fisherman's child,' it was a strange perversity to use such reticence with one who loved her so well."

"You ask why she hid her name from you?" said Ukon. "Can you wonder at it? When could she have been expected to tell you her name (not that it would have meant much to you if you had heard it)? For from the beginning you treated her with a strange mistrust, coming with such secrecy and mystery as might well make her doubt whether you were indeed a creature of the waking world. But though you never told her she knew well enough who you were, and the thought that you would not be thus secret had you regarded her as more than a mere plaything or idle distraction was very painful to her."

"What a wretched series of misunderstandings," said Genji. "For my part I had no mind to put a distance between us. But I had no experience in such affairs as this. There are many difficulties in the path of such people as I. First and foremost I feared the anger of my father the Emperor; and then, the foolish jesting of the world. I felt myself hedged in by courtly rules and restrictions. But for all the tiresome concealments that my rank forced upon me, from that first evening I had so strangely set my heart upon her that though reason counseled me I could not hold back; and indeed it seems sometimes to me that an irresistible fate drove me to do the thing of which I now so bitterly and continually repent. But tell me more about her. For there can now be no reason for concealment When on each seventh day I cause the names of the Buddhas to be written for her comfort and salvation, whom am I to name in my inward prayer?"

"There can be no harm in my telling you that," said Ukon, "and I should have done so before, did I not somehow feel it a shame to be prating to you now about things she would not have me speak of while she was alive. Her parents died when she was quite small. Her father, Sammi Chujo, loved her very dearly, but felt always that he could not give her all the advantages to which her great beauty entitled her; and still perplexed about her future and how best to do his duty by her, he died. Soon afterwards some accident brought her into the company of To no Chujo[*] who was at that time still a lieutenant and for three years he made her very happy. But in the autumn of last year disquieting letters began to arrive from the Great Hall of the Right,[†] and being by nature prone to fits of unreasoning fear she now fell into a wild panic and fled to the western part of the town where she hid herself in the house of her old wet-nurse. Here she was very uncomfortable, and had planned to move to a certain village in the hills, when she discovered that it would be unlucky, owing to the position of the stars since the beginning of the year, to make a journey in that direction; and (though she never told me so) I think, Sir, it troubled her sorely that you should have come upon her when she was living in so wretched a place. But there was never anyone in the world like my lady for keeping things to herself; she could never bear that other people should know what was on her mind. I have no doubt, Sir, that she sometimes behaved very oddly to you and that you have seen all this for yourself."

Yes, this was all just as To no Chujo had described. "I think there was some mention of a child that Chujo was vexed to have lost sight of," said Genji, more interested than ever; "am I right?" "Yes, indeed," she answered; "It was born in the spring of last year, a girl, and a fine child it was." "Where is it now?" asked Genji. "Could you get hold of it and bring it to me here without letting anyone know where you were taking it? It would be a great comfort to me in my present misery to have some remembrance of her near me"; and he added, "I ought of course to tell Chujo, but that would lead to useless and painful discussions about what has happened. Somehow or other I will manage to bring her up here in my palace. I think there can be no harm in that. And you will easily enough find some story to tell to whatever people are now looking after her." "I am very glad that this has entered your head," said Ukon, "It would be a poor look-out for her to grow up in the quarter where

---

[*] Chujo means "Captain"; see above, p. 38.
[†] From To no Chujo's wife, who was the daughter of the Minister of the Right.

she is now living. With no one properly belonging to her and in such a part of the town..."

In the stillness of the evening, under a sky of exquisite beauty, here and there along the borders in front of his palace some insect croaked its song; the leaves were just beginning to turn. And as he looked upon this pleasant picture he felt ashamed at the contrast between his surroundings and the little house where Yugao had lived. Suddenly somewhere among the bamboo groves the bird called iyebato uttered its sharp note. He remembered just how she had looked when in the gardens of that fatal house the same bird had startled her by its cry, and turning to Ukon, "How old was she?" he suddenly asked; "for though she seemed childlike in her diffidence and helplessness, that may only have been a sign that she was not long for this world." "She must have been nineteen," said Ukon. "When my mother, who was her first wet-nurse, died and left me an orphan, my lady's father was pleased to notice me and reared me at my lady's side. Ah, Sir, when I think of it, I do not know how I shall live without her; for kind as people here may be I do not seem to get used to them. I suppose it is that I knew her ways, poor lady, she having been my mistress for so many years."

To Genji even the din of the cloth-beaters' mallets had become dear through recollection, and as he lay in bed he repeated those verses of Po Chü-i.

In the eighth month and ninth month when the nights are growing long
A thousand times, ten thousand times the fuller's stick beats.

The young brother still waited upon him, but he no longer brought with him the letters which he had been used to bring. Utsusemi thought he had at last decided that her treatment of him was too unfriendly to be borne, and was vexed that he should feel so. Then suddenly she heard of his illness, and all her vexation turned to consternation and anxiety. She was soon to set out upon her long journey, but this did not much interest her; and to see whether Genji had quite forgotten her she sent him a message saying that she had been able to find no words in which to express her grief at hearing the news of his illness. With it she sent the poem: "I did not ask for news and you did not ask why I was silent; so the days wore on and I remained in sorrow and dismay." He had not forgotten her, no, not in all his trouble; and his answer came: "Of this life, fragile as the utsusemi's* shell, already I was weary, when your word came, and gave me strength to live anew." The poem was written in a very tremulous and confused hand; but she thought the writing very beautiful and it delighted her that he had not forgotten how, cicada-like, she had shed her scarf. There could be no harm in this interchange of notes, but

---

* Cicada.

she had no intention of arranging a meeting. She thought that at last even he had seen that there could be no sense in that.

As for Utsusemi's companion, she was not yet married, and Genji heard that she had become the mistress of To no Chujo's brother, Kurodo no Shosho; and though he feared that Shosho might already have taken very ill the discovery that he was not first in the field, and did not at all wish to offend him, yet he had a certain curiosity about the girl and sent Utsusemi's little brother with a message asking if she had heard of his illness and the poem: "Had I not once gathered for my pillow a handful of the sedge that grows upon the eaves,* not a dewdrop of pretext could my present message find." It was an acrostic with many hidden meanings. He tied the letter to a tall reed and bade him deliver it secretly; but was afterwards very uneasy at the thought that it might go astray. "If it falls into Shosho's hands," he thought, " he will at once guess that it was I who was before him." But after all Shosho would probably not take that so very hard, Genji had vanity enough to think.

The boy delivered the message when Shosho was at a safe distanced. She could not help feeling a little hurt; but it was something that he had remembered her at all, and justifying it to herself with the excuse that she had had no time to do anything better, she sent the boy straight back with the verse: "The faint wind of your favor, that but for a moment blew, with grief has part befrosted the small sedge of the eaves." It was very ill written, with all sorts of ornamental but misleading strokes and flourishes; indeed with a complete lack of style. However, it served to remind him of the face he had first seen that evening by the lamplight! As for the other who on that occasion had sat so stiffly facing her, what determination there had been in her face, what a steady resolution to give no quarter!

The affair with the lady of the sedge was so unintentional and so insignificant that though he regarded it as rather frivolous and indiscreet, he saw no great harm in it. But if he did not take himself in hand before it was too late he would soon again be involved in some entanglement which might finally ruin his reputation.

On the forty-ninth day after Yugao's death a service in her memory was by his orders secretly held in the Hokedo on Mount Hiyei. The ritual performed was of the most elaborate kind, everything that was required being supplied from the Prince's own store; and even the decoration of the service books and images was carried out with the utmost attention. Koremitsu's brother, a man of great piety, was entrusted with the direction of the ceremony, and all went well. Next Genji sent for his old writing-master, a doctor of letters for whom he had a great liking, and

---

* "Sedge upon the eaves" is *Nokiba no Ogi,* and it is by this name that the lady is generally known.

bade him write the prayer for the dead.* "Say that I commit to Amida the Buddha one not named whom I loved, but lost disastrously," and he wrote out a rough draft for the learned man to amend. "There is nothing to add or alter," said the master, deeply moved. Who could it be, he wondered, at whose death the prince was so distressed? (For Genji, try as he might, could not hide his tears.)

When he was secretly looking through his store for largesse to give to the Hokedo priests, he came upon a certain dress and as he folded it made the poem: "The girdle that today with tears I knot, shall we ever in some new life untie?"

Till now her spirit had wandered in the void.†

But already she must be setting out on her new life-path, and in great solicitude, he prayed continually for her safety.

He met To no Chujo and his heart beat violently, for he had longed to tell him about Yugao's child and how it was to be reared. But he feared that the rest of the story would needlessly anger and distress him, and he did not mention the matter. Meanwhile the servants of Yugao's house were surprised that they had had no news from her nor even from Ukon, and had begun to be seriously disquieted. They had still no proof that it was Genji who was her lover, but several of them thought that they had recognized him and his name was whispered among them. They would have it that Koremitsu knew the secret, but he pretended to know nothing whatever about Yugao's lover and found a way to put off all their questions; and as he was still frequenting the house for his own purposes, it I was easy for them to believe that he was not really concerned in their mistress's affairs. Perhaps after all it was some blackguard of a Zuryo's son who, frightened of To no Chujo's interference, had carried her off to his province. The real owner of the house was a daughter of Yugao's second wet-nurse, who had three children of her own. Ukon had been brought up with them, but they thought that it was perhaps because she was not their own sister that Ukon sent them no news of their mistress, and they were in great distress.

Ukon who knew that they would assail her with questions which her promise to Genji forbad her to answer, dared not go to the house, not even to get news of her lady's child. It had been put out somewhere to nurse, but to her great sorrow she had quite lost sight of it.

Longing all the while to see her face once more though only in a dream, upon the night after the ceremony on Mount Hiyei, he had a vision very different from that for which he prayed. There appeared to

---

* *Gwammon.*

† For forty-nine days the spirit of the dead leads the intermediate existence so strangely described in the *Abhidharma Kosa Sastra;* then it begins its new incarnation.

him once more, just as on that fatal night, the figure of a woman in menacing posture, and he was dismayed at the thought that some demon which haunted the desolate spot might on the occasion when it did that terrible thing, also have entered into him and possessed him.

Iyo no Suke was to start early in the Godless Month and had announced that his wife would go with him. Genji sent very handsome parting presents and among them with special intent he put many very exquisite combs and fans. With them were silk strips to offer to the God of Journeys and, above all, the scarf which she had dropped, and, tied to it, a poem in which he said that he had kept it in remembrance of her while there was still hope of their meeting, but now returned it wet with tears shed in vain. There was a long letter with the poem, but this was of no particular interest and is here omitted. She sent no answer by the man who had brought the presents, but gave her brother the poem: "That to the changed cicada you should return her summer dress shows that you too have changed and fills an insect heart with woe."

He thought long about her. Though she had with so strange and inexplicable a resolution steeled her heart against him to the end, yet each time he remembered that she had gone forever it filled him with depression.

It was the first day of the tenth month, and as though in sign that winter had indeed begun, heavy rain fell. All day long Genji watched the stormy sky. Autumn had hideously bereaved him and winter already was taking from him one whom he dearly loved:

Now like a traveler who has tried two ways in vain
I stand perplexed where these sad seasons meet.

Now at least we must suppose he was convinced that such secret adventures led only to misery.

I should indeed be very loath to recount in all their detail matters which he took so much trouble to conceal, did I not know that if you found I had omitted anything you would at once ask why, just because he was supposed to be an Emperor's son, I must needs put a favorable showing on his conduct by leaving out all his indiscretions; and you would soon be saying that this was no history but a mere made-up tale designed to influence the judgment of posterity. As it is I shall be called a scandalmonger; but that I cannot help.

Murasaki

He fell sick of an ague, and when numerous charms and spells had been tried in vain, the illness many times returning, someone said that in a certain temple on the Northern Hills there lived a wise and holy man who in the summer of the year before (the ague was then rife and the usual spells were giving no relief) was able to work many signal cures: "Lose no time in consulting him, for while you try one useless means after another the disease gains greater hold upon you." At once he sent a messenger to fetch the holy man, who however replied that the infirmities of old age no longer permitted him to go abroad. "What is to be done?" said Genji; "I must go secretly to visit him," and taking only four or five trusted servants he set out long before dawn. The place lay somewhat deep into the hills. It was the last day of the third month and in the Capital the blossoms had all fallen. The hill-cherry was not yet out; but as he approached the open country, the mists began to assume strange and lovely forms, which pleased him the more because, being one whose movements were tethered by many proprieties, he had seldom seen such sights before. The temples too delighted him. The holy man lived in a deep cave hollowed out of a high wall of rock. Genji did not send in his name and was in close disguise, but his face was well known and the priest at once recognized him. "Forgive me," he said; "it was you, was it not, who sent for me the other day? Alas, I think no longer of the things of this world and I am afraid I have forgotten how to work my cures. I am very sorry indeed that you have come so far," and pretending to be very much upset, he looked at Genji, laughing. But it was soon apparent that he was a man of very great piety and learning. He wrote out certain talismans and administered them, and read certain spells. By the time this was over, the sun had risen, and Genji went a little way outside the cave and looked around him. From the high ground where he was standing he looked down on a number of scattered hermitages. A winding track led down to a hut which, though it was hedged with the same small brushwood as the rest, was more spaciously planned, having a pleasant roofed alley running out from it, and there were trim copses set around. He asked whose house it was and was told by one of his men that a certain abbot had been living there in retirement for two years. "I know him well," said Genji on hearing the abbot's name; "I should not like to meet him dressed and attended as I am. I hope he will not hear..."

Just then a party of nicely dressed children came out of the house and began to pluck such flowers as are used for the decoration of altars and holy images. "There are some girls with them," said one of Genji's men. "We cannot suppose that His Reverence keeps them. Who then can they be?" and to satisfy his curiosity he went a little way down the hill and watched them. "Yes, there are some very pretty girls, some of them grown up and others quite children," he came back and reported.

During a great part of the morning Genji was busy with his cure. When at last the ceremony was completed, his attendants, dreading the hour at which the fever usually returned, strove to distract his attention by taking him a little way across the mountain to a point from which the Capital could be seen. "How lovely," cried Genji," are those distances half-lost in haze, and that blur of shimmering woods that stretches out on every side. How could anyone be unhappy for a single instant who lived in such a place?" "This is nothing," said one of his men. "If I could but show you the lakes and mountains of other provinces, you would soon see how far they excel all that you here admire"; and he began to tell him first of Mount Fuji and many another famous peak, and then of the West Country with all its pleasant bays and shores, till he quite forgot that it was the hour of his fever. "Yonder, nearest to us," the man continued, pointing to the sea, "is the bay of Akashi in Harima. Note it well; for though it is not a very out-of-the-way place, yet the feeling one has there of being shut off from everything save one huge waste of sea makes it the strangest and most desolate spot I know. And there it is that the daughter of a lay priest who was once governor of the province presides over a mansion of quite disproportionate and unexpected magnificence. He is the descendant of a Prime Minister and was expected to cut a great figure in the world. But he is a man of very singular disposition and is averse to all society. For a time he was an officer in the Palace Guard, but he gave this up and accepted the province of Harima. However he soon quarrelled with the local people and, announcing that he had been badly treated and was going back to the Capital, he did nothing of the sort, but shaved his head and became a lay priest. Then instead of settling, as is usually done, on some secluded hillside, he built himself a house on the seashore, which may seem to you a very strange thing to do; but as a matter of fact, whereas in that province in one place or another a good many recluses have taken up their abode, the mountain-country is far more dull and lonely and would sorely have tried the patience of his young wife and child, and so as a compromise he chose the seashore. Once when I was travelling in the province of Harima I took occasion to visit his house and noted that, though at the Capital he had lived in a very modest style, here he had built on the most magnificent and lavish scale, as though determined in spite of what had happened (now that he was free from the bother of governing the province) to spend the rest of his days in the greatest comfort imaginable. But all the while he was making great preparations for the life to come and no ordained priest could have led a more austere and pious life."

"But you spoke of his daughter?" said Genji. "She is passably good-looking," he answered, "and not by any means stupid. Several governors and officers of the province have set their hearts upon her and pressed their suit most urgently, but her father has sent them all away. It seems that though in his own person so indifferent to worldly glory, he is determined that this one child, his only object of care, should make amends for his obscurity, and has sworn that if ever she chooses against his will, and when he is gone flouts his set purpose and injunction to satisfy some idle fancy of her own, his ghost will rise and call upon the sea to cover her."

Genji listened with great attention. "Why, she is like the vestal virgin who may know no husband but the King-Dragon of the Sea," and they laughed at the old ex-Governor's absurd ambitions. The teller of the story was a son of the present Governor of Harima, who from being a clerk in the Treasury had last year been capped an officer of the Fifth Rank. He was famous for his love-adventures and the others whispered to one another that it was with every intention of persuading the lady to disobey her father's injunctions that he had gone out of his way to visit the shore of Akashi.

"I fear her breeding must be somewhat countrified," said one; "it cannot well be otherwise, seeing that she has grown up with no other company than that of her old-fashioned parents—though indeed it appears that her mother was a person of some consequence." "Why, yes," said Yoshikiyo, the Governor's son, "and for this reason she was able to secure little girls and boys from all the best houses in the Capital, persuading them to pay visits to the seaside and be playmates to her own little girl, who thus acquired the most polished breeding." "If an unscrupulous person were to find himself in that quarter," said another, "I fear that despite the dead father's curse he might not find it easy to resist her."

The story made a deep impression upon Genji's imagination. As his gentlemen well knew, whatever was fantastic or grotesque both in people and situations at once strongly attracted him. They were therefore not surprised to see him listen with so much attention. "It is now well past noon," said one of them, "and I think we may reckon that you will get safely through the day without a return of your complaint. So let us soon be starting for home." But the priest persuaded him to stay a little longer: "The sinister influences are not yet wholly banished," he said; "it would be well that a further ritual should continue quietly during the night. By tomorrow morning, I think you will be able to proceed." His gentlemen all urged him to stay; nor was he at all unwilling, for the novelty of such a lodging amused him. "Very well then, at dawn," he said, and having nothing to do till bedtime which was still a long way off, he went out on to the hillside, and under cover of the heavy evening mist loitered near the brushwood hedge. His attendants had gone back to the hermit's cave and only Koremitsu was with him. In the western wing, opposite which he was standing, was a nun at her devotions. The blind was partly raised. He thought she seemed to be dedicating flowers to an image. Sitting near the middle pillar, a sutra-book propped upon stool by her side, was another nun. She was reading aloud; there was look of great unhappiness in her face. She seemed to be about forty; not a woman of the common people. Her skin was white and very fine, and though she was much emaciated, there was a certain roundness and fullness in her cheeks, and her hair, clipped short on a level with her eye hung in so delicate a fringe across her brow that she looked, thought Genji, more elegant and even fashionable in this convent guise than if her hair had been long. Two very well conditioned maids waited upon her. Several little girls came running in and out of the room at play. Among them was one who seemed to be about ten years old. She came running into the room dressed in a rather worn white frock lined with stuff of a deep saffron color. Never had he seen a child like this. What an astonishing creature she would grow into! Her hair, thick and wavy, stood out fanwise about her head. She was very flushed and her lips were trembling. "What is it? Have you quarreled with one of the other little girls?" The nun raised her head as she spoke and Genji fancied that there was some resemblance between her and the child. No doubt she was its mother. "Inu has let out my sparrow—the little one that I kept in the clothes-basket," she said, looking very unhappy. "What a tiresome boy that Inu is!" said one of the two maids. "He deserves a good scolding for playing such a stupid trick. Where can it have got to? And this after we had taken so much trouble to tame it nicely! I only hope the crows have not found it," and so saying she left the room. She was a pleasant looking woman, with very long, wavy hair. The others called her Nurse Shonagon, and she seemed to be in charge of the child. "Come," said the nun to the little girl, "you must not be such a baby. You are thinking all the time of things that do not matter at all. Just fancy! Even now when I am so ill that any day I may be taken from you, you do not trouble your head about me, but are grieving about a sparrow. It is very unkind, particularly as I have told you I don't know how many times that it is naughty to shut up live things in cages. Come over here!" and the child sat down beside her. Her features were very exquisite; but it was above all the way her hair grew, in cloudy masses over her temples, but thrust back in childish fashion from her forehead, that struck him as marvelously beautiful. As he watched her and wondered what she would be like when she grew up it suddenly occurred to him that she bore no small resemblance to one whom he had loved with all his being,[*] and at the resemblance he secretly wept.

The nun, stroking the child's hair, now said to her: "It's a lovely mop though you *are* so naughty about having it combed. But it worries me very much that you are still so babyish. Some children of your age are very different. Your dear mother was only twelve when her father died; yet she showed herself quite capable of managing her own affairs. But if I were taken from you now, I do not know what would become of you, I do not indeed," and she began to weep. Even Genji, peeping at the scene from a distance, found himself becoming quite distressed. The girl, who had been watching the nun's face with a strange unchildish intensity, now dropped her head disconsolately, and as she did so her hair fell forward across her cheeks in two great waves of black. Looking at her fondly, the nun recited the poem: "Not knowing if any will come to nurture the tender leaf whereon it lies, how loath is the dewdrop to vanish in the sunny air." To which the waiting-woman replied with a sigh: "O dewdrop, surely you will linger till the young budding leaf has shown in what fair form it means to grow."

At this moment the priest to whom the house belonged entered the room from the other side: "Pray, ladies," he said, "are you not unduly exposing yourselves? You have chosen a bad day to take up your stand so close to the window. I have just heard that Prince Genji has come to the hermit yonder to be cured of an ague. But he has disguised himself in so mean a habit that I did not know him, and have been so near all day without going to pay my respects to him." The nun started back in horror; "How distressing! He may even have passed and seen us..." and she hastened to let down the folding blind. "I am really very glad that I am to have an opportunity of visiting this Prince Genji of whom one hears so much. He is said to be so handsome that even austere old priests like myself forget in his presence the sins and sorrows of the life they have discarded and take heart to live a little longer in a world where so much beauty dwells. But you shall hear all about it..."

Before the old priest had time to leave the house Genji was on his way back to the hermit's cave. What an enchanting creature he had discovered! How right too his friends had been on that rainy night when they told him that on strange excursions such as this beauty might well be found lurking in unexpected quarters! How delightful to have strolled out by chance and at once made so astonishing a find! Whose could this exquisite child be? He would dearly love to have her always near him, to be able to turn to her at any moment for comfort and distraction, as once he had turned to the lady in the Palace.

---

[*] Fujitsubo, who was indeed the child's aunt.

He was already lying down in the hermit's cave when (everything being at very close quarters) he heard the voice of the old priest's disciple calling for Koremitsu. "My master has just learnt," said this disciple, "that you were lodged so near at hand; and though it grieves him that you did not in passing honor him with a visit, he would at once have paid his respects to the Prince, had he not thought that Lord Genji could not be unaware of his presence in the neighborhood of this hermitage, and might perhaps have refrained from visiting him only because he did not wish to disclose the motive of his present pilgrimage. But my master would remind you," continued the man, "that we too in our poor hut could provide you with straw beds to lie on, and should be sorry if you went without honoring us…"

"For ten days," answered Genji from within, "I have been suffering from an ague which returned so constantly that I was in despair, when someone advised me to consult the hermit of this mountain, whom I accordingly visited. But thinking that it would be very disagreeable for a sage of his repute if in such a case as mine it became known that his treatment had been unsuccessful, I was at greater pains to conceal myself than I should have been if visiting an ordinary wonder-worker. Pray ask your master to accept this excuse and bid him enter the cave." Thus encouraged, the priest presented himself. Genji was rather afraid of him, for though an ecclesiastic he was a man of superior genius, very much respected in the secular world, and Genji felt that it was not at all proper to receive him in the shabby old clothes which he had used for his disguise. After giving some details of his life since he had left the Capital and come to live in retirement on this mountain, the priest begged Genji to come back with him and visit the cold spring which flowed in the garden of his hut. Here was an opportunity to see again the people who had so much interested him. But the thought of all the stories that the old priest might have told them about him made him feel rather uncomfortable. What matter? At all costs he must see that lovely child again and he followed the old priest back to his hut. In the garden the natural vegetation of the hillside had been turned to skilful use. There was no moon, and torches had been lit along the sides of the moat, while fairy lanterns hung on the trees. The front parlor was very nicely arranged. A heavy perfume of costly and exotic scents stole from hidden incense-burners and filled the room with a delicious fragrance. These perfumes were quite unfamiliar to Genji and he supposed that they must have been prepared by the ladies of the inner room, who would seem to have spent considerable ingenuity in the task.

The priest began to tell stories about the uncertainty of this life and the retributions of the life to come. Genji was appalled to think how heavy his own sins had already been. It was bad enough to think that he would have them on his conscience for the rest of his present life. But then there was also the life to come. What terrible punishments he had to look forward to! And all the while the priest was speaking Genji thought of his own wickedness. What a good idea it would be to turn hermit and live in some such place... But immediately his thoughts strayed to the lovely face which he had seen that afternoon and longing to know more of her, "Who lives with you here?" he asked. "It interests me to know, because I once saw this place in a dream and was astonished to recognize it when I came here today." At this the priest laughed: "Your dream seems to have come rather suddenly into the conversation," he said, "but I fear that if you pursue your enquiry, your expectations will be sadly disappointed. You have probably never heard of Azechi no Dainagon, he died so long ago. He married my sister, who after his death turned her back upon the world. Just at that time I myself was in certain difficulties and was unable to visit the Capital; so for company she came to join me here in my retreat."

"I have heard that Asechi no Dainagon had a daughter. Is that so?" said Genji at a venture; "I am sure you will not think I ask the question with any indiscreet intention..." "He had an only daughter who died about ten years ago. Her father had always wanted to present her at Court. But she would not listen, and when he was dead and there was only my sister the nun to look after her, she allowed some wretched go-between to introduce her to Prince Hyobukyo whose mistress she became. His wife, a proud, relentless woman, from the first pursued her with constant vexations and affronts; day in and day out this obstinate persecution continued, till at last she died of heartbreak. They say that unkindness cannot kill; but I shall never say so, for from this cause alone I saw my kinswoman fall sick and perish."

"Then the little girl must be this lady's child," Genji realized at last. And that accounted for her resemblance to the lady in the Palace.* He felt more drawn towards her than ever. She was of good lineage, which is never amiss; and her rather rustic simplicity would be an actual advantage when she became his pupil, as he was now determined she should; for it would make it the easier for him to mould her unformed tastes to the pattern of his own. "And did the lady whose sad story you have told me leave no remembrance behind her?" asked Genji, still hoping to turn the conversation on to the child herself. "She died only a short while after her child was born, and it too was a girl. The charge of it fell to my sister who is in failing health and feels herself by no means equal to such a responsibility." All was now clear. "You will think it a very strange proposal," said Genji, "but I feel that I should like to adopt

---

* Fujitsubo, who was Hyobukyo's sister.

this child. Perhaps you would mention this to your sister? Though others early involved me in marriage, their choice proved distasteful to me and having, as it seems, very little relish for society, I now live entirely alone. She is, I quite realize, a mere child, and I am not proposing..." Here he paused and the priest answered: "I am very much obliged to you for this offer; but I am afraid it is clear that you do *not* at all realize that the child in question is a mere infant. You would not even find her amusing as a casual distraction. But it is true that a girl as she grows up needs the backing of powerful friends if she is to make her way in the world, and though I cannot promise you that anything will come of it, I ought certainly to mention the matter to her grandmother." His manner had suddenly become somewhat cool and severe. Genji felt that he had been indiscreet and preserved an embarrassed silence. "There is something which I ought to be doing in the Hall of Our Lord Amida," the priest presently continued, "so I must take leave of you for a while. I must also read my vespers; but I will rejoin you afterwards," and he set out climb the hill. Genji felt very disconsolate. It had begun to rain; a cold wind blew across the hill, carrying with it the sound of a waterfall—audible till then as a gentle intermittent splashing, but now a mighty roar; and with it, somnolently rising and falling, mingled the monotonous chanting of the scriptures. Even the most unimpressionable nature would have been plunged into melancholy by such surroundings. How much the more so Prince Genji, as he lay sleepless on his bed, continually planning and counter-planning! The priest had spoken of "vespers," but the hour was indeed very late. It was clear however that the nun was still awake, for though she was making as little noise possible, every now and then her rosary would knock with a faint click against the praying-stool. There was something alluring in the sound of this low, delicate tapping. It seemed to come from quite close. He opened a small space between the screens which divided the living room from the inner chamber and rustled his fan. He had the impression that someone in the inner room after a little hesitation had come towards the screen as though saying to herself, "It cannot be so, yet I could have sworn I heard..." and then retreated a little; as though thinking, "Well, it was only my fancy after all!" Now she seemed to be feeling her way in the dark, and Genji said aloud, "Follow the Lord Buddha and though your way lie in darkness yet shall you not go astray." Suddenly hearing his clear young voice in the darkness, the woman had not at first the courage to reply. But at last she managed to answer: "In which direction, please, is He leading me? I am afraid I do not quite understand." "I am sorry, to have startled you," said Genji. "I have only this small request to make: that you will carry to your mistress the following poem: 'Since first he saw the green leaf of the tender bush, never for a moment has the dew of longing dried from the traveler's sleeve.'" "Surely you must know that there is no one here who understands messages of that kind," said the woman; "I wonder whom you mean?" "I have a particular reason for wishing your mistress to receive the message," said Genji, "and I should be obliged if you would contrive to deliver it." The nun at once perceived that the poem referred to her grandchild and supposed that Genji, having been wrongly informed about her age, was intending to make love to her. But how had he discovered her granddaughter's existence? For some while she pondered in great annoyance and perplexity, and at last answered prudently with a poem in which she said that "he who was but spending a night upon a traveler's dewy bed could know little of those whose home was forever upon the cold moss of the hillside." Thus she turned his poem to a harmless meaning. "Tell her," said Genji when the message was brought back, "that I am not accustomed to carry on conversations in this indirect manner. However shy she may be, I must ask her on this occasion to dispense with formalities and discuss this matter with me seriously!" "How can he have been thus misinformed?" said the nun, still thinking that Genji imagined her granddaughter to be a grown-up woman. She was terrified at being suddenly commanded to appear before this illustrious personage and was wondering what excuse she would make. Her maids, however, were convinced that Genji would be grievously offended if she did not appear, and at last, coming out from the women's chamber, she said to him: "Though I am no longer a young woman, I very much doubt whether I ought to come like this. But since you sent word that you have serious business to discuss with me, I could not refuse..." "Perhaps," said Genji, "you will think my proposal both ill-timed and frivolous. I can only assure you that I mean it very seriously. Let Buddha judge..." But here he broke off, intimidated by her age and gravity. "You have certainly chosen a very strange manner of communicating this proposal to me. But though you have not yet said what it is, I am sure you are quite in earnest about it." Thus encouraged, Genji continued: "I was deeply touched by the story of your long widowhood and of your daughter's death. I too, like this poor child, was deprived in earliest infancy of the one being who tenderly loved me, and in my childhood suffered long years of loneliness and misery. Thus we are both in like case, and this has given me so deep a sympathy for the child that I long to make amends for what she has lost. It was, then, to ask if you would consent to let me play a mother's part that at this strange and inconvenient hour I trespassed so inconsiderately upon your patience." "I am sure that you are meaning to be very kind," said the nun, "but—forgive me—you have evidently been misinformed. There is indeed a girl living here under my charge; but she is a mere infant and could not be of the slightest interest to you in any way, so that I cannot consent to your proposal." "On the contrary," said

Genji, "I am perfectly conversant with every detail concerning this child; but if you think my sympathy for her exaggerated or misplaced, pray pardon me for having mentioned it." It was evident that he did not in the least realize the absurdity of what he had proposed, and she saw no use in explaining herself any further. The priest was now returning and Genji, saying that he had not expected she would at once fall in with his idea and was confident that she would soon see the matter in a different light, closed the screen behind her.

The night was almost over. In a chapel near by, the Four Meditations of the Law Flower were being practiced. The voices of the ministrants who were now chanting the Litany of Atonement came floating on the gusty mountain-wind, and with this solemn sound was mingled the roar of hurrying waters. "Startled from my dream by a wandering gust of the mountain gale, I heard the waterfall, and at the beauty of its music wept." So Genji greeted the priest; and he in turn replied with the poem, "At the noise of a torrent wherein I daily fill my bowl I am scarce likely to start back in wonder and delight." "I get so used to it," he added apologetically. A heavy mist covered the morning sky, and even the chirruping of the mountain-birds sounded muffled and dim. Such a variety of flowers and blossoming trees (he did not know their names) grew upon the hillside that the rocks seemed to be spread with a many-colored embroidery. Above all he marveled at the exquisite stepping of the deer who moved across the slope, now treading daintily, now suddenly pausing; and as he watched them the last remnants of his sickness were dispelled by sheer delight. Though the hermit had little use of his limbs, he managed by hook or crook to perform the mystic motions of the Guardian Spell[*] and though his aged voice was husky and faltering, he read the sacred text with great dignity and fervor. Several of Genji's friends now arrived to congratulate him upon his recovery, among them a messenger from the Palace. The priest from the hut below brought a present of strange-looking roots for which he had gone deep into the ravine. He begged to be excused from accompanying Genji on his way. "Till the end of the year," he said, "I am bound by a vow which must deprive me of what would have been a great pleasure," and he handed Genji the stirrup-cup. "Were I but able to follow my own desires," said Genji taking the cup,

---

[*] The Guardian Spell (*goshin*) is practiced as follows:

The ministrant holds the palms of his hands together with middle fingers touching and extended, first fingers separated and bent, tips of thumbs and little fingers bunched together, and third fingers in line with middle fingers so as to be invisible from in front. With hands in this sacred pose (*mudra*) he touches the worshipper on forehead, left and right shoulder, heart and throat. At each contact he utters the spell

ON. BASARA GONJI HARAJUBATA. SOHAKA

which is corrupt Sanskrit and means "I invoke thee, thou diamond-fiery very majestic Star." The deity here invoked is Vairocana, favorite Buddha of the Mystic Sect.

"I would not leave these hills and streams. But I hear that my father the Emperor is making anxious enquiry after me. I will come back before the blossom is over." And he recited the verse, "I will go back to the men of the City and tell them to come quickly, lest the wild wind outstripping them should toss these blossoms from the cherry bough." The old priest, flattered by Genji's politeness and captivated by the charm of his voice, answered with the poem: "Like one who finds the aloe-tree in bloom, to the flower of the mountain-cherry I no longer turn my gaze." "I am not after all quite so great a rarity as the aloe-flower," said Genji smiling.

Next the hermit handed him a parting-cup, with the poem: "Though seldom I open, the pine-tree door of my mountain-cell, yet have I now seen face to face the flower few live to see," and as he looked up at Genji, his eyes filled with tears: He gave him, to keep him safe in future from all harm, a magical wand; and seeing this the nun's brother in his turn presented a rosary brought back from Korea by Prince Shotoku. It was ornamented with jade and was still in the same Chinese-looking box in which it had been brought from that country. The box was in an open-work bag, and a five-leafed pine-branch was with it. He also gave him some little vases of blue crystal to keep his medicines in, with sprays of cherry-blossom and wisteria along with them, and such other presents as the place could supply. Genji had sent to the Capital for gifts with which to repay his reception in the mountain. First he gave a reward to the hermit, then distributed alms to the priests who had chanted liturgies on his behalf, and finally he gave useful presents to the poor villagers of the neighborhood. While he was reading a short passage from the scriptures in preparation for his departure, the old priest went into his house and asked his sister the nun whether she had any message for the Prince. "It is very, hard to say anything at present," she said. "Perhaps if he still felt the same inclination four, or five years hence, we might begin to consider it." "That is just what I think," said the priest.

Genji saw to his regret that he had made no progress whatever. In answer to the nun's message he sent a small boy who belonged to the priest's household with the following poem: "Last night indeed, though in the grayness of twilight only, I saw the lovely flower. But today a hateful mist has hidden it utterly from my sight." The nun replied: "That I may know whether indeed it pains you so deeply to leave this flower, I shall watch intently the motions of this hazy sky." It was written in a noteworthy and very aristocratic hand, but quite without the graces of deliberate artistry. While his carriage was being got ready, a great company of young lords arrived from the Great Hall, saying that they had been hard put to it to discover what had become of him and now desired to give him their escort. Among them were To no Chujo, Sachu Ben, and other lesser lords, who had come out of affection for the Prince. "We like nothing better than waiting upon you," they said, rather aggrieved, "it was not kind of you to leave us behind." "But having come so far," said another, "it would be a pity to go away without resting for a while under the shadow of these flowering trees"; whereupon they all sat down in a row upon the moss under a tall rock and passed a rough earthenware wine-jar from hand to hand. Close by them the stream leaped over the rocks in a magnificent cascade. To no Chujo pulled out a flute from the folds of his dress and played a few trills upon it. Sachu Ben, tapping idly with his fan, began to sing "The Temple of Toyora." The young lords who had come to fetch him were all persons of great distinction; but so striking was Genji's appearance as he sat leaning disconsolately against the rock that no eye was likely to be turned in any other direction. One of his attendants now performed upon the reed pipe; someone else turned out to be a skillful *sho** player. Presently the old priest came out of his house carrying a zithern, and putting it into Genji's hands begged him to play something, "that the birds of the mountain may rejoice." He protested that he was not feeling at all in the mood to play; but yielding to the priest's persuasion, he gave what was really not at all a contemptible performance. After that, they all got up and started for home. Everyone on the mountain, down to the humblest priest and youngest neophyte, was bitterly disappointed at the shortness of his stay, and there were many tears shed; while the old nun within doors was sorry to think that she had had but that one brief glimpse of him and might never see him again. The priest declared that for his part he thought the Land of the Rising Sun in her last degenerate days ill-deserved that such a Prince should be born to her, and he wiped his eyes. The little girl too was very much pleased with him and said he was a prettier gentleman than her own father. "If you think so, you had better become his little girl instead," said her nurse. At which the child nodded, thinking that it would be a very good plan indeed; and in future the best-dressed person in the pictures she painted was called Prince Genji, and so was her handsomest doll.

On his return to the Capital he went straight to the Palace and described to his father the experiences of the last two days. The Emperor thought him looking very haggard and was much concerned. He asked many questions about the hermit's magical powers, to all of which Genji replied in great detail. "He ought certainly to have been made Master Magician long ago," said His Majesty. "His ministrations have repeatedly been attended with great success, but for some reason his services have escaped public acknowledgment," and he issued a proclamation to this effect. The Minister of the Left came to meet him on his way from the Presence and apologized for not having come with his sons to bring him

---

* A Chinese instrument; often translated as "mouth-organ."

back from the mountain. "I thought," he said, "that as you had gone there secretly, you would dislike being fetched; but I very much hope that you will now come and spend a few days with us quietly; after which I shall esteem it a privilege to escort you to your palace." He did not in the least want to go, but there was no escape. His father-in-law drove him to the Great Hall in his own carriage, and when the bullocks had been unyoked dragged it in at the gate with his own hands. Such treatment was certainly meant to be very friendly; but Genji found the Minister's attentions merely irritating.

Aoi's quarters had, in anticipation of Genji's coming, just been put thoroughly to rights. In the long interval since he last visited her many changes had been made; among other improvements, a handsome terrace had been built. Not a thing was out of its right place in this supremely well-ordered house. Aoi, as usual, was nowhere to be seen. It was only after repeated entreaties by her father that she at last consented to appear in her husband's presence. Posed like a princess in a picture she sat almost motionless. Beautiful she certainly was. "I should like to tell you about my visit to the mountain, if only I thought that it would interest you at all or draw an answer from you. I hate to go on always like this. Why are you so cold and distant and proud? Year after year we fail to reach an understanding and you cut yourself off from me more completely than before. Can we not manage for a little while to be on ordinary terms? It seems rather strange, considering how ill I have been, that you should not attempt to enquire after my health. Or rather, it is exactly what I should expect; but nevertheless I find it extremely painful." "Yes," said Aoi, "it is extremely painful when people do not care what becomes of one." She glanced back over her shoulder as she spoke, her face full of scorn and pride, looking uncommonly handsome as she did so. "You hardly ever speak," said Genji, "and when you do, it is only to say unkind things and twist one's harmless words so that they seem to be insults. And when I try to find some way of helping you for a while at least to be a little less disagreeable, you become more hopelessly unapproachable than ever. Shall I one day succeed in making you understand...?" and so saying he went into their bedroom. She did not follow him. He lay for a while in a state of great annoyance and distress. But, probably because he did not really care about her very much one way or the other, he soon became drowsy and all sorts of quite different matters drifted through his head. He wanted as much as ever to have the little girl in his keeping and watch her grow to womanhood. But the grandmother was right; the child was too absurdly young, and it would be very difficult to broach the matter again. Would it not however be possible to contrive that she should be brought to the Capital? It would be easy then to find excuses for fetching her and she might, even through some such arrangement as that, become a source of constant delight to him. The father, Prince Hyobukyo, was of course a man of very distinguished manners; but he was not at all handsome. How was it that the child resembled one of her aunts and was so unlike all the rest? He had an idea that Fujitsubo and Prince Hyobukyo were children of the same mother, while the others were only half-sisters. The fact that the little girl was closely related to the lady whom he had loved for so long made him all the more set upon securing her, and he began again to puzzle his head for some means of bringing this about.

Next day he wrote his letter of thanks to the priest. No doubt it contained some allusion to his project. To the nun he wrote: "Seeing you so resolutely averse to what I had proposed, I refrained from justifying my intentions so fully as I could have wished. But should it prove that, even by the few words I ventured to speak, I was able to convince you that this is no mere whim or common fancy, how happy would such news make me." On a slip of paper folded small and tucked into the letter he wrote the poem: "Though with all my heart I tried to leave it behind me, never for a moment has it left me—the fair face of that mountain-flower!" Though she had long passed the zenith of her years the nun could not but be pleased and flattered by the elegance of the note; for it was not only written in an exquisite hand, but was folded with a careless dexterity which she greatly admired. She felt very sorry for him, and would have been glad, had it been in her conscience, to have sent him a more favorable reply. "We were delighted," she wrote, "that being in the neighborhood you took occasion to pay us a visit. But I fear that when (as I very much hope you will) you come here purposely to visit us, I shall not be able to add anything to what I have said already. As for the poem which you enclose, do not expect her to answer it, for she cannot yet write her "Naniwa Zu"* properly, even letter by letter. Let me then answer it for her: 'For as long as the cherry-blossoms remain unscattered upon the shore of Onoe where wild storms blow—so long have you till now been constant!' For my part, I am very uneasy about the matter."

The priest replied to the same effect. Genji was very much disappointed and after two or three days he sent for Koremitsu and gave him a letter for the nun, telling him at the same time to find out whatever he could from Shonagon, the child's nurse. "What an impressionable character he is, thought Koremitsu. He had only had a glimpse of the child; but that had sufficed to convince him that she was a mere baby, though he remembered thinking her quite pretty. What trick would his master's heart be playing upon him next?

The old priest was deeply impressed by the arrival of a letter in the hands of so special and confidential a messenger. After delivering it,

---

* A song the words of which were used as a first writing lesson.

Koremitsu sought out the nurse. He repeated all that Genji had told him to say and added a great deal of general information about his master. Being a man of many words he talked on and on, continually introducing some new topic which had suddenly occurred to him as relevant. But at the end of it all Shonagon was just as puzzled as everyone else had been to account for Genji's interest in a child so ridiculously young. His letter was very deferential. In it he said that he longed to see a specimen of her childish writing done letter by letter, as the nun had described. As before, he enclosed a poem: "Was it the shadows in the mountain well that told you my purpose was but jest?"* To which she answered, "some perhaps that have drawn in that well now bitterly repent. Can the shadows tell me if again it will be so?" and Koremitsu brought a spoken message to the same effect, together with the assurance that so soon as the nun's health improved, she intended to visit the Capital and would then communicate with him again. The prospect of her visit was very exciting.

About this time Lady Fujitsubo fell ill and retired for a while from the Palace. The sight of the Emperor's grief and anxiety moved Genji's pity. But he could not help thinking that this was an opportunity which must not be missed. He spent the whole of that day in a state of great agitation, unable whether in his own house or at the Palace to think of anything else or call upon anyone. When at last the day was over, he succeeded in persuading her maid Omyobu to take a message. The girl, though she regarded any communication between them as most imprudent, seeing a strange look in his face like that of one who walks in a dream, took pity on him and went. The Princess looked back upon their former relationship as something wicked and horrible and the memory of it was a continual torment to her. She had determined that such a thing must never happen again.

She met him with a stern and sorrowful countenance, but this did not disguise her charm, and as though conscious that he was unduly admiring her she began to treat him with great coldness and disdain. He longed to find some blemish in her, to think that he had been mistaken, and be at peace.

I need not tell all that happened. The night passed only too quickly. He whispered in her ear the poem: "Now that at last we have met, would that we might vanish forever into the dream we dreamed tonight!" But she, still conscience-stricken: "Though I were to hide in the darkness of eternal sleep, yet would my shame run through the world from tongue to tongue." And indeed, as Genji knew, it was not without good cause that she had suddenly fallen into this fit of apprehension and remorse. As he left, Omyobu came running after him with his cloak and other

---

* There is here a pun, and a reference to poem 3807 in the *Manyoshu*.

belongings which he had left behind. He lay all day upon his bed in great torment. He sent a letter, but it was returned unopened. This had happened many times in the past, but now it filled him with such consternation that for two or three days he was completely prostrate and kept his room. All this while he was in constant dread lest his father, full of solicitude, should begin enquiring what new trouble had overtaken him. Fujitsubo, convinced that her ruin was accomplished, fell into a profound melancholy and her health grew daily worse. Messengers arrived constantly from the Court begging her to return without delay; but she could not bring herself to go. Her disorder had now taken a turn which filled her with secret foreboding, and she did nothing all day long but sit distractedly wondering what would become of her. When the hot weather set in she ceased to leave her bed at all. Three months had now passed and there was so mistaking her condition. Soon it would be known and everywhere discussed. She was appalled at the calamity which had overtaken her. Not knowing that there was any cause for secrecy, her people were astonished that she had not long ago informed the Emperor of her condition. Speculations were rife, but the question was one which only the Princess herself was in a position definitely to solve. Omyobu and her old nurse's daughter who waited upon her at her toilet and in the bath-house had at once noted the change and were somewhat taken aback. But Omyobu was unwilling to discuss the matter. She had an uncomfortable suspicion that it was the meeting which she arranged that had now taken effect with cruel promptness and precision. It was announced in the Palace that other disorders had misled those about her and prevented them from recognizing the true nature of her condition. This explanation was accepted by everyone.

The Emperor himself was full of tender concern, and though messengers kept him constantly informed, the gloomiest doubts and fancies passed continually through his mind. Genji was at this time visited by a most terrifying and extraordinary dream. He sent for interpreters, but they could make little of it. There were indeed certain passages to which they could assign no meaning at all; but this much was clear: the dreamer had made a false step and must be on his guard. "It was not *my* dream," said Genji, feeling somewhat alarmed. "I am consulting you on behalf of someone else," and he was wondering what this "false step" could have been when news reached him of the Princess's condition. This then was the disaster which his dream had portended! At once he wrote her an immense letter full of passionate self-reproaches and exhortations. But Omyobu, thinking that it would only increase her agitation, refused to deliver it, and he could trust no other messenger. Even the few wretched lines which she had been in the habit of sending to him now and again had for some while utterly ceased.

In her seventh month she again appeared at Court. Overjoyed at her return, the Emperor lavished boundless affection upon her. The added fullness of her figure, the unwonted pallor and thinness of her face gave her, he thought, a new and incomparable charm. As before, all his leisure was spent in her company. During this time several Court festivals took place and Genji's presence was constantly required; sometimes he was called upon to play the *koto* or flute, sometimes to serve his father in other ways. On such occasions, strive as he might to show no trace of embarrassment or agitation, he feared more than once that he had betrayed himself; while to her such confrontations were one long torment.

The nun had somewhat improved in health and was now living in the Capital. He had enquired where she was lodging and sent messages from time to time, receiving (which indeed was all he expected) as little encouragement as before. In the last months his longing for the child had increased rather than diminished, but day after day went by without his finding any means to change the situation. As the autumn drew to its close, he fell into a state of great despondency. One fine moonlit night when he had decided, against his own inclination, to pay a certain secret visit,* a shower came on. As he had started from the Palace and the place to which he was going was in the suburbs of the Sixth Ward, it occurred to him that it would be disagreeable to go so far in the rain. He was considering what he should do when he noticed a tumbled-down house surrounded by very ancient trees. He asked whose this gloomy and desolate mansion might be, and Koremitsu, who, as usual, was with him, replied "Why that is the late Azechi no Dainagon's house. A day or two ago I took occasion to call there and was told that my Lady the nun has grown very weak and does not now know what goes on about her." "Why did you not tell me this before?" said Genji deeply concerned; "I should have called at once to convey my sympathy to her household. Pray go in at once and ask for news." Koremitsu accordingly sent one of the lesser attendants to the house, instructing him to give the impression that Genji had come on purpose to enquire. When the man announced that Prince Genji had sent him for news and was himself waiting outside, great excitement and consternation prevailed in the house. Their mistress, the servants said, had for several days been lying in a very parlous condition and could not possibly receive a visit. But they dared not simply send so distinguished a visitor away, and hastily tidying the southern parlor, they bustled him into it, saying, "You must forgive us for showing you into this untidy room. We have done our best to make it presentable. Perhaps, on a surprise visit, you will forgive us for conducting you to such an out-of-the-way closet…" It was indeed not at all the kind of room

---

* To Lady Rokujo.

that he was used to. "I have been meaning for a long while to visit this house," said Genji, "but time after time the proposals which I made in writing concerning a certain project of mine were summarily rejected and this discouraged me. Had I but known that your mistress's health had taken this turn for the worse..." "Tell him that at this moment my mind is clear, though it may soon be darkened again. I am deeply sensible of the kindness he has shown in thus visiting my deathbed, and regret that I cannot speak with him face to face. Tell him that if by any chance he has not altered his mind with regard to the matter that he has discussed with me before, by all means let him, when the time has come, number her among the ladies of his household. It is with great anxiety that I leave her behind me and I fear that such a bond with earth may hinder me from reaching the life for which I have prayed."

Her room was so near and the partition so thin that as she gave Shonagon her message he could hear now and again the sound of her sad, quavering voice. Presently he heard her saying to someone, "How kind, how very kind of him to come. If only the child were old enough to thank him nicely!" "It is indeed no question of kindness," said Genji to Shonagon. "Surely it is evident that only some very deep feeling would have driven me to display so zealous a persistency! Since first I saw this child, a feeling of strange tenderness towards her possessed me, and it has grown to such a love as cannot be of this world only.* Though it is but an idle fancy, I have a longing to hear her voice. Could you not send for her before I go?" "Poor little thing," said Shonagon. "She is fast asleep in her room and knows nothing of all our troubles." But as she spoke there was a sound of someone moving in the women's quarters and a voice suddenly was heard saying: "Grandmother, Grandmother! Prince Genji who came to see us in the mountains is here, paying a visit. Why do you not let him come and talk to you?" "Hush, child, hush!" cried all the gentlewomen, scandalized. "No, no," said the child; "Grandmother said that when she saw this prince it made her feel better at once. I was not being silly at all." This speech delighted Genji; but the gentlewomen of the household thought the child's incursion painful and unseemly, and pretended not to hear her last remark. Genji gave up the idea of paying a real visit and drove back to his house, thinking as he went that her behavior was indeed still that of a mere infant. Yet how easy and delightful it would be to teach her!

Next day he paid a proper visit. On his arrival he sent in a poem written on his usual tiny slip of paper: "Since first I heard the voice of the young crane, my boat shows a strange tendency to stick among the reeds!" It was meant for the little girl and was written in a large, childish

---

* Arises out of some connection in a previous existence.

hand, but very beautifully, so that the ladies of the house said as soon as they saw it, "This will have to go into the child's copy-book."

Shonagon sent him the following note: "My mistress, feeling that she might not live through the day, asked us to have her moved to the temple in the hills, and she is already on her way. I shall see to it that she learns of your enquiry, if I can but send word to her before it is too late." The letter touched him deeply.

During these autumn evenings his heart was in a continual ferment. But though all his thoughts were occupied in a different quarter, yet owing to the curious relationship in which the child stood to the being who thus obsessed his mind, the desire to make the girl his own throughout this stormy time grew daily stronger. He remembered the evening when he had first seen her and the nun's poem, "Not knowing if any will come to nurture the tender leaf..." She would always be delightful; but in some respects she might not fulfill her early promise. One must take risks. And he made the poem: "When shall I see it lying in my hand, the young grass of the moorside that springs from purple* roots?" In the tenth month the Emperor was to visit the Suzaku-in for the Festival of Red Leaves. The dancers were all to be sons of the noblest houses. The most accomplished among the princes, courtiers and other great gentlemen had been chosen for their parts by the Emperor himself, and from the Royal Princes and State Ministers downward everyone was busy with continual practices and rehearsals. Genji suddenly realized that for a long while he had not enquired after his friends on the mountain. He at once sent a special messenger who brought back this letter from the priest: "The end came on the twentieth day of last month. It is the common lot of mankind; yet her loss is very grievous to me!" This and more he wrote, and Genji, reading the letter, was filled with a bitter sense of life's briefness and futility. And what of the child concerning whose future the dead woman had shown such anxiety? He could not remember his own mother's death at all distinctly; some dim recollection still floated in his mind and gave to his letter of condolence an added warmth of feeling. It was answered, not without a certain self-importance, by the nurse Shonagon.

After the funeral and mourning were over, the child was brought back to the Capital. Hearing of this he allowed a short while to elapse and then one fine, still night went to the house of his own accord. This gloomy, decaying, half-deserted mansion must, he thought, have a most depressing effect upon the child who lived there. He was shown into the same small room as before. Here Shonagon told him between her sobs the whole tale

---

* Purple is *murasaki* in Japanese. From this poem the child is known as Murasaki; and hence the authoress derived the nickname by which she too is known.

of their bereavement, at which he too found himself strangely moved. "I would send my little mistress to His Highness her father's," she continued," did I not remember how cruelly her poor mother was used in that house. And I would do it still if my little lady were a child in arms who would not know where she had been taken to nor what the people there were feeling towards her. But she is now too big a girl to go among a lot of strange children who might not treat her kindly. So her poor dead grandmother was always saying down to her last day. You, Sir, have been very good to us, and it would be a great weight off my mind to know that she was coming to you even if it were only for a little while; and I would not worry you with asking what was to become of her afterwards. Only for her sake I am sorry indeed that she is not some years older, so that you might make a match of it. But the way she has been brought up has made her young even for her age." "You need not so constantly remind me of her childishness," said Genji. "Though it is indeed her youth and helplessness which move my compassion, yet I realize (and why should I hide it from myself or from you?) that a far closer bond unites our souls. Let me tell her myself what we have just now decided," and he recited a poem in which he asked if "like the waves that lap the shore where young reeds grow he must advance only to recede again." "Will she be too much surprised?" he added. Shonagon, saying that the little girl should by all means be fetched, answered his poem with another in which she warned him that he must not expect her to "drift seaweed-like with the waves," before she understood his intention. "Now, what made you think I should send you away without letting her see you?" she asked, speaking in an offhand, familiar tone which he found it easy to pardon. His appearance, which the gentlewomen of the house studied with great care while he sat waiting for the child and singing to himself a verse of the song "Why so hard to cross the hill?" made a deep impression upon them, and they did not forget that moment for a long while after.

The child was lying on her bed weeping for her grandmother. "A gentleman in a big cloak has come to play with you," said one of the women who were waiting upon her; "I wonder if it is your father." At this she jumped up and cried out: "Nurse, where is the gentleman in a cloak? Is he my father?" and she came running into the room. "No," said Genji, "it is not your father; but it is someone else who wants you to be very fond of him. Come…" She had learnt from the way people talked about him that Prince Genji was someone very important, and feeling that he must really be very angry with her for speaking of him as the "gentleman in a cloak" she went straight to her nurse and whispered, "Please, I am sleepy." "You must not be shy of me any more," said Genji. "If you are sleepy, come here and lie on my knee. Will you not even come and talk to me?" "There," said Shonagon, "you see what a little savage she is," and pushed the child towards him. She stood listlessly by his side, passing her hand under her hair so that it fell in waves over her soft dress or clasping a great bunch of it where it stuck out thick around her shoulders. Presently he took her hand in his; but at once, in terror of this close contact with someone to whom she was not used, she cried out, "I said I wanted to go to bed," and snatching her hand away she ran into the women's quarters. He followed her crying, "Dear one, do not run away from me! Now that your granny is gone, you must love me instead." "Well!" gasped Shonagon, deeply shocked. "No, that is too much! How can you bring yourself to say such a wicked thing to the poor child? And it is not much use *telling* people to be fond of one, is it?" "For the moment, it may not be," said Genji. "But you will see that strange things happen if one's heart is set upon a thing as mine is now."

Hail was falling. It was a wild and terrible night. The thought of leaving her to pass it in this gloomy and half-deserted mansion immeasurably depressed him and snatching at this excuse for remaining near her, "shut the partition-door!" he cried. "I will stay for a while and play the watchman here on this terrible night. Draw near to me, all of you!" and so saying, as though it were the most natural thing in the world, he picked up the child in his arms and carried her to her bed. The gentlewomen were far too astonished and confounded to budge from their seats; while Shonagon, though his high-handed proceedings greatly agitated and alarmed her, had to confess to herself that there was no real reason to interfere, and could only sit moaning in her corner. The little girl was at first terribly frightened. She did not know what he was going to do with her and shuddered violently. Even the feel of his delicate, cool skin when he drew her to him, gave her gooseflesh. He saw this; but nonetheless he began gently and carefully to remove her outer garments, and laid her down. Then, though he knew quite well that she was still frightened of him, he began talking to her softly and tenderly: "How would you like to come with me one day to a place where there are lots of lovely pictures and dolls and toys?" And he went on to speak so feelingly of all the things she was most interested in that soon she felt almost at home with him. But for a long while she was restless and did not go properly to sleep. The storm still raged. "Whatever should we have done if this gentleman had not been here?" whispered one of the women; "I know that for my part I should have been in a terrible fright. If only our little lady were nearer to his age!" Shonagon, still mistrustful, sat quite close to Genji all the while.

At last the wind began to drop. The night was far spent; but his return at such an hour would cause no surprise. "She has become so dear to me," said Genji, "that, above all at this sad time in her life, I am loath to leave her even for a few short hours. I think I shall put her somewhere where

I can see her whenever I wish. I wonder that she is not frightened to live in such a place as this." "I think her father spoke of coming to fetch her," said Shonagon; "but that is not likely to be till the Forty-nine Days are up." "It would of course under ordinary circumstances be natural that her father should look after her," admitted Genji; "but as she has been brought up entirely by someone else she has no more reason to care for him than for me. And though I have known her so short a time, I am certainly far fonder of her than her father can possibly be." So saying he stroked the child's hair and then reluctantly, with many backward glances, left the room. There was now a heavy white fog, and hoarfrost lay thick on the grass. Suddenly he found himself wishing that it were a real love affair, and he became very depressed. It occurred to him that on his way home he would pass by a certain house which he had once familiarly frequented. He knocked at the door, but no one answered. He then ordered one of his servants who had a strong voice to recite the following lines: "By my Sister's gate though morning fog makes all the world still dark as night, I could not fail to pause." When this had been sung twice, the lady sent an impertinent coxcomb of a valet to the door, who having recited the poem, "If you disliked the hedge of fog that lies about this place, a gate of crazy wicker would not keep you standing in the street," at once went back again into the house. He waited, but no one else came to the door, and though he was in no mood to go dully home since it was now broad daylight, what else could be done? At his palace he lay for a long while smiling to himself with pleasure as he recollected the child's pretty speeches and ways. Towards noon he rose and began to write a letter to her; but he could not find the right words, and after many times laying his brush aside he determined at last to send her some nice pictures instead.

That day Prince Hyobukyo paid his long-promised visit to the late nun's house. The place seemed to him even more ruinous, vast and antiquated than he remembered it years ago. How depressing it must be for a handful of persons to live in these decaying halls, and looking about him he said to the nurse: "No child ought to live in a place like this even for a little while. I must take her away at once; there is plenty of room in my house. You" (turning to Shonagon) "shall be found a place as a Lady-in-Waiting there. The child will be very well off, for there are several other young people for her to play with." He called the little girl to him and noticing the rich perfume that clung to her dress since Genji held her in his arms, the Prince said, "How nicely your dress is scented. But isn't it rather drab?" No sooner had he said this than he remembered that she was in mourning, and felt slightly uncomfortable. "I used sometimes to tell her grandmother," he continued, "that she ought to let her come to see me and get used to our ways; for indeed it was a strange upbringing for her to live alone year in year out with one whose health and spirits steadily declined. But she for some reason was very unfriendly towards me, and there was in another quarter* too a reluctance which I fear even at such a time as this may not be wholly overcome..." "If that is so," said Shonagon, "dull as it is for her here, I do not think she should be moved till she is a little better able to shift for herself."

For days on end the child had been in a terrible state of grief, and not having eaten the least bite of anything she was grown very thin, but was nonetheless lovely for that. He looked at her tenderly and said: "You must not cry anymore now. When people die, there is no help for it and we must bear it bravely. But now all is well, for I have come instead..." But it was getting late and he could not stay any longer. As he turned to go he saw that the child, by no means consoled at the prospect of falling under his care, was again crying bitterly. The Prince, himself shedding a few tears, did his best to comfort her: "Do not grieve so," he said, "to day or tomorrow I will send for you to come and live with me," and with that he departed. Still the child wept and no way could be found to distract her thoughts. It was not of course that she had any anxiety about her own future, for about such matters she had not yet begun to think at all; but only that she had lost the companion from whom for years on end she had never for a moment been separated. Young as she was, she suffered so cruelly that all her usual games were quite abandoned, and though sometimes during the day her spirits would a little improve, as night drew on she became so melancholy that Shonagon began to wonder how much longer things would go on like this, and in despair at not being able to comfort her, would herself burst into tears.

Presently Koremitsu arrived with a message saying that Genji had intended to visit them, but owing to a sudden command from the Palace was unable to do so, and being very much perturbed at the little one's grievous condition had sent for further news. Having delivered this message, Koremitsu brought in some of Genji's servants whom he had sent to mount guard over the house that night. "This kindness is indeed ill-placed," said Shonagon. "It may not seem to him of much consequence that his gentlemen should be installed here; but if the child's father hears of it, we servants shall get all the blame for the little lady's being given away to a married gentleman. It was you who let it all begin, we shall be told. Now be careful," she said turning to her fellow servants, "do not let her even mention these watchmen to her father." But alas, the child was quite incapable of understanding such a prohibition, and Shonagon, after pouring out many lamentations to Koremitsu, continued: "I do not doubt but that in due time she will somehow become his wife, for so their fate seems to decree. But now and for a long while there can be no talk

---

* His wife.

of any such thing, and this, as he has roundly told me, he knows as well as the rest of us. So what he is after I cannot for the life of me imagine. Only today when Prince Hyobukyo was here he bade me keep a sharp eye upon her and not let her be treated with any indiscretion. I confess when he said it I remembered with vexation certain liberties which I have allowed your master to take, thinking little enough of them at the time." No sooner had she said this than she began to fear that Koremitsu would put a worse construction on her words than she intended, and shaking her head very dolefully she relapsed into silence. Nor was she far wrong, for Koremitsu was indeed wondering of what sort Genji's misdemeanors could have been.

On hearing Koremitsu's report Genji's heart was filled with pity for the child's state and he would like to have gone to her at once. But he feared that ignorant people would misunderstand these frequent visits and, thinking the girl older than she was, spread foolish scandals abroad. It would be far simpler to fetch her to his palace and keep her there. All through the day he sent numerous letters, and at dusk Koremitsu again went to the house saying that urgent business had once more prevented Genji from visiting them, for which remissness he tendered his apologies. Shonagon answered curtly that the girl's father had suddenly decided to fetch her away next day and that they were too busy to receive visits: "The servants are all in a fluster at leaving this shabby old house where they have lived so long and going to a strange, grand place…" She answered his further questions so briefly and seemed so intent upon her sewing that Koremitsu went away.

Genji was at the Great Hall, but as usual he had been unable to get a word out of Aoi and in a gloomy mood he was plucking at his zithern and singing, "Why sped you across field and hill so fast upon this rainy night?"*

The words of the song were aimed at Aoi and he sang them with much feeling. He was thus employed when Koremitsu arrived at the Great Hall. Genji sent for him at once and bade him tell his story. Koremitsu's news was very disquieting. Once she was in her father's palace it would look very odd that Genji should fetch her away, even if she came willingly. It would inevitably be rumored abroad that he had made off with her like a child-snatcher, a thief. Far better to anticipate his rival and exacting a promise of silence from the people about her, carry her off to his own palace immediately. "I shall go there at daybreak," he said to Koremitsu. "Order the carriage that I came here in, it can be used just as it is, and see to it that one or two attendants are ready to go with me." Koremitsu bowed and retired.

---

* The song is addressed by a girl to a suspicious lover; Genji reverses the sense.

Genji knew that whichever course he chose, there was bound to be a scandal so soon as the thing became known. Inevitably gossips would spread the report that, young though she was, the child by this time knew well enough why she had been invited to live with Prince Genji in his palace. Let them draw their own conclusions. That did not matter. There was a much worse possibility. What if Hyobukyo found out where she was? His conduct in abducting another man's child would appear in the highest degree outrageous and discreditable. He was sorely puzzled, but he knew that if he let this opportunity slip he would afterward bitterly repent it, and long before daybreak he started on his way. Aoi was cold and sullen as ever. "I have just remembered something very important which I must see about at home," he said; "I shall not be away long," and he slipped out so quietly that the servants of the house did not know that he was gone. His cloak was brought to him from his own apartments and he drove off attended only by Koremitsu who followed on horseback. After much knocking they succeeded in getting the gate opened, but by a servant who was not in on the secret. Koremitsu ordered the man to pull in Genji's carriage as quietly as he could and himself went straight to the front door, which he rattled, coughing as he did so that Shonagon might know who was there. "My lord is waiting," he said when she came to the door. "But the young lady is fast asleep," said Shonagon; "his Highness has no business to be up and about at this time of night." She said this thinking that he was returning from some nocturnal escapade and had only called there in passing. "I hear," said Genji now coming forward, "that the child is to be moved to her father's and I have something of importance which I must say to her before she goes." "Whatever business you have to transact with her, I am sure she will give the matter her closest attention," scoffed Shonagon. "Matters of importance indeed, with a child of ten!" Genji entered the women's quarters. "You cannot go in there," cried Shonagon in horror; "several aged ladies are lying all undressed...." "They are all fast asleep," said Genji. "See, I am only rousing the child," and bending over her: "The morning mist is rising," he cried, "it is time to wake!" And before Shonagon had time to utter a sound, he had taken the child in his arms and begun gently to rouse her. Still half-dreaming, she thought it was the prince, her father, who had come to fetch her. "Come," said Genji while he put her hair to rights, your father has sent me to bring you back with me to his palace." For a moment she was dazed to find that it was not her father and shrank from him in fright. "Never mind whether it is your father or I," he cried; "it is all the same," and so saying he picked her up in his arms and carried her out of the inner room. "Well!" cried out Koremitsu and Shonagon in astonishment. What would he do next? "It seems," said Genji, "that you were disquieted at my telling you I could not visit her here as often as I wished and would make arrangements for her to go to a more convenient place. I hear that you are sending her where it will be even more difficult for me to see her. Therefore... make ready one or the other of you to come with me."

Shonagon, who now realized that he was going to make off with the child, fell into a terrible fluster. "O, Sir," she said, "you could not have chosen a worse time. Today her father is coming to fetch her, and whatever shall I say to him? If only you would wait, I am sure it would all come right in the end. But by acting so hastily you will do yourself no good and leave the poor servants here in a sad pickle." "If that is all," cried Genji, "let them follow as soon as they choose," and to Shonagon's despair he had the carriage brought in. The child stood by weeping and bewildered. There seemed no way of preventing him from carrying out his purpose and gathering together the child's clothes that she had been sewing the night before, the nurse put on her own best dress and stepped into the carriage. Genji's house was not far off and they arrived before daylight. They drew up in front of the western wing and Genji alighted. Taking the child lightly in his arms, he set her on the ground. Shonagon, to whom these strange events seemed like a dream, hesitated as though still uncertain whether she should enter the house or no. "There is no need for you to come in if you do not want to," said Genji. "Now that the child herself is safely here I am quite content. If you had rather go back, you have only to say so and I will escort you."

Reluctantly she left the carriage. The suddenness of the move was in itself enough to have upset her; but she was also worrying about what Prince Hyobukyo would think when he found that his child had vanished. And indeed what *was* going to become of her? One way or another all her mistresses seemed to be taken from her and it was only when she became frightened of having wept for so long on end that she at last dried her eyes and began to pray.

The western wing had long been uninhabited and was not completely furnished; but Koremitsu had soon fitted up screens and curtains where they were required. For Genji makeshift quarters were soon contrived by letting down the side-wings of his screen-of-honor. He sent to the other part of the house for his night things and went to sleep. The child, who had been put to bed not far off, was still very apprehensive and ill at ease in these new surroundings. Her lips were trembling, but she dared not cry out loud. "I want to sleep with Shonagon," she said at last in a tearful, babyish voice. "You are getting too big to sleep with a nurse," said Genji who had heard her. "You must try and go to sleep nicely where you are." She felt very lonely and lay weeping for a long while. The nurse was far too much upset to think of going to bed and sat up for the rest of the night in the servants' quarters crying so bitterly that she was unconscious of all that went on around her.

But when it grew light she began to look about her a little. Not only this great palace with its marvelous pillars and carvings, but the sand in the courtyard outside which seemed to her like a carpet of jewels made so dazzling an impression upon her that at first she felt somewhat overawed. However, the fact that she was now no longer in a household of women gave her an agreeable sense of security.

It was the hour at which business brought various strangers to the house. There were several men walking just outside her window and she heard one of them whisper to another: "They say that someone new has come to live here. Who can it be, I wonder? A lady of note, I'll warrant you."

Bath water was brought from the other wing, and steamed rice for breakfast. Genji did not rise till far on into the morning. "It is not good for the child to be alone," he said to Shonagon, 'so last night before I came to you I arranged for some little people to come and stay here," and so saying he sent a servant to "fetch the little girls from the eastern wing." He had given special orders that they were to be as small as possible and now four of the tiniest and prettiest creatures imaginable arrived upon the scene.

Murasaki was still asleep, lying wrapped in Genji's own coat. It was with difficulty that he roused her. "You must not be sad any more," he said. "If I were not very fond of you, should I be looking after you like this? Little girls ought to be very gentle and obedient in their ways." And thus her education was begun.

She seemed to him, now that he could study her at leisure, even more lovely than he had realized and they were soon engaged in an affectionate conversation. He sent for delightful pictures and toys to show her and set to work to amuse her in every way he could. Gradually he persuaded her to get up and look about her. In her shabby dress made of some dark grey material she looked so charming now that she was laughing and playing, with all her woes forgotten, that Genji too laughed with pleasure as he watched her. When at last he retired to the eastern wing, she went out of doors to look at the garden. As she picked her way among the trees and along the side of the lake, and gazed with delight upon the frosty flowerbeds that glittered gay as a picture, while a many-colored throng of unknown people passed constantly in and out of the house, she began to think that this was a very nice place indeed. Then she looked at the wonderful pictures that were painted on all the panels and screens and quite lost her heart to them.

For two or three days Genji did not go to the Palace, but spent all his time amusing the little girl. Finally he drew all sorts of pictures for her to put into her copybook, showing them to her one by one as he did so. She thought them the loveliest set of pictures she had ever seen. Then he wrote part of the *Musashi-no* poem.* She was delighted by the way it was written in bold ink-strokes on a background stained with purple. In a smaller hand was the poem: "Though the parent-root† I cannot see, yet tenderly I love its offshoot‡—the dewy plant that grows upon Musashi Moor." "Come," said Genji while she was admiring it, "you must write something too." "I cannot write properly yet," she answered, looking up at him with a witchery so wholly unconscious that Genji laughed. "Even if you cannot write properly it will never do for us to let you off altogether. Let me give you a lesson." With many timid glances towards him she began to write. Even the childish manner in which she grasped the brush gave him a thrill of delight which he was at a loss to explain. "Oh, I have spoiled it," she suddenly cried out and blushing hid from him what she had written. But he forced her to let him see it and found the poem: "I do not know what put Musashi into your head and am very puzzled. What plant is it that you say is a relative of mine?" It was written in a large childish hand which was indeed very undeveloped, but was nevertheless full of promise. It showed a strong resemblance to the late nun's writing. He felt certain that if she were given up-to-date copybooks she would soon write very nicely.

Next they built houses for the dolls and played so long at this game together that Genji forgot for a while the great anxiety§ which was at that time preying upon his mind.

The servants who had been left behind at Murasaki's house were extremely embarrassed when Prince Hyobukyo came to fetch her. Genji had made them promise for a time at any rate to tell no one of what had happened and Shonagon had seemed to agree that this was best. Accordingly he could get nothing out of them save that Shonagon had taken the child away with her without saying anything about where she was going. The Prince felt completely baffled. Perhaps the grandmother had instilled into the nurse's mind the idea that things would not go smoothly for the child at his palace. In that case the nurse with an excess of craftiness might, instead of openly saying that she feared the child would not be well treated under his roof, have thought it wiser to make off with her when opportunity offered. He went home very depressed, asking them to let him know instantly if they had any news, a request which again embarrassed them. He also made enquiries of the priest at the temple in the hills, but could learn nothing. She had seemed to him

---

* "Though I know not the place, yet when they told me this was the moor of Musashi the thought flashed through my mind: 'What else indeed could it be, since all its grass is purple-dyed?'"

† Fujitsubo. The fuji flower is also purple (*murasaki*) in color.

‡ The child Murasaki, who was Fujitsubo's niece. Musashi was famous for the purple dye extracted from the roots of a grass that grew there.

§ The pregnancy of Fujitsubo.

to be a most lovable and delightful child; it was very disappointing to lose sight of her in this manner. The princess his wife had long ago got over her dislike of the child's mother and was indignant at the idea that she was not to be trusted to do her duty by the child properly.

Gradually the servants from Murasaki's house assembled at her new home. The little girls who had been brought to play with her were delighted with their new companion and they were soon all playing together very happily.

When her prince was away or busy, on dreary evenings she would still sometimes long for her grandmother the nun and cry a little. But she never thought about her father whom she had never been used to see except at rare intervals. Now indeed she had "a new father" of whom she was growing every day more fond. When he came back from anywhere she was the first to meet him and then wonderful games and conversations began, she sitting all the while on his lap without the least shyness or restraint. A more charming companion could not have been imagined. It might be that when she grew older, she would not always be so trustful. New aspects of her character might come into play. If she suspected, for example, that he cared for someone else, she might resent it, and in such a case all sorts of unexpected things are apt to happen; but for the present she was a delightful plaything. Had she really been his daughter, convention would not have allowed him to go on much longer living with her on terms of such complete intimacy; but in a case like this he felt that such scruples were not applicable.

The Saffron-Flower

Try as he might he could not dispel the melancholy into which Yugao's sudden death* had cast him, and though many months had gone by he longed for her passionately as ever. In other quarters where he had looked for affection, coldness vied with coldness and pride with pride. He longed to escape once more from the claims of these passionate and exacting natures, and renew the life of tender intimacy which for a while had given him so great a happiness. But alas, no second Yugao would he ever find. Despite his bitter experience he still fancied that one day he might at least discover some beautiful girl of humble origin whom he could meet without concealment, and he listened eagerly to any hint that was likely to put him upon a promising track. If the prospects seemed favorable he would follow up his enquiries by writing a discreet letter which, as he knew from experience, would seldom indeed meet with a wholly discouraging reply. Even those who seemed bent on I showing by the prim stiffness of their answers that they placed virtue high above sensibility, and who at first appeared hardly conversant with the usages of polite society, would suddenly collapse into the wildest intimacy which would continue until their marriage with some commonplace husband cut short the correspondence.

There were vacant moments when he thought of Utsusemi with regret. And there was her companion too; some time or other there would surely be an opportunity of sending her a surprise message. If only he could see her again as he had seen her that night sitting by the chessboard in the dim lamplight. It was not indeed in his nature ever to forget anyone of whom he had once been fond.

Among his old nurses there was one called Sayemon to whom, next after Koremitsu's mother, he was most deeply attached. She had a daughter called Taifu no Myobu who was in service at the Palace. This girl was an illegitimate child of a certain member of the Imperial family who was then Vice-minister of the Board of War. She was a young person of very lively disposition and Genji often made use of her services. Her mother, Genji's nurse, had afterwards married the governor of Echizen and had gone with him to his province, so the girl when she was not at the Palace lived chiefly at her father's.

---

* The events of this chapter are synchronous with those of the last.

She happened one day when she was talking with Genji to mention a certain princess, daughter of the late Prince Hitachi. This lady, she said, was born to the Prince when he was quite an old man and every care had been lavished upon her upbringing. Since his death she had lived alone and was very unhappy. Genji's sympathy was aroused and he began to question Myobu about this unfortunate lady. "I do not really know much either about her character or her appearance," said Myobu; "she is extremely seclusive in her habits. Sometimes I have talked to her a little in the evening, but always with a curtain between us. I believe her zithern is the only companion in whom she is willing to confide." "Of the Three Friends* one at least would in her case be unsuitable," said Genji. "But I should like to hear her play; her father was a great performer on this instrument and it is unlikely that she has not inherited some of his skill." "Oh, I am afraid she is not worth your coming to hear," said Myobu. "You are very discouraging," he answered, "but all the same I shall hide there one of these nights when the full moon is behind the clouds and listen to her playing; and you shall come with me." She was not best pleased; but just then even upon the busy Palace a springtime quiet seemed to have settled, and being quite at leisure she consented to accompany him. Her father's house was at some distance from the town and for convenience he sometimes lodged in Prince Hitachi's palace. Myobu got on badly with her stepmother, and taking a fancy to the lonely princess's quarters, she kept a room there.

It was indeed on the night after the full moon, in just such a veiled light as Genji had spoken of, that they visited the Hitachi palace. "I am afraid," said Myobu, "that it is not a very good night for listening to music; sounds do not seem to carry very well." But he would not be thus put off. "Go to her room," he said, "and persuade her to play a few notes; it would be a pity if I went away without hearing her at all." Myobu felt somewhat shy of leaving him like this in her own little private room. She found the princess sitting by the window, her shutters not yet closed for the night; she was enjoying the scent of a blossoming plum-tree which stood in the garden just outside. It did indeed seem just the right moment. "I thought how lovely your zithern would sound on such a night as this," she said, "and could not resist coming to see you. I am always in such hurry, going to and from the Palace, that do you know I have never had time to hear you play? It is such a pity." "Music of this sort," she replied, "gives no pleasure to those who have not studied it. What do they care for such matters *who all day long run hither and thither in the City of a Hundred Towers?*"† She sent for her zithern, but her heart beat

---

* Wine, zithern and song—in allusion to a poem by Po Chü-i.
† Evidently a quotation.

fast. What impression would her playing make upon this girl? Timidly she sounded a few notes. The effect was very agreeable. True, she was not a great performer; but the instrument was a particularly fine one and Genji found her playing by no means unpleasant to listen to.

Living in this lonely and half-ruined palace after such an upbringing (full no doubt of antiquated formalities and restrictions) as her father was likely to have given her it would be strange indeed if her life did not for the most part consist of memories and regrets. This was just the sort of place which in an old tale would be chosen as the scene for the most romantic happenings. His imagination thus stirred, he thought of sending her a message. But perhaps she would think this rather sudden. For some reason he felt shy, and hesitated.

"It seems to be clouding over," said the astute Myobu, who knew that Genji would carry away a far deeper impression if he heard no more for the present. "Someone was coming to see me," she continued; "I must not keep him waiting. Perhaps some other time when I am not in such a hurry...Let me close your window for you," and with that she rejoined Genji, giving the princess no encouragement to play any more. "She stopped so soon," he complained, "that it was hardly worth getting her to play at all. One had not time to catch the drift of what she was playing. Really it was a pity!" That the princess was beautiful he made no doubt at all. "I should be very much obliged if you would arrange for me to hear her at closer quarters." But Myobu, thinking that this would lead to disappointment, told him that the princess who led so hermit-like an existence and seemed always so depressed and subdued would hardly welcome the suggestion that she should perform before a stranger. "Of course," said Genji, "a thing of that kind could only be suggested between people who were on familiar terms or to someone of very different rank. This lady's rank, as I am perfectly well aware, entitles her to be treated with every consideration, and I would not ask you to do more than hint at my desire." He had promised to meet someone else that night and carefully disguising himself he was preparing to depart when Myobu said laughing: "It amuses me sometimes to think how the Emperor deplores the too strict and domesticated life which he suffers you to lead. What would he think if he could see you disguising yourself like this?" Genji laughed. "I am afraid," he said as he left the room, "that you are not quite the right person to denounce me. Those who think such conduct reprehensible in a man must find it even less excusable in a girl." She remembered that Genji had often been obliged to reproach her for her reckless flirtations, and blushing made no reply.

Still hoping to catch a glimpse of the zithern-player, he crept softly towards her window. He was about to hide at a point where the bamboo-fence was somewhat broken down when he perceived that a man was already ensconced there. Who could it be? No doubt it was one of the princess's lovers and he stepped back to conceal himself in the darkness. The stranger followed him and turned out to be no other than To no Chujo. That evening they had left the Palace together, but when they parted Genji (Chujo had noticed) did not either go in the direction of the Great Hall nor back to his own palace. This aroused Chujo's curiosity and, despite the fact that he too had a secret appointment that night, he decided first to follow Genji and discover what was afoot. So riding upon a strange horse and wearing a hunting-cloak he had got himself up altogether so villainously that he was able to follow Genji without being recognized upon the road. Seeing him enter so unexpected a place, Chujo was trying to imagine what business his friend could possibly have in such a quarter when the music began and he secreted himself with a vague idea of waylaying Genji when he came out. But the Prince, not knowing who the stranger was and frightened of being recognized, stole on tiptoe into the shadow. Chujo suddenly accosted him: "Though you shook me off so uncivilly, I thought it my duty to keep an eye on you," he said, and recited the poem: "Though together we left the great Palace hill, your setting-place you would not show me, Moon of the sixteenth night! Thus he remonstrated, and Genji, though at first he had been somewhat put out by finding that he was not alone, when he recognized To no Chujo could not help being rather amused. "This is indeed an unexpected attention on your part," he said, and expressed his slight annoyance in the answering verse: "Though wheresoever it shines men marvel at its light, who has before thought fit to follow the full moon to the hill whereon it sets?"

"It is most unsafe for you to go about like this," said Chujo. "I really mean it. You ought always to have a bodyguard; then you are all right whatever happens. I wish you would always let me come with you. I am afraid that these clandestine expeditions may one day get you into trouble," and he solemnly repeated the warning. What chiefly worried Genji was the thought that this might not be the first occasion upon which Chujo had followed him; but if it had been his habit to do so it was certainly very tactful of him never to have questioned Genji about Yugao's child.*

Though each of them had an appointment elsewhere, they agreed not to part. Both of them got into Genji's carriage and the moon having vanished behind a cloud, beguiled the way to the Great Hall by playing a duet upon their flutes. They did not send for torchbearers to see them in at the gates, but creeping in very quietly stole to a portico where they could not be seen and had their ordinary clothes brought to them there.

---

* Chujo's child by Yugao.

Having changed, they entered the house merrily blowing their flutes as though they had just come back from the Palace.

Chujo's father, who usually pretended not to hear them when they returned late at night, on this occasion brought out his flageolet, which was his favorite instrument, and began to play very agreeably. Aio sent for her zithern and made all her ladies play on the instruments at which they excelled. Only Nakatsukasa, though she was known for her lute-playing, having thrown over To no Chujo who had been her lover because of her infatuation for Genji with whom her sole intercourse was that she sometimes saw him casually when he visited the Great Hall—only Nakatsukasa sat drooping listlessly; for her passion had become known to Aoi's mother and the rest, and they were being very unpleasant about it. She was thinking in her despair that perhaps it would be better if she went and lived in some place where she would never see Genji at all; but the step was hard to take and she was very unhappy.

The young princes were thinking of the music they had heard earlier in the evening, of those romantic surroundings tinged with a peculiar and inexplicable beauty. Merely because it pleased him so to imagine her, To no Chujo had already endowed the occupant of the lonely mansion with every charm. He had quite decided that Genji had been courting her for months or even years, and thought impatiently that he for his part, if like Genji he were violently in love with a lady of this kind, would have been willing to risk a few reproaches or even the loss of a little reputation. He could not however believe that his friend intended to let the matter rest as it was much longer and determined to amuse himself by a little rivalry. From that time onwards both of them sent letters to the lady, but neither ever received any answer. This both vexed and puzzled them. What could be the reason? Thinking that such images were suitable to a lady brought up in these rustic surroundings, in most of the poems which they sent her they alluded to delicate trees and flowers or other aspects of nature, hoping sooner or later to hit on some topic which would arouse her interest in their suit. Though she was of good birth and education, perhaps through being so long buried away in her vast mansion she had not any longer the wits to write a reply. And what indeed did it matter whether she answered or not, thought To no Chujo, who nonetheless was somewhat piqued. With his usual frankness he said to Genji: "I wonder whether you have had any answer. I must confess that as an experiment I too sent a mild hint, but without any success, so I have not repeated it." "So he too has been trying his hand," thought Genji, smiling to himself. "No," he answered aloud, "my letter did not need an answer, which was perhaps the reason that I did not receive one." From this enigmatic reply Chujo deduced that Genji had been in communication of some kind with the lady and he was slightly piqued by the fact that she had shown a preference between them. Genji's deeper feelings were in no way involved, and though his vanity was a little wounded he would not have pursued the matter farther had he not known the persuasive power of Chujo's style, and feared that even now she might overcome her scruples and send him a reply. Chujo would become insufferably cock-a-hoop if he got into his head the idea that the princess had transferred her affections from Genji to himself. He must see what Myobu could be persuaded to do. "I cannot understand," he said to her, "why the princess should refuse to take any notice of my letters. It is really very uncivil of her. I suppose she thinks I am a frivolous person who intends to amuse himself a little in her company and then disappear. It is a strangely false conception of my character. As you know, my affections never alter, and if I have ever seemed to the world to be unfaithful it has always been because in reality my suit had met with some unexpected discouragement. But this lady is so placed that no opposition from parents or brothers can interrupt our friendship, and if she will but trust me she will find that her being alone in the world, so far from exposing her to callous treatment, makes her the more attractive." "Come," answered Myobu, "it will never do for you to run away with the idea that you can treat this great lady as a pleasant wayside distraction; on the contrary she is extremely difficult of access and her rank has accustomed her to be treated with deference and ceremony." So spoke Myobu, in accordance indeed with her own experience of the princess. "She has evidently no desire to be thought clever or dashing," said Genji; "for some reason I imagine her as very gentle and forgiving." He was thinking of Yugao when he said this.

Soon after this he fell sick of his fever and after that was occupied by a matter of great secrecy; so that spring and summer had both passed away before he could again turn his attention to the lonely lady. But in the autumn came a time of quiet meditation and reflection. Again the sound of the cloth-beaters' mallets reached his ears, tormenting him with memories and longings. He wrote many letters to the zithern-player, but with no more success than before. Her churlishness exasperated him. More than ever he was determined not to give in, and sending for Myobu he scolded her for having been of so little assistance to him. "What can be going on in the princess's mind?" he said; "such strange behavior I have never met with before." If he was piqued and surprised, Myobu for her part was vexed that the affair had gone so badly. "No one can say that you have done anything so very eccentric or indiscreet, and I do not think she feels so. If she does not answer your letters it is only part of her general unwillingness to face the outer world." "But such a way of behaving is positively barbarous," said Genji; "if she were a girl in her "teens and under the care of parents or guardians, such timidity might be pardoned; but in an independent woman it is inconceivable. I would never have written had I not taken it for granted that she had some experience of the world. I was merely hoping that I had found someone who in moments of idleness or depression would respond to me sympathetically. I did not address her in the language of gallantry, but only begged for permission sometimes to converse with her in that strange and lonely dwelling-place. But since she seems unable to understand what it is I am asking of her, we must see what can be done without waiting for her permission. If you will help me, you may be sure I shall not disgrace you in any way."

Myobu had once been in the habit of describing to him the appearance of people whom she had chanced to meet and he always listened to such accounts with insatiable interest and curiosity; but for a long while he had paid no attention to her reports. Now for no reason at all the mere mention of the princess's existence had aroused in him a fever of excitement and activity. It was all very unaccountable. Probably he would find the poor lady extremely unattractive when he saw her and she would be doing her a very poor service in effecting the introduction; but to give Genji no help in a matter to which he evidently attached so much importance, would seem very ill-natured.

Even in Prince Hitachi's lifetime visitors to this stiff, old-fashioned establishment had been very rare, and now no foot at all ever made its way through the thickets which were closing in around the house. It may be imagined then what the visit of so celebrated a person as Genji would have meant to the ladies-in-waiting and lesser persons of the household and with what urgency they begged their mistress to send a favorable reply. But the same desperate shyness still possessed her and Genji's letters she would not even read. Hearing this, Myobu determined to submit Genji's request to her at some suitable moment when she and the princess were carrying on one of their usual uneasy conversations, with the princess's screen-of-honor planted between them. "If she seems displeased," thought Myobu, "I will positively have nothing more to do with the matter; but if she receives him and some sort of an affair starts between them, there is fortunately no one connected with her to scold me or get me into trouble." As the result of these and other reflections, being quite at home in matters of this kind, she sensibly decided to say nothing about the business to anybody, not even to her father.

Late one night, soon after the twentieth day of the eighth month, the princess sat waiting for the moon to rise. Though the starlight shone clear and lovely, the moaning of the wind in the pine-tree branches oppressed her with its melancholy, and growing weary of waiting, she was with many tears and sighs recounting to Myobu stories of bygone men and days.

Now was the time to convey Genji's message, thought Myobu. She sent for him, and secretly as before he crept up to the palace. The moon was just rising. He stood where the neglected bamboo-hedge grew somewhat sparsely and watched. Persuaded by Myobu, the princess was already at her zithern. So far as he could hear it at this distance, he did not find the music displeasing, but Myobu in her anxiety and confusion thought the tune very dull and wished it would occur to the princess to play something rather more up-to-date. The place where Genji was waiting was well screened from view and he had no difficulty in creeping unobserved into the house. Here he called for Myobu, who pretending that the visit was a complete surprise to her, said to the princess: "I am so sorry, here is Prince Genji come to see me. I am always getting into trouble with him for failing to secure him your favor. I have really done my best, but you do not make it possible for me to give him any encouragement, so now I imagine he has come to deal with the matter for himself. What am I to say to him? I can answer for it that he will do nothing violent or rash. I think that considering all the trouble he has taken you might at least tell him that you will speak to him through a screen or curtain." The idea filled the princess with consternation. "I should not know what to say to him," she wailed and as she said the words bolted towards the far side of the room with a bashfulness so infantile that Myobu could not help laughing. "Indeed, Madam," she said, "it is childish of you to take the matter to heart in this way. If you were an ordinary young lady under the eye of stern parents and brothers, one could understand it; but for a person in your position to go on for ever being afraid to face the world is fantastic." So Myobu admonished her and the princess, who could never think of any argument against doing what she was told to do, said at last: "If I have only to listen and need not say anything he may speak to me from behind the lattice-door, so long as it is well locked." "I cannot ask him to sit on the servant's bench," said Myobu. "You really need not be afraid that he will do anything violent or sudden." Thus persuaded, the princess went to a hatch which communicated between the women's quarters and the stranger's dais and firmly locking it with her own hand, stuffed a mattress against it to make sure that no chink was left unstopped. She was in such a terrible state of confusion that she had not the least idea what she should say to her visitor, if she had to speak to him, and had agreed to listen to him only because Myobu told her that she ought to.

Several elderly serving-women of the wet-nurse type had been lying half-asleep in the inner room since dusk. There were however one or two younger maids who had heard a great deal about this Prince Genji and were ready to fall in love with him at a moment's notice. They now brought out their lady's handsomest dress and persuaded her to let them put her a little to rights; but she displayed no interest in these preparations. Myobu meanwhile was thinking how well Genji looked in the picturesque disguise which he had elaborated for use on these night excursions and wished it were being employed in some quarter where it was more likely to be appreciated. Her only consolation was that so mild a lady was not likely to make inordinate demands upon him or pester him with jealousies and exactions. On the other hand, she was rather worried about the princess. "What," thought Myobu, "if she should fall in love with him and her heart be broken merely because I was frightened of getting scolded?"

Remembering her rank and upbringing, he was far from expecting her to behave with the lively pertness of an up-to-date miss. She would be languorous; yes, languorous and passionate. When, half-pushed by Myobu, the princess at last took her stand near the partition where she was to converse with her visitor, a delicious scent of sandalwood* invaded his nostrils, and this piece of coquetry at once raised his hopes. He began to tell her with great earnestness and eloquence how for almost a year she had continually occupied his thoughts. But not a word did she answer; talking to her was no better than writing! Irritated beyond measure he recited the verse: "If with a Vow of Silence thus ten times and again my combat I renew, 'tis that against me at least no sentence of muteness has been passed." "Speak at least one word of dismissal," he continued; "do not leave me in this bewilderment." There was among her ladies one called Jiju, the daughter of her old nurse. Being a girl of great liveliness and intelligence, she could not bear to see her mistress cutting such a figure as this and stepping to her side she answered with the poem: "The bell† had sounded and for a moment silence was imposed upon my lips. To have kept you waiting grieves me, and there let the matter rest." She said the words in such a way that Genji was completely taken in and thought it was the princess who had thus readily answered his poem. He had not expected such smartness from an aristocratic lady of the old school; but the surprise was agreeable and he answered: "Madam, you have won the day," adding the verse: "Though well I know that thoughts unspoken count more than thoughts expressed, yet dumb-crambo is not a cheering game to play."

He went on to speak of one trifle or another as it occurred to him, doing his very best to entertain her; but it was no use. Thinking at last that silence might after all in this strange creature be merely a sign of deep emotion, he could no longer restrain his curiosity and, easily pushing back the bolted door, entered the room. Myobu, seeing with consternation that he had falsified all her assurances, thought it better to know nothing of what followed and without turning her head rushed away to her

---

* Used to scent clothes with.

† The bell which the Zen-master strikes when it is time for his pupils to fall into silent meditation.

own apartments. Jiju and the other ladies-in-waiting had heard so much about Genji and were so anxious to catch sight of him that they were more than ready to forgive his uncivil intrusion. Their only fear was that their mistress would be at a loss how to deal with so unexpected a situation. He did indeed find her in the last extremity of bashfulness and embarrassment, but under the circumstances that, thought Genji, was natural. Much was to be explained by the strict seclusion in which she had been brought up. He must be patient with her...

As his eyes grew used to the dim light he began to see that she was not at all beautiful. Had she then not one quality at all to justify all these hopes and schemes? Apparently not one. It was late. What was the use of staying? Bitterly disappointed he left the house: Myobu, intensely curious to know what would happen, had lain awake listening. She wanted however to keep up the pretence that she had not witnessed Genji's intrusion and though she plainly heard him leaving the house she did not go to see him off or utter a sound of any kind. Stealing away as quietly as possible he returned to the Nijo-in and lay down upon his bed. This time at least he thought he was on the tight path. What a disillusionment! And the worst of it was that she was a princess, a great lady. What a mess he was in! So he lay thinking, when To no Chujo entered the room. "How late you are!" he cried; "I can easily guess the reason." Genji rose: "I was so comfortable sleeping here all alone that I overslept myself," he said. "Have you come here from the Palace?" "Yes," said Chujo, "I was on my way home. I heard yesterday that today they are choosing the dancers and musicians for the celebrations of the Emperor's visit to the Suzaku-in and I am going home to tell my father of this. I will look in here on my way back." Seeing that Chujo was in a hurry, Genji said that he would go with him to the Great Hall. He sent at once for his breakfast, bidding them also serve the guest. Two carriages were drawn up waiting for them, but they both got into the same one. "You still seem very sleepy," said Chujo in an aggrieved tone; "I am sure you have been doing something interesting that you do not want to tell me about."

That day he had a number of important duties to perform and was hard at work in the Palace till nightfall. It did not occur to him till a very late hour that he ought at least to send the customary letter. It was raining. Myobu had only the day before reproached him for using the princess's palace as a "wayside refuge." Today however he had no inclination whatever to halt there.

When hour after hour went by and still no letter came, Myobu began to feel very sorry for the princess whom she imagined to be suffering acutely from Genji's incivility. But in reality the poor lady was still far too occupied with shame and horror at what had happened the night before to think of anything else, and when late in the evening Genji's note at last arrived she could not understand in the least what it meant. It began with the poem: "Scarce had the evening mist lifted and revealed the prospect to my sight when the night rain closed gloomily about me." "I shall watch with impatience for a sign that the clouds are breaking," the letter continued. The ladies of the household at once saw with consternation the meaning of this note: Genji did not intend ever to come again. But they were all agreed that an answer must be sent, and their mistress was for the time being in far too overwrought a condition to put brush to paper; so Jiju (pointing out that it was late and there was no time to be lost) again came to the rescue: "Give a thought to the country-folk who wait for moonlight on this cloudy night, though, while they gaze, so different their thoughts from yours!" This she dictated to her mistress who, under the joint direction of all her ladies, wrote it upon a piece of paper which had once been purple but was now faded and shabby. Her writing was coarse and stiff, very mediocre in style, the upward and downward strokes being of the same thickness. Genji laid it aside scarcely glancing at it; but he was very much worried by the situation. How should he avoid hurting her feelings? Such an affair was certain to get him into trouble of some kind. What was he to do? He made up his mind that at all costs he must go on seeing her. Meanwhile, knowing nothing of this decision, the poor lady was very unhappy.

That night his father-in-law called for him on the way back from the Palace and carried him off to the Great Hall.

Here in preparation for the coming festival all the young princes were gathered together, and during the days which followed everyone was busy practicing the songs or dances which had been assigned to him. Never had the Great Hall resounded with such a continual flow of music. The recorder and the big flute were all the while in full blast; and even the big drum was rolled out on to the verandah, the younger princes amusing themselves by experimenting upon it. Genji was so busy that he had barely time to pay an occasional surreptitious visit even to his dearest friends, and the autumn passed without his returning to the Hitachi Palace. The princess could not make it out.

Just at the time when the music-practices were at their height Myobu came to see him. Her account of the princess's condition was very distressing. "It is sad to witness day by day as I do how the poor lady suffers from your unkind treatment," she said and almost wept as she told him about it. He was doubly embarrassed. What must Myobu be thinking of him since she found that he had so recklessly falsified all the assurances of good behavior that she had made on his account? And then the princess herself... He could imagine what a pathetic figure she must be, dumbly buried in her own despondent thoughts and questionings. "Please make it clear to her," he said, "that I have been extremely busy; that is really the sole reason that I have not visited her." But he added with a sigh, "I hope soon to have a chance of teaching her not to be quite so stiff and shy." He smiled as he said it, and because he was so young and charming Myobu somehow felt that despite her indignation she must smile too. At his age it was inevitable that he should cause a certain amount of suffering. Suddenly it seemed to her perfectly right that he should do as he felt inclined without thinking much about the consequences. When the busy festival time was over he did indeed pay several visits to the Hitachi Palace, but then followed his adoption of little Murasaki whose ways so entranced him that he became very irregular even in his visits to the Sixth Ward;* still less had he any inclination, though he felt as sorry for the princess as ever, to visit that desolate palace. For a long while he had no desire to probe the secret of her bashfulness, to drive her into the light of day. But at last the idea occurred to him that he had perhaps all the while been mistaken. It was only a vague impression gathered in a room so dark that one could hardly see one's hand in front of one's face. If only he could persuade her to let him see her properly? But she seemed frightened to submit herself to the ordeal of daylight. Accordingly one night when he knew that he should catch her household quite at its ease he crept in unobserved and peeped through a gap in the door of the women's apartments. The princess herself was not visible. There was a very dilapidated screen-of-honor at the end of the room, but it looked as if it had not been moved from where it stood for years and years. Four or five elderly gentlewomen were in the room. They were preparing their mistress's supper in Chinese vessels which looked like the famous "royal blue" ware,† but they were much damaged and the food which had been provided seemed quite unworthy of these precious dishes. The old ladies soon retired, presumably to have their own supper. In a closet opening out of the main room he could see a very chilly-looking lady in an incredibly smoke-stained white dress and dirty apron tied at the waist. Despite this shabbiness, her hair was done over a comb in the manner of Court servants in ancient days when they waited at their master's table, though it hung down untidily. He had sometimes seen figures such as this haunting the housekeeper's rooms in the Palace, but he had no idea that they could still actually be seen waiting upon a living person! "O dear, O dear," cried the lady in the apron "what a cold winter we are having! It was not worth living so long only to meet times like these," and she shed a tear. "If only things had but gone on as they were in the old Prince's time!" she moaned. "What a change! No discipline, no authority. To think that I should have lived to see such days!" and she quivered with horror

---

* To Lady Rokujo.
† *Pi-se.* See Hetherington, *Early Ceramic Wares of China*, pp. 71-73.

like one who "were he a bird would take wing and fly away."* She went on to pour out such a pitiful tale of things gone awry that Genji could bear it no longer, and pretending that he had just arrived tapped at the partition-door. With many exclamations of surprise the old lady brought a candle and let him in. Unfortunately Jiju had been chosen with other young persons to wait upon the Vestal Virgin and was not at home. Her absence made the house seem more rustic and old-fashioned than ever, and its oddity struck him even more forcibly than before.

The melancholy snow was now falling faster and faster. Dark clouds hung in the sky, the wind blew fierce and wild. The big lamp had burnt out and it seemed to be no one's business to light it. He remembered the terrible night upon which Yugao had been bewitched. The house indeed was almost as dilapidated. But it was not quite so large and was (to Genji's comfort) at least to some small degree inhabited. Nevertheless it was a depressing place to spend the night at in such weather as this. Yet the snowstorm had a beauty and fascination of its own and it was tiresome that the lady whom he had come to visit was far too stiff and awkward to join him in appreciating its wildness. The dawn was just breaking and lifting one of the shutters with his own hand, he looked out at the snow-covered flowerbeds. Beyond them stretched great fields of snow untrodden by any foot. The sight was very strange and lovely, and moved by the thought that he must soon leave it: "Come and look how beautiful it is out of doors," he cried to the princess who was in an inner room. "It is unkind of you always to treat me as though I were a stranger." Although it was still dark the light of the snow enabled the ancient gentlewomen who had now returned to the room to see the freshness and beauty of Genji's face. Gazing at him with undisguised wonder and delight, they cried out to their mistress: "Yes, madam, indeed you must come. You are not behaving as you should. A young lady should be all kindness and pretty ways." Thus admonished, the princess who when told what to do could never think of any reasons for not doing it, giving her costume a touch here and there, reluctantly crept into the front room. Genji pretended to be still looking out of the window, but presently he managed to glance back into the room. His first impression was that her manner, had it been a little less diffident, would have been extremely pleasing. What an absurd mistake he had made. She was certainly very tall as was shown by the length of her back when she took her seat; he could hardly believe that such a back could belong to a woman. A moment afterwards he suddenly became aware of her main defect. It was her nose. He could not help looking at it. It reminded him of the

---

* *Manyoshu*, 893.

trunk of Samantbhadra's* steed! Not only was it amazingly prominent, but (strangest of all) the tip which drooped downwards a little was tinged with pink, contrasting in the oddest manner with the rest of her complexion which was of a whiteness that would have put snow to shame. Her forehead was unusually high, so that altogether (though this was partly concealed by the forward tilt of her head) her face must be hugely long. She was very thin, her bones showing in the most painful manner, particularly her shoulder-bones which jutted out pitiably above her dress. He was sorry now that he had exacted from her this distressing exhibition, but so extraordinary a spectacle did she provide that he could not help continuing to gaze upon her. In one point at least she yielded nothing to the greatest beauties of the Capital. Her hair was magnificent; she was wearing it loose and it hung a foot or more below the skirt of her gown. A complete description of people's costumes is apt to be tedious, but as in stories the first thing that is said about the characters is invariably *what they wore,* I shall once in a way attempt such a description. Over a terribly faded bodice of imperial purple she wore a gown of which the purple had turned definitely black with age. Her mantle was of sable-skins heavily perfumed with scent. Such a garment as this mantle was considered very smart several generations ago, but it struck him as the most extraordinary costume for a comparatively young girl. However, as a matter of fact she looked as though without this monstrous wrapping she would perish with cold and he could not help feeling sorry for her. As usual she seemed quite devoid of conversation and her silence ended by depriving Genji also of the power of speech. He felt however that he must try again to conquer her religious muteness and began making a string of casual remarks. Overcome with embarrassment she hid her face with her sleeve. This attitude, together with her costume, reminded him so forcibly of queer pompous old officials whom he had sometimes seen walking at funeral pace in state processions, hugging their emblems of office to their breasts, that he could not help laughing. This he felt to be very rude. Really he was very sorry for her and longing to put a quick end to her embarrassment he rose to go. "Till I began to look after you there was no one in whom you could possibly have confided. But henceforward I think you must make up your mind to be frank with me and tell me all your secrets. Your stern aloofness is very painful to me," and he recited the verse: "Already the icicle that hangs from the eaves is melting in the rays of the morning sun. How comes it that these drippings to new ice should turn?" At this she tittered slightly. Finding her inability to express herself quite unendurable, he left the house. Even in the dim light of early morning he noticed that the courtyard

---

* The Bodhisattva Samantabhadra rides on a white elephant with a red trunk.

gate at which his carriage awaited him was shaky on its posts and much askew; daylight, he was sure, would have revealed many other signs of dilapidation and neglect. In all the desolate landscape which stretched monotonously before him under the bleak light of dawn only the thick mantle of snow which covered the pine-trees gave a note of comfort and almost of warmth.

Surely it was such a place as this, somber as a little village in the hills that his friends had thought of on that rainy night when they had spoken of the gate "deep buried in green thickets." If only there were really hidden behind *these* walls some such exquisite creature as they had imagined. How patiently, how tenderly he would court her! He longed for some experience which would bring him respite from the anguish with which a certain hopeless and illicit passion was at that time tormenting him. Alas, no one could have been less likely to bring him the longed-for distraction than the owner of this romantic mansion. Yet the very fact that she had nothing to recommend her made it impossible for him to give her up, for it was certain that no one else would ever take the trouble to visit her. But why, why had it fallen to him of all people to become her intimate? Had the spirit of the departed Prince Hitachi, unhappy at the girl's friendless plight, chosen him out and led him to her?

At the side of the road he noticed a little orange-tree almost buried in snow. He ordered one of his attendants to uncover it. As though jealous of the attention that the man was paying to its neighbor, a pine-tree near by shook its heavily laden branches, pouring great billows of snow over his sleeve. Delighted with the scene, Genji suddenly longed for some companion with whom he might share this pleasure; not necessarily someone who loved such things as he did, but one who at least responded to them in an ordinary way.

The gate through which his carriage had to pass in order to leave the grounds was still locked. When at last the man who kept the key had been discovered, he turned out to be immensely old and feeble. With him was a big, awkward girl who seemed to be his daughter or granddaughter. Her dress looked very grimy in contrast with the new snow amid which she was standing. She seemed to be suffering very much from the cold, for she was hugging a little brazier of some kind with a stick or two of charcoal burning none too brightly in it. The old man had not the strength to push back the door, and the girl was dragging at it as well. Taking pity on them one of Genji's servants went to their assistance and quickly opened it. Genji remembered the poem in which Po Chü-i describes the sufferings of villagers in wintry weather and he murmured the lines: "The little children run naked in the cold; the aged shiver for lack of winter clothes." All at once he remembered the chilly appearance which that unhappy bloom had given to the princess's face and he could not help smiling. If ever he were able to show her to To no Chujo, what strange comparison, he wondered, would Chujo use concerning it? He remembered how Chujo had followed him on the first occasion. Had he continued to do so? Perhaps even at this minute he was under observation. The thought irritated him.

Had her defects been less striking he could not possibly have continued these distressing visits. But since he had actually seen her in all her tragic uncouthness, pity gained the upper hand, and henceforward he kept in constant touch with her and showed her every kindness. In the hope that she would abandon her sables he sent her presents of silk, satin and quilted stuffs. He also sent thick cloth such as old people wear, that the old man at the gate might be more comfortably dressed. Indeed he sent presents to everyone on the estate from the highest to the lowest. She did not seem to have any objection to receiving these donations, which under the circumstances was very convenient as it enabled him for the most part to limit their very singular friendship to good offices of this kind.

Utsusemi too, he remembered, had seemed to him far from handsome when he had peeped at her on the evening of her sudden flight. But she at least knew how to behave and that saved her plainness from being obtrusive. It was hard to believe that the princess belonged to a class so far above that of Utsusemi. It only showed how little these things have to do with birth or station. For in idle moments he still regretted the loss of Utsusemi and it rankled in him yet that he had in the end allowed her unyielding persistency to win the day.

And so the year drew to its close. One day when he was at his apartments in the Emperor's Palace, Myobu came to see him. He liked to have her to do his hair and do small commissions for him. He was not in the least in love with her; but they got on very well together and he found her conversation so amusing that even when she had no duty to perform at the Palace he encouraged her to come and see him whenever she had any news. "Something so absurd has happened," she said, "that I cam hardly bring myself to tell you about it..." and she paused smiling. "I can hardly think," answered Genji, "that there can be anything which you are frightened of telling to me." "If it were connected with my own affairs" she said, "you know quite well that I should tell you at once. But this is something quite different. I really find it very hard to talk about." For a long while he could get nothing out of her, and only after he had scolded her for making so unnecessary a fuss she at last handed him a letter. It was from the princess. "But this," said Genji taking it, "is the last thing in the world that you could have any reason to hide from me." She watched with interest while he read it. It was written on thick paper drenched with a strong perfume; the characters were bold and firm. With it was a poem: "Because of your hard heart, your hard heart only, the sleeves of this my Chinese dress are drenched with tears." The poem must, he thought, refer to something not contained in the letter.

He was considering what this could be, when his eye fell on a clumsy, old-fashioned clothes-box wrapped in a painted canvas cover. "Now," said Myobu, "perhaps you understand why I was feeling rather uncomfortable. You may not believe it, but the princess means you to wear this jacket on New Year's Day. I am afraid I cannot take it back to her; that would be too unkind. But if you like I will keep it for you and no one else shall see it. Only please, since it was to you that she sent, just have one look at it before it goes away." "But I should hate it to go away," said Genji; "I think it was so kind of her to send it." It was difficult to know what to say. Her poem was indeed the most unpleasant jangle of syllables that he had ever encountered. He now realized that the other poems must have been dictated to her, perhaps by Jiju or one of the other ladies. And Jiju too it must surely be who held the princess's brush and acted as writing-master. When he considered what her utmost poetic endeavor would be likely to produce he realized that these absurd verses were probably her masterpiece and should be prized accordingly. He began to examine the parcel; Myobu blushed while she watched him. It was a plain, old-fashioned, buff-colored jacket of finely woven material but apparently not particularly well cut or stitched. It was indeed a strange present, and spreading out her letter he wrote something carelessly in the margin. When Myobu looked over his shoulder she saw that he had written the verse: "How comes it that with my sleeve I brushed this saffron-flower[*] that has no loveliness either of shape or hue?"

What, wondered Myobu, could be the meaning of this outburst against a flower? At last turning over in her mind the various occasions when Genji had visited the princess, she remembered something[†] which she had herself noticed one moonlit night, and though she felt the joke was rather unkind, she could not help being amused. With practiced ease she threw out a verse in which she warned him that in the eyes of a censorious world even this half-whimsical courtship might fatally damage his good name. Her impromptu poem was certainly faulty; but Genji reflected that if the poor princess had even Myobu's very ordinary degree of alertness it would make things much easier; and it was quite true that to tamper with a lady of such high rank was not very safe.

At this point visitors began to arrive. "Please put this somewhere out of sight," said Genji pointing to the jacket; "could one have believed that it was possible to be presented with such an object?" and he groaned. "Oh, why ever did I show it to him?" thought Myobu. "The only result is that

---

[*] *Suyetsumuhana*, by which name the princess is subsequently alluded to in the story.

[†] I.e. the redness of the princess's nose.

now he will be angry with me as well as with the princess," and in very low spirits she slipped out of his apartments.

Next day she was in attendance upon the Emperor and while she was waiting with other gentlewomen in the ladies' common-room Genji came up saying: "Here you are. The answer to yesterday's letter. I am afraid it is rather far-fetched," and he flung a note to her. The curiosity of the other gentlewomen was violently aroused. Genji left the room humming, "The Lady of Mikasa Hill,"* which naturally amused Myobu very much. The other ladies wanted to know why the Prince was laughing to himself. Was there some joke...? "Oh, no," said Myobu; "I think it was only that he had noticed someone whose nose was a little red with the morning cold. The song he hummed was surely very appropriate." "I think it was very silly," said one of the ladies. "There is no one here today with a red nose. He must be thinking of Lady Sakon or Higo no Uneme." They were completely mystified. When Myobu presented Genji's reply, the ladies of the Hitachi Palace gathered round her to admire it. It was written negligently on plain white paper but was nonetheless very elegant. "Does your gift of a garment mean that you wish a greater distance than ever to be kept between us?"†

On the evening of the last day of the year he sent back the box which had contained his jacket, putting into it a court dress which had formerly been presented to him, a dress of woven stuff dyed grape-color and various stuffs of yellow-rose color and the like. The box was brought by Myobu. The princess's ancient gentlewomen realized that Genji did not approve of their mistress's taste in colors and wished to give her a lesson. "Yes," they said grudgingly, "that's a fine deep red while it's new, but just think how it will fade. And in Madam's poem too, I am sure, there was much more good sense. In his answer he only tries to be smart." The princess shared their good opinion of her poem. It had cost her a great deal of effort and before she sent it she had been careful to copy it into her notebook.

Then came the New Year's Day celebrations; and this year there was also to be the New Year's mumming, a band of young noblemen going round dancing and singing in various parts of the Palace. After the festival of the White Horse on the seventh day Genji left the Emperor's presence at nightfall and went to his own apartments in the Palace as though intending to stay the night there. But later he adjourned to the Hitachi Palace which had on this occasion a less forbidding appearance than usual. Even the princess was rather more ordinary and amenable.

---

* A popular song about a lady who suffered from the same defect as the princess.

† Genji's poem is an allusion to a well-known *uta* which runs: "Must we who once would not allow even the thickness of a garment to part us be now far from each other for whole nights on end?"

He was hoping that like the season she too had begun anew, when he saw that sunlight was coming into the room. After hesitating for a while, he got up and went out into the front room. The double doors at the end of the eastern wing were wide open, and the roof of the verandah having fallen in, the sunshine poured straight into the house. A little snow was still falling and its brightness made the morning light yet more exquisitely brilliant and sparkling. She watched a servant helping him into his cloak. She was lying half out of the bed, her head hanging a little downwards and her hair falling in great waves to the floor. Pleased with the sight he began to wonder whether she would not one day outgrow her plainness. He began to close the door of the women's apartments, but suddenly feeling that he owed her amends for the harsh opinion of her appearance which he had formed before, he did not quite shut the door, but bringing a low stool towards it sat there putting his disordered headdress to rights. One of the maids brought him an incredibly battered mirror-stand, Chinese combs, a box of toilet articles and other things It amused him to discover that in this household of women a little male gear still survived, even in so decrepit a state.

He noticed that the princess, who was now up and dressed, was looking quite fashionable. She was in fact wearing the clothes which he had sent her before the New Year, but he did not at first recognize them. He began however to have a vague idea that her mantle, with its rather conspicuous pattern, was very like one of the things he had given her. "I do hope," he said presently, "that this year you will be a little more conversational. I await the day when you will unbend a little towards me more eagerly than the poet longs for the first nightingale. If only like the year that has changed you too would begin anew!" Her face brightened. She had thought of a remark and trembling from head to foot with a tremendous effort she brought out the quotation, "When plovers chirp and all things grow anew." "Splendid," said Genji, "this is a sign that the new year has indeed begun," and smiling encouragingly at her he left the house, she following him with her eyes from the couch on which she lay. Her face as usual was half-covered by her arm; but the unfortunate flower still bloomed conspicuously. "Poor thing, she really *is* very ugly," thought Genji in despair.

When he returned to the Nijo-in he found Murasaki waiting for him. She was growing up as handsome a girl as one could wish, and promised well for the future. She was wearing a plain close-fitting dress of cherry color; above all, the unstudied grace and ease of her movements charmed and delighted him as he watched her come to meet him. In accordance with the wishes of her old-fashioned grandmother her teeth were not blackened, but her eyebrows were delicately touched with stain. "Why, when I might be playing with a beautiful child, do I spend my time with an ugly woman?" Genji kept on asking himself in bewilderment while they sat together playing with her dolls. Next she began to draw pictures and color them. After she had painted all sorts of queer and amusing things, "Now I am going to do a picture for you," said Genji and drawing a lady with very long hair he put a dab of red on her nose. Even in a picture, he thought pausing to look at the effect, it gave one a most uncomfortable feeling. He went and looked at himself in the mirror and as though dissatisfied with his own fresh complexion, he suddenly put on his own nose a dab of red such as he had given to the lady in the picture. He looked at himself in the mirror. His handsome face had in an instant become ridiculous and repulsive. At first the child laughed. "Should you go on liking me if I were always as ugly as this?" he asked. Suddenly she began to be afraid that the paint would not come off. "Oh, why did you do it?" she cried. "How horrible!" He pretended to rub it without effect. "No," he said ruefully, "it will not come off. What a sad end to our game! I wonder what the Emperor will say when I go back to the Palace?" He said it so seriously that she became very unhappy, and longing to cure him, dipped a piece of thick soft paper in the water-jug which stood by his writing-things, and began scrubbing at his nose. "Take care," he cried laughing, "that you do not serve me as Heichu* was treated by his lady. I would rather have a red nose than a black one." So they passed their time, making the prettiest couple.

In the gentle spring sunshine the trees were already shimmering with a haze of new-grown buds. Among them it was the plum trees that gave the surest promise, for already their blossoms were uncurling, like lips parted in a faint smile. Earliest of them all was a red plum that grew beside the covered steps. It was in full color. "Though fair the tree on which it blooms, this red flower fills me with a strange misgiving,"† sang Genji with a deep sigh.

We shall see in the next chapter what happened in the end to all these people.

---

* He used to splash his cheeks with water from a little bottle in order that she might think he was weeping at her unkindness. She exposed this device by mixing ink with the water.

† The reference of course is to the princess. 'Though fair the tree' refers to her high birth.

The Festival of Red Leaves

The imperial visit to the Red Sparrow Court was to take place on the tenth day of the Godless Month. It was to be a more magnificent sight this year than it had ever been before and the ladies of the Palace were very disappointed that they could not be present.* The Emperor too could not bear that Fujitsubo should miss the spectacle, and he decided to hold a grand rehearsal in the Palace. Prince Genji danced the "Waves of the Blue Sea." To no Chujo was his partner; but though both in skill and beauty he far surpassed the common run of performers, yet beside Genji he seemed like a mountain fir growing beside a cherry-tree in bloom. There was a wonderful moment when the rays of the setting sun fell upon him and the music grew suddenly louder. Never had the onlookers seen feet tread so delicately nor head so exquisitely poised; and in the song which follows the first movement of the dance his voice was sweet as that of Kaiavinka† whose music is Buddha's Law. So moving and beautiful was this dance that at the end of it the Emperor's eyes were wet, and all the princes and great gentlemen wept aloud. When the song was over and, straightening his long dancer's sleeves, he stood waiting for the music to begin again and at last the more lively tune of the second movement struck up—then indeed, with his flushed and eager face, he merited more than ever his name of Genji the Shining One. The Princess Kokiden‡ did not at all like to see her stepson's beauty arousing so much enthusiasm and she said sarcastically: "He is altogether too beautiful. Presently we shall have a god coming down from the sky to fetch him away."§ Her young waiting-ladies noticed the spiteful tone in which the remark was made and felt somewhat embarrassed. As for Fujitsubo, she kept on telling herself that were it not for the guilty secret which was shared between them the dance she was now witnessing would be filling her with wonder and delight. As it was, she sat as though in a dream, hardly knowing what went on around her.

Now she was back in her own room. The Emperor was with her. "At today's rehearsal," he said, "the 'Waves of the Blue Sea' went perfectly." Then, noticing that she made no response, "What did you think of it?"

---

* They were not allowed to leave the palace.
† The bird that sings in Paradise.
‡ See above, p. 5.
§ In allusion to a boy-prince of seven years old whom the jealous gods carried off to the sky. See the *Okagami*.

"Yes, it was very good," she managed to say at last. "The partner did not seem to me bad either," he went on; "there is always something about the way a gentleman moves and uses his hands which distinguishes his dancing from that of professionals. Some of our crack dancing-masters have certainly made very clever performers of their own children; but they never have the same freshness, the same charm as the young people of our class. They expended so much effort on the rehearsal that I am afraid the festival itself may seem a very poor affair. No doubt they took all this trouble because they knew that you were here at the rehearsal and would not see the real performance."

Next morning she received a letter from Genji: "What of the rehearsal? How little the people who watched me knew of the turmoil that all the while was seething in my brain!" And to this he added the poem: "When sick with love I yet sprang to my feet and capered with the rest, knew you what meant the fevered waving of my long dancing-sleeve?" Next he enjoined secrecy and prudence upon her, and so his letter ended. Her answer showed that despite her agitation she had not been wholly insensible to what had fascinated all other eyes: "Though from far off a man of China waved his long dancing-sleeves, yet did his every motion fill my heart with wonder and delight."

To receive such a letter from her was indeed a surprise. It charmed him that her knowledge should extend even to the Court customs of a land beyond the sea. Already there was a regal note in her words. Yes, that was the end to which she was destined. Smiling to himself with pleasure he spread the letter out before him, grasping it tightly in both hands as a priest holds the holy book, and gazed at it for a long while.

On the day of the festival the royal princes and all the great gentlemen of the Court were in attendance. Even the Heir Apparent went with the procession. After the music-boats had rowed round the lake, dance upon dance was performed, both Korean and of the land beyond the sea. The whole valley resounded with the noise of music and drums. The Emperor insisted upon treating Genji's performance at the rehearsal as a kind of miracle or religious portent, and ordered special services to be read in every temple. Most people thought this step quite reasonable; but Princess Kokiden said crossly that she saw no necessity for it. The Ring* was by the Emperor's order composed indifferently of commoners and noblemen chosen out of the whole realm for their skill and grace. The two Masters of Ceremony, Sayemon no Kami and Uyemon no Kami, were in charge of the left and right wings of the orchestra. Dancing-masters and others were entrusted with the task of seeking out performers of unusual merit and training them for the festival in their own houses. When at last under the red leafage of

---

* Those who stand in a circle round the dancers while the latter change their clothes

tall autumn trees forty men stood circle-wise with their flutes, and to the music that they made a strong wind from the hills sweeping the pine-woods added its fierce harmonies, while from amid a wreckage of whirling and scattered leaves the Dance of the Blue waves suddenly broke out in all its glittering splendor—a rapture seized the onlookers that was akin to fear.

The maple-wreath that Genji wore had suffered in the wind and thinking that the few red leaves which clung to it had a desolate air, the Minister of the Left* plucked a bunch of chrysanthemums from among those that grew before the Emperor's seat and twined them in the dancer's wreath.

At sunset the sky clouded over and it looked like rain. But even the weather seemed conscious that such sights as this would not for a long while be seen again, and till all was over not a drop fell. His Exit Dance, crowned as he was with this unspeakably beautiful wreath of many-colored flowers, was even more astonishing than that wonderful moment on the day of the rehearsal and seemed to the thrilled onlookers like the vision of another world. Humble and ignorant folk sitting afar on tree-roots or beneath some rock, or half-buried in deep banks of fallen leaves—few were so hardened that they did not shed a tear. Next came the "Autumn Wind" danced by Lady Jokyoden's son† who was still a mere child. The remaining performances attracted little attention, for the audience had had its fill of wonders and felt that whatever followed could but spoil the recollection of what had gone before.

That night Genji was promoted to the First Class of the Third Rank and To no Chujo was promoted to intermediate standing between the First and Second Classes of the Fourth Rank. The gentlemen of the court were all promoted one rank. But though they celebrated their good fortune with the usual rejoicings they were well aware that they had only been dragged in Genji's wake and wondered how it was that their destinies had come to be linked in this curious way with those of the Prince who had brought them this unexpected piece of good fortune.

Fujitsubo now retired to her own house and Genji, waiting about for a chance of visiting her, was seldom at the Great Hall and was consequently in very ill odor there. It was soon after this that he brought the child Murasaki to live with him. Aoi heard a rumor of this, but it reached her merely in the form that someone was living with him at his palace and she did not know that it was a child. Under these circumstances it was quite natural that she should feel much aggrieved. But if only she had flown into an honest passion and abused him for it as most people would have done, he would have told her everything and put matters right. As it was, she only redoubled her icy aloofness and thus led him to seek those very

---

* Reading "Sadaijin," not "Sadaisho."

† Another illegitimate son of the Emperor—Genji's stepbrother.

distractions of which it was intended as a rebuke. Not only was her beauty so flawless that it could not fail to win his admiration, but also the mere fact that he had known her since so long ago, before all the rest, made him feel towards her a tenderness of which she seemed quite unaware. He was convinced however that her nature was not at bottom narrow and vindictive, and this gave him some hope that she would one day relent.

Meanwhile as he got to know little Murasaki better he became the more content both with her appearance and her character. She at least gave him her whole heart. For the present he did not intend to reveal her identity even to the servants in his own palace. She continued to use the somewhat outlying western wing which had now been put into excellent order, and here Genji constantly came to see her. He gave her all kinds of lessons, writing exercises for her to copy and treating her in every way as though she were a little daughter who had been brought up by foster-parents, but had now come to live with him. He chose her servants with great care and gave orders that they should do everything in their power to make her comfortable; but no one except Koremitsu knew who the child was or how she came to be living there. Nor had her father discovered what had become of her.

The little girl still sometimes thought of the past and then she would feel for a while very lonely without her grandmother. When Genji was there she forgot her sorrow; but in the evening he was very seldom at home. She was sorry that he was so busy and when he hurried every evening to some strange place or other she missed him terribly; but she was never angry with him. Sometimes for two or three days on end he would be at the Palace or the Great Hall and when he returned he would find her very tearful and depressed. Then he felt just as though he were neglecting some child of his own, whose mother had died and left it in his keeping, and for a while he grew uneasy about his night excursions.

The priest was puzzled when he heard that Genji had taken Murasaki to live with him, but saw no harm in it and was delighted that she should be so well cared for. He was gratified too when Genji begged that the services in the dead nun's memory should be celebrated with special pomp and magnificence.

When he went to Fujitsubo's palace, anxious to see for himself whether she was keeping her health, he was met by a posse of waiting-women (Myobus, Chunagons, Nakatsukasas and the like) and Fujitsubo herself showed, to his great disappointment, no sign of appearing. They gave a good account of her, which somewhat allayed his anxiety, and had passed on to general gossip when it was announced that Prince Hyobukyo[*] had arrived. Genji at once went out to speak to him. This time Genji thought

---

[*] Fujitsubo's brother; Murasaki's father.

him extremely handsome and there was a softness, a caressing quality in his manner (Genji was watching him more closely than he knew) which was feminine enough to make his connection with Fujitsubo and Murasaki at once uppermost in the mind of his observer. It was, then, as the brother of the one and the father of the other that the newcomer at once created a feeling of intimacy, and they had a long conversation. Hyobukyo could not fail to notice that Genji was suddenly treating him with an affection which he had never displayed before. He was naturally very much gratified, not realizing that Genji had now, in a sense, become his son-in-law. It was getting late and Hyobukyo was about to join his sister in another room. It was with bitterness that Genji remembered how long ago the Emperor had brought her to play with him. In those days he ran in and out of her room just as he chose; now he could not address her save in precarious messages. She was as inaccessible, as remote as one person conceivably could be from another, and finding the situation intolerable, he said politely to Prince Hyobukyo: "I wish I saw you more often; unless there is some special reason for seeing people, I am lazy about it. But if you ever felt inclined to send for me, I should be delighted..." and he hurried away.

Omyobu, the gentlewoman who had contrived Genji's meeting with Fujitsubo, seeing her mistress relapse into a steady gloom and vexed at her belated caution, was all the time doing her best to bring the lovers together again; but days and months went by and still all her efforts were in vain; while they, poor souls, strove desperately to put away from them this love that was a perpetual disaster.

At Genji's palace Shonagon, the little girl's nurse, finding herself in a world of unimagined luxuries and amenities, could only attribute this good fortune to the success of the late nun's prayers. The Lord Buddha to whose protection the dying lady had so fervently recommended her granddaughter had indeed made handsome provision for her. There were of course certain disadvantages. The haughtiness of Aoi was not only in itself to be feared, but it seemed to have the consequence of driving Prince Genji to seek distractions right and left, which would be very unpleasant for the little princess so soon as she was old enough to realize it. Yet so strong a preference did he show for the child's company that Shonagon did not altogether lose heart.

It being then three months since her grandmother died Murasaki came out of mourning at the end of the Godless Month. But it was thought proper since she was to be brought up as an orphan that she should still avoid patterned stuffs, and she wore a little tunic of plain red, brown, or yellow, in which she nevertheless looked very smart and gay.

He came to have a look at her before going off to the New Year's Day reception at Court. "From today onwards you are a grown-up lady," he said, and as he stood smiling at her he looked so charming and friendly that she could not bear him to go, and hoping that he would stay and play with her a little while longer, she got out her toys. There was a doll's kitchen only three feet high but fitted out with all the proper utensils, and a whole collection of little houses which Genji had made for her. Now she had got them all spread out over the floor so that it was difficult to move without treading on them. "Little Inu broke them yesterday," she explained, "when he was pretending to drive out the Old Year's demons, and I am mending them." She was evidently in great trouble. "What a tiresome child he is," said Genji. "I will get them mended for you. Come, you must not cry on New Year's Day," and he went out. Many of the servants had collected at the end of the corridor to see him starting out for the Court in all his splendor. Murasaki too went out and watched him. When she came back she put a grand dress on one of her dolls and did a performance with it which she called "Prince Genji visiting the Emperor." "This year," said Shonagon, looking on with disapproval, "you must really try not to be such a baby. It is time little girls stopped playing with dolls when they are ten years old, and now that you have got a kind gentleman wanting to be your husband you ought to try and show him that you can behave like a nice little grown-up lady or he will get tired of waiting." She said this because she thought that it must be painful for Genji to see the child still so intent upon her games and be thus reminded that she was a mere baby. Her admonishment had the effect of making Murasaki for the first time aware that Genji was to be her husband. She knew all about husbands. Many of the maid-servants had them, but such ugly ones! She was very glad that hers was so much younger and handsomer. Nevertheless the mere fact that she thought about the matter at all showed that she was beginning to grow up a little. Her childish ways and appearance were by no means so great a misfortune as Shonagon supposed, for they went a long way towards allaying the suspicions which the child's presence might otherwise have aroused in Genji's somewhat puzzled household.

When he returned from Court he went straight to the Great Hall. Aoi was as perfect as ever, and just as unfriendly. This never failed to wound Genji. "If only you had changed with the New Year, had become a little less cold and forbidding, how happy I should be!" he exclaimed. But she had heard that someone was living with him and had at once made up her mind that she herself had been utterly supplanted and put aside. Hence she was more sullen than ever; but he pretended not to notice it and by his gaiety and gentleness at last induced her to answer when he spoke. Was it her being four years older than he that made her seem so unapproachable, so exasperatingly well-regulated? But that was not fair. What fault could he possibly find in her? She was perfect in every respect and he realized that if she was sometimes out of humor this was solely the result of his own irregularities. She was after all the daughter of a Minister, and of the Minister who above all others enjoyed the greatest influence and esteem. She was the only child of the Emperor's sister and had been brought up with a full sense of her own dignity and importance. The least slight, the merest hint of disrespect came to her as a complete surprise. To Genji all these pretensions naturally seemed somewhat exaggerated and his failure to make allowances for them increased her hostility.

Aoi's father was vexed by Genji's seeming fickleness, but so soon as he was with him he forgot all his grievances and was always extremely nice to him. When Genji was leaving next day his father-in-law came to his room and helped him to dress, bringing in his own hands a belt which was an heirloom famous far and wide. He pulled straight the back of Genji's robe which had become a little crumpled, and indeed short of bringing him his shoes performed in the friendliest way every possible small service. "This," said Genji handing back the belt, "is for Imperial banquets or other great occasions of that kind." "I have others much more valuable," said the Minister, "which I will give you for the Imperial banquets. This one is not of much account save that the workmanship of it is rather unusual," and despite Genji's protests he insisted upon buckling it round him. The performance of such services was his principal interest in life. What did it matter if Genji was rather irregular in his visits? To have so agreeable a young man going in and out of one's house at all was the greatest pleasure he could imagine.

Genji did not pay many New Year's visits. First he went to the Emperor, then the Heir Apparent and the ex-Emperor, and after that to Princess Fujitsubo's house in the Third Ward. As they saw him enter, the servants of the house noticed how much he had grown and altered in the last year. "Look how he has filled out," they said, "even since his last visit!" Of the Princess herself he was only allowed a distant glimpse. It gave him many forebodings. Her child had been expected in the twelfth month and her condition was now causing some anxiety. That it would at any rate be born sometime during the first weeks of the New Year was confidently assumed by her own people and had been stated at Court. But the first month went by and still nothing happened. It began to be rumored that she was suffering from some kind of possession or delusion. She herself grew very depressed; she felt certain that when the event at last happened she would not survive it and she worried so much about herself that she became seriously ill. The delay made Genji more certain than ever of his own responsibility and he arranged secretly for prayers on her behalf to be said in all the great temples. He had already become firmly convinced that whatever might happen concerning the child, Fujitsubo was herself utterly doomed when he heard that about the tenth day of the second month she had successfully given birth to a boy. The news brought great satisfaction both to the Emperor and the whole court.

The Emperor's fervent prayers for her life and for that of a child which she knew was not his distressed and embarrassed her; whereas, when the maliciously gloomy prognostications of Kokiden and the rest were brought to her notice, she was at once filled with a perverse desire to disappoint their hopes and make them look ridiculous in the eyes of those to whom they had confided their forebodings. By a great effort of will she threw off the despair which had been weighing down upon her and began little by little to recover her usual vigor.

The Emperor was impatient to see Fujitsubo's child and so too (though he was forced to conceal his interest in the matter) was Genji himself. Accordingly he went to her palace when there were not many people about and sent in a note, offering as the Emperor was in such a state of impatience to see the child and etiquette forbad him to do so for several weeks, to look at the child himself and report upon its appearance to the Emperor. She replied that she would rather he saw it on a day when it was less peevish; but in reality her refusal had nothing to do with the state of the child's temper; she could not bear the idea of his seeing it at all. Already it bore an astonishing resemblance to him; of that she was convinced. Always there lurked in her heart the torturing demon of fear. Soon others would see the child and instantly know with absolute certainty the secret of her swift transgression. What charity towards such a crime as this would a world have that gossips if a single hair is awry? Such thoughts continually tormented her and she again became weary of her life.

From time to time he saw Omyobu, but though he still implored her to arrange a meeting, none of his many arguments availed him. He also pestered her with so many questions about the child that she exclaimed at last: "Why do you go on plaguing me like this? You will be seeing him for yourself soon, when he is shown at Court." But though she spoke impatiently she knew quite well what he was suffering and felt for him deeply. The matter was not one which he could discuss except with Fujitsubo herself, and it was impossible to see her. Would he indeed ever again see her alone or communicate with her save through notes and messengers? And half-weeping with despair he recited the verse: "What guilty intercourse must ours have been in some life long ago, that now so cruel a barrier should be set between us?" Omyobu, seeing that it cost her mistress a great struggle to do without him, was at pains not to dismiss him too unkindly and answered with the verse: "Should you see the child, my lady would be in torment; and because you have not seen it you are full of lamentations. Truly have children been called a black darkness that leads the parents' heart astray!" And coming closer she whispered to him, "Poor souls, it is a hard fate that has overtaken you both." Thus many times and again he returned to his house desperate. Fujitsubo meanwhile, fearing lest Genji's continual visits should attract notice, began to suspect that Omyobu was secretly encouraging him and no longer felt the same affection for her. She did not want this to be noticed and tried to treat her just as usual; but her irritation was bound sometimes to betray itself and Omyobu, feeling that her mistress was estranged from her and at a loss to find any reason for it, was very miserable.

It was not till its fourth month that the child was brought to the Palace. It was large for its age and had already begun to take a great interest in what went on around it. Its extraordinary resemblance to Genji was not remarked upon by the Emperor who had an idea that handsome children were all very much alike at that age. He became intensely devoted to the child and lavished every kind of care and attention upon it. For Genji himself he had always had so great a partiality that, had it not been for popular opposition, he would certainly have installed him as Heir Apparent. That he had not been able to do so constantly distressed him. To have produced so magnificent a son and be obliged to watch him growing up a mere nobleman had always been galling to him. Now in his old age a son had been born to him who promised to be equally handsome and had not the tiresome disadvantage of a plebeian mother, and upon this flawless pearl he expended his whole affection. The mother saw little chance of this rapture continuing and was all this while in a state of agonized apprehension.

One day, when as he had been wont to do before, Genji was making music for her at the Emperor's command, His Majesty took the child in his arms, saying to Genji: "I have had many children, but you were the only other one that I ever behaved about in this fashion. It may be my fancy, but it seems to me this child is exactly like what you were at the same age. However, I suppose all babies are very much alike while they are as small as this," and he looked at the fine child with admiration. A succession of violent emotions—terror, shame, pride, and love—passed through Genji's breast while these words were being spoken, and were reflected in his rapidly changing color. He was almost in tears. The child looked so exquisitely beautiful as it lay crowing to itself and smiling that, hideous as the situation was, Genji could not help feeling glad it was thought to be like him. Fujitsubo meanwhile was in a state of embarrassment and agitation so painful that a cold sweat broke out upon her while she sat by. For Genji this jarring of opposite emotions was too much to be borne and he went home. Here he lay tossing on his bed and, unable to distract himself, he determined after a while to go to the Great Hall. As he passed by the flower-beds in front of his house, he noticed that a faint tinge of green was already filming the bushes and under them the *tohonatsu** were already in bloom. He plucked one and sent it to Omyobu with a long letter and an acrostic poem in which he said that he was touched by the likeness of this flower to the child, but also hinted that he was perturbed by the child's likeness to himself. "In this flower," he continued despondently, "I had hoped to see your beauty enshrined. But now I know that being mine yet not mine it can bring me no comfort to look upon it." After waiting a little while till a favorable moment should arise Omyobu showed her mistress the letter, saying with a sigh, "I fear that your answer will be but dust to the petals of this thirsting flower." But Fujitsubo, in whose heart also the new spring was awakening a host of tender thoughts, wrote in answer the poem: "Though it alone be the cause that these poor sleeves are wet with dew, yet goes my heart still with it, this child-flower of Yamato Land." This was all and it was roughly scribbled in a faint hand, but it was a comfort to Omyobu to have even such a message as this to bring back. Genji knew quite well that it could lead to nothing. How many times had she sent him such messages before! Yet as he lay dejectedly gazing at the note, the mere sight of her handwriting soon stirred in him a frenzy of unreasoning excitement and delight. For a while he lay restlessly tossing on his bed. At last unable to remain any longer inactive he sprang up and went, as he had so often done before, to the western wing to seek distraction from the agitated thoughts which pursued him. He came towards the women's apartments with his hair loose upon his shoulders, wearing a queer dressing-gown and, in order to amuse Murasaki, playing a tune on his flute as he walked, he peeped in at the door. She looked as she lay there for all the world like the fresh dewy flower that he had so recently plucked. She was growing a little bit spoilt and having heard some while ago that he had returned from Court she was rather cross with him for not coming to see her at once. She did not run to meet him as she usually did, but lay with her head turned away. He called to her from the far side of the room to get up and come to him, but she did not stir. Suddenly he heard that she was murmuring to herself the lines "Like a sea-flower that the waters have covered when a great tide mounts the shore." They were from an old poem† that he had taught her, in which a lady complains that she is neglected by her lover. She looked bewitching as she lay with her face half-sullenly, half-coquettishly buried in her sleeve. "How naughty," he cried. "Really you are becoming too witty. But if you saw me more often perhaps you would grow tired of me." Then he sent for his zithern and asked her to play to him. But it was a big Chinese instrument‡ with thirteen strings; the five slender strings in the

---

* Another name for the *nadeshiko*, "Child-of-my-heart," see p. 30.

† *Shu-i Shu* 967.

‡ A so no koto.

middle embarrassed her and she could not get the full sound out of them. Taking it from her he shifted the bridge, and tuning it to a lower pitch played a few chords upon it and bade her try again. Her sullen mood was over. She began to play very prettily; sometimes, when there was a gap too long for one small hand to stretch, helping herself out so adroitly with the other hand that Genji was completely captivated and taking up his flute taught her a number of new tunes. She was very quick and grasped the most complicated rhythms at a single hearing. She had indeed in music as in all else just those talents with which it most delighted him that she should be endowed. When he played the Hosoroguseri (which in spite of its absurd name is an excellent tune) she accompanied him though with a childish touch, yet in perfect time.

The great lamp was brought in and they began looking at pictures together. But Genji was going out that night. Already his attendants were assembled in the courtyard outside. One of them was saying that a storm was coming on. He ought not to wait any longer. Again Murasaki was unhappy. She was not looking at the pictures, but sat with her head on her hands staring despondently at the floor. Stroking the lovely hair that had fallen forward across her lap, Genji asked her if she missed him when he was away. She nodded. "I am just the same," he said. "If I miss seeing you for a single day I am terribly unhappy. But you are only a little girl and I know that whatever I do you will not think harsh thoughts about me; while the lady that I go to see is very jealous and angry so that it would break her heart if I were to stay with you too long. But I do not at all like being there and that is why I just go for a little while like this. When you are grown up of course I shall never go away at all. I only go now because if I did not she would be so terribly angry with me that I might very likely die* and then there would be no one to love you and take care of you at all." He had told her all he could, but still she was offended and would not answer a word. At last he took her on his knee and here to his great embarrassment she fell asleep. "It is too late to go out now," he said after a while, turning to the gentlewomen who were in attendance. They rose and went to fetch his supper. He roused the child. "Look," he said," I did not go out after all." She was happy once more and they went to supper together. She liked the queer, irregular meal, but when it was over she began again to watch him uneasily. "If you are really not going out," she said, "why do you not go to sleep at once?" Leaving her at such a moment to go back to his room, he felt all the reluctance of one who is setting out upon a long and perilous journey.

It constantly happened that at the last minute he thus decided to stay with her. It was natural that some report of his new preoccupation should

---

* That hate kills is a fundamental thesis of the book.

leak out into the world and be passed on to the Great Hall. "Who can it be?" said one of Aoi's ladies. "It is really the most inexplicable business. How can he have suddenly become entirely wrapped up in someone whom we had never heard the existence of before? It cannot in any case be a person of much breeding or self-respect. It is probably some girl employed at the Palace whom he has taken to live with him in order that the affair may be hushed up. No doubt he is circulating the story that she is a child merely in order to put us off the scent." And this opinion was shared by the rest.

The Emperor too had heard that there was someone living with Genji and thought it a great pity. "You are treating the Minister very badly," he said. "He has shown the greatest possible devotion to you ever since you were a mere baby and now that you are old enough to know better you behave like this towards him and his family! It is really most ungrateful."

Genji listened respectfully, but made no reply. The Emperor began to fear that his marriage with Aoi had proved a very unhappy one and was sorry that he had arranged it. "I do not understand you," he said, "You seem to have no taste for gallantry and do not, so far as I can see, take the slightest interest in any of the ladies-in-waiting whom one might expect you to find attractive, nor do you bother yourself about the various beauties who in one part of the town or another are now in request; but instead you must needs pick up some creature from no one knows where and wound the feelings of others by keeping her as your mistress!

Though he was now getting on in years the Emperor had himself by no means ceased to be interested in such matters. He had always seen to it that his ladies-in-waiting and palace-servants should be remarkable both for their looks and their intelligence, and it was a time when the Court was full of interesting women. There were few among them whom Genji could not by the slightest word or gesture have made his own. But, perhaps because he saw too much of them, he did not find them in the least attractive. Suspecting this, they would occasionally experiment upon him with some frivolous remark. He answered so staidly that they saw a flirtation would be impossible and some of them came to the conclusion that he was rather a dull, prudish young man.

There was an elderly lady-of-the-bedchamber who, though she was an excellent creature in every other way and was very much liked and respected, was an outrageous flirt. It astonished Genji that despite her advancing years she showed no sign of reforming her reckless and fantastic behavior. Curious to see how she would take it, he one day came up and began joking with her. She appeared to be quite unconscious of the disparity between their ages and at once counted him as an admirer. Slightly alarmed, he nevertheless found her company rather agreeable and often talked with her. But, chiefly because he was frightened of being laughed at if anyone found out, he refused to become her lover, and this she very much resented. One day she was dressing the Emperor's hair. When this was over His Majesty sent for his valets and went with them into another room. Genji and the elderly lady were left alone together. She was fuller than ever of languishing airs and poses, and her costume was to the last degree stylish and elaborate. "Poor creature," he thought, "how little difference it all makes!" and he was passing her on his way out of the room when suddenly the temptation to give a tug at her dress became irresistible. She glanced swiftly round, eyeing him above the rim of a marvelously painted summer-fan. The eyelids beneath which she ogled at his were blackened and sunken; wisps of hair projected untidily around her forehead. There was something singularly inappropriate about this gaudy, coquettish fan. Handing her his own instead, he took it from her and examined it. On paper coated with a red so thick and lustrous that you could see yourself reflected in it a forest of tall trees was painted in gold. At the side of this design, in a hand which though out-of-date was not lacking in distinction was written the poem about the Forest of Oaraki.* He made no doubt that the owner of the fan had written it in allusion to her own advancing years and was expecting him to make a gallant reply. Turning over in his mind how best to divert the extravagant ardor of this strange creature, he could, to his own amusement, think only of another poem† about the same forest; but to this it would have been ill-bred to allude. He was feeling very uncomfortable lest some one should come in and see them together. She however was quite at her ease and seeing that he remained silent she recited with many arch looks the poem: "Come to me in the forest and I will cut pasture for your horse, though it be but of the under leaf whose season is past." "Should I seek your woodland," he answered, "my fair name would be gone, for down its glades at all times the pattering of hoofs is heard," and he tried to get away; but she held him back saying: "How odious you are! That is not what I mean at all. No one has ever insulted me like this before," and she burst into tears. "Let us talk about it some other time," said Genji; "I did not mean..." and freeing himself from her grasp he rushed out of the room, leaving her in great dudgeon. She felt indeed after his repulse prodigiously old and tottering. All this was seen by His Majesty who, his toilet long ago completed, had watched the ill-assorted pair with great amusement from behind his Imperial screen. "I am always being told," he said, "that the boy takes no interest in the members of my household. But I cannot say that he seems to me unduly shy," and he laughed.

---

* "So withered is the grass beneath its trees that the young colt will not graze there and the reapers do not come."

† "So sweet is its shade that all the summer through its leafy avenues are thronged," alluding to the lady's many lovers.

For a moment she was slightly embarrassed; but she felt that any relationship with Genji, even if it consisted of being rebuffed by him in public, was distinctly a feather in her cap, and she made no attempt to defend herself against the Emperor's raillery. The story soon went the round of the Court. It astonished no one more than To no Chujo who, though he knew that Genji was given to odd experiments, could not believe that his friend was really launched upon the fantastic courtship which rumor was attributing to him. There seemed no better way of discovering whether it was conceivably possible to regard the lady in such a light than to make love to her himself.

The attentions of so distinguished a suitor went a long way towards consoling her for her late discomfiture. Her new intrigue was of course carried on with absolute secrecy and Genji knew nothing about it. When he next met her she seemed to be very cross with him, and feeling sorry for her because she was so old he made up his mind that he must try to console her. But for a long while he was completely occupied by tiresome business of one kind and another. At last one very dismal rainy evening when he was strolling in the neighborhood of the Ummeiden* he heard this lady playing most agreeably on her lute. She was so good a performer that she was often called upon to play with the professional male musicians in the Imperial orchestra. It happened that at this moment she was somewhat downcast and discontented, and in such a mood she played with even greater feeling and verve. She was singing the "Melon-grower's Song";† admirably, he thought, despite its inappropriateness to her age. So must the voice of the mysterious lady at O-chou have sounded in Po Chü-i's ears when he heard her singing on her boat at night;‡ and he stood listening. At the end of the song the player sighed heavily as though quite worn out by the passionate vehemence of her serenade. Genji approached softly humming the "Azumaya": "Here in the portico of the eastern house rain splashes on me while I wait. Come, my beloved, open the door and let me in." Immediately, indeed with an unseemly haste, she answered as does the lady in the song, "Open the door and come in,"§ adding the verse: "In the wide shelter of that portico no man yet was ever splashed with rain," and again she sighed so portentously that although he did not at all suppose that he alone was the cause of this demonstration, he felt it in any case to be somewhat exaggerated

---

* The headquarters of the Ladies of the Bedchamber.

† An old folk-song the refrain of which is "At the melon-hoeing he said he loved me and what am I to do, what am I to do?"

‡ The poem referred to is not the famous *Lute Girl's Song*, but a much shorter one (*Works* x. 8) on a similar theme. O-chou is the modern Wu-ch'ang in Hupeh.

§ In the song the lady says: "The door is not bolted or barred. Come quickly and talk to me. Am I another's bride, that you should be so careful and shy?"

and answered with the poem: "Your sighs show clearly that, despite the song, you are another's bride, and I for my part have no mind to haunt the loggias of your eastern house." He would gladly have passed on, but he felt that this would be too unkind, and seeing that someone else was coming towards her room, he stepped inside and began talking lightly of indifferent subjects, in a style which though it was in reality somewhat forced she found very entertaining.

It was intolerable, thought To no Chujo, that Genji should be praised as a quiet and serious young man and should constantly rebuke him for his frivolity, while all the time he was carrying on a multiplicity of interesting intrigues which out of mere churlishness he kept entirely hidden from all his friends. For a long while Chujo had been waiting for an opportunity to expose this sanctimonious imposture, and when he saw Genji enter the gentlewoman's apartment you may be sure he was delighted. To scare him a little at such a moment would be an excellent way to punish him for his unfriendliness. He slackened his pace and watched. The wind sighed in the trees. It was getting very late. Surely Genji would soon begin to doze? And indeed he did now look as though he had fallen asleep. Chujo stole on tiptoe into the room; but Genji who was only half-dreaming instantly heard him, and not knowing that Chujo had followed him, got it into his head that it was a certain Commissioner of Works who years ago had been supposed to be an admirer of the lady. The idea of being discovered in such a situation by this important old gentleman filled him with horror. Furious with his companion for having exposed him to the chance of such a predicament: "This is too bad," he whispered, "I am going home. What possessed you to let me in on a night when you knew that someone else was coming?" He had only time to snatch up his cloak and hide behind a long folding-screen before Chujo entered the room and going straight up to the screen began in a businesslike manner to fold it up. Though she was no longer young, the lady did not lose her head in this alarming crisis. Being a woman of fashion, she had on more than one occasion found herself in an equally agitating position, and now despite her astonishment, after considering for a moment what had best be done with the intruder, she seized him by the back of his coat and with a practiced though trembling hand pulled him away from the screen. Genji had still no idea that it was Chujo. He had half a mind to show himself, but quickly remembered that he was oddly and inadequately clad, with his headdress all awry. He felt that if he ran for it he would cut much too strange a figure as he left the room, and for a moment he hesitated. Wondering how much longer Genji would take to recognize him, Chujo did not say a word but putting on the most ferocious air imaginable, drew his sword from the scabbard. Whereupon the lady crying "Gentlemen! Gentlemen!" flung herself between them in an attitude of romantic supplication. They could hardly refrain from bursting into laughter. It was only by day when very carefully painted and bedizened that she still retained a certain superficial air of youth and charm. But now this woman of fifty-seven or eight, disturbed by a sudden brawl in the midst of her amours, created the most astonishing spectacle as she knelt at the feet of two young men in their teens beseeching them not to die for her. Chujo however refrained from showing the slightest sign of amusement and continued to look as alarming and ferocious as he could. But he was now in full view and Genji realized in a moment that Chujo had all the while known who he was and had been amusing himself at his expense. Much relieved at this discovery, he grabbed at the scabbard from which Chujo had drawn the sword and held it fast lest his friend should attempt to escape and then, despite his annoyance at having been followed, burst into an uncontrollable fit of laughter. "Are you in your right mind?" said Genji at last. "This is really a very poor sort of joke. Do you mind letting me get into my cloak?" Whereupon Chujo snatched the cloak from him and would not give it back. "Very well then," said Genji; "if you are to have my cloak I must have yours," and so saying he pulled open the clasp of Chujo's belt and began tugging his cloak from his shoulders. Chujo resisted and a long tussle followed in which the cloak was torn to shreds. "Should you now get it in exchange for yours, this tattered cloak will but reveal the secrets it is meant to hide," recited To no Chujo; to which Genji replied with an acrostic poem in which he complained that Chujo with whom he shared so many secrets should have thought it necessary to spy upon him in this fashion. But neither was really angry with the other and setting their disordered costumes to rights they both took their departure. Genji discovered when he was alone that it had indeed upset him very much to find his movements had been watched, and he could not sleep. The lady felt utterly bewildered. On the floor she found a belt and a buckle which she sent to Genji next day with a complicated acrostic poem in which she compared these stranded properties to the weeds which after their straining and tugging the waves leave upon the shore. She added an allusion to the crystal river of her tears. He was irritated by her persistency but distressed at the shock to which she had been subjected by Chujo's foolish joke, and he answered with the poem: "At the antics of the prancing wave you have good cause to be angry; but blameless indeed is the shore on whose sands it lashed." The belt was Chujo's; that was plain for it was darker in color than his own cloak. And as he examined his cloak he noticed that the lower half of one sleeve was torn away. What a mess everything was in! He told himself with disgust that he was becoming a rowdy, a vulgar night-brawler. Such people, he knew, were always tearing their clothes and making themselves ridiculous. It was time to reform.

The missing sleeve soon arrived from Chujo's apartments with the message: "Had you not better have this sewn on before you wear your cloak?" How had he managed to get hold of it? Such tricks were very tiresome and silly. But he supposed he must now give back the belt, and wrapping it in paper of the same color he sent it with a riddling poem in which he said that he would not keep it lest he should make trouble between Chujo and the lady. "You have dragged her away from me as in the scuffle you snatched from me this belt," said Chujo in his answering poem, and added "Have I not good reason to be angry with you?"

Later in the morning they met in the Presence Room. Genji wore a solemn and abstracted air. Chujo could not help recollecting the absurd scene of their last meeting, but it was a day upon which there was a great deal of public business to dispatch and he was soon absorbed in his duties. But from time to time each would catch sight of the other's serious face and heavy official bearing, and then they could not help smiling. In an interval Chujo came up to Genji and asked him in a low voice whether he had decided in future to be a little more communicative about his affairs. "No, indeed," said Genji; "but I feel I owe you an apology for preventing you from spending a happy hour with the lady whom you had come to visit. Everything in life seems to go wrong." So they whispered and at the end each solemnly promised the other not to speak of the matter to anybody. But to the two of them it furnished a constant supply of jokes for a long while to come, though Genji took the matter to heart more than he showed and was determined never to get mixed up with such a tiresome creature again. He heard however that the lady was still much ruffled, and fearing that there might be no one at hand to comfort her, he had not the heart quite to discontinue his visits.

Chujo, faithful to his promise, did not mention the affair to anyone, not even to his sister, but kept it as a weapon of self-defense should Genji ever preach high morality to him again.

Such marked preference did the Emperor show in his treatment of Genji that even the other princes of the Blood Royal stood somewhat in awe of him. But To no Chujo was ready to dispute with him on any subject, and was by no means inclined always to let him have his own way. He and Aoi were the only children of the Emperor's sister. Genji, it is true, was the Emperor's son; but though Chujo's father was only a Minister, his influence was far greater than that of his colleagues, and as the son of such a man by his marriage with a royal princess he was used to being treated with the greatest deference. It had never so much as occurred to him that he was in any way Genji's inferior; for he knew that as regards his person at least he had no reason to be dissatisfied; and with most other qualities, whether of character or intelligence, he believed himself to be very adequately endowed. Thus a friendly rivalry grew up between the two of them and led to many diverting incidents which it would take too long to describe.

In the seventh month two events of importance took place. An empress was appointed* and Genji was raised to the rank of Councilor. The Emperor was intending very soon to resign the Throne. He would have liked to proclaim his newborn child as Heir Apparent in place of Kokiden's son. This was difficult, for there was no political faction which would have supported such a choice. Fujitsubo's relations were all members of the Imperial family† and Genji, to whom he might have looked for help owing to his affiliation with the Minamoto clan, unfortunately showed no aptitude for political intrigue. The best he could do was at any rate to strengthen Fujitsubo's position and hope that later on she would be able to exert her influence. Kokiden heard of his intentions, and small wonder if she was distressed and astounded. The Emperor tried to quiet her by pointing out that in a short time her son would succeed to the Throne and that she would then hold the equally important rank of Empress Mother. But it was indeed hard that the mother of the Heir Apparent should be passed over in favor of a concubine aged little more than twenty. The public tended to take Kokiden's side and there was a good deal of discontent. On the night when the new Empress was installed Genji, as a Councilor, was among those who accompanied her to the Middle Palace. As daughter of a previous Empress and mother of an exquisite prince she enjoyed a consideration at Court beyond that which her new rank would have alone procured for her. But if it was with admiring devotion that the other great lords of her train attended her that day, it may be imagined with what fond yet agonized thoughts Prince Genji followed the litter in which she rode. She seemed at last to have been raised so far beyond his reach that scarce knowing what he did he murmured to himself the lines: "Now upon love's dark path has the last shadow closed; for I have seen you carried to a cloud-land whither none may climb."

As the days and months went by the child grew more and more like Genji. The new Empress was greatly distressed, but no one else seemed to notice the resemblance. He was not of course so handsome; how indeed should he have been? But both were beautiful, and the world was content to accept their beauty without troubling to compare them, just as it accepts both moon and sun as lovely occupants of the sky.

---

* The rank of Empress was often not conferred till quite late in a reign. It was of course Fujitsubo whom the Emperor chose in this case.

† And therefore debarred from taking part in political life.

The Flower Feast

About the twentieth day of the second month the Emperor gave a Chinese banquet under the great cherry-tree of the Southern Court. Both Fujitsubo and the Heir Apparent were to be there. Kokiden, although she knew that the mere presence of the Empress was sufficient to spoil her pleasure, could not bring herself to forego so delightful an entertainment. After some promise of rain the day turned out magnificent; and in full sunshine, with the birds singing in every tree, the guests (royal princes, noblemen, and professional poets alike) were handed the rhyme words which the Emperor had drawn by lot, and set to work to compose their poems. It was with a clear and ringing voice that Genji read out the word "spring" which he had received as the rhyme-sound of his poem. Next came To no Chujo who, feeling that all eyes were upon him and determined to impress himself favorably on his audience, moved with the greatest possible elegance and grace; and when on receiving his rhyme he announced his name, rank, and titles, he took great pains to speak pleasantly as well as audibly. Many of the other gentlemen were rather nervous and looked quite pale as they came forward, yet they acquitted themselves well enough. But the professional poets, particularly owing to the high standard of accomplishment which the Emperor's and Heir Apparent's lively interest in Chinese poetry had at that time diffused through the Court, were very ill at ease; as they crossed the long space of the garden on their way to receive their rhymes they felt utterly helpless. A simple Chinese verse is surely not much to ask of a professional poet; but they all wore an expression of the deepest gloom. One expects elderly scholars to be somewhat odd in their movements and behavior, and it was amusing to see the lively concern with which the Emperor watched their various but always uncouth and erratic methods of approaching the Throne. Needless to say a great deal of music had been arranged for. Towards dusk the delightful dance known as the Warbling of Spring Nightingales was performed, and when it was over the Heir Apparent, remembering the Festival of Red Leaves, placed a wreath on Genji's head and pressed him so urgently that it was impossible for him to refuse. Rising to his feet he danced very quietly a fragment of the sleeve-turning passage in the Wave Dance. In a few moments he was seated again, but even into this brief extract from a long dance he managed to import an unrivalled charm and grace. Even his father-in-law who was not in the best of humor with him was deeply moved and found himself wiping away a tear.

And why have we not seen To no Chujo?" said the Heir Apparent. Whereupon Chujo danced the Park of Willow Flowers, giving a far more complete performance than Genji, for no doubt he knew that he would be called upon and had taken trouble to prepare his dance. It was a great success and the Emperor presented him with a cloak, which everyone said was a most unusual honor. After this the other young noblemen who were present danced in no particular order, but it was now so dark that it was impossible to discriminate between their performances.

Then the poems were opened and read aloud. The reading of Genji's verses was continually interrupted by loud murmurs of applause. Even the professional poets were deeply impressed, and it may well be imagined with what pride the Emperor, to whom at times Genji was a source of consolation and delight, watched him upon such an occasion as this. Fujitsubo, when she allowed herself to glance in his direction, marveled that even Kokiden could find it in her heart to hate him. "It is because he is fond of me; there can be no other reason," she decided at last, and the verse, "Were I but a common mortal who now am gazing at the beauty of this flower, from its sweet petals not long should I withhold the dew of love," framed itself on her lips, though she dared not utter it aloud.

It was now very late and the banquet was over. The guests had scattered. The Empress and the Heir Apparent had both returned to the Palace—all was still. The moon had risen very bright and clear, and Genji, heated with wine, could not bear to quit so lovely a scene. The people at the Palace were probably all plunged in a heavy sleep. On such a night it was not impossible that some careless person might have left some door unfastened, some shutter unbarred. Cautiously and stealthily he crept towards Fujitsubo's apartments and inspected them. Every bolt was fast. He sighed; here there was evidently nothing to be done. He was passing the loggia of Kokiden's palace when he noticed that the shutters of the third arch were not drawn. After the banquet Kokiden herself had gone straight to the Emperor's rooms. There did not seem to be anyone about. A door leading from the loggia into the house was standing open, but he could hear no sound within. "It is under just such circumstances as this that one is apt to drift into compromising situations," thought Genji. Nevertheless he climbed quietly on to the balustrade and peeped. Everyone must be asleep. But no; a very agreeable young voice with an intonation which was certainly not that of any waiting-woman or common person was softly humming the last two lines of the *Oborozuki-yo*.*

---

* A famous poem by Oye no Chisato (ninth century): "What so lovely as a night when the moon though dimly clouded is never wholly lost to sight!"

Was not the voice coming towards him? It seemed so, and stretching out his hand he suddenly found that he was grasping a lady's sleeve. "Oh, how you frightened me!" she cried. "Who is it?" "Do not be alarmed," he whispered. "That both of us were not content to miss the beauty of this departing night is proof more clear than the half-clouded moon that we were meant to meet," and as he recited the words he took her gently by the hand and led her into the house, closing the door behind them. Her surprised and puzzled air fascinated him. "There is someone there," she whispered tremulously, pointing to the inner room. "Child," he answered, "I am allowed to go wherever I please and if you send for your friends, they will only tell you that I have every right to be here. But if you will stay quietly here..." It was Genji. She knew his voice and the discovery somewhat reassured her. She thought his conduct rather strange, but she was determined that he should not think her prudish or stiff. And so because he on his side was still somewhat excited after the doings of the evening, while she was far too young and pliant to offer any serious resistance, he soon got his own way with her.

Suddenly they saw to their discomfiture that dawn was creeping into the sky. She looked, thought Genji, as though many disquieting reflections were crowding into her mind. "Tell me your name" he said. "How can I write to you unless you do? Surely this is not going to be our only meeting?" She answered with a poem in which she said that names are of this world only and he would not care to know hers if he were resolved that their love should last till worlds to come. It was a mere quip and Genji, amused at her quickness, answered, "You are quite right. It was a mistake on my part to ask." And he recited the poem: "While still I seek to find on which blade dwells the dew, a great wind shakes the grasses of the level land." "If you did not repent of this meeting," he continued, "you would surely tell me who you are. I do not believe that you want...." But here he was interrupted by the noise of people stirring in the next room. There was a great bustle and it was clear that they would soon be starting out to fetch Princess Kokiden back from the Palace. There was just time to exchange fans in token of their new friendship before Genji was forced to fly precipitately from the room. In his own apartments he found many of his gentlemen waiting for him. Some were awake, and these nudged one another when he entered the room as though to say, "Will he never cease these disreputable excursions?" But discretion forbad them to show that they had seen him and they all pretended to be fast asleep. Genji too lay down, but he could not rest. He tried to recall the features of the lady with whom he had just spent so agreeable a time. Certainly she must be one of Kokiden's sisters. Perhaps the fifth or sixth daughter, both of whom were still unmarried. The handsomest of them (or so he had always heard) were Prince Sochi's wife and the fourth daughter, the one with whom To no Chujo got on so badly. It would really be rather amusing if it did turn out to be Chujo's wife. The sixth was shortly to be married to the Heir Apparent. How tiresome if it were she! But at present he could think of no way to make sure. She had not behaved at all as though she did not want to see him again. Why then had she refused to give him any chance of communicating with her. In fact he worried about the matter so much and turned it over in his mind with such endless persistency that it soon became evident he had fallen deeply in love with her. Nevertheless no sooner did the recollection of Fujitsubo's serious and reticent demeanor come back to his mind than he realized how incomparably more she meant to him than this light-hearted lady.

That day the after-banquet kept him occupied till late at night. At the Emperor's command he performed on the thirteen-stringed zithern and had an even greater success than with his dancing on the day before. At dawn Fujitsubo retired to the Emperor's rooms. Disappointed in his hope that the lady of last night would somewhere or somehow make her appearance on the scene, he sent for Yoshikiyo and Koremitsu with whom all his secrets were shared and bade them keep watch upon the lady's family. When he returned next day from duty at the Palace they reported that they had just witnessed the departure of several coaches which had been drawn up under shelter in the Courtyard of the Watch. "Among a group of persons who seemed to be the domestic attendants of those for whom the coaches were waiting two gentlemen came threading their way in a great hurry. These we recognized as Shii no Shosho and Uchuben,[*] so there is little doubt that the carriages belonged to Princess Kokiden. For the rest we noted that the ladies were by no means looking and that the whole party drove away in three carriages." Genji's heart beat fast. But he was no nearer than before to finding out which of the sisters it had been. Supposing her father, the Minister of the Right, should hear anything of this, what a to-do there would be! It would indeed mean his absolute ruin. It was a pity that while he was about it he did not stay with her till it was a little lighter. But there it was! He did not know her face, but yet he was determined to recognize her. How? He lay on his bed devising and rejecting endless schemes. Murasaki too must be growing impatient. Days had passed since he had visited her and he remembered with tenderness how low-spirited she became when he was not able to be with her. But in a moment his thoughts had returned to the unknown lady. He still had her fan. It was a folding fan with ribs of hinoki-wood and tassels tied in a splice-knot. One side was covered with silver leaf on which was painted a dim moon, giving the impression of a moon reflected in water. It was a device which he had seen many times before, but it had agreeable associations for him, and con-

---

[*] Kokiden's brothers.

tinuing the metaphor of the grass on the moor which she had used in her poem, he wrote on the fan—"Has mortal man ever puzzled his head with such a question before as to ask where the moon goes to when she leaves the sky at dawn?" And he put the fan safely away. It was on his conscience that he had not for a long while been to the Great Hall; but fearing that Murasaki too might be feeling very unhappy, he first went home to give her her lessons. Every day she was improving not only in looks, but also in amiability of character. The beauty of her disposition was indeed quite out of the common. The idea that so perfect a nature was in his hands, to train and cultivate as he thought best, was very attractive to Genji. It might however have been objected that to receive all her education from a young man is likely to make a girl somewhat forward in her manner.

First there was a great deal to tell her about what had happened at the Court entertainments of the last few days. Then followed her music lesson, and already it was time to go. "Oh, why must he always go away so soon?" she wondered sadly, but by now she was so used to it that she no longer fretted as she had done a little while ago.

At the Great Hall he could, as usual, scarcely get a word out of Aoi. The moment that he sat idle a thousand doubts and puzzles began to revolve in his mind. He took up his zithern and began to sing:

Not softlier pillowed is my head
That rests by thine, unloving bride,
Than were those jagged stones my bed
Through which the falls of Nuki stride.

At this moment Aoi's father came by and began to discuss the unusual success of the recent festivities. "Old as I am," he said—"and I may say that I have lived to see four illustrious sovereigns occupy the Throne, have never taken part in a banquet which produced verses so spirited or dancing and music so admirably performed. Talent of every description seems at present to exist in abundance; but it is creditable to those in authority that they knew how to make good use of it. For my part I enjoyed myself so much that had I but been a few years younger I would positively have joined in the dancing!" "No special steps were taken to discover the musicians," answered Genji. "We merely used those who were known to the government in one part of the country and another as capable performers. If I may say so, it was Chujo's Willow Dance that made the deepest impression and is likely always to be remembered as a remarkable performance. But if you, Sir, had indeed honored us, a new luster would have been added to my Father's reign." Aoi's brothers now arrived and leaning against the balustrade gave a little concert, their various instruments blending delightfully.

Fugitive as their meeting had been, it had sufficed to plunge the lady whose identity Prince Genji was now seeking to establish into the depths of despair; for in the fourth month she was to become the Heir Apparent's wife. Turmoil filled her brain. Why had not Genji visited her again? He must surely know whose daughter she was. But how should he know which daughter? Besides, her sister Kokiden's house was not a place where, save under very strange circumstances, he was likely to feel at all at his ease. And so she waited in great impatience and distress; but of Genji there was no news.

About the twentieth day of the third month her father, the Minister of the Right, held an archery meeting at which most of the young noblemen and princes were present. It was followed by a wisteria feast. The cherry blossom was for the most part over, but two trees, which the Minister seemed somehow to have persuaded to flower later than all the rest, were still an enchanting sight. He had had his house rebuilt only a short time ago when celebrating the initiation of his granddaughters, the children of Kokiden. It was now a magnificent building and not a thing in it but was of the very latest fashion. He had invited Genji when he had met him at the Palace only a few days before and was extremely annoyed when he did not appear. Feeling that the party would be a failure if Genji did not come, he sent his son Shii no Shosho to fetch him, with the poem: "Were my flowers as those of other gardens never should I have ventured to summon you." Genji was in attendance upon the Emperor and at once showed him the message. "He seems very pleased with himself and his flowers," said His Majesty with a smile; adding, "as he has sent for you like this, I think you had better go. After all, your half-sisters are being brought up at his house, and you ought not to treat him quite as a stranger." He went to his apartments and dressed. It was very late indeed when at last he made his appearance at the party. He was dressed in a cloak of thin Chinese fabric, white outside but lined with yellow. His robe was of a deep wine-red color with a very long train. The dignity and grace with which he carried this fancifully regal* attire in a company where all were dressed in plain official robes were indeed remarkable, and in the end his presence perhaps contributed more to the success of the party than did the fragrance of the Minister's boasted flowers. His entry was followed by some very agreeable music. It was already fairly late when Genji, on the plea that the wine had given him a headache, left his seat and went for a walk. He knew that his two stepsisters, the daughters of Kokiden, were in the inner apartments of the palace. He went to the eastern portico and rested there. It was on this side of the house that the wisteria grew.

---

* He had no right to such a costume; for though a son of the Emperor, he had been affiliated to the Minamoto clan and no longer counted as a member of the Imperial family.

The wooden blinds were raised and a number of ladies were leaning out of the window to enjoy the blossoms. They had hung bright-colored robes and shawls over the window-sill just as is done at the time of the New Year dancing and other gala days and were behaving with a freedom of allure which contrasted very oddly with the sober decorum of Fujitsubo's household. "I am feeling rather overpowered by all the noise and bustle of the flower party," Genji explained. "I am very sorry to disturb my sisters, but can think of nowhere else to seek refuge..." and advancing towards the main door of the women's apartments, he pushed back the curtain with his shoulder. "Refuge indeed!" cried one of the ladies, laughing at him. "You ought to know by now that it is only poor relations who come to seek refuge with the more successful members of their family. What pray have you come to bother us for?" "Impertinent creatures!" he thought, but nevertheless there was something in their manner which convinced him they were persons of some consequence in the house and not, as he at first supposed, mere waiting-women. A scent of costly perfumes pervaded the room; silken skirts rustled in the darkness. There could be little doubt that these were Kokiden's sisters and their friends. Deeply absorbed, as indeed was the whole of this family, in the fashionable gaieties of the moment, they had flouted decorum and posted themselves at the window that they might see what little they could of the banquet which was proceeding outside. Little thinking that his plan could succeed, yet led on by delightful recollections of his previous encounter, he advanced towards them chanting in a careless undertone the song:

At Ishikawa, Ishikawa
A man from Koma* took my belt away...

But for "belt" he substituted "fan" and by this means he sought to discover which of the ladies was his friend. "Why, you have got it wrong. I never heard of *that* Korean," one of them cried. Certainly it was not she. But there was another who though she remained silent seemed to him to be sighing softly to herself. He stole towards the curtain-of-state behind which she was sitting and taking her hand in his at a venture he whispered the poem: "If on this day of shooting my arrow went astray, 'twas that in dim morning twilight only the mark had glimmered in my view." And she, unable any longer to hide that she knew him, answered with the verse: "Had it been with the arrows of the heart that you had shot, though from the moon's slim bow no brightness came would you have missed your mark?" Yes, it was her voice. He was delighted, and yet...

---

* Korea.

Aoi

The accession of the new Emperor was in many ways unfavorable to Genji's position. His recent promotion* too brought with it heavy responsibilities which sadly interrupted the course of his hidden friendships, so that complaints of desertion or neglect were soon heaped upon him from more than one quarter; while, as though Fate wished to turn the tables upon him, the one being on earth for whose love he longed in vain had now utterly abandoned him. Now that the Emperor was free to live as he chose, she was more constantly than ever at his side, nor was her peace any longer disturbed by the presence of a rival, for Kokiden, resenting the old Emperor's neglect, now seldom left her son's palace. A constant succession of banquets and entertainments, the magnificence of which became the talk of the whole country, helped to enliven the ex-Emperor's retirement and he was on the whole very well content with his new condition. His only regret concerned the Heir Apparent† whose position, unsupported by any powerful influence outside the Palace, he regarded as extremely insecure. He constantly discussed the matter with Genji, begging him to enlist the support of the Minamoto clan. Such conversations tended to be somewhat embarrassing, but they gave Genji pleasure in so far as they enabled him to take measures for the boy's welfare.

An unexpected event now occurred. Lady Rokujo's daughter by her late husband Prince Zembo was chosen to be the new Vestal Virgin at Ise.‡ Her mother, who at the time when the appointment was first announced happened to be particularly aggrieved at Genji's treatment of her, at once determined to make her daughter's extreme youth a pretext for leaving the Capital and settling permanently at Ise. Being at the moment, as I have said, very much out of humor, she discussed the matter openly, making no secret of her real reasons for wishing to leave the City. The story soon reached the ex-Emperor's ears, and sending for Genji he said to him: "The late Prince my brother was, as you probably know, regarded with the utmost affection and esteem and I am profoundly grieved to hear that

---

* We learn in Chapter XXXIV that he was made Commander of the Bodyguard at the age of twenty-one. He is now twenty-two.

† Genji's son by Fujitsubo (supposed by the world to be the Emperor's child) had been made Heir Apparent.

‡ An Emperor upon his succession was obliged to send one unmarried daughter or granddaughter to the Shinto Temple at Ise, another to the Shinto Temple at Kamo.

your reckless and inconsiderate conduct has cast a slur upon his family. For his daughter indeed I feel as much responsible as if she were one of my own children. I must trouble you in future to safeguard to the utmost of your power the reputation of these unfortunate ladies. If you do not learn to keep better control over your frivolous inclinations, you will soon find yourself becoming extremely unpopular." Why should his father be so much upset over the matter? And Genji, smarting under the rebuke, was about to defend himself when it occurred to him that the warning was not at all ill-merited and he maintained a respectful silence.

"Affairs of this kind," the ex-Emperor continued, "must be managed so that the woman, no matter who she is, need not feel that she has been brought into a humiliating position or treated in a cynical and off hand way. Forget this rule, and she will soon make you feel the unpleasant consequences of her resentment." "Wicked as he thinks me already," said Genji to himself while this lecture was going on, "there is a much worse enormity of which he as yet knows nothing." And stupefied with horror at the thought of what would ensue should his father ever discover this hideous secret, he bowed and left the room.

What the ex-Emperor had said about ruining other people's reputations cut him to the quick. He realized that Rokujo's rank and widowed position entitled her to the utmost consideration. But after all it was not he who had made public property of the affair; on the contrary he had done everything in his power to prevent its becoming known. There had always been a certain condescension in her treatment of him, arising perhaps from the inequality of their ages,* and his estrangement from her was solely due to the coldness with which she had for a long time received him. That their private affairs were now known not only to the ex-Emperor but also presumably to the whole Court showed a lack of reticence which seemed to him deplorable.

Among others who heard of the business was Princess Asagao.† Determined that she at least would not submit herself to such treatment, she ceased to answer his letters even with the short and guarded replies that she had been in the habit of sending to him. Nevertheless he found it hard to believe that so gentle-mannered a creature was thinking unkindly of him and continued to regard her with devoted admiration.

Princess Aoi when the story reached her ears was of course distressed by this new instance of his fickleness; but she felt that it was useless, now that his infidelity was open and unabashed, to protest against one particular injury, and to his surprise she seemed to take the matter rather lightly. She was suffering much inconvenience from her condition and

---

* She was seven years older than Genji.

† Daughter of Prince Momozono. See above, p. 36.

her spirits were very low. Her parents were delighted and at the same time surprised to hear of what was to come. But their pleasure and that of all her friends was marred by grave forebodings, and it was arranged that prayers for her health and special services of intercession should be recited in all the temples. At such a time it was impossible for Genji to leave her and there were many who, though his feelings had not in reality cooled towards them, felt that they were being neglected.

The Vestal Virgin of Kamo still remained to be selected. The choice fell upon Kokiden's daughter, San no Miya. She was a great favorite both with her brother the new Emperor and with the Empress Mother. Her retirement from the world was a bitter blow to them; but there was no help for it since she alone of all the royal princesses fulfilled the prescribed conditions.

The actual ritual of investiture could not be altered, but the Emperor saw to it that the proceedings should be attended with the utmost pomp and splendor; while to the customary ritual of the Kamo Festival he added so many touches that it became a spectacle of unparalleled magnificence. All this was due to his partiality for the Virgin Elect.

On the day of her purification the Virgin is attended by a fixed number of noblemen and princes. For this retinue the Emperor was at pains to choose the best built and handsomest of the young men at Court; he settled what colored gowns they were to wear, what pattern was to be on their breeches, and even on what saddles they should ride. By a special decree he ordered that Prince Genji should join this retinue, and so great was everyone's desire to get a good view of the procession that long beforehand people were getting ready special carriages with which to line the route. The scene along the highroad of the First Ward was one of indescribable excitement. Dense crowds surged along the narrow space allotted to them, while the stands which with a wealth of ingenious fancy had been constructed all along the route of the procession, with gay cloaks and shawls hung over the balustrades, were in themselves a spectacle of astonishing beauty.

It had never been Aoi's practice to be present at such occasions as this and in her present state of health she would not have dreamt of doing so had not her gentlewomen pressed round her saying, "Come, Madam! It will be no fun for us to go by ourselves and be hidden away in some corner. It is to see Prince Genji that all these people have come today. Why, all sorts of queer wild men from the mountains are here, and people have brought their wives and children from provinces ever so far away. If all these people who are nothing to do with him have taken the trouble to come so far, it will be too bad if you, his own lady, are not there!" Overhearing this, Aoi's mother joined in. "You are feeling much better just now," she said; "I think you ought to make the effort. It will be so disappointing for your gentlewomen..." At the last minute Aoi changed her mind and announced that she was going. It was now so late that there was no time to put on gala clothes. The whole of the enclosure allotted for this purpose was already lined with coaches which were packed so close that it was quite impossible to find space for the large and numerous carriage of Aoi and her train. A number of grand ladies began to make room for her, backing their coaches away from a suitable space in the reserved enclosure. Conspicuous among the rest were two basket-work carriages of a rather old-fashioned pattern but with curtains such as are used by persons of quality, very discreetly decked with draperies that barely showed beneath the curtains, yet these draperies (whether sleeve-favor, skirt or scarf) all of the handsomest colors. They seemed to belong to some exalted personage who did not wish to be recognized. When it was their turn to move, the coachmen in charge of them would not lift a finger. "It is not for such as we to make way," they said stiffly and did not stir. Among the attendants on both sides there was a number of young grooms who were already the worse for liquor. They were longing for a scuffle and it was impossible to keep them in hand. The staid and elderly outriders tried to call them back, but they took no notice.

The two carriages belonged to Princess Rokujo who had come secretly to the festival hoping for a while to find distraction from her troubles. Despite the steps which she had taken to conceal her identity, it was at once suspected by some of Aoi's gentlemen, and they cried to the grooms that this was not an equipage which could be dealt with so high-handedly, or it would be said that their lady was abusing her position as wife of the Lord Commander. But at this moment a number of Genji's servants mingled in the fray. They knew Rokujo's men by sight, but after a moment's embarrassment they decided not to give assistance to the enemy by betraying his identity.

Thus reinforced Aoi's side won the day and at length her coach and those of all her ladies were drawn up along the front row, while Rokujo's was pushed back among a miscellaneous collection of carts and gigs where she could see nothing at all. She was vexed beyond measure not only at missing what she had come to see but also that despite all her precautions she had been recognized and (as she was convinced) deliberately insulted. Her shaft-rest and other parts of her coach as well were damaged and she was obliged to prop it up against some common person's carriage wheels. Why, she vainly asked herself, had she come among these hateful crowds? She would go home at once. What sense was there in waiting for the procession to come? But when she tried to go, she found that it was impossible to force a way through the dense crowds. She was still struggling to escape when the cry went up that the procession was in sight. Her resolution weakened. She would wait till Genji had passed by.

He did not see her. How should he, for the crowds flashed by him like the hurrying images that a stream catches and breaks. She realized this, yet her disappointment was none the less.

The carriages that lined the route, decked and garlanded for this great day, were crammed to overflowing with excited ladies who though there was no room for them would not consent to be left behind. Peeping out under the blinds of their coaches they smiled at the great personages who were passing quite regardless of whether their greetings were acknowledged. But every now and then a smile would be rewarded by a quick glance or the backward turn of a head. Aoi's party was large and conspicuous. Genji wheeled round as he passed and saluted its members attentively. Rider after rider again as the procession went by would pause in front of Aoi's coach and salute her with the deepest respect. The humiliation of witnessing all this from an obscure corner was more than Rokujo could bear, and murmuring the lines, "Though I saw him but as a shadow that falls on hurrying waters yet knew I that at last my hour of utmost misery was come," she burst into tears. It was hideous that her servants should see her in this state. Yet even while she struggled with her tears she could not find it in her heart to regret that she had seen him in all his glory.

The riders in the procession were indeed all magnificently appareled, each according to his own rank; in particular the young noblemen chosen by the Emperor cut so brilliant a figure that only the luster of Genji's beauty could have eclipsed their splendor. The Commander of this Bodyguard is not generally allotted a Palace-Officer as his special attendant, but as the occasion was of such importance the Imperial Treasurer* rode at Genji's side. It seemed to those who saw so many public honors showered upon him that no flower of fortune could resist the favoring gale which blew towards his side. There were among the crowd women of quite good birth who had dressed in walking-skirts and come a long way on foot. There were nuns and other female recluses who, though in order to see anything of the procession they were obliged to endure being constantly pushed off their feet, and though they commonly regarded all such spectacles with contempt and aversion, were today declaring that they would not have missed it for anything. There were old men grinning through toothless gums, strange-looking girls with their hair poked away under ragged hoods and stolid peasant boys standing with hands raised as though in prayer, whose uncouth faces were suddenly transfigured with wonder and joy as the procession burst into sight. Even the daughters of remote provincial magistrates and governors who had no acquaintances whatever in the City had expended as much coquetry upon the decoration

---

* We learn later that he was a son of Iyo no Kami.

of their persons and coaches as if they were about to submit themselves to a lover's inspection, and their equipages made a bright and varied show. If even these strangers were in such a taking, it may be imagined with what excitement, scattered here and there among the crowd, those with whom Genji was in secret communication watched the procession go by and with how many hidden sighs their bosoms heaved.

Prince Momozono[*] had a seat in one of the stands. He was amazed to see his nephew grown up into such a prodigiously handsome young man and was alarmed lest soon the gods should cast an envious eye upon him. Princess Asagao could not but be touched by the rare persistency with which year after year Genji had pressed his suit. Even had he been positively ugly she would have found it hard to resist such importunity; so small wonder if seeing him ride by in all his splendor she marveled that she had held out so long. But she was determined to know him much better before she committed herself. The young waiting-women who were with her were careful to belaud him in extravagant terms. To the festival itself[†] Aoi did not go. The affray between her servants and those of Rokujo was soon reported to Genji. It vexed him beyond measure that such a thing should have occurred. That the exquisitely well-bred Aoi should have been in any way responsible for this outburst of insolent ruffianism he did not for a moment believe; it must be the work of rough under-servants who, though they had no actual instructions, had imbibed the notion that all was not well between the two houses and imagined that they would get credit for espousing their mistress's cause. He knew well enough the unusual vanity and susceptibility of the affronted lady. Distressed to think of the pain which this incident must have caused her, he hastened to her house. But her daughter, the Virgin Elect of Ise, was still in the house, and she made this a plea for turning him away after the exchange of a few formal words. He had the greatest possible sympathy for her; but he was feeling rather tired of coping with injured susceptibilities.

He could not face the idea of going straight back to the Great Hall. It was the day of the Kamo festival and going to his own palace he ordered Koremitsu to get his coach ready. "Look at her!" he cried, smiling fondly at Murasaki when she appeared in all her finery surrounded by the little children whom he had given her for playmates. "She must needs bring her dames to wait upon her!" and he stroked her lovely hair which today Shonagon had dressed with more than usual care. "It is getting rather long," he said; "today would not be a bad[‡] time to have it cut" and sending for his astrologer he bade him consult his books.

---

[*] Father of Princess Asagao; brother of the ex-Emperor and therefore Genji's paternal uncle.

[†] The clash of coaches took place at the Purification. The actual *matsuri* (Festival) takes place some days later.

[‡] I.e. astrologically.

"The maids-of-honor first!" he cried, nodding at the pretty troupe of babes, and their dainty tresses were trimmed so as to hang neatly over their diapered holiday gowns. "I am going to cut yours myself," he said to Murasaki. "What a lot of it there is! I wonder how much longer it would have grown." Really it was quite hard work. "People with very long hair ought to wear it cut rather short over the temples," he said at last; "but I have not the heart to crop you any closer," and he laid the knife down. Shonagon's gratification knew no bounds when she heard him reciting the prayer with which the ceremony of hair cutting should conclude. There is a seaweed called *miru* which is used in the dressing of ladies' hair and playing upon this word (which also means "to see") he recited a poem in which he said that the miru-weed which had been used in a washing of her hair was a token that he would forever fondly watch it grow. She answered that like the sea-tides which visit the *miru* in its cleft he came but went away, and often her tresses unwatched by him would like the hidden seaweed grow. This she wrote very prettily on a slip of paper and though the verse had no merit in it but the charm of a childish mind it gave him great delight. Today the crowds were as thick as ever. With great difficulty he managed to wedge in his carriage close to the Royal Stables. But here they were surrounded by somewhat turbulent young noblemen and he was looking for a quieter place when a smart carriage crammed full of ladies drew up near by and someone in it beckoned with a fan to Genji's servants. "Will you not come over where we are?" said one of the ladies. "We will gladly make room for you." Such an offer was perhaps somewhat forward, but the place she had indicated was such a good one that Genji at once accepted the invitation. "I am afraid it is very unfair that we should take your place like this..." Genji was beginning to say politely, when one of the ladies handed him a fan with the corner bent down. Here he found the poem: "This flower-decked day of meeting when the great god unfolds his portents in vain have I waited, for alas another is at thy side." Surely the handwriting was familiar. Yes, it was that of the ancient lady-of-the-bedchamber. He felt that it was time she should give up such pranks as this and answered discouragingly: "Not ours this day of tryst when garlanded and passionate the Eighty Tribes converge." This put the lady out of countenance and she replied: "Now bitterly do I repent that for this cheating day my head is decked with flowers; for in name only, is it a day of meeting."

Their carriages remained side by side, but Genji did not even draw up the side-curtains, which was a disappointment to more persons than one. The magnificence of his public appearance a few days ago was contrasted by everyone with the unobtrusive manner in which he now mingled with the crowd. It was agreed that his companion, whoever she might be, must certainly be some very great lady. Genji was afraid that his neighbor was going to prove troublesome. But fortunately some of her companions had more discretion than their mistress, and out of consideration for the unknown sharer of Genji's coach persuaded the voluble lady to restrain herself.

Lady Rokujo's sufferings were now far worse than in previous years. Though she could no longer endure to be treated as Genji was treating her, yet the thought of separating from him altogether and going so far away agitated her so much that she constantly deferred her journey. She felt too that she would become a laughing-stock if it was thought that she had been spurred to flight by Genji's scorn: yet if at the last moment she changed her plans and stayed behind everyone would think her conduct extremely ill-balanced and unaccountable. Thus her days and nights were spent in an agony of indecision and often she repeated to herself the lines, "My heart like the fishers' float on Ise shore is danced from wave to wave."* She felt herself indeed swirled this way and that by paroxysms that sickened her but were utterly beyond her control.

Genji, though it pained him that she should feel it necessary to go so far away, did not attempt to dissuade her from the journey. "It is quite natural," he wrote, "that tiresome creature as I am you should want to put me altogether out of your head. I only beg that even though you see no use in it, you will let me see you once more before you go. Were we to meet, you would soon realize that I care for your happiness far more than you suppose." But she could not forget how when at the River of Cleansing she sought a respite from the torture of her own doubt and indecision, rough waves had dashed her against the rocks,† and she brooded more and more upon this wrong till there was room for no other thought in all her heart.

Meanwhile Princess Aoi became strangely distraught, and it seemed at times as though some hostile spirit had entered into her. The whole household was plunged into such a state of anxiety and gloom that Genji had not the heart to absent himself for more than a few hours. It was only very occasionally that he got even as far as his own palace. After all, she was his wife; moreover, despite all the difficulties that had risen between them he cared for her very much indeed. He could no longer disguise from himself that there was something wrong with her in addition to the discomfort which naturally accompanied her condition, and he was in a state of great distress. Constant rituals of exorcism and divination were performed under his direction, and it was generally agreed that all the signs indicated possession by the spirit of some living person. Many names were tried but to none of them did the spirit respond, and it seemed as

---

* *Kokinshu* 509.
† The clash of the chariots at the Festival of Purification. Probably a quotation.

though it would be impossible to shift it. Aoi herself felt that some alien thing had entered into her, and though she was not conscious of any one definite pain or dread, the sense that the thing was there never for a moment left her. The greatest healers of the day were powerless to eject it and it became apparent that this was no ordinary case of "possession": some tremendous accumulation of malice was discharging itself upon her. It was natural that her friends should turn over in their minds the names of those whom Genji had most favored. It was whispered that only with Lady Rokujo and the girl at the Nijo-in was he on terms of such intimacy that their jealousy would be at all likely to produce a fatal effect. But when the doctors attempted to conjure the spirit by the use of these names, there was no visible response. She had not in all the world any enemy who might be practicing conscious* witchcraft against her. Such indispositions were sometimes attributed to possession by the spirit of some dead retainer or old family-nurse; or again the malice of someone whom the Minister, Aoi's father, had offended might, owing to her delicate condition, have fastened upon her instead of him. Conjecture after conjecture was accepted and then falsified. Meanwhile she lay perpetually weeping. Constantly, indeed, she would break out into fits of sobbing so violent that her breath was stopped, while those about her, in great alarm for her safety, stood by in misery not knowing what to do.

The ex-Emperor enquired after her continually. He even ordered special services to be said on her behalf, and these attentions served to remind her parents in what high estimation she was held at the Court. Not among her friends only but throughout the whole country the news of her illness caused great distress. Rokujo heard of her sufferings with deep concern. For years they had been in open rivalry for Genji's favors, but even after that wretched affair of the coaches (though it must be admitted that this had greatly incensed her) she had never gone so far as to wish evil against the Princess. She herself was very unwell. She began to feel that the violent and distracting emotions which continually assailed her had in some subtle way unhinged her mind and she determined to seek spiritual assistance at a place some miles distant from her home. Genji heard of this and in great anxiety concerning her at once set out for the house where she was reported to be staying. It lay beyond the City precincts and he was obliged to go with the greatest secrecy.† He begged her to forgive him for not having come to see her for so long. "I have not been having a very cheerful time," he said and gave her some account of Aoi's condition. He wanted to make her feel that if he had stayed away

---

* The jealous person is unconscious of the fatal effects which his jealousy is producing.

† Members of the Imperial family were not allowed to leave the Capital without the consent of the Emperor.

it had been from a melancholy necessity and not because he had found more amusing company elsewhere. "It is not so much my own anxiety that unnerves me as the spectacle of the appalling helplessness and misery into which her illness has plunged her wretched parents, and it was in the hope of forgetting for a little while all these sickroom horrors that I came to see you here today. If only just for this once you could overlook all my offences and be kind to me..."

His pleading had no effect. Her attitude was more hostile than before. He was not angry with her, nor indeed was he surprised. Day was already breaking when, unsolaced, he set out for home. But as she watched him go his beauty suddenly made havoc of all her resolutions and again she felt that it was madness to leave him. Yet what had she to stay for? Aoi was with child and this could only be a sign that he had made his peace with her. Henceforward he could lead a life of irreproachable rectitude and if once in a way he came to make his excuse as he had come today, what purpose would that serve, save to keep ever fresh the torment of her desires? Thus when his letter came next day it found her more distraught than before: "The sick woman who for a few days past had shown some improvement is again suffering acutely and it is at present impossible for me to leave her." Certain that this was a mere excuse, she sent in reply the poem: "The fault is mine and the regret, if careless as the peasant girl who stoops too low amid the sprouting rice I soiled my sleeve in love's dark road." At the end of her letter she reminded him of the old song: "Now bitterly do I repent that ever I brought my pitcher to the mountain well where waters were but deep enough to soil my sleeve." He looked at the delicate handwriting. Who was there, even among women of her high lineage and breeding, that could rival the ineffable grace and elegance with which this small note was penned? That one whose mind and person alike so strongly attracted him must now by his own act be lost to him forever, was a bitter thought. Though it was almost dark, he sat down and wrote to her: "Do not say that the waters have but wetted your sleeve. For the shallowness is in your comparison only; not in my affections!" And to this he added the poem: "'Tis you, you only who have loitered among the shallow pools: while I till all my limbs were drenched have battled through the thickets of love's dark track." And he ended with the words: "Had but a ray of comfort lighted the troubles of this house, I should myself have been the bearer of this note."

Meanwhile Aoi's possession had returned in full force; she was in a state of pitiable torment. It reached Lady Rokujo's ears that the illness had been attributed by some to the operation of her living spirit." Others, she was told, believed that her father's ghost was avenging the betrayal of his daughter. She brooded constantly upon the nature of her own feelings towards Aoi, but could discover in herself nothing but intense unhappiness. Of hostility towards Aoi she could find no trace at all. Yet she could not be sure whether somewhere in the depths of a soul consumed by anguish some spark of malice had not lurked. Through all the long years during which she had loved and suffered, though it had often seemed to her that greater torment could not anywhere in the world exist, her whole being had never once been so utterly bruised and shattered as in these last days. It had begun with that hateful episode of the coaches. She had been scorned, treated as though she had no right to exist. Yes, it was true that since the Festival of Purification her mind had been buffeted by such a tempest of conflicting resolutions that sometimes it seemed as though she had lost all control over her own thoughts. She remembered how one night she had suddenly, in the midst of agonizing doubts and indecisions, found that she had been dreaming. It seemed to her that she had been in a large magnificent room where lay a girl whom she knew to be the Princess Aoi. Snatching her by the arm, she had dragged and mauled the prostrate figure with an outburst of brutal fury such as in her waking life would have been utterly foreign to her. Since then she had had the same dream several times. How terrible! It seemed then that it was really possible for one's spirit to leave the body and break out into emotions which the waking mind would not countenance. Even where someone's actions are all but irreproachable (she reflected) people take a malicious delight in saying nothing about the good he has done and everything about the evil. With what joy would they seize upon such a story as this! That after his death a man's ghost should pursue his enemies is a thing which seems to be of constant occurrence, yet even this is taken as a sign that the dead man was of a fiendishly venomous and malignant character and his reputation is utterly destroyed. "What then will become of me if it is thought that while still alive I have been guilty of so hideous a crime?" She must face her fate. She had lost Genji forever. If she were to keep any control at all over her own thoughts she must first of all find some way of putting him wholly out of mind. She kept on reminding herself not to think of him, so that this very resolve led her in the end to think of him but the more.

The Virgin of Ise should by rights have entered upon her duties before the end of the year, but difficulties of various kinds arose and it was not till the autumn of the next year that she could at last be received. She was to enter the Palace-in-the-Fields* in the ninth month, but this was decided so late that the arrangements for her second Purification had to be made in great haste. It was very inconvenient that at this crisis her mother, so far from superintending the preparations, spent hour after

---

* A temporary building erected afresh for each new Virgin a few miles outside Kyoto. She spent several years there before proceeding to Ise.

hour lying dazed and helpless upon her bed. At last the priests arrived to fetch the girl away. They took a grave view of the mother's condition and gave her the benefit of their presence by offering up many prayers and incantations. But week after week she remained in the same condition, showing no symptom which seemed actually dangerous, yet all the time (in some vague and indefinite way) obviously very ill. Genji sent constantly to enquire after her, but she saw clearly that his attention was occupied by quite other matters. Aoi's delivery was not yet due and no preparations for it had been made, when suddenly there were signs that it was close at hand. She was in great distress, but though the healers recited prayer upon prayer their utmost efforts could not shift by one jot the spiteful power which possessed her. All the greatest miracle-workers of the land were there; the utter failure of their ministrations irritated and perplexed them. At last, daunted by the potency of their incantations, the spirit that possessed her found voice and, weeping bitterly, she was heard to say: "Give me a little respite; there is a matter of which Prince Genji and I must speak." The healers nodded at one another as though to say, "Now we shall learn something worth knowing," for they were convinced that the "possession" was speaking through the mouth of the possessed, and they hurried Genji to her bedside. Her parents, thinking that her end being near, she desired to give some last secret injunction to Genji, retired to the back of the room. The priests too ceased their incantations and began to recite the *Hokkekyo*[*] in low impressive tones. He raised the bed-curtain. She looked lovely as ever as she lay there, very big with child, and any man who saw her even now would have found himself strangely troubled by her beauty. How much the more then Prince Genji, whose heart was already overflowing with tenderness and remorse! The plaited tresses of her long hair stood out in sharp contrast to her white jacket.[†] Even to this loose, sickroom garb her natural grace imparted the air of a fashionable gown! He took her hand. "It is terrible," he began, to see you looking so unhappy..." He could say no more. Still she gazed at him, but through his tears he saw that there was no longer in her eyes the wounded scorn that he had come to know so well, but a look of forbearance and tender concern; and while she watched him weep her own eyes brimmed with tears. It would not do for him to go on crying like this. Her father and mother would be alarmed; besides, it was upsetting Aoi herself, and meaning to cheer her he said: "Come, things are not so bad as that! You will soon be much better. But even if anything should happen, it is certain that we shall meet again in worlds to come. Your father and mother too,

---

[*] The Chinese version of the Sanskrit *Saddharma Pundarika Sutra;* see *Sacred Books of the East,* Vol. 21.

[†] The lying-in jacket.

and many others, love you so dearly that between your fate and theirs must be some sure bond that will bring you back to them in many, many lives that are to be." Suddenly she interrupted him: "No, no. That is not it. But stop these prayers a while. They do me great harm," and drawing him nearer to her she went on, "I did not think that you would come. I have waited for you till all my soul is burnt with longing." She spoke wistfully, tenderly; and still in the same tone recited the verse, "Bind thou, as the seam of a skirt is braided, this shred, that from my soul despair and loneliness have sundered." The voice in which these words were said was not Aoi's; nor was the manner hers. He knew someone whose voice was very like that. Who was it? Why, yes; surely only she—the Lady Rokujo. Once or twice he had heard people suggest that something of this kind might be happening; but he had always rejected the idea as hideous and unthinkable, believing it to be the malicious invention of some unprincipled scandalmonger, and had even denied that such "possession" ever took place. Now he had seen one with his own eyes. Ghastly, unbelievable as they were, such things did happen in real life. Controlling himself at last he said in a low voice: "I am not sure who is speaking to me. Do not leave me in doubt..." Her answer proved only too conclusively that he had guessed aright. To his horror her parents now came back to the bed, but she had ceased to speak, and seeing her now lying quietly her mother thought the attack was over, and was coming towards the bed carrying a basin of hot water when Aoi suddenly started up and bore a child. For the moment all was gladness and rejoicing; but it seemed only too likely that the spirit which possessed her had but been temporarily dislodged; for a fierce fit of terror was soon upon her, as though the thing (whatever it was) were angry at having been put to the trouble of shifting, so that there was still grave anxiety about the future. The Abbot of Tendai and the other great ecclesiastics who were gathered together in the room attributed her easy delivery to the persistency of their own incantations and prayers, and as they hastily withdrew to seek refreshment and repose they wiped the sweat from their brows with an expression of considerable self-satisfaction. Her friends who had for days been plunged in the deepest gloom now began to take heart a little, believing that although there was no apparent improvement yet now that the child was safely born she could not fail to mend. The prayers and incantations began once more, but throughout the house there was a new feeling of confidence; for the amusement of looking after the baby at least gave them some relief from the strain under which they had been living for so many days. Handsome presents were sent by the ex-Emperor, the Royal Princes and all the Court, forming an array which grew more dazzling each night.* The fact

---

* These presents (*ubuyashinai*) were given on the third, fifth, and ninth nights.

that the child was a boy made the celebrations connected with his birth all the more sumptuous and elaborate.

The news of this event took Lady Rokujo somewhat aback. The last report she had heard from the Great Hall was that the confinement was bound to be very dangerous. And now they said that there had not been the slightest difficulty. She thought this very peculiar. She had herself for a long while been suffering from the most disconcerting sensations. Often she felt as though her whole personality had in some way suddenly altered. It was as though she were a stranger to herself. Recently she had noticed that a smell of mustard-seed incense for which she was at a loss to account was pervading her clothes and hair. She took a hot bath and put on other clothes; but still the same odor of incense pursued her. It was bad enough even in private to have this sensation of being as it were estranged from oneself. But now her body was playing tricks upon her which her attendants must have noticed and were no doubt discussing behind her back. Yet there was not one person among those about her with whom she could bring herself to discuss such things and all this pent-up misery seemed only to increase the strange process of dissolution which had begun to attack her mind.

Now that Genji was somewhat less anxious about Aoi's condition the recollection of his extraordinary conversation with her at the crisis of her attack kept on recurring in his mind, and it made so painful an impression upon him that though it was now a long time since he had communicated with Rokujo and he knew that she must be deeply offended, he felt that no kind of intimacy with her would ever again be possible. Yet in the end pity prevailed and he sent her a letter. It seemed indeed that it would at present be heartless to absent himself at all from one who had just passed through days of such terrible suffering and from her friends who were still in a state of the gravest anxiety, and all his secret excursions were abandoned. Aoi still remained in a condition so serious that he was not allowed to see her. The child was as handsome an infant as you could wish to see. The great interest which Genji took in it and the zest with which he entered into all the arrangements which were made for its welfare delighted Aoi's father, inasmuch as they seemed signs of a better understanding between his daughter and Genji; and though her slow recovery caused him great anxiety, he realized that an illness such as that through which she had just passed must inevitably leave considerable traces behind it and he persuaded himself that her condition was less dangerous than one might have supposed. The child reminded Genji of the Heir Apparent and made him long to see Fujitsubo's little son again. The desire took such strong hold upon him that at last he sent Aoi a message in which he said: "It is a very long time since I have been to the Palace or indeed have paid any visits at all. I am beginning to feel the need of a little distraction, so today I am going out for a short while and should like to see you before I go. I do not want to feel that we are completely cut off from one another." So he pleaded, and he was supported by her ladies who told her that Prince Genji was her own dear Lord and that she ought not to be so proud and stiff with him. She feared that her illness had told upon her looks and was for speaking to him with a curtain between, but this too her gentlewomen would not allow. He brought a stool close to where she was lying and began speaking to her of one thing or another. Occasionally she put in a word or two, but it was evident that she was still very weak. Nevertheless it was difficult to believe that she had so recently seemed almost at the point of death. They were talking quietly together about those worst days of her illness and how they now seemed like an evil dream when suddenly he recollected the extraordinary conversation he had had with her when she was lying apparently at her last gasp and filled with a sudden bitterness, he said to her: "There are many other things that I must one day talk to you about. But you seem very tired and perhaps I had better leave you." So saying he arranged her pillows, brought her warm water to wash in and in fact played the sicknurse so well that those about her wondered where he had acquired the art. Still peerlessly beautiful but weak and listless, she seemed as she lay motionless on the bed at times almost to fade out of existence. He gazed at her with fond concern. Her hair, every ringlet still in its right plate, was spread out over the pillow. Never before had her marvelous beauty so strangely impressed him. Was it conceivable that year after year he should have allowed such a woman to continue in estrangement from him? Still he stood gazing at her. "I must start for the Palace," he said at last; "but I shall not be away long. Now that you are better you must try to make your mother feel less anxious about you when she comes presently; for though she tries hard not to show it, she is still terribly distressed about you. You must begin now to make an effort and sit up for a little while each day. I think it is partly because she spoils you so much that you are taking so long to get well." As he left the room, robed in all the magnificence of his court attire, she followed him with her eyes more fixedly than ever in her life before. The attendance of the officers who took part in the autumn session was required, and Aoi's father accompanied Genji to the Palace, as did also her brother who needed the Minister's assistance in making their arrangements for the coming political year. Many of their servants went too and the Great Hall wore a deserted and melancholy aspect. Suddenly Aoi was seized with the same choking-fit as before and was soon in a desperate condition. This news was brought to Genji in the Palace and breaking off his Audience he at once made for home. The rest followed in hot haste and though it was Appointment

Evening* they gave up all thought of attending the proceedings, knowing that the tragic turn of affairs at the Great Hall would be considered a sufficient excuse. It was too late to get hold of the abbot from Mount Tendai or any of the dignitaries who had given their assistance before. It was appalling that just when she seemed to have taken a turn for the better she should so suddenly again be at the point of death, and the people at the Great Hall felt utterly helpless and bewildered. Soon the house was full of lackeys who were arriving from every side with messages of sympathy and enquiry; but from the inhabitants of that stricken house they could obtain no information, for they seemed to do nothing but rush about from one room to another in a state of frenzy which it was terrifying to behold.

Remembering that several times already her "possession" had reduced her to a trance-like state, they did not for some time attempt to lay out the body or even touch her pillows, but left her lying just as she was. After two or three days however it became clear that life was extinct.

Amid the general lamentations which ensued Genji's spirit sank with the apathy of utter despair. Sorrow had followed too fast upon sorrow; life as he saw it now was but a succession of futile miseries. The messages of condolence which poured in from all the most exalted quarters in the Court and City merely fatigued and exasperated him.

The warmth of the old ex-Emperor's messages and his evident personal distress at Aoi's death were indeed very flattering and mingled a certain feeling of gratification with her father's perpetual weeping. At the suggestion of a friend various drastic means were resorted to in the hope that it might yet be possible to kindle some spark of life in the body. But it soon became evident, even to their reluctant eyes, that all this was too late, and heavy at heart they took the body to Toribeno. Here, in the great flat cremation-ground beyond the town, the horrors that they had dreaded were only too swiftly begun. Even in this huge open space there was scarcely room for the crowds of mourners who had come from all the great palaces of the City to follow behind the bier and for the concourses of priests who, chanting their liturgies, flocked from the neighboring temples. The ex-Emperor was of course represented; so were the Princess Kokiden and the Heir Apparent; while many other important people came in person and mingled with the crowd. Never had any funeral aroused so universal a demonstration of interest and sympathy. Her father was not present: "Now in my declining years to have lost one who was so young and strong is a blow too staggering..." he said and he could no longer check the tears which he was striving to conceal. His grief was heart-rending. All night long the mournful ceremonies proceeded, but at

---

* The ceremony of investing the newly elected officials.

last only a few pitiful ashes remained upon the pyre and in the morning the mourners returned to their homes. It was in fact, save for its grandeurs, much like any other funeral; but it so happened that save in one case only death had not yet come Genji's way and the scenes of that day haunted him long afterwards with hideous persistency.

The ceremony took place in the last week of the eighth month. Seeing that from Aoi's father all the soft brightness of this autumn morning was hid in the twilight of despair and well knowing what thoughts must be passing through his mind, Genji came to him and pointing to the sky whispered the following verse: "Because of all the mists that wreathe the autumn sky I know not which ascended from my lady's bier, henceforth upon the country of the clouds from pole to pole I gaze with love."

At last he was back in his room. He lay down, but could not sleep. His thoughts went back over the years that he had known her. Why had he been content lazily to assume that in the end all would go right and meanwhile amused himself regardless of her resentment? Why had he let year after year go by without managing even at the very end to establish any real intimacy, any sympathy between them? The bitterest remorse now filled his heart; but what use was it? His servants brought him his light grey mourner's dress and the strange thought floated into his mind, "What if I had died instead and not she? She would be getting into the woman-mourner's deep-dyed robe," and he recited the poem: "Though light in hue the dress which in bereavement custom bids me wear, yet black my sorrow as the gown thou wouldst have worn"; and as thus clad he told his rosary, those about him noted that even the dull hues of mourning could not make him look peaked or drab. He read many sutras in a low voice, among them the liturgy to Samantabhadra as Dispenser of the Dharmadhatu Samadhi, which he recited with an earnestness more impressive in its way than the dexterous intonation of the professional cleric. Next he visited the newborn child and took some comfort in the reflection that she had at least left behind her this memorial of their love. Genji did not attempt to go even for the day to the Nijo-in, but remained buried in recollections and regrets with no other occupation save the ordering of masses for her soul. He did however bring himself to write a few letters, among them one to Rokujo. The Virgin Elect was already in charge of the Guardsmen of the Gate and would soon be passed on by them to the Palace-in-the-Fields. Rokujo accordingly made her daughter's situation an excuse for sending no reply.* He was now so weary of life and its miseries that he seriously contemplated the taking of priestly vows, and might perhaps have done so, had there not been a new bond which

---

* Had she corresponded with someone who was in mourning, she would herself have become unclean and been disqualified from attending upon her daughter the Vestal Virgin.

seemed to tie him irrevocably to the world. But stay, there was the girl Murasaki too, waiting for him in the wing of his palace. How unhappy she must have been during all this long time! That night lying all alone within his royal curtains, though watchmen were going their rounds not far away, he felt very lonely and remembering that "autumn is no time to lie alone," he sent for the sweetest-voiced among the chaplains of the palace. His chanting mingled with the sounds of early dawn was indeed of almost unendurable beauty. But soon the melancholy of late autumn, the murmur of the rising wind took possession of him, and little used to lonely nights he found it hard to keep his bed till morning. Looking out he saw that a heavy mist lay over the garden beds; yet despite the mist it was clear that something was tied to the stem of a fine chrysanthemum not far away. It was a letter written on dark blue paper.* The messenger had left it there and gone away. "What a charming idea!" he was thinking when he suddenly recognized the hand. It was from Rokujo. She began by saying she did not think, having regard to her daughter's situation, that he would be surprised at her long delay in answering his previous note. She added an acrostic poem in which, playing upon the word chrysanthemum (*kiku*) she told him of her distress at hearing (*kiku*) of his bereavement. "The beauty of the morning," she ended, "turned my thoughts more than ever towards you and your sorrow; that is why I could not choose but answer you." It was written even more elegantly than usual; but he tossed it aside. Her condolences wounded him, for after what he had seen he knew that they could not be sincere. Nevertheless he felt that it would be too harsh to break off all communication with her; that he should do so would in fact tend to incriminate her, and this was the last thing he desired. After all, it was probably not *that* at all which had brought about the disaster; maybe Aoi's fate was sealed in any case. If only he had chanced never to see or hear the fatal operation of her spirit! As it was, argue with himself as he might, he doubted whether he would ever be able to efface the impression of what had been revealed to him at that hideous scene.

He had the excuse that he was still in deep mourning and that to receive a letter from him would inconvenience her at this stage of her daughter's Purification. But after turning the matter over in his mind for a long while, he decided that it would be unfeeling not to answer a letter which had evidently been written with the sole object of giving him pleasure and on a paper lightly tinted with brown he wrote: "Though I have let so many days slip by, believe me that you have not been absent from my thoughts. If I was reluctant to answer your letter, it was because, as a mourner, I was loath to trespass upon the sanctity which

---
* Used in writing to people who were in mourning.

now surrounds your home, and this I trusted that you would understand. Do not brood overmuch upon what has happened; for "go we late or soon, more frail our lives than dewdrops hanging in the morning light." For the present, think of it no more. I say this now, because it is not possible for us to meet."

She received the letter at her daughter's place of preparation, but did not read it till she was back in her own house. At a glance she knew at what he was hinting. So he too accused her! And at last the hideous conviction of her own guilt forced itself upon her acceptance. Her misery increased tenfold.

If even Genji had reason to believe in her guilt, her brother-in-law, the ex-Emperor, must already have been informed. What was he thinking of her? Her dead husband, Prince Zembo, had been the brother whom he had loved best. He had accepted the guardianship of the little girl who was now about to be consecrated and at his brother's earnest entreaty had promised to undertake her education and indeed treat her as though she were his own child. The old Emperor had constantly invited the widowed lady and her daughter to live with him in the Palace, but she was reluctant to accept this offer, which indeed was somewhat impracticable. Meanwhile she allowed herself to listen to Genji's youthful addresses and was soon living in constant torment and agitation lest her indiscretion should be discovered. During the whole period of this escapade she was in such a state of mingled excitement and apprehension that she scarcely knew what she was doing. In the world at large she had the reputation of being a great beauty and this, combined with her exalted lineage, brought to the Palace-in-the-Fields, so soon as it was known that she had repaired thither with her daughter, a host of frivolous dandies from the Court, who made it their business to force upon her their fashionable attentions morning, noon, and night. Genji heard of this and did not blame them. He could only think it was a thousand pities that a woman endowed with every talent and charm should take it into her head that she had done with the world and prepare to remove herself to so remote a place. He could not help thinking that she would find Ise extremely dull when she got there.

Though the masses for Aoi's soul were now over, he remained in retirement till the end of the seven weeks. He was not used to doing nothing and the time hung heavy on his hands. Often he sent for To no Chujo to tell him all that was going on in the world, and among much serious information Chujo would often seek to distract him by discussing the strange escapades in which they had sometimes shared.

On one of these occasions he indulged in some jokes at the expense of the ancient lady-of-the-bedchamber with whom Genji had so indiscreetly become involved. "Poor old lady!" Genji protested; "it is too bad to make fun of her in this way. Please do not do it." But all the same he had to admit to himself that he could never think of her without smiling. Then Chujo told him the whole story of how he had followed and watched him on that autumn night, the first after the full moon,* and many other stories besides of his own adventures and other people's. But in the end they fell to talking of their common loss, and agreeing that taken all in all life was but a sad business they parted in tears.

Some weeks afterwards on a gloomy wet evening Chujo strode into the room looking somewhat self-conscious in the light grey winter cloak and breeches which he was today wearing for the first time.† Genji was leaning against the balustrade of the balcony above the main western door. For a long while he had been gazing at the frost-clad gardens which surrounded the house. A high wind was blowing and swift showers dashed against the trees. Near to tears he murmured to himself the line: "Tell me whether her soul be in the rain or whether in the clouds above!"‡ And as Chujo watched him sitting there, his chin resting upon his hand, he thought the soul of one who had been wedded to so lovely a youth would not indeed have borne quite to renounce the scene of her earthly life and must surely be hovering very near him. Still gazing with eager admiration, Chujo come to Genji's side. He noticed now that though his friend had not in any other way abated the plainness of his dress, he had today put on colored sash. This streak of deep red showed up against his grey cloak (which though still a summer one§ was of darker color than that which he had lately been wearing) in so attractive a way that though the effect was very different from that of the magnificent attires which Genji had affected in happier days, yet Chujo could not for a long while take his eyes off him. At last he too gazed up at the stormy sky, and remembering the Chinese verse which he had heard Genji repeat he recited the poem: "Though to rain her soul be turned, yet where in the clouded vault of heaven is that one mist-wreath which is she?" And Genji answered: "Since she whom once we knew beyond the country of the clouds is fled, two months of storm and darkness now have seared the wintry earth below."

The depth of Genji's feeling was evident. Sometimes Chujo had thought it was merely dread of the old Emperor's rebukes—coupled with a sense of obligation towards Aoi's father whose kindness had always been so marked and also towards the Princess her mother, who had cherished

---

* See p. 110.
† Winter clothes are begun on the first day of the tenth month.
‡ From a poem to a dead lady, by Liu Yü-hsi (A.D. 773-842).
  I saw you first standing at the window of Yü Liang's tower;
  Your waist was slender as the willow-trees that grow at Wu-ch'ang.
  My finding you and losing you were both like a dream;
  Oh tell me if your soul dwells in the rain, or whether in the clouds above!
§ A husband in mourning may not wear winter clothes. The mourning lasts for three months.

him with an unfailing patience and fondness—that had made it difficult for him to break off a relationship which was in fact becoming very irksome. Often indeed Genji's apparent indifference to Aoi had been very painful to him. Now it was evident to him that she had never ceased to hold an important place in his affections, and this made him deplore more bitterly than ever the tragedy of her early death. Whatever he did and wherever he went he felt that a light was gone out of his life and he was very despondent.

Among the withered undergrowth in the garden Genji found to his delight a few gentians still blossoming and after Chujo was gone he plucked some and bade the wet-nurse Saiso give them to the child's grandmother, together with the verse: "This gentian flower that lingered amid the withered grasses of the hedge I send you in remembrance of the autumn that is passed." "To you," he added, "it will seem a poor thing in contrast to the flowers that are gone." The Princess looked at her grandson's innocent smiling face and thought that in beauty he was not far behind the child she had lost. Already her tears were pouring faster than a stormy wind shakes down the dry leaves from a tree, and when she read Genji's message they flowed faster still. This was her answer: "New tears, but tears of joy it brings—this blossom from a meadow that is now laid waste,"

Still in need of some small employment to distract his thoughts, though it was already getting dark he began a letter to Princess Asagao who, he felt sore, must long ago have been told of his bereavement. Although it was a long time since he had heard from her he made no reference to their former friendship; his letter was indeed so formal that he allowed the messenger to read it before he started. It was written on Chinese paper tinted sky-blue. With it was the poem: "When I look back upon an autumn fraught with diverse sorrows I find no dusk dimmed with such tears as I tonight have shed." He took great pains with his handwriting and her ladies thought it a shame that so elegant a note should remain unanswered. In the end she reached the same conclusion. "Though my heart goes out towards you in your affliction," she answered, "I see no cause to abandon my distrust." And to this she added the poem: "Since I heard that the mists of autumn had vanished and left desolate winter in your house, I have thought often of you as I watched the streaming sky." This was all, and it was written hastily, but to Genji, who for so long had received no news from her, it gave as much pleasure as the longest and most ingenious epistle.

It is in general the unexplored that attracts us, and Genji tended to fall most deeply in love with those who gave him least encouragement. The ideal condition for the continuance of his affection was that the beloved, much occupied elsewhere, should grant him no more than an occasional favor. There was one[*] who admirably fulfilled these conditions, but unfortunately her high rank and conspicuous position in society brought with them too many material difficulties. But little Murasaki was different. There was no need to bring her up on this principle. He had not during the long days of his mourning ever forgotten her and he knew that she must be feeling very dull without him. But he regarded her merely as an orphan child whose care he had undertaken and it was a comfort to him to think that here at least was someone he could leave for a little while without anxiously wondering all the time whether he would get into trouble.

It was now quite dark, and gathering the people of the house round the great lamp, he got them to tell him stories. There was among them a gentlewoman named Chunagon with whom he had for years been secretly in love. He still felt drawn towards her, but at such a time there could of course be no thought of any closer tie. Seeing now that he was looking despondent she came over to him and when they had talked for a while of various matters at large, Genji said to her: "During these last weeks, when all has been quiet in the house, I have grown so used to the company of you gentlewomen that if a time comes when we can no longer meet so frequently, I shall miss you very much. That was why I was feeling particularly depressed; though indeed whichever way I turn my thoughts I find small matter for consolation!" Here he paused and some of the ladies shed a few tears. At last one of them said: "I know, my Lord, how dark a cloud has fallen upon your life and would not venture to compare our sorrow with yours. But I would have you remember what it must mean to us that henceforward you will never..." "Do not say never," answered Genji kindly. "I do not forget my friends so easily as that. If there are any among you who, mindful of the past, wish still to serve in this house, they may count upon it that so long as I live I shall never desert them." And as he sat gazing into the lamplight, with tears aglitter in his eyes, they felt they were fortunate indeed in having such a protector.

There was among these gentlewomen a little orphan girl who had been Aoi's favorite among all her maids. Well knowing how desolate the child must now be feeling he said to her kindly: "Whose business is it now but mine to look after little Miss Até?" The girl burst into tears. In her short tunic, darker than the dresses the others were wearing, with black neckerchief and dark blue breeches she was a charming figure. "I hope," continued Genji, "that there are some who despite the dull times they are likely to have in this house will choose, in memory of the past, to devote themselves to the care of the little prince whom I am leaving behind. If all who knew his mother are now to be dispersed, his plight

---

[*] Fujitsubo.

will be more wretched than before." Again he promised never to forget them, but they knew well enough that his visits would be few and far between, and felt very despondent.

That night he distributed among these waiting-ladies and among all the servants at the Great Hall according to their rank and condition various keepsakes and trifles that had belonged to their young mistress, giving to each whatever-he thought most likely to keep her memory alive, without regard to his own preferences and dislikes in the household.

He had determined that he could not much longer continue this mode of life and must soon return to his own palace. While his servants were dragging out his coach and his gentlemen assembling in front of his rooms, as though on purpose to delay him a violent rainstorm began, with a wind that tore the last leaves from the trees and swept them over the earth with wild rapidity. The gentlemen who had assembled in front of the house were soon drenched to the skin. He had meant to go to the Palace, then to the Nijo-in and return to sleep at the Great Hall. But on such a night this was impossible, and he ordered his gentlemen to proceed straight to the Nijo-in where he would join them subsequently. As they trooped off each of them felt (though none of them was likely to be seeing the Great Hall for by any means the last time) that today a chapter in his life was closed. Both the Minister and his wife, when they heard that Genji was not returning that night, also felt that they had reached a new and bitter stage in the progress of their affliction. To Aoi's mother he sent this letter: "The ex-Emperor has expressed a strong desire to see me and I feel bound to go to the Palace. Though I shall not be absent for many days, yet it is now so long a time since I left this house that I feel dazed at the prospect of facing the great world once more. I could not go without informing you of my departure, but am in no condition to pay you a visit." The Princess was still lying with closed eyes, her thoughts buried in the profoundest gloom. She did not send a reply. Presently Aoi's father came to Genji's apartments. He found it very hard to bear up, and during the interview clung fast to his son-in-law's sleeve with an air of dependence which was pathetic to witness. After much hesitation he began at last to say: "We old men are prone to tears even when small matters are amiss; you must not wonder then that under the weight of so terrible a sorrow I sometimes find myself breaking into fits of weeping which I am at a loss to control. At such moments of weakness and disarray I had rather be where none can see me, and that is why I have not as yet ventured even to pay my respects to His Majesty your good father. If opportunity offers, I beg you to explain this to him. To be left thus desolate in the last years of life is a sore trial, a very sore trial indeed..." The effort which it cost him to say these words was distressing for Genji to watch and he hastened to assure the old Minister that he would make matters right at the Court. "Though I do not doubt," he added, "that my father has already guessed the reason of your absence." As it was still raining heavily the Minister urged him to start before it grew quite dark. But Genji would not leave the house till he had taken a last look at the inner rooms. His father-in-law followed him. In the space beyond Aoi's curtained seat, packed away behind a screen, some thirty gentlewomen all clad in dark grey weeds were huddled together, forlorn and tearful. "These hapless ladies," said the Minister, turning to Genji, "though they take some comfort in the thought that you are leaving behind you one whose presence will sometimes draw you to this house, well know that it will never again be your rightful home, and this distresses them no less than the loss of their dear mistress. For years they had hoped against hope that you and she would at last be reconciled. Consider then how bitter for them must be the day of this, your final departure." "Let them take heart," said Genji; "for whereas while my lady was alive I would often of set purpose absent myself from her in the vain hope that upon my return I should find her less harshly disposed towards me, now that she is dead I have no longer any cause to shun this house, as soon you shall discover."

When he had watched Genji drive away, Aoi's father went to her bedroom. All her things were just as she had left them. On a stand in front of the bed writing materials lay scattered about. There were some papers covered with Genji's handwriting, and these the old man clasped with an eagerness that made some of the gentlewomen who had followed him smile even in the midst of their grief. The works that Genji had written out were all masterpieces of the past, some Chinese, some Japanese; some written in cursive, some in full script; they constituted indeed an astonishing display of versatile penmanship. The Minister gazed with an almost religious awe at these specimens of Genji's skill, and the thought that he must henceforth regard the young man whom he adored as no longer a member of his household and family must at that moment have been very painful to him.

Among these manuscripts was a copy of Po Chü-i's' Everlasting Wrong"* and beside the words "The old pillow, the old coverlet with whom shall he now share?" Genji had written the poem: "Mournful her ghost that journeying now to unfamiliar realms must flee the couch where we were wont to rest." While beside the words "The white petals of the frost" he had written: "The dust shall cover this bed; for no longer can I bear to brush from it the nightly dew of my tears."

---

* Murasaki quotes the line in the form in which it occurs in Japanese MSS. of Po Chü-i's poem. The Chinese editions have a slightly different text. Cf. Giles's translation, *History of Chinese Literature*, p. 172.

Aoi's ladies were gathered together in groups of two or three in each of which some gentlewoman was pouring out her private griefs and vexations. "No doubt, as his Excellency the Minister told us, Prince Genji will come to us sometimes, if only to see the child. But for my part I doubt whether he will find much comfort in such visits..." So one of them was saying to her friends. And soon there were many affecting scenes of farewell between them, for it had been decided that for the present they were all of them to go back to their homes.

Meanwhile Genji was with his father in the Palace. "You are very thin in the face," said the ex-Emperor as soon as he saw him. "I am afraid you have overtaxed your strength by too much prayer and fasting," and in a state of the deepest concern he at once began pressing all kinds of viands and cordials upon him, showing with regard to his health and indeed his affairs in general a solicitude by which Genji could not help feeling touched.

Late that night he at last arrived at the Nijo-in. Here he found everything garnished and swept; his men-servants and maids were waiting for him at the door. All the gentlewomen of the household at once presented themselves in his apartments. They seemed to have vied with one another which should look the gayest and smartest, and their finery contrasted pleasantly with the somber and dispiriting attire of the unfortunate ladies whom he had left behind him at the Great Hall.

Having changed out of his court dress, he went at once to the western wing. Not only was Murasaki's winter costume most daintily designed, but her pretty waiting-maids and little companions were so handsomely equipped as to reflect the greatest credit on Shonagon's management; and he saw with satisfaction that such matters might with perfect safety be left in her hands. Murasaki herself was indeed exquisitely dressed. "How tall you have grown since last I saw you!" he said and pulled up her little curtain-of-honor. He had been away so long that she felt shy with him and turned her head aside. But he would not for the world have had her look otherwise than she looked at that moment, for as she sat in profile with the lamplight falling upon her face, he realized with delight that she was becoming the very image of her whom from the beginning he had loved best. Coming closer to her side he whispered to her: "Sometime or other I want to tell you about all that has been happening to me since I went away. But it has all been very terrible and I am too tired to speak of it now, so I am going away to rest for a little while in my own room. From tomorrow onwards you will have me to yourself all day long; in fact, I expect you will soon grow quite tired of me."

"So far, so good," thought Shonagon when she heard this speech. But she was still very far from easy in her mind. She knew that there were several ladies of very great influence with whom Genji was on terms of friendship and she feared that when it came to choosing a second wife, he would be far more likely to take one of these than to remember her own little mistress; and she was not at all satisfied.

When Genji had retired to the eastern wing, he sent for a certain Lady Chujo to rub his limbs and then went to bed. Next morning he wrote to the nurses of Aoi's child and received from them in reply a touching account of its beauty and progress; but the letter served only to awaken in him useless memories and regrets. Towards the end of the day he felt very restless and the time hung heavily on his hands, but he was in no mood to resume his secret roving and such an idea did not even occur to him. In Murasaki none of his hopes had been disappointed; she had indeed grown up into as handsome a girl as you could wish to see, nor was she any longer at an age when it was impossible for him to become her lover. He constantly hinted at this, but she did not seem to understand what he meant.

He still had plenty of time on his hands, and the whole of it was now spent in her society. All day long they played together at draughts or word-picking, and even in the course of these trivial pursuits she showed a quickness of mind and beauty of disposition which continually delighted him; but she had been brought up in such rigid seclusion from the world that it never once occurred to her to exploit her charms in any more adult way.

Soon the situation became unendurable, and though he knew that she would be very much upset he determined somehow or another to get his own way.

There came a morning when the gentleman was already up and about, but the young lady was still lying abed. Her attendants had no means of knowing that anything out of the ordinary had happened, for it had always been Genji's habit to go in and out of her room just as he chose. They naturally assumed that she was not feeling well and were glancing at her with sympathy when Genji arrived carrying a writing-box which he slipped behind the bed curtains. He at once retired, and the ladies also left the room. Seeing that she was alone Murasaki slowly raised her head. There by her pillow was the writing-box and tied to it with ribbon, a slender note. Listlessly she detached the note and unfolding it read the hastily scribbled poem: "Too long have we deferred this new emprise, who night by night till now have lain but with a shift between."

That *this* was what Genji had so long been wanting came to her as a complete surprise and she could not think why he should regard the unpleasant thing that had happened last night as in some way the beginning of a new and more intimate friendship between them. Later in the morning he came again. "Is something the matter with you?" he asked. "I shall be very dull today if you cannot play draughts with me."

But when he came close to her she only buried herself more deeply than ever under the bedclothes. He waited till the room was empty and then bending over her he said, "Why are you treating me in this surly way? I little expected to find you in so bad a humor this morning. The others will think it very strange if you lie here all day," and he pulled aside the scarlet coverlet beneath which she had dived. To his astonishment he found that she was bathed in sweat; even the hair that hung across her cheeks was dripping wet. "No! This is too much," he said; "what a state you have worked yourself up into!" But try as he would to coax her back to reason he could not get a word out of her, for she was really feeling very vexed with him indeed. "Very well then," he said at last, "if that is how you feel I will never come to see you again," and he pretended to be very much mortified and humiliated. Turning away, he opened the writing-box to see whether she had written any answer to his poem, but of course found none. He understood perfectly that her distress was due merely to extreme youth and inexperience, and was not at all put out. All day long he sat near her trying to win back her confidence, and though he had small success he found even her rebuffs in a curious way very endearing.

At nightfall, it being the Day of the Wild Boar, the festival cakes* were served. Owing to Genji's bereavement no great display was made, but a few were brought round to Murasaki's quarters in an elegant picnic-basket. Seeing that the different kinds were all mixed up together, Genji came out into the front part of the house and calling for Koremitsu said to him: "I want you to take these cakes away and bring me some more tomorrow evening; only not nearly so many as this, and all of one kind.† This is not the right evening for them." He smiled as he said these words and Koremitsu was quick-witted enough at once to guess what had happened. He did not however think that it would be discreet to congratulate his master in so many words, and merely said: "It is true enough that if you want to make a good beginning you must eat your cakes on the proper day. The day of the Rat is certainly very much to the purpose.‡ Pray how many am I to bring?" When Genji answered, "Divide by three§ and you will get the answer," Koremitsu was no longer in any doubt, and hastily

---

* On the Day of the Boar in the tenth month it was the custom to serve little cakes of seven different kinds, to wit: Large bean, mungo, dolicho, sesamun, chestnut, persimmon, sugar-starch.

† On the third night after the first cohabitation it was the custom to offer up small cake (all of one kind and color) to the god Izanagi and his sister Izanami.

‡ First, because the Rat comes at the beginning of the series of twelve animal signs; secondly, because "Rat" is written with a character that also means "baby."

§ The phrase which I have translated "Divide by three" also means "One of three," i.e. of the Three Mysteries (Birth, Marriage, Death). That is why Koremitsu was "no longer in any doubt." But many other explanations of the passage have been given. It is indeed one of the three major difficulties enumerated by the old-fashioned Genji teachers.

retired, leaving Genji amused at the practiced air with which he invariably handled matters of this kind. He said nothing to anyone, but returning to his private house made the cakes there with his own hands.

Genji was beginning to despair of ever restoring her confidence and good humor. But even now, when she seemed as shy of him as on the night when he first stole her from her home, her beauty fascinated him and he knew that his love for her in past days had been but a particle compared with what he had felt since yesterday.

How strange a thing is the heart of man! For now it would have seemed to him a calamity if even for a single night he had been taken from Murasaki's side; and only a little while ago...

Koremitsu brought the cakes which Genji had ordered very late on the following night. He was careful not to entrust them to Shonagon, for he thought that such a commission might embarrass a grown woman. Instead, he sent for her daughter Miss Ben and putting all the cakes into one large perfume-box he bade her take them secretly to her mistress. "Be sure to put them close by her pillow, for they are lucky cakes and must not be left about the house. Promise me not to do anything silly with them." Miss Ben thought all this very odd, but tossing her head she answered, "When, pray, did you ever know me to be silly?" and she walked off with the box. Being quite a young girl and completely innocent as regards matters of this kind, she marched straight up to her mistress's bed and, remembering Koremitsu's instructions, pushed the box through the curtains and lodged it safely by the pillow. It seemed to her that there was someone else there as well as Murasaki. "No doubt," thought she, "Prince Genji has come as usual to hear her repeat her lessons."

As yet no one in the household save Koremitsu had any knowledge of the betrothal. But when next day the box was found by the bed and brought into the servants' quarters, some of those who were in closest touch with their master's affairs at once guessed the secret. Where did these little dishes come from, each set on its own little carved stand? And who had been at such pains to make these dainty and ingenious cakes? Shonagon, though she was shocked at this casual way of slipping into matrimony, was overjoyed to learn that Genji's strange patronage of her young mistress had at last culminated in a definite act of betrothal, and her eyes brimmed with tears of thankfulness and delight. All the same, she thought he might at least have taken the trouble to inform her old nurse, and there was a good deal of grumbling in the household generally at an outside retainer such as Koremitsu having got wind of the matter first.

During the days that followed he grudged even the short hours of attendance which he was obliged to put in at the Palace and in his father's rooms, discovering (much to his own surprise) that save in her presence he could no longer enjoy a moment's peace. The friends whom he had been wont to visit showed themselves both surprised and offended by this unexplained neglect, but though he had no wish to stand ill with them, he now found that even a remote prospect of having to absent himself from his palace for a single night was enough to throw him quite out of gear; and all the time he was away his spirits were at the very lowest ebb and he looked for all the world as though he were sickening from some strange illness. To all invitations or greetings he invariably replied that he was at present in no fit mood for company (which was naturally taken as an allusion to his recent loss) or that he must now be gone, for someone with whom he had business was already awaiting him.

The Minister of the Right was aware that his youngest daughter[*] was still pining for Prince Genji and he said one day to Princess Kokiden: "While his wife was alive we were bound of course to discourage her friendship with him in every way we could. But the position is now quite changed and I feel that as things are there would be much to be said for such a match." But Kokiden had always hated Genji and having herself arranged that her sister should enter the Palace,[†] she saw no reason, why this plan should suddenly be abandoned. Indeed from this moment onwards she became obstinately determined that the girl should be given to the Emperor and to no one else. Genji indeed still retained a certain partiality towards her; but though it grieved him to hear that he had made her unhappy, he had not at present any spare affection to offer her. Life, he had come to the conclusion, was not long enough for diversions and experiments; henceforward he would concentrate. He had moreover received a terrible warning of the dangers which might accrue from such jealousies and resentments as his former way of life had involved. He thought with great tenderness and concern of Lady Rokujo's distress; but it was clear to him that he must beware of ever again allowing her to regard him as her true haven of refuge. If however she would renew their friendship in quite new terms, permitting him to enjoy her company and conversation at such times as he could conveniently arrange to do so, he saw no reason why they should not sometimes meet.

Society at large knew that someone was living with him, but her identity was quite unknown. This was of no consequence; but Genji felt that sooner or later he ought to let her father Prince Hyobukyo know what had become of her and decided that before he did so it would be best to celebrate her Initiation. This was done privately, but he was at pains that every detail of the ceremony should be performed with due splendor and solemnity, and though the outside world was not invited it was as magnificent an affair as it well could be. But ever since their betrothal Murasaki

---

[*] Oborozukiyo. See above, p. 148.

[†] I.e. become a concubine of the Emperor.

had shown a certain shyness and diffidence in his presence. She could not help feeling sorry that after all the years during which they had got on so well together and been such close friends he should suddenly take this strange idea into his head, and whenever her eyes met his she hastily averted them. He tried to make a joke of the matter, but to her it was very serious indeed and weighed heavily upon her mind. Her changed attitude towards him was indeed somewhat comic; but it was also very distressing, and one day he said: "Sometimes it seems as though you had forgotten all the long years of our friendship and I had suddenly become as new to you as at the start"; and while thus he scolded her the year drew to a close. On New Year's Day he paid the usual visits of ceremony to his father, to the Emperor and to the Heir Apparent. Next he visited the Great Hall. The old Minister made no reference to the new year, but at once began to speak of the past. In the midst of his loneliness and sorrow he was so deeply moved even by this hasty and long-deferred visit that though he strove hard to keep his composure it was more than he could compass to do. Looking fondly at his son-in-law he thought that the passage of each fresh year did but add new beauty to this fair face. They went together into the inner rooms, where his entry surprised and delighted beyond measure the disconsolate ladies who had remained behind. Next they visited the little prince who was growing into a fine child; his merry face was indeed a pleasure to see. His resemblance to the Heir Apparent was certainly very striking and Genji wondered whether it had been noticed.

Aoi's things were still as she had left them. His New Year clothes had as in former years been hung out for him on the clothes-frame. Aoi's clothes-frame which stood empty beside it wore a strangely desolate air. A letter from the Princess her mother was now brought to him: "Today," she said, "our bereavement was more than ever present to my mind, and though touched at the news of your visit, I fear that to see you would but awaken unhappy recollections." "You will remember," she continued, "that it was my custom to present you with a suit of clothes on each New Year's Day. But in these last months my sight has been so dimmed with tears that I fear you will think I have matched the colors very ill. Nevertheless I beg that though it be for today only you will suffer yourself to be disfigured by this unfashionable garb..." and a servant held out before him a second* suit, which was evidently the one he was expected to wear today. The under-stuff was of a most unusual pattern and mixture of colors and did not at all please him; but he could not allow her to feel that she had labored in vain, and at once put the suit on. It was indeed fortunate that he had come to the Great Hall that day, for he could see that she had counted on it. In his reply he said: "Though I came with the hope that

---

* In addition to the one hanging on the frame.

you would be the first friend I should greet at this new springtide, yet now that I am here too many bitter memories assail me and I think it wiser that we should not meet." To this he added an acrostic poem in which he said that with the mourning dress which he had just discarded so many years of friendship were cast aside that were he to come to her* he could but weep. To this she sent in answer an acrostic poem in which she said that in this new season when all things else on earth put on altered hue, one thing alone remained as in the months gone by—her longing for the child who like the passing year had vanished from their sight.

But though hers may have been the greater grief we must not think that there was not at that moment very deep emotion on both sides.

---

* *Kiteba,* "were he to come," also means "should he wear it."

PART TWO
THE SACRED TREE

LIST OF MOST IMPORTANT PERSONS (alphabetical)

Akashi, Lady of . . . . Daughter of the old recluse of Akashi.
Akikonomu, Lady . . . . Vestal Virgin at Ise; daughter of Rokujo.
Aoi, Princess . . . . Genji's first wife.
Asagao, Princess . . . . Genji's first-cousin; courted by him in vain.
Chujo . . . . Short for "To no Chujo."
Chujo, Lady . . . . To no Chujo's daughter by his legitimate wife.
Chunagon . . . . Maid to Oborozuki.
Emperor, The Old . . . . . . Genji's father.
Fujitsubo . . . . The Old Emperor's consort; loved by Genji.
Genji, Prince . . . . The Old Emperor's son by a concubine.
Gosechi, Lady . . . . Dancer at the winter festival; admired by Genji.
Hyobukyo, Prince . . . . Fujitsubo's brother; Murasaki's father.
Iyo no Suke . . . . Husband of Utsusemi.
Jiju . . . . Maid to Suyetsumu.
Jokyoden, Lady . . . . Consort of Suzaku.
Ki no Kami . . . . Son of Iyo no Suke by his first wife.
Kokiden . . . . Original consort of the Old Emperor; supplanted first by Genji's mother, then by Fujitsubo.
Koremitsu . . . . Retainer to Genji.
Murasaki . . . . Genji's second wife.
Oborozukiyo, Princess . . . . Younger sister of Kokiden.
Omyobu . . . . Maid to Fujitsubo.
Reikeiden . . . . Lady-in-waiting at the Old Emperor's Court.
Reikeiden, Princess . . . . . . Niece of Kokiden.
Rokujo, Princess . . . . Widow of the Old Emperor's brother.
Ryozen, Emperor . . . . Son of Genji and Fujitsubo; successor to Suzaku.
Shonagon . . . . Murasaki's old nurse.
Sochi no Miya, Prince . . . Genji's half-brother.
Suyetsumu, Lady . . . . Daughter of Prince Hitachi; the red-nosed
  (Suyetsumuhana)   lady.
Suzaku, Emperor . . . . Genji's half-brother; successor to the Old Emperor.
To no Chujo . . . . Brother of Genji's first wife, Lady Aoi.
Ukon no Jo (Okon) . . . . . Faithful retainer to Genji; brother of Ki no Kami.
Utsusemi . . . . Wife of Iyo no Suke; Courted by Genji.
Village of Falling Flowers,
  Lady from the . . . . Sister of Reikeiden; protected by Genji.

GENEALOGICAL TABLES

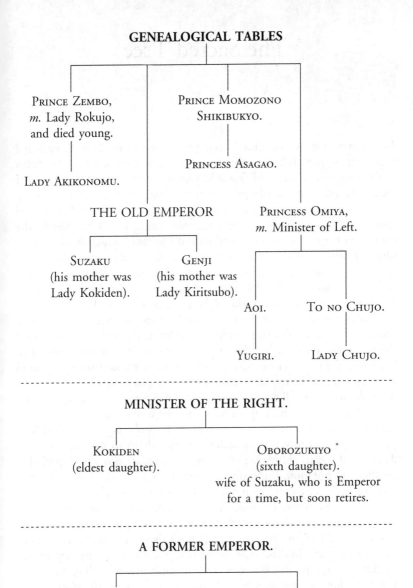

---

* Whom in this volume I call Oborozuki for short.

The Sacred Tree

As the time for her daughter's departure came near, Lady Rokujo fell into utter despair. It had at first been generally supposed that the death of the lady at the Great Hall would put an end to all her troubles and the attendants who waited upon her at the Palace-in-the-Fields were agog with excitement. But their expectations remained unfulfilled. Not a word came from Genji, and this unprecedented treatment on his part finally convinced her that something* had indeed happened which it was impossible for him to forgive. She strove to cast out all thought of him from her heart so that when the time came she might set out upon her journey without misgiving or regret. For a parent to accompany her daughter on such an occasion was in the highest degree unusual; but in this case the Virgin's extreme youth was a convenient excuse, and Rokujo put it about that as the child still needed surveillance she had decided to quit the temporal world in her daughter's company. Even after all that had happened the prospect of parting with her forever was extremely painful to Genji, and as the day drew near he again began to send her letters full of tenderness and solicitude. But he did not propose a meeting, and she herself had by now given up all hope that there could be any question of such a thing. She was certain that (for all his politeness) what had happened must in reality have made her utterly odious to him, and she was determined not to plunge herself, all to no purpose, into a fresh period of conflict and agitation. From time to time she made short visits to her palace, but so secretly that Genji did not hear of it. The Palace-in-the-Fields was not a place where he could see her without inconvenient restrictions and formalities. He fully intended to see her, but put off the visit from day to day till at last months had elapsed since she left the city. Then the ex-Emperor's health began to decline. He had no definitely serious or alarming symptoms, but constantly complained of feeling that there was something wrong with him. Genji's thoughts were therefore a great deal occupied with his father's condition; but he did not want Rokujo to leave with the impression that he had lost all feeling for her, nor did he wish those who knew of their friendship to think that he had treated her heartlessly, and despite all difficulties he set out one day for the Palace-in-the-Fields. It was the seventh day of the ninth month and the departure

---

* Rokujo was still uncertain whether it was her jealousy that had killed Yugao.

of the Virgin for Ise was bound to take place within the next few days. It may be imagined that Rokujo and her maids were in no condition to receive visits, but he wrote again and again begging her to see him even if it were only at the moment of her departure, and at last, despite the fluster into which her whole household was plunged, and feeling all the while that she was acting very imprudently, she could no longer fight against her longing once more to see him and sent word secretly that, if he came, she would contrive to speak to him for a moment from behind her screen-of-state. As he made his way through the open country that stretched out endlessly on every side, his heart was strangely stirred. The autumn flowers were fading; along the reeds by the river the shrill voices of many insects blended with the mournful fluting of the wind in the pines. Scarcely distinguishable from these somewhere in the distance rose and fell a faint, enticing sound of human music. He had with him only a handful of outriders, and his attendants were by his orders dressed so as to attract as little notice as possible. They noted that this lack of show contrasted strangely with the elaborate pains which their master had bestowed upon his own equipment, and as they looked with admiration at the fine figure he cut, the more romantically disposed among them were thrilled at the thought that it had befallen them to accompany him upon a journey, every circumstance of which was calculated to stir to the depth such sensitive hearts as theirs. So delighted was Genji with the scene before him that he continually asked himself why it was that he had deferred this visit for so long; and he regretted that while Rokujo was at the Palace-in-the-Fields he had not made a constant practice of visiting her. They came at last to a group of very temporary-looking wooden huts surrounded by a flimsy brushwood fence. The archways,* built of unstripped wood, stood out black and solemn against the sky. Within the enclosure a number of priests were walking up and down with a preoccupied air. There was something portentous in their manner of addressing one another and in their way of loudly clearing their throats before they spoke. In the Hill of Offering there was a dim flicker of firelight, but elsewhere no single sign of life. So this was the place where he had left one who was from the start in great distress of mind, to shift for herself week after week, month after month! Suddenly he realized with a terrible force all that she must have suffered. He hurried to the place where she had told him he would find her (a room in the northern outbuilding) and sent in a long message contrasting his present quiet and serious existence with his now discarded frivolities. She in return replied with a message, but did not suggest that they should meet. This angered him. "You do not seem to realize," he said, "that such excursions as this are now no part of my

---

* Torii.

ordinary existence and can only be arranged with the greatest difficulty. I had hoped that instead of keeping me beyond the pale, you would hasten to relieve all the anxiety that I have had concerning you in the long months since we met." To this appeal were added the protests of her waiting-ladies who were scandalized at the idea of Prince Genji being left waiting outside the house. At first she pleaded the impossibility of receiving a guest in surroundings so cramped and wretched, her duty towards her daughter at this critical hour, the undesirability of such an interview just on the eve of her permanent departure. But though the prospect of facing him filled her with unspeakable depression, she had not the heart to treat him unkindly, and at last, looking very grave, with sighs and hesitation at every step she came forward to meet him. "I presume that here one is allowed no further than the verandah," he said, and mounting the narrow bamboo platform that surrounded the building he took his seat there. An evening moon had risen and as she saw him moving in its gentle light she knew that all this while she had not been wrong; he was indeed more lovely, more enticing than anyone in the world beside. He began trying to explain why it was that for so many months on end he had not been able to visit her; but he soon got into a tangle, and feeling suddenly embarrassed he plucked a spray from the Sacred Tree[*] which grew outside her room and handing it to her through her blinds-of-state he said: "Take this evergreen bough in token that my love can never change. Were it not so, why should I have set foot within the boundaries of this hallowed plot? You use me very ill." But she answered with the verse: "Thought you perchance that the Holy Tree from whose boughs you plucked a spray was as 'the cedar by the gate'?"[†] To this he replied: "Well knew I what priestess dwelt in this shrine, and for her sake came to pluck this offering of fragrant leaves."

Though the position was not likely to be a very comfortable one, he now thrust his head under the reed blinds and sat with his legs dangling over the wooden framework of the bamboo platform. During all the years when he could see her as often and as intimately as he chose and she on her side withheld nothing from him, he had gone on serenely assuming that it would be always so, and never once in all that time had he felt so deeply moved as at this moment. Suddenly he realized with astonishment that though after that unhappy incident he had imagined it to be impossible for them to meet and had so avoided all risk of his former affection being roused to new life, yet from the first moment of this strange confrontation he had immediately found himself feeling towards

---

[*] The *sakaki*, a species of evergreen oak, is planted at Shinto shrines.

[†] In allusion to the old song, "My home is at the foot of Miwa Hill. If you like me, come some day to visit me. You will know the house by the cedar which grows at the gate."

her precisely as he had before their estrangement. Violently agitated he began to cast his mind rapidly over the long years of their friendship. Now all this was over. It was too horrible. He burst into tears. She had determined not to let him see what she was suffering, but now she could restrain herself no longer and he was soon passionately entreating her not to go down to Ise after all. The moon had set, but the starlit sky was calm and lovely. Pausing often to gaze up into the night he began at last to speak to her of what had lain so heavily on his heart. But no sooner was it openly mentioned between them than all the pent-up bitterness of so many weeks was suddenly released and vanished utterly away. Little by little, in preparation for her final departure, she had at last accustomed herself to think of him almost with indifference. Now in a moment all this was undone, and when she heard Genji himself entreating her to abandon the journey her heart beat violently, and the wildest thoughts agitated her brain. The garden which surrounded her apartments was laid out in so enchanting a manner that the troops of young courtiers, who in the early days of the retreat had sought in vain to press their attentions upon her, used, even when she had sent them about their business, to linger there regretfully; and on this marvelous night the place seemed consciously to be deploying all its charm. In the hours which followed, no secret was withheld on her side or on his; but what passed between them I shall not attempt to tell.

At last the night ended in such a dawn as seemed to have been fashioned for their especial delight. "Sad is any parting at the red of dawn; but never since the world began, gleamed day so tragically in the autumn sky," and as he recited these verses, aghast to leave her, he stood hesitating and laid her hand tenderly in his.

A cold wind was blowing. The pine-crickets in neighboring trees were whispering in harsh despairing tones, as though they knew well enough what was toward. Their dismal voices would have struck a chill to the heart of any casual passer-by, and it may well be imagined what cheer they gave to lovers already at the height of distraction and anguish. She recited the verse, "sad enough already is this autumn parting; add not your dismal song, O pine-crickets of the moor." He knew that it was his neglect that had forced this parting upon them. But now it was too late to make amends. Full of useless regrets, while the grey light of morning spread over the sky, he journeyed back disconsolately to the town, through meadows deep in dew. As she watched him go she could no longer restrain herself, and at the thought that she had lost him forever broke into a fit of reckless weeping. Her gentlewomen, who on the evening before caught a fleeting glimpse of him in the moonlight, enjoyed next morning the excitement of detecting in their mistress's room a lingering fragrance of the princely scent which he had carried.* It may well be imagined that they at any rate were far from condemning the crime to which she had been accessory. "It would have to be a marvelous journey indeed that I was going to take, before I could bring myself to part from such a one as this young prince!" So one of the ladies exclaimed; and at the thought that they had seen him for the last time all were on the verge of tears.

His letter, which arrived during the day, was so full and affectionate that had it been within her power she might have attempted to alter her plans. But matters had gone too far for that and it was useless to think of it. Nor were his feelings towards her (she was convinced) of a sort to warrant such a step. Much of what he had said was inspired simply by pity for her. But the mere fact that he took the trouble to say such things—that he thought it worthwhile to comfort her—showed that he still retained something of his old feeling, and the thought that even upon such remnants of affection as this she must now soon turn her back forever, filled her mind with the most painful longings and regrets. He sent her many costumes and all else of which she could possibly have need upon the journey, with suitable presents to all her ladies. But to these handsome and costly gifts she gave hardly a thought. Indeed as the hour of her departure drew near she sank into a state of utter collapse. It was as though she had never till that moment fully realized the desolation and misery into which an intrigue, undertaken originally in a reckless and frivolous spirit, had at last plunged her. Meanwhile the Virgin, who had to the last been far from certain that her mother really meant to accompany her, was delighted that all was now fixed beyond power of recall. The unusual decision of the mother to accompany her daughter was much discussed in the world at large. Some scented a scandal; a few were touched by so rare an exhibition of family attachment. It is indeed in many ways more comfortable to belong to that section of society whose actions are not publicly canvassed and discussed. A lady in Rokujo's conspicuous position finds her every movement subjected to an embarrassing scrutiny.

On the sixteenth day of the seventh month the Virgin was purified in the Katsura River. The ceremony was performed with more than ordinary splendor, and her escort for the journey to Ise was chosen not from among the Chamberlains and Counselors, but from noblemen of the highest rank and reputation. This was done in compliment to the old ex-Emperor who showed a particular interest in the Virgin, his favorite brother's child. At the moment of her departure from the Palace-in-the-Fields Rokujo was handed a letter. It was from Genji and was couched in all those tender terms that had once been current between them. Remembering the sacred

---

* Princes used rich scents forbidden to commoners.

errand upon which she was bound he tied the letter to a streamer of white bark-cloth.* "Such love as ours," he wrote, "not even the God of Thunder whose footsteps shake the fields of Heaven…"† and added the verse: "O all ye Gods of the Kingdom, Rulers of the Many Isles, to your judgment will I hearken; must needs this parting sever a love insatiable as ours?"‡ Though the letter arrived just when the procession was forming and all was bustle and confusion, an answer came. It was not from Rokujō but from the Virgin herself, and had been dictated by her to her aunt who was acting as Lady Intendant: "Call not upon the Gods of Heaven to sit in judgment upon this case, lest first they charge you with fickleness and pitiless deceit." He longed to witness the presentation of the Virgin and her mother at the Palace,§ but he had a feeling that since it was to avoid him that Rokujō was leaving the City, it would be embarrassing for both of them if he took part in the ceremonies of farewell, and overcoming his desire to see her once more, he stayed in his own palace sunk in idle thoughts. The reply of the Virgin showed a quite astonishing precocity, and he smiled as he read it through again. The girl had begun to interest him. No doubt she was precocious in charm as well as intelligence, and since it was his foible invariably to set his heart upon possessing, even at the cost of endless difficulties, whatever custom and circumstance seemed to have placed beyond his utmost reach, he now began thinking what a misfortune it was that he had in earlier days never once availed himself of his position in the house to make her acquaintance, which would indeed at any time have been perfectly easy. But after all, life is full of uncertainties; perhaps one day some unforeseen circumstance would bring her into his life once more.

The fame of Lady Rokujō brought many spectators to view the procession and the streets were thronged with coaches. The Palace Gates were entered at the hour of the monkey.¶ Lady Rokujō, sitting in the sacred palanquin by her daughter's side, remembered how her father, the late Minister of State, had brought her years ago to these same gates, fondly imagining that he would make her the greatest lady in the land.** Thus to revisit the Palace now that so many changes had come both to her life and to the Court, filled her with immeasurable depression. At sixteen she had been married, at twenty she had been left a widow and now at thirty

---

* Used in making offerings to Shinto gods.

† An allusion to the poem *(Kokinshu* 701), "Can even the God of Thunder whose footfall echoes in the sky put those asunder whom love has joined?"

‡ In reality an appeal to the Virgin (representative of the Gods) to dissuade her mother from accompanying her.

§ Before departing for Ise the Virgin was presented to the Emperor and formally invested.

¶ 4 P.M.

** Prince Zembō, her father, was at that time Heir Apparent.

again she had set foot within the Nine-fold Palisade. She murmured to herself the lines: "Though on this sacred day 'twere profanation to recall a time gone by, yet in my inmost heart a tinge of sadness lurks."

The Virgin was now fourteen. She was extremely handsome and her appearance at the presentation-ceremony, decked in the full robes of her office, made a profound impression. The Emperor, when he came to setting the Comb of Parting in her hair, was deeply moved and it was observed that he shed tears.

Outside the Hall of the Eight Departments a number of gala-coaches were drawn up to witness the departure of the Virgin from the Palace. The windows of those coaches were hung with an exquisitely contrived display of colored scarves and cloaks, and among the courtiers who were to go down to Ise there were many who thought with an especial pang of one who in his honor had added some gay touch of her own to the magnificence of this unprecedented show. It was already dark when the procession left the Palace. When after traversing the Second Wood they turned into the Doi Highway the travelers passed close by Genji's palace. Deeply moved, he sent the following poem tied to a spray of the Holy Tree— "Though today you cast me off and lightly set upon your way, yet surely when at last you ferry the Eighty Rapids of Suzuka Stream[*] your sleeve will not be dry." When this message was brought to her it was already quite dark. This and the noisy bustle of her journey prevented her from answering till the next day. When her reply came it was sent back from beyond the Barrier: "Whether at the Eighty Rapids of Suzuka Stream my sleeve be wet or no, all men will have forgotten me long ere I come to Ise's Land." It was hastily written, yet with all the grace and distinction that habitually marked her hand; but his pleasure in it was marred by the strange bitterness of her tone. A heavy mist had risen, and gazing at the dimly-veiled semblances that were belatedly unfolding in the dawn he whispered to himself the lines: "O mist, I long to follow with my eyes the road that she passed; hide not from me in these autumn days the slopes of Meeting Hill."[†] That night he did not go to the western wing,[‡] but lay sleepless till dawn, brooding disconsolately upon a turn of affairs for which, as he well knew, he alone was responsible. What *she* suffered, as day by day she travelled on through unknown lands, may well be guessed.

By the tenth month the ex-Emperor's condition had become very grave indeed. Throughout the country much concern was felt. The young Emperor was in great distress and hastened to pay him a visit-of-state. Weak though he was the sick man first gave minute instructions as to

---

[*] A river in the Province of Ise.
[†] "Osaka" means Hill of Meeting; a gentle slope on the road from Kyoto to Otsu.
[‡] I.e. to Murasaki.

the upbringing of the Heir Apparent and then passed on to a discussion of Genji's future. "I desire you," he said, "still to look upon him as your guardian and to seek his advice in all matters, whether small or great; as indeed I have accustomed you to do during my lifetime. In the handling of public business he shows a competence beyond his years. There is no doubt that his natural vocation is to administer the affairs of a people rather than to lead the secluded life of a Royal Prince, and when I attached him to a clan devoid of Royal Blood it was that he might the better keep watch for us over the public affairs of our kingdom. I therefore entreat you never to act contrary to his advice." He gave many other parting instructions to his successor, but such matters are not for a woman's pen and I feel I must apologize for having said even so much as this.

The young Emperor, deeply moved, repeatedly signified that he would obey all these instructions in every particular. It gave his father great comfort and pleasure to note that he was already growing up into a fine handsome young fellow. But after a short while Court affairs necessitated the Emperor's immediate presence, and his father, who longed to keep him by his side, was in the end more distressed than comforted by this brief visit. The Heir Apparent was to have come at the same time as the Emperor; but it was thought that this arrangement would be too tiring and the little boy[*] was brought on another day. He was big for his age and very pretty. The old man looked fondly at him and the child, unconscious of the purpose for which he had been summoned, stood watching him with laughter in his face. Fujitsubo, who sat near by, was weeping bitterly; and, suddenly catching sight of her, the ex-Emperor for a while lost his composure. To this little prince also he gave a variety of instructions; but it was evident that he was too young to understand what was being said, and remembering the uncertainties of his future the ex-Emperor gazed at the child with pity and distress. In his final instructions to Genji concerning the management of public affairs he recurred again and again to the question of the Heir Apparent and the importance of giving him due protection and advice. It was now late at night and the Heir Apparent was taken off to bed. A vast number of Courtiers followed in his train, so that his visit created almost as much bustle and confusion as that of the Emperor himself. But this visit had seemed to the sick man only too short and it was with great distress that he watched the procession depart. The Empress Mother, Lady Kokiden, had also intended to come; but hearing that Fujitsubo was at his side she felt somewhat disinclined, and while she was trying to decide whether to go or not, his Majesty passed quietly and painlessly away.

The ex-Emperor's death caused profound consternation in many quarters. Though it was some while since he resigned the Throne, he had

---

[*] Genji's son by Fujitsubo; supposed to be the Emperor's child. He was now four years old.

continued to control the policy of the government just as in former days. The present Emperor was a mere child; his grandfather, the Minister of the Right, was known to be a man of hasty temper and treacherous disposition. Courtiers and noblemen alike regarded with the greatest apprehension a government subjected to his arbitrary power. But among them all none had better reason than Fujitsubo and Prince Genji to dread the coming reign. It was indeed natural that this prince should take a foremost part in the ceremonies of mourning which were performed by the family on each seventh day, and in the Filial Masses for the dead man's soul; but his piety was generally noted and admired. Despite the unbecoming dress which custom required, his beauty made every-where a deep impression; and this, combined with his evident distress, procured him a great share of sympathy.

He had lost in one year his wife and in the next his father. The scenes of affliction through which he had passed weighed heavily upon his spirits and for a while deprived him of all zest for life. He thought much of retiring from the world, and would have done so had he not been restrained by many earthly ties. During the forty-nine days of mourning the ladies of the late ex-Emperor's household remained together in his apartments. But at the expiration of this period they retired to their respective homes. It was the twentieth day of the twelfth month. The dull sky marked (thought Fujitsubo) not only the gloom of the departing year, but the end of all fair prospects. She knew with what feelings Kokiden regarded her and was aware that her existence at a Court dominated by this woman's arbitrary power could not be otherwise than unhappy. Above all it was impossible for her to go on living in a place where, having for so many years enjoyed the old Emperor's company, she found his image continually appearing to her mind. The departure of all his former ladies-in-waiting and ladies-of-the-household rendered her situation unendurable and she determined to move to her mansion in the Third Ward. Her brother Prince Hyobukyo came to fetch her away. Snow was falling, blown by a fierce wind. The old Emperor's quarters, now rapidly becoming denuded of their inhabitants, wore a desolate air. Genji happened to be there when Hyobukyo arrived and they fell to talking of old times. The great pine-tree in front of the Palace was weighed down with snow and its lower boughs were withered. Seeing this, Hyobukyo recited the verses: "Because the great pine-tree is withered that once with wide-spread branches sheltered us from the storm, lo! we the underboughs droop earthward in these last moments of the year." No very wonderful poem, but at that moment it moved Genji deeply, and noticing that the lake was frozen all over he in his turn recited the poem: "Now like a mirror shines the frozen surface of the lake. Alas that it reflects not the form and face we knew so well!" Such was the thought that came to him at the moment, and he gave it utterance well knowing that the prince would think it forced and crude. Omyobu, Fujitsubo's gentlewoman, now interposed with the verse: "The year draws in; even the water of the rock-hewn well is sealed with ice, and faded from those waters is the face that once I saw." Many other poems were exchanged; but I have other things to tell.

Fujitsubo's return to her mansion was carried out with no less ceremony than on former occasions, but to her mind the transit seemed this time a distressing affair and more like a journey to some strange place than a home-coming; and as she approached the house her thoughts travelled back over all the months and years that had passed since this place had been her real home.

The New Year brought with it none of the usual novelties and excitements. Genji, in very dismal humor, shut himself up in his room. At the time when the new appointments were being made, during the old Emperor's reign and to an equal extent even after his retirement, Genji's doors had always been thronged with suitors. But this year the line of horses and carriages waiting outside his palace was thin indeed, and the bags* of courtiers were no longer to be seen at all.

When he looked about him and saw his reception halls frequented only by his personal retainers, who looked as though time were hanging heavily on their hands, the thought that this was but a pretaste of the dreariness and insignificance with which his whole life would henceforth be tinged reduced him to a state of great depression.

In the second month Oborozukiyo was made chief Lady of the Bedchamber, the former occupant of this office having at the ex-Emperor's death become a nun. Her birth and education, together with her unusual charm both of person and disposition, combined to make her much sought after even at a Court where such qualities were to be found in remarkable profusion. Her sister Lady Kokiden was now seldom at Court, and on the rare occasion when she needed a room she lodged in the Umetsubo, resigning her old apartments to the Lady of the Bedchamber. No longer was Oborozukiyo buried away in the inconvenient Tokwaden; she had space and light and a vast number of ladies in her employ, while all about her was in the gayest and newest style. But she could not forget a certain brief and unexpected adventure† which had once befallen her, and was very unhappy. A desultory correspondence was still carried on between them with the greatest caution and secrecy.

He knew well enough how fatal would now be the consequences of discovery; but this, as has often been noted, so far from discouraging him served only to increase his interest in such an affair.

---

* In which they packed the costumes they wore while on duty at the palace.

† Her relations with Genji. See Part I, p. 148. She had now become the Emperor's mistress.

During the late Emperor's lifetime Kokiden had been obliged to behave with a certain restraint. Now she was free to revenge herself with the ferocity of a long-curbed malice upon those who had hitherto been sheltered from her spite. Genji found himself thwarted at every turn. He had expected these intrigues, but having for so long enjoyed a favored and protected existence he was at a loss how to cope with them.

The Minister of the Left felt that his influence was gone and no longer presented himself at Court. Kokiden had never forgiven him for marrying the late princess his daughter to Genji instead of giving her, as had originally been intended, to her son the present Emperor. Moreover there had always been a certain amount of ill-feeling between the families of the two Ministers. During the late Emperor's reign the Minister of the Left had managed things pretty much as he chose, and it was but natural that he now had no desire to take part in the triumph of his rival. Genji continued to visit him as before and was assiduous in his attention to Aoi's maids-of-honor, as also in providing for the education of the little prince her son. This delighted the old Minister and he continued to treat his son-in-law with the same affectionate deference as in old days.

The high position to which Genji had been raised two years ago had entailed much tiresome business and made considerable inroads upon his leisure. He found himself in consequence obliged to discontinue many of the intimacies in which he had been previously engaged. Of his lighter distractions he was now thoroughly ashamed and was glad to abandon them; so that for a while his life became altogether quiet, regular, and exemplary. The announcement of his marriage with Murasaki was very well received by the world at large. Shonagon and her companions naturally attributed their little mistress's success to the prayers of her pious grandmother the late nun, and in secret conclave congratulated themselves on the turn which events had taken. Her father Prince Hyobukyo asked for nothing better than such a match. But his wife, who had not managed to do half as well for her own children on whom she doted, was extremely jealous of her step-child's triumph, and this marriage continued to be a very sore point with her. Indeed, Murasaki's career had been more like that of some stepchild in fiction* than of a real young person.

The Vestal Virgin of Kamo, third daughter of the late Emperor by Lady Kokiden, was now in mourning and had to resign her charge. Her successor was the Princess Asagao.† It had not very often happened that a collateral descendant of the Emperor was chosen for this post; but on this occasion no other princess of suitable age and lineage was available.

---

* The neglected stepchild who in the end triumphs over her pampered rivals is a favorite theme in Japanese stories. Cf. the *Sumiyoshi Monogatari* and the *Ochikubo*.

† See Part I, pp. 36 and 155.

Genji's admiration for this lady had not, in all the years that had passed since he first courted her, in any degree abated, and it was painful to him to learn that she was now to embark upon so different a way of life. She still sent him an occasional message and he had never ceased to write to her. He had known her as a Lady of the Court. Now he must try to picture her to himself as a priestess. This he could not manage to do, and his repeated failure to evoke any image which corresponded to her as she now was bitterly tormented him.

The young Emperor punctiliously obeyed his father's last injunctions and treated Genji with great consideration. But he was still very young, and being somewhat weak and yielding in character he was easily influenced by those about him. Again and again, under pressure from Kokiden or the Minister of the Right, he allowed public measures to be taken of which he did not really in the least approve. Meanwhile Kokiden's sister the Lady Oborozukiyo, though her new position rendered the carrying on of a secret intrigue in the highest degree difficult and perilous, was becoming more and more unhappy, and at last found a means of informing Genji of her unaltered attachment. He would have been glad enough if she had felt otherwise; but after what had passed between them he could not disregard such a message. Accordingly he waited till the Court was immersed in the Celebration at the Five Altars* and went secretly to her apartments. The encounter was brief and dreamlike as on that first occasion, on the night of the Flower-feast.† Her maid Chunagon smuggled him in by the little side door which had before caught his attention. There happened to be a good many people about at the time, and it was with great trepidation that this lady conducted him through the exposed and frequented ante-chambers which led to her mistress's apartments. To look upon Prince Genji was a ceaseless delight even to those who daily served him. It can be imagined then what rapture his visit brought to one who had waited so long for his return. Nor was Genji on his side by any means indifferent to her charms. She was at the height of her youth and good-looks; lively, graceful, confiding. Indeed, save for a certain light-heartedness and inconsequence, there was nothing in her which he would wish to change. Suddenly he heard people stirring in the corridor outside and for a moment thought that it must already be morning. He soon realized however that these were not the people of the house, but members of the Imperial Guard come to report themselves. No doubt some officer of the Guard was known to be spending the night in this part of the Palace; but for a moment Genji had the wild idea that some malicious person

---

* A ritual in honor of the Five Mysterious Buddhas of the Tantric Sect, to wit: Gosanze, Gundari, Dai-itoku, Kongo-yasha and Fudo.

† See Part I, pp. 148 *seq.*

had revealed to the soldiers of the Guard the unexpected presence of their Commander.[*] He was amused at his mistake, but at the same time horrified at the realization of the risks which he was running. Outside in the corridor they could still hear the soldiers tramping up and down looking for their officer and calling out as they went, "First hour of the Tiger Watch, first hour of the Tiger Watch!"[†] Then Oborozukiyo whispered the verse: "Though the watch-man of the night cries out "Enough!" yet seems it from your tears and mine we are not of his mind."[‡] Her plaintive tone touched his heart and he answered with the verse: "Must we, because they say the time is spent, in tears relinquish what our own hearts' reluctance bids us still enjoy?" So saying he left her. Though daylight had not yet come and the setting moon was heavily veiled in mist, he felt very uneasy. And in fact, despite his disguise, his bearing and figure were so notable that he was at once recognized by a brother of Lady Jokyoden[§] who happened, at the moment when Genji passed unsuspecting on his way, to have just left Fujitsubo's old quarters and was now standing in the shadow of a trellis-gate. This gentleman was vastly amused and did not fail to make good use of the episode in his conversation.

So great were the risks he had run that for some time afterwards Genji found himself wishing Fujitsubo's prudence and reserve were more commonly practiced, and at such times he almost applauded her unkindness. At any rate it saved him from these nerve-racking experiences. But such moods did not last long. With the Lady of the Bedchamber his deeper feelings were not involved, whereas he was drawn towards Fujitsubo as though by some secret power, and except at rare moments her coldness caused him nothing but torment and despair.

This princess, though she no longer felt at ease in the Palace and could not bring herself to visit it, was distressed that she was now unable to see her son. It was very awkward that there was no one to advise her about the child except Prince Genji, who unfortunately still persisted in regarding her with the same strange adoration. She was in a continual panic lest he should take advantage of her dependence upon him. True the Emperor had died without betraying the least suspicion concerning the child's parentage. But she shuddered to think of the predicament in which this deception had involved her. Any renewal of their relationship,

---

[*] Genji was Commander of the Imperial Guard. The soldiers of the Guard had to report at 4 A.M. to the senior officer of the Guard who happened on that night to be in the Palace. They had really come to report to some subordinate officer who happened to be lodging close by.

[†] I.e. 4 A.M. They had to go on calling the hour till their officer replied "So be it" to show that he had heard them.

[‡] There is a play of words on *aku* "enough" and *aku* "dawn"; in the next poem between *aku* "enough" and *aku* "open."

[§] Wife of the young Emperor Suzaku.

quite apart from the effect it might have upon her own fortunes, would react disastrously upon her son. So heavily did this matter weigh upon her that when she was supposed to be at her prayers she did nothing but turn over in her mind, a hundred times this way and that, how best she might persuade him to feel differently towards her.

Yet despite all her precautions he managed one night to enter the house and get very near indeed to the room where she was sitting. Not a soul in the house had conspired with him or expected his coming. He seemed to have risen mysteriously up among them like a figure in a dream. He sent her many passionate messages, such as I cannot here transcribe, but she would not let him come to her. At last, worn out by his persistency, she began to feel so faint that Omyobu, Myobu no Ben, and the rest of her favorite waiting-women took fright and were soon busily employed in attending to her. Meanwhile Genji, in a frenzy of irritation and disappointment, scarce knew how he came to be in her antechamber nor thought how he was going to retire from it. So completely had he lost all sense of real things that though broad daylight was come he did not stir from where he stood. The news of her indisposition quickly spread through the house. There was a sound of footsteps, and Genji, still but half conscious, groped his way into a large lumber-room or clothes-cupboard that happened to be near by. An embarrassed lady-in-waiting hastily stowed away a cloak and other effects which she saw lying about.

Fujitsubo herself remained in much distress both of body and mind throughout the night. As she was feeling very giddy, her brothers, who had now arrived upon the scene, sent out for a priest. All this Genji heard from his hiding-place with great grief and alarm. The day was far advanced when she began at last to mend. She had not of course the least idea that he was still in the house and her ladies feared that if they were to tell her of his presence the news might cause a recurrence of last night's attack. At last she dragged herself from her bed to the chair in which she generally sat, and her brothers, thinking that the worst was now over, withdrew and she was left alone. Even her intimate and personal attendants had retired from her dais and could be heard moving away to and fro behind the screens at the other end of the room. The sole preoccupation of Omyobu and the few other ladies who shared the secret of Genji's presence was now how best to get him out of the house. They were certain that if he stayed where he was the same scene would be repeated that night, with the same unhappy effects, and they were whispering together in a tone of great concern when Genji, first cautiously pushing the door a little ajar and then gently slipping out, darted from his hiding-place to the shelter of one of the screens which surrounded her dais. From this point of vantage he was able at last to gaze upon her to his heart's content, and as he did so tears of joy and wonder filled his eyes. "I am wretched,

wretched," she was murmuring; "but soon my misery will end, soon all will be over..." She was looking out towards the center of the room and he caught a profile view of her face which he found inexpressibly charming. Presently Omyobu came with fruit for her breakfast. Though the cover of the fruit-box was of rare and beautiful workmanship she did not so much as glance at it, but sat rigidly staring in front of her, like one for whom life has lost all interest and meaning.

How beautiful she was! And, now that it was possible to compare them on equal terms, how like in every minutest detail of pose and expression to the girl at home! Particularly in the carriage of her head and the way her hair grew there was the same singular charm. For years Murasaki had served to keep Lady Fujitsubo, to some extent at any rate, out of his thoughts. But now that he saw how astonishingly the one resembled the other he fancied that all the while Murasaki had but served as a substitute or eidolon of the lady who denied him her love. Both had the same pride, the same reticence. For a moment he wondered whether, if they were side by side, he should be able to tell them apart. How absurd! Probably indeed, he said to himself, the whole idea of their resemblance was a mere fancy; Fujitsubo had for so many years filled all his thoughts, it was natural that such an idea should come to him. Unable to contain himself any longer, he slipped out of his hiding-place and gently crept between her curtains-of-state, till he was near enough to touch the train of her cloak. By the royal scent which he carried she knew at once that it was he, and overcome by astonishment and terror she fell face downwards upon her couch. "Can you not bear to set eyes upon me?" he cried, and in despair clutched at the skirt of her cloak. She in panic slipped the cloak from her shoulders and would have fled, leaving it in his hands; but by ill luck her hair caught in the buckle and she was held fast. With horror she realized that a fate too strong for her was planning to put her at his mercy. He for his part suddenly lost all dignity and self-restraint. Sobbing violently he poured out to her, scarce knowing what he said, the whole tale of his passion and despair. She was horrified; both the visit and the outburst seemed to her unpardonable, and she did not even reply. At last, hard-pressed, she pleaded illness and promised to see him some other time. But he would not be put off and continued to pour out his tale of love. In the midst of all this talk that so much displeased her and to which she paid no heed at all, there came some phrase which caught her attention and for some reason touched her; and though she was still determined that what had happened on that one unhappy occasion should never, never be repeated, she began to answer him kindly. Thus by skilful parryings and evasions she kept him talking till this night too was safely over. By her gentleness she had shamed him into submission and he now said: "There cannot surely be any harm in my coming occasionally to see you in this way. It would be a great relief to me if I could do so." This and much else he said, now in a far less desperate mood. Even in quite commonplace people such situations produce strange flights of tenderness and fancy. How much the more then in such lovers as Genji and the queen!

But it was now broad daylight. Omyobu and her daughter arrived and soon took possession of their mistress. Genji, retiring from the room, sent her many tender messages. But now she sat staring vacantly in front of her as though she were but half alive. Exasperated by her martyred attitude, he cried out at last: "Answer me, answer me! I cannot live without you. And yet, what use to die? For I know that in every life to come I am doomed to suffer the torment of this same heinous passion." Still, to the alarm of those who waited upon her, she sat staring fixedly in front of her. He recited the verse: "If indeed the foeman fate that parts us works not for today alone, then must I spend Eternity in woe." When she heard him saying that the bonds of her love would hold him back from Paradise, she began to weep and answered with the verse: "If to all time this bond debars you from felicity, not hostile fate but your own heart you should with bitterness condemn." The words were spoken with a tenderness that was infinitely precious to him; yet he knew that a prolongation of the interview could not but be painful to both of them, and he rushed from the room.

He felt that he made himself odious to her. He would never be able to face her again, and contrary to custom he wrote no morning letter. For a long while he paid no visit either to the Emperor or to the Heir Apparent, but lay in his room brooding upon Fujitsubo's unkindness. Misery and longing brought him at last to so pitiable a plight that it was as though with agonizing pain his inmost soul were dissolving within him. Often there ran in his head the lines: "Soon upon causeways of resounding stone my footsteps shall beat out their song!"[*] And indeed the world again seemed to him so cheerless that his decision would soon have been taken had he not remembered that there was one over whose happiness he was pledged to watch. So exquisite, so trustful a creature he could not abandon, and the project was soon put aside.

Fujitsubo too reflected upon what had taken place with great uneasiness of mind. She had now learnt how he had concealed himself for a whole day in her house without giving her the slightest intimation of his presence. This fact Omyobu and the rest had not, in their indignation at his plight, managed to restrain themselves from revealing to her. Such conduct she could not tolerate. Yet she well knew that if she showed her displeasure Genji would feel a disinclination towards the Heir Apparent,

---

[*] I.e. in a monastery.

and this she was above all things anxious to avoid. In a fit of despair he might even take some step which could not be rectified, and that thought, despite the torment of his importunity, filled her even now with horror. If such an occurrence as that of last night were often to be repeated it was certain that both their reputations would soon be irrecoverably destroyed. She felt that it would in a way disarm the censures of the world if she were to give up the rank of Empress, the bestowal of which had been received with such caustic comments by Lady Kokiden. She remembered with what intention and with what explicit injunctions this title had been granted her by the late Emperor. But she felt herself no longer bound by his instructions; for since his death the whole position at Court had utterly changed. She had no fear of suffering the fate of Lady Chi,[*] but she had every reason to suppose that her position as Empress would henceforth be both ludicrous and humiliating. She felt no inclination to struggle against ridicule and opposition. Soon her mind was made up. She must renounce the world. But first she must visit her son. She could not bear that he should never again see her as he had known her in days of old. She drove to the Palace without public escort. On many occasions when she had travelled in even less state than this, Genji had attended her and arranged every detail of her progress. This time he pleaded sickness and was not present. Previously he had been in the habit of sending constantly to enquire after her health. The fact that he had discontinued this practice was cited by the sympathetic Omyobu as a proof that he must be now plunged in the utmost misery.

The little prince[†] had grown into a handsome boy. His mother's visit surprised and delighted him and he was soon telling her all his secrets. She looked at him sadly. The step that she contemplated seemed unendurably hard to take. Yet a glance at the Palace reminded her how great were the changes and upheavals that had taken place, how insecure had now become her own position at the Court. The Lady Kokiden still showed the same unrelenting hostility, finding at every turn some means to inconvenience or humiliate her. Her high rank, so far from protecting her, now imperiled both herself and her son. For a long while she hesitated, torn by many conflicting feelings. At last she succeeded in saying to the child: "What would you think if I were to go away for a long while and, when at last I came back to see you, were to look quite different, almost as though it were another person?" She watched his face while she spoke. "What would happen to you?" he said, very much interested. "Would you become like old Lady Shikibu? Why do you want to be like that?" and

---

[*] Who, after the death of her lover, the Chinese Emperor Kao Tsu, was tortured and mutilated (c. B.C. 200) by his wife.

[†] Genji's child by Fujitsubo; supposed by the world to be the late Emperor's son.

he laughed. It was very difficult to tell him. She began again: "Shikibu is ugly because she is so old. That is not what I mean. I shall have even less hair than Shikibu and I shall wear a black dress, like the chaplain whom you have seen coming to say prayers here in the evenings; but it will be a long while before they let me come here to see you." He saw that she was crying and at once said very decidedly: "If you do not come for a long while, I shall miss you terribly." He too began to cry, and ashamed of his tears, turned his head away. As he did so his long hair fell rippling across his cheek. The eyes, the brow—all was as though a cast had been taken from the face she knew so well. He had not yet lost his baby-teeth. One or two of them were a little decayed, their blackness amid a row of white giving to his smile a peculiar piquancy and charm. As she watched him standing there in his half-girlish beauty and suddenly realized how like he was to his father, she became more than ever unhappy. But if the resemblance was painful to her and seemed to her at that moment almost to spoil his beauty, it was only because she dreaded the gossip to which this likeness would give rise.

Genji too was longing to see his son, but while Princess Fujitsubo was at Court he was resolved to keep away. Perhaps this would make her realize how completely he had been frustrated by her harshness; for she would certainly be expecting to meet him in the young prince's apartments.

He was in very ill humor and the time hung heavily on his hands. It was now autumn and it seemed a pity not to be in the country. He decided to spend a little while at the Temple in the Cloudy Woods.* Here in the cell of his mother's elder brother, a master of the Vinaya,† he spent several days reading the sacred texts and practicing various austerities. During this time much happened both to move and delight him. The maple leaves in the surrounding forests were just turning and he remembered Sojo's song written in the same place: "Proud autumn fields..." In a little while he had almost forgotten that this quiet place was not his home. He gathered about him a number of doctors famous for their understanding of the Holy Law and made them dispute in his presence. Yet even in the midst of scenes such as these, calculated to impress him in the highest degree with the futility of all earthly desires, one figure from the fleeting world of men still rose up importunately before him and haunted every prayer. One day at dawn by the light of a sinking moon the priests of the temple were making the morning offering of fresh leaves and flowers before an image that stood near by. He could hear the clink of the silver flower-trays as they scattered chrysanthemum and maple leaves of many hues around the Buddha's feet.

---

* The Unrinin, near Kyoto.
† Books on monastic discipline, and morality in general.

It seemed to him then that the life these people led was worthwhile, not merely as a means to salvation but for its own pleasantness and beauty. Again and again he marveled that he could have for so long endured his own aimless existence. His uncle, the Vinaya-master, had an extremely impressive voice and when he came to the passage, "None shall be cast out, but take unto him all living things that call upon his name," Genji envied him the assurance with which he uttered the Buddha's promise. Why should not he too avail himself of this promise, why should not he too lead this sanctified existence? Suddenly he remembered Murasaki and his home. What must she be thinking of him? It was many days since he had seen her, and he hastened to repair this neglect: "I came here as an experiment," he wrote, "that I might decide whether it would not be better for me to withdraw forever from the world. Since I have been here it has been gradually becoming clearer to me that my present way of life can bring me nothing but misery; and today I heard something read out loud which made a deep impression upon me and convinced me that I ought not any longer to delay..." The letter was written on sandalwood paper of Michinoku, informally but with great elegance. With it he sent the poem: "Because I left you in a home deep-girt with dewy sedge, with troubled mind I hear the wild winds blow from every side." This he said and much else beside. She cried when she read it. Her answer was written on a white slip: "First, when the wild wind blows, flutters the dewy web that hangs upon the wilting sedge-row in the fields." He smiled to himself with pleasure as he read it, noting how swiftly her hand had improved. He had written her so many letters that her writing had grown to be very like his, save that to his style she had added some touches of girlish delicacy and grace. In this as in all else she at least had not disappointed him.

It occurred to him that Kamo was not so very far off and he thought he would send a message to the Vestal Virgin.[*] To Chujo her maid he sent the letter: "That here among strangers in deep affliction I languish unconsoled, your mistress cannot know." To this he added a long tale of his present woes and to the Virgin herself addressed the poem: "Goddess Immaculate, the memory of other days has made me bold to hang this token at thy shrine!" And to this, quoting an old song, he added the words: "Would that like a ring upon the hand I might turn Time around till 'then' was 'now.'" He wrote on light green paper, and with the letter was a twig of the Sacred Tree festooned with fluttering tassels of white as befitted the holy place to which it was addressed. In answer the maid Chujo wrote: "There is so little here to break the sameness of the long empty days that sometimes an idle memory of the past will for a moment

---

[*] Princess Asagao.

visit the Virgin's heavenly thoughts. Of you she has spoken now and again, but only to say that now all thought of you is profitless." The gentlewoman's letter was long and written with great care. On a small strip tied to a white ritual tassel the Virgin herself had written the poem: "Full well you know that in those other days no secret was between us for you to hang as ritual-token at your heart." It was not written with much pains, but there was an easy flow in the cursive passages which delighted his eye and he realized that the Court had lost one who would in time have grown to be a woman of no ordinary accomplishments.

He shuddered. How pitiless is God! Suddenly he remembered that only last autumn the melancholy gateway of the Palace-in-the-Fields had filled him with just such an indignation and dismay. Why should these Powers be suffered to pursue their hideous exactions?

That strange trait of perversity, so often noted, was indeed at work again under the most absurd circumstances. For in all the years when Asagao was within reach he had not made one serious effort to win her, but had contented himself with vague protestations and appeals. But now that she was utterly unattainable he suddenly imagined that he had never really cared for anyone else! Believing him to be the victim of an inconsolable passion, the Virgin had not the heart to leave his letters unanswered, and a correspondence of a rather strange and unreal kind was for some while carried on between them.

Before he left the Temple in the Cloudy Woods he read the whole of the Sixty Chapters,[*] consulting his uncle on many obscure points. The delight of the priests, down to the humblest servitor, may well be imagined. It seemed as though the Lord Amida must hold their poor country temple in especial favor, or he would not have vouchsafed that such a radiance should shine among them.

But soon Genji began to grow restless. His mind strayed constantly to mundane affairs, and though he dreaded the return, there was one whom it was not in his heart any longer to neglect. Before his departure he ordered a grand chanting of the Scripture to be held and gave suitable presents to all the resident priests both high and low, and even to the peasants of the surrounding country. Then, after many other rituals and benefactions, he drove away. The country people from far and near crowded round the gates to see him go, uncouth figures strangely gnarled and bent. His carriage was draped with black and he himself was still dressed in the drab unbecoming robes of mourning. Yet even the momentary glimpse of him that they caught as he entered his carriage sufficed to convince them that a prince of no ordinary beauty had been dwelling near to them and many were moved to tears.

---

[*] The canonical book of the Tendai Sect.

It seemed to him when he was back in his palace that Murasaki had in these last months become far less childish. She spoke very seriously of the changes at Court and showed great concern for his future. That in these last weeks his affections had been much occupied elsewhere could hardly have escaped her notice. He remembered with a pang that in the last poem she had sent him there was some reference to "the wilting sedge-row," and full of remorse he treated her with more than ordinary kindness. He had brought her a branch of autumn leaves from the country temple where he had been staying. Together they compared it with the trees in his palace garden, and found when they set them side by side that the country leaves were dyed to a yet deeper red. There was one who was at all times paramount in his thoughts, and the sight of these leaves, tinged with so strong a hue that they eclipsed whatever colors were set beside them, reminded him that to her alone he had given no token of his return. The desire to have news of her so tormented him that at last he wrote a letter to Omyobu announcing that he had left the temple: "I heard with surprise and joy of your Lady's visit to the Court. I longed for news both of her and of the young prince; but though I was uneasy on their account, I could not interrupt my appointed course of penance and study. Thus many days have passed since last I gave you any news. Here are some sprays of autumn leaf. Bid your Lady look at them when she feels so disposed, lest unregarded they should waste their beauty 'like silken stuffs spread out by night.'"

They were huge, leaf-laden boughs, and when she looked closer, Fujitsubo saw that the usual tiny strip of paper, such as he always used in writing to her, was tied to one of them. Her gentlewomen were watching her, and as she examined the offering she felt herself blushing. So he was still in the same deplorable state of mind! Surely he must realize that it was very embarrassing for her to receive offerings of this kind from one who was known to be her admirer! Wishing that he would show more regard for her feelings and reputation she bade a servant put the boughs in a vase and stand it against one of the pillows on the verandah, as far out of the way as possible.

In her reply she confined herself to matters of business upon which she needed his advice. Her cold and impersonal tone deeply wounded him. But as it was his usual practice to assist her in every difficulty, he felt that his absence on the day of her departure from Court would give rise to unwelcome speculations, and hearing that the day had been fixed he hastened to the Palace. He went first to the apartments of the young Emperor and finding him at leisure settled down to a long conversation. In person His Majesty much resembled the late Emperor, but he was of a quicker and livelier disposition. He was very easy to get on with and they were soon exchanging recollections of their late father. The Emperor had heard that Genji was still on intimate terms with his aunt the Princess Oborozuki, and had on his own account observed many signs of such an attachment. If the affair had begun since the Princess's arrival at Court he would have felt bound to take cognizance of it. But he knew that the friendship between them was of very old standing and felt that under these circumstances there was no great impropriety in it.

They discussed all manner of affairs together, including their Chinese studies, and the Emperor consulted him about the interpretation of various difficult passages. They then repeated to one another such poems of gallantry as they had lately addressed to ladies of the Court, and it was in the course of this conversation that the Emperor mentioned his admiration of the Lady Rokujo's daughter and his distress on the occasion of her departure for Ise. This emboldened Genji, and soon he was telling the Emperor about his own visit to the Palace-in-the-Fields and all the sad circumstances attending it. The waning moon had begun at last to rise. "It is at such moments as this," said the Emperor sadly, "that one longs for music"*

Genji now took his leave, explaining that he must wait upon the ex-Empress before she retired again to her own home. "You will remember," he said, "that the late Emperor our father committed the Heir Apparent to my guardianship and protection. There happens unfortunately to be no one else to watch over his interests, and as I am very uneasy concerning his future I am obliged to take counsel fairly frequently with his mother." "Our father certainly asked me to retain him as Heir Apparent," replied the Emperor, "and I have always tried to help him in any way I could. But there is really nothing much that I can do for him. I hear he has made astonishing progress with his handwriting and is in every way satisfactory. I am afraid he is more likely to be a credit to me than I a help to him." " He does indeed seem to be in most ways very forward and intelligent," said Genji, "but his character is still quite unformed." And after some further description of the child's attainments he proceeded to the Heir Apparent's apartments.

There was a certain To no Ben, a son of Kokiden's elder brother To Dainagon. Being young, good-looking and popular he had grown somewhat out of hand. This young man was now on his way to the rooms of his sister Princess Reikeiden. For a moment Genji's servants who were preceding him to the Heir Apparent's rooms blocked his path and forced him to stand waiting till they had passed. In a low voice, but quite distinctly enough for Genji to hear every word, the young courtier chanted the lines,

---

* The Court was still in mourning and music was not allowed.

"When a white rainbow crossed the sun the Crown Prince[*] trembled." Genji flushed, but it was obviously best to let the matter pass.

That Kokiden should have succeeded in infecting her whole clan with her venomous hostility towards him was both vexatious and alarming. Genji was indeed much disquieted; but he contrived on all such occasions to conceal his discomfiture.

In arriving at Fujitsubo's rooms he sent in a message to explain that he had been detained in the Presence. It was a moonlit night of unusual beauty. It was at such times as this that the old Emperor would call for music. Fujitsubo remembered those dazzling midnight parties. Here were the old courtyards, the old gardens and rooms, and yet this was not the Palace after all! Through Omyobu her maid she sent to him the poem: "Though now dark exhalations hide from sight the Palace of the Ninefold Wall, yet goes my heart to the bright moon[†] that far above the cloud-bank dwells." She did not in this message give any hint that she wished to see him; yet her tone was not unkind, and forgetting all his rancor he wrote with tears in his eyes: "Though lovely still as in past years the moonbeams of this night, for me in vain their beauty, since now in shadows of unkindness they are wrapped."

She was to leave the Palace at dawn and was much preoccupied with the young prince her son. In her anxiety for his future she overwhelmed him with warnings and instructions. The child understood but little of what she was saying, and seeing that his attention had wandered, she felt more than ever that he was of no age to shift for himself. He usually went to bed very early, but on this occasion he had asked to sit up till his mother started. It was evident that he was very much upset by her departure, but he was very brave about it, and this made her feel more than ever remorseful at leaving him.

Genji could not banish from his mind the thought of To no Ben's insolent behavior. It spoilt all his enjoyment in life and for a long while he wrote to no one, not even to Oborozuki. The autumn rains set in and still no word came from him. She began to wonder what could be amiss, and at last sent him the poem: "While leaf by leaf autumn has stripped the trees, all this long windy while have I in sadness waited for the news that did not come." Doubtless it had cost her some trouble to communicate with him in secret; moreover the poem itself was not at all displeasing. Genji detained the messenger, and going to his desk opened the drawer where he kept his Chinese writing-paper and chose the prettiest piece he could find. Mending his pen with the greatest care, he indited a note so

---

[*] The Crown Prince sent an assassin to murder the King of Ch'in; whereupon the above phenomenon was observed and the Crown Prince felt convinced that the plot would fail. The young courtier vaguely hints that Genji is meditating treason.

[†] I.e. the late Emperor.

elegant even in its outside appearance that on its arrival there was quite a stir among the ladies who were at her side. Who could be the sender of such a missive? Significant glances were exchanged. "I have for some while, for reasons about which it would be useless to speak, been in the last depths of depression." So he wrote and to this he added the poem: "Why, think you, fell the rains of autumn yet faster than of yore? It was my tears that swelled them, my tears because we could not meet." He told her too that if the path of their friendship were but clear, he should soon forget the rain and his depression and all that was amiss in the world. He took much pains with this letter. There were several other people who had written to complain of his neglect, but though he sent them all encouraging replies there were some of them about whom he did not feel very strongly one way or the other.

On the anniversary of the Emperor's death, in addition to the usual ceremonies, he caused the Service of the Eight Recitals* to be celebrated with particular magnificence. The day of national mourning was the first of the eleventh month. A heavy snow was falling. He sent to Fujitsubo the poem: "Though once again the time of his departure has come back, not yet dare hope we for the day when we shall meet."† It happened that on that day she felt in utter despair, seeing no hope of happiness on any side. She answered: "Though sad to have outlived him for so long, yet in this day's return found I some peace; it was as though the world again were in his rule."

It was not written with very great display of penmanship, but there was (or Genji fancied that there was) a peculiar distinction and refinement in the writing. It was not quite in the fashion of the moment; but that did not matter, for she had a style that was completely of her own invention.

But this, he remembered, was the day of the great masses for his father's soul. He must put Fujitsubo out of his thoughts; and wet through by the perpetual downpour of rainy snow, he played his part in the elaborate rituals and processions.

The Service of the Eight Recitals was to be celebrated in Fujitsubo's house on the tenth of the twelfth month and the four succeeding days. She was at great pains to render the ceremony as impressive as possible. The tents to be used on each of the five days were wound on rods of ivory; they were backed with thin silk and laid in cases of woven bamboo. All was ordered with a splendor such as had seldom been seen before. But under her management even the most trivial daily arrangements became invested with a singular beauty and completeness. It did not therefore

---

* Of the Hokkekyo.
† Ostensibly the poem refers to the late Emperor, but it has a hidden reference to the meeting of Fujitsubo and Genji. There is a pun on *yuki,* "snow," and *yuki,* "go."

surprise Genji that the Recitals were carried out with unequalled impressiveness and dignity. The adornments of the Buddha, the coverings of the flower-altars, all were of a beauty that made him dream he was indeed a dweller in Amida's Land of Bliss.

The first day's Recital was dedicated to the memory of her father;[*] the next was on behalf of her mother, the deceased Empress; the third day was in memory of her husband, the late ex-Emperor. It is on this day that the fifth book is read; despite the disapproval of Kokiden and her flatterers, the ceremony was attended by the greater part of those about the Court. The readers of this third day had been chosen with especial care, and when they came to the passage: "Then he gathered sticks for firewood and plucked wild berries and the fruit of the mountains and trees," the words that all had heard so many times before took on a strange significance. It fell to the lot of the dead man's sons to officiate at the altar, circling it with gold and silver dishes held aloft in their hands, and these dishes piled high with offerings of many kinds. This rite was performed by Genji with a grace and deftness that was not equaled by any of his companions. You will say that I have noted this superiority many times before; that is true, and I can only plead in excuse that people were actually struck by it afresh each time they saw him.

The last day's Recital was on behalf of her own salvation. To the astonishment of all present it was announced that she herself wished to take this opportunity of abandoning the world, and had desired the clergy to intimate her renunciation to the Lord Buddha. It may well be imagined with what consternation both Prince Hyobukyo her brother and Genji himself received this utterly unexpected announcement. It was made in the middle of the service, and Hyobukyo, without waiting for the Recital to end, left his seat and went at once to her side. But all his pleading was in vain. At the end of the service she sent for the Head of the Tendai Sect[†] and told him that she was ready to receive the Rules forthwith. Her uncle the High Priest of Yogawa thereupon ascended the dais and shaved her head. A murmur of horror ran through the hall; there was a sound of sobbing. There is something strangely moving in the spectacle of such a renunciation, even when some decrepit old woman decides at last that it is time to take her vows. But here a lady in the prime of her beauty, who till now had given the world no inkling of her intention, was suddenly casting herself away. Her brother found himself weeping with the rest; and even strangers who had come merely for the sake of the service felt, under the spell of the reader's solemn voice and of this sudden declaration, that a personal calamity had befallen them. The sons

---

[*] Of whom we are vaguely told that he was "a former Emperor."
[†] The bishop of the Enryakuji on Mount Hie.

of the late Emperor who remembered her proud bearing at their Father's Court were particularly distressed, and all of them intimated their regret at the step which she had taken. Only Genji stood rooted to the spot in speechless horror and dismay. At last he realized that his behavior must be attracting attention, and when all the princes had left her he made his way to her dais.

Most of the people had cleared off and only a few ladies-in-waiting, all of them on the verge of tears, sat here and there in small disconsolate groups. An unclouded moon heightened the sparkling radiance of the fresh snow which lay around the house. Old memories crowded to his mind and for a moment he feared that he would break down. But at last controlling himself he said very quietly, "What made you suddenly decide to do this?" "I have been meaning to for a long while, but so many things were happening and I had not time to think about it quietly..." He was standing outside her curtains-of-state. This answer was not spoken directly to him, but was brought by Omyobu, her maid. Within the curtains he knew that her favorites were gathered round her. He could hear a faint, reiterated rustling, as though a company of silent mourners were swaying in inconsolable grief, how well he understood their utter despair! From the hanging incense-burner behind her curtain-of-state there rose a heavy perfume of *kurobo*,[*] carried through the room by the fierce snow-wind which had blown since dusk; and with it mingled a faint remnant of the holy incense which the priests had that day been burning in the house. Add to this the princely scent which Genji wore and you may well imagine that the night air was fragrant as the winds of Paradise.

A messenger came from the Heir Apparent's household. There rose before her mind the memory of the child's pretty speeches and ways, that last morning in the Palace. It was more than she could bear, and lest she should break down altogether she left the message unanswered. Seeing the messenger go away empty-handed, Genji wrote a few words on her behalf. It was now time for him to take his leave; but both he and she were in a state of agitation which they could barely control, and he dared not utter the thoughts that were at that moment passing through his mind. Through Omyobu he sent her this poem: "Though fain I too would seek that stainless tract whither the moon has climbed, yet how unguided in the darkness should those small feet not go astray?"[†] He spoke of his regret at the step she had taken, but only in formal terms, for he knew that she was not alone. Of the tumultuous thoughts which surged through his brain there was not one to which he could at such

---

[*] An incense made of sandal-wood, cloves, etc.

[†] I should like to become a priest, but I must stay and look after the child. There is an allusion to the famous poem on the death of a child: "Because in Death's dark land he will not know the way, I will make offerings to the Guardian of Souls that on his shoulders he may carry him."

a time give vent. And answer came: "Though now upon life and all its sorrow I have looked my last, yet are there certain earthly things I shall not soon forget... The stain of the world clings fast to me..." This and much else was in the answer; but he guessed that a great part of it had been supplied by those who were about her.

There was no more to be done, and heavy at heart he left the house. At the Nijo-in he lay alone upon his bed, never once closing his eyes. He was now firmly convinced that if it were not for his duty to Fujitsubo's son he would certainly retire from the world. The late Emperor had hoped that by investing Lady Fujitsubo with definite public rank he would assure the boy's future. But now, by becoming a nun, she had upset all his calculations; for it was almost certain that she would not continue to hold her present position in the State. Were Genji also now to desert the child, what would become of him? These were the thoughts that still perplexed him when morning came. He remembered that Fujitsubo would now have to provide herself with such articles as appertain to a nun's life. In this matter at least he could assist her, and he hastened to send to her palace before the end of the year a suitable provision of rosaries, prayer-desks and the like. He heard that Omyobu also had renounced the world that she might keep her mistress company, and to this gentlewoman he sent a message of affectionate condolence. In this letter he touched on many incidents of their common past, and a correspondence ensued, of such length that it would not be possible to record it. As was natural on so affecting an occasion many poems were exchanged between them, and as these were of considerable merit I regret that they must be omitted.

Now that Fujitsubo had definitely embraced the religious life she felt that there was less impropriety in her receiving him, and on several occasions she no longer conversed through an intermediary, but actually admitted him to her presence. His feelings towards her were absolutely unchanged, but now that there could be no question of intimacy between them he could face her with some degree of tranquility.

The close of that year ended the period of Court mourning, and the New Year was celebrated at the Palace with the usual festivities, including the Imperial Banquet and the Dance Songs.* But of these things no echo reached Fujitsubo's house. Day after day was spent in prayers, penances, and meditations on the life to come, and he who had been at once her comfort and despair no longer found any place in her thoughts. She continued to use the old palace-chapel for her daily observances; but for the celebration of more elaborate rites she built a new chapel in front of the west wing, but at some distance from the house.

---

* Performed by girls on the 16th day and by young men on the 14th and 15th days of the first month.

He visited her on New Year's Day. Nowhere was there a sign of renewal or rejoicing. The house was very quiet and seemed almost deserted. Here and there stood a few of her most devoted retainers, looking (or was it only his fancy?) very downcast and depressed. Of the usual New Year offerings from the Palace only the white horse[*] had this year arrived. The gentlewomen of the house could not but remember how at this season in former years princes and courtiers had thronged these halls. Now they drove straight past, making one and all for the great palace in the next Ward.[†]

This was under the circumstances perfectly natural and Fujitsubo had fully expected it. Yet when it happened she became very depressed. But now the arrival of one whom she would not have exchanged for a thousand visitors put all this chagrin out of her head.

So great were the changes that had taken place since he was last in her room that for a while he could do nothing but stare about him in bewilderment.

The canopy of her dais and the hangings of her screen-of-state were now of dark blue; here and there behind the curtains he caught a glimpse of light grey and jasmine-colored sleeves. The effect was not displeasing and he would gladly have studied it more closely.

The ice on the lake was just beginning to break up. The willows on the banks showed a faint tinge of green; they at least remembered that a new season had begun. These and other portents of the approaching spring he watched till it grew dark. From behind the curtains Fujitsubo gazed at him as he sat singing softly to himself the song: "Happy the fisher-folk[‡] that dwell…"; she thought that in all the world there could be no one so beautiful.

She remained all the while behind her curtains, but a great part of the room was taken up by images and altars, so that she was obliged to let him sit very near the dais and he did not feel wholly cut off from her.

A number of elderly nuns were installed at her side, and fearing lest in their presence his parting words might betray too great an emotion he stole in silence from the room. "What a fine gentleman he has grown up to be!" they exclaimed after Genji's departure. "One might have thought that it would have spoiled him always having things his own way as he did in his Father's time, and being first in everything. How little can he then have guessed that he would ever come to know the world's ingratitude! But you can see that he bears his troubles manfully, though there is a graver look in his face now than there was in the old days. Poor gentle-

---

[*] Twenty-one white horses were offered to the Emperor on the 7th day, and afterwards distributed by him among members of his family.

[†] The residence of the Minister of the Right, Kokiden's father.

[‡] *Ama*, "fishermen," also means "nun."

man, it makes one's heart bleed to see him so sad!" So the old ladies whispered together, shaking their heads and calling blessings upon him, while to Fujitsubo herself came many painful recollections.

It was the time when the yearly distribution of honors took place. Fujitsubo's kinsmen and retainers were entirely passed over. This was quite natural and she did not resent it; but she noticed that even the usual bounties were withheld, and promotions which had always been taken as a matter of course were in many cases not granted. There was a great deal of disappointment and annoyance. Moreover on the ground that she would shortly have to give up her official rank and would not then be able to maintain so large an establishment,* many other changes and readjustments were made.

All this she had expected. It was indeed the inevitable consequence of her retirement from secular life; but when she saw her former pensioners and retainers going about with dismal faces and in many instances left without proper support, she was very much upset. But above all her thoughts were centered on one persistent desire; that, even though she herself should come to utter ruin, the Heir Apparent might in due course come peacefully to the Throne, and it was to this end that she caused perpetual services to be celebrated in the chapel attached to her house.

To what secret peril was the young prince's life exposed? Those who were called upon to officiate at these incessant litanies could themselves form no conjecture. But her own prayers were more explicit. Again and again she called upon the Buddha to save the young prince from the ruin which would immediately overtake him should the true story of his birth be known; and she prayed with all her heart that, if retribution must needs come, it might fall upon herself rather than upon the child. These prayers had at least the effect of bringing her to a calmer state of mind. Genji, for his part, regarded them as by no means superfluous.

His own servants and retainers had in the recent distribution of honors fared little better than hers and were in very ill humor. Thoroughly discontented with the march of public affairs both they and their master henceforward appeared but seldom at Court. About this time the Minister of the Left decided to send in his resignation. The changes in his home as well as the decline of his own political influence had recently told very much upon his spirit and he no longer felt equal to his charge. The Emperor remembered the unbounded confidence which his father had placed in this Minister's sagacity, and how in his last hours the old Emperor had said that to dispense with such a man's counsel must needs endanger the security of the Throne. He was therefore very reluctant to give this resignation effect and for a while attempted to ignore it. But the

---

* The State grant allowed to an ex-Empress was sufficient to maintain 2,000 dependants.

Minister stuck to his point and, though his retirement had not been formally accepted, no longer appeared at Court.

Henceforward the whole government of the country fell into the hands of a single family, that of Kokiden's father, the Minister of the Right. The powerful influence of the retired Minister had indeed been the last check upon the complete dominance of this ascendant faction, and his withdrawal from public affairs was regarded with grave apprehension both by the young Emperor himself and by all right-thinking people.

The late Minister's sons, who had hitherto enjoyed a consideration in the world somewhat beyond that to which their own abilities would have entitled them, were mortified to discover that they could no longer have everything their own way. The most crestfallen of them all was To no Chujo, who through his connection[*] with the family which was now dominant, might have been expected to fare rather better than the rest. Unfortunately he was still on very bad terms with his wife, and his neglect of her had deeply offended the Minister, who no longer received Chujo as a son-in-law. No doubt as a punishment for his misdemeanor, his name had been altogether omitted from the list of New Year honors and promotions. Such things however did not much interest him and he was not nearly so disappointed as the Minister had hoped. He could indeed hardly expect to enjoy much influence when even Genji's fortunes were so obviously on the decline, and leaving public business to look after itself he would go off to Genji's palace, where the two of them spent the time in the study of music and letters. Often they would remind one another of the many absurd exploits in which they had once been rivals; and even in their present quiet pursuits the old rivalry continued. Genji was much occupied with the readings of Holy Scripture which are appointed for spring and autumn, and with the performance of various other annual observances.[†] He also gathered round him a number of scholars who seemed, no doubt owing to the present state of public affairs, to be out of employment, and put them to writing Chinese poems and essays. He also spent many hours in playing literary games such as rhyme-covering and the like. He soon became so interested in these trivial pursuits that for a month on end he never once set foot in the palace. This incivility, together with his enthusiasm for what were considered frivolous and undignified occupations, was commented upon very unfavorably in many quarters.

The summer rains had set in, and one day when a steady downpour made other amusements impossible Chujo arrived at the palace with a great pile of books. Genji too opened his library, and after exploring several cases which had not been unlocked for a long time he produced some

---

[*] His wife was the fourth daughter of the Minister of the Right.

[†] Such as Buddha's birthday, Maya's birthday, Buddha's Nirvana day, etc.

very remarkable collections of ancient Chinese poetry. There happened to be with him that day several friends who, though they were not scholars by profession, had a very considerable knowledge of such matters. From among these gentlemen and the learned doctors who were present Genji picked sides, and ranging them to left and right of the room instituted a grand competition with very handsome prizes. In the course of the rhyme-covering contests they came across some most unusual and puzzling rhyme-words, and even well-known scholars were occasionally at a loss. More than once Genji was able to come to their rescue. They were astonished at his knowledge. How, they wondered, did he find time to pick up so many accomplishments? There seemed to be no art or pastime in which he did not show the same marvelous proficiency. The "right" won easily and it fell to Chujo's lot to provide the winners with a feast. This took place on the following day. It was not an elaborate affair, but consisted of a collation served in elegant luncheon boxes.

Various prizes were also given and when this was over the doctors of literature were again called upon to divert the company with essays. The rose-trees at the foot of the steps were in full bloom and coming as they did in a somewhat dull season, when the brightness of spring is over and the riot of autumn colors has not yet begun, these flowers gave Genji an especial pleasure.

Chujo's son, a little boy of eight or nine who had only that year been introduced at Court, was present that day. He sang well and could play the *sho*. Genji was very fond of him and they used often to practice together. He was Chujo's second son by his wife, the sister of Kokiden, and as grandson of the all-powerful Minister of the Right he was treated by everyone at Court with great deference. But he was also not only handsome but extremely intelligent, and in the present company his performance received so much encouragement that he was soon singing that rather noisy song the *Ballad of Takasago,* which he got through with great credit and applause. As a reward for this song Genji laid his own cloak on the boy's shoulders, and as he sat flushed with the excitement of the party and wearing only an unlined shirt of thin gauze that showed the delicate texture of his skin beneath, the old doctors of literature stared at him with delight and amazement from the distant part of the room where they had respectfully taken up their stand; and many of them shed tears of wonder and delight. At the close of the stanza: "May I be there where lilies bloom," Chujo picked up the wine-bowl and handed it to Genji, reciting as he did so the poem: "Not the first rose, that but this morning opened on the tree, with thy fair face would I compare." Laughing, Genji took the cup and whispered the poem: "Their time they knew not, the rose-buds that today unclosed. For all their fragrance and their freshness the summer rains have washed away." Then Chujo, who had become somewhat excited, accused Genji of toying with the wine-bowl and forced him to drink what he considered a proper draught.

Much else happened before the banquet closed. But to describe in detail all that was said and done on an occasion such as this would, I think, be very unfair to the persons concerned. I will therefore observe Tsurayuki's warning and refrain from tiring you with any further particulars. Suffice it to say that the company made a great many poems both in Chinese and Japanese, all of them containing flattering references to their host, and Genji soon began to feel in very good humor with himself. He could not help thinking of the passage in Chinese history where the Duke of Chou boasts that he is "the son of King Wen and the brother of King Wu." These were very good names and fitted his case exactly. "Son of King Wen, brother of King Wu." Suddenly, as he murmured these words, he remembered that the Chinese duke had added "and uncle of King Ch'eng." But here he was on difficult ground; something seemed to have gone wrong with the parallel. The "King Ch'eng"* of his case, though something more than a nephew, was still a very long way from being a king!

Prince Sochi no Miya† frequently joined these gatherings, and as he was not only a man of taste and fashion but also an excellent performer on various instruments, his presence added greatly to the pleasure of the company.

About this time Princess Oborozuki left the Court for a while and went to stay at her father's house. She had for some time been suffering from slight attacks of malaria and it was thought that she could be treated for this illness more conveniently at her home than amid the bustle of the Court. Priests were summoned and their incantations were at once effective. Among the many people who wrote to congratulate her upon her recovery Genji was naturally one, and as both of them happened for the moment to have a good deal of time on their hands, a correspondence ensued which led in the end to his paying her a somewhat reluctant visit. This was followed by others and he was soon seeing her every night. She was well made, tending even to plumpness, so that the slight pallor and thinness which had ensued from her recent indisposition only enhanced her charm. It happened that at the time Kokiden was also staying in the house. This made Genji's visits particularly imprudent, but it was just this added risk which attracted him and induced him to repeat them. It was not of course long before several inmates of the house became aware that something of this kind was going on, but they were too frightened of Kokiden to say anything to her about it, nor had the Minister of the Right any suspicion whatever.

---

* The Heir Apparent, Genji's son by Fujitsubo, supposed to be the old Emperor's child.

† One of Genji's stepbrothers.

One night when Genji was with her a violent storm suddenly came on. The rain fell in such torrential floods as to be quite alarming and just after midnight tremendous crashes of thunder began. Soon the whole place was astir. The young princes and Kokiden's gentlemen-in-attendance seemed to be wandering all over the house, while the ladies-in-waiting, terrified by the thunderstorm, were clinging to one another hysterically in the passage just outside. There were people everywhere and Genji began to wonder how he was ever going to escape.

It was now broad daylight. Oborozuki's maids had entered the room and seemed to be crowding round the great curtained bed. Genji was appalled by the situation. Among these ladies there were two who knew the secret, but they quite lost their heads in this emergency and were unable to be of any use. The thunderstorm was over and the rain was now less violent. The Minister was now up and about. He first paid his elder daughter a visit, and then, just at a moment when the rain was falling rather heavily, stepped lightly and briskly into Oborozuki's room. The rain was making such a noise that they did not hear him and it was not till a hand was thrust through the bed-curtains that they realized what had happened. "We have had a very bad thunderstorm," he said, pulling the curtain slightly aside as he spoke. "I thought of you in the night and had half a mind to come round and see how you were getting on, but somehow or other I didn't. Your brothers were on duty at the Palace last night. Just fancy..." So he went on, speaking in an excited inconsequent manner which, even in his present quandary, Genji could not help contrasting with the gravity and good sense of that other Minister, Aoi's father, and he smiled to himself. Really if he had so much to say he had better come right inside and have done with it. Oborozuki, determined to screen her lover if she could, now crept to the edge of the bed and issued cautiously from between the curtains. Her face was so flushed and she looked so very ill at ease that her father was quite alarmed. "What have you been doing?" he said, "you are not looking at all well. I am afraid we stopped the treatment too soon. These attacks are very troublesome to get rid of..." As he spoke his eye suddenly fell upon a man's pale violet-colored belt that had got mixed up with her clothes, and at the same time he noticed a piece of paper with writing upon it lying near the bed. How did these things come to be in his daughter's room? "Whose is this?" he asked, pointing at the paper. "I think you had better give it to me; it may be something important. I shall probably know the writing." She looked where he was pointing. Yes, there was Genji's paper lying conspicuously upon the floor. Were there no means of heading her father away from it? She could think of none and did not attempt to answer his question. It was evident that she was acutely embarrassed, and even though she was his own child he ought to have remembered that she was now a lady of some consequence, whose feelings, however reprehensible might be her conduct, he was bound in some measure to respect. Unfortunately there was not in his nature a particle either of moderation or restraint. He stooped to pick up the paper, and as he did so, without the slightest hesitation or compunction he opened the bed-curtains and peered right in. There full length upon the bed and apparently quite at his ease lolled a charming young man, who when the curtain stirred merely rolled quietly over and hid his face in the pillows. Enraged, astonished as the Minister was, even he had not quite the courage to press the discovery home. Blind with fury he thrust the paper into his pocket and rushed out of the room.

Genji was indeed extremely concerned about the consequences of this incident, coming as it did in the wake of so many other indiscretions: But his first care was to comfort his companion, which he did as best he could.

Self-restraint had never been a characteristic of the lady's father and now that he was getting old he found it more than ever impossible to keep anything to himself. It was therefore only to be expected that without considering the consequences or turning the matter over in his mind for a single moment, he went and told the whole story to his daughter Kokiden.

"Well, there it is," he wound up, "and you will not be surprised to hear that the handwriting was that of no less a person than Prince Genji! Of course I know quite well that this affair has been going on for a long time. A good deal of license is allowed to people in his position and unfortunately I was weak-minded enough to let the matter pass. Then came the death of his wife, and it seemed certain that he would now legitimize his relations with your sister. Instead of doing so he suddenly abandoned her in the most heartless and disgraceful fashion. I was very uneasy about what had happened, but there was nothing to do except to make the best of a bad business, and I sent her to Court, fully trusting that His Majesty would not regard this one escapade as a fatal objection. Unfortunately he looked upon her as still more or less betrothed to Genji and left her severely alone. One would have thought she had suffered enough already! It is really disgusting, after what has happened, that he should have the face to start the thing all over again. You may say that a young man is bound to have his fling; but this Prince Genii goes a great deal too far. I hear that he has been behaving very badly with the Vestal Virgin of Kamo, carrying on a secret correspondence with her, and according to some people going a good deal further than that. If he has no respect for her holy calling he might at least realize that this kind of thing does his own reputation no good. How anyone holding an important and responsible position in the State can bring himself to behave in this way I simply cannot imagine..." Kokiden had always detested Genji and she now burst out angrily: "They call him their Emperor, but from the very beginning they have gone out of their way to heap every sort of indignity upon him. Even before he came to the Throne they had already begun to treat him abominably. Remember how the Minister of the Left behaved about the marriage of his cherished only daughter! He insisted forsooth in giving her to this wretched Prince Genji instead of to my son, though my boy was older and had already been proclaimed Heir Apparent, while Genji did not count as a member of the royal family at all and was so young that the wedding took place on the same day as his Initiation! We too, you may remember, were planning to give my sister to Genji when we were outwitted by this hasty wedding, of which till the last minute no one was given the slightest intimation. Everyone was indeed astonished that we should allow ourselves to be tricked in this unscrupulous fashion. We should all much have preferred to see her married to this young man, but when that fell through there was nothing for it but to do the best we could for her at Court. It is really extraordinary that after all the painful experiences she has had with this wretch she should still imagine she can make a permanent conquest of him. I have no doubt he is treating the Vestal Virgin in just the same way; and his behavior in this matter, as indeed in many others, is causing His Majesty the greatest anxiety; which is not to be wondered at, seeing that the heir to the Throne is entirely in this Prince Genji's hands."

She went on in this strain for so long and with so much rancor that her father, who never remained angry for more than a short time, soon began to sympathize with Genji rather than with her and was sorry that he had mentioned the matter at all. "I think that for the present," he said, "you had better not speak of this to anyone, not even to His Majesty your son. Prince Genji's conduct is certainly outrageous; but you are very fond of your sister and you cannot denounce him without getting her too into trouble. Leave the matter to me. I intend to speak to her very seriously, and if this has no effect, then we shall have done our best and she must take the consequences." But it was too late to mend matters; she was indeed only further exasperated by his attempt to conciliate her. That Genji should have been carrying on this intrigue in her own house, and that too at a time when he knew she was in residence, showed an impudent contempt for her authority which deeply wounded her, and all that she now thought of was how best she might use this discovery to his undoing.

The Village of Falling Flowers

The outlook was very black. Not only were his private affairs in a state of grievous entanglement, but also his position at Court was being made every day more difficult. So despondent did he become that he had serious thoughts of giving everything up and quitting the Capital. But this was by no means easy now that so many persons were dependent upon him. For example there was Lady Reikeiden, a lady of his father's Court. She had no children to look after her and had, since the old Emperor's death, been living in very bad circumstances. But for Genji's assistance she would never have pulled through. With her lived a sister much younger than herself with whom he had once had a fugitive affair when both of them were living at the Palace. He never forgot anyone to whom he had stood, even for the briefest period, in such a relation as this. Their friendship had never been resumed; but he had reason to suppose that on her side the attachment was still as strong as ever. During the period of emotional tumult through which he had just passed he had many times brooded upon his relations with this lady. At last he felt that he could neglect her no longer, and the rains of the fifth month having given place to an enchanting spell of fine warm weather, he set out for her sister's house. He went without any outriders and took care that there should be nothing to distinguish his coach from that of an ordinary individual. As he was nearing the Middle River he noticed a small house standing amid clumps of trees. There came from it the sound of someone playing the zithern; a well-made instrument, so it seemed, and tuned to the eastern mode.* It was being excellently played. The house was quite near the highway and Genji, alighting for a moment from the carriage, stood near the gate to listen. Peeping inside he saw a great laurel-tree quavering in the wind. It reminded him of that Kamo festival long ago, when the dancers had nodded their garlands of laurel and sunflower.† Something about the place interested him, seemed even to be vaguely familiar. Suddenly he remembered that this was a house which he had once visited a long while before. His heart beat fast... But it had all happened too long ago. He felt shy of announcing himself. All the same, it seemed a pity to pass the house without a word, and for a while he

---

* I.e. as a *wagon* or Japanese zithern, not in the Chinese style.
† See Part I, p. 158.

stood hesitating. Just when he was about to drive away, a cuckoo flew by. Somehow its note seemed to be an invitation to him to stay, and turning his chariot he composed the following poem, which he gave into Koremitsu's hands: "Hark to the cuckoo's song! Who could not but revisit the hedge-row of this house where once he sung before?" There seemed to be several people sitting together in a room on the left. This must be the lady's own apartment. Several of the voices Koremitsu thought he could remember having heard before. He made a slight noise to attract attention and delivered the poem. He could hear it being discussed within by a number of young women who seemed somewhat puzzled by it. Presently a reply was brought: "That to my garden Cuckoo has returned, his song proclaims. But how, pray, should I see him, caged behind the summer rain?" Koremitsu made sure that they were only pretending not to know who their visitor was. The lady indeed, though she hid her feelings from the rest, was very loath to send Koremitsu away with this hollow message. But so long a time had elapsed since her adventure with Genji that she may very well have had good reasons for doing so. Suddenly, as he drove away, there came into his mind a picture of this lady dancing with four others at the Palace. Yes, that was who she was. She had been one of the Gosechi dancers one winter long ago. How much he had admired her! And for a moment he felt about her exactly as he had felt before. It was this strange capacity of his for re-creating in its full intensity an emotion suspended for months or even years and overlaid by a thousand intervening distractions, that gained for him, faithless though he was, so large a number of persistent admirers.

At last he arrived at Lady Reikeiden's house. Noting that it wore an aspect fully as cheerless and deserted as he had feared, he hastened at once to the elder lady's room. They talked much of old times and the night was soon far advanced. It was the twentieth day and the moon had now risen, but so tall were the surrounding trees that the garden still looked dark and gloomy as before. The lady herself sat in a room pervaded by the fragrance of orange-trees. She was no longer young, but still preserved much dignity and charm. Though she had never been singled out as a particular favorite with the late Emperor, they had been on very familiar terms and she was able to entertain Genji with many intimate recollections of his father's life and habits. Indeed so vivid a picture of those old days soon rose before his mind that the tears came into his eyes. A cuckoo was suddenly heard in the garden outside, perhaps the very same that had sung when he was waiting at the gate of the little house; its note at any rate seemed strangely similar. Had it followed him? Pleased with this idea he sang softly to himself the old song, "Knows the cuckoo when he sings?" Presently he handed to her this poem: "It is the scent of orange-trees that draws the cuckoo to the village of falling flowers." "I knew you would remind me of many things that I would not gladly forget; that is why I made my way straight to your room. Though life at Court gives me much both to think of and to feel, there are often times when I should like to have about me people who would talk of the past, and now that the world has given its allegiance to new powers such people are hard to find. But if I, amid the bustle of the town, feel this deprivation, how much the more must you in your long hours of tedious inactivity!"

His prospects had indeed changed very much for the worse since she had first known him, and he certainly seemed to feel those changes deeply. But if her heart went out to him it was perhaps rather because of his youth and beauty than because she regarded his position in the world as calling for any particular commiseration. She answered him with the poem: "To these wild gardens and abandoned halls only the scent of orange-trees could draw the traveler's steps!" She said no more and he took his leave. Yes, despite the fact that greater beauties had overshadowed her at his father's Court, this lady had a singular charm and distinction of her own.

Her sister was living in the western wing. He did not hide from her that he was only calling upon her on his way from Lady Reikeiden's rooms. But in her delight at his sudden arrival and her surprise at seeing him under circumstances so different she forgot to take offence either at his having visited her sister first or having taken so long in making up his mind to come at all. The time that they spent together was in every way successful and agreeable, and she can scarcely have thought that he did not care for her.

It was often thus with those whom he met only in this casual way. Being women of character and position they had no false pride and saw that it was worthwhile to take what they could get. Thus without any ill will on either side concerning the future or the past they would enjoy the pleasure of each other's company, and so part. However, if by chance anyone resented this kind of treatment and cooled towards him, Genji was never in the least surprised; for though, as far as feelings went, perfectly constant himself, he had long ago learnt that such constancy was very unusual. The lady in the little house by the roadside was clearly an example of the latter class; she had resented the infrequence of his visits and no longer felt disposed to receive him.

Exile at Suma

The intrigue against him was becoming every day more formidable. It was evident that he could not in any case go on living much longer where he was, and by a voluntary withdrawal he might well get off more lightly than if he merely allowed events to take their course.

There was Suma. It might not be such a bad place to choose. There had indeed once been some houses there; but it was now a long way to the nearest village and the coast wore a very deserted aspect. Apart from a few fishermen's huts there was not anywhere a sign of life. This did not matter, for a thickly populated, noisy place was not at all what he wanted; but even Suma was a terribly long way from the Capital, and the prospect of being separated from all those whose society he liked best was not at all inviting. His life hitherto had been one long series of disasters. As for the future, it did not bear thinking of! Clearly the world held in store for him nothing but disappointment and vexation. But no sooner had he proved to himself convincingly that he was glad to leave the Capital than he began to recollect a thousand reasons for remaining in it. Above all, he could not imagine what would become of Murasaki if he were to leave her. Even when for one reason or another he was obliged to pass a few days away from his palace, he spent so much of the time wondering how she was getting on without him that he never really enjoyed himself and in the end dreaded even these short absences almost as much as she did. Now he was going away not for a fixed number of days or even years, but for a huge, incalculable period of time; perhaps (for who knew what might not happen either to him or her?) forever. The thought that he might never see her again was unendurable and he began to devise a scheme for hiding her in his retinue and secretly taking her with him. He soon saw however that this was quite impracticable. First there was the difficult sea-journey; and then, at Suma, the total lack of amusements and society. The waves and winds of that desolate shore would make poor companions for one used to the gaieties of a fashionable house. It would moreover be utterly impossible in such a place to make adequate provision for the comfort of a fastidious and delicately-nurtured lady. Her presence would soon involve him in all sorts of difficulties and anxieties. She herself felt that she would rather face every danger, every hardship, than be left behind at the Nijo-in, and that he should doubt her courage wounded her deeply.

The ladies at the "village of falling flowers," though in any case they saw him but seldom, were dismayed at the news of his departure, not for personal reasons only, but also because they had come to depend in numerous ways on his patronage and support. Many others whose acquaintance with him was very slight, were, though they would not have confessed it, shattered at the prospect of his disappearance from the Court. The abbess[*] herself feared that if she showed him any open mark of sympathy at this turn in his fortunes she would give new life to rumors which had already been used against him by his enemies. But from the time when his decision was first announced she contrived to send him constant secret messages. He could not help reflecting with some bitterness that she might sometimes have shown an equal concern while it was still possible for her to console him in more concrete ways. But it seemed to be fated that throughout all this long relationship each, however well disposed, should only cause torment to the other. He left the City about the twentieth day of the third month. The date of his departure had not been previously disclosed and he left his palace very quietly, accompanied only by some seven or eight intimate retainers. He did not even send formal letters of farewell but only hasty and secret messages to a few of those whom he loved best, telling them in such words as came to him at the moment what pain it cost him to leave them. Those notes were written under the stress of deep emotion and would doubtless interest the reader; but though some of them were read to me at the time, I was myself in so distracted a state of mind that I cannot accurately recall them. Two or three days before his departure he paid a secret visit to Aoi's father. He came in a rattan-coach such as women use, and heavily disguised. When they saw that it was indeed Prince Genji who had stepped out of this humble equipage the people at the Great Hall could hardly believe that this was not some strange dream. Aoi's old room wore a dismal and deserted air; but the nurses of his little boy and such of Aoi's servants as were still in the house soon heard the news of his unexpected arrival and came bustling from the women's quarters to gaze at him and pay him their respects. Even the new young servants who had not seen him before and had no reason to take his affairs particularly to heart were deeply moved at this farewell visit, which brought home to them so vividly the evanescence of human grandeurs. The little prince recognized him and at once ran up to him in the prettiest and most confiding way. This delighted Genji; taking the child on his knee he played with it so charmingly that the ladies could hardly contain their emotion. Presently the old Minister arrived: "I have often meant," he said, "during these last months when you have been living so much at home, to come round and

---

[*] Fujitsubo.

talk over with you various small matters connected with the past; but first I was ill and for a long time could not attend to my duties, and then at last my resignation was definitely accepted. Now I am merely a private person, and I have been afraid that if I came to see you it would be said that it must be to promote some personal intrigue that I was bestirring my aged bones. As far as I am concerned I am out of it all, and have really nothing to be afraid of. But these new people are very suspicious and one cannot be too careful... I am distressed beyond measure that you should be obliged to take the course which you are now contemplating; I would gladly not have lived to witness such a day. These are bad times, and I fully expected to see a great deal of mischief done to the country. But I confess I did not foresee that you would find yourself in such a situation as this, and I am heartbroken about it, utterly heartbroken..." "We are told," answered Genji, "that everything which happens to us in this life is the result of our conduct in some previous existence. If this is to be taken literally I suppose I must now accept the fact that in a previous incarnation I must have misbehaved myself in some way. It is clear, at any rate, that I am in bad odor at Court; though, seeing that they have not thought it necessary to deprive me of my various offices and titles, they cannot have very much against me. But when the Government has shown that it mistrusts a man, he is generally considered much to blame if he continues to flaunt himself at Court as though nothing were amiss. I could cite many instances in the history both of our own and other countries. But distant banishment, the penalty which I hear is contemplated in my case, has never been decreed except as the penalty of scandalous and open misdemeanor. My conscience is of course perfectly clear; but I see that it would be very dangerous to sit down and await events. I have therefore decided to withdraw from the Capital, lest some worse humiliation should befall me." He gave the Minister many further details of his proposed flight. The old man replied with a multitude of reminiscences, particularly of the late Emperor, with anecdotes illustrating his opinions and policies. Each time that Genji tried to go his father-in-law gripped his sleeve and began a new story. He was indeed himself deeply moved by these stories of old days, as also by the pretty behavior of his little son, who while they were talking of policies and grave affairs constantly ran up to one or the other with his absurd, confiding prattle. The Minister continued: "Though the loss of my dear daughter is a sorrow from which to my dying day I shall not recover, I find myself now quite thankful that she did not live to see these dreadful days. Poor girl, she would have suffered terribly. What a nightmare it all is! More than anything else I am distressed that my grandson here should be left with us elderly people and that for months or even years to come you will be quite cut off from him.

"As you say, exile has hitherto been reserved as a punishment for particularly grave offences. There have indeed been many cases both here and in China of innocent persons being condemned to banishment, but always in consequence of some false charge being made against them. But against you a threat of exile seems to have been made without any cause being alleged. I cannot understand it..."

To no Chujo now joined them and wine was served. It was very late, but Genji showed no signs of going, and presently all the gentlewomen of the household collected round him and made him tell them stories. There was one among them, Chunagon by name, who, though she never spoke of it, had always cared for Genji far more deeply than did any of her companions. She now sat sad and thoughtful waiting to say something to him but unable to think of anything to say. He noticed this and was very sorry for her. When all the rest had gone to their rooms he kept her by him and talked to her for a long while. It may perhaps have been for her sake that he stayed so long. Dawn was beginning to come into the sky and the moon, which had not long risen, darted its light among the blossoms of the garden trees, now just beyond their prime. In the courtyard leafy branches cast delicate half-shadows upon the floor, and thin wreaths of cloud sank through the air till they met the first flicker of the white grass-mists which, scarcely perceptible, now quivered in the growing light.

He hung over the balustrade outside the corner room and for a while gazed in silence at this scene, which transcended even the beauty of an autumn night. Chunagon, that she might watch him go, had opened the main door and stood holding it back. "I shall return," Genii said, "and we shall surely meet again. Though indeed, when I think about it, I can find no reason to suppose that I shall ever be recalled. Oh, why did I not make haste to know you in better days, when it would have been so easy for us to meet?" She wept but made no answer.

Presently Aoi's mother sent a message by Saisho, the little prince's nurse: "There are many things that I want to talk over with you, but my mind is nowadays so clouded and confused that I hesitate to send for you. It is kind of you to have paid us so long a visit and I would ask you to come to me; but I fear that to talk with you would remind me too much of all that is now so changed. However, pray do not leave the house till your poor little son is awake." He answered with the poem: "To a shore I go where the tapering smoke of salt-kilns shall remind me of the smoke that loitered by her pyre." He wrote no letter to go with the poem, but turning to the nurse he said: "It is sad at all times to leave one's friends at dawn. How much the more for one such as I, who goes never to return!" "Indeed," she answered, "'farewell' is a monster among words, and never yet sounded kindly in any ear. But seldom can this word have had so sinister an import as to all of us on this unhappy morning."

Touched by her concern at his departure he felt that he must give her what she evidently expected—some further message for her mistress, and he wrote: "There is much that I should like to say, but after all you will have little difficulty in imagining for yourself the perplexity and despair into which my present situation has plunged me. I should indeed dearly like to see the little prince before I go. But I fear that the sight of him might weaken my resolution to forsake the fleeting world, and therefore I must force myself to leave this house without further delay."

The whole household was now awake and everyone was on the watch to see him start. The moon shone red at the edge of the sky, and in its strange light he looked so lovely, *yet* so sad and thoughtful, that the hearts of wolves and tigers, nay of very demons, would have melted at the sight of him. It may be imagined then with what feelings those gentlewomen watched him drive away, many of whom had known and loved him since he was a child. But I had forgotten to say that Aoi's mother replied with the poem: "Seek not another sky, but if you love her,* stay beneath these clouds with which her soul is blent." When he reached his own palace he found that none of the gentlewomen there had slept a wink. They were sitting a few here, a few there, in frightened groups, looking as though they would never lift their heads again. Those officers of his household and personal retainers who had been chosen to go with him to Suma were busy preparing for their departure or saying good-bye to their friends, so that the retainers" hall was absolutely deserted; nor had the gentlewomen whom he was leaving behind dared to present themselves on the occasion of his departure, for they knew that any demonstration of good will towards an enemy of those in power would be remembered against them by the Government. So that instead of his doors being thronged, as once they had been, by a continual multitude of horsemen and carriages, he found them that morning utterly deserted and realized with bitterness how frail is the fabric of worldly power. Already his great guest-tables, pushed against the wall, were looking tarnished and dusty; the guest-mats were rolled up and stowed away in corners. If the house looked like this now, what sort of spectacle he wondered would it present when he had been absent for a few months?

On reaching the western wing he found the partition door still open. Murasaki had sat there watching till dawn. Some of the little boys who waited upon her were sleeping on the verandah. Hearing him coming they now shook themselves and rose with a clatter. It was a pleasant sight to see them pattering about in their little pages' costumes; but now he watched them with a pang at his heart, for he could not help remembering that while he was away they would grow up into men and in the end

---

* The dead Aoi, Genji's first wife.

have to seek service elsewhere. And indeed during those days he looked with interest and regret on many things which had never engaged his attention before. "I am so sorry about last night," he said. "One thing happened after another, and by the time I was free to come back it would not have been worth while. You must have thought it horrid of me. Now that there is so little time left, I hate to be away from you at all. But my departure from the Court naturally involves me in many painful duties, and it would be quite impossible for me to remain shut up here all the time. There are other people, some of whom I may very likely never see again, who would think it unkind of me if I did not even bid them good-bye…" "It is your going away that matters," she answered; "nothing else is of any consequence now…" She said no more, but sat staring before her in an attitude of the profoundest despair. And indeed, as Genji realized, she had every possible reason to dread his departure. Her father Prince Hyobukyo had never put himself out for her, and since Genji's disgrace he stopped writing and no longer even enquired about her. She was ashamed of his worldly caution and dreaded lest others should notice it. For her part she was resolved that, since he showed no interest in her, she would be the last to remind him of her existence. Someone told her that her stepmother* went about saying: "This is what comes of trying to get on too quickly in the world. Look how she has been punished! All her relatives expire and now her lover takes flight!" She was deeply distressed and felt that she could not ever communicate with her stepmother again. There was indeed no one to whom she could turn for help, and her position was likely to be in every way unhappy and difficult. "I promise," said Genji to comfort her, "that if my exile seems likely to last for a considerable time, I will send for you to join me, even if I can offer you nothing better to live in than a hole in the rocks. But it would be considered most improper for me to take you with me now. People who are disapproved of by the Government are expected to creep about miserably in the dark, and if they try to make themselves happy and comfortable it is considered very wicked. I have not of course done anything wrong, but my misfortune must certainly be due to some sin in a previous life, and I am sure that if I did anything so unusual as to take my lady into exile with me, fate would find some yet more cruel way to punish me for the presumption."

He then lay down and slept till noon. Later in the day his half-brother Prince Sochi no Miya and To no Chujo called and offered to help him, dress. He reminded them that he had resigned his rank and they brought him a cloak of plain silk without any crest or badge. This costume had an informal air which became him better than they had expected.

---

* Hyobukyo's wife. Murasaki was his illegitimate daughter.

When he went to the mirror that his servants might do his hair he could not help noticing how thin his face had lately grown, and he said, "What a fright I look! Can I really be such a skeleton as this? It is indeed a bad business if I am." Murasaki, her eyes full of tears, came and peeped at the mirror. To distract her he recited the poem: "Though I wander in strange lands and far away, in this mirror let me leave my image; that it may never quit your side." "That, yes, even so little as that, would comfort me, if indeed this mirror might hold the image of your distant face." So she answered, and without another word sank into a seat behind the roof-pillar, that her tears might not be seen. His heart went out to her, and he felt at this moment that among all the women he had known she was indeed the most adorable.

His stepbrother now fell to reminding him of scenes in their common childhood, and it was already growing dark when he left Genji's room. The lady at the "village of falling flowers" had written to him constantly since she heard the news of his approaching departure. He knew that she had many reasons for dreading his absence and it seemed unfeeling not to pay her one more visit before he left. But if he spent another evening away from his palace Murasaki would be very disappointed, and he therefore did not start till late in the night. He went first to the room of Princess Reikeiden, who was flattered and delighted beyond measure that hers should be the only house to which he paid the honor of a farewell visit. But what passed between them was not of sufficient interest to be recorded. He remembered that it was only through his help and protection that she had managed to overcome the difficulties and anxieties of the last few years. Now matters would go from bad to worse. In the house nothing stirred. The moon had risen and now shimmered faintly through the clouds. The lake in front of the building was large and wild, and dense thickets of mountain-trees surrounded it. He was just thinking that there could hardly in all the world be a lonelier, stranger place, when he remembered the rocky shore of Suma—a thousand times more forbidding, more inaccessible!

The younger sister had quite made up her mind that Genji was going to leave the house without visiting her, and she was all the more surprised and delighted when at last, more lovely than ever by moonlight and in the grave simplicity of his exile's dress, he stole into her room. At once she crept towards the window and they stood together gazing at the moonlight. They talked for a while, and found to their astonishment that it was nearly day. "How short the night has been," said Genji. "Yet even such a hasty meeting as this may never be ours again. Why did I not know you better in all those years when it would have been so easy to meet? Never have such misfortunes befallen an innocent man before, nor ever will they again. I go from torment to torment. Listen..." and he was beginning to recount to her the disasters and miscalculations of the past when the cock crowed, and fearing detection he hastened away.

The moon was like last night, just on the point of setting; it seemed to him a symbol of his own declining fortunes. Shining through the dark purple of her dress the moonlight had indeed, as in the old poem, "the leaden look of those who weep," and she recited the poem: "Though to the moonlight my sleeve but narrow lodging can afford, yet might it dwell there for ever and for ever, this radiance* of which my eyes can never tire." He saw that she was deeply moved by this parting and in pity sought to comfort her with the poem: "In its long journeying the moon at last shall meet a clearer sky; then heed not if for a while its light be dimmed." "It is foolish," he added, "to spoil the present with tears for sorrows that are still to come," and with that he hurried away, that he might be out of the house while it was still dark.

At home he had a great many things to arrange before his departure. First of all he had to give instructions concerning the upkeep of his palace to the few faithful retainers who had taken the risk of remaining in his service. When these had at last all been assigned their functions, difficulties arose about some of the attendants who were to have gone with him into exile, and a fresh choice had to be made. Then there was the business of deciding how much luggage he should take with him to his mountain fastness. Some things were obviously indispensable; but even when he cut down his equipment to the barest possible necessities there were still all kinds of odds and ends, such as writing-materials, poems, Chinese books, which all had to be fitted into the right sort of boxes. And then there was his zithern; he could not leave that behind. But he took no large objects of furniture nor any of his more elaborate costumes, having resigned himself to the prospect of a completely bucolic existence. Finally he had to explain to Murasaki all the arrangements he had made about the servants who were to stay behind, and a hundred other matters. Into her charge too he put all the documents concerning his various estates and grazing-lands in different parts of the country. His granaries and storehouses he put into the keeping of the nurse Shonagon whose vigilance and reliability he had often noted, giving her the help of one or two trusted household officers. And here again there were numerous arrangements to be made.

With the gentlewomen of his palace he had never been on intimate terms. But he kept them in a good humor by sending for them occasionally to talk with him, and he now summoned them all, saying to them: "I am afraid it will be rather dull here while I am away. But if any of you care to stay in my service on the chance that I may one day return

---

* Genji.

to the Court, which if I live long enough is indeed certain to happen sooner or later—please consider yourselves at the disposition of the Lady in the western wing." So saying he sent for all the other servants, high and low, and distributed suitable keepsakes among them.

No one was forgotten; to the nurse of Aoi's little son and even to the servants at the "village of falling flowers" he sent tokens of his appreciation, chosen, you may be sure, with the greatest taste and care.

To Oborozuki, despite a certain reluctance, he wrote at last: "That after what happened between us you should have ceased to communicate with me was both natural and prudent. But I would now have you know that the unparalleled ferocity of my enemies has at last driven me from the Court. The rising torrent of your reproachful tears has carried me at last to the flood-mark of exile and disgrace. I cannot forget that this folly alone was the instrument of my undoing." There was some danger that the letter might fall into wrong hands before it reached its destination, and for that reason he made it brief and vague.

The lady was heart-stricken, and though she strove to hide her tears, they flowed in a torrent that her sleeve was not broad enough to dam. She sent him the poem: "Long ere I reach the tide of your return shall I, poor scum upon the river of tears, be vanished out of sight." She was weeping violently when she wrote it, and there were many blotches and mistakes, but her writing was at all times elegant and pleasing. He would very much have liked to see her once more before his departure, and he many times thought of arranging it. But she was too intimately connected with just those people who had been chiefly responsible for his undoing, and somewhat regretfully he put the idea aside.

On the evening of the day before his departure he went to worship at his father's tomb on the Northern Hills. As the moon did not rise till after midnight he found himself with time on his hands, and went first to visit the Abbess Fujitsubo. She allowed him to stand close up to her curtain, and on this occasion spoke to him with her own mouth. She naturally had many questions to talk over concerning the future of her son, which was now more than ever uncertain. But apart from this, two people who had once lived on such terms as this prince and princess, could not now fail to have much to say to one another of a far more intimate and tender character. He thought her every bit as charming and graceful as in old days, and this made him allude with bitterness to her heartless treatment of him. But he remembered in time that her present state made any such complaints in the highest degree unseemly and inappropriate. He was allowing his feelings to get out of hand, and withdrawing for a while into his own thoughts, he said at last: "This punishment has come upon me quite unexpectedly, and when I try to account for it, one possible explanation of a most alarming character presents itself to my mind. I am not thinking of the danger to myself should a certain fact be known, but of the disastrous consequences of such a disclosure upon the career of the young prince, your son..." The same possibility had of course occurred to her. Her heart beat wildly, but she did not answer. The many painful scenes in which he had recently taken part had broken his spirit and he now wept unrestrainedly. "I am going to the Royal Tombs," he said at last. "Have you any message?" She answered with the poem: "He that was, is not; and he that is, now hides from the afflictions of the world. What increase but of tears did my renunciation bring?"

At last the moon rose, and he set out. Only five or six attendants were with him, men of low rank, but all of them deeply attached to him. Genji himself rode on horseback like the rest. This was quite natural on such an occasion, but his companions could not help contrasting this melancholy cavalcade with the splendors of his retinue in former days. Among them the most downcast was Ukon,[*] who had formed part of his special escort on the occasion of the Kamo festival a few years ago. This gentleman had since that time seen himself repeatedly passed over at the annual distribution of honors, and finally his name disappeared altogether from the lists. Being without employment he had been obliged to go into service, and was now acting as Genji's groom. As they rode along Ukon's eye lighted on the Lower Shrine of Kamo which lay quite near their road, and remembering that wonderful day of the festival he leapt from his horse and holding Genji's bridle he recited the verse: "Well I remember how, crowned with golden flowers, we rode together on that glorious day! Little, alas, they heed their worshippers, the churlish gods that in the Shrine of Kamo dwell."

Genji well knew what was passing through the man's mind. He remembered with indignation and pity how Ukon had been the gayest, the most resplendent figure among those who had ridden with him on that day. Genji too alighted from his horse and turning his face towards the Shrine repeated this parting poem: "Thou who art called the Righter of Wrongs, to Thee I leave it to clear the name that stays behind me, now that I am driven from the fleeting haunts of men." Ukon was a very impressionable youth, and this small episode thrilled and delighted him beyond measure.

At last they reached the Tombs. Genji's mind was full of long-forgotten images. He saw his father seated on the throne in the days of his prime, the pattern of a kindly yet magnificent king. Who could then have guessed that death would in an instant deface all memory of that good and glorious reign? Who could have foreseen that the wise policies which, with tears in his eyes, he had time and again commended to those

---
[*] See Part I, pp. 156 *seq*.

about him, would in an instant be reversed, and even his dying wishes contemptuously cast aside? The path to the Royal Tomb was already overgrown with tall thick grass, so that in pressing his way along it he became soaked with dew. The moon was hidden behind clouds, dank woods closed about him on either hand, such woods as give one the feeling one will never return through them alive. When at last he knelt at the tomb, his father's face appeared so vividly before him that he turned cold with fear. Then murmuring the verse: "How comes it that thy vanished image looms before me, though the bright moon, symbol of thy high fortunes, is hidden from my sight?" he set out towards the town, for it was now broad daylight. On his return he sent a message to the Heir Apparent. Omyobu had taken charge of the child since Fujitsubo's retirement and it was through her that Genji now addressed his son: "I leave the City today. That I have been unable to visit you once more is the greatest of my many vexations. You indeed know better than I can tell what thoughts are mine in this extremity, and I beg you to commend me to your little master in such terms as you deem best." With this letter he enclosed a spray of withered cherry-blossoms to which was tied the poem: "When again shall I see the flowers of the City blossoming in Spring, I whom fortune has cast out upon the barren mountains of the shore?" This she passed on to the boy who, young though he was, quite well understood the import of the message, and when Omyobu added, "It is hard at present to say when he will return ...!" the young prince said sadly, "Even when he stays away for a little while I miss him very much, and now that he is going a long way off I do not know how I shall get on... Please say this to him for me."

She was touched by the simplicity of his message. Omyobu often called to mind all the misery which in past days had grown out of her mistress's disastrous attachment. Scene after scene rose before her. How happy they might both have been, if only... And then she would remember that she and she alone had been the promoter of their ruin. She had pleaded for Genji, arranged those fatal meetings! And a bitter remorse filled her soul. She now sent the following reply: "His Highness dictated no formal answer. When I informed him of your departure, his distress was very evident..." This and more she wrote, somewhat incoherently, for her thoughts were in great confusion. With the letter was the poem: "Though sad it is to mark how swift the flowers fall, yet to the City Spring will come again and with it, who can tell..." "Oh, if that time were come!" she added, and spent the hours which followed in recounting such moving tales of Genji's wisdom and kindness that everyone in the Palace was soon dissolved in tears. If these people who but seldom caught sight of him were distressed at the prospect of his departure, it may be imagined what were the feelings of those whose duties brought them constantly into his presence. At the Nijō-in everyone down to the mere scullery-maids and outdoor servants, who could never hope to exchange a single word with him and had thought themselves very lucky if they obtained an occasional glance or smile, had always been in despair when it was known that he would be absent from the palace even for a few days. Nor was his downfall by any means welcome in the country at large. Since his seventh year he had enjoyed the privilege of running in and out of the old Emperor's rooms just as he felt inclined. Everything he asked for had been granted without question, and there were few who had not at one time or another found themselves beholden to his boundless good nature and generosity. Even among the great nobles and Ministers of the Crown there were some who owed their first promotion to Genji's good offices; and countless persons of less importance knew quite well that they owed everything to him. But such was their dread of the present Government, with its ruthless methods of persecution and suppression, that not one of them now came near him. Expressions of regret were everywhere heard; but it was only in the secrecy of their own hearts that these sympathizers dared blame the Government for happenings which they universally deplored. After all, what was the good of risking their own positions by showing to the exiled prince civilities which could be of no real use to him? There was some sense in this, but on Genji their prudence made a most painful and dispiriting impression. He suddenly felt the world was inhabited by a set of mean and despicable creatures, none of whom were worth putting oneself out for in any way at all.

He spent the whole of that day quietly with Murasaki at his palace. He was to start soon after midnight. She hardly knew him as he stood before her dressed in his queer travelling clothes. "The moon has risen," he said at last. "Come out to the door and see me start. I know that at the last minute I shall think of all kinds of things I meant to say to you today. Even when I am only going away for a few nights, there are always so many things to remember..." He raised the curtain-of-state behind which she was sitting and drew her with him towards the portico. She was weeping bitterly. Her feet would not obey her and she stumbled haltingly at his side. The moonlight fell straight upon her face. He looked down at her tenderly. The thought came to him that he might die at Suma. Who would look after her? What would become of her? He was indeed no less heart-broken than she; but he knew that if he gave way to his feelings her misery would only be increased and he recited the verse: "We who so long have sworn that death alone should part us, must suffer life for once to cancel all our vows." He tried to speak lightly, but when she answered: "Could my death pay to hold you back, how gladly would I purchase a single moment of delay," he knew that she was not speaking idly. It was terrible to leave her, but he knew that by daylight it would be harder still, and he fled from the house. All the way down to the river her image haunted him and it was with a heart full to bursting that he went aboard the ship. It was a season when the days are long, and meeting with a favorable wind they found themselves at Suma between three and four o'clock in the afternoon.* It was indeed a trifling journey, but to Genji, who had never crossed the sea before, the experience was somewhat alarming, though his fears were mingled with wonder and delight. As they came in sight of that wild and lonely headland where stands the Hall of Oye† marked by its solitary pine, he recited the verse: "A life more outcast shall be mine among these hills than all those exiles led whose sufferings the books of Kara‡ have rehearsed." He watched the waves lapping up over the sands and then creeping back again. It put him in mind of the ancient song: "Oh would that like the tides I went but to return!" Those who were with him knew the song well enough, but never before had it moved them as now when Genji murmured to himself the long-familiar words. Looking back he saw that the mountains behind them were already melting into the hazy distance, and it seemed to him that he had indeed travelled the classical "three thousand leagues" of which the Chinese poets so often speak. The monotonous dripping of the oars now became almost unendurable. "Now is my home hid from me by the mist-clad hills, and even the sky above me seems not the lovely cloud-land that I knew." So he sang, being for the moment utterly downcast and dispirited.

His new home was quite close to the place where in ancient days Ariwara no Yukihira§ once lived in exile, "trailing his water-buckets along the lonely shore." At this point the sea bends back, forming a shallow inlet, encompassed by desolate hills.

He proceeded to inspect the hut which had been prepared for his reception. Never had he seen such a place before. Even the hedge was built in quite a different way from what he was used to; and the hut itself, with its thatched roof and wide-spreading gables covered with wattled bull-rushes, seemed to him the most extraordinary place to live in. But he could not help admiring the ingenuity with which it was constructed, and he knew that if he had come there under different circumstances the prospect of staying in such a cottage would have fascinated and delighted him. How, in the old days, he had longed for such an experience!

---

* The distance is about 60 miles. It could, says Moto-ori, in no circumstances have been covered in one day. He therefore concludes that the travelers spent a night at Naniwa (the modern Osaka) on the way. A much more probable solution is that Murasaki was herself rather vague about the time which such a journey would take.

† Near Naniwa. It was here that the returning Vestals of Ise lodged on their way back to the Capital.

‡ China.

§ For the story of his exile, see the Noh play *Matsukaze* in my *Noh Plays of Japan,* p. 204.

Many repairs and alterations were necessary, and Genji sent at once for the bailiffs of some of his estates which lay in the neighborhood. They and their workmen, directed by the faithful Yoshikiyo, soon carried out Genji's plans, and the place began to assume a much more habitable air. The pond was dredged and deepened, plantations were laid out. Soon he settled down to his new life in a way that he would never have dreamed to be possible. The Governor of the province had formerly been attached to his household, and though he did not dare to give him a public welcome, he made it clear in private that his sympathies were on Genji's side. Thus even in this remote spot he was not entirely deprived of society; but there was no one with whom he was really intimate and such conversation as he could get was of the most superficial and uninteresting kind. He felt almost as isolated as if he had been cast up on a desert island, and the prospect of spending months, nay years, buried away amid these uncivilized surroundings still appalled him. He was just beginning to reconcile himself a little to his rustic employments when the summer rains set in. During this tedious period of inactivity he thought much of his friends at the Capital. Often he called to mind the picture of Murasaki's misery in those last hours, of the Heir Apparent's infant beauty or the heedless antics of Aoi's little son. He determined to send a courier to the City, and began writing letters to everybody. While he wrote to the Lady of his palace and again while he wrote to Fujitsubo in her cloister he wept so bitterly that the letters had many times to be put aside. To Oborozuki he dared not write direct, but as he had sometimes done before enclosed a message to her in a letter to Lady Chunagon, with the acrostic poem: "That I, though cast like weed upon the barren margin of the sea, am unrepentant still, how should they guess—these fisher folk that tend their salt-kilns on the shore?" To the retired Minister and to Nurse Saisho he sent many instructions concerning the upbringing of the child. It may well be imagined that the arrival of his post-bag in the City set many hearts a-flutter.

The condition of Murasaki after his departure had gravely alarmed her attendants. She lay for many days utterly overcome by the shock of his departure. Every effort to cheer her was in vain. The sight or mention of things which she connected with him, a zithern which he had once played, the perfume of a dress which he had left behind, threw her at once into a new paroxysm of grief. She behaved indeed for all the world as though he were not merely exiled but already in his grave. At last Shonagon, becoming seriously alarmed, sent for her uncle the priest and begged his aid. The liturgy of intercession which he conducted had for its aim both the recovery of Lady Murasaki from her present prostration and the early recall of Genji himself. For a while she was somewhat calmer and began to go about the house again. She spent much time at her devotions, praying fervently that he might soon return and live with her as before. She sent him sleeping-clothes and many other comforts which she feared he might not otherwise be able to secure. Among the garments which she packed were a cloak and breeches of plain homespun. She folded them with a sigh, remembering his Court apparel with its figured silks and glittering badges. And there was his mirror! He had left it behind as in his poem he had jestingly promised to do; but his image he had taken with him, and much good was a mirror that reflected another face than his! The places where he used to walk, the pinewood pillar against which he used to lean—on these she could still never look without a bitter pang. Her situation might well have dismayed even a woman long inured to the world; for an inexperienced girl the sudden departure of one who had taken the place of both father and mother, to whom she had confided everything, to whom she had looked on every occasion for comfort and advice, was a blow from which it could hardly be expected that she would quickly recover. Deep down in her heart there was the haunting fear that he might die before his recall. But apart from this dread (which did not bear thinking of), there was the possibility that gradually, at such a distance as this, his affection for her would cease. True, she could write to him, and had his absence been fixed at a few weeks or months she would have had no great anxiety. But as it was, year might follow year without the slightest change in his prospects, and when he found that this was so who knew what might not come…?

The Lady Abbess too was at this time in great distress. The sin of the Heir Apparent's birth was a constant weight upon her heart. She felt that she had up to the present escaped more lightly than her *karma* in any degree warranted and that a day of disastrous reckoning might still be at hand. For years she had been so terrified lest her secret should become known that she had treated Genji with exaggerated indifference, convinced that if by any sign or look she betrayed her partiality for him their attachment would at once become common knowledge at Court. She called to mind countless occasions when, longing for his sympathy and love, she had turned coldly away. The result of all her precautions did indeed seem to be that, in a world where everything that anyone knows sooner or later gets repeated, this particular secret had, so far as she could judge by the demeanor of those with whom she came in contact, remained absolutely undivulged. But the effort had cost her very dear, and she now remembered with pity and remorse the harshness which this successful policy had involved. Her answer to the letter which he sent from Suma was long and tender; she sought indeed to explain and expiate her seeming heartlessness in former days.

An answer also came from Oborozuki: "Not even to fishers that on the shore of Suma their faggots burn must we reveal the smoldering ashes of pure love." "More I have no heart to write," she added in the margin of this poem, which was on a tiny strip of paper discreetly hidden between the pages of a note from Lady Chunagon. In her own letter this lady gave a most melancholy account of her mistress's condition. All these tales of woe made the arrival of Genji's return post-bag a somewhat depressing event.

Murasaki's letter was full of the tenderest allusions and messages. With it was the poem: "Look at the sleeves of the fisher folk who trail salt-water tubs along the shore: you will not find them wetter than mine were on the night you put out to sea." The clothes and other odds and ends which she sent him were all of the most delicate make and color. She had evidently taken immense trouble, and he reflected that she could now have little indeed to employ her. No doubt she had in her loneliness deliberately prolonged this task. Day and night her image floated before him and at last, unable to endure any longer the idea of her remaining by herself in that dull lonely palace, he began to make fresh plans for bringing her out to join him. But after further reflection he changed his mind. Such a step would at once bring down upon him the full retribution of his offences, and putting the idea out of his head he took to prayer and fasting, in the hope that Buddha would have pity on him and bring his exile to a speedy end. He was also somewhat distressed at being separated from Aoi's son. But here the case was different from that of older people. There was every probability that he would eventually see the child again, and meanwhile he had the comfort of knowing that it was in excellent hands.

But stay! There has been so much to tell that one important matter had quite escaped me. I ought to have told you that before his departure he sent a message to Ise with a letter informing Lady Rokujo of the place at which she must in future address him. An envoy now arrived at Suma with her reply. It was long and intimate. Both the handwriting and mode of expression showed just that extraordinary distinction and fineness of breeding which he had always admired in her. "I find it impossible," she wrote, "to conceive of you in such a place as that at which you bid me to address you. Surely this must be some long, fantastic dream! I cannot but believe that I shall soon hear of you as again at the Capital; alas, even so it will be far longer before *my* fault is expiated and we can meet face to face. 'Forget not those who for salvation dredge their misery by Ise's shore, while you with fisher folk drag dripping buckets to the kiln.'" This and much more was written, not as it seemed at one time, but bit by bit as fresh waves of feeling prompted her. There were altogether four or five large sheets of white Chinese paper, and there were many passages which in the handling of the ink were quite masterly. This woman, whom he once so passionately admired, had, after the fatal outcome of her jealousy, become utterly distasteful to him. He knew well enough that she was not to blame for what had occurred and that his own feelings towards her were utterly unreasonable, and now that he was himself suffering the penalty of exile he felt more than ever ashamed of having driven her away by his sudden coldness. Her present letter moved him so deeply that he detained the messenger for several days, questioning him upon every detail of the life at Ise. The man was a young courtier of good family and was enchanted at the opportunity of living in the company of this famous prince at such close quarters as the limited accommodation of the cottage made necessary. In his reply Genji said: "Had I known that I was to be driven from the Court, I might have done well to join you in your journey. Were I but in the little boat that the men of Ise push along the wave-tops of the shore, some converse would at least be mine. Now, alas, there is less prospect even than before that we shall ever meet again…"

He had now acquitted himself of all his epistolary duties, and no one had any right to complain. Meanwhile a letter arrived from the lady in the "village of falling flowers," or rather a journal in which she had from time to time noted down her impressions since his departure. The manner in which she recorded her despondency at his absence was both entertaining and original. The letter was a great distraction and aroused in him a quite new interest in this lady. It had come to his ears that the summer rains had done considerable damage to the foundations of her house and he sent word to his people at the Capital to get materials from such of his farms as were nearest to the ladies' home and do whatever was necessary in the way of repairs.

The Emperor still showed no signs of summoning Princess Oborozuki to his side. Her father imagined that she felt her position and, since she was his favorite daughter, was most anxious to get matters put right. He spoke about it to Kokiden, begging her to use all her influence, and indeed went so far as to mention his daughter's disappointment to the Emperor himself. It was hoped that he might be prevailed upon to install her, if not as a regular mistress, at any rate in some dignified capacity in his immediate entourage. The Emperor had hitherto neglected her solely because of her supposed attachment in another direction. When at last, yielding to the persuasion of her relatives, he summoned her to him, she was as a matter of fact more than ever absorbed in her unlucky passion. She moved into the Inner Palace during the seventh month. As it was known that the Emperor had previously been very much in love with her, no surprise was felt when he began immediately to treat her as a full lady-in-waiting. From the first he showered upon her a multitude both of endearments and reproaches. He was by no means distasteful to her either in person or character, but a thousand recollections crowded to her mind and continuously held her back. He did not fail to notice this, and once when they were at music together he said to her suddenly:

"I know why you are unhappy. It is because that man has gone away. Well, you are not the only one who misses him; my whole Court seems to be plunged in the darkest gloom. I see what it is; I ought never to have let him go. The old Emperor on his death-bed warned me of all this, but I took no notice, and now I shall suffer for it." He had become quite tearful. She made no comment, and after a while he continued: "I get very little pleasure out of my life. I am fast realizing that there is no point in any of the things I do. I have the feeling that I shall probably not be with you much longer... I know quite well that you will not be much upset; certainly much less than you were recently. That poet was a fool who prayed that he might know what happened to his mistress after he was gone. He cannot have cared much about her, or he would certainly rather not have known." He really seemed to set such store by her affection and spoke in so bitter and despondent a tone that she could bear it no longer and burst into tears. "It is no good your crying like that," he said peevishly, "I know well enough that your tears are not in any way connected with me." For a while he was silent. Then he began again: "It is so depressing not to have had any children. Of course I shall keep Lady Fujitsubo's son as my Heir Apparent, since the old Emperor desired it. But there is sure to be a great deal of opposition, and it is very inconvenient..."

In reality, the government of the country was not in his hands at all; at every turn he saw his own wishes being violated and a quite contrary policy pursued by men who knew how to take advantage of his inexperience and weakness of character. All this he deplored but was powerless to alter.

At Suma autumn had set in with a vengeance. The little house stood some way back from the sea; but when in sudden gusts the wind came "blowing through the gap" (the very wind of Yukihira's poem*) it seemed as though the waves were at Genji's door. Night after night he lay listening to that melancholy sound and wondering whether in all the world there could be any place where the sadness of autumn was more overwhelming. The few attendants who shared the house with him had all gone to rest. Only Genji lay awake, propped high on his pillow, listening to the storm-winds which burst upon the house from every side. Louder and louder came the noise of the waves, till it seemed to him they must have mounted the foreshore and be surging round the very bed on which he lay. Then he would take up his zithern and strike a few notes. But his tune echoed so forlornly through the house that he had not the heart to continue and, putting the zithern aside, he sang to himself the song:

---

* See *Noh Plays of Japan*, p. 204.

"The wind that waked you,
Came it from where my Lady lies,
Waves of the shore, whose sighs
Echo my sobbing?"

At this his followers awoke with a start and listened to his singing with wonder and delight. But the words filled them with an unendurable sadness, and there were some whose lips trembled while they rose and dressed.

What (Genji asked himself) must they think of him? For his sake they had given up their homes, parents, brothers, friends from whom they had never been absent for a day; abandoned everything in life which they had held dear. The thought that these unfortunate gentlemen should be involved in the consequences of his indiscretion was very painful to him. He knew that his own moodiness and ill humor had greatly contributed to their depression. Next day he tried to cheer them with jokes and amusing stories; and to make the time pass less tediously he set them to work to join strips of variegated paper into a long roll and did some writing practice, while on a piece of very fine Chinese silk he made a number of rough ink sketches which when pasted on to a screen looked very well indeed. Here before his eyes were all those hills and shores of which he had so often dreamed since the day long ago when they had been shown to him from a far-off height.* He now made good use of his opportunities and soon got together a collection of views which admirably illustrated the scenery of this beautiful coast-line. So delighted were his companions that they were anxious he should send for Chiyeda and Tsunenori† and make them use his sketches as models for proper-colored paintings. His new affability soon made them forget all their troubles, and the four or five retainers who habitually served him felt that the discomforts of exile were quite outweighed by the pleasure of waiting upon such a master.

The flowers which had been planted in front of the cottage were blooming with a wild profusion of color. One particularly calm and delightful evening Genji came out on to the verandah which looked towards the bay. He was dressed in a soft coat of fine white silk with breeches of aster-color. A cloak of some dark material hung loosely over his shoulders. After reciting the formula of submission ('such a one, being a disciple of the Buddha Sakyamuni, does obeisance to him and craves that in the moonlit shelter of the Tree of Knowledge he may seek refuge from the clouds of sorrow and death") he began in a low voice to read a passage from the

---

* See Part I, pp. 81 *seq.*

† Tsunenori was a famous painter, c. 950 A.D. So presumably was Chiyeda. Some people say Chiyeda was a name used by Tsunenori.

Scriptures. The sunset, the light from the sea, the towering hills cast so strange a radiance upon him as he stood reading from the book, that to those who watched he seemed like some visitant from another world. Out beyond the bay a line of boats was passing, the fishermen singing as they rowed. So far off were these boats that they looked like a convoy of small birds afloat upon the high seas. With the sound of oars was subtly blended the crying of wild geese, each wanderer's lament swiftly matched by the voice of his close-following mate. How different his lot to theirs! And Genji raised his sleeve to brush away the tears that had begun to flow. As he did so the whiteness of his hand flashed against the black wooden beads of his rosary. Here indeed, thought those who were with him, was beauty enough to console them for the absence of the women whom they had left behind.

Among his followers was that same Ukon who had gone with him to the old Emperor's tomb. Ukon's father had become Governor of Hitachi and was anxious that he should join him in his province. He had chosen instead to go with Genji to Suma. The decision cost him a bitter struggle, but from Genji he hid all this, and appeared to be quite eager for the journey. This man, pointing to the wild geese above, now recited the poem: "Like flocks that unafraid explore the shifting highways of the air, I have no fear but that my leader should outwing me in the empty sky."

About this time the Secretary to the Viceroy came back to Court. As he was travelling with his wife, daughters, and a very large staff of attendants he preferred to make the whole journey by water. They were proceeding in a leisurely fashion along the coast and had intended to stop at Suma which was said to be the most beautiful bay of all, when they heard that Genji was living there. The giddy young persons in the boat were immediately in the wildest state of excitement, though their father showed no signs of putting them ashore. If the other sisters, who did not know Genji, were in a flutter, it may be imagined what a commotion was going on in the breast of Lady Gosechi.* She could indeed hardly restrain herself from cutting the tow-cord, and when the boat put in so near the shore that a faint sound of string-music could be heard floating down from Genji's cottage, the beauty of the shore, the proximity of so interesting a personage and the interrupted strains of the tune combined to make a powerful impression upon the imaginations of these young people, and the tears came into their eyes. The Secretary sent the following letter ashore: "I had hoped that after my long absence it would be from your lips that I should first hear all the gossip of the Capital. I now learn to my intense surprise and, if you will allow me to say so, to my deep regret, that you are at present living in retirement in this

---

* See above, p. 224.

remote place. As we are a large and mixed party, I must excuse myself from troubling you, but I hope to have the pleasure of your society upon some other occasion." This letter was brought by his son the Governor of Echizen, a nobleman who had been one of Genji's equerries and had been treated by him with particular kindness. He was distressed at his former master's ill fortune and did not wish to seem ungrateful; but he knew that there were persons in his father's train who had their eye upon him and would, if he lingered in Genji's company, denounce him to the authorities. He therefore handed in the letter and at once hurried away. "You are the first of my friends to visit me since I left the Capital," said Genji. "I cannot sufficiently thank you for sparing me so much of your time..." His reply to the Viceroy's letter was couched in much the same terms. The young Governor returned in very low spirits, and his account of what he had seen and heard provoked loud expressions of sympathy not only from the ladies of the party but also from the Viceroy himself. Lady Gosechi contrived to send a short message on her own account, together with the poem: "Little you guessed that at the sound of your distant lute one hand was near indeed to severing the tow-cord of the boat." "Do not think me forward if under these strange circumstances I have ventured once more to address you," she added. He smiled as he read the letter. She seemed to have become very demure. "Had you in truth been minded to visit me, what easier than to cut the cable that drags you past this shore?" So he wrote and again: "You are a little taken aback, I think, to find me 'among the fishers at their toil.'" So much did he long for some distraction that he would indeed have been delighted if she had found courage to come ashore; nor is this strange when we remember how not far away from this same place a mighty exile[*] found solace in the company of an ostler.

In the Capital Genji's absence was still universally deplored. His stepbrothers and some of the noblemen with whom he was most intimate had in the early days of his exile sent sometimes to enquire about him and had composed elegies in his honor, to which he had replied. This soon reached Kokiden's ears. She was furious at this proof of his continued popularity: "It is unheard of," she burst out angrily, "that a man condemned of offences against the Government of his country should be allowed to live as he pleases and even share in the literary pastimes of the Court. There he sits (by the way I hear he has got a very pretty house!) railing all day at the Government, and no doubt experimenting on loyal servants of the Crown for all the world like that man in the History Book who declared that a stag was a horse."[†] Henceforward Genji received no letters from Court.

---

[*] The great statesman Sugawara no Michizane, 845-903.

[†] Chao Kao was plotting to overthrow the Second Emperor (3rd cent. B.C.). He brought his

The lady at the Nijo-in remained inconsolable. The servants in the eastern wing had at first been somewhat reluctant to transfer their services to her; but after a while her charming manners and amiable disposition completely won their hearts, and none of them showed any signs of seeking service elsewhere. Their employment had given them opportunity of observing, albeit at a distance, most of the great ladies of the Court. They were soon willing to allow that in beauty of character Murasaki far excelled them all, and they well understood why Genji had singled her out to be his pupil.

He, meanwhile, longed more and more to have her with him. But apart from the fact that the roughness of life at Suma would be utterly unsuited to her, he knew that his sending for her would be regarded as an impudent challenge to those who had achieved his downfall.

They were within easy distance of Akashi, and Yoshikiyo naturally thought of the strange lady whom he had once courted there, daughter of the eccentric recluse* who had made his home near the Bay. He wrote to her several times, but received no reply. Finally a note came not from her but from her father, saying that he had something to tell Yoshikiyo and would be glad if he could find time to call. It was quite clear what this meant. The old man merely wanted to tell him that his suit was unwelcome. Yoshikiyo saw no point in going to the house on purpose to be snubbed, and left the letter unanswered. As a rule provincial governors seem to think that there are no reputable families in the land except those of other provincial governors, and it would never occur to them to marry their daughters into any other class. But this ex-Governor was a man who not only had ideas of his own but clung to them with passionate obstinacy. For years past, the sons of provincial officials had been courting his daughter, and one and all he had sent them about their business. His own notion of a husband was very different. Then came Genji's arrival at Suma. So soon as he heard of it, the ex-Governor said to his wife: "I hear that Lady Kiritsubo's boy, Prince Hikaru Genji, has got into some sort of trouble with the authorities and has come to live at Suma. I confess I am delighted to hear it. What a splendid opportunity for our girl..."

"You must be mad!" broke in the mother. "I have been told by people at Court, that he already keeps several ladies of the highest rank as his mistresses; and not content with that, it appears that he has now got into trouble about some lady in the Imperial Household. I cannot imagine why you suppose that a coxcomb of this kind is likely to take any interest in a simple, country girl..." You know nothing whatever about it," inter-

---

majesty a stag, telling him it was a horse. The Emperor laughed, but some of the Courtiers were so much afraid of Chao Kao that they sided with him and insisted that it was indeed a horse. Then Kao knew that they feared him more than the Emperor and definitely decided to revolt.

* See Part I, p. 82.

rupted the father testily. "I have very good reasons for thinking as I do, and I must trouble you to fall in with my plans. I intend to invite Prince Genji over here at the earliest possible opportunity." He now spoke in a gentler tone, but it was evident that he meant to have his own way, and to his wife's consternation he began to make the most lavish preparations for Genji's entertainment. "I cannot imagine," she said, "why you are so set upon marrying our daughter to this man. However exalted his position may once have been, that does not alter the fact that he has now been expelled from the City as a criminal. Even if by any chance he did take a fancy to her, the idea of accepting such a person as our son-in-law is one which you cannot surely entertain even as a joke..." "What is all this about criminals?" he growled. "Surely you know that some of the most distinguished men in history both here and in China have been forced at one time or another to retire from Court. There is nothing disgraceful about it. Just consider for a moment who this prince is. His mother was the daughter of my own uncle, the late Inspector of Provinces, who having made a name for himself by his public services was able to obtain for her a position in the Imperial Palace. Here she at once became the idol of our beloved Monarch, and although the very exceptional favor with which she was treated aroused a good deal of jealousy and in the end brought about her undoing, her career cannot be considered unsuccessful, since she became the mother of His Majesty's most cherished son. In short, the family with which his august father was not ashamed to ally himself is surely good enough for this young prince, and though our daughter is a country-bred girl, I do not think you will find he turns up his nose at her..."

The young woman in question was not remarkably handsome, but she had considerable distinction and charm. Indeed many of the greatest ladies at Court had, so far as good looks went, far less to boast of. She was painfully conscious of her own deficiencies and had made up her mind that no one of good position would ever take any notice of her. Men of her own rank in life she knew that she had no opportunity of meeting. Sooner or later her parents would die, and then she would either become a nun or else drown herself in the sea; she was not sure which. Her father brought her up with extreme strictness, and her only outings were pilgrimages to the Shrine of Sumiyoshi, whither he brought her regularly twice a year, secretly hoping that the God would be moved to assist his ambitious designs.

The New Year had begun. The days were growing longer and already there was a faint show of blossom on the cherry-trees which Genji had planted in his garden at Suma. The weather was delightful, and sitting idly in the sunshine he recalled a thousand incidents that were linked in his mind with former springs. The twentieth day of the second month!

It was just a year ago that he left the Capital. All those painful scenes of farewell came back vividly to his mind, bringing with them a new access of longing. The cherry-trees of the Southern Hall must now be in full bloom. He remembered the wonderful Flower Feast of six years ago, saw his father's face, the elegant figure of the young Crown Prince; and verses from the poems which he had himself made on that occasion floated back into his mind.

All this while To no Chujo had been living at the Great Hall, with very little indeed to amuse him. He had been put down again into the Fourth Rank and was very much discouraged. It was essential to his prospects that he should not come under any further suspicion, but he was an affectionate creature and finding himself longing more and more for Genji's society, he determined, even at the cost of offending the Government, to set out at once for Suma. The complete unexpectedness of his visit made it all the more cheering and delightful. He was soon admiring Genji's rustic house, which seemed to him the most extraordinary place to be living in. He thought it more like some legendary hermit's hut in a Chinese book than a real cottage. Indeed the whole place might have come straight out of a picture, with its hedge of wattled bamboo, the steps of unhewn stone, the stout pine-wood pillars and general air of improvisation. Chujo was enchanted by the strangeness of it all. Genji was dressed in peasant style with a grey hunting-cloak and outer breeches over a suit of russet-brown. The way in which he played up to this rustic costume struck Chujo as highly absurd and at the same time delighted him. The furniture was all of the simplest kind and even Genji's seat was not divided off in any way from the rest of the room. Near it lay boards for the games of go and *sugoroku,* and chessmen, with other such gear as is met with in country houses. The meals, which were necessarily of a somewhat makeshift character, seemed to Chujo positively exciting. One day some fishermen arrived with cockles to sell. Genji sent for them and inspected their catch. He questioned them about their trade and learned something of the life led year in and year out by those whose homes were on this shore. It was a story of painful unremitting toil, and though they told it in a jargon which he could only half understand, he realized with compassion that their feelings were, after all, very much like his own. He made them handsome presents from his wardrobe and they felt that these shells had indeed been lifegiving.*

The stable was quite close by and in full view of the cottage. It amused Chujo to watch the laborers fetching rice-husks from a queer building which seemed to be a sort of store-house or granary and using

---

* There is here a play on words. The other meaning is: "That life was indeed worth living."

them as provender for the horses; and he would sing the ballad: "Sweet is the shade…"*

He had of course a great deal to tell to his friend, and it was sometimes with laughter, sometimes with tears that they went step by step over all that had happened in the long months of their separation. There were many stories of Aoi's little son, happily still too young to understand what was going on in the world around him, of the old Minister, who now was sunk into a state of unremitting melancholy, and of a thousand other happenings at the Great Hall and Court, which could not possibly be recounted in full and would lose all interest if told incompletely. Neither of them had any inclination to sleep, and at dawn they were still exchanging Chinese odes.

Though Chujo had said that he no longer cared what the authorities thought of him, he was reluctant to aggravate his offence by lingering on this forbidden shore, and he now announced that he must start for home again immediately. This was a terrible blow to Genji who knew that so short a visit would leave him even more wretched than before. Wine was brought and as they drank the farewell cup they murmured in unison the words of Po Chü-i's parting poem:

> "Chin on hand by the candle we lay at dawn
> Chanting songs of sadness, till the tears had splashed
> Our cup of new-made wine…"

Chujo had brought with him some delightful presents from the Capital. With many apologies Genji offered him in return a black colt, saying as he did so: "I fear that it may be embarrassing for you to receive even so poor a gift as this from one in my position. But I beg of you to accept it as a symbol of my longing to return, for in the *Old Poem* it is written:

> 'The Tartar horse neighs into the northern wind;
> The bird of Yüeh nests on the southern bough.'"

It was in fact a magnificent horse and could hardly have been matched in all the kingdom. Among the presents brought by Chujo was a celebrated flute which had long been in his possession, and many other small but beautiful objects such as could easily be secreted and would serve as tokens of his affection without exciting troublesome comment.

The morning was well advanced before Chujo set out. He could hardly believe that the long-dreamed-of meeting was already over and looked

---

* "Sweet is the shade, the lapping waters cool, and good the pasture for our weary steeds. By the well of Asuka, here let us stay." See Part 1, p. 23.

back again and again to where his friend was standing. The sight of Genji gazing after him as the boat drew away made it more difficult than ever to endure so speedy a parting, and he cried out, "When, when shall we meet again? I cannot think that they will let you go on much longer..." At which Genji answered him with the poem: "O crane, who travellest at will even to the very margin of the Land on High, look well upon me, whether in intent I be not cloudless as this new day of Spring."* "Sometimes for a while I have hope," he added; "but of those who before have been in my case even the most grave and virtuous have seldom managed to repair their fortunes. I fear I shall not see the precincts of the Capital again." "Hapless in cloudland shall your crane's solitary voice re-echo till with his lost friend, wing to wing again, he can renew his flight." This was the poem that Chujo now recited as his boat left the shore.

The third month was now beginning and someone who was supposed to be well up in these matters reminded Genji that one in his circumstances would do well to perform the ceremony of Purification on the coming Festival Day.† He loved exploring the coast and readily consented. It happened that a certain itinerant magician was then touring the province of Harima with no other apparatus than the crude back-scene‡ before which he performed his incantations. Genji now sent for him and bade him perform the ceremony of Purification. Part of the ritual consisted in the loading of a little boat with a number of doll like figures and letting it float out to sea. While he watched this, Genji recited the poem: "How like these puppets am I too cast out to dwell amid the unportioned fallows of the mighty sea." These verses he recited standing out in the open with nothing but the wind and sky around him, and the magician, pausing to watch him, thought that he had never in his life encountered a creature of such beauty. Till now there had not been the least ripple on the face of the sea. Genji, wondering what would in the end become of him, began to review the whole course of his past life and the chances of better fortune in the future. He gazed on the quiet aspects of both sky and sea. "The Gods at least, the myriad Gods look kindly on my fate, knowing that sinful though I be, no penalty have I deserved such as I suffer in this desolate place." As he recited these words, the wind suddenly rose; the sky grew dark and without waiting to finish the ceremony everyone began hastily preparing to make for home. Just when they had decided to return as quickly as possible, a squall of rain commenced, beginning so unexpectedly that there was no time even to put up umbrellas. The wind was now blowing with unparalleled violence and things which the

---

* I.e. You have access to the Emperor, put in a word on my behalf.

† The third day of the third month.

‡ *Zesho,* a screen or in some cases curtain with a pine-tree painted on it; used as a background to sacred performances.

calmness of the morning had tempted them to leave carelessly lying about the shore, were soon scattered in every direction. The sea too was rapidly advancing and they were obliged to run for their lives. Looking back they saw that the whole surface of the bay was now covered with a blanket of gleaming white foam. Soon the thunder was rolling and great flashes of lightning fell across the sky. It was all they could do to make their way home. The peasants had never witnessed such a gale before. "It blows pretty stormy sometimes," they said, "but you can generally see it coming up a long while before." Of such a storm as this, coming on without a moment's warning, they could make nothing at all. Still the thunder crashed, and the rain fell with such violence that each shaft struck deep into the earth. It seemed indeed as though the end of the world were come. Some of Genji's servants became very restless and uneasy; but he himself settled quietly in his chair and read out loud from the Scriptures. Towards evening the thunder became less violent, but the wind remained very high all night. It was soon apparent that if the wind did not change, the waves would carry away their house. Sudden high tides had often before done great damage on the coast, but it was agreed that such a sea as this had never been seen before. Towards dawn everyone went off to get a little rest. Genji too began to doze a little. There appeared to him in his dream a vague and shadowy figure who said: "I have come from the Palace to fetch you. Why do you not follow me?" He tried to obey the command, but suddenly awoke. He realized that the "Palace" of his dream did not mean, as he had at first supposed, the Palace of the Emperor, but rather the dwelling of the Sea God. The whole import of the dream was that the Dragon King* had taken a fancy to him and wished to detain him yet longer on the shore of his domains. He became very depressed and from this time onwards took a dislike to the particular part of the coast in which he had chosen to reside.

---

* Sovereign of the Ocean.

Akashi

The bad weather continued; day after day nothing but rain, wind and repeated thunderstorms, bringing with them countless troubles and inconveniences. So depressing was the past to look back upon and so little hope did the future hold out for him that, try as he might, Genji could no longer keep up even the appearance of cheerfulness. His prospects were indeed dark. It was just possible that he might some day be permitted to return to the Capital. But with the dominant faction at Court still working against him he would be subject to unendurable slights and vexations. He thought more than once of withdrawing from the coast and seeking shelter at some point well back among the inland hills. But he knew that if he did so it would be said he had been scared away by a few days of foul weather. The smallest actions of people in his position are recorded, and he did not care to figure in the history-books as the Prince who ran away from a storm. Night after night he had the same dream of a messenger summoning him to the realms below the sea. It seemed as though the Dragon of the Ocean had indeed set his heart upon him.

Day followed day without the least break showing in the sky. It was now a long time since he had heard any news from the Capital, and he was becoming very anxious. To be immured for weeks on end in his small house was to the last degree enervating and depressing; but in this villainous weather there was no question of so much as even sticking one's head out of doors for two minutes. Needless to say no one came to visit him. At last a pitifully bedraggled figure hove into view, fighting its way through the storm. A messenger from the Nijo-in. So he announced himself; but the journey had reduced him to such a plight that Genji would scarce have known that this tattered, dripping mass was a human being at all. He was indeed a common peasant, such a one as in old days would have been unceremoniously bundled out of Genji's path. Now Genji found himself (not without some surprise at the degree of condescension to which his misfortunes had brought, him) welcoming the fellow as an equal, and commiserating with him upon his plight.

In her letter Murasaki said: "In these odious days when never for a single instant has the least gleam or break pierced our sodden sky, the clouds have seemed to shut you off from me and I know not behind which part of this dark curtain to look for you. 'How fiercely must the tempests be blowing on your shore, when even here my sleeves are drenched with ceaseless spray!'"

The letter was full of sad and tender messages. He had no sooner opened it than a darkness spread before his eyes and tears fell in floods, "belike to swell the margin of the sea."

He learnt from the messenger that at Kyoto too the storm had raged with such violence and persistency that it had been proclaimed a national Visitation, and it was said that the great Service of Intercession* had been held in the Palace. So great were the floods that the officers of the Court were unable to reach the Inner City, and all business was at a standstill. He told his story confusedly and in a broken jargon that was very hard to follow. But what matter? Such as it was, his news came from Kyoto, from the City, and that in itself was enough to make Genji catch eagerly at every word. He had the messenger brought to his own room and was soon plying him with questions. It seemed that the same continuous downpour had gone on day after day without a moment's break, varied only by occasional hurricanes of wind. Thunder they had not had, nor the alarming hailstorms which along the coast were of such violence that the hailstones had penetrated far down into the earth. Such horror came into the man's face as he recalled the scenes through which he had passed, and so lamentable was his present condition that even those who had taken the storm somewhat lightly now began to feel seriously alarmed. It seemed indeed as though a continuance of the present deluge must speedily wash the world away; but worse was to come, for next day, from dawn onwards, an even more violent wind raged, causing a tremendous flood-tide along all the shore. Soon the breakers were crashing with a din so stupendous that you would have thought the rocks, nay the very hills, could not long resist them. Suddenly a blaze of lightning, inexpressibly fierce and dazzling, rushed earthward. They realized that something must have been struck, and there was now no longer anyone who even pretended to take the situation lightly. Each of Genji's servants was wondering in his heart what he had done to deserve at the hand of Fate so hideous an experience. Here, it seemed, they were all to die; never again to meet mother or father, far from the pitying faces of wife, of children, or of friends. Genji himself had no desire to end his existence on this inhospitable shore, but he managed to control his feelings and did his best to introduce some order among his followers. This proved to be by no means easy. At last he set them to offering up prayer-strips and ribbons to the God of Sumiyoshi and himself called upon the God to save from

---

* Instituted in China in the 6th century. It centered round the reading of the *Jen Wang Ching* (Nanjio No. 17) in which Buddha instructs the great kings of the earth how to preserve their countries from calamity.

calamity a shore that was so near his own Holy Abode and, if indeed he were a Present Deity, to prove it now by his aid. So he prayed, with many other vows and supplications. And his servants, as they heard him, forgot for a while the peril that threatened their own lives, and could think only of the calamity which would befall their country should such a prince be lost amid the waters of this deserted shore. Then one, who was of greater courage than the rest and had now somewhat regained the use of his faculties and better feelings, began to call upon the God to take his life and welcome, so be it Genji was saved. And after this, all began in chorus to invoke both Buddhas and Gods of their own land; and presently one said: "Though nurtured in a palace of princes and inured from infancy to softness and delights, our master has not hidden his face from common men; for in every corner of the Eight Islands his patience and kindness are known. How many that were downcast and obscure has he not helped upward to greatness? Tell us now. Heaven, tell us, Earth, of what crime has he been guilty, that he should be cast away, a victim to the winds and seas? Guiltless he has been punished, has been robbed of rank and office, has been torn from home and country, nor has been suffered to be at peace either by day or night…" Genji himself prayed again to the gods, saying: "With such sights and sounds about us we cannot but wonder whether the end of our days is come. Do ye now, O Powers, put an end to this grievous visitation, whether it be the fruit of *karma* or the punishment of present crimes; lest we should doubt if Gods and Buddhas can indeed make manifest their will." Then turning in the direction of the Sumiyoshi Shrine he uttered many further prayers to that God, to the Dragon King of the Ocean and to a thousand and one other Gods and Spirits. Suddenly, however, while he was in the midst of these prayers, there was a louder thunderclap than ever, and at the same time lightning struck a pent-house which actually adjoined Genji's room. Flames shot up and that part of the building was soon in ashes. His men were now without exception in such a state of panic that they could do nothing. Finally Genji got them to move his things into a sort of shed at the back of the house, which had sometimes been used as a kitchen. Here, huddled with all his followers and grooms, he spent the rest of the day, wearied by their ceaseless lamentations, which indeed bid fair to out-din the thunder. The sky was still black as ink when night fell. However, the wind began to subside and presently the rain grew a little less heavy; and at last an occasional star began to twinkle. The thought of their master spending the night in so strange and undignified a situation was very perturbing to his attendants and they began trying to make his proper bedroom habitable again. This, however, did not prove to be feasible, for although a great part of it had not been actually touched by the fire, "the Storm God in his boisterous passage" had left a terrible havoc behind him and the room was strewn with the tattered wreckage of furniture, screens, and bedding. It was agreed that nothing could be done till next day.

Genji said his prayers and began to consider the situation. It was indeed sufficiently alarming. So high had the tide risen that, now the moon was up, the line of the incoming waves was plainly visible from his house, and standing at the open wicker door he watched the fierce breakers plunge and recoil. Such conditions of storm and tide had not occurred in recent times and no one was prepared to say how far matters were likely to go. This being the only gentleman's house in the neighborhood many of the fishing people and peasants who lived along the shore had now collected in front of it. Their queer, clipped dialect and the rustic topics of their conversation were alike very strange to him; but he would not suffer them to be driven out of earshot. "If this wind does not go down," one of them was saying, "we shall have the sea right on top of us before the tide turns. God's help alone can save us." It may be imagined that these predictions were far from disposing the townsmen towards a quiet night's rest. A brisk sea wind was again driving onward the swollen tide, and though he tried to reassure his men Genji was himself in considerable anxiety; when suddenly and quite unexpectedly he fell into a doze and dreamed that his father, looking exactly as in the old days when he was on the throne, stood beside the crazy bed which had been improvised for him in this disordered place. "How comes it that you are sleeping in such a place as this?" the vision asked, and taking his hand made as though to drag him from the bed. And again, "Put your trust in the God of Sumiyoshi. Leave this place, take to your ship and He will show you where to go." What joy it was to hear that voice once more! "Father," Genji answered, "since your protection was taken from me nothing but sorrow and ill-fortune have befallen me, and now I am fully expecting to perish miserably upon this forsaken shore." "It is not to be thought of," answered the Emperor. "Your offence was not so great that you must needs be driven to such a place as this. Unfortunately I myself am at present expiating a few small offences (such as it is indeed impossible to avoid; for the Judges of the Dead have not managed to prove that during my whole reign I did serious harm to anyone). However, for the present this expiation keeps me very busy, and I have not been able to keep an eye upon what is happening here. But your late misfortunes have been such as I could not bear to think of, and though it cost me great labor, I have made my way through the depths of ocean and up again on to the shore, that I might be with you in your suffering. Yet this time I must not stay longer, but will go straight to the Palace and tell these things to him who is now Ruler there." So he spoke, and turned to fly away. "Let me go with you. Do not leave me!" cried Genji in his dream. But looking up he found that there was no one there at all. The full-faced moon stared down at him, cold and undreamlike; a cloud trailed across the sky, shaped to the dim semblance of a figure in flight.

It was many years since he had dreamed of his father, though in his waking hours he had never ceased to mourn for him and long for his company. This sudden vision which, though so brief, had all the vividness of a real encounter, brought him great comfort. The thought that at the hour of his greatest despair, nay when death itself seemed close at hand, his father's spirit had hastened through the air to succor him, made him almost glad that Fate had brought him to the extremity which had moved his father's compassion. So full was he of new hope and comfort that in his exultation he utterly forgot the perils that encompassed him, and lay trying to recall stray fragments of his father's dream-speech which had faded from his waking mind. Thinking that the dream might be repeated, he tried to sleep again; but this time all his efforts were in vain, and at daylight he was still awake.

Next morning there landed at a point in the bay opposite to Genji's house a little boat with two or three persons aboard her. It proved on enquiry that, they had come from the Bay of Akashi and that the boat belonged to the ex-Governor of the province, now turned lay-priest. The messenger explained that his master was himself aboard and desired to have a word in private with the Genshonagon* Yoshikiyo, if he were at present to be found at Suma. Yoshikiyo thought this very peculiar. The ex-Governor was perfectly well aware of all that went on in the district; but though he had been acquainted with Yoshikiyo for years, he had not during all the while they had been at Suma paid the slightest attention to him. It seemed indeed (thought Yoshikiyo) as if he were definitely in the old man's bad books. And now, in the middle of an atrocious storm, he took it into his head to pay a call. It was all very queer. But Genji, who saw in this new happening a possible fulfillment of his dream, said at once, "You had better go," and Yoshikiyo accordingly accompanied the messenger back to the boat. How they had ever managed to launch it at all, under the conditions which must have prevailed at the time they left Akashi, was a complete mystery to him. "On the first day of this month," the old man began, "I had a most singular and interesting dream. What it portended seemed to me at the time very improbable; but part of the dream was that if I wished to see the promise fulfilled, I must get ready a boat and on the thirteenth day, so soon as there was the slightest lull in the storm, make straight for this coast. As this injunction was several times repeated I had the boat manned and at the appointed time waited for a chance of getting to sea. There was a fearful gale blowing; rain was

---

* A Court title. Yoshikiyo was son of the Governor of Harima and had courted the Lady of Akashi. See Part I, p. 82, where, following another text, I have called him Yoshizane.

falling in torrents and a thunderstorm was in progress. It certainly did not seem a very good moment to start. But there are many instances in foreign history of people saving a whole country from peril by obeying an apparently senseless dream. I feared that if I delayed my departure beyond the day which had been named my journey would be of no service to anyone. And so, determined that you should know of the divine indication which had been vouchsafed to me, I launched my boat. What was my surprise to discover that we had a quite moderate wind blowing nicely in our wake! We had this wind behind us all the way, and I cannot but regard the whole affair as a clear instance of divine intervention. It is possible that on your side too there has been some warning or message which fits into the revelations which I have received. I am very sorry to disturb His Highness; but I should be obliged if you would tell him of what has passed." Yoshikiyo accordingly went back to Genji and told him the whole story. The matter needed some consideration. Here was a chance which it would not be wise to let pass. Both actual events, such as the destruction of his bedroom, and a general restlessness induced by his own singular dream, with its warning to quit this place, inclined him to make use of the ex-Governor's visit. No doubt that if he retired to Akashi his move would become the subject of a great many scurrilous jokes;[*] but on the other hand he would look even more foolish if it turned out that he had not availed himself of a genuine warning from the Gods. And this must be a very dangerous thing to do; for even human beings are extremely annoyed if one disregards their advice. His situation could hardly be worse than it was already. The old Governor was many years his senior; was even, as things went now, his superior in rank, and was certainly viewed by the authorities in a very different light from that in which Genji was regarded. In fact it would be most unwise not to take advantage of his visitor's evident friendliness and desire to be connected with him. To go to Akashi would be to beat a retreat. But a wise man[†] of ancient times has told us that "to retreat is no disgrace." And then there was his own dream, in which his father had begged him to leave this place. He had made up his mind about it. He would ask if he might go back with them to Akashi. He therefore sent a message to his visitor saying: "Though I am living in a strange land, under circumstances in the highest degree painful and depressing, from the direction of my own home there does not come a single message of enquiry or condolence. Here all is unfamiliar to me; save the stars and sun there is not one being or thing that recalls to me the life I used to know. You can imagine then with what joy I saw your fishing-boat

---

[*] It would be said that he was running after the Lady of Akashi, the old recluse's daughter.

[†] Lao Tzu, say the commentators; but this saying does not occur in the *Tao Te Ching*.

draw near. Tell me, is there not on your shore some corner where I could hide myself and be at peace?"

This was just what the old gentleman wanted, and in high delight he hastened to welcome Genji's suggestion. A great bustle commenced; but before daybreak all Genji's effects had been stowed away in the boat and, with his usual band of chosen retainers, he at last set sail. The wind had veered and was behind them on the return journey too, so that the little ship flew to Akashi like a bird. The distance is of course not great and the voyage does not in any case take more than a few hours. But so assiduously did the wind follow them on this occasion that it really seemed as though it were doing it on purpose.

Akashi was evidently a very different sort of place. Indeed his first impression was that, if anything, it would be difficult here to find seclusion enough. The ex-Governor's estate comprised not only the foreshore, but also a considerable extent of mountain-land behind. And everywhere, in creeks and hill-folds and on river-shores, were felt-roofed huts so situated that the old recluse might not lack an agreeable place of retirement at any season of the year.

On all sides there rose groups of substantial granaries and barns, which looked as though they must contain rice and corn enough to last for the rest of his present existence. But though so careful to provide for his earthly needs, he had by no means forgotten the life to come. On a site which, commanding as it did a magnificent panorama, was calculated to inspire him with the sublimest thoughts, he had built a handsome temple, where part of his time was spent in the performance of penances and mystic meditations.

During the recent storms he had moved his wife and daughter to a lodge on the hillside and was therefore able to place his seaside residence entirely at Genji's disposal. It was still dark when they left the boat; but as they drove along the shore, the growing daylight at last gave him an opportunity of taking a good look at his guest. So delighted was he by the young man's appearance and by the rapid success of his expedition that his usually severe and formidable countenance relaxed into a perfect efflorescence of smiles and affability. But even in this state of preoccupation and excitement he did not forget to offer up a prayer of thankfulness to the God of Sumiyoshi. To the old man it was as though the sun and moon had been taken down from the sky and entrusted to his keeping. It may easily be imagined that he left no stone unturned to make Genji comfortable and contented. Not only was the place one of great natural beauty, but it had been laid out with unusual taste and skill. Copses had been planted, rock-gardens constructed and flower-beds made—all this around the mouth of a little creek that ran in from the sea. The charms of the place were such as a very skilful landscape-painter might possibly manage to convey; to describe them in words would, I fear, be quite useless. The contrast with the uncomfortable quarters where he had been cooped up for months was immense. The house was equipped with every possible elegance and convenience; it scarcely fell short of the great mansions which he had been used to frequent at the Capital; and indeed in many respects surpassed them. Thus admirably served and lodged Genji began to regain some of his equanimity and was soon engaged in writing letters to his friends at the Capital. The messenger who had brought Murasaki's letter was far too much shaken by his previous experiences to be sent back immediately to the City and Genji had left him behind at Suma. He now sent for him and entrusted to him a letter in which he described all that he had recently been through and with many tender messages explained the reasons which had led him to his new abode. He also sent private intimation of his whereabouts and present condition to various holy men who were charged to pray for his welfare. To Fujitsubo he sent an account of the thunderstorm and his own almost miraculous escape from harm. He had tried to write an answer to Murasaki's letter during the melancholy period when he was still at Suma, but had never managed to finish it, for his tears fell so fast that he was for ever putting the letter aside. And it was indeed a piteous sight to see him stop again and again to wipe away the tears that soiled his page. In this letter he said: "More than once my misery has become so intense that I was fully determined to give up my career and end my days in some cloister cell. But then I always remembered your little poem;[*] and felt that it was impossible to leave the world, at least till I had seen you once again.

"Swift as before
My thoughts fly back to thee,
Though now from unknown shore
To stranger and more distant shores I flee..."

Forgive this letter which, written as in a dream, may well say much which a waking mind can scarcely apprehend." It was written distractedly and with a shaking hand: but those who were with him could not forbear from peeping a little as he wrote, such was their curiosity to know what he would say to one who held so great a sway over his affections. And presently, having seen what they could, his servants too began their own letter writing, each of them having some dear one at the City from whom he was anxious to obtain news.

The bad weather in which for so many weeks there had not been a single break, had now completely vanished. Out came all the fishing-

---
[*] The mirror-poem, p. 232.

boats, eager to make up for lost time. The complete desertedness of Suma, which apart from a few fishermen who lived in caves under the cliff, had no inhabitants at all, was very depressing. Akashi could certainly not be complained of on that score; indeed, he feared at first that it might prove somewhat too populous. But the beauty of the place was so great and afforded him so many surprises that he was soon perfectly contented. His host seemed to be exclusively absorbed in religious exercises. Only one other matter occupied his thoughts; it was clear from stray allusions in his conversation that he lived in a state of continual agitation about his only daughter, to whom he was evidently attached with an almost morbid degree of concentration. Genji had not forgotten the favorable account of this lady which had been given him some years ago. Her presence had of course been no part of his reason for coming to this place; but the fact that accident had finally brought him so near her was in a way intriguing. However, his misfortunes were still weighing heavily upon his mind and he was in a mood for prayer and fasting rather than for any gallant diversions. Moreover his thoughts were, for the time being, more than ever turned towards the City, and he would not have dreamed of doing anything that the girl whom he had left in his palace might feel to be a betrayal of his promises. He was therefore careful not to show the slightest interest in the topic to which his host so often returned. But various indications had already convinced him that the lady in question was a person of very unusual and attractive qualities, and despite this assumed indifference he could not help feeling a certain curiosity with regard to her. The ex-Governor showed himself to be an ideal host. He stationed himself at the far end of the house, in a wing which was completely cut off from Genji's quarters. Here he was always to be found when wanted, but never obtruded himself. The self-effacement was the more remarkable seeing that he was all the time longing to be in Genji's company, and he was continually praying Gods and Buddhas for guidance as to how he might best win the confidence of his exalted guest. Although he was not much over sixty a constant habit of watching and fasting had told much upon him, so that in appearance he was wizened and almost decrepit. But he was by no means a dull companion, for owing to the influential circles in which his youth had been passed he was extremely well-informed concerning all the principal events of a period which had hitherto lain outside Genji's ken, and his anecdotes were a considerable source of distraction. Genji found indeed that he had started a veritable landslide of information about a generation which his own distractions, both social and political, had never left him time to study. So pleased was he both with his host and with his new place of residence that he thought with horror how easily it might never have occurred to him to pay this visit.

Though he had now become so intimate with his guest, the old man was still daunted by a certain reserve and distance in Genii's manner towards him; and whereas in the first few days of their acquaintance he had sometimes mentioned his daughter, he now hardly ever referred to her. But all the while he was trying to discover some way of unfolding his project and his complete failure to do so distressed him beyond measure. He was obliged at last to confess to his wife that he had made no progress; but she was not able to offer him any useful advice. The girl herself had been brought up in a neighborhood where there was not a single male of any description whom she could possibly think of as a lover. At last she had a chance of convincing herself that such creatures as men of her own class did actually exist. But this particular one was such an exalted person that he seemed to her in his way quite as remote as any of the local people. She knew of her parents' project, which indeed distressed her greatly, for she was convinced they were merely making themselves ridiculous.

It was now the fourth month. A dazzling summer outfit was supplied for Genji's use; magnificent fresh hangings and decorations were put up in all his apartments. The attentions of his host were indeed so lavishly bestowed that they would have proved embarrassing, had not Genji remembered that he was in the hands of an eccentric, whose exalted notions were notorious and must, in a man of such distinction, be regarded with indulgence. About this time he began to have a fresh distraction; for messengers again began to arrive from the Capital, and came indeed in a pretty constant stream. One quiet moonlit night, when a cloudless sky stretched over the wide sea, Genji stood looking put across the bay. He thought of the lakes and rivers of his native land. This featureless expanse of sea awakened in him only a vague and general yearning. There was no intimate mark round which his associations might gather, no bourne to which his eyes instinctively turned. In all the empty space before him only the island of Awaji stood out solidly and invited attention. "Awaji, from afar a speck of foam," he quoted, and recited the acrostic verse: "Oh, foam-flecked island that wast nothing to me, even such sorrow as mine is, on this night of flawless beauty thou hast power to heal!"

It was so long since he had touched his zithern that there was a considerable stir among his followers when they saw him draw it out of its bag and strike a few random notes. Presently he began trying that piece which they call the "Koryo"* and played the greater part of it straight through. The sound of his zithern reached the house on the hillside near by, mingled with the sighing of pine-woods and the rustling of summer waves. The effect of all this upon the imagination of the impressionable

---

* Evidently a Chinese tune. Attempts to identify it have hitherto been very unconvincing.

young lady in the house above may well be guessed. Even gnarled old peasants, whom one would not have expected to make head or tail of this Chinese music, poked their noses out of their cottage-doors and presently came to take an airing along the shore, The Governor could not contain himself, and breaking off in the middle of his prayers, hastened to Genji's rooms. "How this brings back to me the old days at Court, before I turned my back on all the pleasures of the world," he exclaimed: "But surely the enchantment of such music as this is not all earthly! Does it not turn our thoughts towards those celestial strains which will greet us when we come at last to the place of our desires?" To Genji too the sound of the zithern brought recollections of many music-makings at the Capital. He remembered with just what turns and graces such a one had played the zithern at a particular banquet or another had played the flute. The very intonations of some singer's voice came back to him from years ago. He remembered many an occasion of his own triumph or that of his friends; the acclamations, the compliments and congratulations of the Court, nay, the homage of everyone from the Emperor downwards; and these shadowy memories imparted to his playing a peculiar tinge of melancholy and regret. The old recluse was deeply moved and sent to his house on the hill for his own lute and large zithern. Then, looking for all the world like a *biwa* priest,* he played several very admirable and charming pieces. Presently he handed the large zithern to Genji, who struck a few chords, but was soon overcome by the tender memories which this instrument† evoked. The poorest music may gain a certain interest and beauty from the circumstances in which it is performed. It may be imagined then how enchanting was the effect of Genji's touch as the notes sped across the bay. Nor indeed could any flowering groves of spring nor russet winter woods have made a better setting for his music than this huge space of open sea. Somewhere in the region of soft, vague shadows along the shore, shrike were making that strange tapping sound with their bills. It sounded as though someone had been locked out and were rapping, rapping, rapping in the desperate hope that those within might at last relent of their unkindness. The old recluse then played so delightfully on both instruments that Genji was fascinated. "This large zithern," he said to the old man presently, "is usually supposed to be a woman's instrument and requires a very delicate, fluttering touch." He meant this quite generally, and not as an apology for his own playing; but the old man answered with a deprecatory smile: "I cannot imagine a touch more suitable to this instrument than yours. This zithern was

---

* Priests who collected money for their community by going round playing the *biwa* at street-corners.

† Which he had taught to Murasaki.

originally a present from the Emperor Engi[*] and has been in my family for three generations. Since my misfortunes and retirement I have had little taste for such distractions as this, and have lost what small skill I ever possessed. But in times of great spiritual stress or deep depression I have occasionally turned to this instrument for solace and support. And indeed there is in my household one who from watching me at such times has herself developed a strange proficiency, and already plays in a manner which would not, I venture to think, displease those departed princes to whom the zithern once belonged. But perhaps by now, like the mountain-hermit in the old story, I have an ear that is better attuned to the rushing of wind through the treetops than to the music of human hands. Nevertheless I wish that, yourself unseen, you might one day hear this person's playing; and his eyes moistened in fond paternal recollection. "I had no idea," answered Genji, "that I was in the neighborhood of genius such as you describe. I fear my playing will have sounded to you indeed as a 'mere rushing of wind through the tree-tops,'" and he hastened to put back the zithern in the old priest's hands. "It is indeed a curious fact," Genji continued, "that all the best players of this instrument have been women. You will remember that the Fifth Princess became, under the instruction of her father the Emperor Saga,[†] the most famous performer of her whole generation. But none of her descendants seems to have inherited her talent. Of all the players who in our own time have achieved a certain reputation in this line, there is not one who is more than an intelligent amateur. That in this remote place there should be someone who is really a skilled performer excites me beyond measure. Do please lose no time in arranging…" "As for that," the priest answered, "I do not see why there should be any great difficulty about it, even if it meant bringing the player down here to meet you. Was not one that had sunk into ignominy and made herself a merchant's drudge once summoned to a great man's[‡] side, because she could still play upon her lute the music that long ago he had loved? And speaking of the lute, I should tell you that the person to whom I refer is also a remarkable lute-player, though this instrument too is one which is very rarely mastered completely. Such absolute fluency, such delicacy of touch, I assure you! And such certainty, such distinction of style! Shut away for so long on this shore, where one hears no sound but the roaring of the sea, I sometimes fall a prey to dark and depressing thoughts; but I have only to listen for a while to this delightful performer and all my sorrows disappear." He spoke with so much enthusiasm and discernment that Genji was charmed

---

[*] 898-930. Sixtieth Emperor of Japan.

[†] 810-823. Fifty-second Emperor of Japan.

[‡] Po Chü-i. The reference is to his poem *The Lute Girl's Song*.

with him and insisted upon his playing something on the large zithern. The old man's skill was astonishing. True, his handling of the instrument was such as is now considered very old-fashioned, and his fingering was all entirely in the discarded "Chinese" style, with the left-hand notes heavily accentuated. But when (though this was not the sea of Ise) he played the song "Let us gather shells along the clean seashore," getting one of his servants, who had an excellent voice, to sing the words, Genji enjoyed the performance so much that he could not refrain from beating the measure and sometimes even joining in the words. Whereupon the priest would pause in his playing and listen with an expression of respectful rapture.

Fruit and other refreshments were then served, all with the greatest taste and elegance. The old priest insisted upon everyone present drinking endless cups of wine, though the night itself was of a beauty so intoxicating that the dull realities of life, had long ago faded from their minds. As the night wore on a cool wind began to blow among the trees, and the moon, who in her higher course had been somewhat overcast, now at her setting shone out of a cloudless sky. When the company was grown a little quieter, the priest began gradually to tell the whole story of his life on this shore, together with his reasons for settling there and a voluminous account of his vows and religious observances; when without difficulty he led the conversation towards the topic of his daughter. She certainly sounded very interesting, and despite the old man's volubility Genji found himself listening with pleasure at any rate to this part of the discourse. "It seems a strange thing to say," his host went on, "but I sometimes wonder whether, humble old cleric though I be, my own prayers are not really responsible for your Highness's excursion to these remote parts! You will say that if this is so I have done you a very bad turn... But let me explain what I mean. For the last eighteen years I have put myself under the special protection of the God of Sumiyoshi. From my daughter's earliest childhood I have been very much exercised in mind regarding her future, and every year in the spring and autumn I have taken her with me to the shrine of that deity, where praying day and night I have performed the offices of the Six Divisions,* with no other desire at heart save that, whether I myself should be reborn upon a Lotus Throne or no, to her at least all might be given that I asked. My father, as you know, was a Minister of State; while I, no doubt owing to some folly committed in a former life, am become a simple countryman, a mere yokel, dwelling obscurely among the hills. If the process continued unchecked and my daughter was to fall as far below me in estate as I am now below my illustrious father, what a wretched fate, thought I, must be in store for her! Since the day of her birth my whole object has been

---

* A service performed at dawn, sunrise, midday, sunset, dusk, and nightfall.

to save her from such a catastrophe, and I have always been determined that in the end she should marry some gentleman of good birth from the Capital. This has compelled me to discourage many local suitors, and in doing so I have earned a great deal of unpopularity. I am indeed, in consequence of my efforts on her behalf, obliged to put up with many cold looks from the neighboring gentry; but these do not upset me at all. So long as I am alive to do it, I am determined to afford her what little protection my narrow sleeve can give. When I am no longer there to watch over her, she will no doubt do as she thinks best. But I confess I would rather hear she were drowned in the sea than that she had settled herself in the sphere of life to which my folly has for the time reduced her." He went on thus for a long while, pausing now and again to shed a few tears; but most of what he said would not be worth repeating. Genji was for various reasons also in a very emotional and discursive mood, and presently he interrupted: "I could never make out why I had suddenly fallen into disgrace and been compelled to live in these remote regions; for I have certainly done nothing in my whole life to deserve so stern a punishment as this. But at last you have furnished me with the explanation, and I am perfectly well satisfied. No doubt it was, as you suggest, entirely in answer to your prayers that all this has happened to me. I only regret that, since you must all the time have been aware of this, you did not think fit to tell me about it a little sooner. Since I left the City I have been so much obsessed by the uncertainty of human life that I have felt no inclination towards any save religious employments. I am now so worn out by months of penance and fasting that no worldly impulse or desire is left in any corner of my being. I had indeed been told long ago that a grown-up daughter lived here with you; but I knew nothing more, and assumed that the society of a disgraced and exiled man could only be distasteful to one of her birth and breeding. But since you thus encourage me, I ask for nothing better than to make her acquaintance as soon as possible. I do not doubt that her company will prove a solace to my loneliness." His prompt acceptance was more than the old man had dared to expect and in high delight he answered with the verse: "You too have learnt to know it, the loneliness of night upon Akashi shore, when hour and listless hour must yet be filled before the dawn can come." "And when you consider the anxiety in which I have for all these years been living…," the old man added: and though he trembled somewhat affectedly at the recollection of what he had been through, Genji was willing to concede that to have lived all one's life in such a place must indeed have been very disagreeable: However he would not be too sympathetic and answered: "You at any rate have the advantage of being used to the coast…" and he recited the poem: "What know you of sorrow, who wear not the traveler's cloak, nor on an unaccustomed pillow rest, groping for dreams till dawn?" For the first time Genji was treating him without the slightest formality or reserve. In his gratitude and admiration the old man poured out an endless stream of inconsequent but flattering remarks, which would be wearisome to read. I am conscious indeed that the whole of this section is rather a bundle of absurdities. But how else could I display the vanity and eccentricity of the old recluse?

At last everything seemed to be turning out just as he desired. He was already beginning to breathe more freely when, to crown his satisfaction, very early on the morning of the next day a messenger from Prince Genji arrived at the house on the hill. The letter which he carried was written with a certain embarrassment, for the lady had grown up in very different surroundings from those whom he was used to address. But the very fact of discovering such talent and charm hidden away in a place where one would least have expected it was enough to kindle his fancy. He took unusual pains with the letter, writing it on a *kurumi-iro*** paper from Korea. In it was the poem: "Long wandered my lonely gaze with naught to rest on save the drifting pathways of the clouds, till the mists divided and I saw the tree-tops by your house." "Love has vanquished discretion…" he ended, quoting from the old song.

Anxious to be on the spot in case such a letter arrived, the old priest had already installed himself in the mansion on the hill before the messenger started. He imagined that his presence in the house was entirely unsuspected. But Genji's man, had he not already been perfectly well aware that the old recluse had preceded him, would certainly have guessed it by the almost embarrassing attentions which were paid to him when he reached the house. Despite the distracting refreshments with which he was being regaled the messenger could not but wonder why the lady was taking such an immense while in composing her reply. The truth was that though her father had gone through into the women's apartments and was giving her all the assistance in his power, she found herself utterly at a loss to frame a reply. Despite the trouble that Genji had taken with his letter, there was an uneasiness about it which made her feel that it was not spontaneous; and even had she known in what terms to reply there was still the question of handwriting. She guessed that in this matter he would be a severe critic and felt utterly incapable of pleasing him. No! The gulf between them was too great. Pretending that she was unwell she sank helplessly upon a couch. There was nothing for it but to reply in her stead, and the old priest wrote as follows: "You will think it very peculiar that I should answer your letter in my daughter's stead. Pray attribute her inability to frame a reply not to any want of gratitude or respect, but rather to the bashfulness engendered by country breeding; pray reflect

---

* A double paper; light blue on a white ground.

also that she has never yet had the privilege of finding herself in your company. She has however ventured to compose the following poem, which she bids me communicate to you: 'That I too for long years have gazed upon these selfsame pathways of the sky is token of some strange kinship in the course of our desires.' She is, as you will observe, deeply affected by the arrival of your message. Pray do not think her answering poem impertinently bold."

This was written on Michinoku paper, and although the style of the writing was quite out of fashion it had a certain dignity and elegance of its own. The poem did strike Genji as somewhat forward in tone, and this surprised him.

He sent back the messenger loaded with handsome stuffs for dresses. Next day he wrote to her again protesting that he was not used to receive, in reply to a private letter, an answer dictated as though to a Palace Secretary. And he added the verse: "This surely is a dismal and outrageous thing, to greet a passerby and get no friendly nod nor 'Say, how goes the world with you?'" This time he wrote on a very soft thin paper, with great delicacy and care. The appearance of the letter was such that a young girl who did not admire it must needs have been rustic, nay brutish indeed. The lady to whom it was addressed was by no means insensible; but she felt that the writer of it was too far removed from her in rank and influence for any interchange of affection to be thinkable. The discovery that a world existed which was populated by such dazzling creatures, so far from giving her pleasure, merely left her more unhappy and discontented than before. Again she found herself utterly at a loss how to reply, and it was only the persistence of her father which forced her at last to indite the poem: "'How goes the world?' is said to friends. That one whom you have never seen should greet more stiffly, can do small outrage to the feelings of your heart." It was written in sharply contrasted light and heavy strokes on a deep-brown paper, in a masterly style which would not have disgraced a lady of the Court. Genji was naturally very pleased; but he did not want it to be reported at the Capital that he had committed himself to a fresh entanglement. He was therefore careful henceforward always to leave several days' interval between his letters to her. He wrote in fact only when it chanced that the evening hours hung heavy on his hands, or upon the pretext of some particularly beautiful sunrise or other natural effect; at such times in short as he guessed that she might be under the influence of the same impressions as himself. In such a correspondence it seemed to him that there could not be any impropriety. He had heard so much about her pride that he felt sorely tempted to put it to the test. But he remembered that his retainer Yoshikiyo had spoken of her very much as though she were his own property. Should Genji now by any chance succeed where the devotion of years had brought no reward, he would certainly feel that he had treated his gentleman very badly and suffer the discomfort of remorse. But on reflection he decided that as she had been so reluctantly thrust upon his notice, there could be no harm in pursuing a guarded correspondence with her. She did indeed turn out in the course of this correspondence to be possessed of a pride and aloofness which rivalled that of the greatest princesses whom he had known and, on such occasions as he pitted his own pride against hers, it was generally she who came out on top.

Though now yet another range of hills separated him from the Capital, his mind was more constantly than ever occupied with thoughts of his friends at home. His longing for Murasaki often became unendurable. What was there to be done? In such moments he could not resist making plans for bringing her secretly from the Capital. But quiet reflection would show him that it was unlikely he would go on living for more than a year or two longer at Akashi and no step was worthwhile which might merely provoke a fresh outburst on the part of his adversaries.

That year the Court was troubled by a succession of disquieting portents and apparitions. On the thirteenth day of the third month, during a night marked by violent thunderstorms and a fierce wind with torrents of rain, the Emperor dreamed that he saw His Majesty the late Emperor standing at the foot of the step before his throne, wearing an expression of extreme displeasure, indeed glaring at him, as it seemed, with an angry and astonished eye. The Emperor having assumed an attitude of respectful attention, the apparition proceeded to deliver a long discourse, part of which was concerned with Genji's present plight. The Emperor was very much frightened, and being in any case somewhat uneasy at Genji's prolonged absence, he hastened to communicate his dream to Kokiden. She was not at all sympathetic. "These stormy nights are very disturbing," she said. "It is quite natural that you should have had bad dreams; the rain alone would have accounted for it. You must not allow such trifles to upset you." About this time the Emperor began to suffer from a pain in his eyes. Remembering his dream, he could not get out of his head the idea that this pain was in some way caused by the wrathful glance of the apparition which had rebuked him. His sufferings became more and more acute, despite the fact that continual services of intercession were held both in the Palace and at Kokiden's house.

Next came the death of Kokiden's father, the Grand Minister of the Right. There was nothing unexpected in this, for he had reached a very great age. But coming as it did on top of various other public calamities it caused widespread consternation. Kokiden herself, though she had no definite malady, was also very far from well. As time went on she seemed gradually to lose strength. A general gloom spread over the Court. It was felt that if, as was alleged by his friends, Prince Genji had indeed been banished without any sufficient cause, the present misfortunes of the nation might well have been sent as punishment for this injustice. Again and again the Emperor thought of restoring Genji to his previous rank and appointments; but whenever he mentioned this project to Kokiden, that lady would answer: "To do so would be to incur the public charge of inconsequence and frivolity. He was banished and if, when less than three years have elapsed, he is suddenly recalled to the Capital, a pretty figure you and I shall cut in history!" She spoke with such fierce conviction that the Emperor was completely overawed. So the months went by, and meantime both he and Kokiden were gradually sinking under the burden of their respective maladies.

At Akashi, as frequently happens in autumn, heavy winds were blowing in the bay. Genji began to find the long evenings very monotonous and depressing. Sometimes he would allow the priest to come and talk to him, and in the course of one of these conversations Genji said: "I am longing for a little diversion. Could you not manage, without attracting too much attention, to bring your daughter here one day to see me?" It seemed somehow to be accepted that for Genji to pay a visit to the house on the hill was entirely out of the question. Unfortunately the lady herself was equally averse to making any move. She knew that gentlemen who visited the provinces on Government business would often take up with some wretched peasant girl and, for so long as they happened to be in the district, carry on a purely frivolous affair with her. The Lady of Akashi was convinced that Genji regarded her in just such a light. To accept his advances could only render her in the end more wretched than before. Her parents, she knew, were still clinging to the idea that all those long years of watchfulness and isolation had at last borne fruit. To them the inevitable disillusion would be a crushing blow. Her mind was quite made up; so long as this prince remained at Akashi she would continue to correspond with him, but further than that she would not go.

His name had been known to her for years past, and she had sometimes wondered whether it would ever fall to her lot to meet, even in the most superficial way, some such magnificent personage as he. Now, astonishing though it seemed, he was actually living a stone's throw away. She could not be said exactly to have met him, but she constantly caught glimpses of him, heard his inimitable zithern-playing, and knew, one way and another, all that there was to know about his daily comings and goings. That such a person should even be aware of her existence was more than, as an inhabitant of this remote fishing-town, she had any right to expect. As time went on it seemed to her less than ever possible that any closer relationship should be established between them. Meanwhile her parents were far less confident about the situation than she supposed. They felt that in their anxiety to see the prayers of half a lifetime at last fulfilled they had perhaps acted somewhat precipitately. If Genji did not after all seem to regard their daughter as "counting," her feelings would have been upset for nothing. True he was a great catch and was worth certain risks, but that only made it harder to lose him. They had an uneasy feeling that while they had been placing all their trust in "Gods whom no eye seeth" they had paid too little attention to the dispositions of the human beings for whose future they had schemed.

"A little music," said Genji to the old priest one evening, "would mingle pleasantly with the sound of these autumn waves. It is only as a background to music that the sound of the sea is tolerable."

The time for action had come. The old priest looked in his calendar, chose a lucky day, and despite the misgivings of his wife began to prepare the house on the hill for Genji's visit. Not even to his most intimate acolytes and disciples did he explain the object of these elaborate preparations. The visit was to take place on the thirteenth day of the month. It turned out to be a resplendent moonlit night. The old man came to Genji's room and recited the line: "Is this a night to lose?" Genji at once understood that this was an invitation to the house on the hill. Suddenly what had seemed impossible became perfectly simple. He set his cloak to rights and left the house. His host had provided him with a magnificent coach, but the narrow lanes would have made its use inconvenient and Genji preferred to go on horseback. He was accompanied only by Koremitsu and one or two of his other trusted servants. The house stood a little way back from the shore and while he climbed to it he was all the time looking down over the bays that spread out on every side. He remembered the verse: "Would that to one who loves what I love I now might show it, this moon that lies foundered at the bottom of the bay!" For the first time since he had agreed to set out upon this excursion he remembered the lady at his palace far away, and at that moment he could hardly resist turning his horse's head and riding straight to the Capital. "O thou, my milk-white pony, whose coat is as the moon-beams of this autumn night, carry me like a bird through the air that though it be but for a moment I may look upon the lady whom I love!" So he murmured as he approached the house, which was thickly girt with an abundance of fine timber. It was indeed a house impressively situated and in many ways remarkable; but it had not the conveniences nor the cheerful aspect of the house on the shore. So dark and shut-in an appearance did it present as he drew near, that Genji soon began to imagine all its inhabitants as necessarily a prey to the deepest melancholy and felt quite concerned at the thought of what they must suffer through living in so cheerless a place. The Hall of Meditation stood close by and the sound of its bell blent mournfully with the whispering of the pine-trees that on the steep uneven ground grew precariously out of a ledge of rock, their roots clutching at it like some desperate hand. From the plantations in front of the house came a confused wailing of insect voices.

He looked about him. That part of the house which he knew to be occupied by the lady and her servants wore an air of festive preparation. Full in the moonlight a door stood significantly ajar. He opened it. "I wish to rest for a few minutes," he said; "I hope you have no objection to my coming in?" She had in fact the greatest objection, for it was against just such a meeting as this that she had resolutely set her face. She could not actually turn him away, but she showed no signs of making him welcome. He thought her in fact the most disagreeable young person whom he had ever met. He was accustomed to see women of very much greater consequence than this girl show at any rate a certain gratification at being thought worthy of his attentions. She would not, he felt, have dared to treat him so rudely but for the present eclipse of his fortunes. He was not used to being regarded so lightly, and it upset him. The nature of the circumstances was obviously not such that he could carry off the situation with a high hand. But though violence was out of the question, he would certainly cut a very ridiculous figure in the eyes of the girl's parents if he had to admit that she showed no signs of wanting to be acquainted with him. He felt embarrassed and angry. Suddenly one of the cords of the screen-of-state behind which she was sitting fell across her zithern, making as it did so a kind of casual tune. As she bent over the instrument he saw her for an instant just as she must have looked before his entry had made her stiffen; just as she must look when carelessly and at ease she swept an idle plectrum over the strings. He was captivated. "Will you not even play me something upon this zithern of which I have heard so much?" he added, and he recited the poem: "Were it but from your zithern that those soft words came which your lips refuse, half should I awaken from the wretched dream wherein I am bemused." And she: "A night of endless dreams, inconsequent and wild, is this my life; none more worth telling than the rest." Seen dimly behind her curtains she recalled to him in a certain measure the princess[*] who was now in Ise. It was soon evident that though she had answered his poem she was no nearer than before to treating his visit as otherwise than an impertinence. She had been sitting there so comfortable and happy, when suddenly this tiresome person burst in upon her without apology or warning. However, the remedy lay in her own hands, and rising to her feet she fled into a neighboring closet, fastening the door behind her with ostentatious care. You might have supposed that this was the end of the matter, for she had evidently no mind to return, nor he any intention of forcing bolts and bars. Curiously enough, however, this was not the end of the matter. The

---

[*] Rokujo.

difficulties that ensued may well be imagined if we remember the lady's unusual shyness and pride. Suffice it to say that from this night's meeting, which seemed at first to have been forced upon him by chance and other people's intrigues, sprang an intimacy which was grounded in the deepest feeling. The night, generally so long and tedious at Akashi, passed on this occasion all too quickly. It was essential that he should leave unobserved, and at the first streak of dawn, with many last endearments and injunctions, he crept stealthily from the room. His next day's letter was sent very secretly, for he was haunted by the fear that some story of this adventure might find its way back to the Capital. The lady for her part was anxious to show that she was to be trusted, and deliberately treated Genji's messenger without ceremony of any kind, as though he were bound on some errand of merely domestic import. He paid many subsequent visits to the house on the hill, always with the greatest secrecy. Unfortunately the way there led nowhere else, and knowing that fisher-folk are notorious gossips he began to fear that his addiction to this particular road would be noticed and commented upon. His visits now became far less frequent, and the lady began to think that her early fears were soon to be fulfilled. The old priest's thoughts were, if the truth must be told, for the time being much more frequently occupied with the coming of Genji than with the coming of Amida.* He could not make out what had gone wrong, and was in a terrible state of agitation. To make matters worse he knew that such earthly considerations ought to leave him quite unmoved and he was ashamed to discover how little his pious observances had availed to render him indifferent to the blows of fortune.

Genji would not for all the world have had the news of his latest adventure reach Murasaki as a piece of current gossip, even though it were represented in the most harmless light. Her hold upon him was indeed still strong as ever, and the mere idea of such a story reaching her, of her feeling that she had been superseded, of a possible quarrel or estrangement, filled him with shame and dismay. She was not indeed given to jealousy; but more than once she had shown plainly that his irregularities, so far from passing unobserved, were indeed extremely distressing to her. How bitterly he now regretted those trivial gallantries, so profitless to him, yet to her so miserably disquieting! And even while he was still visiting the lady of the hillside, since there was no other way of quieting his conscience concerning Murasaki, he wrote to the Nijō-in more frequently and more affectionately than ever before. At the end of one of these letters he added: "How it grieves me to remember the many occasions when I have spoilt our friendship for the sake of some passing whim or fancy in which (though you could not believe it) my deeper feelings were not

---

* Buddha.

at all engaged. And now I have another matter of this kind to confess, a passing dream, the insignificance of which you can guess by the fact that I tell you of it thus unasked. 'Though with the shining seaweed of the shore the fisherman a moment toys, yet seeks he but assuagement of a sorrow that long ere this has filled his eye with burning tears.'"

Her answer showed no resentment and was couched in the tenderest terms. But at the end, in reference to his disclosure, she wrote: "As regards the 'dream' which you could not forbear telling me, I have experience enough in that direction to enable me to draw several conclusions. 'Too downrightly, it seems, have I obeyed it, our vow that sooner would the Isle of Pines by the sea-waves be crossed…'" But though her tone was good-humored, there was in all her letter an undercurrent of irony, which disturbed him. He carried it about with him for a long while and constantly re-read it. During this time his secret nocturnal excursions were entirely abandoned, and the Lady of Akashi naturally imagined that all her fears had now come true. He had amused himself to his fill and had no longer any interest in what became of her. With no support, save that of parents whose advanced age made it improbable that they could much longer be of any assistance, she had long ago given up hope of taking her place in the world with those of equal rank and attainments. But she did now bitterly regret the waste of all those empty months and years during which she had been so conscientiously guarded and kept—for what? At last she had some experience of the usages which prevailed in the "grand world" outside, and she found them even less to her liking than she had anticipated. She indulged however in no outburst of spleen or disappointment, nor in her letters did she ever reproach him for his long absence. He had indeed as time went on become more and more attached to her, and it was only his desire to be able to allay the anxiety of one who had after all a prior claim upon him that induced him to suspend his visits to the lady on the hill. Henceforward his nights at Akashi were again spent in solitude.

He amused himself by making sketches upon which he afterwards scribbled whatever thoughts happened to be passing through his mind. These he sent to Murasaki, inviting her comments. No method of correspondence could have been better calculated to move and interest her. The distance between them seemed in some sort to have been annihilated. She too, at times when she was feeling out of spirits or at a loss for employment, would also make sketches of the scenes around her, and at the same time she jotted down all that was happening to her day by day in the form of a commonplace book or diary.

What, she wondered, would she have to write in her diary? And he in his?

The New Year had come. At the Palace nothing was now talked of save the Emperor's illness, and the Court was full of restless speculation.

The only child of the present Emperor was a boy born to him by Princess Jokyoden, daughter of the new Minister of the Right. But he was only two years old and therefore of no particular account. The Heir Apparent, Fujitsubo's son, was also a minor. The Emperor was fully determined to resign the Throne to him at the earliest opportunity, but should he do so it would be necessary to appoint a regent. There were so few people to whom it would be in any way possible to entrust the affairs of government that it seemed a pity Genji should be out of the running. His presence was indeed becoming in every way more and more imperative, and at last the Emperor decided to recall him, whether Kokiden approved or not. Since the end of the year her illness had taken a more serious turn.* The Emperor too—although for a time thanks to the immense efforts made on his behalf in consequence of certain disastrous omens which had engendered something in the nature of a natural panic, although for a time his eyes showed some improvement—was soon in as bad a way as ever, and feeling very uncertain of the future, he dictated an edict in which Genji was commanded to return to the Capital by the end of the seventh month. That sooner or later there would be a turn in his fortunes Genji had always been convinced. But the shortness and uncertainty of life made him little inclined to settle down quietly and wait for events to take their course. This swift recall came therefore as an intense relief. And yet, for one reason at any rate, he was by no means anxious to leave the coast so soon. The priest too had never expected that Genji would be with him very long; but the news of his immediate departure came as something of a shock. However, it was a consolation to feel that Genji was now definitely re-embarking upon the path of prosperity, and that his partiality, should it continue, would be in the future even more valuable than before. Genji now began again to visit the upper house almost every evening. Since the beginning of the sixth month the Lady of Akashi had been slightly indisposed and it was now certain that she was with child. No sooner had a definite term been put to their friendship than Genji's feeling for her redoubled: surely in those last days she was more charming than she had ever been before! Here indeed, rash though his courtship had been, was one whom under no circumstances he would ever feel that he had loved and cherished beyond her deserts! She for her part sat in absolute silence before him, lost in her own thoughts. Poor soul, he could not blame her.

When three years ago he had set out so reluctantly upon that miserable journey to Suma, his only consolation had been to imagine the joy and excitement with which on some far distant yet inevitable day he would retrace his steps to the City. Now that day had come, and to

---

* There is some doubt about the punctuation of this and the following sentence.

be returning was indeed very pleasant. But all the while, mingled with delightful anticipations, was the strange fear that he might never be able to revisit the place of his banishment! His servants however were all in high spirits, and this, combined with the bustle of numerous friendly deputations from the Capital, created an atmosphere of general liveliness and excitement, despite the obvious depression that all these signs of departure brought to the host under whose roof the numerous visitors were lodged. The seventh month had begun, and the summer weather was even more delightful than usual. Why, wondered Genji, was he, who took such pleasure in quiet and harmless pursuits, doomed on every occasion to find himself involved in the most harrowing and disastrous situations? It had not indeed escaped the notice of those who knew him best that a fresh complication, of the kind they already knew only too well, had arisen in his life. For several months on end he had never once mentioned the lady's name, and they began to hope that the affair had run its course. But the curiously subdued state of his spirits on the very eve of departure told them only too plainly that this hope was premature. It was whispered that all this trouble had arisen from Yoshikiyo's indiscreet eloquence upon the occasion when after Genji's cure they had climbed the mountain summit and looked down towards the western seas.* Yoshikiyo himself, as indeed he had every reason to be, was very much irritated by the whole affair.

Two days before his departure Genji visited the house on the hill some hours earlier than was his wont. He had never before seen the lady by full daylight, and her beauty astonished him. Such dignity of bearing, such an air of proud decision he had not in the least expected. This fresh discovery of her, this last-hour revelation filled him with new longings and regrets. Must he lose her? Could not some excuse be formed for bringing her to the Capital, for installing her at Court? And to ease his feelings he began to discuss with her the wildest plans as though they had been perfectly simple and practicable.

The austerities which he had practiced during the earlier days of his exile had left him still looking somewhat worn and thin. Yet such was his beauty that while, touched by her misery, he sat beside her and with tears in his eyes whispered the tenderest words of pity and endearment, for a moment she felt that even if there had been but one such night as that and after it he had disappeared forever, she would still feel his love for her to have been the greatest happiness of her life.

But for all his kindness he was a prince—the inhabitant of a world peopled not by creatures like herself, but by a remote and superior order

---

* See Part I, pp. 82 *seq*. Some texts call Yoshikiyo "Yoshizane," as I have done in Part I. See above p. 237.

of beings. Such was the thought that even at moments like this would obtrude itself with painful persistency. Oddly enough, though the promise that she would play to him had been the excuse for his first visit, she had never once touched her zithern since he had known her. For this he had often scolded her, and now he determined to make a last attempt. "Will you not play one small tune, so that I may carry it away in my head to remember you by," he said, and sent to the lower house for the zithern which he had brought with him from the Capital. He tuned it with special care, and the few chords that he struck while he did so floated with a strange distinctness through the still midnight air. The old priest heard these sounds, and unable to contain himself came bustling round to the women's quarters with his Chinese zithern in his arms and deposited it in the room where his daughter was receiving her guest. Then he discreetly withdrew. Genji now renewed his entreaties and at last she could resist no longer. He guessed at once, by the way that she handled and tuned the instrument, that she would prove to be a remarkable performer. Lady Fujitsubo used generally to be considered the best zithern player of the day, and though the applause of the fashionable world was in part a tribute to her rank and beauty, she was without question a very fine musician. But the Lady of Akashi, in addition to a complete command of her instrument, played with an intensity of feeling and a power of expression utterly unknown to the princess. Such indeed was her playing that even he, who could now so seldom get from music a pleasure that he had not experienced many times before, was utterly taken aback. He could have listened forever, and his only regret was that he had not forced her to play to him months ago. Of course he must not lose her! And handing to her his own zithern he begged her to keep it for him till they should play together again. She answered with an acrostic poem in which she prophesied that this loan was likely to remain forever on her hands. And he, in indignation—"Steadfast am I as the middle strings* of this my zithern that I leave with you until we meet." "Who knows that it may not be soon," he added. "Perhaps before these very strings have fallen out of tune." Thus he sought to comfort her; but to her mind one thought only was present—that he was going away. She began to sob bitterly.

On the day of his departure he was up long before sunrise. The setting out of so large a party (for the house was now full of friends who had come to escort him back to the City) occasioned a tremendous bustle. Genji too was much preoccupied, but in the midst of these distractions he found time to send her a message: "Because they have left the sea behind them, the rising waves creep listlessly across the sand. But I, a sinking wave, cast back disconsolate thoughts towards the shore whence I retreat."

---

* Which remained unaltered whatever tuning was adopted.

And she: "My cabin by the shore the winds have sheltered, and gladly now amid the receding wreckage of the storm would I drift out to sea." His friends from the Capital noticed that he was in great distress, and could only suppose that, despite the untoward circumstances which had brought him to this place, he had in the course of years become so attached to it that the actual moment of parting was somewhat of a wrench. But they could not help thinking that such a display of emotion was very excessive. On the other hand Yoshikiyo and the rest saw their worst fears confirmed. This was evidently a serious business, and they foresaw all kinds of complications that might arise from it. These gentlemen were delighted to be going home, but when it came to the actual moment of departure they felt a certain regret at leaving this extremely agreeable coast, and there were naturally many among them who had on their own account to face somewhat painful scenes of farewell. Many affecting poems were written and tearful speeches made; but what use would it be to record them all?

In his preparations for the departure of the travelers the old priest had surpassed himself. For every single person connected with the expedition, down to the humblest carriers and menials, the most sumptuous equipment was provided. It was indeed hard to imagine how in these few weeks such elaborate preparations could possibly have been made. The arrangements for Genji's own comfort were of the most extraordinary ingenuity; in fact the luxuries forced upon him filled so many boxes that it required quite an army of porters to carry all his luggage. Genji was indeed equipped more like a traveler setting out from the Capital than like one returning from the provinces. There seemed to be no imaginable contingency which the old priest had not thought of. To the travelling cloak which had been specially designed for that day's journey the Lady of Akashi attached the poem: "That this cloak of travel, cut and folded by the salt seashore, should bear a stain or two of spray, you will not take amiss!" Despite the noise and confusion of departure, he found a moment in which to write the answer: "Though for a while I must wear it in remembrance, yet soon as certain days and months are safely passed, once more no garment shall divide us." This message he sent privately, and when he put on the new cloak he was at pains to tell those about him that it was a present from the old priest and worn at his especial desire. The cloak which he had previously been wearing he sent to the house on the hill, where for long afterwards the sight of it and the smell of the fair scent with which it was perfumed awakened tantalizing memories in those from whose thoughts he would in any case seldom have been absent.

The priest excused himself from accompanying the expedition even so far as the frontier of the province, saying that in his present state of grief and agitation he did not feel equal to so great an exertion. "Pray do not think me impertinent," he added, "but I ought perhaps to remind you… in fact, we none of us doubt for an instant… But quite at your own time and convenience, of course!" He did not dare go beyond these brief, disjointed hints; but Genji, so far from taking offence, was extremely sorry for the old man, who, it was evident, had taken the business to heart in the most unfortunate way. "There is now a particular reason why I should cherish and remember her," said Genji presently; "you may be sure that in a very little while I shall see to it that she has her due. To leave you all at such a moment grieves me more than I can say. But what would you have me do?" The lady herself was in a strange state of mind. She was still convinced that the difference in rank between them precluded any lasting union and was certain that in the long run she had no more chance of happiness at the City than she had if left behind here in the wilds. But when it came to his actually starting, she could not bear to be left behind. Try as she might, she could not control herself. His image perpetually haunted her and every effort to banish it ended in a wild fit of sobbing. "It would have saved the poor girl untold misery," said the mother, having in vain tried every means to distract her, "if this wretched business had never begun. And how unnecessary it all is! Nothing of the kind need ever have entered the child's head, but for the odious and perverse advice which certain people…" "Hold your tongue," the old priest said angrily. "This will all come right in the end; he has told me so himself. He knows about her condition and will do all that he can for her." "Come, child," he said, bringing her a basin of hot water in his own hands; "you must get up at once and let yourself be dressed. You really must not go on like this. It is terrible, you know, terrible," and he stood at the corner of the bed looking at her encouragingly. Not only the mother, but the girl's old nurse and most of the confidential servants were in a state of indignation against their master and went about saying that his misguided promptings had brought them all into this terrible trouble. But the old man's evident misery soon dismissed their anger. He went about muttering to himself: "To think that I should have waited all these years for a chance to do something that would help her! And just when I thought everything was going so well, I find I have only made the poor thing unhappy…"

So much did his mistake (for such he was now convinced that it was) afflict the old man that he became a little queer in the head. During the day he did little but doze; but at night he would suddenly get up and seated in an attitude of prayer would fumble with his hands as though he had forgotten even how to use his rosary. One night his disciples managed to persuade him to go for a walk in the moonlight. Mumbling prayers as he went and quite unaware of his surroundings he stumbled and fell headlong into the moat. He was soon fished out; but in falling he had caught his leg against a large stone and done himself considerable injury. During the illness which followed, his mind, strangely enough, seemed to be somewhat easier and he appeared to be worrying less about the unfortunate situation of his daughter.

Meanwhile Genji was on his homeward way. At Naniwa he halted to perform the customary ceremony of Purification. He did not on this occasion go to the Shrine of Sumiyoshi himself but sent a messenger to inform the authorities that he was intending to perform his devotions there quietly on some future occasion. He was now travelling so hurriedly and with so large a retinue that a personal visit was impossible. Apart from the halt at Naniwa he made no unnecessary discursions or digressions, but pressed on with all possible speed to the Capital.

Upon his arrival the Nijo-in presented an extraordinary spectacle. The friends who had accompanied him on the journey were here joined by numerous others who had awaited him in the City. All of them now surged in wild excitement through the Palace, some hurraying lustily, some weeping with joy, and the scene soon became one of indescribable noise and disorder.

And now Murasaki, who at the moment of his departure had vowed in her poem that "could it but purchase an hour of respite, life itself was a price she would not grudge to pay," was glad that the gift which in her despair she had bartered so lightly had not indeed been taken from her!

In these three years she had grown even handsomer than before. At first he could not make out in what way it was that her appearance was altered. But when they were alone together he noticed that her hair, which even before he went away had begun to be almost too thick, had been cleverly thinned out. He had to confess that this new way of wearing it became her very well. But suddenly, while he watched her with fond satisfaction, the pleasant thought that she would always be near him was interrupted by a very different image. There rose before his mind the figure of the lady whom he had left behind in that sad mansion above the bay. Plainly as though she were with him he saw her loneliness, her misery, her despair. Why was it that time after time he of all people should find himself in this odious position? Lest Murasaki should feel that things were passing through his mind which he must hide from her, he began telling her about the lady of the shore. But he took such evident pleasure in dilating upon this subject that his frankness had the effect of convincing her that the matter was a far more serious one than she had before supposed. "It is not for myself I mind,"* she quoted, only half meaning him to understand. How terrible that he had lost three whole

---

* "It is not for myself I mind; but since the Gods are just, for him who is forsworn I am indeed afraid." No. 38 of the *Hundred Poems;* it is by Lady Ukon, 10th century.

years of her company, and lost them, too, in punishment for those very infidelities which he would now have given so much to undo!

Soon after his return all his original titles were restored and he was accorded the rank of supernumerary President of Council; while his supporters were re-established in offices equivalent to those of which they had been deprived. Indeed so wide an amnesty was proclaimed that the Court soon wore the aspect of a withered tree that one spring morning suddenly begins to sprout again.

A message came summoning Genji to the Palace. Great excitement prevailed among the Court attendants. It seemed to them that he looked more handsome and flourishing than ever. Had he really spent the last three years under such harrowing conditions as rumor had reported? Among the gentlewomen present were some who had served the old Emperor his father and these old ladies, who had always taken his side, now pressed round him chattering and weeping. The Emperor had been somewhat nervous about this interview. Anxious to make a good impression, he had spent an immense while over his toilet. On this particular day he was feeling somewhat stronger; but for a long while he had been seriously out of health and he was looking sadly altered. They talked quietly till nightfall. It was the fifteenth day of the month. The weather was calm and fine and, as he sat in the moonlight, such a host of memories crowded to the young Emperor's mind that he shed a few tears. He was indeed at that time full of the darkest forebodings. "Nothing entertaining has happened here," he said at last. "I used to like it when you played to me; but of course it is a long time since you did that..." Genji answered with the poem: "For as many years as the leech-baby* could not stand upon its feet have I been set adrift upon the wide plains of the sea." The Emperor, who felt the sting of this allusion, skillfully parried the thrust with the verse: "Round the Palace Pillar† long enough have we played hide-and-seek; let us forget the rancor of wasted spring times that we in amity might better have employed."

After this visit Genji's first care was to perform the ceremonial Eight Readings of the Lotus Sutra in memory of his father the late Emperor. He next visited the Crown Prince and found him grown almost beyond recognition. The child was surprised and delighted to recover his old playmate, whom he perfectly well remembered. Genji was relieved to discover that the boy was unusually quick at his studies and promised, so far as could at present be judged, to make a very satisfactory successor to the Throne.

---

* The Royal Gods Izanagi and Isanami bore a leech-child; as at the age of three it could not stand they cast it adrift in a boat.

† After a sort of game of hide-and-seek round the Pillar of the Palace of Heaven these Gods met face to face and Izanagi exclaimed: "I have met a lovely maiden"; whereupon they became husband and wife and bore the leech-child.

His agitation upon being admitted to Fujitsubo was not indeed such as it would have been some years ago; but the meeting was an affecting one and they had much to discuss together. One thing I had almost forgotten: by one of the priest's servants who had come with them all the way to the Capital he sent a number of letters to Akashi, among them a long one to the priest's daughter, in which, as he was able to convey it to her secretly, he did his best, by dint of tender messages and allusions, to comfort and console her. In it was the poem: "At Akashi is all night spent* in weeping? And do the mists of morning hide the long-looked-for light of day?"

At last Lady Gosechi,† who silently and unknown to all the world had been grieving bitterly at Genji's exile, was able to relieve her feelings by taking action. It was natural and proper that she should write to congratulate him upon his recall. She did so, but left him to guess from whom the letter came. With it, was the poem: "A seafarer that with reluctant heart floated past Suma's shore would fain you saw her sleeve that since that day has never once grown dry." Her fine handwriting at once betrayed her and he replied: "With better cause might I make tearful plaint, to whom you steered so close, yet would not stay your course." Brief as their meeting had been, he still preserved the happiest recollections of it and this sudden reminder of her made him for a moment hope that their friendship might one day be renewed. But what was he thinking of! Now and henceforward there were to be no more frivolities of that kind. Thus he cautioned himself, and the result was that even the Lady at the Village of Falling Flowers received only a formal intimation of his return. To know that he was to be seen and not to see him was worse than his being utterly out of reach, and the poor lady was unhappier than ever now that he was again at the Nijo-in.

---

* *Akashi* means "spending the whole night."
† See p. 245.

The Flood Gauge

Since the night of his so vivid and disquieting dream, the late Emperor had been constantly in Genji's thoughts. He longed to succor his father's soul, weighed down as it was (if the words of that nightly apparition were indeed to be trusted) by a load of earthly sin. Now that he was back in the City he was anxious to lose no time, and the great ceremony of the Eight Readings, for which he had begun to make arrangements soon after his return, was duly carried out in the Godless Month.* The manner in which this function was attended showed that Genji had fully regained his former ascendancy.

Ill though she was, Kokiden still had sufficient interest in what went on about her to be furious at this recrudescence of a force which she confidently supposed herself to have annihilated. But the Emperor, much as he stood in awe of her, was now obsessed by the idea that if he again disobeyed the late Emperor's injunction some terrible calamity would overtake him. The feeling that he had successfully insisted upon Genji's recall quite braced him; and the pain in his eyes, which had till recently been very troublesome, now began to show signs of improvement. But he did not somehow feel that he was likely to be very much longer on the Throne. There were many matters which he desired to see satisfactorily settled while he was still capable of attending to them, and he constantly summoned Genji to the Palace to consult him upon the most confidential affairs of policy and state. In doing so he was but following his real inclination; this was very well understood in the country and the public at large was delighted to see the Emperor once more asserting himself.

As the time drew near when he intended to renounce the Throne, the Emperor became increasingly concerned with regard to the effect that this step would have upon Lady Oborozuki's career. "My poor grandfather, the late Chief Minister, is gone," he said to her one day; "and it does not look as though my mother† would be with us much longer. I myself have no intention of remaining on the Throne. I am afraid you will be left in a most tiresome position. I know that there is someone whom you have always liked better than me. But I do not think anyone could possibly

---

* Tenth month. The Shinto gods become inaccessible during this month; but the Buddhas are, apparently, still available.
† Lady Kokiden.

be more attached to you than I am, and it distresses me continually to think what will become of you when I am gone. Even if your former friend is willing to look after you again, however kind he is to you, I am quite certain he will take far less trouble about you than I do." The color rushed to her cheeks and her eyes filled with tears. He saw that he had wounded her and, moved to sudden pity by the spectacle of her humiliation and remorse, he forgot all her misdeeds and continued in a gentler tone: "What a pity that we have never had any children! I am sure you and he will have some later on, and it will be a pity that they are his and not mine, because they will only be commoners, you know." He went on for some while discussing what would happen after he was dead, her distress and remorse increasing at every word. Her charm was such that, despite his jealousy, the Emperor had grown steadily more attached to her in the years that had passed. But though his partiality had raised her to a position of undisputed pre-eminence at Court, she had not at any time been happy. At first she brooded incessantly upon Genji's comparative indifference towards her, but later, as her sense of responsibility increased, she marveled more and more at the childish recklessness which had led her into that miserable adventure and, besides destroying her own good name, had reacted so disastrously upon her seducer.

In the second month of the new year the Initiation Ceremony of the Crown Prince was performed. He was only eleven years old but was big for his age, and it was already apparent that he was developing an extraordinary resemblance to his guardian, Prince Genji. In this the world saw nothing to complain of; their future monarch could not, they felt, have chosen a better model. But the Lady Abbess, his mother, watched the growing resemblance with very different feelings and could not but imagine that it was arousing the blackest suspicions.

The Emperor himself was greatly relieved to see that the boy was shaping so well, and he now began to prepare Lady Kokiden for the news that he intended to vacate the Throne. His actual resignation came suddenly, indeed before the end of the second month, and Kokiden was very much upset. To put matters right he assured her that his abdication had but one motive: namely, that he might be free to devote his poor abilities to looking after her. At this she was naturally somewhat mollified.

Fujitsubo's son accordingly became Emperor under the title Ryozen, and Lady Jokyoden's little son became Crown Prince. The new regime bore somewhat the character of a Restoration and was marked by a return to all the gaieties and festivities of the old Emperor's reign. From being President of Council, Genji became Palace Counselor; it was intended that he should fulfill the functions of Chief Minister, and it was only because the two ministerial posts were already filled that this less imposing title was given him. Genji however professed himself quite unable to cope with the duties of so arduous a function, and proposed that Aoi's father, the Minister of the Left, should be asked to assume control. But the old man pointed out that illness had long ago obliged him to forgo the executive part of his duties. Since then he had not grown any younger, and feared that his head was no longer clear enough to deal with complicated affairs. Genji replied that in the Other Land,* at times of change and uncertainty, even those who had retreated far away among the hills had sometimes been prevailed upon to return and lend their aid to a government that showed itself to be well-disposed. Nor had such men ever considered that their white hairs constituted a bar, but had come forward gladly to take office under the new regime. And indeed for doing so they had always been deemed true paladins of wisdom. "It is my desire," Genji concluded, "and that of the Council that you should resume the position which you held before your health obliged you to withdraw, and we feel that in doing so you may be sure of incurring no hostile criticism from any quarter." It was quite true that retired Ministers had sometimes been known to resume their functions. The old man withdrew his opposition and allowed them to make him Grand Minister with Plenary Powers. He was now sixty-three. Since the decline of his public influence, his whole family had lived very much under a cloud. But now that he was again in the ascendant they began to resume their old place in society. His sons were soon once more entrusted with positions of great importance; in particular, To no Chujo became Privy Counselor of the Second Class. Chujo's daughter, who was now twelve years old, was being trained for the Court, whither she was to be sent as soon as she was old enough. The boy who had sung the Ballad of Takasago so prettily some years ago, was already installed as one of the Emperor's pages and was thought to be doing very well. Besides these he had a number of other children, all of them very promising, and Genji, whose exiguous progeny was of small comfort to him, quite envied Chujo the size and prosperity of his young family.

Yugiri, Genji's son by Aoi, was a fine little fellow. He was already attached to the suite of the new Crown Prince. The princess, Aoi's mother, remained entirely unmoved by the renewed good fortunes of her husband and family. Indeed, this return to happier days only served to awaken fresh memories of the daughter whose loss had marked the beginning of all their troubles. Her one consolation had been that by her death Aoi had been spared the torture which Genji's disgrace and banishment would have inflicted upon her proud and fastidious nature. Now that he was restored to his former glories not even this consideration remained valid. Genji continued to show her the same attentions as before his exile and lost no opportunity of going over to the Great Hall.

---

* China.

Yugiri's old nurse and other members of the household had during all these years remained faithfully at their posts, and Genji contrived, in one way and another, to show each of them how much he appreciated her patience and fidelity. The recipients of these small favors were in a state of rapturous gratitude and delight.

He was also deeply touched by the conduct of the gentlewomen at the Nijo-in, in whom he had formerly shown so little interest. He determined henceforward to take more pains about them. He soon found himself so much occupied in paying small attentions to Miss Chujo, Madam Nakatsukasa and other good ladies of his household, that he scarcely ever had time to leave the house. He was also much taken up with the rebuilding of a lodge which stood to the east of his palace, on an estate which had belonged to his father. He took great trouble over the work and had the place put in splendid order, for it was his intention to lend it to unfortunate or unprotected persons, such as the lady at "the village of falling flowers," whom he could best assist if he had them near at hand.

Meanwhile he often wondered how the Lady of Akashi was faring, but he was at this time so much occupied both with private and national affairs that he could not get news of her as often as he would have liked to do. He reckoned that her delivery was likely to take place early in the third month, and about that time he contrived to send a secret courier to Akashi and learnt that the event had already taken place sixteen days ago. It was a girl, and everything had gone well. This was Genji's first daughter, and he felt quite excited. But how callous he had been to let her go through all this alone! Why had he not brought her with him to the City and looked after her while this was happening? He felt, indeed, a sudden outburst of tenderness towards her and of remorse at his own hardness of heart.

Astromers had once told him that he would have three children, of whom the eldest and youngest would eventually ascend the Throne, while the middle one would rise to be Chief Minister. They had further said it would be the lowest-born of the three mothers who would give birth to the future Empress. All that had happened so far fitted in very well with their prognostications. The prophecy that his children would attain Imperial rank and lead the Government of the country had been repeatedly made by sign-readers of all kinds; but during the difficult times from which Genji had just emerged it appeared to be wildly improbable that any of these hopes would be fulfilled. But now the safe accession of Ryozen to the Throne made him feel that everything would happen as the soothsayers had foretold. That he himself was not destined to achieve such honors had been generally recognized and he had long ago given up regarding such a thing as within the bounds of possibility. So well had this been recognized by his father, the old Emperor, that although Genji was his favorite son he had given special instructions that he was to remain a commoner. As regards Ryozen, it was not of course recognized in the world that His Majesty was Genji's son; but that, after all, did not in any way invalidate the truth of the sign-readers' prognostications.

But if this new child were really going to be empress it seemed almost disrespectful to have allowed her to be born at so strange a place. He must make amends to this future sovereign, and that he might soon be able to lodge both mother and child in proper comfort, he ordered his bailiffs to push through the rebuilding of the eastern lodge as rapidly as possible.

It occurred to him that it would be very difficult for her to secure a suitable wet-nurse at Akashi. He chanced to hear of a young woman, a child of the old Emperor's Lady-in-Attendance, who had recently, under distressing circumstances, been left with an infant on her hands. Both the Lady-in-Attendance and her husband, who had been one of the Royal Chamberlains, were dead, and the girl had been left entirely to her own devices; with the result which I have mentioned above. His informant undertook to interview the girl and, if possible, persuade her to take service at Akashi. She did not in point of fact need very much persuasion. She was young and thoughtless and thoroughly tired of sitting all day in a large tumble-down house with nothing to do but stare in front of her. She could not imagine any service which she would better like to enter than his, and at once agreed to go. Genji was of course delighted; though he felt somewhat uncomfortable at sending away a young girl to a place where she would enjoy so few distractions. There were certain matters which it was necessary to talk over with her, and in complete secrecy, with many precautions against his absence being noticed at home, he contrived to visit the young woman's house. She did not actually withdraw her consent; but she was now feeling very nervous about the whole business. Genji, however, took so much trouble in explaining to her what she had to do and in removing all her doubts and apprehensions that in the end she put herself entirely at his disposal. It happened to be a lucky day, and with many apologies for giving her so little time he asked her to get ready for the journey. "It seems very hard," Genji said, "that you should be packed off to the country like this to look after someone else's child. But I am particularly anxious that someone should be there. I know by experience that it will be rather dull; but you must make up your mind to put up with it for a time, just as I did." Having thus encouraged her, he gave a detailed description of the place and all that belonged to it.

She had sometimes done service at the Palace and this was not the first time Genji had seen her. But her misfortunes had brought her very low and she looked years older than when he saw her last. The house was in a hopeless state of disrepair and its vast size, together with the carefully planned copses and avenues which surrounded it, made the place only the more depressing. How had she contrived to hold out there so long? His sympathy was aroused. The charm of youth had not after all entirely deserted her, and she was intelligent. He felt inclined to prolong the interview and said laughing: "Now that it is all arranged I feel quite sorry that you have agreed to go. What do you feel about it?" She felt indeed that if she were destined to enter Genji's service at all, it would have been agreeable to find herself consigned to a rather less remote part of his household. He now recited the verse: "Can this one moment of farewell indeed have been the sum of all our friendship, whose separation seems now like the parting of familiar friends?" Smiling she answered him: "Your chagrin, I suspect, is not that I must leave you, but springs from envy that *I* not *you* should go whither your heart is set." Her quickness delighted him and, whatever truth there may have been in her ironic exposure of his feelings, he was really sorry that she was going.

He sent her as far as the boundary of the City in a wheeled carriage,* under the care of his most trusted personal servants, upon whom he had enjoined absolute silence concerning this affair. Among the baggage was a vast number of presents, from the Guardian Sword† down to the most trifling articles such as might possibly be useful to the Lady of Akashi at this crisis; upon the young nurse too he lavished every small attention which his ingenuity could devise, determined to mitigate so far as was possible the discomfort of her long journey. It amused him to picture to himself the extravagant fuss which the old priest, at all times so comically preoccupied with his daughter's fortunes, must be making in this latest crisis. Not but what he was himself filled with the tenderest concern for the Lady's welfare. Above all, he must not let her feel at such a minute that there was now or ever could be any obstacle to his fulfilling the promises concerning which she herself had always been so skeptical, and in the letter which he now sent he spoke in the most definite manner of his intentions towards the child and his plans for her future life at the Capital.

The travelers proceeded as far as the borders of Settsu by boat, and thence on horseback to Akashi with all possible speed, where their arrival was welcomed by the old recluse with boundless gratitude and delight. With raised hands he solemnly made obeisance in the direction of the Capital, and the mother and child, marked henceforward with this new and unhoped-for sign of princely favor, became invested in his eyes with an almost alarming degree of sanctity. The child was indeed a most exquisite creature, and the young nurse felt, from the moment it was presented to her, that Genji's care and anxiety on its behalf were by no means ill-bestowed. In an instant the discomforts and perils of her long journey

---

* As opposed to a Sedan-chair. A carriage drawn by oxen is meant; this was a great luxury.

† Used at the birth-ceremonies of a Princess.

seemed like an evil dream, from which she had suddenly awaked to find this pretty and enticing infant lying in her arms. Henceforward she had no thought but how best to tend and succor it.

The mother, it seemed, had for many months past been in very low spirits. Her confinement had left her in a condition of extreme weakness, and she was herself convinced that she would not recover. These fresh tokens of Genji's affection and concern could not fail somewhat to revive her. For the first time she raised her head from the pillows and received the messengers with every sign of interest and delight. They informed her that they had been ordered to return to the Capital without a moment's delay. She contrived to write a few hasty lines, in which little indeed could appear of all that at that moment she was thinking and feeling. Yet these few words made an impression upon their recipient the violence of which surprised and disquieted him.

He had not himself told Murasaki about the birth of his child at Akashi, nor was it likely that anyone else would in so many words have done so. But he feared that some inkling of the matter might reach her, and he finally made up his mind that it would be better for her to know all about it. "I had far rather that this had not happened. It is all the more irritating because I have for so long been hoping that you would have a child; and that, now the child has come, it should be someone else's instead is very provoking. It is only a girl, you know, which really makes it rather a different matter. It would perhaps have been better from every point of view if I had left things as they were, but this new complication makes that quite impossible. I think, indeed, of sending for the child. I hope that when it arrives you will not feel ill-disposed towards it." She flushed: "That is just the sort of thing you always used to say," she answered. "It seems to me to show a very strange state of mind. Of course I ought to put up with it, but there are certain things which I do not see how I can be expected to get used to…" "Softly, softly," he answered, laughing at her unwonted asperity, "who is asking you to get used to anything? I will tell you what you are doing. You are inventing all sorts of feelings for me such as I have never really had at all, and then getting cross with me for having them. That is not a very amiable proceeding, is it?" And having gone on in this strain for some while, he became quite cheerful.

She thought of how they had longed for one another during the years of his exile, of his constant letters and messages. This whole affair at Akashi—what had it been but a pastime, a momentary distraction in the midst of his disappointments and troubles? "You will understand then," Genji continued, "that I was anxious to hear how things were going on. I sent to enquire and have just heard that everything is still as well as one can hope for. But if I start telling you about it now I know we shall soon be at cross purposes again…" "She is of course very charming," he added presently, "but I think my feeling for her had a good deal to do with the place and the circumstances…" He began to describe how exquisitely the smoke from the salt-kilns had tapered across the evening sky; he spoke of the poems which they had exchanged, of his first glimpse of her by night, of her delightful playing on the zithern. Upon all these themes he enlarged with evident satisfaction. Murasaki while she listened could not but remember how particularly unhappy she had been just at the very time when the episodes which Genji was now recalling with such relish were taking place at Akashi. Even if this affair were, as he represented it to be, a mere pastime of the moment, it was clear that he had been singularly successful in his search for distraction. "Come," he said at last, "I am doing my best to show you that I am fond of you. You had best be quick, if you are ever going to forgive me at all; life does not last forever. Here am I trying so hard just now not to give you the slightest cause for one speck of jealousy or suspicion. And now just because of this unfortunate affair…" So saying he sent for his large zithern and tried to persuade her to play it with him as they were used to do. But Murasaki could not help remembering his enthusiasm for the playing of the Lady at Akashi. With such virtuosity she did not care to compete, and say what he would he could not persuade her to play a note.

It sometimes happened that her usual good temper and gentleness would thus all at once desert her, giving place to a fit of wild jealousy and resentment. To Genji these outbursts were by no means unattractive.

It occurred to him that the fifth day of the fifth month would be the fiftieth day of the child's life, and he knew that his absence from the Prayers which would be held on that day would be extremely painful to the mother. If only he had them with him in the Capital, what a delightful affair he could make of this Fiftieth Day Ceremony! It was really too bad that a daughter of his should have come into existence in such an outlandish place as this. He ought never to have allowed it. And this was his first daughter. If it had been a boy he did not think he would have minded nearly so much. But this girl seemed very important, for he felt that in a sense all his misfortunes had come to him as a preliminary to her birth, and had, if one could put it so, no other goal or object. He lost no time in sending a messenger to Akashi with strict injunctions to arrive there on the fifth day without fail. The messenger duly arrived, bearing with him the most touching and gratifying tokens of Genji's anxiety for the welfare of his friends. To the Lady of Akashi he sent an acrostic poem, lamenting that he should have left her to dwell, like the pine-tree that grows beneath the northern cliff, in a place of shadows, to which not even the rejoicings of the Fiftieth Day would bring an altering gleam. "My anxiety for you both," his letter continued, "is becoming too great a torment for me to bear. Things cannot go on like this and I have quite decided to bring you to the Capital. Do not however think that my care for you will end merely with that..." She told her father of Genji's decision, and this time at any rate the old man had good cause for that mixture of joy and weeping to which he was at all times prone. Looking round at Genji's Fiftieth Day presents which lay about in astonishing profusion she realized how dark a day this would have been for her but for the coming of this messenger from the City. As a second consolation she had for the first time, in the nurse whom Genji had sent to her, someone to whom she could confide the affairs of her heart, and this changed her whole life. Her father had gathered about her, picking them up one by one as opportunity offered, a collection of dames who, as regards birth and upbringing, were quite the equals of the new nurse. But the mountain solitudes of Akashi did not offer much scope for choice and the poor ladies were one and all the most tottering and antiquated relics of bygone Courts. Among them the new arrival felt incredibly brisk and smart and in this gloomy company her opinion of herself went up by leaps and bounds. She had endless stories about life at the Capital; and when these failed, she had only to describe some occasion at which Genji had figured or some incident showing the affection in which he was held or the extent of the power which he now wielded (subjects to which she continually returned with remarkable zest): at once the Lady of Akashi's cheeks would glow with pride. She ought indeed to be happy that such a Prince as this should deign even to undo and abandon her, leaving nothing to show for their love save the child that had been begotten of it. The nurse was allowed to read Genji's letters, and though she did so with passionate interest, she could not but feel somewhat jealous of her mistress's strange and unforeseen good fortune. At such times it would seem to the nurse that to her alone of all mankind nothing good ever happened, till suddenly in Genji's letter she would come across some reference to herself: "What about the nurse? How is she turning out?" and so forth, or sometimes even more personal enquiry about her health and spirits. Then for a long while the girl, usually so despondent, would feel perfectly happy and contented.

To Genji's Fiftieth Day letter the Lady of Akashi sent the following reply: "Alas that to the little crane who calls to you from among the numberless islands of the deep, you do not come, though the Fiftieth Day* be come." "I am for a thousand reasons," she continued, "in great despondency concerning our future; and for that very reason occasional kindnesses such as you have today shown to me are all the more precious. As for myself I do not rightly know what will become of me. But I

---

* *Ika*—Fiftieth Day; but also "Why do you not come?"

earnestly hope that our daughter at any rate may live to be a consolation to you rather than an embarrassment and anxiety."

Genji carried this letter about with him and constantly re-read it half aloud to himself, pausing over every sentence with fond deliberation; Murasaki could not fail to notice his preoccupation and once, hearing him thus employed, she murmured the song: "Far from me have you drifted as those boats that, starting from Mikuma shore, now row far out at sea." She had not meant him to hear. But he looked up and said sharply: "Do you really think that it is so bad as that! I should have thought you would understand exactly what such a letter as this must mean to me. It is perfectly natural that I should be interested, deeply interested in an occasional budget of news from a place where I spent so long a time, and if in reading it I come across references which remind me suddenly of some interesting event or experience of those days, I think it is quite natural that I should occasionally break out into an exclamation, or something of that sort. It would be much better if you simply pretended not to hear. But here is the letter." He held it out to her, but in such a way that she could only see the outer fold upon which the address was written. Examining the writing she saw at once that it was a flawless hand, such as the greatest lady in the land would have had no cause to disown. From that moment she knew what was in store for her; this would assuredly prove no fleeting fancy.

In spite of these preoccupations his thoughts sometimes turned towards the Lady in the Village of Falling Flowers and he realized with dismay that he had not once been near her since his return to the Capital. For one thing, his new position in the Government had given him so much business to look after and was attended by formalities and restrictions which made it more than ever difficult for him to go about as he chose. Part of the fault however was certainly hers; for, inured to a life that offered few novelties or distractions, she was willing to accept without ill-temper or complaint such treatment as others would have found insufferable. But the fifth month at last brought him a little leisure. Once more he thought of his obligation, and this time he actually managed to slip away and make the long-deferred visit. It was a comfort that here at least he was certain of not being treated to any exhibition of fashionable tantrums, coquettishly withering glances or well-calculated resentment; for he knew that, seldom as she saw him, his interest in her was by far the most important fact in her life, and a visit from him was not lightly to be sacrificed to some useless outburst of jealousy or irritation.

The house had in these last years grown rapidly more and more dilapidated and had indeed become a most melancholy-looking place. After paying his respects to the elder sister he hastened to the main entrance of the western wing and stood in the porch. It was near midnight; the moon had sunk behind a bank of light clouds. It was with feelings of inexpressible joy and agitation that she suddenly saw his figure dimly outlined in the darkness. She had been sitting at the lattice and, in her shyness, did not rise when she saw him. They continued to converse thus, he in the porch and she at her window, but there was in her manner no hint of unfriendliness or reprobation. What a relief to encounter at last a disposition so grateful and unexacting! Some water-fowl were clamoring quite close to the house. She recited the verse: "Dare I admit you to a house so desolate that even the shy water-birds regard it as their home?" Her voice died away to a whisper as she reached the last words in a way which he found strangely alluring. What a lot of nice people there seemed to be in the world, thought Genji. And the odd part of it was that it was just this very fact which made life so difficult and fatiguing. He answered with the verse: "If the cry of the water-fowl brings you always so promptly to your door, *some* visitor there must be whom it is your pleasure to admit." This was of course mere word-play. He did not for a moment suppose that any such agreeable adventures ever fell to her lot; nor indeed that she would welcome them. For though she had had to wait years for this visit, he felt confident that her fidelity had never once wavered. She reminded him of his poem: "Gaze not into the sky..." and of all that had befallen at that farewell scene on the eve of his departure for Suma. "It seems strange," she said at last, "that I of all people should so much have minded your being away, considering how seldom I see you when you are here!" But even this was said with perfect gentleness and good humor. His reply to this charge was, you may be sure, both prompt and conciliatory, and it was not long before he had managed, by kindness of one sort or another, to make her, for the moment at any rate, as happy as it is possible for any woman to be.

He often thought during these days of Lady Gosechi, and would very much have liked to see her again; but the difficulties seemed too great and he did not attempt it. Her parents saw plainly enough that she had not got over her unfortunate attachment and did their best to settle her future in some other way. But she for her part declared she had given up all thought of lovers or marriage. "If only, I had some large convenient building," thought Genji, "where I could house these friends of mine and be able to keep an eye not only on them, but on any babies that might chance to get born, how much simpler life would be!" The new eastern wing was indeed promising to prove a very handsome affair and thoroughly in the style of the moment. He was impatient to get it finished, and now appointed special foremen to superintend the different branches of the work and get it put through as quickly as possible.

Not infrequently something would happen to remind him of the Lady Oborozuki and despite all that had happened a fresh wave of longing would beset him. She for her part had not only suffered but learnt her lesson and utterly refused to have any dealings with him, which made him feel very irritated and depressed. Now that the ex-Emperor Suzaku was relieved of the cares of Government, he became somewhat more animated and showed a certain amount of interest in music and other Court diversions. It was curious that among all his Ladies-in-Waiting and Ladies-of-the-Wardrobe it was to Lady Jokyoden, the mother of the Crown Prince, that he paid the least attention. Not even the singular chance which made her mother of the Heir Apparent seemed able to restore to her any particle of the ascendancy which she had lost when Lady Oborozuki was taken into favor. She had indeed left the Emperor's Palace and now lived in apartments attached to those of the Crown Prince, her son. Genji's rooms at Court were in the old Shigeisa; the Crown Prince was occupying the Nashitsubo, which was not far away. Thus Genji, as a near neighbor, was constantly consulted by the Prince's staff and was often able to be of considerable assistance to them.

As Fujitsubo had become a nun, her full rank could not be restored; but she received a Royal Grant equivalent to that of an Empress Mother,[*] together with the services of such State officers as usually wait upon an ex-Empress. The whole of these additional resources went in the celebration of those religious functions which had now become her whole employment in life. For many years she had felt that it was impossible for her to appear at Court and to her great distress her son, the present Emperor, had grown up a stranger to her. Now that he was safely on the Throne she could come and go as she pleased; and indeed her constant presence at Court now became the greatest grievance of her old rival Kokiden, who saw in it the frustration of all the schemes to which her whole life had been devoted. Genji bore Kokiden no malice and, without thrusting his services upon her, did what he could to help her. The fact that these magnanimous overtures were met with unrelenting hostility was observed by all at Court and made a most painful impression.

Prince Hyobukyo had treated Genji with marked coldness in the period before his exile. Now that Genji's fortunes were again on the ascendant he appeared anxious to renew their former friendship; but Genji felt little inclined to do so. That at a time when so many animosities were in abeyance and so many broken friendships had been renewed Genji and her brother should be on these very indifferent terms was to Fujitsubo a source of great disappointment and anxiety.

Power was now pretty equally divided between Genji himself and his father-in-law, the old Minister at the Great Hall. In the eighth month of this year To no Chujo's daughter came to Court. Her grandfather,

---

[*] The taxes paid by 2,000 households.

the old Minister, was a conspicuous figure at the Presentation and saw to it that the ceremony should lack no jot of its traditional grandeur. It was well known that Prince Hyobukyo would very much have liked to see his second daughter in a similar position. But Genji did not feel sufficiently friendly towards him to second this design, particularly as there were many other young ladies who were quite as well qualified to fill the post. Prince Hyobukyo saw nothing for it but to submit.

In the autumn Genji made his pilgrimage to the Shrine of Sumiyoshi, where, as will be remembered, he had various vows to fulfill. The occasion was made one of public importance and the splendor of his cortege, in which all the greatest noblemen and courtiers of the day vied with one another to take part, made a deep impression throughout the kingdom. The Lady of Akashi had been unable to pay her accustomed visit to the Shrine either last autumn or during the spring of this year. She determined to renew the practice, and it so happened that she arrived by boat at Sumiyoshi just as Genji's magnificent procession was passing along the shore. She saw throngs of servitors, laden with costly offerings; she saw the Eastern Dancers,* in companies of ten, riding by on horseback, men of picked stature, conspicuous in their strange blue-striped dress. Not a word concerning Genji's visit to Sumiyoshi had reached her, and turning to someone who was standing near she asked what procession this might be. "What procession?" the man exclaimed in astonishment. "Why, the Chief Minister's!" and a shout of laughter went up at the notion that there could possibly exist anybody in the world who had not heard of this all-important event, laughter in which a number of rough scalawags who were standing by joined as heartily as the rest.

She was confounded. That after all these long months of waiting it should be thus she met him showed indeed to what a different world he really belonged! Yet after all they were not quite strangers, he and she. She was at least of more account in his eyes than these wretches who had scoffed at her ignorance, than all this rabble who cared nothing for him and had come here only that they might boast of having shared in his triumph. How cruel an irony that she who thought of him and him only, who painfully gathered together every scrap of intelligence concerning his health and movements, should all unwittingly have chosen this disastrous day for her journey, while all the rest of the world resounded with the news of his coming; she hid her face and wept. The procession moved on its way—innumerable green cloaks, with here and there a scarlet one among them, bright as an autumn maple-tree amid a grove of pines. In cavalcade after cavalcade the varying colors flashed by, now dark,

---

* These men accompanied a Minister of State on pilgrimages to the great Shinto shrines, danced in front of the shrine and afterwards took part in horse-races round it.

now light.* Among the officers of the Sixth Grade there was one whose sheriff's coat of gold and green made him conspicuous; this was Ukon, the gentleman who upon the occasion of Genji's visit to the Imperial Tombs had recited the verse: "Little, alas, they heed their worshippers…"† He had become captain of the Quiver Bearers, and as such was attended by more numerous officers than any other of the sheriffs. Among these attendants was Yoshikiyo, who in a resplendent crimson cloak, worn with an air of the utmost nonchalance, was perhaps the handsomest figure in all the throng.

Here, prosperous and happy, were all the knights and gentlemen whom she had seen at Akashi; then a pitiable band, now scattered amongst a vast cohort of partisans and retainers. The young princes and courtiers who rode with the procession had vied with one another in the magnificence of their accoutrement. Such gorgeous saddles and trappings had rarely been seen; and it may be imagined how they dazzled the eye of a country girl, fresh from her hillside retreat. At last came Genji's coach. She could catch but a momentary glimpse of it; and of the face for which she yearned with so ardent a longing she could see nothing at all. Imitating the example of the great Toru‡ he was attended by boy outriders. They were charmingly dressed, their hair looped at the sides and tied with purple ribbons. The ten of them were arranged according to their height, and a very pretty sight they were as they filed past in their dainty costumes. A boy rode by, clad in the dress of a Court page, a person of some consequence evidently, for he was obsequiously watched over and assisted, while a posse of boy grooms; each differently dressed, yet forming between them a carefully designed pattern, rode in his train. She was told that this was Prince Yugiri, Genji's son by Lady Aoi. She thought of her own daughter for whom so different a fate seemed to be reserved, and in sad submission bowed her head towards the Shrine. The Governor of the Province had now appeared, his arrival being attended by greater pomp than had ever before marked his intercourse with a Minister on pilgrimage. The Lady of Akashi saw clearly that even should she succeed in forcing her way through the crowd, there was little chance that in the midst of all these excitements the God would pay any attention to her insignificant offering. She was on the point of going home again, since there seemed to be no object in staying any longer, when it occurred to her that she might at any rate row over to Naniwa and perform the ceremony of Purification. This she did, while Genji, still unaware that she had been so near him, spent the rest of the evening performing his vows within the Shrine.

---

* The higher officers wore cloaks of deeper hue, i.e. dipped more often in the dye and therefore more costly.

† See above, p. 235.

‡ For the extravagances of this statesman, see *Noh Plays of Japan*, p. 232.

At last, thinking that by now the God ought to be thoroughly content, Genji determined to enjoy himself a little into the bargain; and the rest of the night was spent by the whole company in the most lively fashion imaginable. Koremitsu and the rest made a mental note that for certain kinds of religious observance there was much to be said. It happened that Genji went outside for a little while and Koremitsu, who was with him, recited an acrostic verse in which he hinted that beneath the pine-trees of Sumiyoshi a less solemn stillness now prevailed than when the Gods first ruled on earth. This could not be denied, and indeed to Genji too a joyful time had succeeded to an age of sadness. He therefore answered with the verse: "That from wild waves whose onslaught drove me from my course this God delivered me, I shall not soon forget." Koremitsu then went on to tell him how the boat from Akashi, dismayed by the crowds that flocked the Shrine, had put out again to sea. He hated to think that she had been there without his knowing it; besides, he felt now that it was this very God of Sumiyoshi who had given her to him for a bride. He could not let her go back without a word from him to cheer her. To think that she had come and gone without his even hearing that she was at hand would certainly grieve her worst of all. But for the moment she had gone further up the coast and there was nothing to be done.

After leaving Sumiyoshi he visited several places in the neighborhood. At Naniwa he too underwent the ceremony of Purification, together with other ceremonies, particularly the Ablution of the Seven Streams. As he passed the estuary of Horiye he murmured, "Like the Tide-gauge at Naniwa...,"[*] hardly knowing why the lines had come into his head. Koremitsu, who was near his coach, overheard these words, and regarding them as a command to him to produce writing materials (a duty for which he was often in request) he whipped out a short-handled pen from the folds of his dress and as soon as Genji's coach came to a standstill handed it in to him. Genji was amused by his promptness and on a folded paper wrote the lines: "That once again our love to its flood-mark shall rise, what better presage than this chance meeting by the tide-gauge of the shore?" This he sent across to Naniwa by the hand of an underling who, from conversation with her servants, knew at what address she was to be found. Much as she had suffered at seeing him pass her by, it needed only this trifling message to allay all her agitation. In a flutter of gratitude and pride she indited the answer: "How comes it[†] that to the least of those who bide as pilgrims in this town you bear a love that mounts so high upon the flood-gauge of your heart?" She had that day been bathing in

---

[*] "As to the tide-gauge at Naniwa that now lies bare, so to our love the flood tide shall at last return."

[†] Pun on Naniwa, name of town and *nani wa* "How comes it?" Here and in the preceding poem there is also a play on *miozukushi* = tide-gauge, and *mi wo tsukushi* = "with all one's heart and soul."

the Holy Waters at the Shrine of Rain-coat Island; and she sent him her poem tied to a prayer-strip which she had brought from the Shrine. When the message reached Genji it was already growing dark; the tide was full, and the cranes along the river-mouth had with one accord set up their strange and moving cry. Touched by the beauty of the place and hour, he suddenly lost all patience with the crowds that surged around him. Could he but banish them all from his sight and find himself with only the writer of this diffident poem at his side!

The journey back to the City was enlivened by many excursions and entertainments, but all the while his thoughts continually returned to the strange coincidence of that unhappy meeting. Quantities of dancing girls had attached themselves to his retinue. Despite their total lack of sense or breeding, their company appeared to afford a vast deal of satisfaction to the hot-blooded young gentlemen who formed Genji's escort. This seemed to him very strange. One cannot enjoy beautiful scenery or works of art in the company of any but the right person; and surely if, in such matters as that, one is so easily put off by commonness or stupidity, it must make some difference *whom* one chooses as partner in these far more intimate associations. He could not indeed contrive to take the slightest interest in these creatures. They on their side quickly perceived that they were not being a success, and at once redoubled their efforts, with the consequence that he found them only the more repulsive.

Next day was marked a "good day" in the calendar, and Genji's party being safely on its way back to the Capital, the Lady of Akashi was able to return to Sumiyoshi and pursue her devotions in peace, now at last finding occasion to fulfill the many vows that had accumulated since her last visit to the Shrine. Her recent glimpse of Genji in all his glory had but increased the misgivings which day and night beset her: amid such surroundings as that it was impossible that so insignificant a person as herself should not rapidly sink into obscurity and contempt. She did not expect to hear from him again till he was back at Court. She was counting the days, when to her surprise a messenger appeared. In a letter, which had evidently been written during the journey, he named the actual date at which he should send for her to the City. Once more he sought to dispel all her doubts and anxieties; she could rely upon him implicitly; her position in his household would, he besought her to believe, be neither equivocal nor insecure. Nevertheless, she felt that she was embarking upon a perilous voyage under skies which, however promising an aspect they might now be wearing, might at any moment change to the threat of a hideous disaster. Her father too, when it came to the prospect of actually releasing her from his care, was exceedingly perturbed; indeed he dreaded her departure for the Capital even more than he had feared the prospect of her remaining forever buried in her rustic home. Her answer to Genji was full of reservations and misgivings concerning her fitness for the position which he promised her.

The retirement of the Emperor Suzaku had necessitated the appointment of a new Vestal at Ise, and Lady Rokujo had brought her daughter back again to the City. Genji had written the usual congratulations and this had given her immense pleasure; but she had no desire to give him the opportunity of once more distracting her as he had done in those old days, and she had answered only in the most formal terms. Consequently he had not, since her return, made any attempt to visit her. He did indeed make some vague suggestion of a meeting; but these hints were very half-hearted and it was a relief to him that they were not taken. He had recently decided not to complicate his life by outside relationships even of the most harmless kind: he simply had not time. And particularly in a case of this sort he saw no object in forcing his society upon someone who did not desire it. He was however extremely curious to see how the Vestal Virgin, now known as Lady Akikonomu, had grown up. Rokujo's old palace in the Sixth Ward had been admirably repaired and redecorated, and life there was in these days by no means intolerable. Rokujo herself had gifts of character and intelligence which the passage of years had not obliterated. Her own personality and the unusual beauty of many of her gentlewomen combined to make her house a meeting place for men of fashion, and though she was herself at times very lonely, she was leading a life with which she was on the whole by no means ill-contented, when her health gave way. She felt at once that there was no hope for her, and oppressed by the thought that she had for so long been living in a sinful place,* she resolved to become a nun. This news was a great blow to Genji. That he would ever again meet her as a lover, he had long felt to be impossible. But he thought of her as a friend whose company and conversation would always be among his greatest pleasures. That she should have felt it necessary to take this solemn and irrevocable step was a terrible shock, and on hearing what had happened he at once hastened to her palace. It proved to be a most harrowing visit. He found her in a state of complete collapse. Screens surrounded her bed; his chair was placed outside them, as near as possible to her pillow, and in this manner they conversed. It was evident that her strength was rapidly failing. How bitterly he now repented that he had not come to her sooner; had not proved, while yet there was time, that his passion for her had never expired! He wept bitterly, and Rokujo on her side, amazed to realize from the very intensity of his grief that during all the years when she had imagined herself to be forgotten, she had never been wholly absent from his thoughts, in a moment discarded all her bitterness, and seeing that

---

* A Shinto shrine, offensive to Buddha.

his distress was unendurable began with the utmost tenderness to lead his thoughts to other matters. She spoke after a while about her daughter, Lady Akikonomu, the former Virgin of Ise, begging him to help her on in the world in any way he could. "I had hoped," she said, "having cast the cares of the world aside, to live on quietly at any rate until this child of mine should have reached an age when she could take her life into her own hands…" Her voice died away. "Even if you had not mentioned it, I should always have done what I could to help her," answered Genji, "but now that you have made this formal request to me, you may be sure that I shall make it my business to look after her and protect her in every way that lies in my power. You need have no further anxiety on that score…" "It will not be so easy," she answered. "Even a girl whose welfare has been the sole object of devoted parents often finds herself in a very difficult position if her mother dies and she has only her father to rely upon. But your task will, I fear, be far harder than that of a widowed father. Any kindness that you show the girl will at once be misinterpreted; she will be mixed up in all sorts of unpleasant bickerings and all your own friends will be set against her. And this brings me to a matter which is really very difficult to speak about. I wish I were so sure in my own mind that you would *not* make love to her. Had she my experience, I should have no fear for her. But unfortunately she is utterly ignorant and indeed is just the sort of person who might easily suffer unspeakable torment through finding herself in such a position. I cannot help wishing that I could provide for her future in some way that was not fraught with this particular danger…" What an extraordinary notion, thought Genji. How could she have got such a thing into her head? "You are thinking of me as I was years ago," he answered quickly. "I have changed a great deal since then, as you would soon discover if you knew more about me…"

Out of doors it was now quite dark. The room where he was sitting was lit only by the dim glow that, interrupted by many partitions, filtered through from the great lamp in the hall. Someone had entered the room. He peeped cautiously through a tear in one of the screens which surrounded the bed. In the very uncertain light he could just distinguish Rokujo's form. Her hair was cropped, as is customary with novices before the final tonsure; but elegantly and with taste, so that her head, outlined against the pillows, made a delicate and charming picture. On the far side of the bed he could distinguish a second figure. This surely must be Lady Akikonomu. There was a point at which the screens had been carelessly joined, and looking through this gap he saw a young girl sitting in an attitude of deep dejection with her chin resting on her hand. So far as he could judge from this very imperfect view she was exceedingly good-looking. Her hair that hung loose to the ground, the carriage of her head, her movements and expression—all had a singular dignity and grace; yet despite this proud air there was something about her affectionate, almost appealing. But was he not already beginning to take just that interest in her person against which her mother had a few moments ago been warning him? He hastily corrected his thoughts. Lady Rokujo now spoke again: "I am in great pain," she said, "and fear that at any moment my end may come. I would not have you witness my last agonies. Pray leave me at once." This she said with great difficulty, her women supporting her on either side. "How glad I should have been," said Genji, "if my visit had made you better. I am afraid it has only made you worse. I cannot bear to leave you in such pain. Tell me what it is that hurts so much?" And so saying he made as though to come to her side. "Do not come to me!" she cried out in terror, "I am grown hideous; you would not know me. Does what I say seem to you very strange and disjointed? It may be that my thoughts wander a little, for I am dying. Thank you for bearing patiently with me at such a time. I am much easier in my mind now that, I have had this talk with you. I had meant to for a long time…" "I am touched," replied Genji, "that you should have thought of me as a person to whom you could confide these requests. As you know, my father the late Emperor had a very large number of sons and daughters; for my part, I am not very intimate with any of them. But, when his brother died, he also regarded Lady Akikonomu here as though she were his own child and for that reason I have every right to regard her as my sister and help her in just those ways which a brother might. It is true that I am a great deal older than she is; but my own family is sadly small,* and I could well afford to have someone else to look after…"

After his return he sent incessantly to enquire after her progress and constantly wrote to her. She died some eight days later. He was deeply distressed, for a long while took no interest in anything that happened and had not the heart to go even so far as the Emperor's Palace. The arrangements concerning her funeral and many other matters about which she had left behind instructions fell entirely upon him, for there was no one else to whom her people could apply. Fortunately the officers who had been attached to Lady Akikonomu's suite while she was at Ise still remained in her service and they were able to give her a certain amount of assistance. Before the funeral Genji called in person and sent in a note to the bereaved lady of the house. A housekeeper (one of the people from Ise) brought back word that her mistress was completely overwhelmed by her loss and could not reply to him. He sent in a second message reminding Lady Akikonomu that her mother had solemnly committed her to his care and begging her not to regard him as an alien intruder into her affairs. He then sent for the various members of the household

---

* Aoi's son Yugiri was his only acknowledged child.

and gave them their instructions. He did so with an air of confidence and authority which surprised those who remembered for how long he had absented himself from that house. The funeral was carried out with the utmost pomp, the bier being attended not only by her servants, but by all Genji's servants and retainers.

For a long while afterwards he was immersed in prayers and penances and but seldom emerged from the seclusion of a thickly curtained recess. To Lady Akikonomu he sent many messages of enquiry, to which she now answered in her own hand. She had at first been too shy to do so; much to the dismay of her old nurse, who explained to her that not to answer letters is considered very uncivil. One day as he sat watching the wild storms of sleet and snow that were sweeping in a confused blizzard across the land, he could not help wondering how Lady Akikonomu was faring in this rough weather and sent a messenger to her palace. "I wonder how you like this storm," he wrote, and added the poem: "I see a house of mourning; dark tempests threaten it, and high amid the clouds hovers a ghost with anxious wing." It was written on light blue paper tinged with grey; the penmanship and make-up of the note were indeed purposely intended to be such as would impress a young girl. So much did this elegant missive dazzle her inexperienced eye that she again felt utterly unable to reply, and it was only when one member of her household after another reproached her for such rudeness and ingratitude that she at last took up a sheet of heavily scented dark grey paper and in brushstrokes so faint as to be scarcely distinguishable wrote the poem: "Would that like the snowflakes when they are weary of falling I might sink down upon the earth and end my days." There was nothing very remarkable about the writing, but it was an agreeable hand and one which bore unmistakable traces of the writer's lineage. He had formed a high opinion of her at the time when she first went to Ise and had very much regretted her withdrawal from the world. Now she was an ordinary person again, and, if he wished to cultivate her acquaintance, entirely at his disposal; but this very fact (as was usual with him) caused a revulsion of feeling. To go forward in the direction where fewest obstacles existed seemed to him to be taking a mean advantage. Although he was, in his attentions to Lady Akikonomu, merely fulfilling her mother's request, he knew quite well how everyone at Court was expecting the story to end. Well, for once in a way their expectations would be disappointed. He was fully determined to bring her up with the utmost propriety and, so soon as the Emperor reached years of discretion, to present her at Court; in fact, to adopt her as his daughter—a thing which, considering the smallness of his family, it was natural for him to do. He constantly wrote her letters full of kindness and encouragement, and occasionally called at her palace. "What I should really like," he said one day, "would be for you to look upon me, if you will forgive my putting it in that way, as a substitute for your dear mother. Can you not sometimes treat me as though I were an old friend? Can you not trust me with some of the secrets you used to confide to her?" Such appeals merely embarrassed her. She had lived so secluded a life that to open her mouth at all in a stranger's presence seemed to her a terrible ordeal, and her gentlewomen were in the end obliged to make such amends as they could. It was a comfort that many of her officers and gentlewomen were closely connected with the Imperial Family and would, if his project for installing her in the Palace did not come to naught, be able to help her to assert herself. He would have been glad to know more about her appearance, but she always received him from behind her curtains, and he neither felt justified in taking the liberties that are accorded to a parent nor did he feel quite sure enough of himself to wish to put his parental feelings to the test. He was indeed very uncertain with regard to his own intentions, and for the present mentioned his plans about her to nobody. He saw to it that the Memorial Service was carried out with great splendor, devoting to the arrangement of it a care that deeply gratified the bereaved household. Life there was becoming more and more featureless and depressing as the weeks went by. One by one Lady Akikonomu's servants and retainers were finding other employment. The Palace stood at the extreme outer edge of the Sixth Ward, in a district which was very little frequented, and the melancholy bells which went on tolling and tolling in innumerable adjacent temples reduced her every evening to a state of abject misery. She had always been used to spend a great deal of time in her mother's company, and even when she was sent to Ise, though no parent had ever before accompanied the Vestal Virgin, they still remained unseparated. It can be imagined then that her mother's loss left her peculiarly helpless and desolate; and the thought that Rokujo, who had travelled so far for her sake, should now set out upon this last journey all alone, caused her unspeakable pain. Many suitors both high and low, under cover of paying attentions to one or other of her gentlewomen, now began to frequent the house. Genji however had in his best fatherly style exacted a promise from the lady's old nurse that she would allow no matchmaking to go on in the house. Above all he feared that some of her women might wish for their own ends to keep these gentlemen hanging about the premises. It soon however became apparent that there was no danger of this. The ladies concerned knew that their doings would probably reach Genji's ears, and they were far too anxious to stand well with him to dream of abusing their position. The suitors soon found that their advances were not met with the slightest encouragement.

It will be remembered that at the time of Lady Akikonomu's departure for Ise the retired Emperor Suzaku had, when presiding at the magnificent farewell ceremony in the Daigoku Hall, been greatly struck with her beauty. This impression had remained with him, and on her return to the Capital he begged Rokujo to let her daughter come to him, promising that she should take her place as the equal of his sister, the former Vestal of Kamo, and the other princesses, his sisters and kinswomen whom he sheltered under his roof. This proposal did not please her. She feared that where so many exalted personages were gathered together her daughter would be likely to receive but scant attention. Moreover Suzaku was at the time in very bad health, and if he should fail to recover, his dependants might be left in a precarious position. Now that her mother was dead it was all the more desirable to establish her in a manner which offered some prospect of security. When therefore Suzaku repeated his invitation, this time in somewhat insistent terms, Lady Akikonomu's friends were placed in an awkward position. Genji's private plan of affiancing her to the boy-Emperor would, now that Suzaku had displayed so marked an inclination towards her, be difficult to pursue without too deeply offending his brother. Another consideration weighed with him: he was becoming more and more fascinated by the girl's beauty and he was in no hurry to commit her to other hands. Under the circumstances he thought the best thing he could do was to talk the matter over with Lady Fujitsubo. "I am in great difficulties over this business," he said. "As you know, the girl's mother was a woman of singularly proud and sensitive temperament. I am ashamed to say that, following my own wanton and selfish inclinations, I behaved in such a way as to do great injury to her reputation, with the consequence that henceforward she on her side harbored against me a passionate resentment, while I on mine found myself branded not only by her but also by the world at large as a profligate and scamp. Till the very last I was never able to recover her confidence; but on her death-bed she spoke to me of Akikonomu's future in a way which she would never have done had she not wholly regained her good opinion of me. This was a great weight off my mind. Even had these peculiar relations not existed between us, her request was one which even to a stranger I could hardly have refused. And as it was, you may imagine how gladly I welcomed this chance of repairing, even at this late hour, the grievous wrong which my light-mindedness had inflicted upon her during her lifetime. His Majesty is of course many years younger than Akikonomu;[*] but I do not think it would be a bad thing if he had some older and more experienced person in his entourage. However, it is for you to decide…" "I am of the same opinion," Fujitsubo replied. "It would of course be very imprudent to offend the retired Emperor. But surely the mother's wishes are a sufficient excuse. If I were you I should pretend you know nothing about the retired Emperor's inclination towards her and present her at the Palace without

---

[*] Akikonomu was now nineteen; the boy-Emperor Ryozen, seven.

more ado. As a matter of fact, Suzaku now cares very little about such matters. What energy he still possesses is spent on prayers and meditation. I do not think you will find that he minds very much one way or the other..." "All the same, I think it will be best under the circumstances if the request for Akikonomu's Presentation came from you," said Genji. "I could then seem merely to be adding my solicitations to yours. You will think that in weighing the pros and cons of the matter with such care I am over-scrupulous; and indeed I fear that you have found me rather tedious. It is simply that I am extremely anxious people should not think me lacking in respect towards my brother..." It soon became apparent that, in accordance with Fujitsubo's advice, he had decided to disregard the retired Emperor's wishes. But it was in Genji's own palace and not, for the moment at any rate, in the Emperor's household that Lady Akikonomu was to be installed. He explained the circumstances to Murasaki. "She is just about your age," he said, "and you will find her a very agreeable companion. I think you will get on famously together..." Murasaki at once took to the idea and was soon busy with preparations for the reception of the visitor.

Fujitsubo was all this while extremely exercised in mind concerning the future of her niece, the youngest daughter of Prince Hyobukyo, for Genji's estrangement from the father seemed to block every avenue of advancement. To no Chujo's daughter, as the grandchild of the Senior Minister, was treated on all sides with the utmost deference and consideration, and she had now become the Emperor's favorite playmate. "My brother's little girl is just the same age as the Emperor," said Fujitsubo one day; "he would enjoy having her to play at dolls with him sometimes, and it would be a help to the older people who are looking after him." But quite apart from affairs of state, Genji had (as Fujitsubo knew) such a multiplicity of private matters to attend to and was plagued from morning till night by such a variety of irritating applications and requests that she had not the heart to keep on bothering him. It was something that a person like Lady Akikonomu would soon be at the Emperor's side; for Fujitsubo herself was in very poor health and, though she sometimes visited the Palace, she could not look after her son's education as she would have liked to do. It was necessary that there should be someone grown-up to keep an eye on him, and though she would dearly like to have seen her niece installed as his playmate, she was extremely glad of the arrangement whereby a sensible creature like Lady Akikonomu was to have him in her constant care.

The Palace in the Tangled Woods

While Genji, like Yukihira of old, "dragged his leaky pails" along the shore of Suma, his absence had been mourned, in varying ways and degrees, by a very large number of persons in the Capital. Even those who stood in no need of patronage or protection and had through his departure lost only the amenities of a charming friendship were deeply distressed. For some of them, such as Murasaki, this sad time was mitigated by constant messages from his place of exile; some were privileged to busy their needles upon such garments as his altered state prescribed, or were allowed the consolation of rendering him other small services such as in his present difficulties he was likely to require. But there were others who, though they had received his favors, had done so unknown to the world, and these ladies now learned of Genji's last hours at the Capital from the casual gossip of some friend who had no idea that the matter was of any particular concern, to them. Needless to say they feigned a like indifference; but such concealment costs one dear and not a few hearts were broken in the process.

Among those who fared worst during his absence was the lady at the Hitachi Palace.* During the period after her father's death there had been no one to take care of her and she had for a while led a very wretched existence. But then came the unexpected apparition of Genji. His letters and visits, which to him in the crowded days of his glory were insignificant acts of courtesy, implying no more than a very mild degree of interest and affection, were to their recipient, with her narrow and unvarying life, like the reflection of a star when it chances to fall into a bowl of water. It was but natural, she thought, that when the outcry against him began Genji should no longer find time for an attachment which had in any case played only a very subordinate part in his life, particularly as the attacks upon him were part of a widespread movement which could not but be causing him the greatest anxiety. Then came his exile and at last his triumphant return. But still she heard no word from him.

In old days when she heard nothing from him for a week or two she would become a little tearful it is true, but she still managed to carry on her ordinary existence. Now months, years had passed; long ago she had given up all hope, and sank into a condition of settled apathy and

---

* Suyetsumuhana. See Part I, ch. VI. I shall henceforward call her Suyetsumu.

gloom. "Poor princess!" said the elderly gentlewomen who waited upon her. "Really she has had the worst possible luck! To see this glorious apparition suddenly descending upon her like a God or Buddha out of the sky—not that he meant very much by it; but she, poor lady, could never get over the surprise of his noticing her at all—and then for him to disappear without a word! She knows of course that it is not from her that he has run away to Suma; it all comes of this new government! But still, one cannot help being very sorry for the poor young creature." She had indeed during the time after her father's death become gradually inured to a life of extreme monotony and isolation; but Genji's visits had awakened in her quite new ambitions; for the first time in her life she began to feel herself drawn towards the world of taste and fashion. This made her renewed state of poverty and isolation all the more difficult to bear. The fact that Genji frequented the house had for the time being induced a certain number of other visitors to present themselves. But since his departure one visitor after another, having grown more and more remiss in his attentions, finally ceased to come at all. Her father's ladies-in-waiting were all very advanced in years and every now and then one of them would die; the other servants, both indoors and out, were continually seeking better service, and hardly a month passed but some member of her staff either died or drifted away. The palace grounds, which had for long years past been allowed to sink into a sad state of neglect, had now become a mere jungle. Foxes had made their lairs in the garden walks, while from the ornamental plantations, now grown into dank and forbidding woods, the voice of the screech-owl sounded day and night alike; so little was there now any sign of human habitation in that place, so dim was the daylight that pierced those tangled thickets. The few servants who still lingered on in the midst of all this desolation began to declare that tree-spirits and other fearsome monsters had established themselves in the palace grounds and were every day becoming more open and venturesome in their habits. "There is no sense in continuing to live like this," one of these ladies said. "Nowadays all the government officials are building themselves handsome houses. Several of them have for a long time past had their eye on all your timber and have been making enquiries in the neighborhood whether you might not be prevailed upon to part with it. If only you would consent to do so, you might with the proceeds easily buy some newer place that would be less depressing to live in. You are really asking too much of the few servants that remain with you..." "Hush, how can you suggest such a thing!" answered the princess. "What would people think if they heard you? So long as I am alive no such disrespect to my poor Father's memory shall ever be committed. I know quite well that the grounds have become rather wild and dismal; but this was his home, his dear spirit haunts the place, and I feel that so long as I am here I am never far off from him. That has become my only comfort..." She broke off in tears, and it was impossible to allude to the subject again. Her furniture too, though entirely out of fashion, was much of it very beautiful in an old-world way, and enquiries were constantly coming from those who made it their business to understand such matters and had heard that she possessed a work by such and such a master of some particular time and school. Such proposals she regarded merely as an ill-bred comment upon her poverty and indeed complained of them bitterly to the aforementioned gentlewoman. "But, Madam," the lady protested, "it is not at all an unusual thing..." And to convince her mistress that funds must somehow or other be procured she began to call her attention to various dilapidations, the repair of which could not safely be deferred for a single day. But it made no difference. The idea of selling any of her possessions seemed to the princess utterly untenable. "If he had not meant me to keep them, he would not have put them here," she said; "I cannot bear to think of them becoming ornaments in ordinary, worldly people's houses. I do not think he would wish me to..." and that was all that could be got out of her.

Visitors and even letters were now absolutely unknown at the Hitachi Palace. True, her elder brother the Zen priest on the rare occasions when he came up to the Capital, usually visited the palace. But he did little more than poke his head in and go away. He was a particularly vague and unpractical sort of man, who even among his fellow clerics ranked as unusually detached from all worldly considerations. In fact he was a saint, and consequently very unlikely to notice that the whole place was overgrown with weeds and bushes, still less to suggest any means of clearing them away.

Meanwhile, the state of affairs was becoming very acute. The once elegant courtyard was thickly overgrown with weeds; the lusty hemlock clumps were fast destroying the gables and eaves of the roof. The main eastern and western gates of the park were barricaded by huge masses of mugwort and it was impossible to open them. This might have given the inhabitants of the palace a certain comforting sense of security, had it not been for the fact that the walls which surrounded the estate were everywhere either broken down or upon the point of falling. Horse and oxen from the neighboring pastures soon found their way through these gaps, and when the summer came they began to make free with the palace lawns in a way which scandalized the little herd-boys who were in charge of them. At the time of the autumn equinox there were very heavy gales, and one day the main roof of the servants' wing was blown right away, leaving only a ceiling of thin match-boarding, a mere shell, which would not have withstood the mildest shower of rain. At this the under servants left in a body. Henceforward the few inhabitants of the palace led a pitiable existence, not even getting enough to eat, for there was no one to make up the fires or prepare their food. Thieves and vagabonds had the place completely at their mercy; but fortunately it never occurred to them to go near it. How could so desolate a ruin contain anything worth meddling with? They shook their heads and trudged on. But strangely enough, had he penetrated those savage thickets, an enterprising burglar would have found, amid a tangled mass of wreckage, a drawing-room* perfectly appointed in every detail, each ornament, each screen and article of furniture still standing exactly where the late prince had left it. True, there was no longer anyone to dust this last-surviving room, and it needed dusting badly. Never mind, it was a real room; not just a living-place, but a noble apartment with everything in it handsome and dignified just as it ought to be. And here, year in and year out, her whole life was spent.

Solitary people with a great deal of time on their hands seem usually to turn to old ballads and romances for amusement and distraction, but for such employments the princess showed little inclination. Even in the lives of those who have no particular interest in poetry there are usually periods of inactivity during which they take to exchanging verses with some sympathetic correspondent—verses which, if they are young, generally contain affecting references to various kinds of plant and tree. But the princess's father had imbued her with the belief that all outward display of emotion is undignified and ill-bred; she felt that what he would really have liked best would have been for her to communicate with no one at all, and she had long given up writing even to the few relations with whom she might have been expected occasionally to correspond.

At rare intervals she would open an old-fashioned chest and fiddle for a while with a number of ancient picture-scrolls, illustrations of such stories as *The Chinese Prefect, The Mistress of Hakoya, Princess Kaguya*† and the like. Then there were some poems which, though all of very ancient date, were excellently chosen, with the names of the poets and the titles of the poems written in a nice clear hand at the side, so that one could really tell what one was reading. They were written on the best Kanya and Michinoku papers, now grown somewhat puffy with age,‡ and though it cannot be supposed that she could derive much pleasure from reading the same familiar pages over and over again, yet it was noticed that in

---

* Such a term must only be taken as a rough equivalent.

† Of these three romances the first is quite unknown; the second must have been a Taoist fairy story, for "Hakoya" is the "Miao-ku-she" of Chuang Tzu, Chapter I—a divine mountain inhabited by mysterious sages. The third is either identical with the *Taketori Monogatari* ("The Bamboo-cutter's Story") or at any rate treated the same theme.

‡ Kanya River ("Paper-makers' River") is between Hirano and Kitano, near Kyoto. Michinoku paper, from the province of that name, was made of spindle-wood. These stout Japanese papers become thick and fluffy with age.

her hours of deepest depression she would often sit with the books spread open before her. As for reading the Sutras or performing those Buddhist ceremonies which have now become so indispensable an element in fashionable life, she would have shuddered at the thought, and would not have dreamed of so much as touching a rosary, even though no one was there to see. Such was the arduous standard of conduct which this lady imposed upon herself.

Of her old servants only Jiju, the daughter of her foster-nurse, had survived the general exodus of the last few years. Jiju's friend, the former Vestal of Kamo, whose company had been one of her distractions, was dead, and the poor lady's existence had become such as no one could reasonably be expected to endure. A sister of the princess's mother had fallen on evil days and ended by marrying a provincial official. She now lived at the Capital, and as she had daughters, together with a bevy of unusually agreeable young waiting-women, Jiju occasionally visited the house, where indeed she was quite at home, for both her parents had been friends of the family. But the princess herself, with her usual unsociability, absolutely refused to hold any communication with her aunt's household. "I am afraid the princess looks upon me as a very vulgar person," the aunt said to Jiju one day. "She still thinks, despite the wretched manner in which she now lives, that to have such relations as we is a disgrace to her. At any rate I suppose that is why she is so careful never to come near us." It was in this somewhat malicious tone that she always discussed her niece's behavior.

I have noticed that people of quite common origin who have risen in the world can in a very short time achieve a perfect imitation of aristocratic importance. And similarly, if through some accident an aristocrat falls into low company, he generally exhibits a meanness so thoroughgoing that it is hard to believe he has been at any pains to acquire it. Of this second tendency the princess's aunt was a good example. She knew that after her unfortunate marriage the people at the Hitachi Palace had regarded her as a disgrace to the family. Now that the prince was dead and Suyetsumu herself was in circumstances of such difficulty, there seemed to be quite a good chance that the princess might eventually have to take shelter under her aunt's roof. This was what the aunt herself was looking forward to. It was her revenge. She saw the princess installed as a dependant, fetching and carrying for her daughters. And what an ideal drudge she would make, being so priggish and strait-laced that it would never be necessary to keep an eye upon her! "You ought to bring her round to see us sometimes," the aunt would say to Jiju, "and if you could get her to bring her zithern, so much the better; we have heard so much about her playing." Jiju did her best, and the princess, docile as usual, admitted that there was everything to be said in favor of paying an occasional visit.

But when it came to the point, panic overwhelmed her. She would do anything, anything that Jiju asked; but she would not make friends. And so, greatly to the aunt's discomfiture, the matter was dropped.

About this time her uncle was appointed treasurer to a provincial district. He intended to take his family with him, and was anxious to equip his daughters with attendants whom it would be pleasant to name in the cars of provincial visitors. The chance of being able to exhibit a real princess as a member of their staff was not to be thrown away and the aunt returned once more to the attack. "I am very worried at having to go so far away from you," she sent word by Jiju. "We have not had the pleasure of seeing you much lately; but it was a great comfort to me to feel that I was near at hand and could help you if anything went wrong. I am most anxious that, if possible, we should not be separated..." All this had no effect whatever. "The conceited little fool! I have no patience with her," the aunt cried out at last. "She may have these grand ideas about herself if she chooses; but no one else is going to take much notice of a creature that goes on year after year living in the hole-and-corner way that she does; least of all this famous Prince Genji, with whom she pretends to be so intimate."

At last came Genji's pardon and recall, celebrated in every part of the kingdom by riotous holiday-making and rejoicing. His friends of either sex were soon vying with one another in demonstrations of good will and affection. These testimonies to his popularity, pouring in from persons of every rank and condition in life, naturally touched him deeply, and in these stirring days it would have been strange indeed if many minor affairs had not escaped his memory. But for her the time of his restoration was far harder to bear than that of his exile. For whereas she had before confidently looked forward to his return, counting upon it as we count upon the winter trees to bud again in spring, this glorious home-coming and restoration, when at last they came, brought joy to every hut and hovel in the land, but to her only a hundredfold increase of her former misery. For of what comfort to her were his triumphs, if she must hear of them from other lips?

The aunt had the satisfaction of seeing her prophecies fulfilled. It was of course out of the question that anyone would own to an acquaintance with a person living in such miserable squalor as now surrounded the princess. There are those, says the *Hokkekyo*,* whom even Buddha and his saints would have hard work to redeem; and certainly this lady had allowed her affairs to drift into a disorder which the most generous patron would shrink from attempting to set straight. This contempt for all the rest of the world, this almost savage unsociability, was of course

---

* *The Saddharmapundarika Sutra.*

no invention of her own; it was merely an attempt to perpetuate the haughty demeanor of the late prince and princess, her parents. But this did not make the young princess's attitude any less irritating and ridiculous. "There is still time to change your mind," said her aunt one day. "A change of scene—a journey through the mountains, for example, is often very beneficial to people who have some trouble on their minds. I am sure you think that life in the provinces is very uncomfortable and disagreeable, but I can assure you that while you are with us you will never have to stay anywhere quite so higgledy-piggledy…" The wretched old women who still dragged on their existence in the palace eagerly watched the princess's face while their fate was being decided. Surely she would not throw away this opportunity of escape! To their consternation they soon saw that her aunt's appeal was not making the slightest impression upon her. Jiju, for her part, had recently become engaged to a young cousin of the provincial treasurer's, who was to accompany him to his province, and she was therefore pledged to go down to Tsukushi, whether the princess joined the party or not. She was however deeply attached to her mistress and very loath indeed to leave her in her present condition. She therefore discussed the matter with her again, and did everything in her power to persuade the princess to accompany them; only to make the extraordinary discovery that Suyetsumu was still from day to day living in the hope that the visitor from whom she had for all those years had no word would suddenly reappear and put everything to rights again. "He was very fond of me," she said. "It is only because he has been unhappy himself that he has not remembered to write to me. If he had the slightest idea of what is happening to us here, he would come at once…" So she had been thinking for years, and though the general structure of the house fell every day into a more fantastic state of dilapidation, she still persisted as obstinately as ever in retaining every trifling article of furniture and decoration in exactly the place where it had always been. She spent so much of her time in tears that a certain part of her face had now become as red as the flower which the hillman carries over his ear; so that her appearance, particularly when she showed her face in profile, would have struck a casual visitor as somewhat forbidding. But of this I will say no more; it is perhaps always a mistake to enter into matters of that kind.

As the cold weather came on, existence at the Hitachi Palace rapidly became more and more difficult. The princess sat staring in front of her, plunged in unbroken gloom. Meanwhile Genji celebrated the ritual of the Eight Readings, in memory of his father, the old Emperor. He took great trouble in choosing the priests for this ceremony and succeeded finally in assembling a notable band of dignitaries. Among them none was more renowned for the sanctity of his life and the wide range of his studies than Princess Suyetsumu's brother, the Abbot of Daigoji. On his way back from the ceremony, he looked in for a moment at the Hitachi Palace. "I have just been celebrating the Eight Readings in Prince Genji's palace," he said; "a magnificent ceremony! It is a pleasure to take part in such a service as that! I cannot imagine anything more beautiful and impressive. A veritable paradise—I say it in all reverence—a veritable paradise on earth; and the prince himself, so calm and dignified, you might have thought him an incarnation of some holy Buddha or Bodhisat. How came so bright a being to be born into this dim world of ours?" So saying, he hurried off to his temple. Unlike ordinary, worldly men and women he never wasted time in discussing sordid everyday affairs or gossiping about other people's business. Consequently he made no allusion to the embarrassed circumstances in which his sister was living. She sometimes wondered whether even the Saints whom he worshipped would, if they had found someone in a like situation, really have succeeded in behaving with so splendid an indifference.

She was indeed beginning to feel that she could hold out no longer, when one day her aunt suddenly arrived at the palace. This lady was quite prepared to meet with the usual rebuffs; but having on this occasion come in a comfortable travelling coach stored with everything that the princess could need during a journey she did not for an instant doubt that she would gain her point. With an air of complete self-confidence she bustled towards the front gate. No sooner had the porter begun trying to open it than she realized into what a pitch of decay her niece's property had fallen. The doors were off their hinges, and as soon as they were moved tottered over sideways, and it was not till her own men-servants came to the rescue that, after a tremendous shouldering and hoisting, a passage was cleared through which she could enter the grounds. What did one do next? Even such a heap of gimcrack ruins as this presumably had some apertures which were conventionally recognized as doors and windows. A lattice door on the southern side of the house was half open and here the visitors halted. It did not seem possible that any human being was within; but to their astonishment, from behind a smoke-stained, tattered screen-of-state the maid Jiju suddenly appeared. She was looking very haggard, but though age and suffering had greatly changed her, she was still a well-made, pleasing woman; "at any rate far more presentable than her mistress," thought the visitors. "We are just starting," cried out the aunt to the lady of the house, who, as she guessed, was seated behind this sooty screen: I have come to take Jiju away. I am afraid you will find it very difficult to get on without her, but even if you will not design to have any dealings with us yourself, I am sure you will not be so inconsiderate as to stand in this poor creature's way..." She put in so moving a plea on behalf of Jiju that there ought by rights to have been tears in her eyes. But she was in such high spirits at the prospect of travelling as a provincial governor's wife that a smile of pleasant anticipation played upon her lips all the while. "I know quite well," she continued," that the late prince was not at all proud of his connection with us, and I am sure it was quite natural that when you were a child you should pick up his way of thinking and feeling. But that is a long time ago now. You may say that it was my fault we did not meet. But really while celebrities such as Prince Genji were frequenting the house I was not at all sure that humble people like ourselves would be welcome. However, one of the advantages of being of no importance is that we humdrum creatures are not subject to the same violent ups and downs as you exalted people. I for my part was very sorry to see your fortunes declining so rapidly as they have done of late, but so long as I was near at hand I was quite happy about you and did not consider it my duty to interfere. But now that I am going away to another part of the country, I confess I feel very uneasy…" "It would be delightful to go with you. Most people would be very glad indeed… But I think that as long as the place holds together at all I had better go on as I am…" That was all that could be got out of her. "Well, that is for you to decide," said the aunt at last, "but I should not think that anyone has ever before buried himself alive in such a god-forsaken place. I am sure that if you had asked him in time Prince Genji would have been delighted to put things straight for you; indeed, with a touch here and there no doubt he would soon have made the place more sumptuous than the Jade Emperor's* Palace. But unfortunately he is now entirely preoccupied with this young daughter of Prince Hyobukyo, and will do nothing for anyone else. He used to lead a roving life, distributing his favors in all sorts of directions. But now that has all stopped, and under these circumstances it is very unlikely to occur to him that a person living buried away in the middle of such a jungle as this, is all the time expecting him to rush round and take her affairs in hand." The princess knew that this was only too true and she now began to weep bitterly. Yet she showed no signs of changing her mind, and the Chancellor's wife, after wasting the whole afternoon in tormenting her, exclaimed at last: "Well then, I shall take Jiju. Make haste, please, please; it is getting late!" Weeping and flustered Jiju drew her mistress back into the alcove: "I never meant to go," she whispered, "but this lady seems so very anxious to take me. I think perhaps I will travel with them part of the way and then come back again. There is a great deal of truth in all that she has been saying. But then, on the other hand, I do not like to upset you by leaving. It is terrible to have to decide so quickly…" So she whispered; but though the princess loved her dearly and was stung to the quick that even this last friend should be making ready to desert her, she said not a word to encourage Jiju to stay, but only sobbed more bitterly

---

* The sovereign divinity of the Chinese Taoists.

than before. She was wondering what she could give to her maid to keep in remembrance of her long service in the family. Perhaps some cloak or dress? Unfortunately all her clothes were far too worn and soiled to give away. She remembered that somewhere in the house was a rather pretty box containing some plaited strands of her own hair, her fine glossy hair that grew seven feet long. This would be her present, and along with it she would give one of those boxes of delicious clothes-scent that still survived from the old days when her parents were alive. These she handed to Jiju together with an acrostic poem in which she compared her departure to the severing of this plaited tress of hair. "Your Mama told me always to look after you," she said, "and whatever happened to me I should never dream of sending you away. I think however that you are probably right to go, and only wish that someone nicer were taking charge of you..." "I know Mama wished me to stay with you," said Jiju at last through her tears. "But quite apart from that, we have been through such terrible times together in these last years that I cannot bear to go off heaven knows where and leave you here to shift for yourself. But, Madam, 'By the Gods of Travel to whom I shall make offering upon my way, I swear that never can I be shorn from you like this tress of severed hair.'" Suddenly the voice of the aunt broke in upon them shouting impatiently: "What has become of Jiju? Be quick, now, it is getting quite dark!" Hardly knowing what she did, Jiju climbed into the coach and as it drove away stared helplessly at the dilapidated house.

So at last Jiju had left her; Jiju who for years past, though in sore need of a little pleasure and distraction, had never once asked for a single day's holiday! But this was not the end of the princess's troubles; for now even the few old charwomen who still remained in the house—poor doddering creatures who could never have persuaded anyone else to employ them— began threatening to leave. "Do you think I blame her?" said one of them, speaking of Jiju's departure. "Not I! What had she to stay for, I ask you. And come to that, I should like to know why we go on putting up with it all." And they began with one accord remembering influential patrons who had at one time or another promised to employ them. No, decidedly they would not stay in the place any longer.

These conversations, which took place in the princess's hearing, had the most disquieting effect upon her. The Frosty Month* had now come. In the open country around, though snow and hail frequently fell, they tended to melt between-whiles. But in the wilderness that surrounded the Hitachi Palace vast drifts of snow, protected by the tangled overgrowth from any ray of sunlight, piled higher and higher, till one might have fancied oneself in some valley among the Alps of Koshi. Through these

---

* Eleventh month.

arctic wastes not even the peasants would consent to press their way and the palace was for weeks on end entirely cut off from the outer world.

The princess sat staring at the snow. Life had been dull enough before, but at any rate she had someone at hand whose chatter at times broke in upon her gloom. But now Jiju's laughter, Jiju's tears were gone, and as she lay day and night alike behind her crumbling curtains-of-state the princess was consumed by a loneliness and misery such as she had never known before.

Meanwhile, at the Nijo Palace, Genji remained wholly absorbed in the girl from whom he had so long been separated, and it was only a few very particular friends who heard any news of him at all. He did sometimes think of the Hitachi Palace and wondered whether the princess could still be living there all alone. But he was in no great hurry to discover, and the New Year passed without his having taken any steps about her. In the fourth month he decided to call upon the ladies in the Village of Falling Flowers, and having obtained Murasaki's permission he set out one evening, clad in his usual disguise. For days it had rained unceasingly. But now, just at the moment when the heavy rain stopped and only a few scattered drops were falling, the moon rose; and soon it was one of those exquisite late spring nights through whose moonlight stillness he had in earlier years so often ridden out on errands of adventure. Busy with memories of such excursions he had not noticed where he was driving, when suddenly looking up he saw a pile of ruined buildings surrounded by plantations so tangled and overgrown that they wore the aspect of a primeval jungle. Over a tall pine-tree a trail of wisteria blossoms was hanging; it quivered in the moonlight, shaken by a sudden puff of wind that carried with it when it reached him a faint and almost imperceptible odor of flowers. It was for orange-blossom that he had set out that night; but here too was a flower that had a fragrance worth enjoying. He leaned out of the carriage window. They were passing by a willow whose branches swept the ground; with the crumbling away of the wall which had once supported it the tree had fallen forward till its trunk was almost prostrate. Surely he had seen these grounds before? Why, yes, this must be—suddenly it all came back to him. Of course it was that strange lady's house. He was driving past the Hitachi Palace. Poor creature, he must discover at once what had become of her; and stopping his carriage and calling to Koremitsu, who as usual on occasions of the kind was in attendance upon him, he asked him whether this was not indeed Princess Suyetsumu's place. "Why certainly!" said Koremitsu. "In that case," said Genji, "I should like to find out whether the same people are still living there. I have not time to pay a personal visit now, but I should like you to go in and enquire. Make sure that you discover exactly how things stand. It looks so silly if one calls on the wrong people."

After a particularly dismal morning spent in staring blankly in front of her the princess had fallen asleep and dreamed that her father, the late prince, was still alive and well. After such a dream as that she woke up more miserable than ever. The window side of the room had been flooded in the recent rains; but taking a cloth she began mopping up the water and trying to find a place where she could put her chair. While she did so the stress of her sufferings stirred her to a point of mental alertness which she did not often reach. She had composed a poem, and suddenly she recited the lines: "To the tears I shed in longing for him that is no more, are added the ceaseless drippings that patter from my broken roof!"

Meanwhile Koremitsu had made his way into the house and was wandering this way and that looking for some sign of life. He spent a long while in poking into all sorts of corners and at last concluded that the place had been abandoned as uninhabited. He was just setting out to report this to Genji when the moon came out from behind a cloud, lighting up the front of the house. He then noticed a trellis roll-door which was half pulled up. A curtain behind it moved. It almost seemed as though someone were there. Koremitsu, feeling oddly enough quite nervous, turned back and approached this door, clearing his throat loudly as he did so. In answer to this signal a very aged, decrepit voice answered from within the room. "Well, what is it? Who are you?" "It is Koremitsu," he answered, "could you tell Jiju that I should like to speak to her?" "Jiju?" the aged voice answered, "you cannot speak to her, she has gone away. But would not I do just as well?" The voice was incredibly ancient and croaking, but he recognized it as that of one of the gentlewomen whom he used to meet here in former days. To those within, inured as they were to years of absolute isolation, the sudden apparition of this figure wrapped in a great hunting cloak, was a mystery so startling and inexplicable that for a while it did not occur to them that their visitor could be other than some fox-spirit or will-o-the-wisp masquerading in human form. But the apparition behaved with reassuring gentility and coming right up to the doorway now addressed them as follows: "I must make it my business to find out exactly how matters stand. If you can assure me that, on your mistress's side, nothing has changed since the time when we used to come here, then I think you will find His Highness my master no less ready to help you than he was in days gone by. Can I trust you to let her know that we halted here tonight? I must be able to report to my master that his message is in safe hands…" The old lady and her companions burst out laughing. "Listen to him!" they cried, "asking whether Madam has altered her way of life, whether she has taken to new friends! Do you suppose, young man, that if she were not waiting day and night for this famous prince of yours, she would still be living in this wilderness? Why, if there had been a soul in the world to help us, we should have shifted from these tumble-down quarters a long while ago. Just let Prince Genji have a look at the place for himself; he'll soon know how things stand! Yes, and we have been living like this for years; I shouldn't think anyone in the world has ever been through such times as we have in this house. I tell you it's a wonder we've been able to bear it for so long, such a life as we and our poor young lady have been leading..." They soon got launched upon a recital of their sufferings and misfortunes, which wandered so far from the purpose in hand that Koremitsu, growing impatient, at last interrupted them. "Enough, enough," he cried; "that will do to go on with. I will go to Prince Genji at once and tell him of this."

"What a long time you have been!" exclaimed Genji, when Koremitsu finally reappeared. "Are things in the palace much as they used to be? The whole place is so overgrown with creepers and bushes that I hardly recognize it." Koremitsu described how he at last discovered signs of life in the house and finally recognized the voice of Shosho, Jiju's old aunt, who had told him the lamentable tale which he now repeated.

Genji was horror-stricken at what he heard. How she must have suffered, buried away month after month amid all this disorder and decay! He was appalled at his own cruelty. How was it conceivable that he should have left her all this while to her own devices? "Now then, what am I to do?" he said at last. "If I am to visit the poor lady I had much rather it was not at this time of night; but if I do not go in now, I may not get another chance for a long while. I am afraid that what the old ladies said is only too true; if she were not counting upon my return, she would scarcely have gone on living such a life as you have just heard described..." He was about to go straight into the house, but suddenly he hesitated. Would it not be better first of all to send in a very nice friendly note and discover whether she really insisted upon seeing him? But then he remembered the extraordinary difficulty with which she penned an answer. If she had not very much improved in this respect since his last dealings with her, he might easily spend the rest of the night waiting for his messenger to return with her reply. He had just dismissed that idea as impracticable when Koremitsu broke in: "Pardon me, you have no notion how difficult it is to force a way through the brambles. Let me go first and shake the dew off the long branches. Then you will not get quite so wet."

Accordingly Koremitsu went in front lashing the bushes with his riding-whip. But when they got under the trees such showers shook down on them from the branches (for the woods were still wet with the recent rains) that Koremitsu was obliged to go and fetch his master's umbrella, quoting as he held it aloft the old song about the dense forests of Miyagi-no, where "the drippings from wet boughs are worse than rain." Even so, the ends of Genji's trousers became dripping wet before he reached the house. It was by no means easy even in old days to distinguish which was supposed to be the front door. By now such architectural features as doors and lobbies had long ago become merged in the general dilapidation. Genji's entry, though effected by a somewhat undignified scramble, had at any rate the advantage of being completely private and unobserved. At last, just as she had always predicted, Genji had come back! But in the midst of her elation a sudden panic seized her. How could she meet him in the miserable dress that she was wearing? All seemed lost, when she remembered the clothes that her aunt had brought for her to travel in. She had thought at the time that her father would have considered them very unsuitable and had put them aside after a mere hasty glance. The servants had packed them in a scented Chinese trunk and now brought them out; smelling deliciously fragrant. She could not receive him in what she was wearing and she had nothing else to change into. Much as she disapproved of her aunt's taste, what could she do but let them dress her in these new-fangled clothes? Thus equipped she took her seat behind the smoky curtains-of-state and waited. Presently Genji entered the room. "It is a long time since we have held any communication, is it not?" he said, "but on my side at any rate that does not mean that there has been any change of feeling. I was all the while expecting to hear from you and was determined that I would not be the first to give a sign of life. At last however the sight of the familiar tree-groups by your gate overcame this resolution and I could not forbear..." So saying he lifted one corner of the curtains that surrounded her dais and peeped in. As in old days she was utterly overcome by confusion, and sat for some while unable to make any kind of rejoinder. At last, almost inaudibly, she murmured something about its being "kind of him to have found his way...through all those wet bushes...such a scramble!"

"I am afraid you have been having a very dull time," he went on, "but pray give me credit for tonight's persistence. It showed some devotion, did it not, that I should have forced my way into the heart of this tangled, dripping maze, without a word of invitation or encouragement? I am sure you will forgive me for neglecting you for so long when I tell you that for some while past I have seen absolutely no one. Not having received a word of any kind from you, I could not suppose that you were particularly anxious to see me. But henceforward I am going to assume, whether you write to me or no, that I shall not be unwelcome. There now! After that, if I ever behave badly again you will really have some cause to complain." So unhappy was he at the thought of all that she must have suffered during those years of penury and isolation that, in his desire to make amends, he soon began saying things which he did not quite mean. He even had thoughts of giving up his intended excursion and staying here for the night. But the princess seemed to be so painfully conscious of the deficiencies in her domestic arrangements and in general so completely overwhelmed by the presence of a visitor, that after passing some time in rather unsuccessful efforts to make further conversation, he began looking for an opportunity to slip quietly away. There came into his mind the old song: "The tree I planted spreads its boughs so high."* He had not indeed planted those great pine-trees that closed about the ruined palace on every side, but it seemed to him that they had shot up surprisingly since he first visited the place. How quickly the years had sped! And from the thought of what she must have been through during all this time he passed naturally to the recollection of his own misfortunes and adventures. "Yes, when one comes to think of it, it is indeed a long time," he said at last. "At Court there have been great changes, many of them for the worse. Some day when I have plenty of time I must tell you of my exile and the strange outcast life we led on those deserted shores. You too, no doubt, have much to tell of all that has befallen you in these last dull and dreary days. I could wish indeed that you had many friends to whom you could confide your sorrows. But if for the moment I am the only one, make what use of me you can. You will find that, whatever my faults may be, as a listener I have much to recommend me."

The moon was now sinking. The main western door stood wide open, and as the covered gallery which had formerly run along that side of the house had now completely crumbled away, the moonlight streamed unimpeded into the room where they were sitting. Looking about him he recognized one after another the familiar fittings and ornaments. Not a thing was missing from its place. It was strange indeed to contrast the absolutely unchanged aspect of this corner of the house with the surrounding wreckage and desolation. He remembered the old story of the unfilial son who so much enjoyed pulling down the pagoda which his poor father had erected. The princess could not indeed prevent the outward fabric of her father's palace from falling into decay; but it was astonishing how little trace the passage of time had left upon the inner room in which he had once taken such pride.

Genji's thoughts returned to the princess herself. She was the shyest, the most awkward creature he had ever met; and yet there was something extraordinarily distinguished about her movements and bearing. She interested him, as indeed she had always done; so much so that he had fully intended not to lose sight of her. How should he ever forgive himself for allowing her affairs to drift into this deplorable condition? The truth was, he had been entirely absorbed in his own troubles and projects. But that was no excuse.

---

* "I knew it not; but an old man must I be indeed; the pine-tree that with my hands I planted spreads its boughs so high."

Had his ultimate destination that night been some scene of lively modern entertainment, the contrast would have been fatal. But the Village of Falling Flowers struck him on this occasion as particularly staid and dreary, and he left with the impression that the latter hours of the night had been by no means more agreeably spent than the former.

The time of the Kamo Festival had come. On the eve of the festival-day Genji was to undergo the ritual of Purification and the presents which are customary in connection with this occasion began pouring in thick and fast. Much of his time was spent in acknowledging them; but he did not forget his promise to the lady at Hitachi. The first thing to do was to make her palace habitable; and sending for his most reliable bailiffs he explained to them what he wanted done. Soon a host of workmen were clearing away the undergrowth, while carpenters went round with planks and stays, here patching a hole, there shoring up a tottering wall or replacing some rotten beam, till at last all was tolerably weather-tight and secure. The mere fact that Genji's men were at work upon the building at once set the gossips talking and the most absurd stories were circulated. Somewhat embarrassed by all this Genji himself remained at a distance, but he wrote a long letter to the princess, telling her of the new rooms which he was now adding to his palace and offering her accommodation in them, so soon as the place was ready. "You had better be looking round for a few nice young maids and pages to bring with you," he told her. Nor did he forget to enquire individually after each of the queer old waiting-ladies, an attention which put them into such high spirits that the old palace had hardly room enough to hold them, as now gazing up at the sky, now staring in the direction from which the messenger had come, they gave unbridled vent to their gratitude and admiration. It was well known in society that Genji took little interest in the common run of women. Even the mildest flirtation with such persons seemed to hold no attraction for him; their conversation would have bored him and indeed he scarcely seemed to notice their existence. Those few favored persons with whom he was generally known to have been on terms of intimacy were in every case women of entirely exceptional qualities. That one who in general showed such discrimination should single out as the recipient of his attentions a creature who could not lay claim to a single merit either of person or intellect, caused universal astonishment. This much at any rate was agreed, that though no one had heard anything about it, the affair must in reality be of very long standing.

The retainers and dependants who, thinking that the Hitachi Palace would never see better days, had a short while ago been in such a hurry to seek other employment, now one after another came begging to re-enter the princess's service. She at any rate knew how to behave towards those who waited upon her—treated them even with perhaps an exaggerated consideration. Whereas in the houses to which they had betaken themselves, belonging for the most part to wholly uncultured and undistinguished members of the petty bureaucracy, their experiences had been such as they would never have imagined to be possible; and they made no secret of the fact that they heartily repented of their recent experiment.

Prince Genji's influence was now greater than it had ever been in the days before his disaster. The mere fact that he was known to take an interest in the Hitachi Palace was enough to invest the place with a certain glamour. Visitors began to make their appearance, and soon the once deserted hills presented quite a busy and animated scene. One thing which had made the house so depressing was the fact that it was wholly shut in by bushes and trees. This jungle Genji now ordered to be reduced to tolerable dimensions; he had the ponds cleared and pleasant streams were made to run in and out among the flower-beds. All this work was performed with remarkable dispatch, for even the lowest laborers and serfs knew that it was in their interest to please a lady who, for whatever reason it might be, evidently stood high in Genji's esteem.

She lived for two years more in the old palace, at the end of which time she moved into the new Eastern Wing that Prince Genji had been building. He did not spend much time in her company, but she was well content merely to feel that they inhabited, the same domain, and whenever he had occasion to visit that part of the house he would look in upon her for a few minutes, that she might not feel she was wholly neglected. Her aunt's astonishment when in due time she returned to the Capital—Jiju's delight at her mistress's good fortune and shame at the thought that she had not held out a little longer in the princess's service—all this remains yet to be told. I would indeed have been glad to carry my story a little further, but at this moment my head is aching and I am feeling very tired and depressed. Provided a favorable opportunity presents itself and I do not forget to, I promise I will tell you all about it on some future occasion.

A Meeting at the Frontier

It will be remembered that the year after the old Emperor's death Iyo no Suke* was sent as governor to a distant province and that his wife, the lady of the Broom-tree episode, was prevailed upon to accompany him. Vague rumors reached her concerning Genji's banishment; it was said that he was in disgrace and was living somewhere along the shores of Suma. Though obliged to feign indifference, she was indeed naturally very much distressed and longed to write to him. But though " the wind sometimes blew across the Tsukubane hills"† she dared not trust her secret to so fickle a breeze, and while she waited for some securer messenger the months and years went swiftly by. It had at one time seemed as though Genji's banishment might last indefinitely, far longer in any case than Iyo no Suke's short term of office. But in the end it so turned out that Genji had already been back in the Capital for a year when Iyo's governorship expired. By an odd chance it happened that on the very day when the ex-governor and his party were to enter the Barrier at Osaka, Genji was to pass through this same barrier on his way to Ishiyama where he was to attend a service in the Temple of Kwannon. Ki no Kami and various other friends and relations of the ex-governor had come out from the City to meet him, and from them the returning provincials learnt that Genji with a vast ceremonial procession would shortly be passing along their road. Iyo no Suke, wishing to reach the Barrier while things were still quiet, set out with his party long before daylight. But his wagons crowded with women and their luggage jolted along so slowly that when daylight came they were still trailing along the coast-road at Uchi-ide. News now came that Genji's procession had crossed the Awata Road. Already his first outriders were in sight. So dense was even this vanguard of the great procession that to press past it was out of the question. Accordingly, at the foot of the Frontier Hill Iyo called a halt. The wagons were drawn up along the wayside, and the oxen released from the yoke were soon browsing here and there among the fir-trees. Meanwhile the travelers sat in the shelter of a neighboring copse, waiting for the procession to pass.

---

* Utsusemi's husband. See Part I, chapters II and III.
† "The wind that blows across the ridge, that blows across the hills would that it might carry a message to him that I love."

Although this was but a portion of Iyo no Suke's train, for he had sent some wagons on in advance while others were still to follow, it seemed a very large party; no less than ten coaches, with such a blaze of shawls, scarves and gaily colored favors protruding from their windows that they looked more like the coaches from which ladies of fashion view the departure of Vestals to Ise or Kamo than the workaday vehicles in which rustic persons are usually conveyed to the Capital.

In honor of Genji's return to public life the pilgrimage to Ishiyama was on this occasion carried out with unusual solemnity, and at the head of the procession rode vast throngs of noblemen and courtiers, most of whom stared with considerable curiosity at this cluster of gay equipages drawn up along the roadside.

It was the last day of the ninth month, and autumn leaves in many tints of red and brown stood out against a dull background of colorless winter grass. Suddenly from behind the frontier guardhouse there burst forth a blaze of many-colored travelling cloaks, some richly embroidered, some batik-dyed, of every pattern and hue. Genji's coach was passing. He too scanned the party by the roadside, but instantly lowered the carriage blind. He had recognized, among those who had come out to meet the travelers, his page and message-carrier, Utsusemi's brother—a child in those old days but now Captain of the Guard. He bade one of his equerries call this young man to his side and when he arrived said to him laughingly: "I hope your sister notices how attentive I am to her. It is not often that I go all the way to the Barrier to meet my friends!" He spoke lightly, but his heart beat fast and there rose up in his mind a host of tender memories to which in this hasty message it would have been useless to allude.

It was years since Utsusemi had spoken of Genji; yet she had never forgotten what had passed between them and it needed only these few words from him to renew all the misery in which her yearning for him had plunged her long ago.

When Genji returned from Ishiyama, Utsusemi's brother, the Captain of the Guard, came out towards the Barrier to meet him and made his excuses for having taken a day's leave in honor of his sister's return. As a boy he had been very good-looking and Genji had taken a great fancy to him. But despite the fact that he owed everything to Genji, without whose patronage he would never have been able to enter the Imperial Guard at all, still less to obtain promotion, no sooner had his master's fortunes begun to decline than this young man, fearing to offend those in power, entered the service of his brother-in-law, the provincial governor. Genji, though, he showed no resentment at the time, found this dereliction very hard to forgive. Their old relations were never resumed; but the Captain was still numbered among the favorite gentlemen of his household. Iyo no Suke's son; Ki no Kami, had become governor of Kawachi and was consequently no longer on the spot. The younger son, Ukon no Jo, had, as will be remembered, followed Genji into exile and now stood very high in his favor. His position was envied not only by this young Captain of the Guard but by many another who in the days of Genji's adversity had thought it wiser to leave him to his fate.

Soon after this Genji sent for the Captain* and gave him a letter to be taken to his sister. "So was this affair, which he thought had come to an end long ago, still dragging on after all these years?" the young man asked himself as he carried the letter to Iyo no Suke's house. "Did not our meeting of the other day seem almost as though it had been arranged by Fate? Surely you too must have felt so." With the letter was the acrostic poem: "Though on this lake-side Fate willed that we should meet, upon its tideless shore no love-shell† can we hope to find." "How bitterly I envied the Guardian of the Pass,"‡ he added.

"I hope you will send an answer," said the Captain. "He has got it into his head that I behaved badly to him some time ago. I should be very glad if I could get back on to the old terms with him. I do not myself, see much point in correspondences of this kind; but when anyone writes to me such a letter as I suppose this to be, I take care to write a civil answer. No one blames me for that; and still less is a woman thought the worse of for showing that a little harmless flattery does not altogether displease her."

She was still the same shy, inexperienced girl of years ago; her brother's tone profoundly shocked her and she had no intention of carrying on a flirtation for his benefit. But naturally enough she *did* feel flattered at the reception of such a note and in the end consented to reply. With her letter was an acrostic poem in which she said that the Barrier of Osaka had been no barrier to her tears, nor the Hill of Osaka a true hill of meetings.§

She was connected in his mind with the most delightful and also perhaps the most painful moment in his life. Hence his thoughts tended frequently to recur to her, and he continued to write to her from time to time.

Meanwhile Iyo no Suke, who was now a very old man, began to decline in health, and feeling that his end was near, he called his sons to him and discussed with them the disposition of his worldly affairs. But what evidently concerned him above all was the future of his young wife. They must promise him to yield to her wishes in everything and to treat her exactly as they had done during his lifetime. Still unsatisfied by their assurances he sent for them over and over again at every hour of the

---

* Utsusemi's brother; the "boy" of Part I, ch. III.
† *Kai-nashi* = "no shell"; but also "no profit."
‡ I.e. Iyo no Suke.
§ O-saka means "Hill of Meeting"; *seki* means a barrier, but also a flood-dam.

night and day and exacted fresh promises. But Utsusemi, after all that she had suffered already, could not believe that happiness of any kind could ever be in her fate. She saw herself, so soon as her husband was dead, bandied about unwanted from one relation's house to another, and the prospect appalled her. Iyo knew only too well what was passing in her mind. He desired so persistently to comfort and protect her that, could life be prolonged by mere anxiety to live, he would never have deserted her. For her indeed he would gladly have foregone the joys of Paradise that his ghost might linger on earth and keep her from all harm. Thus, profoundly distrusting the intention of his sons and full of the blackest forebodings, he died at last after a bitter struggle against fate, and only when his will could no longer hold out against the encroachments of sickness and old age.

For a while, with their father's dying injunctions fresh in their ears, the stepsons treated her with at any rate superficial kindness; but this soon wore off and she began to find her position in the house exceedingly unpleasant. This no doubt lay rather in the nature of the circumstances themselves than in any particular ill will on the part of her guardians. But she felt herself to be the object of a deliberate persecution and her life became one continual succession of tears and lamentations. The only one of the brothers who seemed to have any sympathy with her was Ki no Kami: "Please keep nothing back from me," he said. "My father was so anxious that I should help you and how can I, unless you entrust your secrets to me?" Then he took to following her about. She remembered how amorous he had always been. Soon his intentions became perfectly apparent. She had suffered enough already in her life; why should she sit down and wait quietly for the fresh miseries which fate had now in store for her? Without a word to anybody she sent for her confessor and took the vows of a nun. Her waiting-women and servants were naturally aghast at this sudden step. Ki no Kami took it as a personal affront. "She did it simply to spite me," he told people; "but she is young yet and will soon be wondering how on earth she is going to support such an existence for the rest of her life"—sagacity which did not impress his hearers quite as he intended.

The Picture Competition

It will be remembered that after Rokujo's death Genji decided that her daughter, Princess Akikonomu, had best come and live with him till the time came for her Presentation at Court. At the last minute, however, he altered his mind, for such a step seemed too direct a provocation to Princess Akikonomu's admirer, the young ex-Emperor Suzaku. But though he did not remove her from her palace in the Sixth Ward he felt his responsibilities towards this unfortunate orphan very keenly and paid her many lengthy visits. He had now definitely arranged with Fujitsubo that Akikonomu was soon to enter the Emperor's Palace; but he was careful not to betray in public any knowledge of this plan, and to the world at large he seemed merely to be giving the girl such general guidance and support as might be expected from a guardian and family friend.

Suzaku was indeed bitterly disappointed at the intelligence that the Princess had been handed over to a mere infant such as the present Emperor. He often thought of writing to her but at the same time dreaded the scandal which would ensue if his attachment became known. When however the day of Presentation at last arrived his caution suddenly deserted him, and he sent to Akikonomu's palace an assortment of the most costly and magnificent gifts which his treasury could supply—comb-boxes, scrap-boxes, cases for incense-jars; all of the most exquisite workmanship and material; with these was a supply of the most precious perfumes both for burning and for the scenting of clothes, so that the bales in which these gifts arrived scented the air for a full league on every side. This extravagant magnificence, besides relieving Suzaku's feelings, had another very definite object. It was particularly intended to annoy the lady's guardian, to whom, as Suzaku very well knew, the contents of these packages would immediately be shown. It so happened that Genji was actually at Akikonomu's palace when the scented bales arrived; her servants at once showed them to him and told him whence they came. He picked up at random one of a pair of comb-boxes; it was a work of fascinating elegance and delicacy. Near it was a box for combs such as are worn in the hair, decorated with a pattern of flowers. In the very center of one petal was an inscription. Looking closer he read the poem:

"Come not again!"* Because it fell to me,
Who least would have it so,
At Heaven's command your exile to ordain;
To others, not to me who bade you go,
You come again!

Somehow or other, in cases of this kind, Genji could never help imagining what he himself would feel if he were in the same position. Supposing that he had fallen in love with someone all those years ago and that the beloved person had gone away immediately to some far-off place; and suppose that he, instead of forgetting all about her as might have been expected, had waited patiently year after year and, when at last she returned, had been told that she was to be handed over to someone else—he saw on reflection that the situation was really very painful. Judging from his own experience he knew that Suzaku's complete lack of employment, now that he had resigned all his official duties, would gravely aggravate the case. Yes, he must indeed be passing through a period of terrible agitation! He was now extremely sorry that he had ever suggested the Presentation of the young Princess. He had indeed in the past good reason to resent his brother's conduct towards him. But lately Suzaku had shown nothing but affability...He stood for a long while lost in thought. It was all very perplexing. Turning at last to Akikonomu's gentlewomen who were inspecting these magnificent presents, he asked whether their mistress had already composed her answering poem. "And surely a letter must also have come with these things?" he added. There was indeed a letter and the gentlewomen had read it, but they very much doubted whether it was fit for Genji's eyes and made no offer to produce it. The Princess herself was distressed by this exhibition of devotion on the part of one with whom she could no longer have any dealings. What answer could she possibly contrive? But her maids were pressing round her, insisting that it would be intolerably rude to allow the messengers to depart without handing to them a word of thanks, and Genji was telling her that not to reply was out of the question; a few words would suffice. No doubt they were right. She felt very much embarrassed by Suzaku's attentions; but she remembered distinctly how handsome, how distinguished he had seemed to her on that day of the farewell ceremony. There had been tears in his eyes, and though it all happened so many years ago she could recall as distinctly as if it were yesterday the vague feelings of childish sympathy and admiration which her meeting with the young Emperor had aroused in her on that last morning when she went to the Palace for her Crowning. With these memories were blended others;

---

* The formula with which the Emperor dispatches the Vestal of Ise.

thoughts, for example, of her mother Lady Rokujo and of the long exile which they had shared. She wrote no letter, but only the poem:

"Come not again!" I wept to hear those words,
Thinking you willed it so,
When Heaven's command my exile did ordain;
Now hearing that it grieved you I should go,
I weep again.

The messengers who had brought the presents were richly rewarded and sent upon their way. Genji would very much have liked to see her reply, but she refused to show it to him.

She was small and frail. How well Suzaku, with his almost girlish beauty, would have suited her; while as for the Emperor, he was years her junior, scarcely out of the nursery. Did she too (though she certainly breathed no word of complaint) secretly resent the steps which he had taken for her worldly advancement? This idea troubled him sorely; but it was by now far too late to undo the arrangement, and the best he could do was to stay with her for a little while and advise her as kindly and discreetly as possible how to conduct herself in the new life that was before her. He then interviewed the Court chamberlains who were to arrange her Presentation, and having settled everything satisfactorily with them he made his way to the Inner Palace. He did not wish it to appear that he was himself standing sponsor for the new arrival nor that he was in the Palace as her relative or guardian. He therefore gave his coming the appearance of an ordinary ceremonial visit.

Princess Akikonomu's palace was famous for the unusual number of good-looking gentlewomen who were in service there. Many of these had recently been living at their homes, but they now assembled in full force, and arriving with their mistress at Court created a most dazzling impression. Were Rokujo alive, with what solicitude would she be watching over that day's momentous proceedings, thought Genji, as he saw the procession arrive; and remembering her singular gifts and lively intelligence, he felt how great a loss she was not to himself only, but to the whole life of the Court. So rare indeed (as it now seemed to him) was her perfection both of mind and person that he seldom encountered among his acquaintance talent or accomplishment of any kind without immediately recalling how slender these attainments would seem if set beside those of Lady Rokujo.

On the day of the Presentation Fujitsubo was at the Palace. When she told the Emperor that someone new was coming to see him, he listened very earnestly and attentively. He was an intelligent and lively child, very forward for his age. After telling him all about the princess, "so you see she is rather an important lady," Fujitsubo continued, "and when she comes this evening you must be very polite to her and not play any of your tricks..." The Emperor said nothing, but he thought to himself that if the lady were indeed so grown-up and so important, far from wanting to tease her he would be very frightened of her indeed. Great was his delight then when very late that evening there arrived at the Palace a very shy, shrinking girl, very small and fragile, not indeed looking like a grown-up person at all. He thought her very pretty; but he was much more at his ease with Chujo's little daughter, who had lived at the Palace for some while and was very sociable and affectionate, while the new princess was terribly silent and shy. Still, though he found her rather difficult to get on with, he felt, partly owing to the deference with which, as Prince Genji's ward, she was treated by everyone else at Court, and partly owing to the magnificence with which she was served and appareled—he felt that she was in some way which he did not understand a person of very great importance. In the evenings indeed he allowed the one to wait upon him as often as the other; but when he wanted a partner in some game or someone to amuse him in the early part of the day, it was seldom Akikonomu for whom he sent.

To no Chujo had presented his daughter at Court with the express intention that she should one day share the Throne. The presence of this formidable rival at the Palace could not fail to cause him considerable anxiety.

The poem with which Princess Akikonomu had acknowledged the ex-Emperor's gifts had but served to increase his agitation. He knew that he must now banish all thought of her from his mind; but it was hard indeed to do so. He was brooding now over his loss, when Genji arrived on a visit. They talked for a long while about many different matters, and in the course of this conversation mention was made of the ceremonies upon the occasion of Lady Akikonomu's departure for Ise. This was a subject which they had often discussed before; but now, as on previous occasions, the conversation terminated without Suzaku making the slightest allusion to the real reason why this topic so much interested him. Genji naturally did not betray his knowledge of the secret; but he was curious to know exactly how far this mysterious passion went, and he could not restrain himself from experimenting upon his brother with various anecdotes concerning the lady in question and her recent admission to the Emperor's suite. It was apparent in a moment that Suzaku suffered acutely while these subjects were being discussed, and Genji, ashamed of his unkindness, hastily turned the conversation to other matters.

At such a ceremony as that of the crowning of the Vestal the Emperor meets the lady whom he is to initiate face to face and during the whole proceedings no curtain or screen divides them. Suzaku must therefore at least know what Princess Akikonomu looked like; which was more than Genji did, for she had till this day never received him except in an unlighted room or behind her curtains-of-state. In what exactly did her charm consist? What was it that had kindled in the ex-Emperor's heart a passion that had survived the lapse of so many years? The problem intrigued him and he almost envied his brother the knowledge which he must possess on the subject. She was indeed evidently of a very melancholy, indolent disposition. If only she would sometimes forget herself, show a little of the impetuosity of youth, then in course of time he might hope for a moment to catch a glimpse of her as she really was! But while her gravity and reticence seemed to become every day more pronounced, all his dealings with her tended only to confirm his conviction that underneath all this reserve was concealed an interesting and admirable character.

Now that all the Emperor's time was divided between the two princesses of his retinue, Prince Hyobukyo had given up all idea of presenting his second daughter at Court. Perhaps an opportunity would occur later on when the Emperor was of an age to perceive for himself that such a match was by no means to be despised. Meanwhile his favor seemed to be pretty equally divided between the two existing claimants. He was particularly interested in pictures and had as a result of this taste himself acquired considerable skill. It happened that Lady Akikonomu painted very charmingly, and so soon as he discovered this the Emperor began constantly sending for her to paint pictures with him. Among the serving-women in the Palace he had always taken an interest in any who were said to be fond of pictures; and it was natural that when he discovered painting to be the favorite occupation of the pretty princess he should become very much attached to her. Hers were not solemn pictures, but such clever, quick sketches; so that just to watch her do them was an exciting game. And when, sitting so charmingly beside him on the divan, she paused and held her brush in the air for a moment wondering where to put the next stroke, she looked so daring that the little Emperor's heart was completely captivated. Soon he was going to her rooms at all hours, and To no Chujo became seriously alarmed lest his own daughter should lose her primacy. But he was determined not to be outdone, and being of an extremely ingenious and resourceful nature he soon had a plan for putting an end to this menacing situation. He sent for all the most skilful painters in the land and under strict bond of secrecy set them to work upon a collection of pictures which was to be like nothing that had ever been seen before. They were to be illustrations to romances, which would be preferable to purely ingenious subjects, the significance being more easily grasped by a young mind and all the most interesting and exciting stories were chosen. In addition to these illustrations there was to be a set of "Months," a very attractive subject, with texts specially written for the occasion. In due time Princess Chujo* showed them to the Emperor, who was naturally very much interested and soon afterwards asked for them again, saying that he thought Princess Akikonomu would like to see them. At this Princess Chujo began to make difficulties, and though His Majesty promised to show them to no one else and carry them with the greatest care straight to the other princess's apartments, she refused to part with them. Genji heard of this and was amused to see that To no Chujo could still throw himself into these absurd conspiracies with the same childish excitement as in their young days. "I am very sorry," he said to the Emperor, "to hear that Princess Chujo hides her pictures from you and will not let you take them away and study them at your ease. It seems, too, that she was quite cross and quarrelsome about it, which was most reprehensible. But I have some very nice pictures, painted a long while ago. I will send them to you."

At the Nijo-in there were whole cupboards full of pictures both old and new. Taking Murasaki with him he now inspected their contents and together they went through the whole collection, putting on one side those which were most likely to appeal to modern taste. There were naturally many illustrations of the *Everlasting Wrong*† and the story of Wang Chao-chün,‡ both of them very interesting and moving subjects, but unfortunately quite inappropriate to the present occasion. These therefore had to be excluded. But it occurred to Genji that his own sketches made during his sojourn at Suma and Akashi might be of interest, and sending for the box in which they were kept he took advantage of this occasion to go through them with Murasaki. Even someone seeing them without any knowledge of the circumstances under which they were painted would, if possessed of the slightest understanding of such matters, have at once been profoundly moved by these drawings. It may be imagined then with what emotion they were examined by one to whom each scene came as an answer to the questionings and anxieties of some evil dream from which it seemed there could be no awakening. She told him more of what she had suffered in those unforgettable days than she had ever done before. Why had he not sometimes sent such pictures as these? How they would have comforted and reassured her! And she recited the verse: "Better had it been for me when I was alone to look at pictures of the realms where fishers dwell, than stare at nothing, as I did all day long!" Genji was deeply moved and with tears in his eyes he answered with the verse:

---

* Chujo's daughter. Actually she is called Kokiden, but this is a name of another character in the book, and as the use of it would lead to confusion, I have given her a name which links her to her father.

† The story of Ming Huang and Yang Kuei-fei; a long poem by Po Chü-i.

‡ A Chinese princess given to a Tartar king in marriage and carried away into the north.

"It was an evil time; yet never once in all those days was my heart sore as now when, hand in hand, we view the pictured past."

To one other person only had he shown them—the ex-Empress Fujitsubo. Going through the whole collection sketch by sketch, in order to choose out the best and also to give as good an idea as possible of the different estuaries and bays, he could not help wondering all the time how things were faring in the house of his host at Akashi.

On hearing of the preparations that were taking place at the Nijo-in, To no Chujo went through his pictures again and had them all fitted out with the most elegant ivory-rollers, backings, and ribbons.[*] It was about the tenth day of the third month. The weather was delightful, things were looking at their best and everyone was in a good temper; moreover it was a time at which no particular fetes or ceremonies occupied the Court, so that uninterrupted attention could be now given to those lighter pastimes in which the Emperor so much delighted, and whole days were spent unrolling painting after painting. The one ambition of everyone at Court was to rout out and bring to the Palace some picture which should particularly catch the young Emperor's fancy. Both Akikonomu's partisans and those of Lady Chujo had brought forward vast numbers of scrolls. On the whole, illustrated romances proved to be the most popular. Akikonomu's side was strongest in ancient works of well-established reputation; while Lady Chujo patronized all the cleverest modern painters, so that her collection, representing as it did all that most appealed to the fashionable tastes of the moment, made at first sight a more dazzling impression. The Emperor's own ladies-in-waiting were divided in opinion. Some of the most intelligent were on the side of the ancients; others favored the present day. But on the whole modern works tended to win their approval.

It happened that Fujitsubo was paying one of her periodical visits to the Court, and having given a casual inspection to the exhibits of both parties she decided to suspend her usual religious observances and devote herself to a thorough study of all these works, for painting was a matter in which she had always taken a deep interest. Hearing the animated discussions which were taking place between the supporters of modern and ancient art, she suggested that those present should be formed into two teams. On Lady Akikonomu's side the principal names were Hei-naishi no Suke, Jiju no Naishi, Shosho no Myobu; on Lady Chujo's—Daini no Naishi no Suke, Chujo no-Myobu and Hyoye no Myobu. These were considered the cleverest women of the day, and Fujitsubo promised herself very good entertainment from such an interchange of wit and knowledge as their rivalry was likely to afford.

---

[*] For tying up the rolls.

In the first contest that archetype and parent of all romances, *The Bamboo-Cutter's Story*,* was matched against the tale of Toshikage in *The Hollow Tree*. The partisans of antiquity defended their choice as follows: "We admit that this story, like the ancient bamboo-stem in which its heroine was found, has in the course of ages become a little loose in the joints. But the character of Lady Kaguya herself, so free from all stain of worldly impurity, so nobly elevated both in thought and conduct, carries us back to the Age of the Gods, and if such a tale fails to win your applause, this can only be because it deals with matters far beyond the reach of your frivolous feminine comprehensions." To this the other side replied: "The Sky Land to which Lady Kaguya was removed is indeed beyond our comprehensions, and we venture to doubt whether any such place exists. But if we regard merely the mundane part of your story, we find that the heroine emanated from a bamboo joint. This gives to the story from the start an atmosphere of low life which we for our part consider very disagreeable. We are told that from the lady's person there emanated a radiance which lit up every corner of her foster-father's house. But these fireworks, if we remember aright, cut a very poor figure when submitted to the august light of His Majesty's palace. Moreover the episode of the fireproof ratskin ends very tamely, for after Abe no Oshi† had spent thousands of gold pieces in order to obtain it, no sooner was it put to the test than it disappeared in a blaze of flame. Still more lamentable was the failure of Prince Kuramochi† who, knowing that the journey to Fairyland was somewhat difficult, did not attempt to go there but had a branch of the Jewel Tree fabricated by his goldsmith; a deception which was exposed at the first scratch."

The picture was painted by Kose no Omi‡ and the text was in the hand of Ki no Tsurayki.§ It was on Kanya paper backed with Chinese silk. The cover was of a reddish violet tinge, the rollers being of sandalwood—by no means an extraordinary get-up. The moderns then proceeded to defend their own exhibit; "Toshikage,"¶ they said, "though buffeted by wind and wave, pitched headlong into a stormy sea and in the end cast up upon an unknown shore, pursued, undaunted by suffering and disaster, the purpose which he had set before him, and succeeded at last in displaying,

---

* A 9th-century story about a fairy who was found in a bamboo-stem, set various fantastic ordeals to her lovers and finally disappeared in the Land Above the Sky. It is written in a rather disjointed style. Translated by Victor Dickins in *Japanese Texts*.

† One of the suitors.

‡ Also called Aimi. Successor of Kose no Kanaoka, who founded the Kose school in the 9th century.

§ 883-946 A.D. Editor of the *Kokinshu*, the first official anthology of poetry.

¶ Having set out from Japan to China he was wrecked on the coast of Persia, where he acquired a magic zithern and the knowledge of unearthly tunes, armed with which he won great fame as a musician in China and Japan. See Aston's *History of Japanese Literature*, p. 76.

both at the foreign court* and in our own country, the marvelous talent which it had cost him so much to acquire. The adventures of so dauntless a character, affording as they do a comparison between the manners of the Land Beyond the Sea and of our own Land of Sunrise, cannot fail to be of interest; moreover the same contrast has been maintained in the style of the pictures as in the matter of the text."

It was painted on thick white paper such as poem-slips are made of; the outer cover was of blue paper and the roller of yellow jade. The artist was Tsunenori;† the scribe, Ono no Michikaze‡—a combination that could hardly have been more dazzling in its fashionableness and modernity. Against such claims as these the partisans of the antique were quite unable to prevail and Lady Chujo's side scored the overwhelming victory.

In the next contest the *Tales of Ise*§ were pitted against the story of *Sho Sammi*.¶ A long discussion ensued; but here again the fact that *Sho Sammi* deals with persons in a comfortable and prosperous situation, presents scenes of court life and shows the world as we know it today could not fail to render this work far more attractive to the majority of these young critics. An opposite opinion was voiced by Heinaishi, who recited the verse: "Shall we leave the deep heart of Ise's waters unexplored till time shall have effaced their secret, like a footprint that the tide washes from the shore?" "Shall the fame of Narihira,"** she added, "be eclipsed by modern tittle-tattle dressed up in the finery of a specious style?" To this Daini no Naishi no Suke replied with the verse: "Upon the topmost regions of the sky†† our hero's heart is set; with scorn he views your shoals, upon which, heavy as a thousand watery fathoms, the ages rest."

"Well," said Fujitsubo, "ambition such as that of Prince Hyoye‡‡ is no doubt a very valuable quality; but I sincerely hope that admiration for him and his like will never cause us to let the fame of Captain Laigo§§ sink into decay!" And she recited the verse: "Has the old fisherman of Ise shore, like seaweed that the ebbing tide reveals, so long been flattered by the public eye, only to sink at last beneath the rising sea of scorn?"

These feminine discussions are capable of continuing, more or less at cross-purposes for an indefinite length of time. It would indeed be impossible to record all the arguments and counter-arguments that were

---

* China.
† Asukabe Tsunenori, flourished about 964 A.D.
‡ Also called Ono no Dofu, the most celebrated calligraphist of Japan.
§ A collection of short love-episodes, each centering round a poem or poems. See Alton's *History of Japanese Literature*, p. 80.
¶ Already lost in the 15th century.
** Hero of the *Tales of Ise*.
†† I.e. upon promotion at Court. Courtiers were called "men above the clouds."
‡‡ Presumably the hero of the tale of *Sho Sammi*.
§§ Narihira, hero of the *Tales of Ise*.

expended over even one of these pictures. Moreover the younger and less considered of the gentlewomen present, though any one of them would have given her eyes not to miss any of the paintings that were being unrolled, were hustled into the background, even though they belonged to the Emperor's own or to Lady Fujitsubo's household, and were scarcely able to see anything at all. This occasioned much jealousy and heart-burning.

Presently Genji arrived at the Palace and was greatly diverted by the spectacle of this disorderly and embittered combat. "If you will get up another competition," he said, "I will arrange for the Emperor to be present and will myself make the awards." In preparation for this event, which he had indeed been contemplating for some time, he made a further selection from the pictures which he had recently put aside, and having done so he could not resist inserting among them the two scrolls of his sketches made at Suma and Akashi. To no Chujo meanwhile, determined not to be outdone, was straining every nerve in preparation for the new contest. It was indeed a moment in the history of our country when the whole energy of the nation seemed to be concentrated upon the search for the prettiest method of mounting paper-scrolls. In arranging the conditions of the contest Genji had said: "My idea is that it should be confined to paintings already in existence; we do not want a lot of new work hurriedly executed for this special purpose…" But To no Chujo could not resist the temptation to set some of his favorite masters to work, and improvising a little studio with a secret door he strove to steal a march on his rivals. The secrecy was not however as well maintained as he could have desired; even Suzaku, in his secluded apartments, heard the story and determined to put his own collection at the service of Princess Akikonomu. He had a series of "Festivals All the Year Round," painted by various famous old masters; texts explaining these pictures had been added by no less a hand than that of the Emperor Daigo.* Why should he not order a series of paintings illustrating the principal events of his own reign? Among these subjects one would naturally be the crowning of the Vestal at the Daigoku Hall upon the day of her departure for Ise. He entrusted this scene to Kose no Kimmochi† and it may be imagined with what care and insistence he discussed every detail of a work so dear to his heart. It was encased in a delicately fretted box of aloes wood. The pattern on the wrappings and decorations of the roll was a heart-shaped crest formed by leaves of the same tree. Nothing could have been more delightfully up-to-date. He sent it by the hand of the Captain of the Senior Bodyguard, who was one of his retainers. There was no message, save for a poem written on

---

* 898-930, a great patron of literature, and himself an important poet and calligrapher.

† Grandson of the great Kose no Kanaoka. Flourished about 960 A.D.

the picture just by where the Vestal was shown arriving in her litter at the Daigoku Hall: "Though I no longer within the Circle of the Gods a place may take, yet unforgotten is the concourse which in those hours with bright Divinities I held."

To return no answer would show too great a disrespect towards one who had once occupied the Throne, and though these attentions distressed her she broke off a piece of the ritual comb which he had fastened in her hair on that day long ago, and tying to it the verse, "Not yet forgotten is that high converse, and once again within the Precinct of the Gods oh were it but my lot to stray!" she wrapped the broken comb in Chinese paper of deep color and gave it to the messenger, whom she rewarded with many handsome presents. The ex-Emperor when he opened the packet was deeply moved, and for the first time regretted that he had so soon resigned the Throne. Not unnaturally he was feeling somewhat bitterly against Prince Genji; but he realized that he had himself, in past days, deserved none too well at his brother's hands. Most of the ex-Emperor's pictures had belonged to his mother, the Empress Kokiden; unfortunately a considerable part of her collection had however come into the possession of Lady Chujo, who was her granddaughter.

The ex-Emperor's wife, Lady Oborozuki, was also extremely interested in painting and had shown the utmost discrimination in forming her collection.

When the great day came, though there had not been much time for preparation everything was arranged in the most striking and effective manner. The ladies-in-waiting belonging to the two sides stood drawn up in line on either side of the Imperial Throne; the courtiers, very much on the alert, were ranged up in the verandah of the small back room. Lady Chujo's party (the left) exhibited their pictures in boxes of purple sandalwood mounted on sapanwood stands, over which was thrown a cover of Chinese brocade worked on a mauve ground. The carpet on which the boxes stood was of Chinese fine-silk, dyed to the color of grape-juice. Six little girls were in attendance to assist in handling the boxes and scrolls; they were dressed in mantles with white scarves lined with pink; their tunics were of scarlet, worn with facings blue outside and light green within.

Akikonomu's boxes were of aloes wood arranged on a low table of similar wood, but lighter in color. The carpet was of Korean brocade on a blue-green ground. The festoons hanging round the table and the design of the table-legs were carefully thought out and in the best taste. The little girls in attendance wore blue mantles, with willow-colored scarves; their tunics, brown outside and yellow within. When all the boxes were duly arranged on their stands, the Emperor's own ladies took up their places, some with Lady Chujo's supporters, some with the opposing side. At the summons of the herald Genji and To no Chujo now appeared and with them Genji's half-brother, Prince Sochi no Miya, who among the various arts which he cultivated was particularly fond of painting. He had received no official summons on this particular occasion, but had in the end yielded to Genji's entreaties that he would come and help him in his difficult task. Prince Sochi was at once called to the Emperor's side and appointed part-umpire in the coming contest. An amazing collection of paintings had been assembled and assuredly the task of the judges was no light one. A great impression was made when Akikonomu's side produced the famous series of "Four Seasons" by noted masters of antiquity. Both the charming fancy displayed in the choice of episodes for illustration and the easy, flowing character of the brush-strokes rendered these works highly attractive; and the modern paintings on paper, being necessarily limited in size, sometimes, especially in landscape, made a certain impression of incompleteness. Yet the far greater richness both of brushwork and invention gave even to the more trivial of these modern works a liveliness which made them compare not unfavorably with the masterpieces of the past. Thus it was very difficult indeed to reach any decision, save that today, as on the previous occasion, both sides had produced many works of absorbing interest.

The sliding-screen of the breakfast-room was now pushed aside and Lady Fujitsubo entered. Remembering how learned she was in these matters Genji felt somewhat shy, and contented himself henceforward as exhibit after exhibit was produced with an occasional comment or suggestion, discreetly thrown in only when some point of especial difficulty threatened an indefinite delay. The contest was still undecided when night fell.

At last the moment arrived when there was only one more picture to show on each side. Amid intense excitement Princess Akikonomu's side produced the roll containing Genji's sketches at Suma. To no Chujo was aghast. His daughter's side too had reserved for their last stroke one of the most important works at their disposition; but against the prospect of so masterly a hand working at complete leisure and far from the distracting influences which beset an artist in town, Lady Chujo's supporters at once knew that they could not hope to prevail. An additional advantage was given to Genji's paintings by the pathos of the subject. That during those years of exile he had endured a cheerless and monotonous existence those present could well conjecture. But when they saw, so vividly presented, both the stern manner of his life and in some sort even the feelings which this rustic life had aroused in one used to every luxury and indulgence, they could not but be deeply moved, and there were many (Prince Sochi no Miya among them) who could scarcely refrain from tears. Here were presented in the most vivid manner famous bays and shores of the Suma coast, so renowned in story yet to these city folk so utterly unknown and unimagined. The text was written in cursive Chinese characters, helped out here and there with a little native script, and unlike the business day-to-day journals that men generally keep it was varied by the insertion of an occasional poem or song. The spectators now clamored only for more specimens of Genji's handiwork, and it would have been impossible at that moment to interest them in anything else. It seemed to them as though all the interest and beauty of the many pictures which they had been examining had in some strange manner accumulated and attached themselves to this one scroll. By universal and ungrudging consent Princess Akikonomu's side was awarded the victory.

It was already nearing the dawn when Genji, feeling somewhat discursive, sent round the great tankard and presently began telling stories to the company. "From my earliest childhood," he said at last, "I have always been fond of books; and my father the late Emperor, fearing that I might become wholly absorbed in my studies, used to say to me: 'Perhaps learning carries with it inevitably so great a share of the world's esteem that, to redress the balance, the scholar, once he advances beyond a certain stage of learning, is doomed to pay for his enviable attainments either by ill health or poverty. Those who are born to greatness may be certain that, whether they exert their minds or not, the advantages of noble birth will suffice to distinguish them from their fellows; and for you of all men the acquisition of such ill-starred accomplishments would be entirely superfluous. I sincerely hope that you will not allow them to occupy too much of your time.' He arranged that most of my lessons should be in practical subjects connected with national administration and economy. I got on fairly well, but there was no branch in which I showed any particular aptitude. It was only in painting, which my preceptors considered a very trivial and unbecoming pastime, that I displayed any unusual talent. Often I used to wonder whether I should ever get the chance of using this gift to the full, for the time allotted to these lighter distractions was very short. At last, with my unexpected retirement to a remote shore, the longed-for opportunity arrived. On every side the great sea spread about me; I began to learn its secrets, became so intimate with its every mood and aspect that where these sketches fail it is not for lack of understanding, but because there came at last a point where my brush could no longer keep pace with the visions that beset my brain. Not having previously had any opportunity of showing these sketches to His Majesty, I took advantage of this occasion to display them. But I fear that my action in using them for this competition will when reflected upon provoke very unfavorable comments…" The conversation was carried on by Prince Sochi no Miya: "I know, of course," he said, "that mere industry will not carry one far in any art; his heart must be in the matter. But all the same there is a great deal which can simply be learnt from masters; so that a man, without any understanding of what is really important, will often easily succeed in imitating the outward forms and procedures of an art. But painting and draughts demand an extraordinary degree of natural equipment and also furnish us with the strangest surprises; for some apparently half-witted fellow, who does not seem capable of any useful activity, will turn out to be a genius at draughts or painting! On the other hand I have occasionally come across instances where intelligent children of good family have possessed what I may term a general superiority, showing an unusual capacity in every form of art and learning.

"My father the late Emperor gave personal attention to the training of all his children, both girls and boys, in every imaginable art and accomplishment. But it was in your education, Genji, that he took by far the greatest interest, and it was to you, whom he considered most likely to profit by it, that he was at pains to hand on the great store of information which in the course of his long life he had here and there acquired. In literature of course you were far ahead of any of us; just as you were in other less important matters, such as playing upon the zithern, which was indeed perhaps your principal accomplishment. But I remember that, in addition to this, you played reasonably well on the flute, guitar, and great zithern; as indeed your father often mentioned with wonder. These talents of yours were well known at Court, and I for my part had heard that you occasionally amused yourself with brushes and paints. But I had always supposed that this was a mere pastime, and I confess that the masterpieces which you have exhibited before us today took me completely by surprise. I assure you that even the great ink-painters of antiquity would feel no small uneasiness should their works be set beside these sketches of yours. You are indeed a prodigy!" He spoke rather thickly and indistinctly, for he was already a little bit fuddled with wine; and being for the same reason somewhat lachrymose, when mentioning his late father's name he suddenly burst into tears.

It was towards the end of the month and the late moon had at last risen. The rooms where they were assembled were still dark, but the sky outside was already aglow with dawn. The Keeper of Books and Instruments was asked to bring out the zitherns. To no Chujo took the *wagon*,[*] which he played, if not so well as Genji, at any rate in a very distinguished manner. Sochi no Miya took the great zithern and Genji the *kin*.[†] The lute was played by Akikonomu's gentlewoman Shosho no Myobu. There was a certain courtier who had a genius for beating time;

---

[*] Japanese zithern.
[†] Chinese zithern.

he was now sent for and a most agreeable concert ensued. Dawn was spreading fast. Color began to come into the flowers, and the features of those sitting by became dimly discernible in the growing light. The birds were singing lustily; a pleasant morning had begun.

Presents were now distributed to the guests by Lady Fujitsubo on behalf of the Emperor; Prince Sochi no Miya received in addition the special tribute of a cloak from the wardrobe, in recognition of his services as umpire.

Genji gave instructions that the Suma scroll should be left with Fujitsubo. Hearing that it was only one of a series, she begged to be shown the rest. "You shall see them all in good time," Genji said; "there are far too many of them to go through at one sitting." The little Emperor, too, seemed to have thoroughly enjoyed the proceedings, which was a great comfort to those who had engineered them.

When To no Chujo saw with what zest Genji supported his ward Princess Akikonomu even in such trifling matters as this contest he again became a little uneasy about Lady Chujo's position. But observing the situation closely, he noted that the young Emperor, who certainly began by being very deeply attached to his little playmate, after the first excitement of recognizing this new companion with her interesting grownup accomplishments had passed away, settled down again quite happily to his old love. For the present at any rate there was no need for anxiety.

Genji had a strong presentiment the Court ceremony and festivals of the reign were destined to be taken as a model in future times. It was for this reason that even in the matter of private pastimes and receptions he took great pains that everything should be carried out in the most perfectly appropriate and pleasurable manner. Hence life at Court during this period became one long series of exquisitely adjusted pomps and festivities.

Genji was still haunted by the impermanence of worldly things, and now that the Emperor was beginning to reach years of discretion he often thought quite seriously of embracing a monastic life. It seemed to him that in history one so often reads of men who at an immature age rose to high position and became conspicuous figures in the world only to fall, after a very short time, into disaster and ignominy. With regard to himself he had felt since his exile that if the position in which he now found himself was beyond that to which he was properly entitled, this was only fate's kind compensation for the indignities to which in his early life he had suddenly been exposed. But now the debt which fortune owed him was fully discharged and he could not believe that he was far from the brink of some fresh disaster. He would have liked to shut himself away in some retired corner and devote himself to meditations upon the life to come; he did indeed choose a quiet site on a hill near the City and build a hermitage there, which he even went so far as to furnish with images and holy books. But so many questions arose concerning the education of his children and their future at Court that there could be no question of his actually taking his vows, at any rate for some considerable time; and what exactly he had in mind when he began building this hermitage it would be hard to say.

The Wind in the Pine-Trees

The new quarters which Genji had built to the east of his palace were now ready and the lady from the Village of Falling Flowers was duly installed there. The western wing and connecting galleries of the Nijo-in had been arranged in offices for the clerks whom he employed in his capacity as Grand Minister. In the eastern wing he intended to establish the Lady of Akashi. The women's quarters at the back of the palace he enlarged considerably, making several sets of very agreeable and comfortable apartments; these he destined for those ladies who having in the past received some mark of favor which, though fleeting, had generally been coupled with handsome promises, now looked to him for recognition and support. He kept the Grand Bedchamber of the Palace open, and though he lived chiefly in the new building, he continued to use the other from time to time and none of the necessary furniture was removed.

He wrote frequently to Akashi and many times begged her to come up to the Capital. But she had heard so many stories of how others had suffered at his hands—how he had again and again toyed with the affections not only of humble creatures such as herself, but of the greatest ladies in the land, only to cast them aside a few months later with the most callous indifference. Surely it would be foolish not to take warning. If this was his conduct towards person of rank and influence, what sort of treatment could she, a friendless girl, expect? What part could she hope to play save the humiliating one of a foil to the young princess who was Genji's lawful bride? Suppose she accepted his offer, suppose she let him install her in this new house, how often would he come near her? Sometimes perhaps on his way to Murasaki's room he might look in casually for a moment; more she could not expect. She saw herself the butt of every lewd wit in his palace. No; she would never consent.

But there were other considerations. Should she continue to bring up her baby daughter in this sequestered spot, how could the child ever hope to take its place among the princes and princesses of the Blood? Little as she trusted Genji, she must not cut off her child from all possibility of an ultimate transference to the Capital. Her parents too realized with dismay that her prospect at the City was none too bright; but on the whole they inclined towards a move.

There was a certain estate near the Oi River* which her mother had inherited (it had belonged to Nakatsukasa no Miya, the mother's paternal grandfather). Successive heirs failed to claim it and for two years the place had been falling into decay. A fresh plan had occurred to the old recluse and his wife. They summoned the caretaker of the place, a descendant of the man whom Nakatsukasa had originally left in charge and said to him: "We had intended to quit the world forever and end our earthly days in this inaccessible retreat. But certain unexpected events in our family have made it necessary that we should again seek a residence within easy reach of the Capital. After our long absence from the Court we should feel utterly lost and bewildered were we to plunge straight into the bustle of the town, and it occurred to us that while we are looking for some quiet, old house to live in permanently, it might be a good thing to use this place at Oi which you have been looking after for us!" "I am afraid you will be very disappointed when you see it," said the man. "For years past no one has been in possession and everything is tumbling to pieces. I have been making shift myself to live in a room which has indeed a kind of ceiling, but no roof! And since the spring they have been building this new hermitage for Prince Genji close by, and this has changed the whole character of the district. The place is crowded with workmen; for the hermitage, by what I can make out, is going to be a very grand affair. If what you are looking for is a quiet, unfrequented spot you will certainly be badly disappointed." His remarks had the opposite effect to that which he had intended. To learn that at Oi they would be living as it were under Genji's very wing was an astonishing piece of news. He ordered the man to put the large repairs in hand at once; what wanted setting to rights indoors they could see to at leisure later on. This did not at all suit the caretaker. "If you want to know," he said sulkily, "I reckon this place belongs to me as much as to anyone. I have been living there quietly all these years and this is the first I have heard of anybody putting in a claim to it. When I first took things in hand the pastures and rice-fields were all running to waste, and his lordship Mimbu no Tayu told me before he died that I could have them for my very own and do what I could with them as payment of certain sums which he then owed me." What he was really frightened of was that if the family came into residence, they would lay claim to some of the livestock and grain that their land had produced. He had suddenly grown very red in the face, his voice quivered with anger and his whole aspect was so grim and even menacing that the old recluse hastened to reassure him: "I am not in any way interested in the farm or its produce," he said; "with regard to them

---

* Also called the Katsura River. Runs near Saga (to the east of Kyoto) where Genji was building his hermitage.

please go on just as before. As a matter of fact I *have* got the title-deeds somewhere here, but it is a long time since I attended to business matters of any kind and it might take me a long while to find these papers. I will remember to look into the question and see how it stands..." The steward soon cooled down. He noted that the old priest was evidently on friendly terms with Genji. This decided him to be civil. And after all, even if the presence of his masters might for the moment be rather inconvenient, he would later on have plenty of opportunities for reimbursing himself. Mollified by these reflections he set the repairs in hand at once.

Genji meanwhile had no notion of what was afoot and could not understand why, after all his entreaties, the Lady of Akashi still hung back. He did not at all like the idea of their child being brought up amid such uncivilized surroundings. Moreover, if the story afterwards became known, it would certainly seem as though he had been reluctant to acknowledge the child and had behaved with great heartlessness in making no proper provision for it or for the mother.

But at last the house of Oi was ready and a letter came from Akashi describing how, with no idea that he was building in the district, they had suddenly remembered the existence of the place and were making plans for living there. He understood quite well the object of this move. The lady of Akashi was determined that if their intercourse was to be resumed it must be in a place where she would not be subjected to a humiliating contact with her rivals. To avoid this she was evidently prepared to make every conceivable sacrifice. He was curious to know more about her future plan of retreat and sent Koremitsu, who was always employed in confidential missions of this kind, to investigate the place a little and let him know if there was anything he could do to assist the newcomers at Oi. Koremitsu reported that the house was in a very agreeable situation which somehow reminded one of the seaside. "It sounds just the place for her," said Genji. The hermitage which he was building was to the south of Daikakuji, which temple, in the beauty of its groves and cascades, it even bid fair to rival. The house where the family from Akashi was coming to live was right on the river, among the most delightful pine-woods, and the unpretentious way in which it was planned, in one long building without galleries or side-wings, gave it rather the air of a farmhouse than of a gentleman's mansion. As regards furniture Koremitsu told him what was most needed and he saw to it that these wants were supplied.

A number of Genji's personal servants now arrived at Akashi to assist the family in their removal. When she found herself actually faced with the prospect of leaving these shores and inlets, near which so great a part of her life had been spent, the Lady of Akashi was filled with consternation. The present plan was that her father should stay on at Akashi alone, and the idea of leaving him made her very unhappy. Looking back over the whole affair, with all its consequences, she was amazed to think that she had ever drifted into this miserable union, which had brought nothing but trouble and confusion upon herself and those for whom she cared. She found herself envying those whose fortune it had been never to cross this prince's path. Her father, seeing the house full of the servants and retainers whom Genji had sent from the Capital, could not deny to himself that here indeed was the fulfillment of his every dream and prayer. He had secured his daughter's future. But what about his own? How would his life be endurable without her? He brooded on this night and day, but never showed what was passing in his mind, save for saying once or twice to his wife: "Do you think even if I went with you I should see much of the little girl?"* The mother was also much distressed. For years past her husband had slept in his little hermitage and had lived an entirely separate life, engrossed in his meditations and devotions. There was little reason to suppose that, even should she stay behind, he would give her very much of his society, and virtually she would be living without any companionship or support. But though he was a spectator of their lives rather than a participator in them, his casual exits and entrances had become the rock in which her whole existence was rooted; the prospect of separation appalled her. He was a strange creature; but she had long ago given up expecting him to play in any sense a husband's part. His odd appearance, his eccentric opinions, their lonely life—all these she had learnt to tolerate in the belief that this at any rate was the last stage of her disillusionment, the final and unalterable ordeal which death alone would end. Suddenly she found herself face to face with this undreamed-of parting, and her heart shrank. The wet-nurse and other young persons whom at the time of the child's birth Genji had sent from the Capital were beginning to become very restive and the prospect of the coming journey delighted them. Yet even the most frivolous among them could not leave these creeks and sandy bays without a pang; and there were some who, knowing that it might never be their lot to visit such scenes again, came near to adding the salt of tears to sleeves already splashed by the breakers of the rising tide.

Autumn had begun and the country was at its loveliest. At dawn upon the day fixed for their departure a chill wind was blowing and insects filled the air with their interminable cry. The Lady of Akashi, already awake, kept going to her window and looking out across the sea. Her father had returned early from celebrating the night service in his chapel; it was with trembling lips that he had performed the familiar ceremonies. But now that the day of parting had come no words of sorrow or ill omen must be spoken. So each was determined, but it was no easy matter to keep things going. The child was brought in, its infant beauty shining like a jewel in

---

* The Lady of Akashi's child.

the grayness of the dawn. The grandfather never wearied of holding it in his arms and, young as it was, an understanding seemed to have grown up between them. He was indeed astonished by the readiness with which the child accepted a companion whose appearance and manners, so different from those of its regular attendants, might have been expected to have alarmed it in the highest degree. Moreover there seemed something inappropriate, almost sinister in their alliance. Yet for long he had scarcely let it be a minute out of his sight. How should he live without it? He did not want to spoil the journey by an outburst of unrestrained grief; yet utterly silent he could not remain, and reciting the verse: "While for good speed upon their road and happiness to come I pray, one thing the travelers will not deny me, an old man's right to shed a foolish tear or two," he tried to hide his tears with his sleeve, exclaiming: "No, I ought not to; I should not do it!"

His wife stood weeping at his side; there was one thing that she could not disguise from herself; after long years both of his life and her own that had been spent in an unceasing protest against the pleasures and frivolities of the world, it was to those same frivolities and in pursuit of the most worldly ambitions that her husband was sending her away from him: "Together we left the City," she cried; "how all alone shall I refind the paths down which you led me over heath and hill?" The Lady of Akashi also recited a poem in which she said that even to those who seem to have parted forever, life with its turns and chances brings strange reunions to pass. She besought her father to come at least part of the way with them; but he seemed to regard it as utterly impossible that he should venture away from his seaside retreat, and it was evident that he regarded the negotiation even of the short road down to the sea as the most venturesome and nerve-racking business.

"When I first put worldly ambitions aside," said the old man, "and contented myself with a mere provincial post, I made up my mind that, come what might, you, my dear daughter, should not suffer from my having sacrificed my own prospects; and how best, despite the remoteness of our home, to fit you for the station of life to which you properly belonged became my one thought and care. But my experience as Governor taught me much; I realized my incapacity for public affairs, and knew that if I returned to the City it would only be to play the wretched part of ex-Governor. My resources were much diminished and were I to set up house again at the Capital it would be on a very different scale from before. I knew that I should be regarded as a failure both in my private and public life, a disgrace to the memory of my father who occupied the highest station in the State; moreover my acceptance of a provincial governorship had everywhere been regarded as the end of my career, and as for myself, I could not but think that it was indeed best it should be so. But you were now growing up and your future had to be thought of. How could I allow you to waste your beauty in this far corner of the earth like a brocade that is never taken from the drawer? But no better prospect seemed to present itself, and in my despair I called upon Buddha and all the gods to help me. That, living as we did, any fresh acquaintances should ever be formed by us seemed out of the question. Yet all the time I believed that some strange chance would one day befall us. And what indeed could have been more utterly unforeseen than the circumstance which at last brought so distinguished a guest to our home? In this I could not but see the hand of Heaven, and my only anxiety was lest too great an inequality of rank should divide you. But since the birth of this child, that fear has not so much troubled me, for I feel that your union is fated to be a lasting one. A child of Royal Blood cannot, we must allow, pass all its days in a village by the sea, and though this parting costs me dear I am determined never again to tamper with the world that I have renounced. Princes are the lamps that light this world, and though they may for a time be destined to cast confusion upon the quiet of rusticity, soon they must perforce return to their true firmament; while those whom they have left smile back, as I do now, into the lowly Sphere* from whence they sprang. Should you hear that I am dead, do not tease yourselves concerning the welfare of my soul, and above all, while less than death divides us, do not worry over what may be befalling me." Thus he poured out all that was passing through his mind and at last he added in conclusion: "You may be sure that each of the six times of Prayer, till the day when the smoke rises from my pyre, I shall pray with all my heart for the happiness of the little princess…"

Hitherto he had spoken with great self-possession; but now his face began to pucker.

There was so much baggage to be transported that a vast quantity of wagons would have been required had the whole party proceeded by road. To send some of the stuff by road and the rest by sea was in many ways inconvenient; moreover Genji's retainers did not wish to be recognized on the journey, and for all these reasons it seemed best that the whole party should proceed by water. They set sail at the hour of the Dragon, and soon their ship, like that of the old poet's story,† was lost amid the morning mists far out across the bay. The old priest stood gazing after it lost in a bewildered trance of grief from which it seemed as though he would never awake. The wind was fresh and favorable, and they arrived at the City punctually at the hour they had announced. Wishing to attract no notice they left their large baggage on board and

---

* The metaphor of souls sinking back into lower incarnations.
† See Waley, *Japanese Poetry* (Oxford, 1920), p. 56.

travelled inland as quickly as possible. The house at Oi at once took their fancy and was, as Koremitsu had noticed, in some curious way very reminiscent of the seaside, so that they soon felt quite at home. The mother had known this place as a girl and moving recollections crowded to her mind at every turn. By Genji's orders a covered gallery had been added to the house, which was a great improvement, and the course of the stream had also been very successfully altered. Much still remained to be done, but for the most part only such small jobs as could easily be finished off later on, when they had got things straight and settled in. On their arrival they found that entertainment had been prepared for them at Genji's command by one of his confidential servants. He intended to come himself at the earliest opportunity, but many days passed before he could contrive an excuse for slipping away. The Lady of Akashi had made sure that he would be there to welcome her. She therefore spent the first days at Oi in the deepest depression, regretting her old home and quite at a loss how to occupy her time. At last she took out the zithern which Genji had given to her at Akashi. She was feeling at the moment particularly desperate, and as she had the part of the house where she was sitting entirely to herself she gave vent to her feelings in a somewhat wild improvisation, which soon startled her mother from the couch where she was lying and brought her to the player's side. With the music of the zithern was blended the sighing of the wind in the great pine-woods that lay behind the house. "An altered and a lonely woman to this my native village I return. But still unchanged the wind blows music through the trees." So the mother sang, and the daughter: "Far off now is the dear companion of my happier days, and none is here who comprehends the broken language of my lute."

While things were going thus dismally at Oi, Genji was feeling very uneasy. To have established the people from Akashi so close to the Capital and then neglect them entirely was indeed a monstrous way to behave; but circumstances made it very difficult for him to escape unobserved. He had not said anything to Murasaki about the move to Oi, but such things have a way of getting round, and he decided that it would be better not to explain his absence in a note. He therefore wrote to her one morning as follows: "There are various matters at Katsura* which I ought to have looked into a long while ago; but I did not at all want the bother of going there and have kept on putting it off. Some people whom I promised to visit have settled near by and I am afraid I shall have to go and see them too. Then I ought to go over to my hermitage at Saga and see the Buddha there before it is painted. So I am afraid I shall have to be away for two or three days."

---

* Where Genji had an estate.

Some faint echo of the business at Oi had reached her, but in a very garbled form. She heard that Genji was hurriedly building a large new mansion on his estate at Katsura. This was of course quite untrue. Murasaki at once concluded that the mansion at Katsura was intended for the Lady of Akashi and depressed by this she wrote in answer: "Do you know the story of the woodman* who waited so long that leaves sprouted from the handle of his axe? Do not imagine that I shall be quite so patient as that..." It was evident that she was out of humor with him! "How crotchety you are!" he said. "In the past you did indeed have some excuse; but now I have entirely changed my habits. Anyone who knows me would tell you as much." It took the whole morning to coax her back into a reasonable frame of mind. At last very secretly, with no outriders of any kind save for a few intimate personal attendants, and taking every precaution lest he should be spied on or followed, he set out for Oi and arrived there just as it was growing dark. Even when dressed in the plain hunting clothes that he wore at Akashi he had seemed to the Lady of the Shore a figure of unimaginable brilliance; and now when he appeared in full Court dress (he had indeed made himself as splendid as possible for the occasion) she was completely overwhelmed by his magnificence and soon, in contemplating this dazzling spectacle, the whole household recovered from the gloom into which they had been plunged. The little princess had of course to be fetched and it was naturally with considerable emotion that he now saw his child for the first time. It was indeed a pity that he should make its acquaintance in this belated manner. What nonsense people talk about children, he thought. Everyone used to make such a fuss about Yugiri, Princess Aoi's child, and pretend it was so remarkably handsome. Such people were mere time-servers and flatterers. If it had not been the Prime Minister's grandchild no one would have seen anything remarkable about it at all. But here was a very different story. If this little creature did not grow up into a woman of quite exceptional beauty, he was indeed very much mistaken. The child smiled at him with such innocent surprise and had such a perfect little face and air that he at once took an immense fancy to it. The nurse who when he had first sent her to Akashi was already losing her looks, had now grown quite middle-aged. He asked her many questions about her experiences in these last months, to which she replied frankly and without any shyness. He felt sorry that he had sent her to waste the last hours of her vanishing youth in so dull a place and now said sympathetically: "Here too you are a long way from everything and it is not at all easy

---

* A Chinese named Wang Chih. He watched a couple of hermits playing chess in a cave. The game absorbed his attention so completely that it seemed to him to last only a few minutes; but when it was over he found that years had elapsed and leaves had actually sprouted from the wood of his axe.

for me to come over. I wish you would persuade your mistress to make use of the apartments I originally offered her..." "We must see how we get on," the Lady of Akashi interposed.

That night at least she had no reason to complain of neglect and day came only too swiftly. During the morning he gave fresh instructions to the retainers who were responsible for the redecoration of the house, and presently a number of people who farmed on and around his Katsura estate came to pay their respects, having heard beforehand that he was about to visit his properties in this neighborhood. As they were there, he thought he had better make them useful and set them to work repairing some places in the Lodge where the shrubs had been trodden down. "I see," he said, "that some of the artificial rocks have rolled over and almost disappeared under the grass. I must get my people to hoist them up again into some position in which they will not look quite so pointless. However this is not the kind of garden that looks the better for too much trouble being taken with it; and you may not be staying here very long. It will not do to make everything here too nice or it will soon be as hard to go away from here as it was to leave Akashi." Soon they fell to talking of those old days, now laughing, now weeping, but all the time divinely happy. Once her mother came and peeped at them as they sat talking and the sight of their happiness made her forget that she herself was old, was wretched. Wreathed in smiles she hobbled away from the room. A little later she was watching him standing in his shirt-sleeves instructing the workmen how to utilize the little spring of water that issued near the gallery of the eastern wing. He had no idea that he was being watched, till happening to come across a tray for flower-offerings and other religious gear lying about the house, he suddenly thought of the pious old lady and said to his companion: "By the way, did your mother come with you? I had quite forgotten she might be here or I should not be going about the house dressed in this fashion." He sent for his cloak and going up to the curtain-of-state behind which he was told the old lady would probably be sitting, he said in a gentle tone: "Madam, I have come to thank you; for it is your doing that the little girl thrives so well. Your prayers and devotions it is that have lightened the load of her *karma* and caused her to grow up so fine and healthy a child. I know well enough what it must have cost you to leave the house which had become your sanctuary and mingle once more with the follies of this transitory world. I know too what anxiety you must be in concerning the husband whom you have left... For this and much else, Madam, I have come to thank you..." "That you should guess how dear it cost me to come back to the turmoil of the world, and that in these kind words you should tell me my exertions have not been made in vain, is in itself sufficient reward for all that I have endured, and justifies a life drawn out beyond the allotted span." So the pious old lady spoke and then continued, weeping: "I have been in great anxiety concerning this 'twin leaved pine,'* and while we dwelt under the shadow of those wild cliffs I scarce dared hope that it would at last find room to spread and grow. But now I pray more confidently—though still afraid that from roots† so lowly no valiant stem can ever spring..."

There was in her speech and bearing a courtly dignity which pleased him, and he led her on to talk of the time when her grandfather, the old Prince, was living at the house. While she spoke the sound of running water reached them. It came from the buried spring near the eastern wall of the house; the workmen had just finished clearing it. It seemed like the voice of one suddenly aroused from lethargy by the mention of old familiar names. "I, that was mistress here, scarce know the way from room to room; only this crystal spring remembers still and meditates the ancient secrets of the house." She murmured this poem softly to herself and did not know that he had heard what she said. But it had not escaped him; indeed, he thought it by no means lacking in beauty and power of expression.

As he stood looking down at her, full of interest and compassion, the aged lady thought him more beautiful than anything she could have ever dreamed would exist in the world. He now drove over to his hermitage at Saga and arranged for the Reading of the *Samantabhadra Sutra* and the meditations on Amitabha and Shakyamuni to take place every month on the fourteenth, fifteenth, and last days respectively, together with other rituals for which he now made the final arrangements. The decoration of the Buddha Hall and the provision of the necessary altars and furniture were then discussed and various duties assigned to those in charge of the place. He returned to Oi by moonlight. It was strangely like those nights of old when he used to visit her at the house on the hill. It seemed natural enough that, as in those days, she should bring out a zithern (it was indeed his own, which he had given her), and soon, stirred by his presence and the beauty of the night, she began to finger the instrument. He noticed at once that true to her promise she had not altered the tuning since that last night at Akashi, and it seemed as though all that had happened since were obliterated and he were still listening to that farewell tune.

He was conscious of no inequality between herself and him. Despite her mixed descent and rustic upbringing there was about her an air of personal distinction which made ample amends for her lack of breeding and worldly experience. Her looks had indeed greatly improved since he

---

* Two-year-old child.
† Referring to the Lady of Akashi's comparatively humble birth.

knew her, and as he gazed, now at her, now at the lovely child, he felt that both of them were destined to occupy henceforward a very large share of his attention. But what was he to do? It would indeed be a great pity that the child should grow up in an obscure country-house. Most people would no doubt think him perfectly justified in taking it away with him to the Nijō-in and bringing it up in whatever way he chose. But he knew that this would be a terrible blow to the mother and could not bring himself to suggest it. He sat watching the two of them with tears in his eyes. The little creature had at first been rather shy with him. But now it was quite at its ease, prattled and laughed in his face and in fact showed every sign of wanting to make friends with him. The infant in this expansive mood seemed to him more entrancing than ever. He took it up in his arms, and watching the tenderness with which he held it the mother felt that its fortunes were indeed secure. Next day he was to return to the Capital. He therefore returned to rest for a while; but the news that he was shortly to leave this house spread with disconcerting rapidity to his tenants at Katsura and the ante-rooms were soon full of visitors waiting to escort him on his journey. A number of courtiers had also discovered his whereabouts and were waiting to pay their respects. While he was being dressed, Genji said petulantly: "This is intolerable. If I am being tracked down even to such a place as this, where can I ever hope to hide my head?" And with a mob of visitors pressing round him he was swept away to his carriage. At a window by which they had to pass, stationed there as though by accident, was the child's nurse with the infant in her arms. Stroking its face tenderly as he passed, Genji said to her: "I should have been sorry not to see this child. But it has all been so hurried... Better than nothing perhaps... But 'your village is so far away...'"* "We shall expect rather more from Your Highness than we did in the old days when we really were a long way off," the nurse replied. The little princess stretched out her hand as though trying to hold him back. Pausing for a while he turned and said: "It is terrible to have such a sentimental disposition as mine. I cannot bear to part from those I am fond of even if it be only for a single day. But where is your mistress? Why did not she too come to bid me good-bye? Tell her that it is barbarous..." The nurse smiled and withdrawing into the house delivered the message. But so far from being unconcerned at his departure, the Lady of Akashi was so much agitated that she had sunk helpless upon her bed, and it was some while before she could muster enough strength to rise. At last, after Genji, not knowing what was amiss, had in his heart passed severe censure upon her coyness, she arrived in the front-room supported by her ladies

---

* Quoting the old song: "Your village is so far away that I must go back almost as soon as I come. Yet short as our meetings are perhaps we should be still unhappier without them."

and sank into a seat where, though she was partly hidden by a curtain, he got a fair view of her face. Such delicacy of feature, such distinction, such grace would not he thought have done discredit to an Emperor's daughter. He went up to the window, pulled aside the curtain and whispered a few words of farewell. Then he hastened to rejoin his companions; but looking back for an instant over his shoulder he saw that, though all this time she had remained motionless and silent, she was following him intently with her eyes. He had in old days been somewhat too slender for his height; now he had filled out a little and she found this slightly robuster air very becoming. He must indeed have expended considerable thought upon his appearance, every detail down to the elegantly adjusted billowing of his wide, puffy trousers being calculated with the nicest eye for effect. Such at any rate was her impression as he passed out of sight that morning—a view perhaps somewhat colored by partiality.

Ukon, the brother of Ki no Kami, had relinquished his office of Treasurer, and having been appointed Quiver-bearer to His Majesty had this year been formally invested as an officer of the fifth rank. He now came to relieve Genji of his sword, and looking in the direction from which his master had come saw the Lady of Akashi's form dimly outlined at the window. He had himself formed some slight acquaintance with her during the period of Genji's exile and wished to discover whether she still had a liking for him. He therefore drew one of her maids-of-honor aside and said: "I have not forgotten those hours of pleasant intercourse, but fear to give offence. Sometimes when, waking before the dawn, I hear the rustling of the wind among the trees, I think for a moment that I am back at Akashi, or listening again to the waves that beat upon the shore. At such moments I long to break the silence with some message or token; but till now no proper means has come to hand..." He purposely spoke in such a way that she might not understand him unless she were already aware of his feelings towards her mistress. "The clouds that hang eightfold about this lonely hillside screen us from the world no less securely than the mist-wreaths of that sequestered bay. I for my part thought that of my friends in those days 'none save the ancient pine-tree'* remembered me, and it is good news indeed to hear that by you at least..." She could not have been wider of the mark!† He was now very sorry that he had in old days so scrupulously avoided all reference to this attachment. He would have explained himself further, but Genji was waiting; and calling out with an assumed cheerfulness, "Let us talk of this another time," he hastened to rejoin his master. Already the outriders were clearing intruders

---

* Allusion to an old poem.
† The lady was unaware that he had been in love with her mistress and imagined it was of his feelings for herself that Ukon was speaking.

from the road and amid great clatter and bustle the procession started on its way. Two officious gentlemen, the Captain of the Guard and a certain Hyoye no Kami, rode at the back of Genji's coach. "I object to being tracked down like this," said Genji wearily, "when I go to pay a quiet visit to private friends." "The moonlight was so exquisite last night," they said in self-defense, "that we could not bear having been left behind, and this morning we groped our way through the early mist to find you. The maple-leaves in the Capital are not yet quite at their best; but in the open country the colors are marvelous. We should have been here sooner, had we not become involved in a hawking party that one of the chamberlains has got up." "I must go back to Katsura first," said Genji; and accordingly the party set out in that direction. It was no easy matter on the spur of the moment to provide entertainment for so large a number of persons. However, the cormorant-fishers who ply their trade on the Katsura river were hastily sent for, and promised to secure food enough for the whole party. Their strange, clipped talk reminded Genji of the fishermen at Suma and greatly diverted him. The falconers, who had decided to camp in the open country, sent a present of small snipe, each bird tied to a bunch of sedge-leaves. They played at the game* of floating wine-cups down the stream. So many times were the cups set afloat and so steep were the banks of the stream that the game proved somewhat dangerous. But the wine made them reckless and they were still shouting out their couplets long after it grew dark. At last the moon rose and it was time for the music to begin. The most skilful performers on zithern, lute, *wagon,* and various wind instruments were called upon and were soon playing such tunes as were best suited to the place and hour. A gentle breeze blew down the stream blending its whisperings with the music of pipe and string. Higher and higher the moon rose above them; never had night been so radiant and still. It was already very late when a band of four or five courtiers made their appearance. They had come straight from the Palace where the Emperor had been giving a concert. "This is the first of the Six Fast Days," His Majesty had suddenly exclaimed. "I expected that Genji would be here. What has become of him?" Someone then informed His Majesty of Genji's present whereabouts and messengers were at once dispatched to Katsura bearing a letter in which the Emperor declared himself envious of the pleasant excursion in which his Minister had found time to indulge. With this letter was the poem: "How pleasantly the shadow of the laurel-tree must fall upon the waters in the village beyond the stream!"† Genji answered with due humility and respect. The messengers found this moonlight concert even

---

* Each competitor had to improvise a verse before the cup reached him.

† Many puns. *Katsura* = "laurel." Also, a *katsura*-tree was supposed to grow in the moon.

more agreeable than the one which they had left and had soon settled down to drink and listen for the second time that night. When at last they rose it was proper that they should not be sent away empty-handed. As there was nothing here to give to them Genji sent a note to Oi: "Have you anything that would do to give to some messengers from the Court?" After looking round for a little they sent such objects as they could lay hands on. There were two boxes full of clothes. For the chief messenger, who was now anxious to return to the Palace, he selected a lady's dress of very handsome stuff.

The company now became extremely animated. Poem followed poem in a swift exchange, and even Genji's conversation, usually equable and restrained, began to take so extravagant a turn that his hearers would gladly have kept him talking thus till the end of the time. As for things at home, he reflected—the harm was already done. The rishi's axe must by now have blossomed, aye, and withered too. Why not one more day? But no; that would never do; and the party broke up hastily.

They set out for the Capital, each wearing on his head the bright colored scarf with which, according to his rank and station, he had been presented the night before and with these gay patches that bobbed up here and there in the morning mist blended the colors of the flowers in the gardens through which they passed.

There was with them a certain member of the Night Watch famous for his singing of ancient ballads, and to cheer the company he now sang with great spirit the ballad "Ho, my pony"; whereupon his companions doffed their scarves and wound them round the singer's head. The wind fluttered through the many-colored ends that dangled about his shoulders, weaving as gay a brocade as that with which the storms of autumn carpet a forest floor.

The news of his swift return or at least some faint echo of it reached the Lady of Akashi in her chamber, making her feel more than ever desolate. To Genji it suddenly occurred that he had never written the customary[*] letter. Other things had indeed been occupying his attention, but he wished he had remembered.

On his return to the Nijo-in he rested for a little while and then went to tell Murasaki about his country visit. "I am very sorry that I was away longer than I led you to expect," he said. "Those wretched fellows hounded me down and, try as I might, I could not get rid of them. I am very tired this morning. I think, if you will excuse me, I must get some more sleep," and so saying he retired to his own room. When they met later he saw that things were not going well, but for a time pretended not to notice. At last she became so tiresome that he said somewhat sharply:

---

[*] The "next morning" letter.

"This is ridiculous. You know quite well that there can never be any comparison between her position and yours. Surely you had better drop this absurd affectation and make the best of me now I am here."

He had promised to be at the Palace before nightfall, and now rose to go. But before he left the room she saw him go into a corner and scribble a hasty note. She guessed at once to whom it was addressed. What a long time it was taking! He seemed to have a great deal to say. Her women saw him giving it to a messenger with many whispered instructions and they were duly indignant.

He was supposed to be on duty all night at the Palace. But he was impatient to put matters right, and though it was very late indeed before he could get away he hurried back to Murasaki at the first opportunity of escape. While he was with her, the messenger returned from Oi with an answer in his hand. Genji read it without any attempt at concealment, and finding it to be of the most harmless description, he handed it to her saying: "Please tear it up when you have read it, and do not leave the pieces lying about; pieces make such a bad impression. In my position one has to be so careful."

He came and sat by her couch; but he was thinking all the time of the Lady at Oi and wishing he could be with her. For a long while he sat gazing into the lamp and did not speak a word.

The letter which he had handed to Murasaki was spread open before her, but she was not reading it. "I am sure you have been peeping," he said at last. "That way of reading letters is very tiring," and he smiled at her with such evident affection that the tears welled to her eyes. "There is something I want to talk to you about," he said, bending over her; "I have seen the little girl and, as a matter of fact, taken a great fancy to her. I naturally want to do as well for her as I can, but under the circumstances that is far from easy, and I am rather worried about it. I want you to think about the matter a little, and see if you cannot help me. What can be done? For example, would you be willing to have her here and bring her up as your own child? She is almost three years old, and at that age they are so pretty and innocent that it is very hard indeed to harden one's heart against them. It is getting to be time that she came out of her long clothes. Would you be very much upset if I asked you to take charge of the ceremony?"* "I was cross just now," she said, "but I knew you were thinking all the while about other things, and there seemed to be no use in pretending we were friends if we were not. I should love to look after the little girl. She is just the age I like best." She laughed with joy at the thought of having such a creature in her arms, for she was passionately fond of children. Should he try to secure the child? Genji was still very

---

* The *mogi* or "First Putting on of the Skirt."

doubtful. Visits to Oi were very difficult to arrange, and he seldom contrived to get there except on the two days in each month when he went over to hear the service at his chapel near Saga.

Thus though the Lady of Akashi fared considerably better than the Weaving Lady* in the story and though her expectations were of the most modern description, it would have been strange had these hurried visits contented her.

---

* The two stars, Weaving Lady and Plough Boy, meet only on the seventh day of the seventh month.

PART THREE
A WREATH OF CLOUD

LIST OF MOST IMPORTANT PERSONS (alphabetical)

Akashi, Lady of .... Whom Genji courted during his exile.
Akashi, Princess from .... Daughter of the above by Genji.
Akikonomu, Empress .... Daughter of Rokujo.
Aoi .... Genji's first wife.
Asagao, Princess .... Daughter of Prince Momozono Shikibukyo, courted by Genji since his boyhood, without success.
Ateki .... Daughter of Tamakatsura's old nurse.
Bugo no Suke .... Brother of the above.
Chujo, Lady .... To no Chujo's eldest daughter (called Kokiden in the original, but this renders her liable to confusion with Genji's stepmother).
Emperor, The Old ...... Genji's father.
Falling Flowers, Lady from the Village of ... Sister of one of the Old Emperor's Court ladies under Genji's protection.
Fujitsubo .... Consort of the Old Emperor; loved by Genji.
Genji .... Son of the Old Emperor by a lady-in-waiting.
Higekuro .... Brother of Suzaku's consort Lady Jokyoden.
Hyobukyo, Prince .... Murasaki's father.
Kashiwagi .... Eldest son of To no Chujo.
Kobai .... Brother of the above.
Kokiden .... Consort of the Old Emperor; Genji's wicked "stepmother."
Koremitsu .... Genji's retainer.
Koremitsu's Daughter .... Gosechi dancer, admired by Yugiri.
Kumoi .... Younger daughter of To no Chujo.
Momozono, Prince ...... Brother of the Old Emperor. Father of Asagao.
Murasaki .... Second "wife" of Genji (never, technically speaking, his *kita no kata* or formal wife).
Nyogo, Princess .... Younger sister of the Old Emperor.
Oborozuki .... Consort of the ex-Emperor Suzaku. Loved by Genji.
Omi, Lady of .... Bastard of To no Chujo, reclaimed by him in error while searching for Tamakatsura.
Omiya, Princess .... Mother of Aoi and To no Chujo. Sister of the Old Emperor.
Rokujo .... Widow of a brother of the Old Emperor.

Ryozen, The Emperor	Reputed son of the Old Emperor, but really son of Genji and Fujitsubo.
Sanjo	Yugao's maid.
Shoni	Husband of Tamakatsura's nurse. Father of Ateki and Bugo no Suke.
Sochi, Prince	Genji's stepbrother.
Suyetsumu	Fantastic lady with red nose, daughter of Prince Hitachi.
Suzaku, The Ex-Emperor	Genji's stepbrother; son of Kokiden.
Tamakatsura	Child of To no Chujo by Yugao.
Tayu	Swashbuckler in Tsukushi.
Utsusemi	Wife of a provincial governor; loved by Genji.
Yoshikiyo	Faithful retainer of Genji; followed him into exile.
Yugao	Loved first by To no Chujo, then by Genji. Dies in a deserted mansion.
Yugiri	Genji's son by Aoi.

A Wreath of Cloud

As winter drew on, the Lady of Akashi in her house by the Oi river became very dispirited. Formerly the prospect of a visit from Genji was sufficient to rouse her from her melancholy; but now he found her always in the same dejected posture morning, noon, and night: "How much longer is this to go on?" he cried impatiently. "Do, I beg of you, make up your mind to come to my palace and use the quarters I have reserved for you." But he could never persuade her that she would not be thus exposing herself to a hundred indignities and affronts. It was of course impossible to be quite sure how things would go, and if, after all his assurances, the move did not turn out well, her vague resentment against him would henceforth be transformed into a definite and justified grievance. "Do you not feel," he said, "that it would be unfair to your child to keep it here with you much longer? Indeed, knowing as you do what plans[*] I have made for its future, you must surely see that you are behaving towards it with a lack of proper respect... I have constantly discussed this matter with my wife and she has always shown great interest in the child's future. If it is put for a while under her care, she will no doubt be willing to stand sponsor to it; so that it will be possible to carry out the Initiation ceremony and other rituals of induction[†] with full publicity." So far from being convinced by his arguments, she saw herself now being inveigled into doing precisely what she had always suspected with horror that he would one day ask of her. "Take the child away from me if you like," she said at last, "and give her to these grand people to bring up as though she were their own. But just when you think you have repaired the accident of her birth, someone will let out the secret, and where will you be then?" "Yes, we must be careful about that," answered Genji. "But you need have no fear that the child will not be properly looked after. As you know, though we have been married for many years, Lady Murasaki has no children of her own, and this very much distresses her. She badly needs companionship, and when at one time there was some question of her adopting Lady Akikonomu, the former Vestal Virgin, she was obviously delighted at the prospect, though this lady was already a

---

[*] Genji had promised in due course to marry the child to the Heir Apparent, son of the Emperor Ryozen.
[†] Buddhist ceremonies corresponding to the Christian "Confirmation."

grown-up person. But when it comes to a child—at an age, too, when such creatures have an irresistible charm—it is quite certain that she will welcome it with alacrity and henceforward devote all her time to its care. Of that there is no doubt at all..." and he proceeded to a general eulogy upon Murasaki's docility and charm. But while he was speaking the Lady of Akashi recalled the stories of Genji's adventurous past, and of numerous other attachments with which rumor credited him. It seemed on the one hand very unlikely that Lady Murasaki would not ultimately suffer the fare of her predecessors, and why should her child be entrusted to a favorite who might soon be forgotten or thrust aside? If on the other hand Murasaki were indeed endowed with such pre-eminent qualities that she alone of all her rivals, and predecessors was destined to enjoy permanent favor, then as long as mother and child remained in their present obscurity there was little danger that this magnificent lady would regard them as worth a moment's thought. But as soon as one or both should make an appearance in the Nijo palace, Murasaki's pride would be affronted and her jealousy aroused... Her mother, however, was a woman who looked beyond the difficulties of the moment, and she now said with some severity: "You are behaving very foolishly. It is natural enough that you should dislike parting with the child; but you must make up your mind to do what will be best for it. I feel certain that His Highness is perfectly serious in his intentions concerning its future, and I advise you to entrust it to him at once. You need have no misgivings. After all, even Royal Princes are of very varying stock on the mother's side. I seem to remember that Prince Genji himself, who is reckoned the greatest gentleman in the land, could not be put forward as a successor to the Throne because his mother was so far inferior to the other ladies of the Court; and indeed, judged from that point of view, he is a mere waiting-woman's son. If such disadvantages are not fatal even in the most exalted spheres, we lesser folk certainly need not trouble ourselves about them..." The Lady of Akashi took the advice of several other persons who had a reputation for sagacity in such matters, and also consulted various soothsayers and astrologers. In every case the answer was the same: the child must go to the Capital. In face of such unanimity she began to waver. Genji, for his part, was still as anxious as ever that his plan should be carried out. But the subject was evidently so painful to her that he no longer attempted to broach it, and in the course of his next letter merely asked what were her wishes concerning the Initiation ceremony. She answered: "I see now that, being what I am, I cannot keep the child with me without injuring its prospects. I am ready to part with it; but I still fear that amid such surroundings..." He was very sorry for her; but all the same he ordered his clerks to search the calendar for a suitable day, and began secretly to make preparations for the child's arrival.

To hand over her own child to another woman's keeping was indeed a bitter trial; but she kept on repeating to herself that, for its own sake, this sacrifice must sooner or later be made. The nurse whom Genji had originally sent to Akashi would of course go to take charge of it at the palace, and the prospect of losing this lady, to whom she had long confided all her sorrows, finding in her society the one solace of her monotonous and unhappy existence, added greatly to her present distress. "Madam," the nurse would say to her, "I shall never forget your kindness to me ever since the day when, so unexpectedly, yet as I think not without the intervention of some kind fate, it fell to my lot to serve you. You may be sure that I shall all the while be longing to have you with me. But I shall never regard our separation as more than an expedient of the moment. In the end I am convinced that all will come right. Meanwhile, do not think that I look forward with any pleasant anticipations to a life that will take me so far from your side." She wept; and thus day after day was spent in sad forebodings and preparations till the twelfth month was already come.

Storms of snow and hail now made the situation at Oi more than ever depressing and uncomfortable. It appalled the Lady of Akashi to discover what manifold varieties of suffering one can be called upon to endure at one and the same time. She now spent every moment of the day in tending and caressing her little girl. One morning when the fast-falling snow was piling up high on every side she sat with the child in her arms, again and again going back in her mind over all the miseries of the past, and picturing to herself the yet more desolate days that were to come. It was long since she had gone into the front of the house. But this morning there was ice on the moat, and she went to the window to look. She was clad in many wraps of some soft, white, fluttering stuff, and as she stood gazing before her with hands clasped behind her head, those within the room thought that, prince's daughter though her rival was, she could scarce be more lovely in poise and gesture than their lady in her snowy dress. Raising her sleeve to catch the tears that had now begun to fall, the Lady of Akashi turned to the nurse and said: "If it were upon a day such as this,* I do not think that I could bear it..." And she recited the poem: "If country roads be deep in snow, and clouds return, tread thou the written path, and though thyself thou contest not, vouchsafe a sign."† To comfort her the nurse answered through her tears: "Though the snow-drifts of Yoshino were heaped across his path, doubt not that whither his heart is set, his footsteps shall tread out their way." The snow was now falling a little less fast. Suddenly Genji appeared at

---

* That Genji fetched the child.

† There is a play on words: *fumi* = "letter"; also "treading." *Ato* = "the tracks of feet," but also "tracks of the pen," σήματα.

the door. The moments during which she waited to receive him put her always into a state of painful agitation. Today guessing as she did the purpose of his visit, his arrival threw her immediately into an agonizing conflict. Why had she consented? There was still time. If she refused to part with the child, would he snatch it from her? No, indeed; that was unthinkable. But stay! She had consented; and should she now change her mind, she would lose his confidence forever. At one moment she was ready to obey; a moment afterwards, she had decided to resist by every means in her power.

She sat by the window, holding the little girl in her arms. He thought the child very beautiful, and felt at once that her birth was one of the most important things that had happened in his life. Since last spring her hair had been allowed to grow* and it was now an inch or two long, falling in delicate waves about her ears like that of a little novice at a convent. Her skin too was of exquisite whiteness and purity, and she had the most delightful eyes. To part with such a creature, to send her away into strange hands—he understood well enough what this must mean, and suddenly it seemed to him that it was impossible even to suggest such a sacrifice. The whole matter was reopened, and a discussion followed which lasted the better part of the day. "Whether it is worth while depends on you," she said at last. "It is in your power to make amends to the child for the disadvantages of its birth. And if I thought that you meant to do so..." He was worn out by the long discussion, and now burst into tears. It was terrible to witness such distress. But the child, heedless of what was going on about it, was lustily demanding "a ride in the nice carriage." The mother picked it up and carried it in her own arms to the end of the drive. When she had set it down, it caught at her sleeve and in the prettiest, baby voice imaginable begged her to "come for a ride too." There framed themselves in the lady's heart the lines: "Were all my prayers in vain, or shall I live to see the two-leaved pine from which today I part spread mighty shadows on the earth?" but she could scarce speak the words, and seeing her now weeping wildly Genji strove to comfort her with the verse: "Like the little pine-tree that at Takekuma from the big one grows, grafted to my deep roots long shall this stripling thrive secure." "Wait patiently," he added. She strove hard to persuade herself that he was right, that all was for the best. But now the carriages were moving away...

With the child rode the nurse and also a gentlewoman of good family called Shosho, holding on their knees the Sword, the Heavenly Children,† and other emblems of royalty. In the next carriage followed a band of

---

* Babies' heads were shaved, save for two tufts.

† The sword was the emblem of the child's royal blood. The Heavenly Children were dolls which were intended to attract evil influences and so save the child from harm.

youths and little girls whom he had brought to form the child's escort on the homeward way. All the time they were driving to the Capital Genji was haunted by the image of the sorrow-stricken figure that had watched their departure. Small blame to her if at the moment she was feeling bitterly towards him!

It was quite dark when they arrived. So soon as the carriages had been drawn in, Shosho and the nurse began looking about them at the splendors amid which they were now destined to reside. They felt indeed (coming as they did from rural and quite unpretentious surroundings) somewhat awestruck and ill at ease. But when they were shown the apartments which had been set aside for the new arrival, with a tiny bed, screens-of-state, and everything which a little lady could require, all beautifully set out and arranged, they began to take heart. The nurse's own room was in the corridor leading to the western wing, on the north side of the passage.

The child had fallen asleep during the journey and while she was carried into the house had not cried or seemed at all put out. She was taken straight to Murasaki's room and there given her supper. After a while she began to look round her.

She evidently wondered why her mother was nowhere to be seen, and after a further search her little lips began to tremble. The nurse was sent for and soon succeeded in distracting her attention. If only, thought Genji, who had witnessed this scene—if only the mother in that slow country home could be as easily comforted! But now there was no way to make amends to her, save to see to it that never in one jot should the child's care and upbringing fall short of what its mother might in her wildest dream have craved for it. For the moment indeed he accounted it a blessing that Murasaki had not borne him a child of her own, and was thus free to devote herself to the reparation of the wrong which he had inflicted upon this little newcomer by the circumstances of its birth. For some days the child continued occasionally to ask for its mother or some other person whom it had been used to see daily at Oi, and when they could not be produced it would have a fit of screaming or of tears. But it was by nature a contented, happy little thing, and soon struck up a friendship with its new mother, who for her part was delighted to take charge of a creature so graceful and confiding. She insisted on carrying it about in her own arms, attended herself to all its wants and joined in all its games. Gradually the nurse became a personal attendant upon Lady Murasaki rather than the under-servant she had been before. Meanwhile a lady of irreproachable birth happened to become available as a wet-nurse and was accordingly added to the establishment. The ceremony of her Initiation did not involve any very elaborate preparations, but the child's little companions were naturally aware that something was afoot.

Her outfit, so tiny that it looked as though it came out of a doll's-house, was a charming sight. So many people came in and out of the house all day even at ordinary times that they hardly noticed the guests who had assembled in their little mistress's honor. It was only when she raised her arms for the Binding of the Sleeves that the unwonted gesture caught their attention; they had never seen her in so pretty a pose before.

Meanwhile the mother at Oi was all the more wretched because she now felt that her misery was self-inflicted. Had she been firm, the child might still be with her and life in some measure endurable. She could not believe that so extreme a course could really have been indispensable to its interests and bitterly repented of her docility. Even the grandmother, who had been foremost in urging the sacrifice, missed the baby sadly and went about the house with tears in her eyes. But news had reached them of the pains which Genji was bestowing upon its upbringing, and she felt no doubt that she had advised for the best.

A peculiar compunction prevented the Lady of Akashi from sending any gift or message to the child which was no longer hers, but she took immense pains in contriving presents for all its companions and attendants from the nurse downwards, and would spend hours in the matching of colors and the choosing of stuffs.

Genji did not at all want her to think that, now she had parted with the child, his visits were going to become any the less frequent, and though it was very difficult to arrange, he made a point of going out to Oi before the turn of the year. It must at the best of times, he thought, be an uninteresting place to live in; but at any rate she had had the child to look after, and (what with getting it up and putting it to bed) that seemed to occupy a good deal of time. How she managed to get through the day now he could not imagine, and coming away from this visit with a heavy heart he henceforward wrote to her almost daily. Fortunately Murasaki no longer showed any jealousy on this score, feeling, as it seemed, that the surrender of so exquisite a child needed whatever recompense Genji found it in his heart to bestow.

The New Year* was ushered in by a spell of bright, clear weather. At the Nijo-in everything seemed to be going particularly well and, now that all the improvements were completed, an unusually large number of guests was entertained during the period of festivities. The older, married visitors came, as is customary, on the seventh day, bringing with them their children to assist in the ceremonies of congratulation; and these young visitors all seemed to be in excellent health and spirits. Even the lesser gentlemen and retainers who came to pay their respects, though no doubt many of them had worries and troubles enough of their own,

---

* Genji must now have been thirty.

managed to keep up, during these few days at any rate, an outward appearance of jollity.

The lady from the Village of Failing Flowers, who was now installed in the new eastern wing, seemed completely satisfied by her new surroundings. She had her work cut out for her in keeping up to the mark all the waiting-women and young girls whom Genji had allotted to her service. Nor could she feel that she had gained nothing by her present proximity; for whenever he had a few moments to spare, he would come round and sit with her. He did not however visit her by previous appointment or stay at all late at night in her apartments. Happily she was by nature extremely unexacting. If what she wanted did not come her way, she at once assumed that this particular thing was not "in her destiny," and ceased to worry about it. This habit of mind made her quite unusually easy to handle, and he for his part lost no opportunity of publicly showing by his manner towards her that he regarded her as of scarcely less consequence than Murasaki, with the result that those who came to the house felt they would be displeasing him if they did not pay their respects to her as well as to his wife; while stewards and servants saw that she was a person whom it would not be advisable to neglect. Thus everything seemed to be working very smoothly, and Genji felt that the arrangement was going to be a great success.

He thought constantly of the country house at Oi and of the dull hours which the Lady of Akashi must be passing there at this season of festivity. So soon as the New Year celebrations both at his own house and in the Palace were drawing to a close, he determined to pay her another visit, and with this object in view he put on his finest clothes, wearing under his cherry-colored cloak a matchless vesture of deep saffron hue, steeped in the perfumes of the scented box where it had lain. Thus clad he went to take his leave of Murasaki, and as he stood in the full rays of the setting sun, his appearance was so magnificent that she gazed at him with even greater admiration than was her wont. The little princess grabbed at the ends of his long wide trousers with her baby hands, as though she did not want him to go. When he reached the door of the women's apartments she was still clinging to him and he was obliged to halt for a moment in order to disentangle himself. Having at last coaxed her into releasing him, he hurried down the corridor humming to himself as he did so the peasant-song, "Tomorrow I will come again."* At the door he met one of Murasaki's ladies and by her he sent back just that message, "Tomorrow I will come again." She instantly recognized whence the words came

---

* "Stop your boat, oh cherry-man! I must sow the ten-rood island field. Then I will come again. Tomorrow I will come again!" The lady answers: "Tomorrow, forsooth! Those are but words. You keep a girl upon the other side, and tomorrow you will not come, no, not tomorrow will you come."

and answered with the poem: "Were there on the far shore no person to detain your boat, then might I indeed believe that tomorrow you will come again." This was brought to him before he drove away, and smiling at her readiness of wit he answered: "In truth I will but look to my business and come back again; come back tomorrow, though she across the waters chide me as she will." The little girl did not of course understand a word of all this; but she saw that there was a joke, and was cutting the strangest capers. As usual the sight of her antics disarmed all Murasaki's resentment, and though she would much rather there had been no "lady on the far shore," she no longer felt any hostility towards her. Through what misery the mother must be passing, Murasaki was now in a position to judge for herself. She continually imagined what her own feelings would be if the child were taken from her, never for an instant let it go out of her sight, and again and again pressed it to her bosom, putting her lovely teats to its mouth, and caressing it for hours together.

"What a pity that she has never had one of her own!" her ladies whispered. "To be sure if this were hers, she could not wish it different..."

Meanwhile the Lady of Akashi was setting herself to face with resolute calm the dullness and monotony of country life. The house had a curious charm of its own, which appealed very much to Genji during his visits, and as for its occupant—he was astonished at the continual improvement in her looks. Indeed, had not that queer father of hers taken such extraordinary pains to prevent her ever mixing with the world, he believed there was no reason why she should not have done extremely well for herself. Yes, all she had needed was an ordinary father; even a rather shabby one would not have mattered. For such beauty and intelligence as hers, if once given the chance, could not have failed to pull her through. Each visit left him restless and unsatisfied, and he found himself spending his time in continual goings and comings, his life "a tremulous causeway linking dream to dream."

Sometimes he would send for a zithern and remembering the exquisite music with which she had beguiled those nights at Akashi, he begged her to play to him upon her lute. She would not now play alone; but she sometimes consented to accompany him, doing so with a mastery he could not imagine how she had contrived to acquire. The rest of the time was generally spent in minute recital of the little princess's sayings and doings. Often he had come over on business connected with his new oratory at Saga or his estate at Katsura; and then there would perhaps be only time enough to eat a little fruit and dried rice with her at Oi before he hurried back to town. On such occasions there was not time for intimacies of any kind; but the mere fact that he snatched at every chance of seeing her and that he did so without any attempt at concealment, marked her as one who held a not inconsiderable place in his affections.

She was quite aware of this; but she never presumed upon it, and without any tiresome display of humility she obeyed his orders and in general gave him as little trouble as possible. By all that she could hear, there was not one of the great ladies at Court with whom he was on so intimate a footing as with herself; indeed, he was said to be somewhat stand-offish and difficult of approach. Were she to live closer at hand he would perhaps grow weary of her, and in any case there would certainly be unpleasant rivalries and jealousies. Thus or in some such way may we suppose the Lady of Akashi to have reconciled herself to these brief and accidental visits. Her father, despite his disavowal of all worldly interests, was extremely anxious to hear how Genji was behaving towards his daughter and constantly sent messengers to Oi to pick up what news they could. Much of what he heard distressed and disappointed him; but frequently too there were signs and indications of a more encouraging kind, and he would grow quite elated.

About this time Lady Aoi's father died. His name had carried great weight in the country and his death was a heavy loss to the present government. It so happened that the period during which he took part in public life had been marked by much disorder and unrest. A renewal of these upheavals was now expected and general depression prevailed. Genji too was much distressed, both for personal reasons and because he had been in the habit of delegating to the old Minister most of the public business which fell to his lot. He had thus managed to secure a reasonable amount of leisure. He saw himself henceforward perpetually immersed in a multiplicity of tiresome affairs, and the prospect greatly depressed him. The Emperor, though still only twelve years old, was extremely forward for his age both in body and mind, and although it was not to be expected that he should act alone, the task of supervising his work was not a difficult one. But for some years such supervision would still be needed, and unfortunately there was no one else to whom Genji could possibly entrust such a task. Thus the prospect of being able to lead the retired life which alone appealed to him was still remote, and he frequently became very discontented."

For some while he was occupied with the celebration of rituals and services on behalf of the dead man's soul; these he carried out even more elaborately than did the sons and grandsons of the deceased. This year, as had been predicted, was marked by a number of disorders and calamities. The Palace was frequently visited by the most disagreeable and alarming apparitions, the motions of the planets, sun, and moon were irregular and unaccountable, and clouds of baleful and significant shape were repeatedly observed. Learned men of every school sent in elaborate addresses to the Throne, in which they attempted to account for these strange manifestations. But they were obliged to confess that many of the reported happenings were unique, and of a very baffling character. While speculation thus reigned on every side, Genji held in his heart a guilty secret* which might well be the key to these distressing portents.

Lady Fujitsubo had fallen ill at the beginning of the year and since the third month her malady had taken a serious turn. The august visit of the Emperor to her bedside and other unusual ceremonies had already taken place. He was a mere child when she relinquished the care of him, and he had grown up without any very strong feelings towards her. But he now looked so solemn as he stood by the bedside that she herself began to feel quite sad. "I have for some while felt certain," she said to him calmly, "that this would be the last year of my life. But as long as my illness did not prevent me from going about as usual, I gave no hint to those around me that I knew my end was near; for I dreaded the fuss and outcry that such a confession would have produced. Nor did I alter in any way my daily prayers and observances. I longed to visit you at the Palace and talk with you quietly about old days. But I seldom felt equal to so great an exertion... And now it is too late."

She spoke in a very low, feeble voice. She was thirty-seven years old, but seemed much younger. The Emperor, as he looked at her, was overwhelmed by pity and regret. That just as she was reaching an age when she would need his care, she should, unknown to him, have passed through months of continual suffering without once having recourse to those sacred expedients which alone might have saved her—this thought made the most painful impression upon him; and now, in a last attempt to rescue her from death, he set in motion every conceivable sort of ritual and spell. Genji too was dismayed at the discovery that for months past she had been worn out by constant pain, and now sought desperately to find some remedy for her condition. But it was apparent that the end was at hand; the Emperor's visits became more and more frequent and many affecting scenes were witnessed. Fujitsubo was in great pain and seldom attempted to speak at any length. But lying there and looking back over the whole course of her career, she thought that while in the outward circumstances of life few women could have been more fortunate than herself, inwardly scarce one in all history had been more continually apprehensive and wretched. The young Emperor was of course still wholly ignorant of the secret of his birth. In not acquainting him with it she felt that she had failed in the discharge of an essential duty, and the one matter after her death in which she felt any interest was the repair of this omission.

---

* The secret that the Emperor was his son. The safety of the State depended upon the cult of ancestors. This could only be performed by their true descendants. Moreover the occupation of the throne by one who was not by birth entitled to it would arouse the wrath of the Sun, from whom the Emperor of Japan claims descent.

Merely in his position as head of the government it was natural that Genji should be gravely concerned by the approaching loss to his faction of so distinguished a supporter, coming, as it seemed likely to, not many months after the death of the old Grand Minister. This public concern could indeed be openly displayed. But concealed from all those about him there was in his inmost heart a measureless sorrow, to which he dared give vent only in perpetual supplication and prayer. That it was no longer possible to renew even such casual and colorless intercourse as had been theirs in recent years was very painful to him. He hurried to her bedside at the first news of the serious turn which her condition had taken.

To his surprise she did, in a faint and halting manner, contrive to speak a few words to him when she realized that he was near. First she thanked him for carrying out so scrupulously the late Emperor's wishes with regard to the surveillance of his present Majesty. Much had happened in the last years for which she had cause to be grateful to him, and she had often meant to tell him how sensible she was of his kindness. And there was another matter of which she had meant for some time to speak... to the Emperor himself. She was sorry she had never... Here her voice became inaudible, and tears for a while prevented him from making a reply. He feared that this display of emotion would arouse comment among those who were standing by; but indeed anyone who had known her as she used to be might well have been overcome with grief to see her in so woeful a condition. Suddenly he looked up. No thought or prayer of his could now recall her; and in unspeakable anguish, not knowing whether she heard him or no, he began to address her: "In spite of the difficulties into which I myself have sometimes fallen, I have tried to do my best for His Majesty, or at any rate, what then seemed to me best. But since the death of the old Grand Minister, everything has gone wrong; and with you lying ill like this I do not know which way to turn. Were you now to die, I think I should soon follow you..." He paused, but there was no reply; for she had died suddenly like a candle blown out by the wind, and he was left in bewilderment and misery.

She was, of all the great ladies about the Court at that time, the most tender-hearted and universally considerate. Women of her class do not as a rule expect to compass their own ends without causing considerable inconvenience to ordinary people. Fujitsubo on the contrary invariably released even her servants and retainers from any duty which she felt to be an undue infringement of their liberty.

She was devout; but unlike many religious persons she did not display her piety by impressive benefactions paid for out of funds which other people had collected. Her charities (and they were considerable) were made at the expense of her own exchequer. The ranks, titles, and benefices which were at her disposal she distributed with great intelligence and care, and so many were her individual acts of generosity that there was scarcely a poor ignorant mountain-priest in all the land who had not reason to lament her loss. Seldom had the obsequies of any public person provoked so heart-felt and universal a sorrow. At Court no color but black was anywhere to be seen; and the last weeks of spring lacked all their usual brilliance and gaiety.

Standing one day before the great cherry-tree which grew in front of the Nijo-in Genji suddenly remembered that this was the season when, under ordinary circumstances, the Flower Feast would have been held at the Emperor's Palace. "This year should'st thou have blossomed with black flowers,"* he murmured and, to hide the sudden access of grief that had overwhelmed him, rushed into his chapel and remained there weeping bitterly till it began to grow dark. Issuing at last, he found a flaming sun about to sink beneath the horizon. Against this vivid glow the trees upon the hill stood out with marvelous clearness, every branch, nay every twig distinct. But across the hill there presently drifted a thin filament of cloud, draping the summit with a band of grey. He was in no mood that day to notice sunsets or pretty cloud-effects; but in this half-curtained sky there seemed to him to be a strange significance, and none being by to hear him he recited the verse: "Across the sunset hill there hangs a wreath of cloud that garbs the evening as with the dark folds of a mourner's dress."

There was a certain priest who had for generations served as chaplain in Lady Fujitsubo's family. Her mother had placed extraordinary confidence in him, and she herself had instilled the young Emperor Ryozen with deep veneration for this old man, who was indeed known throughout the land for the sanctity of his life and the unfailing efficacy of his prayers. He was now over seventy and had for some time been living in retirement, intent upon his final devotions. But recently the occasion of Lady Fujitsubo's death had called him back to the Court, and the Emperor had more than once summoned him to his side. An urgent message, conveyed by Prince Genji, now reached him. The night was already far advanced, and the old man at first protested that these nocturnal errands were no longer within his capacity. But in the end he promised, out of respect for His Majesty, to make a great effort to appear, and at the calm of dawn, at a moment when, as it so happened, many of the courtiers were absent and those on duty had all withdrawn from the Presence, the old man stepped into Ryozen's room. After talking for a while in his aged, croaking voice about various matters of public interest, he said at last: "There is one very difficult matter which I wish to discuss with you. I fear I may not have the courage to embark upon it, and I am still more afraid that if I suc-

---

* Quoting a poem of Uyeno Mine-o's upon the death of Fujiwara no Mototsune, 891 A.D.

ceed in broaching this topic I may give you great offence. But it concerns something which it would be very wrong to conceal; a secret indeed such as makes me fear the eye of Heaven. What use is there, now that I am so near my end, in locking it up so tightly in my heart? I fear that Buddha himself might cast me out should I approach him defiled by this unholy concealment." He began trying to tell the Emperor something; but he seemed unable to come to the point. It was strange that there should be any worldly matter concerning which the old priest retained such violent emotions. Perhaps, despite his reputation, he had once secretly pursued some hideous vendetta, had caused an innocent person to be entrapped, done away with... a thousand monstrous possibilities crowded to the Emperor's mind. "Reverend Father," he said at last, "you have known me since I was a baby, and I have never once hidden anything from you. And now I learn that there is something which you have for a long time past been concealing from me. I confess, I am surprised." "There is nothing that I have kept from you," the old man cried indignantly. "Have I not made you master of my most secret spells, of the inner doctrines that Buddha forbids us to reveal? Do you think that I, who in these holy matters reposed so great a confidence in Your Majesty, would have concealed from you any dealing of my own?

"The matter of which I speak is one that has had grave results already and may possibly in the future entail worse consequences still. The reputations concerned are those of your late august mother and of someone who now holds a prominent place in the government of our country... it is to Prince Genji that I refer. It is for their sake, and lest some distorted account of the affair should ultimately reach you from other sources, that I have undertaken this painful task. I am an old man and a priest; I therefore have little to lose and, even should this revelation win me your displeasure, I shall never repent of having made it; for Buddha and the Gods of Heaven showed me by unmistakable signs that it was my duty to speak.

"You must know, then, that from the time of Your Majesty's conception the late Empress your mother was in evident distress concerning the prospect of your birth. She told me indeed that there were reasons which made the expected child particularly in need of my prayers; but what these reasons were she did not say; and I, being without experience in such matters, could form no conjecture. Soon after your birth there followed a species of convulsion in the State; Prince Genji was in disgrace and later in exile. Meanwhile your august mother seemed to grow every day more uneasy about your future, and again and again I was asked to offer fresh prayers on your behalf. Strangest of all, so long as Prince Genji was at the Capital he too seemed to be acquainted with the instructions I had received; for on every occasion he at once sent round a message bidding me add by so much to the prayers that had been ordered and make this or that fresh expenditure on some service or ritual..."

The disclosure* was astonishing, thrilling, terrifying. Indeed so many conflicting emotions struggled for the upper hand that he was unable to make any comment or reply. The old priest misunderstood this silence and, grieved that he should have incurred Ryozen's displeasure by a revelation which had been made in His Majesty's own interest, he bowed and withdrew from the Presence. The Emperor immediately ordered him to return. "I am glad that you have told me of this," said Ryozen. "Had I gone on living in ignorance of it I see that a kind of contempt would have been attached forever to my name; for in the end such things are bound to be known. I am only sorry that you should have concealed this from me for so long; and tremble to think of the things that in my ignorance I may have said or done.† Tell me, does anyone besides yourself know of this... anyone who is likely to have let out the secret?" "Besides myself and your mother's maid Omyobu there is no one who has an inkling of the matter," the priest hastened to assure him. "Nevertheless the existence of such a secret causes me grave misgivings. Upheavals of nature, earthquakes, drought, and storm, have become alarmingly frequent; and in the State, we have had constant disorder and unrest. All these things may be due to the existence of this secret. So long as Your Majesty was a helpless infant Heaven took pity on your innocence; but now that you are grown to your full stature and have reached years of understanding and discretion, the Powers Above are manifesting their displeasure; for, as you have been taught, it frequently happens that the sins of one generation are visited upon the next. I saw plainly that you did not know to what cause our present troubles and disorders are due, and that is why I at last determined to reveal a secret which I hoped need never pass my lips." The old man spoke with difficulty, tears frequently interrupted his discourse, and it was already broad daylight when he finally left the Palace.

No sooner had he realized the full significance of this astonishing revelation than a medley of conflicting thoughts began to harass Ryozen's mind. First and foremost, he felt indignant on behalf of the old Emperor, whom he had always been taught to regard as his father; but he also felt strangely uncomfortable at the idea that Genji, who had a much better right to the Throne than he, should have been cast out of the Imperial family, to become a Minister, a mere servant of the State. Viewed from whatever standpoint, the new situation was extremely painful to him, and overcome by shock and bewilderment he lay in his room long after the sun was high. Learning that His Majesty had not risen, Genji assumed that he

---

* That Ryozen was in reality Genji's son.
† See above, note on p. 371, and below, note on p. 377.

was indisposed and at once called to enquire. The Emperor was in tears, and utterly unable to control himself even in the presence of a visitor. But this was after all perhaps not so very surprising. The young man had only a few weeks ago lost his mother, and it was natural that he should still be somewhat upset. Unfortunately it was Genji's duty that morning to announce to His Majesty the decease of Prince Momozono.* It seemed to Ryozen as though the whole world, with all its familiar landmarks and connections, were crumbling about him. During the first weeks of mourning Genji spent all his time at the Palace and paid an early visit to the Emperor every day. They had many long, uninterrupted conversations, during the course of which Ryozen on one occasion said: "I do not think that my reign is going to last much longer. Never have I had so strong a foreboding that calamity of some stupendous kind was at hand; and quite apart from this presentiment, the unrest which is now troubling the whole land is already enough to keep me in a continual state of agitation and alarm. Ever since this began I have had great thoughts of withdrawing from the Throne; but while my mother was alive I did not wish to distress her by doing so. Now, however, I consider that I am free to do as I choose, and I intend before long to seek some quieter mode of life..." "I sincerely hope you will do nothing of the kind," said Genji. "The present unrest casts no reflection upon you or your government. Difficulties of this kind sometimes arise during the rule of the most enlightened government, as is proved by the history of China as well as by that of our own country. Nor must you allow yourself to be unduly depressed by the demise of persons such as your respected uncle, who had, after all, reached a time of life when we could not reasonably expect..." Thus Genji managed, by arguments which for fear of wearying you I will not repeat, to coax the Emperor into a slightly less desperate state of mind. Both were dressed in the simplest style and in the same somber hue. For years past it had struck the Emperor, on looking at himself in the mirror, that he was extraordinarily like Prince Genji. Since the revelation of his true parentage, he had more frequently than ever examined his own features. Why, of course! There was no mistaking such a likeness! But if he was Genji's son, Genji too must be aware of the fact, and it was absurd that the relationship should not be acknowledged between them. Again and again he tried to find some way of introducing the subject. But to Genji, he supposed, the whole matter must be a very painful one. He often felt that it was impossible to refer to such a thing at all, and conversation after conversation went by without any but the most general topics being discussed, though it was noticeable that Ryozen's manner was even more friendly and charming than usual. Genji who was extremely sensitive to such changes did not fail to notice

---

* Prince Momozono Shikibukyo, brother of the old Emperor and father of Princess Asagao.

that there was something new in the young Emperor's attitude towards him—an air of added respect, almost of deference. But it never occurred to him that Ryozen could by any possibility be in possession of the whole terrible secret. At first the Emperor had thought of discussing the matter with the maid Omyobu and asking her for a fuller account of his birth and all that had led up to it. But at the last moment he felt that it was better she should continue to think herself the only inheritor of the secret, and he decided not to discuss the matter with anyone. But he longed, without actually letting out that he knew, to get some further information from Genji himself. Among other things he wanted to know whether what had happened with regard to his birth was wholly unexampled, or whether it was in point of fact far more common than one would suppose. But he could never find the right way to introduce such a subject. It was clear that he must get his knowledge from other sources, and he threw himself with fresh ardor into the study of history, reading every book with the sole object of discovering other cases like his own. In China, he soon found, irregularities of descent have not only in many cases been successfully concealed till long afterwards, but have often been known and tolerated from the beginning. In Japan he could discover no such instance; but he knew that if things of this kind occurred, they would probably not be recorded, so that their absence from native history might only mean that in our country such matters are hushed up more successfully than elsewhere.

The more he thought about it, the more Genji regretted that Ryozen should have discovered (as from His Majesty's repeated offers of abdication he now felt certain to be the case) the real facts concerning his birth. Fujitsubo, Genji was sure, would have given anything rather than that the boy should know; it could not have been by her instructions that the secret had been divulged. Who then had betrayed him? Naturally his thoughts turned towards Omyobu. She had moved into the apartments which had been made out of the old offices of the Lady-of-the-Bedchamber. Here she had been given official quarters and was to reside permanently in the Palace. Discussing the matter with her one day, Genji said: "Are you sure that you yourself, in the course of some conversation with His Majesty, may not by accident have put this idea into his head?" "It is out of the question," she replied. "I know too well how determined my lady was that he should never discover... indeed, the fear that he might one day stumble upon the facts for himself was her constant torment. And this despite the dangers into which she knew that ignorance might lead him.* And they fell to talking of Lady Fujitsubo's scrupulous respect for propriety, and how the fear of scandals and exposures which another

---

* Into performing ceremonies at the grave of his supposed father which unless performed by a true son, were sacrilegious and criminal.

woman would in the long run have grown to regard with indifference, had embittered her whole life.

For Lady Akikonomu he had done all and more than all that he led her to expect, and she had already become a prominent figure at Court. During the autumn, having been granted leave of absence from the Palace, she came to stay for a while at the Nijo-in. She was given the Main Hall, and found everything decked with the gayest colors in honor of her arrival. She assumed in the household the place of a favorite elder daughter, and it was entirely in this spirit that Genji entertained and amused her. One day when the autumn rain was falling steadily and the dripping flowers in the garden seemed to be washed to one dull tinge of grey, memories of long-forgotten things came crowding one after another to Genji's mind, and with eyes full of tears he betook himself to Lady Akikonomu's rooms. Not a touch of color relieved the dark of his mourner's dress, and on pretext of doing penance for the sins of the nation during the recent disorders he carried a rosary under his cloak; yet he contrived to wear even this dour, penitential garb with perfect elegance and grace, and it was with a fine sweep of the cloak that he now entered the curtained alcove where she sat. He came straight to her side and, with only a thin latticed screen between them, began to address her without waiting to be announced: "What an unfortunate year this is! It is too bad that we should get weather like this just when everything in the garden is at its best. Look at the flowers. Are not you sorry for them? They came when it was their turn, and this is the way they are welcomed." He leant upon the pillar of her seat, the evening light falling upon him as he turned towards her. They had many memories in common; did she still recall, he asked, that terrible morning when he came to visit her mother at the Palace-in-the-Fields? "Too much my thoughts frequent those vanished days," she quoted,* and her eyes filled with tears. Already he was thinking her handsome and interesting, when for some reason she rose and shifted her position, using her limbs with a subtle grace that made him long to see her show them to better advantage... But stay! Ought such thoughts to be occurring to him? "Years ago," he said, "at a time when I might have been far more happily employed, I became involved, entirely through my own fault, in a number of attachments, all of the most unfortunate kind, with the result that I never knew an instant's peace of mind. Among these affairs there were two which were not only, while they lasted, far more distressing than the rest, but also both ended under a dark cloud of uncharitableness and obstinacy. The first was with Lady Rokujo, your mother. The fact that she died still harboring against me feelings of the

---

* From a poem by Ono no Komachi's sister, say the commentaries; but such a poem is not to be found in her surviving works.

intensest bitterness will cast a shadow over my whole life, and my one consolation is that in accordance with her wishes, I have been able to do something towards helping *you* in the world. But that by any act of mine the flame of her love should thus forever have been stifled will remain the greatest sorrow of my life." He had mentioned two affairs; but he decided to leave the other part of his tale untold and continued: "During the period when my fortunes were in eclipse I had plenty of time to think over all these things and worked out a new plan which I hoped would make everyone satisfied and happy. It was in pursuance of this plan that I induced the Lady from the Village of Falling Flowers to take up residence in the new eastern wing. Her own resources are quite inadequate, and I used to feel very uncomfortable about her; it is a great relief to know that she is getting all she needs. Fortunately she is very easy to deal with, we understand each other perfectly and there is (or at any rate I hope so) complete satisfaction on both sides. Soon after I came back a great deal of my time began to be taken up in looking after the young Emperor and helping him to conduct the business of the State. I am not particularly interested in that sort of thing, but I was glad to be of use. It was only when it came to filling his household that I found myself confronted with a task that was definitely uncongenial. I wonder whether you realize what very strong impulses of my own I had to overcome before I surrendered you to the Palace? You might at least tell me that you feel for me and are grateful; then I should no longer think that this sacrifice was made quite in vain..." She was vexed. Why must he needs start talking in that strain? She made no reply. "Forgive me," he said; "I see that I have displeased you..." and he began hastily to talk of other matters: "How much I should like to retire to some quiet place—to know that for the rest of my life on earth I should have no more anxieties or cares and could devote myself for as long as I liked each day to preparation for the life to come. But of course all this would be very dull if one had nothing interesting to look back upon. There are many things to be thought of first. For example, I have young children, whose place in the world is very insecure; it will be a long time before I can establish them satisfactorily. And here you can be of great use to me; for should you—forgive me for speaking of such a thing—one day bring increase to His Majesty's house, it would be in your power to render considerable services to my children, even though I should chance no longer to be with you..." It was evident that this sort of conversation was far more to her liking. She did not indeed say more than a word or two at a time; but her manner was friendly and encouraging, and they were still immersed in these domestic projects when darkness began to fall. "And when all these weighty matters are off my hands," said Genji at last, "I hope I shall have a little time left for things which I really enjoy—flowers, autumn leaves, the sky, all those day-to-day changes and wonders that a single year brings forth; that is what I look forward to. Forests of flowering trees in spring, the open country in autumn... Which do you prefer? It is of course useless to argue on such a subject, as has so often been done. It is a question of temperament. Each person is born with 'his season' and is bound to prefer it. No one, you may be sure, has ever yet succeeded in convincing anyone else on such a subject. In China it has always been the springtime with its 'broidery of flowers' that has won the highest praise; here however the brooding melancholy of autumn seems always to have moved our poets more deeply. For my own part I find it impossible to reach a decision; for much as I enjoy the music of birds and the beauty of flowers, I confess I seldom remember at what season I have seen a particular flower, heard this or that bird sing. But in this I am to blame; for even within the narrow compass of my own walls, I might well have learnt what sights and sounds distinguish each season of the year, having as you see not only provided for the springtime by a profusion of flowering trees, but also planted in my garden many varieties of autumn grass and shrub, brought in, root and all, from the countryside. Why, I have even carried hither whole tribes of insects that were wasting their shrill song in the solitude of lanes and fields. All this I did that I might be able to enjoy these things in the company of my friends, among whom you are one. Pray tell me then, to which season do you find that your preference inclines?" She thought this a very difficult form of conversation, but politeness demanded some sort of reply and she said timidly: "But you have just said you can never yourself remember when it was you saw or heard the thing that pleased you most. How can you expect me to have a better memory? However, difficult as it is to decide, I think I agree with the poet[*] who found the dusk of an autumn evening 'strangest and loveliest thing of all.' Perhaps I am more easily moved at such moments because, you know, it was at just such a time..." Her voice died away, and knowing well indeed what was in her mind Genji answered tenderly with the verse: "The world knows it not; but to you, oh Autumn, I confess it: your wind at night-fall stabs deep into my heart."[†] "Sometimes I am near to thinking that I can hold out no longer," he added. To such words as these she was by no means bound to reply and even thought it best to pretend that she had not understood. This however had the effect of leading him on to be a little more explicit; and matters would surely have come a good deal further had she not at once shown in the most unmistakable manner her horror at the sentiments which he was beginning to profess. Suddenly he pulled himself up. He had been behaving with a childish lack of restraint.

---

[*] Anon., in *Kokinshu,* No. 546.

[†] He identifies Akikonomu with the autumn.

How fortunate that she at least had shown some sense! He felt very much cast down; but neither his sighs nor his languishing airs had any effect upon her. He saw that she was making as though to steal quietly and unobtrusively from the room, and holding her back, he said: "I see that you are terribly offended; well, I do not deny that you have good cause. I ought not to be so impetuous; I know that it is wrong. But, granted I spoke far too suddenly—it is all over now. Do not, I beg of you, go on being angry with me; for if you are unkind..."* And with that he retired to his own quarters. Even the scent of his richly perfumed garments had become unendurable to her; she summoned her maids and bade them open the window and door. "Just come over here and smell the cushion that His Highness was sitting on!" one of them called to another. "What an exquisite fragrance! How he contrives to get hold of such scents I simply cannot imagine. 'If the willow-tree had but the fragrance of the plum and the petals of the cherry!' So the old poet wished, and surely Prince Genji must be the answer to his prayer, for it seems that in him every perfection is combined."

He went to the western wing; but instead of going straight into Murasaki's room, he flung himself down upon a couch in the vestibule. Above the partition he could see the far-off flicker of a lamp; there Murasaki was sitting with her ladies, one of whom was reading her a story. He began to think about what had just occurred. It was a sad disappointment to discover that he was still by no means immune from a tendency which had already played such havoc with his own and other people's happiness. Upon what more inappropriate object could his affections possibly have lighted? True, his chief offence in old days had been of far greater magnitude. But then he had the excuse of youth and ignorance, and it was possible that, taking this into consideration, Heaven might by this time have forgiven the offence. But on this occasion he could hardly plead inexperience; indeed, as he ruefully admitted to himself, he ought by now to have learnt every lesson which repeated failure can teach.

Lady Akikonomu now bitterly repented of having confessed her partiality for the autumn. It would have been so easy not to reply at all, and this one answer of hers seemed somehow to have opened up the way for the distressing incident that followed. She told no one of what had occurred, but was for a time very much scared and distressed. Soon however the extreme stiffness and formality of address which Genji henceforth adopted began somewhat to restore her confidence.

On entering Murasaki's room at a later hour in the day of the incident, he said to her: "Lady Akikonomu has been telling me that she likes

---

* "If you are unkind, I too by unkindness will teach you the pain that unkindness can inflict." Anonymous poem.

autumn best. It is a taste which I can quite understand, but all the same, I am not surprised that you should prefer, as you have often told me that you do, the early morning in spring. How I wish that I were able to spend more time with you! We would pass many hours in the gardens at all seasons of the year, deciding which trees and flowers we liked the best. There is nothing which I more detest than having all my time taken up by this endless succession of business. You know indeed that if I had only myself to consider I should long ago have thrown up everything and retired to some temple in the hills..."

But there was the Lady of Akashi; she too must be considered. He wondered constantly how she was faring; but it seemed to become every day more impossible for him to go beyond the Walls of his palace. What a pity she had got it into her head that she would be miserable at Court! If only she would put a little more confidence in him and trust herself under his roof as anyone else would do, he would prove to her that she had no reason for all these reservations and precautions. Presently one of his accustomed excursions to the oratory at Saga gave him an excuse for a visit to Oi. "What a lonely place to live in always!" he thought as he approached the house, and even if the people living there had been quite unknown to him he would have felt a certain concern on their behalf. But when he thought how she must wait for him day after day and how seldom her hopes could ever be fulfilled, he suddenly felt and showed an overwhelming compassion towards her. This however had only the effect of making her more than ever inconsolable. Seeking for some means of distracting her mind, he noticed that behind a tangle of close-set trees points of flame were gleaming—the flares of the cormorant-fishers at work on Oi River; and with these lights, sometimes hardly distinguishable from them, blended the fireflies that hovered above the moat. "It is wonderful here," said Genji; "you too would feel so, were not one's pleasure always spoiled by familiarity." "Those lights on the water!" she murmured. "Often I think that I am still at Akashi. 'As the fisher's flare that follows close astern, so in those days and in these has misery clung to my tossing bark, and followed me from home to home.'" "My love," he answered, "is like the secret flame that burns brightly because it is hidden from sight; yours is like the fisherman's torch, that flares up in the wind and presently is spent. No, no; you are right," he said after a pause; "life (yours and mine alike) is indeed a wretched business." It happened to be a time at which he was somewhat less tied and harassed than of late, and he was able to devote himself more wholeheartedly than usual to the proceedings at his oratory. This kept him in the district for several days on end, a circumstance which did not often occur and which he hoped would, for the moment at any rate, make her feel a little less neglected.

Asagao

The death of Prince Momozono meant, of course, the return to Court of the Kamo Vestal, Lady Asagao; and Genji followed up his letter of welcome by numerous other notes and messages. For it was, as I have said before, a peculiarity of his character that if he had once become fond of anyone, neither separation nor lapse of time could ever obliterate his affection. But Asagao remembered only too well the difficulty that she had before experienced in keeping him at arm's length, and she was careful to answer in the most formal and guarded terms. He found these decorous replies exceedingly irritating. In the ninth month he heard that she had moved into her father's old residence, the Momozono Palace, which was at that time occupied by Princess Nyogo, a younger sister of the old Emperor.[*] Here was an opening; for it was perfectly natural and proper that Genji should visit this princess, who had been his father's favorite sister and with whom he had himself always remained on excellent terms. He found that the two ladies were living in opposite wings of the Palace, separated by the great central hall. Though old Prince Momozono had so recently passed away the place had already assumed a rather decayed and depressing air. Princess Nyogo received him immediately. He noticed at once that she had aged very rapidly since he last saw her. She was indeed quite decrepit, and it was difficult to believe that she was really younger than Aoi's mother, who seemed to him never to have changed since he had known her; whereas in the quavering accents and palsied gait of the aged lady who now greeted him it was well nigh impossible to recognize the princess of former days.

"Everything has been in a wretched way since the old Emperor, your poor father, was taken from us, and as the years go by the outlook seems to grow blacker and blacker; I confess, I never have an easy moment. And now even my brother Prince Momozono has left me! I go on, I go on; but it hardly seems like being alive, except when I get a visit like yours today, and then I forget all my troubles..." "Poor thing," thought Genji, "how terribly she has gone to pieces!" But he answered very politely: "For me too the world has been in many ways a different place since my

---

[*] Consequently an aunt both of Asagao and Genji, who were first cousins; Prince Momozono, Asagao's father, being a brother of Genji's father, the old Emperor. Asagao was the one lady whom Genji had courted in vain. See Part 1, p. 36.

father died. First, as you know, came this unexpected attack upon me, followed by my exile to a remote district. Then came my restoration to rank and privilege, bringing with it all manner of ties and distractions. All this time I have been longing to have a talk with you, and regret immensely that there has never before been an opportunity..." "Oh, the changes, the changes," she broke in; "such terrible destruction I have seen on every side. Nothing seems safe from it, and often I feel as though I would give anything to have died before all this began. But I do assure you I am glad I have lived long enough to witness your return. To die while you were still in such trouble, not knowing how it was all going to end—that would indeed have been a melancholy business." She paused for a while and then went on in her quavering, thin voice: "You know, you have grown to be a very handsome man. But I remember that the first time I saw you, when you were only a little boy, I was astonished at you, really I was. I could never have believed that such loveliness would be seen shining in the face of any mortal child! And every time I see you I always feel just as I did then. They say that his present Majesty, the Emperor Ryozen, is the image of you; but I don't believe a word of it. He may be just a little like; but no one is going to persuade me that he is half as handsome as you." So she rambled on. Coming from anyone else such flattery would have very much embarrassed him. But at this strange old lady's outpourings one could only be amused. "Since my exile I have quite lost whatever good looks I may once have possessed," he said; "one cannot live for years on end under those depressing conditions without its changing one very much. As for the Emperor, I assure you that his is a beauty of an altogether different order. I should doubt if a better-looking young man has ever existed, and to assert that he is less handsome than I is, if you will forgive my saying so, quite ridiculous." "If only you came to see me every day I believe I should go on living for ever," she burst out. "I am suddenly beginning to feel quite young, and I am not at all sure that the world is half so bad a place as I made out just now." Nevertheless it was not long before she was again wailing and weeping. "How I envy my sister Princess Omiya,"* she cried; "no doubt, being your mother-in-law, she sees a great deal of you. I only wish I were in that position. You know, I expect, that my poor brother often talked of affiancing his daughter to you and was very sorry afterwards that he did not do so." At this Genji pricked up his ears. "I desired nothing better," said he, "than to be connected on close terms with your family, and it would still give me great pleasure to be on a more intimate footing in this house. But I cannot say that I have hitherto received much encouragement... He was vexed that he had not discovered this at the time. He looked towards

---

* Aoi's mother.

the other wing of the house. The garden under the younger princess's windows was carefully tended. He scanned those borders of late autumn flowers, and then the rooms behind; he pictured her sitting not far from the window, her eyes fixed upon these same swiftly-fading petals. Yes, he must certainly contrive to see her; and bowing to Princess Nyogo he said: "I naturally intend to pay my respects to your niece today; indeed, I should not like her to regard my visit as a mere afterthought, and for that reason I shall, with your permission, approach her apartments by way of the garden instead of going along the corridor and through the hall." Skirting the side of the house he came at length to her window. Although it was now almost dark, he could see, behind grey curtains, the outline of a black screen-of-state. He was soon observed, and Asagao's servants, scandalized that he should have been left standing even for a moment in the verandah, hurried him into the guest-room at the back of the house. Here a gentlewoman came to enquire what was his pleasure, and he handed to her the following note: "How this carries me back to the days of our youth—this sending in of notes and waiting in ante-chambers! I had hoped, I confess, that my reticence during the years of your sacred calling would have won for me, still your ardent admirer, the right to a somewhat less formal reception." It would be hard indeed if she gave him no more encouragement than this! Her answer was brought by word of mouth: "To come back to this house and find my father no longer here, is so strange an experience that it is difficult to believe those old days were not a mere dream from which I now awake to a fleeting prospect of the most comfortless realities. But in a world where all is changed, it would, I confess, be ungracious not to cherish and encourage a devotion so undeviating as that which you have described."

She need not, he thought, remind him of life's uncertainties. For who had in every circumstance great and small more grievously experienced them than he? In reply he sent the poem: "Have I not manfully held back and kept cold silence year on year, till the Gods gave me leave?" "Madam," he added, "you are a Vestal no longer and cannot plead that any sanctity now hedges you about. Since last we met I have experienced many strange, vicissitudes. If you would but let me tell you a little part of all that I have seen and suffered..." The gentlewoman who took his answer noticed that his badges and decorations were somewhat more dazzling than in old days; but though he was now a good deal older, his honors still far outstripped his years.

"Though it were but to tell me of your trials and sorrows that you have made this visit, yet even such tidings the Gods, my masters till of late, forbid me to receive." This was too bad! "Tell your lady," he cried peevishly, "that I have long ago cast my, offence* of old days to the winds of Shinado; or does she think perhaps that the Gods did not accept my vows?"† The messenger saw that though he sought to turn off the matter with these allusions and jests he was in reality very much put about; and she was vexed on his behalf. She had for years past been watching her mistress become more and more aloof from the common interests and distractions of life, and it had long distressed her to see Prince Genji's letters so often left unanswered. "I did ill to call at so late an hour," he said; "I can see that the purpose of my visit has been wholly misunderstood." And sighing heavily he turned to go, saying as he did so: "This is the way one is treated when one begins to grow old... It is useless, I know, after what has passed, even to suggest that Her Highness should come to the window for a moment to see me start..." And with that he left the house, watched by a bevy of ladies who made all the usual comments and appraisements. Not only was it delightful weather, but at this moment the wind was making a most agreeable music in the neighboring trees, and these ladies soon fell to talking of the old days when Prince Momozono was alive; particularly of Genji's visits long ago and the many signs he had given of a deep and unaltering attachment to their mistress.

After his return from this unsuccessful expedition, Genji felt in no mood for sleep, and soon he jumped up and threw open his casement. The morning mist lay thick over the garden of flowers, which, at the season's close, looked very battered and wan. Among them, its blossoms shimmering vaguely, was here and there a Morning Glory,‡ growing mixed in among the other flowers. Choosing one that was even more wilted and autumnal than the rest, he sent it to the Momozono Palace, with the note: "The poor reception which you gave me last night has left a most humiliating and painful impression upon me. Indeed, I can only imagine it was with feelings of relief that you so soon saw my back turned upon your house, though I am loath to think that things can even now have come to such a pass: 'Can it be that the Morning Glory, once seen by me and ever since remembered in its beauty, is now a dry and withered flower?'" Does it count with you for nothing that I have admired you unrequited, year in year out, for so great a stretch of time? That at least might be put to my credit..." She could not leave so mannerly an appeal quite unheeded, and when her people pressed round her with ink-stone and brush, she yielded to their persuasion so far as to write the poem: "Autumn is over, and now with ghostly flower the Morning Glory withers on the mist-bound hedge." "Your comparison," she added, "is so just

---

* I.e. making love to her.

† Allusion to the poem: "By the River of Cleansing I tied prayer-strips inscribed "I will love no more"; but it seems that the Gods would not accept my vow."

‡ *Asagao.*

that the arrival of your note has brought fresh dewdrops to the petals of the flower to whom this reminder was addressed." That was all, and it was in truth not very interesting or ingenious. But for some reason he read the poem many times over, and during the course of the day found himself continually looking at it. Perhaps what fascinated him was the effect of her faint, sinuous ink-strokes on the blue-grey writing-paper which her mourning dictated. For it often happens that a letter, its value enhanced to us either by the quality of the writer or by the beauty of the penmanship, appears at the time to be faultless. But when it is copied out and put into a book something seems to have gone wrong... Efforts are made to improve the sense or style, and in the end the original effect is altogether lost.

He realized the impropriety of the letters with which he had in old days assailed her and did not intend to return to so unrestrained a method of address. His new style had indeed met with a certain measure of success; for whereas she had formerly seldom vouchsafed any answer at all, he had now received a not unfriendly reply. But even this reply was far from being such as to satisfy him, and he was unable to resist the temptation of trying to improve upon so meager a success. He wrote again, this time in much less cautious terms, and posting himself in the eastern wing[§] of his palace he sent a carriage to fetch one of Asagao's ladies, and presently sent her back again with the letter. Her gentlewomen would themselves never have dreamed of discouraging far less distinguished attentions, let alone those of such a personage as Prince Genji, and they now urged his claims upon their mistress as one "for whose sake a little virtue was surely worth sacrificing." But after all her efforts in the past to keep free of such an entanglement, this was hardly the moment to give in; for she felt that both he and she had now reached an age when such things are best put aside. She feared that even her inevitable allusions to the flowers and trees of the season might easily be misinterpreted, and even if Genji himself was under no misapprehension, there are always those who made a business of getting hold of such things and turning them to mischief, and in consequence she was careful to avoid the slightest hint of anything intimate or sentimental. About this time a rumor ran through the Court to the effect that Genji was in active correspondence with the former Vestal, abetted and encouraged by Princess Nyogo and the lady's other relatives. The pair seemed very well suited to one another and no one expressed any surprise at the existence of such an attachment. The story eventually reached Murasaki's ears. At first she refused to credit it, making sure that if he were indeed carrying on any such intrigue it would be scarcely possible for him to conceal it from her. But observing him with

---

§ Where Murasaki would not be likely to come.

this tale in her mind she thought that he seemed unusually abstracted and depressed. What if this affair, which he had always passed off as a mere joke between himself and his cousin, were to turn out after all to be something important—the beginning of what she dreaded day and night? In rank and in accomplishments perhaps there was little to choose between Asagao and herself. But he had begun to admire and court this princess long, long ago; and if an affection grounded so far back in the past were now to resume its sway over him, Murasaki knew that she must be prepared for the worst. It was not easy to face what she now believed to threaten her. For years past she had held, beyond challenge or doubt, the first place in Genji's affections—had been the center of all his plans and contrivings. To see herself ousted by a stranger from a place which long use had taught her to regard as her own by inalienable right—such was the ordeal for which she now began silently to prepare herself. He would not, of course, abandon her altogether; of that she was sure. But the very fact that they had for so many years lived together on terms of daily intimacy and shared so many trifling experiences made her, she felt, in a way less interesting to him. So she speculated, sometimes thinking that all was indeed lost, sometimes that the whole thing was her fancy and nothing whatever was amiss. In his general conduct towards her there was not anything of which she could reasonably complain. But there were from time to time certain vague indications that he was not in the best of tempers, and these were enough whenever they occurred to convince her that she was undone for good and all—though she showed no outward sign of the despair which had now settled upon her. Genji, meanwhile, spent much of his time in the front[*] of the house and was also frequently at the Emperor's Palace. His leisure was employed in writing endless letters. Murasaki wondered how she could have ever doubted the rumors that were now rampant throughout the Court. If only he would tell, give even the slightest hint of what was in these days passing through his mind!

Winter drew on, and at last the eleventh month came round. But this year there were none of the usual religious festivals and processions[†] to distract him, and Genji became more and more restless. One evening when the delicate twilight was sprinkled with a few thin flakes of snow, he determined to set out for the Momozono Palace. All day he had been more than usually preoccupied with thoughts of its occupant, and somehow he could hot help feeling that she too would on this occasion prove less unyielding. Before starting, he came to take leave of Murasaki in the

---

[*] In the men's quarters.

[†] During the tenth month the Gods withdraw themselves and cannot hear our prayers; their return in the eleventh month is celebrated with rejoicing; but this year, owing to the National Mourning for Fujitsubo's death, these ceremonies were omitted.

western wing. "I am sorry to say Princess Nyogo is very unwell," he said; "I must go and offer her my sympathy." She did not even look round, but went on playing with her little foster-child as though determined not to be interrupted. Evidently there was going to be trouble. "There has been something very strange in your manner lately," he said. "I am not conscious of having done anything to offend you. I thought we understood one another well enough for me to be able to spend a day or two now and then at the Emperor's Palace without your taking offence. But perhaps it is something else?" "I certainly understand you well enough," she answered, "to know that I must expect to put up with a great deal of suffering..." and she sank back upon the divan, her face turned away from him. He could never bear to leave her thus, and knew he would be wretched every step of the way to Princess Nyogo's house. But the hour was already late, and as he had promised beforehand that he would call there that evening, it was impossible to defer his departure.

Murasaki meanwhile lay on her couch, continually debating within herself whether this affair might not really have been going on for years past—perhaps ever since his return—without her having any suspicion of it. She went to the window. He was still dressed chiefly in grey; but the few touches of color which his mourning permitted showed up all the more brightly, and as she watched his handsome figure moving against a background of glittering snow, the thought that she might be losing him, that soon, very soon perhaps, he would vanish never to return, was more than she could endure. His cortege consisted only of a few favorite outriders, to whom he said: "I am not feeling inclined just now to go about paying calls; indeed, you will have noticed that apart from a few necessary visits to Court, I have hardly left home at all. But my friends at the Momozono Palace are passing through a very trying time. Her Highness has for years relied upon her brother's aid and, now that he is taken from her, the least I can do is to help her occasionally with a little encouragement and advice..." But his gentlemen were not so easily deceived and whispered among themselves as they rode along: "Come, come, that will not do. Unless he has very much changed his ways it is not to chatter with old ladies that His Highness sets out at this hour of a winter night. There is more here than meets the eye," and they shook their heads over his incurable frivolity.

The main gate of the palace was on the north side; but here there was usually a great deal of traffic, and not wishing to attract attention he drove up to a side-entrance, the one which Prince Momozono himself commonly used, and sent in a servant to announce his arrival. As he had promised to appear at a much earlier hour Princess Nyogo had by now quite given up expecting him, and, much put about by this untimely visit, she bade her people send the porter to the western gate. The man made his appearance a moment later, looking wretchedly pinched and cold as he hastened through the snow with the key in his hand. Unfortunately the lock would not work, and when he went back to look for help no other manservant could anywhere be found. "It's very rusty," said the old porter dolefully, fumbling all the while with the lock that grated with an unpleasant sound but would not turn. "There's nothing else wrong with it, but it's terribly rusty. No one uses this gate now."

The words, ordinary enough in themselves, filled Genji with an unaccountable depression. How swiftly the locks rust, the hinges grow stiff on doors that close behind us! "I am more than thirty," he thought; and it seemed to him impossible to go on doing things just as though they would last... as though people would remember... "And yet," he said to himself, "I know that even at this moment the sight of something very beautiful, were it only some common flower or tree, might in an instant make life again seem full of meaning and reality."

At last the key turned and with a great deal of pushing and pulling the gate was gradually forced open. Soon he was in the Princess's room, listening to her usual discourses and lamentations. She began telling a series of very involved and rambling stories about things all of which seemed to have happened a great while ago. His attention began to wander; it was all he could do to keep awake. Before very long the Princess herself broke off and said with a yawn: "It's no good; I can't tell things properly at this time of night, it all gets mixed up..."

Then suddenly he heard a loud and peculiar noise. Where did it come from? What could it be? His eye fell upon the Princess. Yes; it was from her that these strange sounds proceeded; for she was now fast asleep and snoring with a resonance such as he would never have conceived to be possible.

Delighted at this opportunity of escape he was just about to slip out of the room when he heard a loud "Ahem," also uttered in a very aged and husky voice, and perceived that someone had just entered the room. "There! What a shame! I've startled you. And I made sure you heard me come in. But I see you don't know who in the world I am. Well, your poor father, the old Emperor, who loved his joke, used to call me the Grandam. Perhaps that will help you to remember..." Could this be... Yes, surely it was that same elderly Lady-of-the-Bedchamber who had flirted with him so outrageously years ago, at the time of the Feast of Red Leaves.* He seemed to remember hearing that she had joined some lay order and become a pensioner in the late prince's household. But it had not occurred to him that she could possibly still be in existence, and this sudden encounter was something of a shock. "I am distressed to

---

* See Part I, p. 140.

find," he answered, "that those old days are becoming very dim in my mind, and anything that recalls them to me is therefore very precious. I am delighted to hear your voice again. Pray remember that, like the traveler whom Prince Shotoku[*] found lying at the wayside, I have "no parent to succor me" and must therefore look to old friends such as you for shelter from the world's unkindness." It was extraordinary how little she had changed in appearance, and her manner was certainly as arch and coquettish as ever. Her utterance, indeed, suggested that she now had very few teeth left in her head; but she still managed to impart to her words the same insinuating and caressing tone as of old. It amused him that she spoke of herself as though she had been a mere girl when they first met and that she continually apologized for the changes which he must now be noticing in her. He was amused, but also saddened. For he could not help thinking that of all the gentlewomen who had been this lady's rivals scarce one was now left at Court. Most were dead; others had fallen into disgrace and were eking out a miserable existence no one knew where. Or again, that a creature such as Lady Fujitsubo should vanish so soon, while this absurd grandam, even in her younger days totally devoid of charm or intelligence, should be left behind! And judging by her appearance, there was every prospect that she would go on happily pottering about and telling her rosary for another twenty years. No, there was no sense, no purpose in all this.

She saw that thoughts which moved him deeply were passing through his mind and at once assumed that he was recalling the details of what she was pleased to think of as their "love affair" and now in her most playful voice she recited the poem: "Though your father called me Granny, I am not so old but that you and I were sweethearts long ago." He felt somewhat embarrassed but he answered kindly: "Such motherly care as yours not in this life only but in all lives to come none save a scapegrace would forget." "We must meet again at a more convenient time and have a good talk," he said; and with that he hastened towards the western wing. The blinds were drawn and everything was shut up for the night, save that at one window she[†] had left a lattice half-unclosed, feeling that to show no light at all on the evening of his visit would be too pointedly uncivil. The moon had risen and its rays blended with the glitter of the newly fallen snow. It was indeed a most charming night. "An old woman in love and the moon at midwinter," he remembered the saying that these are the two most dismal things in the world; but tonight he felt this collocation to be very unjust. He sent in an urgent letter: if despite her scruples she intended ever to admit him for a few moments to her presence, why not

---

[*] 572-621 A.D.

[†] Asagao.

take advantage of this excellent opportunity and not subject him to the irritation of purposeless delays?

She did not doubt the reality of his feelings; but if at a time when they were both young enough to be forgiven a few indiscretions, when moreover her father was actually seeking to promote an alliance between them, she had without a moment's hesitation refused to yield herself to him—what sense could there be, now that they were both past the age to which such irresponsible gallantries by right belong, what sense (she asked herself) could there be in parleying with him, indeed, in admitting him into her presence at all? He saw that she was absolutely unmoved by his appeal, and was both astonished and hurt. She meanwhile disliked intensely this frigid interchange of messages and notes, but for the moment saw no way of bringing it to a close. It was now getting late, a fierce wind had begun to blow and Genji, feeling a very real disappointment and distress, was about to make his way homeward, flinging out as he did so the parting verse: "No penance can your hard heart find save such as you long since have taught me to endure." As usual her gentlewomen insisted that she must send a reply, and reluctantly she wrote the verse: "Is it for me to change, for me who hear on every wind some tale that proves you, though the years go by, not other than you were?"

He burst into a great rage when he received her note, but a moment afterwards felt that he was behaving very childishly, and said to the gentlewoman who had brought it: "I would not for the world have anyone know how I have been treated tonight. Promise me, I beg of you, that you will speak of it to no one; stay, you had best even deny that I was here at all..." He whispered this in a very low voice; but some servants who were hanging about near by noticed the aside, and one of them said to another: "Look at that now! Poor gentleman! You can see she has sent him a very stinging reply. Even if she does not fancy him, she might at least treat him with common civility. For he does not look at all the kind of gentleman who would take advantage of a little kindness..."

As a matter of fact, she had no distaste for him whatever. His beauty delighted her and she was sure that she would have found him a most charming companion. But she was convinced that from the moment she betrayed this liking he would class her among the common ruck of his admirers and imagine that she would put up with such treatment as they were apparently content to endure. A position so humiliating she knew that she could never tolerate. She was resolute, therefore, in her determination never to allow the slightest intimacy to grow up between them. But at the same time she was now careful always to answer his letters fully and courteously, and she allowed him to converse with her at second hand whenever he felt inclined. It was hardly conceivable that, submitted to this treatment, he would not soon grow weary of the whole affair.

For her part she wished to devote herself to the expiation of the many offences against her own religion* that her residence at Kamo had involved. Ultimately she meant to take orders; but any sudden step of that kind would certainly be attributed to an unfortunate love-affair and so give color to the rumors which already connected her name with his. Indeed, she had seen enough of the world to know that in few people is discretion stronger than the desire to tell a good story, and she therefore took no one into her confidence, not even the gentlewomen who waited daily upon her. Meanwhile she devoted herself more and more ardently to preparation for the mode of life which she hoped soon to embrace.

She had several brothers; but they were the children of Prince Zembo's first wife† and she knew very little of them. Other visitors at the Momozono Palace became increasingly rare; but the fact that no less a person than Genji was known to be Princess Asagao's admirer aroused a widespread curiosity concerning her.

As a matter of fact, he was not very desperately in love with her; but her apparent indifference had piqued him and he was determined to go on till he had gained his point. He had recently gathered from several sources of information, including persons of every rank in society, but all of them in a position to know what they were talking about, that his own reputation now stood very high in the country. He felt indeed that his insight into affairs had very greatly improved since old days, and it would certainly be a pity if a scandal once more deprived him of popular confidence. Nevertheless, if gossip were to concern itself with the matter at all, he could not help feeling he should prefer to figure in the story as having succeeded than as having been ignominiously repulsed.

Meanwhile his frequent absences from the Nijo-in had already convinced Murasaki that the affair was as serious as it could possibly be. She tried to conceal her agitation, but there were times when it was evident that she had been secretly weeping, and Genji said to her one day: "What has come over you lately? I cannot imagine any reason why you should be so depressed"; and as he gently stroked the hair back from her forehead they looked such a pair as you might put straight into a picture.

"Since his mother's death," Genji went on presently, "the Emperor Ryozen has been in very low spirits and I have felt bound to spend a good deal of time at the Palace. But that is not the only thing which takes up my time in these days; you must remember that I have now to attend personally to a mass of business which the old Minister of the Left used formerly to take off my hands. I am as sorry as you are that we see

---

* Buddhism. She had been Vestal in the Shinto temple at Kamo, where no Buddhist prayers or observances were allowed.

† Rokujo was his second.

so much less of one another; but I do my best, and you must really try henceforward to bear with me more patiently. You are no longer a child; yet you make as little effort to enter into my feelings and see my point of view as if you were still in the nursery." And with that, just as though she were indeed a small child, he put back in its place a lock of her hair that had become disordered while she was weeping.

But still she turned away from him and would not speak a word. "This is quite new," he said; "who has been teaching you these pettish airs and graces?" He spoke lightly; but how long, he wondered, was this going to last, how much time were they going to spend in this dismal fashion, while at any moment one of those countless horrors that life perpetually holds over us might suddenly descend upon them and reconciliation be no longer possible? Determined to bring the matter to a head, he said at last: "I think you have perhaps been misled by very foolish rumors concerning my friendship with the former Vestal. As a matter of fact, it is of the most distant kind, as in the end you will yourself probably realize. She has always, since I first got to know her years ago, treated me with an exaggerated coldness. This hurts me, and I have more than once remonstrated with her on the subject. As very little now goes on at the Momozono Palace, she has a good deal of time on her hands and it amuses her to keep up a desultory correspondence. This is all that has happened between us; and even you will surely admit that is not worth crying about! If it is really this affair that has been on your mind, I assure you that there is no cause whatever for anxiety..." He spent the whole day in trying to win back her confidence, and his patience was at last rewarded.

By this time the snow was lying very deep, and it was still falling, though now very lightly. So far from obliterating the shapes of pine-tree and bamboo, the heavy covering of snow seemed only to accentuate their varying forms, which stood out with strange distinctness in the evening light. "We decided the other day," said Genji to Murasaki, "that Lady Akikonomu's season is autumn, and yours spring. This evening I am more sure than ever that mine is winter. What could be more lovely than a winter night such as this, when the moon shines out of a cloudless sky upon the glittering, fresh-fallen snow? Beauty without color seems somehow to belong to another world. At any rate, I find such a scene as this infinitely more lovely and moving than any other in the whole year. How little do I agree with the proverb that calls the moon in winter a dismal sight!" So saying he raised the window-blind, and they looked out. The moon was now fully risen, covering the whole garden with its steady, even light. The withered flower-beds showed, in these cold rays, with painful clearness the ravages of wind and frost. And look, the river was half-choked with ice, while the pond, frozen all over, was unutterably strange and lonesome under its coat of snow. Near it some children had been allowed to make a monster snowball. They looked very pretty as they tripped about in the moonlight. Several of the older girls had taken off their coats and set to in a very business-like way, showing all sorts of strange under-garments; while their brothers, coming straight from their tasks as page-boys and what not, had merely loosened their belts, and there was now a sight of smart coat-tails flapping and long hair falling forward till its ends brushed the white garden floor—an effect both singular and delightful. Some of the very little ones were quite wild with joy and rushed about dropping all their fans and other belongings in their mad excitement. The glee imprinted on these small faces was charming to behold. The children made so big a snowball that when it came to rolling it along the ground they could not make it budge an inch, and the sight of their frantic endeavors to get it moving provoked much jeering and laughter from another party of children which had just made its appearance at the eastern door.

"I remember," said Genji, "that one year Lady Fujitsubo had a snow-mountain built in front of her palace. It is a common enough amusement in winter time; but she had the art of making the most ordinary things striking and interesting. What countless reasons I have to regret her at every moment! I was during the greater part of her life not at all intimate with her and had little opportunity of studying her at close quarters. But during her residence at the Palace, she often allowed me to be of service to her in various small ways, and I frequently had occasion to use her good offices. In this way we were constantly discussing one piece of business or another, and I discovered that though she had no obvious or showy talents, she had the most extraordinary capacity for carrying through even quite unimportant and trivial affairs with a perfection of taste and management that has surely never been equaled. At the same time she was of a rather timid disposition and often took things too much to heart. Though you and she both spring from the same stem and necessarily have much in common, I have noticed that you are a good deal less even in temperament than she.

"Lady Asagao, now, has a quite different nature. If in an idle moment I address to her some trifling fancy she replies with such spirit that I have hard work not to be left lagging. I know no one else at Court to compare with her in this respect."

"I have always heard," said Murasaki, "that Lady Oborozuki is extremely accomplished and quick-witted. I should have thought, too, from all I know of her that she was very sensible and discreet; and that makes me all the more surprised at certain stories that I have heard repeated…"

"You are quite right," said Genji. "Among all the ladies now at Court she is the one I should pick out both for liveliness and beauty. As to the rumors you speak of—I know quite well what you are referring to. I bitterly regret what happened; as indeed I regret much else that belongs to that part of my life. And what quantities of things most people must begin to repent of as the years go by! For compared with almost any of my friends, I have led a very quiet and decorous life." He paused for a moment; the mention of Oborozuki seemed to have moved him deeply. Presently he continued: "I have a feeling that you look down upon country people such as the Lady of Akashi. I assure you that, unlike most women in that station of life, she is extremely cultivated and intelligent; though of course people of her class are bound in many ways to be very different from us, and I admit she has certain strained and exaggerated ideas of which I cannot approve.

"About women of the common sort I know nothing; but among our own people it has always seemed to me that few indeed were in any way remarkable or interesting. An exception however is our guest in the new wing;[*] she remains charming as ever. But though such beauty and intelligence are very rare, she has never cared to parade them; and since the time when I first realized her gifts and hastened to make her acquaintance, she has always continued to show the same indifference to the worldly conquests which she might so easily have secured. We have now been friends for so long that I do not think we are ever likely to part; I at any rate should be very sorry if she were to leave my house." While he thus talked of one thing and another, it grew very late. The moon shone brighter and brighter, and a stillness now reigned that, after the recent wintry storms, was very agreeable. Murasaki recited the verse: "The frozen waters are at rest; but now with waves of light the moonbeam ebbs and flows." She was looking out at the window, her head a little to one side, and both the expression of her face and the way her hair fell reminded him, as so often before, of her whom he had lost. Suddenly his affections, which for many weeks past had to some small extent been divided, were once more hers, and hers alone.

Just then a love-bird[†] cried, and he recited the verse: "Does it not move you strangely, the love-bird's cry, tonight when, like the drifting snow, memory piles up on memory?" Long after he and Murasaki had retired to rest, recollections of Lady Fujitsubo continued to crowd into his mind, and when at last he fell asleep, a vision of her at once appeared to him, saying in tones of deep reproach: "It may be that you on earth have kept our secret; but in the land of the dead shame cannot be hid, and I am paying dearly for what you made me do..." He tried to answer, but fear choked his voice, and Murasaki, hearing him suddenly give a strange muffled cry, said rather peevishly: "What are you doing that for?

---

[*] The lady from the Village of Falling Flowers.
[†] Generally called by the ugly name "Mandarin Duck."

You frightened me!" The sound of her voice roused him. He woke in a terrible state of grief and agitation, his eyes full of tears which he at once made violent efforts to control. But soon he was weeping bitterly, to the bewilderment of Murasaki, who nevertheless lay all the time stock-still at his side. He was now too miserable and distracted to think of sleep, and slipping out of bed presently began writing notes to various temples in the district, directing that certain texts and spells should be recited; he did not however dare to state on whose behalf these things were to be done.

Small wonder that in the dream she turned upon him so bitter and reproachful a gaze, feeling (as by her words he judged she did) that this one sin had robbed her of salvation. He remembered her constant devotions; never since that fatal day had she omitted one single prayer, penance or charity that might serve as atonement for her guilt. Yet all had been in vain, and even in the world beyond, this one crime clung to her like a stain that could not be washed away. In the past he had never thought clearly about such things; but now they lived in his mind with a terrible vividness and certainty. Were there but some spell, some magic that could enable him to seek her out in the obscure region where her soul was dwelling, and suffer in her stead the penalties of his own offence! Yet the truth was that he could not so much as have a few poor Masses said for her soul; for, had he named her, the suspicions of the Court would at once have been aroused.

Concerning the Emperor, too, Genji's conscience was very uneasy; for had Ryozen indeed discovered the true story of his birth, he must now be living in a state of continual apprehension. It was at about this time that Genji put himself under the especial protection of Amida, Buddha of Boundless Light, beseeching the Blessed One that in due time his soul and that of the lady whom he had undone might spring from the same lotus in His holy Paradise. But of such an issue he had little hope, and often he would disconsolately recite the verse: "Fain would I follow her, could I but hope to thread my way among the sunless Rivers of the World Below."*

---

* Through each of the Three Evil Realms (of Animals, Hungry Ghosts, and Demons) runs a meandering river.

The Maiden

IN THE spring of the next year[*] the National Mourning for Lady Fujitsubo came to an end. Gay colors began to appear once more at Court, and when the time for summer dresses came round it was seen that the fashions were smarter than ever; moreover, the weather was unusually agreeable and there was every prospect of a fine spell for the Kamo Festival.[†] Lady Asagao gave no outward sign of what reflections passed through her mind while she witnessed the ceremonies in which she herself had a few years ago taken the leading part. But she gazed fixedly at the laurel tree[‡] in front of her window; and though there was much beauty in those lank branches, swept to and fro by the roving winds, yet it seemed as if it must be for some other cause that again and again her eyes returned to it. In her ladies, at any rate, the sight of this tree aroused a host of reminiscences and suitable reflections.

From Genji came a note in which he said: "Does it not give you a strange feeling to witness a Day of Cleansing in which you take no part?" And remembering that she was still in mourning for her father, he added the poem: "Little thought I that, like a wave in the swirl of the flood, you would come back so soon, a dark-robed mourner swept along time's hurrying stream."

It was written on purple paper in a bold script, and a spray of wisteria[§] was attached to it. Moved by all that was going on around her she replied: "It seems but yesterday that I first wore my somber dress; but now the pool of days has grown into a flood wherein I soon shall wash my grief away."[¶] The poem was sent without explanation or comment and constituted, indeed, a meager reply; but, as usual, he found himself constantly holding it in front of him and gazing at it as though it had been much more than a few poor lines of verse.

When the end of the mourning actually came, the lady who acted as messenger and intermediary in general was overwhelmed by the number

---

[*] Genji is now thirty-three.
[†] In the fourth month.
[‡] The laurel and the hollyhock form the garlands worn by worshippers at this festival.
[§] Her mourning was of dark blue wisteria color.
[¶] Her period of mourning is almost over. There is a play of words; *fuji* = wisteria, and *fuchi* = pool.

of packages* from the Nijo-in which now began to arrive. Lady Asagao expressed great displeasure at this lavishness and, if the presents had been accompanied by letters or poems of at all a familiar or impertinent kind, she would at once have put a stop to these attentions. But for a year past there had been nothing in his conduct to complain of. From time to time he came to the house and enquired after her, but always quite openly. His letters were frequent and affectionate, but he took no liberties, and what nowadays troubled her chiefly was the difficulty of inventing anything to say in reply.

To Princess Nyogo, too, Genji sent good wishes on the occasion of her coming out of mourning. This delighted her, and the old lady observed to her maids, whilst reading the letter: "How strange it is to get this very nice letter from Prince Genji! Why, it seems only yesterday that he was a baby-in-arms, and here he is, writing such a sensible, manly letter! I had heard that he had grown up very good-looking; but what pleases me is that he evidently has a quite exceptionally nice disposition." These outbursts of praise were always greeted with laughter by the younger ladies-in-waiting, among whom Princess Nyogo's weakness for Genji was a standing joke.

The old lady next bustled off to her niece's rooms. "What do you say to this?" she asked, holding out the letter; "could anything be more friendly and considerate? But he has always regarded this house as a second home. I have often told you that your poor father was bitterly disappointed that the circumstances of your birth made it impossible for him to offer your hand to this Prince. It was indeed definitely arranged that he should do so, and it was with the greatest reluctance that he consented to your departure. He talked to me about this constantly in after years, and it was obvious that he bitterly regretted not having arranged the marriage at a much earlier period in your life. What held him back from doing so was that my sister Princess Omiya had already arranged for the marriage of her daughter, Lady Aoi, to Prince Genji and, frightened of giving offence, he let time slip by without doing anything towards the accomplishment of this favorite project. But Lady Aoi's death has removed the one insurmountable obstacle which before made it out of the question that any person of consequence should offer to this Prince his daughter's hand. For though there are now several ladies in his household, none of them is of the highest rank. Such a person as yourself, for example, would necessarily assume the foremost place, and I confess I cannot see why, if an offer came your way, it would be such a bad thing for you to accept it. At any rate, that is how I feel. He must be very fond of you,

---

* The presents of gay clothing which are customarily made to a person who has just emerged from a period of mourning.

or he certainly would not have started writing again directly you came back from Kamo..."

Princess Asagao thought her aunt's way of looking at things very old-fashioned and mistaken: "Having held out for so long against the reproaches of my father, who was, as you will remember, by no means used to being gainsaid, it would be a strange thing if I were now to yield, after all that has happened since, to your or anyone else's friendly persuasions." She looked so reluctant to discuss the subject further that her aunt did not proceed. The whole staff of the Palace, from dames-of-honor down to kitchen-maids, being all of them more or less in love with Genji themselves, watched with great interest to see how he would fare at Princess Asagao's hands, the majority prophesying for him a heavy discomfiture. But Genji himself firmly believed that if only he went on quietly displaying his devotion, sooner or later there would come some sign that she was ready to yield. He had long ago realized that she was not a person who could ever be hustled into acting against her own better judgment and inclination.

It was high time to be thinking about the Initiation of Yugiri, Aoi's son, who was now twelve years old. It would in many ways have been better that the ceremony should be performed in Genji's palace. But it was natural that the boy's grandmother should be anxious to witness it, and in the end it was decided that it should be performed at the Great Hall. Here the boy had the support of his uncle To no Chujo and of Aoi's other brothers, all of whom were now in influential positions, and as the function was to take place under their own roof they were additionally ready to do whatever they could to help in making the occasion a success. It was an event which aroused very wide interest throughout the country, and what with visitors pouring in from all sides and a mass of preparations to be made for the actual ceremony, there was hardly room to turn round for days beforehand.

He had thought at first of placing Yugiri in the Fourth Rank; but he was afraid that this would be considered an abuse of power, and there was indeed no hurry; for the boy was still very immature, and affairs being now entirely in Genji's hands he could easily promote him by small steps, till within a comparatively short time it would be possible to put him in the Fourth Rank without attracting an undue amount of attention. When, however, Yugiri made his appearance at the Great Hall in the light blue decorations of the Sixth Rank, this was more than his grandmother Princess Omiya could bear. Genji fortunately realized that she would very likely be somewhat upset. When he went to call upon her she at once began voicing her grievance. "You must remember," replied Genji, "that he is far too young to begin his public career. I would not indeed have performed his Initiation so early save that I designed to make a scholar of him. This will give him profitable employment during two or three years which might otherwise have been completely thrown away. As soon as he is old enough to take public office, he is certain to come quickly to the fore.

"I myself was brought up at the Palace in complete ignorance of the outside world. Living as I did continually at my father the Emperor's side I could not but pick up a certain vague familiarity with writing and books; it was, however, of the most meager kind. For I could not at the best learn more than he chanced himself to have picked up in the same casual way, so that in every subject I only knew disconnected scraps and had no notion of how they ought to be fitted together. This was the case particularly as regards literature; but even in music my knowledge was hopelessly incomplete, and I acquired no real command over either zithern or flute. It may turn out that he is quicker than I; but on the whole it seems far commoner for children to have less natural aptitude than their parents; and I determined that this child of mine should be educated in a far more thorough way. For if I merely handed on to him the scraps of information which I in my day had picked up from the old Emperor I feared that knowledge might reach him in so attenuated a form as would stand him in very poor stead for the future.

"I have noticed that children of good families, assured of such titles and emoluments as they desire, and used to receive the homage of the world however little they do to deserve it, see no advantage in fatiguing themselves by arduous and exacting studies. Having then in due time been raised to offices for which they have qualified themselves only by a long course of frolics and indiscretions, they are helped out of all their difficulties by a set of time-servers (who are all the while laughing at them behind their backs), and they soon imagine themselves to be the most accomplished statesmen on earth. But however influential such a one may be, the death of some relative or a change in the government may easily work his undoing, and he will soon discover with surprise how poor an opinion of him the world really has. It is *then* that he feels the disadvantages of the desultory education which I have described. For the truth is, that without a solid foundation of book learning this 'Japanese spirit' of which one hears so much is not of any great use in the world.

"So you see that, though at the present moment I may seem to be doing less for him than I ought, it is my wish that he may one day be fit to bear the highest charges in the State, and be capable of so doing even if I am no longer here to direct him. For the moment, though you think that I do not adequately use my influence on his behalf, I will at any rate see to it that he is not looked down upon as a mere starveling aspirant of the Schools." But the Princess would not part with her grievance: "I am sure you have thought it all out very carefully," she said, "but his uncles and most other people will not understand a word of this, and will merely think he is being badly treated; and I am sure the poor boy himself is very disappointed. He has always been brought up with the idea that To no Chujo's children and his other little cousins are in some way inferior to him, and now he sees them all going steadily upwards in rank, while he is treated like this... I assure you he found it very painful wearing that light blue dress, and my heart went out to him." Genji could not help laughing: "You must not take these things so seriously," he said. "What does it all matter? Please remember that you are talking about a child of twelve years old. You may be sure he understands nothing whatever of all this business. When he has been at his studies for a little while, you will see how much improved he is and be angry with me no longer."

The ceremony of bestowing the School-name took place in the new part of the Nijo-in palace, a portion of the eastern wing being set aside for the purpose. As such a function seldom takes place in the houses of the great, the occasion was one of great interest, and Princes and Courtiers of every degree vied with one another for the best seats; the professors who had come to conduct the proceedings were not expecting so large and distinguished an audience, and they were evidently very much put out. "Gentlemen," said Genji, addressing them, "I want you to perform this ceremony in all its rigor, omitting no detail, and above all not in any way altering the prescribed usages either in deference to the company here assembled or out of consideration for the pupil whom you are about to admit into your craft." The professors did their best to look business-like and unconcerned. Many of them were dressed in gowns which they had hired for the occasion; but fortunately they had no idea how absurd they looked in these old-fashioned and ill-fitting clothes which saved them from a great deal of embarrassment. Their grimaces and odd turns of speech, both combined with a certain mincing affability which they thought suitable to the occasion—even the strange forms and ceremonies that had to be gone through before any one of them could so much as sit down in his seat—all this was so queer that Yugiri's cousins, who had never seen anything of the sort in their lives before, could not refrain from smiling. It was therefore as well that, as actual participators in the ceremony, only the older and steadier among the princes of the Great Hall had been selected. They at least could be relied upon to control their laughter, and all was going smoothly, when it fell to the lot of To no Chujo and his friend Prince Mimbuyko to fill goblets out of the great wine-flagon and present them to their learned guests. Being both of them entirely unversed in these academic rites they paused for a moment, as though not quite certain whether they were really expected to perform this task with their own hands. So at any rate the professors interpreted their hesitation, and at once broke out into indignant expostulations:

"The whole proceeding is in the highest degree irregular,"* they cried. "These gentlemen possess no academic qualifications and ought not to be here at all. They must be made to understand that we know nothing of the distinctions and privileges which prevail at Court. They must be told to mend their manners..." At this someone in the audience ventured to titter, and the professors again expostulated: "These proceedings cannot continue," they said, "unless absolute silence is preserved. Interruptions are in the highest degree irregular, and if they occur again we shall be obliged to leave our seats." Several more testy speeches followed, and the audience was vastly entertained; for those who had never witnessed such performances before were naturally carried away by so diverting a novelty; while the few who were familiar with the proceedings had now the satisfaction of smiling indulgently at the crude amazement of their companions. It was long indeed since Learning had received so signal a mark of encouragement, and for the first time its partisans felt themselves to be people of real weight and consequence. Not a single word might anyone in the audience so much as whisper to his neighbor without calling down upon himself an angry expostulation, and excited cries of "disgraceful behavior!" were provoked by the mildest signs of restlessness in the crowd. For some time the ceremony had been proceeding in darkness, and now when the torches were suddenly lit, revealing those aged faces contorted with censoriousness and self-importance, Genji could not help thinking of the Sarugaku† mountebanks with their burlesque postures and grimaces. "Truly," he thought, looking at the professors, "truly in more ways than one an extraordinary and unaccountable profession!" "I think it is rather fun," he said, "to see everyone being kept in order by these crabbed old people," and hid himself well behind his curtains-of-state, lest his comments too should be heard and rebuked.

Not nearly enough accommodation had been provided, and many of the young students from the College had been turned away for lack of room. Hearing this, Genji sent after them with apologies and had them brought back to the Summer House where they were entertained with food and drink. Some of the professors and doctors whose own part in the ceremony was over had also left the palace, and Genji now brought them back and made them compose poem after poem. He also detained such of the courtiers and princes as he knew to care most for poetry; the professors were called upon to compose complete poems‡ while the company, from Genji downwards, tried their hands at quatrains, Teachers of Literature being asked to choose the themes. The summer night was so

---

* The professors speak in a mixture of antiquated Japanese and classical Chinese the effect of which I do not attempt to reproduce.

† See my *Noh Plays,* p. xxi *seq.*

‡ In eight lines.

short that before the time came to read out the poems it was already broad daylight. The reading was done by the Under-secretary to the Council, who, besides being a man of fine appearance, had a remarkably strong and impressive voice, so that his recitations gave everyone great pleasure.

That mere enthusiasm should lead young men of high birth, who might so easily have contented themselves with the life of brilliant gaieties to which their position entitled them, to study "by the light of the glow-worm at the window or the glimmer of snow on the bough,"* was highly gratifying; and such a number of ingenious fancies and comparisons pervaded the minds of the competitors that any one of these compositions might well have been carried to the Land Beyond the Sea without fear of bringing our country into contempt. But women are not supposed to know anything about Chinese literature, and I will not shock your sense of propriety by quoting any of the poems—even that by which Genji so deeply moved his hearers.

Hard upon the ceremony of giving the School-name came that of actual admittance to the College, and finally Yugiri took up residence in the rooms which had been prepared for him at the Nijo-in. Here he was put in charge of the most learned masters that could be procured, and his education began in earnest. At first he was not allowed to visit his grandmother at all; for Genji had noticed that she spoiled him shockingly, treating him, indeed, as though he were still a little child, and there seemed a much better chance that he would settle down to his new life if it were not interrupted by constant treats and cossetings at the Great Hall. But Princess Omiya took the boy's absence so much to heart that in the end three visits a month were allowed.

Yugiri found this sudden restriction of liberty very depressing, and he thought it unkind of his father to inflict these labors upon him, when he might so easily have allowed him to amuse himself for a little while longer and then go straight into some high post. Did Genji think him so very-stupid as to need, before he could work for the Government, a training with which everyone else seemed able to dispense? But he was an amiable, good-natured boy, who took life rather seriously, and seeing that he was not going to be allowed to mix in the world or start upon his career till he had read his books, he determined to get through the business as quickly as possible. The consequence was that in the space of four or five months he had read not only the whole of the *Historical Records*† but many other books as well. When the time came for his Examinations, Genji determined to put him to the test privately a little while beforehand.

---

* Like Ch'e Yün and Sun K'ang, two Chinese scholars who had not money enough to buy candles (4th century A.D.).

† By Ssu-ma Ch'ien, 1st century B.C., a book somewhat longer than Gibbon's *Decline and Fall*; by far the most distinguished Chinese historical work.

He was assisted by To no Chujo, by the Chief Secretary of Council, the Clerk of the Board of Rites and a few other friends. The chief tutor was now sent for, and asked to select passages from the *Historical Records*. He went through every chapter, picking out the most difficult paragraphs—just such parts indeed as the College Examiners were likely to hit upon—and made his pupil read them out loud. Yugiri not only read without the slightest stumbling or hesitation but showed clearly in every doubtful or misleading passage that he understood the sense of what he was reading. Everyone present was astonished at his proficiency and it was generally agreed that he had the makings of a first-rate scholar. "If only his poor grandfather could see him!" said To no Chujo with a sigh; and Genji, unable to restrain his feelings, exclaimed with tears in his eyes: "All this makes me feel very old! Before it has always been other people over whom one shook one's head, saying that they were 'getting on in life' or 'not so active as they were.' But now that I have a grownup child of my own, I feel (though I am still fortunately some way off my second childhood) that henceforward he will every day grow more intelligent, and I more stupid." The tutor listened attentively to this speech and felt much comforted by it. To no Chujo had been helping him liberally to wine, and the learned man's gaunt, rugged features were now suffused with smiles of joy and pride. He was a very unpractical man and his worldly success had never been proportionate to his great attainments. At the time when Genji first came across him he was without patronage or any means of subsistence. Then came this sudden stroke of good fortune; he of all people was singled out and summoned to this all-important task. Ever since his arrival he had enjoyed a degree of consideration far in excess of what, in his capacity of tutor, he had any right to expect, and now that the diligence of his pupil had procured for him this fresh ground for Genji's esteem, he looked forward at last to a distinguished and prosperous career.

On the day of the actual examination the College courtyards were crammed to overflowing with fashionable equipages; it seemed indeed as though the whole world had turned out to witness the ceremony, and the princely candidate's entry at the College gates wore the air of a triumphal procession. He looked very unfit to mingle with the crowd (shabby and uncouth as such lads generally are) among whom he now had to take his place, sitting right at the end of the bench, for he was the youngest scholar present; and it was small wonder that he came near to wincing as he took his place amid his uncouth classmates.

On this occasion also the presence of so large and profane an audience sorely tried the nerves of the academic authorities, and it was to the accompaniment of constant appeals for silence and good manners that Yugiri read his portion. But he did not feel in the least put out and performed his task with complete success.

This occasion had an important effect upon the fortunes of the College. It began to recover much of its old prestige, and henceforward the students were drawn not only from the lower and middle, but also to a considerable degree from the upper classes, and it became more and more frequent for the holders of high office to have received a certain amount of education. It was found that the possession of Degrees, such as that of Doctor of Letters or even Bachelor, was now an advantage in after life and frequently led to more rapid promotion. This incited both masters and pupils to unprecedented efforts. At Genji's palace too the making of Chinese poems became frequent; both scholars and professors were often his guests, and learning of every kind was encouraged and esteemed in a manner seldom before witnessed at Court.

The question of appointing an Empress now became urgent.

The claims of Akikonomu were considerable, since it was the dying wish of Fujitsubo, the Emperor's mother, that her son should be guided by this lady's counsel; and in urging her claims Genji was able to plead this excuse. The great disadvantage of such a choice was that Akikonomu, like Fujitsubo before her, was closely connected with the reigning family, and such alliances are very unpopular in the country. Lady Chujo* had the merit of priority, and to her partisans it appeared that there could be no question of anyone else being called upon to share the Throne. But there were many supporters of Lady Akikonomu who were equally indignant that her claims should for an instant be questioned.

Prince Hyobukyo† had now succeeded to the post of President of the Board of Rites, previously held by Asagao's father; he had become a figure of considerable importance at Court and it was no longer deemed politic that his daughter should be refused admittance to the Imperial Household.

This lady, like Akikonomu, had the disadvantage of a close connection with the ruling House; but on the other hand her elevation to the Throne was just as likely to have been supported by the Emperor's late mother as that of Akikonomu, for the newcomer was her brother's child, and it was thought by many people not to be unreasonable that this elder cousin should be called upon to take Fujitsubo's place, as far as watching over the health and happiness of the young Emperor was concerned. The claims, then, were pretty equally divided, and after some hesitation Genji followed his own inclinations by appointing Akikonomu to share the Throne. How strange that in the end this lady should have risen to an even higher position than her celebrated mother! Such was the comment of the world, and in the country at large some surprise was felt

---

* The eldest daughter of To no Chujo.
† Murasaki's father, who was anxious to place his younger daughter at Court.

at the announcement of her good fortune, for little was known of her outside the Court.

About this time To no Chujo became Palace Minister and Genji began to hand over to him most of the business of state. Chujo had a vigorous and rapid mind, his judgment tended to be very sound, and his natural intelligence was backed by considerable learning. Thus, though-it will be remembered that at the game of "covering rhymes"* he was badly defeated, in public affairs he carried all before him. By his various wives† he had some ten children, who were now all grown-up and taking their places very creditably in the world. Besides the daughter whom he had given in marriage to the Emperor there was another, Lady Kumoi by name, who was a child of a certain princess with whom he had at one time carried on an intrigue. This lady then was not, as far as birth went, in any way her sister's inferior; but the mother had subsequently married a Provincial Inspector who already had a large number of children. It seemed a pity to allow the girl to be brought up by a stepfather among this promiscuous herd of youngsters, and To no Chujo had obtained leave to have her at the Great Hall and put her under his mother Princess Omiya's keeping. He took far less interest in her, it is true, than he did in Lady Chujo; but both in beauty and intelligence she was generally considered to be at least her sister's equal. She had during her childhood naturally been brought much into contact with Yugiri. When each of them was about ten years old they began to live in separate quarters of the house. She was still very much attached to him; but one day her father told her that he did not like her to make great friends with little boys, and the next time they met she was careful to be very distant towards him. He was old enough to feel puzzled and hurt; and often when she was in the garden admiring the flowers or autumn leaves or giving her dolls an airing he would follow her about, entreating to be allowed to play with her. At such times she could not bring herself to drive him away, for the truth was that she cared for him quite as much as he for her. Her nurses noticed her changed manner towards him, and could not understand how it was that two children who for years had seemed to be inseparable companions should suddenly begin to behave as though they were almost strangers to one another. The girl was so young that the relationship certainly had no particular meaning for her; but Yugiri was a couple of years older, and it was quite possible (they thought) that he had tried to give too grown-up a turn to the friendship. Meanwhile the boy's studies began, and opportunities for meeting were rarer than ever. They exchanged let-

---

* See Part II, p. 218. The rhyme-words at the end of the verses were covered and the competitors had to guess them.

† His first wife was a daughter of the Minister of the Right.

ters written in an odd childish scrawl which nevertheless in both cases showed great promise for the future. As was natural with such juvenile correspondents they were continually losing these letters and leaving them about, so that among the servants in both houses there was soon a pretty shrewd idea of what was going on. But there was nothing to be gained by giving information and, having read these notes, the finders hastened to put them somewhere out of sight.

After the various feasts of congratulation were over things became very quiet at Court. Rain set in, and one night when a dank wind was blowing through the tips of the sedges, To no Chujo, finding himself quite at leisure, went to call upon his mother, and sending for Lady Kumoi asked her to play to them on her zithern. Princess Omiya herself performed excellently on several instruments and had taught all she knew to her granddaughter. "The lute," said To no Chujo, "seems to be the one instrument which women can never master successfully; yet it is the very one that I long to hear properly played. It seems as though the real art of playing were now entirely lost. True, there is Prince So-and-so, and Genji..." And he began to enumerate the few living persons whom he considered to have any inkling of this art. "Among women-players I believe the best is that girl whom Prince Genji has settled in the country near Oi. They say that she inherits her method of playing straight from the Emperor Engi, from whom it was handed on to her father. But considering that she has lived by herself in the depths of the country for years on end, it is indeed extraordinary that she should have attained to any great degree of skill. Genji has constantly spoken to me of her playing and, according to him, it is absolutely unsurpassed. Progress in music more than in any other subject depends upon securing a variety of companions with whom to study and rehearse. For anyone living in isolation to obtain mastery over an instrument is most unusual and must imply a prodigious talent." He then tried to persuade the old princess to play a little. "I am terribly stiff in the fingers," she said; "I can't manage the 'stopping' at all." But she played very nicely. "The Lady of Akashi," said To no Chujo presently, "must, as I have said, be exceptionally gifted; but she has also had great luck. To have given my cousin Genji a daughter when he had waited for one so long was a singular stroke of good fortune. She seems moreover to be a curiously self-effacing and obliging person; for I hear that she has resigned all claim to the child and allows her betters to bring it up as though it were their own." And he told the whole story, so far as the facts were known to him. "Women," he went on, "are odd creatures; it is no use trying to advance them in the world unless they have exactly the right temperament." After naming several examples, he referred to the failure of his own daughter, Lady Chujo: "She is by no means bad-looking," he said," and she has had every possible advantage.

Yet now she has managed things so badly that she is thrust aside in favor of someone* who seemed to have no chance at all. I sometimes feel that it is quite useless to make these family plans. I hope indeed that I shall be able to do better for this little lady;† and there did at one time seem to be a chance that so soon as the Crown Prince‡ was almost old enough for his Initiation I might be able to do something for her in that direction. But now I hear that the little girl from Akashi is being spoken of as the future Empress Presumptive, and if that is so I fear that no one else has any chance. "How can you say such a thing?" asked the Princess indignantly. "You have far too low an opinion of your own family. The late Minister, your father, always believed firmly that we should one day have the credit of supplying a partner to the Throne, and he took immense pains to get this child of yours accepted in the Imperial Household at the earliest possible moment. If only he were alive, things would never have gone wrong like this." It was evident, from what she went on to say, that she felt very indignant at Genji's conduct in the matter.

It was a very pretty sight to see little Lady Kumoi playing her mother's great thirteen-stringed zithern. Her hair fell forward across her face with a charming effect as she bent over her instrument. Chujo was just thinking how graceful and distinguished the child's appearance was when, feeling that she was being watched, Lady Kumoi shyly turned away, showing for a moment as she did so a profile of particular beauty. The poise of her left hand, as with small fingers she depressed the heavy strings, was such as one sees in Buddhist carvings. Even her grandmother, who had watched her at her lessons day by day, could not hold back a murmur of admiration.

When they had played several duets the big zithern was removed, and To no Chujo played a few pieces on his six-stringed Japanese zithern, using the harsh "major"§ tuning which was appropriate to the season. Played not too solemnly and by so skilful a hand as Chujo's, this somewhat strident mode was very agreeable. On the boughs outside the window only a few ragged leaves were left; while within several groups of aged gentlewomen clustering with their heads together behind this or that curtain-of-state, moved by Chujo's playing were shedding the tears that people at that time of life are only too ready to let fall upon any provocation. "It needs but a light wind to strip the autumn boughs," quoted Chujo, and continuing the quotation, he added: "'It cannot be the music of my zithern that has moved them. Though they know it not,

---

* Akikonomu.

† Kumoi

‡ The ex-Emperor Suzaku's little son.

§ Using "major" and "minor" as translations of *Yo* and *In*. The six strings were tuned to the 1st, 5th, 9th, and 3rd, 7th, 11th, semitones of the diatonic scale.

it is the sad beauty of this autumn evening that has provoked their sudden tears.' But come, let us have more music before we part." Upon this Princess Omiya and her daughter played *The Autumn Wind* and To no Chujo sang the words with so delightful an effect that everyone present was just thinking how much his presence added to the amenity of any gathering, when yet another visitor arrived. Yugiri, thinking that such an evening was wasted if not spent in agreeable company, had come over from Genji's palace to the Great Hall. "Here she is," said To no Chujo, leading the boy towards the curtain-of-state behind which Kumoi was now sitting. "You see she is a little shy of you and has taken refuge behind her curtains." And then looking at Yugiri: "I don't believe all this reading is suiting you. Your father himself agrees with me; I know that learning easily becomes a useless and tedious thing if pushed beyond a reasonable point. However, in your case he must have had some particular reason for supposing that academic honors would be useful. I do not know what was in his mind, but be that as it may, I am sure it is bad for you to be bending all day over your books!" And again: "I am sure that you ought sometimes to have a change. Come now, play a tune on my flute. Your masters can have no objection to that, for is not the flute itself the subject of a hundred antique and learned stories?" Yugiri took the flute and played a tune or two with a certain boyish faltering, but with very agreeable effect. The zitherns were laid aside and while Chujo beat the measure softly with his hands, Yugiri sang to them the old ballad "Shall I wear my flowered dress?" "This is just the sort of concert that Genji so much enjoys," said To no Chujo, "and that is why he is always trying to get free from the ties of business. Nor do I blame him; for the world is an unpleasant place at best, and surely one might as well spend one's time doing what one likes, instead of toiling day after day at things that do not interest one in the least."

He passed round the wine-flagon, and as it was now getting dark, the great lamp was brought in, soon followed by supper. When the meal was over, To no Chujo sent Lady Kumoi back to her room. It did not escape the notice of Princess Omiya's gentlewomen that Chujo was anxious to keep Yugiri and his little daughter as far as possible apart. "Why, he has sent her away," they whispered, "because he does not want her to hear the little gentleman play on the zithern. There will be a sad awakening for him one day, if he goes on treating them like that..." When To no Chujo at length withdrew, he remembered that he had not given certain instructions to one of the Princess's ladies, and stealing back into the room he delivered his message as quietly as possible and was on his way out of the room again, when he caught the sound of his own name. A group of ancient gentlewomen at the far end of the apartment had not noticed his return and their whispering had gone on uninterrupted. He stood still and, listening intently, heard the words: "He is supposed to be a very clever man. But people are always fools when it comes to dealing with their own children. I could never see any sense at all in that proverb—you know the one I mean—'No one knows a child but its parents.' All nonsense, I say," and she nudged her neighbor expressively. This was a shock to Chujo. It meant, he realized as he hurried from the room, that the friendship between these two children, which he had hoped to keep within bounds, had already, in the eyes of the household, taken on a romantic tinge. The old ladies within suddenly heard the sharp cry of Chujo's outriders. "Well! What do you think of that?" they said. "He's only just starting! Where has he been hiding all this time? I'll tell you what. He's up to some of his old tricks again, you mark my words!" And another: "I thought a fresh puff of scent blew this way; but little Prince Yugiri has got some just like it, and I fancied it was his. Do you think His Excellency was anywhere round here? It would be a terrible thing for all of us if he heard what we said after we thought he had gone away. He's got a hasty temper..." "Well, after all, there is really nothing to worry about," thought To no Chujo, as he drove to the Palace. "It is perfectly natural that they should have made friends." But it really would be very galling if after the failure of Lady Chujo to get herself made Empress, Lady Kumoi should through this boy-and-girl affair lose her chance of becoming Empress Presumptive.

Now as always, he was really on very good terms with Genji; but, just as in old days, their interests sometimes clashed, and Chujo lay awake a long while calling to mind their boyish rivalry and later jealousies. The old princess saw all that was going on; but Yugiri was her favorite grandchild, and whatever he did she accepted as perfectly justified. But she too was very much irritated by various conversations that she overheard, and henceforward watched over the situation with all the concentration of which her vigorous and somewhat acrid nature was capable.

Only two days later To no Chujo came to his mother's rooms again. The princess was extremely flattered and pleased; it was seldom that he honored her with two visits in such rapid succession. Before receiving him she had her hair set to rights and sent for her best gown; for though he was her own child he had become so important that she never felt quite sure of herself in his presence, and was as anxious to make a good impression as if he had been a complete stranger. It was soon evident on this occasion that he was in a very bad temper: "I hesitated to come again so soon," he said; "I am afraid your servants must think it very strange. I know I am not so competent as my father and cannot look after you as he did; but we have always seen a great deal of one another and, I hope, always shall. Look back over all that time, and I do not think you will be able to recall one occasion upon which there has been any sort of breach or misunderstanding between us. It never occurred to me as possible that I should ever come here with the express purpose of scolding you, least of all about an affair of this particular sort; but that is why I am here..." The old princess opened her eyes very wide and, under all the powder and paint that she had hurriedly applied when she heard of his coming, she visibly changed color. "To what are you alluding?" she asked. "It would indeed be surprising if you suddenly insisted upon picking a quarrel with a woman of my age. I should like to hear what it is all about." He quite agreed; it would be lamentable if after so many years of unbroken affection a difference should arise between them. Nevertheless he proceeded: "The matter is quite simple. I entrusted to your care a child from whom I myself had unfortunately been separated during her early years. I was at the time very much occupied with the future of my other daughter and was much exercised in mind to discover that, despite all my efforts, I could not do for her all that I had planned. But I had absolute confidence that this other child at any rate could be coming to no harm. I now find that quite the opposite is the case, and I think I have every right to complain. You will tell me, I know, that the young gentleman in question is a very fine scholar. He may for all I know be on his way to becoming the most learned man in the world; but that does not alter the fact that these two are first-cousins and have been brought up together. Should it become known that they are carrying on an intrigue, it would look as though very lax standards prevailed in your house. Such a thing would be considered scandalous even in any ordinary family... I am thinking of Yugiri's future quite as much as that of my own child. What both of them need is a connection with quite new people; they would in the end find such an alliance as this too obvious and uninteresting. And if I on my side object to the match on these grounds, you may be sure that Genji, when he hears of it, will insist upon the boy looking further afield. If you could yourself do nothing to forestall this attachment, you might at least have informed me of its existence. I could then have had a chance of arranging the match, despite all its disadvantages, before the matter became the talk of the whole town. You could not have done worse than to leave these young people to their own devices."

That the matter was so serious as this had never occurred to Princess Omiya at all, and she was horrified. "I entirely agree with you," she said. "But how could I possibly know what was going on all the while in the minds of these two children? I am sure I am very sorry it has happened; indeed I have quite as much reason to lament over it as you have. But I think it is the young pair themselves, and not I, who ought to bear the blame for what has happened. You have no idea of all that I have done for this girl since you first sent her to me. She has had advantages such as it would never have occurred to you to suggest, and if, through a blindness very natural in a grandmother, I have too long regarded the boy's friendship for her as a matter of no particular consequence, what reason is there to think that any harm has as yet been done? All your information on the subject is founded on the chatter of good-for-nothings who take a pleasure in damaging the reputations of everyone round them. If you were to look into these stories you would probably find they were pure inventions, and stupid inventions at that!" "Not at all!" said To no Chujo hotly. "It is not a question of slanders or lies. The way in which these two carry on together is a common matter for jest among your own ladies-in-waiting. It is a most disagreeable situation and I am worried about it"; and with that he left the room.

The news of all this rumpus soon went the round of the aged servants at the Great Hall and there was much wringing of hands. In particular the ladies whose conversation had been overheard felt that, without meaning any harm, they had done irreparable damage, and could not imagine how they could have been so rash as to begin discussing such a subject directly His Excellency left the room.

To no Chujo next looked in upon the young lady herself, and could not help being somewhat melted by her innocent and appealing air. He therefore passed on and went to look for her nurse. "I understood when I engaged you," he said, "that you were young; but one can be young without being infantile, and I supposed you had your wits about you like other people. I seem to have made a great mistake..." To these sarcastic remarks it was impossible to make any reply; but the nurse said afterwards to one of her assistants: "How is one expected to prevent these things? Just the same might have happened if she had been the Emperor's favorite daughter! In old stories the lovers are generally brought together by some go-between, but we certainly cannot be accused of having played any such part as that, for these two have been allowed to be together as much as they chose for years past; and if my lady thought they were so young that there was no harm in it, what reason was there for us to interfere? But they have been seeing much less of each other for some while past, and the last thing in the world I should have suspected was that anything wrong could possibly have been going on. Why, the little gentleman looks quite a child; I can't believe such things have ever entered his head."

So the nurse afterwards declared. But while she was actually being scolded she merely hung her head, and To no Chujo said at last: "That will do. I am not going to mention this business to anyone else at present. I am afraid a good many people must have heard about it, but you might at least contradict any rumors that you hear going about... As for the young lady, I intend to have her moved to my palace as soon as I can arrange it. I think my mother has acted very imprudently;

but she could not possibly have foreseen that you nurses would behave with such imbecility."

So they were all going to move to the Prime Minister's palace! Such was the young nurse's first thought, and she found this prospect so attractive that, though she knew the loss of Lady Kumoi would be a sad blow to the old princess, she could not feel otherwise than elated. "There now, only think of it!" she said, harping back to To no Chujo's injunction to secrecy. "And I had half a mind to go round to the Inspector's house and tell the little lady's mama! I should have thought this Prince Yugiri was good enough for anyone; but of course he does not count as a member of the Royal Family, and they say Lady Kumoi's mama has very grand ideas indeed." It was clearly no use saying any more to such a featherhead as this, and Kumoi herself was so young that it would be mere waste of breath to lecture her.

The old princess was upset by the affair; but she was fond of both her grandchildren, perhaps especially of Yugiri, and at the bottom of her heart she was extremely gratified at their having taken such a fancy to each other. On reflection it seemed to her that To no Chujo had been very heartless about the matter and had also treated it far more seriously than it deserved. After all he had taken very little trouble about this girl himself, and had never once indicated that he had any ambitious plans for the future. Indeed, it really seemed as though the idea of offering her to the Imperial Household never occurred to him till this trouble arose, and had been invented, thought the old princess indignantly, merely in order to furnish To no Chujo with a colorable grievance. He had certainly never really counted on this Palace plan; and granted that it was only an afterthought, he must often have contemplated the possibility of the child marrying a commoner. If so, where could a better match be found? Yugiri was certainly, as regards birth and general advantages, more than the equal of Kumoi; indeed, she could not conceive that any lady would not feel proud to have him as her husband. This no doubt was due to a certain grandmotherly partiality on Omiya's part; but be that as it may, she felt very cross with To no Chujo. She was however determined not to let him know it, lest he should become even further incensed against the young people.

Quite unconscious of all the fuss that had been going on at the Great Hall, Yugiri a few days afterwards again presented himself at his grandmother's apartments. On the last occasion there had been so many people about that he had not managed to get a word in private with Lady Kumoi, and he now arrived very late in the evening, hoping that things would be quieter at such an hour. Old Lady Omiya was usually delighted to see him, and full of jokes and nonsense. But today she was terribly grave. "I am very much upset," she said at last, after talking stiffly of various indifferent matters, "because your uncle is displeased with you. It is unkind of you to take advantage of us all like this, because naturally I get the blame just as much as you. But that is not why I am talking about it. I mention the matter because you might not otherwise discover that you are in disgrace..." The affair was so much on his mind already that after she had spoken two words he guessed all that was coming. The color mounted to his cheeks: "I don't know what he means," he said. "Since I began my lessons I have been shut up all the time and have scarcely seen anyone. Certainly nothing has happened that my uncle could possibly object to..." It went to her heart to see what pain it cost him to discuss the subject with her. "There, there," she said kindly. "Be careful for the future that is all I ask," and she turned the conversation on to other matters.

Since in the last month he had done little more than exchange notes with his sweetheart, Yugiri supposed that even this was considered improper and was very depressed. Supper was served, but he would not eat, and presently it seemed that he had fallen asleep. But in truth he was very wide awake indeed, listening with all his ears till the last sounds of people retiring and settling down for the night had everywhere ceased. Then he stole softly to the door of Lady Kumoi's room, which was usually fastened on a latch, but not bolted or barred. Tonight it would not yield an inch. No sound was audible within. With beating heart he leant close up against the door. Despite his care, he had made a certain amount of noise, and this woke her. But now, as she lay listening, she could hear no other sound save that of the wind rustling among the bamboos, and very faint and far away, the mournful cry of wild geese overhead. Perhaps because, young though she was, the events of the last few weeks had left her far more unhappy than her elders knew, there now came into her head the lines:[*] "The wild geese that with sorrowful cry..." and thinking that no one could hear her, she repeated the poem to herself aloud, causing Yugiri's heart to beat yet more wildly than before. By what stratagem could he prevail upon her to open the door? "I am Kojiju," he said in a feigned childish voice. "Do let me in!" This Kojiju was the child of Kumbi's old wet-nurse; so desperate was he that any ruse seemed justifiable if he could but bring her to the door. But now all was silent, for Kumoi, ashamed that he should have heard her speaking to herself, lay with her face pressed deep into the pillows. His ruse had not deceived her, and it was misery to picture him standing behind the bolted door. Presently some of the servants in an adjoining room began moving about, and for a moment both he, standing without, and she on her bed within remained rigidly motionless. Soon however all was quiet

---

[*] "Some such sorrow as mine they too must know, the wild geese that with sorrowful cry trail through the country of the clouds."

again and he made his way back to his own bedroom. As he passed by Princess Omiya's apartments he heard the noise of someone sighing heavily. Evidently she was still awake; most likely indeed she had heard all that had happened! He crept past the door with the utmost caution and it was with feelings of intense shame and guilt that he at last reached his room. He rose early and wrote a letter to Kumoi which he hoped to convey to her by the hand of that same Kojiju whose voice he had counterfeited in the night. But the child was nowhere to be seen, and Yugiri left the house in great distress.

What Kumoi on her side could not endure was being scolded by her father and grandmother, and she did all she could to avoid it. But she had not the least idea what they meant when they talked about her "future" or her "reputation." To be whispered about by nurses and servants flattered her vanity and was in itself far from acting as a deterrent. One thing about which her guardians made terrible scenes seemed to her most harmless of all; this was the writing of letters and poems. But though she had no idea why they forbad it, she saw that it led to scoldings, and henceforward Yugiri did not receive a single line from her. Had she been a little older she would have found out some way of circumventing these restrictions; and Yugiri, who already possessed far more capacity to shift for himself, was bitterly disappointed by her tame surrender.

To Princess Omiya's great distress To no Chujo no longer paid his customary visits to the Great Hall. Nor did he ever discuss the matter with his wife,[*] who was only able to guess, from his general ill-humor and irritability, that something had gone amiss. He did however one day allude to his disappointment concerning their own daughter, Lady Chujo: "I think," he said, "that during the ceremonies of Investiture[†] it would be better that our daughter should not be at Court. A quiet time at home would not do her any harm; and although she has been passed over on this occasion she really stands very well with the Emperor. Indeed, she is in such constant attendance upon him that it is a great strain on her gentlewomen who are kept running about at every hour of the day and night ..."; and he applied for her release. The Emperor Ryozen was extremely loath to part with her and at first refused. But To no Chujo seemed to attach such extreme importance to the matter that in the end he agreed to let her spend a short holiday at home. "I am afraid it will be rather dull for you," he said to his daughter when she arrived; "but I have arranged for Kumoi to visit us, so you will have someone to play with. They have been very good to her at her grandmother's, but I find that the house is frequented by a certain rather undesirably precocious

---

[*] A sister of Kokiden.
[†] Of Akikonomu as Empress.

child, with whom, as was inevitable, she has struck up a great friendship. She is far too young for that kind of thing..." And he began at once to arrange for Lady Kumoi's removal from the Great Hall.

Princess Omiya whose one consolation, since the death of her daughter Aoi, had been the arrival of Lady Kumoi, was appalled at this sudden loss. No hint had been given to her that it was not final, and she saw herself deprived at a stroke of the one happiness which promised to alleviate the miseries of old age and decay. And added to all this was the fact that her own son had taken sides against her and become quite indifferent to her sufferings. She charged him with this, but he hotly denied it. "No, no," he said, "it is nonsense to say that I have turned against you. I think that you have behaved foolishly in one particular matter, and shall continue to think so. Lady Chujo is going through rather a difficult time at Court just now and I have thought it best to withdraw her for a little while. It is very dull at my house and it is a great comfort for her to have a young companion. This is only a temporary measure..." and he added: "Do not think that I am ungrateful for all your kindness to the child. I know that I can never thank you enough..."

Such speeches did little to reassure her. But it was evident that he was determined to part the two children and it was no use arguing about that. "How heartless men are!" she said. "Whatever may have been your reasons for acting like this, the chief result has been that I have lost the confidence of both these children. Perhaps that has not occurred to you? Besides, even if Kumoi is no longer here, Prince Genji, though he is far from being an unreasonable man, is certain to feel that my house is no safe place for young people, and now that he has got Yugiri at the Nijo-in, he will keep him there permanently."

Soon afterwards Yugiri called again at the Great Hall. He was far exceeding the number of visits for which his grandmother had stipulated; but he still hoped that by some accident he might get the chance of speaking a word or two to the playmate who had been so cruelly wrested from him. To his disgust the first thing he saw when he approached the Great Hall was To no Chujo's carriage. He stole away to his old room, which was still kept in readiness for him, and remained in hiding for some while. Not only To no Chujo but all his sons were there—Kashiwagi, Kobai, and the rest, but Princess Omiya would not receive any of them behind her curtains-of-state. Sayemon no Kami and Gon Chunagon, who were not her own children but had been born to the late Minister of the Left by another wife, were also in the habit of calling, out of respect to their father's memory, and on this occasion, thinking to please and interest their stepmother, they had brought their little sons with them. But the only result was that, comparing them in her mind with her favorite Yugiri, she thought them very ugly, unattractive little boys. Yugiri and Kumoi, these were the only grandchildren for whom she really cared. And now the little girl who had been her delight, upon whom she had lavished so much tenderness and care—Kumoi, who for all these years had never left her side, was to be taken from her and put into a stranger's hands.

"I have to go to the Palace now," said To no Chujo quickly. "I will come back towards nightfall and fetch Kumoi away."

He had thought the matter out very carefully and decided that even if it should afterwards prove necessary for him to consent to this match, it was not one which he would ever be able to regard with any satisfaction. However, when Yugiri had begun his career it would be possible to see of what stuff he was made and also to judge the strength of his feeling for Kumoi. If the boy still remained anxious to marry her the betrothal could be announced in a proper way and the whole affair be carried through without discredit to anybody. But so long as they were allowed to frequent the same house, however much they were scolded and watched, it was, considering their age, only to be expected that they would get into a scrape. He could not put it like this to his mother, because to do so would have hurt her feelings; and wishing to avoid any suggestion that Princess Omiya had been to blame, he used both at the Great Hall and at his own house the convenient excuse that Lady Chujo was at home and needed a companion.

Soon after To no Chujo left, Kumoi received a note from Princess Omiya: "Your father is going to take you home with him this evening. I hope you understand that this is entirely his doing. Nothing that happens will ever change my feelings towards you... Come and see me at once..."

The child presented herself immediately. She was dressed in her smartest clothes and, though only eleven and still undeveloped, she had quite the gracious air of a little lady paying a farewell call. She felt very uncomfortable while Princess Omiya told her how lonely she would be without anyone to play with, and how (though the houses were not far apart) it would seem as though she had gone to live a long, long way off. All this trouble, the child felt dimly, as she listened to the recital of Omiya's woe, came from having made friends with that little boy, and hanging her head, she began to weep bitterly. At this moment Yugiri's old nurse happened to come in. "Well, I *am* sorry you are going away from us!" she said to Kumoi. "I always thought of you as *my* lady, just as much as Prince Yugiri was *my* little gentleman. We all know what His Excellency means by taking you away like this; but don't you let him down you!" The girl felt all the more wretched and ashamed, but did not know how to reply. "Don't say such things to the child!" cried Princess Omiya. "It may all come right in the end, without any need to upset the poor little thing like that!" "The truth is," answered the nurse indignantly, "that all of you think my young gentleman is not good enough for her. You and

His Excellency may take it from me that Yugiri is going to be the finest gentleman in the land..." Just as the outraged nurse was voicing this opinion Yugiri entered the room. He at once recognized the figure of Kumoi behind her curtains-of-state; but there seemed only a very remote chance of getting any conversation with her, and he stood upon the threshold looking so disconsolate that his old nurse could not bear it. A long, whispered consultation took place. At last Omiya yielded and under cover of a fading light, at a moment when the movements of the other guests created a useful diversion, Yugiri was smuggled behind the little princess's curtains-of-state. They sat looking at one another with nothing to say; they felt very shy and the eyes of both of them began to fill with tears. "Listen," said Yugiri at last. "Your father thinks that by taking you away from me he can make me stop caring for you. But by all his cruelty he has only made me love you far more than before. Why have I not seen you for so many weeks? Surely we could have found some way..." He spoke childishly; but there was a passion in his voice that strangely stirred her. "Darling, I wanted to see you," was all she could say in reply. "Then you still love me?" She answered with a quick, childish nod.

But now the great lamp was brought in, and a moment afterwards there was a shouting and clatter of hoofs in the courtyard outside. "There are the outriders, he'll be here in a minute!" cried one of the maids in great alarm, and Kumoi shuddered from head to foot. She attempted indeed to rush from the room; but Yugiri held her fast. The nurse, who was to go with her to the Prime Minister's Palace, now came to fetch her and to her dismay saw the outline of a boy's figure behind the curtains-of-state. What folly to allow this kind of thing at the last moment! The old princess must suddenly have taken leave of her wits! "Well, you ought to be ashamed of yourself," she muttered to Yugiri as she dived behind the curtains to fetch her charge away. "I don't know what your uncle would say if he knew this. I have half a mind in any case to tell Madam Inspector,[*] and you'll catch it then. You may be Prince Genji's boy and I don't know what else, but you are only in the Sixth Rank, and have no right to meddle with such a little lady as this!" It was true enough. He had been kept back, while everyone else was promoted; and awakening suddenly to an intense indignation against the powers which had put this affront upon him, he recited the lines: "Pale was the robe they made me wear; but tears of blood long since have stained it to a hue no tongue should dare deride." "Hard driven as we are and thwarted at every hour, how can our love spring upward and put on a deeper hue?" So Kumoi answered; but she had scarcely said the lines when someone announced that His Excellency was waiting, and the nurse bustled her

---

[*] Kumoi's mother.

out of the room. There were three coaches altogether to carry away To no Chujo, the little girl and her belongings. Yugiri heard them start one after another. Princess Omiya presently sent for him to come to her, but he pretended to be asleep. All night he lay sobbing bitterly, and very early next morning, through a world white with frost, he hurried back to the Nijo-in. His eyes were swollen with weeping and he feared that if he stayed longer at the Great Hall his grandmother would insist upon seeing him. All the way home the most melancholy ideas came one after another into his mind. Thick clouds covered the sky and it was still quite dark: "Unbroken is my misery as this dull sky that day on day has bound the waters of the earth in ice and snow."

It fell to Genji's lot to supply a dancer for the Gosechi Festival, and though he was merely supposed to choose the girl from among the children of his retainers and leave the rest to her parents, he went much further than this, taking a great interest even in the costumes of the little girls who were to wait upon the dancer and hurrying on the seamstresses when he found that they were leaving things to the last moment. The Lady from the Village of Falling Flowers was put in charge of the dresses of those who were to be present at the Early Levee before the ceremony. Genji determined that the dancer supplied by his household should make a brave show, and he equipped her with a body of pages and attendants such as the Empress herself might well have been proud of. Last year, owing to the National Mourning for Fujitsubo, there had been no public festivals or amusements of any kind, so that people looked forward to the coming occasion with an unusual zest, and the families whose turn it was to supply a dancer vied with one another in the pains they took over her training and equipment. One came from the household of the Inspector, one from that of To no Chujo's stepbrother Sayemon no Kami, and one from Yoshikiyo, who was now Governor of Omi. This year the Emperor had expressed a desire to retain all the dancers in his service at the Palace, and consequently both these gentlemen had chosen daughters of their own to send to the Festival. The dancer from Genji's household was the daughter of Koremitsu, who had now become Governor of the province of Tsu. She had the reputation of being a particularly lively and good-looking child. When Genji first suggested it, Koremitsu did not at all take to the idea, feeling that his family had no claim to such an honor. But everyone pointed out to him that the Inspector had shown no hesitation, though he was only offering a bastard daughter; and in the end Koremitsu reluctantly consented, believing like the others that it would give his daughter a chance of permanent service at the Palace. He trained the girl at home, taking endless trouble in teaching her dance-steps and also in selecting the attendants who were to look after her, and on the night before the ceremony he took her to the Nijo-in himself.

Meanwhile Genji was inspecting the little train-bearers and pages. They had been chosen from among the prettiest children in the service of the various ladies in his household, and seldom can so engaging a troupe have been collected. His next business was to teach them the curtsey which they would have to make when they were presented to the Emperor, and each one of them showed such readiness and perfect grace in executing the unaccustomed movements that Genji said, laughing: "We should have no difficulty in producing a second dancer from this household, if one were wanted!" There were still however more of them than were actually required for the ceremony, and since all seemed equally good-looking and equally intelligent, he was obliged to select them according to the rank of their parents.

All this while Yugiri sat hour after hour in his room, giving no heed to what was going on in this busy house. He was too depressed to work at his books, and lay all day on his couch staring blankly in front of him. But at last he grew tired of doing nothing, and thinking that a little company might distract him, he strolled out to join the throngs who filled the palace.

He was well-born, handsome, and, in a subdued way, very agreeable in his manners. The gentlewomen of the household took no small interest in him, but he remained somewhat of a mystery to them. With Murasaki he had few dealings and was indeed barely acquainted with her. Why it was that he held aloof from her he would have been at a loss to explain. Was it that some dim instinct warned him against a repetition of his father's disastrous entanglements?*

The Gosechi dancer had already arrived and a space had been screened up for her to rest in while she was waiting for her rehearsal. Yugiri sauntered towards the screens and peeped to see what was behind them. There she lay or rather crouched in her corner, looking very miserable. She seemed about the same age as Kumoi but rather taller, and was indeed far more obviously good-looking. It was growing dark and he could not see her features very clearly, but there was certainly something about her which reminded him of the girl he loved. The resemblance was not enough to make him feel in any way drawn towards her; but his curiosity was aroused, and to attract her attention he rustled the train of her skirt. She looked up startled and on the spur of the moment he recited the lines: "Though you become a servant of Princess Hill-Eternal† who dwells above the skies, forget not that tonight I waited at your door." She heard that he had a pleasant voice, and evidently he was young. But she had not

---

* With Fujitsubo, his father's concubine.

† There is a legend which tells how certain dancing-maidens took the fancy of the gods and were snatched up to the sky.

the least idea who he was, and was beginning to feel somewhat nervous when her attendants came bustling along with her dancing-clothes, and as there were now several other people in the room, Yugiri was obliged to slip away as unobtrusively as he could. He did not like to show himself at the Festival in that wretched blue dress and was feeling very disconsolate at the prospect of being left all alone, when he heard that by Imperial permission cloaks of any color might be worn at today's ceremony, and set off to the Palace. He had no need to hide; for he had a charming young figure upon which, slender though he was, his man's dress sat very well indeed, and everyone from the Emperor downwards noticed him on this occasion with particular pleasure and admiration.

At the ceremony of Presentation the dancers all acquitted themselves very creditably and there was little to choose between the children in any way, though Koremitsu's and the Inspector's were generally voted to have the best of it as regards good looks. But pretty as they all were, none of the others was handsome to anything like the same degree as the girl from Genji's household.* She had been brought up in a far humbler way than the others and at any ordinary gathering would have been quite eclipsed by them. But now, when all were dressed for the same part, her real superiority became evident. They were all a little older than the Gosechi dancers usually are, which gave to this year's ceremony a character of its own. Genji was present at the ceremony of Introduction, and the spectacle at once recalled to his mind that occasion, years ago, when he had so much admired one of the Gosechi maidens—the daughter of the Provincial Secretary.† And now on the evening of the Festival Day he sent a messenger to her house with the poem: "Be thankful that upon the maidens of the Sky time leaves no mark; for upon me, to whom long since you waved your dancing-sleeve, age and its evils creep apace."

She began to count the years. What a long time ago it had all happened! She knew that this letter did but betoken a brief moment of reminiscent tenderness; but it gave her pleasure that he had succumbed to this feeling, and she answered: "It needed but your word to bring them back, those winter days; though long since faded is the wreath that crowned them with delight." Her answer was written on a blue diapered paper in a boldly varied hand, heavy and light strokes being dashed in with an almost cursive sweep—a somewhat mixed style but, considering the writer's position in life, highly creditable, thought Genji as he examined the note.

Meanwhile with *his* Gosechi dancer Yugiri made no further progress, though he thought a good deal about her and would have cultivated her

---

* Koremitsu's daughter.
† See Part II, pp. 224 and 245.

acquaintance, had it been possible to do so without attracting attention. Unfortunately she seemed as a rule to be under extremely close surveillance and he was as yet wholly inexperienced in the art of circumventing such precautions. But he had certainly taken a great fancy to her; and though no one could replace Kumoi, a friendship with this girl might, he felt, do something towards distracting him from his misery.

All four dancers were to be retained at the Palace; but for the moment they had to retire from Court in order to perform the ceremony of Purification. Yoshikiyo's daughter was taken off to Karasaki, Koremitsu's to Naniwa, and soon the dancers had all left Court. A post in the Lady-of-the-Bedchamber's office was vacant, and when the Emperor suggested that Koremitsu's daughter might care to take it Genji naturally accepted for her with alacrity. This was bad news for Yugiri. Young and unimportant as he was, he could not possibly try to restrain her from accepting such a post; but it would be too bad if she never even found out who it was that had made friends with her that evening at the Nijo-in; and though Kumoi still occupied the chief place in his thoughts, there were times when this subsidiary failure weighed heavily upon him. The girl had a brother who was a page at Court and had also often waited upon Yugiri at Genji's palace. "When is your sister going into residence at Court?" he asked the page one day, after making conversation with him for some time. "I do not know; some time this year, I suppose," the boy answered. "She has an extraordinarily beautiful face," said Yugiri. "I envy you for seeing her so constantly. I wish you would arrange for me to meet her again." "How can I?" said the boy. "I am much younger than she. We have not been brought up together, and I do not myself see her except on special occasions. I have no chance of introducing her to gentlemen such as you..." "But a letter, surely you could manage a letter?" and Yugiri handed him a note. The boy had been brought up to consider this kind of thing very underhand; but Yugiri was so insistent that, much against his will, he at last consented. The girl had more taste in such matters than is usual at her age, and the appearance of the note greatly delighted her. It was on a greenish paper, very thin and fine, laid down on a stout backing. The hand was naturally still somewhat unformed; but it did not promise ill for the future. With the letter was a poem: "Hidden though I was, surely the Maid of Heaven perceived with what enthrallment I witnessed the waving of her feathery sleeves?"

Brother and sister were reading the note together when Koremitsu suddenly entered the room and snatched it out of their hands. The girl sat motionless, while the blood rushed to her cheeks. But her brother, indignant at Koremitsu's high-handed manner of dealing with the situation, strode angrily out of the room. "Who sent this?" Koremitsu called after him. "Prince Genji's son," the boy answered, turning back; "the one who is studying for the College. At any rate it was he who gave me the note and asked me to bring it here." Koremitsu, who regarded Yugiri as a mere child, burst into a hearty laugh. "Well, you have chosen a pretty little prince for your sweetheart," he said; "I thought this letter came from some grown-up person. Of course there can be no harm in fun of that sort...," and showing the letter to his wife he proceeded to tell her what a nice child Yugiri was. "If it ever should happen," he said to her in an aside, "that one of these young princes took a fancy to our daughter, we should do much better for her that way than by keeping her at the Palace, where she can never play more than a very humble part. There's this comfort about it, that if Prince Yugiri is anything like his father he will continue to show an interest in her when he grows up. You know I have always told you that once Prince Genji takes a fancy to people, he never forgets them, come what may. Look at what he has done for that girl from Akashi." Nevertheless they hurried on the preparations for their daughter's departure to Court.

After this brief diversion Yugiri became more than ever preoccupied with his main misfortune. To Kumoi it was impossible even to send a letter, and all his time was now spent in endless speculations as to where and how he should ever see her again. He no longer visited the Great Hall, for the sight of the rooms where they used to play together evoked memories that he could not endure. But he was almost equally miserable at home, and shut himself up for days on end in his own room. Genji now put him under the care of the Lady from the Village of Falling Flowers. "His grandmother is not likely to live very long," Genji said to her. "You have known him since he was quite small and will be much the best person to look after him." She always accepted with docility whatever duties he put upon her, and now did her best to look after the boy, of whom she was indeed very fond. Yugiri liked her, but he did not think she was at all pretty. It seemed to him that Genji, who had gone on being fond of this uninteresting lady for so many years, would surely be able to understand that if one fell in love with a handsome creature, like Kumoi one was not likely to give her up all in a minute. No doubt the Lady from the Village of Falling Flowers had quite other qualities to recommend her. She was docile and equable, and Yugiri saw that it would be very convenient only to fall in love with people of that sort. However, if they were as plain as the lady who had been commissioned to look after him, love would be a painful business. But perhaps his father thought her beautiful or intelligent? The question was hard to answer, but one thing was certain: Genji managed not to spend much time alone with her. "No," said Yugiri to himself, "I cannot remember his doing more than bring her some little present or chat with her for a few moments from outside her screen ever since I have been in the house."

About this time old Princess Omiya took her vows, and though this necessitated a change of costume, it did not prevent her being as anxious as ever to make a good impression, and she continued to take the greatest possible pains with her appearance. Yugiri had indeed always known people with whom appearances counted for a great deal; while the lady who had been put in charge of him, having never been particularly handsome, had, now that she was no longer quite young, grown somewhat angular, and her hair was becoming scanty. These things made a disagreeable impression upon him.

As the year drew towards a close, Princess Omiya's whole attention became occupied with the delightful task of making ready the young scholar's New Year clothes. It was a splendid costume, that he could not deny. But it did not seem to interest him very much. "I don't know why you have ordered all these clothes," he said at last; "I have no intention of going to Court at all on New Year's day. Why did you suppose I meant to?" "What a way to talk!" she said in bitter disappointment. "One would think you were already an old gentleman hardly able to drag yourself about!" "One can have the feeling that one's life is over, without being old," he muttered, his eyes filling with tears. She knew quite well what was on his mind, and felt very sorry for him. But she thought it better not to discuss the matter and said gently: "A man ought to bear himself with pride even if he knows that he deserves a higher rank than that which for the moment has been accorded to him. You must not let it depress you so much. Why do you go about looking so wretched nowadays? It really becomes quite insufferable." "I don't know what you are talking about," answered Yugiri. "Why should I go to Court if I do not choose to? As a matter of fact, it is very unpleasant to be only in the Sixth Rank. People notice it and make remarks. I know it is only for the present; but all the same I had rather stay at home. I am sure that if my grandfather were alive, he would never allow me to be treated like this. One would think my father might do something about it; but he does not seem to care what becomes of me. I saw little enough of him before; but now he has put me to live right away in the new eastern wing, and never comes near me at all. The only person who takes any trouble about me is this "Falling Flowers" whom he keeps there..." "Poor child," said Princess Omiya, "it is a terrible misfortune to have no mother, in whatever rank of life one may be. But before long you will be old enough to go out into the world and shift for yourself. Then people will soon learn to respect you. Meanwhile you must try to be patient and not take these things so much to heart. Your grandfather would indeed have done more for you if he were here. For though your father holds the same position, he does not seem to have the same influence over people as your poor grandfather did. They still tell me that your uncle To no Chujo is a man of very remarkable talents, and I used to think so myself. But I have noticed a change in him lately, and it becomes greater every day. However, things must indeed be in a bad way if a young boy like you, with all his life before him, can talk so gloomily about the future..."

On New Year's day Genji, being Grand Minister Extraordinary, did not go to Court, but following the precedent set by Fujiwara no Yoshifusa[*] celebrated the rites of the season at his own palace. On the seventh day a White Horse was presented to the Grand Minister with exactly the same ceremonies as to the Emperor at Court; indeed, in many respects the festivities arranged by Genji exceeded in their magnificence anything that had ever been seen on such occasions save at the Palace itself. Towards the end of the second month came the Imperial Visit to the ex-Emperor Suzaku. It was too early for the blossoms to be quite at their best, but immediately afterwards came the "month of fasting" in memory of the Emperor's mother, so the Visit could not be postponed. Fortunately the cherry blossom was unusually early this year and in Suzaku's gardens it already made a delightful show. A tremendous cleaning and polishing was set afoot at his palace in preparation for the Emperor's arrival; and meanwhile the noblemen and princes who were to accompany His Majesty thought of nothing but their new clothes. They had been ordered to wear dove-grey lined with pale green; the Emperor himself was to be dressed all in crimson. By special command Genji was also in attendance on the day of the Visit, and he too wore red; so that frequently during the day the figure of the Emperor seemed to merge into that of his Minister, and it was as though the two of them formed but one crimson giant. Everyone present had taken unusual pains with his appearance, and their host, the ex-Emperor, who had grown into a far better-looking man than at one time seemed possible, evidently took much more interest in such matters than before, and was himself magnificently appareled.

Professional poets had not been summoned for the occasion, but only some ten scholars from the College who had the reputation of being able to turn out good verses.

The subjects chosen were modeled on those given out to the competitors for posts in the Board of Rites. It was thought that it would be a good thing to give Yugiri some idea of the themes given out at Palace examinations. That his mind might not be disturbed, each poet was set adrift on the lake all by himself, and it was with considerable alarm that these timid scholars, few of whom had ever set foot in a boat before, saw their moorings loosed and felt themselves gliding further and further away from the shore. As dusk drew on, boats with musicians on board began to circle the lake, and their tunes mingled agreeably with the sighing of the

---

[*] 804-872 A.D.

mountain wind. Here, thought Yugiri, was a profession which brought one into pleasant contact with the world and at the same time entailed studies far less arduous than those to which he had been so heartlessly condemned; and he wandered about feeling very discontented.

Later on, the dance called "Warbling of the Spring Nightingales" was performed, and Suzaku, remembering that famous Feast of Flowers* years ago said to Genji with a sigh: "What wonderful days those were! We shall not see their like again." There were indeed many incidents belonging to that time which even now Genji looked back upon with considerable emotion, and when the dance was over, he handed the wine bowl to Suzaku, reciting as he did so: "Spring comes, and still the sweet birds warble as of old; but altered and bereft† are they that sit beneath the blossoming tree." To this Suzaku replied: "Today the nightingales have come to tell me of the spring. Else had no sunshine pierced the mists that hide my hermit's dwelling from the world's pomp and pride." It was now the turn of Prince Sochi no Miya, who had recently become President of the Board of War, to present the bowl. He did so, reciting the verse: "Speak not of change; unaltered through all ages‡ shall the flute preserve their song, the nightingales that in the springtime warble on the swaying bough." This was said with a glance towards the Emperor, and in loud clear voice, that the compliment might not be missed. Ryozen was indeed gratified by the graceful allusion, but as he took the bowl he answered modestly: "If birds still sing and a few faded blossoms deck the tree, it is but in remembrance of those happier days when Virtue ruled the world." This was said with great earnestness and humility. All the above poems were exchanged privately and only overheard by a few privileged persons, and there were others which did not get recorded at all. The pavilion of the musicians was some way off, and Suzaku suggested that those about him should send for their instruments and make a little music of their own. Sochi no Miya accordingly played on the lute, To no Chujo on the Japanese zithern, while Suzaku himself played to the Emperor on the thirteen-stringed zithern. The Chinese zithern was as usual played by Genji. It was seldom that so gifted a band of performers chanced to meet in one place, and the concert that followed was of unforgettable beauty. Several of the courtiers present had good voices, and the songs "Was ever such a day!" and the "Cherry Man"§ were now performed. Finally torches were lit all round the edge of the island in the lake, and so the feast at last came to an end. But late as it was, Ryozen felt that it

---

* See Part I, p. 147 seq.

† Allusion to the death of the old Emperor, Genji's and Suzaku's father.

‡ The song and dance "Warbling of the Spring Nightingales" are attributed to the mythical Chinese Emperor Yao, third millennium B.C.

§ See above, p. 368.

would be uncivil on his part if he went away without paying his respects to Suzaku's mother, Lady Kokiden, who was living in the same house with him. Genji was naturally obliged to accompany him. The old lady received them in person and was evidently very much gratified by the visit. She had aged immensely since he last saw her; but here she still was, and it irritated him to think that she should hang on to life in this way, when a much younger woman like Fujitsubo was already in her grave. "My memory is not so good as it was," said Kokiden, "but this visit of yours has brought back the old days to my mind more clearly than anything that has happened to me for a long time past." "Those upon whom I leaned have now been taken from me one after another," the Emperor replied, "and hitherto the year has had no springtime for me. But my visit to your house today has at last dispelled my grief; I hope you will permit me to come here often..." Genji too had to make a suitable speech, and had even to ask if he also might venture to call again. The procession left the house amid great scenes of popular enthusiasm, which painfully reminded the old lady of her complete failure to injure Prince Genji's career. To govern he was born, and govern he would despite all her scheming. "Well, such is fate," she thought, and was almost sorry that she had wasted time contending against it.

It was natural that this visit should bring Oborozuki to his mind. Not that he had altogether ceased corresponding with her; for lately whenever an opportunity occurred, he had sent her a word or two of greeting. And now there rose before him on his way home many delightful recollections of the hours they had spent together.

As for Kokiden, despite her professions of good will she did as a matter of fact intensely dislike all contact with the present Emperor and his government. But it was sometimes necessary to communicate with them concerning her own salary, or the preferment of her friends, and on such occasions she often wished that she had not lived to see an age which was in all respects the reversal of what she herself had striven for. Old age had not improved her temper, and even Suzaku found her very difficult to get on with, and sometimes wondered how much longer he would be able to endure so trying a partnership.

So greatly had Yugiri distinguished himself in the literary competitions which marked that day's festivity, that upon the strength of them alone he was awarded the Doctor's degree. Among those who had competed were many who were far older than he and some who were thought to possess remarkable ability. But besides Yugiri only two others were passed. When the time of the autumn appointments came round he received the rank of Chamberlain. He longed as much as ever to see Lady Kumoi. But he knew that To no Chujo had his eye upon him, and to force his way into her presence under such circumstances would have been so very disagreeable that he contented himself with an occasional letter. She, meanwhile, was fully as wretched as her young lover.

Genji had long had it in his mind, if only he could find a site sufficiently extensive and with the same natural advantages as the Nijo-in, to build himself a new palace where he could house under one roof the various friends whose present inaccessibility, installed as they were in remote country places, was very inconvenient to him. He now managed to secure a site of four *machi** in the Sixth Ward close to where Lady Rokujo had lived and at once began to build.

The fiftieth birthday of Murasaki's father Prince Hyobukyo was in the autumn of the following year. The preparations for this event were of course chiefly in her hands; but Genji too, seeing that on this occasion at any rate he must appear to have overcome his dislike of the Prince, determined to give the affair an additional magnificence by holding the celebrations in his new house; and with this end in view he hurried on the work of construction as fast as he could. The New Year came, and still the place was far from finished. What with spurring on architects and builders, arranging for the Birthday Service, choosing the musicians, the dancers and the like, he had plenty to keep him busy. Murasaki herself had undertaken the decking of the scripture-rolls and images that would be used at the Service; as well as the customary distribution of presents and mementos. In these tasks she was aided by the Lady from the Village of Falling Flowers, and it was at this time that an intimacy sprang up between them such as had never existed before.

The rumor of these preparations soon reached Prince Hyobukyo's ears. After the general amnesty which succeeded his return from Suma, Genji in general made no difference between those who had remained loyal to his cause and those who had stood aloof from him. But from the first Hyobukyo felt that in his case an exception was made. Over and over again he found himself treated with marked coldness, and the refusal to accept his younger daughter as a candidate for the Emperor's hand, together with a number of other small but vexatious incidents, finally convinced him that he must at some time have given Genji particular offence. How this had occurred he was at a loss to conjecture; it was indeed the last thing in the world which he would have wished to happen. The fact that, among the many women upon whom Genji had bestowed his favors, it was Murasaki who had been chosen to be the mistress of his house, gave to Hyobukyo, as her father, a certain worldly prestige. But it could by no means be said that he had hitherto taken a personal share in any of his daughter's triumphs. This time, however, a celebration in which Hyobukyo necessarily played the foremost part was being planned

---

* A *machi* is 119 yards.

and prepared by Genji himself on a scale which had set the whole country talking. The Prince began to hope that his old age would be lightened by a period of belated conspicuity, and he began to feel very well pleased with himself. This intensely irritated his wife, who could not endure that honors should come to him through the influence of her stepchild, and saw no reason why Genji should so quickly be forgiven his obstructive attitude concerning the Presentation of her own little daughter.

The new palace was finished in the eighth month. The portions corresponding to the astrological signs Sheep and Monkey* were reserved for Lady Akikonomu's occasional use, for they stood on ground that her own suite of rooms had once occupied. The Dragon and Snake quarters were for Genji himself; while the Bull and Tiger corner was to be used by the Lady from the Village of Falling Flowers. Finally the Dog and Wild Boar quarters were made ready for the Lady from Akashi, in the hope that she would at last consent to install herself under his roof.

He effected great improvement in the appearance of the grounds by a judicious handling of knoll and lake, for though such features were already there in abundance, he found it necessary here to cut away a slope, there to dam a stream, that each occupant of the various quarters might look out of her windows upon such a prospect as pleased her best. To the southeast he raised the level of the ground, and on this bank planted a profusion of early flowering trees. At the foot of this slope the lake curved with especial beauty, and in the foreground, just beneath the windows, he planted borders of cinquefoil, of red-plum, cherry, wisteria, kerria, rock-azalea, and other such plants as are at their best in springtime; for he knew that Murasaki was in especial a lover of the spring; while here and there, in places where they would not obstruct his main plan, autumn beds were cleverly interwoven with the rest.

Akikonomu's garden was full of such trees as in autumn-time turn to the deepest hue. The stream above the waterfall was cleared out and deepened to a considerable distance; and that the noise of the cascade might carry further, he set great boulders in mid-stream, against which the current crashed and broke. It so happened that, the season being far advanced, it was this part of the garden that was now seen at its best; here indeed was such beauty as far eclipsed the autumn splendor even of the forests near Oi, so famous for their autumn tints.

In the northeastern garden there was a cool spring, the neighborhood of which seemed likely to yield an agreeable refuge from the summer heat. In the borders near the house upon this side he planted Chinese bamboos, and a little further off, tall-stemmed forest-trees whose thick

---

* The points of the compass indicated by these animal designations are successively, S.W., S.E., N.E., N.W. Houses were planned with reference to Chinese astrological conceptions.

leaves roofed airy tunnels of shade, pleasant as those of the most lovely upland wood. This garden was fenced with hedges of the white deutzia flower, the orange tree "whose scent rewakes forgotten love," the briar-rose, and the giant peony; with many other sorts of bush and tall flower so skillfully spread about among them that neither spring nor autumn would ever lack in bravery.

On the east a great space was walled off, behind which rose the Racing Lodge;[*] in front of it the race-course was marked off with ozier hurdles; and as he would be resident here during the sports of the fifth month, all along the stream at this point he planted the appropriate purple irises.[†] Opposite were the stables with stalls for his race-horses, and quarters for the jockeys and grooms. Here were gathered together the most daring riders from every province in the kingdom. To the north of Lady Akashi's rooms rose a high embankment, behind which lay the storehouses and granaries, screened also by a close-set wall of pine-trees, planted there on purpose that she might have the pleasure of seeing them when their boughs were laden with snow; and for her delight in the earlier days of the winter there was a great bed of chrysanthemums, which he pictured her enjoying on some morning when all the garden was white with frost. Then there was the mother-oak[‡] (for was not she a mother?) and, brought hither from wild and inaccessible places, a hundred other bushes and trees, so seldom seen that no one knew what names to call them by.

The move was to take place about the time of the Festival of the Further Shore.[§] He had at first intended to transfer all the occupants at one time. But it soon became apparent that this would be too vast an undertaking, and it was arranged that Lady Akikonomu should not arrive till somewhat later than the rest. With her usual amiability and good sense the Lady from the Village of Falling Flowers readily fell in with the suggestion that she and her party should not form a separate cortege, but should join with Murasaki in the ceremony of removal. Genji regretted that the latter was not going to see her new domain at the season for which it had been principally designed; but still, the move itself was a diverting experience. There were fifteen coaches in the procession and almost all the outriders were gentlemen of the fourth or fifth rank. The ordering of the procession was not so elaborate as might have been expected, for it seemed likely at the moment that too lavish a display might try the temper of the common people, and some of the more ostentatious forms and ceremonies were either omitted or abridged.

---

[*] Used for residence during the Kamo Festival.

[†] Plucked on the fifth day of the fifth month.

[‡] *Queicus dentala.*

[§] Lasts for a week, centering round the autumnal equinox. The Further Shore is Nirvana, to which Buddha carries us in the Ship of Salvation. The festival is peculiar to Japan.

But Genji was careful not to let it seem that any of these restrictions had been carried out to the detriment of one lady rather than another. The Lady from the Village of Falling Flowers had indeed nothing to complain of, for Yugiri had been told off to wait upon her exclusively during the whole ceremony. The gentlewomen and maids found their quarters in the new house admirably fitted out with every comfort and convenience and they were louder than ever in Genji's praises. About six days later the Empress Akikonomu arrived from the Palace. The ceremony of her arrival, though it had been intended that the whole move should be as little ostentatious as possible, was necessarily a very sumptuous and imposing affair. Not only had she risen from obscurity to the highest place which a woman can hold in the land, but she had herself advanced so much in beauty and acquired so great a dignity of carriage and mien that she now figured very large in the popular imagination, and crowds flocked the road wherever she was to pass.

The various quarters of which the New Palace was composed were joined by numerous alleys and covered ways, so that access from one to another was easy, and no one felt that she had been bundled away into a corner. When the ninth month came and the autumn leaves began to be at their best, the splendors of Akikonomu's new garden were at last revealed, and indeed the sights upon which her windows looked were indescribably lovely. One evening when the crimson carpet was ruffled by a gusty wind, she filled a little box with red leaves from different trees and sent it to Murasaki. As messenger she chose one of the little girls who waited upon her. The child, a well-grown, confident little thing, came tripping across the humped wooden bridge that led from the Empress's apartments with the utmost unconcern. Pleased though Murasaki was to receive this prompt mark of friendship, she could for a while do nothing but gaze with delight at the messenger's appearance, and she quite forgot to be resentful, as some in her place would have been, that an older and more dignified messenger had not been entrusted with the Empress's gift. The child wore a silk shirt, yellow outside and lined with green. Her mantle was of brown gauze. She was used to running about on messages in the Palace, had that absolute faultlessness of turn-out and bearing which seems never to be found elsewhere, and was far from being overawed at finding herself in the presence of such a person as Lady Murasaki. Attached to the box was the poem: "Though yours be a garden where only springtime is of price, suffer it that from my house autumn should blow a crimson leaf into your hand." It was amusing to see how while Murasaki read the missive, her ladies crowded round the little messenger and plied her with refreshments and caresses. For answer, Murasaki placed in the lid of the box a carpet of moss and on it laid a very little toy rock. Then she wrote on a strip of paper tied to a sprig of five-pointed pine:

"The light leaf scatters in the wind, and of the vaunted spring no tinge is left us, save where the pine-tree grips its ledge of stone."

The Empress thought at first that it was a real pine-branch. But when she looked closer she saw that, like the rock, it was a work of art—as delicate and ingenious a piece of craftsmanship as she had ever encountered. The readiness of Murasaki's answer and the tact with which, while not exalting her own favorite season above that of Akikonomu's choice, she had yet found a symbol to save her from tame surrender, pleased the Empress and was greeted as a happy stroke by all the ladies who were with her. But Genji when she showed it to him pretended to think the reply very impertinent, and to tease Murasaki he said to her afterwards: "I think you received these leaves most ungraciously. At another season one might venture perhaps upon such disparagement; but to do so now that the Goddess of Tatsuta[*] holds us all in sway seems almost seditious. You should have bided your time; for only from behind the shelter of blossoming boughs could such a judgment be uttered with impunity." So he spoke; but he was in reality delighted to find these marks of interest and good will being exchanged between the various occupants of his house, and he felt that the new arrangement was certain to prove a great success.

When the Lady of Akashi heard of the removal to the New Palace and was told that only her own quarters, as spacious and handsome as any of the rest, now remained untenanted, she determined at last to hold aloof no longer. It was the Godless month when she arrived. She looked around her and, mistrustful though she was, she certainly could see no sign here that as regards either elegance or comfort she would be expected to put up with less than her neighbors. And indeed Genji saw to it that on all occasions she should rank in the eyes of the household rather as mother of the little princess for whom so brilliant a future was in store, than as the scion of a poor and undistinguished provincial family.

---

[*] Goddess of the autumn; here compared to Akikonomu. The secondary meaning is "You must be more civil to Akikonomu now that she is Empress."

Tamakatsura

Though seventeen years had now passed since Yugao's death,* Genji had not by any means forgotten her. He had indeed since those early days seen much of the world and encountered the most divers temperaments. But he had yet to find a disposition such as hers; and it was with feelings of longing and contrition that he looked back upon their intimacy.

Though Ukon was not a creature of much account, she was the one person to whom he could speak of the dead lady. He felt a considerable degree of affection towards her, and during the years after Yugao's death Ukon had practically lived at the Nijo-in, being allowed to spend most of her time with the older servants in the housekeeper's room. Then came the exile, and with Genji's other servants she went across to the western wing and entered Murasaki's service. She gave the impression of being a harmless, self-effacing creature, and it would have surprised everyone very much to know what was all the while going on in her mind. For Ukon, particularly after the move to the New Palace, was constantly appraising the relative positions of the great ladies who ruled the house, and deciding what place her own dear mistress would now be occupying, were she still alive. "Certainly," said Ukon to herself, looking critically at the Lady of Akashi, "my poor lady would not have been eclipsed by such as you!" And indeed Ukon had seen for herself that even where his feelings were far less strong than in Yugao's case, there never came a time when Genji turned aside from those who had opened their hearts to him, or behaved as though his obligations towards them were at an end. However full might be the cup of his affections, he did not allow a drop to spill; and though Yugao might not perhaps have been able to vie with so great a personage as Murasaki, yet it was certain that were she alive she would now be occupying one of the main apartments in the newly finished house.

Such were the sad reflections that dwelt constantly in this solitary lady's heart. She had never attempted to get into communication with the family of her late mistress, nor ever to discover the present whereabouts of the child† whom Yugao had left behind at the house in the Fifth Ward; partly through fear of being questioned concerning her own part in the

---

* See Part I, Chapter IV.
† To no Chujo's child by Yugao. Her name was Tamakatsura.

unhappy affair, partly because there seemed to be no object in doing so. Moreover, Genji had strictly forbidden her to mention the story to anybody, and though she had sometimes thought of writing to the people at the house, she felt that it would be disloyal to him to do so, and was entirely without news. She did, however, hear long afterwards a report that the husband of the nurse in whose care the child had been left was now working in a provincial Treasury and that his wife was with him. It seemed probable that they had also taken the child.

This was indeed the case. Tamakatsura was four years old when she made the journey to Tsukushi. The nurse, after months of vain endeavor to discover Yugao's whereabouts, during which she had trudged weary and weeping from quarter to quarter and house to house without finding the least glimmer of news, had at last given up all hope. She would have been glad enough for her own sake to keep the child, to whom she had become fondly attached, as a remembrance of the mistress whom she must now regard as forever lost. But there were also the little girl's own interests to consider. "We are humble people," thought the nurse, "and Tsukushi* is a long way off. Perhaps it is my duty to tell her father† of what has happened and give him the chance of making some more suitable provision for her future." But it was difficult for such people to communicate with a young gentleman of To no Chujo's quality. "If I mention the child to its father," she said to her husband one day, "he is certain to ask at once how I could have been so foolish as to let our poor young lady out of my sight. And indeed, I don't know how I should answer him. Then again, it isn't as if he had ever seen much of the little creature. It would be like handing her over to strangers, and I do not think that, when the time came, I should ever find it in my heart to let her go. He may of course refuse to do anything for her himself; but one thing is certain: if he hears we are going off to Tsukushi, he will never give me leave to take her with us!" So the nurse declared to her husband and companions. Though Tamakatsura was not much over three years old when her mother disappeared, she had acquired all the airs and graces of a little lady; she was remarkably good-looking and it was apparent that she already had a strong will of her own. But now she was bundled on to a common trading-ship in which no provision whatever had been made for the comfort of the passengers; and as they rowed out into the bay, she began to look very disconsolate. She still thought a great deal about her mother, and, to reassure herself, she said out loud: "I know why we are travelling on this ship; we are going to see mother!" She returned to this idea again and again, but it received no confirmation on any side, and

---

* The large southern island upon which the modern town of Nagasaki stands.
† To no Chujo.

at last she burst into tears. Two young women sitting near by were also weeping, though they suddenly ceased to do so when one of the sailors reminded them that "tears bring bad luck at sea."

Skirting along the coast they passed much lovely scenery, and the nurse, remembering what delight her young mistress had taken in such sights as these, wished for a moment that she were here to see them. But then she remembered that but for Yugao's disappearance she and her husband would never have been driven to accept this wretched post in the provinces, and she gazed regretfully in the direction of the City, envying even the waves that stole back so peacefully towards shores "that she, perhaps, would never tread again." Soon the rowers began chanting in their rough, wild voices the song "Over the distant waves," and the two young women, who were sitting face to face, again began to weep bitterly. At last the ship rounded the Golden Cape, and knowing that the coast which now came into view belonged not to the mainland, but to the island of Tsukushi, the travelers felt that exile had indeed begun. The old nurse's heart sank; but she had her little charge to see to and was most of the time far too busy to think of anything else. Now and again she would drop off to sleep and then, as for some time past, she would at once dream that her mistress appeared before her. But always at Yugao's side there stood the figure of another woman, who seemed to follow her wherever she went. The nurse woke from these dreams sickened and afraid, and she felt, after each such occasion, more certain than ever that Yugao was no longer alive.

Shoni, the nurse's husband, had only been appointed to his post in Tsukushi for a term of five years. But the position he held was a very humble one and when the time came, he found it difficult to meet the expenses of a long journey. Thus their departure for the capital had to be postponed again and again. At last, after many months of disappointment and delay, Shoni fell seriously ill. Tamakatsura was now ten years old and was growing handsomer every day. Shoni, who knew that his end was near, kept asking himself what would become of her in this desolate place. He had always felt that in bringing her with them they had acted somewhat unfairly to the child. For after all she was To no Chujo's daughter, and her birth entitled her to better surroundings than the cramped and dingy home of a provincial clerk. But five years is not a very long time, and he had always confidently expected that when his term of office ran out he would be able to take her with him to Kyoto and put her into touch with her father. True, it was possible that Chujo would refuse to acknowledge her. But the City is a big place, and Shoni made no doubt that, once he had settled her there, a girl such as this would not have to wait very long before a satisfactory opening occurred. For this reason he had done everything in his power to raise funds for the journey. But now the last expedient had failed and he knew that for his part he was fated never to leave Tsukushi. During his last days he worried much over the injustice which had been done to the child in detaining her so long away from the Capital, and sending for his sons he said to them: "As soon as this is over I want you to take Tamakatsura back to the City. The same day. Don't wait for the funeral..."

It was only known to the members of Shoni's family that the little girl was To no Chujo's daughter. To the other government clerks and to the world in general she was a granddaughter of Shoni's whose parents were in trouble of some kind and had left her in his charge. But in the family she continued to be treated as "the young lady," and every sacrifice was made that she might have, so far as possible, the upbringing to which her birth entitled her. Shoni's sudden illness and death naturally threw his wife into a piteous state of distraction; but in the midst of her grief, one thought obsessed her; would they ever be able to secure a passage back to the City and restore the little girl to her relations? Unfortunately Shoni had been unpopular with the local people and none of them would give any assistance. Thus the time dragged on, wretched years full of anxiety and discouragement; and still there seemed no prospect of return.

Meanwhile Tamakatsura grew to womanhood. She had all her mother's beauty, and something more besides; for she seemed to have inherited from her father's side a singular air of high breeding, an aristocratic fineness of limb and gesture, that in Yugao, whose beauty was that of the by-street rather than of the palace, had been entirely lacking. She was of a very generous disposition, and in every way a most delightful companion. Her fame soon spread through the island, and hardly a day passed but some local squire or farmer attempted to get into correspondence with her. These letters, written for the most part in a rustic sprawling hand and very crudely expressed, were thrust upon every member of the household in turn in the hope that he or she would consent to act as a go-between. Clumsy documents of this kind were calculated to arouse nothing but disgust in the breast of anyone save an islander, and no attention whatever was paid to them. At last the persistence of her suitors became a nuisance, and the nurse put it about that though the girl looked just like other people, she suffered from a secret deformity which made it impossible for her ever to marry. It had indeed (so the story ran) already been decided that she was to live quietly with her "grandmother" till the old lady died, and after that was to enter a nunnery. But it soon became so irritating to hear everyone saying: "Isn't it sad about poor Shoni's granddaughter? They say she has got some terrible deformity," that the old nurse could bear it no longer and again began racking her brains to discover some way of getting the girl back to her father. Was it conceivable that he would refuse to look after her? After all, he had made quite a fuss over her when she was a baby. The old lady prayed fervently to every Buddha and God that some way might present itself of taking Tamakatsura to Kyoto. But the chance of any member of her family getting away from Tsukushi was now remoter than ever. Her daughters had married local people and her sons were employed in the neighborhood. In her heart of hearts she still cherished all sorts of schemes for compassing the return of the whole family; but every day it became more and more impossible that anything of the kind would ever happen. Thus Tamakatsura grew up amid continual lamentations and repinings and learnt to look upon life as one long succession of troubles and disappointments, varied only by three great bouts of penance and fasting, each January, May, and September. The years went by. She was now twenty; her beauty was at its height, and still it was being wasted in this barbarous and sequestered land.

Some while after Shoni's death the family had moved along the coast from Chikuzeri to Hizen, hoping for a more peaceful existence in a place where they were not known. But Tamakatsura's reputation had preceded her and, little inclined to credit the stories about her deformity, the notabilities of the neighboring countryside began pestering her guardians with such assiduity that life soon became as harassing as before.

Among these suitors there was a certain Tayu no Gen who held a small position under the Lord-Lieutenant of Tsukushi. He came of a family that was very influential in Higo and the surrounding country, and on this side of the island he ranked as a person of considerable importance. He had, moreover, greatly distinguished himself in a campaign against the insurgents. To a singular degree of hardihood and endurance there was added in his nature more than a fair share of sensuality. Women were his hobby; he kept a prodigious quantity of them always about him, and was continually on the lookout for opportunities of adding to the collection. The story of the beautiful Tamakatsura and of the secret deformity which prevented her marriage soon reached Tayu's ears. "Misshapen, is she?" he cried. "Frightened that people will stare? She need not worry about that if she comes to me. I'll keep her locked up all right!" and he wrote at once to Shoni's wife. The old lady, who knew his reputation, was sadly put about. She replied that her granddaughter was destined for the convent and that no proposals of this kind could be entertained on her behalf. Tayu was not used to be put off like this and, determined at all costs to get his way, he came galloping over to Hizen at full speed. He immediately summoned Shoni's three sons to his lodging and said to them: "Let me have that girl, and you may count on me as a friend for life. My name goes for something on the Higo side..." Two of the sons were easily won over and promised to do as Tayu asked. They had, it is true, a moment's qualm at the thought of handing over To no Chujo's child to this lawless provincial swashbuckler. But they had their own way to make in the world, and they knew that Tayu had by no means exaggerated the value of his own friendship and protection. On the other hand, life on this part of the island with Tayu against one was a prospect not to be faced with equanimity. If the girl had failed to take in the world the place to which her rank entitled her, that was her father's fault, not theirs. She ought to be grateful that such a man as this (after all, he was the principal person in the neighborhood) should have taken such a fancy to her. In Tsukushi at any rate there was no prospect of doing better for her, and Tayu, angered by the refusal of his proffered patronage, would certainly stick at nothing... So they argued, doing their best to scare their mother into assent by stories of Tayu's violence and implacability. Only the second brother, Bugo no Suke, stood out: "I know a good deal about this fellow," he said. "It's too much of a shame. We simply cannot hand her over to him... Somehow or other one of us ought to do what our father asked us to—take her back to Kyoto. There must be some way of managing it..." Shoni's two daughters stood by weeping. Their mother was utterly heartbroken. What had become now of all her plans for the girl's happy future? Of what use had been all these years of isolation and subterfuge, if at the end Tamakatsura must be handed over to this coarse and unscrupulous barbarian?

It would indeed have astonished Tayu to know that anyone in Hizen considered him in such a light as this. He had always regarded his attentions to women as favors bestowed, he flattered himself, moreover, that he knew as well as any man how to conduct a gallant correspondence, and his letters began to arrive thick and fast. They were written in a clean, bold hand on thick Chinese paper, heavily scented. It was evident indeed that he regarded himself as no mean calligrapher. His style of composition was not an agreeable one, being very tortuous and affected. Soon he made up his mind that the time had come for him to call in person, and he arranged with the brothers to meet him at their mother's house. Tayu was a man of about thirty, tall and solidly built. He was far from ill-looking; but he had the power (which he frequently exercised) of assuming the most repulsively ferocious expression. This, however, was reserved for his followers and opponents. When in a good temper and engaged upon errands of love he adopted an entirely different voice and manner. You would have thought indeed that some little bird was chirruping, so dexterously did he reduce his rough bass to a small silvery fluting: "As a lover, I ought to have come after dark, ought I not? Isn't that what courting means—coming at night? So I was always told. What extraordinary weather for a spring evening! In autumn of course one expects it..."

Upon a strict undertaking that she would not provoke Tayu in any way, the old lady's sons had allowed her to see him. He now turned to her saying: "Madam, though I never had the pleasure of meeting your late husband, I knew him to be a kind-hearted and upright gentleman. I always hoped that I might one day have an opportunity of showing him how much I appreciated his excellent qualities, and it was with deep regret that I heard of his untimely decease. But though I can no longer do him any service, I hope that you will allow me to show my regard for him in some practical way. There is, I think, a young lady here (I am right, am I not?) a ward of yours, or relative of some sort? If I venture to speak of her, it is with the greatest deference and respect; for I understand that she is of extremely high birth. I assure you that, were I ever privileged to make the acquaintance of such a person, I should kneel before her like a slave, dedicate my life to her service, humbly petition her... But I see that you are looking at me somewhat askance. You have heard stories no doubt... Believe me, there is no truth in them. I have in the past admired one or two of our simple country girls; but surely you can understand that *this* would be a very different matter. Should you admit me to the friendship of your exalted kinswoman, I would set her up as my paragon, my empress, my all-in-all..." He made many fair speeches of this kind. At last the old nurse answered: "I should indeed consider my granddaughter singularly fortunate to have aroused the interest of so distinguished a gentleman as yourself, were it not for the fact that nature has played upon her a cruel trick at birth... Sir, I have seldom spoken of this to anyone before; but I must assure you that the poor girl's unhappy condition has for years past been a sore trouble to me. As for offering her hand in marriage to anyone—that is entirely out of the question..." "Pray don't make so many apologies," cried Tayu. "Were she the most bleareyed, broken-legged creature under Heaven, I'd have her put right for you in a very short while. The truth of the matter is, the Gods and Buddhas in the temples round here owe a good deal to me, and I can make them do pretty much whatever I choose..." So he bragged; but when, assuming that his offer had already been accepted, he began pressing the old lady to name a day, she hastily changed the subject, saying that summer would soon be coming, that the farmers were needing rain, plying him in fact with all the usual topics of the countryside. He felt that before he left he ought to recite a few verses of poetry, and after a long period of silent meditation, he produced the following:

If she does not want to be married,
I shall go to the pine-tree Bay
And complain to the God of the Mirror;*
Then I need hardly say
That I shall get my way.

---

* The God of the Sacred Mirror, at Matsura, in Hizen.

"I don't think that's such a bad poem," he said smiling awkwardly. The nurse was in far too agitated a condition to indulge in literary pastimes. Utterly unable to produce any sort of reply, she begged her daughters to answer in her stead. "But mother darling," the young ladies protested, "if *you* cannot think of anything to say, still less can we..." At last after much painful cogitation, the old lady recited the following poem, speaking as though she were addressing herself as much as him: "Unkind were it indeed should the Guardian of the Mirror frustrate the prayers of one[*] who year on year hath been his and his alone." "What's that?" cried Tayu rushing towards her. "How dare you say such a thing?" So sudden was his onrush that Shoni's wife jumped almost out of her skin, and she turned pale with fright. Fortunately her daughters were not so easily scared, and one of them, laughing as though an absurd misunderstanding had occurred, at once said to Tayu: "What mother meant was this: she hopes that after all the trouble she has taken praying to the Gods of Matsura on our little niece's behalf, they will not allow the poor girl's deformity to turn you against her. But dear mother is getting old and it is not always easy to make out what she is saying." "Oho! Yes, yes, I see," he said, nodding his head reflectively. "I don't know how I came to misunderstand it. Ha! ha! Very neatly expressed. I expect you look upon me as a very uncultivated, provincial person. And so I should be, if I were at all like the other people round here. But I've been very fortunate; you would not find many men even at the City who have had a better education than I. You'd be making a great mistake if you set me down as a plain, countrified sort of man. As a matter of fact, there's nothing I have not studied." He would very much have liked to try his hand at a second poem; but his stock of ideas was exhausted and he was obliged to take leave.

The fact that two of her sons had openly sided with Tayu increased the old lady's terror and despair. All she could now think of was to spirit the girl away from Tsukushi as rapidly and secretly as possible. She besought the other son, Bugo no Suke, to devise some means of conducting the girl to Kyoto, but Bugo no Suke answered: "I wish I could; but I do not see how it is to be done. There is not a soul on the island who will help me. We three used to hang together in old times; but now they say I am Tayu's enemy and will have nothing to do with me. And with Tayu against one it is a difficult thing in these parts to stir hand or foot, let alone take passage for several persons in an outgoing ship. I might find I was doing Lady Tamakatsura a very ill turn..."

But though no one had told the girl of what was going on, she somehow or other seemed to know all about it. She was in a state of the wildest agi-

---

[*] Herself.

tation, and Bugo no Suke heard her declare in tones of the utmost horror that she intended to take her own life rather than accept the fate which was in store for her. Bugo was certain that this was no empty threat, and by a tremendous effort he managed to collect a sum sufficient to cover the expenses of the journey. His mother, now getting on in years, was determined not to end her days in Tsukushi. But she was growing very infirm, and it would be impossible for her to accompany them did not one of her daughters consent to come and look after her. The younger sister, Ateki, had been married for several years; but Bugo no Suke prevailed upon her at last to abandon her home and take charge of their mother on the journey. The elder sister had been married much longer; her family was already large and it was obviously impossible for her to get away. The travelers were obliged to leave home hastily late one night and embark at once; for they had suddenly heard that Tayu, who had gone home to Higo, was expected back in Hizen early next day (the twelfth of the fourth month), and he would doubtless lose no time in claiming his bride.

There were distressing scenes of farewell. It seemed unlikely that the elder sister would ever see her mother again. But Ateki took the parting much more calmly; for though Tsukushi had been her home for so long, she was by no means sorry to leave the place, and it was only when someone pointed back to the Matsura temple and Ateki scanning the quay-side recognized the very spot where she had said goodbye to her sister, that she felt at all downcast at the thought of the journey before her. "Swiftly we row," she sang; "the Floating Islands vanish in the mist and, pilotless as they, I quit life's anchorage to drift amid the tempests of a world unknown." "No longer men but playthings of the wind are they who in their misery must needs take ship upon the uncertain pathways of the deep." So Tamakatsura replied, and in utter despair she flung herself face downward upon her seat, where she lay motionless for many hours.

The news of her flight soon leaked out, and eventually reached Tayu's ears. He was not the man to let his prey slip from him in this manner, and though for an instant he was so angry and surprised that he could do nothing at all, he soon pulled himself together, hired a light skiff and set out in pursuit. It was a vessel specially constructed for swift launching, and the wind was blowing hard from shore. He shot across the harbor at an immense speed, with every inch of sail spread, and a moment later was through the Clanging Breakers. Launched upon the calmer waters of the open sea his craft scudded along more swiftly than ever. Seeing a small boat chasing after them at reckless speed the captain of the pursued vessel imagined that pirates were on his track and pressed on towards the nearest port. Only Tamakatsura and her companions knew that in that rapidly approaching craft there was one who, by them at any rate, was far more to be dreaded than the most ruthless pirate. Louder and louder beat the poor girl's heart; so loud indeed that the noise of the breakers seemed to her to have stopped. At last they entered the bay of Kawajiri. Tayu's vessel was no longer in sight, and as their ship approached the harbor, the fugitives began to breathe again. One of the sailors was singing a snatch of the song:

So I pressed on from China Port to Kawajiri Bay
With never a thought for my own sad love or the babe that wept on her knee.

He sang in an expressionless, monotonous voice, but the melancholy tune caught Bugo no Suke's fancy and he found himself joining in: "With never a thought..." Yes, he too had left behind those who were dearest to him, with little thought indeed of what was to become of them. Even the two or three sturdy youths who worked for him in the house would have been some comfort to his wife and babes. But these young fellows had clamored to go with him and he weakly consented. He pictured to himself how Tayu, maddened by the failure of his pursuit, would rush back to Hizen and wreak his vengeance upon the defenseless families of those who had worked against him. How far would he go? What exactly would he do? Bugo no Suke now realized that in planning this flight he had behaved with the wildest lack of forethought; all his self-confidence vanished, and so hideous were the scenes which his imagination conjured up before him that he broke down altogether and sat weeping with his head on his knees. Like the ransomed prisoner in Po Chü-i's poem,* though returning to his native place, he had left wife and child to shift for themselves amid the Tartar hordes. His sister Ateki heard him sobbing and could well understand his dismay. The plight of those who had remained at Hizen was indeed a wretched one. Most of all she pitied the few old followers and servants who had consented to come with them from the Capital long ago, believing that in five years they would be back again in their homes. To leave these faithful old people in the lurch seemed the basest of treacheries. They had always (she and her brother) been used to speaking of the City as their "home"; but now that they were drawing near to it they realized that though it was indeed their native place, there was not within it one house where they were known, one friend or acquaintance to whom they could turn. For this lady's sake they had left what for most of their lives had been their world, their only true home—had committed their lives to the hazard of wind and wave; all this without a moment's reflection or misgiving. And now that their precious cargo was within hail of port, what were they to do with her?

---

* See my *170 Chinese Poems*, p. 130.

How were they to approach her family, make known her presence, prove her identity? Endlessly though they had discussed these points during the journey, they could arrive at no conclusion, and it was with a sense of helplessness and bewilderment that they hurried into the City.

In the Ninth Ward they chanced to hear of an old acquaintance of their mother's who was still living in the neighborhood, and here they managed to procure temporary lodgings. The Ninth Ward does indeed count as part of Kyoto; but it is an immense distance from the center, and no one of any consequence lives there. Thus in their effort to find some influential person who would help them to fulfill their mission, the brother and sister encountered only the strangest types of market-women and hagglers. Autumn was coming on, they had achieved nothing and there seemed no reason to suppose that the ensuing months would be any more profitable than those which they had just wasted. Ateki who had relied entirely upon her brother and imagined him capable of dealing with any situation that arose, was dismayed to discover that in the City he was like a water bird on shore. He hung about the house, had no notion how to make enquiries or cultivate fresh acquaintances, and was no better able to look after himself than the youths he had brought with him from Tsukushi. These young fellows, after much grumbling, had indeed mostly either found employment in the neighborhood or gone back to their native province. It grieved Ateki beyond measure that her brother should be thus stranded in the Capital without occupation or resource, and she bewailed his lot day and night. "Come, come, Sister," he would say to her, "on my account you have no cause to be uneasy. I would gladly come a good deal further than we have travelled and put up with many another month of hardship and waiting, if only I could get our young lady back among the friends who ought to be looking after her. We may have spoilt our own prospects, you and I; but what should we be feeling like today, if we consented to let that monster carry her off to his infamous den? But it is my opinion that the Gods alone can help us in our present pass. Not far from here is the great temple of Yawata where the same God is worshipped as in our own Yawata Temples at Hakozaki and Matsura, where mother used to take the young lady to do her penances. Those two temples may be a long way off, but the same God inhabits all three, and I believe that her many visits to Hakozaki and Matsura would now stand her in good stead. What if she were to go to the Temple here and perform a service of thanksgiving for her safe journey to the Capital?" Bugo no Suke made enquiries in the neighborhood and found out that one of the Five Abbots, a very holy man with whom Shoni had been well acquainted, was still alive. He obtained an interview with the old priest and arranged that Tamakatsura should be allowed to visit the Temple.

After this they visited a succession of holy places. At last Bugo no Suke suggested a pilgrimage to the Temple of the Hasegawa Kwannon. "There is no deity in Japan," he said, "who has in recent times worked so many miracles as this Goddess of Hatsuse. I am told that the fame of her shrine has spread even to China,* and far off though Tsukushi is, I know that Lady Tamakatsura has for years past been deeply interested in the achievements of this Divinity and shown an exemplary piety towards her. I believe that a visit to Hatsuse would do more for our young lady than anything else." It was decided that, to give it a greater significance, the pilgrimage should be made on foot and, despite her great age and infirmity, the old nurse would not be left behind. Tamakatsura, wholly unused to such experiences, felt scared and wretched as, pilgrims in front and behind, she tramped wearily on, turning to right or left when she was bid, but otherwise too deeply buried in her own thoughts to notice what went on around her. What had she done, she asked herself over and over again, to deserve this downtrodden existence? And as she dragged foot after foot along the dusty road she prayed earnestly to Buddha, saying "O Much-Honored One, if my mother is indeed no longer in this world, grant that, wherever it be, her soul may look upon me with compassion and her prayers bring me quick release, that I may take refuge in the place where her spirit dwells. And if she is still alive, grant, O Buddha, that I may one day meet her face to face." So she prayed, and while she did so suddenly remembered that it was a useless prayer. For she was very young when Yugao disappeared, had only the haziest recollection of her appearance, and even if the prayer were answered, would certainly pass her mother unrecognized! Dismal as these reflections would at any time have been, they were doubly so now, worn out as she was by the fatigue of the journey. The party had indeed travelled at a very leisurely pace and it was not till the hour of the Snake, on the fourth day, that they at last reached Tsuba Market.† Tamakatsura was by this time more dead than alive; they attempted to improvise a carrying-chair, but the pain in her legs was so great that she could not bear to be moved, and there was nothing for it but to let her rest at the inn.

The party consisted of Bugo no Suke, two bowmen, and three or four very rough-looking boys to carry the luggage. The three ladies had their skirts tucked in at the belt like country-women, and were attended only by two aged crones who looked like broken-down charwomen.

---

* There is a story in Japan that the wife of the Chinese Emperor Hsi Tsung (874-888 A.D.) was so ugly that she was nicknamed "Horse-head." In obedience to a dream she turned to the East and prayed to the Kwannon of Hasegawa in Japan. Instantly there appeared before her a figure carrying Kwannon's sacred water-vessel. He dashed the water over her face and she became the most beautiful woman in China.

† A short distance from the Hasegawa Temple.

It would indeed have been impossible to guess that any person of quality was among them.

They spent the time till dusk in trimming their holy lamps and preparing such other emblems and offerings as are brought by pilgrims to the Hasegawa Shrine.

Going his rounds at nightfall the priest who owned the inn came upon the two decrepit old serving-women calmly making a bed for Tamakatsura in a corner of the best room of the house. "These quarters have been engaged for the night by a gentlewoman who may arrive at any minute," he said in consternation. "Be off with you at once! Just fancy, without so much as a 'by your leave'!" They were still staring at him helplessly, when there was a noise at the door and it became evident that the expected guests had actually arrived. They too seemed to have come on foot. There were two gentlewomen, very well-conditioned, and quite a number of attendants both male and female. Their baggage was on the backs of some four or five horses, and though they wore plain liveries it was evident that the grooms were in good service. The landlord was determined that the newcomers should have the quarters which he had intended for them; but the intruders showed no signs of moving, and he stood scratching his head in great perplexity. It did indeed go to the hearts of Tamakatsura's old servants to turn her out of the corner where she was so comfortably established and pack her away into the back room. But it was soon apparent that the only alternative was to seek quarters in a different inn, and as this would have been both humiliating and troublesome they made the best of a bad job and carried their mistress to the inner room, while others of the party either took shelter in the outhouses or squeezed themselves and their belongings into stray angles and corners of the main house.

The new arrivals did not after all seem to be of such rank and consequence as the priest had made out. But it was hard to guess what manner of people they might be; for they concealed themselves scrupulously from the gaze of their fellow-guests and hardly spoke to one another at all.

In point of fact, the person to whom Lady Tamakatsura had been thus unceremoniously compelled to give place was none other than her mother's faithful maid, Ukon! For years past it had been the one comfort of the solitary and grief-stricken old lady's existence to make this pilgrimage, and Genji had always assisted her to do so with as much comfort as possible. So familiar was the journey that it no longer seemed to her in any way formidable; but having come on foot she was quite ready for a rest, and immediately lay down upon the nearest couch. Beside her was a thin partition of plaited reeds. Behind it she could hear people moving about, and presently someone entered who seemed to be carrying a tray of food. Then she heard a man's voice saying: "Please take this to my lady. Tell her I am very sorry it is so badly served; but I have done the best I can." From the tone in which he spoke it was evident that the lady to whom these apologies were to be conveyed was a person far above him in social position. Ukon's curiosity was aroused. She peeped through a crack in the partition, and at once had the impression that she had seen the young man before. Who could it be? She racked her brains, but could not imagine. It would indeed have been strange had she been able to identify Bugo no Suke, who was a mere child when she last saw him, while now he was a full-grown man, much bronzed from exposure to the sun and winds of Tsukushi, and dressed in the poorest clothes. "Sanjo, my lady is asking for you." So Bugo no Suke now cried, and to her astonishment Ukon saw that the old woman who answered to this name was also certainly someone whom she had once known. But here there could be no mistake. This Sanjo was the one who had been in service with Ukon in Yugao's house, and had afterwards (like Ukon herself) been one of the few servants whom Yugao took with her to the house in the Fifth Ward. It seemed like a dream. Who was the lady whom they were accompanying? She strained her eyes; but the bed in the room behind the partition was surrounded by screens and there was no possibility of seeing its occupant. She had made up her mind to accost the maid Sanjo and question her when part of her doubt resolved itself spontaneously: the man must be that boy of Shoni's... the one they used to call Hyotoda, and the lady towards whom they showed such deference could be no other than Tamakatsura, Yugao's child by To no Chujo. In wild excitement she called to Sanjo by name; but the old woman was busy serving the supper and for the moment she took no notice. She was very cross at being called away from her work like this, but whoever it was that wanted her seemed to be in a great hurry, and presently she arrived, exclaiming: "I can't make it out. I've spent the last twenty years in service on the island of Tsukushi, and here's a lady from Kyoto calling for me by my own name, as though she knew all about me. Well, Madam, I am called Sanjo. But I think it must be another Sanjo that you are wanting." As she drew near Ukon noticed that the old woman was wearing the most extraordinary narrow-sleeved overall on top of her frumpy old dress. She had grown enormously stout. The sight of her brought a sudden flush of humiliation to Ukon's cheeks, for she realized that she herself was an old woman, and as Sanjo now looked to her, so must she, Ukon, for years past have appeared to all eyes save her own. "Look again! Do you not know me?" she said at last looking straight into Sanjo's face. "Why, to be sure I do!" cried the old lady, clapping her hands, "you were in service with my lady. I was never so glad in my life. Where have you been hiding our dear mistress all this while?... Of course she is with you now?" and in the midst of her excitement Sanjo began to weep; for the encounter had brought back to her mind the days when she was young. What times those had been! And how long, how cruelly long ago it all was! "First," answered Ukon gravely, "you must give me a little of your news. Is nurse with you? And what has happened to the baby girl... and Ateki, where is she?" For the moment Ukon could not bear to dash Sanjo's hope to the ground; moreover it was so painful to her to speak of Yugao's death that she now listened in silence to Sanjo's tale: mother, brother and sister were all there. Tamakatsura was grown to be a fine young lady and was with them too. "But here I am talking," said Sanjo at last, "when I ought to have run straight in to tell nurse..." and with this she disappeared. After their first surprise the chief feeling of Ateki and her mother, upon the reception of this news, was one of indignation against Ukon, whom they supposed to have left their mistress in hiding all these years, callously indifferent to the suspense and misery of all her friends. "I don't feel that I want to see her," said the old nurse at last, nodding in the direction of Ukon's room, "but I suppose I ought to go." No sooner, however, was she sitting by Ukon's couch, with all the curtains drawn aside, than both of them burst into tears. "What has become of her, where is my lady?" the nurse sobbed. "You cannot imagine what I have been through in all these years. I have prayed again and again that some sign, some chance word, some dream might tell me where she was hiding. But not one breath of news came to us, and at last I thought terrible things—that she must be very far away indeed. Yes, I have even imagined that she must be dead, and fallen then into such despair that I hated my own life and would have ended it too, had not my love for the little girl whom she left with me held my feet from the Paths of Night. And even so, you see for yourself what I am... It is but a faint flicker of life..."

In this strain the nurse spoke on, supposing all the while that Lady Yugao herself was somewhere not far away. "How shall I tell her? What am I to say?" The same questions that tormented Ukon's brain during those first days after the funeral returned to her now with redoubled urgency. But this could not go on; it was impossible not to speak; and Ukon suddenly broke in upon the old nurse's outpourings: "Listen!" she said. "It is no use my telling you how it happened... But Lady Yugao died a long while ago."

After this there was silence, broken at last by the agonized and convulsive sobbing of these three old women."

It was growing dark, and now with lamps lit and offerings in their hands the pilgrims were about to start for the temple. The women clung to one another till the last moment and, still scarce knowing what they did, were about to set out upon the road together, when Ukon suddenly bethought herself of the astonishment which her attendants must be feeling at this strange addition to the party; moreover Bugo no Suke had as yet heard nothing of the meeting, and for the moment the old nurse had not the heart to enter into a long explanation of what had occurred. The two parties accordingly separated, Ukon scanning with curiosity the pilgrims who filed past her into the street. Among them was a girl, very poorly dressed; her hair was caught up in a thin summer scarf, which held it tight but did not conceal it. In the procession she walked some way ahead, but even the momentary back view which Ukon was thus able to obtain convinced her that the girl was not only of exceptional beauty, but also of a rank in life very different from that of the shabby pilgrims who tramped beside her. When at last they arrived the service was already in full swing and the temple crowded to overflowing; for most of the pilgrims in whose company the party from Tsukushi had set out from the city were sturdy-legged peasants and working people who had pressed on through Tsuba without a moment's rest and long ago secured their places in the holy building. Ukon, being an habitual visitor to the temple, was at once conducted to a place which had been reserved for her immediately to the right of the Main Altar. But Tamakatsura and her party, who had never been there before and had, moreover, the misfortune to fall into the hands of a very unenterprising verger, found themselves bundled away into the western transept. Ukon from her place of privilege soon caught sight of them and beckoned to them to join her. After a hasty consultation with her son, during the course of which the nurse appeared to be explaining, so far as was possible in a few words, who Ukon was and why she had beckoned, the women of the party pushed their way towards the altar, leaving Bugo no Suke and his two followers where the incompetent sacristan had placed them. Though Ukon was in herself a person of no consequence, she was known to be in Genji's service, and that alone, as she had long ago discovered, was sufficient to secure her from interference, even in such a place as this. Let the herd gape if they chose and ask one another with indignation why two ill-dressed women, from the provinces, who had arrived at the last minute, were calmly seating themselves in places reserved for the gentry. Ukon was not going to have her young lady wedged into a corner or jostled by the common crowd. She longed to get into conversation at once; but the critical moment in the service had just arrived and she was obliged to remain kneeling with head lowered. So it had come at last, this meeting for which she had prayed year in and year out! And now it only remained that Genji, who had so often begged her to find out what had become of Yugao's child, should welcome the discovery (as she felt sure he would) and by his influence restore to this unhappy lady the place at Court to which her birth entitled her. Such indeed was the purport of her prayer as she now knelt at the altar by Tamakatsura's side.

In the crowded temple were pilgrims from every province in the land. Among them the wife of the Governor of Yamato Province was conspicuous for her elegance and consequential air, for most of the worshippers were simple country people, very unfashionably dressed. Sanjo, who, after so many years passed in barbarous Tsukushi, had quite forgotten how town people get themselves up for occasions such as this, could not take her eyes off the magnificent lady. "Hark ye," she said at last in an awe-struck whisper to the nurse, "I don't know what you're a-going to pray for to our Lady Kwannon. But I'm a-praying that if our dear young lady can't be wife to the Lord-Lieutenant* (as I have always hoped she might be), then let her marry a Governor of this fine province of Yamato. For a grander lady than that one there I'm sure I've never seen! 'Just do that,' I said to Lady Kwannon in my prayer, 'and you'll be surprised at the wonderful offerings poor old Sanjo will bring to your altar.'" And smiting her forehead with her hand, she began again to pray with immense fervor. "Well," said Ukon, astonished by this extraordinary speech. "You *have* become a regular countrywoman; there's no doubt about it. Don't you know that Madam is To no Chujo's own daughter? That's enough in itself; but now that Prince Genji, who for her mother's sake, would do anything for her, has come into his own again, do you suppose there is any gentleman in the land who would be too good for her? It would be a sad come-down indeed if she were to become some paltry Governor's wife!" But Sanjo was not thus to be put out of countenance. "Pardon me," she said hotly; "I don't know much about your Prince Genjis or such-like. But I do know that I've seen the Lord-Lieutenant's wife and all her train on their way to the temple of Our Lady Kwannon at Kiyomizu, and I can tell you the Emperor himself never rode out in such state! So don't try to put *me* in my place!" and unabashed the old woman resumed her attitude of prayer.

The party from Tsukushi had arranged to stay three days within the precincts of the temple, and Ukon, though she had not at first intended to stay for so long, now sent for her favorite priest and asked him to procure her a lodging; for she hoped that these days of Retreat would afford her a chance of talking things over quietly with the old nurse. The priest knew by long experience just what she wanted written on the prayer-strips which he was to place in the holy lamps, and at once began scribbling "On behalf of Lady Fujiwara no Ruri I make these offerings and burn..." "That is quite right," said Ukon (for Fujiwara no Ruri was the false name by which she had always referred to Tamakatsura in discussing the matter with her spiritual adviser); "all the usual texts will do, but I want you to pray harder than ever today. For I have at last been fortunate enough to meet the young lady and am more anxious than ever that my prayer for her happiness may be fulfilled."

---

* Of Tsukushi.

"There!" said the priest triumphantly. "Was there ever a clearer case? Met her? Dear Madam, of course you have. That is just what I have been praying for night and day ever since you were here last." And much encouraged by this success he set to work once more and was hard at it till daylight came. Then the whole party, at Ukon's invitation, moved to the lodgings that her *daitoko** had reserved for her. Here if anywhere she felt that she would be able to embark upon the story which she found so difficult to tell.

At last she was able to have a good look at the child for whose happiness she had prayed during so many years. Tamakatsura was undeniably ill-dressed and somewhat embarrassed in the presence of strangers whom she felt to be taking stock of her appearance; but Ukon was unfeignedly delighted with her, and burst out: "Though I am sure I never had any right to expect it, it so happens that I have had the good luck to see as much of fine ladies and gentlemen as any serving-woman in the City. There's Prince Genji's own lady, Madam Murasaki—I see her nearly every day. What a handsome young thing! I thought there could be no one to compare with her. But now there's this little daughter from Akashi.† Of course she is only a child at present. But she grows prettier every day, and it would not surprise me if in the end she put all our other young ladies to shame. Of course they dress that child in such fine clothes and make such a fuss of her that it is hard to compare her with other children. Whereas our young lady (she whispered to the nurse), dressed as she is at this very minute, would hold her own against any of them, I dare swear she would. I have sometimes heard Prince Genji himself say that of the many beauties whom he has known, whether at Court or elsewhere since his father's time, the present Emperor's mother‡ and the little girl born at Akashi stand apart from all the rest. Not one other has he known of whom you could say without fear of contradiction from any living soul that she was perfection itself from tip to toe. Those were his words; but for my own part I never knew Lady Fujitsubo; and charming though the little princess from Akashi may be, she is still little more than a baby, and when Prince Genji speaks of her in these terms, he is but guessing at the future. He did not mention Lady Murasaki at all in this conversation, but I know quite well that in his heart of hearts he puts her above all the rest—so far indeed that he would never dream of mentioning her in such a reckoning as this; and, great gentleman though he is, I have heard him tell her again and again that she deserves a husband a thousand times better than he. I have often thought that

---

* I hesitate to use the word "Confessor."

† Now about six years old.

‡ Fujitsubo.

having had about him at the start such peerless ladies as those whom I have mentioned, he might well chance to end his days without once finding their like. But now I see that I was wrong; for Madam here is fully their match. Trust me, I shall not say anything high-flown, nor would he listen to fine phrases such as 'The light that shines from her countenance is brighter than Buddha's golden rays.' I shall just say 'See her, and you will not be disappointed.'" So said Ukon, smiling benevolently at the company. But the nurse, who knew nothing, it must be remembered, of Genji's connection with Yugao nor of any reason why he should interest himself in Tamakatsura, was somewhat disconcerted. "I am sure I thank you very heartily for suggesting this," she said; "and indeed you will believe that no one cares more for this young lady's future than I do, when I tell you that I gave up house and hearth, quitted sons, daughters and friends, and came back to the City which is now as strange to me as some foreign town—all this only for Lady Tamakatsura's sake; for I hated to see her wasting her youth in a dismal place where there was not a soul for her to speak to... No indeed! I should be the last person to interfere with any plan that promises to bring her to her own again; and I am sure that among the grand people whom you have mentioned she would have a much better chance of doing something for herself in the world... But I must say that, with her father at Court all the while, it seems to me a queer thing to quarter her on a perfect stranger. Perhaps I do not quite understand what you propose... but wouldn't it be more natural to tell her father that she is here and give him a chance of acknowledging her? That is what we have been trying to do, and we shall be very glad if you would help us." The conversation was overheard by Tamakatsura; she felt very uncomfortable at being thus publicly discussed and, shifting impatiently in her seat, sat with her back to the talkers. "I see you think I am taking too much upon myself," said Ukon. "I know quite well that I am no one at all. But all the same Prince Genji often sends for me to wait upon him and likes me sometimes to tell him about anything interesting that I have seen or heard. On one occasion I told him the story of Madam here—how she had been left motherless and carried off to some distant province (for so much I had heard). His Highness was much moved by the story, begged me to make further enquiries and at once let him know all that I could discover..." "I do not doubt," said the nurse, "that Prince Genji is a very fine gentleman. But it seems from what you tell me that he has a wife of whom he is fond and several other ladies living with him as well. He may for the moment have been interested in your story; but I cannot imagine why you should suppose he wants to adopt her, when her own father is so close at hand. It would oblige me if you would first help us to inform To no Chujo of Madam's arrival. If nothing comes of that..."

Ukon could keep up her end no longer. Unless she told the nurse of Genji's connection with Yugao, further conversation would be impossible. And having got so far as to confess that Genji had known Yugao, Ukon plunging desperately on finally managed to tell the whole terrible story. "Do not think," she said at last, "that Genji has forgotten all this, or will ever do so. It has been his one desire since that day to find some means of expiating, in however small a degree, the guilt which brought my lady to her unhappy end; and often I have heard him long that he might one day be able to bring such happiness to Lady Yugao's child as would in some sort make amends for all that she had lost. Indeed, having few children, he has always planned, if she could but be found, to adopt her as his own, and he begged me to speak of her always as a child of his, whom he had placed with country folk to be nursed.

"But in those days I had seen very little of the world and was so much scared by all that had happened that I dared not go about making enquiries. At last I chanced one day to see your husband's name in a list of provincial clerks. I even saw him, though at some distance, the day he went to the Prime Minister's palace to receive confirmation of his new appointment. I suppose I ought to have spoken to him then; but somehow or other I could not bring myself to do so. Sometimes I imagined that you had left Lady Tamakatsura behind, at the house in the Fifth Ward; for the thought of her being brought up as a little peasant girl on the island was more than I could endure..."

So they spent the day, now talking, now praying, or again amusing themselves by watching the hordes of pilgrims who were constantly arriving at the temple gate. Under their windows ran a river called the Hatsuse, and Ukon now recited the acrostic poem: "Had I not entered the gate that the Twin Fir-Trees guard, would the old river of our days e'er have resumed its flow?" To this Tamakatsura answered: "Little knew I of those early days as this river knows of the hill from whence it sprang." She sat gently weeping. But Ukon made no effort to comfort her, feeling that now all was on the right path. Considering Tamakatsura's upbringing no one would have blamed her if there had been a little country roughness, a shade of over-simplicity in her manner. Ukon could not imagine how the old nurse had achieved so remarkable a feat of education, and thanked her again and again for what she had done. Yugao's ways had till the last been timid, docile, almost child-like; but about her daughter there was not a trace of all this. Tamakatsura, despite her shyness, had an air of self-assurance, even of authority. "Perhaps," thought Ukon to herself, "Tsukushi is not by any means so barbarous a place as one is led to suppose." She began thinking of all the Tsukushi people she had known; each individual she could recall was more coarse-mannered and uneducated than the rest. No, nurse's achievement remained a mystery.

At dusk they all went back to the temple, where they stayed that night and most of the following day, absorbed in various spiritual exercises. A cold autumn wind was blowing from the valley, and at its cruel touch the miseries of the past rose up one by one before Shoni's widow as she knelt shivering at the Main Altar. But all these sad memories vanished instantly at the thought that the child upon whom she had lavished her care would now take the place that was her birth-due. Ukon had told her about the careers of To no Chujo's other children. They seemed all of them to be remarkably prosperous, irrespective of the rank of their various mothers, and this filled the old lady with an additional sense of security.

At last the moment came to part. The two women exchanged addresses and set out upon their different ways: Ukon to a little house Genji had given her, not far away from his new palace; the others to their lodgings in the Ninth Ward. No sooner had they parted than Ukon was suddenly seized with a panic lest Tamakatsura should attempt to evade her, as Yugao had fled from Chujo in days of old; and constantly running between her house and theirs, she had not a moment's peace of mind. It was soon time for Ukon to be back at the new palace, and she was not loath to end her holiday, for she was in a hurry to obtain an interview with Genji and inform him of her success. She could not get used to this new mansion, and from the moment she entered the gates she was always astonished by the vastness of the place. Yet so great was nowadays the number of coaches driving* in and out, that the crush was appalling and Ukon began to wonder if she would ever get to the house.

She was not sent for that night, and lay tossing about on her bed, thinking how best to make known her discovery. Next day, though it so happened that a large number of ladies-in-waiting and other young people had just returned from their holidays, Murasaki sent specially for old Ukon, who was delighted by this compliment. "What a long holiday you have been having!" cried Genji to her when she entered. "When you were last here you looked like some dismal old widow-lady, and here you are looking quite skittish! Something very nice must have happened to you; what was it?" "Sir," she answered, "it is quite true that I have been away from the City for a whole week; but I don't know whether anything has happened that you would call nice. I have been over the hills to Hatsuse (on foot too!) and came across someone whom I was glad to meet again." "Who was that?" asked Genji quickly, and she was about to tell him when it occurred to her that it would be much better to tell him separately, on some occasion when Murasaki was not present. But then perhaps the whole thing would come round to Murasaki's ears and her mistress would be offended that Ukon had not told her first...

---

* Pulled by servants, the oxen being unyoked at the Gate.

It was a difficult situation. "Well then if you must know..." Ukon was beginning, when suddenly there was a fresh incursion of visitors, and she was obliged to withdraw. But later in the day, when the great lamp had been brought in and Genji was sitting quietly with Murasaki, he said that he would soon be ready for bed, and sent for Ukon to give him his evening massage.

Lady Murasaki was now almost twenty-eight, but never (thought the old woman when she arrived) had she looked so handsome. It seemed indeed as though her full charm had only just matured. Ukon had not seen her mistress at close quarters for some months past, and could now have sworn that even in that short space of time Lady Murasaki had grown twice as handsome. And yet Ukon had no fears for Yugao's daughter. There was indeed an undeniable difference between this splendid princess and the shy girl from Tsukushi. But it was only the difference between obscurity and success; a single turn of fortune would quickly redress the balance.

"I do not like being massaged by the new young maids," Genji said to Ukon when she arrived. "They let me see so plainly how much it bores them to do it. I much prefer someone I have known for a long time... you, for example." No such preference had ever been noticed by those about him, and smiles were secretly exchanged. They realized that Genji had only said this in order to please and flatter the old lady. But it was far from true that any of them had ever been otherwise than delighted at the reception of such a command, and they thought the joke rather a tiresome one. "Would you be angry with me if I took to consorting with elderly ladies?" he whispered to Murasaki. "Yes," she nodded, "I think I should. With you one never knows where one is. I should be very much perturbed..." All the while she was at work Genji amused the old lady with his talk. Never had Ukon seen him so lively and amiable. He had now placed the whole direction of public affairs in To no Chujo's hands; the experiment was working well, and such was Genji's relief at escaping from the burden which had so long oppressed him that he found it impossible to be serious for a minute. To joke with Ukon, a very matter-of-fact old lady, was found by most people to be out of the question. But Genji had a peculiar gift of sympathy, which enabled him to penetrate the most obstinate gloom, the most imperturbable gravity.

"Tell me about the interesting person whom you have discovered," he went on. "I believe it is another of your holy men. You have brought him back here, and now I am to let him pray for me. Have I not guessed right?" "No, indeed," Ukon answered indignantly; "I should never dream of doing such a thing!" And then, lowering her voice: "I have become acquainted with the daughter of a lady whom I served long ago... The mother came to a miserable end... You will know of whom it is I am speaking." "Yes," said Genji... "I know well enough, and your news is indeed very different from anything I had imagined. Where has the child been during all these years?" "In the country," answered Ukon vaguely; this did not seem a good moment for going into the whole story. "Some of the old servants took charge of the child," she continued, "and are still in her service now that she has grown up. They of course knew nothing of the circumstances under which their former mistress... It was torture to speak of it; but I managed at last to tell them..." "I think we had better talk about this some other time," Genji interrupted, drawing Ukon aside. But Murasaki had overheard them. "Pray do not trouble about me," she said with a yawn. "I am half-asleep in any case; and if it is something I am not to hear..." So saying she covered her ears with her sleeves.

"Is she as handsome as her mother?" Genji then asked. "I did not at all expect that she would be," answered Ukon. "But I must say that I have seldom seen..." "I am sure she is *pretty,*" he said. "I wonder whether you mean anything more than that. Compared with my lady...?" and he nodded towards Lady Murasaki. "No, indeed," said Ukon hastily; "that would be going too far..." "Come," he said, "it would not be going much farther than you go yourself. I can see that by your face. For my part, I must own to the usual vanity of parents. I hope that I shall be able to see in her some slight resemblance to myself." He said this because he intended to pass off the girl as his own child, and was afraid that part of the conversation had been overheard. Having learnt so much, he could not resist the temptation to hear the whole of Ukon's story, and presently he took her into a side-room, where they could discuss the matter undisturbed. "Well," he said, when Ukon had satisfied his curiosity, "I have quite made up my mind what to do with her. She shall come and live with me here. For years past I have constantly wondered what had become of her, and dreaded lest she should be throwing away her youth in some dismal, unfrequented place. I am delighted indeed that you have rediscovered her. My only misgiving concerns her father. I suppose I ought at once to tell him of her return. But I do not quite see how to set about it; for he knows nothing of my connection with Lady Yugao, and I have never been able to see that there was any use in enlightening him. He has already more children than he knows what to do with, and the arrival in his house of a fully-grown girl, whom he has not set eyes on since she was a child-in-arms, would merely be a nuisance to him. It seems much simpler that I, who have so small a family, should take charge of her; and it is easy enough to give out that she is a daughter of mine, whom I have been educating in the quiet of the country. If what you say of her is true, it is certain that she will be a great deal run after. The charge of such a girl needs immense tact and care; I do not think it would be fair to saddle To no Chujo with so great a responsibility." "That shall be as Your Highness decides," answered Ukon. "I am sure, at any rate, that *if you* do not tell To no Chujo, no one else will. And for my part I had rather she should go to you than to anyone else. For I am certain you are anxious to make what amends you can for your part in leading Yugao to her miserable fate; and what better way could there be to do this, than by promoting her daughter's happiness by every means in your power?" "The fact that I ruined the mother might to some people seem a strange reason for claiming custody of the child," said Genji smiling; but his eyes were filled with tears. "My love for her still fills a great part of my thoughts," he said after a pause. "You must think that a strange thing for me to say, considering how my household is now arranged... And it is true that in the years since her death I have formed many deep attachments. But, believe it or not as you will, by no one has my heart ever been stirred as it was by your dear mistress in those far-off days. You have known me long enough to see for yourself that I am not one in whom such feelings lightly come and go. It has been an unspeakable comfort to me during all these years that to you at least I could sometimes talk of your mistress, sometimes ease my longing. But that was not enough. I yearned for some object dear to her upon which I could lavish ceaseless pains and care. What could be more to my purpose than that this orphaned child of hers should thus be entrusted to my protection?"

His next step must be a letter to Tamakatsura herself. He remembered Suyetsumu's extreme incapacity in this direction, and feared that Tamakatsura, after her strange upbringing, might prove to be a hundred times more hesitating and inefficient. It was therefore in order to know the worst as soon as possible that he now lost no time in addressing her. His letter was full of the friendliest assurances; in the margin was written the poem: "It shows not from afar; but seek and you shall find it, the marsh-flower of the Island. For from the ancient stem new shoots forever spring."

Ukon herself was the bearer of this letter; she also reported much of what Genji had said to her, especially such expressions of cordiality and good will as would tend to allay Tamakatsura's apprehensions. He also sent many handsome stuffs and dresses, with presents for her nurse and other members of the party. With Murasaki's consent the Mistress-of-Robes had gone through all the store-cupboards and laid out before him an immense display of costumes, from which he chose those that were most distinctive in color and design, thinking to astonish and delight an eye used to the homespuns of Tsukushi.

Had all this kindness, nay even the smallest part of it, proceeded from her own father, Tamakatsura would indeed have been happy. But to be thus indebted to someone whom she had never seen and upon whom she had not the smallest claim, was an uncomfortable experience. As for taking up residence in his house—the prospect appalled her. But Ukon insisted that such an offer could not be refused; and those about her argued that so soon as she was decently set up in the world, her father would repent of his negligence and speedily lay claim to her. "That a mere nobody like old Ukon should be in a position to do any service at all is in itself a miracle," they said, "and could not have happened were not some God or Buddha on our side. For her to send a message to To no Chujo is, compared with what she has already done, the merest trifle, and so soon as we are all more comfortably settled..." Thus her friends encouraged her. But, whether she accepted his invitation or not, civility demanded that she must at least reply to his poem. She knew that he would regard her cadences and handwriting very critically, expecting something hopelessly countrified and out-of-date. This made the framing of an answer all the more embarrassing. She chose a Chinese paper, very heavily scented. "Some fault there must be in the stem of this marshflower. Else it had not been left unheeded amid the miry meadows by the sea." Such was her poem. It was written in rather faint ink and Genji, as he eagerly scanned it, thought the hand lacking in force and decision. But there was breeding and distinction in it, more indeed than he had dared to look for; and on the whole he felt much relieved.

The next thing was to decide in what part of the house she was to live. In Murasaki's southern wing there was not a room to spare. The Empress Akikonomu was obliged by her rank to live in considerable state. Etiquette forbade that she should ever appear without a numerous train of followers, and her suite had been designed to accommodate an almost indefinite number of gentlewomen. There was plenty of room for Tamakatsura here; but in such quarters she would tend to become lost amid the horde of Akikonomu's gentlewomen, and to put her in such a place at all would indeed seem as though he expected her to assist in waiting upon the Empress. The only considerable free space in the house was the wing which he had built to contain his official papers. These had for the most part been handed over to To no Chujo, and what was still left could easily be housed elsewhere. The advantage of those quarters was that Tamakatsura would here be the close neighbor of the Lady from the Village of Falling Flowers, whose sensible and affectionate nature would, he was sure, prove a great comfort to the new arrival. And now that all was ready, it seemed to him impossible to install Tamakatsura in his household without revealing to Murasaki the whole truth about the girl's identity and his own dealings with her mother. No sooner had he begun the story than he saw plainly enough that she was vexed with him for having made a mystery of the matter for so long. "I see that you are vexed," he said, "that I did not tell you about all this before, But you have always known quite well that I had many such attachments as this in the days before I knew you, and I have never seen that there was any point in mentioning them, unless some special circumstance made it necessary to do so. In the present case, it is essential that someone should be acquainted with all the facts, and I chose you rather than another merely because you are a thousand times dearer to me than any of the rest." Then he told her the whole story of his dealings with Yugao. It was apparent to her that he was deeply moved, and at the same time that he took great pleasure in recalling every detail of their relationship. "Conversation turns often upon such matters," he said at last, "and I have heard innumerable stories of women's blind devotion, even in cases where their love was in no degree reciprocated. Passion such as this is indeed rarely long withstood even by those who have gravely determined to rule out of their lives every species of romance; and I have seen many who have instantly succumbed. But such love as Yugao's, such utter self-forgetfullness, so complete a surrender of the whole being to one single and ever-present emotion—I have never seen or heard of, and were she alive she would certainly be occupying no less important a place in my palace than, for example, the Lady of Akashi is occupying today... In many ways, of course, she fell short of perfection, as indeed is bound to be the case. She was not of great intelligence, nor was her beauty flawless. But she was a singularly lovable creature..." "Were she as much in your good graces as the Lady of Akashi, she would have nothing to complain of..." broke in Murasaki suddenly; for the Akashi episode still rankled sore. The little princess,[*] who constantly visited Murasaki's rooms, was playing with her toys not far away, and Murasaki seeing her look so innocent and pretty, in her childlessness forgave Genji the infidelity which had brought to her so charming a little playmate and companion.

These things happened in the ninth month; but Tamakatsura's actual arrival could not take place for some while afterwards, for though her quarters had been chosen she still lacked attendants. The first thing was to find her some pretty pages and serving-girls. Even in Tsukushi the old nurse had managed to procure some very passable children to wait upon her; for it sometimes happened that someone from the City, having fallen upon evil days, would get stranded on the Island and be glad to place his boy or girl in a respectable home. But in the sudden flight from Tsukushi all these young people had been left behind. Orders were given to market-women and trades-people to keep their eyes open and report upon any suitable children whom they came across; and in this way, as could scarcely fail to happen in so vast a town, a fine batch of attendants was quickly brought together. Nothing was said to them about Tamakatsura's rank, and they were mustered in Ukon's own house,

---

[*] The Lady of Akashi's daughter.

whither Tamakatsura herself now repaired, that her wardrobe might be finally inspected, her staff fitted out with proper costumes and instructed in their duties. The move to Genji's Palace took place in the tenth month. He had already visited the Lady from the Village of Falling Flowers and prepared her for the arrival of her new neighbors: "A lady to whom I was much attached, being seized with a sudden melancholy, fled from the Court and soon afterwards ended her days in a remote country place. She left behind a daughter, of whom I could for years obtain no news. All this happened many years ago and this daughter is now of course a full-grown woman; but though I have been making enquiries ever since, it was only quite recently (and in the most accidental way) that I at last obtained a clue. I at once determined to invite her to my palace, and I am going to give her quarters close to yours, in the unused Record Office. To one motherless child of mine you have already shown infinite kindness, and have not, I think, found the care of him unduly irksome. If you will do for this newcomer what you have been doing for Prince Yugiri, I shall be deeply thankful to you. She has been brought up in very humble and rustic surroundings. In many ways she must be ill-prepared for the life which she will lead in such a place as this. I hope that you will instruct her..." and he made many suggestions for Tamakatsura's polite education. "I had no idea," the Lady replied, "that you had more than one daughter. However, I am extremely glad, if only for the Akashi child's sake. I am sure she will be delighted to find that she has a sister..." "The mother," said Genji, "was the most gentle and confiding creature I have ever encountered. This girl, Lady Tamakatsura, doubtless resembles her; and since you yourself are the easiest person to get on with..." "I have so much time on my hands," she answered quickly. "Someone of my own sort to look after and advise a little... That is just what I long for."

Genji's own servants and retainers had been told nothing save that a strange lady was shortly to arrive. "I wonder whom he has picked up this time?" one of them said. "I don't believe this is a fresh affair," said another. "In all probability she is only some discarded mistress who needs looking after for a time..."

The party arrived in three carriages. As Ukon had superintended every detail, the whole turn-out was quite adequately stylish, or at any rate did not betray such rusticity as to attract attention. On their arrival they found their quarters stacked with all sorts of presents from Genji. He gave them time to settle in, and did not call till late the same night. Long, long ago Tamakatsura used often to hear him spoken of in terms of extravagant admiration; "Genji the Shining One," that was what people had called him. All the rest she had forgotten; for hers had been a life from which tales of Courts and palaces seemed so remote that she had scarcely heeded them. And now when through a chink in her curtains-of-state she caught a glimpse of him—vague enough, for the room was lit only by the far distant rays of the great lamp beyond the partition—her feeling was one of admiration, but (could it be so, she asked herself) of downright terror.

Ukon had flung open both halves of the heavy main door and was now obsequiously ushering him into the room. "You should not have done that," he protested. "You are making too much of my entry. No such ceremonies are necessary when one inmate of this house takes it into his head to visit another," and he seated himself alongside her curtained chair. "This dim light too," he continued, addressing Ukon, "may seem to you very romantic. But Lady Tamakatsura has consented to make believe that she is my daughter, and family meetings such as this require a better illumination. Do you not agree?" And with this he slightly raised one corner of her curtain. She looked extremely shy and was sitting, as he now discovered, with face half-turned away. But he knew at once that as far as looks were concerned she was not going to cause him any anxiety. "Could we not have a little more light?" he said, turning again to Ukon. "It is so irritating..." Ukon lit a candle and came towards them holding it aloft in her hand. "It is rather heavy work to get started!" he whispered, smiling. "Things will go better presently." Even the way she hung her head, as though frightened of meeting his eyes, reminded him so vividly of Yugao that it was impossible for him to treat her as a stranger; instinctively indeed he began to speak to her in a tone of complete familiarity as though they had shared the same house all their lives: "I have been hunting high and low for you ever since you were a baby," he said, "and now that I have found you, and see you sitting there with a look that I know so well, it is more than I can bear. I wanted so much to talk to you, but now..." and he paused to wipe the tears from his eyes, whilst there rushed to his mind a thousand tender recollections of Yugao and her incomparable ways. "I doubt," he said at last, reckoning up the years since her death, "whether true parent has ever reclaimed a child after so long a search as I have made for you. Indeed so long a time has passed that you are already a woman of judgment and experience, and can tell me a far more interesting story of all that has befallen you on that island of yours than could be told by a mere child. I have that compensation at least for having met you so late..."

What would she tell him? For a long while she hung her head in silence. At last she said shyly: "Pray remember that like the leech-child,* at three years old I was set adrift upon the ocean. Since then I have been stranded in a place where only such things could befall me as to

---

* The Royal Gods Izanagi and Izanami bore a leech-child; as at the age of three it could not stand, they cast it adrift in a boat. It made a song which said: "I should have thought my daddy and mammy would have been sorry for me, seeing that at three years old I could not stand." See Part II, p. 281.

you would seem nothing at all." Her voice died away at the end of the sentence with a half-childish murmur, exactly as her mother's had done long ago, "I was 'sorry for you' indeed," he said, "when I heard whither you had drifted. But I am going to see to it now that no one shall ever be sorry for you again." She said no more that night; but her one short reply had convinced him that she was by no means a nonentity, and he went back to his own quarters feeling confident that there could be no difficulty in launching her upon a suitable career. "Poor Tamakasura has lived in the country for so long," he said to Murasaki later, "that it would not at all have surprised me to find her very boorish, and I was prepared to make every allowance... But on the contrary she seems very well able to hold her own. It will be amusing to watch the effect upon our friends when it becomes known that this girl is living in the house. I can well imagine the flutter into which she will put some of them—my half-brother Prince Sochi no Miya for example. The reason that quite lively and amusing people often look so gloomy when they come here is that there have been no attractions of this kind. We must make as much play with her as possible; it will be such fun to see which of our acquaintances become brisker, and which remain as solemn as ever." "You are certainly the strangest 'father'!" exclaimed Murasaki. The first thing you think of is how to use her as a bait to the more unprincipled among your friends. It is monstrous!" "If only I had thought of it in time," he laughed, "I see now how splendidly you would have served for the same purpose. It was silly of me not to think of it; but, somehow or other, I preferred to keep you all to myself." She flushed slightly as he said this, looking younger and more charming than ever. Sending for his ink-stone Genji now wrote on a slip the poem: "Save that both she and I have common cause to mourn, my own is she no more than a false lock worn upon an aged head."* Seeing him sigh heavily and go about muttering to himself, Murasaki knew that his love for Yugao had been no mere boyish fancy, but an affair that had stirred his nature to its depths.

Yugiri, having been told that a half-sister (of whose existence he had never heard) was come to live with them in the palace, and that he ought to make friends with her and make her feel at home, at once rushed round to her rooms, saying: "I do not count for very much, I know, but since we are brother and sister, I think you might have sent for me before. If only I had known who you were, I would have been so glad to help you to unpack your things. I do think you might have told me..." "Poor young gentleman," thought Ukon, who was close at hand; "this is really too bad. How long will they let him go on in this style, thinking all the while she is his sister? I don't think it's fair..."

---

* *Tarnakazura* = jeweled wig.

The contrast between her present way of life and the days at Tsukushi was staggering. Here every elegance, every convenience appeared as though by magic; there the simplest articles could be procured only by endless contriving, and when found were soiled, dilapidated, out-of-date. Here Prince Genji claimed her as his daughter, Prince Yugiri as his sister... "Now these," thought old Sanjo, "really are fine gentlemen. However I came to have such a high opinion of that Lord-Lieutenant I do not know!" And when she remembered what airs a miserable creature like Tayu had given himself on the Island, she almost expired with indignation.

That Bugo no Suke had acted with rare courage and wisdom in planning the sudden flight from Tsukushi was readily admitted by Genji when Ukon had laid all the circumstances before him. It was unlikely that any stranger would serve Tamakatsura with such devotion as this foster-brother had shown, and in drawing up for her a list of gentlemen-in-attendance, Genji saw to it that Bugo no Suke's name should figure among them.

Never in his wildest dreams had it occurred to Bugo no Suke that he, a plain Tsukushi yeoman, would ever set foot in a Minister's palace; nay, would in all his living days so much as set eyes on such a place. And here he was, not merely walking in and out just as he chose, but going with the lords and ladies wherever they went, and even arranging their affairs for them and ordering about their underlings as though they were his own. And to crown his content, no day passed but brought to his mistress some ingenious intention, some well-devised if trifling act of kindness from their host himself.

At the end of the year there took place the usual distribution of stuff for spring clothes, and Genji was determined that the newcomer should not feel that she had come off worse than the greatest ladies in the house. But he feared that, graceful and charming though she was, her taste in dress must necessarily be somewhat rustic, and among the silks which he gave her he determined also to send a certain number of woven dresses, that she might be gently guided towards the fashions of the day. The gentlewomen of the palace, each anxious to prove that there was nothing she did not know about the latest shapes of bodice and kirtle, set to work with such a will that when they brought their wares for Genji's inspection, he exclaimed: "I fear your zeal has been excessive. If all my presents are to be on this scale (and I have no desire to excite jealousy), I shall indeed be hard put to it." So saying he had his storerooms ransacked for fine stuffs; and Murasaki came to the rescue with many of the costly robes which he had from time to time given her for her own wardrobe. All these were now laid out and inspected. Murasaki had a peculiar talent in such matters, and there was not a woman in all the world who chose her dyes with a subtler feeling for color, as Genji very well knew. Dress after dress was now brought in fresh from the beating-room, and Genji would choose some robe now for its marvelous dark red, now for some curious and exciting pattern or blend, and have it laid aside. "This one in the box at the end," he would say, handing some dress to one of the waiting-women who were standing beside the long narrow clothes-boxes; or "Try this one in your box." "You seem to be making a very just division, and I am sure no one ought to feel aggrieved. But, if I may make a suggestion, would it not be better to think whether the stuffs will suit the complexions of their recipient rather than whether they look nice in the box?" "I know just why you said that," Genji laughed. "You want me to launch out into a discussion of each lady's personal charms, in order that you may know in what light she appears to me. I am going to turn the tables. You shall have for your own whichever of my stuffs you like, and by your choice I shall know how *you* regard *yourself.*" "I have not the least idea what I look like," she answered, blushing slightly; "after all, I am the last person in the world to consult upon the subject. One never sees oneself except in the mirror..." After much debating, the presents were distributed as follows: to Murasaki herself, a kirtle yellow without and flowered within, lightly diapered with the red plum-blossom crest—a marvel of modern dyeing. To the Akashi child, a long close-fitting dress, white without, yellow within, the whole seen through an outer facing of shimmering red gauze. To the Lady from the Village of Falling Flowers he gave a light blue robe with a pattern of sea-shells woven into it. Lovely though the dress was as an example of complicated weaving, it would have been too light in tone had it not been covered with a somewhat heavy russet floss.

To Tamakatsura he sent, among other gifts, a close-fitting dress with a pattern of mountain-kerria woven upon a plain red background. Murasaki seemed scarcely to have glanced at it; but all the while, true to Genji's surmise, she was guessing the meaning of this choice. Like her father To no Chujo, Tamakatsura (she conjectured) was doubtless good-looking; but certainly lacked .his liveliness and love of adventure. Murasaki had no idea that she had in any way betrayed what was going on in her mind and was surprised when Genji suddenly said: "In the end this matching of dresses and complexions breaks down entirely and one gives almost at hazard. I can never find anything that does justice to my handsome friends, or anything that it does not seem a shame to waste on the ugly ones... and so saying he glanced with a smile at the present which was about to be dispatched to Suyetsumu, a dress white without and green within, what is called a "willow-weaving," with an elegant Chinese vine-scroll worked upon it.

To the Lady of Akashi he sent a white kirtle with a spray of plum-blossom on it, and birds and butterflies fluttering hither and thither, cut somewhat in the Chinese fashion, with a very handsome dark purple lining. This also caught Murasaki's observant eye and she augured from it that the rival of whom Genji spoke to her so lightly was in reality occupying a considerable place in his thoughts.

To Utsusemi, now turned nun, he sent a grey cloak, and, in addition, a coat of his own which he knew she would remember—jasmine-sprinkled, faced with Courtier's crimson and lined with russet. In each box was a note in which the recipient was begged to favor him by wearing these garments during the Festival of the New Year. He had taken a great deal of trouble over the business and could not imagine that any of the presents was likely to meet with a very bad reception. And indeed the satisfaction which he had given was soon evidenced not only by the delighted letters which came pouring in, but also by the handsome gratuities given to the bearers of these gifts. Suyetsumu was still living at the old Nijo-in palace, and the messenger who brought her present, having a quite considerable distance to travel, expected something rather out of the ordinary in the way of a reward. But to Suyetsumu these things were matters not of commerce, but of etiquette. A present such as this was, she had been taught long ago, a species of formal address which must be answered in the same language, and fetching an orange-colored gown, very much frayed at the cuffs, she hung it over the messenger's shoulders, attaching to it a letter written on heavily scented Michinoku paper, which age had not only considerably yellowed, but also bloated to twice its proper thickness. "Alas," she wrote, "your present serves but to remind me of your absence. What pleasure can I take in a dress that you will never see me wear?" With this was the poem: "Was ever gift more heartless? Behold, I send it back to you, your Chinese dress—worn but an instant, yet discolored with the brine of tears." The handwriting, with its antique flourishes, was admirably suited to the stilted sentiment of the poem. Genji laughed afresh each time he read it and finally, seeing that Murasaki was regarding him with astonishment, he handed her the missive. Meanwhile he examined the bedraggled old frock with which the discomfited messenger had been entrusted, with so rueful an expression that the fellow edged behind the bystanders and finally slipped out of the room, fearing that he had committed a grave breach of etiquette in introducing so pitiful an object into the presence of the Exalted Ones. His plight was the occasion of much whispering and laughter among his fellow servants. But laugh as one might at the absurd scenes which the princess's archaic behavior invariably provoked, the very fact that adherence to bygone fashions could produce so ludicrous a result suggested the most disquieting reflections. "It is no laughing matter," said Genji. "Her 'Chinese dress' and 'discolored with the brine of tears' made me feel thoroughly uncomfortable. With the writers of a generation or two ago every dress was 'Chinese,' and, no matter what the occasion of the poem, its sleeves were invariably soaked with tears. But what about your poems and mine? Are they not every bit as bad? Our tags may be different from those of the princess; but we use them just as hard and when we come to write a poem are as impervious as she is to the speech of our own day. And this is true not only of amateurs such as ourselves, but of those whose whole reputation depends on their supposed poetical gifts. Think of them at Court festivals, with their eternal *madoi, madoi*.[*] It is a wonder they do not grow tired of the word. A little while ago *adabito* "Faithless one" was used by well-bred lovers in every poem which they exchanged. They declined it ("of the faithless one," "from the faithless one," and so on) in the third line, thus gaining time to think out their final couplet. And so we all go on, poring over nicely stitched *Aids to Song*, and when we have committed a sufficient number of phrases to memory, producing them on the next occasion when they are required. It is not a method which leads to very much variety.

"But if we need a change, how much more does this unfortunate princess whose scruples forbid her to open any book except these old-fashioned collections of standard verse, written on dingy, native paper, to which her father Prince Hitachi introduced her long ago? Apart from these the only other reading which he seems to have permitted her was the *Marrow of Native Song*. Unfortunately this book consists almost entirely of "Faults to be avoided"; its comminations and restrictions have but served to aggravate her natural lack of facility. After such an education as this it is no wonder that her compositions have a well-worn and familiar air."

"You are too severe," said Murasaki, pleading for the princess. "Whatever you may say, she managed this time to send an answer, and promptly too. Pray let me have a copy of her poem that I may show it to the Akashi child. I too used to have such books as the *Marrow of Poesy*, but I do not know what has become of them. Probably bookworms got into them and they were thrown away. I believe that to anyone unfamiliar with the old phrase books Suyetsumu's poem would seem delightfully fanciful and original. Let us try..." "Do nothing of the kind," said Genji. "Her education would be ruined if she began to take an interest in poetry. It is an accepted principle that however great the aptitude which a girl may show for some branch of science or art, she must beware of using it; for there is always a risk that her mind may be unduly diverted from ordinary duties and pursuits. She must know just so much of each subject that it cannot be said she has entirely neglected it. Further than this, she can only go at the risk of undermining the fortress of chastity or diminishing that softness of manner without which no woman can be expected to please."

---

[*] "I go astray."

But all this while he had forgotten that Suyetsumu's letter itself required a reply; indeed, as was pointed out by Murasaki, the princess's poem contained a hidden meaning which might be construed as a direct plea for further consolation. It would have been very unlike him not to have heeded such an appeal, and feeling that the standard she had set was not a very exacting one, he dashed off the following reply: "If heartlessness there be, not mine it is but yours, who speak of sending back the coat that, rightly worn, brings dreams of love."[*]

---

[*] A coat worn inside out brings dreams of one's lover.

The First Song of The Year

WITH the morning of the New Year's* Day began a spell of the most delightful weather. Soft air, bright sunshine, and not a cloud to be seen in the whole sky. In every garden, on the humblest piece of waste ground, young shoots that formed each day a clearer patch of green were pushing up amid the snow; while over the trees hung a mist, stretched there, so it seemed, on purpose that the wonders it was hiding might later come as a surprise. Nor was this pleasant change confined to garden and wood; for men and women also, without knowing why, suddenly felt good-humored and hopeful. It may be imagined then what an enchantment these first spring days, everywhere so delightful, cast upon the gardens of Genji's palace, with their paths of jade-dust, their groves and lakes. It would be impossible here to describe in any way that would not be both tedious and inadequate the beauties of the four domains which Genji had allotted to his favorites. But this I may say, that the Spring Garden,† with its great orchards of fruit trees at this moment far excelled the rest, and even behind her screens-of-state Murasaki breathed an atmosphere that was heavily laden with the scent of plum blossom. Indeed the place was a Heaven upon earth; but a Heaven adapted to human requirements by the addition of numerous comforts and amenities. The Princess‡ from Akashi was still living in Murasaki's apartments. The younger among the gentlewomen-in-waiting had been placed at her disposal; while the older among them, and such as had distinguished themselves in any way, were retained by Murasaki. On the third day they were already gathered together in front of the Mirror Cake§ reciting "for a thousand years may we dwell under thy shadow" and other New Year verses, with a good deal of laughter and scuffling, when Genji's unexpected entry suddenly caused many pairs of hands to fly back into an attitude of prayer. The ladies looked so uncomfortable at having been caught treating the ceremonies of the day with undue levity, that Genji said to them laughing: "Come now, there is no need to take the prayers on our behalf so seriously. I am sure each of you has plenty of things she would like to pray for on her own account. Tell me, all of you, what you most desire in the com-

---

* The year began in the spring. Genji was now thirty-six.
† Murasaki's.
‡ The child born at Akashi.
§ Served on the evening of the third day of the year, with radish and oranges.

ing year, and I will add my prayers to yours." Among these ladies was a certain Chujo,* one of his own gentlewomen, whom he had transferred to Murasaki's service at the time of his exile. She knew well enough, poor lady, what thing *she* most desired. But she only said: "I tried just now to think of something to pray for on my own account; but it ended by my saying the prayer: 'May he endure long as the Mountain of Kagami in the country of Omi.'"†

The morning had been occupied in receiving a host of New Year visitors; but now Genji thought he would call upon the various inhabitants of his palace, to give them his good wishes and see how they looked in their New Year clothes. "Your ladies," he said to Murasaki, "do not seem to take these proceedings seriously. I found them romping together, instead of saying their prayers. You and I will have to hold a service of our own." So saying he recited the prayer, not without certain additions which showed that he took the business only a trifle more seriously than the ladies whom he had just criticized. He then handed her the poem: "May the course of our love be clear as the waters of yonder lake, from which, in the spring sunshine, the last clot of ice has melted away." To this she answered: "On the bright mirror of these waters I see stretched out the cloudless years love holds for us in store." Then (as how many times before!) Genji began telling her that, whatever was reported of him or whatever she herself observed, she need never have any anxiety. And he protested, in the most violent and impressive terms, that his passion for her underlay all that he felt or did, and could not be altered by any passing interest or fancy. She was for the moment convinced, and accepted his protestations ungrudgingly.

Besides being the third of the year it was also the Day of the Rat‡ and therefore as fine an occasion for prayers and resolutions as could possibly have been found.

His next visit was to the little girl from Akashi. He found her maids and page-boys playing New Year games on the mound in front of her windows, and pulling up the dwarf pine-trees, an occupation in which they seemed to take a boundless delight. The little princess's rooms were full of sweetmeat boxes and hampers, all of them presents from her mother. To one toy, a little nightingale perched upon a sprig of the five-leaved pine, was fastened a plaintive message: "In *my* home the nightingale's voice I never hear,..."§ and with it the poem:

---

* She had always been in love with Genji.
† Kagami = "Mirror."
‡ The first of the cyclical signs.
§ You are silent as this toy bird and send me no New Year greetings.

> O nightingale, to one that many months,
> While strangers heard you sing,
> Has waited for your voice, grudge not today
> The first song of the year!

Genji read the poem and was touched by it; for he knew that only under the stress of great emotion would she have allowed this note of sadness to tinge a New Year poem. "Come, little nightingale!" he said to the child, "you must make haste with your answer; it would be heartless indeed if in the quarter whence these pretty things come you were ungenerous with your springtime notes!" and taking his own ink-stone from a servant who was standing by, he prepared it for her and made her write. She looked so charming while she did this that he found himself envying those who spent all day in attendance upon her, and he felt that to have deprived the Lady of Akashi year after year of so great a joy was a crime for which he would never be able to forgive himself. He looked to see what she had written. "Though years be spent asunder, not lightly can the nightingale forget the tree where first it nested and was taught to sing." The flatness of the verse had at least this much to recommend it—the mother would know for certain that the poem had been written without grown-up assistance!

The Summer Quarters* were not looking their best; indeed at this time of year they could hardly be expected not to wear a somewhat uninteresting air. As he looked about him he could see no object that was evidence of any very pronounced taste or proclivity; the arrangements betokened, rather, a general discrimination and good breeding. For many years past his affection for her had remained at exactly the same pitch, never flagging in the slightest degree, and at the same time never tempting him to the extremer forms of intimacy. In this way there had long ago grown up between them a relationship far more steady and harmonious than can ever exist between those who are lovers in the stricter sense of the term. This morning he spoke to her for a while from behind her curtains-of-state. But presently he cautiously raised a corner of one curtain, and he looked in. How little she had changed! But he was sorry to see that the New Year's dress he had given her was not a great success. Her hair had of late years grown much less abundant, and in order to maintain the same style of coiffure, she had been obliged to supplement it by false locks. To these Genji had long ago grown accustomed. But he now began trying to imagine how she appeared to other people, and saw at once that to them she must seem a very homely, middle-aged person indeed. So much the better, then, that he who loved her had this strange power of seeing her

---

* Allotted to the Lady from the Village of Falling Flowers.

as she used to be, rather than as she was now. And she on her side—what if she should one day grow weary of him, as women often did of those who gave them so little as he had done!

Such were the reflections that passed through Genji's mind while he sat with her. "We are both singularly fortunate," he concluded to himself. "I, in my capacity for self-delusion; she in hers for good-tempered acceptance of whatever comes her way." They talked for a long while, chiefly of old times, till at last he found that he ought to be on his way to the western wing.

Considering the short time that Tamakatsura had been in residence she had made things look uncommonly nice. The number and smartness of her maids gave the place an air of great animation. The large and indispensable articles of furniture had all arrived; but many of the smaller fittings were not yet complete. This was in a way an advantage; for it gave to her rooms a look of spaciousness and simplicity which had a peculiar charm. But it was the mistress of these apartments who, when she suddenly appeared upon the scene, positively confounded him by her beauty. How perfectly she wore that long, close-fitting robe, with its pattern of mountain-kerria! Here, he thought, contrasting her inevitably with the lady to whom he had just said farewell, here was nothing that it might be dangerous to scrutinize, nothing that kindness bade him condone; but radiance, freshness, dazzling youth from tip to toe. Her hair was somewhat thinned out at the ends, in pursuance, perhaps, of some vow made during the days of her tribulation; and this gave to her movements an ease and freedom which strangely accorded with the bareness of her quarters. Had he chosen any but his present role,[*] he would not now be watching her flit unconstrainedly hither and thither across her room... She, however, having by this time grown used to his informal visits, enjoyed his company to the full and would even have had him treat her with a shade less deference... when suddenly she remembered that he was only a make-believe father after all, and then it seemed to her that she had already countenanced far greater liberties than their situation demanded. "For my part," said Genji at last, "I feel as though you had been living with us for years, and am certain that I shall never have cause to repent your coming. But you have not progressed so fast in friendship with the other inmates of my household as I have done in mine with you. I notice you do not visit Lady Murasaki. I am sorry for this, and hope that in future you will make use of her apartments without formality of any sort whenever you feel inclined. You could be of great help to the little girl who lives with her. For example, if you would take charge of her music-lessons... You would find everyone in that quarter most affable and

---

[*] That of father.

forthcoming... Do promise me to try!" "If you wish it," was all she said; but in a voice which indicated that she really meant to obey.

It was already becoming dark when he arrived at the Lady of Akashi's rooms. Through an open door a sudden puff of wind carried straight towards him from her dais a blend of perfumes as exquisite as it was unfamiliar. But where was the Lady herself? For a while he scanned the room in vain. He noticed a writing-case, and near it a great litter of books and papers. On a long flat cushion bordered with Chinese brocade from Lo-yang lay a handsome zithern; while in a brazier which, even in the dim light, he could see to be an object of value and importance, there burned some of that incense which is known as "The Courtier's Favorite." This was the scent which pervaded the whole room and, blending with a strong odor of musk, created the delicious perfume which Genji had noticed when he first turned into the corridor. Coming close enough to examine the papers which lay scattered about the dais, he saw that though there were many experiments in different styles, some of them quite interesting, there were no efforts towards the more extravagant and pretentious forms of cursive. Her child's letter of thanks for the toy bird and tree had already arrived, and it was evident that, in her delight, she had just been copying out a number of classic poems appropriate to such an occasion. But among these was written a poem of her own: "Oh joy untold! The nightingale that, lured by the spring flowers, to distant woods was gone, now to its valley nest again repairs." She had also copied out the old poems: "I waited for thy song" and "Because my house is where the plum tree blooms," and many other snatches and fragments such as were likely to run in the head of one to whom a sudden consolation had come. He took up the papers one by one, sometimes smiling, yet ashamed of himself for doing so. Then he wetted the pen and was just about to write a message of his own, when the Lady of Akashi suddenly appeared from a back room. Despite the splendors by which she was now surrounded she still maintained a certain deference of manner and anxiety to please which marked her as belonging to a different class. Yet there was some thing about the way her very dark hair stood out against the white of her dress, hanging rather flat against it, that strangely attracted him. It was New Year's night. He could not very well absent himself from his own apartments, for there were visitors coming and Murasaki was expecting him...

Yet it was in the Lady of Akashi's rooms that he spent the night, thus causing considerable disappointment in many quarters, but above all in the southern wing, where Murasaki's gentlewomen made bitter comments upon this ill-timed defection.

It was still almost dark when Genji returned, and he persuaded himself that, though he had stayed out late, it could not be said that he had been absent for a night. To the Lady of Akashi, on her side, it seemed that he was suddenly rising to leave her just as the night was beginning. Nevertheless, she was enraptured by his visit. Murasaki would no doubt have sat up waiting for him, and he was quite prepared to find her in rather a bad humor. But one never knows, and in order to find out he said: "I have just had the most uncomfortable doze. It was too childish... I fell asleep in my chair. I wish someone had woken me. It was the most mistaken kindness..." But no! She did not reply, and seeing that for the moment there was no more to be done, he lay back and pretended to be asleep, but as soon as it was broad daylight got up and left the room.

Next day there was a great deal of New Year's entertaining to be done, which was fortunate, for it enabled him to save his face. As usual, almost the whole Court was there—princes, ministers, and noblemen. There was a concert and on Genji's part a grand distribution of trinkets and New Year presents. This party was an occasion of great excitement for the more elderly and undistinguished of the guests; and it may be imagined with what eagerness it was this year awaited by the younger princes and noblemen, who were perpetually on the lookout for adventure and flattered themselves that the new inmate* of Genji's palace was by no means beyond their reach. A gentle evening breeze carried the scent of fruit-blossom into every corner of the house; in particular, most fragrant of all, the plum-trees in Murasaki's garden were now in full bloom. It was at that nameless hour which is neither day nor night: The concert had begun; delicate harmonies of flute and string filled the air, and at last came the swinging measure of "Well may this Hall grow rich and thrive,"† with its animated refrain "Oh, the saki-grass so sweet," in which Genji joined with excellent effect. This indeed was one of his peculiar gifts, that whatever was afoot, whether music, dancing or what not, he had only to join in and everyone else was at once inspired to efforts of which they would not have imagined themselves capable.

Meanwhile the ladies of the household, in the seclusion of their rooms, heard little more than a confused din of horse-hoofs and carriage-wheels, their plight being indeed much like that of the least deserving among the Blest, who though they are reborn in Paradise, receive an unopened lotus-bud as their lodging.‡ But still worse was the position of those who inhabited the old eastern wing; for having once lived at any rate within earshot of such festivities as this, they now saw themselves condemned

---

* Tamakatsura.

† "Well may this house grow rich and thrive —
Oh, the saki-grass, the saki-grass so sweet —
Of the saki-grass, three leaves, four leaves, so trim
Are the walls of this house made."

‡ And consequently cannot see the Buddha nor hear his Word.

to an isolation and lack of employment which every year would increase. Yet though they might almost as well have renounced the Court and ensconced themselves "by mountain paths where Sorrow is unknown," they did nothing of the kind nor, real though their grievances were, did the slightest complaint ever cross their lips. Indeed, save that they were left pretty much to their own devices, they had little else to complain of. They were housed in the utmost comfort and security. Those of them who were religious had at least the certainty that their pious practices would not be interrupted; while those who cared for study had plenty of time to fill a thousand copybooks with native characters. As regards their lodging and equipment, they had only to express a desire for it to be immediately gratified. And sometimes their benefactor actually called upon them, as indeed happened this spring, so soon as the busy days of the New Festival were over.

Suyetsumu was after all the daughter of Prince Hitachi, and as such was entitled to keep up a considerable degree of state. Genji had accordingly provided her with a very ample staff of attendants. Her surroundings indeed were all that could be desired. She herself had changed greatly in recent years. Her hair was now quite grey, and seeing that she was embarrassed by this and was evidently wondering what impression it would make upon him, he at first kept his eyes averted while he spoke to her. His gaze naturally fell upon her dress. He recognized it as that which he had given her for New Year; but it looked very odd, and he was wondering how he had come to give her so unsuitable a garment when he discovered that the fault was entirely that of the wearer. Over it she had put a thin mantle of dull black crepe, unlined, and so stiff that it crackled when she moved. The woven dress which he had given her was meant to wear under a heavy cloak, and naturally in her present garb she was, as he could see, suffering terribly from the cold. He had given her an ample supply of stuff for winter cloaks. What could she have done with it all? But with Suyetsumu nothing seemed to thrive, every stuff became threadbare, every color turned dingy, save that of one bright flower...* But one must keep such things out of one's head; and he firmly replaced the open flap of her curtain.

She was not offended. It was quite enough that year after year he should preserve the same unmistakable signs of affection; for did he not always treat her as an intimate and equal, taking her completely into his confidence and addressing her always in the most informal manner imaginable? If this were not affection, what else could it be?

He meanwhile was thinking what a uniquely depressing and wearisome creature she was, and deciding that he must really make up his mind to

---

* *Hana* = "nose" and "flower."

be a little kinder to her, since it was certain that no one else intended to take the business off his hands.

He noticed that while she talked her teeth positively chattered with cold. He looked at her with consternation. "Is there no one," he asked, "whose business it is to take charge of your wardrobe? It does not seem to me that stiff clumsy over-garments are very well suited to your present surroundings. This cloak of yours, for example. If you cannot do without it, then at any rate be consistent and wear it over a dress of the same description. You cannot get yourself up in one style on top and another underneath." He had never spoken to her so bluntly before, but she only tittered slightly. "My brother Daigo no Azari," she said at last, "promised to look after those warm stuffs for me, and he carried them all off before I had time to make them into dresses. He even took away my sables.* I am so cold without them..." Her brother evidently felt the cold even more than she did, and Genji imagined him with a very red nose indeed. Simplicity was no doubt an engaging quality; but really this lady carried it a little too far. However, with her it was certainly no affectation, and he answered good-humoredly: "As far as those sables are concerned, I am delighted to hear what has become of them. I always thought they were really meant to keep out the rain and snow. Next time your brother goes on a mountain pilgrimage... But there is no need for *you* to shiver. You can have as much of this white material as you like, and there is nothing to prevent your wearing it sevenfold thick, if you find you cannot keep warm. Please always remind me of such promises. If I do not do things at once, I am apt to forget about them. My memory was never very good and I have always needed keeping up to the mark. But now that there are so many conflicting claims upon my time and attention, nothing gets done at all unless I am constantly reminded..." And thinking it safest to act while the matter was still in his mind, he sent a messenger across to the New Palace for a fresh supply of silks and brocades.

The Nijo-in was kept in perfect order and repair; but the fact that it was no longer the main residence somehow or other gave it an air of abandonment and desolation. The gardens, however, were as delightful as ever. The red plum-blossom was at its best, and it seemed a pity that so much beauty and fragrance should be, one might almost say, wasted. He murmured to himself the lines: "To see the springtide to my old home I came, and found within it a rarer flower than any that on orchard twigs was hung!"

She heard the words; but luckily did not grasp the unflattering allusion.†

---

* See Part I, p. 121.
† *Hana* = "flower" and "nose." See above.

He also paid a brief visit to Utsusemi, now turned nun. She had installed herself in apartments so utterly devoid of ornament or personal touches of any kind that they had the character of official waiting-rooms. The only conspicuous object which they contained was a large statue of Buddha, and Genji was lamenting to himself that somber piety, to the exclusion of all other interest, should have possessed so gracious and gentle a spirit, when he noticed that the decoration of her prayer-books, the laying of her altar with its dishes of floating petals—these and many another small sign of elegance seemed to betray a heart that was not yet utterly crushed by the severities of religion. Her blue-grey curtains-of-state showed much taste and care. She sat so far back as scarcely to be seen. But one touch of color stood out amid the gloom; the long sleeves of the gay coat he had sent her showed beneath her mantle of grey, and moved by her acceptance of this token he said with tears in his eyes: "I know that I ought not now even to remember how once I felt towards you. But from the beginning our love brought to us only irritation and misery. It is as well that, if we are to be friends at all, it must now be in a very different way." She too was deeply moved and said at last: "How can I doubt your good will towards me, seeing at what pains you have been to provide for me, protect me... I should be ungrateful indeed..." "I daresay many another lover suffered just as I did," he said, attempting a lighter tone; "and Buddha condemns you to your present life as a penance for all the hearts you have broken. And how the others must have suffered if their experience was anything like mine! Not once but over and over again did I fall in love with you; and those others... There, I knew that I was right. You are thinking, I am sure, of an entanglement beside which our escapade pales into insignificance." His only intention was to divert the conversation from their own relationship, and he was speaking quite at random. But she instantly imagined that he had in some circuitous way got wind of that terrible story...* and blushing she said in a low voice: "Do not remind me of it, The mere fact that you should have been told of it is punishment enough..." and she burst into tears.

He did not know to what she referred. He had imagined that her retirement from the world was merely due to increasing depression and timidity. How was he to converse with her, if every chance remark threw her into a fit of weeping? He had no desire to go away; but he could not think of any light topic upon which to embark, and after a few general enquiries he took his leave. If only it were Lady Suyetsumu who was the nun and he could put Utsusemi in her place! So Genji thought as on his way back he again passed by the red-nosed lady's door. He then paid short visits to the numerous other persons who lived upon his bounty,

---

* Her relations with Ki no Kami, her stepson. See Part II, p. 326.

saying to such of them as he had not seen for some time: "If long intervals sometimes elapse between my visits to you, you must not think that my feelings towards you have changed. On the contrary, I often think what a pity it is that we so seldom meet. For time slips away, and bound up with every deep affection is the fear that Death may take us unawares..." Nor was there anything the least insincere in these speeches; in one way or another he did actually feel very deeply about each of the persons to whom they were made. Unlike most occupants of the exalted position which he now held, Genji was entirely devoid of pomposity and self-importance. Whatever the rank of those whom he was addressing, under whatever circumstances he met them, his manner remained always equally kind and attentive. Indeed, by that thread and that alone hung many of his oldest friendships.

This year there was to be the New Year's mumming.* After performing in the Imperial Palace the dancers were to visit the Suzaku-in† and then come on to Genji's. This meant covering a good deal of ground, and it was already nearing dawn when they arrived. The weather had at first been somewhat uncertain, but at dusk the clouds cleared away, and bright moonlight shone upon those exquisite gardens, now clad in a thin covering of snow. Many of the young courtiers who had recently come into notice showed unusual proficiency on instruments of one kind or another. There were flute-players in abundance, and nowhere that night did they give a more admirable display than when they welcomed the arrival of the mummers in front of Genji's palace. The ladies of the household had been apprised of the ceremony, and they were now assembled in stands which had been set up in the cross-galleries between the central hall and its two wings. The lady of the western side‡ was invited to witness the proceedings in company with the little princess from Akashi, whose windows looked out onto the courtyard where the dancing was to take place. Murasaki was their neighbor, being separated from them only by a curtain. After performing before the ex-Emperor the dancers had been summoned to give a second display in front of Kokiden's apartments. It was consequently even later than had been anticipated when they at last arrived. Before they danced, they had to be served with their "mummers" portions. It was expected that, considering the lateness of the hour, this part of the proceedings, with its curious rites and observances, would be somewhat curtailed. But on the contrary Genji insisted upon its being carried out with even more than the prescribed elaboration. A faint light was showing in the east, the moon was still shining, but it had begun to

---

* A band of young noblemen going round dancing and singing in various parts of the Palace and at the houses of the great on the 14th day of the 1st month. See Part I, p. 126.

† The residence of the ex-Emperor and his mother, Kokiden.

‡ Tamakatsura.

snow again, this time harder than ever. The wind, too, had risen; already the tree-tops were swaying, and it became clear that a violent storm was at hand. There was, in the scene that followed, a strange discrepancy; the delicate pale green cloaks of the mummers, lined with pure white, fluttered lightly, elegantly to the movements of the dance; while around them gathered the gloom and menace of the rising storm. Only the cotton plumes of their headgear, stiff and in a way graceless as they were, seemed to concord with the place and hour. These, as they swayed and nodded in the dance, had a strangely vivid and satisfying beauty.

Among those who sang and played for the dancers Yugiri and To no Chujo's sons took the lead. As daylight came the snow began to clear, and only a few scattered flakes were falling when through the cold air there rose the strains of *Bamboo River.** I should like to describe the movements of this dance—how the dancers suddenly rise on tiptoe and spread their sleeves like wings—and with how delightful an effect voice after voice joins in the lively tune. But it has truly been said that such things are beyond the painter's art; and still less, I suppose, can any depiction of them be expected of a mere storyteller.

The ladies of the household vied with one another in the decoration of their stalls. Gay scarves and favors hung out on every side; while shimmering New Year dresses now dimly discovered behind drawn curtains-of-state, now flashing for a moment into the open as some lady-in-waiting reached forward to adjust a mat or rescue a fan, looked in the dawning light like a meadow of bright flowers "half-curtained by the trailing mists of Spring." Seldom can there have been seen so strange and lovely a sight. There was, too, a remote, barbaric beauty in the high turbans of the dancers, with their stiff festoons of artificial flowers; and when at last they intoned the final prayer, despite the fact that the words were nonsense and the tune apparently a mere jangle of discordant sounds, there was in the whole setting of the performance something so tense, so stirring that these savage cries seemed at the moment more moving than the deliberate harmonics by which the skilled musician coldly seeks to charm our ear.

After the usual distribution of presents, the mummers at last withdrew. It was now broad daylight, and all the guests retired to get a little belated sleep. Genji rose again towards midday. "I believe that Yugiri is going to make every bit as good a musician as Kobai,"† he said, while discussing the scenes of the night before. "I am astonished by the talent of the generation which is now growing to manhood. The ancients no doubt far excelled us in the solid virtues; but our sensibilities are, I venture to assert, far

---

* "In the garden of flowers at the end of the bridge that crosses Bamboo River—in the garden of flowers set me free, with youths and maidens round me."

† To no Chujo's son, famous for the beauty of his voice. See Part II, p. 218.

keener than theirs. I thought at one time that Yugiri was quite different from his companions and counted upon turning him into a good, steady-going man of affairs. My own nature is, I fear, inherently frivolous, and not wishing him to take after me I have been at great pains to implant in him a more serious view of life. But signs are not wanting that under a very correct and solemn exterior he hides a disposition towards just those foibles which have proved my own undoing. If it turns out that his wonderful air of good sense and moderation are mere superficial poses, it will indeed be annoying for us all." So he spoke, but he was in reality feeling extremely pleased with his son. Then, humming the tune* that the mummers sing at the moment when they rise to depart, Genji said: "Seeing all the ladies of the household gathered together here last night has made me think how amazing it would be if we could one day persuade them to give us a concert. It might be a sort of private After Feast."† The rumor of this project soon spread through the palace. On every hand lutes and zitherns were being pulled from out the handsome brocade bags into which they had been so carefully stowed away; and there was such a sprucing, polishing, and tuning as you can scarcely imagine; followed by unremitting practice and the wildest daydreams.

---

* The *Bansuraku* or "Joy of Ten Thousand Springs."
† The After Feast is held in the Emperor's palace.

The Butterflies

Towards the end of the third month, when out in the country the orchards were no longer at their best and the song of the wild birds had lost its first freshness, Murasaki's Spring Garden seemed only to become every day more enchanting. The little wood on the hill beyond the lake, the bridge that joined the two islands, the mossy banks that seemed to grow greener not every day but every hour—could anything have looked more tempting? "If only one could get there!" sighed the young people of the household; and at last Genji decided that there must be boats on the lake. They were built in the Chinese style. Everyone was in such a hurry to get on board that very little time was spent in decorating them, and they were put into use almost as soon as they would float. On the day when they were launched the Water Music was played by musicians summoned from the Imperial Board of Song. The spectacle was witnessed by a large assembly of princes, noblemen, and courtiers, and also by the Empress Akikonomu, who was spending her holidays at the New Palace.

Akikonomu remembered Murasaki's response to her present:[*] it had been tantamount to saying "Do not visit me now, but in the springtime when my garden will be at its best." Genji too was always saying that he wanted to show her the Spring Garden. How simple it would all have been if she could merely have walked across to Murasaki's domain when the fancy seized her, enjoyed herself among the flowers and gone away! But she was now an Empress, an August Being hedged round by sacred statutes and conventions. However, if such liberties were hers no longer, there were in her service many who could enjoy them in her stead, and sending for one of the new boats she filled it with some of the younger and more adventurous of her gentlewomen. It was possible to go by water all the way to the Spring Garden, first rowing along the Southern Lake, then passing through a narrow channel straight towards a toy mountain which seemed to bar all further progress. But in reality there was a way round, and eventually the party found itself at the Fishing Pavilion. Here they picked up Murasaki's ladies, who were waiting at the Pavilion by appointment. The boats were carved with a dragon's head at the prow and painted with the image of an osprey at the stern, completely in the Chinese style; and the boys who manned them were all in Chinese cos-

---

[*] The box of autumn leaves. See above, p. 432.

tume, with their hair tied up with bright ribbons behind. The lake, as they now put out towards the middle of it, seemed immensely large, and those on board, to whom the whole experience was new and deliciously exciting, could hardly believe that they were not heading for some undiscovered land. At last however the rowers brought them close in under the rocky bank of the channel between the two large islands, and on closer examination they discovered to their delight that the shape of every little ledge and crag of stone had been as carefully devised as if a painter had traced them with his brush. Here and there in the distance the topmost boughs of an orchard showed above the mist, so heavily laden with blossom that it looked as though a bright carpet were spread in mid-air. Far away they could just catch sight of Murasaki's apartments, marked by the deeper green of the willow boughs that swept her courtyards, and by the shimmer of her flowering orchards, which even at this distance seemed to shed their fragrance amid the isles and rocks. In the world outside, the cherry-blossom was almost over; but here it seemed to laugh at decay, and round the Palace even the wisteria that ran along the covered alleys and porticos was all in bloom, but not a flower past its best; while here, where the boats were tied, mountain-kerria poured its yellow blossom over the rocky cliffs in a torrent of color that was mirrored in the waters of the lake below. Water-birds of many kinds played in and out among the boats or fluttered hither and thither with tiny twigs or flower sprays in their beaks, and love-birds roamed in pairs, their delicate markings blending, in reflection, with the frilled pattern of the waves. Here, like figures in a picture of fairyland, they spent the day gazing in rapture, and envied the woodman[*] on whose axe green leaves at last appeared.

Many trifling poems were interchanged, such as: "When the wind blows, even the wave-petals, that are no blossoms at all, put on strange colors; for this is the vaunted cape, the Cliff of Kerria-Flowers."[†] And "To the Rapids of Idé[‡] surely the channels of our spring lake must bend; for where else hang the kerria-flowers so thick across the rocks?" Or this: "Never again will I dream of the Mountain[§] on the Tortoise's Back, for here in this boat have I found a magic that shall preserve both me and my name for ever from the onset of mortality." And again: "In the soft spring sunshine even the spray that falls from the rower's oars sinks soft as scattered petals onto the waveless waters of the lake."

So captivated were they by this novel experience that they had soon lost all sense of whither they were faring or whence they had come. It was indeed as though the waters had cast a spell of forgetfulness upon

---

[*] See Part II, p. 350.

[†] Yamabuki no Saki, a place in Omi, referred to in the *Gossamer Diary*.

[‡] A place in Yamashiro, also famous for its kerria-flowers.

[§] Horai, fairyland, the Immortal Island.

their hearts, and when evening came they were still, as it seemed to them, gliding away and away across the lake, to the pleasant strains of the tune called *The Royal Deer*... Suddenly the boats halted, the ladies were invited to go ashore, and to their complete surprise found that they were back again at the Fishing Pavilion.

This place was finished in a manner which combined elegance with extreme simplicity. The rooms were indeed almost bare, and as now the rival parties pressed into them, spreading along the empty galleries and across the wide, deserted floors, there was such an interweaving of gay colors as would have been hard to outdo. The musicians were again called upon, and this time played a sequence of little-known airs which won universal applause. Soon they were joined by a troupe of dancers whom Genji had himself selected, drawing up at the same time a list of pieces which he thought would interest such an audience.

It seemed a pity that darkness should be allowed to interfere with these pleasures, and when night came on, a move was made to the courtyard in front of the Palace. Here flares were lit, and on the mossy lawn at the foot of the Great Steps not only professional musicians, but also various visitors from Court and friends of the family performed on wind and string, while picked teachers of the flute gave a display in the "double mode."* Then all the zitherns and lutes belonging to different members of the household were brought out onto the steps and carefully tuned to the same pitch. A grand concert followed, the piece *Was ever such a day?* being performed with admirable effect. Even the grooms and laborers who were loitering amid the serried ranks of coaches drawn up outside the great gates, little as they usually cared for such things, on this occasion pricked up their ears and were soon listening with lips parted in wonder and delight. For it was indeed impossible that the strange shrill descants of the Spring Mode, enhanced as they were by the unusual beauty of the night, should not move the most impercipient of human creatures.

The concert continued till dawn. As a return-tune† *Gay Springtide Pleasures* was added to the program, and Prince Sochi no Miya carried the vocal music back very pleasantly to the common mode by singing *Green Willows*‡ in the words of which Genji also joined.

Already the morning birds were clamoring in a lusty chorus to which, from behind the curtains, the Empress Akikonomu listened with irritation.

---

* The mode of the second, beginning on alto A. Being so high it was very difficult to play. It symbolized Spring.

† The tune which marked the return from the unusual "Spring" tuning to the ordinary mode.

‡ "With a thread of green from the willow-tree—Ohé
The nightingale has stitched himself a hat—Ohé!
A hat of plum-blossom, they say—Ohé!"

It would have been hard in these days to find a mote in the perfect sunshine of Genji's prosperity and contentment. But it was noticed with regret by his friends, as a circumstance which must of necessity be painful to him, that Murasaki still bore him no child. It was felt, however, that this misfortune was to some extent remedied by the arrival of his handsome natural daughter (for so Tamakatsura was regarded by the world at large). The evident store which Genji himself set by this lady, becoming a matter of common report, together with the tales of her almost unbelievable beauty, soon induced a large number of suitors to seek her hand; which was precisely what he had anticipated. Those of them whose position in life entitled them to confidence had, through suitable channels, already gone so far as to make hints in this direction; while there were doubtless many petty courtiers the flame of whose love burned secretly as a campfire buried under a pile of stones.*

To no Chujo's sons were, of course, like everyone else, under the delusion that she was Genji's child and took a considerable interest in her. But the principal suitor was Genji's half-brother Prince Sochi no Miya. It so happened that he had been a widower for three years; he was tired of this comfortless state of life and had made it clear not only that he considered himself a suitable match for Lady Tamakatsura, but also that he should like the wedding to take place immediately. This morning he was still in a very emotional condition; with a wreath of wisteria flowers about his head, he was indulging in languorous airs which confirmed Genji's previous suspicion that this prince had lately fallen seriously in love. Till now, however, Genji had deliberately pretended not to notice that anything was wrong. When the great tankard was handed round, Prince Sochi said in a doleful voice to Genji: "You know, if I were not so fond of you, I should long ago have left this entertainment. It has been a terrible night for me..." and he recited the poem: "Because my heart is steeped in a dye too near to its own blood,† life do I prize no longer and in the surging stream shall shortly cast myself away." So saying he took the wreath of wisteria from his own head and laid it on Genji's, quoting the poem: "My wreath shall be thine." Genji laughingly accepted it and replied: "Watch by the flowers of spring till the last petal be unfolded; then will be time enough to talk of whirlpools and despair." So saying he caught hold of his brother and held him fast in his seat, promising that if he would but stay, he should today witness a performance far more entertaining than what had gone before.

---

* Lest the enemy should see it.

† He thinks that Tamakatsura is Genji's daughter, and therefore his own niece. Union with a brother's child was ill-viewed. There are numerous puns, which it would be tedious to explain.

It so happened that this day marked the opening of the Empress Akikonomu's Spring Devotions. Most of the visitors, not wishing to miss the ceremonies connected with this occasion, asked leave to stay on, and retiring to the guest-rooms, changed into their morning clothes. A few who had urgent business at home reluctantly withdrew from the Palace; but on returning later they found that they had missed nothing, for it was close upon noon before the actual ceremony began. The visitors reached the Empress's apartments in a long procession, headed by Genji himself. The whole Court was there, and though the magnificence of the occasion was partly due to Akikonomu's own position, it was in large measure a tribute to Genji's influence and popularity. At Murasaki's request an offering of flowers was to be made to the presiding Buddha. They were brought by eight little boys disguised some as birds, some as butterflies. The Birds carried cherry-blossom in silver bowls; the Butterflies, mountain-kerria in golden bowls. They were in reality quite ordinary flowers such as you might find in any country place; but in this setting they seemed to acquire an unearthly glint and splendor. The boys arrived by water, having embarked at the landing-stage in front of Murasaki's rooms. As they landed at the Autumn domain a sudden gust of wind caught the cherry-blossom in the silver bowls and some of it scattered along the bank. The day was cloudless and it was a pretty sight indeed to see the little messengers come out into the sunshine from behind a trailing patch of mist.

It had not been found convenient to set up the regular Musicians' Tent; but a platform had been constructed under the portico that ran in front of the Empress's apartments, and chairs had been borrowed that the musicians might be seated in foreign fashion.* The little boys advanced as far as the foot of the steps, their offerings held aloft in their hands. Here they were met by incense-bearers who conveyed the bowls to the grand altar and adding their contents to that of the holy flower-vessels, pronounced the ritual of dedication. At this point Yugiri arrived, bearing a poem from Murasaki: "Lover of Autumn, whom best it pleases that pine-crickets should chirp amid the withered grass, forgive the butterflies that trespass from my garden of flowers." The Empress smiled. To her own gift of autumn leaves these festive birds and butterflies were the belated response.

Her ladies, who were at first loyal to the season with which their mistress was identified, had been somewhat shaken in their allegiance by yesterday's astonishing excursion and came back assuring the Empress that her preference would not survive a visit to the rival park.

---

* The Japanese, as is well known, squat cross-legged on the ground. But the use of chairs had spread with Buddhism from Central Asia.

After the acceptance of their offerings, the Birds performed the Kalyavinka* Dance. The accompanying music was backed by the warbling of real nightingales; while afar off, with strangely happy effect, there sounded the faint and occasional cry of some crane or heron on the lake. All too soon came the wild and rapid passage which marks the close.

Now it was the turn of the Butterflies, who after fluttering hither and thither for a while, settled at the foot of a tangled thorn-hedge, over which the yellow kerria streamed down in splendid profusion, and here executed their dance.

The Comptroller of the Empress's household, assisted by several courtiers, now distributed largesse to the boy-dancers on her behalf. To the Birds, cherry-colored jackets; to the Butterflies, cloaks lined with silk of kerria hue. These were so appropriate that they could hardly have been produced on the spur of the moment, and it almost seemed as though some hint of Murasaki's intention had reached the Empress's quarters beforehand. To the musicians were given white, unlined dresses, and presents of silk and cloth according to their rank. Yugiri received a blue jacket for himself and a lady's costume for his store-cupboards. He was also charged to carry a reply from the Empress: "I could have cried yesterday at missing it all... But what can I do? I am not my own mistress. 'If anything could tempt me to batter down the flowery, eightfold wall of precedent, it would be the visit of those butterflies who fluttered from your garden into mine.'"

You may think that many of the poems which I here repeat are not worthy of the talented characters to whom they are attributed. I can only reply that they were in every case composed upon the spur of the moment, and the makers were no better pleased with them than you are.

On looking back, I see that I have forgotten to mention the presents which Murasaki distributed among her visitors after the ceremonies of the day before. They were, as you may well imagine, very handsome indeed; but to describe all such matters in detail would be very tiresome. Henceforward communication between the Spring and Autumn quarters was of daily occurrence, joint concerts and excursions were constantly planned, and the two parties of gentlewomen began to feel as much at home in one domain as in the other.

Tamakatsura, after that first encounter on the night when the mummers danced in front of the Palace, had continued her friendship with Murasaki. The newcomer's evident desire for cordial relations would in any case have been hard to withstand. But it was also apparent that she was extremely intelligent and at the same time very easy to get on with; so that she was soon a general favorite in the Palace.

---

* One of the magical birds in Amida Buddha's Paradise.

As has been said, her suitors were numerous; but Genji had not as yet shown any sign of encouraging one rather than another. His feelings upon the subject were indeed very fluctuating. To begin with, he had no confidence in his own capacity to go on playing his present fatherly part with success. Something must be done soon; and he often thought that the first step must be to enlighten To no Chujo as to the girl's identity. So long as he hesitated to do so, the situation was very embarrassing. For whereas Yugiri had formed the habit of going constantly in and out of her room in a manner which very much embarrassed her, but which it was impossible to criticize, since all the world believed him to be her brother (and it must be confessed that he never attempted to behave with anything else than brotherly affection), To no Chujo's sons whose intimacy with Yugiri brought them frequently to the house, pressed upon her attentions of an unmistakable sort, which she, knowing her true relationship to these young men, was at a loss how to receive. She would very much have liked her real father at any rate to know of her present position; but she made no attempt to get into communication with him, for she had complete confidence that Genji, who would not do so much for her unless he wished her well, must know far better than she what policy it was best to pursue. Her docility touched and delighted him; for though it did not by any means equal Yugao's, it served constantly to remind him of her. But Tamakatsura was, as he soon discovered, a person of very much stronger character than he had supposed.

The summer came round, bringing with it the distraction of new clothes and an uncertain yet on the whole extremely agreeable weather. Genji had very little business at this season, and there was a great deal of music and entertaining at the New Palace. He heard that love-letters were pouring into the western wing[*] and with the pleasure that one always feels at discovering that one's anticipations are being fulfilled he hastened thither to examine these missives. He took upon himself not only to read all her correspondence, but also to advise her which letters ought to be neglected and which acknowledged with civility. To this advice she listened somewhat coldly. By far the most passionate and profuse of her correspondents seemed to be Prince Sochi no Miya, and Genji smiled as he looked through the thick packet into which that prince's letters had been collected. "Sochi and I," he said, "have always been great friends. With none of the royal princes have I ever been so intimate, and I know that he has always been devoted to me. The only subject upon which we have ever had any difference of opinion is just this matter of love-making. He allowed it to play far too important a part in his life. I am amused and at the same time, in a way, distressed to find him after all these years

---

[*] Tamakatsura's quarters.

behaving exactly as he did when we were both boys. However, I should like you to answer him. I know of no other person about the Court with whom it would so well become a lady of consequence to correspond. He is a remarkable man in many ways. His appearance alone would entitle him..." and more to this effect, designed of course not to blacken Sochi's character, but to portray him in just such a light as would interest an inexperienced girl. These remarks had, however, an exactly opposite effect to that which Genji intended.

Then there was Prince Higekuro. He had always seemed to be a steady-going, capable fellow, successful in everything he undertook. But glancing at his letters Genji feared that upon the hill of Love, where, let it be remembered, even Confucius stumbled,[*] this wise prince too might easily find his undoing. By far the most elegant letter in the whole collection was one written on very dark blue Chinese paper, heavily perfumed with some delicious scent. It was folded up very small, and Genji, whose curiosity would have been aroused by this fact alone, now spread it out, displaying the poem: "Of my love perchance you know not, for like a stream that is buried under the ground, a moment it springs into the sunlight; then sinks into the cavern whence it sprang."

It was very well written, in a hand which combined fanciful originality with adherence to the latest fashions. "Who wrote this?" he asked, but he received only the vaguest replies. Ukon had now joined them and addressing her, Genji said: "I want you to give your mistress some guidance in the answering of such letters of this kind as may in future arrive. For the unfortunate situations which sometimes result from our present freedom of manners we men are not always to blame. It often happens that a little timely severity on the lady's part would avert the quandaries into which we are led by our determination to treat love as our principal pastime and distraction. At the time (who should know it better than I?) such severity is of course resented by the gentleman, who will rail in the accepted style at his lady's 'cruelty' and 'insensibility.' But in the end he will be grateful that the matter was not allowed to go further.

"On the other hand it may happen that some suitor, whose rank is not such that he can be considered as a possible husband, may entertain very serious feelings indeed, yet through fear of giving offence may go no further in his communications than to make a few conventional remarks about the weather or the garden. In such a case, if the lady, insisting upon seeing in such epistles more than is actually expressed, administers a rebuff, the result will only be that the affair is henceforward on a footing of passion, not (as hitherto) of formality. A civil answer, couched in the same conventional terms as the original letter, may instead dispel the

---

[*] The married life of Confucius, like that of Socrates, was very unhappy.

lover's romantic notions and lead him to abandon the quest. But whatever happens the lady has done all that ought to be expected of her.

"On the other hand to mistake the idle compliments and attentions which it is now fashionable to scatter in such profusion, and to treat these courtly formalities as signs of genuine feeling, is even more dangerous than to ignore them altogether, and though such a course may lead to a little momentary excitement, it is bound in the long run to produce a disagreeable situation.

"It often happens that a young girl will cast aside all reserve and pursue without thought of the consequences some quite trivial inclination, merely in order to convince the world that she is a woman of feeling. At first the discovery of a new pleasure is in itself sufficient to carry her through; but repetition palls, and after a few months excitement gives place to tedium or even disgust.

"I have, however, reason to believe that both my stepbrother and Prince Higekuro are in this case completely sincere, and whatever her own feelings may be it is improper that anyone in your mistress's position should deal too curtly with offers such as these. As for the rest, I assume that their rank is not such as to make acceptance conceivable, and there can therefore be no objection to your mistress meting out among them such varying degrees of kindness or severity as her fancy dictates."

While this exposition was in progress at the far end of the room, Tamakatsura sat with her back towards the speakers, occasionally glancing across her shoulder with a turn of the head that showed off her delicate profile to great advantage. She was wearing a long close-fitting robe, pink plum-blossom color without, and green within; her short mantle matched the flower of the white deutzia, then in full bloom. There was to her style of dress something which made it seem homely without being dowdy or unfashionable. If in her manners any trace of rusticity could still be found, it lay perhaps in a certain lack of self-assurance which she seemed to have retained as a last remnant of her country breeding. But in every other respect she had made ample use of the opportunities afforded her by life at the New Palace. The way she dressed her hair and her use of make-up showed that she observed those around her with an acute and intelligent eye. She had, in fact, since her arrival at Court, grown into a perfectly well turned-out and fashionable beauty, all ready to become, alas, not his own (reflected Genji with chagrin) but some fortunate young man's immaculate bride. Ukon, too, was thinking, as she watched them, that Genji looked much more fit to be her lover than her father. Yes, they were surely made for one another; and Ukon doubted whether, however long he searched, Genji would find her a partner whose looks matched her so well. "Most of the letters that come," said the old lady, "I do not pass on at all. The three or four that you have been looking at, you will agree I could not possibly have returned. But though I delivered them to my mistress, she has not answered them, and though of course she will do so if you insist upon it..." "Perhaps you can tell me," broke in Genji, "who sent this curious note. Despite its minute size there seems to be a great deal of writing in it." "Ah, that one..." said Ukon, "if I returned it once I returned it a hundred times! But there was no getting rid of the messenger. It comes from Captain Kashiwagi, His Excellency To no Chujo's eldest son. This gentleman knows little Miruko, my lady's chambermaid, and it was through her that the messenger was first admitted. I assure you no one else but this child Miruko knows anything about the matter at all..." "But how delightful!" said Genji, much relieved. "Kashiwagi of course holds a rather low rank, and that is a disadvantage. But no child of such a man as To no Chujo is to be scorned; and there are, in point of fact, a great many important officials who in public esteem occupy a far lower place than these young men. Moreover, Kashiwagi is generally considered to be the most serious and competent of the brothers. To receive compliments from such a man is very gratifying, and though he must of course sooner or later learn of his close relationship to you, for the present I see no need to enlighten him." And still examining the letter, he added, "There are touches in his handwriting, too, which are by no means to be despised." "You agree with everything I say," he continued, "but I feel that inwardly you are raising objections all the while. I am very sorry not to please you; but if you are thinking that I ought to hand you over to your father without more ado, I simply do not agree with you. You are very young and inexperienced. If you were suddenly to find yourself in the midst of brothers and sisters whom you have never known, I am certain you would be miserable. Whereas if you will only wait till I have settled your future (in such a way as your father, upon whom there are so many claims, could not possibly manage), there will be time enough afterwards to disclose the story of your birth."

Though he did not say in so many words that he would far rather have kept her for himself, he more than once came perilously near to hinting something of the kind. Such indiscretions she either misunderstood or ignored. This piqued him; but he enjoyed the visit and was quite unhappy when he discovered that it was high time for him to go back to his own quarters. Before he left she reminded him, in guarded language, of his promise to tell her real father what had become of her. He felt at this more conscience-stricken than he need have done. For in her heart of hearts Tamakatsura was by no means in a hurry to leave the New Palace. She would have been glad to have the inevitable introduction to her real parent safely behind her, chiefly because the prospect of it destroyed her peace of mind. However kind her father might be, it was impossible that he should take more trouble about her than Prince Genji was doing; indeed, To no Chujo, not having once set eyes on her since she was a mere infant, might well have ceased to take any interest in her whatever. She had lately been reading a number of old romances and had come across many accounts of cases very similar to her own. She began to see that it was a delicate matter for a child to force itself upon the attention of a parent who had done his best to forget that it existed, and she abandoned all idea of taking the business into her own hands.

Genji arrived at Murasaki's rooms full of enthusiasm for the lady whom he had just been visiting: "What a surprising and delightful creature this Tamakatsura is!" he exclaimed. "Her mother, with whom I was so intimate years ago, had almost too grave and earnest a character. This girl will, I can see, be more a 'woman of the world,' but she is at the same time evidently very affectionate. I am sure she has a brilliant future before her..." From his manner Murasaki instantly saw that his interest in Tamakatsura had assumed a new character. "I am very sorry for the girl," she said. "She evidently has complete confidence in you. But I happen to know what you mean by that phrase 'a woman of the world,' and if I chose to do so, could tell the unfortunate creature what to expect..." "But you surely cannot mean that I shall *betray* her confidence?" asked Genji indignantly. "You forget," she replied, "that I was once in very much the same position myself. You had made up your mind to treat me as a daughter; but, unless I am much mistaken, there were times when you did not carry out this resolution very successfully..." "How clever everyone is!" thought Genji, much put out at the facility with which his inmost thoughts were read. But he hastened to rejoin: "If I were in love with Tamakatsura, she would presumably become aware of the fact quite as quickly as you would." He was too much annoyed to continue the conversation; however, he admitted to himself in private that when people come to a conclusion of this kind, it is hardly ever far from the mark. But surely, after all, he could judge better than she. And Murasaki, he reflected, was not judging this case on its merits, but merely assuming, in the light of past experience, that events were about to take a certain course... .

To convince himself that Murasaki had no ground for her suspicions he frequently went across to the side wing and spent some hours in Tamakatsura's company.

During the fourth month the weather was rather depressing. But one evening, when it had been raining heavily all day, he looked out and saw to his relief that at last the sky was clearing. The young maples and oak-trees in the garden blent their leafage in a marvelous curtain of green. Genji remembered the lines "In the fourth month the weather grew clearer and still..."* and thence his thoughts wandered to the girl in the western wing. He felt a sudden longing, on this early summer evening, for the sight of something fresh, something fragrant; and without a word to anyone he slipped away to her rooms. He found her practicing at her desk in an easy attitude and attire. She was in no way prepared to receive such a visit, and upon his arrival rose to her feet with a blush. Caught thus unawares and informally dressed, she was more like her mother than he had ever seen her before, and he could not help exclaiming: "I could not have believed it possible! Tonight you are simply Yugao herself. Of course, I have always noticed the resemblance; but never before has it reached such a point as this. It so happens that Yugiri is not at all like his mother, and consequently I am apt to forget how complete such resemblances can sometimes be."

A sprig of orange-blossom was stuck among some fruit that was lying on a tray near by. "As the orange-blossom gives its scent unaltered to the sleeve that brushes it, so have you taken on your mother's beauty, till you and she are one." So he recited, adding: "Nothing has ever consoled me for her loss, and indeed, though so many years have passed I shall die regretting her as bitterly as at the start. But tonight, when I first caught sight of you, it seemed to me for an instant that she had come back to me again—that the past was only a dream... Bear with me; you cannot conceive what happiness was brought me by one moment of illusion. But now it is over..." and so saying he took her hand in his. She was somewhat taken aback, for he had never attempted to do such a thing before; but she answered quietly: "Wretched will be my lot indeed, should the flower's perfume prove hapless as the flower that was destroyed."

She felt that things were not going well, and sat staring at the floor, her chin propped on her fist. This was just the attitude in which she most attracted him. He noticed the plumpness of her hand, the softness of her skin, the delicacy of her whole figure. Such beauty could not, at these close quarters, in any case have failed to move him; coupled with the memories which every feature inspired, it proved irresistible, and today his discretion broke down as never before. True, he did no more than make a somewhat vague avowal of his feelings towards her. But Tamakatsura was instantly terror-stricken; of this there could be no doubt, for she was trembling from head to foot. "Come!" he said, "you need not look so horrified. There is no harm in my having such feelings, so long as only you and I are aware of them. You have known for some time past that I was very fond of you, and now you have learnt that I care for you even

---

* From a poem written by Po Chü-i in 821, describing the pleasure of returning to his own house after a spell of duty in the Palace: "I sit at the window and listen to the wind rustling among the bamboo; I walk on the terrace and watch the moon rising between the trees."

more than you supposed. But were I drawn towards you by the blindest passion that has ever darkened the heart of man, this would not damage your chances with Sochi no Miya, Higekuro and the rest. For in their eyes you are my daughter, and it would never occur to them that my affection for you could in any way hinder their courtship. My only fear is that you will never find a husband who cares for you half as much as I do. Such feelings as mine for you are not as common in the world as you perhaps imagine them to be..."

He spoke all the while as though what he had said to her implied nothing more than an unusual access of paternal feeling. It had now quite stopped raining; "the wind was rustling in the bamboos,"* and the moon was shining brightly. It was a lovely and solemn night. Tamakatsura's ladies, seeing that the conversation was beginning to take a somewhat intimate turn, had tactfully withdrawn from her presence.

His visits had for some while been very frequent; but circumstances seldom favored him as they did tonight. Moreover, now that he had, quite without premeditation, confessed to these feelings, they seemed suddenly to have taken a far stronger hold upon him. Unobtrusively, indeed almost without her being aware of what was happening, he slipped from her shoulders the light cloak which she had been wearing since summer came in, and lay down beside her. She was horrified, but chiefly through the fear that someone might discover them in this posture. Her own father, she ruefully reflected, might refuse to admit his responsibilities towards her and even order her out of his sight, but she could be certain that he would not submit her to such ordeals as she was here undergoing... She did her best to hide her tears, but before long they burst forth in an uncontrollable flood. Genji was dismayed. "If that is what you feel about it," he said, "you must really dislike me very much indeed. I have not attempted to do anything that the world would consider in the least reprehensible, even were I in no way connected with you. But as it is, we have been friends for almost a year. Surely there is nothing very strange in the way I have behaved? You know quite well that I should never force you to do anything you would be sorry for afterwards. Do not, please, be angry with me. Now that you have grown so like your mother, it is an immense comfort to me simply to be with you..." He spoke then for a long while, tenderly, caressingly. For now that she was lying beside him the resemblance to Yugao was more than ever complete. But happy though he would have been to remain far longer at her side, he was still able to see that his behavior had been in the highest degree rash and inconsiderate. It was growing late; at any moment someone might return to the room and discover them. "Do not think the worse

---

* See note on p. 490.

of me for what has happened this evening," he said at last, rising from the couch; "it would distress me very much if you did. I know quite well that there are people who never allow their feelings to get the better of them. I can only say that I am differently made. But of this at least I can assure you: whatever you may think of me, such outbursts are not due in my case merely to some frivolous impulse of the moment. Once my affections are aroused they are boundless both in time and extent. You need not fear that I shall ever act in such a way as to harm your good name. All I ask is that I may sometimes be allowed to talk as I have talked tonight; and perhaps I may even hope that you will occasionally answer me in the same spirit."

He spoke gently, reasonably, but she was now beside herself with agitation, and made no intelligible reply.

"I see that I have made a great mistake," he said at last. "I always thought that we got on unusually well together; but it is now clear that the friendship was all on my side. For I cannot think that my showing a little affection would so much perturb you unless you definitely dislike me..." He broke off, and left the room with a final entreaty that she would speak to no one of what had occurred.

Though Tamakatsura was no longer very young, she was still entirely innocent, and this made her judge Genji's conduct more harshly than she would otherwise have done. He had indeed merely lain down on the same couch; but she, in her inexperience, imagined that in so doing he had taken advantage of her to the utmost possible extent. On returning to the room her gentlewomen at once noticed that she was looking very distraught, and pestered her with tiresome enquiries about her health. No sooner had they withdrawn than Ateki,[*] the daughter of her old nurse, began (irritatingly enough) to congratulate her upon her guardian's extraordinary kindness: "How gratifying it is," she said, "that His Excellence is so admirably attentive to you! With all respect to your own father, I very much doubt whether he would put himself to half as much trouble on your account... Prince Genji seems to take a positive pleasure in looking after you." But Tamakatsura had been too much surprised and shocked by Genji's conduct to feel, for the moment, any gratitude for the more than parental solicitude by which Ateki was so deeply impressed. She had no desire whatever to see him again, and yet in his absence felt strangely lonely and depressed.

---

[*] See above, p. 442. Ateki of course knew the secret of Tamakatsura's birth.

The Glow-Worm

Genji was now in a singularly fortunate position. The government of the country lay wholly in his hands; but though his power was supreme, he was now seldom troubled by the uninteresting details of public business; for he had some while ago delegated all such minor decisions to To no Chujo, and the arrangement continued to work very successfully. In varying ways and degrees his dependants naturally benefited by his increased leisure and security. Not only was he able to devote far more time to looking after their affairs, but they could also feel that, such as it was, their position was now something permanent and dependable; whereas in the old days, when the powers arrayed against him were still unshaken, they knew quite well that he might at any moment find himself far more in need of patronage than able any longer to dispense it. Most of them, even those who received a very small share of his attentions, were nowadays fairly well content with their lot; but the Princess[*] in the western wing continued to view with great apprehension the imprudent turn which her guardian had lately given to their relationship, and different as were his manners from those of her persecutor[†] on the Island, she was now scarcely less alarmed than in the weeks which preceded her flight. She felt that in first insisting on their playing the part of father and daughter, and then suddenly revealing himself in another character, he had taken advantage of her in a very mean way, and despite his protestations it seemed vain to suppose that, out of consideration for her at any rate, he would restrain himself sufficiently to avoid an open scandal. She had no one to whom she could turn, and now that she was face to face with the actual difficulties of life she realized far more acutely than she had even done as a child the irreparable loss which she had sustained in her mother's death.

Genji, on his side, was exceedingly vexed with himself for having acted so imprudently. He had not breathed a word about the matter to anyone, and being anxious to convince himself that his behavior on that unlucky night had been altogether exceptional, he visited her frequently and, apart from a few rather ambiguous remarks (which however he was careful never to let fall in the presence of her gentlewomen and attendants) he behaved in a manner to which exception could not be taken. Each time

---

[*] Tamakatsura.
[†] Tayu.

that he began to venture on dangerous ground she felt her heart beat violently and, if he had been anyone else, would have cut him short and sent him about his business. But as it was she merely pretended not to notice what he was saying.

She was naturally of a very cheerful and lively disposition, so that she made friends easily. Prince Sochi and her other suitors, though they themselves had obtained so little encouragement from her, continued to hear on all sides nothing but praises of her good looks and general charm. They therefore redoubled their efforts; but to their chagrin the rains of the fifth month* had already set in without any sign that their industry was likely to be rewarded.

Among some letters which Tamakatsura was showing to him Genji found one from Prince Sochi: "If you could but find it in your heart to admit me for one single moment to your presence, you would earn my undying gratitude, even though I should never see you again. For I should thus enjoy a respite, the first for many months, from the tortures which I now endure..." "I have never seen Prince Sochi making love," said Genji as he read the letter. "It would be a sight worth seeing. Please tell him he may come," and he began suggesting the terms in which she should reply. But the idea did not at all appeal to her, and alleging that she was feeling giddy and could not, at the moment, possibly handle a pen, she attempted to lead the conversation into other channels. "But there is no need that you should write yourself," said Genji, returning to his project; "we will dictate a letter between us."

Among Tamakatsura's gentlewomen there was none in whom she placed any great confidence. The only exception was a certain Saisho no Kimi, a daughter of her mother's younger brother, who seemed to have far more sense than most young women. Hearing that this girl was in difficult circumstances Tamakatsura had sent for her to see what could be done; and finding that Saisho was not only the sort of person whom it would be useful in a general way to have about her, but was also an unusually good penwoman, she retained this young cousin in her service. Genji, who knew that Tamakatsura often used the girl as her amanuensis, now sent for Saisho and proceeded to dictate a letter. For he was consumed by an overwhelming curiosity to see how his half-brother, with whose conduct in all other situations he was so familiar, would conduct himself at such an interview as this. As for Tamakatsura, she had, since the occasion of Genji's unpardonable indiscretion, begun to pay a good deal more attention to the communications of her suitors. She had no reason to give any preference to Prince Sochi; but he, as much as any other husband, represented a way of escape from the embarrassment in

---

* It is unlucky to marry in the fifth month.

which she found herself. She was, however, far from having ever thought of him seriously in this connection.

Little knowing that his success was due to a whim of Prince Genji's rather than to any favorable impression that his own suit had made, Sochi no Miya in great elation rushed round to the New Palace and presented himself at Tamakatsura's door. He could not complain of his treatment; for he was at once accommodated with a divan which was only a few paces from her curtains-of-state. He looked about him. On every side he recognized such presents and appurtenances as far more commonly emanate from a lover than from a parent. The air was laden with costly perfumes. There were hangings, brocades, a thousand trifles any one of which would have been enough to arouse in Sochi's heart the suspicion that Genji, from whom he was convinced that those bounties flowed, was not her father. And if he was not her father, then inevitably, as Sochi ruefully recognized, he must be reckoned with as a serious rival. Tamakatsura herself made no effort to converse with him or even answer his questions. Her maids seemed quite incapable of replying on her behalf, and when even Saisho, reputed to be so capable in every emergency, continued to sit in awkward silence, Genji whispered: "What is the matter with you all? Have you become rooted to your seats? Get up, do something... Be civil!" But all this had no effect. They merely stared helplessly in front of them.

The evening was now drawing in, and as the sky was very much overcast the room was almost dark. Beyond her curtains Tamakatsura could just discern the motionless form of her suitor, gracefully outlined against the gloom, while from her side a stirring of the evening air would occasionally carry towards him a fragrance enhanced by a strange perfume[*] which, though it was familiar to him, he could not then identify. The room seemed full of diverse and exquisite scents that inflamed his imagination, and though he had previously pictured her to himself as handsome, he now (as these perfumes floated round him) thought of her as a hundred times more beautiful than he had ever done before. Her curtains were thick and it was now quite dark. He could not see her and could only guess that she was still near him; but so vividly did she now appear before his mind's eye that it was as though no barrier were between them, and he began to address her in the most passionate terms. There was now in his style no longer anything of the professional courtier or hardened man-of-the-world. The long outpouring to which Genji, ensconced in his corner of her curtained dais, now listened with considerable emotion, was natural, direct—almost boyish. When it was over, Prince Sochi was rewarded by a note from Saisho, informing him that her mistress had

---

[*] The rare perfume which Genji wore.

some time ago retired to the inner room!* "This is too bad!" whispered Genji, creeping to the door of her refuge (he had himself been so intent upon his brother's eloquence that he had not seen her slip away). "You cannot simply disappear while people are talking to you. You are governed by absurd preconceived notions, and never stop to consider the merits of the case in question. To treat any visitor, and above all a person of Prince Sochi's standing, in the manner I have just witnessed would not be tolerated in a child; and in your case, seeing that you are a grown woman not without some experience of Court life, such behavior is insufferable. Even if you are too shy to converse with him, you might at least sit within reasonable distance..." Genji had never yet pursued her into the inner room; but she had no doubt that on the present occasion, in his eagerness to reform her manners, he would have no scruple in doing so; and reluctantly she left her place of retreat and once more seated herself near the edge of her curtained dais. Sochi now attempted to begin a more general conversation, but no topic seemed to arouse her interest. Suddenly her attention was distracted by a light which had begun to glimmer quite close to where she sat. It seemed to move when Genji moved. She now saw him go to her curtains-of-state and, at a certain point, hook back the inner curtain, leaving only a single thickness of light transparent stuff. Here he suspended something bright that looked like a paper candle... What was he doing? She was dumbfounded.

The fact was that on his way to her apartments earlier in the evening Genji had encountered an unusual number of glow-worms. Collecting them in a thin paper bag he had concealed this improvised lantern under the folds of his cloak and, on his arrival, disposed of it in a safe corner. Startled by the sudden glow of light, Tamakatsura snatched up her fan and buried her face behind it, not before Sochi had caught an enchanting glimpse of her beauty. This was just what Genji had intended. The attentions which his brother had hitherto paid to Tamakatsura were, he suspected, due solely to the fact that Sochi had accepted the current story and imagined her indeed to be Genji's daughter. He knew that, despite her fame as a delightful accession to the Court, Prince Sochi could have but a vague conception of her charm; and in order that he might the sooner escape from his own dilemma he was determined that Sochi should no longer merely pay formal court to the girl, but should really lose his head about her. He imagined that he was now at any rate indisputably playing the part of a fond and disinterested parent. A strange delusion! For had he reflected for a moment he would have seen that nothing

---

* Sochi had been addressing her through her curtains-of-state. She crept away in the darkness as an animal at the Zoo might slink into its back cage. Genji was, of course, all the time with her behind her curtains.

would ever have induced him so crudely to thrust his own daughter, the Princess of Akashi, upon a suitor's notice. He now stole away by a back door and returned to his own apartments.

Sochi was feeling much encouraged. He now discredited Saisho's note and imagined that the lady had been sitting during the whole time of his discourse in the position where the light of the glow-worms revealed her. "After all," he thought to himself, "I have interested her. She listens patiently and apparently even likes to be near me." And with that he pulled back the light gauze flap at the part of her curtains where Genji had removed the thick inner hanging. She was now but a few feet away from him, and though a bag of glow-worms makes no very famous* illumination, he saw enough by this fitful and glimmering light to confirm his impression that she was one of the most beautiful women he had ever seen. In another moment Tamakatsura's maids, summoned hastily to the scene, had detached the strange lantern and carried it somewhere out of sight.

Genji's stratagem was indeed abundantly successful. This momentary vision of Tamakatsura huddled disconsolately upon her couch had profoundly disturbed him. "Does the harsh world decree that even the flickering glow-worm, too shy for common speech, must quench the timid torchlight of its love!" So he now recited; and she, thinking that if she appeared to be taking much trouble about her reply, he would suppose she attached more importance to the matter than was actually the case, answered instantly: "Far deeper is the glow-worm's love that speaks in silent points of flame, than all the passions idle courtiers prate with facile tongue." She spoke coldly; moreover she had now withdrawn to the far side of her dais. For some while he pleaded in vain against this inhospitable treatment. But he soon saw that he would gain nothing, even should he stay where he was till dawn; and though he could hear by the water dripping from the eaves that it was a most disagreeable night, he rose and took his leave. Despite the rain the nightingales were singing lustily; but he was in no mood to enjoy their song and did not pause an instant to hear them.

On the fifth day of the fifth month, business at the Stables brought Genji in the direction of her apartments, and he availed himself of this opportunity to discover what had happened on the night of Sochi's visit. "Did the prince stay very late?" he asked. "I hope you did not let him go too far. He is the sort of man who might very easily lose control of himself... not that he is worse than others. It is really very unusual indeed to meet with anyone who is capable of acting with self-restraint under such circumstances." And this was the match-maker who on the very occasion to which he was now referring, had driven her into Prince Sochi's arms!

---

* *Qhoye-naki* "fame-less." I retain this idiom as it corresponds curiously with ours.

She could not help being amused at his unblushing inconsistency. But all the while he was warning her against the very man for whose visit he had himself been responsible. Tamakatsura scanning him in his holiday clothes thought that he could not, by any imaginable touch of art or nature, have looked more beautiful. That thin cloak—what a marvelous blend of colors! Did fairies preside over his dyeing-vats? Even the familiar and traditional patterns, she thought, on such days as this take on a new significance and beauty. And then looking again at Genji: "If only we were not on this tiresome footing," she said to herself, "I believe I should long ago have fallen very much in love with him."

A letter arrived. It was from Prince Sochi, written on thin white paper in a competent hand, and couched in terms which at the time seemed very spirited and apposite. I fear, however, that were I to reproduce it here, this admired letter would seem in no way remarkable, and I will only record the poem which accompanied it: "Shall I, like the flower that grows unnoticed by the stream though holiday-makers in their dozens pass that way, find myself still, when this day closes, unwanted and passed-by?" The letter was attached to the tallest and handsomest flag-iris* she had ever seen. "He is quite right," said Genji; "today there is no escape for you." And when one after another of her gentlewomen had pleaded with her that this once at any rate she should answer him with her own hand, she produced the following reply, which had, however, very little to do with what was going on in her mind: "Better had the flower remained amid the waters, content to be ignored, than prove, thus swiftly plucked, how feeble were the roots on which it stood."

It was an idle repartee, and even the handwriting seemed to Prince Sochi's expectant eye somewhat vague and purposeless. He was, indeed, not at all sure, when he saw it, that he had not made a great mistake... Tamakatsura, on the other hand, was disposed to be in rather a good humor with herself. She had this morning received Magic Balls† of the utmost variety and splendor from an unprecedented number of admirers. A more complete contrast than that between her poverty-stricken years on the island and her present pampered existence could hardly be imagined. Her ideas on a variety of subjects were becoming far less rigid than when she first arrived at the New Palace; and she began to see that provided her relationship with Genji could be maintained upon its present harmless footing she had everything to gain from its continuance.

Later in the day Genji called upon the lady in the eastern quarter.‡ "The young men in the Royal Bodyguard are holding their sports here

---

* Irises were plucked on the fifth day of the fifth month.
† Balls made of colored stuffs, with scent-bags in the middle. Supposed to ward off disease.
‡ The Lady from the Village of Falling Flowers.

today," he said. "Yugiri will be bringing them back with him to his rooms and is counting on you to prepare for their entertainment. They will arrive just before sunset. There will also probably be a great deal of company besides; for ever since a rumor spread round the Court that we were secretly harboring in the New Palace some fabulous prodigy of wit and beauty, an overwhelming interest has been taken in us, and we have not had a moment's peace. So be prepared for the worst!"

Part of the race course was not far away from this side of the Palace and a good view could be obtained from the porticos and outer galleries. "You had better throw open all the garden-doors along the passage between this wing and the main house," he said. "The young people will see very well from there. The Bodyguard of the Right is exceptionally strong this year. In my opinion they are a far more interesting lot than most of the present high officers at Court." This whetted, as it was intended to do, the curiosity of the young people in that part of the house, and the galleries were soon thronged. The pages and younger waiting-women from Tamakatsura's wing also came to see the sights and were accommodated at the open doors along the passage, the persons of quality being ensconced behind green shutters or curtains dyed in this new-fashioned way according to which the color is allowed to run down into the fringe. Among the dresses of the visitors were many elaborate Chinese costumes, specially designed for the day's festivity, the color of the young dianthus leaf tending to prevail. The ladies who belonged to this wing had not been encouraged to make any special effort for the occasion and were for the most part in thin summer gowns, green without and peach-blossom color within. There was a great deal of rivalry and harmless self-display, which was rewarded from time to time by a glance from one of the young courtiers who were assembled on the course.

Genji arrived on the scene at the hour of the Sheep,[*] and found just such a concourse of distinguished visitors as he had predicted. It was interesting to see the competitors, whom he knew only in their official uniforms, so differently arrayed, each with his following of smartly dressed squires and assistants. The sports continued till evening. The ladies, although they had a very imperfect understanding of what was going on, were at least capable of deriving a great deal of pleasure from the sight of so many young men in elegant riding-jackets hurling themselves with desperate recklessness into the fray. The finish of the course was not so very far from Murasaki's rooms, so that her gentlewomen too were able to get some idea of what was going on. The races were followed by a game of polo played to the tune of Tagyuraku.[†] Then came a

---

[*] 1 P.M.
[†] "Hitting the Ball Tune."

competition of rival pairs in the Nasori.* All this was accompanied by a great din of bells and drums, sounded to announce the gaining of points on one side and another. It was now getting quite dark and the spectators could barely see what was going on. The first part of the indoor entertainment which came next consisted in the distribution of prizes among the successful riders. Then followed a great banquet and it was very late indeed when the guests began to withdraw. Genji had arranged to sleep that night in the eastern wing. He sat up a long while, talking to the Lady from the Village of Falling Flowers. "Did you not think today," he said, "that Prince Sochi was immeasurably superior to any of the other visitors? His appearance is of course not particularly in his favor. But there is something in his manners and mode of address which I at any rate find very attractive. I was able recently to observe him on an occasion when he had no reason to believe that he was being watched, and came to the conclusion that those who so loudly praise his wit and ingenuity have no idea what constitutes his real charm." "I know that he is your younger brother," she answered; "but he certainly looks considerably older than you. I am told that he has visited here very frequently during the last few months. But as a matter of fact I had not till today once set eyes on him since I saw him years ago when my sister was at Court. I confess I then had no idea that he would turn out so well as he has done. In those days it was his younger brother, the Viceroy of Tsukushi, whom I used to admire. But I see now that he had not the same princeliness of air and carriage which you rightly attribute to Prince Sochi." He saw that, brief as was the time she had spent in Prince Sochi's company that day, she had already completely succumbed to his charms. He smiled, but did not draw her on into a general discussion of his guests and their merits or defects. He had always had a great dislike of those who cannot mention an acquaintance without immediately beginning to pick his character to pieces and make him seem utterly contemptible. When he heard the Lady from the Village of Falling Flowers going into raptures over Prince Higekuro, he did indeed find it hard not to disillusion her, particularly as he was just then beginning to be somewhat alarmed lest this prince, whom he regarded as rather unsuitable, should in the end turn out to be the strongest candidate for Tamakatsura's favor.

He and the Lady from the Village of Falling Flowers had for years past been on terms merely of ordinary confidence and friendliness. It was assumed on this occasion as on others that they would presently retreat each to a separate resting-place. How and why had this assumption first begun? He could not remember, and felt that tonight he would very gladly have broken the rule. But she seemed to take for granted that he

---

* A Korean dance.

would presently wish to retire, and so far from resenting this or seeming to be at all depressed, she evidently felt highly gratified that her own quarters had been selected as the scene of a festivity the like of which she had not witnessed in person for a very great number of years. "The withered grass that even the woodland pony left untouched, today with the wild iris of the pool-side has been twisted in one wreath." Thus she expressed her gratitude and pride. He was touched that so small an event should mean so much to her, and answered with the verse: "The colt whose shadow falls upon the waters close where the wild swan's wing is mirrored in the lake, from iris and sweet marsh-marigold shall ne'er be far away." How easily was she now contented, and how vague had his own compliments become! "Though I so seldom manage to see you," he said, "I assure you I am never happier than when I am here." It would have been unlike her to take him to task for the insincerity of this last speech. She merely accepted it quietly and they parted for the night. He found that she had given up her own bed to him, and had all her things carried to another place. Had she not seemed so convinced that anything in the way of greatest intimacy was out of the question, he might have felt inclined on this occasion to suggest a different arrangement.

This year the rainy season lasted much longer than usual, and whereas the monotony of the downpour is usually relieved by an occasional day of sunshine, this time there was nothing but one continuous drizzle for weeks on end. The inhabitants of the New Palace found it very hard to get through the day and tried one amusement after another. In the end they mostly betook themselves to reading illustrated romances. The Lady of Akashi had, among her other accomplishments, a talent for copying out and finely decorating such books as these; and being told that everyone was clamoring for some occupation which would help them to get through the day, she now sent over a large supply to the Princess, her daughter. But the greatest enthusiast of all was Lady Tamakatsura, who would rise at daybreak and spend the whole day absorbed in reading or copying out romances. Many of her younger ladies-in-waiting had a vast stock of stories, some legendary, some about real people, which they told with considerable skill. But Tamakatsura could not help feeling that the history of her own life, should it ever come to be told, was really far more interesting than any of the tales with which her ladies sought to entertain her. True, the sufferings of the princess in the *Sumiyoshi Tale*[*] had at certain points a resemblance to her own experiences. But she could see no reason why for generations past so many tears of indignation and pity should have been shed over the fate of this princess at the hands of

---

[*] The story of a misused stepchild. It is no longer extant, the text which bears this name being merely a 15th-century adaptation of the *Room Below Stairs*.

her unscrupulous lover.* Judged as an episode, thought Tamakatsura, her own escape from the violence of Tayu was quite as exciting.

One day Genji, going the round with a number of romances which he had promised to lend, came to Tamakatsura's room and found her, as usual, hardly able to lift her eyes from the book in front of her. "Really, you are incurable," he said, laughing. "I sometimes think that young ladies exist for no other purpose than to provide purveyors of the absurd and improbable with a market for their wares. I am sure that the book you are now so intent upon is full of the wildest nonsense. Yet knowing this all the time, you are completely captivated by its extravagances and follow them with the utmost excitement: why, here you are on this hot day, so hard at work that, though I am sure you have not the least idea of it, your hair is in the most extraordinary tangle... . But there; I know quite well that these old tales are indispensable during such weather as this. How else would you all manage to get through the day? Now for a confession. I too have lately been studying these books and have, I must tell you, been amazed by the delight which they have given me. There is, it seems, an art of so fitting each part of the narrative into the next that, though all is mere invention, the reader is persuaded that such things might easily have happened and is as deeply moved as though they were actually going on around him. We may know with one part of our minds that every incident has been invented for the express purpose of impressing us, but (if the plot is constructed with the requisite skill) we may all the while in another part of our minds be burning with indignation at the wrongs endured by some wholly imaginary princess. Or again we may be persuaded by a writer's eloquence into accepting the crudest absurdities, our judgment being as it were dazzled by sheer splendor of language.

"I have lately sometimes stopped and listened to one of our young people reading out loud to her companions and have been amazed at the advances which this art of fiction is now making. How do you suppose that our new writers come by this talent? It used to be thought that the authors of successful romances were merely particularly untruthful people whose imaginations had been stimulated by constantly inventing plausible lies. But that is clearly unfair..." "Perhaps," she said, "only people who are themselves much occupied in practicing deception have the habit of thus dipping below the surface. I can assure you that for my part, when I read a story, I always accept it as an account of something that has really and actually happened."

So saying she pushed away from her the book which she had been copying. Genji continued: "So you see as a matter of fact I think far better of this art than I have led you to suppose. Even its practical value

---

* A disagreeable old man to whom her stepmother tried to marry her.

is immense. Without it what should we know of how people lived in the past, from the Age of the Gods down to the present day? For history-books such as the Chronicles of Japan show us only one small corner of life; whereas these diaries and romances which I see piled around you contain, I am sure, the most minute information about all sorts of people's private affairs..." He smiled, and went on: "But I have a theory of my own about what this art of the novel is, and how it came into being. To begin with, it does not simply consist in the author's telling a story about the adventures of some other person. On the contrary, it happens because the storyteller's own experience of men and things, whether for good or ill—not only what he has passed through himself, but even events which he has only witnessed or been told of—has moved him to an emotion so passionate that he can no longer keep it shut up in his heart. Again and again something in his own life or in that around him will seem to the writer so important that he cannot bear to let it pass into oblivion. There must never come a time, he feels, when men do not know about it. That is my view of how this art arose.

"Clearly then, it is no part of the storyteller's craft to describe only what is good or beautiful. Sometimes, of course, virtue will be his theme, and he may then make such play with it as he will. But he is just as likely to have been struck by numerous examples of vice and folly in the world around him, and about them he has exactly the same feelings as about the pre-eminently good deeds which he encounters: they are important and must all be garnered in. Thus anything whatsoever may become the subject of a novel, provided only that it happens in this mundane life and not in some fairyland beyond our human ken.

"The outward forms of this art will not of course be everywhere the same. At the Court of China and in other foreign lands both the genius of the writers and their actual methods of composition are necessarily very different from ours; and even here in Japan the art of storytelling has in course of time undergone great changes. There will, too, always be a distinction between the lighter and the more serious forms of fiction... Well, I have said enough to show that when at the beginning of our conversation I spoke of romances as though they were mere frivolous fabrications, I was only teasing you. Some people have taken exception on moral grounds to an art in which the perfect and imperfect are set side by side. But even in the discourses which Buddha in his bounty allowed to be recorded, certain passages contain what the learned call Upaya or "Adapted Truth"—a fact that has led some superficial persons to doubt whether a doctrine so inconsistent with itself could possibly command our credence. Even in the scriptures of the Greater Vehicle,[*] there are,

---

[*] The Mahayana, the later development of Buddhism which prevailed in China and Japan.

I confess, many such instances. We may indeed go so far as to say that there is an actual mixture of Truth and Error. But the purpose of these holy writings, namely the compassing of our Salvation, remains always the same. So too, I think, may it be said that the art of fiction must not lose our allegiance because, in the pursuit of the main purpose to which I have alluded above, it sets virtue by the side of vice, or mingles wisdom with folly. Viewed in this light the novel is seen to be not, as is usually supposed, a mixture of useful truth with idle invention, but something which at every stage and in every part has a definite and serious purpose."

Thus did he vindicate the storyteller's profession as an art of real importance.

Murasaki, who had first taken to reading romances in order to see whether they were suitable for her adopted daughter, the Princess from Akashi, was now deeply immersed in them. She was particularly fond of the *Tale of Komano** and showing to Genji an illustrated copy of it she said one day: "Do you not think that these pictures are very well painted?" The reason that she liked the illustrations so much was that one of them showed the little girl in the story lying peacefully asleep in her chair, and this somehow reminded Murasaki of her own childhood. "And do you mean to tell me," asked Genji, "that such an infant as that has already, at this early point in the story, been the heroine of gallant episodes? When I remember the exemplary way in which I looked after you during your childhood I realize that my self-restraint is even more unusual than I supposed." It could not be denied that his conduct was in many ways unusual; but hardly, perhaps, exemplary in the common sense of the word. "I hope you are very careful not to allow the little princess to read any of the looser stories," he continued. "She would realize, I am sure, that the heroines of such books are acting very wrongly in embarking upon these secret intrigues; but I had much rather she did not know that such things go on in the world at all." "This is really too much!" thought Murasaki. "That he could come straight from one of his interminable visits to Tamakatsura and at once begin lecturing me on how to bring up young ladies!"

"I should be very sorry," she said," if she read books in which licentious characters were too obviously held up to her as an example. But I hope you do not wish to confine her reading to *The Hollow Tree*.† Lady Até certainly knows how to look after herself, in a blundering sort of way; and she gets her reward in the end, but at the expense of so grim a tenacity in all her dealings that, in reading the book, we hardly feel

---

* Now lost.

† Lady Até refuses suitor after suitor. Finally she marries the Crown Prince and lives happily ever after. The book seemed as old-fashioned to Murasaki as Hannah More's novels do to us.

her to be a woman at all." "Not only did such women actually exist in those days," replied Genji, "but I can assure you that we have them still among us. It comes of their being brought up by unsocial and inhuman people who have allowed a few one-sided ideas to run away with them. The immense pains which people of good family often take over their daughters' education is apt to lead only to the production of spiritless creatures whose minds seem to grow more and more childlike in proportion to the care which is lavished on their upbringing. Their ignorance and awkwardness are only too apparent; and after wondering in what, precisely, this superior education consisted, people begin to regard not only the children as humbugs but the parents as well.

"On the other hand if the children happen to have natural talents, parents of this kind at once attribute the faintest sign of such endowment to the efficacy of their own inhuman system, and become distressingly pleased with themselves, using with regard to some very ordinary girl or stripling terms of the most extravagant eulogy. The world consequently expects much more of the unfortunate creatures than they can possibly perform, and having waited in vain for them to do or say something wonderful, begins to feel a kind of grudge against them..."

"Over praise," he added, "does a great deal of harm to the young. Servants are very dangerous in this respect..." Nevertheless he did not object, as Murasaki had often noticed, to the little Princess from Akashi being praised by anyone who came along, and he often put himself to immense trouble in order that she might escape a scolding which he knew she thoroughly deserved.

Stepmothers in books usually behave very spitefully towards the children entrusted to them. But he was now learning by his own experience that in real life this does not always happen. In choosing books for Murasaki and her charge he was therefore careful to eliminate those that depict stepmothers in the traditional light; for he feared she might otherwise think he was trying to give her a quite unnecessary warning.

Yugiri, as has been said before, saw very little of Murasaki; but it was natural that he should sometimes visit his little sister, the Princess from Akashi, and Genji did not discourage this. On the contrary he was anxious to establish an affectionate relationship between them. For Genji, young though he still was, often thought of what would happen after his death, and he could imagine circumstances in which the princess might stand sorely in need of her brother's help. He therefore gave the boy permission to visit her and even go behind her curtains-of-state as often as he chose, though he still forbad him to enter into conversation with Lady Murasaki's gentlewomen. So few were the children of the house that a great deal more trouble was taken about them than is usually the case. Yugiri certainly seemed to have repaid this care. In the ordinary affairs of life he showed great judgment and good sense, and Genji had the comfortable feeling that whatever went amiss, Yugiri at least could always be relied upon.

The little girl was only seven years old and dolls were still her principal interest. Yugiri, who a year or two ago used so often to play just such games with his little companion at the Great Hall, made an excellent major-domo of the doll's house, though the part, bringing as it did a host of recollections to his mind, was often a painful one. Indeed more than once he was obliged to turn away for an instant, his eyes full of tears. During these visits he naturally met many of the princess's other playmates, and a great deal of chattering took place on every conceivable subject. He took his share in these conversations; but he did not get to know any of the little girls at all well, nor did they, so far as he could see, take any particular interest in him. "Was all that side of life forever to be closed to him?" Yugiri asked himself. But though this was the thought which instantly recurred to him during these meetings, his outward behavior seemed only to betoken complete indifference. His green badge!* Yes, it was that which lay at the bottom not only of these smaller troubles but also of the great disaster† which had wrecked all his chances of happiness.

Sometimes the idea came to him that if he simply went straight to Kumoi's father and tackled him about the matter—insisted, shouted, made a great scene—To no Chujo would suddenly give in. But he had suffered enough already in private; there was nothing to be gained by also making himself publicly ridiculous. No, the better way was to convince Kumoi herself by his behavior, above all by a complete and obvious indifference to the rest of the world, that so far as his own feelings were concerned nothing was altered by one jot or tittle since the day when he first told her of his love.

Between him and her brothers slight difficulties were always arising which resulted, for the time being, in a certain coldness. For example, Kashiwagi, Kumoi's eldest brother, in ignorance of the fact that Lady Tamakatsura was his sister, continued to pay his addresses to her, and finding that his letters often failed to reach their destination, naturally turned to Yugiri for assistance. Never once did he offer to perform a similar service in return, though it was presumably as easy for him to see Kumoi as it was for Yugiri to see Tamakatsura. The request irritated him and he firmly refused. Not that they ceased to be friends; for their relationship, like that of their fathers, had always been built up of small rivalries and feuds.

To no Chujo had an unusually large number of children, most of whom had amply fulfilled, as regards both popularity and attainments, the

---

* The mark of the sixth rank. Genji, it will be remembered, had refused to promote him.

† His failure to win To no Chujo's daughter, Lady Kumoi.

high promise of their early years. His position in the State had enabled him to do extremely well for all his sons. As regards his daughters (who were, however, not so numerous) he had been less fortunate. His plans for the future of the eldest girl had entirely miscarried;* he had signified his desire to present Lady Kumoi at Court, but had hitherto received no command to do so. He had not in all these years ever forgotten the little girl who, along with her mother, had so mysteriously disappeared, and sometimes spoke of her to those who had at the time been aware of his attachment to that unhappy lady. What had become of them both? He imagined that her strange timidity had driven the mother to take flight with that exquisite child into some lonely and undiscoverable place. He fell into the habit of staring hard into the face of every girl whom he met; and the commoner, the more ill-clad and wretched the creature was, the surer he became that this was his lost child. For the lower she had sunk, the less likely it was that she would be able to persuade anyone that she was indeed his daughter. It was impossible, he felt, that sooner or later one or other of his agents should not get news of her, and then what reparation he would make for the down-trodden existence that she must now be leading! He told his sons her child-name and begged them to report to him immediately if they should ever come across anyone who bore it. "In my early days," he said, "I am afraid I became involved in a great many rather purposeless intrigues. But this was quite a different matter. I cared for the mother very deeply indeed, and it distresses me intensely that I should not only have lost the confidence of the lady herself, but also have been able to do nothing at all for the one child that bore witness to our love."

For long periods, especially if nothing happened to remind him of the matter, he succeeded in putting it out of his head. But whenever he heard of anyone adopting a stray girl or taking some supposed poor relation into their house, he at once became very suspicious, made innumerable enquiries and was bitterly disappointed when it was finally proved to him that his supposition was entirely unfounded.

About this time he had a curious dream, and sending for the best interpreters of the day asked them what it meant. "It seems to mean," they said, "that you have at last heard what has become of a child that you had lost sight of for many years, the reason that you have failed to discover her being that she is thought by the world at large to be someone else's child." Heard what has become... he faltered. "No, on the contrary, I have heard no such thing. I cannot imagine what you are talking about."

---

* He had hoped to get Lady Chujo made Empress.

A Bed of Carnations

One very hot day Genji, finding the air at the New Palace intolerably close, decided to picnic at the fishing-hut on the lake. He invited Yugiri to come with him, and they were joined by most of the courtiers with whom Genji was on friendly terms. From the Western River on his estate at Katsura *ayu* had been brought, and from the nearer streams *ishibushi* and other fresh-water fish, and these formed the staple of their repast. Several of To no Chujo's sons had called to see Yugiri, and hearing where he was to be found, joined the picnic. "How heavy and sleepy one has felt lately!" exclaimed Genji. "This is certainly a great improvement." Wine was brought; but he sent for iced water as well. A delicious cold soup was served, and many other delicacies. Here by the lake there was a certain amount of movement in the air; but the sun blazed down out of a cloudless sky, and even when the shadows began to lengthen there was a continual buzzing of insects which was very oppressive. "I have never known such a day," said Genji. "It does not after all seem any better here than it was indoors. You must excuse me if I am too limp to do much in the way of entertaining you," and he lay back against his cushions. "One does not feel much inclined for music or games of any kind in such weather, and yet one badly needs something to occupy the mind. I have sometimes wondered lately whether the sun was ever going to set... All the same, the young people on duty at the Emperor's Palace are in a much worse position than we. Imagine not being able to loosen one's belt and ribbons on a day like this! Here at any rate we can loll about just as we please. The only difficulty is to avoid going to sleep. Has not any of you got some startling piece of news to tell us? You need have no fear that I may have heard it already, for I am becoming quite senile; I never hear about anything till everyone else has forgotten about it." They all began wracking their brains to think of some exciting piece of intelligence or entertaining anecdote, but without success; and presently, since their host had invited them to be at their ease, one after another of the visitors somewhat timidly took up a position with his back planted against the cool metal railings of the verandah. "Well," said Genji at last, "as a matter of fact, rarely though this now happens, I myself have picked up a small piece of information. It seems that His Excellency To no Chujo has lately rediscovered and taken to live with him a natural daughter of whom he had lost sight for many years.

Come, Kobai," addressing Kashiwagi's younger brother, "you will be able to tell me if there is any truth in this." "Something of the kind has happened," answered the young man, "though there is a good deal of exaggeration in many of the stories which are being put about. The facts are that last spring, in consequence of a dream, my father asked us to enquire carefully into every case we could discover of a child claiming paternity by him. My brother Kashiwagi did finally hear of a girl who seemed to possess absolute proof that she was an illegitimate child of our father's, and we were told to call upon her and verify this, which we accordingly did. That is all I know about it; and I am sure that there is no one present who has not something a great deal more interesting than that to talk about. I am afraid what I have just told you cannot possibly be of interest to anyone but the people actually concerned." "So it is true!" thought Genji, wondering whether To no Chujo could have been so misled as to suppose that it was Yugao's child whom he had rediscovered. "There are so many of you in the family already," he said to Kobai, "that I wonder your father should search the sky for one stray swallow that has not managed to keep pace with the flock. I, who nurture so small a brood, might be pardoned for such conduct; but in your father it seems somewhat grasping. Unfortunately, though I should feel proud to acknowledge my children, no one shows the slightest inclination to claim me as a father. However, it is no mere accident that To no Chujo is more in request than I am. The moon's image shows dimly in waters that are troubled at the bottom." Your father's early adventures were of a most indiscriminate character, and if you know all your brothers and sisters, you would probably realize that, taken as a whole, you are a very queer family..." Yugiri, who knew a mass of stories which amply confirmed Genji's last statement, could not help showing his amusement to an extent which Kobai and his brothers thought to be in exceedingly bad taste. "It is all very well for you to laugh, Yugiri," continued Genji, "but you would be much better employed in picking up some of those stray leaves than in making trouble for yourself by pressing in where you are not wanted. In so large a garland you might surely find some other flower with which to console yourself?" All Genji's remarks about To no Chujo wore superficially the aspect of such friendly banter as one old friend commonly indulges in concerning another. But as a matter of fact there had for some while past been a real coolness between them, which was increased by Chujo's scornful refusal to accept Yugiri as his son-in-law. He realized that he had just been somewhat spiteful; but so far from being uncomfortable lest these remarks should reach his old friend's ears, he found himself actually hoping that the boys would repeat them.

This conversation about the waif whom To no Chujo had recently acknowledged and adopted reminded Genji that it was becoming high time he should himself make a certain long-intended revelation. Tamakatsura had now lived for over a year at the New Palace; she was definitely accepted as a member of the Court circle, and there was now no fear that her father would be in any way ashamed of her. But the views of To no Chujo were in some ways peculiar. He made an absolutely hard and fast distinction between the "right" and the "wrong" people. To those who satisfied his very exacting standards he was extraordinarily helpful and agreeable. As for the others, he ignored them with a sublime completeness that no other Grand Minister had ever equaled. Was it quite certain in which class he would place his own daughter? Then a brilliant idea occurred to Genji. He would introduce To no Chujo to Tamakatsura immediately, but not reveal her identity until Chujo had once and for all classed her as "possible."

The evening wind was by this time delightfully fresh, and it was with great regret that the young guests prepared to take their leave. "I should be perfectly contented to go on sitting here quietly in the cool; but I know that at your age there are many far more interesting things to be done," and with that he set out for the western wing, his guests accompanying him to the door.

Knowing that in an uncertain evening light all people in Court cloaks look very much alike, Genji at once summoned Tamakatsura to him and explained in a low voice why he had arrived with so large an escort. "I have been entertaining To no Chujo's sons," he said, "Kashiwagi, Kobai and the rest. It was obvious that they were very anxious to come on here with me and Yuguri is such an honest soul, it would have been unkind not to let him come too. Those poor young men, To no Chujo's sons, must really soon be told you are their sister. I am afraid they are all more or less in love with you. But even in the case of quite ordinary families the sudden arrival of some unknown young lady causes endless speculation among those who frequent the house, and though there is intense curiosity to see her, it is apparent that everyone has long beforehand made up his mind to fall in love. Unfortunately, even before your arrival, my palace had an undeserved reputation for harboring bevies of incomparable creatures. Every visitor who comes here seems to arrive primed up with compliments and fine speeches, only to discover, that there is no quarter in which they could be employed without impertinence.* But you have often asked me about those particular young men and lamented that you never get an opportunity yourself of judging whether they are as intelligent as everyone makes out. So I thought you would not mind me bringing them here, and would perhaps like to have a word with one or the other of them..."

---

* Akikonomu, for example, had become Empress.

While this whispered conversation was going on, the young men were standing in the garden outside. It was not planted in formal borders; but there was a great clump of carnations and a tangled hedge of tall flowering plants, both Chinese and Japanese, with great masses of blossom that stood out vividly in the fading light. True, they had come that evening hoping to pluck a very different flower; but as they sat resting in front of the house they could scarcely restrain themselves from stretching out a hand and filling their laps with these resplendent blossoms.

"They are really very remarkable young men," Genji went on. "There is not one of them but in his way shows unmistakable signs of genius, and this is true even of Kashiwagi, who in outward manner is particularly quiet and diffident. By the way, has he written to you again? I remember we read his poem together. You cannot, of course, under the circumstances risk giving him any definite encouragement; but do not be too hard upon him."

Even amid these very exceptional young men Yugiri looked surprisingly handsome and distinguished, and Genji, pointing to him, said to Tamakatsura in a whisper: "I am terribly disappointed that To no Chujo should take up his present attitude about that boy. It has come to this nowadays, that those people will not look at anyone who is not part and parcel of their own gang.* A drop of other blood, even if it be that of the Royal House, seems to them a painful blemish..." "That was not the way Royal Princes were regarded once upon a time," said Tamakatsura, and quoted the old folk-song *Come to my House*.† "They certainly seem in no hurry to make ready a banquet for poor Yugiri," admitted Genji. "I am extremely sorry for those two. They took a fancy to each other when they were mere children and have never got over it. I know quite well that they have suffered a great deal through this long separation. If it is merely because of Yugiri's low rank that To no Chujo refuses his consent, he might on this occasion be content to disregard the comments of the world and leave the matter in my hands. He surely does not suppose that I intend the boy to remain in the Sixth Rank forever..." Again he was speaking of To no Chujo with asperity and, like her brothers a few hours ago, Tamakatsura was perturbed to discover that the breach between them was widening, partly because such a state of affairs made it all the less probable that Genji would in the near future reveal her identity to To no Chujo.

As there was no moon that night, the great lamp was presently brought in. "It is now just comfortably warm," said Genji, "and the only thing we need is a little more light." He sent for a servant and said to him:

---

* I.e. the Fujiwaras, the clan to which the writer herself belonged.

† "In my house the awnings are at the doors and curtains are hanging about the bed. Come, my Prince! you shall have my daughter for your bride, and at the wedding-feast you shall have the fish you like best, be it *awabi*, oyster, or what you will."

"One tray of bamboo flares! In here, please." When they were brought he noticed a very beautiful native zithern and drawing it towards him struck a few chords. It was tuned to the difficult *ritsu* mode, but with remarkable accuracy. It seemed indeed to be an exceptionally fine instrument, and when he had played on it for a little while he said to her: "I have all these months been doing you the injustice of supposing that you were not interested in these things. What I like is to play such an instrument as yours on a cool autumn evening, when the moon is up, sitting quite close to the window. One then plays in concert with the cicadas, purposely using their chirruping as part of the accompaniment. The result is a kind of music which is intimate, but at the same time thoroughly modern. There is, of course, a go-as-you-please, informal quality about the Japanese zithern which makes it unsuitable for use on ceremonial occasions. But when one remembers that almost all our native airs and measures originated on this instrument, one cannot help regarding it with respect. There are stray references which show that its history stretches back into the dimmest past; but to hear people talk nowadays one would think it had been specially invented for the benefit of young ladies, in whom an acquaintance with foreign arts and usages is considered unbecoming. Above all, do make a practice of playing it in concert with other instruments whenever you get the chance. This will immensely improve your command over it. For though the Japanese zithern is a far less complicated instrument than its rivals, it is by no means so easy to play as most people imagine. At the present time there is no better performer than your father, To no Chujo. You would be astonished at the variety of tone he can get out of a mere succession of open strings; it is as though by some magic he were able in an instant to change his zithern into whatever instrument he pleases. And the volume of sound which he obtains from those few slender strings is unbelievable!"

Tamakatsura had reached a certain point of proficiency herself. But she knew that she had much to learn, and longed to meet with a first-rate performer. "Do you think I might one day be allowed to hear him?" she asked, not very hopefully. "I suppose he sometimes plays when he comes here to entertainments. Even among those outlandish people on the Island there were several teachers, and I always supposed that they knew all about it. But from what you have just said I see that such playing as my father's must be something quite different..."

"It is indeed," he said, "and you shall certainly hear him play. You know, I expect, that though it is called the Eastern zithern and is said to have come from the other side of the country, it is always played at the beginning of every Imperial concert, being solemnly carried in by the Mistress of the Rolls. As far as our country is concerned (about the history of music in other lands I know very little) it is certainly the parent of all other instruments, and that perhaps the best performer upon it who has ever lived should be your own father is certainly a great stroke of luck for you. He does, as you suggested, play here and at other people's houses from time to time, when there is music afoot; but chiefly on other instruments. It is really very difficult to make him play on the Japanese zithern. Often he begins a tune and then, for some reason, will not go on. It is the same with all great artists. They cannot perform unless they are in the right mood, and the right mood seldom comes. But later on you will, of course, certainly be hearing him..." So saying, he began trying over a few usual chords and runs. Already she wondered how she had managed to tolerate the clumsy twanging of the island-professors. How exciting it would be to live with a father, who, according to Genji's own showing, played far, far better even than this! It was intolerable to feel that all the while she might have been hearing him day after day, in his own home, with nothing to disturb or interrupt him. When, oh when, would this new life begin?

Among other old ballads Genji now sang "Not softlier pillowed is my head," and when he came to the line "O lady parted from thy kin" he could not help catching her eye and smiling. Not only did she find his voice very agreeable, but his improvisations between verse and verse delighted her beyond measure. Suddenly he broke off, saying: "Now it is your turn. Do not tell me you are shy; for I am certain that you have talent, and if that is so you will forget that there is anyone here, once you have become interested in what you are playing. The lady* who was "too shy to do anything but go over the tune in her head" wanted all the time to sing the *Sojuren*,† and that is a very different matter. You must get into the habit of playing with anyone who comes along, without minding what he thinks of you..." But try as he might, he could not persuade her to begin. She was certain that her teacher on the Island, an old lady of whom it was reported that she had once been in some vague way connected with the Capital and even that she was distantly related to the Imperial Family, had got everything wrong from beginning to end. If only she could persuade Genji to go on playing a little while longer, she felt sure she could pick up enough of the right method to prevent a complete catastrophe, and she sat as near as possible to the zithern, watching his fingers and listening intently. "Why does it not always produce such lovely sounds as that?" she said laughing. "Perhaps it depends which way the wind is blowing..." She looked very lovely as she sat leaning towards him, with the lamplight full upon her face. "I have sometimes known you by no means so ready to listen," he said, and to her disappointment

---
* In some story now lost.
† Literally: "Thinking of a man, and yearning."

pushed the zithern from him. But her gentlewomen were passing in and out of the room. Whether for this or other reasons his behavior tonight continued to be very serious and correct. "I see no sign of those young men I brought with me," he said at last. "I am afraid they grew tired of gazing at every flower save the one they came to see, and went away in disgust. But it is their father's visit to this flower-garden that I ought all the while to be arranging. I must not be dilatory, for life is full of uncertainties... How well I remember the conversation in the course of which your father first told me how your mother had carried you away, and of his long search for you both. It does not seem long ago..." And he told her more than he had ever done before about the rainy night's conversation and his own first meeting with Yugao.

"Gladly would I show the world this Child-flower's beauty, did I not fear that men would ask me where stands the hedge on which it grew."*

"The truth is, he loved your mother so dearly that I cannot bear the thought of telling him the whole miserable story. That is why I have kept you hidden away like a chrysalis in a cocoon. I know I ought not to have delayed..." He paused, and she answered with the verse: "Who cares to question whence was first transplanted a Child-flower that from the peasant's tattered hedge was hither brought?" Her eyes filled with tears as in a scarcely audible voice she whispered this reply.

There were times when he himself took fright at the frequency of his visits to this part of the house, and in order to make a good impression stayed away for days on end. But he always contrived to think of some point in connection with her servants or household affairs which required an endless going and coming of messengers, so that even during these brief periods of absence she was in continual communication with him. The truth is that at this period she was the only subject to which he ever gave a thought. Day and night he asked himself how he could have been so insensate as to embark upon this fatal course. If the affair was maintained upon its present footing he was faced with the prospect of such torture as he felt he could not possibly endure. If on the other hand his resolution broke down and she on her side was willing to accept him as a lover, the affair would cause a scandal which his own prestige might in time enable him to live down, but which for her would mean irreparable disaster. He cared for her very deeply; but not, as he well knew, to such an extent that he would ever dream of putting her on an equality with Murasaki, while to thrust her into a position of inferiority would do violence to his own feelings and be most unfair to her. Exceptional as was the position that he now occupied in the State, this did not mean that it was any great distinction to figure merely as a belated appendage to

---

* A reference to To no Chujo's poem, Part I, p. 30.

his household. Far better, he very well knew, to reign supreme in the affections of some wholly unremarkable Deputy Councilor! Then again there was the question whether he ought to hand her over to his stepbrother Prince Sochi or to Prince Higekuro. Even were this course in every way desirable, he gravely doubted his own capacity to pursue it. Such self-sacrifices, he knew, are easier to plan than to effect. Nevertheless, there were times when he regarded this as the plan which he had definitely adopted, and for a while he could really believe that he was on the point of carrying it out. But then would come one of his visits to her. She would be looking even more charming than usual, and lately there were these zithern lessons, which, involving as they did a great deal of leaning across and sitting shoulder to shoulder, had increased their intimacy with disquieting rapidity. All his good resolutions began to break down, while she on her side no longer regarded him with anything like the same distrust as before. He had indeed behaved with model propriety for so long that she made sure his undue tenderness towards her was a thing of the past. Gradually she became used to having him constantly about her, allowed him to say what he pleased, and answered in a manner which though discreet was by no means discouraging. Whatever resolutions he may have made before his visit, he would go away feeling that, at this point in their relations, simply to hand her over to a husband was more than the most severe moralist could expect of him. Surely there could be no harm in keeping her here a little longer, that he might enjoy the innocent pleasure of sometimes visiting her, sometimes arranging her affairs? Certainly, he could assure himself, his presence was by no means distasteful to her. Her uneasiness at the beginning was due not to hostility but to mere lack of experience. Though "strong the watchman at the gate," she was beginning to take a very different view of life. Soon she would be struggling with her own as well as his desires, and then all her defenses would rapidly give way...

To no Chujo was somewhat uneasy about his newly discovered daughter.[*] The members of his own household seemed to have a very poor opinion of her, and at Court he had overheard people whispering that she was not quite right in the head. His son Kobai told him, of course, about Genji's questions, and To no Chujo laughed, saying: "I can quite understand his interest in the matter. A year or two ago he himself took over a daughter whom he had by some peasant woman or other, and now makes an absurd fuss over her. It is very odd: Genji says nothing but nice things about everyone else. But about me and everyone connected with me he is careful to be as disagreeable as possible. But I suppose I ought to regard it as a sort of distinction even to be run down by him." "Father,

---

[*] The rustic creature unearthed by Kobai in his search for Tamakatsura.

if you mean the girl who lives in the western wing," said Kobai, "I can assure you she is the most beautiful creature you can possibly imagine. Prince Sochi and many of the others have completely lost their hearts to her... Indeed, everyone agrees that she is probably one of the handsomest women at Court." "You surely do not yourself believe such stories?" said To no Chujo. "The same thing is always said about the daughters of men in such a position as Genji's; and so oddly is the world made that those who spread such reports really believe in them. I do not for a moment suppose she is anything out of the ordinary. Now that Genji is Grand Minister, faced by an opposition that has dwindled to a mere speck and esteemed as few Ministers before, I fancy the one flaw in his happiness must be the lack of a daughter to lavish his care upon and bring up to be the envy and admiration of the whole Court. I can well imagine what a delight the education of such a child would be to him. But in this matter Fate seems to be against him. Of course, there is the little girl who was born at Akashi. Unfortunately her mother's parents are quite humble people and she can never play the part that would naturally have been taken by a child of my sister Lady Aoi or of his present wife, Lady Murasaki. All the same, I have reason to believe that his schemes for her subsequent career are of the most ambitious nature.

"As for this newly-imported princess, it would not surprise me to discover that she is not his child at all. You know as well as I do what Genji's failings are... It is far more probable that she is merely some girl whom he is keeping." After other somewhat damaging remarks about Genji's habits and character, he continued: "However, if he continues to give out that she is his daughter, it will soon be incumbent upon him to find her a husband. I imagine his choice will fall upon Prince Sochi, with whom he has always been on particularly good terms. She would certainly be fortunate in securing such a husband; he is a most distinguished character..."

Nothing more exasperated To no Chujo at the present moment than the endless speculations concerning Lady Tamakatsura's future which were now the staple of every conversation at Court. He was sick of hearing people ask, "What are Prince Genji's intentions?" "Why has he changed his mind?" and so on, while the future of his own daughter, Lady Kumoi, seemed for some reason not to arouse the slightest curiosity. Why should not a little of the energy which Genji expended in dangling this supposed daughter of his before the eyes of an expectant Court be used on Lady Kumoi's behalf? A word whispered by Genji in the Emperor's ear would suffice to secure her future; but that word, it was very evident, had never been spoken.

If Genji (and this seemed hardly credible) were waiting to secure Kumoi for his own son Yugiri, let him raise the boy to a decent rank.

Then, provided suitable overtures were made on Genji's side, he was quite willing to consider the possibility of such a match. As to what the young man's feelings in the matter might be—he did not give the question a moment's thought, having always regarded Yugiri merely as a nuisance.

One day when he had been reflecting upon this problem more earnestly than usual, To no Chujo determined to thresh the matter out with the girl herself, and taking Kobai with him he went straight to her room. It so happened that Kumoi had fallen asleep. She was lying, a small and fragile figure, with only a single wrap of thin diaphanous stuff thrown carelessly across her. It was certainly a pleasure on such a day to see anyone looking so delightfully cool! The delicate outline of her bare limbs showed plainly beneath the light wrap which covered her. She lay pillowed on one outstretched arm, her fan still in her hand. Her loosened hair fell all about her, and though it was not remarkably thick or long, there was something particularly agreeable in its texture and in the lines it made as it hung across her face. Her gentlewomen were also reposing, but at some distance away, in the room which opened out behind her curtained dais, so that they did not wake in time, and it was only when To no Chujo himself rustled impatiently with his fan that she slowly raised her head and turned upon him a bewildered gaze. Her beauty, enhanced by the flush of sleep, could not but impress a father's heart, and To no Chujo looked at her with a pride which his subsequent words by no means betrayed. "I have told you often before," he said, "that even to be caught dozing in your seat is a thing a girl of your age ought to be ashamed of; and here I find you going to bed in broad daylight... you really must be a little more careful. I cannot imagine how you could be so foolish as to allow all your gentlewomen to desert you in this way. It is extremely unsafe for a young girl to expose herself, and quite unnecessary in your case, since I have provided you with a sufficient number of attendants to mount guard on all occasions. To behave in this reckless manner is, to say the least of it, very bad form. Not that I want you to sit all day with your hands folded in front of you as though you were reciting the Spells of Fudo.[*] I am not one of those people who think it a mark of refinement in a girl to stand on ceremony even with her everyday acquaintances and never to address a word to anyone except through a barricade of curtains and screens. So far from being dignified, such a method of behavior seems to me merely peevish and unsociable. I cannot help admiring the way in which Prince Genji is bringing up this future Empress[†] of his. He takes no exaggerated precautions of any kind, nor does he force her talent in

---

[*] Of these there are several, the shortest of which runs (in Sanskrit) Namas samanta-vajranam ham. "Praise be to all the Thunderbolt-bearers. Ay verily." Its impressiveness was partly due to the fact that very few Japanese knew what it meant.

[†] The Princess from Akashi.

this direction or that; but at the same time he sees to it that there is no subject in which she remains wholly uninitiated. Thus she is able to choose intelligently for herself where other girls would be obliged merely to do as they were told. For the time it may seem that the energies of the mind have been somewhat diffused and extenuated, but in later life, given the best balanced and broadest system of education in the world, idiosyncrasies both of character and behavior will inevitably reappear. At the present moment the Princess from Akashi is in the first and less interesting stage. I am very curious to see how she will develop when she arrives at Court." After these preliminaries he embarked at last upon the subject which he had really come to discuss. "You know," he said, "that I have not been very successful in my plans for your own future. But I still hope that we may be able to arrange something not too contemptible. I promise you at any rate that you shall not be made ridiculous. I am keeping my ears open and have one or two projects in mind, but for the moment it is exceedingly difficult to arrive at a decision. Meanwhile, do not be deceived by the tears and protestations of young men who have nothing better to do than amuse themselves at the expense of confiding creatures such as you. I know what I am talking about"... and so on, speaking more and more kindly as he went along.

In old days the scoldings which she had received on account of her intimacy with Yugiri had been the more distressing to her because she had not at that time the least idea what all this fuss was about. But now that she was a little better acquainted with such matters, she recalled with burning shame time after time when she had mentioned to her elders things which she now saw it was the wildest folly ever to have repeated. The old Princess* frequently complained that Kumoi never came to see her. This put the child in great embarrassment, for the truth was that she dared not go, for To no Chujo would be sure to think that she was using her duty towards the old lady as a pretext for clandestine meeting with her lover.

But another question was at this time occupying a good deal of To no Chujo's attention. What was to be done with this new daughter of his, the Lady from Omi? If, after going out of his way to track her down, he were now to send her home again merely because certain people had said disobliging things about her, he would himself figure as intolerably capricious and eccentric. To let her mix in general society was, judging by what he had heard and seen of her already, quite out of the question. But if he continued to keep her, as he had hitherto done, in the seclusion of her own rooms, it would soon be rumored at Court that she was some paragon who, just at the right moment, would be produced with dazzling

---

* To no Chujo's mother, Kumoi's grandmother.

effect and carry all before her. This, too, would be very irritating. Perhaps the best that could be done under the circumstances was to put her into touch with his daughter Lady Chujo,* who happened at the moment to be home from Court. It would then be possible to discover whether, when one got to know her better, this Lady from Omi were really such a monster as some people made out. He therefore said to Lady Chujo one day: "I am going to send this new sister of yours to see you. It seems that her manners are rather odd, and I should be very much obliged if you would ask one of your older gentlewomen to take her in hand. Young girls are useless in such a case. They would merely lead her on to greater absurdities in order to amuse themselves. Her manner is at present, I gather, somewhat too boisterous"; and he smiled as he recollected some of the anecdotes which had already reached him. "I will gladly do all I can," answered Lady Chujo. "I see no reason to suppose that the poor creature is anything like so outrageous as people are making out. It is only that Kobai, wishing to gain credit for his discovery, tended to exaggerate her charms, and people are a little disappointed. I do not think there is any need for you to take alarm. I can quite understand that coming for the first time among surroundings such as these, she feels somewhat lost, and does not always quite do herself justice..." She spoke very demurely. This Lady Chujo was no great beauty; but there was about her a serene air of conscious superiority which, combined with considerable charm of manner, led most people to accept her as handsome, an impression shared at this moment by her father as he watched her lips part in a smile that reminded him of the red plum-blossom in the morning when its petals first begin to unfold. "I daresay you are right," he replied; "but all the same I think that Kobai showed a lack of judgment such as I should have thought he had long ago outgrown..." He was himself inclined to think that the Lady from Omi's defects had probably been much exaggerated, and as he in any case must pass her rooms on his way back he now thought he had better go and have another look at her. Crossing the garden he noticed at once that her blinds were rolled back almost to the top of the windows. Clearly visible within were the figures of the Lady herself and of a lively young person called Gosechi, one of last year's Winter Dancers. The two were playing Double Sixes,† and the Lady of Omi, perpetually clasping and unclasping her hands in her excitement, was crying out "Low, low! Oh, how I hope it will be low!" at the top of her voice, which rose at every moment to a shriller and shriller scream. "What a creature!" thought To no Chujo, already in despair, and signaling to his attendant, who were about to enter the apartments and

---

* On leave from the Palace; she was one of the Emperor's consorts.

† Sugoroku, a kind of backgammon.

announce him, that for a moment he intended to watch unobserved, he stood near the double door and looked through the passage window at a point where the paper* did not quite meet the frame. The young dancer was also entirely absorbed in the game. Shouting out: "A twelve, a twelve. This time I know it is going to be a twelve!" she continually twirled the dice cup in her hand, but could not bring herself to make the throw. Somewhere there, inside that bamboo tube, the right number lurked, she saw the two little stones with six pips on each... But how was one to know when to throw? Never were excitement and suspense more clearly marked on two young faces. The Lady of Omi was somewhat homely in appearance; but nobody (thought To no Chujo) could possibly call her downright ugly. Indeed, she had several very good points. Her hair, for example, could alone have sufficed to make up for many shortcomings. Two serious defects, however, she certainly had; her forehead was far too narrow, and her voice was appallingly loud and harsh. In a word, she was nothing to be particularly, proud of; but at the same time (and he called up before him the image of his own face as he knew it in the mirror) it would be useless to deny that there was a strong resemblance.

"How are you getting on?" he asked on being admitted to the room. "I am afraid it will take you some time to get the hang of things here. I wish I could see you more often, but, as you know, my time is not my own..." "Don't you worry about that," she answered, screaming as usual at the top of her voice. "I'm here, aren't I? And that's quite enough for me. I haven't had the pleasure of setting eyes on you at all for all these years... But I'll own that when I came here and found I shouldn't be with you all the time, like what I'd expected, I was as vexed as though I had thrown a 'double-one' at dice." "As a matter of fact," said To no Chujo, "I have not anyone at present to run my messages and look after me generally; I had it in mind that, when you were a little more used to things here, I might train you to help me in that way. But I am not at all sure that such a post would suit you. I do not mean that as a lady-in-waiting in some other family you would not get on very nicely. But that would be different... There would be a lot of other young women... People would not notice so much... I am afraid I am not expressing myself very happily. I only mean that a daughter or sister is bound to attract attention. People who come to the house ask, "Now which of them is the daughter?" "Show me which of them is your sister!" and so on. That sort of thing sometimes makes a girl feel awkward, and it may even be rather embarrassing for the parents. Of course, in your case..." He broke off.

Despite all his ingenuity he was in the end saying just what he had determined on no account to say. He was merely telling her that he was

---

* Japanese windows are made of translucent paper, not of glass.

ashamed of her. But fortunately she did not take it in bad part. "That's quite right," she said. "If you was to put me down among all the fine ladies and gentlemen, I shouldn't know which way to look. I'd far rather you asked me to empty their chamber-pots; I think I might be able to manage that." "What odd ideas do come into your head!" laughed To no Chujo. "But before we go any further, I have a small request to make: if you have any filial feeling whatever towards a father whom you see so seldom, try to moderate your voice a little when you address him. Seriously, you will take years off my life if you persist in screaming at me in this way..." How delightful to find that even a Minister could make jokes! "It's no good," she said. "I've always been like that. I suppose I was born so. Mother was always going on at me about it ever since I can remember, and she used to say it all came of her letting an old priest from the Myoho Temple into her bedroom when she was lying-in. He had a terrible loud voice, and all the while he was reading prayers with her, poor mother was wondering whether, when I was born, I shouldn't take after him. And sure enough I did. But I wish for your sake I didn't speak so loud..." It was evident that she was sorry to distress him, and touched by this exhibition of filial affection he said to her kindly: "The fault, then, is evidently not yours but your mother's for choosing her associates among the pious at so critical a moment in her existence. For it is written: 'The tongue of the blasphemer shall tremble, his voice shall be silenced,' and it seems that, conversely, the voices of the pious generally tend to become more and more resonant."

He himself stood somewhat in awe of his daughter Lady Chujo. He knew that she would wonder what had induced him to import, without further enquiries, so incongruous a resident into his household. He imagined, too, the pleasantries at his expense which would be exchanged among her people and soon repeated broadcast over the whole Court. He was on the verge of abandoning the plan, when he suddenly decided that it was too late to withdraw: "I wish you would sometimes go out and see your sister Lady Chujo while she is staying here," he said. "I fancy she could give you one or two useful hints. It is, after all, only by mixing in the society of those who have had greater advantages than themselves, that ordinary people can hope to make any progress. I want you to bear that in mind when you are with her..." "Well, that will be a treat!" she cried delightedly. "I never thought in my wildest dreams that, even if you one day sent for me, you would ever make me into a great lady like my sister. The best I hoped for was that I might wheedle you into letting me carry pitchers from the well..." The last words were spoken in a tiny, squeaky voice like that of a new-fledged sparrow, for she had suddenly remembered her father's injunctions. The effect was very absurd; but there was no use in scolding her any more, and he said good-humoredly: "I see no reason why you should draw water, or hew wood either. But if I send you to Lady Chujo, you must promise me that you have made up your mind never again to model yourself on that pious personage from the Myoho Temple." She took this very seriously. "I'll do my best," she said. "When may I go and see her?" To no Chujo was now an important person; indeed, he was reckoned to be the most formidable enemy to the then Minister of State. But the Lady from Omi appeared quite unconscious of the subduing effect which his presence had upon everyone else, and for her part spoke to him with the utmost confidence and composure. "I will enquire which day will be the best," he said. "But come to think of it, probably one day is quite as good as another. Yes, by all means go today..." and with that he hastened from the room.

She gazed after him. He was attended by officers of the fourth and fifth ranks, who made a brave show as they escorted him towards the main building. But why were they all nudging one another and laughing? "Well," she said at last, "I have got a fine gentleman for my papa, and no mistake. It does seem queer to think what a funny little house I was brought up in, when by rights I ought to have been in this palace all the while." "If you ask my opinion," said her friend the dancer, "I think he is far too grand for you. You'd be a great deal better off if you had been claimed by some decent hard-working sort of man, who wouldn't be ashamed of you..." This was too bad! "There you go again," the Lady from Omi cried, "trying to put a body down whenever she opens her mouth. But you shan't do it any more, indeed you shan't; for they've made me into a lady now, and you'll have to wait till I choose to let you speak. So there!"

Her face was flushed with anger. Seen thus, showing off in the presence of one whom she now regarded as an inferior, she became suddenly handsome and almost dignified. Only her manner of speech, picked up from the absolute riff-raff among whom she had been educated, remained irredeemably vulgar.

It is indeed a strange thing that a perfectly ordinary remark, if made in a quiet, colorless voice, may seem original and interesting; for instance, in conversations about poetry, some quite commonplace piece of criticism will be accepted as very profound merely because it is made in a particular tone of voice. Or again, half a verse from the middle of some little-known poem can make, if produced in the right tone of voice, a deep impression even among people who have no notion what the words imply. Whereas if someone speaks in a disagreeable voice or uses vulgar language, no matter how important or profound are the thoughts which he expresses, nobody will believe that it can possibly be worth while to pay any attention to him. So it was with the Lady from Omi. She had a loud rasping voice and in general behaved with no more regard for the impression she was making on those around her than a child screaming in its nurse's lap. She thus seemed far sillier than she really was. Indeed, her facility in stringing together poems of thirty-one syllables, of the kind in which the beginning of any one poem might just as well be the end of any other, was quite prodigious.

"But I must be getting ready," she now exclaimed. "My father told me I was to call on Lady Chujo, and if I don't go at once, Her Ladyship will think I don't want to meet her. Do you know what? I think I'll go this very night, for though I can see that my papa thinks the world of me, I shall never get on in this palace unless the ladies are on my side..." Which again shows that she had more good sense than one would have supposed.

She now sat down at once and addressed the following letter to Lady Chujo: "Honored Madam, though we have been living these many days past with (as the saying goes) scarce so much as a hurdle between us, I have not hitherto, as they say, ventured to tread upon your shadow, for to tell the honest truth I was in two minds whether I should not find 'No Admittance' in large letters on your door. But though I hardly like to mention it, we are (in the words of the poet) both 'tinged with the purple of Musashi Moor.' If I am being too bold, pray tell me so and do not take offence." All this was written in a rather speckly hand. On the back was the postscript: "By the way, I have some thoughts of inflicting myself upon you this very same evening. And please forgive these blots, which (as the saying goes) all the waters of Minasé River would not wash away, so what is the use of trying?" In the margin was the following extraordinary poem: "I wonder with as big a query as How Cape on the Sea of Hitachi where the grasses are so young and green, when, oh when, like the waves on the shore of Tago, shall we meet face to face?"

"I'll write no more," she added at the side of the poem, "for I declare I feel as flustered as the foam on the great River at Yoshino..."

It was written on a single sheet of blue poetry-paper, in a very cursive style, copiously adorned with hooks and flourishes which seemed to wander about at their own will and stand for nothing at all. The tails of her "*shi's*" were protracted to an inordinate length, and the lines slanted more and more as the letter went on, till in the end they seemed in danger of falling over sideways. But so delighted was she with her own composition that she could hardly bear to part with it. At last, however, she gave it a final look of admiration, folded it up very small and attaching it to a carnation-blossom, handed it to her favorite messenger, a little peasant-boy who did the dirty work in her part of the Palace. He was a good-looking child, and though he had only been in service for a very short while, he had made himself quite at home. Sauntering into Lady

Chujo's apartments, he found his way to the servants' sitting-room and demanded that the note should at once be taken to Her Ladyship. For a moment they surveyed him with astonishment, but presently one of the under-servants exclaimed: "Why, it's the little boy from the northern wing!" and took the letter, which ultimately reached the hands of a certain gentlewoman named Tayu no Kimi. This lady actually carried it into Lady Chujo's presence, unfolded it at her bidding and then held it in front of her. The great lady glanced at it, smiled, and indicated that it might now be removed. It happened that a certain Lady Chunagon was at the moment in attendance. She caught a side view of the letter where it lay, and hoping to be allowed to read it properly, she remarked: "At a distance, Madam, that looks an uncommonly fashionable note." Lady Chujo motioned her to take the letter: "I cannot make head or tail of it," she said; "you will be doing me a service if you can tell me what it is about. Perhaps I am being stupid over these cursive characters..." And a few minutes later: "How are you getting on? If my answer has no connection with the contents of her letter, she will think me very discourteous. I wish you would write an answer for me, I am sure you would do it very nicely..." The young ladies-in-waiting, though they dared not openly show their amusement, were now all tittering behind their sleeves. Someone came to say that the boy was still waiting for an answer. "But the letter is just one mass of stock phrases that none of them seem to have anything to do with what she is trying to say," exclaimed Chunagon in despair. "How can I possibly answer it? Besides, I must make it seem to come from you, Madam, not from a third person, or the poor creature's feelings will be terribly hurt."

"It vexes me," wrote Chunagon in her mistress's name, "to think that we should have been at close quarters for so long without arranging to meet. By all means come..." And at the side she wrote the poem: "Upon the shore of Suma, that is on the sea of Suruga in the land of Hitachi, mount, O ye waves, to where the Headland of Hako with pine-woods is clad."*

"I think you have gone too far," said Lady Chujo when she saw the letter. "I certainly hope she will not think it was I who wrote this ridiculous nonsense..." "I assure you, Madam," replied Chunagon, "there is more sense in it than you think; quite enough at any rate to satisfy the person to whom it is addressed." And with that she folded the note and sent it on its way. "How quickly these great ladies take one's meaning!" exclaimed Omi, as she scanned the reply. "Look, too, how subtly she expresses herself! Merely by mentioning those pine-trees she lets me know, as plain as

---

* The Lady of Omi's poem contained three irrelevant place-names. This one contains four, and is intentionally senseless, for Chunagon had not been able to make out what Omi's rigmarole was about.

could be, that she is waiting for me at this minute..." There was no time to be lost. She scented herself by repeated exposure to the fumes of an incense, which seemed to contain far too generous an admixture of honey, daubed her cheeks with a heavy rouge, and finally combed out her hair, which being, as I have said, unusually fine and abundant, really looked very nice when she took sufficient trouble about it.

The subsequent interview can hardly have been otherwise than extremely diverting.

The Flares

IT was now the turn of Lady Omi's eccentricities to become the sole topic of conversation at Court. "All this is very puzzling," said Genji. "Her father gave orders that she was to be kept in close confinement; how comes it, then, that everyone seems to know so much about her? One hears nothing but stories of her ridiculous behavior. So far from keeping the poor half-witted creature out of harm's way he seems to be positively making an exhibition of her. Here again I think I see the consequences of his obstinate belief in the impeccability of his own family. He sent for her without making the slightest enquiry, convinced that since his blood ran in her veins she must necessarily be beyond reproach. Finding her an exception to this rule he has taken his revenge by deliberately exposing her to derision. However, I can hardly believe that after all the trouble he has taken, it can really give him much satisfaction that the mere mention of her name should evoke peals of laughter..."

The fate of Omi seemed, incidentally, to afford some justification for Genji's reluctance to part with Tamakatsura, a fact which she herself recognized. It was by no means safe to assume that To no Chujo would treat a second long-lost daughter any better than the first. The old nurse Ukon, who daily collected for her mistress's benefit some fresh anecdote of Omi's discomfiture, vigorously supported the view that To no Chujo was not a father to be lightly adopted. "True," thought Tamakatsura, "Genji's attitude towards me is not quite such as I could wish. But I am bound to confess that hitherto he has never tried to go further than I intend he should, and in practical ways no one could possibly be more kind and considerate." Thus gratitude was slowly replaced by friendship and even by a certain semblance of intimacy.

Autumn had now come, and with it a bitterly cold wind—the "first wind" whose chill breath "only a lover's cloak can nullify." He made great efforts to keep away from the western wing, but all to no purpose; and soon, on the pretext of music-lessons or what not, he was spending the greater part of every day at Tamakatsura's side.

One evening when the moon was some five or six days old he came suddenly to her room. The weather was chilly and overcast, and the wind rustled with a melancholy note through the reeds outside the window. She sat with her head resting against her zithern. Tonight, too, as on so many previous occasions, he would make his timorous advances, and at the end of it all be just where he started. So Genji grumbled to himself, and continued to behave in a somewhat plaintive and peevish manner during his whole visit. It was however already very late when the fear of giving offence in other quarters drove him from the room. Just as he was leaving he noticed that the flares outside her window were burning very low, and sending for one of his men, he had them kindled anew; but this time at a little distance from the house, under a strangely leaning spindle-tree which spread its branches in the form of a broad canopy, near to the banks of a deep, chilly stream. The thin flares of split pine-wood were placed at wide intervals, casting pale shadows that flickered remotely upon the walls of the unlighted room where she and Genji sat. He caught a glimpse of her hand, showing frail and ghostly against the dark background of her hair. Her face, suddenly illumined by the cold glare of the distant torches, wore an uneasy and distrustful air. He had risen to go, but still lingered. "You should tell your people never to let the flares go out," he said. "Even in summer, except when there is a moon, it is not wise to leave the garden unlighted. And in autumn... I shall feel very uneasy if you do not promise to remember about this. 'Did but the torches flickering at your door burn brightly as the fire within my breast, you should not want for light!'" And he reminded her of the old song in which the lover asks: "How long, like the smoldering watch-fire at the gate, must my desire burn only with an inward flame?"

"Would that, like the smoke of the watch-fires that mounts and vanishes at random in the empty sky, the smoldering flame of passion could burn itself away!" So she recited, adding: "I do not know what has come over you. Please leave me at once or people will think..." "As you wish," he answered, and was stepping into the courtyard, when he heard a sound of music in the wing occupied by the Lady from the Village of Falling Flowers. Someone seemed to be playing the flute to the accompaniment of a Chinese zithern. No doubt Yugiri was giving a small party. The flute-player could be none other than To no Chujo's eldest son Kashiwagi; for who else at Court performed with such marvelous delicacy and finish? How pleasant would be the effect, thought Genji, if they would consent to come and give a serenade by the streamside, in the subdued light of those flickering torches! "I long to join you," he wrote, "but, could you see the pale, watery shadows that the watch-flares are casting here in the garden of the western wing, you would know why I am slow to come..." He sent this note to Yugiri, and presently three figures appeared out of the darkness. "I should not have sent for you," he called to them, "had you not played 'The Wind's voice tells me...' It is a tune that I can never resist." So saying he brought out his own zithern. When he had played for a while, Yugiri began to improvise on his flute in the Banshiki mode.[*] Kashiwagi attempted to join in, but his thoughts were evidently employed elsewhere,[†] for again and again he entered at the wrong beat. "Too late," cried Genji, and at last Kobai was obliged to keep his brother in measure by humming the air in a low monotone like the chirping of a meditative grasshopper. Genji made them go through the piece twice, and then handed his zithern to Kashiwagi. It was some while since he had heard the boy play and he now observed with delight that his talent was not by any means confined to wind-instruments. "You could have given me no greater pleasure," he said, when the piece was over. "Your father is reckoned a fine performer on the zithern; but you have certainly more than overtaken him... By the way, I should have cautioned you that there is someone seated just within who can probably hear all that is going on out in this portico. So tonight there had better not be too much drinking. Do not be offended, for I was really thinking more of myself than of you. Now that I am getting on in years I find wine far more dangerous than I used to. I am apt to say the most indiscreet things..."

Tamakatsura did, as a matter of fact, overhear every word of this, as indeed she was intended to, and was thankful that he at any rate saw the necessity of keeping himself in hand. The near presence of the two visitors could not fail to interest her extremely, if for no other reason than merely because they were, after all, though themselves entirely unaware of the fact, so very closely related to her; and for long past she had surreptitiously collected all possible information concerning their characters and pursuits. Kashiwagi was, as to her distress she had frequently ascertained, very deeply in love with her. Again and again during the course of the evening, he was on the verge of collapsing altogether; but never was the state of agitation through which he was passing for a moment reflected in his playing.

---

[*] Corresponding roughly with the white notes from D to D.
[†] He was in love with Tamakatsura.

The Typhoon

THIS year great pains had been taken to improve the Empress Akikonomu's domain; and by now her gardens were aglow with the varied tints of innumerable frost-stained leaves and autumn flowers. Above all, the new pergolas made an admirable show, now that their timber, here stripped of bark, there used in its natural state, was thickly interwoven with blossoming boughs. And when at morning and evening the sun slanted across the dewy gardens, it was as though every flower and tree were decked with strings of glittering pearls. Those who but a few months back had been carried away by the springtime loveliness of the Southern Garden, could not fail, as they gazed upon the colder beauty of this autumnal scene, with one accord to resume their earlier preference. The lovers of autumn have, I am persuaded, at all times embraced the larger part of mankind; and in thus returning to their allegiance the Empress's companions were but following their natural bent.

So delighted was Akikonomu with the scene I have described that she asked for leave of absence from the Emperor and settled for a while in her own establishment. Unfortunately the anniversary of the late Prince Zembo's[*] death fell in the eighth month, and it was with great anxiety that she watched autumn's almost hourly advance; for she feared that the best month would be over before she came out of mourning. Meanwhile she was confined to the house and all amusements were suspended.

The equinoctial gales were this year particularly violent. Then came a day when the whole sky grew black, and an appalling typhoon began. It would have been bad enough wherever one had been to see every tree stripped of its leaves just when they were at their loveliest, every flower stricken to the earth; but to witness such havoc in an exquisite garden, planned from corner to corner with endless foresight and care, to see those dew-pearls unthreaded in an instant and scattered upon the ground, was a sight calculated, to drive the onlooker well nigh to madness. As time went on the hurricane became more and more alarming, till all was lost to view in a blinding swirl of fog and dust. But while she sat behind tightly closed shutters in a room that rocked with every fresh blast, it was with thoughts of autumn splendors irrevocably lost rather than with terror of the storm that the Empress's heart was shaken.

---

[*] Her father, Rokujo's husband, who died early.

The Southern Gardens were just being laid out with wild plants from the countryside when the high winds began, and that impatient longing which the poet attributes to the young lespidezas[*] was indeed fulfilled in all too ample measure. Morning after morning Murasaki too saw the dew roughly snatched from leaf and flower. She was sitting thus one day on watch at her window while Genji played with the little princess in a neighboring room. It happened that Yugiri had occasion to come across from the eastern wing. When he reached the door at the end of the passage he noticed that the great double-doors leading into Murasaki's room were half-open. Without thinking what he was doing, he paused and looked in. Numerous ladies-in-waiting were passing to and fro just inside, and had he made any sound they would have looked up, seen him and necessarily supposed that he had stationed himself there on purpose to spy upon those within. He saw nothing for it but to stand dead still. Even indoors the wind was so violent that screens would not stand up. Those which usually surrounded the high dais were folded and stacked against the wall. There, in full view of anyone who came along the corridor, reclined a lady whose notable dignity of mien and bearing would alone have sufficed to betray her identity. This could be none other than Murasaki. Her beauty flashed upon him as at dawn the blossom of the red flowering cherry flames out of the mist upon the traveler's still sleepy eye. It was wafted towards him, suddenly imbued him, as though a strong perfume had been dashed against his face. She was more beautiful than any woman he had ever seen. The hangings of her dais had broken away from the poles and now fluttered in the wind like huge flags. Her ladies made vain attempts to recapture these flapping curtain-ends, and in the course of the struggle (only half-visible to Yugiri) something very amusing evidently occurred, for Murasaki suddenly burst into peals of laughter. Soon however she became serious again. For here, too, though in a lesser degree, the wind was working irreparable havoc, and at each fresh blast he saw her turn a despairing gaze towards her newly-planted beds. Several of her gentlewomen, thought Yugiri, as his eye accustomed itself to the scene, were noticeably good-looking; but there was not one whose appearance could for more than an instant have distracted his attention from the astonishing creature at whose command they served. Now he understood why it was that Genji had always taken such pains to keep him away from her. His father was wise enough to know that no one could possibly see her thus without losing all control of himself. Genji had indeed, in forbidding him all access to her rooms, foreseen just such a contingency as had at this moment occurred. The boy, suddenly

---

[*] "I await your coming eagerly as waits the young lespedeza, so heavy with dew, for the wind that shall disburden it."

realizing the extreme insecurity of his hiding-place and at the same time overwhelmed with shame at the mere thought of being discovered in such a situation, was about to dart into safety, when a door on the left opened and Genji himself entered the room. "What a wind!" he said as he surveyed the exposed condition of her dais. "It would really be better just now if you left all the shutters closed. You probably do not realize that you and your ladies are at this moment exposing yourselves completely to the view of any gentleman who may happen to come this way..." Yugiri had already withdrawn his eye from the crack; but the sound of Genji's voice aroused in him an invincible curiosity, and he returned to his former position. His father was bending over Murasaki and whispering something in her ear; now he was laughing. It seemed to Yugiri very odd that this high-spirited, handsome, quite young-looking man should really be his father. As for Genji's companion—he could not imagine that she could ever have been more beautiful than at this moment. He gazed spellbound, and would certainly have crouched at his chink for hours to come, had not the door on the opposite side of the passage suddenly blown wide open, thus leaving his hiding-place embarrassingly exposed. Reluctantly he withdrew (as was now possible, for Murasaki's attendants had all retired to the far end of the room), and working his way round to the verandah, he called to Genji as though he had just arrived from the eastern wing. His father answered the greeting and presently joined him, saying to Murasaki as he left the room something which evidently referred to the imperfectly fastened passage-door. "Look there!" Genji was saying crossly; "is not that just what I told you? You must really be more careful..." "This," thought Yugiri, "is indeed a tribute to the devotion of her guards during all these years! Only a tempest capable of hurling rocks through the air and uprooting whole forests can so far disarm their vigilance that for a few seconds she is exposed to the curiosity of the passerby." He was bound to confess that towards him at any rate the dreaded hurricane had done its best to act a benevolent part.

Several retainers now arrived, reporting that the typhoon was assuming a very serious aspect. "It is from the northeast," they said, 'so that here you are comparatively protected and have no notion of its real violence. Both the racing-lodge and the fishing-pavilion are in great danger..." While those people were busy making fast various doors and shutters, and repairing the damage of the previous night, Genji turned to Yugiri and said: "Where did you arrive from just now?" "I spent the night at my grandmother's," he replied. "But everyone says that we are in for a very bad storm, and I felt I ought to come back here and see if I could be of any use... But as a matter of fact it is far worse in the Third Ward than here in the Sixth. The mere noise of the wind, quite apart from everything else, is terrifying at my grandmother's, and if you do not mind I think it would be a good thing if I went back there at once. She is as frightened as though she were a child of two, and it seems unkind to leave her..." "Yes, by all means go back at once," answered Genji hastily. "One sometimes thinks that the notion of old people slipping back into a second childhood is a mere fable; but I have learnt lately from instances in my own family that it does really happen. Tell her, please, that I have heard how bad things are in the Third Ward and should certainly come myself, were I not satisfied that you will be able to do quite as much for her as I could."

Yugiri had a high sense of duty. It was his practice at this time to visit his grandmother at least once a day, and it would have been a ferocious wind indeed that could deter him either from setting out for the Third Ward or returning thence at the hour when his father usually asked for him. There were of course "times of observance" when he was obliged to remain shut up in the Emperor's Palace for several days on end. But otherwise neither pressure of public business nor attendance at state ceremonies and festivals, however much they might impinge upon his leisure, ever prevented him from calling first at the New Palace and the upon the old Princess, before he dreamt of embarking upon any amusement of his own. Still less upon such a day as this, when, bad as the storm was already, there seemed every prospect that it would soon develop into something more alarming still, could he have brought himself to leave the old lady in solitude.

She was, indeed, delighted that he had not failed her. "This is the worst typhoon there has ever been in my lifetime," she said; "and I can assure you I have seen a good many." She was trembling from head to foot. Now and again came a strange and terrifying sound; some huge bough that a single breath of the hurricane had twisted from its trunk, crashed in splinters to the ground. Apart from all other dangers, showers of tiles were falling from every roof. To go into the streets at all on such a day was indeed no very safe undertaking, and for a while she listened with mingled gratitude and alarm to the recital of his perils and escapes.

The old Princess's lonely and monotonous existence contrasted strangely with the brilliant scenes amid which she had moved during the days of her husband's remarkable ascendancy. Indeed, that the visits of this staid young grandson should mean so much to her showed only too plainly how far she had fallen from the days when her antechambers were thronged by the fashionable world. True, her name was still widely known and even revered in the country at large; but this was small consolation for the fact that her own son, To no Chujo, had for some time past been far from cordial in his manner towards her. It was very good of Yugiri to come on such an evening. But why was it that he looked so thoughtful? Perhaps the noise of the hurricane distracted him. It was certainly very alarming.

If Yugiri fell into a meditative mood in this house, it was generally with memories of his little playmate[*] that his mind was employed. But tonight he had not, as a matter of fact, thought of her once; nor did the tempest disturb him. It was the face he had seen this morning, in the course of his unintended eavesdropping, which now continually haunted him, till he suddenly checked his imagination and asked himself remorsefully what had come over him that in this of all places another face than Kumoi's should have filled his thoughts during a whole evening. And if it was a crime in him that he should presume to court To no Chujo's daughter, what view would his elders take if they should discover that he spent his leisure in thinking of Genji's wife? He tried hard to think of other things; but after a moment or two the recollection of what he had seen that morning sprang back into his mind. Was all this a mere aberration on his part? He could not believe it; surely her beauty was indisputably of the kind that occurs only once or twice in a century—that a whole epoch may utterly lack? There was nothing to be wondered at in the impression which the sight of her had made upon him; if there was anything strange in the matter at all, it was that Genji, having such a wife as this, could ever have taken any interest in such creatures as the lady in the eastern wing.[†] That did indeed require some explanation. It was heart-rending that the most beautiful woman of her generation should fall to the lot of one whose other intimacies proved him so completely lacking in discrimination.

It was characteristic of Yugiri's high sense of propriety that when in his imaginings he became better acquainted with this lovely creature, it was not with Murasaki herself but with someone in every respect exactly like her that he pictured himself spending hours of enchanted bliss. Yes, that was what he needed; without it life, he had begun to discover, was not worth living at all.

Towards dawn the wind became somewhat dank and clammy; before long sheets of rain were being swept onward by the hurricane. News came that many of the outbuildings at the New Palace had been blown to the ground. The main structure was so solidly built as to defy any storm. In the quarters inhabited by Genji there was, too, a continual coming and going, which served to mitigate the strain of those alarming hours. But the side wings of the Palace were very sparsely inhabited. Yugiri's own neighbor, for example—the Lady from the Village of Falling Flowers—might easily be by this time in a pitiable state of panic. Clearly it was his duty to give her his support, and he set out for home while it was still dark. The rain was blowing crossways, and no sooner had he seated himself in his

---

[*] Kumoi

[†] The Lady from the Village of Falling Flowers.

litter, than an icy douche poured in through the ventilator and drenched his knees. The town wore an inconceivably desolate and stricken air. In his own mind too there was a strange sensation; it was as though there also, just as in the world outside, the wonted landmarks and boundaries had been laid waste by some sudden hurricane. What had happened to him? For a moment he could only remember that it was something distressing, shameful... Why, it was hideous! Yesterday morning... That was it, of course. He was mad; nothing more nor less than a raving lunatic. He had fallen in love with Murasaki!

He did indeed find his neighbor in the eastern wing sadly in need of a little support and encouragement. He managed however to convince her that the worst danger was over, and sending for some of his own carpenters had everything put to rights. He felt that he ought now to greet his father. But in the central hall everything was still locked and barred. He went to the end of the passage and leaning on the balustrade looked out into the Southern Garden. Even such trees as still stood were kneeling over in the wind so that their tops almost touched the ground. Broken branches were scattered in every direction and what once had been flowerbeds were now mere rubbish heaps, strewn with a promiscuous litter of thatch and tiles, with here and there a fragment of trellis-work or the top of a fence. There was now a little pale sunshine, that slanting through a break in the sky gleamed fitfully upon the garden's woe-begone face; but sullen clouds packed the horizon, and as Yugiri gazed on the desolate scene his eyes filled with tears. How came it, he asked himself, that he should be doomed time and again to long precisely for what it was impossible for him to obtain. He wiped away his tears, came close to Genji's door and called. "That sounds like Yugiri's voice," he heard Genji say. "I had no notion it was so late..." He heard his father rise. There was a pause, and then Genji laughed, perhaps at some remark that had been inaudible. "No indeed," he said. "You and I have fared better than most lovers. We have never known what it was to be torn from each other at the first streak of dawn, and I do not think that after all these years we should easily reconcile ourselves to such a fate." Even to overhear such a conversation as this gave Yugiri a certain kind of pleasure. He could not make out a word of what Murasaki said in reply and judging from the laughter with which the conversation was constantly interrupted it was not of a very serious description. But he felt he could say to himself, "That is what happens when they are alone together," and he went on listening. Now, however, there was a noise of swift footsteps. Evidently Genji was about to unbolt the door with his own hands. Conscious that he was standing far closer to it than was natural Yugiri stepped back guiltily into the corridor. "Well," asked Genji, "was the Princess pleased to see you last night?" "Yes, I think she was," answered Yugiri. "She seems to be very much upset about something that has happened between her and my uncle Tō no Chūjō. She cried a great deal and I was very sorry for her." Genji smiled. "Oh, I know all about that business," he said. "She will soon get over it. You must persuade her not to brood upon such matters. He thinks she has been indiscreet, and is doing his best to make her feel uncomfortable about it. He cares immensely about the impression which his conduct makes on other people; and as regards his mother—he has always gone out of his way to convince the world that he is a paragon of filial devotion. So far as outward show is concerned, this is true enough. But I fancy that it is all done chiefly for the sake of appearances. The truth of the matter is that he has no very deep feelings towards anybody. This may seem a hard thing to say; but, on the other hand, I freely admit his good qualities. He is extremely well-informed and intelligent; he is musical to an extent which has become very rare in these days. In addition to all that, he is good-looking. As I have said, I think his feelings somewhat superficial. But we all have defects of one sort or another... By the way, I ought to find out how the Empress has been getting on during this appalling hurricane. I wish you would find out if there is anything I can do for her..." and he gave Yūgiri a note in which he said: "I am afraid the wind prevented you from getting much sleep. I myself find it a great strain and am feeling rather shaky; otherwise I should have come round to see you long ago..."

On approaching the Empress's apartments he saw a little girl with a cage in her hand trip lightly into the garden; she had come to give the tame cicadas their morning sip of dew. Further off several ladies were wandering among the flower-beds with baskets over their arms, searching for such stray blossoms as might chance to have survived the tempest. Now and again they were hidden by great wreaths of storm-cloud that trailed across the garden with strange and lovely effect. Yūgiri called to the flower-gatherers. They did not start or betray the least sign of discomposure, but in an instant they had all disappeared into the house.

Being still a mere boy at the time when Akikonomu came to Genji's house, he had been allowed to run in and out of her rooms just as he chose, and had thus become very intimate with several of her gentlewomen. While he was waiting for the Empress's reply, two of these old acquaintances, a certain Saishō no Kimi, and a lady called Naishi, came into view at the end of the passage. He hailed them and had a long conversation. He used to think Lady Akikonomu a very splendid person; and he was still obliged to confess, as he now looked about him, that she lived in very good style and had shown excellent taste in the furnishing of her quarters. But since those days he had learnt to judge by very different standards, and a visit to this part of the Palace no longer interested him in the slightest degree.

On his return to Murasaki's rooms, he found all the shutters unbarred. Everything had resumed its normal course. He delivered the Empress's reply, in which she said: "It may be very childish, but I own I have been much upset by the storm. I made sure that you would come and see to things here... It would still be a great help to me if you could spare a moment..." "I remember," said Genji, "that she was always very easily upset by anything of this kind. I can imagine what a panic she and her ladies must have worked themselves up into during the course of the night! It was wrong of me not to see after her..." and he started off towards the Empress's apartments. But he found he had forgotten his cloak, and turning back to the high dais he raised a corner of the curtain and disappeared within. For a moment Yugiri caught sight of a light-colored sleeve; his heart began to beat so loud that it seemed to him everyone else in the room must be able to hear it, and he quickly averted his eyes from the dais. There was an interval during which Genji was presumably adjusting his cloak at the mirror. Then Yugiri heard his father's voice saying: "I cannot help thinking that Yugiri is really looking quite handsome this morning. No doubt I am partial, and to everyone else he looks a mere hobbledehoy; for I know that at the between-stage he has now reached young men are usually far from prepossessing in appearance." After this there was a pause during which he was perhaps looking at his own countenance in the mirror, well content that the passage of time had as yet done so little to impair it. Presently Yugiri heard him say very thoughtfully: "It is strange; whenever I am going to see Akikonomu I suddenly begin to feel that I am looking terribly shabby and unpresentable. I cannot think why she should have that effect on one. There is really nothing very remarkable about her, either in intellect or appearance. But one feels, I think, that she is all the while making judgments, which if they ever came to the surface, would seem oddly at variance with the mild femininity of her outward manner..." With these words Genji reappeared from behind the curtains. The look of complete detachment with which Yugiri imagined he met his father's gaze was perhaps not so successfully assumed as the boy supposed; for Genji suddenly halted and returning to the dais whispered to Murasaki something about the door which had been left unfastened yesterday morning. "No, I am sure he didn't," answered Murasaki indignantly. "If he had come along the corridor my people would have noticed. They never heard a sound..." "Very queer, all the same," murmured Genji to himself as he left the room. Yugiri now noticed that a group of gentlemen was waiting for him at the end of the cross-gallery, and he hastened to meet them. He tried to join in their conversation and even in their laughter; but he was feeling in no mood for society, and little as his friends expected of him in the way of gaiety, they found him on this occasion more obdurately low-spirited than ever before.

Soon however his father returned and carried him off to the eastern wing. They found the gentlewomen of this quarter engaged in making preparations to meet the sudden cold. A number of grey-haired old ladies were cutting out and stitching, while the young girls were busy hanging out quilts and winter cloaks over lacquered clothes-frames. They had just beaten and pulled a very handsome dark-red under-robe, a garment of magnificent color, certainly unsurpassed as an example of modern dyeing—and were spreading it out to air. "Why, Yugiri," said Genji, "that is your coat, is it not? I suppose you would have been wearing it at the Emperor's Chrysanthemum Feast; but of course this odious hurricane has put a stop to everything of that sort. What a depressing autumn it is going to be!"

But Yugiri could not summon up much interest in the round of visits upon which his father had embarked, and slipped away to the rooms of his little sister, the Princess from Akashi. The child was not there. "She is still with Madam," her nurse said. "She went later than usual today. She was so frightened of the storm that it was a long time before she got to sleep, and we had a job to get her out of bed at all this morning." "When things began to be so bad," said Yugiri, "I intended to come round here and sit up with her; but then I heard that my grandmother was very much upset, and thought that I had better go to her instead. What about the doll's house? Has that come to any harm?" The nurse and her companions laughed. "Oh, that doll's house!" one of them exclaimed. "Why, if I so much as fanned myself the little lady would always cry out to me that I was blowing her dolls to bits. You can imagine, then, what a time we had of it when the whole house was being blown topsy-turvy, and every minute something came down with a crash... You'd better take charge of that doll's house. I don't mind telling you I'm sick to death of it!"

Yugiri had several letters to write, and as the little girl was still with her stepmother he said to the nurse: "Might I have some ordinary paper. Perhaps from the writing-case in your own room..." The nurse however went straight to the little Princess's own desk and taking the cover off her lacquered writing-case laid upon it a whole roll of the most elegant paper she could find. Yugiri at first protested. But after all, was not a rather absurd fuss made about this young lady and her future? There was nothing sacrosanct about her possessions; and accepting the paper, which was of a thin, purple variety, he mixed his ink very carefully and, continually inspecting the point of his brush, began writing slowly and cautiously. The air of serious concentration with which he settled down to his task was very impressive; more so, indeed, than the composition itself, for his education had been chiefly upon other lines.

The poem was as follows: "Not even on this distracted night when howling winds drive serried hosts of cloud across the sky, do I for an instant forget thee, thou Unforgettable One." He tied this to a tattered spray of miscanthus that he had picked up in the porch. At this there was general laughter. "It's clear you haven't read your Karano no Shosho*" said one of the nurses, "or you would at least choose a flower that matched your paper..." "You are quite right," he answered rather sulkily, "I have never bothered my head about such matters. No doubt one ought to go tramping about the countryside looking for an appropriate flower, but I have no intention of doing so..." He had always seemed to the nurses and other such ladies of the household very difficult to get anything out of. Apparently he did not care what impression he made upon them; and as a matter of fact they were beginning to think him rather priggish and stuck-up.

He wrote a second letter, and sending for his retainer Uma no Suke put this and the original note into the man's hand. But evidently the two letters were to go in quite different directions.† For Uma no Suke, having scanned the addresses, entrusted one to a page boy and the other to a discreet, responsible-looking body-servant. These proceedings were accompanied by a great many whispered warnings and injunctions. The curiosity of the young nurses knew no bounds; but it remained wholly unsatisfied; for hard though they strained their ears, they could not catch a word.

Yugiri was now tired of waiting and made his way to his grandmother's house. He found her quietly pursuing her devotions, surrounded by gentlewomen not all of whom were either old or ill-looking. But in dress and bearing they formed a strange contrast to the chattering, frivolous young creatures from whom he had just parted. The nuns, too, who had come to take part in the service, were by no means decrepit or disagreeable in person, a fact which gave an additional pathos to their assumption of this somber and unbecoming guise.

Later in the day To no Chujo called, and when the great lamp had been brought in, he and the old Princess had a long, quiet talk. At last she screwed up her courage to say: "It is a very long time since I saw Kumoi..." and she burst into tears. "I was just going to suggest sending her round here in a day or two," said To no Chujo. "I am not very happy about her. She is certainly thinner than she used to be, and there is sometimes a peculiar expression in her face... It is almost as though she had something on her mind. I do not understand how it is that, while I have never had a moment's anxiety over my boys, with these daughters of mine something goes wrong at every turn. And never through any fault of mine..." He said this with an intonation that clearly showed he had not

---

* A tale of the "perfect lover," very popular in Murasaki's day, but now lost. Cf. Part I, p. 18.

† One to Kumoi, one to Koremitsu's daughter.

entirely forgiven her. She was sorely wounded by this obstinate injustice, but did not attempt to defend herself.

"Talking of daughters," he went on, "you have probably heard that I have lately made a very unsuccessful addition to my household. You have no idea what worries I am going through..." He spoke in a doleful tone, but no sooner were the words uttered than he burst out laughing. "I cannot bear to hear you talking in that way," said the old Princess. "Of one thing I am quite sure: if she is really your daughter she cannot be so bad as people are making out." "I think, all the same," said To no Chujo, "that it might be possible to put too great a strain upon your habitual indulgence towards everything connected with me. That being so, I have no intention whatever of introducing her to you."

PART FOUR
BLUE TROUSERS

LIST OF MOST IMPORTANT PERSONS (alphabetical)

Akashi, Lady of.........Brought back by Genji from his place of exile.
Akashi, Princess........Daughter of the above.
Akikonomu............Daughter of Rokujo. Consort of the Emperor Ryozen.
Aoi..................Genji's first wife. Her death is recorded at the end of Part I.
Asagao, Princess........Courted in vain by Genji.
Chujo, Lady...........Daughter of To no Chujo. Concubine of the Emperor Ryozen.
Chujo no Omoto.......Maid in service of Higekuro.
Crown Prince, The......Son of Suzaku. Afterwards ascends the Throne. "The New Emperor."
Emperor, The New.....See Crown Prince.
Falling Flowers.........Lady from the Village of. A mild and patient lady, entrusted with Yugiri's upbringing.
Fujitsubo..............Genji's stepmother. Secretly loved by him.
Genji, Prince...........The hero.
Higekuro..............Husband to Makibashira, who goes mad. Subsequently marries Tamakatsura.
Hyobukyo, Prince.......Murasaki's father.
Jokyoden, Princess......Consort of Suzaku.
Kaoru................Son of Nyosan and Kashiwagi. Supposed by the world to be Genji's son.
Kashiwagi.............Son of To no Chujo. In love with Nyosan.
Kobai................Kashiwagi's brother.
Kojiju................Maid to Nyosan.
Koremitsu.............Genji's favorite retainer.
Koremitsu's Daughter..."The Gosechi dancer." Yugiri takes a fancy to her at the time when he cannot get access to Kumoi.
Kumoi................To no Chujo's daughter. Yugiri's wife.
Makibashira...........Higekuro's mad wife.
Moku no Kimi.........Maid in service of Higekuro.
Murasaki..............Genji's wife. The low rank of her mother prevented her ever being installed as kita no kata or "legitimate spouse."
Niou.................Son of the New Emperor and the Akashi Princess. Genji's grandson.
Nishi no Miya.........Murasaki's eldest sister.

Nyosan	Favorite daughter of the ex-Emperor Suzaku. Accepted by Genji as his kita no kata, in deference to Suzaku's wishes. Loved by Kashiwagi.
Oborozuki	Consort of Suzaku. Formerly loved by Genji.
Ochiba	Daughter of Suzaku. Married to Kashiwagi; after his death, loved by Yugiri.
Omi, Lady from	Illegitimate daughter of To no Chujo.
Omiya, Princess	To no Chujo's mother. Yugiri's maternal grandmother.
Rokujo, Lady	Loved by Genji in his early day. Violently jealous of his other attendants.
Ryozen, Emperor	Thought by the world to be the son of the Old Emperor (Genji's father); but in reality son of Genji and the Old Emperor's consort, Lady Fujitsubo.
Saisho	Maid to Tamakatsura.
Sochi, Prince	Genji's half-brother.
Suzaku, Ex-Emperor	Genji's half-brother. Father of Nyosan and Ochiba.
Tamakatsura	Daughter of To no Chujo and Yugao. Adopted by Genji.
To no Chujo	Genji's great friend. Brother of Genji's first wife, Aoi.
Yamato, Governor of	Nephew of Ochiba's mother.
Yugao	Loved by Genji in his youth. Withered by Rokujo's jealousy. Dies in the deserted mansion (see Part I, Chap. IV).
Yugiri	Genji's son by Aoi.

The Royal Visit

Genji's mind was still occupied with the question of Tamakatsura's future. He was, as he put it to himself, exploring various possibilities—honestly endeavoring to discover a plan that would ensure her happiness. But meanwhile the girl's reputation had, true to Murasaki's prediction, already begun to suffer. The fact that rumors connecting Genji's name with hers were now generally current made his situation with regard to her true father more than ever embarrassing. Where other people's conduct was concerned To no Chujo's standards were singularly exacting. The moment he heard that the subject of all this gossip was his own daughter Chujo's moral indignation would know no bounds, and he would certainly not consider it any part of his duty to save Genji's face or lighten the consequences of his equivocal behavior. Was it, Genji now began to ask himself, of any advantage either to the girl or her father that their relationship should be disclosed? Far better, surely, to find her a suitable husband as soon as possible, or best of all, induce the Emperor to admit her into the Palace.

This year the Emperor was to take part in the Oharano Festival.[*] People came from all over the country to witness the ceremony, and the sightseers included several parties from the New Palace.[†] The procession left the Suzaku gate at the hour of the Hare,[‡] turning to the right when it reached the Great Highway of the Fifth Ward. All through the town, and beyond it as far as the Katsura river, the road was thickly lined by coaches. The procession was, strictly speaking, an Imperial Progress; but on this occasion the Palanquin was followed by most of the younger princes and noblemen, on horses sumptuously saddled and equipped. Their retainers, also on horseback, were all men of fine stature and appearance, clad in magnificent costumes, so that the general effect was one of extraordinary splendor. All the great Ministers of State were there, from the Ministers of the Right and Left, the Palace Minister and Chancellors downwards. Even the lower officers, including those of the Sixth Rank, were as a special privilege allowed to wear the dove-grey cloak and wine-red tunic. There had been a slight fall of snow, but

---

[*] A religious ceremony which took place in the twelfth month. The Oharano shrine was situated in the hills to the west of Kyoto.
[†] Genji's palace.
[‡] 5 A.M.

during the time of the procession the weather was perfect. Such of the courtiers as had been taking part in the recent hunting expeditions were still in their strange falconers' costumes. They were attended by the hawk-trainers drawn from the falconries of the Six Bodyguards. These men, in their rather wild-looking, patterned dresses, quite unfamiliar to most residents of the Capital, attracted a great deal of attention. Though there was much in the proceedings that lay outside the scope of what young ladies are supposed to understand, the mere interest and beauty of the sight brought them to the scene in their thousands, and it was touching to observe how many crazy, tottering conveyances just managed to creak and lumber to the spot in time to see the procession pass. The most fashionable viewpoint was just before the Bridge of Boats. Here the really smart equipages were seen in greatest abundance; among them, that of Lady Tamakatsura. It was of course towards the open window of the Emperor's Palanquin that she at once turned a fascinated gaze. Clad in a bright scarlet cloak, he sat motionless, not for an instant turning his young face to right or left. Never in her life had she seen so many handsome faces and fine clothes; but the Emperor could hold his own. She could not help casting a secret glance towards her father as he rode by with the other Ministers. He was a finely built man, and wore an air of vigor and enterprise that marked him out from among all the other commoners in the train. But it was not for long that she diverted her gaze from the scarlet-robed figure in the Palanquin. As for such or such a young prince whose conversation or appearance she had heard praised, this or that chamberlain or courtier who had plied her with love letters— though her friends kept pointing them out, she did not pay the slightest attention, but continued to gaze at the figure in the red cloak, who was not only her Sovereign, but also the handsomest young man in all the throng. In cast of countenance he was, she thought, extraordinarily like Prince Genji, though the august position which he held had given to these same features a sternness, an imperturbable dignity very different from the habitual expression of her guardian's face.

By the lesser figures in the procession she was, she must needs confess, very much disappointed. Used to Genji and Yugiri, she had fallen into the habit of supposing that beauty was the common property of all wellborn gentlemen; and it was with some consternation that she today encountered such chins and noses as she could scarcely believe to be varieties of the organs with which she was familiar. She recognized Prince Hyobukyo;[*] and also her own suitor Prince Higekuro, who, though not usually very particular about his appearance, was today quite smart in his guardsman's dress, with a stylish Persian quiver across his shoulders. He

---

[*] Murasaki's father.

was dark-skinned and very hairy. This disgusted her, though she knew that men cannot be expected to have faces as smooth and complexions as delicately graded as those of a lady fresh from her toilet-table. No doubt she was unreasonable; but she could not help it. Argue with herself as she might, the appearance of such people as Prince Higekuro distressed her. Her thoughts went back to the Emperor. Genji had spoken lately about the possibility of her being summoned to the Palace. She did not want to become the Emperor's concubine. That kind of thing did not appeal to her; moreover she did not think herself sufficiently presentable, and could not imagine that she would ever stand a chance of being chosen for such a purpose. But to be attached to the Palace in some general capacity, and if not actually to enjoy the Emperor's friendship, at any rate often to see him in a far less fleeting manner than she had done today—such a notion pleased her, and henceforward her mind frequently dwelt upon it.

At last the procession arrived at Oharano, the Palanquin halted, and a great banquet was served in the Imperial Tent. While such of the guests as had arrived in Court dress were changing into their cloaks and hunting-jackets, a great hamper of wine and fruit arrived as a present from the New Palace. The Emperor had expressed a wish that Genji should be present at today's proceedings; but he had excused himself, saying the day fixed for the ceremony clashed with a religious observance* which it was impossible for him to neglect. His Majesty, upon the receipt of Genji's hamper, sent a lieutenant of the Guard back to the New Palace with a return present of game—a dozen or so partridges strung to the bough of a tree. With it was a prose message of the usual kind, which I will not here reproduce, for the pronouncements of Royalty on such occasions are not necessarily of great interest. The Imperial Poem was as follows: "The tracks these woodland birds imprinted on the snowy hill would guide you safely on the path that Precedent decrees." By this he meant that the Grand Minister had never before been absent on the occasion of the Royal Visit.

Genji entertained the messenger with suitable respect, and finally sent him back with the poem: "So thick this morning's snow that, where I seek my way, no ancient track remains upon the wind-drifts of the desolate hill."† I have, as a matter of fact, heard a good deal more of what took place on this occasion; but there are still several gaps that I have not been able to fill in, and I shall therefore at present say nothing further about it.

Next day Genji wrote a note to Tamakatsura in which he said: "How did you get on yesterday? Were you able to see the procession properly?

---

* Perhaps the anniversary of Lady Rokujo's death?

† This Royal Visit is so much more splendid than any previous one that precedents do not count. There is a play of words: *mi-yuki* means "deep snow," but also "Royal Visit."

I am sure that, if you were, you now take a very different view about my recent proposal...." She was at first amused by the notion that a fleeting, glimpse through the window of a palanquin could have altered her decision about serving at the Palace. But after a moment's reflection she realized that this was precisely what had happened. How clever he always was at guessing what went on in other people's heads!

In reply she sent the poem: "How think you I could have seen the Light of Heaven when snow-clouds dimmed the morning with their sullen breath?"* Genji showed the letter to Murasaki, and explained the situation. "I have been suggesting that she should apply for a post at the Palace," he said. "But I am not sure that I could get her accepted. You see, it was from my house that Lady Akikonomu entered the Imperial service, and it might be thought that I was asking too much in trying to establish a second ward of mine in a high position at the Palace. Nothing would be gained if I restored her to her father; for he too has already supplied His Majesty with a consort.† It is all very difficult and confusing.... The Emperor is extremely attractive. Now that she has seen him, were she only a few years younger and somewhat less diffident about her own powers to please, she would not, I am sure, rest content till she secured a footing in his household...." "How horrible you think everyone is," Murasaki answered, laughing. "Even if she admired the Emperor (and there is no reason to suppose that she did), a girl such as she would never dream of putting herself forward... We women are really far less immodest than you suppose." "Possibly," replied Genji. "But on the other hand the Emperor is far handsomer than you suppose, as you will admit when you have seen him."

Another difficulty was now beginning to present itself. So long as she continued to live quietly in the New Palace the question of Tamakatsura's clan-rights was not likely to be raised. She would pass as a member of the Minamoto, Genji's own clan, and be admitted without further scrutiny to the worship of his family gods. But supposing he succeeded in getting her into the Palace or in finding her a husband, it would then be necessary to come into the open about which clan she belonged to. He would, of course, if he intended to pass her off as his own child, have to pretend that she was a Minamoto. If this only meant depriving the Kasuga Deity‡ of a worshipper, it would not be of much consequence. But there was always the risk that the true facts might one day come to light, and then his own conduct towards those who had accepted her at his hands would appear so discreditable that he would never be able to face them again.

---

* Again there is a play on the two senses of *mi-yuki*.

† Lady Chujo, To no Chujo's eldest daughter.

‡ Clan god of the Fujiwaras, the family to which To no Chujo and consequently Tamakatsura belonged.

He knew of course that ordinary upper-class people changed over from one clan to another without the slightest compunction; it was, indeed, rather a fashionable thing to do so...

No, it was no use arguing in this way. Such adoptions did not alter the facts of the case. Tamakatsura was not his child, but To no Chujo's. Sooner or later her father would become aware of this, and that being so it was far better that he should learn the truth from Genji's own lips He accordingly wrote to To no Chujo, and without giving any explanation asked him to be sponsor* for the girl at the long-deferred ceremony of her Initiation, which was fixed for the second month of the new year.

The old Princess, To no Chujo's mother, had been very unwell all the winter, and though custom demanded that, if To no Chujo were sponsor, the ceremony should take place in her house, Genji feared that this would be putting her to too much inconvenience. He noticed that Yugiri, who was constantly with her, looked more and more care-worn every day. This was a bad sign; probably the old lady would not last out many weeks more. But if she died before his intended conversation with To no Chujo had taken place, Tamakatsura would not be able to wear mourning for her, and would thus, through no fault of her own, be guilty of a serious offence. Accordingly he set out for the Third Ward, calling first at the old Princess's apartments. He was obliged to act with great secrecy, for he had pleaded only yesterday that a religious obligation confined him to his rooms. But lest she should be disappointed, he robed himself for the visit quite as magnificently as he would have done for the recent procession. Her joy at the sight of this dazzling spectacle knew no bounds. Ill though she was, she immediately cast away all her troubles, dragged herself from her couch and received him, propped up on an easy chair.

She was evidently very much enfeebled; but she was perfectly well able to carry on a conversation. "I always know how things are going here by watching Yugiri," Genji said to her. "Lately he has been very absent-minded and depressed, and sometimes I have heard him sighing heavily when he was by himself. I knew this meant that he was worrying about you, and I felt I must come and enquire on my own account. Nowadays I do not even visit at the Palace except on very special occasions. I still hold the position of Grand Minister; but you would not find a single business document on my table. I live shut away in my own house, and am quite out of touch with everything that goes on in the outside world. You probably think it very reprehensible of me to withdraw from all public responsibilities at so early an age; and I know that you could

---

* The sponsor was usually the father; but also sometimes an uncle, brother-in-law, or the like. The Initiation, frequently mentioned in the *Tale,* was a religious ceremony corresponding to our Confirmation.

quote to me cases, both ancient and modern, of indomitable old men who have gone on tottering to their government offices every day of their lives till their backs were bent double. If I do not manage to supply the world with so edifying a spectacle, it is partly because I feel myself wholly lacking in capacity for such matters, partly because I am by nature in curably indolent..." "You're only making excuses because it's a very long time since you have been to see me," she answered. "Well, I haven't been getting on so badly. Till this year I had nothing to complain of, except the usual inconveniences of old age. But now they have not much hope for me. I have been wondering lately whether I should ever see you again. As a matter of fact, I am better than usual today, and do not feel at all as though my time were up. I have never thought there was much to be said in favor of dragging on long after all one's friends were dead, and for my part I was ready and anxious to be gone. If I have hung on till now, it has really been chiefly because of Yugiri's extraordinary kindness and devotion. I can see that the idea of losing me upsets him terribly..." She cried a good deal while she spoke, and her voice was so tremulous that he found it hard to catch her words; but the emotion which lay behind her quavering and often incoherent phrases was always such as he could most easily comprehend and share. In the course of this conversation Genji said: "I suppose To no Chujo comes to see you several times a day? I should be glad to have a word with him, if he looks in while I am here. There is something I have been wanting to tell him about for a long time. I should be sorry to miss this opportunity; for nowadays we seem very seldom to meet." "I don't know how it is," the old Princess replied; "it may be that he is very busy, or it may be that he simply does not want to come. I can only tell you that he has not been here once since my illness began. I wonder what sort of thing it is you want to discuss with him? I wish he were not so set against poor Yugiri. I have said to him ever so many times: 'It's no good arguing about how it all began. The harm is done now; they've got themselves talked about, and if you go on keeping them apart, you will only turn everyone against you.' But once he gets an idea into his head there is no doing anything with him. He was always the same..." Genji smiled at her assumption that whatever was to be said must necessarily concern her darling Yugiri. "I am afraid I was partly to blame," he said. "I was led to suppose that To no Chujo did not regard the affair as worth his interference, and took the same line myself. Afterwards, when I discovered how angry he was, I wished I had not meddled in the matter at all.

"However, that is not what I want to talk to him about now... Some while ago I happened quite by chance to discover the whereabouts of a person in whose fate I imagine him to be deeply interested. I ought of course to have spoken to him at once; but there were reasons that made me very reluctant to go into the whole matter. A home had to be found for her immediately, and having a very small family myself, I took her into the New Palace, never intending this to be more than a temporary measure...I was seeing very little of To no Chujo at this time, and month after month went by without my having a chance to discuss the matter with him, as I fully intended to do as soon as an opportunity arose...

"It now appears that the Emperor is looking for a Lady-of-the-Wardrobe. The position has been allowed to remain vacant far too long, the work being entrusted to mere housekeepers and lower servants, with the result that everything is in a state of hopeless confusion. In old days there seemed to be no difficulty in filling the post. All that is required is a lady free from domestic ties, who is also of good birth and tolerable character. But now, quite apart from birth and breeding, it seems impossible to produce anyone who even as regards previous conduct and experience is in any way qualified for the position. Having seen several applicants who came with the highest recommendations, the Emperor decided that he must look for someone of quite a different class.

"I at once thought of Lady Tamakatsura, the girl whom I have taken into my house. So far as I can make out, she is just the sort of person His Majesty is looking for. Service at the Palace has, I know, usually been regarded solely as an avenue to Imperial notice and favor, with the result that the work of such offices as the Wardrobe has been treated as something to scramble through with as little effort as possible. But it is not intended that this shall continue, and Lady Tamakatsura seems to me just the right person to put things upon a more sensible footing.

"However, I can do nothing till I have seen her father and talked the matter over with him. I have already asked him to stand sponsor at her Initiation, and now that you are feeling stronger I hope that the ceremony will soon be able to take place at your house." "If I understand you rightly," said the old lady, "this is some child of To no Chujo's. Your story very much surprises me. He was rather wild in his younger days, but he never failed to make provision for his children, and, indeed, he has in his time collected some very queer waifs and strays who succeeded in convincing him he was their father. I think it is most unaccountable that, if this girl is really his daughter, he should have completely lost touch with her and allowed you to pass her off as your child. What strange things you are telling me! But now I come to think of it, there was some story that I heard years ago..."

"It may sound to you very improbable," he replied, "but all that I have told you is true so far as it goes. I shall necessarily be telling To no Chujo a good deal more about it, and you can get the details from him. It is a long and rather sordid story, and you would soon wish I had not begun it. Even Yugiri still knows nothing, and believes that the girl is my daughter. You will not of course allow the matter to go any further." So he cautioned her. Meanwhile To no Chujo heard that Prince Genji was at his mother's house. "Of course my mother will be delighted," said he, "but I wish he had let us know that he was coming. Only Yugiri is with her... It is most unfortunate. There will be no one to receive him or see to it that his escort is properly entertained." Much agitated, To no Chujo began routing out such of his own sons and of Genji's particular acquaintance as could be procured at such short notice, and sent them round post-haste to the old lady's apartments, begging them to make sure that the distinguished guest was not being shamefully neglected. "The wine!" he called after them. "Be sure that he is offered wine and a little fruit. I would come with you myself, were I not afraid of giving trouble..."

Just then a note from his mother was handed him. "Genji is here," she said. "Of course I was delighted to see him. But I knew well enough that he had not come merely to chatter with me. It now appears that he counted on finding you here. There is something he wants to discuss with you." It was quite clear what had happened. The Princess, thinking that her end was near, had again been beseeching Genji to champion Yugiri's cause. "He himself," thought To no Chujo, "is probably tired of seeing the boy moping about day after day with the same lovelorn expression. He no doubt imagines that a word from him, preceded by a little judicious flattery, will suffice to alter all my views. If more is required, there is always the plea that, in her present condition, my mother must at all costs be allowed to have her way. At this moment, I suppose, they are putting their heads together and deciding how to propitiate me...under the circumstances it will be very difficult not to give way; and yet I don't at all see why I should!" So he wavered, feeling very much irritated by the whole affair, and extremely disinclined to obey the summons. But he valued civility very highly, and he could not without great rudeness refuse his mother's invitation just on the one occasion when Genji was in the house. It would be better not to put himself in the wrong... It was evident, indeed, that he had decided to go; for he began dressing in his finest clothes, and soon afterwards he set out, with only a handful of outriders, but accompanied by all the gentlemen of his household. The party was an imposing one as it swept along, dominated by the resplendent figure of To no Chujo himself, who was noticeably taller than the rest and broad chested to match, fulfilling in dignity of mien and gait all that the popular imagination expects of a great political leader. He was magnificently dressed in long trousers of wine-red silk and a lined cloak, white outside and red within, with a very long and sumptuous train. His costume contrasted in the strangest manner with that of Genji, who had changed into a plain cloak of Chinese silk thrown about him with just that touch of negligence which is proper to a great lord on a small occasion. But the contrast, which would have put anyone else at a disadvantage, only served to show that Genji at his very shabbiest could hold his own against the most grandiose display of trains and trappings.

The friendship of To no Chujo's sons with Yugiri made it natural that they should accompany their father on this visit. It happened that Chujo's two younger brothers, sons of a different mother, holding now the positions of Tutor to the Crown Prince and Representative of the Fujiwara Family on the Grand Council, were also at hand; and though no particular meeting of the Government had been called, circumstances had obliged some ten or twelve of the great officers of State (the Chief Treasurer, the Treasurer of the Fifth Rank, the Colonel of the Bodyguard and others) to foregather in To no Chujo's house that morning. They too, with a number of squires and commoners, joined the throng, and it was an impressive concourse of courtiers and gentlemen that was now entertained in the old Princess's Reception Hall. The great tankard went round again and again, everyone became very much elated, and scenes took place which (as was generally observed) far exceeded in brilliance and gaiety what is usually witnessed in an antiquated dowager's apartments. Genji and To no Chujo were soon engaged in an animated conversation. When they were apart it seemed to each that an exasperating accumulation of small grievances was all that now remained of their ancient alliance. But from the first moment of this unpremeditated and almost accidental meeting all consciousness of these recent jars and irritations utterly vanished. No sooner were they seated side by side than a host of common memories crowded to the mind of each. What miseries they had suffered together, what delights they had enjoyed! It seemed impossible that such trivial incidents as those of the last few months could have sufficed to raise a barrier between them. But so it had been; and for that very reason there was more to talk about now than there could possibly else have been. Enquiries, recollections, allusions followed hard upon one another, and when dusk fell the two friends had still not come to a pause in their conversation. At last To no Chujo remembered that the guest must be in need of refreshment, and handing him the tankard he said: "It has for a long while past distressed me very much to see so little of you; and I felt that it would indeed mark a disastrous climax in our estrangement if you should come today without my being here to receive you. I imagined that, had you not expressly desired to avoid me, you would certainly have told me of your intended visit. Fortunately, however, I decided that to come unwanted would endanger our friendship less than to stay away when I knew that you were honoring my mother's house..." "If anyone has been endangering our good relations, it is I answered Genji. "Did you but know it, I stand in need of all the charity and forbearance that you can muster."*

To no Chujo was puzzled by this; but he naturally assumed that it referred to the trouble concerning Kumoi and Yugiri, and certain that something very disagreeable was coming, he waited for Genji to continue. "In old days it was very seldom that we differed about any matter of importance, whether it concerned our own lives or the affairs of the country, and for this reason I felt perfectly confident in handing over to you the direction of the Government. It seemed as little likely that our views would clash as that a bird's two wings should start flying in different directions. If lately I may seem to you sometimes to have acted in a way at variance with this old concord, you cannot claim that it has been in matters of any wide or general importance. But that is not enough; as I grow older I feel all the more anxious that not even these small domestic difficulties should continue to mar our friendship or in any way alter it from what it was in earlier days. You seemed to avoid me; but I knew from experience that the duties I myself had thrust upon you leave little time for friendship, and had I been merely an acquaintance I should not have been surprised at your becoming somewhat difficult of access. But despite all that had arisen between us our relationship was merely of a somewhat different kind..."

To no Chujo had not the least idea what all this was going to lead up to. "Certainly we were very intimate at one time," he answered. "It is possible that I presumed too much upon our friendship—ignored too completely the great distance that separated us. You have compared us to the two wings of a bird. Such was never our position. You were always far above me, and if I have risen from insignificance to high rank and office I know quite well that it is entirely your doing. Perhaps I ought more frequently to have acknowledged this obligation, but as one grows older one tends more and more to take things for granted..." To no Chujo, who had arrived in such ill humor, was now speaking almost apologetically. It was at this point that Genji ventured upon an allusion to the rainy night's conversation,† then to Yugao, and last to To no Chujo's little daughter, Tamakatsura. "I have news concerning her which will very much surprise you," Genji said at last, and, without going into the whole story, broke to To no Chujo the news that Yugao was long ago dead, and that Tamakatsura had for some while been living with him.

Tears sprang to Chujo's eyes. "I think that at the time when I first lost sight of her," he said at last, "I told you and some of my other friends about my endeavors to trace Yugao and her child. It would have

---

* Genji is of course referring to his sequestration of Tamakatsura.
† See Part I, p. 18 Seq.

been better not to speak of the matter, but I was so wretched that I could not contain myself. However, the search brought no result, and at last I gave up all hope. It was only recently, when my accession to high office induced all kinds of odd and undesirable creatures in every quarter to claim relationship with me, that I began to think once more about this true child of mine. How much more gladly would I have acknowledged and welcomed Yugao's daughter than the band of discreditable and unconvincing claimants who henceforward thronged my gates! But now that I know she is in good hands..." Gradually the conversation drifted back to that rainy night and to the theories which each of them had then put forward. Had life refuted or confirmed them? And so, between tears and laughter, the talk went on, with not a shade of reproach or coolness on either side, till morning was almost come. "I have no desire to go away," said Genji, rising at last. "The things of which we have been speaking happened so long ago that they are already ancient history, and I thought that they no longer much concerned me. But this meeting of ours tonight has brought them back out of the past, and..." Perhaps it was partly because he had been drinking (some special reason there must have been, for it was very seldom indeed that he betrayed his emotion), Genji at this point broke down completely and burst into a flood of tears.

Nor was he the only person in the house to weep that night. For the old Princess, seeing Genji so far increased in dignities and power since the time of Aoi's death, could not help picturing to herself the impression that the more consequential Genji of today would undoubtedly have made upon her fastidious daughter. A year or two longer, a little more experience on either side, and all might have been well.

The matter of Yugiri and Kumoi had not been so much as mentioned during To no Chujo's visit. Genji was by no means anxious to start the subject, for he knew that the girl's family considered that he had been remiss in not putting in a word for her at Court, and he felt no inclination to defend himself; while Chujo, not venturing to embark upon a topic which Genji seemed deliberately to avoid, gave the impression that upon this point he still harbored a grievance. "I shall not escort you to your palace tonight," he said to Genji. "Our joint cavalcades, suddenly let loose upon the sleeping town, would cause an uncomfortable commotion. But next time we meet here we will let it be known in advance that I am going to escort you..."

It now seemed certain that the old Princess would by the appointed day be sufficiently recovered to allow of the Initiation* taking place in her house. "On that occasion, if not before," said Genji, "we may count on meeting again."

---

* See above, p. 547.

It was noticed by the companions who waited for them that when Genji and To no Chujo at last reappeared they were both smiling with evident satisfaction, as though some difficult negotiation had been successfully arranged between them. What was it all about? With what new powers could To no Chujo have been invested? Many wild guesses were made, nor would it have occurred to anyone that politics had not once been mentioned between them.

The news of Tamakatsura's whereabouts came as such a shock to To no Chujo that he was at first quite unable to decide whether he was glad or sorry at what had happened. Only one reason (not referred to by Genji in his account of the affair) could possibly have induced him to adopt the girl. Nothing had been said about restoring her to her real father, and To no Chujo was certain that under the circumstances Genji would make every possible effort to avoid doing so. If he had not openly accepted her as his concubine, it was through fear of Murasaki and the rest. Certainly it was most unfortunate (the real situation being such as To no Chujo guessed) that Genji should have insisted upon spreading this ridiculous report about the girl being his daughter. After all, in the mere fact of his taking a fancy to her there was nothing discreditable either to her or himself, and only this stupid pretence would make the attachment, should it become known, seem in any way reprehensible.

Should Genji decide to escape from his dilemma by presenting Tamakatsura at Court, she might prove (thought To no Chujo) a formidable rival to his eldest daughter, who already had difficulties enough at the Palace. But in any case, having now resumed his old relations with Genji, he was determined to let no matter of this kind endanger them, and was quite prepared to do whatever Genji seemed to expect of him.

The reconciliation took place early in the second month. The sixteenth of this month, being the first day of the Higan* Festival, seemed particularly favorable for the holding of Tamakatsura's Initiation Ceremony. An inspection of the calendar showed that there would not be another suitable day for a long time, and as the old Princess maintained her improvement, there seemed a good chance that the ceremony would be able to take place at her house on the sixteenth.

The next time Genji visited his ward he was able to inform her that he had at last arranged the long-promised meeting with her father, and had told him, if not the whole story, at any rate as much of it as it was necessary for him to know. He seemed in the end to have chosen his time so well, and managed the disclosure with so much tact, that she felt no real father could possibly handle her affairs with more judgment and devotion, and she had no desire to change her lot. But all the same

---

* In Sanskrit, Paramita. The festival is held in autumn and spring, apparently in Japan only.

it was a weight off her mind to know that To no Chujo had been duly informed of her existence. While he was about it Genji thought that he had better tell Yugiri too, for it was awkward that he should still imagine the girl to be his sister. The news that she was not Genji's daughter hardly came as a surprise to him, for his father's manner towards her had in the course of the last months continually aroused his suspicion. But when he remembered the glimpse he had caught of her on the morning of the typhoon (he was obliged to admit to himself that he thought her handsomer even than the lady from whom a cruel fate divided him), for a moment he felt that he had been a fool not to guess the truth and use the opportunities that chance had provided. But no sooner had this idea crossed his mind than he rejected it with horror. Could it be that even in thought he had for an instant been disloyal to the love upon which his whole life was founded?

When the day of the ceremony came round, a messenger arrived from the Sanjo palace bearing presents from the old Princess. There was the usual lacquered box in which to lay the severed lock, and though there had been very little time for preparation, both this and the other presents were of the handsomest kind imaginable. In her letter she said: "I am not certain that it is proper* for me even to write upon such an occasion as this. I should not in any case have been able to witness the proceedings, for I am far too ill to leave my bed; and if a few presents and a letter from me are unprecedented in such a case, so too is the age which I have now reached, and it is clear that the ordinary rules must not be applied to me. In accordance with surprising and delightful information which I have just received, I long to address you as my granddaughter, but hesitate to do so except at your express command... 'Since son and son-in-law both claim you, a double reason have I to greet you as a long-lost scion of my race.'"†

Letter and poem were written in a very aged and trembling hand. Genji was present when the messenger arrived, having come across to Tamakatsura's apartments to make the final arrangements for the ceremony. "The style to which she was brought up looks to us very quaint and old-fashioned," he said, inspecting the writing; "but I have been told that in her day she was considered the best pen woman at Court. One is apt to forget that she is now, poor thing, a very old lady indeed. Look at that line. How terribly her hand shook!" Then, after reading the poem through a second time: "What ingenuity! There is in the whole poem not a single phrase which has not some special application to

---
* She had taken Buddhist orders, and this was a Shinto occasion.

† An ingenious poem in which every word has some allusion to the ceremony in hand. For example *futa* = "both" and "cover of the box"; *kakego* = "hidden child" and "nest of boxes, fitting one into the other."

today's ceremony. It would be difficult to imagine lines in which so little space was wasted," and he smiled.

Even a man of far less hasty disposition than To no Chujo would, after such a revelation as that which had recently taken place at the old Princess's house, have awaited the day of the Initiation Ceremony with the utmost impatience. It was evident, when the time came, that the proceedings were to be attended with every possible pomp and formality. In fact the whole complexion of the affair only served to convince To no Chujo more firmly than ever that his daughter had from the start been Genji's mistress. In his capacity as Sponsor he was admitted behind her screens at the Hour of the Swine.* Over and above the equipment that is customary on such occasions he noticed that her dais was furnished with a magnificence such as he had never witnessed. When the main ritual was ended and food had been served behind the screen, Genji saw to it that the Great Lamp was so disposed as to illumine this corner of the room far more clearly than usual; and it was in a flood of lamplight that father and daughter now met face to face. But merely to see her was not enough; he longed to pour upon her a thousand questions concerning her own childhood and later adventures, concerning her mother's death, and all that had led up to the present extraordinary situation. However, it was clear that for the moment any such conversation was impossible, and he had the strange experience of being called upon to tie the girdle of his daughter's dress without having yet exchanged a single word with her. "I have not yet publicly announced that you are her father," whispered Genji, "so please behave as though you were standing Sponsor to her as my friend." "You need not worry about that," whispered To no Chujo in reply; "it will be difficult enough under the best of circumstances suddenly to begin addressing her as my daughter, and at the present minute..." While the tankard was going round he added: "I am so overwhelmed by the splendor of today's proceedings and the trouble which you have evidently taken to make them a success, that I feel it would be ungrateful of me to ask why I was not taken into your confidence before. But you will admit, I am sure, that it would be strange if I were not somewhat puzzled..." Genji made no reply.

Most of the Royal Princes were waiting in the anteroom, among them several of Tamakatsura's suitors, who were curious to know why the two Ministers were so long in reappearing from behind the screen. Of To no Chujo's sons, only the two eldest, Kashiwagi and Kobai, had been let into the secret. Their feelings about the matter were necessarily somewhat mixed; for with the disappointment of finding that Tamakatsura was their sister was mingled a feeling of intense relief that their courtship

---

* 9 P.M.

had hitherto remained secret. "I may tell you," whispered Kobai, leaning across to Kashiwagi, "that I have had a very lucky escape. I was on the point of giving myself away over this. But as it is, I don't think anyone knows about it." "There's something very odd about Genji," whispered Kashiwagi in reply. "This is really the second time that he has adopted a girl apparently because he had himself taken a fancy to her, and has then pressed her into the arms of anyone who cared to take her...

Genji, as a matter of fact, overheard both these remarks, and going to To no Chujo, he said: "I must beg of you to be very careful for a little while; otherwise both our reputations are likely to suffer. Were we ordinary citizens we should only have our own consciences to satisfy, and if our mutual affairs got into rather a mess it would concern no one but ourselves. Unfortunately, however, we both of us hold positions in which the good opinion of all sorts of people (some of whom judge by standards quite different from ours) is of the greatest importance to us, and can only be disregarded at the risk of disagreeable consequences. It would be fatal, for example, if this situation were suddenly sprung upon the world in all its details. But allowed to leak out piecemeal, it will do very little harm. What matters is that people should have plenty of time to get used to one part of a scandal before the next is allowed to leak out." "I had no intention of putting her under your wing," replied To no Chujo; "but I must confess that it has worked out very well. In fact, it seems as though she were intended by Fate to be your child rather than mine; you may count upon me to do exactly as you think best."

Great efforts were made to hush up for a little while longer the true facts concerning Tamakatsura's birth. But talking about other people's affairs is so indispensable an occupation that such efforts are commonly of little avail; and in this case it was not long before every detail was known. Being a great gossip; the Lady from Omi was soon in possession of the secret, and one day in Lady Chujo's room, when Kashiwagi and Kobai were both present, she screamed out: "Here's news for you! My father's found another new daughter! What do you think of that? And she's a luckier girl than I am, for before father found her Prince Genji said she was *his* daughter, and made no end of a fuss over her. And listen now, this is the queer part of it: that girl's mother was no better than mine!" All this was blurted but at her usual high pitch, and without a thought of the effect which she was producing. Lady Chujo, upon whom these outbursts made a painful impression, did not answer. Kashiwagi thought it his duty to say severely, "It is quite true that Lady Tamakatsura is our father's child. There were reasons why it was more convenient that she should be brought up by Prince Genji. But it is undesirable that this should be talked about. I cannot understand how you came to hear of it at all; and still more surprised that you should regard it as a piece of news that can be shouted all over the house. However, as I know by experience, several of our gentlewomen are particularly bad at holding their tongues, and one of them might possibly have overheard..." The Lady from Omi laughed boisterously: "Well, I never!" she said. "What a silly fuss to make! Why, no one talks of anything else! And look here! They say she thinks she's going to be Lady-of-the-Bedchamber. Now listen to me all of you. I wouldn't ever have come to fetch and carry for my sister in these grand rooms and do all the jobs that the rest of you thought yourselves too good for, if I hadn't been told she would put in a word for me when she got the chance. I could be Lady-of-the-Bedchamber tomorrow, yes, so I could, if my sister didn't choose to let a stranger get off with the job." This outburst provoked peals of laughter. "I don't know why you should have got it into your head," said someone at last, "that if there was a vacancy for the post of Lady-of-the-Bedchamber, the choice should lie between you and Lady Tamakatsura." "It's no good your trying to make fun of me," she shouted angrily. "I know quite well what it is: you think I'm not fit to live among such grand people as you. And whose fault is it, pray, that I came at all? Master Kashiwagi here thought it was a very clever thing to take a poor girl away from her village and make a joke of her in this fine house. Yes, you're very grand people, Prime Ministers and I don't know what! I do you reverence..." And with this she retreated to a corner, stepping backwards in mock obeisance.

Kashiwagi surveyed her as she crouched panting in her corner. She was not such a bad-looking creature. But at the present moment, with her face contorted by rage and her eyeballs extended to twice their proper size, she cut so fantastic a figure that he was obliged to agree with her own dictum: it was indeed a mistake on his part ever to have brought her here. He now made vain efforts to calm her, which were seconded by his brother Kobai, who said: "It is quite true that our sister Lady Chujo has a certain influence in such matters, and I am sure she will do her best for you. But you must first calm yourself down a little. At the present you look for the world like the Sun Goddess,[*] when she 'stamped on the hard stones of her courtyard till the chips flew like snow.' Be patient a little while longer, and you will find that Lady Chujo is most anxious to do what she can for you." "If you go on like this," Kashiwagi could not help observing, "we shall all hope that, like the Sun Goddess, you will end by shutting yourself up in a cave." At this point he and Kobai withdrew.

"Your brothers would never dare come here and make fun of me like this unless you put them up to it," Omi now gasped to Lady Chujo

---

[*] When the God Susano-o returned from the Nether World, his sister the Sun Goddess was enraged at his presumption and "stamped on the stones of her courtyard till the chips flew like snow." Later on she was so much upset by her brother's conduct that she retired to a cavern and the Earth was plunged in darkness.

between her tears. But she still did not despair of winning her sister's good graces, and to that end she now flung herself with alacrity into all the odd jobs which the charwomen and scullery-maids would not touch. She could be seen at any hour of the day running at full speed hither and thither (but generally in the wrong direction) with a zest never equaled in the annals of this ancient house. Whenever she met her sister she called out to her: "Now you will recommend me, won't you, for that post at Court?" Lady Chujo resented this continual persecution, but thought it better to make no reply.

The story of Omi's misguided aspiration reached To no Chujo's ears and diverted him extremely. He went straight to Lady Chujo's apartments and called for the Lady of Omi to be sent to him. She was not far off, and hearing her own name uttered she at once replied with a loud whoop and came flouncing into the room. "You seem to have plenty to do nowadays," he said. "If you put the same energy into this Palace work that I hear you are asking for, you would certainly be setting a new precedent! But why did you not tell me before that you wanted this place? I have only this moment heard about it." Her father at any rate was not making fun of her, she said to herself with great satisfaction. "I did hope you would hear about it," she answered To no Chujo; "but Madam my sister or someone else promised me they would tell you, and I thought it was all in safe hands. Indeed, I'd counted on it so, that" when I found out this Lady Tamakatsura was after my place and everyone seemed to think she'd get it, I felt like the poor tinker who dreamed of millions, and was so put about I didn't know, as the saying goes, whether my hands grew out of my arms or my chest." There was no denying that she expressed herself with considerable vigor. To no Chujo found it hard to maintain his gravity, but he succeeded in saying at last: "I wish you had taken me into your confidence. If only I had known that you wanted this post I could have put in for it before there was any other candidate in the field. Of course Lady Tamakatsura has considerable claims. But I am sure that if I had known in good time I could easily have convinced His Majesty that you were something not to be missed. Even now I dare say it is not too late. You had better make haste and compose your letter of application, and write it out in your best hand. When His Majesty sees that it is full (as no doubt it will be) of conceits from the Long Poems and other such archaic compositions, he will certainly give your case very serious consideration. For he is particularly open to impressions of that sort." She had not the least idea that she was being made game of by a heartless and facetious parent. "If that's all I have got to do," she answered gaily, "I shall manage famously. I can make Japanese poems one after another; there's no stopping me. I get a bit mixed up about these terms of respect. But if you'll just give me a little help with those, I'll manage to work in something nice about you into the bargain." So saying she rubbed her hands with delight at the prospect of being allowed to exercise her wonderful powers of composition. The gentlemen who were in attendance upon Lady Chujo heard the whole of this conversation, and nearly died of suppressed laughter. Several were afflicted by so terrible a fit of the giggles that they had to be removed from the room. Lady Chujo herself, so far from being amused, merely went hot and cold all over while this painful exhibition was in progress. To no Chujo insisted upon treating the matter as a joke. "Whenever I feel at all depressed," he said to Lady Omi, "I shall come to you for distraction. You are an unfailing source of entertainment." It was, however, said at Court that To no Chujo was in reality very much distressed by the girl's silliness, and only made a joke of it in order to cover up his disappointment.

Blue Trousers

Though both Genji and To no Chujo strongly urged her to accept the post of Lady-of-the-Bedchamber, Tamakatsura still hesitated. The position did not necessarily imply that she would have personal contact with the Emperor or be in any way under his protection. But since so many people (even her supposed "father") seemed to find her interesting, she now assumed, without any very good reason for doing so, that the Emperor too would doubtless become attached to her, and she foresaw endless conflicts of the most disagreeable kind with both Akikonomu and Lady Chujo, not to mention other minor favorites. Her own rapid rise to fame and the deference with which she, a mere foundling from the hedge side, was treated by both the Chief Ministers, had inevitably aroused hostility in many quarters; among her female acquaintances there were many (she was sure) who regarded her as a pampered upstart, and would with the greatest pleasure in the world have seen her placed in a painful and undignified position. She was old enough to be fully aware of the disadvantages and dangers of every course which lay open to her, and though she concealed her troubles from those about her, she was during all this time in a condition of great depression and perplexity.

Many people would not have regarded her present situation as anything to be complained of. Genji's behavior towards her was still beyond reproach, and in many respects her life at the New Palace was obviously a very enviable one. But she felt that their relation was equivocal, the subject for months past of many jests and speculations. She was occupying a position which was in its essence utterly distasteful to her, and longed to clear herself finally of the suspicions which were bound to hang over her as long as she stayed under this roof.

To no Chujo, anxious to remain on good terms with Genji, and certain that, whatever might be his friend's professions, he could not really wish to part with the girl, made no effort to remove her from her present quarters or in any way assert his parental authority.

The extraordinary position which she occupied, thus hung as it were precariously between two rival parents, naturally caused her name and story to become more than ever notorious in the City; and to make matters worse, just at the moment when all eyes were turned upon her, Genji began once more, as the summer drew on, to be far less discreet in his behavior; as though, having heroically discharged his duty by informing her father of her whereabouts, he were exempt from any further obligation to play a sober and paternal part. How she longed at this time for some female confidant, mother or sister, with whom she could discuss even some small part of the difficulties which now beset her! Unfortunately, her most frequent visitors during all these months were Genji and To no Chujo, precisely the two persons in whom it was least possible that she should confide.

Tamakatsura's mourning* was now over; but until the end of the month,† there could be no question of her formal affiancement. The Emperor was impatient to get the matter settled, and her various lovers pressed their claims more vehemently than ever upon those whom they imagined to be responsible for her decision. But in whatever quarter they applied, the answer was the same: nothing could be done until the tenth month had begun.

Her new brothers‡ received no encouragement to visit her. But it would be their business to look after her affairs should she take service at Court, and they were anxious to discuss with her several matters in connection with this. Kashiwagi had been much attracted by Genji's daughter. The rapidity with which he had adjusted himself to the new situation caused a good deal of amusement. This embarrassed him, and it was only at his father's request that he visited the New Palace. Outwardly, there was no change in the manner of his reception. When he first arrived, announcing that he had a message to deliver, he was left waiting in the garden, and as he had been instructed to perform his commission secretly, he was obliged to hide in the shadow of a laurel-tree, for a bright moon was shining. Having protested that his message was of a very private nature, he was at last allowed to address Tamakatsura through the curtains of the southern window. But in her nervousness she did not feel capable of speaking to him herself, and her replies were made through her maid Saisho. "When my father chose me to deliver this message, I am sure he took for granted that you would do me the honor of replying to it with your own lips. The matter will require a certain amount of further discussion, and I fear we shall find this roundabout method very inconvenient. Even though you do not consider me worth putting yourself out for in the usual way, you must remember that we are now recognized to be children of the same father. I may be old-fashioned, but I came here hoping that a brother counted with you for a good deal..."

She felt that she must make some concrete excuse, and said to her maid: "Tell him that I should very much like to thank him for all his

---

* For the old Princess, To no Chujo's mother, and consequently her grandmother, whose death is here assumed, though not actually referred to till three chapters later. The blue trousers, after which the chapter is named, were worn in sign of mourning.

† The ninth month, in which no marriages could be celebrated.

‡ Kashiwagi, Kobai, and To no Chujo's other sons.

kindness to me during the last year or so; but unfortunately I am feeling very unwell and cannot leave my couch. I should not feel justified in treating him with such informality but for the family tie which now unites us." This, repeated to him by the maid Saisho, sounded very stiff and unaccommodating. "If your mistress is unwell," he said, "would it not be better if I came and stood at her bedside? The matter is an important one, and I do not at present feel as though I were getting into touch with her at all. But I will not insist..." and he began in a low voice to read out his father's message. Kashiwagi was as well turned-out as any prince at Court, and the maid by no means regretted her mistress's obduracy. "I have heard nothing more from you" (the message ran) "about our Palace project. It is high time that a decision were reached, and I should like to have another talk with you. But I think that, for obvious reasons, it is better for me to keep away at present. There can, however, be no objection to your sending me an occasional note, and your complete silence is somewhat perplexing." "Tell your mistress," Kashiwagi added on his own account, "that however distasteful to her my conversation may in the past have been, it cannot in our altered circumstances be of a nature to cause her the slightest offence. I am still at a loss to know why my previous advances, made in ignorance of our true relation, were so coldly and unfeelingly rejected. Still less do I understand why now, when I can no longer be suspected of coming as a lover, she should insist upon putting the whole breadth of her apartments between us. Never again shall I consent to be treated in this way. Polite society, please point out to her, will have to change a great deal before such discourtesy is tolerated..."

How was she to pacify him? "The change in our relationship is not generally known," she said in her reply; "moreover, I do not think that having left me to rusticate for so many years amid the savagery of Tsukushi, your family ought to expect of me the last refinements of urban demeanor." So she rallied him, and with complete success.

"Forgive me for intruding," said the maid, "but I think Madam's difficulty today has been that she did not know whether you came as a suitor or a brother. She is extremely sensitive to what is thought of her by the world at large; that, I am sure, is the only reason she did not come and converse with you at close quarters. But such behavior is quite unlike her, and you will find that next time you come..." "No, thank you," he cried; I fancy I might have to come a great many times and sit here a very long while before your mistress would own that my service had redeemed me from her ban." So saying, he left the house.

Prince Higekuro served in the same Guard Regiment as Yugiri, and was continually seeking him out in order to have long and emotional conversations about Tamakatsura. He always hoped that Yugiri would plead his cause with Genji. A more suitable husband for her than himself could not, Higekuro felt sure, possibly be imagined. He was amiable, good-looking, qualified by rank and birth to secure for her at Court a far higher place than that to which she had any right to aspire. What more could Genji want? But, as Yugiri pointed out, the main difficulty was that, as things now stood, she was in a few months' time to take service in the Palace; this was Genji's idea, and To no Chujo, convinced that it was part of some subtle plan, did not think it wise to interfere.

Prince Higekuro was the elder brother of the ex-Emperor Suzaku's Consort, Lady Jokyoden. With the exception of Genji and To no Chujo, he was by far the most influential man in the country. He was now about thirty-two or three. His wife, an elder sister of Murasaki, was four years his senior. In many cases such a disparity of age would not much have mattered; but Lady Makibashira* seemed far older than her actual years. He nicknamed her "granny," and in this there was something more than a jest, for soon her old-maidish ways began to annoy him, and they had not been together many months before he was wondering how long he should be able to go on enduring her society.

It was the existence of this unfortunate entanglement that had discouraged Genji from furthering Prince Higekuro's suit. The Prince had not, indeed, by any means the reputation of leading a disorderly or even frivolous existence. True, he was seldom at home; but apart from his courtship of Tamakatsura herself, his time seemed to be devoted entirely to practical affairs. Having heard that To no Chujo thought well of him and also that the lady herself was by no means anxious for a career at the Palace, Higekuro, who had almost lost hope, again plucked up heart. Genji, he admitted to himself, was evidently against him. But everyone knew why Genji was so reluctant to part with her.

One morning in the ninth month, when the whole world lay glittering in the first frost of the year, messenger after messenger began to arrive with the usual fancifully decked and folded love-letters. Tamakatsura refused even to look at them, and only reluctantly consented to hear them read aloud.

From Higekuro came a note in which he said: "The changing skies tell me that the time of my respite† is almost spent. 'Lived I in hope, so were this Month of Fasting my despair; but being what I am, I hang my life upon the weak thread of its dwindling days.'" He seemed to assume that a decision had been reached and would irretrievably take effect at the beginning of the next month. She herself knew nothing of this.

Another suitor, Prince Sochi, was equally despondent: "Why am I writing?" he said in his letter. "I have lost you, and there is no more to be said.

---

* Not named in the book. But in English she needs a name. Makibashira is the name of her little girl, who appears so seldom as not to need one, so I have used this name for the mother.

† The ninth month, during which no such step as the affiancement of Tamakatsura or her presentation at Court could take place. See above, p. 563.

But "Though you be standing in the radiance of the Morning Sun, perchance one drop of dew may linger of those your sleeve once gathered in shadowy garden walks." Did I but think you knew how much it costs me to lose you, I should derive some trifling comfort..." The note containing this poem was attached to an ice-cold spray of bamboo, plucked from near the ground and carried with such care that it was still thickly covered with hoarfrost. The messenger was on this, as upon every occasion, a person whose quality matched the elegance of the letter.

Yet another suitor, whose communications were of the most pressing nature, was Prince Hyobukyo's son, Sahyoye. Being Murasaki's brother, he was constantly at her apartments, and his present despondency seemed to prove that, according to the information to be gathered in that quarter, Lady Tamakatsura's fate was already decided. His messenger now brought a letter in which Sahyoye said: "Even though I should at last forget you, how, oh how, shall I learn to support the dreariness of a life into which no thought of you may find its way?..." And so on.

These letters were a source of great interest and pleasure to Tamakatsura's gentlewomen, who discussed with unfailing relish the color of the paper, the style of penmanship, the various kinds of scent with which the letter was perfumed, and many kindred questions. "I hope Madam will not make up her mind for a long while to come," said one of them. "We shall be bored to death when this is all over."

Her reply to Prince Sochi was short and vague, but not altogether discouraging; for in her poem she said: "The sunflower, that seems so willingly of its own nature to turn towards the Light of Day, would fain enough (who knows?) have kept the bright frost glittering on its leaves." This could be interpreted in several ways; but Prince Sochi was very agreeably surprised by even so faint a flicker of regret. That in entering the Palace she was acting against her own will and judgment he did not at all believe, and he could only regard her reply as a sign of well-bred gratitude for his patient courtship; yet it gave him a considerable degree of pleasure.

In the course of the morning lovelorn communications arrived from a number of less distinguished suitors. For most of them she had no special feeling one way or the other, and dealt with each of these protestations as her guardians informed her that the position of the writer required. She showed indeed throughout the whole business (as both Genji and To no Chujo were forced to admit) a good sense and docility that other members of her sex might have done well to imitate.

Makibashira

I am very much perturbed by what you have just told me," said Genji to Prince Higekuro some months later. "It will very likely upset all my plans. I hope you are not telling everyone about it..." That is precisely what Higekuro *was* doing; the temptation to brag of such a success was one indeed which he could hardly be expected to resist. Some time had now elapsed since the episode to which Genji referred. Tamakatsura had then yielded less to his importunity than to a feeling that this man, from whose touch she still shrank with horror, was not so much a lover as an instrument of Fate, no more to be avoided than were those other strokes of destiny that had pursued her so relentlessly since her earliest years. He hoped at first that she would grow used to him, and pretended not to notice her depression. But as time went on matters only became worse, and Higekuro was already beginning to regard the situation as hopeless, when it became clear that she was with child. This gave him fresh courage; he felt that Heaven had set its seal upon their union, and determined to bear with patience her present wayward humor. For the mere sight of her beauty gave him an increasing pleasure, and the thought that he had still no hold upon her and might any day wake to find that she had fled from him to the Emperor's Palace, perhaps even into His Majesty's arms, was more than he could bear. He attributed his momentary success quite as much to the astuteness of Ben no Omoto* as to the compassion of the Ishiyama Buddha, to whom his prayers had for long been addressed. But his human ally was now in deep disgrace for the part she had played in the affair and was at present a prisoner in the servants' rooms. "Though all the blame falls upon me," thought this unfortunate creature, "it is clear that the Blessed Buddha is really responsible. For I have played the go-between without a grain of success for a score or so of my mistress's lovers; and if I did better this time it was only because the Buddha of Ishiyama knows an honest gentleman when he sees one..."

Genji would have given worlds that this thing should not have happened; but both he and To no Chujo had encouraged Higekuro's suit, and though they had every right to complain of the unfortunate manner in which he had urged it, it was now too late to scold him or send him about his business. Indeed, if the girl's reputation were to be saved, the

---

* One of Tamakatsura's maids.

only possible course was to treat Higekuro as an approved and accepted lover; and henceforward on his visits to the New Palace he was openly received with every mark of consideration and respect. Higekuro for his part was anxious to go through the necessary formalities and establish the young bride in his own palace at the earliest possible moment. But Genji was determined that this should not take place if there was any chance that the girl's reception there would in any quarter be an unfavorable one. Such at least was the pretext which he used for delaying Tamakatsura's departure. "Do, I beg of you, make sure," he said to her father, "that she is not suddenly plunged into scenes of jealousy and intrigue. Anything in the shape of scandal or bickering would be extremely painful to her." "On the contrary," said To no Chujo, "I should be much more uneasy if she were going to the Palace, which I imagine to be now out of the question. His Majesty has an undoubted partiality for her; and anyone in that position, unless backed up by the most powerful family connections, is apt to have a very disagreeable time. I should certainly do all I could for her. But you see for yourself what difficulties I am having over Lady Chujo's Palace career..." There was much truth in this. The Emperor had himself suggested her application for the vacant post. But his interest in her, if it existed at all, was based only on one brief glimpse, and so casual an approbation by no means implied that he would protect her with the full weight of Imperial authority against the contemptuous hostility of her rivals.

In the formal letter of committal sent by To no Chujo to the husband on the third day after the wedding, he purposely laid great stress on the part played by Genji in her upbringing, expressing in the warmest terms his gratitude for her foster-father's unceasing care and kindness; for he was certain that the content of the letter would end by reaching Genji's ears. The marriage was of course concluded with the utmost secrecy; but the news of it was too interesting a piece of gossip to remain long concealed. It was whispered, in strictest confidence, from ear to ear; before long it had reached the Palace, and was finally recounted to the Emperor himself.

He was very nice about it. "I am extremely sorry that we are to lose her," he said. "But of course, if her thoughts have been occupied elsewhere, that quite explains her long hesitation... I can easily understand that at such a moment as this she would not be willing to take up permanent duties at Court. But if she cares to assist us occasionally..."

It was now the eleventh month. Tamakatsura had agreed to discharge the functions of Lady-of-the-Bedchamber from her apartments in Genji's palace. It was a time of year when a great many religious ceremonies take place at Court, and the new Lady-of-the-Bedchamber had not a moment's leisure. Her subordinates were continually coming over from the Palace to ask her advice, and her rooms were full of bustle and youthful chatter. Much to her annoyance, Prince Higekuro was no longer content to pay long evening visits, but had now installed himself permanently in her quarters. Prince Sochi and the other suitors, who were still unaware that a secret wedding had taken place, were naturally indignant at the liberties which they saw accorded to their rival. One of them, indeed, had a double reason for annoyance. This was Sahyoye, the brother of Lady Makibashira. Not only was his own suit ignominiously unsuccessful, but his sister was being made publicly ridiculous by the continued presence of her husband in another woman's house. The young man was furious, but at present saw no means of bringing his brother-in-law[*] to book.

The situation was really rather comic. Higekuro had for years past been held up as a model of regularity, industry, sobriety; and now his hectic courtship, with its secret journeyings at dead of night and break of dawn, was the talk of half the Court. Romantic touches were added to the story, and in the end it really seemed to Higekuro's astonished friends that he must have undergone some mysterious transformation. Tamakatsura, too, was by nature sociable, good-humored and full of high spirits; but in Higekuro's presence her whole being underwent a profound change: she became gloomy, irritable, sharp-tempered, to a degree that must have made it sufficiently apparent to everyone that she did not care in the least for him. But she constantly wondered whether Genji thought that she was really enjoying herself with this repulsive man, and blushed at the low opinion he must now have formed of her taste. She remembered too Prince Sochi's attractive warmth and liveliness of disposition. What could have possessed her?... And she became more disagreeable to Higekuro than ever.

Genji was much relieved at having put an end once for all to a situation which had involved him in much unpleasant suspicion. Feelings beyond his control might sometimes lead him into odd and equivocal positions, but (Genji assured himself) his natural tendency was to shrink from such entanglements. He was with Murasaki when these reflections passed through his mind, and said to her suddenly: "Do you remember how suspicious you were when Tamakatsura first came to us? You see now that there was no reason for your alarm..." Yes, he could at last be certain that he was quite safe. Even if circumstances should bring them together again and some part of their former intimacy revive, there would never be the same danger as before... And he began to recall the time when he was most in love with her, when he had even persuaded himself that he could find a way of keeping her for his own. But stay! Had things changed so much after all? Could the thought of parting with her ever have been

---

[*] Prince Higekuro.

more painful to him than at this very minute it was? Henceforward the image of Tamakatsura haunted his mind more constantly than ever.

One morning, hearing that Prince Higekuro had for a short while quitted her apartments, Genji once more paid her a visit. He found her looking extremely depressed and unwell. He was told that for some time past she had seemed incapable of making the slightest exertion. But his arrival seemed to give her a little strength, for she raised herself on her couch and had her screens drawn partly back. Genji was careful to behave with the utmost restraint, and for some while they conversed rather stiffly about the general news of the day. What a relief it was to be in the company of someone really good-looking, after such a long spell of Higekuro's society! Her husband, it was true, had a straightforward, well-meaning sort of face, but how commonplace, how ordinary! She felt bitterly ashamed at the choice that Genji and the world at large must be thinking her to have made, and the tears welled into her eyes. Gradually their conversation became less strained, he moved to a low stool which he drew up quite close to her couch. She was much thinner in the face than when he last saw her, but this showed her features to even better advantage, and the prospect of losing her entirely was unendurably painful to him.

"Though when I stooped I drew no draught, yet never thought I that at the Shallows of the Stream of Death another would stretch out his hand to claim what I had lost."* He looked at her more tenderly than she could bear. She hid her face, murmuring as she did so the lines: "Long ere he guide me across the Shallows of Death's Stream, may my life, a foam-fleck on the Waters of Trouble, have vanished quite away." "Come," he said smiling, "the River has got to be crossed; we cannot escape it by 'vanishing.' However, I promise you I will be there too to hold your other hand. But let us be serious. You know, I am sure, how wretched I am at what has happened. Clearly, when I struggled as I did to overcome my feelings for you, it was not that you might be free to yield yourself in this rash way to one who, after all, cares far less for you than I did. It seems to me now incredible that I should ever have placed such confidence in his discretion; but who could foresee...?"

He saw that the whole matter was too painful for her to discuss; and to change the subject he continued hastily: "The Emperor is very much disappointed that you have not once been seen at Court. How would it be if you were to stay at the Palace for a little while after you leave us? It will not be so easy for you to get away, once you have settled in your new home. The Emperor will in any case think that I have behaved in a very inconsistent way. But I am glad to say your father is quite satisfied at what has happened..." So he spoke, trying to distract her by such

---

* The soul of a woman is helped across the Stream of Death by the specter of her first lover.

comfortable considerations as occurred to him. But it was all of no avail, and she was soon hopelessly involved in tears. He was aghast to discover into what depths of misery her own inexplicable act had plunged her; but it was clear that sympathy could not help her, and in as sensible and dispassionate a tone as he could muster he began to give her advice concerning her immediate future, insisting above all that, as things were,* there could be no question of her living at Higekuro's house.

Prince Higekuro himself was at first very averse to the idea of her going to the Palace at all. But in the end he saw that it would be easier to move her thence to his own palace than to snatch her straight from Genji's hands, and he at last consented to her spending a few weeks at Court.

His present mode of existence, stowed away in a corner of Tamakatsura's apartments, was very cramped and inconvenient; but even should he persuade her to return with him to his own palace, much required to be done before he could house her with even tolerable comfort. In the last year he had allowed everything to go to ruin, and there was hardly a corner in the whole building that did not urgently need repairs. For many months he had ceased to make any enquiry concerning his wife's present condition of mind, and even his children, of whom he had always been particularly fond, seemed no longer to interest him. But he was at bottom a kind-hearted and even rather sentimental man; he realized in a vague and general way that this refurnishing of the house in honor of another woman's arrival was probably rather painful to her, and he did his best to spare her any unnecessary inconvenience or humiliation. But his thoughts were all the time so entirely occupied with other things that his precautions were not in the least successful; indeed, everything seemed to happen in the way most calculated to wound her susceptibilities.

Lady Makibashira had not been brought up in a way to prepare her for servility or self-effacement. The daughter of a Royal Prince, and herself not lacking (at least in girlhood) either charm or good looks, she had been universally flattered and applauded. But in recent years a change had come over her; she had been subject to some strange possession or spiritual disorder. Her behavior became more and more peculiar, and at times she seemed barely conscious of what was going on around her. For these and other reasons there had for a long time past been no question of Higekuro living with her as a wife in the ordinary sense of the word. But he continued to treat her in the way that her rank demanded, and nothing had occurred till now which could suggest to the world at large that she did not occupy the foremost place in his affections.

News of these preparations for Tamakatsura's arrival reached Prince Hyobukyo's ears: "So it has come to this!" he said with a sigh. "I hear she

---

* While Makibashira, Higekuro's mad wife, was still there.

is extremely handsome and intelligent. No doubt he will make arrangements to keep her out of sight; but once this girl gets a foothold in the house, my daughter's position will become such as no woman of her quality should be called upon to endure. I shall at once take steps to protect her from this humiliation; if Higekuro cannot be brought to reason, she must leave this house immediately. After all, so long as I am alive, she will not lack a home..." and he began setting to rights an unoccupied wing in his own palace.

But Lady Makibashira had been a married woman for many years. Though Prince Hyobukyo was her father, she had long since ceased to think of his palace as her "home," and so far from reassuring her, the news that he intended her to come back to him completely overwhelmed her already distracted brain. She became first desperately violent and irrational, and then for days on end lay stretched out motionless upon her bed in a state of complete exhaustion.

She was by nature very quiet, and even-tempered, seeming at times more like a child on its best behavior than a full-grown woman. But for some while past she had suffered from sudden attacks, during which she played upon those about her the most unaccountable and repulsive tricks. Lately she had allowed no one to come near her, and her room had fallen into an indescribable state of filth and disorder. Such a scene would have at any time disgusted Prince Higekuro, to whom the least sign of slovenliness was an unforgivable offence. But coming as he now did straight from Tamakatsura's scrupulously clean and well-ordered apartments, he was appalled at the slatternly scene that lay before him.

But he had shared his life with her for year upon year, and even now pity soon prevailed over disgust. She seemed to know him and be quite capable of carrying on a conversation. After a while he said: "It is obvious, is it not, that the relation between two people cannot go on being always exactly the same. But it is only among savages or quite uneducated persons that this leads to wranglings and altercations. People of our sort know how to control themselves, show a reasonable amount of forbearance so long as they choose to put up with the situation; and when there is obviously nothing to be gained by holding out any longer, they part good-humouredly. You, on the contrary, have worked yourself up into such a state over this business that you are quite ill, and though I have wanted to talk things over with you, I did not know whether you were in a fit state to take part in such a conversation. Not that there is anything new to say. We agreed about all this some time ago. For a long while after you first began to suffer from these attacks I waited patiently and was careful to do nothing that might distress you. But you always admitted that I could not be expected to wait forever; sooner or later someone fresh would have to be called in to manage the household.

Well, that's what is now going to happen; you must try not to be cross with me about it. Quite apart from my affection for you, if it were only for our little people's sake, you may be quite sure I should never ill-treat or neglect you. This continual state of grievance and jealousy in which you now live is simply due to your abandoning yourself unresistingly, morbidly to wild dreams and imaginings. I can quite understand that while all this was still undecided you passed through a very anxious and agitated time. But now everything is settled, and you must make up your mind to give the new arrangements a trial before you decide that you are being treated unkindly. I hear that your father is full of indignation at my alleged barbarity, and intends to remove you to his own house. Do you think he really means anything by it, or is it only a threat by which he hopes to bring me to my senses?" He laughed as he said this, but in reply she only stared at him with an expression of reproach and anguish. Even Higekuro's personal servants, the maids Moku no Kimi and Chujo no Omoto, were against him in this matter, and expressed loud indignation at the prospect of Tamakatsura's arrival.

One day when Makibashira, apparently better than she had been for some time, lay quietly weeping, she suddenly said to Chujo no Omoto: "If he told me straight out that he is ashamed of me because I look so old and do odd things, I should not mind. But I cannot bear his dragging in my father's name. He would not dare say such things to my father's face, and if they were to get round... What he says to me does not much matter. I have heard it all before, and it does me no harm to hear it again. But my father..." At this moment Prince Higekuro entered. She quickly turned on the couch so that her face was hidden from him. She was very lightly built, and emaciated as she now was by months of constant illness, she presented as she lay there a spectacle of almost unconceivable fragility. Her hair was long and fine; but it had lately been falling out rapidly, and had in places become very thin. It was now in a hopeless tangle and pitiably bedraggled with tears. She could never have been very strikingly handsome, but there was enough of her father in her to give her face great distinction and charm, which, however, in her present uncared-for and haggard condition, had not much chance to take effect.

"What is this you are saying about your father?" asked Higekuro as he entered. "You will make terrible mischief between us, if you put it about that I speak slightingly of him. Besides, it is quite untrue..." Then more kindly: "I have never felt at my ease in that magnificent palace of Prince Genji's, and should not care to stay there for long at a time. But I am determined to go on seeing the lady whom I have just been visiting, and as I am not suited either by age or temperament to these perpetual runnings to and fro, I have arranged for her to come and live with us here. This will certainly be much pleasanter for her and me, and, I think, for you too. The fact that she is at such a distance and in so closely scrutinized a place makes the whole affair far more conspicuous than it need be. Prince Genji, as you know well enough, is a very important person; he has made himself responsible for this lady's happiness, and if he hears that you are being unkind to her, he will be very angry both with you and with me. So please be as nice to her as you can... But of course if you feel you would rather go and live with Prince Hyobukyo for a little while, by all means do so, I promise to come and see you frequently. But in either case you need not be afraid that I shall cease to care for you and look after you. I wish I could be as sure that you, on your side, will begin to take things a little more quietly and sensibly. You do not realize, I am sure, that all this outcry (which presumably you would not make unless you were fond of me) is doing me a great deal of harm. For years past I have done all that was in my power to make you happy, and you may rest assured that I shall continue to do so..." He tried to soothe her, speaking somewhat as he would have spoken to a cross child. "There is no need for you to tell me about your love affairs," she answered. "I am not interested in them. You know quite well what is worrying me. My father has been terribly upset by my illness ever since it began. What the effect upon him would be if I were to go home in my present condition, I dread to think. It distresses him immeasurably to see me suffer... I cannot do it... My father says that, after all, Lady Murasaki is my own sister, and it is very wrong of her to spoil my happiness by introducing you to this girl. But I do not at all agree with him. Let her introduce you to anyone she likes. It is no affair of mine..."

She spoke quite calmly and sensibly. But Higekuro had seen her in this mood before, and knew only too well that it might at any moment terminate in an outburst of the wildest irrationality. "You are quite mistaken about Lady Murasaki," he said. "She had no hand whatever in this. She lives locked away in her bower like an Enchanted Princess in a fairy-story, and would never dream of interfering in the affairs of persons such as you or I. She regards us all, I can assure you, with complete contempt. Certainly nothing would distress her more than that it should be thought she had tried to interest me in Lady Tamakatsura. Please do not spread such a report; it might do a great deal of harm."

He stayed chatting with her all the afternoon. By dusk his attention had already begun to wander, and he was conscious that his replies were often somewhat at random. For he was trying to decide whether he could contrive, without too much hurting her feelings, not to spend the whole of the evening in her society. Just as he was about to rise, a violent snowstorm began. To insist upon leaving at such a moment would have shown with too painful a clearness how anxious he was to escape from her company. Had she spoken one word of complaint or showed the slightest sign of ill humor, it would have been easy enough for him to flare up on his side and so escape from his predicament. But she had, on the contrary, been a marvel of tolerance, reasonableness, and amiability. It seemed too cruel to leave her, but he had not yet quite made up his mind, and stood with his hand on the door, staring out into the dusk. "I am afraid it is going to be a very heavy storm," she said, watching him. "You will never find your way. It has suddenly grown quite dark..." Suddenly her expression changed. He knew exactly what was passing in her mind. "That is all over now," she was thinking. "If he does stay, what will be the use?..." "I will wait till it clears a little," he said to her. And later: "Another time I shall be able to stay here as long as you like. But tonight there are reasons... It might be misunderstood... Both Genji and To no Chujo particularly desired that I should not miss... But there is no need to explain. You are so good and patient that I am sure you will forgive me. Tonight will be the last time. When Lady Tamakatsura is living here everything will be easier... But really, you are so much better tonight that there seems no reason to have anyone else in the house at all." "I know you would not really like to stay here tonight," she said gently. "I shall be happier if you go. So long as I know you are thinking kindly of me I do not mind where you go. I promise not to cry any more. Look! My sleeve is almost dry..."

Then she sent for her incense-burner, poured in fresh perfumes one upon another, and with her own hands scented his great riding-cloak from tip to toe. Her own dress was of a soft yielding stuff, and as she bent over her work, this dress fell in loose folds that gave her figure a homely, useful air. But how thin, how frail she had grown! She seemed like some pale phantom flickering across the winter night. Her eyes were swollen with weeping, yet her face, he thought, was beautiful. He felt a sudden tenderness towards her. She had never been to blame. Ought he not to have waited months, years if need be, before he inflicted this terrible suffering upon her? For he knew in that moment all that she had suffered since his dereliction of her began. But in the midst of his remorse the image of Tamakatsura rose up before him, and sighing deeply he began to put on his cloak, perfuming it once more with a miniature brazier that he held for a moment inside each sleeve. He was not as handsome as Genji, but he was magnificently built; and as he stood there handling his great riding-coat he looked a man not lightly to be trifled with. One of his retainers remarked loud enough to be heard, though not speaking directly to the Prince, that it had "almost stopped snowing and was getting very late." The maids Chujo no Omoto and Moku no Kimi were lying on a couch in the corner telling one another dismal stories and sighing, "What a sad world it is to be sure!" at regular intervals. Makibashira herself was lying calm and still at Higekuro's feet, her head resting on a low stool.

Suddenly she leapt up, seized a large brazier that was used for drying damp clothes, and coming up from behind, emptied it over his head.

The thing was done in a moment; so swiftly indeed that Higekuro had no idea what had happened. He only knew that suddenly his eyes and nostrils were full of fine, penetrating dust. Blind, choking, and still but dimly aware of what had happened to him, he found himself shaking ashes out of his coat, his breeches, his shirt, his hair. Her ladies stood by terror-stricken. Would he understand that this was one of her fits, one of those strange accesses of perversity in which her frenzy drove her to play the most revolting tricks precisely on those whom she most wished to please? If he thought that she had acted deliberately, was in possession of her senses when she played this odious prank, it was inconceivable that he would ever come near her again. They pressed round, dusting him, sponging him, offering him fresh clothes; but nothing took away this dry, gritty sensation that pervaded his whole person, so that he still felt as though he were smeared with ashes to the very roots of his thick, stubborn hair.

He could not present himself at Tamakatsura's immaculate apartments in this condition, and dismissing his followers, he prepared to settle in for the night.

Makibashira was now in her gentlewomen's hands. He knew that it was impossible to hold her responsible for what she had done. Yet the look of complete unconcern with which she surveyed the havoc she had just created stung him to a sudden fury, and he felt that he would have shouted abuse at her, had he not been terrified of provoking on her part a fresh outburst of devilry. It was now midnight, but he sent for priests and exorcists, and soon a service of Intercession was in full swing. The mad woman was now cursing and raving in the most horrifying manner. All night long she was cudgeled and pulled about by the priests;[*] dawn found her still maundering and weeping, but after a little while she became somewhat quieter, and Higekuro took this opportunity of sending his apologies to the New Palace. "Someone here was suddenly taken ill last night," he wrote, "and it was impossible for me to get away. Besides, it looked as though we were in for a very heavy fall of snow, and it would have seemed to my friends very odd if I had insisted upon setting out. Time after time I was on the point of starting, and at this moment I am chilled to the bone with waiting about for a chance to escape... I know well enough that you will not be heart-broken at my failure to appear; but I fear that others may have taken advantage of my discourtesy..."

He was right. His absence had certainly not caused Tamakatsura the slightest concern, and the letter of apology, which he had penned with

---

[*] In order to drive the "possession" out of her.

such agitation in the midst of a scene of utmost horror, she did not open or in any way acknowledge.

Next day Higekuro's wife was still in a very distracted condition, and further incantations were performed. His own secret prayer was that she might at least recover her reason for a sufficient length of time to permit of his installing Tamakatsura in the house. For at present any such step was clearly impossible. He who knew her as she ought to be could realize that her present savagery and malice were merely the result of her illness; but a stranger would be terrified and disgusted.

At dusk he set out as usual for Tamakatsura's rooms. Since his wife's illness his wardrobe had been much neglected, and he was continually complaining that the garments put out for his use were so badly cut as to make him an object of ridicule as he drove through the streets. Today a new cloak had been put out, which fitted him so ill that he refused to appear in it. The one he had worn on the night of the catastrophe was full of small holes made by fragments of red-hot charcoal, and though it had been carefully cleaned, there still clung to it a most unpleasant smell of burning. Yet in all his clothes the fragrance of the incense with which she had perfumed them that night was still distinctly perceptible. To arrive in this charred and smoldering condition at the New Palace was not to be thought of. He threw off all these garments, sent them to the washhouse, and once more had them thoroughly cleaned and set to rights. When they came back, Moku no Kimi was sent for to give them a good final perfuming. At last he was ready to start.

Even this one night's absence made her seem to him more marvelously lovely than ever. To be with her drove the thought of what was going on in his own house completely out of his head. And some such solace was needed, for the scene which he had just left had been agonizing in the extreme. He stayed at the New Palace till far into the next day. Spells and incantations seemed powerless against the spirit which had possessed the sick woman, and she continued to rave in an unabating frenzy. Terrified lest she should attempt to disfigure him, or, at the best, play upon him some other sinister prank, Higekuro for the next few days kept as far away from her rooms as possible. When from time to time business compelled him to spend an hour or two at his house, he established himself at the farthest possible end of the building, and it was here that with great precautions he sent for his children to come and see him. The eldest was a girl of twelve; the two boys were younger. They had grown gradually used to the fact that their father and mother did not often meet; but till now there had never been any question of their mother's place being usurped by someone else, and primed by their nurses with the notion that Tamakatsura's projected arrival was part of a dark and monstrous conspiracy, they obeyed his summonses very sullenly.

Hearing what had taken place, Prince Hyobukyo's first thought was to get his daughter as quickly as possible out of Higekuro's house. "This is certain to lead to a definite and final breach," he said. "She cannot with any dignity remain a day longer under his roof. After all, so long as I am alive, she can have a very good time here... There is no need to take this business too tragically..." And without any warning he arrived at Higekuro's to fetch her away. It so happened that she was on this occasion enjoying an interval of comparative quietness and lucidity; though on recovering her self-possession, and realizing to some extent what had been passing, she was seized with a terrible fit of melancholy.

When informed that her father was at the door she knew at once what this implied, and determined to offer no resistance. To stay meant only to witness the last remnants of her husband's affection for her dwindle and disappear. In the end she would probably be forced out of the house, under circumstances of even greater humiliation. Thinking that it would give her a feeling of support, her father had brought with him all her brothers; both the elder ones, Sahyoye and the rest, all of whom were now great officers at Court, and had come uniformed and attended as though for a state ceremony; and also her younger brothers, who by now were making their way in the world, one of them being a Captain in the Bodyguard, another a Lieutenant; a third, Assistant in the National Board. The whole party filled no less than three coaches. That if her father ever came to fetch her, it would be in this cumbersome and ceremonious way, both she and her gentlewomen had long anticipated. But the sight of the formidable cortège which was to put an end forever to her married life completely overwhelmed her. To make matters worse, it was announced that the part of his palace which Hyobukyo could put at her disposal could not possibly house both her and all her gentlewomen. Hasty consultations followed. It was arranged that about half the maids should go back to their own homes. There was much weeping, whispered promises of reinstatement "when Madam recovers herself," and hasty sorting out of small personal belongings. Then there was the sick woman's own baggage to be considered, and heated discussions as to what she would need in her new home. Amid this scene of tears and confusion the three children strayed about, apparently quite unmoved. Calling to them, their mother now said: "I have been in great trouble for a long time; but now everything is over, and I do not care what becomes of me. But you three still have all your lives before you, and I do not want you to be dragged down with me in my ruin. You, my little girl, I shall keep with me, come what may. But I shall let the boys go to their father as often as he wants them— indeed, I would leave them with him altogether if I thought he would go on taking any interest in them. Their grandfather will give them all the usual advantages and make them as happy as he can; but when they grow up they will find it a great handicap to have been connected with him; for nothing can nowadays be done except through Prince Genji, and your grandfather is on very bad terms with him. What I should really like would be to take you all to some forest far away in the mountains where no one could ever find us... But I know that would be a crime..." and she burst into tears. The children had very little idea what all this was about, but they too began quietly weeping. "Poor little things," said the nurses. "One knows from old stories that the kindest father will turn against his children if his heart is set upon another woman; and a man so barbarous as our master, who puts his own wife out of his house when she is ailing, is not likely to show much pity towards these defenseless creatures..." It was now getting late. It looked as if more snow were coming, and was indeed a most cheerless and uninviting evening. "Make haste," someone shouted from outside, "it's blowing up for a storm." Wiping her eyes, Makibashira went to the window and looked out. She was ready for the journey; but the little girl, who had always been a great favorite with her father, could not believe that he would wish her to go away without even having said good-bye to him and she now flung herself upon a couch and declared that the carriage must start without her. Her mother tried to coax her, saying that things were bad enough as it was, and it was very unkind of her to be disobedient at such a time. But the child was all the while hoping that her father would come back to say good-bye to her, and was determined not to start until she had seen him. But the storm had now commenced, and she at last saw for herself that there was not the remotest chance of his stirring on such a night.

There was a certain pillar on the right as you went into the women's rooms. Here it was that the little girl generally had her seat; and now, hating to think that this favorite corner of hers might soon become some stranger's sitting-place, she took a folded sheet of dark-brown paper, and hastily scribbling something upon it, she pushed it into a crack in the pillar with the point of her long hairpin. What she wrote was: "Though I say good-bye to this house and shall never see it again, do not forget me, O pillar of the Steadfast Tree!" As the carriage drove away the maids looked wistfully at the familiar haunts that they would in all likelihood never set eyes on again. At this last moment many a tree, never noticed before, seemed the one place where it would be pleasant to seek shade when the summer-time came round; and neither Lady Makibashira nor her ladies ceased to gaze behind them till the topmost bough of the last tree had faded out of sight. For this place had been their home for year upon year, and even though they had been leaving under very different circumstances, they must needs have forsaken it with many a bitter pang.

Meanwhile their arrival was awaited at Prince Hyobukyo's palace with great trepidation. His wife, sharp-tongued as ever,[*] was bitterly reproaching him for having fallen out with Genji, whose hostility (she now made sure) was at the bottom of all their present trouble. "It all began with your miserable cowardice over that Suma affair. You did not write to him once all the time he was away from Court, and then were surprised that he would not help you to make an Empress of our younger daughter. You know quite well why it was that he would do nothing for you, as you confessed to me at the time and everyone agreed. However, I did think that you had learnt your lesson and would take the first opportunity of re-establishing yourself in his good graces. But nothing of the kind. Prince Genji was completely under the sway of this bastard of yours, Lady Murasaki. Everything is easy for you. You had only to interest the girl in her sisters—people in her privileged position are expected to do something for their relations—and we could have got anything we liked to ask for. Instead of that, having got into a scrape with this supposed "daughter" of his, and being under the necessity of passing her off on anyone who was fool enough to take her, he hit upon this simpleton Higekuro, whose wife, being your daughter, could easily be hustled out of the way. Upon my honor, I wonder you are willing to sit down under it all..."

"Silence, woman," he broke in. "Prince Genji is our lord and master, and must be spoken of in this house with proper respect. A man of his intelligence is not as easily wheedled into friendship by one whom he believes to have done him an injury. My blunder at the time of his exile has turned out to be a great misfortune for us all. But I was not the only person to make that mistake. Indeed, if you look round the Court and note who has gone under and who has kept afloat, you will see that in every case it depended on what line they took in those Suma and Akashi days. So meticulous a scheme of punishments and rewards has surely never before been put into practice. I certainly have not fared worse than the rest. On the contrary, when a year or two ago I celebrated my fiftieth birthday,[†] Prince Genji's interest in the affair gave it an importance far beyond what my rank and birth demanded; and this was solely due to his affection for my daughter Murasaki, a feeling which you accuse me of never having turned to proper account."

But his wife's bitterness only became more intense than ever; moreover, she began to spread the most scandalous stories about Genji's conduct in the affair. And it may be imagined that in these inventions he did not

---

[*] For this woman's character see Part I, p. 86. She had pursued her rival, Murasaki's mother, "with constant vexations and affronts; day in and day out this obstinate persecution continued, till at last she died of heart-break."

[†] See Part III, p. 429.

come off lightly; for hers was the most dangerous tongue in the whole Court. The removal of his wife and children came as a complete surprise to Higekuro. He assumed that Lady Makibashira had, in a sudden fit of childish spleen, implored her father to take this drastic step. But Prince Hyobukyo must himself be held largely to blame, for Makibashira's mind was in an entirely volatile condition, and if her father had exercised a little tact she would a few hours later have been begging him to leave her where she was. "This has come as rather a shock," he said to Tamakatsura when he heard the news. "Of course, in a way it makes it much easier for you to come and live with me. But in any case she is in a condition which would soon have made it absolutely necessary to shut her up in some outlying wing of the house; and then you could have lived with me quite comfortably. I resent her being carried off so suddenly. It implies that I am not looking after her properly. I shall go at once to her father and complain."

He was wearing a very handsome cloak lined with willow-green and blue-grey silken breeches. The costume became him particularly well, and the waiting-women who saw him pass out on the way to Hyobukyo's palace could not for the lives of them make out why their mistress was so down upon him.

The news that she had just heard convinced Tamakatsura more firmly than ever of the folly that she had committed in blindly yielding herself to such a man, and as he left the room she did not even raise her eyes to watch him go.

On the way to Prince Hyobukyo's he called at his own house. He was met by Moku no Kimi, who being his personal servant had been left behind, and from her lips he heard the full story of his wife's departure. His distress was obvious, and when she was telling him of the little girl's reluctance to leave the house without saying good-bye to him Moku no Kimi feared that her master would altogether lose his self-possession. "Hyobukyo," he said at last, "does not in the least realize all that I patiently endured during the earlier stages of my wife's insanity. I do not think there are many men in the world who would have sacrificed themselves as I did. As regards her happiness, it is doubtful if this change of residence will make any difference at all, for her mind is now breaking down entirely. But in any case what sense can there be in letting her carry off those unfortunate children?..." Just then his eye fell upon the little girl's favorite pillar. He saw that something was poked into the crack, and grasping at once who had put it there, he rescued the folded note and put it in his sleeve. On the way to Prince Hyobukyo's palace he read it, obliged to wipe the tears from his eyes while he did so, for though the handwriting had as yet no beauty, the sentiment expressed in the child's poem could not fail to move him.

On his arrival he found that there was no question of his wife or daughter being allowed to see him. From her parents he received this message: "If your neglect of our daughter were of recent origin, we might be willing to listen to your protestations, and if satisfactory assurance were forthcoming might consider the possibility of permitting her return. But we are fully aware that your affections have for a long time past been engaged in another quarter, and we see no reason to suppose that time would bring any amendment to your ways. We therefore decided to act without delay, and are persuaded that by so doing we have saved you from much annoyance and discomfort." He replied that they had taken advantage of him in an extremely unfair way. They knew how great was his affection for the children, and might have assumed that his feelings towards the mother were at least sufficiently humane to make it worth while discussing this matter with him (many times, if necessary) before taking so drastic a measure. As it was, the world at large, which knew nothing of the real facts, must inevitably be led to the most damaging and at the same time erroneous conclusions.

So he justified himself, but with no effect; and Hyobukyo would not even allow the little girl to come out and talk to him. The elder boy, now ten years old, had already become a page at Court. He was a fascinating child and much beloved; not exactly handsome, but very quick-witted and alert. The other, a boy of eight, was particularly good-looking and bore a strong resemblance to his sister. This child was now brought to Higekuro, and patting it on the head, he said sadly: "It is well that you are so like your sister, for you are all that I shall see to remind me of her in the years that are to come." He begged Prince Hyobukyo to accord him even a few moments' interview. But the prince excused himself on the ground that "he had caught cold and was at present avoiding all exertion." There was nothing for it but to drive away. His two sons had climbed into the carriage to talk to him. They now begged for a drive, but as he was going straight to Tamakatsura's, this was rather embarrassing. "You had better stay here," he said. "I will come and see you again soon." They gazed after the carriage, and when they presently saw that instead of going in the direction of their father's house it had turned towards the New Palace, they looked at one another in bewilderment. But once he was back again in Tamakatsura's presence, the picture of these two children staring after him in consternation, the memory of his unhappy wife's ravings and contortions, all vanished completely from his mind, and it was long before he again attempted to get news from his father-in-law's house. He felt indeed that he could hardly be expected to risk the repetition of such a welcome as he had met with last time he called; but Hyobukyo insisted upon regarding this abstention as a fresh offence, and made many caustic remarks concerning Higekuro's callous indifference.

"Even *I* have been getting into trouble over this business," said Murasaki to Genji one day. "My stepmother says I ought not to have let you upset her daughter's domestic arrangements!" "It has been very difficult to know what to do," he replied. "If it had rested with me only, I should never have encouraged her to marry Higekuro. But her father was bent upon it, and I fell in with his desire. The Emperor was not at all pleased, and one naturally hears it said that all the other suitors are in a rage with me; though I can hardly believe this of Prince Sochi, who is such a sensible fellow, that I am sure as soon as he sees that I have really given Tamakatsura up he will not, despite his disappointment, be so unreasonable as to pick a quarrel with *me*. I am very glad that the true nature of my relations with her is now known. For though I think that in general it is better for people to keep their private affairs to themselves, there are cases where, unless all be known, far worse things will be imagined than there is any warrant for assuming."

Meanwhile Tamakatsura was taking less trouble than ever to pretend that Higekuro's caresses were agreeable to her. But his efforts to overcome her distaste for him were untiring, and when the time came for her to spend a few days at the Palace in order to be presented to the Emperor, Higekuro did his best to prevent or at least postpone this separation. But it was evident that the Emperor would regard any further refusal as an act of discourtesy; Genji and To no Chujo both strongly urged him to obey at once, and Higekuro himself discovered, on looking into the matter, that there were numberless precedents for the Emperor's request. Accordingly he yielded, and in the spring of the next year she was brought to the Palace. There was a dancing festival going on at the time, and consequently the ceremonies connected with her Presentation attracted very little notice. But it was known that Genji, To no Chujo and Higekuro, the three most powerful men in the country, were her sponsors; while she was actually attended at the time of her arrival by Yugiri and several of her elder brothers, so that it was by no means likely that she would be overlooked. The room that was allotted to her was separated only by a covered gallery from the apartments of Lady Nishi no Miya, Prince Hyobukyo's eldest daughter; but though their habitations were divided by so small a space, their interests and sympathies could hardly have been farther apart, and no civilities were exchanged between them.

It happened to be a moment when the scene at Court was simplified by the absence of lowborn favorites or clandestine mistresses. Four great ladies, Akikonomu, Lady Chujo, Nishi no Miya (whom I have just mentioned), and finally a daughter of the Minister of the Left held absolute sway. Apart from them, two young girls, daughters of the Junior State Secretary and the Chancellor, enjoyed a certain prominence; but on the whole the field was remarkably clear.

This year the Mummers visited all the apartments at Court where they had kinswomen or connections of any kind, and the whole affair was far more animated and interesting than usual. The reception given to the dancers in the various quarters they visited was of the most magnificent kind, such a display of hangings and gay-colored favors seldom having been witnessed. One of the most dazzling displays took place in the rooms of the Crown Prince's mother, Lady Jokyoden. The Prince was still a mere child,[*] but his nursery had already become a center of fashionable activities.

After performing before the Emperor, the Mummers visited the quarters of Lady Akikonomu, and finally finished their round very late in the day at the ex-Emperor Suzaku's palace. There had been some talk of their going on to Genji's; but it would have been inconvenient to receive them at such an hour, and he discouraged the visit. On their way back from Suzaku's, already much enlivened by the hospitality which they had received during the course of the evening, they went the round of the Crown Prince's apartments, singing the "Bamboo River"[†] at the tops of their voices. Faint streaks of light were already appearing in the sky when they were joined by a band of young men, which included some of To no Chujo's sons and a number of courtiers famous for the beauty of their voices. The youngest among them all was Chujo's eighth son, who being the child of his legitimate wife, had been brought up to regard himself as a little person of considerable consequence. He was a good-looking child, about the same age as Higekuro's eldest boy, with whom he was often favorably compared. Unlike many of the other children who saw the sights that day, he was not at all overawed by the first appearance at Court of this much-talked-about lady, but on the contrary stared at her to his fill.

Tamakatsura had not so much experience of Court festivities as was possessed by most of her rivals and neighbors. She wisely refrained from venturing upon any unusual or particularly ambitious combinations of color. But upon the general lines laid down by the taste of her competitors, she often achieved a success considerably greater than theirs. Both she and her gentlewomen found this sojourn at the Palace a most welcome distraction, and only wished that it might be indefinitely prolonged.

Wherever they went the Mummers were received with presents of costly wadded cloaks and a profusion of good things both to eat and drink. Though it was not at Tamakatsura's that they were to have their set banquet, the entertainment she gave them was, by Higekuro's help, on so generous a scale that it was hard to recognize in it the mere "passing

---

[*] He must by now be about eleven, having been born shortly before Genji's exile.
[†] See Part III, p. 478.

refreshments,"* which it was supposed to represent. Higekuro was himself on duty at the Palace that day, and said to his wife more than once during the course of the festivities, "There is no need whatever for you to sleep here a second night; it would look as though you had changed your mind and meant to stay on in the Palace." She did not answer. But her gentlewomen protested that Genji had only allowed her to leave the New Palace on the express understanding that she should pay a leisurely visit to the Emperor, which, considering she had never once been to Court before and might not go again for a long time, was the least that ordinary good breeding demanded. To leave so soon as this would be far too precipitate...

He noted with pain her obvious reluctance to leave a place the chief charm of which, as he conjectured, lay in the fact that it afforded her a refuge from his embraces.

Prince Sochi was present when the Mummers performed at the Palace, and his heart beat wildly as he pressed near the Lady-of-the-Bedchamber's† office. Knowing that if she recognized a note as coming from him she would not open it, he found an excuse for going to Higekuro's official quarters and sent a messenger from there. Tamakatsura naturally thought that the note came from her husband, and reluctantly opened it: "Hate-fullest of seasons for me has Spring become, who must stand by and watch the birds of the deep forest folded wing in wing." So ran his poem. She blushed crimson as she read it, and was just thinking how she could possibly reply, when the Emperor himself came that way. The moon had risen, and in its full light she scanned his countenance. He was, she at once noticed, extraordinarily like Genji, and it was a relief to her to discover that there were perhaps people in the world who possessed Genji's beauty yet at the same time were not cut off from her by fictitious parental ties. But her guardian had been extremely fond of her, of that there could be no doubt; whereas this young man unfortunately showed no signs whatever of feeling for her one particle of the affection which Genji had attributed to him. His Majesty expressed in a very good-tempered and considerate way his regret that she had decided not to live permanently at the Palace. This made her feel extremely uncomfortable; she hid her face in her sleeve and did not reply. "I should like so much to know what is going on in your mind," he said at last. "I have a small piece of news for you which I flattered myself would not be unwelcome. But I now remember that not answering is a peculiarity of yours." He then handed her an acrostic poem in which he at the same time asked

---

* "Mizu-umaya," or water-stabling, as it was technically called by the dancers. The regular banquet was called "ii-umaya," or rice-stabling.

† Tamakatsura.

what previous affection on her side had for so long delayed their meeting, and also announced that she had been promoted to the Third Rank. "I had hoped that in time we might become very close friends," he added. "But I see that you hold a different view." There came into his voice as he said these few words a new tone, which proved to her in an instant that the Emperor's feelings as well as his outward appearance were after all uncommonly like those of Genji. Her heart leapt, and she replied with the poem: "Of what former love you speak I know not; but henceforward him alone I serve who put the purple on my sleeve."* "It is now my duty to earn what hitherto I have done so little to deserve," she said timidly. At this he laughed. "No," he said, "you have got your reward, and you had better make the most of it. I did not mean it as a bribe. But I think that any reasonable person would admit I had come very badly out of the business..." He spoke lightly, but it was evident that he was genuinely piqued. "This is dreadful," thought poor Tamakatsura. "Will a handsome man never fall in love with me without saying in the same breath that we must part forever?" Evidently he regarded her marriage as a fatal bar to friendship. She became very staid in her manner. Noting this, the Emperor feared that he had shocked her, and made up his mind (for he had by no means abandoned the idea of continuing the acquaintance) henceforth to advance more cautiously.

Meanwhile it reached Higekuro's ears that the Emperor was with her, and falling into a panic he again began scheming to carry her home at the earliest possible moment. Nor did she attempt to dissuade him, for repeated disasters had at last destroyed in her all capacity for resistance. Higekuro invented one pretext after another for her instant removal, and when each in turn had been easily disposed of, he tried to enlist the help of To no Chujo and others of the Court Council. At last the Imperial sanction was obtained. "I see that I had better let her go," said the young Emperor good-humoredly. "If I keep her now, Higekuro will not allow her to come here again and I am hoping for frequent visits. I think I am right in saying that I first began to take interest in her long before Prince Higekuro set eyes upon her. But he got to work much more quickly than I, and fully deserves the advantage which he has gained... I have an idea that there was a famous case† of this kind in years gone by, but cannot now recall the names." When he had seen her in the distance years ago his curiosity had been aroused, and he had felt that she might be worth getting to know. But at close quarters he found her far more attractive

---

* Promoted her to the Third Rank.

† In the 9th century Fujiwara no Tokihira carried off a lady who had for some time been admired by Taira no Sadabumi. When reproached by Sadabumi for her fickleness, the lady replied: "What in waking hours I may have promised I know not; but now I wander in the mazes of a dream; or *someone* wanders, for I scarce think it can be I."

than he had imagined or been led by those who knew her to suppose. He could not now forgive himself for having handled the affair so incompetently. Having at one moment determined to give her confidence by slow stages, he felt at the next that he had not made his sentiments sufficiently plain, and plunged into the most impassioned and hectic avowals. She could not help thinking how well her own state of mind matched that of the lady to whose story the Emperor had already referred.

Meanwhile the letters of several public men who were seeking audience with His Majesty had for some time been waiting in the corridor, and just outside the door Higekuro stood officiously mounting sentry over the apartment. "I know he is an officer in the Bodyguard," said the Emperor, annoyed by his persistency, "but I think that on this occasion he is performing his professional duties rather too thoroughly."

At parting he gave her the poem: "Because the Ninefold Hedge of royalty girds me about, not even the scent of the plum-blossom, nay; not even so much* is carried to the steps of my Throne." Not a very remarkable poem, as on later reflection she would easily have perceived; but at the time it seemed to her a masterly performance. "Higekuro," the Emperor added, "is like the man who 'went to gather violets'; I cannot expect that he should be willing even for the briefest space to 'quit the fields of Spring.'† Nor have I the heart to ask it of him. Henceforward I shall not attempt to approach you..."

She could not but admire his delicacy of feeling: "Though the scent of this blossom be not as that of others that grow upon the tree, yet even so much let the wind carry to and from your Throne."‡ It cost him much to part from her for the last time as he supposed, and it was with many backward glances that he now left her room.

Higekuro was determined that she should not sleep another night at the Palace. He knew that if he broached the matter beforehand to his colleagues on the Council they would certainly refuse to countenance so precipitate a step. Accordingly, without mentioning the matter to anybody, he went straight to Tamakatsura and said: "I have suddenly caught a severe chill, and it is essential that I should go at once to some place where I can be properly looked after. There is nothing so awkward as being ill in other people's houses." He spoke in such a weak, plaintive tone that she felt quite sorry for him. A few hours later she was already installed in Higekuro's house.

Her father To no Chujo soon heard of this. He was not best pleased, for he feared that the Emperor would regard so sudden a flight as very

---

* *Kabakari* means "so much," and also "only the scent."

† Allusion to a poem by Yamabe no Akahito (8th century).

‡ I.e. write to me sometimes.

discourteous. But on the whole he was glad he had not been consulted, for he had no desire to quarrel with Higekuro over so small a matter. In fact, as he usually did when things went wrong, he chose to regard it as Genji's affair rather than his own; and Genji, although this sudden termination of his tutelage over the girl came as a great shock to him, naturally did not feel called upon to interfere.

Higekuro, though in his heart of hearts he knew that Tamakatsura had no more chosen this destiny than the smoke from the salt-kilns chooses to be blown back across the hill, was so much elated by his success that for the moment her contempt for him did not in the least spoil his pleasure. His state of mind was indeed that of some brigand chief who has carried off an unwilling bride at his saddle-croup. He did indeed scold her for having remained closeted so long with the Emperor. This seemed to her insufferably petty and vindictive on Higekuro's part. Henceforward she took less and less pains even to keep up in public the appearance of being on any kind of terms with him. He was also cut off from all intercourse with Prince Hyobukyo's family. He tried to give the impression that he regarded this as no great loss; but in reality he felt this isolation acutely. However, he did not attempt to communicate with the Prince, and henceforward spent the whole of his time in lavishing unwanted attentions upon his new-won prize.

To Genji, who had for months past been preparing himself for Tamakatsura's departure, her loss came as a far greater blow than he had ever anticipated. It was not indeed her departure (he explained to himself) that he found difficult to bear, but the suddenness and completeness with which Higekuro had taken possession. But be that as it may, he could not for an instant stop thinking about her, and soon fell into a condition of absent-mindedness and melancholy that was observed by all who met him. It is said that whatever happens to us is ruled by our conduct in previous existences, or, as others would express it, by Fate. But it seemed to Genji that for the miseries into which he constantly found himself plunged, no other person or power could possibly be held responsible. They sprang from his own excessive susceptibility, and from no other cause whatever. He longed to write to her; but it seemed impossible, now that she was in the hands of the grim, unbending Higekuro, to address to her the small humors and absurdities of which their correspondence was usually composed. In the second month a period of heavy rain set in; after the ceremonies of the New Year this season is apt to seem rather flat and stale, and, desperately in need of distraction, Genji broke all his resolutions and called at Prince Higekuro's house. He knew, however, that there was no chance of his seeing her personally, and though it was painful to him, who had been used to spend hour after hour in her company, merely to send in a note, this was the most he dared to attempt. And even so, despite the fact that he was able to get hold of the old nurse Ukon and send the letter through her, he thought it unwise to send a closed note and was therefore obliged to express himself in the most guarded manner, trusting that she would be able to read between the lines. "In these dull days when hour on hour the spring rain spills upon the quiet earth, do you at times recall the people and the palace whence you came?" So he wrote, adding: "This is a dreary season at best; and worse than ever for me, who am tormented by longings and recollections of which I cannot now speak." Ukon took the letter and succeeded in conveying it to Tamakatsura at one of the rare moments when Higekuro was absent from her side. The old woman, of course, knew nothing of Genji's sentiments towards her mistress, who had never breathed to anyone a word concerning his occasional indiscretions and excesses; but watching Tamakatsura's face as she read the letter Ukon now guessed a good deal of the truth. But exactly how much had happened between them? That was a question about which Ukon henceforward frequently puzzled her head; but she was unable to reach any conclusion.

Throughout this time Genji was constantly reminded of his separation from Oborozuki* at the time when she became Consort of the Emperor Suzaku. She too was Lady-of-the-Bedchamber; she too was carried away and locked up in a place whither it was impossible for him to pursue her. He remembered having been very unhappy then, but nothing like so miserable as he was now. Was it that he was becoming more and more sentimental, he asked himself, or merely that the sufferings of the moment always seem more acute than those which we conjure up out of the past? But whether or no the miseries of today were really worse than those of yesterday, of this much he was sure, that from none of his divagations had anything but torment and agitation ever ensued. Well, it was all over now; henceforward his existence would be free from these devastating entanglements, and no doubt he would be a great deal happier than ever before. But for the moment it was not so very easy as he had imagined to begin this new life of resignation and tranquility. He thought he would make use of the bad weather to practice a little on his zithern; but no sooner did he take it into his hands than he began to recall how Tamakatsura had played this and that phrase or run at the time when he was giving her a lesson every day. To break the spell of these recollections he tuned his instrument to the Eastern Mode and played the old song "Let the weeds grow."† Could she have seen him as he sat playing that lovely air, it would have been strange indeed if she had not wished herself back in her late home.

---

* Part II, p. 197.

† "The water-weeds that grow in the pool on the plain of Oshitaka where wild doves feed—do not cut them at the root, for they will not grow again. Do not cut them at the root."

The young Emperor too, though their acquaintance had been so brief, could not get Tamakatsura out of his head. "As she went by, trailing the skirts of her crimson gown..."* For some reason these words haunted him, though the poem could scarcely be more ill sounding and crude than it is; and he too began to contrive secret ways of communicating with her. But she had long ago made up her mind that happiness was not to be her fate, and could not bring herself to toy with it by the familiar interchange of pretty thoughts and images. Letter after letter arrived; but in her replies she never went beyond a formal acknowledgment. Often she remembered with gratitude Genji's untiring devotion to her interests and comforts. What matter if he fell between the two extremes of parent and lover? No one, she felt sure, would ever look after her as he had done.

It was now the third month. The wisteria and mountain-kerria in the gardens of the New Palace were in full bloom, loveliest of all at evening, when the light of the setting sun slanted through the hanging sprays of delicate blossom. This was a moment of the year that had always given him an intense delight; but now it hardly seemed to move him. He left Murasaki's domain and made his way to the western garden.† Here too the mountain-kerria was in magnificent bloom. In especial he noticed a great trail of it that hung across a clump of Chinese bamboos and recited to himself the poem: "O mountain flower that lovest to grow upon the rocks,‡ thou shalt teach me to endure in silence, the love that I must hide." Never before had he repented so bitterly of his determination to surrender the girl into other hands. It had seemed while she was with him so easy to be wise, to make self-sacrificing resolutions. But now that he had lost her it was incredible that he could ever have deliberately planned and executed so terrible a disaster. He happened to notice that there were a lot of eggs in the pigeon-house, and arranging them prettily in a basket along with oranges and lemons he sent it as a present to Tamakatsura, not with any very definite intention.§ When Higekuro saw the basket with its accompanying note, he burst out laughing: "What an extraordinary man this Genji is!" he said. "Why, even if he were your real father he could not now that you are married expect to meet you except on particular occasions. What does he want? He seems, in one way or another, to be always complaining that he does not see you." She did not seem to have any intention of acknowledging the gift, and as the messenger was still

---

* "Outdoors I think, at home I think of how she looked that day as she went by trailing the skirts of her crimson gown." *Manyoshu* 2550. A very rough, primitive poem.

† Tamakatsura's former apartments.

‡ *Iwa*—"rock" and "silent."

§ But there is a hint that Tamakatsura is shut away in Higekuro's palace like a tame bird in a cage. The bird mentioned is really a kind of duck, but much smaller. "Duck's eggs" would give a wholly wrong visual impression.

waiting, Higekuro said: "Let me answer it for you." "I am not minded that any should reclaim her, this fledgling that was not counted among the brood of either nest." Such was the poem he sent, and he added: "My wife was surprised at the nature of your gift, and was at a loss how to reply without seeming to attach an undue importance to it..."

Genji laughed when the note was brought to him. "I have never known Higekuro stoop to concern himself in such trifles as this," he said. "What is the world coming to?" But in his heart he was deeply offended by the arrogantly possessive tone of Higekuro's letter.

As the months went by Lady Makibashira became more and more deeply buried in her own dark and frightful thoughts. Soon she seemed to be gradually lapsing into complete helplessness and imbecility. Higekuro enquired after her constantly and did everything in his power to make her comfortable, incurring considerable outlay on her behalf, and indeed watching over her practical interests exactly as he would have done if she had still been at home. He continued to be devotedly attached to his children, but Prince Hyobukyo would not allow him to see the little girl. The boys, however, were constantly at their father's house, and came back chattering about "such a nice, new lady" who had come to live there. "She knows all sorts of lovely games and plays with us all day," they said. The little girl stared at them open-eyed, having formed in her mind a very different picture of the woman whom her present guardians represented always as the unscrupulous monster who had ruined their father's home. But in reality it was not surprising that Tamakatsura should have won the boys' hearts, for she possessed an extraordinary faculty for making herself liked by people of all sorts and ages wherever she went.

In the eleventh month of that year she bore Higekuro a handsome boy. The father's delight knew no bounds, and the solicitude with which he watched over both mother and child can easily be imagined. To no Chujo too rejoiced that the match should be turning out so unqualified a success and felt that he had acted very wisely in recommending it. And certainly, he said to himself, she deserved a success, for she possessed quite as much charm as the sisters over whom he had taken a great deal more trouble. Kashiwagi too was glad that all seemed to be going well, for he had settled down into the position of an extremely helpful and admiring brother. Perhaps, however, he still cared for her with something more than brotherly affection; he had a feeling that he would have preferred the child to be someone else's rather than Higekuro's; for example, if only she had borne such a child (so he reflected as he gazed at the infant) to the Emperor Ryozen, who constantly lamented that he had no children, what a future might have been in store for it!

After her recovery Tamakatsura continued to administer the business of the Bedchamber from her husband's house, and seemed to show no intention of ever again appearing at the Palace. There were precedents for such an arrangement as this, and no exception could well be taken to it.

But to go back a little, in the autumn of this year To no Chujo's eccentric daughter, foiled in her ambition to become Lady-of-the-Bedchamber, added to the embarrassment of her relations by a series of the most flutter-brained flirtations. Her sister Lady Chujo lived in a constant state of agitation, convinced that sooner or later this Lady of Omi would get into some scrape of a kind which might seriously compromise the whole family. She saw no reason why she should be saddled with so needless a responsibility and begged her father to intervene. To no Chujo accordingly sent for her and warned her as impressively as he could that she must in future stay in her sister's rooms and not wander all over the house, as she had lately developed the habit of doing. This remonstrance, however, had no-effect, and she was soon causing as much anxiety as ever to her unwilling sponsors.

It happened one day that a number of distinguished courtiers had come to the house; it was an autumn night of exceptional beauty, music was in progress, and everyone was in uncommonly good spirits. Even Yugiri, usually so quiet and orderly, was talking in rather an excited manner. Someone amid the group of ladies at the end of the room pointed him out to her neighbor and made some remark to the effect that she had never seen him look so handsome. "Handsome! Who's handsome?" screamed a piercing voice, the owner of which suddenly craned her neck in the direction indicated; and before anyone could stop her the Lady of Omi had pressed her way to the front of the throng, where she stood staring at Yugiri open-mouthed, while everyone present wondered what hideous piece of folly or impertinence would shortly issue from those ecstatically parted lips. But all she did was to point at the embarrassed Yugiri and say in a voice which, though it was meant to be a whisper, was audible all over the room: "Look at that one, now, just look at him!" And she recited in a ringing voice the poem:

> If your ship is lost at sea
> And you cannot land where you'd like to be,
> You'd better come aboard of me.*

"Like the man who lost his rudder said, when he found himself at the same place where he started: 'It all comes to the same thing in the end,'" she added encouragingly.

Who on earth could this extraordinary madcap be, wondered poor Yugiri, when suddenly he recollected the queer stories that had a little

---

* If you can't have Kumoi, why not marry me?

while ago been current about some odd girl whom To no Chujo had adopted. This of course must be she, and laughing, he answered her with the poem:

> Though my good ship should split in two,
> I'd rather be drowned with all my crew
> Than trust my life to one like you.

That does not sound very kind, she thought.

The Spray of Plum-Blossom

Although it was early days to begin thinking about the little Akashi Princess's Initiation, Genji seemed bent upon celebrating it immediately. The Heir Apparent's Putting on of the Trousers was to take place in the second month, and it was perhaps Genji's wish that the girl should go to the Palace as soon as the little prince set up a separate establishment. Towards the end of the first month, a moment when there is very little going on at home or abroad, Genji held an inspection of the perfumes and incenses that were to be used at the Initiation. He first looked through the scents that had recently been forwarded to the Capital by the Governor of Tsukushi. He soon came to the conclusion that these modern importations fell far behind what used to reach this country in former times, and opening his storehouses at the Nijo-in he brought out all the old Chinese perfumes he could find and had them carried to his New Palace. "With perfumes," he said, "it is just as it is with embroideries and woven brocades: The old ones are far better workmanship than anything that is turned out today." So saying, he began to look out for likely pieces of embroidery and gold brocade; for many would be wanted to fringe the box-covers, carpets, and cushions used in the ceremony of Presentation at the Palace. Luckily he came upon some particularly fine pieces presented to his father, the late Emperor, by the Korean soothsayers who had come to Court in the earlier part of his reign.* These so far excelled what was now imported that he determined to make use only of ancient pieces, and distributed among his friends† the stuffs sent in for the occasion by the Governor of Tsukushi. But with the perfumes to be used at the Initiation such a method was impossible, for the stock of ancient perfumes would soon have run out. In distributing a supply of perfumes to the various members of his household, he therefore ordered that new and old should be mixed. Then there were the presents to be got ready, for no one who came to the Initiation could be allowed to go away without some small gift; and in addition to these there were the particular rewards granted to the princes and noblemen who took the leading part in the affair. Both at the New Palace and at the Nijo-in there was such a bustle as seldom before accompanied, in

---

* At the time of Genji's birth. See Part I, p. 17.
† Instead of using them for the ceremony.

every quarter of each establishment by a continual jingling of pestle and mortar.* Meanwhile Genji, who by some means or other had contrived to get hold of two secret recipes very jealously guarded by the Emperor Nimmyo,† and thought never to have been transmitted to any of his descendants, was locked away in his own rooms, completely absorbed in certain mysterious experiments. Murasaki, not to be outdone, succeeded in discovering a recipe that had belonged to Prince Motoyasu, the son of Nimmyo, and ensconcing herself in a secret closet behind the double-doors of the Great Bedroom, refused to give any information as to what was afoot, though, as Genji remarked, he would soon know how she was getting on by the scent that emanated from her hiding-place. Indeed they both threw themselves into the thing with such abandon that it was hard to believe they were to play the part of dignified elders at the coming ceremony. Both he and she were obliged to seek the assistance of a few chosen attendants; for even when the perfumes were made there was still a great deal of work to be done. Such exquisite scents could not be crammed into any stray vessel that lay handy. Hours were spent in selecting jars of appropriate shape, incense-burners incised with an exactly suitable flower-pattern, boxes that would not disgrace the marvels they were to contain. And to add to their difficulties, there must be a touch of novelty, a suggestion of surprise, about every article. Meanwhile similar scenes were in progress throughout the New Palace and the Nijo-in, each competitor straining every nerve to produce a blend which should attract the notice of her fastidious patron.

On the tenth day of the second month there was a little rain, not more than was needed to bring to perfection the smell and color of the red plum-blossom in front of Genji's palace. Prince Sochi had heard of the existing preparations which were afoot, and being on intimate terms with the household, ventured to call, though he knew that everyone must be very busy. After talking of one thing and another, he went out with Genji to look at the flowers; suddenly a messenger arrived, bearing a letter tied to a spray of half-scattered plum-blossom. He announced that he came from Princess Asagao, the former Vestal Virgin. Sochi had heard of Genji's admiration for this lady: "What does she say?" he asked. "I hope you are beginning to make a little progress." Genji smiled. "It is a business letter," he said. "She has heard that we are all making perfumes, and as she has had a good deal of experience in that line, she gives me a few hints." So saying, he quickly hid the letter. But there was evidently some truth in his account, for the messenger had also brought a cedar-wood box containing two glass bowls, each filled

---

* The ingredients of the perfumes were pounded in metal mortars.
† 9th century.

with large balls of incense. One was of blue glass, and on this there was a five-pointed pine-leaf pattern; the other was of white glass, carved with a plum-blossom spray. Even the cord with which the box was tied had evidently been chosen with the greatest care, and was delightfully soft to the touch. "What an elegant affair!" exclaimed Prince Sochi, staring hard at the box. He was able as he did so to decipher the poem which was attached to it: "Though, like the plum-branch that I send, these perfumes have small fragrance of their own, yet worn by you they will not lack for regal scent..." The entertainment of the messenger was entrusted to Yugiri, who plied him with drink, and as payment for his trouble gave him a close-fitting Chinese lady's gown, red plum-blossom color without, yellow within. For his reply Genji chose paper of the same color as the blossom she had sent, and attached the letter to a spray from the aforementioned trees in front of his own window. "I can imagine what sort of thing he is writing," thought Sochi as he watched Genji compose the answer. "But I really wonder that, after all the confidences we have exchanged, he should think it necessary to be so secretive," and he wondered whether there were not some additional mystery beyond what he could possibly surmise. "I can see you think you have scented a mystery," said Genji. "You are quite wrong; there is no corner of my heart which I am not willing you should explore." Genji's poem ran: "Only too profoundly does the scent of your blossoms stir me, though lest the world should see my weakness I have hidden their fragrance deep within the folds of my dress."

"You will think," he said, turning to Prince Sochi, "that we are making a great deal too much fuss over the coming celebration. For my part I excuse myself on the ground that she is my only daughter. I am under no delusions about her looks or intelligence, and did not like to trouble any outside person to come and stand sponsor for her at the ceremony. The Empress Akikonomu, who is staying here on leave from the Palace, has kindly consented to undertake the task, and it is in deference to her position that I am doing everything in proper style." "I am so glad you got hold of the Empress," said Prince Sochi; "I think it is a very good idea; for we all hope that your little girl will one day occupy the position that Akikonomu holds now." At this moment messengers arrived from all the various quarters of the establishment where the blending of perfumes had been in progress, for Genji had decided that the last time to make trial of them was when the evening air began to grow damp. "You must help me to judge these perfumes," said Genji to his brother. "I am sure there is no one who knows more about it than you." The incense-burners were brought, and though Prince Sochi protested that this was not at all in his line, he was soon amazing everyone present by the incredible delicacy of his perceptions. He would say of some perfume the ingredients of which were quite unknown to him: "There is a fraction too much cloves in this," or of another: "Just a trifle too little aloes." He never made any sweeping criticism, but established a sufficient number of small points to allow of arranging the competitors, all of whom would to any common critic have seemed equally unimpeachable, in a definite and justified order of precedence.

When this was over, Genji's two secret blends were at last submitted to the light of day. Just as the Emperor Nimmyo had on a famous occasion buried his incense at the edge of the moat near the barracks of the Bodyguard of the Right, so Genji had now buried his two secret compounds under the bank of a little stream that ran out near the western cross-gallery of his palace. Koremitsu's son Hyoye no Jo was now sent to dig them up, and they were finally laid before Prince Sochi by Yugiri. "No, no," said Sochi. "The room is getting too smoky. In such an atmosphere it is quite impossible to go on judging..." But nothing could be done, for in every quarter of the house the manufacture of incense had been proceeding so busily that the air was laden with perfume. The Prince went on sniffing bravely, and the subtlety with which, even under such adverse circumstances, he detected small merits and defects, won universal applause. Though there was very little to choose between the different *kurobo* submitted, on the whole Princess Asagao's was declared to be the best, for it combined the strong fragrance usual to this species with a delightful delicacy and mildness. Among the various *jiju* incenses, Genji's easily came out on top, for it was indeed an extraordinarily delightful and intriguing mixture. Murasaki had submitted three kinds. It was agreed that her *baikwa* was a more distinctive and ingenious blend than the other two; Prince Sochi was full of enthusiasm for it, saying he could imagine no incense that would mix so well with the prevailing scent of the air at this season.

The Lady from the Village of Falling Flowers, thinking that if she allowed the gentlewomen under her control to send in a variety of perfumes the task of the judges would be tiresomely complicated and lengthy (for even in such a matter as this she did not fail to show her usual modesty), sent in only one kind of incense, the sort called Lotus Leaf, but of a very delicate and subtle variety, which seemed to Genji characteristic of her unassuming personality. The Lady from Akashi, who presided over the Winter Garden, and might have been expected to offer an incense appropriate to her own season, was not inclined to risk so direct a challenge to the mistresses of Summer and Spring. Fortunately she remembered a recipe that had been invented by Minamoto no Kintada* with

---

* Grandson of the Emperor Uda. A famous poet and aesthete.

the help of notes inherited from the Emperor Uda.* This by itself would, have sufficed to win considerable approbation; but she also succeeded in recollecting the ingredients of the famous Hundred Steps Incense,† and Sochi was obliged to pronounce each of those contributions deserving of the highest honors. "Our judge is losing his subtlety," complained Genji, "and is obliged to fall back upon praising everything indiscriminately."

The moon had now risen. Supper was served, and afterwards stories were told by various members of the party. A slight mist veiled the moon with the most entrancing effect. The rain of the morning had left a slight breeze in its trail, that continually wafted into the already thickly perfumed rooms of the house fresh perfumes from the trees in the garden. From the Music Room came sounds of flute and string, for a practice was in progress, music being destined to play an important part in the ceremonies of the ensuing day. Many courtiers had arrived, and there was a noise of zithers being got into tune, and an agreeable meandering of flutes. To no Chujo's sons Kashiwagi and Kobai had come merely to make the formal announcement of their intention to take part in tomorrow's proceedings. But they were now prevailed upon to stay and join in the music, Genji himself providing the instruments. At the same time he set a lute in front of Prince Sochi, and himself sent for his great Chinese zithern. Kashiwagi played upon the *wagon*,‡ and so a quite interesting combination was possible. Yugiri then played upon the cross-flute, choosing airs appropriate to the season; away went the shrill notes on their journey to the country of the clouds. It will be remembered that Kashiwagi's brother Kobai was famous for his voice. It was he who as a boy sang the Ballad of Takasago at the time of the rhyme-covering competitions. He now sang *Umegaye:* "Look, to a bough of the plum-tree the nightingale has come to tell us that Spring is here. But though he sings, but though he sings, the snow is falling fast." Genji and his brother joined in the refrain, and though more practice would have been required to make the thing a complete success, it afforded a very agreeable evening's entertainment. When the wine was handed round Prince Sochi recited the verse: "To an ecstasy the 'song of the nightingale' has carried us, who by the beauty of the snow-white boughs already were enthralled." To which Genji replied: "Prince, if this springtime no other beacon guide you to my house, let these frail flowers suffice to bring you back before their time is passed." So saying he handed the cup to Kashiwagi, who addressing Yugiri recited the verse: "Play shrilly once again the flute-songs of the night, lest on his bed of flowers the weary

---

* A.D. 889–897.

† So called because it could be smelt a hundred feet away.

‡ Japanese zithern.

nightingale should fall asleep." And Yugiri: "Ask me not to shake with the shrill blast of piping those flowers that even the wild Spring wind had not the heart to stir." At this whimsical excuse everyone laughed. When it came to Kobai's turn, he sang: "Did not the mists of Spring enfold both earth and sky, the birds that sleep so sound had long ago burst out into their clamorous daybreak song." And true enough, the first streaks of light were already appearing in the eastern sky. Sochi announced that he must go at once. As a reward for his services in judging at the competition Genji gave him a cloak from his own wardrobe and two jars of incense which had been left unopened during the trials. These were put in his carriage, and finding them there, Sochi improvised the poem: "Incense and fine clothes! What gifts are these for an honest man to carry home at dawn?" "You must not be so frightened of your family," laughed Genji, waiting beside the carriage while the bulls were being yoked; and he answered Sochi with the poem: "Well can I believe it, dear friend, that your family will rub their eyes at seeing you come home with so decent a coat upon your back." Sochi, who thought himself a very well dressed man, did not take this in very good part. The other guests also received small presents in memory of the occasion—a gown, a brocaded under-robe, or the like.

The ceremony of Initiation took place in Akikonomu's rooms in the evening of the next day. The company arrived at the hour of the Dog.[*] The Empress herself was in the small side-room behind the double-doors at the western end of the corridor, and here she was soon joined by the gentlewomen entrusted with the dressing of the Initiate's hair. For this room had been set apart as her dressing-place. Murasaki was also there, and as both ladies were attended by a full complement of gentlewomen-in-waiting, there was not much room to spare. The little Princess herself did not arrive till the hour of the Rat,[†] when the actual Tying of the Belt took place. The room was lit only by the flickering rays of the great lamp in the corridor outside; but, from what she could see of the child, Akikonomu (who happened not to have come across her before) made her out to be very good-looking. Genji, however, whispered many apologies for her. "I knew you would help me," he said. "But of course the child is nothing out of the ordinary, and it seems a shame to give you all this trouble. You are doing what I suppose no Empress has ever done before..." "I thought nothing of coming, and indeed imagined it would be a mere family affair. If it is on my account that you have done things on this grand style, I assure you it is not you who ought to feel embarrassed." She looked so charming and still so young as she made this polite speech

---

[*] 7 P.M.

[†] 11 P.M.

that Genji congratulated himself upon an occasion which, if it possessed no other importance, had at least the merit of bringing together in one room so many delightful women.

He would very much have liked the child's mother to take part in the ceremony, for he knew that it would pain her deeply not to be invited; but as the girl had been formally adopted by Murasaki, it was hard to see in what capacity the Lady from Akashi could be summoned, and very reluctantly he abandoned the idea.

For To no Chujo it was extremely galling to hear the accounts of all these preparations and festivities. His own daughter Lady Kumoi was now at the height of her beauty, and to see her wasting her youth and charm in the dull seclusion of the home, while the Akashi girl's success was being bruited on every side, was naturally very hard for him to bear. Yugiri's attachment to her seemed neither to have ripened nor, on the other hand, declined. To do anything that savored of a wish to negotiate with him might now only lead to a humiliating rebuff—a risk that had not existed in the days when Yugiri's passion was still open and declared. He felt that he had let things drift too far, and was indeed in these days more angry with himself than with Yugiri.

The young man heard that his uncle no longer spoke of him with any asperity; but the harshness of years was not so easy to forget, and Yugiri could not bring himself to plead for the termination of a quarrel which had been entirely of Chujo's making. He therefore continued to behave exactly as before. Not but what his fidelity suffered at one time and another from considerable strains and stresses. Naturally it did; but he could never forget the day upon which her nurses had taunted him with his light-blue dress, and he was determined that until he could come forward as a full-blown Counselor he would make no further advances.

Genji disapproved extremely of the boy's solitary and unsettled mode of existence. Some time ago he had received a hint from the Minister of the Right that a proposition from Yugiri would not be unwelcome; and now a similar intimation had come from a certain Prince Nakatsukasa... Surely the boy would not allow a childish attachment to stand in the way of such solid alliances as these? He told Yugiri of the two offers. "One or the other you must certainly accept," he said. "Try to make up your mind as quickly as you can." Yugiri did not answer, but merely waited respectfully for his father to continue. "I know that, in a way, it is rather absurd for me to advise you about things of this kind," Genji said after a pause. "I remember how tiresome I used to find my father the old Emperor's lectures on these and similar subjects. But I assure you that, irritating as it was at the time, his advice generally turned out to be perfectly sound, and I wish I had more often followed it... But what I wanted to say to you now was this: your present unsettled way of living is doing your reputation a great deal of harm. Naturally everyone assumes that a previous attachment of some kind is holding you back, and the impression most people are likely to get is that you have got tied up with someone so lowborn or discreditable that you cannot possibly introduce her into your family. I know that this idea is the opposite of the truth; indeed no one could possibly accuse you of aiming too low. But it is now perfectly clear that you cannot get what you want... Under such circumstances the only thing to do is to take what one can get, and make the best of it...

"I myself had just the same sort of trouble at your age. But things were even worse; for in the Palace one is hedged round by all kinds of rules and restrictions. All eyes were upon me, and I knew that the slightest indication on my part would be eagerly seized upon and exploited by those who stood to gain by my undoing. In consequence of this I was always extremely careful... Yes. In spite of all my precautions I did once get into trouble, and it even looked at one time as though I had ruined myself for good and all. I was still low in rank then and had not particularly distinguished myself in any way. I felt that I was free to do as I chose, and that if things went wrong I had not much to lose. As a matter of fact it is just at such a moment in life that one makes the most far-reaching and irreparable mistakes; for it is then that passion is at its strongest, while the checks and restraints, that in middle age inevitably protect us against the wilder forms of folly, have not yet come into play. To suggest that you need advice on this subject is in no way derogatory to your intelligence; for in their relations with women people who show the utmost good sense in other matters seem constantly to get into the most inextricable mess. One of the difficulties is that we tend to be attracted precisely by those people with whom it is most impossible that we should be permanently connected. I can think of a case in which the lady's reputation was fatally injured and the man's happiness destroyed, not only in this world but probably in the next, by the fierce resentment which she bore against him in consequence of this youthful indiscretion.

"And one thing more: suppose you get married and find that the match is not altogether a success. There will be moments at which you will be tempted to throw the whole thing over. But do not act rashly. Think out the situation afresh each time that it appears to you insupportable. Probably you will find that there is a very good reason for hanging on a little longer. Even if you have lost all affection for the lady herself, you may perhaps feel that for the sake of her parents you ought to make one more effort... Or even if she has no parents or other supporters to whom you are under an obligation, you will very likely find on reflection that she has some small trick of speech or manner that still attracts you.

It will in the end possibly be best both for you and for her if you can keep things going even in the most precarious way."

So at moments of leisure used Genji to admonish the young man, never with any note of asperity in his tone. Nor did he once go beyond the vaguest general reflections and reminiscences.

The suggestion that at his father's advice he should at once transfer his affections to some quarter where they would be more acceptable struck Yugiri as the most gratuitous piece of folly imaginable. Let them compel him if they chose, but at least refrain from insulting his love by veiling such senseless propositions under the cloak of kindness.

Meanwhile Kumoi noticed that her father, who for a long time past had eyed her with a strangely sorrowful look, now gazed at her more mournfully than ever. She felt that through her own fault something had gone wrong with her life, and ceased soon to hope for any kind of happiness; but outwardly she showed no signs of this despair and seemed content to let her youth slip by unmarked. Yugiri's letters, written at moments when a sudden access of longing compelled him to seek an outlet for his emotion, were as passionate as at the first day of their separation. But did they represent his true feelings? Sometimes she came near to doubting it, and had she possessed other lovers who gave more tangible proof of their devotion, it would have been easy for her to assume that Yugiri's outpourings were utterly insincere. But an inexperienced girl cannot afford to doubt—that privilege is reserved for those with whom love has become a familiar distraction. His letters were her only interest, and she read them again and again. It soon reached To no Chujo's ears that Prince Nakatsukasa had offered his daughter, and that the suggestion had not been ill received by Genji. He drew Kumoi aside and spoke of this, with evident agitation. "I am afraid this means that the young man has given way," he said. "No doubt Genji is offended at my not having accepted Yugiri at the start, and is anxious to show that it is now too late for me to change my mind. For your sake I should be willing to humble myself before him to any extent; but I am afraid we should only be making ourselves ridiculous." There were tears in his eyes while he spoke. Embarrassed, for she had never seen him weep before, Kumoi turned away her head, thus managing also to conceal her own tears, which by now were beginning gently to fall. What should he do? It was unendurable to watch her misery. And determined to make a last desperate appeal to Genji, he fled abruptly from the room. At the sound of his departure she turned her head, and coming to the window stood gazing after him. What would her lover think, what would he do, could he but have seen her father's strangely belated tears? It was not thus, she felt sure, that Yugiri pictured the tyrant who stood between them. Just at this moment a messenger arrived. A letter from Yugiri! Her first thought was that it would announce his engagement to this daughter of Prince Nakatsukasa, and for a while she had not the heart to open it. But when at last she did so she found that it was couched in terms as passionate as ever before. His poem ran: "Now faithlessness, that once was held a crime, rules all the world, and he a half-wit is accounted whose heart is steadfast for an hour." There was not in the letter a hint of any intention such as her father had referred to, but the more she thought about it the more convinced she became that the rumor could not be without foundation. "It seems that you, who preach so much of steadfast faith, yourself will soon be following the world's new treacherous way." He had no notion what this could mean, and puzzled over it fruitlessly for many an hour.

Fuji no Uraba

Despite his friendship for the little Princess, Yugiri had shown no interest in the recent proceedings at the New Palace. He had indeed lately heard that the "watchman of the gate,"* worn out by a vigil so unexpectedly prolonged, already showed signs of collapse. The boy, extremely sensitive to rebuffs, would far rather that the first step should be taken by the other side, and though constantly planning to approach his uncle, he felt when it came to the point unable to do so unless Chujo's manner towards him in some way indicated that the rumored change of attitude had really taken place.

Meanwhile Kumoi, convinced that Yugiri's engagement to the Nakatsukasa girl would soon be announced, was doing her best to wipe out from her thoughts all memory of the lover who had betrayed her. Thus, though in effect the way was now clear, a tangle of misunderstandings made it impossible for either side to advance. Her father, whose ill-judged obstinacy was responsible for the whole situation, was by now willing to make any compromise. Above all it was essential, at the cost of whatever humiliation, to forestall Prince Nakatsukasa's definite and final offer, which did not seem yet to have been made. For after all that had happened it might be exceedingly difficult to procure the girl an even tolerable alliance. Despite all the precautions of her family Kumoi's early friendship with Yugiri had become known, and innocent though it had been, she would inevitably share in the discredit which attaches to the jilted. He foresaw indeed that belated efforts to find her a husband would involve both him and the girl herself in even greater humiliations than would ensue from an immediate surrender. This time he determined to approach the boy himself; but though they occasionally met and were to outward appearances on perfectly good terms, he found it very difficult to embark suddenly upon such a subject as this. To send for Yugiri on purpose to discuss the matter seemed to be making altogether too much fuss about it, and would indeed mark a point of surrender beyond what, even in his present mood, he was prepared to bring himself to. At last, however, circumstances afforded just such an occasion as he sought. On the twentieth day of the third month, the anniversary of his mother's†

---

* To no Chujo. Reference to a passage in the *Ise Monogatori*.
† Princess Omiya.

death, a memorial service was held at the Gyokurakuji.* There was a great gathering of princes and noblemen, among whom Yugiri, now grown to his full stature and today magnificently accoutered, cut no discreditable figure. The presence of To no Chujo, who was of course in charge of the proceedings, always had the effect of damping Yugiri's spirits, and his particularly subdued, cautious manner did not today escape his uncle's notice. A special recitation of the scriptures was also held at Genji's expense, and Yugiri himself, as grandson of the deceased, was naturally responsible for many of the arrangements. They were all going home late in the afternoon amid a shower of falling blossoms, when To no Chujo, overcome by the memories which had crowded to his mind during this melancholy celebration, paused for a moment to gaze upon the scene about him. Yugiri too was deeply moved by the beauty of the evening and had also halted. There was a rainy feeling in the air, and some of their companions shouted to them to come on quickly if they did not want to catch a wetting. Turning round To no Chujo saw that, like himself, Yugiri was spellbound by the sadness of the closing day, and pulling him gently by the sleeve he said: "What does this mean? All day you have been doing your best to avoid me. I should have thought that on such an occasion you would have been willing to call a truce. I feel that today I have reached a turning point in my life. I am beginning to be an old man, and I cannot afford to lose the affection of those who are growing up around me..." "I remember," Yugiri answered, "that before she died my grandmother begged me if I were ever in trouble to come first to you for advice. And I would gladly have done so, had you not made it clear that you had no wish at all to see me..." But there the conversation ended; for the wind had suddenly risen, bringing with it a violent storm of rain, and the whole party were obliged to make for home as fast as they could.

Never before had To no Chujo addressed such words to him; and though there was no direct allusion to the trouble over Kumoi, he could not help feeling that they were meant as a definite hint of encouragement. For Yugiri's thoughts were continually occupied by this subject, and he was apt to see a reference to it in the most ordinary remarks. Of this he was conscious, and all night long he turned over in his mind what Chujo had said to him.

But in point of fact Yugiri's years-long patience had at last triumphed completely. If there was a slight further delay it was only because To no Chujo was waiting for a not too inappropriate occasion upon which to make his full and unqualified surrender.

Early in the fourth month, one evening when the unusual magnificence of the wisteria in his courtyard (it had never been so profuse in blossom

---

* The mausoleum of the Fujiwara family.

or so splendid in color as this year) induced him to invite a few friends with whom to feast and make music, when the dusk was already gathering and the beauty of the flowers, as they gleamed in the half-night, was even more dazzling than before, To no Chujo plucked a spray of the blossom and asked his son Kashiwagi to deliver it to Yugiri with the message: "I should very much like to continue our conversation of a few days ago, and if you have nothing better to do, please come round and see me..." Attached to the wisteria spray was the poem: "The wisteria in my garden is at its deepest hue, and now not many nights are left in which to see it shining through the dusk." Yugiri could not for a moment doubt that this was the signal he had waited for. He thanked Kashiwagi for bringing the message and handed to him the poem: "Alas, I fear lest groping through the dusk I now may miss the hour when these deep-colored blossoms shed their splendor on the night." "I am ashamed of this poem," he said to Kashiwagi, "and beg you to amend it in any way you can." "Are you not coming straight back with me?" said the other. "No," answered Yugiri decisively. "My retainers would be a trouble to you," and he sent Kashiwagi away. This took place in Genji's presence, and looking at the poem, he said: "This of course is all you could desire. Well, I am glad it has happened at last. No doubt the other day's proceedings awakened in him the feeling that he had often treated his mother very badly, and his present surrender is a sort of propitiation..." This confident, off hand tone jarred on Yugiri. "I don't think this invitation means anything out of the ordinary," he replied, blushing. "The wisteria is in bloom and they are having some music in the courtyard. It is quite natural that he should send for me..." "Well, in any case," replied Genji, "he is evidently anxious to have you there, or he would not have sent Kashiwagi on purpose. You had better go at once." To a casual observer Yugiri would have appeared at this moment apathetic—impassively obedient. But his heart within staggered with excitement, and in sheer intensity of expectation he almost fainted away. "Wait a minute!" his father called after him. "That dark cloak will not do at all! It was well enough while you were a young nobody and did not attend the Council. But now you have every right to make a better show... Let me lend you something," and sending a servant to his wardrobe, he presently displayed a whole pile of the most magnificent Court cloaks, one of which Yugiri carried off to his own room. By the time his toilet was complete, twilight had turned to darkness. He hurried to his uncle's house, arriving just when To no Chujo, to his chagrin, had decided that it was useless to expect him. He was led into the house by a band of some seven or eight young men, headed by Kashiwagi. A seat of honor had been set apart for him by To no Chujo, who for the moment was absent, having gone to change his Court hat for a more comfortable form of headdress. His wife and some young ladies-in-waiting helped him to change. "You must take a peep at our new guest," he said to them. "I saw him arriving a moment ago. He has really grown up into a most distinguished-looking young man; and he dresses admirably. He looks to me as though he would turn out to have more strength and decision of character than his father. Genji of course was always very good company; when one is with him, one is indeed so completely carried away by his high spirits and charm that the worries and difficulties of everyday life seem suddenly to lose all reality. But in public affairs he seems to me to suffer from a certain lack of earnestness, of gravity... However, that may be a fault on the right side. Certainly this son of his has not inherited any such defect; I hear that he is a better scholar than his father, and is indeed a most serious and persevering character..." To no Chujo now rejoined his guests, and after the usual compliments had been exchanged he said to Yugiri: "You should have come when the spring flowers were at their best. It was an astonishing sight this year. Every imaginable color. But the spring treated us badly; never has its stay been so short. And now all that is left us to console ourselves with is these wonderful blossoms here, which are already almost in summer bloom. For my part I take an immense delight in them, and I hope that to you as well their color has tonight a special significance..."* and he smiled reassuringly. The moon had now risen, and having admired by its light what little was to be seen of the wisteria blossom, they settled down again to music and drink. Seeing that Yugiri's shyness required overcoming by some more drastic procedure than mere friendly encouragement, To no Chujo affected to be more drunk than he actually was, and under cover of this pretence pressed the drink upon Yugiri with a boisterous insistence. But the boy was determined to keep all his wits about him, and over and over again refused. "I hear," said To no Chujo, "that you are becoming such a scholar as in these latter days we never hoped to see again. Perhaps that is why you are so cold towards your old acquaintances who can boast no such worldwide reputation. But even in your learned books I fancy there is a good deal about 'family visits,'" and there is a certain person,† very dear to those of your persuasion, who made such small formalities the groundwork of his teaching. You must know far more about all this than I do, and it can only be for some very particular reason that you so determinedly avoid your uncle's house..." Such a complaint came quite naturally amid the general sentimentality induced by wine and music. "Come," answered Yugiri, "did nothing else attach me to you, the memory of my mother and grandmother would alone make me ready to serve you with my last breath, and I cannot conceive what I have done to merit such a reproach.

---

* Purple, a presage of high rank.
† Confucius.

It was you who in the first place gave me to understand that I was not welcome..." To no Chujo held his peace; but when a suitable opportunity occurred he rose to his feet and sang the old song: "If like the leaf..."* while Kashiwagi, evidently at his father's bidding, plucked a spray of wisteria blossom, the deepest-colored and longest he could find, and twined it round the guest's wine-cup. Yugiri modestly protested; whereupon To no Chujo recited the verse: "That as token of kinship this flower you should invoke I waited† till the blossom hung lower than the pine-boughs; then at last I humbled my pride."

Yugiri, holding the cup, made a slight obeisance, and answered: "Strange that through so many dewy springtimes I was doomed to pass before I met the season when this flower for me its blossom should unfold." So saying he handed the cup to Kashiwagi, and as it went the round everyone in turn produced the best he could in the way of a poem. But amid the confused revel it was not likely that anything very good should come to light, and the verses that followed were even more ragged than those I have already quoted. The moon was only seven days old, and across the mirror of the silent lake hung a thin veil of mist. The trees still lacked their full profusion of summer green, and it was over bare and lonely-looking boughs that the wisteria, not merged as at a later season in the general mass of leafage, hung its heavy loads of blossom. Kobai, whose voice was always in request upon such occasions, sang "The Hedge of Reeds"‡ very charmingly. "Come," broke in To no Chujo, "no one has broken down any hedges here!" and next time the refrain came he drowned it with the words: "Welcome to this ancient house!"§ Soon all trace of embarrassment on either side had completely disappeared, and the party was kept up with a great deal of noisy singing and other merriment till a very late hour in the night. At last Yugiri thought the time had come for a hint on his side, and pretending to be much more drunk than he really was, he said to To no Chujo: "I am afraid I am not good for much more of this. Could you possibly allow me to sleep here tonight? My head goes round, and I doubt whether, even if I managed to set out for home, I should ever get there safely." "Kashiwagi!" cried To no Chujo, "a bed for Yugiri! I would see to it myself, but I am already far more drunk than an old person of my age has any right to be, and I must ask you to continue the concert without me." So saying, he went straight to his room.

---

* "If like the leaf of the wisteria through which the sun darts his rays transparently you give your heart to me, I will no more mistrust you."

† The usual pun: *matsu* = "pine-tree," and "wait."

‡ "About that broken place in the reed-hedge, in the front hedge, someone has told my mother. I think it was that chatterbox, my younger brother's wife. For she saw you climbing over, and she it must have been who told."

§ From another old song.

"I know what it is," said Kashiwagi, turning to Yugiri. "You came to see the flowers, and with the flowers you would stay." I'll do what I can for you. But it may not be so easy as you suppose." "This is no wild fancy of the moment," answered Yugiri. "Is not the pine-tree called "the lover of these flowers," and does he not all the year "wait changeless till at their own time the blossoms come"? Bring me to her...

Kashiwagi was not sure that this was what his father had intended, and was somewhat loath to take so great a responsibility; but he greatly admired Yugiri and had always hoped that matters would end in this way. It was therefore without any great misgiving that he now led the way to his sister's room...

Next day was the Festival of Buddha's Baptism.[*] The priests carrying the sacred image arrived somewhat late, and it was evening when the little girls sent from the various quarters of Genji's household arrived with their thank-offerings and alms. This part of the ceremony was carried out in Genji's palace exactly as at Court, while Genji's levée on the evening of the festival was even better attended than that held by the Emperor; so that the priests in charge of the image, who had got through the ordeal of appearing before the Emperor pretty comfortably, felt much less sure of themselves at this second and, as it seemed to them, far more critical gathering. But these proceedings did not in the least interest Yugiri, who at an early hour put on his best clothes and hurried away towards To no Chujo's house. Several of the younger ladies-in-waiting at the New Palace, without being actually in love with him, had always taken a considerable interest in his doings, and were not best pleased to hear that his prolonged bachelordom had at last come to a close.

The accumulated longing of years, satisfied at last in a manner beyond the wildest dreams of either, made the union of these two young people into a basket[†] that certainly let no water through. To no Chujo, too, liked Yugiri more and more as he got to know him better, and lavished upon him every sort of attention. He could not help still feeling a little sore at having had to surrender in so abject a manner. At the same time he had a great respect for the tenacity and single-heartedness which Yugiri had displayed in the face of every discouragement during these last years, and he bore the boy no grudge at all. There was a certain feeling against him in the household, for Kumoi had now grown to be indubitably prettier and in every way more interesting than her sister, Lady Chujo. This had for some time past excited the jealousy of Lady Chujo's mother and of

---

[*] Eighth day of the fourth month. Images of the Infant Buddha (four inches high, with right hand raised towards the sky) are carried in procession and sprinkled with water. The festival commemorates the occasion when the Rain Dragons sprinkled the head of the Infant Buddha.

[†] There is a proverb "It is no use pouring water into a basket." *Augo* means "union," and also "basket," "wicker panier."

such gentlewomen as sided with her; and this faction in the household did its best to keep Yugiri in his place. But Kumoi's mother* and many other people were delighted to hear of the engagement.

The Akashi Princess's actual move into the Crown Prince's palace was fixed for the twentieth of the fourth month. Meanwhile Murasaki expressed a desire to visit the August Birthplace.† The other ladies of the household were eager to accompany her; but she did not like the idea of a huge miscellaneous excursion, and in the end she confined the party to her own gentlewomen and servants. Even as it was there were twenty coaches, but everything was done as unostentatiously as possible, and the number of outriders was extremely small. The visit to the Shrine was made very early in the morning of the Festival,‡ and Murasaki was back in time to view the processions from the usual Stand. There was a good deal of rough hustling and pushing among the grooms and outriders of various ladies, each of whom was determined to secure a prominent place for her equipage; but as soon as Murasaki's carriage came in sight the rest fell back respectfully to let her pass. Genji, who was already waiting in the Stand, could not but recollect how at that other Kamo Festival years ago there had been an awkward clash of coaches. "I am glad you got through without any trouble," he said. "There is often a good deal of ill-feeling on these occasions. I am afraid the favorite of the moment is apt to abuse her power, sweeping mercilessly aside all who stand in her path. Yugiri's mother was by no means given to self-assertion. Yet her death was due to the resentment she incurred by allowing her servants to behave with insolence during one of these holiday encounters. It was the present Empress's mother who suffered upon that occasion; and it is strange that whereas her child has reached the highest position to which any lady can aspire, poor Aoi's son has only just begun to get on, even in the most modest way. We must never forget how uncertain everything in this world is. I have no reason to suppose that things will not now go smoothly with me to the end. But should you survive me, you might easily find yourself in a very precarious position ..."

A number of princes and noblemen had now assembled near Murasaki's Stand to pay her their respects, and Genji joined them. Kashiwagi was today the representative§ of the Imperial Bodyguard, and it was at his father's house that the gentlemen who now accompanied him had that morning assembled.

---

* A princess with whom To no Chujo had had an intrigue in early days. Subsequently she morganatically married a Provincial Inspector.

† The place at the Kamo Shrine where the Goddess Tamayorihime gave birth to Wakeikazuchi, the Thunder God. It is this event which the Kamo Festival commemorates.

‡ Fourth month.

§ Each of the Palace departments was officially represented at the Kamo Festival.

Koremitsu's daughter, who, as will be remembered, now held a post in the Bedchamber, was also present as representative of her office. She was just now having a prodigious success at Court, and today her coach was attracting as great a throng of admirers as that of any lady from the Palace, the Crown Prince's apartments, or the Sixth Ward.* Among those who paid their respects to her this morning was Yugiri. He had courted her in old days, in a somewhat half-hearted way it is true, but the news of his sudden engagement to the daughter of so eminent a house piqued her more than she would have expected. "If on no other day, then surely with this wreath† about your brow, lady, you call to mind that once we met!"‡ Such was the poem that he handed into her coach, and distracted though she was by the importunities of her admirers, she was touched that he should remember her at such a moment, and despite the fact that a carriage-seat is no place for writing verse, she answered him with the poem: "That 'hollyhock' spells 'meeting' is for scholars to conclude. They know it not who pluck the flowers, nor they that weave them as a crown about their brow." It was not meant seriously; but Yugiri felt that it was a snub and retired, somewhat surprised to find that in his present happiness any other woman's reply could make the slightest difference to him.

It was usual, when the Heir Apparent's consort was of very immature age, for her to be accompanied at Court by her mother or guardian. Murasaki had adopted the Akashi Princess in its infancy, and according to the usual practice it would now be she who followed the girl to the Eastern Palace. But Genji would not sanction a plan that involved continual and prolonged absence from home, and the opportunity seemed an excellent one for restoring the child to the care of her true mother, the Lady of Akashi. Murasaki had long felt that the separation of the girl from her mother, though from a worldly point of view advantageous to her, was an arrangement too inhumane to be otherwise than temporary. The little Princess herself, now that she was of an age to understand the situation, was obviously becoming more and more dissatisfied with it. To stand in the way of a reunion which promised so much happiness on both sides was out of the question, and on her own initiative Murasaki said to Genji: "Would it not be possible for the Lady from Akashi to go with the child to the Eastern Palace? She still needs a lot of looking after, and almost all her ladies are far too young to be much use in that respect. She has her nurses, of course, who will do all they can. But there are many points which people of that kind cannot reasonably be expected

---

* Genji's palace.
† Wreath of hollyhock, *ao-hi;* also means "Day of meeting."
‡ *Katsu,* once; *katsura,* "laurel," also used for festival wreaths.

to, decide. Were I myself to take charge of her I could not possibly be on the spot all the time. I would much rather she had someone who could give undivided attention..." What a comfort that she took so sensible a view! Genji hastened to inform the mother of this decision, and her delight was touching to behold. Indeed, her only anxiety was lest after all these years of retirement she should herself have become too dowdy to mingle with the bevy of resplendent young creatures who had been chosen for her daughter's service, and she began hastily providing herself with a new outfit.

Her mother, the old recluse's wife, heard with profound relief that the little girl's prospects were now finally assured, and henceforward she clung desperately to life, despite many infirmities and troubles, in the one hope that she might see her grandchild again before she went down into the grave. But she lived a long way from the Court, and at last began to wonder disconsolately whether the meeting would ever really take place.

On the night of the actual Presentation Murasaki accompanied the child in the hand-litter which was to convey her to the Eastern Palace. It was open to the Lady of Akashi to follow on foot, and as far as she herself was concerned she would have been ready enough to do so. But she feared that her presence would spoil the effect of the Princess's entry, and remained for the time being in her own apartments, feeling, as may well be imagined, very unwanted and forlorn. The ceremony of introduction was, at Genji's request, performed with as little publicity as possible. But it is in any case an elaborate affair, such as is bound to arouse a good deal of interest. While dressing the little Princess in all the finery that this trying occasion demanded, Murasaki could not help passionately wishing that this lovely child were really hers. And to Genji as well as to Yugiri the same thought occurred: if only this one thing were not lacking, surely Lady Murasaki would be the happiest, the most fortunate woman on earth!

After three days she left the Palace, and on the way out met the child's own mother, who had now come to take charge. They got into conversation, and Murasaki said: "Seeing the little Princess in these grownup clothes has reminded me how long it is since you first came to live with us. I think, having been neighbors all these years, we ought by now to know one another a little better than we do..." It was not an easy conversation to get started, but Murasaki's manner was so obviously kindly and sympathetic that a friendship was soon struck up between them. Murasaki, for her part, was so much attracted by the other's manner and way of speaking that she soon well understood Genji's admiration for her; while the Lady of Akashi could not fail to be delighted by Murasaki's noble bearing and faultless beauty. She felt it to be perfectly natural that among all the women who had received Genji's favors, this lady should always have held the unquestioned supremacy; she thought indeed at this moment that even to have been set beside her as the humblest participant in Genji's affection was an honor of which she might justly be proud.

Murasaki's return was attended by great pomp and solemnity. She was permitted the use of a hand-litter, a privilege usually restricted to the Emperor's consorts, and the Lady of Akashi, as she watched her leave the Palace, once more felt for a moment painfully conscious of her own utter inferiority.

The sight of her lovely child, waiting for her with a doll-like and neat composure, was more than she could bear, and so near are the outward signs of grief and joy that no one seeing her then could have guessed that the tears which now rushed to her eyes were those of the purest and tenderest delight. For years it had seemed as though fate were utterly against her, and she were destined to drift on only into greater depression and obscurity. But now a brighter prospect had opened, and remembering her pious father's constant prayers and oblations she could not but think that it was the God of Sumiyoshi who had at last set her fortunes on a fairer course.

The little Princess had been so carefully brought up by Murasaki that she needed very little guidance. Everyone in the Eastern Palace was at once charmed by her beauty and friendly disposition, not least the Crown Prince himself. For, mere child though he was, he could not fail to perceive that she far outshone all other companions whom fate had put in his way. Those whose designs had been frustrated by the little Princess's arrival made a point of speaking disparagingly in His Highness's presence of the child's mother, saying with mock sympathy that it would be a great handicap to her at Court to have so homely a creature always at her side. But such remarks had no effect. Not only was the child unusually quick-witted, but it soon became apparent that she already possessed considerable will and character of her own. Her every whim was now gratified, and as many of her ladies had admirers among the most fashionable young noblemen at Court, her rooms became the scene of the most dazzling fetes and receptions. It was indeed all the Lady of Akashi could do to keep the ladies-in-waiting in proper trim for all these festivities, after she had attended to the Princess's outfit and made the necessary household arrangement. Murasaki managed occasionally to visit them, and was delighted to find that there was in the Lady of Akashi's manner towards her no longer any of the distrust and coldness which had for so long made it well nigh impossible for them to meet.

Genji, who could never think of himself as living to any great age, was profoundly thankful that he had now provided for his daughter in a manner which seemed to make her happiness assured. And even Yugiri, whose excellent qualities of heart had seemed at one time likely to condemn him to a state of permanent unsettledness and despondency, was now happily provided for... It seemed in fact to Genji at this time that all the worst dangers and difficulties of his life had been successfully over-mounted, and that he might now even manage to arrive at the finish without any very serious disaster. Were he to die now his only anxiety would be on Murasaki's behalf; but so long as Akikonomu, who had always regarded her as a second mother, retained her influence, Murasaki was not likely to come to any great harm. Moreover, as foster-mother of a future Empress she would be certain of a considerable position at Court even in the event of Akikonomu's death or retirement.

He sometimes had qualms about the Lady from the Village of Falling Flowers. She, poor thing, certainly did not have a very gay time of it; but for the moment she had Yugiri to keep an eye on her. Generally speaking, he could remember no time at which his affairs had been in such hopeful trim.

Next year would see his fortieth birthday, and he heard that both at Court and in the country at large great preparations were afoot for celebrating this event. Already in the autumn of the present year he was proclaimed equal in rank to an Imperial Parent, and his fiefs and patronage were correspondingly increased. His actual power had for a long time past been absolute and complete, so that these changes brought him no great advantage. Indeed, in one respect they were inconvenient; for in defiance of a very well-established precedent he was burdened with the special retinue of his new rank, which, magnificent though it made his public appearances, rendered his comings and goings in the Palace very burdensome, and he was no longer able to meet the Emperor so often as he desired.

Ryozen still felt acutely the illegality of his own position and would at any moment have been prepared to resign the Throne, had not Genji refused to sanction such a step, pointing out that it would have a disastrous effect on public opinion if it became known that the true line of succession had been impaired.

To no Chujo of course succeeded to the position which Genji had vacated, and Yugiri at last became a Palace Counselor. On the day when the new officers went to Court to receive their Investiture To no Chujo was greatly struck by the improvement in the boy's carriage and appearance. For the first time he felt that Kumoi would after all be far better off with this young man as her devoted slave and protector than she would ever have been in the Palace, where she could not at best hope for more than a perfunctory share of the Emperor's attention.

Yugiri's new estate required more spacious quarters than were available in his father's palace, and soon after his promotion he moved into his grandmother's old house in the Third Ward. It was somewhat out of repair, but the damage was soon put to rights, and the Princess's former apartments were modified to suit the requirements of the newly married pair. For both of them the place was full of old and tender memories. They could remember as clumps of scraggy, freshly planted trees, plantations that now yielded an ample shade, and one bed of miscanthus, planted by the old Princess herself, had by now grown so thick and tangled that they were obliged to thin it out and cut it back, lest it should keep the sun off the plants around. The moat too needed clearing out and, when fresh water-plants had been set in it, looked very inviting. One lovely autumn evening the young pair stood by the water, talking of their childhood and of all the tribulations that were now happily overcome. Kumoi, among much that it was delightful to recall, could not help remembering several small incidents that had seemed to her of no significance at the time, but now made her somewhat uncomfortable in the presence of her grandmother's old servants, most of whom had joyfully welcomed the opportunity of returning to their old positions. Yugiri, gazing into the water, recited the poem: "Guardian of secrets, thou only could'st tell whither her soul is fled, but speakest not, O rock-fed wellspring of our house." To this Kumoi answered: "Of her that is departed no shadow haunts thy waters, O springlet, as calm and unrepentant thy waves flow onward to their goal!"

At this moment To no Chujo, drawn hither by the beauty of the autumn leaves, came into the garden for a while on his way back from the Palace. The house, full once more of movement and life, looked (thought To no Chujo) just as he had known it on many an autumn day in his parents' lifetime, and as he wandered from one familiar spot to another it affected him strangely to find those whom he had recently thought of as mere children playing the part of dignified masters and possessors amid the scenes where he himself had once submitted to his elders' rule. Yugiri too seemed slightly embarrassed by the situation; he blushed noticeably when giving orders, and his manner was oddly subdued. They were, thought To no Chujo, a singularly handsome and well-matched pair. Kumoi, indeed, was no very exceptional beauty; but the boy was certainly as graceful and well built as any young man he knew. Glancing among some papers covered with practice writing, Chujo noticed the poems about the wellspring which the young pair had just composed. Deeply moved, he said: "I too have it in my heart to invoke the spirit of this familiar stream; but for one who stands so near the margin of the grave..."* Nevertheless, he took a brush and wrote the verse: "Long must it be indeed since the old tree withered; for already its seedlings spread their green roots across the shaded earth." Some of

---

* He speaks of himself as though he were an old man.

the old Princess's aged servants were sitting in a group near by, croaking mysterious tales of vanished wonders. Among them was Yugiri's old nurse. She had never forgiven To no Chujo for his former harshness towards her young master, and overhearing the recital of his "seedling" poem, she was unable to restrain her indignation and burst out with the lines: "Some of us have tended these two seedlings since first they put forth leaf, and have not only at this last hour discovered that they cast upon the earth a pleasant shade." This encouraged several of the other aged dames to vent their views, and Yugiri for his part was much amused by their quaint impromptus. But Kumoi found their fulsome compliments somewhat embarrassing, and was glad when their inspiration ran out.

Late in the tenth month the Emperor declared his intention of visiting Genji in the New Palace. Knowing that the maple leaves would be particularly lovely at this season, he invited the ex-Emperor Suzaku to accompany him. The visit of a reigning sovereign and his predecessor to the house of a subject had seldom if ever occurred before, and the event aroused great interest throughout the country. The simultaneous reception of two such august visitors was a matter that required much forethought, and the dazzling preparations which Genji set afoot cost him hours of deliberation.

The guests arrived at the hour of the Serpent.[*] The first ceremony was a parade of the Bodyguards of the Right and Left, who lined up beside their horses exactly as at the Imperial Race-meeting in the fifth month. Early in the afternoon the Emperor proceeded to the Main Hall. All the plank bridges and galleries along which he passed were carpeted with costly brocades, and his progress was screened from the public gaze by heavy canvas curtains painted with landscape scenery. At the Eastern Lake the party embarked on boats, and the head cormorant-fisher from the Palace, combined with Genji's men, gave a display with his birds, who brought up a number of small gibel in their beaks. This fishing display was not part of the original programme, but was improvised at the last moment, lest the royal personages should be bored on the way from the parade ground to the main palace. Every knoll in the gardens was crowned by the scarlet of maple leaves; but nowhere were they in better color than in Akikonomu's Western Garden, and in order that His Majesty might in passing have a better view of them, part of the wall that divided her domain from the Great Gardens had been hastily removed.

The seats of the two visitors had been placed side by side in the Great Hall, with Genji's at a considerable distance; but at the Emperor's request Genji's seat was brought into line with theirs. This treatment, which to those present appeared in the highest degree flattering, was indeed far less

---

[*] 9 A.M.

than the Emperor would have liked to do for Genji, before whom the laws of filial piety demanded that he should kneel in humble reverence. The fish caught on the lake were to be submitted to the Emperor's approval by the Colonel of the Bodyguard of the Left. Meanwhile Genji's falconers returned from the Northern Fields with a string of birds which were handed over to the Colonel of the other Guard, who entering the Main Hall by the eastern doors submitted the game kneeling at one side of the steps,* while the fish were displayed on the other side. To no Chujo, at His Majesty's command, directed the cooking of these viands, which were served to the Emperor himself, while the princes and noblemen in attendance were offered a repast of the most appetizing kind, in which every dish was served in a manner to some degree out of the ordinary. When everyone had had as much as he wanted and dusk was setting in, the musicians were sent for. It was not a formal concert, but there was some very lively dancing by various young pages from Court. The ex-Emperor Suzaku could not but remember the dancing at the Festival of Red Leaves years ago, an occasion which often came back to his mind. When the Ga-o-on† was played, To no Chujo's sons, ten in all, danced to it with such success that the Emperor rewarded them with the gift of his own cloak, which To no Chujo received on their behalf with an elaborate *budo*.‡ Genji was meanwhile recalling the day when he had been To no Chujo's partner in the Dance of the Blue Waves, and plucking a chrysanthemum he addressed to him the poem: "Though like this flower you have as time goes by put on a deeper hue, do you recall a day when in the autumn wind your sleeve flapped close to mine?" Yes, then indeed (thought To no Chujo) they were partners, and there was little to choose between them in rank and prospects. But now, despite the very important position he held, he knew well enough that, compared with Genji, he was in popular estimation a very insignificant person indeed. "Not to a flower shall I compare thee, who hidest amid the pomp of regal clouds, but to a star that shines out of an air stiller and clearer than our own." Such was To no Chujo's answer. By now the evening wind was stirring among the red leaves that lay heaped upon the courtyard floor, weaving them into patterns of brown and red. Here some pretty little boys, children of various noble houses, were imitating in play the dances of their elders. They wore blue and crimson tunics, and shirts of yellow with dark-red facings. Apart from their little Court hats they had no formal insignia, and it was a pretty sight to see them capering about amid the maple leaves, through which the setting sun now slanted its last rays. The professional musi-

---

* Of the Imperial Dais.
† "Thanking for the Prince's Favor," a Chinese dance.
‡ A form of obeisance so elaborate as to be almost a dance.

cians were not called upon to give any very exacting performance, and at an early hour the private playing began, led by the Emperor, who sent to the Palace Library for a selection of zitherns. Prompted by the beauty of the season and hour, one after another of the great personages there present called for his instrument and gave vent upon it to the feelings of the moment. Suzaku was deeply moved at hearing the familiar tones of Uda no Hoshi.* Turning to the Emperor he recited the verse: "Though, watcher of the woods, through many rainy autumns I have passed, such tints as these it never was my lot in any devious valley to behold." He said this in his usual tone of gentle complaint. The Emperor answered: "You speak as though mere leaves were on the ground; here rather has autumn woven a brocade that, could it be an heirloom, after-ages would covet to possess."

Now that he was grown to full manhood the Emperor's likeness to Genji was astonishingly complete. Equally striking was his resemblance to Yugiri. The latter of course had not that complete self-possession and authority of manner which His Majesty had naturally acquired during his years of rule; but Yugiri had distinctly the better complexion. He was now called upon to play the flute; among the courtiers who, drawn up along the steps, were singing the words of the tune was To no Chujo's son Kobai, long famous for the beauty of his voice. It was indeed a memorable occasion, and one which it seemed that some special Providence must have contrived.

---

* Name of a famous Japanese zithern.

Wakana
("Young Shoots")

PART ONE

For years past the ex-Emperor Suzaku had been ailing, though it was hard to say exactly what was wrong with him. Soon after his visit to Genji's palace he became much worse, and began preparing himself for admission to the priesthood. He would indeed long ago have entered a monastery, had not his mother Lady Kokiden, masterful as ever in her extreme old age, obstinately opposed such a step. But now she was dead, and the only remaining difficulty was the question of his family.

Oborozuki remained childless; but Lady Jokyoden had borne him four children: one boy (the present Heir Apparent) and three girls. But he had another daughter, born to him by a certain Princess Wisteria, a younger sister of Lady Fujitsubo. Suzaku was extremely fond of this princess, and their daughter, Princess Nyosan, was undoubtedly his favorite child. But under the influence of Kokiden, who had subsequently thrust Oborozuki upon him, he kept Nyosan's mother very much in the background. After his abdication her life became more than ever dull and purposeless. In a short while she pined away and died.

Nyosan was, at the point we have reached in our story, about thirteen years old. Already the retreat that Suzaku had built for himself on the Western Hills was nearing completion; soon he would be immured forever, and his one anxiety was to get his child started in life before he disappeared. The first consideration was her Initiation, which could not any longer be delayed. When Suzaku gave his children toys, it was always Nyosan who had the first choice, the others never getting the smallest trinket unless she had first refused it. You may imagine then with what care he now ransacked his treasury for rare and costly objects that might add splendor to the coming celebration.

Hearing that Suzaku was on the point of departure from the City, his son, the Heir Apparent, accompanied by Lady Jokyoden, came to pay him a farewell visit. Suzaku had never cared much for this Lady Jokyoden, who had indeed been imposed upon him solely out of political considerations; but as mother of the future sovereign she was a person of great consequence at Court, and there were now many matters that he was glad to talk over with her. Having discussed his son's future, about which he felt no forebodings, he said to his visitors: "It is the girls that I am worried about. I cannot imagine what will become of them. I have so often seen this sort of thing happen before. It is torture to foresee in every detail how they will be taken advantage of and insulted. When I say "they," of course all this does not really apply to your children, you will no doubt see to it that they get properly settled. It is about Nyosan that I am chiefly troubled. I wish you would undertake to look after her..." But this was asking a good deal. Nyosan's mother, for whom the Emperor cared far more than for Jokyoden, had behaved very disagreeably to her when their rivalry was at its height, and though Jokyoden had no intention of avenging herself upon a defenseless orphan, she saw no reason why she of all people should be expected to assume responsibility in the matter.

Day and night Suzaku brooded over the future of this favorite child. Meanwhile his weakness steadily increased and by the end of the year he was no longer able to leave his bed. To visitor after visitor he poured out the same tale of perplexity, and received much sympathy, though nothing in the way of practical suggestions. Genji sent frequently to enquire and even promised to come in person, but ultimately sent his son Yugiri instead. "I am afraid your father has a grudge against me," said Suzaku. "I have myself always regarded him with the utmost affection; but at one time the powers arrayed against him were very strong, and I allowed certain measures to be taken... People are always coming here and warning me to be on my guard... 'Some day he will find a way of getting even with you,' they say. 'Many a man has waited far longer than this to settle an old score,' and so on. But I am bound to say nothing comes of it. I cannot remember a single occasion on which Genji has shown me the slightest trace of ill will. It is of course to him that I should most naturally turn for help in my present difficulties. But I know how trying people are when they talk about their own children; and so I have ended by discussing the matter with all and sundry, rather than with Genji, whose sympathy I was particularly anxious not to lose. But my visit to his palace this autumn made me feel how unfortunate it is that I see him so seldom. I wish you could persuade him to come here one day..." "I am sure he would be delighted to come," answered Yugiri. "Of course I know nothing of what happened between you in the past. But lately he has frequently discussed political affairs with me, and I have never heard him mention you in a way to suggest that he bears you ill-will for what happened in the past..." While Yugiri spoke, a new idea entered the ex-Emperor's head. How would it be to confide to this competent and agreeable young man the care of the daughter whose future was causing him so much anxiety? "I hear you have now got a house of your own," he said to Yugiri. "I have known for a long time past of your difficulties over this matter and was extremely sorry for you. However, now your troubles have all ended in a manner completely satisfactory to you, I suppose. But what I feel about it is that really, after all that happened, To no Chujo hardly deserves you as his son-in-law. Indeed, I must confess, in that respect I feel somewhat jealous of him..." For a moment Yugiri was mystified; but then he remembered having heard that Suzaku was in a great state about one of his daughters... However, he was shy of letting it be seen that he understood this hint, and only answered: "I am sure you need not be jealous of anything that concerns me. As you know well enough, I am a very insignificant person..."

That was the end of the conversation. Some of the gentlewomen who had caught a glimpse of Yugiri as he passed were loud in their admiration of his costume and person. But an older lady-in-waiting croaked out indignantly: "Nothing to what his father was at that age! You don't see such men nowadays. He really *was* a handsome young gentleman." "She is quite right," said Suzaku, overhearing this outburst. "There will never be anyone like Genji. He has aged, of course; but I think that the extraordinary vividness and radiance of his expression—the quality which in his infancy won for him the name of Hikaru[*]—has if anything increased as time goes by. His face when in repose has now a nobility and dignity that in his younger and more irresponsible days were lacking; but I still think that he is never so attractive as when laughing and talking sheer nonsense. Then he is the real Genji whose like has never been seen in the world before."

One day when the little princess had been brought to his bedside, seeing her so childlike and helpless, the ex-Emperor exclaimed: "What I should really like would be for someone to take a fancy to her and bring her up privately, with a view to making her his wife later on. Then I should feel that both her education and her subsequent career were safely provided for..." He called the head nurse to him, and having discussed one or two matters connected with Nyosan's Initiation, he said to her presently: "You have probably heard the story of Lady Murasaki's upbringing. I wish I could find someone who would adopt my little girl in that fashion. Outside the Imperial Family it is difficult to think of anyone suitable; and in the Palace, Akikonomu has everything so much her own way that the other ladies of the Household come off very badly. If Nyosan had strong backing at Court, I might risk it; but as things are... I wish, by the way, I had thought of approaching this young Yugiri while he was still available. I feel certain that he has a great future before him." "You would have had to think of this a very long time ago if you wished to secure Prince Yugiri," the nurse assured him. "For years past he has been waiting for this daughter of To no Chujo, and I do not think you would have found it an easy matter to interest him in any other proposal. Genji himself is far more promising. Of one thing you may be quite certain: if he once took a fancy to our young lady he would never abandon her.

---

[*] The Shining One.

Why, I hear that despite all his other preoccupations he still goes on visiting Princess Asagao and all those other ladies about whom we used to hear so much in early days." "Come," said Suzaku, "the fact that so many youthful affairs are still in his hands does not particularly recommend him for our present purpose..." But the idea stuck in his head. Although Nyosan would in Genji's household grow up as one among many, she would at least enjoy the advantage of having come there as a child; an orphan whose interests Genji was pledged to defend. "If anyone were looking for a place where a young girl could be sent to pick up a little knowledge of the world, I cannot imagine anywhere better than Genji's palace. I only wish that I could spend the little that remains to me of life in surroundings half so pleasant and entertaining! Were I a girl I should certainly have fallen in love with Genji. Indeed, when I was young I did feel something of the kind; and I entirely understand how it is that he carries everything before him..." Suzaku paused. Perhaps he was thinking of his own failure with Oborozuki.*

The longer Suzaku reflected, the more difficult did it appear to find anyone more promising than Genji. There was certainly no one else who could do more for her if he chose. And as for the other ladies in Genji's household—their presence would not necessarily be a disadvantage; Genji could easily prevent that, if he was by way of taking any trouble about her at all. A man living in retirement with plenty of time on his hands, of rare charm, settled habits—what more could be asked? One or two other names did, however, cross his mind. There was Prince Sochi. No one could say she was marrying beneath her, for he too was the child of an Emperor, and there was indeed in that way nothing to choose between them. But Suzaku regarded him as weak, frivolous, irresponsible; and there were stories... No; certainly he would not do.

His mind roamed from possibility to possibility. For a moment he even considered To Dainagon, the Superintendent of his household, who would himself never have dreamed of applying for the Princess's hand, but had offered "to look after her affairs," in the event of her being left an orphan. And admirably he would do it, Suzaku felt sure, for this gentleman was a model of painstaking devotion. But he was, after all, a mere junior official, without influence or distinction of any kind. Things had indeed come to a pretty pass if for an Emperor's daughter no better match than this could be found! His thoughts again took a more ambitious turn. Oborozuki told him that her sister's son Kashiwagi was secretly anxious to form a connection with the Imperial House. Perhaps it was this ambition that kept him still unmarried, and though many people would have laughed at such aspirations, Suzaku was by no means ready

---

* See Part II, p. 245.

to condemn them. They showed at least that Kashiwagi had definite aims in life, and this fact alone sufficed to mark him out from among the ordinary run of easy-going young courtiers who lived solely for the pleasures of the moment.

As a scholar his talents were respectable, and in the natural course of things he would one day be at the head of the Government... A brilliant match for any other woman; but when it came to imagining him as Nyosan's husband, Kashiwagi (as indeed everyone else of whom Suzaku thought) seemed somehow hopelessly inadequate. Indeed, he worried a thousand times more over Nyosan, who had already received numerous flattering offers, than over the other sisters who could scarcely muster one wretched suitor apiece.

The ex-Emperor might never have reached a decision at all, had not the Crown Prince taken a very firm line on the subject. The young man did not of course openly venture to advise his father on such a point; but it came round to Suzaku that his son was in the strongest possible way opposed to Nyosan's marrying a commoner.* The matter was one that did not merely concern her happiness, but would create a precedent and thus affect the stability of the Imperial Family.

The only course the Crown Prince favored was one that had already occurred to Suzaku: Genji must be persuaded to take charge of the girl.

At last Suzaku allowed his mind to be made up for him, and employed Sachuben,† the brother of Nyosan's head nurse, to obtain Genji's views on the matter. Genji had of course for some while past known that the question of Nyosan's future was tormenting the ex-Emperor, and was anxious to assist him. "But there can be no suggestion of my adopting the child," he said. "The ex-Emperor is, I fear, failing rapidly, and no doubt in the ordinary course of things I shall survive him by a certain number of years. In that case I shall be glad to do what I can in a general way to help all his children. But I cannot accept a special responsibility for any particular child... As for taking her as a concubine, considering the difference of age between us, the question is too absurd to discuss. However, there is no necessity for so strange a choice. Yugiri, for example, has not got far at present; but he has a brilliant future before him... However, I quite see the difficulty there. Yugiri is a faithful fellow, and perhaps at present he would be unwilling. No doubt Suzaku is right not to suggest it."

Not to be put off by this first refusal, Sachuben now gave so harrowing a picture of the effect such a reply would have upon the ex-Emperor's already precarious condition that Genji could not help smiling: "I know that he is ill and she is his favorite child," he said. "But that surely does

---

* I.e. not a member of the Imperial Family.

† One of Genji's retainers.

not give him the right to impose her willy-nilly on anyone he pleases. Am I to have no say in the matter at all? But for my part I do not see wherein lies his difficulty. Why not simply send her to the Palace? She would have competitors, of course; but the last arrival does not always do worst. His own mother's[*] career was a case in point. While my father was Crown Prince, and during the early part of his reign, Kokiden carried all before her; but later on she was completely superseded by Lady Fujitsubo. Lady Wisteria, Nyosan's mother, was a sister of Fujitsubo. I hear the child is exceedingly good-looking, rather in Fujitsubo's style, they say; though of course to a far less remarkable degree... Why should not the same thing happen again? With birth and good looks both on her side it would be strange indeed if she did not make her way..."

But even while giving this advice he felt a certain curiosity to see the child for himself.

Three days after Nyosan's Initiation the ex-Emperor received the tonsure. However commonplace, however uneventful a man's life has been, this final ceremony is always painful to witness. But here was one, who had formerly stood upon the highest pinnacle of glory, ready now to obliterate at a stroke all that remained to him of comeliness and youth. A murmur of horror ran through the ranks of his gentlemen and attendants as the priests began to set about their fatal work. Oborozuki was at his side, and unable to bear the sight of her woe, Suzaku said: "I always thought the hardest thing would be parting with my children; but they, fortunately, seem cheerful enough on their side—which is a great help to me. Whereas you, with your tearful faces..."

Though he was not fit to be out of bed, they had carried him to a chair, where despite great weakness and discomfort he remained till the Abbot of Hiyeizan, attended by three senior priests, had administered to him the rules of the Tendai Sect, arrayed him in the habit of their order and performed such other rites as mark a final severance from the world. During these proceedings even the officiating priests could not restrain their tears, and such a storm of sobbing broke out among the princesses, consorts and miscellaneous gentlewomen who thronged the room, that Suzaku devoutly wished he were already safely installed in his mountain retreat. It now seemed unlikely, however, that he would ever be able to perform the journey. And if he had thus irrevocably deprived himself of the quiet monastic days with which he had always hoped to close his life, it was (as he now confessed to himself) solely his perpetual worrying about Nyosan's future that had kept him in the Capital till too late.

After the ceremony he received numerous visitors, including the reigning Emperor. As the result of all this excitement Suzaku rallied slightly,

---

[*] Kokiden.

and hearing of this Genji went to pay his long promised visit. He was received quite informally and accommodated in the seat commonly used by Suzaku when in health, a few extra hangings and ornaments having been added to smarten it. For a moment it was a great shock to Genji to see the companion of his youth arrayed in this solemn and penitential garb. Controlling himself by an effort, he said at last: "Ever since my father's death, which for the first time impressed me strongly with the shortness and futility of human existence, I have been making plans to compass what you have now successfully achieved. I wish I had your strength of mind. The sight of you in those robes makes me feel thoroughly disgusted with my own continual procrastination. If you, who have known what it is to be lord of all the land, can bring yourself to take this step, there is certainly no reason why a humble person like myself should shrink from it. But every time I think that the last obstacle has been removed, some fresh difficulty crops up..." They talked much of old times, and finally Suzaku said: "You have no need to apologize in my presence for your slowness in breaking with the world. I myself have delayed from day till day, until it looks as though the better part of my plan will never be fulfilled. But though I doubt whether I shall ever reach my retreat among the Western Hills, I hope I may live long enough to get through a few quiet prayers here in my own house. What now bothers me is that I have not been nearly so strict in my observances as I might have been, though all the while my thoughts were certainly turned to holy things, for it was only in the hope of spending a few last years in a sacred place that I struggled on against all this illness and pain..." Having mentioned several small matters concerning which Genji could be useful to him, Suzaku continued: "You have heard no doubt that I am very much exercised in mind over the future of my daughters. There is one in particular I should feel profoundly thankful to leave in the charge of some responsible person who would really give proper attention to her..."

"Surely he is not going to start that business all over again?" thought Genji in alarm. Yet in a way he was not sorry to return to the subject, for he had a certain secret curiosity concerning this little princess. "I quite understand," he said, "that a girl of Nyosan's rank needs, far more than anyone of ordinary birth, to be provided from the outset with a settled home. But failing this, she will surely come to very little harm with her brother the Crown Prince to keep an eye upon her. He is a young man of remarkable abilities, and the whole country looks up to him with confidence and respect. He would in any case consider it his duty to take so near a relative under his especial protection; and if you mention the matter to him in advance, still less will you have any need to worry about her future. Later on your son will of course succeed to the Throne, and if to provide for a woman's happiness were as easy as to make new laws, Nyosan would indeed be assured of perfect felicity. But I admit that in the last resort there is very little that even an Emperor can do for women, save to admit them to his household, which in this case does not come into question. So if you want here and now to make a permanent provision for her whole future, you must arrange with someone to adopt her after your death, and either marry her himself or promise to effect her marriage with someone previously selected by you. Then you surely need not fear that any misgivings will disturb you in the life beyond the grave..." "What is the use of telling me this?" Suzaku asked. "Naturally I have thought of it all long ago. But it is not so easy as you make out. It is a difficult matter even for a reigning Emperor to find suitable alliances for several daughters. And for me, who have not only long ago resigned the Throne, but am on the verge of retiring to a monastery (if indeed I do not die before I succeed in getting there), the whole business is so perplexing that I verily believe half my illness is due to worrying about it... I cannot afford to let another day go by without getting this thing settled... I know it is asking a great deal of you, but do, I beseech you, consent to taking this one daughter of mine under your protection. As to finding her a husband, I will leave that to you. I am sure your choice would be all that I could desire. Were Yugiri still available, his is the name I should suggest. But unfortunately To no Chujo has anticipated me..."

"Yugiri," replied Genji, "has a great deal of steady-going good sense, and I think he would have made her an excellent husband. But he has had very little experience, and I doubt whether in any case I could recommend him as sole protector to a girl in Nyosan's position. As regards myself, I think it is quite true that if she is left an orphan she would under my care suffer the smallest possible inconvenience from the change in her position. Well, if I have hesitated to say 'yes,' it is only because it is likely enough, after all, that I shall not long survive you."

It was unbelievable. Genji had consented; and apparently in the most whole-hearted way, for it was henceforward assumed on both sides that he would in due course marry* Nyosan himself.

Murasaki had already heard some rumor of Suzaku's intention. Her first feeling was one of alarm. But then she reminded herself of all the groundless and unnecessary misery she had suffered on finding that Genji was still visiting Princess Asagao. So determined was she not to attach undue importance to the affair that on his return she refrained even from asking him whether the subject had been discussed. He meanwhile naturally assumed that she knew nothing about the matter, and was wondering what line she would take. If there were to be difficulties, they could only last for

---

* Since Aoi's death Genji had no wife, Murasaki being technically only a chief concubine, her mother's low rank making it impossible for her to be a *kita no kata* or "legitimate consort."

a very short time. Murasaki would soon realize that the presence of this girl in the house, even as his wife, would make no difference whatever to her own position. But he knew that promises and assurances on his side would be of no avail. Time alone would convince Murasaki that nothing could change his feelings towards her; meanwhile, it was possible that a rather troublesome period was ahead. It was now so long since the slightest difficulty or suspicion had arisen between them that the idea of saying anything likely to upset her or interfere even for a few moments with the habitual tenderness of the hours they spent alone together was extremely painful to him. That night at any rate, he thought, matters might be left as they were, and he made no reference to his conversation with Suzaku.

Next day the weather was wretched, and while storms of snow swept a sullen sky he sat with Murasaki, laying plans for the future, and recalling many episodes of their common past.

"I thought I had better go and see the ex-Emperor before it was too late," said Genji at last. "It was in many ways a painful meeting. He seems unable to think about anything but who is going to look after this daughter of his, little Princess Nyosan. He at once attacked me on the subject, and considering the pitiable state he was now in, I felt it was impossible to refuse... I know that tiresome stories will be put about, I cannot help that... As a matter of fact he made a similar proposal to me some time ago, but indirectly, through a servant of mine. On that occasion I refused unhesitatingly, for I did not at all like the idea of taking on fresh responsibilities at my age. But when, during my visit, he returned (as I had thought it impossible he should do) to the same subject, and besought me passionately not to persist in my refusal, I could not help feeling that it would be inhuman to hold out... She will not in any case come here until Suzaku moves into his mountain retreat. I can quite understand that you would rather I had not consented. But please believe me that, at the worst, nothing can happen which will make the slightest difference to you. Try to enter into Suzaku's feelings. I am sure that if you do so, you will be glad that I am helping him in this way. With a little tact and forbearance on both sides, I do not see why there should be any great difficulty..."

He had only to tease her a little—pretend jokingly to admire some quite absurd and impossible individual, and instantly Murasaki would fall into a panic, certain that here was the beginning of a final disastrous episode. Yet now, for some reason, she felt that at all cost he must not see what was passing through her mind, and she answered quietly: "Poor Suzaku! I do not see how under such circumstances you could possibly have refused. Nor should I dream of raising any objection on my own account. Indeed, I shall be very unhappy if I do not quickly succeed in convincing her that, as far as I am concerned, she is doubly welcome here.

For not only am I touched by her father's plight, but I also recollect a fact of which she no doubt is fully aware, though you have not mentioned it: her mother, Lady Wisteria, was my father's sister. I should be thought churlish indeed if I did not make a cousin feel at home in my house..."

He knew her too well not to guess that, behind this tone of complete reasonableness and accord, there might easily be hidden quite other thoughts and feelings. But if this did indeed, quite contrary to what he had expected, turn out to be her real attitude, if she managed both to make the little princess feel at her ease, and at the same time to be happy herself, then he would have more reason than ever to prize her as the greatest treasure that life had yielded to him. "There are sure to be all sorts of absurd rumors..." he said. "Do not pay any attention to them. Remember that, as regards matters of this kind, the most circumstantial accounts frequently lack the slightest foundation in fact. It is best to observe for oneself, and not let outside stories affect one's judgment. So whatever you may hear, wait till your own experience confirms it before you decide that I am not treating you as I should..."

After all, she thought to herself afterwards, the care of this girl was a duty that he could not possibly have avoided. It had fallen upon him as it were from the sky, and to be cross with him for accepting it would be ridiculous. If Nyosan had been some girl that he had taken a fancy to or gone out of his way to befriend, the case would have been different. But it was perfectly true that this step had been imposed upon him; and Murasaki was determined to show the world that she was not going to lose her head. But she knew that once people take a dislike to one, it does not make much difference how one behaves... For example, her stepmother had even held her responsible for Makibashira's fall; it was Murasaki's jealousy (so this woman asserted) that had forced Genji to plant Tamakatsura in Higekuro's way! No doubt her tortuous imagination would not fail to supply equally complicated slanders in the present case. For though generous and long-suffering, Murasaki was capable of making judgments that were by no means devoid of sharpness. And now, though as yet all was well, there came back to her again and again the thought that perhaps the dreaded turning point had come. His confidence, his devotion, the whole sovereignty in his affections that had been so long her pride, would begin to slip away from her...

But during all this time there was nothing in her behavior which could have suggested to her companions that any such fears were passing through her mind.

So the year drew to a close. Suzaku was still lying bed-ridden in the Capital, but he had now made up his mind that Nyosan was to move into the New Palace at once. Not only were the various aspirants to her hand much put out at hearing that Genji was to take possession of her, but the Emperor himself, who had counted on being given a chance of adding her to his establishment, was distinctly disappointed. However, he did not think it worthwhile disputing the matter, and decided to let things take their course. This year, as has already been said, Genji was to celebrate his fortieth birthday, and resolutions were passed by the Government concerning the festivities that were to mark this event. The prospect was a formidable one for Genji, who had always disliked pompous anniversaries and commemorations. The whole country seemed bent upon devising elaborate and costly methods of disturbing his peace, all of which he discouraged firmly.

But there was one small attention which he had no chance of forestalling. On the third day of the first month, being a day of the Rat, Tamakatsura determined to take upon herself the customary Presentation of Spring Shoots.* She allowed no breath of this intention to leak out beforehand; but as wife of a State Minister she could not appear without a considerable escort, and her arrival at Genji's palace made far more of a stir than she desired.

Genji's seat was in the side-room opening out of the great Front Hall. His dais was surrounded by newly-painted screens, and there were fresh white canvas hangings round the walls; but the special stools, tables, and stands used in the formal celebration of a fortieth birthday had all been dispensed with. The forty little mats laid out around him, his cushions and seat—indeed all the details of his installation were very daintily chosen. The four boxes containing the customary presents of clothing were displayed upon two stands of mother-of-pearl inlaid with enamel. These clothes (complete outfits for both winter and summer), together with the incense jars, medicine boxes, inkstand, hair washing appliances, comb boxes, and such things were all of the finest. The mirror-stand was of cedar wood, and the mirror itself, though no other substance was inlaid the metal nor was any sort of coloring applied to it, was grained on the back with a delicate leaf-pattern. All these arrangements had been devised by Tamakatsura herself, who had a particular gift for the happy ordering of such small elegancies. The whole affair was very quiet and informal. Tamakatsura had audience with him before he took his place on the birthday throne. It was a long while since they had met, and, in the mind of each, recollections of a curious, possibly even of an embarrassing kind must have arisen. He seemed to her very young to be celebrating such an anniversary, and looking at him she found herself wondering for a moment whether there had not been some mistake! Could this be the head of a household, the founder of a family? It was very difficult after all these months of separation to know what tone to take up or even

---

* A Chinese custom, imitated by the Japanese Court.

what to talk about. But soon she found herself carrying on very much the same sort of conversation as in the old days. She had brought with her her two little boys.* Genji had often asked to see them, but hitherto she had refused, and on this occasion it was only in obedience to her husband's absolute command that she had brought them to the New Palace. They were handsome little fellows, both dressed exactly alike in miniature Court cloaks and breeches, with their hair parted in the middle and done up in a loop on either side. Speaking of growing old, he said to her: "Please do not think that I do it on purpose. I should have been perfectly content to remain just as I was; and indeed I could keep up the pretence fairly well, did not such creatures as these, whom I now see springing up on every side, convict me of being, in age at any rate, a grandfather. Perhaps indeed I really am one; for I hear very little of Yugiri nowadays, and am not at all sure he would think it worthwhile to tell me. However, I had quite made up my mind to go on being young for a little while longer, when you of all people come to warn me that I have overstepped the fatal mark... "

She too had outwardly suffered very little from the passage of the years, though she seemed less diffident and retiring.

At the Presentation of the Spring Shoots, which followed a few minutes later, she recited with great dignity and composure the congratulatory poem:

"With these new shoots fetched from the green hillside, young pine-boughs have I brought to crown your fortunes with eternal spring." The young shoots were presented for his inspection on four trays of sandalwood. Taking the great wine flagon in his hand, he recited the answer: "Though loath to pile the years about my head, not lightly shall I quit the field where spring by spring these pines spread wider shade."

A number of visitors were assembled in the southern side-room. Prince Hyobukyo had made up his mind to stay away; but his absence being noted, a special messenger was sent to summon him. Being nearly related to so many of those who were concerned in today's ceremony, he could not, without marked discourtesy, have persisted in his refusal, and towards noon he at last arrived. The spectacle of his son-in-law Higekuro flaunting his new bride in the face of the company was more than he could have been expected to bear with equanimity. But Makibashira's two children were there, and for their sakes he did his best to be friendly, taking a hand, whenever he was wanted, in the small arrangements of the ensuing ceremony. The presents, in forty baskets and forty boxes, were offered by a band of noblemen and courtiers, led by Yugiri. The great flagon went round, and Genji tasted the broth that had been brewed with Tamakatsura's

---

* They must have been about four and three years old.

offering. The August Cup and other utensils were daintily laid out on four low tables of sandalwood. The ex-Emperor was still thought to be in danger, and consequently no professional musicians were employed. But the flute-music was in charge of To no Chujo, who was determined that an occasion of such importance should not be marred by lack of music, and had drawn up an excellent programme. As for other instruments, he saw to it that the rarest and oldest of every kind should be produced, setting the example himself by bringing out a Japanese zithern that had for centuries been one of the most treasured possessions in his family. He, the greatest performer of the time, played on it himself, with delightful but somewhat embarrassing effect. For everyone else suddenly became shy, and when Genji asked Kashiwagi to play something, the young man for a long while refused. But at last he overcame his reluctance, which was a good thing, for his performance was by no means inferior to that of his father. Everyone was both pleased and surprised; for such talent is very rarely inherited. And here must be noted a point that is often overlooked: it is far easier to learn ancient Chinese tunes, though every note has to be played exactly as it is handed down, than to improvise upon the Japanese zithern, where one has complete freedom, save for the necessity of giving scope to the accompanying players. It was just in this way that Kashiwagi excelled. He was now playing in concert with a full orchestra; but managed in the most astonishing way to keep in touch with all the other instruments.

To no Chujo had, in his solo, played with his zithern tuned very low, so that the strings vibrated with a dull, rumbling sound. But Kashiwagi's was tuned to the ordinary high pitch, and this (by contrast) gave to his playing a quality of lightness and gaiety. Never had the company heard him in such good form.

About the middle of the second month Nyosan moved into the New Palace. Great preparations were made for her reception; the room where the Presentation of Young Shoots had taken place was set apart for her own use, while several rooms in the neighboring wing and galleries were made ready for her attendants, after a great sweeping and scrubbing. She brought her own furniture with her, just as is done by a new arrival at the Emperor's Palace. Her coming took on the aspect of a great public ceremony, being attended by the whole Court. Genji (though, his rank being equal to that of a retired Emperor, he was under no obligation to do so) went out to assist her in alighting from her coach.

The exchange of compliments* on the third day was carried out in the most formal manner. Murasaki had naturally not been slow to realize—what Genji had not hitherto definitely disclosed—that Nyosan had come

---

* On the third day after the arrival of a bride the husband notified the bride's father that the marriage had been consummated and was likely to prove a success.

as a bride. The discovery came as a cruel blow, yet even so there was no reason to suppose that the newcomer was likely in any sense to take Murasaki's place. After all, this was not the first time that she had been called upon to suffer the presence of a rival in the house. But hitherto these rivals had been without exception her inferiors in birth, and not much less than her equals in age; whereas Nyosan was a person of quite as much social consequence as herself, and, into the bargain, was just entering upon that season of sunshine and flowers to which Murasaki was already bidding farewell.

But she did not show, or hoped she did not show, any of these feelings, and in the preparations for Nyosan's arrival she gave Genji all the help she could. While side-by-side they were devising plans for these new household arrangements, she seemed to enter with the greatest interest into every detail, and looking at her fondly, Genji wondered whether any other woman in the world would have done the same. The little princess, though now well on in her thirteenth year, was very small for her age, and indeed still looked a mere child. Her conversation and behavior also savored solely of the nursery, and Genji could not help remembering how lively, how full of character and imagination little Murasaki had been when twenty years ago he had carried her to his home. But perhaps it was a good thing that the newcomer was, except in actual years, so very much of a child. She would certainly be less likely to get into scrapes. But unfortunately, Genji reflected, people who do not get into scrapes are a great deal less interesting than those who do.

During the first three nights Murasaki saw nothing of him, and though this was quite natural under the circumstances, she felt it deeply; for it was now several years since they had thus been separated. Each evening she perfumed his clothes with more than ordinary care. Never had she seemed to him more complete, more all sufficing than at these moments; and watching her grave, eager face as she bent over the work, he wondered that a dying man's pleadings and lamentations should have sufficed to lead him into such a course. But stay! Did not his own restlessness, his own insatiable curiosity have something to do with this rash consent? There was Yugiri. Young though he was, it had been justly assumed that it was not worth while even approaching him with the proposal to which Genji had so readily consented. "Just once more," he said on the third night. "After this I shall not have to desert you again; or, if I ever do so, you may be certain it will not be at my own desire. I must not give Suzaku the impression..."

His predicament seemed to her a strange and rather absurd one. "If it is Suzaku and not yourself whom you are trying to please," she said, smiling, "I am sure you can judge better than I can what will suffice to keep him happy."

In the end it was at Murasaki's persuasion that, far later than he had intended, he made his way to Nyosan's room. But it was with aching heart that she watched him cross the threshold, clad in the soft, fine cloak that she had scented with her own hands.

If all this had happened a few years ago, at the time when she lived constantly on the watch for the first signs of some such trouble, she would have been better able to meet it. But lately she had grown used to life running in an even tenor that seemed incapable of change, and even if it had been a mere matter of rumor or suspicion, her sense of security would have received a rude shock. As it was, she knew that henceforward, come what might, she would not have many easy moments; but of this she did not breathe a word to anyone. Not so her gentlewomen, among whom there was tonight a great deal of indignant nudging and whispering: "Who would have thought we should ever live to see such a day!" "Well, this isn't the first time he's taken a fancy to someone…" "Of course not, but none of the others was anything to worry about, so far as I ever heard. I don't mean that even now there is any real danger. But small difficulties are bound to crop up now and again. It is not going to be any too pleasant a time for most of us…" Murasaki affected to be unconscious of these dialogues, and sat talking, spiritedly enough, till a late hour in the night. Anxious that her women should have no excuse for spreading in the world at large the impression that she was taking up a hostile line towards Nyosan, she said at last: "I am so glad that this young princess has come to live with us. For though we are already so large a household, His Highness badly needs new society. I think he will get on very well with her, and she will make a fresh interest in his life. I too shall be delighted to have her here, for since the Akashi Princess went away there has been no one for me to play games with, and oddly enough I still enjoy them just as much as when I was a child. It is too bad that people are saying I am opposed to her living here. Nothing could be further from the truth. Perhaps if His Highness were to take someone of my own rank, or someone whom I regarded as very inferior, too much into his confidence, I might for a time feel a little bit jealous. But as it is, I am glad that he should have found any way of assisting this unfortunate creature…"

With such sentiments as these it was hard for Nakatsukasa and Chujo no Kimi to keep patience, and they exchanged glances which clearly meant: "Sympathy can be carried too far!" Formerly they had both been in Genji's personal service; but for a long while past they had waited upon Murasaki, and were both devotedly attached to her.

Meanwhile speculation was rife among the other ladies of the household as to how this new development would affect Murasaki's position; and for the first time they felt a certain satisfaction in their own poor estate, which, humdrum though it was, could never land them in one of these humiliating predicaments... To each of them separately it occurred that it would be kind to call upon Murasaki, and they arrived in rapid succession, thus bringing home to her in the most painful fashion the fact that she had become an object of sympathy.

Again and again Murasaki told herself that life was very short. Soon this and all else would be over; what sense could there be in minding things so much? But when night came she felt she could not rest, and it was only to avoid the comments of those about her that at last she crept under the bedclothes. And though such nights as the one I am describing had become common enough since Nyosan's arrival, Murasaki still felt awkward and lopsided as she tried to arrange herself in bed. This reminded her of the days when he was at Suma. She found herself, strangely enough, wishing that he were now equally far away. Simply to know that he was alive—that was all she asked; and she afflicted herself afresh by imagining him at the ends of the earth, while she remained alone in the Capital. To vary this, she imagined her own death, rapidly followed by his. Here she checked herself. A pretty pass things had come to when she had to conjure up such visions in order to allay the torment of reality!

A dismal wind was howling. She tried in vain to sleep, lying dead still, that the gentlewomen who were near her might think she was asleep despite the storm; and she was lying thus when a dreary cock-crow seemed to tell that the night was past. But opening her eyes she saw that it was still dark.

She had not all this while thought of Genji with any rancor or hostility, but her distress was vivid enough to find a way into his dreams, and it was after a terrifying vision of her that he woke up with a start and hearing the cock crow told Nyosan he must be gone, for it had been agreed that he should leave at daybreak, and now, in his anxiety to discover whether Murasaki was in some special need of him, he affected not to notice that, despite the crowing of the cock, it was still black night. Nyosan was still so young that she liked to have her nurses sleeping close at hand, and when Genji opened the passage-door, they sat up and craned their necks after him. In the east a faint semblance of light was beginning to show, dimly reflected by the snow that lay on the path. The perfume of his dress lingered where he had passed, and one of the nurses whispered, "Though black the night..."*

The snow only remained in patches here and there, but the sand of the garden-paths was very white, and often he was in doubt whether he was

---

* "Though black this night of spring, what guide need we save the scent of their blossoms to guide us whither the plum-trees bloom?"

going to tread on sand or snow. While he knocked at the outer door of Murasaki's room, he murmured to himself those lines of Po Chu-i:

> In broken places of the Castle wall snow is still left;
> Down streets unwoken by the morning drum no foot has yet stirred.

It was a long time before there was any answer to his summons, for her people were quite unused to answering the door at such an hour, and when at last they undid the bolts, he grumbled: "You have kept me standing here till I am half frozen. A poor reward for hurrying home so early! I wish now that I had not bestirred myself..."

He came to Murasaki's bedside and pulled back the coverlet. As he did so, with a quick movement she hid the sleeve of her dress, that was still wet with the tears she had shed during the night. He began treating her as though nothing were amiss, speaking with the utmost tenderness and affection. But coax and pet as he might, she remained serious and preoccupied, turning from him sorrowfully as though she felt he had no right to have come. He sat watching her, full of admiration and delight. Certainly it was not in search of beauty that he had need to go abroad at night! He spent all day with her, recalling a thousand tender passages in their past life together, begging her not to shut her thoughts away from him. When night came he sent a note to Nyosan's quarters saying that the snowy weather had upset him and that it was thought best he should remain where he was. The nurse, who took his message, knew very well what to make of it, and came back in a minute or two, saying curtly: "I have told my Lady." Evidently Nyosan's people were not best pleased with the excuse. What if they should carry their complaint to the ex-Emperor? This was only the fourth night after the marriage. Perhaps after all it was rather soon to begin suspending his nightly visits; he had better invent some fresh excuse and go to Nyosan at any rate this one time more. But a moment later, looking at Murasaki, he wondered how it could ever have occurred to him as possible to leave her. Meanwhile she on her side felt that he had treated Nyosan almost contemptuously, and wished that he would take the trouble to manage things a little better...

Next morning he sent a note of apology to Nyosan's apartments, and though it was not to be supposed that at her age she was very critical in such matters, he trimmed his brush with the utmost care and wrote on exquisitely white paper: "No deep drift bars my path, but with their whirling these thin, parched snowflakes have bewitched my dizzy brain." This he tied to a sprig of plum-blossom, and sending for one of his servants, bade him take it not across the garden,* but by way of the

---

* That Murasaki might not see.

western gallery. The answer was long in coming, and tired of waiting he went back to Murasaki in the inner room. He was still carrying in his hand the rest of the plum-branch from which he had detached the spray, and conscious that Murasaki was looking at it curiously, he said: "How pleasant it would be if all flowers had so delightful a scent as this! However, it is a good thing for the other flowers that the cherry-blossom cannot borrow this smell. The rest would seem to us mere weeds, and we should never give them another thought again. The plum-flower, however, has this advantage over the others, that it comes first. Our eyes have not yet been sated with blossom, and we accord to this earliest comer what is perhaps an undue attention. Then, wisely, it vanishes, before the cherry has reached its prime..."

At this moment (when he had almost given up expecting it) Nyosan's answer at last arrived. It was on thin crimson paper, and the extreme ingenuity and daintiness with which it was folded made his heart beat fast as he opened it. Alas, her writing was still quite unformed, and he wished that it had been possible to prevent Murasaki from seeing it some while longer. Not that the letter contained anything in the slightest degree intimate. But considering the writer's rank and what would naturally be expected of her, it seemed a shame to show so childish a production. But to conceal it from Murasaki would be sure to lead to misunderstandings, so he let her read what she could see of it over his shoulder as she lay beside him. The poem ran: "So light the last spring snow that, should the least waft of unkindness come, those thin flakes soon would vanish down the windy cross-roads of the sky."

It was indeed a childish, scrawling hand, far behind what one would have expected in a girl of Nyosan's years; but Genji merely glanced at it and put the letter away. If it had come from anyone else he would certainly have discussed this strangely backward letter with Murasaki and attempted to account for its inefficiency. As it was, he merely said with a sigh: "Well, well! That at any rate must prove to you that you have small ground for anxiety."

During the day he paid a short visit to Nyosan's rooms. He had taken more trouble than ever with his costume, wishing her to feel that his failure to appear last night was not due to carelessness or disrespect. Her younger gentlewomen were easily mollified by the magnificence of his get-up; but the head nurses regarded last night's non-appearance as a very grave omen. "Come, come," they said. "It's no use his trying to mend matters by wearing his smartest clothes." The little princess was certainly very pretty; but all her surroundings were so exquisitely appointed and she herself so marvelously dressed, that looking at her one began to wonder whether, apart from her clothes and grand belongings, she had any existence at all. It could not be said that she was particularly shy; but her friendliness and composure were those of a child that barely distinguishes between friends and strangers, rather than of a young lady to whom experience has taught the art of self-possession. Her father Suzaku, though always somewhat effeminate and over-sensitive, or at any rate constantly criticized on this score by his subjects, was assuredly not lacking in feeling for the elegancies of life, and to Genji it was incomprehensible that he should have allowed his favorite child to grow up backward in just those accomplishments to which he himself had always paid the greatest attention. Genji was upset, for the girl's deficiencies were such as must inevitably make her an uninteresting associate for some while to come. However, he did not take an actual dislike to her, and soon began attempting to draw her into conversation. She agreed with everything he said, but did not succeed in introducing any fresh topic of her own, and not so many years ago he would have set her down as a hopeless simpleton. But recently he had grown much more tolerant. If one was going to dismiss people because of a single shortcoming, there would soon be no one left. He had made up his mind henceforward to get as much pleasure as possible out of what was interesting in the people he met and forget about their bad points. To be bored by this girl, for whose hand in marriage the whole Court would in a short while have been scrambling, was really too perverse. Yet far more than at any time before Nyosan's arrival he now felt how unique Murasaki was. Surely his adoption of her was the one step in his life that he would never have cause to regret. Such time as he spent with Nyosan (whether by day or night) he found himself grudging more and more, till he was frightened at his own increasing inability to live more than an hour or two on end in any but Murasaki's company.

The Crown Prince had taken an immense fancy to his little bride from Akashi, and never allowed her out of his sight. One day she announced that she was tired of Court and had decided to go home for a while to Genji's palace. But the Crown Prince would not hear of it. She was obliged to give way; not however without considerable resentment, for this was the first time in her life that she had ever failed to get her way. In the summer she was not very well, and it was agreed in principle that she should be allowed a short leave of absence. But day after day her departure was deferred, and she began to feel as though her marriage had sentenced her to perpetual captivity. Presently it became clear that there was a special reason for her indisposition. Her attendants would indeed have reached this conclusion sooner had she not been so very young;[*] but as soon as it was apparent that she needed rest and care, leave of absence was granted, and she moved into the New Palace. Her old rooms were no

---

[*] Barely fourteen.

longer available, and she was put into a suite that opened out of Princess Nyosan's quarters, her mother of course accompanying her. This was the first time that the Lady of Akashi had inhabited the New Palace without being separated from her child, and her delight knew no bounds.

One day when Murasaki and Genji were about to visit the Crown Princess's rooms, Murasaki said to him: "Would not this be a good opportunity for me to make Nyosan's acquaintance? That dividing-door could so easily be opened... I have for some time past been meaning to visit her, but it has always been very difficult to arrange. This seems the best chance that is likely to turn up..." "Certainly, nothing could be easier," replied Genji, "you have only to walk in. It is impossible to treat her otherwise than as a child. So far from standing on ceremony with her, I hope you will help me to correct her faults. It is the kindest thing you can do..." He went to Nyosan, and in the course of conversation said to her: "Later on this evening Lady Murasaki will be visiting your neighbor, the Crown Princess. It is an excellent opportunity for you to make her acquaintance, and I hope you will allow her to come straight through into these rooms. Murasaki is a delightful person, and she is just as fond of games as you are. I believe you would have great fun together." Nyosan looked rather scared. "I should not know what to say to her..." she answered helplessly. "Oh, that would be all right," he hastened to assure her. "She would talk, and you are quite good at finding things to say if someone helps you out by leading the way. In any case, make friends with her. That is all I ask."

So anxious was he for them to get on well together that he had for some time past been positively dreading the inevitable encounter, and had done nothing on his side to promote it. For he feared that Murasaki would, when it came to the point, find Nyosan's childish ways merely tiresome and her insipid conversation exasperating. However, this time it was Murasaki herself who had suggested the meeting, and there could be no sense in opposing it.

Meanwhile Murasaki went to her room to get ready for the visit. Even while she did so she assured herself that, despite all the care she was taking in her preparations and the feeling (dictated by all the circumstances of the visit) that she was about to pay her court to a reigning power, Nyosan was neither her superior in this household, nor to any considerable extent in the world at large. While waiting for Genji to fetch her, she began doing a little writing-practice, not composing the poems, but writing old ones that she knew by heart. She was not feeling depressed, but only the most desolate and love-lorn verses came into her head, and by an odd accident each seemed in some special way to fit her own case.

Coming from the presence of younger women, such as Nyosan, Genji always expected that Murasaki would appear to him inevitably (and he was willing to make allowance for it) a little bit jaded, a trifle seared and worn. Moreover, he had lived with her so long, knew her, as he supposed, so well by heart that, even had not age touched her charms, it would scarcely have been strange if they no longer had power to excite him. But as a matter of fact it was just these younger women who failed to provide any element of surprise, whereas Murasaki was continually astounding him, as indeed she did tonight, dressed in all the splendor that the coming visit demanded, her clothes scented with the subtlest and most delicious perfumes, her whole person ever more radiant this year than last year, today than yesterday.

Seeing him enter, she hid the papers on which she had been writing under the inkstand; but he rescued them before she could protest. Hers was not a hand of the sort that occurs once in a generation, and is remembered forever afterwards. But there was great beauty in it, and scanning the papers he found the verse: "Is autumn* near to me as to those leafy hills, that even while I watch them grow less green?" Taking her brush he wrote beside her poem: "Look to the moat! Sooner shall yon bird's emerald wings grow white, than autumn bind its frosts about my Love."

Again and again, from small indications that she gave him unintentionally and unawares, he saw that she was very unhappy. If he made no allusion to this, it was not either that he failed to observe it, or that he did not know what struggles she made to conceal her pain.

With Murasaki the Crown Princess was quite as much at home as with her own mother, and this part of the visit naturally passed off agreeably enough. The girl had grown very good-looking, and Murasaki, to whom her existence had once been a reminder of unpleasant things, no longer felt in her society anything but the most unfeigned pleasure. After a short conversation she proceeded through the dividing door into Nyosan's apartments. The little princess's childish lack of conventional small-talk proved to be the reverse of embarrassing, for it enabled Murasaki from the start to treat her as a young relative who had been put into her care. It was necessary first of all to explain the rather complicated chapter of family history which made them cousins. Sending for Nyosan's head nurse, she said: "We have been working things out, and it certainly seems beyond doubt that your mistress and I are connected by family ties in many directions. I hope you do not think it rude of me to have been so long in coming. It seemed so difficult to arrange. But your mistress and I have now made great friends, and I hope you will not only allow me to visit you again, but also bring her to my rooms. Please consider henceforward that, if we do not frequently come together, the fault will lie on your side." "Well, madam," replied the nurse, "what with her

---

* *Aki* means "autumn," but also "to be tired of" and there is the secondary meaning: "Is the day when Genji will grow tired of me near at hand?"

mother dead and her father shut away in a monastery, I am sure my little lady would have a sad time of it, were it not for kindness such as yours. But I know quite well that her father would never have brought himself to leave the City if he had not been certain that you would welcome us as you have done today, and make it your business to watch over our young lady with a friendly eye. For, madam, as you see, she is very young in her ways, and not only needs your help, but is used to being guided by those about her, and fully expects you to take her under your wing." "The ex-Emperor's appeal was couched in such terms," answered Murasaki, "that Prince Genji could never have dreamed of rejecting it; and I for my part was only sorry that it lay in my power to do so little for this poor child's happiness." Then turning abruptly from this serious conversation, to which Nyosan had herself paid very little attention, Murasaki began talking about picture-books and dolls with such knowledge and enthusiasm, that Nyosan at once decided she was not so dull as most grown-up people, nor indeed like one at all. Henceforward they met very often, or when that was impossible, exchanged little notes concerned exclusively with the behavior of Nyosan's dolls and the fortunes or reverses of her other toys.

At the first news of Nyosan's removal to the New Palace, people had hastened to make the obvious prediction that Murasaki's day would soon be over. When, however, as time passed, it became abundantly clear that Genji, so far from being exclusively interested in the new arrival, was treating Murasaki with an even greater consideration than before, they waxed indignant on Nyosan's behalf, and said that if Murasaki had him so completely in her power he ought never to have taken the little princess into his house. Now came the news (disconcerting to gossip of either kind) that perfect harmony prevailed between the two ladies, and to these outside observers the situation lost all further interest.

The Crown Princess was now nearing her time. From the beginning of the next year a service of continual intercession was kept up in Genji's palace, and in every Buddhist temple or shrine of the old faith throughout the land prayers were said on her behalf. A previous experience[*] had made Genji particularly nervous about such events, and though it was a grief to him that Murasaki had never borne a child, he was in a way relieved that he had never been called upon to endure the agonies of suspense that such an event would have inflicted upon him. The Princess's extreme youth was another source of anxiety, and when at the beginning of Kisaragi[†] her strength showed signs of failing, not only Genji but all those in charge of her began to take serious alarm. After careful investigation, the magi-

---

[*] Aoi's death in childbirth.
[†] The second month.

cians decided that the situation of her present room was unfavorable, and insisted upon a change. To move her away from the Palace altogether would clearly be a very risky undertaking, and she was carried to the central hall of her mother's former apartments in the northern wing. These had the advantage of being surrounded on every side by passages and covered galleries in which it was possible to accommodate the huge band of priests (with their altars and other gear) that had now assembled in the palace. For every healer of any repute in the country had been summoned to work his spells.

The Lady of Akashi, quite apart from the anxiety that she must in any case feel at such a time, was in a state of the utmost suspense; for the safe delivery of an heir would mean that all her sacrifices had not been made in vain. On this occasion her mother, now a very old lady indeed, had come up from the country, unable to bear the anxiety of being at a distance from all news.

The Crown Princess knew very little about the circumstances of her birth; but once admitted to her bedside, the old grandmother was soon pouring out a tremulous flood of anecdotes and lamentations that, confused though it was, for the first time did something towards enlightening her. The girl had at first stared at this extraordinary visitor, wondering who on earth she could be; but she was just aware of the fact that she possessed a grandmother, and when it became evident that this talkative old woman was certainly she, the Princess tried to be as civil as she could. The visitor began describing Genji's life at Akashi, and the despair into which they had fallen at the time of his sudden recall. "We never thought we should any of us set eyes on him again," she said. "Oh dear, oh dear! If only I could have known then that it was all going to work out for the best... It was your coming into the world that saved us. I don't believe that but for you we should ever have heard a word from him after he went away." And she burst into tears of gratitude and joy. The Princess also wept, partly because it always moves one to hear about one's childhood, partly because this revelation of the true facts about her birth had come to her as something of a shock. She had always known that her mother was not quite of the same class as the people with whom she now associated. But the careful education she had received at Murasaki's hands, combined with the admiring attitude of all her companions at Court, had destroyed in her the last trace of diffidence or timidity. She had long felt herself to be in every way on an equality with the greatest ladies in the land. With burning cheeks she recalled occasion upon occasion when she had spoken scornfully of persons who were (as she now realized) very far indeed from being her inferiors. The true facts about her origin were probably known to most people at Court, and though in her presence no sarcastic comment had ever been made, she could imagine the mirth that (behind the scenes) had always been provoked by her ignorant self-conceit. Akashi!* Born at Akashi! What a hideous thought! That things were as bad as that she had never for a moment suspected; for it was her nature to turn away instinctively from enquiries that were likely to yield unpleasant information. Well, here indeed was a disagreeable and humiliating surprise. She wondered how she would ever be able to hold up her head again.

She was obliged next to listen to a long account of her grandfather's odd ways; he had become, it seemed, a kind of rishi, living in the world but not of it. A queer place she came from and queer people she belonged to, thought the Princess, remembering the high line she had always taken on questions of birth and breeding. At this moment her mother entered, and noticed at once that she was looking very rueful indeed. In the passages outside there was a great stir, for the priests and magic-workers drawn from every quarter of the land were just assembling to recite the Rites of the Day. But actually in the Princess's room all was quiet, and availing herself of this opportunity the old nun had installed herself at the bedside and seemed to have taken complete possession of her granddaughter and all that appertained to her.

"I wish she wouldn't do that," thought the Lady of Akashi as she entered. "She might at least put up a small screen. Anyone seeing her planted at the bedside like that will wonder how on earth she got there. You would think she was the herb-doctor come to give the child a pill. How tiresome people do become at that age." The old lady saw in a moment that she was thought to have taken too much upon herself. But she was getting very hard of hearing, and, as was usual when she was afraid she had missed some remark, she cocked her head on one side: "Eh? Eh?" "Really, she's not so old as all that," thought the Lady of Akashi. "She can't be more than sixty-five, or at the most sixty-six." The old lady looked very neat and respectable, even dignified, in her nun's robe; but her appearance was spoilt for the moment by the fact that her eyes were red and swollen with weeping. The Lady of Akashi knew only too well what this meant: her mother had been reminiscing, and turning to the Princess she said nervously: "I can see that grandmother has been telling all sorts of extraordinary tales about the days of long ago. You must not believe everything she says; for she is apt to mix up all sorts of fairy-stories, legends, and marvels with things that really happened. I am sure she has been treating you to the oddest extracts from our family history." Her suspicions were confirmed by the Princess's extreme quietness; it was only too evident that the old nun had chattered with the greatest

---

* Not to be born in the City was regarded as a severe social disqualification, whoever the parents might be. In the narrative she is called the Princess from Akashi; but it must not be supposed that she was ever so addressed.

possible indiscretion. The Lady of Akashi had long ago decided that the moment of the Crown Prince's ascent to the Throne would be the right occasion for revealing to the Princess in their entirety the painful facts concerning her birth. As Empress she would have reached the utmost limit of a woman's ambition, and intelligence such as this, disagreeable though it might be, could not greatly depress her. But at the present moment it might have a very upsetting effect, and she regretted that her mother should have thought fit to take such a liberty.

The Rites of the Day were now over, and there was a great clatter as the priests left their work. To distract the Princess's thoughts her mother now brought her some fruit, coaxing her with: "Could you not manage just one of these?" and such-like motherly phrases. The old nun's delight in the presence of her lovely grandchild manifested itself in the most curious way. For whereas tears streamed from her eyes and her brows were contracted into what looked like the most disapproving frown, her lips were parted in a perpetual smile of delight, revealing a painfully toothless mouth. So truly alarming was the old lady's expression that she was positively afraid of the effect it might have upon the invalid, and tried to catch her mother's eye, apparently without success.

Presently, however, the old nun recited the verse: "Blame not the tears of love that like a running tide have stranded this old bark upon a profitable shore." "When I was young," she added, "people of the age I am now were privileged to weep as often as they felt inclined."

"Following the pathway of that bark across the foam, I would retrace its course and find the felt-roofed hut whence it was launched upon the deep." Thus the young Princess wrote upon the sheet of paper that was topmost in her writing-case; and the Lady of Akashi: "Though he that lingers on that shore long since of every worldly thought has cleared his breast, perchance of the heart's darkness* a little clings to him and clouds his nature still."

There was then talk of the morning upon which they had parted with the old recluse. The Princess, who was at that time a mere infant, had not the haziest remembrance of this episode, but she could well believe that it had been very affecting.

About the middle of the third month she had an extremely painless and easy delivery, strangely at variance with what seemed to be portended by her previous weakness and distress. It was with intense relief that Genji heard of this event. The child was a boy; so that everything had turned out in the happiest manner possible. Her present temporary quarters were inconveniently far from the front of the house, but it was pleasant for her to be so near her mother, and pleasant too for

---

* "The heart's darkness," *kokoro no yami,* is the love of parent for child.

the old nun to watch the arrival of the presents which poured in from every side. She could indeed feel that the storm-tossed voyage of her life had cast her up at last upon "a profitable shore," as she herself had said. But this arrangement could not continue, as it was too much at variance with traditional practice, and it was decided that the Princess must be moved back into her own apartments. Here she was visited by Murasaki, who found her sitting up in her white jacket, holding the little boy in her arms. It was a pretty sight; but it was hard indeed for Murasaki to accustom herself to the idea that the little Princess from Akashi was a mother!

Not only was she herself without experience of this kind; but it so happened that she had never before been brought into contact with such events, for this was the first child to be born in the house. Her delight in handling and attending to the child was so obvious that the Lady of Akashi had not the heart to deprive her of these offices, contenting herself with the bathing of the infant. She even consented to play this part on the official occasion when the Crown Prince's envoy came to administer the Bath of Recognition,* and the man, who had some general notion concerning the true state of affairs, thought how disagreeable it must be for the Princess to be continually reminded by her mother's shortcomings of this flaw in her lineage. But to his surprise he found during the performance of his duties that the Lady from Akashi had dignity and high breeding enough to be the mother of the grandest imaginable Princess.

Any further account of the birth-ceremonies would not be of special interest, and I shall therefore hurry on with my story. It was on the sixth night after the child's birth that the Princess moved back into her own quarters. On the seventh night the Emperor himself sent his presents. Suzaku's vows forbad that any gift from him should figure on such an occasion; but it was generally understood that a magnificent largesse from the Public Treasury, brought by To no Ben and Senji, two officials of the Imperial Purse, was due to Suzaku's instigation. Presents of silk came in abundance, the Empress Akikonomu's offering exceeding that of the Emperor himself. The various princes and Ministers vied with one another in the magnificence of their gifts, and even Genji, who hated display and was apt to cut down all public demonstrations to the minimum, this time saw to it that everything should be carried through with the utmost splendor. Indeed the whole Court was in such a state of chatter and excitement that my head was in a whirl, and I forgot to make any note of the many beautiful and interesting ceremonies that took place in the Palace at the time of this little Prince's birth.

---

* By sending this representative the Crown Prince acknowledged paternity of the child.

Genji, too, constantly took the child in his arms. "Yugiri," he once said, "has never invited me to make the acquaintance of his children, so that it is a great treat for me to be allowed to handle this pretty fellow..."

The child was filling out fast. It was high time to find nurses for him, but Genji, rather than employ persons whom he did not know, spent some time searching round among those in his employ for ladies of good birth and intelligence with whose record he was thoroughly familiar. Through all this period the behavior of the Lady of Akashi provoked universal admiration. She had shown dignity without touchiness, humility without disagreeable self-abasement. Hitherto Murasaki had always continued to feel a slight discomfort in her presence. But after the birth of the Prince they became much better friends. Though childless herself, she was extremely fond of children. She made the Guardian Dolls[*] and other toy figures with her own hands, and would sit for hours working their joints and making them do tricks.

During the third month there was a spell of delightful weather, and on one of these bright, still days Prince Sochi and To no Chujo's son Kashiwagi called at the New Palace. "I am afraid things are very quiet here," Genji said to them. "At this time of the year, when there are no public or private festivities of any kind, it is harder than ever to keep people amused. I wish I could think of some way to distract you... Yugiri was here just now. I cannot think what has become of him. I suppose we shall have to watch some more of this shooting on horseback; though I confess that for my part I am sick to death of it. I expect Yugiri caught sight of some of the young men who always clamor for it, and that was why he vanished so soon." "I saw Yugiri," someone said. "He is in the fields near the Race-course, playing football. There are a lot of them there..." "I am not myself very fond of watching football," said Genji. "It is a rough game. But I feel that today we all need something to wake us up..." and he sent a message to Yugiri asking him to come round to the front of the house. The young man presently appeared accompanied by a band of courtiers. "I hope you have not left your ball behind," he said to them. "How have you arranged the teams?" Yugiri told him how they had been playing, and promised to find a fresh ground where the game could be seen from the windows of the house. The Crown Princess having now rejoined her husband, her apartments were vacant, and as there was a large stretch of ground not intersected by rivulets or in any other way obstructed, this seemed the best place to set up the posts. To no Chujo's sons, both young and old, were all expert players. Neither the hour nor the weather could have been bettered, for it was the late afternoon, and there was not a breath of wind. Even Kobai abandoned

---

[*] The original object of dolls is to divert evil influences from the child.

himself with such excitement to the game that Genji said: "Look at our Privy Counsellor!* He has quite forgotten all his dignities. Well, I see no harm in a man shouting and leaping about, whatever his rank may be, provided he is quite young. But I am afraid I have long passed the age when one can go through such violent contortions without becoming ridiculous. Look at that fellow's posture now. You must admit it would suit a man of my years very ill."

Yugiri soon induced Kashiwagi to join in the game, and as, against a background of flowering trees, these two sped hither and thither in the evening sunlight, the rough, noisy game suddenly took on an unwonted gentleness and grace. This, no doubt, was in part due to the character of the players; but also to the influence of the scene about them. For all around were great clumps of flowering bushes and trees, every blossom now open to its full. Among the eager group gathered round the goal-post, itself tinged with the first faint promise of green, none was more intent upon victory than Kashiwagi, whose face showed clearly enough that there was a question of measuring his skill against that of opponents, even in a mere game; it would be torment to him not to prove himself in a different class from all the other players. And indeed he had not been in the game for more than a few moments when it became apparent, from the way in which he gave even the most casual kick to the ball, that there was no one to compare with him. Not only was he an extremely handsome man, but he took great pains about his appearance and always moved with a certain rather cautious dignity and deliberation. It was therefore very entertaining to see him leaping this way and that, regardless of all decorum. The cherry-tree† was quite near the steps of the verandah from which Genji and Nyosan were watching the game, and it was strange to see how the players, their eye on the ball, did not seem to give a thought to those lovely flowers even when they were standing right under them. By this time the costumes of the players were considerably disordered, and even the most dignified amongst them had a ribbon flying loose or a hat-string undone. Among these disheveled figures a constant shower of blossom was falling. Yugiri could at last no longer refrain from looking up. Just above him was a half-wilted bough. Pulling it down, he plucked a spray, and taking it with him, seated himself on the steps with his back to the house. Kashiwagi soon joined him, saying: "We seem to have brought down most of the cherry-blossom. The poet‡ who begged the spring wind 'not to come where orchards were in bloom' would have been shocked by our wantonness..." He turned his head and

---

* Kobai was now a member of the Grand Council.
† The four goal-posts were a pine-tree, a maple, a willow, and a cherry-tree, growing in tubs.
‡ Fujiwara no Yoshikaze, 9th century.

looked behind him to where Nyosan and her ladies were dimly visible beyond their curtains.

Kashiwagi had been on intimate terms with the ex-Emperor Suzaku, and at the time when her future was still in question had corresponded occasionally with Nyosan. Suzaku was aware of this, and seemed on the whole to encourage it. Kashiwagi was therefore both surprised and disappointed when her marriage with Genji was announced. He had become very much interested in her, and through one of her gentlewomen with whom he happened to be acquainted he still heard a great deal about her. This, however, was but a poor consolation; and to make his chagrin the greater, he heard rumors that Nyosan was very inadequately appreciated at the New Palace, Lady Murasaki still retaining an undiminished hold over His Highness's affections. Kashiwagi might be her inferior in birth and thus unsuited to claim her as a wife; but at any rate she would not in his house have been subjected to the humiliations that he supposed her now to be enduring. Tired of merely hearing news about her health and employments, he made friends with a certain Kojiju, the little daughter of Nyosan's nurse, and tried to persuade her to carry messages. One never knew what might not happen. After all, Genji was always talking of retiring to a monastery. Some day he might really do so, and then would come Kashiwagi's second chance. Meanwhile he continued to plot and scheme for a renewal of the acquaintance.

And now on the day of the football match he found himself not many steps away from her. As usual, her gentlewomen were not under very good control, and a patch of bright sleeve or skirt constantly obtruded, as some spectator, in her excitement, tugged back a corner of the curtains through which the ladies of the house were watching the game. And behind the curtains there showed all the time gay strips of color, flashing like prayer-strips at the roadside on a sunny spring day. The Princess's screens-of-state were carelessly arranged; she was not in the least protected on the side from which she was most likely to be seen. Still less was she adequately prepared for such an accident as now occurred; for suddenly a large cat leapt between the curtains in pursuit of a very small and pretty Chinese kitten. Immediately there was a shuffling and scuffling behind the screens, figures could be seen darting to and fro, and there was a great rustling of skirts and sound of objects being moved. The big cat, it soon appeared, was a stranger in the house, and lest it should escape it had been provided with a leash, which was unfortunately a very long one, and had now got entangled in every object in the room. During its wild plunges (for it now made violent efforts to get free) the creature hopelessly disarrayed the already somewhat disorderly curtains, and so busy were those within disentangling themselves from the leash that no one closed the gap. In the foreground was plainly visible a group of ladies in a state of wild excitement and commotion. A short way behind them was a little figure standing up, dressed in a long robe without mantle. It was a red plum-blossom gown, with many facings, that showed one overlapping another, in different tinges of the same color, like the binding of a book. Her hair, shaking like a skein of loose thread, was prettily trimmed and thinned out at the ends, but still reached to within a few inches from the ground. The contrast between the numerous overlapping thicknesses of her dress and her own extreme slimness and smallness was very alluring, her movements were graceful, and her hair, above all when seen with her head in profile, was unusually fine. Kashiwagi, as he peered through the growing darkness, wished that the accident had happened somewhat earlier in the evening. At this moment the cat gave a frenzied scream, and Nyosan turned her head, revealing as she did so a singularly unconcerned and confident young face. Yugiri feared that he would be held responsible for this indiscretion, and was on the point of going up to the window and protesting; but he felt that this would draw further attention to the incident, and contented himself with clearing his throat in a loud and significant manner. Nyosan immediately vanished amid the shadows, rather too rapidly to suit the taste of Yugiri, who had a considerable curiosity about the girl, and would, had he dared, gladly have availed himself of this opportunity to look at her for a little while longer. But by now the cat had been extricated; the screens and curtains were restored to proper order, and there was no chance that the intriguing vision of a moment ago would be repeated. And if it was with a slight feeling of disappointment that Yugiri saw his hint so rapidly obeyed, it may be imagined how loud Kashiwagi's heart had all this while been beating. From the first moment of her appearance there had been no doubt which was she, for she was differently dressed from any of the ladies about her, they wearing Chinese cloaks, and she an under-robe without cape or mantle. He hid, or hoped that he hid, the excitement through which he was passing. But Yugiri guessed easily enough what impression such an episode was likely to have made, and being still in a way identified with this house, he blushed for Nyosan's immodesty. The cat was now straying at large, and to distract his thoughts Kashiwagi called it to him. The creature jumped into his lap and began purring complacently. It had not long ago been in Nyosan's own arms; of this he was sure, for its soft fur still exhaled a strong perfume of the royal scent that only she could wear. At this moment Genji arrived, and seeing Kashiwagi fondling the Princess's cat with an expression of dreamy tenderness, he said sharply to the young men on the steps: "You had better not sit so close to the house. It is embarrassing for the people in the room behind... Won't you come in here?" and he led them through a neighboring door. They were soon joined by Prince Sochi, and a lively conversation began.

The football players now began to arrive, taking their seats on straw cushions lined up along the verandah, and refreshments were served, first and foremost the usual Camellia cakes,* then pears, oranges, and other such fruits, the exhausted players stretching for them greedily as the tray came their way. Finally, the great wine-flagon went round, accompanied only by dried fish.

Kashiwagi took very little part in the conversation and gazed all the while straight in front of him, apparently at the flowering trees in the garden. But Yugiri knew well enough what vision it was that floated before his friend's eyes. The whole episode was very unfortunate. It must certainly have given Kashiwagi the impression that the Princess was extremely loose in her ways. He could not imagine Murasaki allowing herself to be exposed like this, and the fact that such things could happen showed plainly how right the world was in declaring Genji to be reprehensibly inattentive to his new wife. Of course the Princess's lack of precaution was not due to shamelessness, but rather to the unsuspecting and serene self-confidence of extreme youth. All this no doubt was very attractive; but if he were in Genji's place he should find it also somewhat perturbing.

Kashiwagi for his part was not occupied in censoring either Nyosan or her attendants for the carelessness to which he owed his vision of her. Rather he regarded the affair as a happy accident—an omen, if one liked to consider it so, that his attachment was destined to ripen into something less shadowy than had hitherto seemed probable.

Genji began talking to Kashiwagi of his early rivalries with To no Chujo: "At football," he said, "your father was always far ahead of me. I do not suppose that you have actually learnt your skill from him, for such things cannot be taught; but no doubt you inherit an aptitude for the game. This evening you certainly gave us a masterly display..." Kashiwagi laughed. "I am afraid," he said, "that of all my father's talents this is the only one I have inherited. I am sorry for my descendants; apart from this one trifling gift, they will have nothing to inherit at all." "Never mind," said Genji, "so long as there is something at which you are better than other people, you deserve a place in history. You shall figure in your family records as a footballer; that would be rather amusing..."

While they talked and laughed the conviction was borne in upon Kashiwagi that no one in the world could possibly turn from Genji to him. Nyosan might like him, but there was no conceivable way in which she would not be the loser by such an exchange. His hopes, so high a moment before, suddenly sank to nothingness. She who had been so near in a moment became in his thoughts utterly inaccessible and remote, and he left the New Palace in the depths of despair.

---

* Always served to footballers.

He drove away in the same carriage as Yugiri, and said to him presently: "One ought really to visit Genji more often; particularly at this time of year, when there is so little to do. He said he hoped we should come again before the blossom was all gone. It is getting very near the end of Spring now. Do meet me here one day this month, and bring your bow..." A day was fixed upon, but this was not what was really in his mind. He was trying to find some way of introducing Nyosan's name into the conversation, and presently he said: "Genji does not seem to worry much about anyone except Lady Murasaki. I wonder how the young Princess feels about it. She is used to being made such a fuss of by her father that I cannot help thinking she must find her new life rather wretched." "You are entirely wrong," Yugiri replied. "My father's relations with Murasaki are of a kind it is difficult for outside people to understand. He adopted her when she was still a child, and there is naturally a great intimacy between them. He would not for the world do anything to hurt her feelings; but if you suppose this means he does not care for Nyosan, you are very much mistaken." Yugiri had raised his voice. "Don't talk so loud," Kashiwagi rebuked him, "the grooms can hear every word you say. For my part I am certain that she is often very unhappy, and I do not think anyone has a right to put a girl of her birth and breeding into such a position as this..." He seemed to take the matter very much to heart.

Kashiwagi still lived in his father's house, all alone in the eastern wing. It was not a very lively form of existence for a man of his age, but this solitude was entirely of his own seeking. Sometimes he felt wretched, and thought of marrying the first girl who came his way. But then he remembered that his father was Grand Minister. There was no reason at all why he should content himself with a plebeian marriage, and he determined to remain as he was until he obtained the bride to whom he considered himself in every way entitled. Tonight he sat all alone in his room puzzling till his head ached... How should he ever manage to see her again, how contrive to catch even so hasty and unsatisfying a glimpse as he had enjoyed today? With other women it was different. There was always the chance that some religious vow or omen of the stars might drive them into the open. And if such things did not spontaneously occur, they could easily be arranged... But with Nyosan these simple and recognized expedients would be of no avail. Nothing was more improbable than that she should ever leave her apartments; and it was difficult enough even to let her know of his feelings. However, he wrote a letter (by no means the first with which Nyosan's maid Kojiju had in recent days been entrusted): "Madam, one day not long since, the springtime lured me to trespass within the barrier that hides your sovereign precincts from the grosser world, an audacity for which I fear you condemn me with the bitterest scorn. On that occasion, Madam, like the poet* of old, "I saw, yet did not see." Since when such a turmoil has reigned in my heart as only the vision of what those baffling shadows hid from me can ever put to rest." With this was the poem: "Though flowers of sorrow only, my hand could reach on the high tree, would I were back amid the shadows of that provoking night."

Kojiju knew nothing about the "day not long since," and thought that the letter was an unusually pointless collection of stock lamentations. Waiting for a moment when Nyosan was alone she brought in the letter, saying: "I wish your Kashiwagi were a little less faithful. I am tired of bringing these continual messages. Why then do I accept them? you ask. I suppose it is because I can see that he would be in despair if I refused. But why should I mind his being in despair? Really, I have not the least idea..." and she burst out laughing. "What odd things you say," replied Nyosan, taking the letter. By the allusion to "seeing yet seeing not" she understood at once that he had caught sight of her during that unfortunate accident with the curtains. She blushed, not however at the idea of Kashiwagi's having seen her, but at the recollection that Genji had more than once warned her not to expose herself in Yugiri's presence. Now she remembered that Yugiri had on that occasion been sitting at Kashiwagi's side. What one saw, the other too would have seen. Her sole concern was lest Yugiri should mention her carelessness to Genji, and then she would get a scolding. As had often occurred before, the task of writing an answer fell to Kojiju. Only a conventional acknowledgment was necessary, and she dashed off the following: "Why you should speak of 'seeing, yet not seeing' passes my comprehension. Despite the embarrassment in which your proximity placed us, you certainly posted yourself at a point of vantage where nothing was likely to escape you." With this was the poem: "Feel what you will, but tell not to the world that where no hand may reach, upon the mountain cherry's topmost bough your heart you fain would hang."

The promised archery meeting at the New Palace took place on the last day of the third month. Kashiwagi felt very little inclined for company, and if he accepted the invitation it was only in the vague hope of some second accident such as that which had occurred at the football match. Yugiri at once noticed that his friend was still particularly silent and distracted. He knew well enough what this meant, and was genuinely distressed not only at the prospect of unpleasant scenes in which he would himself be involved, but also on Kashiwagi's account. For Yugiri was extremely fond of him, and could never bear to see him, even for small everyday reasons, depressed or in ill humor.

---

* In section 99 of the *Tales of Ise* the poet "sees, yet does not see," a lady in her carriage at the summer race meeting.

On this occasion Kashiwagi had come with the firm intention of behaving with perfect propriety, for not only did he stand in great awe of Genji, but also was extremely sensitive to public opinion in general, and nothing was more painful to him than the idea of his name figuring in the scurrilous gossip of the Court. If he had designs of any kind, they were not upon Nyosan but upon her cat. A fancy seized him that it would make him less miserable if he could get possession of this creature and have it always about him. But even this, as he well knew, was a mad idea, and under the circumstances to purloin the cat was not much easier than to make off with its mistress. The archery meeting proved uneventful. But a few days afterwards he was reminded of his project by seeing in the Crown Prince's rooms a very handsome kitten which had just arrived as a present from the Emperor's Palace. His Majesty's court-cat had just given birth to a large family of kittens, which had been distributed among his acquaintances. "I happened the other day," said Kashiwagi casually, "to catch sight of a remarkably fine cat belonging to one of the ladies at Genji's palace. I never saw so handsome a creature. By the way, I think they said that it is your sister Nyosan's..." This was a very good move, for the Crown Prince had a passion for cats, and the subject was one that he was willing to converse upon for any length of time. He began questioning Kashiwagi about this marvelous cat of Nyosan's, which he did not remember to have seen. "You have some of the same breed here," said Kashiwagi, "but there was something uncommon about that particular creature. It seemed so much more friendly and intelligent than any that I have ever known." Thus began a long conversation upon the merits of different cats. The Crown Prince first of all borrowed those belonging to his wife, the Akashi Princess, and finally sent a message to his sister Nyosan asking if she would mind lending him hers. Upon its arrival everyone agreed that it was undoubtedly a very fine cat. Kashiwagi, who knew the Crown Prince would give his sister a full account of the reception that her favorite had received, thought it better on this occasion not to display any great interest in the animal. But some days later he called again, on the pretext of giving the Prince a long promised lesson upon the zithern. "Which is the fellow I saw at Genji's?" he asked, in the course of conversation. "Is he still here? You have so many that I find it hard to keep them apart..." But as a matter of fact he had already recognized Nyosan's cat, and was soon fondling it upon his lap. "Isn't he behaving beautifully?" said the Crown Prince. "Considering you only saw him in the distance the other day, it is extraordinary that he should recognize you. But he certainly does, for they are by nature very distrustful creatures, and will not let anyone touch them unless they remember having seen him before. However, our cats often remember someone who has only been here for a moment and took no particular notice of them."

"They may not have reasoning powers such as we have," answered Kashiwagi, "but I am convinced that some of them at any rate have souls like ours." Presently he added: "Perhaps, as you have so many delightful cats of your own here, you would lend me this one of Nyosan's for a little while?" It was only after he had made this request that he realized how eccentric it must appear.

The cat lay close by him all night, and the first thing he did in the morning was to see to its wants, combing it and feeding it with his own hand. The most unsociable cat, when it finds itself wrapped up in some one's coat and put to sleep upon his bed—stroked, fed, and tended with every imaginable care—soon ceases to stand upon its dignity; and when, a little later, Kashiwagi posted himself near the window, where he sat gazing vacantly before him, his new friend soon stole gently to his side and mewed several times as though in the tenderest sympathy. Such advances on the part of a cat are rare indeed, and smiling, he recited to the animal the following verse: "I love and am not loved. But you, who nestle daily in my dear one's arms—what need have you to moan?" He gazed into the cat's eyes as he spoke, and again it began mewing piteously, till he took it up into his lap, and he was still nursing it thus when the first visitors of the day began to arrive. "This is very sudden," they whispered to one another. "He used not to take the slightest interest in such creatures." Presently a messenger arrived from the Crown Prince, asking that the cat might be sent back at once. But Kashiwagi refused to part with it.

Wakana
("Young Shoots")
PART TWO

So time* went by, bringing with it remarkably few changes either at home or in the world at large. Even so important an event as the abdication of the Emperor Ryozen seemed to make very little difference, for though he had no heir of his own, his nephew the Crown Prince had now reached manhood, and would, it was confidently expected, merely carry on his predecessor's policy. The actual resignation came very suddenly, ill health being given as a pretext. But during the eighteen years of his reign Ryozen had never ceased ardently to long for an opportunity of escaping from a position that entailed at every turn the most dangerous concealments and deceptions.† He had many friends with whom it would be possible for him as a private person to associate in a far freer and more interesting way; moreover his childlessness (decreed, as he thought, by Heaven as a punishment for his unwilling impiety), would not weigh upon him so heavily when the future of the Throne was no longer involved.

As sister to the new Emperor, Nyosan naturally became more prominent than ever both at Court and in the estimation of the populace. But she was still very far from occupying a position anything like that of Murasaki, upon whom, as the years went by, Genji seemed to become more and more dependent. Yet it was from time to time clear that, despite his unchanging tenderness and confidence, Murasaki was not wholly contented with her present position. "There are too many people in this house," she would sometimes say; "I wish I lived in some quieter place, where I could pursue my devotions undisturbed. I have reached an age when one cannot expect much more pleasure in this world, and had better spend the time in preparing oneself for the next." But Genji always assured her that he too intended quite soon to quit the Court, and indeed would long ago have done so, had he not feared to leave her in solitude. "Life here would be intolerable without you," he said. "Will you not wait till I have arranged to take my vows?"

One night, on going to Murasaki's apartments, Genji found she was not there. It was already long past midnight when she returned. There had been music, it appeared, in Princess Nyosan's rooms, and afterwards

---

* About three and a half years. This jump, which may read as though it were a "cut" made by the translator, exists in the original.

† He was really Genji's son, not the old Emperor's. In sacrificing at the Imperial tomb, etc., he was committing an outrage upon the dead.

Murasaki had stayed talking to her. "What did you think of Nyosan's playing?" Genji asked. "It seems to me that she has really improved very much lately." "When she first came to live with us," Murasaki answered, "and I used to hear her playing in the distance, I confess I was rather surprised by her incompetence. But it is quite true that she now plays very nicely. This no doubt is all due to your frequent lessons." "Very likely," he replied. "The truth of the matter is, hardly anyone gets properly taught nowadays. Giving music-lessons, if one really does it properly, correcting every mistake and continually guiding the pupil's hands, is a troublesome, exhausting business. Moreover it takes up an immense amount of time. But both Suzaku and her brother the present Emperor evidently counted upon me to take charge at any rate of her zithern lessons, and I had not the heart to disappoint them. Well, I am glad you think that, if in other ways she has got no great advantage through coming to live here, she has at least made progress in her music. When you were at a learner's stage I was unfortunately far busier than at present, and was never able to give you such long and thorough lessons, and lately one thing after another seems to have prevented our practicing together. I was delighted, therefore, to hear from Yugiri, the other day, the most enthusiastic accounts of your progress."

It seemed to him strange indeed that Murasaki, whom he was still apt to regard as his "little pupil," should now in her turn be giving lessons to his grandchildren. But such was the case, at any rate as regards music. Nor for the matter of that was there any side of their education of which she would not have been well qualified to take charge. For she had always mastered fresh subjects with astounding ease and quickness, showing a versatility which often disquieted him, in view of the common opinion that such brilliance and rapidity of attainment often presage an early death. His only consolation was that her knowledge, however quickly garnered, was always solid and complete; whereas in the cases of precocity that he heard quoted a merely superficial variety of talents seemed to be the rule. She had recently celebrated her thirty-seventh birthday, and after talking for a while of their life together during all those years, Genji said: "You must be very careful this year. You have reached a dangerous age* and ought to have special prayers said on your behalf. I will help you so far as I can; but probably there are all sorts of contingencies that it would never occur to me to provide against. Just think things over, and if there is any particular form of intercession that you would like to be used, let

---

* The soothsayers taught that there were several "dangerous ages" in the lives both of men and women. A few centuries later thirty-three was commonly regarded as a woman's most dangerous age. Nowhere else is thirty-seven mentioned; but it is to be noted Fujitsubo died at the age of thirty-seven.

me know, and I will arrange it for you. What a pity that your uncle* is no longer alive. For the ordinary, everyday prayers he would have done excellently..." For a while he was silent; but presently he said: "What a strange life mine has been! I suppose few careers have ever appeared outwardly more brilliant; but I have never been happy. Person after person that I cared for has in one way or another been taken from me. It is long since I lost all zest for life, and if I have been condemned to continue my existence, it is (I sometimes think) only as a punishment for certain misdeeds† that at all times still lie heavily on my mind. You alone have always been here to console me, and I am glad to think that, apart from the time when I was away at Akashi, I have never behaved in such a way as to cause you a moment's real unhappiness. You know quite well that I do not care for grand society. Women with whom one has to behave according to set forms and rules are in my opinion simply a nuisance. It is only with people such as you, whom I have known all their lives, that I am really happy. But you know all this quite well, and there is no use in my repeating it. About Princess Nyosan—of course it was tiresome for you that I was obliged to have her here, but since she came, I have grown even fonder of you than before; a change you would have noticed quickly enough, if it had been my affection towards someone else that was on the increase! However, you are very observant, and I cannot believe you are not perfectly well aware..." "I cannot explain it," she said. "I know that to any outside person I must appear the happiest of women—fortunate indeed far above my deserts. But inwardly I am wretched...Every day..." She felt it would take a long time to explain, and had not the courage. "As a matter of fact," she said at last, "I do not feel as though I should live much longer. You yourself have told me that this is a dangerous year. Let me meet the danger by doing what I have long been wanting to do. Then you will have less need for anxiety about me." As usual, he declared that such a thing was out of the question; the mere thought of separation was unendurable; their daily meetings, the only semblance of happiness that remained to him. "Surely, you would rather that I did not want you to go?" he asked, seeing her disappointment. She was now weeping bitterly, and he knew that the only way of putting a stop to this was to go on steadily for some while talking of indifferent topics. He began telling her about various people whom he had known years ago. It was natural that he should mention, among other acquaintances of old days, Lady Rokujo, the Empress Akikonomu's mother. "Despite all that happened," he said, "I always think of her as the most brilliant creature that was ever at Court. Never have I encountered a sensibility

---

* See Part I, Chap. V.

† His intrigue with Fujitsubo.

so vivid and profound, and this, as you can imagine, made her at first a most fascinating companion. But there can never have been anyone with whom it was more impossible to have relations of a permanent kind. It is natural that people should sometimes feel out of temper or aggrieved, and equally natural that, after a time, the feeling should wear off. But in her mind the smallest sense of injury grew deeper from day to day, till it had presently become colored with emotions, the violence of which I cannot describe. The circumstances were such that it was, as she well knew, impossible for me to go to her whenever I wanted to, and equally impossible for her to receive me. But her pride demanded that every absence should be treated as a delinquency on my part, requiring prolonged coldness on her side, and on mine an abject apology. In the end, all dealings with her became impossible. Unfortunately the secret of my relations with her was not well kept. Considering her temperament, nothing could have been more disastrous. The idea that her name was being bandied about the Court was torture to her, and though all the difficulties had arisen through her inordinate jealousy, and not through any fault of mine, I was extremely sorry for her, and in the end felt quite as wretched as though I had in fact been to blame. That is why I have taken so much trouble over Akikonomu's career, incurring thereby, as I well know, a great deal of unpopularity. But what does it matter if I am accused of favoritism and I know not what, so long as I feel that, in the grave, her mother can no longer doubt my good will? But I own that far too often in my life I have yielded to the impulse of the moment—have sought pleasures of which I afterwards bitterly repented." He went on to discuss the characters of various other women whom he had known, and said after a while: "I used to think that the Lady of Akashi, always conscious of her humble origins, was content with very little; and indeed the difficulty seemed to consist in persuading her to put herself forward at all. But I found out one cannot judge her by what appears on the surface. Modest, docile, self-effacing though she may seem to be, somewhere in the hidden depths of her nature there is more than a suspicion of self-will and pride."

"Most of the people about whom you have talked," answered Murasaki, now calm and composed, "I never saw, and therefore do not know whether you are right about them or no. But with the Lady of Akashi I am now fairly well acquainted, and I confess that her extreme sensitiveness and pride, so far from being hidden away in some secret corner of her being, have always seemed to me extremely conspicuous. Indeed, when with her I feel myself to be, in comparison, singularly lacking in reserve and sensibility. But though her shyness has often baffled me, I have persevered in the knowledge that the child understands me, and would put things right." Here was a wonderful change! Genji could remember the time when it was impossible for him so much as to mention the Lady of Akashi's name; and here was Murasaki singing her praises. He knew that this had come about through her affection for the little Princess, and he felt thankful for the existence of the child. "I do not think that you have any reason to feel over-sensitive or too easy-going in whatever company you may find yourself," he replied. "My experience has at least had the effect of teaching me how rare it is to find anyone who so successfully steers the middle course. You are indeed a prodigy... But I must go to Nyosan and congratulate her on the progress she has made with her music"

To Nyosan it never occurred that any other woman could be inconvenienced by her presence in the house. She flung herself with childish absorption into the distractions of the moment. Just now it was her zithern that occupied her thoughts, and nothing else seemed of any importance. "You have earned a holiday," Genji said. "I hope your teacher will always be as pleased with you as he is today. We have had some arduous times together, haven't we, and it is a comfort that something has come of it all at last. For the first time I really feel quite confident about you"; and so saying he pushed the zithern from him and fell fast asleep.

On the nights when Genji was away, Murasaki used to make her women read to her. She thus became acquainted with many of the old-fashioned romances, and she noticed that the heroes of these stories, however light-minded, faithless, or even vicious they might be, were invariably represented as in the end settling down to one steady and undivided attachment. If this were true to life, then Genji was, as he himself so often said, very differently constituted indeed from the generality of mankind. Never, she was convinced, never as long as he lived would his affections cease to wander in whatever direction his insatiable curiosity dictated. Say what he might, wish what he might, the future would be just what the past had been. With such thoughts going round and round in her head she fell asleep very late one night, only to wake a few hours later, long before it was light, with a violent pain in her chest. Her people did what they could for her, but with little effect. They were anxious to summon Genji; but she would not allow it, saying she did not wish him to be disturbed. She bore her pain as best she could till daylight came. She was now in a high fever and very restless. Again her maids begged her to let them summon His Highness. But Genji was still in the other part of the house, and she would not let them go to him. Presently, however, there came a note from the Crown Princess, and in the answer that she dictated Murasaki mentioned that she was unwell. The Princess felt alarmed, and guessing that Genji might not have heard, she sent a note to him, repeating the little that Murasaki had told her. In a moment he was at her bedside in a state of the utmost concern. "Are you better?" he asked; but laying his hand upon her burning forehead he knew that she was not. At once he remembered their conversation of the other day. What if this were the very danger against which he had warned her? He was terrified.

Presently, seeing that he would not leave her, his people brought him his breakfast on a tray; but he did not touch it, and all day long he sat motionless by the bedside, gazing at her as though stupefied with grief. Thus many days passed. She was evidently in great pain, not a morsel of food would she eat, nor did she once raise her head from the pillows. Meanwhile his messengers set out at top speed in all directions, arranging for prayers on her behalf to be said in every important temple throughout the land, and priests were sent for to work their spells at the bedside. She was now in great general distress and discomfort. The pain in her chest was no longer continual, but at each fresh attack was so severe that she hardly knew how to bear it. Every known remedy was tried, but nothing brought her any relief. It was apparent that she was very ill indeed, but Genji tried to find encouragement in the fact that there were now considerable intervals between these severe attacks. This showed, he thought, some natural resistance to the disease; perhaps in time the intervals would gradually become long enough for health to reassert itself. But he was still in the greatest agitation and anxiety. He ought at this very time to have been supervising the arrangements for the celebration of Suzaku's fiftieth birthday. But he was utterly unable to give his mind to any outside subject, and left the business in other hands. Suzaku in his monastery heard the news of Murasaki's illness, and constantly sent messages of enquiry.

Week after week passed without any improvement. The only expedient which now remained untried was a change of scene, and, as this was recommended, Genji, with extreme reluctance, moved her into his old palace, the Nijo-in.

Often she was hardly conscious of what went on around her; but once during a moment of comparative calm and lucidity she reproached Genji for not having allowed her to seek the consolations of religion while there was still time. But if it was terrible to see her thus carried from him by a stroke of fate, by this cruel sickness against which she struggled in vain, how much worse would it have been to see her deliberately proclaim as worthless the love he bore her, to stand by while she cast away her beauty, her talents, her charm, and in preference to living with him chose as a more tolerable lot the gloom and squalor of a convent? "Long, long before you ever thought of it," he said, "I earnestly desired to take my vows, and if I did not do so, it was wholly for your sake. Think, what I should have felt if, after all, you had deserted me first..."

She was now so weak that small hope of her recovery could be entertained. Again and again it seemed as though the end were come, and Genji lived in so continual an agony of suspense that during this whole time he never once went near Nyosan's rooms. There were no more music lessons, and week after week her lute and zitherns lay packed away in their wrappers. Many of the servants belonging to the New Palace had followed Murasaki to the Nijo-in, so that, what with her own rooms empty and so little stir of any kind going on, the place wore a strangely crepuscular air, and it seemed as though the whole life of this once so brilliant and joyous house had depended on Murasaki's presence, and on that alone.

One day Genji brought the Akashi Princess[*] to see her. "Come quickly!" she called to them. "Strange visions haunt me, and I am afraid to be alone." The Princess had brought her little boy, Prince Niou, with her, and seeing him Murasaki burst into tears. "I longed to watch him growing up," she sobbed. "Now he will not even remember me." "No, no," Genji interrupted her, "we must not let you talk like that. You are going to get well. Everything depends on what we think. If our thoughts are large and courageous, all kinds of good things will come our way; but if they are small and timid, then ill-luck will always attend us. And it is just so with health. Even people of the highest birth, surrounded by every comfort, often worry themselves into the grave by fretting over every trifle, and never learning to take life as it comes. But you have always been so sensible and even-tempered. That is sure to stand you in good stead..." And in his prayers to Buddha and to the Gods of our land he mentioned her great beauty of character, begging them to spare one who in her dealings with others had always shown such gentleness and forbearance. The priests and miracle-workers, who were on duty night and day, being told that her condition had reached a very critical phase, now redoubled their efforts, and for five or six days she seemed to be a little better. After that she had another bad attack; but things had gone on thus for so long that it seemed quite probable she would again rally. Of her final recovery Genji no longer had any expectation. Those in attendance upon her could discover no sign of any actual possession,[†] nor was it clear where the principal seat of her malady lay. But she was growing steadily weaker, and knowing that at any moment the end might come, Genji watched by her bedside hour after hour in an agony of continual suspense.

Among those whom recent changes in the government had tended to bring to the fore was Kashiwagi. He had for long past been one of the new Emperor's most intimate friends, and it was evident that, should he choose to take advantage of his position, a great future was in store for him. Realizing at last the hopelessness of his designs upon Nyosan, he had been prevailed upon to take as a concubine her elder sister, Lady Ochiba,

---

[*] She was now Consort of the Emperor; but had not been proclaimed Empress.

[†] By spirits, demons, or the like.

who being the child of a waiting-woman and thus at a great disadvantage in the world, was glad-enough to accept the position now offered to her by a very half-hearted lover. She was quite good-looking. Indeed, many would have regarded her as extremely attractive. But Kashiwagi was under no delusion that this alliance would in any way console him for his failure with the younger sister. His own old nurse was a sister of Nyosan's nurse (the mother of Kojiju, whose assistance had proved so fruitless before). It was through the relationship of these two old ladies that Kashiwagi had first heard of Nyosan. Indeed, while the Princess was still a child, his old nurse had whenever he visited her regaled him with continual stories of the little girl's clever sayings and pretty ways, and of Suzaku's extraordinary attachment to her; and it was these tales, repeated from her nurse to his, that had first aroused his curiosity. It was now long since Kashiwagi had attempted to hold any communication with her; but seeing the New Palace almost deserted (for since Murasaki's illness Genji was always at the Nijo-in and most of the servants had followed him), Kashiwagi felt that the time for a further attempt had come, and sending for Kojiju he begged her to assist him. "I feel no compunction in the matter," he said, "for Genji is neglecting her scandalously. Indeed, he ought never to have accepted such a responsibility, for his affections were already engaged in many other quarters, and it was clear from the beginning that she would be left entirely to her own devices. Months pass without his ever going near her, and she leads (I gather) the dullest life imaginable. Suzaku has heard something of this, and is now extremely sorry that he did not give her to some commoner who would have appreciated the honor and devoted himself to making her happy. I am afraid he thinks that in providing for Ochiba he has found just such a steady going, conscientious husband in me! I wish it were so; but though they are sisters and in some ways very much alike, Ochiba is Ochiba and Nyosan is Nyosan. That is all there is to be said about it..." Kojiju was horrified. "Come now!" she said. "That beats all. You have just promised to devote your life to one sister, and now you tell me that the only person in the world you care for is the other." "I know it seems very odd," said Kashiwagi, smiling. "But I believe both Suzaku and His Present Majesty would really have liked to give me Nyosan. And even now, since it is clear that Genji does not take any interest in her, I gather they are by no means displeased that I should feel as I do. They have her happiness to consider, and at present she is leading a miserable existence... Come! I think you might oblige me by having one more try." "You are asking a great deal more than you suppose," said Kojiju heatedly. "To begin with, she knows that you have just married someone else. And then, do you really think you have reached such a position in the world that you can afford to make an enemy of Prince Genji? I may be mistaken, but it does not seem so very long..." She was beginning to remind him how recent was his present promotion, but so indignant was she at his audacity that the words tripped over one another and she suddenly broke off. "That will do," he said. "Let us stick to the point. All I ask is that one day when you and she are alone together you should mention me. This surely cannot be very difficult now that so little is going on at the New Palace. I only want her to know that I have not forgotten her. I am not asking you to arrange a meeting, or indeed to say anything that could possibly bring a blush to the most modest cheek." "You are asking me to do precisely what is most likely to lead you both into trouble. Besides which, how can I suddenly begin talking about you? And for the matter of that, how am I to get at her when she is alone? It is hardly ever possible..." So she fenced, trying her best to put him off. "You are simply inventing difficulties," he said impatiently at last. "And why all this fuss? Is it so strange a thing for a lady to be admired? Queens, I seem to remember, and Empresses too have sometimes been known to have their lovers. And who is Nyosan that you should think it sacrilege for anyone to dream of her? Certainly the way she is treated at present does not suggest that Genji considers her to be of any great importance. You must learn to be less rigid in your ideas..." "If you think that Nyosan feels herself to be imperfectly appreciated and is on the lookout for someone to rescue her from her humiliations, you are very much mistaken. It was clearly understood from the beginning that this was not to be an ordinary marriage. She was extremely young, and came to the New Palace that, after her father's retirement from the City, she might have a fixed home and gain a little experience of polite life. All your talk of her being neglected or maltreated is beside the point." She was beginning to lose her temper; but by adroit flattery he managed to prevent her flinging out of the room, and at last she said: "If I ever do find myself alone with my lady, I will speak of this. But even when Genji is away at the Nijo-in there are always a lot of people gathered round her curtains-of-state, and even by her chair there is generally someone in attendance. So don't ask me to make any promises."

Day after day he badgered her, and at last, about the middle of the fourth month, there came from her a hurried note bidding him at once repair to the New Palace. He set out heavily disguised. His expectations were of an agreeable but by no means exorbitant kind. He did not for a moment suppose that she would admit him within her curtained dais. But she would, he hoped, be willing to converse with him, and if he were fortunate he might catch a glimpse of her sleeve, her fan, the train of her dress.

The Purification of the new Kamo Vestal was to take place next day. Twelve of the ladies who were to attend her were in service at the New Palace and were now in their own rooms busily engaged in trimming and sewing. The other gentlewomen of the household were to be present at tomorrow's show and were busy with their preparations, so that in Nyosan's part of the house there were very few people about; and even her confidential maid Azechi was absent, for she had received a sudden summons from a certain young captain (a member of the Minamoto clan, who had been paying her attentions for some time) and Nyosan had given her a holiday. Indeed, only Kojiju was in attendance, and she now led him noiselessly to a seat close by the side of her mistress's dais. Well, he thought, even should matters go no further, this was already a great deal more than he had expected when he set out.

Nyosan was asleep, and presently waking to find a man's form outlined against the curtains of her dais she naturally thought that it was Genji. But it was certainly not at all like Genji to sit nervously at the end of his chair in an attitude of constrained obeisance. For a moment she thought herself haunted by a ghost and hid her face in her hands; but finding courage to look up once more she saw clearly enough that the visitor, though not Genji, was a person quite as real. Seeing that she was now awake, Kashiwagi began explaining his presence. Protestations, entreaties, apologies... Who was he, and what did it all mean? More terrified now than when she had thought him a ghost, Nyosan called for help. But no one came, for there was no one to hear her call. She was now trembling from head to foot and drops of perspiration stood out on her brow. In this exhibition of childish panic there was something that fascinated him; but he was at the same time ashamed of having terrified her, and again began rather confusedly apologizing for his intrusion: "My rank does not, I know, entitle me to address you as an equal. But I had hoped all the same you would not consider me quite outside the pale of possible acquaintance. This claim at least I have upon your interest: that for years past you have occupied my thoughts to the exclusion of all else, as your father could bear witness. For utterly unable to lock up these feelings in my own breast (where indeed they were already grown rank with keeping) I long ago made confession of them, and found him by no means discouraging. But I was soon disillusioned. For weighed in the balance against one who had never given a moment's thought to you I, who loved you so dearly, was found wanting merely for lack of governmental dignities and royal pedigree. So soon as your lot was cast I determined to banish all thought of you forever from my heart. But love had burnt down too deep into the core. Months, years passed, and still I thought of you, longed for you, wept for you; until, unable for an instant longer to support my misery, I rushed thus uncivilly into your presence, showing, as I fully perceive, a lack of consideration for your feelings that makes me blush for shame. But now that I am here, let me make amends by assuring you that you shall at least have no cause to repent of my having been admitted." While he spoke she kept on asking herself who he was, and it was only gradually that it dawned upon her he could not very well be anyone but Kashiwagi. This realization made her feel more than ever scared, and she did not manage to bring out a word in reply. "You know so little of me," he went on, "that I am not surprised you should be somewhat nervous. But after all, such visits as this of mine tonight are of fairly frequent occurrence! If you persist in treating it as an affront, my misery will drive me to... But no! Have pity on me, say one kind word, and I will leave you." Her complete lack of self-importance had, however, somewhat upset his calculations. He had expected to find her haughty, stiff, unapproachable—in a word, all that women of such rank are generally supposed to be. Consequently it had never occurred to him that on this first visit he would by any conceivable chance get beyond the stage of a little stiff and unadventurous conversation. But to his surprise she was not grand, not proud, not contemptuous. She was only a singularly handsome girl, looking up at him with a shy, questioning yet almost trustful air. His good resolutions suddenly broke down. Soon the world and its inhabitants seemed nothing to him, nor would he have stretched out a hand to save them from instant destruction.

At last, lying by her side, he did not exactly fall asleep, or certainly had no mind to do so; but must indeed have dozed a little. For suddenly there appeared before him the cat which he had once contrived to steal from her. It advanced towards him purring loudly, and wondering in his dream how it had got there, he supposed that he must have brought it with him. What had made him do that?... So he was asking himself in his dream, when he woke with a start. There was of course no cat anywhere to be seen, and he wondered why he should have had so curious a dream.

The Princess felt that something terrible had befallen her; and yet, so sudden had it all been, she could scarcely believe that anything had happened at all. "This was in our destinies," he whispered. "Surely you too will admit that it could not but come," and he began to tell her about the evening of the football match, and how he had seen her through the gap in her ill-fastened curtains, thanks partly to the plunging and tugging of the runaway cat.

So he *had* seen her—everyone had seen her on that unfortunate night! But what happened then was a small disgrace indeed compared with what had followed as the direct consequence of that unguarded moment. How should she ever face Genji again? So she asked herself, and burst into agonized tears—the tears of a child that is at the same time sorry and afraid. Tenderly, almost respectfully he helped her to wipe those tears away. It was growing light, and Kashiwagi, whose one thought for months past had been how to get into her rooms, was now face to face with the much more difficult problem of how to escape from them. However, he was determined not to go till he had obtained from her some sign that she did not altogether detest him. "All this time you have hardly spoken a word," he said. "Do say something—no matter how unkind—that I may not go away from you forever without even knowing the sound of your voice. For, having shown so plainly that I am distasteful to you, you need not fear that I shall ever trouble you again."

In vain he entreated her. She was far too scared and penitent to utter a single syllable. "You need not think that by prolonging your silence you will reduce me to any greater pitch of misery," he said at last. "More downcast than I am at this minute no human being could ever be." Still she remained mute, and maddened by her obstinacy, he burst out: "I see it is no use. Well, that decides matters for me. This is my last night on earth. It was the thought of you that alone gave life any value in my eyes, and now that I must think of you no more... But stay, are you so heartless that, knowing I have scarce an hour to live, you grudge me the gift of one kind word to take with me as my prize to the grave?" So saying he picked her up in his arms and carried her back to the outer room. The door by which he had entered last night was still open. Why did he not leave her? She watched him with consternation. Surely he did not intend to wait till some fresh harm was done? The house was still quite dark. But midnight must by now be long past; and thinking that out of doors there might already be a little light, he gently raised the shutter, and turning round caught (as he had hoped to) a clearer view of her form and face.

"I cannot think, I cannot move," he cried, looking at her desperately. "If you wish me to recover my senses, to be calm, to leave you, let me hear you say one word. Speak, though it be only in pity..." Never had she seen anyone behave like this; what could it matter to him whether she spoke or not? At this point, however, she did try to say something; but so violently was she trembling that the words turned into meaningless jangle of sound. The room was growing lighter every moment. "Listen!" he said excitedly, "I had a wonderful dream last night. I know what it means and wanted to tell you, but how could I, when I found you hated me so? Well, you shall not hear it. But time will show me whether I read it right or no." He stumbled towards the door.

It was early summer, but never had autumn sky looked to him colder and sadder than that which now met his eyes. "So dim to me the dawning world, I know not whither I go; nor whence I came, save that the place was dank with showers of dew." Such was his parting poem, and as he spoke it he held up the sleeve with which he had wiped her tears. Now that he was really going she plucked up heart a little, and managed in a faint voice to murmur the reply: "Would that with the shadows of this dawn my grief might vanish, and of last night no token but a dream be left behind." Her soft, half-childish voice was echoing in his ears as he left the room, and for the first time in his life he knew that it was no mere phrase when the poet said: "Though the body move, the soul may stay behind."

Instead of going home he went to his father's house, slipping in quietly without being seen. He lay down and tried to sleep, but did not succeed. That dream... It was, as a matter of fact, very unlikely that it could signify what it is generally supposed to,* and looking back in detail upon all that had happened he felt that there was no need to worry. He even, with a certain pleasure, recalled the details of his dream. But whether his dreaming of a cat really signified anything or no, he had committed what the world would consider a terrible crime. For many days afterwards he was haunted by a shame and fear that made it impossible for him to set foot outside his own door. These feelings indeed were gradually assuming an intensity quite out of proportion (as Kashiwagi kept telling himself) to the magnitude of his offence. No doubt he had behaved indiscreetly, and should the meeting have certain consequences the girl might conceivably find herself in an embarrassing position. But that was only a remote chance, and in all probability no harm of any kind had been done. Why was it that such a weight of shame and contrition had settled upon him? If he had seduced the Empress herself and his crime were already known, he could not have been in a greater panic—a state of mind all the more unreasonable since he was convinced that no punishment, not even death itself, could be more terrible than the torture that he was now enduring.

Long before Nyosan could possibly have shown any outward sign such as might betray her, he began to fancy that Genji was looking at him with a peculiar expression, and those supposedly accusing eyes filled him with terror and shame.

There is in many highborn women an abundance of natural appetite that the good manners instilled into them from childhood render invisible to the common eye. But upon the mildest provocation this tendency will manifest itself in the most surprising ways. With Nyosan, however, this was not the case. Her innocence was every bit as great as it seemed. The experiences of that fatal night had left in her mind no impression but that of the most abject terror. She could not convince herself that all was safely over, that no one had betrayed them, and hardly daring to appear even among her own people she spent week after week in the darkness of the back room. She felt that something had gone wrong with her, and at last, unaided by any outside person, she realized what was amiss.

Genji heard that she was indisposed and hurried round in alarm to the New Palace. Had a fresh burden now been added to the already

---

* Dreaming of a cat signifies that a child will be born.

unbearable load of his anxiety? He was glad to find her, to all appearances, uncommonly well. All he noticed was that she looked very much ashamed of herself and persistently refused to meet his gaze. No doubt she was cross with him for having left her so long to her own devices, and in order that she might better understand how he had come thus to neglect her, he began describing Murasaki's illness. "I do not think she can last much longer now," he said after a while, "and you may be certain that you will never find yourself neglected like this again. But Murasaki has been with me since she was a child, she has become an inseparable part of my life, and you will guess, I am sure, that during these last weeks I have been in no condition to think or speak of anything else. I am sure you are not so unreasonable as to be cross with me..." He was gone again. Evidently her people had not told him the nature of her malady. But in the long run he would have to know, and as soon as she was alone Nyosan burst into a flood of tears.

So seldom did Genji now visit the New Palace that he had much to do there and did not intend to return immediately. He was wondering uneasily what condition affairs would be in when he got back to the Nijo-in. Suddenly a messenger arrived announcing that Murasaki appeared to be sinking fast. In a moment all else was forgotten, and with darkness closing about his heart he rushed round to his old palace. It seemed to take an interminable time to get there. At last, coming into view of the house, he saw that something terrible must indeed have happened, for the whole space between the main building and the highway was filled with a surging throng of people, while from within came a continual sound of weeping.

Not looking to right or left, he tore towards her apartments, where he was met by one of her maids. "All day she had seemed much better," said the lady. "This faintness came upon her quite suddenly." Within, all was weeping and confusion. Many of those that had served her longest, frantic with grief, were calling upon death not to leave them behind; while such of the priests and miracle-workers whose duty for the day was over were noisily dismantling their altars and making ready to depart. There was nothing unusual in this; their places would soon be taken by newcomers and the long services of intercession would continue. But to Genji there seemed on this particular day to be an air of finality in the methodical clatter of their departure. He rushed towards them, sharply bidding them make their exit more quietly. Murasaki was now unconscious, but he was convinced that this was merely a trance, due to "possession" by some evil influence, and so far from allowing the priests to slacken their efforts, he now sent for a number of celebrated miracle-workers from all parts of the land, and bade them preside over a grand service of exorcism. The form of their prayer was that, even though the sick woman's days were numbered, she might in accordance with the Promise of the Immovable One,* be granted a half-year of reprieve. The priests, intent upon their ritual, bent so close over the burnt offering that it seemed as though the smoke was rising not from the altar but from their very heads. The most Genji now hoped for was that she might for a brief spell recover consciousness before she died. The thought that she would perhaps never know him again, that he would never be able to ask her forgiveness for all that he had done amiss, threw him into such a state of agitation and despair as those about him had seldom witnessed, and they felt it was impossible he should survive her loss. Perhaps the sight of so deep a sorrow touched even Buddha's heart; be that as it may, signs of a definite "possession"— the first that had been visible for many months—now became manifest in the patient, and the exorcists were soon able to transfer this possessing spirit to the body of a small boy whom they had brought with them to act as medium. While, through this boy's mouth, the spirit railed against the priests who had forced it to do their bidding, Murasaki gradually regained consciousness, and it was with mingled feelings of joy and horror that he watched on the one hand her slow recovery, and on the other the ravings and contortions of the boy. At last, subdued to reason by the spells and passes of the exorcists, the spirit still speaking through the boy's mouth said quietly: "Let everyone save Prince Genji leave the room. What I must now say, no one else but he must hear. You have plagued me this long time past with your spells and incantations. I do not love you for it, of that you may be sure. And I would here and now take my vengeance on you all; it is not that I lack the power... rather, I have chosen of my own free will to postpone the task; for strange though you may think it, we ghosts love as we loved on earth; and when I saw Prince Genji frantic with grief, shattered by long days of watching and apprehension—when I saw that, did I not leave my work a while, he too would fall beneath my blow— then I was sorry for him; I, that have become a foul and fiendish thing, pitied him as tenderly as any living creature can pity. That is why I have shown myself to you. I did not mean that you should ever know..."

The hair stood upright on the boy-medium's head, while at the same time huge tears trickled down his cheeks. Where had he seen before this strange blending of rage and misery? Yes. Such had been the face of the apparition that had appeared at Aoi's bedside. He was dumbfounded. Nothing then, not death itself, could alter the hideous trend of evil that the passionate agony of those old days had set upon its course. All else was fading, slipping away. But this terrible thing had never changed.

He took the medium by the hand, and leading him to a safe distance from Murasaki's bed, he said: "Give me some proof... Speak of something

---

* Fudo.

that I shall remember, but no one else could possibly know about. Then I shall believe that you are she. But not till then; for fox-spirit and the like often cause great harm by passing themselves off as the spirits of our dead friends, and I must be on my guard." While Genji spoke thus, the medium was shaken by violent sobbing. At last a voice sounded amid the sobs, and though distorted by anguish, it was, past all denying, the proud passionate voice of Rokujo: "You know me well enough; for changed though I may be, I still remember what it means when you put on that stupid, innocent air. You at least are what you always were—heartless, dishonest..." Again the voice was choked by sobs. He was filled with pity, but, at the same time, a kind of repulsion, and made no attempt to reply. Presently the medium spoke again: "Do not think that, even in my most distant wanderings, banished amid the realms of outer space, I have ever for a moment been ignorant of what was passing here on earth. All that in penitence you have done for my daughter, the Empress's sake, is known to me, and I thank you for it. And yet—it is strange—nothing now seems the same to me. She is mine, I have not forgotten her. But do not think that I love her as a living woman loves her child. Nothing, not one thought nor feeling, have I brought with me unaltered into the world of death, save this insensate passion, that even on earth made my own nature loathsome and despicable to me. Rage, jealousy, hatred—they alone cling to my soul and drag it back each moment closer to the earth.

"And do you know what hurt me more than all your cruelty to me when I was alive? It was to hear you entertaining this friend of yours with stories of my "bad temper," my "grievances," my "inordinate jealousy."[*] I should have thought that the dead at least might be spared such insults and lies! A thousand times I have asked myself how you of all men, you with your fine breeding, could speak of me thus to another woman. Bad as I was before, this fresh insult has worked in me a ghastly change. Never before have I done harm to those on earth, but now—Listen! If you think I have any desire to prey upon this woman on the bed, you are wrong. I want to leave her, to leave you all; but if you wish to be rid of me, put an end to all these spells and incantations, that can but keep me at a little distance, and use these mighty miracle-workers and priests, whom you have set like a hedge about you, to pray for my soul's release, for the cancelling of all my sins. Do not think that because for the moment I could stand your dronings and buzzings no longer—your prayers and scripture-readings that beset me like tongues of flame—do not think that I am conquered. Back I shall come and back again, till in your liturgies I hear some word of comfort for my own soul. Say masses for me, read them night and day. Tell my daughter the Empress to pray

---

[*] See above, p. 657.

for me with all her heart; and bid her never for one instant, though she may fall from favor and another be set in her place, never so much as in a dream to let one envious or jealous thought creep into her heart. She has guilt enough on her conscience, having spent many months at Ise,* where the name of the Blessed One may not be spoken."

The medium continued to rave; but this conversation with a ghost was too eerie to be prolonged. Already those who had been asked to retire from the room must be asking themselves what was happening. He readmitted them, had the boy-medium placed in a sealed romo,† and Murasaki carried secretly to a different part of the house.

Somehow or other a rumor got started that Murasaki was dead, and Genji had the painful experience of receiving innumerable letters of condolence. It was the day of the Kamo festival, and among the courtiers returning from the Shrine many jokes were made on the topic of Murasaki's sudden fall and eclipse. Someone said that since she had lost her power to charm the sunlight‡ it was not to be wondered at that the rain should have washed her away. And another: "Prodigies of that kind never last long, and perhaps it is as well for them that they do not. Otherwise they might tend to fare like the cherry-blossom in the proverb.§ Did they not so quickly retire from the scene they would end by getting all the fun into their own hands and spoiling things for everyone else. It is nice to think of that poor little Princess Nyosan coming into her own again. I am sure it was high time..."

Kashiwagi had stayed at home on the previous day, but had found the time hang so heavily on his hands that today he set out for the Festival, taking his brothers with him in the back of the carriage. On the way home they heard the rumor that was being bandied from coach to coach. The brothers were by no means convinced of its truth, and to offer premature condolences would be very embarrassing. But they decided that there could be no harm in paying an ordinary visit, as though in ignorance of what was being said. Their first impression upon arriving at the New Palace was that the end had indeed come. On every side rose the sound of weeping and wailing. No sooner had they entered than Murasaki's father Prince Hyobukyo rushed past them into the house, obviously in a state of frenzied agitation.

Presently Yugiri came out, wiping the tears from his eyes, and Kashiwagi said to him: "Tell us quickly what has happened. We heard very bad news

---

* As it was a Shinto shrine, the rival religion (Buddhism) could not be mentioned there.

† Partly with the idea of securing Murasaki's safety; partly lest the words spoken by Rokujo through the boy's mouth should be overheard.

‡ A pun on Genji's name Hikaru, "The Shining One."

§ "If it were in our power to keep the cherry-blossom on the tree, we should cease so much to admire it."

on the road, but were loath to believe it, and have come, as we intended to do in any case, merely to enquire... We hoped for some improvement. This has been going on for so long..." "She has indeed been in a very serious condition for some weeks past," said Yugiri. "Finally, early this morning, she lost consciousness altogether. However, at this point the presence of a 'possession' became obvious, and when this had been dealt with, she came to, and is now, I hear, considered not to be in any immediate danger. Of course, this is a great relief to us all. But I am afraid there is not really much hope..." It was obvious that he was deeply moved. He must have been crying a great deal, for his eyes were quite swollen. "Why should he mind so much?" Kashiwagi asked himself, remembering that Yugiri had been brought up by his mother's family, and had, ostensibly at any rate, always been kept at a distance from his stepmother. And at once, suspecting others (as we always do) of harboring the same guilty secrets as ourselves, he began imagining that Yugiri not Genji had been the partner of Murasaki's great romance.

A message now came from Genji asking the visitors to excuse him from appearing in person. "You will forgive me, I know," he said, "when I tell you that we have all been taking part in what had every appearance of being an actual death-scene. Our gentlewomen have not yet had time to recover their composure, and I myself am still, I confess, far too agitated to receive you properly. I hope you will do me the honor of repeating your visit at some time when I am better able to appreciate it." The mere mention of Genji's name filled Kashiwagi with shame and embarrassment; he for his part was glad it was upon so distracted an occasion that he had come to the house. As for repeating the experiment, the others might come if they chose, but he most assuredly would not be with them.

Meanwhile Murasaki remained conscious; but the services of intercession were continued, and to them Genji added secret masses for the release of Rokujo's soul. And he had reason enough of every kind to hope ardently that these would be successful. Even during her lifetime he had experienced in fashion sinister enough the evil potency of her rage; and now that she was in another world, changed into a thing devoid of all human pity or compunction, it was hideous to think that her malice towards him was still unappeased. Apparently all that he had done for Akikonomu was useless! But what was the good of trying to please women? If they were not fundamentally evil, they would not have been born as women at all.[*] Perhaps he ought not to have spoken of her to Murasaki. But he remembered the occasion perfectly well; it was the night before Murasaki's illness began, and really he had not said anything very bad... It was difficult enough to satisfy the living; but existence was intol-

---

[*] A Buddhist doctrine.

erable if even one's most intimate conversations might at any moment let loose the vindictive fury of the dead.

Murasaki still longed to receive the tonsure, and thinking that the ceremony might help her to rally a little, Genji at last consented. Her reception into the Order was more a semblance than a reality, for no attempt was made to do more than cut away a lock or two from the crown of her head, and only five of the Ten Vows were administered. During the whole ceremony Genji, regardless of convention, sat by her side, and with tears in his eyes helped her to repeat her responses.

The fifth month was now closing, and the weather was exceedingly hot. She began again to have frequent fainting-fits, and grew much weaker. But though her mind often wandered, she was perfectly well aware of the tense anxiety with which Genji watched her progress. She had herself no desire or hope of recovery, and if she now occasionally forced herself into a sitting posture or managed to swallow a little broth, it was that Genji might feel her to be still a living creature, rather than (as she knew, herself to be) a strangely lingering ghost. At the beginning of the sixth month she astonished and delighted him by even looking about her a little. But he was still in great alarm, and did not once succeed in getting across to the New Palace.

Nyosan's condition was now quite definitely established; but she was not by any means in bad health. Indeed, save for the fact that her complexion was rather sallow and her appetite not so good as usual, she had not much to complain of. Kashiwagi had not been able to restrain himself from several times repeating his visit, but the girl had made it abundantly plain that she would much rather he left her in peace. The truth was that Kashiwagi had made no such impression upon her as could outweigh her fear of getting into trouble with Genji. True, her lover was one of the handsomest and most talented figures at Court, and many a girl's head would have been completely turned by his advances; but to Nyosan, used as she was to Genji's far more striking looks and personality, this young man seemed almost insipid in character, no more than passable in appearance, and (Palace Counselor though he was) none the more impressive on that account to one whose upbringing had been such as hers.

Her old nurse and gentlewoman had, of course, long ago discovered the condition she was in. "Do you remember exactly when it was that His Highness was last here?" one of them said. "It seems to me as though it were a very long time ago." They felt rather uneasy about the matter, but thought it their duty to inform Genji. He at once came round to the New Palace.

It was as a matter of fact (Genji remembered this quite clearly) more than a year... Surely there must be some mistake? He said nothing to her about the reason of his visit. She did, he thought, perhaps look a trifle out of sorts, and he treated her with every mark of tenderness and concern. Really, she was a charming girl. Now that, after being so many times obliged to postpone his visit, he had at last managed to get here, he ought to stay for a night or two. And so he did; but he was all the while in such a state of anxiety about Murasaki that he could think of nothing else, and spent most of the time in writing messages to her. "That's good!" said one of Nyosan's ladies indignantly. "He saves up all his letter-writing till he comes here. We appreciate the compliment, I am sure!" Kojiju for her part only wished that Kashiwagi took a like view of Genji's visit. No sooner did the young man hear of it than he fell into a state of violent agitation and began pouring in upon Nyosan a stream of letters, couched in the most hectic terms of jealousy and desperation—all of which it fell to Kojiju's lot to deliver.

"Don't show me these tiresome things," said Nyosan, when Kojiju, seeing Genji go to fetch something from Murasaki's old rooms, hastily produced one of these frenzied epistles. "I do wish you would just read what he says here in the margin," Kojiju pleaded. "I am sure you would feel sorry for him..." So saying, she unfolded the letter and had just placed it in Nyosan's hands, when there was a noise of footsteps. A sudden panic descending upon her, Kojiju glided from the room. There was no time to destroy the letter or lock it up in a safe place. Her heart beating wildly, Nyosan stuffed it under the mattress of the couch upon which she lay.

Next morning he rose early, wanting to go back to the Nijo-in before the sun became unpleasantly strong. "Where is that fan I had yesterday?" he asked his servant. "This one is no good at all. I think I must have left it where I was sitting with the Princess yesterday evening. I had better go and look." Having hunted high and low, he went towards the couch where Nyosan had lain, and suddenly noticed that a piece of light blue paper was sticking out from under her mattress, which was pushed slightly out of place. Without paying any particular attention to what he was doing, he pulled out this piece of paper, and glancing at it, saw that it was covered with writing in a man's hand. He noticed too that it was heavily scented, and in every way as elegantly devised as a note could possibly be. Moreover, oddly enough he knew the writing (of which there was plenty, for it covered both sides of a double sheet). There could be no mistake. This was Kashiwagi's hand. His servant, who had brought a mirror into the room and now began to do his master's hair, was not in any way surprised to see him take possession of the note, for he supposed it to be one that Genji and Nyosan had been reading together, on the day before. But Kojiju, who was also present, was startled to observe that it was of the same color as the letter she had herself delivered. While serving Genji's breakfast she never for an instant took her eye off this blue letter, that lay folded beside his bowl. Of course, it could not be the same.

Lots of people wrote on paper like that. The mere fact that it had been left lying about showed that it must be something quite different. The Princess would never have been so mad...

Meanwhile Nyosan was quietly sleeping. What a feather-hearted little creature she was. He had always suspected that expressions of feeling conveyed nothing to her mind whatever; and from the way in which she left such a letter as this (for he had already cast an eye over it) lying where anyone might find it, he was convinced that its contents had no meaning for her at all. It was fortunate indeed that it was he who had found it, and not some outside person, upon whom the fact that she was receiving such letters would make a wholly erroneous impression.

"What did you do with that note I brought yesterday?" Kojiju said, when Genji left the room. "I saw His Highness looking just now at a letter that looked very much like it." Nyosan immediately remembered only too well what she had done with it. "Where did you put it?" went on Kojiju, seeing that her eyes had suddenly filled with tears. "When we heard someone coming, I thought it might look as though there were a secret between us if I were found alone with you, and to be on the safe side I made off as fast as I could. But as a matter of fact it was some while before His Highness actually entered the room, and I supposed that during this time you would have managed to find somewhere safe to put the letter." "I had only that very moment begun reading it when he came in," she sobbed. "I just stuffed it away anywhere I could; and then I forgot about it..." Helplessly she indicated the place under the mattress. Kojiju went and examined it. "There's nothing there now," she said. "This is an awful business. I would give anything that it should not have happened. It was only the other day that Kashiwagi begged me to make you be more careful. He is terrified of Prince Genji getting wind of this. And now, no sooner do I put a letter in your hands than you leave it just where it was most likely to catch His Highness's eye. However, it is all of a piece with the way you have always carried on. I shouldn't say it, but you have no more idea how to behave than a baby. First of all you leave all your screens in disorder and let him see you. Then you allow him to go on for month after month writing desperate letters to you, and finally drive him to such a pitch of madness that he insists upon being allowed to see you. It was I who arranged it, I own; but I don't mind telling you I would never have dreamed of bringing him, if I had supposed that you could look after yourself no better than you did. Well, I'm sorry for you both!" So she scolded the girl, speaking to her as though she were a person of her own class; for Nyosan was so completely lacking in self-consequence that it was difficult for those about her to remember she was Genji's favorite and the Emperor's sister.

At Kojiju's harsh words she only wept the more. During the course of the day her people noticed that she was in very low spirits and ate nothing at all. "Instead of fussing all the while about Lady Murasaki, who, if she was ever ill at all, is now perfectly recovered, His Highness might give a little more attention to our young lady, who really has got something the matter with her," they said.

As soon as he was alone Genji pulled out the letter and studied it more attentively. He did not now feel so certain that it was written by Kashiwagi. The writing indeed looked to him much more like an attempt to imitate Kashiwagi's hand, and he came to the conclusion that it must be the work of some waiting-woman, who had concocted the letter as a practical joke. But the style did not in the least bear out this supposition. Granted the document was genuine, several facts emerged: the writer had been in love with Nyosan for several years, he had once at any rate obtained access to her, but now something had gone wrong, and the writer of the letter was evidently very ill at ease. All this could have been deduced without difficulty by anyone who saw the letter. Since when (Genji wondered) had people taken to writing in this reckless and inconsiderate manner? For letters are ticklish things; one never knows into whose hands they may fall—as he himself had good reason to remember.[*] But, after all, there are ways of protecting oneself. Never had Genji in his life (or so he now felt convinced) addressed a woman whom he loved in terms so crude, so tactless, so flatly incriminating; and he was filled not so much with anger at Kashiwagi's presumption as contempt for his stupidity.

Genji's thoughts ran on. What must he do with Nyosan? Of course there was no longer any doubt how she came to be in her present condition. The simplest thing would be to go on as if nothing had happened. This, he felt, would have been impossible if the knowledge of their intrigue had come to him from outside. But having made the discovery for himself, he was free to use it as he chose. Yet was he free? He tried to imagine himself visiting her, joking, pretending to know nothing... It was easy enough to decide on such a course, but utterly impossible to carry it out. He knew that when he was merely amusing himself with someone, without really being in love, the discovery that this person was receiving attentions from another man at once made it impossible for him to continue his own mild dalliance. In such cases it galled him that another should receive what he himself had never even claimed. And now Nyosan... No, this was something that he could never forgive. As for Kashiwagi, his conduct had been of an insolence and treachery such as Genji would not have imagined any human being to be capable of. Suddenly it occurred to him that there was a certain resemblance between

---

[*] Cf. Part II, p. 221.

this episode and another, in which he himself had figured. But that was a very different affair. There is something special about an Emperor's concubines. To begin with, many of them hold their position for reasons of State; no personal tie attaches them to their Master, and it is assumed that they are free to seek distraction elsewhere. Then again, the ladies and gentlemen of the Emperor's entourage are through the very nature of their service thrown together in a way peculiar to the Court, and intimacies, such as could not without the gravest scandal be divulged, are constantly springing into existence, to be suspended at a moment's notice if they are in any danger of being observed. Nor in the promiscuous life of the Palace are such shifts and changes, such sudden alliances and dissolutions, likely to attract the slightest attention. But the seduction of Nyosan was an entirely different matter. She, on her side, knew quite well all the circumstances that had induced him to take charge of her, knew that he had expended infinite pains in her education and improvement, had risked on her behalf a breach with the one being to whom his whole heart was drawn. Such ingratitude was unthinkable! That anyone who belonged to him should turn elsewhere for affection—and to a person such as Kashiwagi—was more than he could be expected to endure. And yet, unless he were willing to make himself ridiculous, the alternatives to enduring it were not very obvious.

Suddenly it occurred to Genji to ask himself whether perhaps his father, the Old Emperor, had not been in just the same fix. No doubt he too (though Genji had never before suspected it) knew perfectly well what was going on, and had merely pretended not to see. There was no denying it: that was a disgraceful affair, as indeed he had always known; though all that his father might have suffered through it he had never till this moment guessed.

Murasaki at once saw, when he arrived, that something was on his mind. She thought that he had reluctantly left the New Palace merely out of pity for her, and was worried at being obliged to spend so much time out of Nyosan's company. "You really need not have come back so soon," she said. "I am much better now, while Nyosan, they tell me, is very poorly."

"She looks a little bit out of sorts," he answered. "But there is nothing serious the matter with her, and I do not feel there is any need for me to remain there. But her family makes a great fuss. The Emperor is always sending to enquire after her. A messenger came while I was there today. I do not think he is really worried, but his father* expects it of him, and is always keeping him up to the mark. They both of them have their eye on me, and so I have to be extremely careful." "I don't mind

---

* Suzaku.

what the Emperor thinks," Murasaki replied. "But I should be very sorry indeed if my illness caused Nyosan to think you were neglecting her. And even if she understands, I am so afraid that some of her gentlewomen may make mischief..." "You are evidently far more solicitous concerning Nyosan than I am myself," he said, laughing. "And for your sake I must try to take my responsibilities more seriously. But I fear I shall never succeed in working out what effect my actions may have on her maids and dependants. You may think me heartless, but I confess that if I avoid getting into trouble with the Emperor, I shall be quite satisfied. I am hoping that next time I go to the New Palace you will be able to come with me." "I am afraid that will not be for some while yet," she answered. "Do, I beg of you, go and live there again at once. It would be such a comfort to Nyosan. I will follow when I can." But days passed without his making the move.

Nyosan regarded his absence as a sign that she was in disgrace. True, he had often before deserted her for weeks on end; but in those days she had done nothing bad, and it had therefore not occurred to her that his staying away might be meant as a punishment. She was also terrified lest her father should hear that Genji never came to see her; for she had got it into her head that Suzaku too would at once think she had done something wicked.

The next time Kashiwagi tried to send a letter, Kojiju, rather glad of an opportunity to bring the business to an end, told him flatly what had happened to his last note. Kashiwagi was appalled.

If such an affair as this went on for a considerable time it was almost inevitable (he knew) that some rumor of it should eventually leak out. But there was no reason why any actual proof should exist; and if the parties concerned chose to deny it stoutly enough, people often ended by believing that nothing much had really happened. And here was Nyosan, after the infinite care that he had taken not to arouse the faintest suspicion on any side, leaving under the very nose of the person principally concerned a document of the most incriminating kind. It was the hottest time in the year; but at the receipt of this news he turned so icy cold from head to foot that he veritably thought he would freeze to death. It was not as though Genji had been a stranger (though even then it would have been bad enough, considering his rank and influence). Always, for years past, it had been for Kashiwagi that he had sent whenever either pleasure or business demanded the presence of some chosen friend whom he liked and could trust. And this obvious partiality of Genji for his company had been one of the greatest joys in Kashiwagi's life. There could now be no question of their ever being friends again. That was of course the worst; but the actual and immediate question of how to behave towards Genji for the moment fretted Kashiwagi till he became positively ill.

If he stayed away altogether everyone would want to know the reason, and Genji himself, if by any chance he had failed to be absolutely convinced of Kashiwagi's guilt, would then no longer be in doubt. Beset by continual panic and forebodings he shut himself up indoors. Constantly he assured himself that this overwhelming sense of guilt was put of all proportion to the magnitude of his crime. But he could not get out of his head the idea that by this one act he had forfeited all right to exist.

He felt now that it was madness on his part not to have foreseen what would happen. From the moment she exposed herself on that ill-fated evening of the football match he ought to have known she would prove utterly undependable. No doubt Yugiri, to whom he had certainly betrayed his excitement on the way home that night, had known quite well what was in store for him, should he attempt to carry on a secret intrigue with a creature so completely lacking in the most elementary sense of responsibility or even loyalty (for he could hardly imagine that anyone could merely *forget* to put a note of that kind somewhere out of sight). But though he tried at times to escape from his own sense of guilt by reflections of this kind, he was all the while extremely sorry for Nyosan and fully conscious of the terrible predicament in which he had landed her.

At last Genji visited the New Palace. Of course there could be no question now of his ever again feeling any affection for her; yet, so much sympathy did her obvious wretchedness and terror arouse in him, that he found himself longing to console her, caress her—to pretend, in fact, that everything was the same as before. But this lasted for a very short while. Expenditure on her behalf, solicitude for her comfort—these were easy enough; but when it came to speaking to her in such a manner that those present would not detect any embarrassment or frigidity, then he was hard put to it indeed, and by his own unavailing struggles knew something of what her misery must be. It soon became clear that he did not intend to refer in any way to what had happened; but this, so far from giving Nyosan confidence, seemed only to imprint a more abject look of shame and contrition upon her downcast face. She could not be certain how much he had discovered or what conclusions he had drawn; and to look as though she were being scolded, when precisely the opposite was happening, in itself betrayed her guilt. Such behavior was indeed part and parcel of the same utter childishness that had brought about this whole catastrophe.

Meanwhile the news of Nyosan's condition reached Suzaku in his mountain retreat. He was of course delighted. He knew that during the worst period of Murasaki's illness Genji had for months on end been absent from the New Palace; but this, under the circumstances, was perfectly natural. It appeared that even after her partial recovery Genji had continued to be perhaps unduly nervous of leaving her; and this protracted neglect, for which Nyosan would see no adequate cause, had no doubt tried her patience. Not that in any of her letters she had ever complained. But it was only too likely that some of her people had, in their indiscreet zeal, talked against Genji at Court or in social gatherings elsewhere. Suzaku could only hope that Nyosan had herself done nothing to countenance such gossip. He had lost interest in all other worldly matters; but his affection for his daughter remained as keen as ever. The letter that he now wrote to her happened to arrive on one of the rare occasions when Genji was at the New Palace. "I am afraid it is a long time since you heard from me," he said; "but I always think about you a great deal. As soon as I heard of your condition I put a special supplication on your behalf into my prayers. Please be sure to let me know how you get on. I am afraid that, through no one's fault, you have been left a great deal alone in the last few months. Remember that, even if this should continue, it is no fault of Genji's; and above all things avoid giving him or anyone else the impression that you are in the slightest degree resentful of these long absences."

The position was a very difficult one. Genji had not intended ever to speak to Suzaku of what had happened. But sooner or later the girl's father would see that Murasaki's illness was quite unconnected with the present estrangement. Unless he were told the truth Suzaku would think that Genji had broken all his promises in the cruelest and most treacherous manner. "How are you going to reply?" he said, turning to Nyosan. "I wonder who told him that I was neglecting you? If we are nowadays on rather distant terms, it is certainly through no fault of mine." Blushing deeply, she turned away her head. "I think what most bothers your father," he continued, "is the knowledge that you are so childish and entirely unable to look after yourself. You must try in future to show him that he need no longer worry about you on that account. I had not meant to tell him about this business. But it is clearly impossible that you and I should be on the same terms as before; and if he is going to interpret this change as a dereliction on my part, I should be obliged to explain matters to him. I had not meant to discuss this even with you; but while we are on the subject, I may as well say that if you have found someone who can make you happier than I do, by all means go to him... I think that from your own point of view you are behaving very imprudently; but whether that is so, events will prove.

"It does not in the least surprise me that you should feel as you do. For one thing, novelties are inevitably more interesting, and you have known me since you were a child. But the real trouble is that I am too old for you. It is true. I am hideously old. Indeed, what in the world could be more natural than that an infant like you should desire to escape from me? I only make one condition. So long as your father is alive we must keep up the pretence, tiresome old person though you may find me, that I am still your husband. Afterwards you may do as you like. But I cannot bear that Suzaku should know what has in reality been the end of this wonderful marriage of ours, upon which he built all his hopes. It is not at all likely that he will live much longer. If you do not wish to add to his sufferings, please let us for the present have no more episodes of this kind."

But as he said the words he caught in his own voice a familiar intonation. How often, years ago, those responsible for his upbringing had adopted just this tone, and how dreary, how contemptible he had thought their self-righteous homilies. "Boring old man!" That was what she must be thinking, and in sudden shame he relapsed into a complete silence, during which he drew her writing-case towards him, carefully mixed the ink and arranged the paper. But Nyosan was by now sobbing bitterly, and her hand shook so much that at first she was unable to write. How very differently must her pen have flowed, Genji mused, when she sat down to answer the letter he had found under her cushion! But now, even when her hand ceased to tremble, she was quite unable to frame her sentences, and he was obliged to dictate the whole letter.

The celebration of Suzaku's fiftieth birthday, again and again deferred, had now been fixed for the middle of the twelfth month. Arrangements for the dancing and music were already in active progress at the New Palace, and Murasaki, who had meant to put off her return some time longer, suddenly took it into her head that all this bustle would help to distract her from her sufferings. She was accordingly moved into her old apartments without further delay. The Akashi Princess was also in residence at the New Palace, with her little boy, Niou, and her second child, also a boy. They were both delightful children, and it was a great pleasure to have them in the house. Genji, who had not taken at first kindly to the idea of being a grandfather, now played with them for hours on end.

Kashiwagi was of course invited to the rehearsal. He knew that if he stayed at home on such an occasion he would feel extremely bored and miserable; moreover his absence would be remarked upon by everyone and might arouse unwelcome suspicions. But when the invitation arrived he wrote that he was to ill to come. Genji was certain that only a very serious and definite illness would have kept him away upon such an occasion, and wrote again, begging him to accept. His father To no Chujo pointed out that Genji would certainly be offended. "Everyone knows that there is nothing serious the matter with you," he said, "and on musical occasions of this kind your help is very much needed." Finally Kashiwagi promised to go. He arrived before the other princes and courtiers who were expected, and was at once admitted behind Genji's screens-of-state. He did indeed not look at all well. He was thin, pale, utterly lacking in the buoyancy and high spirits that were the common possession of his family. He wore a thoughtful, serious air, like one who is over-conscious of his responsibilities. Just the kind of person, thought Genji, whom one would hit upon to put in charge of a flighty young princess. Probably they were very well suited to one another, and if only such an arrangement had been thought of before... Indeed it was not so much what had happened, as the way in which it had taken place, that he would never be able to forgive. If only either of them had behaved with the slightest consideration...

But he spoke to Kashiwagi without a trace of coldness or disapproval. "What a long time it is since we last met!" he said. "And there has really been no particular reason. I have, of course, a great deal of illness in the home. Things are better; but the arrangements connected with Suzaku's birthday have kept me very busy, and I have also been obliged to have services read on behalf of his daughter, who, as you know, is now living here with me. Suzaku has taken his vows, and it would be unseemly to celebrate his birthday with the same festivities that we should use were he a layman. But it so happens that there are at present in my house a number of young boys, and I know that it would give Suzaku great pleasure if I trained them to do a few dances in his honor on the day of the celebration. There is no one who can be so useful to me in this matter as yourself, and I am very grateful to you for having forgiven my long neglect and thus hurried to assist me." While these words were being spoken Kashiwagi felt his color continually come and go. It was some time before he could master his feelings sufficiently to reply. At last he said: "I was very sorry to hear of all your troubles. Since the spring I myself have been very unwell. I think it is really an attack of beriberi. I have often been almost unable to walk. It is months since I got even so far as the Palace, and I feel as though I had been utterly shut off from the world. No one owes more to Suzaku than I do; but I am afraid that, had not my father reminded me, I should have entirely forgotten about his fiftieth birthday. If you will forgive my suggesting it, I do not think that a very elaborate ceremony would be at all to Suzaku's taste. When the deputation visits him, a few unambitious songs and dances, with plenty of time afterwards for quiet conversation with his guests—that, I think, is what would give him most pleasure." "I entirely agree with you," answered Genji. "Of course, we must not cut things down so much as to seem disrespectful; but if you are in charge I shall have no anxiety on that score. Yugiri is now thoroughly competent as regards public ceremonies and the like; but he has never understood much about art. Suzaku is so good a critic in all such matters, particularly as regards music and dancing, that what little we do must at all costs be done properly. That is why I want you to help Yugiri in arranging the little boys' dances.

The professional dancing-masters are hopeless. Each of them has his own set of tricks, and nothing can persuade him to vary them."

It would have been impossible for anyone to speak more kindly than Genji had just spoken; but Kashiwagi, though fully sensible of this fact, still felt as uncomfortable as when he first entered the room. Once this business about the rehearsal had been settled, there seemed nothing else to talk about, and after a few unsuccessful attempts to begin their usual sort of conversation, Kashiwagi quietly withdrew.

The rehearsal took place in the Music Room that opened out of the Fishing Pavilion, the dancers appearing at the foot of a high mound. There was a thin sprinkling of snow upon the ground; but the air had in it a softness which suggested that spring was camping somewhere close at hand, and already the orchards were whitening with the first faint tinge of bloom.

As the day wore on, the scene grew somewhat riotous. Everyone drank heavily, and the older men, at the sight of their grandchildren's performance (which was indeed a very pretty one, the dancers all being of minute size), tended to become rather maudlin. "All right, Kashiwagi; don't look so contemptuous!" Genji shouted across to him. "Just wait a few years, and you'll find a little wine will make your tears flow quite as fast as ours!" Kashiwagi made no reply, and Genji, looking at him more attentively, saw that he was not only (alone among the whole company) entirely sober, but also extremely depressed. Surely, thought Kashiwagi, everyone can see that I am far too ill to take part in such a scene as this. How inconsiderate of Genji (who was certainly not nearly so drunk as he pretended) to call attention to him by shouting across the room in that way! No doubt it was meant as a joke; but Kashiwagi found it quite impossible to be amused. He had a violent headache, and each time the flagon came round he merely pretended to drink out of it. Genji presently noticed this, and sending it back, pressed him again and again to take his share.

At last he could endure the banquet no longer, and though the proceedings showed no signs whatever of coming to a close, he dragged himself to his feet and left the room. He had such difficulty in walking that he at first imagined he must have drunk far more than he intended. But this explanation would not hold, for he could clearly recollect all that had happened, and was quite certain that he had not taken enough to cause any such effect as this. He definitely connected his present sensations with the strain of appearing in Genji's presence. But embarrassing though the ordeal had been, it would scarcely account for the fact that he was in his present state of complete collapse.

It soon became apparent that his was ho mere migraine or surfeit, but the beginning of a desperate malady. His mother proposed to remove him to his father's house, where she thought he could be better looked after. Kashiwagi knew that such a step would be extremely painful to his wife Princess Ochiba, who had for months past endured his complete neglect of her with exemplary patience, always hoping that he would in the end recover from his present disastrous infatuation. The assumption that now, at the onset of a serious illness, she was not the proper person to take charge of him, would seem (as Kashiwagi was well aware) to mark the end of their brief and unhappy relationship. Ochiba's mother was also present. "They ought never to have suggested such a thing," she said indignantly. "Under no possible circumstances have the parents any right to separate a man from his wife. Even if Kashiwagi only stays there till he recovers, the separation will be a most painful one for my daughter. She is perfectly capable of looking after him, and I can see no reason why he should not remain here, at any rate until it is proved that he is not making sufficient progress." Kashiwagi heard all this, and he felt that she was right. "I knew from the first," he said to Ochiba's mother, "that as regards birth I was hopelessly inferior to the Princess. But I hoped as time went on to climb high enough in the Government to compensate for this inequality. However, since this terrible illness came upon me I have lost all hope of justifying myself in that way, and all I care about now is that she should not feel I have been altogether unkind to her. Shall I have time ever to do so much as that? Who knows? In any case, I have no desire to move..." The upshot was that for the present he stayed in his own house. But his mother could not believe he was being properly looked after. "I am very sad about Kashiwagi," she said. "He does not any longer care to have me with him. In old days, if he was the least bit unwell or out of spirits, I would always leave my other children and come to look after him. And he liked me to be there; I know he did..." She went to her son's house and made another attempt to bring him away. This time he relented. It was quite true that his mother had been fonder of him than of the rest. Perhaps it was only because he was her first child. But be that as it may, her devotion to him both in the past and since his marriage had been such that he felt it would be cruel to the point of wickedness not to let her take him to a place where she could during those last days be always at his side. He said to Ochiba: "Do not worry about me. As soon as I am any worse I will let you know, and you can come round quietly to my father's house. Forgive me for having treated you as I have done. I cannot understand now how I came to behave so foolishly. If only I had known that I had so short a time ahead of me..." Weeping bitterly, he was carried to his father's house; Ochiba remained behind, in a state of unspeakable agitation and suspense. The arrival of Kashiwagi in this condition was a great shock to his father To no Chujo. But he reflected that the illness was not so sudden as people were making out. He had noticed for months that the boy was hardly eating anything, often taking no more than a paltry orange, and sometimes refusing even that. Under such circumstances he could not fail to lose his strength.

The sudden collapse of so well known and talented a figure provoked in all quarters the liveliest regret. Everyone at Court came to enquire after his progress; the Emperor and Suzaku both sent frequent messengers, while the grief of his parents need not be described. Genji too was very much upset, sent constant messages of enquiry, and wrote several letters of encouragement and sympathy to To no Chujo. Above all, Yugiri, who had been his closest friend, was in great distress, and now spent most of his time at Kashiwagi's bedside.

The celebration of Suzaku's birthday was fixed for the twenty-fifth of the twelfth month. The serious illness of so prominent a person, casting a gloom not only over his own family, but also over so great a part of the higher circles at Court, made the time chosen a singularly unfortunate one. But the affair had for so long been postponed from month to month, that to defer it on account of an illness that might go on indefinitely was out of the question. Moreover, Nyosan, who had already spent much time in planning the arrangements, would (he thought) be grievously disappointed. The ceremony accordingly took place on the appointed day; prayers were said in the usual fifty temples, and in Suzaku's own retreat the Scripture of the Great Sun Buddha[*] was solemnly recited.

---

[*] In Sanskrit, Maha-vairocana; in Japanese, Dainichi. The chief Buddha of the Mystical (Tantric) Sect.

Kashiwagi

The New Year brought with it no change in Kashiwagi's condition. A fatal issue seemed certain, and on his own account he had not the slightest wish to avoid it. If indeed from time to time he seemed to be struggling against his fate, it was because he dared not reveal to his parents how little he dreaded a separation, the prospect of which manifestly caused them so bitter an affliction.

From his early childhood the one thing that he had never been able to endure was the feeling of inferiority. In small things and great it had always been the same: if he could not gain the prize, win the game, receive the highest appointment, he at once conceived the profoundest contempt for himself and felt his whole life to be utterly useless. And now, when things had indeed gone far more wrong with him than ever before, this feeling of self-contempt was so overwhelming that all thought of his earthly existence became intolerable to him. He would have been happiest had it been possible to end his days in some country temple; but he knew only too well that his parents' distress at such a step would be continually present in his mind, and utterly destroy the peace which such a place would otherwise afford. Supposing he did after all recover from this illness? Worse than the general scandal and discredit, worse than the spectacle of Nyosan's misery and disgrace, would be the knowledge that Genji no longer respected him. They had been friends for so long, were bound together by so many ties of common recollection and experience; and only in this one matter had he ever betrayed this friendship. He knew that when he was dead, nay, so soon as it was apparent that he was dying, his final act of treachery would be forgotten, and the long years of their intimacy be cherished and remembered. So sure was he of this that it made the prospect of death doubly welcome to him.

One day, being left alone for a little while, he wrote a letter to Nyosan, in which he said: "I imagine you heard that I had fallen dangerously ill. You have, since then, shown no sign of wanting to know what has become of me. Perhaps that is quite natural under the circumstances, but it makes me sad to feel..." His hand trembled so much that he could not write all he meant to, and closed suddenly with the poem: "Even amid the smoke that hangs above my smoldering pyre shall burst into new brightness the unquenchable glitter of my love." "Give me one kind word," he added, "to light my steps through the darkness that my own folly has cast about the path where I must walk." This he sent by the hand of Kojiju along with many last messages and injunctions. The servant-girl, though she was well enough used to being employed on these errands (for the affair had begun when she was a mere child), had since Kashiwagi's abuse of her good offices been in a state of violent indignation against him. But now, hearing such phrases as "for the last time" and "never again," she at once lapsed into tears, and when she delivered the letter, besought Nyosan to answer it while there was still time. "I am sorry that he is ill," said Nyosan; "but I am far too wretched now all day long to feel very differently because this thing or that has gone wrong. Kashiwagi has made enough mischief already, and I am not going to make more by being caught in correspondence with him." Such resolutions on her part were never the result of firmness, but rather of fear that Genji, who had still only referred in vague terms to her escapade, might again find it necessary to speak to her upon this shameful subject—a prospect that filled her with the utmost misery and dismay. But Kojiju began quietly preparing the Princess's writing things, and presently, with many hesitations, she produced an answer, which Kojiju under cover of night managed to convey secretly to To no Chujo's house.

The quiet of Kashiwagi's apartments now began to be rudely disturbed; for To no Chujo, still desperately clinging to the hope that his son's life could be saved, was continually bringing to the bedside some new miracle-worker or healer. Ascetics from Mount Katsuragi, famous clerics from the great temples and priests from obscure village shrines, holy men of every rank and description filled the house. Among the magic-workers whom, at their father's bidding, Kobai* and the rest brought back from the hills, were some Yamabushi† of the most repulsive and ferocious aspect; nor were the priests from nearer at hand much less uncouth in appearance, as with wildly rolling eye and harsh voice they intoned their Sanskrit spells. The soothsayers and diviners were for the most part agreed that the evil influence at work upon the sick man was of a feminine kind. But they did not succeed in detecting any actual "possession," and it was in the hope of finding someone who could dislodge this mysterious influence that To no Chujo had collected this motley crowd of clerics and healers. "How I hate this noise!" cried Kashiwagi at last. "It may be because of my sins—I do not know—but so far from giving me any comfort this jangle of holy words dismays me, and I feel I should live longer were it utterly to cease." So saying, he dragged himself into the inner room. His real object was to meet Kojiju, but to To no Chujo it was given out that Kashiwagi was asleep. Chujo was no longer young; but he was still for

---

* Younger brother of Kashiwagi.
† Mountain ascetics.

the most part very lively and amusing in his conversation. To see him now solemnly and endlessly discussing Kashiwagi's symptoms with these grim practicants was a strange and saddening spectacle. Listening from the inner-room Kashiwagi overheard him saying: "I am convinced there is a definite 'possession,' and I implore you not to rest till you have detected it." "What is that he is saying?" said Kashiwagi to Kojiju. "I suppose the soothsayers have discovered that it is a female influence; for I am sure my father still knows nothing of the real story. Well, if indeed her spirit clings to mine I am proud to die from such a cause. But as for my offence itself, we make too much of it. Such things have happened often enough in the past, and will happen again. What makes me glad to die is not remorse for my guilt, but a strange terror that comes over me when I think that Prince Genji knows my secret. In some way it is his glamor, his dazzling ascendancy that, after what has happened, make life impossible for me. From the moment I met his gaze on the night of the music-practice some sudden cleavage took place in my soul, and its brighter element floated away from me, far off, perhaps to her side, leaving only the dull dross behind. Kojiju, should you find a soul at large in the New Palace, bind it fast to your girdle and bring it back to me." He was now very weak, and said this half-laughing, half-crying. Kojiju then told him Nyosan had received his message. Her shame, her contrition, her downcast gaze, and sunken cheeks—all appeared so vividly before him that he did indeed feel as though, at the mere mention of her name, his soul was torn from him and drawn irresistibly to her side. "So soon as I have heard that she has passed safely through her present danger," Kashiwagi continued, "I shall be ready to depart. You remember that dream I had—of a cat following me into the room? I never consulted anyone about it, but in my heart of hearts I always knew what it foretold." The intensity of his passion, which seemed, while he lay here inactive, continually to gather fresh depth and concentration, struck Kojiju usually as something morbid and terrifying. But now she could not withhold her sympathy and began weeping bitterly. Kashiwagi now sent her to fetch a paper candle and by its light examined Nyosan's reply. Her hand was still unformed, but was beginning to have certain good points in it. "Do not suppose," she wrote, "that I have all this while been indifferent to your sufferings. But was it easy for me to express my sympathy? Put yourself for a moment into my position. As for your poem, 'May the smoke of my ashes mingle with the flame of your pyre, for to evade the torment of condemning thoughts my need is as great as yours.'" Never had she addressed him in such a tone; this at least was something to carry into the other world. His reply looked much as though birds with wet feet had walked over the paper; for he wrote it lying on his back, and the ill-guided pen strayed weakly in every direction. "Though naught of me remains save smoke drawn out across the windless sky, yet shall I drift to thee unerringly amid the trackless fields of space."

That evening Nyosan was much indisposed, and the more experienced among her gentlewomen at once recognized that her delivery was at hand. They sent hastily for Genji, who, as he made his way to the New Palace, could not help reflecting how happy and excited this news would have made him, if only the child had indisputably been his. As it was, he must show not only the elation but all the solicitude of an expectant father. Services of intercession must be ordered, priests and miracle-workers summoned to the Palace, spells and incantations set at work. Her travail lasted all night. At the first ray of morning sunlight a child was born. It was hard indeed for Genji to receive this news, and to be told too that the child was a boy, with all the paternal pride and thankfulness that the occasion (if he were not to betray his secret) so urgently demanded. As things were, he was certainly glad that it was a boy; for with a girl's upbringing he would have been expected to take much more trouble, whereas a boy can be left to his own devices. But should the child, when it grew up, show a striking resemblance to Kashiwagi, this would be far more likely to attract notice in a boy than in a girl. With how strange an appropriateness he had been punished for the crime* that never ceased to haunt his conscience! The only consolation was that sins for which we are punished in this world are said to weigh less heavily against us in the life to come. In point of fact he did for the child all that those who believed it to be his own could possibly expect of him. The Birth Room was fitted out with the utmost prodigality and splendor, and the usual trays, magic boxes,† and cake-stands poured in from every side, the donors vying with one another in the elegance and ingenuity of the designs with which these customary gifts were adorned. On the night of the fifth day there arrived from the ex-Empress Akikonomu a present of delicacies for the young mother, and gifts for each of her ladies chosen according to their rank and standing, the presentation of which was carried out in the most formal and imposing manner. On the seventh night the Emperor's presents arrived and were delivered by his State messengers with all the solemnity of a public occasion. To no Chujo was anxious to show his good will towards Genji upon what appeared to be so auspicious an occasion; but owing to Kashiwagi's alarming condition he was unable to appear in person. However, the callers included almost every other figure of importance whether at the Palace or in the Government. It may be imagined, however, that all these ceremonies, in which to outward appearances Genji was intimately concerned, gave him in reality nothing but

---

* His relations with his father's mistress, Fujitsubo.
† Sets of boxes fitting one into the other.

awkwardness and discomfort. There was even talk of a grand feast and concert; but with these he managed to dispense.

Nyosan was completely shattered by the ordeal through which she had just passed, the alarming experience of a first childbirth having come upon her at a time when she was already in a very enfeebled and morbid condition. She would not take even so much as a cup of broth; the presence of the child only served to remind her of her disaster, and she heartily wished that she might never recover. Genji did what he could to give those about him the impression that he took an interest in the child; but days passed without his ever asking to see it, and this one fact was enough to set the older nurses gossiping: "You'd think he would show more feeling than that," they said. "Such a lovely child as Madam has given him, and he never chooses so much as to set eyes on it!" These remarks were overheard by Nyosan. This, she felt, was only a foretaste of the attitude that he was about to take up towards herself and the child. Under such circumstances life at the Palace would not, she well knew, be endurable; and she determined so soon as she was strong enough to enter a nunnery.

He did not spend the night in her apartments, but every morning he looked in to see how she was getting on. "I am sorry I have spent so little time with you," he said. "The truth is, I have lately been much absorbed in various penances and devotions. I feel that I have not much time left in which to make ready for the life to come—and in any case there was no use in visiting you when all the ceremonies, with their attendant bustle and disturbance, were going on in your part of the house. But I am very anxious to know how you are. Do you feel quite strong again?" So saying he bent over her couch and gazed at her. Raising her head, Nyosan replied, not in the childish voice that he knew, but in a strangely sobered and disillusioned tone: "I do not think I should have lived through it, had I not known that to die in such a way* is reckoned shameful in the world to come. I am going to enter a nunnery and see whether I cannot live on there long enough to lighten the burden of my sins." "Do not say such things," he answered. "That the experience through which you have just passed should have tried you severely is natural enough; but surely it was not so terrible as to deprive you of all wish to live?" Did she really mean what she had said? He was appalled at the idea of her carrying out such a resolution. And yet he knew well enough all the difficulties that would arise if they attempted to go on living as though nothing had happened. He knew his own feelings, knew that no effort of his own could alter them, and that, try as he might to forget the past, Nyosan would suffer at every instant from the knowledge that in his heart of hearts he had not forgiven her. And other people, her father for example, would

---

* Those who die in childbirth are much handicapped in spiritual progress beyond the grave.

inevitably notice the change in their relations. If, on the other hand, she insisted upon taking her vows, it would be far better that she should do so at once, making her ill-health the pretext. Otherwise the step would certainly be attributed to his unkindness. But then his eye fell upon her long, lovely hair, that should by rights have delighted his eyes for so many years longer; and the idea of its being shorn from her by the cleric's knife was intolerable to him. "Come, come," he said; "you must pluck up your courage. Things are not so bad as that. Look at Murasaki, she was much worse than you have been; but now she is quite out of danger." He persuaded her to drink a little of her soup. She was certainly very thin and pale, indeed in every way alarmingly fragile. But nevertheless, as he looked at her lying motionless on the bed, he thought her singularly beautiful, and at that moment all thought of her unfaithfulness vanished from his mind. To such beauty all things could be forgiven.

The ex-Emperor Suzaku was much perturbed by the accounts of Nyosan's slow recovery. She on her side had, since her extreme physical weakness set in, felt the need of his support far more than she had ever done during the early years of their separation, and her women constantly heard her moaning to herself, "If only my father were here! I cannot bear to die without seeing him once again." A messenger was sent to Suzaku's mountain temple, it being thought right he should know that she was continually asking for him. Immediately upon this the ex-Emperor did what he had thought never in his life to do again—he left the precincts of the temple, and under cover of night made his way to the New Palace. Genji was quite unprepared for this sudden arrival, but hastened to thank the august visitor for the singular honor he had conferred upon them by his coming. "Well," said Suzaku, "a few weeks ago no one would have been more surprised than myself if it had been suggested that I should ever appear in your midst again. But I have lately been so much perturbed by the accounts of Nyosan's health that I find it impossible to go on with my ordinary round of prayers and devotions. The thought that she, a mere child, may go first, and I, old and enfeebled, be left behind without even the consolation of having seen her these many months past, is so terrible to me, that though I well know my sudden reappearance may easily give great offence,* it was without a moment's hesitation that I thus hastened to her side." Even in his monastic garb Suzaku was still a graceful and attractive figure; and though, to escape attention, he had dressed in the simple black robes of a common priest, his bearing gave to them a certain dignity and grace of line that made the sight of his altered guise less saddening than is usually the case. Genji's eyes indeed filled with tears when Suzaku first entered the room; but they were tears

---

* Suggest that he was meditating a *coup d'état*.

of envy rather than sorrow. "I do not think there is much the matter with her," he said. "Considering how little proper nourishment she has taken in the last few weeks it would be strange if she were not feeling out of sorts. But if you do not mind putting up with a rather uncomfortable seat..." So saying, he led the ex-Emperor to her bed and motioned him to a low divan that had been pushed alongside of it. With the help of her people she shifted a little towards the near side of the bed. He raised the bed-curtain and said gently: "I am afraid I look very much like the household chaplain arriving to read the evening incarnations. But it does not seem that I shall ever make much of a name for myself in that line, for all my prayers on your behalf appear to be singularly unsuccessful. If I have come, it was not in the belief I could be of any use to you, but merely because I could not endure to stay away." "If you had not come," she answered amid her tears, "I do not think I should have lived for many hours. But now that you are here, let me take my vows before it is too late." "This is a very serious matter," he answered. "Of course, if you have considered it properly and are certain that you would not repent of such a step, I should be the last person in the world to oppose it. But you are very young. Should you survive this illness, you have in all probability a long while yet to live. Your renouncement of the world at such an age would cause great astonishment, and hard things would inevitably be said of those on whom your happiness here is supposed to depend. I hope you have reflected upon these points..." Then turning to Genji: "I think we ought to consider whether such a step would not in any case be a great help to her. Even if, as she fears, she has only a very short time to live, her wishes in such a matter ought to be respected." "She has been saying this for days past," said Genji. "But I had the impression that the evil influence which has possessed her was causing her to speak thus in order that we might be deceived, and I paid no attention." "Doubtless," answered Suzaku, "when spirits suggest evil courses to us it is better not to obey them. But when someone who is obviously in the last stages of weakness and exhaustion asks us to take a certain step, we are likely afterwards to suffer from great remorse if we pay no attention to the request." This then, thought Suzaku to himself, was Genji's attitude towards the loved being whose happiness he had so confidently entrusted to his keeping. It was evident, from the way in which Genji spoke, that Nyosan's wishes had long ceased to have any importance to him. Indeed, the tone of what he had just heard fitted in only too well with rumors that had been reaching him for years past. Well, if Genji's treatment of her was such that she preferred the rigors of the cloister, much scandal would certainly be avoided were she to take her vows now, when her illness offered a reasonable excuse. However unsatisfactory Genji might have proved as a husband, he had certainly provided very handsomely for her in material ways. This fact would under ordinary circumstances have made it difficult to remove her from his control. But if she took orders Suzaku could establish her very comfortably in that roomy pleasant palace in the Third Ward, which his father, the old Emperor, had once presented to him. While he was alive, he could keep an eye upon her himself; and Genji, whatever might be his other preoccupations, would surely not be so unfeeling as wholly to abandon her. But as to that, events would show.

On finding that Suzaku was not averse to Nyosan's project, Genji (with now no thought in his head of the wrong that she had done him) rushed to her bedside, beseeching her at least to wait until she was stronger. "At present and for a long while to come you would be far too weak to perform the offices of a nun. Eat, drink, recover your strength, and then will be time to talk more about this." But she shook her head, hating the hypocrisy (as it seemed to her) that forced him to act thus in Suzaku's presence. He saw at once that she thought his forgiveness only a pretence; but how was he to convince her? It was now nearing dawn, and as Suzaku wished to be back in his monastery before daylight, it was necessary to act at once. Choosing from among the priests who were on night-duty in her apartments those who seemed to him most suitable for the task, he brought them to her, bade them administer the vows and shave her head. To see those long and lovely tresses cast aside, to hear her recite the dismal vows, was more than Genji could bear, and he wept bitterly during the whole of the ceremony. Nor could Suzaku stand by unmoved while the child for whom he had desired every worldly blessing, upon whom he had lavished a hundred times more care than upon any of the rest, made that renouncement of which none would dream who hoped for further happiness in this earthly life. "You can say the prayers when you are stronger," he said hastily and drove away. For it was growing rapidly lighter. Nyosan was now so weak as to be but half-conscious of what was going on, and she did not bid him farewell or, apparently, even notice his departure.

During the course of the early morning rituals a "possession" declared itself, and presently, in tones of laughing malice, a voice was heard to say: "Ha, ha! you thought you were done with me. No such thing. When number one turned me off, I took service with my lady here, and, unsuspected of you all, have been giving her my very best attention ever since. Now I shall go back..."

The news that Nyosan had taken her vows was the final blow to Kashiwagi's last flickering desire of recovery. He thought often of Ochiba, and wished that he could have had her with him. But his parents had now taken such complete possession of him that he feared she would feel her position more acutely here than at home, and instead he made the hopeless suggestion that he should be moved for a while back into his own house. To this they naturally refused consent. He discussed Ochiba's future with various people. Her mother had always been strongly opposed to the match, and had only yielded to the insistence of To no Chujo, and also of Suzaku himself, who thought that he had found in Kashiwagi the straightforward, steady-going husband that Nyosan's disaster had taught him to prefer—a man who would be so flattered by the offer of this connection with the Imperial Family that all his energies would be spent in proving himself worthy of the honor! Kashiwagi blushed when he remembered what had been expected of him. "I hope," he said to his own mother one day, "you will do what you can for Ochiba when I am gone. I know it is wretched for her to be left like this, and though it is not my fault that our life together has lasted for so short a time, she will have the feeling that she has got very little out of this alliance." "It's no good your asking such things of me," said his mother. "I shall be in my grave almost as soon as you." It was evident that she did not mean to be of any use, and he turned to his brother Kobai, to whom he gave a number of detailed instructions about this and his affairs in general. Kashiwagi had always been regarded in the family as a model of solidity and good sense. His brothers and other young men of the household had looked upon him as a kind of general parent and protector, so that the prospect of his loss was a shattering blow to them all.

The Emperor, too, was greatly distressed, and being told that Kashiwagi was not expected to live much longer, he thought he might safely confer upon him the rank of Counselor Extraordinary. He hoped that perhaps the excitement of receiving this promotion might act as a spur to Kashiwagi's failing strength, and even bring him back once more on a final visit to the Palace. Kashiwagi was of course delighted; but was obliged to reply that it was impossible for him to receive the investiture in person.

The first visitor who came to congratulate him on this honor was Yugiri, with whom he had always been on particularly intimate terms. The gate nearest Kashiwagi's apartments was thronged with riders and coaches; but since the turn of the year he had been too weak even to sit up in bed, and was able to receive none of these visitors. But the very fact of his extreme weakness warned him that, if he were ever to see Yugiri again, it would be as well not to let this opportunity pass, and asking him to forgive the untidy condition of the room, he dismissed the priests and attendants who were at his bedside, that he and Yugiri might enjoy this final visit undisturbed. "I hoped to find you a little stronger today. I thought that perhaps this promotion..." Yugiri said, pulling aside the bed-curtains. The white bedclothes and (despite his apologies) the neatness and cleanliness of all his surroundings made Kashiwagi's abode seem positively enviable in its brightness and peace. Pleasant perfumes had just been burnt in the room, and it was evident that the sick man was determined, though he could do nothing for Yugiri's entertainment, not to let the visit remain in his memory as a disagreeable experience. Yugiri bent close down over the pillow, but Kashiwagi was so weak that his voice was scarcely audible, and it seemed as though he had great difficulty in breathing. "You do not look nearly so bad as I had expected," said Yugiri. "One would never guess you had been laid up for so long." But as he said these words he was obliged to pause and dry his tears. "Tell me about this illness of yours," he went on. "When did it first begin to be so serious? Though I know you so well, I feel very much in the dark about it all." After telling him a good deal about the outward course of his illness, Kashiwagi said: "But it is all connected with something that has been very much on my mind. I ought perhaps to have spoken about this before; but there cannot be any use in doing so now. I have often longed to speak to someone, to my brothers, for example. But whenever I was on the point of talking about it, there seemed some reason why that particular person was out of the question as a confidant on such a subject. It was—how shall I say?—a kind of awkwardness that had arisen between Genji and me. For weeks past I had been meaning to go into it with him, and already the thing had begun to weigh so much upon me that life was becoming quite unendurable, when suddenly he sent for me of his own accord. It was the night of the music-rehearsal. The moment I entered his presence I felt that in his heart he was condemning me, and when I met his eyes there was something in them that robbed me of all courage, of all desire to face my shame; and since that day I have not known an instant's happiness or peace. Of course, Genji must always have regarded me as in every way far beneath him; but ever since I was a boy he had always shown the greatest confidence in me. I felt I must have all this out with him; for if I died with it on my conscience I should be held back from Salvation in the life to come. However, it is too late now... But the greatest kindness you could do me would be to explain matters to him when I am gone. I know quite well that he will at once forgive me then. If you would only consent to do that..." Obscure as this request was, Yugiri had some notion what it was about. However, he dared not assume that he had guessed correctly, and only replied: "I think your fears are entirely imaginary. My father invariably speaks of you with the greatest good will, and since your illness he has been very anxious about you, and shown quite clearly again and again how heavy a loss to him your death would be. If there has been any sort of misunderstanding between you, why did you not tell me about it before? I am sure I could easily have cleared it up for you." "Perhaps it would have been better if I had," he answered. "But every day I thought that next day I should be stronger and more able to tell about such a thing as this, and so in the end I have left it till too late. Of course, it is essential that not a hint of this business should go any farther. I only spoke to you because I was sure you would one day contrive to bring up the subject and do your best to make him see the thing in its true light.

"And there is something else. Do what you can for Ochiba. I do not want Suzaku to think that I have left her with no one to keep an eye upon her." There was much more that he eagerly desired to say. But his voice had quite given out, and when he was finally furnished with paper and a brush, all he had strength to write was: "Please go away!"

Once more the miracle-workers crowded round the bed, his parents were hastily summoned, as also his sisters, Lady Chujo and Yugiri's wife, Kumoi. Tamakatsura, too, who did not forget that Kashiwagi had been her suitor before he became her brother, was extremely upset by the news of his condition, and had many services on his behalf read in her favorite temples. Yet all was to no purpose, for he now expired in the presence of his family; but so suddenly that there was no time to fetch Lady Ochiba from the house in the First Ward. Though he had never really given her his affection, he had always treated her with the greatest possible consideration and outward kindness, and she had no feeling of grievance against him. She was only sad at being left a widow at so early an age, after having been married to a husband who seemed, as she thought when looking back upon it, to have taken no pleasure in life at all.

Nyosan, who since his unhappy exploit had often thought that death would not be too bad a punishment for him, was aghast to hear of his end. She remembered how he had predicted the birth of her child. Perhaps he had not come that day intending to do any harm. Some meetings (her religion taught her) are ordained by Fate.* Had she after all judged his transgression too harshly?

Yugiri thought again and again of Kashiwagi's mysterious request. That the trouble to which he had alluded was in some way connected with Princess Nyosan he could not doubt. To begin with, Kashiwagi had repeatedly betrayed by signs of one sort or another the fact that he took a particular interest in her. This in the case of Kashiwagi, usually so reticent, so perfectly in command of himself, meant that some tremendous force was at work within, and it was not difficult to imagine that such a passion might have broken out in some painful scene or indiscreet declaration. Indeed, it was almost certain that a definite scandal had occurred; if not, why had Genji permitted the Princess to take her vows at such a ridiculously early age, and upon the pretext of an illness that appeared to be of very little consequence?

He did not mention the matter to anyone, not even to Kumoi, who shared all his secrets. But he was determined, next time an opportunity

---

* Karma.

occurred, simply to repeat to Genji what Kashiwagi had said, and see whether Genji could make sense of it all, or no. Meanwhile there was another visit he must pay. For Ochiba, alone with her mother in that vast, empty palace, the days passed in cheerless fashion enough. Occasionally one of her brothers-in-law would look in; but apart from this she had no company and no distractions. From time to time she would catch sight of his favorite hawk or horse, or merely of some falconer or groom moping disconsolately about, and note how man and beast alike wore the same cast-off, ownerless air, and a like impression of gloom was created by the sight of his other possessions—his lute and zithern above all, which looked so forlorn with their strings detached.[*] Over the trees in front of the house there hung already a thick haze of blossom. These things, she thought, as she gazed out of the window, went on just as before; and amid her women who crept to and fro in their dark mourning dress she was feeling very lonely, when suddenly there was a sound of shouting and a great ringing of hoofs in the road outside. She expected the sounds to pass by and fade away into the distance. But to her surprise the cavalcade drew up at her own door. For a moment she forgot everything, and thought this was Kashiwagi driving back from the Palace. A note was brought in. It must of course be Kobai or one of his brothers. Who else indeed ever came near her? It caused her some perturbation to discover that the visitor was no less a person than Yugiri. She was on the point of sending her women to make him welcome, when she reflected that this was not the sort of treatment to which he was probably used, and in the end her mother ushered him into the side-room of the great hall. He expressed his sorrow at her daughter's bereavement and told her how, shortly before his death, Kashiwagi had committed Princess Ochiba to his care. "I hope before very long to have an opportunity of showing you that I take this duty very seriously indeed. I should have come to talk the matter over with you before, had not this last month been crowded with Court functions which etiquette obliged me to attend. You can imagine that, as far as my own inclinations were concerned, I have not been feeling at all in the mood for such junketings, and would far rather have remained quietly at home. I can judge something of what poor Ochiba's feelings must be by what I have seen and heard at To no Chujo's house. The loss is after all a far heavier one for her than for his parents." Ochiba's mother had at first been rather shy of this unwonted visitor; but his tone was friendly and reassuring. "Poor thing!" she said. "We older people do our best to keep up her courage. After all, she is not the only young widow in the land. She must try to remember that. I have lived long enough myself to know that loss and sorrow are what we must expect as our portion in this life.

---

[*] In sign of mourning.

If happiness comes in, it is only by the way. And I do indeed wish she would try to be more cheerful. If she goes on like this she will soon follow him to the grave. You, I know, were Kashiwagi's great friend; but I must tell you that I was opposed to this match from the start. I don't know why Suzaku was so pleased about it. I suppose he wanted to do To no Chujo a good turn. But it now seems that, though the reasons I gave may have been very bad ones, I was perfectly right in my objection, and I only wish I had not let them talk me down. Not that I foresaw what would happen. I was merely old-fashioned enough to disapprove in any case of a marriage outside the Imperial Family. It turned out, however, to be something even worse than such an alliance. For her life with Kashiwagi was such that you could call her neither wife nor maid. That she should now pine to death at the loss of such a husband may be very good for his reputation in the world outside; but as her mother I cannot be expected to applaud the sacrifice."

It was growing late, and as he was due at To no Chujo's house he was obliged to retire. Ochiba did not put in an appearance. But this was by no means his last visit to the Palace in the First Ward.

It was the fourth month; and the same level shade of green lay upon every thicket and wood. The grief-stricken palace and those in it who had been committed to his charge recurred constantly to Yugiri's thoughts during these enjoyable summer days. One afternoon, finding the time hang heavy on his hands, he set out earlier than usual upon his visit to the First Ward. He noticed that a film of grass was already spreading across the courtyards, and here and there where the sand had worn thin or in sheltered crannies along the walls, clumps of motherwort had already squeezed themselves a place. Ochiba's seat was today for the first time surrounded by thin, summer curtains-of-state, which, as the wind and light of the early afternoon filtered through them, looked delightfully fresh and cool. He was met by a little girl, whose exquisitely poised head pleased him, though she, like everyone else in the house, wore garments that by their drab color told the same sad tale. While he waited to learn whether Ochiba could receive him (her mother was unwell and was said to be lying down) he was looking at the copses in front of the house and thinking that they at least knew nothing of what had befallen its inmates and did not scruple to flaunt their gay summer tints, when he noticed an oak and a maple, both conspicuous for the brightness of their fresh foliage, standing side by side, their branches intertwined. "I wonder how they became such friends?" he said to one of Ochiba's ladies, and approaching the curtains-of-state, he recited the verse: "What to the oak you gave, now to its trusted friend the maple-tree, ungracious Goddess of the Woods, will you deny?" "Those soft summer clothes look very well on him," whispered the ladies-in-waiting, as Yugiri bent over the curtains.

"What elegance! What grace!" A maid called Shosho presently brought the answer: "Though the oak be fallen, not yet to a chance comer shall I give the small twigs of the roof." Ochiba's mother now appeared, and Yugiri hastily moved further away from the curtains. "All these weeks of sorrow and disturbance have upset my health," she said, "and I am very shaky. But really, it is so good of you to keep on coming like this, that I felt I must make an effort to thank you in person." She did certainly look very unwell. "I am afraid you are having a very difficult time with Ochiba," he said. "It is of course natural that she should be upset; but there is a limit to all things. We must accept what Fate sends, and make the best of it. After all, life is short—our sorrows will soon be over." But what he was really thinking was that this Ochiba had obviously a great deal more in her than people had led him to suppose. Why was it that she mourned so inconsolably for someone whom she had scarcely known? He was determined to probe the mystery, and asked all manner of questions about her. Perhaps she felt now, more than during his lifetime, that her marriage had rendered her ridiculous in the eyes of society. Poor thing! She was far from being a great beauty. Yet she was not downright ugly, or certainly did not appear to be so from what he had been allowed to see of her. But even if she were, one ought not to be unkind to a woman merely on account of her plainness, any more than one had a right to take liberties with her merely because she was handsome. "Please sometimes try to be quite frank with me and confide your difficulties to me as you would have done to Kashiwagi." There was nothing actually improper in this speech of Yugiri's, but it was said in so impassioned a tone of voice as to be somewhat embarrassing.

Meanwhile Kashiwagi's loss continued to be severely felt in the country and at Court. He had been unusually popular in every class of society, and among people of all ages and professions. Even the most unlikely kitchen-men and tottering dames at Court continually bemoaned his loss; while the young Emperor, whose constant companion he had been at all concerts, feasts, and excursions, felt a bitter pang whenever he thought of the past. And indeed there were few occasions upon which some did not suddenly exclaim: "O Kashiwagi, poor Kashiwagi!" Only Genji knew that he had not quitted the world without leaving one small keepsake behind him, a fact that would have interested the friends of the deceased, but unfortunately could not be communicated to them.

Nor was this memento of Kashiwagi's career any longer so insignificant a creature. For by the time autumn came round it was already crawling on the floor, and was destined soon to learn other accomplishments.

The Flute

The first anniversary of Kashiwagi's death had come. Every day Genji felt his loss more keenly. The number of persons with whom he was on easy and informal terms was in any case none too great. But Kashiwagi had been something more than this. They had shared each other's lives and thoughts—at least until the disastrous episode which Genji now did his best to forget. Besides the masses that on his own account he caused to be said in Kashiwagi's memory, he set apart a sum of a hundred golden pieces which he spent on services that in his own heart he regarded as being performed in the name of Kaoru, the dead man's child. But this must of course remain a secret; for he continued to bring up the boy as though he were his. Yugiri not only celebrated the anniversary in the most solemn manner, but was upon this sad occasion so prodigal in his attentions to the ladies in the First Ward* that To no Chujo could not help remarking it. "Yugiri," he said, "is taking a far larger share in managing my poor son's affairs than I should ever have expected. Kobai and the rest are not nearly so active. He must have been far more intimate with Kashiwagi than I supposed." Yugiri's zeal and all the other marks of the affection and esteem in which the deceased had been held, served but to make his parents feel more bitterly the pang of his untimely loss.

To Suzaku, had not the affairs of this world been by now of shadowy import to him, the tragic outcome of all his paternal solicitude would indeed have been a shattering blow. Here was Ochiba left stranded, after a short experience of a marriage that had from the first been mere mockery; and Nyosan, his beloved Nyosan, for whom he had hoped such splendid things, dead—at least to all the friendly and human part of life. As it was, however, it gave him considerable pleasure to think that his daily occupations—his own round of prayers, penances, and offerings—had now become hers, and he constantly wrote to her upon small matters connected with the religious life. One day he sent her a bamboo sprout taken from a wood near his retreat and some *tokoro*† dug up on the neighboring hillside, and in the margin of his letter, which was a very long one, he wrote: "I send you these tokens of a hermit's life, none too easy to come by, now that the spring mist lies so thick upon the hills. 'Though far behind me

---

* Kashiwagi's widow (Princess Ochiba) and her mother.
† A bitter root.

you walk upon Salvation's path, go boldly on and let my goal be yours.'"*
She was reading this poem with tears in her eyes, when Genji entered. What were those strange objects reposing in the lacquer bowls which she usually kept filled with fruit? Then he saw that she was reading a letter from Suzaku, which she handed to him. It was very long, contained many reflections upon his own approaching death, and lamenting the impossibility of their ever meeting again. The passage about the *tokoro* came oddly from Suzaku's pen, belonging as it did to pietism rather than to poetry; but Genji read it with a feeling of deep remorse. No doubt Suzaku had suffered great anxiety and disappointment over Nyosan's marriage; and though Genji could not regard this as his own fault, "I do indeed hope," he said, "that you have no intention of taking your father's hint. That you should dream of scaling these mountain fastnesses is a terrible idea." Now that his relation to her could only be of the slenderest kind, he began to be more than ever struck by her rather childish beauty, the effect of which seemed only to be enhanced by the way her hair was cut at the sides, so that its ends lay flat against her cheeks. It had all been his fault. It was he who had allowed her to drift away from him; and as though in a futile effort to repair the remissness of past years he now came very close to her curtains and spoke to her almost caressingly.

The little boy was asleep in his nurse's quarters; but presently he was waked, and crawling into the room made straight for Genji and grabbed at his sleeve. He was dressed in a little shirt of white floss, over which was a red coat with a Chinese pattern finely worked upon it. The skirts of this garment were remarkably long and trailed behind him in the quaintest way; but it was (as is usual with children of that age) quite open at the front, showing his little limbs, white and smooth as a fresh-stripped willow wand. There was certainly in his smile and the shape of his brow something that recalled Kashiwagi. But where had the child got his remarkably good looks? Not from his father, who was passable in appearance, but could not possibly have been called handsome. To Nyosan, curiously enough, he could see no resemblance. Indeed the expression that chiefly gave character to the boy's face (or so Genji contrived to fancy) was not at all unlike his own.

The child was just beginning to walk. As soon as he entered the room he caught sight of Suzaku's strange-looking roots lying in the fruit-dish, and toddled in that direction. Anxious to discover what sort of things they were, he was soon pulling at them, scattering them over the floor, breaking them in pieces, munching them, and in general making a terrible mess both of himself and the room. "Look what mischief he is up to,"

---

* *Tokoro* also means "place, destination." "Seek out the same *Tokoro* as I have done," i.e. leave the City and take refuge in a mountain retreat.

said Genji. "You had better put them somewhere out of sight. I expect one of the maids thought it a good joke to tell him they were meant to eat." So saying, he took up the child in his arms, "What an expressive face this boy has!" he continued. "I have had very little to do with children of this age, and had got it into my head that they were all much alike and all equally uninteresting. I see now how wrong I was. What havoc he will live one day to work upon the hearts of the princesses that are growing up in these neighboring apartments!* I am half sorry that I shall not be there to see. But 'though Spring comes each year...'"† "How can you talk of such a thing?" everyone said with horror. Little Kaoru was cutting his teeth, and thinking that one of Suzaku's bamboo shoots would be just the thing to press against his swollen gums, he managed to grab at them, and dribbling monstrously, thrust one into his mouth. "Now he's really enjoying himself," said Genji. "What depraved tastes children do have! 'Though there be that in its stem which is bitter to recall, yet from this bamboo-shoot no more my heart can I withhold.'" Reciting this acrostic poem, he took the child by the hand and tried to persuade him to put the thing down. But Kaoru, smiling broadly, took not the slightest notice, and with a great clatter crawled away with his prize as fast as his arms and legs could carry him.

As the weeks went by, the child grew more and more attractive, and before long even the "touch of bitterness" that its existence had been wont to lend to Genji's thoughts utterly disappeared. He felt that the child, now a source of so much delight to him, was destined to be born in that way and no other. Kashiwagi had but been the instrument of Fate. Among the strange inconsistencies of his apparently enviable lot, none (thought Genji) was more curious than this, that the one lady in his household who was of faultless lineage, young, beautiful, in every way immaculate, should after a short spell of marriage with him declare her preference for the convent! At such moments some of the old bitterness against Kashiwagi would for a while return.

All this time Yugiri had been turning over in his mind what Kashiwagi had said to him on his deathbed. Had he been entirely ignorant of what it referred to, he would probably have discussed the matter with Genji long ago. But as it was, he knew just enough to feel that the subject was a very embarrassing one, and he wondered whether he should ever have the courage to embark upon it.

One melancholy autumn evening when he went to pay his accustomed visit to the ladies in the First Ward, he found Ochiba busily engaged

---

* The little daughter of the Akashi Princess.

† "Though Spring comes back each year and fresh flowers bloom, we shall be there to see them only so long as Fate gives us leave."

in playing upon her zithern. She did not wish to be disturbed, and he was shown into the southern or side-room. As he took his seat he heard the swish of retreating skirts and caught a pleasant whiff of scent, those things denoting (as he guessed) that a bevy of ladies had, at the news of his arrival, hastened to take cover in the inner room. The visit began by his usual conversation with Ochiba's mother. While they were talking together of old times he could not help contrasting the utter stillness and desolation of this house with the lively stir and bustle that went on from dawn to dusk in his own palace, teeming as it did with unruly children and their innumerable attendants. There was a dignity, a severity about the place; and looking round him he felt that he who broke in upon this flat tranquility with so much as a hint of common passions and desires, who fluttered this decorous stillness by any coarse vehemence or unwarranted familiarity, would be guilty of a breach of taste, for the condemnation of which no word could be strong enough. He was given a zithern, and recognized it to be Kashiwagi's. After playing a few chords he said to Ochiba's mother: "I know the tone of this instrument; it is the one that Kashiwagi used, is it not? How I wish that your daughter would play something on it. They say that a dead man's touch lingers in the instruments that he played, and can be recognized even after his death." "I fear that cannot be so in this case," the mother replied, "for after his death the strings were removed, and those are new ones. Ochiba has played very little lately, and is, I am sorry to say, in danger of forgetting all that her father taught her. Suzaku, who, as you know, took a lot of trouble with his daughters' music, often said Ochiba was the one that showed the greatest promise. But since all this trouble came, I fear her playing has gone utterly to pieces..." She begged him to play again; but he refused, saying that if any hand could waken the echoes of Kashiwagi's touch, it would be that of Ochiba; and he insisted upon the zithern being laid near her chair. But she seemed disinclined to comply with his wish, and he did not press her.

The moon was shining out of a cloudless sky; a flight of wild geese passed over the house, wing to wing, in faultless line. How she, companionless, must envy that blissful troop!* At last, moved by the beauty of the autumn evening, with its sudden stirrings of light wind, cool to the skin, she took up a large Chinese zithern and played a few chords, which by their passionate intensity stirred his feelings far more than mere words could have done. But she showed no inclination to play in concert with him, and as it was now very late, he made ready to depart. Just as he was leaving, the mother handed him a flute. "This had been in his family for years," she said; "but there is no use in its lying idle in this

---

* The male and female wild goose were supposed to fly wing interlocked with wing.

deserted house. He used to play it as he sat in his coach, and its music blended with the cries of his outriders. I long to hear it played so again, even in another's hand..." He saw at once that it was Kashiwagi's familiar flute, and remembered having often heard him express the hope that it would fall into the hands of someone who could make good use of it, and not merely be treated as a keepsake when he was gone. Yugiri played a few runs upon it and then suddenly stopped. "You let me play on his zithern," he said, "and encouraged by you I felt no compunction. But somehow when it comes to playing on this flute..." He broke off, and Ochiba's mother recited the poem: "Tonight at last has the voice of the cicada sounded as of old in the dewy bushes round my house." "Though hole for hole, unaltered are the notes the flute gives forth, what should these fingers conjure from it now, save the choked sound of tears?" So Yugiri answered, and after many hesitations and delays, at last, far on into the night, went back to his own house.

The shutters were closed and everyone was asleep. Kumoi had heard the extraordinary trouble he was taking in arranging the affairs of the two ladies in the First Ward. It seemed to involve his coming home very late at night; and though Kumoi distinctly heard him arrive on this occasion, she felt in no mood for conversation, and pretended to be asleep. "Why have you locked yourselves in like this?" he cried, when he was at last admitted. "I should have thought that with such a moon as this abroad in the heavens no one would have the heart to shut their windows." So saying he threw back the shutters, and rolled up the blinds of her divan, while he himself took a seat at a point from whence he could see the beauties of the night. "How anyone can lie a-bed when there are such sights to be seen, I cannot imagine," said Yugiri. "Do come here and look. I hate your not seeing it!" But she was in a bad temper, and pretended not to hear. The apartments seemed to be littered with children, their little faces blank with the vacancy of infant slumber, and wherever he turned were bevies of dames-in waiting, nurses and the like—a perfect tangle of sleeping forms. Again he contrasted this crowded scene with the death-like mansion that he had just left. Taking the flute out of his pocket he played a few notes. Were they already asleep in the First Ward, or was Ochiba at any rate thinking of him, wishing he were still in the house? Perhaps she was at this very instant playing upon the zithern that he had placed within her reach. Had she changed the tuning?[*] And her mother too, she was a fine player on the Japanese zithern. So his thoughts rambled on as he lay in bed. Why was it, he asked himself, that Kashiwagi had seemed to take so little interest in Ochiba? Though no one could say he had actually

---

[*] In sign of dislike for him.

ill-treated her. The idea that if one possessed Ochiba one could ever grow tired of her seemed to him preposterous. Yet he knew that such things did happen, and indeed it was rarely enough that any attachment subsisted unaltered through the years—his own relation to Kumoi was the one example that occurred to him. And the result was that by this exclusive fidelity he had spoilt her. She had grown a trifle touchy and exacting... At this point he fell asleep. He dreamt that Kashiwagi appeared to him, and picking up the flute examined it curiously. It occurred to Yugiri even in his dream that it had been unwise of him to play on it, for this had certainly drawn Kashiwagi's ghost to his side. "Could I, like the wind among the reed-stems, blow where I would, then into the hands of a true heir should fall the music of this flute." So the dream-figure recited; and Yugiri was about to question it concerning the meaning of this strange verse, when he woke with a start. One of his children was crying. The piercing noise went on and on. It would not take its milk, and the nurses were scurrying about, evidently in great concern. Presently Kumoi took the child in her own arms and sat with it near the lamp, her hair thrown back behind her ears and her dress open in front, showing the pretty curves and undulations of her breast. She did not attempt to feed the child, but let it put its lips to her breasts, and by one device and another had soon stopped its tears. Yugiri was now standing by her side. "Is there anything amiss with the child?" he asked, and to show his concern began scattering handfuls of rice and reciting spells of protection; an activity which, if it did not greatly help the child, served at least to dispel the impression of his own dream. "It is no use your doing that," she said. "The boy is ill. Probably he caught some infection when you insisted upon opening the window. You come back like this, after amusing yourself I don't know how or where, and flood the house with unwholesome night air, merely that you may have the pleasure of staring at the moon." But he saw from her face that she was no longer cross, and was now only teasing him. "I am certainly very much to blame," he said, "if it is true that 'infections' can only enter through doors and windows. Had anyone else suggested this I should have thought it a rather infantile view. But coming from the mother of half a dozen children it must of course be treated with respect." After that he sat silently watching her in a manner that Kumoi found very disconcerting, and she said at last: "Had not you better go to bed? I am afraid I am not dressed for show." She was conscious that, sitting in the full glare of the lamp, she did not look her best. So far from being irritated by this coquetry, Yugiri felt touched that she should still care so much what impression she made upon him. The child did indeed seem to be very much indisposed. It continued to cry at intervals all through the night, and no one in the house got much sleep.

Yugiri was worried about this flute. The dream seemed clearly to indicate that it had not reached its right destination. Kashiwagi certainly could not have wanted it to go to a woman. What good could it be to her? And there was no man who seemed to come into question. Recollecting his late interview with Kashiwagi, Yugiri became more than ever convinced that he had died with some desperate entanglement clinging about his soul, some secret or remorse such as might forever hold him back from release; and turning over in his mind what were generally considered the best ways of dealing with such a case, he arranged for all manner of services to be said on behalf of Kashiwagi's soul at Otagi[*] and at the various temples with which the dead man's family had been connected. He thought of dealing with the flute by offering it as present to some Buddhist shrine; but on reflection he saw that this would be less than civil to the lady who had just given it to him, and he determined to consult his father upon the subject. Genji, he was told, was with the Akashi Princess. As he was passing through Murasaki's apartments Yugiri was greeted by little Niou, now three years old. He was Murasaki's great favorite, and perhaps the prettiest of all the children in the palace. "Will you pick me up, please," he said, "and do yourself the honor to carry me back to my mummy?" He still got his words mixed up, and applied to himself the terms of respect that he heard his nurses use when they spoke of him. "Come up then," said Yugiri, laughing. "But we shall have to pass in front of Lady Murasaki's screen. Won't she think that very rude?" "She can't see you now," said Niou, covering Yugiri's face with his little sleeve; and thus, guided by the child, Yugiri arrived blindfolt at the Akashi Princess's door. Here Kaoru was playing along with the other Akashi children. Seeing Niou being deposited upon the threshold, his elder brother, Ni no Miya, rushed up to Yugiri, crying: "Me too, a ride!" But Niou tried to stop Yugiri from taking the other child in his arms. "No, no," he said, "he's my uncle Yugiri, not yours. I want him for my own." "Behave yourselves, children," cried Genji, who was standing near by. "Yugiri does not belong to either of you. As a matter of fact, he is the Emperor's gentleman, and if His Majesty were to hear that either of you had stolen the Colonel of his Bodyguard, he might be very angry. As for you, Niou, you're a little rascal. You are always trying to get the better of your elder brother!" "Ni no Miya," said Yugiri, "is already beginning to forgo his rights with quite an elderly resignation. In a child of his age such unselfishness is alarming." Genji thought he had never seen three such charming children, and despite the hubbub they were creating, smiled indulgently upon them all. At last, however, he said: "But this is no place to receive a visitor; let us go somewhere where we can talk more comfortably." So saying he

---

[*] Where Kashiwagi had presumably been buried.

led the way to his own room. But they had hard work to escape, for the three little princes clung to them tightly and would not leave go. It was of course quite wrong that Kaoru, the child of a commoner, should be brought up with the Akashi Princess's children. But, as Genji well knew, the slightest sign on his part that he was conscious of this impropriety would be taken by Nyosan as a reproach. He was indeed, as has before been noted, particularly good at guessing what effect his actions would have upon the feelings of others; and he therefore lost no opportunity of showing that the child ranked with him on exactly the same plane as his own grandchildren.

Yugiri had often watched Kaoru from a distance, but had never made friends with him. Seeing the little boy now peeping at him through a chink in the screen, he picked up a spray of cherry-blossom that had fallen to the floor and, holding it out, called the child to him. Instantly he came toddling along, in his dark blue overall, that contrasted so strongly with the even pallor of his skin. He was, thought Yugiri, a far handsomer child than the two Akashi boys. Was it only his fancy—the fruit of a suspicion that had long ago formed in his mind—or did Kaoru really bear a certain resemblance to poor Kashiwagi? In the expression of the eyes and the way they were set (though in the child this peculiarity was far more marked) there was something that he could not remember to have met elsewhere. And that smile too... Was he imagining? No. Surely Genji could not see that smile without at once thinking of Kashiwagi. And if so, what did he make of it all? The Akashi princes were a pair of sturdy, quite ordinary good-looking boys. But Kaoru had about him something refined, distinguished, that would have marked him out among a hundred other well-born children. "What a terrible pity it is," thought Yugiri, "that To no Chujo, who is so heartbroken at Kaskiwagi not even leaving a child behind to continue his name, should not know the truth about this little one—always supposing that it is the truth..." And despite all To no Chujo's past hostility, Yugiri felt a longing to give him this great pleasure; though when he came to think how he should do so, he saw that the idea was quite impracticable. Meanwhile, he was making friends with Kaoru, who was not in the least shy, and they were soon having wonderful games together.

Genji listened with a slightly ironical smile to Yugiri's description of his recent visit to the First Ward, and after a few enquiries about such parts of the story as concerned old friends and acquaintances, he said suddenly: "I hope you are not behaving in such a way as to give Princess Ochiba a false impression. I know by bitter experience that there is a grave risk of this. No doubt you are acting entirely out of regard for the memory of your friend; but anyone who hears of these numerous visits is likely to draw a very different conclusion. For your own sake as well as hers you must be careful to make it clear that you have completely disinterested motives for frequenting the house." Advice on this sort of subject was, thought Yugiri, his father's specialty. How high-minded were Genji's principles, and how unsuccessful he was in applying them! "So far from being censured for my attentions to those two ladies," he answered, "I should certainly be thought to have behaved very badly if I had not taken their affairs a little in hand. I daresay my description of these visits might easily give the impression that either she or I had not been very discreet. But everything depends upon the circumstances under which things are said or done. A remark that might be very impertinent at one moment may be perfectly harmless at another. Much again (as I am sure you will admit) depends upon the character and age of the people concerned. Ochiba is no longer very young, and I am by no means given to miscellaneous flirtations. If our relation sounds to you to be somewhat too informal, it is because I know that she takes life seriously, and she, that I am to be trusted." Hence he led on the conversation to a point at which it was quite natural that he should recount his dream. Genji listened without making any comment; but he perfectly well understood the meaning* of the dream. "I know the flute of which you speak," he said at last. "As a matter of fact it ought, properly speaking, to be in this house, for it belonged to Murasaki's father. He allowed Kashiwagi to take it away one day after the Lezpideza Concert, knowing that he was such a fine player. Of course, Ochiba's mother would not know anything of this; it was quite natural that she should give it to you." This was a mere invention, and Genji was fairly certain that Yugiri recognized it as such, and all the time knew quite well who was this mysterious "heir" spoken of by Kashiwagi in the dream. But until Yugiri made some more definite sign of being in the secret, Genji was not going to give himself away. Yugiri, seeing that his father was not at all inclined to take him into his confidence, thought he had better postpone the attempt (long overdue) to deliver Kashiwagi's cryptic deathbed message. But the temptation to get the thing over was too much for him, and he said at last, as though it were a casual recollection: "Soon before Kashiwagi died he gave me various instructions concerning the disposition of his affairs, and at the same time charged me with some mission that was connected with his devotion towards you; or so it seemed. But though he made several attempts to explain the matter I never succeeded in discovering what it was, nor on subsequent reflection have I ever been able to make out exactly what he meant." He rather overdid these protestations of bewilderment, with the result that Genji became more certain than ever of his having learnt the whole secret. But he was still determined not to commit himself.

---

* That the flute should be given to Kashiwagi's son Kaoru.

"I certainly know no reason why Kashiwagi should ever have thought that I was cross with him," he said. "As for the dream, I will think it over quietly and let you know how you should act. There is a saying among old women that dreams should only be discussed by daylight!" It was evident that nothing was to be got out of him. But the story Yugiri had just told must have made *some* impression upon his father. What precisely was going on in Genji's mind, he respectfully wondered.

Yugiri

So high was Yugiri's reputation for prudence and fidelity that his constant visits to the First Ward gave rise to no scandal whatever, and were merely regarded as a touching proof of his attachment to Kashiwagi's memory. And hitherto his behavior had indeed been beyond reproach; but down underneath his thoughts was a feeling that things would not always go on like this. Ochiba's mother was at a loss how to thank the young man for his extraordinary kindness. She was now less and less able to distract herself, and his continual letters and visits were her chief source of pleasure. In his relation towards Ochiba there had at the beginning been nothing of gallantry or sentiment, and this had become so much a matter of habit that a sudden change on his part would, for both of them, have been very embarrassing. But sooner or later circumstances would surely arise such as would put their friendship naturally and imperceptibly onto a less formal footing. Such circumstances certainly did occur; but watching Ochiba closely he was obliged to confess that she seemed singularly unwilling to avail herself of them. Tired of these experiments, he was just beginning to think it would be better to tell her straight out that he was in love with her, and see how she took it, when the mother fell seriously ill and was moved away from the City to her estate on the hills. Her former chaplain, a man of great sanctity, who had frequently been successful in exorcising demonic seizures and possessions, was now living in the hills, under a strict vow never to leave the village. But fortunately his place of retreat was quite near to her estate, and it was with a view to securing his services that she now left the City. The outriders and the carriage in which she travelled were supplied by Yugiri. It might have been supposed that this would offend Ochiba's brothers-in-law whose business it clearly was to supply such assistance. But as a matter of fact they were fully occupied with their own affairs, and it never even occurred to them to offer their services. The only one that took any personal interest in Ochiba was Kobai, but he had always found her so discouraging that in the end he gave up going to the house.

There seemed to be no end to Yugiri's thoughtfulness. When he heard that services of intercession were being held at the old lady's bedside, he sent alms for the priests and new vestments. The letter of thanks was written by Ochiba herself, for the mother was too ill to write, and everyone agreed that it would be uncivil to send a letter dictated to an ordinary amanuensis. The handwriting pleased him uncommonly, and so agreeable was it to receive such a letter, even though the writer was merely transmitting another's sentiments, that he wrote to Ochiba's mother even more often than before, in the hope of receiving similar replies. He longed, of course, to visit them in their country home; but he knew that Kumoi would regard this as a confirmation of her worst suspicions, and he decided, for the present at any rate, that it would be a mistake to go.

But as the autumn drew on he longed more and more to find out how things were going. Moreover, he knew that on the hills the leaves would be changing, and he had a burning desire to get out into the country.

The excuse he made was that the old chaplain, who seldom left his solitary and unapproachable retreat, had consented to visit his former patron. "There are various points, about which I should like to consult him," said Yugiri. "Such an opportunity may never occur again, and I shall be able at the same time to find out how Ochiba's mother is really getting on." He made the journey with only a few outriders and half a dozen personal servants, all clad in hunting-dress. The place lay only a little way into the hills; but the colors of Oyama, near Matsugasaki, though doubtless not to be compared with the wild and rocky country farther on, excited him far more than the cunningly contrived autumn effects of the great palace gardens at home. The house was surrounded merely by a low brushwood fence, but looked very trim and neat. Inside, though all the arrangements were of a temporary nature, there was everything that the most exacting taste could require. The altar of intercession had been put up in a side-wing opening out of the main hall. The sick woman herself was at the back of the house, and her daughter occupied the western side. It was thought that the malady might be catching, and Ochiba had been advised to stay in the City. But nothing would induce her to do so, and the utmost precaution she would take was to remain at the other end of the house. There were no guest-rooms, and Yugiri was brought straight to Ochiba's quarters. From here he conducted the usual interchange of messages with the old Princess. Ochiba was certainly at the far end of the room, for from behind the curtains of her dais (which having been put up hastily on her arrival was a very flimsy affair) he heard the soft rustling of a skirt, and caught the outline of a form that could only be hers. His heart beat wildly; but the business of communicating with the sick woman was a very slow one, as she was at the far end of the house, and in the intervals, while the messengers were going to and fro, he fell into conversation with one of the old Princess's gentlewomen. "Considering it is now more than a year since I took your mistress's affairs in hand," he said, "it is extraordinary that Ochiba should still affect to treat me as a complete stranger. She must have heard me arrive; yet she does not send a word of greeting. I have never known such a thing before. It is the height of absurdity in my case; and people who know the sort of man I am must really find it hard not to laugh in her face. Just think of it, a steady-going married man of my age, who even when he was younger certainly displayed little of the wildness of youth! How do you explain her attitude?" The lady was in any case at no loss to explain Yugiri's present indignation. She went and urged Ochiba to show a little more hospitality; but the Princess replied: "I was obliged to write to him occasionally on my mother's behalf. But he must not take this as a sign on my part that I desire to correspond with him. At the present moment I am far too much taken up with my mother's illness to want to see anybody." "This is all very senseless," he replied, when these words were reported to him. "She is obviously fretting so much over her mother's illness that she will soon destroy her own health. If you don't mind my saying so, I think your mistress's illness has been largely caused by the distressing spectacle of Ochiba's persistent brooding. I believe that if she could rouse herself a little, it would have an extraordinary effect on her mother, and be the best thing for Lady Ochiba herself. This pretence that my relations are solely with her mother is very tiresome." To this everyone agreed.

Towards sunset a heavy mist began to rise and the hill at the foot of which the house stood now hung above it in dark, featureless bulk; from among the child-flowers growing along the hedge (their color subdued to a strange grayness by the mist) came unabated the ceaseless murmuring of insects; while from among the wild and tangled plantations sounded, cold and clear, the noise of running water. From time to time a melancholy gust of dank wind swept the hills above, shaking the deep woods; and at intervals there sounded the "booming of the gong which marked the close of one service and at the same time the beginning of the next—the new voices striking in almost before the closing notes had died away. Though these sounds and the whole aspect of the place were of a nature to subdue the rovings of an idle fancy, they served but to heighten the passion that was mounting in Yugiri's breast. The noise of spells and chanting rose more and more insistent from the sick woman's apartments. A rumor spread that she was sinking, and everyone trooped off in that direction. A better opportunity to declare his feelings could not, thought Yugiri, possibly have arisen. The house was now completely shut in by mist. "It is no use my starting at present," he said, "I should never be able to find my way back." And he sent her the poem: "Lovelier in their coat of mist, the hills shut out for me the pathway of escape." "To hide our country hedge this mist arose; not to detain the idle-hearted guest." So she answered. That she should reply at all was unusual, and the mere fact that she had done so put out of his head any notion of returning to the City that night. "But in sober truth," he said, "I cannot possibly find my way back. And you will not let me stay here. What do you expect me to do?" Hitherto his indiscreet speeches had always been of such a nature that it was possible to ignore them. But she considered this plea impertinent, and was so much vexed that she refused to continue the discussion. He was all the more disappointed because he realized that such an opportunity might never occur again. He hated her to feel that he was taking advantage of her loneliness; but it could do her no harm to hear once and for all from his lips exactly what were his emotions towards her. He sent for one of his gentlemen who served under him in the Guard and in whom he had complete confidence. "I cannot go away until I have seen the chaplain," he said. "Hitherto he has not for a moment left the Princess's side; but I imagine that he will soon be taking a rest. I shall stay here and try to get a word with him when the night service is over. I wish you and the other officers to stay where you are. But send some of the men to my farm at Kurusuno, which is not far from here, I think. They will be able to get together some fodder for the horses. And there must be no talking among those of you who remain here. If your voices are heard, people will know I have stayed here for the night, and spread a false impression of my object in coming." "It is useless for me to think of returning," he then said to Ochiba in an off hand manner, "and I may as well wait here as anywhere else. I hope this will not disturb you. When the chaplain leaves your mother's room, I shall join him." Never before had he behaved in this impertinent manner. The only effective answer to his insolence would have been to seek shelter in her mother's rooms. But such a course seemed under the circumstances too extreme, and she sat motionless in her chair, wondering what would come next. Nor had she long to wait. For a few minutes afterwards a gentlewoman came with a message, and Yugiri, upon some excuse or other, accompanied her behind the curtains. The fog was now so thick, even inside the house, that despite the lamp it was almost dark. In sudden terror she made for a sliding door at the back of the room. Dark though it was, he darted unerringly upon her tracks, and was just in time to seize the train of her dress before she closed the door. She shook herself free; but there was no bolt or catch on her side, and holding the door to, she stood trembling like water. "Is it really so very shocking that I should venture behind your curtains?" he asked. "I may not be of much importance in your eyes, but I have known you for some while, and rendered you, perhaps, a few small services." He now spoke calmly and reasonably of his feelings towards her; but she could only think of his impertinent behavior in securing this interview, and in her indignation at his intrusion she was scarcely conscious of what were the sentiments that he was patiently laboring to express. "If to feel as I do," he continued, "is an offence, then I have indeed merited your displeasure. But do not for a moment fear that I could possibly be guilty of any other misdemeanor. I am here to speak, and only to speak. Surely

I have the right to tell you of thoughts that, unexpressed, would by their violence soon shatter my heart to dust. I have tried again and again to let you know in other ways of the torment I was enduring, but you would not listen to me. Is it so surprising that I should have seized this kindly opportunity? Do not, however, think me worse than I am. Provoke me as you may, I swear to you that I will do no more than frame in words the turmoil that I can no longer lock up unuttered in my breast." She was still holding the door, but it was clear that he could easily open it if he chose; and he made no attempt to do so. "Might you not save yourself this trouble?" he asked at last, with a laugh that somehow convinced her he meant no further harm. Her hand fell; he pushed back the door and entered. "I do not think you know what I am enduring for your sake," he said presently. "I am beginning to think that, though you were a wife, you do not understand even the rudiments of love."

To this and many other remarks that he had made she could think of no reply. He had indeed charged her before with not "understanding" love; but so far as it meant anything at all the phrase seemed to imply merely a readiness to yield oneself at demand, irrespective of one's own principles or inclinations. "You are quite wrong," she said between her tears. "I know a good deal more than you suppose—enough to be sure that such cruelty as you have displayed tonight has little indeed to do with love."

He tried to lead her into the moonlight, for a great wind was now blowing, and the mist had cleared away. But she still held aloof. "Surely I have proved to you by now that I mean no harm," he said earnestly. "Trust me, and you will find that I do nothing without your leave. Come..." and he drew her to him. It was now nearing dawn. The moon was shining out of a cloudless sky, its light penetrating even the last hovering remnants of the mist. They were sitting on an open verandah, so shallow that the moon seemed to thrust its face into theirs. He began to talk about Kashiwagi, and she now joined in the conversation quite calmly and happily.

He could not, however, forbear from reproaching her for showing more tenderness to the memory of Kashiwagi, who neglected her, than kindness to himself, who offered her an unbounded admiration. She did not reply, but silently reflected that though there was not much to recommend Kashiwagi either in rank or birth, he was at least a legitimate husband, approved both by her father and his, and able to give her the place that was her due. If even an alliance that seemed so certain of success had failed thus disastrously, what could she expect from an intrigue that would be carried on in the teeth of endless opposition and obstruction? It was not as if Kumoi were a stranger; she was Kashiwagi's sister, and Ochiba had made great friends with her. And To no Chujo, too! What would he think of it all? Wherever her thoughts turned, they fell upon some person neat and dear to her whom the news of this liaison would profoundly shock and offend. And if she herself, who alone knew that, despite appearances, her conduct had been irreproachable—if she herself were already so much horrified what would be the view of those whose ignorance left them free to make the blackest conjectures? Nor was it any consolation that, for the moment, her mother knew nothing of what was going on. For she would certainly find out in the end, and the fact that it had been kept from her would give the affair in her eyes an even more guilty turn.

Ochiba's mother, though she showed no real signs of recovery, was on certain days perfectly conscious and rational. On one such occasion, when the daily Intercession was over, the chaplain remained behind and sat by the bed reading incantations. He felt extremely gratified at the patient's improvement. "The vows of the Great Sun Buddha[*] were not made in vain," he said. "I knew well enough that the spells we have worked at so hard could not fail to have their effect. The evil spirit that possesses you has fought well; but it is, after all, a frail wretched thing, shackled with such a load of sin as will never let it prevail against weapons of holiness." In mentioning the evil spirit he spoke in a stern and angry voice. Then, with a curtness that is often assumed by men of uncompromising piety, he suddenly asked: "How long has your daughter been going with Yugiri?" "I don't know what you are talking about," said the old lady indignantly. "He was a great friend of Kashiwagi's, and in memory of their friendship has helped us in one way or another from time to time. I hear he has been here constantly to enquire after me during my illness, and I am sure it is very kind of him..." "This is all quite unnecessary," broke in the priest. "There is no question of concealing the matter from me. This morning as I was going to early service I distinctly saw an extremely handsome young man go out at the door of the western wing. There was a good deal of mist about, and I should not myself have recognized him. But I heard my servitors saying to one another: "There goes Prince Yugiri. The same business as before. When his carriage came he sent it away, and settled in for the night!" As a matter of fact I should have guessed for myself who it was by the smell he left behind him. It made my head ache. But that young man has always used too much scent.

"This will never do. You must not think I am prejudiced against him. On the contrary, I have been under obligations to his family for a long while. His grandmother always made use of me when she required prayers to be said on his behalf, and since she died he has frequently sent for me himself. But I am not going to countenance an intrigue of this kind. His wife, Lady Kumoi, is not a person with whom it is safe

---

[*] See above, p. 684.

to trifle. What important office of state is there now which one or the other of her relatives does not hold? Moreover, she has borne him eight (or is it nine?) children. You surely do not imagine that your daughter is going to oust her from her place? There will be endless jealousies and bickerings, leading at last to just such shameless and frenzied passions as all too commonly prove to be a woman's undoing, when it is her fate at last to enter into the Long Darkness. And even though your daughter herself may give way to no violent feelings, the jealousy that her situation arouses in this young man's wife will in the end prey equally on Lady Ochiba's soul, and gravely endanger her salvation. In a word, this must stop at once. I insist upon it."

He became more and more excited and violent in his denunciation of the supposed intrigue, and it was only with difficulty that the old lady at last obtained his attention. "I was absolutely unaware that anything of the kind was taking place," she said. "There was one occasion when my people told me he had been unwell and was resting here so that he might visit me next day. Perhaps that is what has given rise to these rumors. He has always been so serious-minded, so reliable, that I really cannot think..." But she had as a matter of fact noticed one or two queer things, and though Yugiri was so punctilious, so scrupulously careful to avoid anything that might give rise to gossip, so deferential and courtly in his treatment of women, she yet could imagine from various small indications that, left to himself, with no strange eye upon him to criticize or make note, he might quite well have taken the most unwarranted liberties. And for the last few weeks Ochiba's part of the house had been almost deserted. However, there was one person who must certainly know the truth about the matter: she sent for the maid Koshosho, who was reluctantly obliged to tell all she knew. "I was given to understand, Madam," she said, "that Prince Yugiri merely desired to unburden his heart upon some question that has been occupying him since the end of last year. He left before dawn, and I can answer for it that nothing of any consequence took place. I don't know what can have put this idea into people's heads." She was racking her brain to think who had been the talebearer. It never occurred to her that the chaplain might have played this part.

The old lady was extremely upset by these revelations, and began to weep so bitterly that Koshosho wished a thousand times that she had not been so simple as to tell the truth. She now tried to repair her error by putting the matter in as good a light as possible. "But, Madam, there was a screen between them..." "But, Madam, they were not together more than a moment," and so on. "What difference does that make?" groaned Ochiba's mother. "No girl with any common sense or decency would have received him at all. Maybe they did no harm together at all. But that's not the way the story will be told among the priests here, nor in the kitchens and sculleries either. If only there were some way of explaining to people what really happened! But unfortunately no one in this house can be trusted to do anything..." So she gasped, being now seized upon by a fresh paroxysm of pain.

Very reluctantly Yugiri decided to spend the next night at home. An immediate repetition of his visit would only serve to strengthen any suspicion that might have been aroused on this last disastrous occasion. Irritable as he had been for months past, he was now a thousand times more restless and gloomy. Kumoi knew, or at any rate could very well conjecture, where he had spent the night. But she did not allude to the matter, and disguised her chagrin by taking part in the games of her children. Late in the evening came a note from Ochiba's mother. It was written in so shaky a hand that he found it hard to read, and was obliged to hold it close to the great lamp. Though Kumoi was behind her curtains-of-state, she instantly became aware of what he was doing, and slipping up behind him, took the letter out of his hand. "What are you doing?" he cried, starting violently. "That is not the way to behave. As a matter of fact; this letter is of no interest. It is from Her Ladyship in the eastern wing.* She was not very well this morning, and after my audience† I ought to have called upon her. But being pressed for time I sent a note to enquire how she was. You can see for yourself that it does not look much like a love-letter! You really must not grab at things in that fashion. You are allowing your rudeness to go further and further every day. You might at least behave properly when there are people in the room." "If anyone is going 'further and further every day' at the present moment, it is surely you," was all she answered. But she forced herself to speak lightly, hoping at all costs to dispel his present grimness. He laughed. "Perhaps you are right," he said. "But have you really anything to complain of? Everyone must be allowed an occasional distraction; and surely there is not another man in the world who has used this right so sparingly as I. The fidelity of a husband who seemed incapable of venturing one step further afield would in the long run become a very slight satisfaction to you. Indeed, you lose by my particularity. For surely the position of a woman who stands first among many rivals is far more distinguished than that of one who stands alone? Moreover, the affection of the husband is far more likely to be permanent if he is allowed a certain amount of variety and diversion. You would not set much store by my admiration, if it merely meant I were too dull to see the beauty of other women." He hoped thus to divert her attention and quietly regain possession of the letter. But she laughed at him outright, and presently said: "You have made these kind

---

* The Lady from the Village of Falling Flowers.
† With his father, Genji.

provisions for my happiness at a time when I am too old to profit by them. Perhaps if I had more experience in that direction, your present preoccupation would not depress me so much as it does. If ever before I had received unkindness at your hands..."* The allusion was apt; but he would not accept it. "Come," he said, "to hint at 'dereliction' is absurd. You must have been hearing stories that are utterly untrue. It is strange; but some of your people have never lost the spite they felt against me at the beginning—you remember—when I was in the Sixth Rank, and they thought I was not good enough for you. I am sure that now they have been trying to turn you against me by some lie or other. It is too bad. I feel it on Ochiba's account as much as my own." But though Kumoi had probably heard things which were, at the moment, still untrue, the hope he felt that they would soon be true prevented him from protesting very effectively. He discovered that Kumoi's old nurse had indeed been speaking to her very bitterly about him; but he let the matter pass and did not attempt to justify himself.

As regards the letter, it would have been very unwise to show too much interest in it, and he went to bed without attempting to get it back. But it was very worrying not to know what it contained. He managed unobtrusively, under some pretext or other, to get up and look for it under the couch where she had been lying; but nothing was there. Having passed a troubled night, he lay in bed late into the morning, and it was only when Kumoi was called away to look after the children that, under cover of dressing and so on, he set to work upon a fresh search. Kumoi, on her side, seeing that he did not press her for the return of the letter, concluded that it was indeed of the dull nature he had described, and even forgot that she had taken it. All the morning she was busily occupied in making dolls, giving first writing-lessons, and romping with high-spirited babies, so that it was small wonder if the matter never entered her head. But Yugiri was still thinking of nothing else. It had now become imperative that he should send an answer. But if it was apparent by his reply that he had not got the letter with him (and he had really only managed to make out a few words here and there) the old lady would at once suspect that he had left it lying about.

Breakfast was followed by a quiet morning. Suddenly Yugiri said: "What happened to that letter you took from me yesterday? You saw I had scarcely read it; I wonder you did not give it back to me. I feel rather tired today and though I ought really to visit her,† I do not think I shall even call upon my father. The least I can do is to write her a note.

---

* "If ever before I had received unkindness at your hands, this sudden dereliction would be less hard to bear."

† The Lady from the Village of Falling Flowers. Yugiri is pretending that it was from her the letter came.

What did she say?" He managed to pass this off so well that she felt she had behaved ridiculously over the letter, and said (keeping up her end as best she could): "You have a very good excuse. You can say you caught cold when exposing yourself to the mountain air the other night." "I did think we had heard the last of that business," he answered. "I wonder you are not ashamed to talk of me as though I were a vulgar pleasure-seeker. Your waiting-women, among whom my rigid domesticity has long been a standing joke, would be excessively amused if they could hear the line you are now taking." Then, breaking off, he suddenly exclaimed: "Well, anyway, where is that letter?" She promised to find it, but did not immediately do so; and after a little further talk, he went to take a rest, for it was already growing dark. He was soon disturbed by the din of the crickets in the garden outside. This set him thinking of how noisily they had cried on that mist-bound evening at Ono.[*] He must not let another day go by without answering. He got up quickly and began grinding his ink. Surely there must be some way of framing a reply so that she would not realize he had not kept her letter? As he sat pondering, he felt a slight unevenness in the cushion under him, and pulling it up to see what was amiss, to his delight and also, as it proved, to his embarrassment, he discovered the missing letter. For it was no less committal than in his most gloomy forebodings he had imagined it. "Your last letter," she wrote, "came at a time when my daughter was visiting my bedside, and was brought to her here. As she seemed at a loss how to reply, I am now writing in her stead: 'Full clearly have you shown that in your eyes a place for one night's dallying is the moorside where droops the Lady-flower.'"

"One night." It was quite clear what the writer meant to imply. And what must be the conclusion that she had drawn from his protracted silence! It was obvious to him on a second inspection of the letter that it had been written in great distress of mind. He could not help feeling somewhat bitterly against Kumoi, whose foolish trick had inflicted such suspense. But after all, a year or two ago she would never have dreamt of doing such a thing. It was his own changed conduct that had altered hers. He thought for a moment of going straight to Ono. But he felt certain Ochiba would not receive him, even though her mother countenanced his visit. As a matter of fact, it was hopeless in any case; for today was his Black Day.[†] Perhaps it was a good thing that circumstances thus conspired against him, he thought virtuously, and hastened to answer the letter. "The sight of your letter delighted me in more ways than one," he wrote. "But the hint of reproof which it contains is rather mysterious. What is

---

[*] Ochiba's house in the mountains.
[†] According to the astrologers.

it that people have been telling you? 'In truth, I lay amid the thickets of the autumn heath; yet by no dalliance of pillowing leaves was my rest comforted.' I do not in general think there is much sense in replying to such reproofs; but on this occasion I must protest that you have jumped to conclusions somewhat too rapidly..."

There was a separate letter for Ochiba, and both were given to Tayu, the principal retainer who had been with him on his last visit to Ono, the man being instructed to use the swiftest horse in the stable, with a light Chinese relay-saddle. "Say that I have been detained at my father's palace," he whispered, "and have only just returned."

Meanwhile things at Ono were not going well. Rather recklessly, as she felt, Ochiba's mother had taken matters into her own hands and protested against Yugiri's light-minded and casual escapade. And now it was clear that she had offended him. Hour after hour went by; it grew quite dark and still no answer came. This so much upset her that her apparent convalescence was soon a thing of the past, and before the end of the day her condition was as serious as ever. Ochiba, on the other hand, so far from being perturbed by his failure to reappear, regretted nothing save that she had not been a little curter with him on that one occasion. Seeing her mother's distress, she attributed it to horror at the things which were supposed to have taken place on that unfortunate night; and she began trying to explain how little had really happened. But the subject was not easy to talk about. Confusion overcame her, and she left off in the middle. Seeing the girl's embarrassment, her mother was doubly distressed: "Poor creature!" she thought. "Has anyone of similar talents and position ever been so consistently unfortunate?" At last she said rather bitterly: "I am going to be disagreeable—a thing which I thought I had long ago done for the last time. It may not have been your fault... But really, from what I hear, it seems as though your behavior had been incredibly childish. This particular matter is at an end; for it is clear that he does not mean to come near us again. But do, I beg you, be on your guard about this sort of thing in future. I am sure I have taken immense pains with your upbringing. And after all, with regard to affairs of that kind, you are not without experience... Perhaps it was foolish of me, but I assure you this, of all ways, is not the one in which I thought you would get into trouble. A little firmness, good sense, decision—nothing more was required. I see that you are far indeed from being capable of looking after yourself, and it perturbs me beyond measure to think that I must leave you so soon. Even among commoners there is a feeling —at any rate among the better sort of people—that flippancy does not become a widow; still less should anyone of your rank dream of allowing admirers to go in and out in that fashion. I am very sorry your married life brought you so little happiness. You know that the choice always seemed to me singularly inappropriate;

but your father, the ex-Emperor, and Kashiwagi's father pressed me so hard that in the end I came over to their side, convinced for the moment that this quite unnecessary match was preordained by Fate. It turned out to be a terrible misfortune, the results of which you will feel all your life. But you had at any rate the satisfaction of knowing that you yourself were in no way to blame, and could reproach Heaven without fear of retort. Such feelings you can no longer entertain; but if you could manage to take no notice of all the unpleasant things that were being said around you, I suppose you might find considerable solace in relations with this young man—if he made a practice of coming here, which I am certain he has not the least intention of doing!"

To this cruelly faithful picture of her predicament she could find no reply. She now sat gently sobbing. Her mother, watching her intently, was moved this time by a sudden outburst of affectionate admiration. "How handsome you are!" she said. "There is no one like you. What kink is it in your fate that made such beauty the rallying point of every imaginable check and disappointment?" Her agitation soon reduced her to a state in which she fell an easy prey to the next onslaught of the "possession" that had for long past been assailing her. In a moment she had lost consciousness, and an icy coldness had settled upon her limbs. The chaplains hastily assembled and with frantic supplications sought to revive her. They were all holy men, drawn from inaccessible mountain temples, which they had vowed never to leave till death. The entreaties of Ochiba and her friends had induced them to break their vows; and if they should now pull down their altars and return to their cells defeated, surely (they protested to Buddha) the Faith would suffer a grave discredit.

It was at this moment that Yugiri's letter arrived. The sick woman was able, in a fleeting interval of consciousness, to comprehend that Yugiri made no suggestion of repeating his visit. All, then, was as bad as she had feared. He had on this occasion merely been heartlessly amusing himself. "And," remembered Ochiba's mother—it was her last conscious thought—"whatever scandal is talked about this at Court will as likely as not be founded on my own letter."[*]

Her people were slow to realize that the end had come. She had often before suffered from seizures during which life appeared to be extinct. But now the usual spells had no effect, and at last it was apparent that all was over.

The ninth month had come. Storms were raging in the hills. Not a leaf on any tree; the whole country wore its most desolate air; and Ochiba, sensitive to the changing aspects of nature, was in a more wretched state than ever before. So gloomy indeed were her thoughts that she longed

---

[*] See above, p. 717.

continually for death to terminate the terrible monotony of her lonely existence. True, Yugiri wrote almost every day. His enquiries and the presents he sent gave great satisfaction to the resident priests, whose long seclusion made such distractions exceedingly welcome. But Ochiba, though he sent the most solicitous messages, and sometimes long notes in which he enquired after every item of her health with the utmost concern, gave no sign of gratification. This was the man she reasoned, whose heartlessness had preyed upon her mother's mind so that she had died unquietly and carried with her to the grave a burden that would endanger her salvation.* It nowadays sufficed merely for his name to be mentioned, and Ochiba's tears would break out afresh. Her people did their best to assist Yugiri's cause, and when he failed even to obtain a single line in reply he at first attributed this to the mental confusion caused by her mother's death. But as time went by it was apparent that there must be some other cause for what he regarded as her crudely insulting conduct. Had he written letters in which her loss was ignored, letters devoted to the pageants and frivolities of the day, he could have understood her irritation. But he was conscious of having shown the tenderest sympathy, the most delicate appreciation of all she must be feeling. He remembered how when his grandmother had died he had been for a time very much dispirited; more so, he thought, than his uncle To no Chujo, who had taken the death of his mother very much as a matter of course, and while anxious to do everything that the public would think proper, obviously regarded the whole business as a tiresome waste of time. Even Genji, who was only a son-in-law, had shown much more concern. Among Yugiri's own contemporaries, the one, strangely enough, who most entered into his feelings was the quiet, almost stolid Kashiwagi. How glad he had been to see him during those days, and how precious his sympathy had been! And it seemed to Yugiri exceedingly odd that Ochiba showed no desire for similar consolation.

Kumoi still remained in the same uncertainty as to what was going on. The frequent letters to Ono were all supposed to be connected with Ochiba's recent loss. But the death of this excellent lady was not in itself sufficient to account for Yugiri's listlessness and preoccupation. One evening when he lay on his couch, gazing at the evening sky, she sent one of the children to him with a scrap of paper on which was written: "Gladly would I console you did I but know whether for the dead you mourn, or for the living thus consume your heart." He smiled. Why (he asked himself) did it please her to give him this loophole? She knew well enough that, greatly though he had liked the old Princess, her death could not conceivably weigh much on his mind after all these months. Swiftly and

---

* Those who died with anything on their minds cannot enter Paradise.

negligently he dashed off the reply: "Nor this, nor that. Who grieves that one particular dewdrop vanishes into the morning air?" This was all very well; but putting aside general considerations as to the fate of dewdrops, it was evident that he had no intention of taking her into his confidence; and Kumoi was very unhappy.

Yugiri had thought of waiting till the period of mourning was over before he attempted another visit to Ono. But he found himself unable to hold out so long, and reasoning that, so far as her reputation was concerned, no more harm could happen than had been done already, he was determined not to abandon the quest till his full purpose was achieved. Kumoi might think what she pleased. And however little encouragement he received from Ochiba herself, that phrase about "one night only" in her mother's letter gave his renewed attentions a sort of sanction, and would in the last resort make it difficult for her to dismiss him altogether.

It was about the middle of the ninth month. The grandeur of the scenes through which Yugiri passed was such as could not have failed to awe the dullest, the most unimpressionable visitor. His way lay through forests in which not merely every leaf, but every bough had been caught by the tempest and hurried earthwards, to toss amid the whirling wreckage from the heights above. As he approached the house, the noise of distant chanting mingled with the clamor of the storm. Close under the fence a group of deer was sheltering from the blasts of the storm, their hoofs pressing upon the brown rice-stalks; nor did even the harsh tones of the bird-clapper* drive them from their refuge. They stood together, crying with a pitiful air. The noise of the torrent startled Yugiri from his thoughts, bursting upon his ear with its thunderous clang. Only the crickets, their arbors laid low by the storm, were strangely quiet. But one flower, the blue Dragon's Gall, was now rewarded for its long patience, and shining out all dewy amid the dead grass, triumphed at last in its desolate supremacy.

In all this there was nothing out of the ordinary; but given the nature and circumstances of his visit, these commonplaces of the autumn landscape moved him to an almost unendurable sadness.

Remembering Shosho no Kimi's gay laugh and handsome face, he felt that to be with her for a little might help to drive away this intolerable depression, and it was for her that he sent when he arrived at the usual western door.

"Closer," he said. "If I am obliged to raise my voice we may be overheard, and I want to talk with you seriously. Surely you count it to my credit that I have made my way through the hills at such a season." He glanced towards the mountain. "And now the mist is rising," he said.

---

* A rattle used by peasants to scare away birds from the crops.

"Look how thick..." "Closer, closer," he whispered. She pressed forward the curtain behind which she sat, till it obtruded a little way beyond the edge of the reed-blind. She kept pulling her skirts to one side. This Shosho no Kimi was a sister of the Governor of Yamato, and consequently a cousin of Ochiba, with whom she had been brought up on terms of complete equality. She was therefore wearing the deepest mourning.

"I am sure it is natural enough that Lady Ochiba should be very much upset," said Yugiri at last, "but I still do not understand why this should involve such persistent rudeness to *me*. I am exasperated to the verge of madness by her refusal to grant me a single word of reply. My mind is going to pieces altogether; everyone notices it." So he went on, and presently mentioned the old Princess's last letter, breaking into tears as he did so. "Your slowness in replying," said Shosho no Kimi, weeping even more bitterly than he, "seemed to have a disastrous effect upon her. She had been much stronger lately; but that one day's suspense undid all the good work. The evil influences that had before possessed her saw their opportunity and were quick to use it. She was in a bad way on one or two occasions at the time of her son-in-law's death, and we sometimes thought it was all over with her. But she had only to remember Lady Ochiba's need, and she would at once make an effort to recover herself. I wish indeed we had someone like her to comfort my cousin Ochiba. She's in such a state she hardly seems to know her own name, and so it goes on from one day's end to another." So, amid her sobs, she somewhat inconsequently sought to explain Ochiba's silence. "That's all very well," he said, "but it leaves me as puzzled as ever by her mystifications. I am, I hope I may say without rudeness, the one person who can be of use to her at present. Her father* is buried away in the clouds on some distant mountain peak, and if he ever gives a thought to family affairs, he is too far off to be of any practical assistance. There is no reason why you yourself should not remonstrate with her when you get the chance. It is really turning into a kind of obstinacy. However, it will all come right in the end. She feels at present that she will never want to return into society; but people do not remain in that state of mind indefinitely. Nor do things happen as one plans..." But Shosho no Kimi gave him no help, and to his repeated messages Ochiba sent only the reply that upon some future occasion, when feeling less dazed by her loss, she would attempt to thank him for his repeated visits.

Back in his palace, he mooned about in so vague and distracted a manner, that the ladies of the household said to one another in shocked tones: "What a wretched sight the man is! And the last person too whom one would have expected to see in this state." As for Kumoi, he remem-

---

* Suzaku.

bered how often he had praised in her hearing the pleasant relations that prevailed between the members of Genji's household. If she showed any signs of resentment at his interest in Ochiba, he would at once think her a most disagreeable, ungenerous creature. She, too, Kumoi felt, could have endured rivals well enough if she had been used to them and if those around her had learnt to take them as a matter of course. But from the very beginning her father, her brothers—everyone had quoted Yugiri as an unparalleled example of single-minded devotion; and that even this prodigy of steadfastness should grow tired of her was a humiliation indeed.

So they lay till it was almost dawn, neither heeding the other or showing the least disposition to make friends; and long before the mists had cleared he irritated Kumoi by getting up and writing his usual letter to Ono. This time, however, she played no trick upon him. He wrote at considerable length, and then pushing the letter away from him, began humming a poem to himself. He did this very softly; but Kumoi heard the words: "No message will you send me save that no message you will send till an unending night its dreams shall end?" "The Silent Waterfall[*] that from Mount Ono drops..." she thought she heard him quote.

The answer came later in the morning. It was a solid-looking epistle, written on stout, brownish paper; and as usual the writer was Shosho no Kimi. Kumoi watched his face while he read it. Had Princess Ochiba at last broken her silence? As a matter of fact the letter contained nothing but remonstrations from Shosho upon the uselessness of his continuing to write. "To prove my point," she said, "I enclose your last letter to her, just as it was when I rescued it." And here was his letter indeed, torn in pieces and covered all over with random scribblings. His first feeling, however, was not so much of pique at the use to which it had been put, as of delight that she had seen and handled it. Piecing together the fragments, he thought he could make put a poem somewhat in this style: "Ceaseless as the waters of Mount Ono, day and night my silent tears flow." It was only the old Ono poem twisted a little to suit her own plight; but there were points of interest in the penmanship.

How often had Yugiri watched other men falling into the helpless state in which he now found himself! There had always seemed to him something unreal in their languishings; and he had spoken of such people with considerable severity, feeling that with a little effort they might at any moment have escaped from their difficulties. But no, there was no escape; nothing to do but to endure.

It was not long before Genji heard what was going on. It had always been a comfort to him that Yugiri possessed so much good sense and moderation. It was pleasant, for instance, to feel that whatever scandals

---

[*] Otonashi no Taki.

had to be investigated, Yugiri's name would never be involved; and the more so because Genji himself had suffered from the effects of a quite opposite reputation. This attachment with Ochiba in any case could bring little happiness to either of them. But it would not have been quite so bad if she had been someone quite outside their circle. As it was, what must To no Chujo and the rest be feeling about it? However, Yugiri was quite capable of seeing all this for himself. There was nothing that Genji could usefully say. He did not indeed think so much about Yugiri as about the two ladies. For them he could not help being extremely sorry. He mentioned the affair to Murasaki one day when he was talking things over with her, and spoke of his own anxiety as to what would become of her when he, like Kashiwagi, should have passed away. She blushed and a look of pain crossed her face; for she knew well enough how unlikely it was that she would survive him. She pitied all women. How impossibly difficult was their position! If they shut themselves away, ignored the existence of beauty, tenderness—of all emotion—what was left, save to sit thinking of darkness and the grave? Nor was it, in the end, of the slightest satisfaction to the parents who bore one, that one should grow up into an inexperienced nonentity; on the contrary, they were extremely disappointed. Was there not a story about the Silent Prince?* That was the kind of life women were expected to lead. They must lock everything up in their hearts. But even the clergy regarded silence as one of the hardest penances; and it was only by consenting to speak at last that the Silent Prince, despite all his "knowledge of good and evil," managed to avoid being buried alive. And even if one could settle, to one's own satisfaction, on a correct middle course, the difficulties of pursuing it were immense... It was not of herself, of course, that she was thinking, but of her adopted child, the Akashi Princess.

Curious to see how he would take it, Genji began speaking of their friends at Ono next time Yugiri came to his palace. "So the mourning for Ochiba's mother will soon be over," he said. "It must be just thirty years since Suzaku first took her under his protection... A lifetime, yes, that is what a whole lifetime looks like when one sees it stretched out! The night is soon over, the dewdrops vanish in the sun, and 'what worth gaining, to hold so short a while?' But after she had taken her vows and turned her back on the world, I fancy she settled down into a not too uncomfortable existence. I am sorry she is gone. A great misfortune, a

---

* A Buddhist story. The Prince, being endowed with knowledge of good and evil, and memory of his past existences, remembered that in the last but one he had spoken an angry word, and consequently spent his next existence in Hell. Having now been born as a prince, he determined to be on the safe side, and did not speak at all. When he was thirteen, the King lost patience with him and gave orders that he was to be buried alive. Upon which the Silent Prince at last spoke. For a version of the story see Chavannes, *Cinq Cent Contes et Apologues,* i, 126.

very great misfortune." "Yes, indeed," said Yugiri, "when one sees what useless and unimportant people are spoken of at their decease as 'losses to the country.'" "The ceremonies on the Forty-ninth Day," he continued, "are left entirely in the hands of her nephew, the Governor of Yamato. It is a wretched business; and somehow her evident loss of all influence and proper support makes a more painful impression now that she is gone than ever during her lifetime."

"It has no doubt been a great shock to Suzaku," said Genji. "But I am chiefly sorry for the daughter. I hear, by the way, that she is pretty; after Nyosan, she was certainly her father's favorite." "About the daughter," said Yugiri, "I know very little. But I believe the mother was a very agreeable woman. I did not know her well; but on one or two occasions I was able to be of some slight service to her." If his son had lied less flatly, Genji would have felt it possible to continue the conversation. But such an attitude betokened a state of mind that was far removed from either inviting or accepting advice. He felt in any case the absurdity of such a person as himself taking a high line about these questions, and changed the subject.

In point of fact the arrangements for the service of the Forty-ninth Day were made almost entirely by Yugiri, who took the utmost pains in planning every detail. The reason for all this zest on his part was naturally the subject of much speculation. To no Chujo, when the matter was mentioned to him, was disinclined, from what he knew of Yugiri's character, to credit the existence of any scandal, and chiefly blamed Ochiba for allowing an outside person to play so prominent a part in the proceedings.

It reached Suzaku's ears that she intended to stay at Ono and become a nun. "I hope you will do nothing of the kind," he wrote. "It is, I know, generally considered creditable for a widow to remain in retirement. But there are circumstances under which, for a girl like you, with no one to take her side, such a course might have an opposite effect, both in this life and the next, to that which you imagine. At this moment I do not think you can either withdraw from the Court without giving countenance to undesirable rumors, or embrace the religious life in a suitable state of mind. If you are really bent upon religion, pray do nothing irretrievable till you have given your feelings time to subside..." He wrote several times to this effect. It was evident that he had heard her name coupled with Yugiri's, and was afraid it would be thought that she was leaving the world in a fit of pique at the affair's not having gone as she wished.

The news that Ochiba was soon returning to Court put Yugiri in a difficult position. If he acted as one already having claims upon her, it would give the impression that the late Princess had not exercised her functions with proper strictness—an aspersion which, even though it were not taken very seriously, he did not care to inflict upon the dead woman's reputation. But to convince the world that the attachment had just commenced, to re-enact all the familiar stages of incipient attraction, courtship, and melancholy was more than could be expected of him.

As soon as the day of her arrival had been fixed, he sent for the Governor of Yamato and consulted with him as to what could be done to make the palace in the First Ward less uncomfortable. Even before the removal to Ono the place had for so long been inhabited by women only that everything had run very much to seed. He now gave orders for a general cleaning up of the rooms and a complete new set of hangings, screens, curtains-of-state, and the like, seeing to every detail himself. It was arranged that these fittings should be made as quickly as possible in the Governor's own house.

When the day came Yugiri sent his carriage and outriders to fetch her, but did not go himself. To her protestations that she had no intention of leaving Ono, her cousin, the Governor of Yamato, replied: "Madam, in this matter you must bow to my judgment. I feel for you deeply, and have for some time past done everything in my power to assist you. But I have my province to think of; urgent affairs await me, and I must return at once. Fortunately things are not so bad as they might be. I am handing on the direction of your household to a most loyal and painstaking successor. I am not suggesting that you should accept him in any capacity other than mine has lately been. But should you choose to do so, you would have many precedents in your favor; nor would anyone have a right to blame you, even though it were known that the attachment were solely on his side. For a lady's intentions, however determined she may be, cannot be put into practice without the aid of some admirer who is ready to place his influence and resources at her disposal. Do not think that I mistrust your intelligence. Your decisions, I am sure, will always be excellent; I merely question your ability to carry them out." And then turning to Ochiba's ladies: "I regard you all as very much to blame in this matter. You set the whole thing going, and now, I have reason to believe, you are refusing to carry messages or give the unfortunate gentleman any reasonable assistance." Thus reproached, her waiting-women gathered round her and began to attire her in the new clothes into which she was to change for the journey. She was prevailed upon at last to let them dress the hair—full six feet of it—that she longed so ardently to sacrifice.* It grew a little thinner than formerly, though not to an extent that anyone else would have noticed. But Ochiba now surveyed it with dismay. How altered she was, in this and every way! Never again would she dare to show herself..." "Come now," her ladies cried, "we should have been on the road hours ago. It will soon be getting dark." One had slipped out

---

* I.e. to become a nun.

with a toilet-case, another with a clothes-box. Hampers, sacks one by one had been laid upon the wagons. There was no one left in the house, and at last, since she could not stay there all alone, weeping bitterly she climbed into the carriage that Yugiri had sent.

At last they arrived. What had happened to her mother's house? Who were all these people that crowded the passages? Whence this strange air of festivity? And hardly able to believe that this was indeed her old home, Ochiba sat motionless in the carriage long after it had halted.

Yugiri was waiting in the eastern wing of the Palace. He had brought so many possessions with him that Kumoi's people concluded he was about to make a long stay. "He might have given us a little warning," they said. "When, pray, did the ceremony* take place?" It was assumed that a relationship had been going on in secret for years past. To no one did it occur that the attachment was not mutual; a state of affairs very unfortunate for Ochiba.

When supper was over and everything had quieted down, Yugiri went to Shosho no Kimi and commenced his usual appeal. "Surely you can make up your mind to let her alone for a day or two," the girl said. "We can all trust you to remain faithful for as long as that. Madam, so far from being any more cheerful today, has felt this homecoming very bitterly, and it is no use trying to approach her. I must ask you, on my own behalf, to show a little consideration; for if anything puts her out, all the burden falls on me. It really is not possible to do anything with her when she is in this state." "That is very odd," said Yugiri. "I should never have supposed, from what I know of her, that she was so churlish and unmanageable..." and he began to advance every reason why it must inevitably be not only to his advantage but also to hers—why no one could possibly blame them, till Shosho no Kimi interrupted impatiently: "You might as well ask me to bring messages to a corpse. I tell you she is half out of her wits, and were I to talk to her all night, she would not at the end of it have understood a word I said. I am sure, Sir, you would not wish to take advantage of her while she is in such a condition." And she wrung her hands. "This is unheard of," he cried. "No one can ever have been insulted in so brutal a manner before. It would surprise her to learn how any outside person would be struck by such conduct." "You have very little experience of the world," she laughed, "if this is what you call 'unheard of.' And as for appealing to outsiders, I think the less said about that the better. I am not at all sure that they would be on your side." But though she stood up to him so well, she could not, as he was now in charge of the household, close doors against him, and presently the two of them together entered the Princess's room. How could one combat such

---

* The formal betrothal.

impertinence, such callous lack of consideration? Ochiba did something which she knew would be thought childish and undignified. Picking up a mattress, she rushed into the storeroom and locked the door from within. How long would she have to stay here? There was no knowing. All her people seemed now to be on Yugiri's side; and in utter wretchedness she settled down there for the night. He for his part, when he had got over his first indignation and surprise, felt calmer. This was decisive; there could be no question of any completer rebuff. Here they were for the night, for all the world like those unfortunate birds the *yamadori*,* one on each side of the door. At last the dawn broke, and as he was not anxious to publish too widely the fact that *this* was the way in which they had spent the night, he now left the house, after once more attempting in vain to induce her to open the door even so much as a crack.

He went to his father's palace to rest, and there got into conversation with the Lady from the Village of Falling Flowers. "What does Kumoi think of Ochiba's return to the First Ward?" she asked in her mild, tranquil voice. "So people are making a story out of that, are they?" he said. "The truth is quite simple. At first Ochiba's mother was adverse to my taking charge of her daughter. But in her last hours she felt very anxious as to what would become of Ochiba, were she left with no one to manage her affairs, and as I had been a great friend of Kashiwagi, she withdrew her objection and begged me to help Ochiba in every way. There was nothing scandalous or surprising in my having brought her back to the First Ward; all such ideas are the mere invention of gossips and busy-bodies. As for Ochiba"—and here he laughed slightly—"she talks of nothing but becoming a nun, which shows that my devotion is not of much interest to her. Perhaps it would be the best thing, after all, if she did go into a nunnery; for at present my position both with her and with Kumoi is an impossible one. But till she does so, I must continue to help her as best I can—to do what her mother would have wished.

"Next time my father comes to see you, please explain all this to him, if you get the chance. I have been frightened to mention it, lest he should think that, after all this time, I have suddenly become frivolous in my behavior... Though as a matter of fact in things of that kind there is no reason for me to fear reproach, either from others or from my own conscience." "I always thought," she answered, "that a quite wrong account had been given of the matter; and now I see that I was right. And really, there is no reason why you should not have two wives if you want to. I am only sorry for the poor little princess. She has had things all her own way for so long." "'Poor little princess,' indeed!" exclaimed Yugiri indignantly. "It is hard to recognize her in such a description. She is

---

* The copper pheasant; the male and female are supposed to sleep one on each side of the valley.

very well able to look after herself, I assure you. 'Little demon' would describe her better, when she fancies her rights are being infringed. And why should you suppose I am going to ill-treat her? If you will forgive my saying so, I should have thought your own case showed how much was to be gained in the end by a little patience and self-restraint. A man may for the moment be hustled by tears and demonstrations, but promises exacted in that way are broken immediately, and at the same time leave behind them a disagreeable feeling on both sides. As you know, I have always admired my stepmother in many ways; but nothing about her has ever struck me as more admirable than her forbearance with regard to you." She was not deceived by this flattery. "That is only your way of making clear how little so insignificant a person as myself can know of such a situation," she said, smiling. "But I cannot believe that Genji, of all people, would dare to make any fuss about a matter of this kind, even to me in private. That would really be more than one could tolerate..." "You are quite wrong," answered Yugiri. "He has often held forth to me about such matters; and naturally, however bad his advice may be, I am bound to appear impressed. I know the situation is rather absurd."

But to return to the palace in the First Ward, "Madam," said Ochiba's maids, "you cannot continue to shut yourself up every time he calls. Would it not be better to receive him once in the usual way, and if you wish to break with him, tell him so properly, and have done with the business for good and all?" But she did not feel that she owed any consideration to one who had shown none to her and had already inflicted upon her reputation injuries which it would take years to efface.

"Our mistress says that if later on, when she is feeling more inclined for conversation, you are still kind enough to remember her, she will see whether she cannot arrange to talk with you. But at present, while the memory of her mother's death is still so recent, she begs to be excused." So reported one of the maids. "But the fact of the matter is," she went on, "that everyone already regards you as a married pair, and this naturally annoys her extremely." "But it is not as though on any previous occasion I had taken advantage of her, as many men would have done... Tell her that if she will come out into her room, I will make no objection to there being a screen between us, so long as I am allowed to tell her of what I am suffering—which will certainly not break her heart to hear! Let her grant me this, and she shall hear no more from me for many a long month." So Yugiri pleaded; and when all other arguments proved vain, he put it at last to Shosho no Kimi that if he were now to absent himself altogether, it would be thought that he had tired of Ochiba—an assumption more wounding to her pride than any of the rumors that were already afoot.

This was undeniable, and Yugiri (it was evident) would be so abjectly grateful for a mere glimpse of the princess, that Shosho no Kimi weakened, and finally showed him how to enter the storeroom by a secret door that led into the maids' rooms on the north side. That one of the ordinary servants should be talked round into betraying her was natural enough, the world being as it is, but here was Shosho no Kimi, her kinswoman, the one person whom she believed to be really on her side, handing her over to the enemy without a moment's compunction. Yugiri was now addressing to her every conceivable form of specious argument and entreaty. But though he spoke with what she recognized to be great eloquence and spirit, she remained entirely unmoved, sitting before him with her robe (for she was wearing no mantle) clutched tightly to her. Her determination to thwart him was evidently so intense, and her whole attitude expressed such profound horror at his proximity, that for the first time he began to think this was no mere shyness or widowly discretion. Almost any woman, he felt, would have shown some response to such a courtship as his had been. But she, through it all, had been unbending as an oak. He had heard of intense, unreasoning dislikes, for which no cause, save an adverse experience in some previous life, could be assigned. But so dear a case as this he never thought to have discovered. Was this all that he had got in return for so much that he had thrown away? And he remembered the time before any difficulties grew up between him and Kumoi—all the small secrets and confidences that had made those years so delightful. Suddenly he lapsed into silence; his pleading was at an end. They both sat waiting for the dawn.

Though called a storeroom, the place where they sat was not much encumbered. There were a few chests, full of perfumes, and some tray-stands, all pushed well out of the way, so that the effect was that of a small and rather cozy room. It had hitherto been quite dark; but now a ray of daylight suddenly darted in at the open door. She had buried her head in the folds of her robe. He leant forward and pulled the dress. Her hair fell in a tangle about her face, and it was only when he had pushed it back that he could at last make out her features in the growing light. It was an interesting, lively face that met his gaze; aristocratic, yet soft and womanly. And what did she think of him? In truth, she liked him as she saw him now far better than when he was dressed up for company. But it was impossible that he should see anything in her. Had not Kashiwagi (who had far less right to be particular) found her utterly unattractive? And that was years ago, when she was very different indeed from what she was now... Thus she reasoned with herself. And what would her father and To no Chujo think? Then there was her mother's death... If only the period of mourning were over... It took Yugiri a long time to contend with all these arguments.

When breakfast was served (not in the storeroom, I need hardly say!) it was thought that the dark furniture used during her mourning would strike a jarring note, and a space was divided off at one end of the room, her screen-of-state being of clove-grey, and the furniture in general of not too sumptuous a nature. The meal was served on a two-shelved sideboard of plain sandal-wood, all these things having been provided beforehand by the Governor of Yamato.

The attendants were dressed in inconspicuous shades of yellow, plum-color, grey, and brown, with a few in lighter and gayer color mixed among them. As the union had taken place in a woman's establishment, there were many details in the traditional rite which could not be observed; nor had there been anyone except the Governor to arrange matters and instruct the under-servants in their duties. On hearing that so distinguished a guest was settled in the house, many family retainers who were not for the moment on duty hastened to the palace, and were received by Yugiri in what I think is called the estate-office.

When Kumoi found that he showed no signs of returning from the palace in the First Ward, she felt that she had gone on long enough defending him. People were right. He was no longer the same steady, unchanging Yugiri of former days. Of that Yugiri not a scrap was left; and seeing no reason why she should put up with further humiliation at his hands, she called at To no Chujo's house, and alleging an unfavorable conjunction of the stars, established herself there apparently for the night. It so happened that Lady Chujo was home on a visit. Kumoi found considerable comfort in her sister's company, and prolonged her stay.

To no Chujo had heard rumors of Yugiri's new attachment, and was not surprised that the affair should have come to a head. He thought Kumoi's flight an unnecessarily violent form of protest; but then she had always been quick-tempered and headstrong.

However, if Kumoi was difficult to deal with, her father was ten times more so. No one had ever insisted so punctiliously upon his rights as head of the family. He seemed almost to take pleasure in parading his intractability. Yugiri was convinced that if he presented himself at the Great Hall, his father-in-law would behave in the most unreasonable way. "Disgraceful. Not a word. Out of my sight!" That was his style, and Yugiri felt he could not face such a scene.

Kumoi had left some of the children behind; but the little girls, who were mere babies, she had taken with her to To no Chujo's palace. Upon Yugiri's first return to his home the little boys were wild with delight and clustered round him. One of them, however, began to cry, saying he was unhappy without his mother, which Yugiri found very harassing. He wrote letter after letter begging Kumoi to return, and even sent a carriage to fetch her; but all to no effect. Her obstinacy was beginning to irritate him, and he felt very much inclined to leave things as they were. But this, he feared, might make a bad impression upon her father, and towards evening he called in person at the house. He went at once to the quarters she usually occupied when on a visit here. Kumoi was nowhere to be seen; but he eventually found some of her ladies, and the little girls with their nurse. From them he learned that Kumoi was living in the central building with her sister. "You establish yourself in your sister's apartments, as though you were not yet of age, leaving some of your children at home and the rest in a distant wing of this palace. Pray tell me what all this means. I have realized for a long time past that your head was full of the most ridiculous notions; but I did not think that, after all the devotion I have shown you in past times, you would fly both from me and our large family of children upon what is after all so flimsy a pretext." This was the rather testy note he sent in to her. She replied: "What good can come of my returning to you? At present you are tired of me, and I see no reason to suppose that this feeling is not permanent. As for the children, I am delighted to find that you take such an interest in them."

He made no further effort to bring her back with him, and spent the night alone. What kind of man can he have been (Yugiri asked himself) who started the notion that love was an agreeable business? To distract himself he had the little boys put to sleep where he could see them. But he got little rest; for no sooner had he stopped thinking about the disastrous flight of Kumoi than he began worrying about Ochiba. How much would she be upset by his absence tonight? Would all his work in that quarter have to be begun over again?

Next morning he wrote to Kumoi: "I think your decision will be regarded by everyone as very unreasonable; but such as it is I am willing to accept it. The children you have left behind with me are naturally much distressed at your absence. But I presume you had reasons of your own for deserting them as you did, and you must leave it to me to make such provision for them as I think best." There seemed in this to be hidden some form of threat. Did he mean to hand them over to a stepmother? Monstrous as such a demand would be, she thought him quite capable of it. Later on he even asked that the girls might be sent back to him. "It will henceforward be very difficult for me to have any dealings with your father," he wrote, "and I shall probably never see the little girls at all, unless they come here. Surely it would be better to bring up all the children together?" The boys were pretty creatures, still quite small. "Do not listen to your mother," he said to them. "There are many things which she does not properly understand, and this has given her some harsh ideas, that are doing us all great harm."

So far from being indignant with Yugiri, To no Chujo thought that his daughter was merely making herself ridiculous by this sudden decampment. "You might have waited a little," he said to Kumoi, "to see how things would go. Yugiri is after all a man of considerable good sense. Such headstrong and precipitate behavior does not sit at all well upon a woman. However, since you have adopted this line, you must stick to it for the present. We shall see later on what steps he will take to get you back.

To Ochiba To no Chujo sent the poem: "Because of the bond that was between us I will keep you a place in my heart. But for sympathy you must ask me no longer—you who now have more than your share!" As messenger he chose his son Ben no Shosho, who had known the house very well in Kashiwagi's time, and walked straight in. He was given a seat on the verandah outside the women's quarters; but none of the ladies seemed much inclined for conversation. In Ochiba his visit naturally awakened painful memories. He was the best-looking and most promising of To no Chujo's sons, and as she watched him from within, Ochiba was astonished by his resemblance to Kashiwagi. "Can it be," he wrote, "that you intend to treat me, who came so often to this house, as an utter stranger?"

She found To no Chujo's poem very hard to answer. Her maids insisted that it could not be dealt with by proxy. If only her mother were there to help her with it. She perhaps would be vexed at the circumstances that had called forth To no Chujo's protest. But her mother had always been ready to help her out of a difficulty, even to screen her misdoings.

"How can I, that am but one person, at the same time merit both sympathy and reproach?" Such was the tenor of her reply, and merely folding it up she sent it out to Ben no Shosho unsealed. "For a person who used to know the house," he was saying to her ladies, "it is rather dispiriting to be left on the verandah in this way. I see that if I am to be regarded as a privileged person I must come here often. Full admittance is no doubt only granted as the reward of long assiduity. So expect to see me there frequently," and with this attempt at levity he withdrew.

At the time when Ochiba was giving him no encouragement and Yugiri's distraction was most trying to those who lived with him, Kumoi suddenly received a letter from Koremitsu's* daughter. Kumoi, this lady supposed, had always regarded her with complete indifference. Yet somehow the news of what was going on at Ono moved her to write a letter of sympathy, and it was followed by others. In her poem she said: "I that am nothing, not for my own sake but for yours with tear-wet sleeve lament that love grows cold." Kumoi thought this perhaps a trifle impertinent; but receiving it as she did at a time of profound discouragement, she was by no means displeased to discover sympathy even in so humble a quarter. "How often have I grieved for others in this same plight, and little dreamed how soon it would be mine." This was all that she sent in

---

* Genji's retainer. See Part I, *passim*. Yugiri had fallen in love with her when she was at the Palace as a Gosechi dancer. See Part III, p. 422.

reply; but simple though the words were, Koremitsu's daughter did not doubt their sincerity.

It should be explained that during the period when To no Chujo kept Yugiri away from Kumoi, he had carried on a secret affair with this daughter of Koremitsu. After his marriage he saw her only on very rare occasions. By Kumoi he had four boys and four girls; by Koremitsu's daughter two boys and two girls. All twelve were handsome and well-grown children, particularly the four born to him in this secret union, who were also very intelligent. The younger girl and younger boy were left with Koremitsu's daughter. But the older boy and girl were educated by the Lady from the Village of Falling Flowers, who made a great fuss of them. Here they were often seen by Genji and became great favorites with him.

And so for the present we may leave Yugiri and his affairs.

The Law

Though Murasaki was apparently no longer in immediate danger, her illness had now lasted so many months that there appeared to be little hope of recovery. To Genji it seemed that her strength was gradually ebbing away. The thought of surviving her appalled him; and she herself, without anxiety for the future* (she was indeed to a singular extent devoid of such fetters as commonly bind us to the world), had no misgiving, save the thought of what her death would mean to one who had been her companion so long.

Her thoughts, as was natural, turned much upon the life to come, and her time was spent in numerous charities and consecrations. Best of all, she would still have liked to spend the remaining moments of her life in some place where they could be wholly devoted to religion, but Genji would not give her leave. However, he had himself often expressed an intention of pursuing the same course. Why should they not then do so together? But certain though their faith might be that in Amida's Paradise the same lotus would be their throne, in the meanwhile, he in his convent and she in her nunnery, however near they might be, would not be able to meet. His anxiety, if she should grow suddenly worse, the mere thought that she was in pain, would (Genji well knew) make havoc of his meditations. Yes, he must content himself to lag behind, where so many frail creatures† had gone forward unafraid.

She might indeed have acted without his permission; but to have obtained her end by such a course would, she knew, give her no satisfaction, and she felt aggrieved that her wish was still denied. Perhaps, however (she reflected), it was not his fault. No doubt some sin of her own was weighing upon her and holding her back from spiritual progress.

Some while ago she had caused a thousand copies of the Lotus Scripture to be made, and she now hastened to give them as an offering. The ceremony was to take place in the Nijo-in, which she had come to regard as her home. The robes for the seven ministrants were also her gift, and every detail, down to the stitching of the seams, was designed according to her directions. She had not told Genji what was afoot, but he naturally saw something of the preparations, and admired the taste and knowledge

---

* She had married off her adopted child, the Akashi Princess, to the Emperor.
† Utsusemi, Fujitsubo, Nyosan, etc.

that marked her handling of religious as well as of all other activities; and he managed, while not knowing exactly what was needed, to make a few such general contributions as could not come amiss. Yugiri was in charge of the dancers and music. Presents and contributions poured in from the Emperor, the Crown Prince, the Empress, and all the great ladies at Court, in such numbers that the messengers would at any time have packed the corridors almost to overflowing. It may be imagined then what was the scene when they were added to the throngs that were already assembled for the Service.*

It was the tenth day of the third month. The trees were all in blossom, the weather mild and calm; indeed it seemed as though Paradise itself were not far away, and even an unbeliever could not but have regained his innocence. The Woodman's Song, resounding from so many lips, moved Murasaki intensely, as indeed it would have done at any time in her life. But today the words had a new significance. "Though in life no prize awaits me, yet am I sad to know the firewood is burnt out and soon the flame will sink." So she wrote, and sent the poem to the Lady of Akashi, by the hand of little Prince Niou. To answer in the same strain would be thought unfeeling, should anyone chance to hear of it, and though the reply seemed to her somewhat forced, the Lady of Akashi wrote: "For a thousand years did the Blessed One that hermit serve; and shall your flame so soon amid the faggots of his Law expire?"

All night long the chanting continued, to the perpetual beatings of gongs and drums. As dawn began to break and the colors of the flowers showed forth again where the morning air had rent the mist, Murasaki felt that spring, the season she had loved, still had the power to call her back. And while from every branch came a twittering of birds that made even the shrill music of the flutes seem dumb, the dancer stepped the dance of Prince Ling.† The effect of the final movement, especially of the gay, rapid passage at the end (given the place and hour), was tremendous. Gifts poured in upon the performers, those present in their excitement stripping the cloaks off their own backs and heaping them before the dancers and musicians. Then followed a concert in which all the notable players at Court took their part. Everyone seemed happy and excited.

---

* The service consisted of the reading of the Lotus Scripture; this required eight sittings. There was also the drama of the Woodman, one priest playing the part of Shakyamuni when he was a woodman, and the rest walking round him in circle and chanting the *Woodman's Song:* "Had I not cut firewood and drawn water for the rishi, would you now possess the Scripture of the Lotus Flower?"

This refers to a legend that in a previous incarnation Buddha obtained the doctrine of the Lotus Scripture from a rishi whom he served as henchman.

† *The Ranryo-o*. Prince Ling had a face of womanish beauty and found that in battle his enemies were not afraid of him. He therefore took to wearing a ferocious mask. But some say he wore it to protect his complexion.

"A little longer," thought Murasaki; and she felt there were after all many things that it was sad to lose.

But she had on the day before exerted herself far more than usual, and was now very fatigued. When she thought that all these people, whom she had for so many years past seen at similar gatherings, such a one always with his flute, another with his zithern, were before her for the last time, she raised herself with an effort and looked fixedly at each one. And then there were the ladies with whom, at the summer and winter festivals, she had carried on a kind of rivalry. Sometimes, over these concerts and sports, there had even been, underneath the outward show of good manners, a certain element of jealousy and bitterness. Yet she loved them all; and now they, for a time at any rate, would stay behind, while she, all alone, set out she knew not whither.

So grave was her condition during the summer heats that the Akashi Princess obtained leave of absence from the Palace, and settled in the Nijo-in. She was to occupy the eastern wing, but ceremonies of reception took place in the Main Hall. The procedure was the same as that which Murasaki had witnessed many times before. But today it moved her strangely, for she felt it to be her last glimpse of the outside world; and as the names of the attendant officers were called, her ear strained eagerly for the response of this or that long-familiar voice. It was some, while since she had seen the Princess and there was much to say. "I am so glad you have come here first," Murasaki greeted her. "I hear you are to be quartered far off in the eastern wing. Once you are settled there, it will be tiresome for you to come over here; and I am afraid I shall scarcely be able to visit you..."

The Princess remained with her a long while, and they were presently joined by the Lady of Akashi. During the conversation that followed, Murasaki made no allusion to her own approaching death. But she let fall now and then a few words, spoken very seriously and quietly, which showed that the transience of all human things ran constantly through her thoughts. Seeing the Akashi Princess's children she shed a few tears. How dearly she would have loved to see what became of them! Her tear-stained face was so lovely, and she looked in every way so far the reverse of haggard or ailing, that the Princess could hardly believe the truth of the dismal reports she had heard. This mysterious and ever-growing weakness—whence came it and how had it begun? Murasaki did at last refer to her death, but in a quite matter-of-fact way, saying in the course of conversation: "There are one or two servants who have been here for years past. I do not like to think of their being left without support. Perhaps, when I am no longer here, you would not mind keeping an eye upon them," and she named several of such officers and retainers to the Akashi Princess.

Presently, when the others had retired, to prayers or what not, Murasaki, during a respite of her malady, sent for little Niou, who was her favorite among all the royal children, and said to him: "If I were not here, would you sometimes think about me?" "Yes, indeed I would," he said. "I love my father, the Emperor, and Madam my mother too; but not half as much as I love my dear granny. Without you I should be very sad," and trying to hide his tears, he hastily brushed his sleeve across his face with so pretty a gesture that she could not help smiling. "When you are grown up," she said, "you shall have this house for your own, and in the flower-season you will have the red plum and cherry-tree in front of your window. Enjoy them, and sometimes, should you think of it, offer a spray or two of blossom to the Lord Buddha." He watched her face earnestly while she spoke, and nodded at the end. Then, feeling that he could no longer check his tears, he left the room.

The cool of autumn brought her a certain measure of relief; but the slightest exertion was sufficient to cause a relapse. The weather was at no time very severe; but as the season wore on she suffered from a continual sense of damp and chill. The time for the Princess's return to Court had come. Murasaki longed to beg for an extension of her visit, but the Emperor was already chafing at her long absence. Messengers were continually arriving from Court, and it would have been impertinent to detain her for more than a few hours longer. Since it was utterly out of the question that Murasaki should pay the customary visit to the Princess's quarters, the Princess, contrary to all precedent, condescended to visit her. The sick woman felt embarrassed at causing this difficulty; but she longed passionately to see the girl once more, and finally all the royal gear was carried to the Main Hall.

A cold wind had sprung up towards evening; but Murasaki, wanting to get a better view of the garden, had been helped onto a couch by the window. Genji was delighted to see her capable of so much exertion. "You seemed to get on much better today," he said. "I believe it has given you new strength to have the Princess so near you." His delight at her supposed improvement only brought home to her all the more poignantly how terrible was the blow that awaited him. "Hopes then the dewdrop upon the wind-swept grasses of the heath to build a safe abode?" Such was the acrostic* poem she recited; and he: "Where all things race so madly to their doom, why think one fragile dewdrop will be first to reach the destined goal?"

"Now," she said presently, "you had better go back to your rooms. I am feeling very giddy; and though I know you would forgive me if I did not entertain you properly, I do not like to feel that I have been

---

* Play on *oku,* "to settle" (of dew) and *oku,* "to rise from bed."

behaving badly." Her screens-of-state were drawn in close about the couch. The Princess stood holding Murasaki's hand in hers. She seemed indeed to be fading like a dewdrop from the grass. So certain seemed the approach of death that messengers were sent in every direction to bid the priests read scriptures for her salvation. But she had more than once recovered from such attacks as these, and it was hoped that this was merely another onslaught of the "possession" that had attacked her years before. All night long various prayers and incantations were kept going, but in vain; for she died next morning soon after sunrise.

The Akashi Princess was profoundly thankful that she had stayed to witness the end. The event, though so long expected, left all her people in a state of dazed bewilderment. Genji himself broke down completely, and when Yugiri arrived, felt disposed to put all arrangements into his son's hands. Summoning him to where she lay, Genji said: "You know that it was always her desire to take Orders before she died; but not realizing how swiftly the end would come, I would not give her leave—which I now deeply regret. The chaplains who were on duty during the night have apparently all left the house, or at least I hear no sound of them. But there is probably still some priest or other to be found. It is not too late to do what may, with Buddha's help, aid her on the dark road she must tread."*

"I have known many cases," said Yugiri, "in which a possessing spirit was thwarted by such a course, and it might well have been so in her case. They say that to have joined a holy Order for a single day or night brings great benefit in the life hereafter. But now that she is dead, what sense can there be in administering the tonsure? You will only be making the scenes which must ensue more depressing for yourself, without affording any assistance to her in the journey beyond the grave." Certain priests had, it was found, stayed behind to watch the body, and sending for them Yugiri now instructed them in their duties. It was many years since his thoughts about Murasaki had been other than he could publish to all the world. But since he caught sight of her on the morning of the typhoon, he had often wondered whether they would ever again be brought together. Her voice he now knew he would never hear; but there was still a chance to see her once again, and while scolding one of the maids for the loudness of her sobbing, as though absent-mindedly, he pulled up a corner of the curtains. The daylight was still feeble, and he could see very little. But at that moment Genji† himself held up the great lamp, bringing it so close to the couch that Yugiri suddenly saw her in all her loveliness. "And why should he not see her?" thought Genji, who

---

* Administer the tonsure; this was often done to the dying, and occasionally to the dead.
† From inside the curtains.

knew that Yugiri was peeping. But in a moment he covered his eyes with his sleeve. "It is almost worse to see her now while she is still unchanged," he said. "One thinks that she will speak, move..." Yugiri brushed away the tears that kept on dimming his eyes. Her hair lay spread across the pillows, loose, but not tangled or disorderly, in a great mass, against which in the strong lamplight her face shone with a dazzling whiteness. Never, thought Genji, had her beauty seemed so flawless as now, when the eye could rest upon it undistracted by any ripple of sound or motion. Yugiri gazed astounded. His spirit seemed to leave him, to float through space and hover near her, as though it were he that was the ghost, and this the lovely body he had chosen for his habitation.

As neither Genji nor any of the ladies who had been long in Murasaki's service were in a condition to make the final arrangements, all this, as well as the duty of encouraging and consoling the bereaved, fell upon Yugiri. His life had brought him occasion to witness many scenes of sorrow, but none so pitiful as those that now ensued; nor did he imagine that it could ever fall to his lot again.

For many days afterwards he remained in close attendance upon his father, trying by every means he could think of to distract and console him. The equinoctial gales had begun to blow, and tonight it came back vividly to Yugiri's mind how he had caught sight of her on the morning of the great typhoon. And then again on the day she died. That Genji should mourn was well enough; but what right had Yugiri to this grievous pain? And to hide his sorrow he drew a rosary towards him, and clicking the beads loudly he muttered, "Amida, Amida, Amida Buddha," so swiftly that the falling of his tears could not be heard.

Day and night Genji wept, till it seemed that a veil of tears hung between him and the world. A thousand times he asked himself what use they had ever been to him—this beauty, of which so much had been said, these talents that were supposed to raise him above all his peers? No sooner did he come into the world than loneliness and sorrow fell to his share. And then as though Buddha feared that even now he might harbor some remnant of trust in life and its joys, loss upon loss was visited upon him, from all of which he had in the end recovered. But now at last this greatest of imaginable sorrows had indeed effected what all previous afflictions had failed to achieve. No longer did he ask for a day more in the world, save that he might devote it to penances and fasting. And yet, if anything stood between him and the demands of religion, it was this very sorrow, which by its insensate violence had so unarmed him that he knew himself to be in no fit state to take his vows. Often he prayed earnestly that a moment of oblivion might come in which he could embrace the life he craved for. There were times too when another consideration weighed with him. If he were at once to enter an Order, it would be thought that he had done so yielding weakly to an impulse of the moment—had been unhinged by the shock of a sudden bereavement; and this was an impression that he by no means wished to create.

Thus the struggle between his desire to embrace a different life, and his distaste for the impression he would create by doing so, further increased his agitation.

Even in the matter of condolences To no Chujo made a point of never going beyond what, in his view, the occasion strictly demanded. And it indicated on his part a very high view of Murasaki's worth that he now not merely paid the formal visit of sympathy, but followed it by numerous letters. He remembered that it had been just this time of year, the middle of the eighth month, when his sister Aoi died; and of those who had then mourned her, how many had since followed in her tracks! So he was reflecting one cheerless evening, when autumn had more than ever set its mark upon the sky. Sending for his son Ben no Shosho, he wrote a long letter to Genji, and in the margin: "An autumn of the past seems like today, and adds fresh dewdrops to a sleeve already drenched with, tears." Memories of the past, not only of the time when Aoi died, but of a thousand episodes in which he and To no Chujo had been linked together, now crowded to his mind, and it was through a stream of tears that he wrote the reply: "This grief and that are mingled in my thoughts, and only this I know: that hateful is this season and all its ways." In the letter that he wrote with this poem there might have been, had he expressed the half of what he felt, a passionate outpouring of misery and despair. But he knew that To no Chujo was apt to regard the expression of such feelings as a sign of reprehensible weakness, and promising to write again later, he now merely said: "I cannot thank you enough for the sympathy that your many enquiries have shown." "Though light in hue the dress..." So had Genji once[*] written. But custom could no longer restrain him, and he now wore what was not far removed from full mourning.

Nor indeed was grief confined to the immediate circles of the Court. It frequently happens that those who by favor have risen to such an eminence as that which Murasaki enjoyed are subjected to a good deal of general spite. Often they are felt, even when showing themselves most affable, to be so conscious of their superiority, that what they mean as kindness has merely the effect of making ordinary people additionally timid and uncomfortable. In Murasaki there was no suspicion of this. The rare loveableness of her nature had in one way or another made its impression even in the most unlikely quarters, and her partisans were as warm as they were ubiquitous. There were many who, though they

---

[*] At the time of Aoi's death. See Part I, p. 169. Full mourning was worn for a parent, but not for a wife.

belonged to a class of society very different from hers, could not during these autumn days hear with dry eyes either the rush of the wind or the cry of insects.

The Empress Akikonomu wrote constantly to Genji at this time. In one of her poems she said: "Rightly she judged (no more will I gainsay it) who to dead leaves and weary autumn fields gave but a grudging praise."

This letter, listless though he was, he read many times, and felt that if anyone's company could serve at this moment to distract him a little from his misery, it would be hers. "You that in far-off countries of the sky can dwell secure, look back upon me here; for I am weary of this frail world's decay." So he answered, and having folded the paper, sat for a long while gazing abstractedly before he sent it on its way.

So little could he trust himself to behave with proper dignity and restraint, that he altogether avoided the more public parts of the Palace, spending most of his time in a room near the women's apartments at the back. Here he was able to pursue his devotions undisturbed. One thing only mattered to him now: to attain the certainty that, parted though they were upon earth, in Paradise they would for ever be refreshed by the dew of the same lotus.

The ceremonies of the Forty-ninth Day, for which (in his distraction) Genji had omitted to give any instructions, were arranged by Yugiri. And so time passed, Genji constantly thinking that he would tomorrow take the step for which he longed... But somehow he did not do so. For one thing, he longed first to see the Akashi Princess and her children.

Mirage

Spring shone once more upon the world; and as in other years his doors were thronged by visitors. But he pleaded illness, and remained behind the screens-of-state. It was only when his half-brother, Prince Sochi, came that he felt inclined for a less formal salutation, and calling him into the screened recess, Genji recited the verse: "Seek not in this domain the gladness of the year; for gone is she with whom 'twas joy to praise the shining boughs of Spring." Prince Sochi answered: "Think not that I have come in quest of common flowers; but rather to bemoan the loss of one whose scent has vanished from the air." And when later on Genji watched his brother walking away beneath boughs of red plum-blossom, he felt that if anyone could this year incite him to take pleasure in the beauty of the garden, it would be this Prince Sochi, to whom his heart always warmed. The flowers were not yet fully open; but that is just the time when their scent is sweetest. But this year there were no concerts or picnics; indeed, all was changed.

Those of Murasaki's ladies who had been long in her service were still dressed in deep mourning and were inconsolable as ever for her loss. Their only comfort was that Genji had quite ceased to pay any visits, and they were thus able to distract themselves by continually waiting upon him. It was long since he had had any serious dealings with people such as this. But there were some of them to whom he had at one time or another taken a fancy. If any of these now hoped to profit by the situation, they were sadly mistaken. He slept alone; and those ladies who were retained for night service went on duty several at a time and were posted at a considerable distance from where he lay. Sometimes he would talk to them about old days. It seemed that, despite the increasing earnestness of her convictions, small matters (likely to have no lasting effect upon their relations) had at the time very much disturbed her; and it was intolerable to him that, trivial or ridiculous though the occasion might have been, he should ever have caused her to suffer. And much more when he came to think of the few more serious occasions... How often, while perfectly understanding all that was going on in his mind, had she refrained from any reproach or complaint! But there must all the same have been times when, at any rate for the moment, it was quite impossible for her to foresee how this affair or that would turn out in the end; and he bitterly regretted that he should ever have caused her to watch him with anxiety and misgiving. He sometimes talked this over with those who had known her best in those days. There was the time when Nyosan first came to live with them. Murasaki had never been openly hostile; but she had certainly suffered very much. He remembered that snowy morning, when coming back to their room at dawn he found that she had been weeping. How gentle, how forbearing she had been, how she struggled to hide from him what she was enduring! And now he lay all night long, hoping against hope that he might so much as see her for an instant in his dreams. "There's been quite a heavy fall of snow." He woke up to hear someone saying this—no doubt one of the ladies, going back to her own quarters. More vividly than ever did he remember that other snowbound morning, and his loneliness became unendurable. To distract himself he dressed hastily and was soon absorbed in his devotions. Presently the dead ashes were swept from his fire-stand, the buried flame shot up again and burned brightly in his room. Chunagon and Chujo, two of Murasaki's ladies, were with him. "You may well imagine," he said, "that last night was no very good one for sleeping all alone. Why, when every circumstance seems aimed to wean me from the world, I should still cling to this sort of life, is more than I can explain." But he was really thinking that to these ladies of hers the task of waiting upon him did afford some small comfort, and he wondered what would become of them when he was gone.

He had known Chujo since she was a child, and there had at one time been an intimacy between them. This, while Murasaki was alive, made Chujo very shy in Genji's presence. But since her death, they had (on quite different terms) again become friends. For the girl had been a great favorite of Murasaki's, and this reason alone sufficed to make her dear to him; he grafted her on to his life, like the pine-tree that grows on the green barrow of a tomb.

The princes with whom he had been most intimate, his brothers and cousins, called constantly; but he would see none of them. For despite all the efforts he made to get himself into a fit state for company, months of despondency had, he felt, worked such havoc with him, that if he were again to receive his friends, they would remember him as he now was, and not as they had once known him. But merely to hide would defeat his end; for if it got about that he was ashamed to be seen, or was so broken by sorrow that he could not maintain a rational conversation, an even worse impression might get abroad than was warranted by the truth. And lest it should be said that he had ended his days in decrepitude and imbecility, he began again to admit Yugiri and a few others to his presence. But he spoke to them always from behind his curtains-of-state. About one thing he was determined: he must recover himself sufficiently to meet people and show a good face to the world before he took the final step that he was contemplating. He attempted several times to visit the various ladies of his household; but he found himself unable to control his grief, and hastening home determined in future not to make any further effort to keep in touch with the world.

The Akashi Princess was now back at the Imperial Palace; but Genji persuaded her to let Prince Niou stay with him for a while. The child showed a great interest in the red plum-tree in front of his room, constantly trotting out to see that no harm came to it. His granny, he said, had told him to. It was only the second month, and though the flowering trees were all in bloom, they were not fully out, so that the shimmer of the blossoms hung like a delicate mist along the boughs; and when a nightingale began to sing in full voice upon a branch of Niou's tree, Genji could not refrain from coming out to listen. "Knows he that she who built his shining bower hears him no more—the nightingale upon the red plum-tree?" So he murmured as he walked.

Spring advanced, and Murasaki's gardens took on their wonted splendor; but the sight of them gave him no pleasure, and indeed he longed to be in some place far off among the mountains, so bare and desolate that neither sight of flower nor song of bird would sharpen his sorrow. First the globe-flower reached its glory in a tangle of dewy blossom. Then when the single cherry had fallen and the eight-fold giant cherry was almost over, the birch-cherry began to open, while the wisteria was still but faintly coloring, and held all its treats in store. How skillfully she had contrived her planting, so that wherever one turned there were later flowers to follow those that were early over, and others and ever more to take their place.

Little Niou, who had not yet discovered that the Nijo-in and the New Palace* were separate places, cried out in delight: "Look, my cherry-tree is in bloom. I know what we'll do to prevent its losing the flowers. We'll put screens-of-state all round it, and then if no one opens the flaps, the wind cannot possibly get in." This was certainly a good idea, and Genji smiling asked him if he knew the poem: "Would that my sleeve were wide enough to cover..."† "But yours is a much more sensible plan," he added. This little prince was the only person in whose company he now took pleasure. "I am afraid we shall not be able to play together much longer," he now said to the child. "I do not mean that I am going to die; but I shall be living at a place where we cannot meet." "At a place where we cannot meet? That is what my granny said too..." and Niou lowered his eyes.

---

* Genji's old palace (where Murasaki died) and the New Palace in the Sixth Ward, where the child now was.

† "Would that my sleeve were wide enough to cover the spaces of the sky; then should the wind no longer at his pleasure scatter the flowers in Spring."—Anon.

One evening when a faint haze mingled with the fading light, Genji at last set out to visit the Lady of Akashi. His visit took her completely by surprise; for it was a very long while since he had been near her. But she managed all the same to receive him in good style, and to make so agreeable an impression that he found himself wondering whether she were not after all the most charming person in the world. But then there came into his face an expression, the meaning of which she was perfectly well able to decipher: he was thinking how little she had ever interested him compared with Murasaki, and how useless it was to seek consolation in this or any other quarter.

"Even during my exile at Suma," he said, when they had talked quietly for a while, "I was already thinking of entering some monastic retreat far away from all human habitation, and there ending my days. And at the time there was not much reason why I should not do so. But in my latter years a thousand ties and duties have made such a prisoner of me that I could no longer dream of escape. But I feel ashamed that, while it was still possible, I had not firmness enough to take this step." "I do not think anyone is likely to reproach you," she answered. "Even those whom no one would miss are often prevented from leaving the world by ties and affections that exist only on their side. And how much the less can you, upon whom so many persons depend, be expected to take such a step without misgiving? I think you are much more likely to be blamed for taking Orders in a rash and inconsiderate manner than for continuing your present life too long. I remember many cases of people leaving the world because they were upset about something; but I have always considered that a very foolish course. I feel sure you had better wait until the little princes are older and things have been settled in a manner that will rid you of all agitation and anxiety." How wise such advice sounded! "I fear," he said, "that such extreme circumspection as you recommend seems to me more culpable than any rashness." He talked for a while about their own long friendship, and then said: "Do you remember the Spring when Lady Fujitsubo died? Then I did indeed feel that 'if the cherry-tree had any heart, it would flower with black blossom.' I admired her for her taste and elegance; beside, we had been brought up together as children, so that it was natural I should feel her loss. But this is a very different business. It is not only as a wife that I miss her. She came to me so young, and it seemed as though we had so many years before us... When I consider her charm, her talents, her wit, I am overwhelmed at the thought of what has befallen me..."

They sat talking of old times till late that night. He would indeed have, in a way, been happy to stay there till morning. But nonetheless, he went home, though he knew that this would disappoint her. "What a change from the Genji of old days!" he thought, as he left her rooms.

Going straight to his day quarters he resumed his devotions, taking no more repose than a few minutes' rest upon his couch.

The time of the Festival* came round, and Genji, thinking of the lively throngs that would soon be gathering at the Shrine, sent all Murasaki's people back to their families. "They will be disappointed if they miss the sights," he said. "Let them go quietly home and attend the Festival from there." It so happened that as Genji came along towards the eastern wing he found Chujo no Kimi taking a hurried sleep. She rose quickly when she heard his step, and in the moment that elapsed before she hid her face in the wide sleeve of her gown he had time to note the liveliness of her features, the fine poise of her head. Her hair, ruffled during her nap, spread down in a wide tangle, as she now stood with bent head. Her trousers were red, with faint markings in yellow. Her robe, of somber purple, with patterns in very dark colors, was folded all awry, and her Chinese cloak had slipped from her shoulders. While setting herself to rights she laid down the hollyhock† she had been carrying in her hand, and picking it up Genji said: "What is this thing? I have positively forgotten what they are called." "On this day of all days, when the water plant is set in the pot to which the God descends, can you forget the garland's name?" Such was the acrostic poem with which she answered him, and he: "Nothing, I thought, in the wide world could tempt me. But lo, the hollyhock has shown that in my fancy lurk treacheries unsubdued."

During the heavy rains of the fifth month he grew weary of sitting day after day with nothing to distract him, and towards the middle of the month, one night when the rain had stopped and the moon appeared in marvelous splendor between the clouds, he called Yugiri to him. The orange-blossom glowed in the moonlight, and an exquisite fragrance was wafted towards them where they sat. They were hoping every moment to hear "the voice that eternally revisits those changeless haunts,"‡ when huge clouds came rolling, rain began to pelt, and a sudden gust of wind almost blew out the lamp. "I am getting used to solitude," he said to Yugiri; "but tonight for some reason I was feeling very lonely. My life here is certainly such that I shall be in very good practice when I arrive at my mountain temple!" He remembered that Yugiri had not been offered anything. "One of the ladies can bring the fruit," he said. "We shall not require any gentlemen in attendance tonight. They would only be a worry to us." Yugiri meanwhile, watching his father's face, wondered whether he were really so well prepared for the cloister as he imagined. It was clear that his thoughts were still at every moment centered on the one

---

* The Kamo Festival in the fourth month.

† Worn by worshippers at the Kamo Festival. Its name also means "day of meeting," and there is a play on this in both poems.

‡ The cuckoo.

subject of his loss, and this was hardly a state of mind that promised him much success in his devotions. But Yugiri, who was still haunted by the glimpse of her he had caught on that unforgettable morning, felt that he could understand his father's condition. "The anniversary will soon be here," he reminded Genji. "Have you any instructions to give?" "I do not know," replied Genji, "that there is much point in doing anything out of the ordinary. But I think this would be the right time to dedicate that picture of Amitabha's Paradise which she ordered before she died. I know that she gave one of her chaplains full instructions about the dedication, and if there is anything else that requires doing, you had better go to him for advice." "I am sure we shall have no difficulty about anything of that kind," answered Yugiri, "for she went into all these matters with the minutest care; indeed, if any soul ever deserved salvation, I am sure it is hers. But what a pity it is that, dying so young, she left behind her no real heir to her beauty and talents! It is a thing I have always regretted…" "The fault," said Genji, "lay perhaps not so much in her destiny as in mine. Look how few children I have had altogether! You are the one whom Fate has endowed with a fine brood of heirs! There is no fear of your house shrinking into oblivion." He knew that if the conversation turned upon the past, he might at any moment display his weakness in a manner that he wished above all things to avoid. Suddenly the long-expected voice of the Cuckoo came to his rescue, and with singular appropriateness he quoted the poem, "How can the Cuckoo have known?"

"Come you in quest of her that is no more, O Cuckoo,
Who through the drenching rain did hurry from your hill?"

So Genji now sang, and Yugiri answered him: "Search rather in your Dark Land,* O Cuckoo, and tell her that the tree she planted is in bloom."

Yugiri remained at his father's disposition all night; and it gave him a strange sensation to move without restraint in these quarters which, during Murasaki's lifetime, had been surrounded by so much mystery.

During the Gosechi dancing† that year Yugiri's two older boys acted as pages at the Court. They were about the same height, and looked very pretty together. Kurodo and his brothers,‡ who had been chosen to act as heralds at the Tasting of the New Rice and were wearing the magnificent blue-printed robes of their office, took charge of the boys and introduced them into the Presence. What, Genji asked himself as he watched the boys, lay behind that wondering and innocent expression? And once

---

* The cuckoo is called Headman of the Hill of Death.
† In the eleventh month.
‡ Younger sons of To no Chujo.

more he vividly recalled the little Gosechi dancer who had caught his own fancy years ago.

As the day drew near when his present life of seclusion in the midst of the Court was to reach its close, he spent his time chiefly in going through his possessions and deciding what was to become of them after his departure. Much of his property he now dispersed in a succession of small gifts, avoiding any such considerable transference as would excite attention; for up till now his retainers knew nothing of the disaster that awaited them. But it was known that his heart was set upon retirement, and they awaited the turn of the year with great apprehension.

One task that now devolved upon him was the destruction of letters such as it would be embarrassing to leave behind. Many he had torn up long ago; but often he had put a letter aside meaning to destroy it, and then had never brought himself to do so. Now, as opportunity offered, he took them out a few at a time, and went through them carefully. Among those that he had received at Suma, most of which he now tore up or threw away, there were a lot of Murasaki's letters carefully tied up in a bundle. It must indeed have been he himself who did up the packet, though so long a time had passed that he had no recollection of doing so. The ink was as fresh as on the day when they were written, and looked as if it would remain so for hundreds of years. But what was the use of such a keepsake? He could not take it with him... He sent for two or three of the ladies with whom she had been most intimate and began handing them the letters, one after another, to tear up. But soon, while he held the letters, his tears flowed so fast upon each page that fresh tracks were added to those the pen had made, and at last, unwilling to display his weakness, he pushed the bundle of letters away from him, reciting as he did so the verse: "So longs my heart for her that past the Hill of Death is gone, not even upon the tracks she left can I endure to gaze."* The ladies did not, of course, unfold the pages that were handed to them; but they caught sight of a phrase here and there—sufficient to tell them what the letters were; and it was with a pang that they now destroyed them. They remembered several of those letters being written. And if then, when she and Genji were separated only by a few miles and there was every prospect of their soon meeting again, Murasaki's misery had been such as they well remembered, could they wonder that now the sight of them was more than he could bear?

He took one from the bundle, and without stopping to read it, he wrote in the margin: "Go, useless leaves, well steeped in brine, to join the smoke that through the pathways of the sky trailed from her smoldering pyre"; and forthwith he had the whole lot burnt.

---

* *Ato* means "tracks" and also "handwriting."

He celebrated the Festival of Buddha's Names[*] with unusual solemnity, for he knew that it was the last he would see in his Palace. Never had been heard such jangling of shakujo[†] as on those nights. It was strange to hear the priests repeating the usual prayer that he "might long enjoy his present high estate," and he hoped that the Lord Buddha would know how far this prayer was removed from his real desires. Snow lay deep on the ground and was still falling. When the services were over, he sent for the leader of the procession, and having gone through the usual forms of handing him the wine-cup and so on, made handsome presents to all who had taken part in the ceremony.

The leader had for years past been employed at the Imperial Palace; he had been well known to the Old Emperor,[‡] and Genji noted with emotion how grey the old man's head had grown in the service of his family. There was the usual levée of princes and courtiers. On a few plum-trees there was already a faint hint of blossom, all the lovelier for the snow that lay heaped upon their boughs. There should have been feasting and music in the Palace; but even this year his grief still stifled in him all desire for song, and he arranged that only a few Chinese verses, appropriate to the season, should be recited at his levée.

But I had forgotten to mention the poem he made when he handed the wine-cup to the head priest. It was as follows: "Who knows in winter if the springtime he shall see? Wait not for blossom, but take the budding spray and wear it at your brow." "For naught else have I prayed, save that a thousand springtides you might see; till silver snow has blossomed on my brow." So the priest replied, and many other poems were made, which need not be here recorded.

This was the first occasion since Murasaki's death upon which Genji had mingled with his guests. They thought him more beautiful than ever, and the aged priest could not refrain from tears of joy.

Remembering that this was the end of the year, little Niou went scampering about saying everyone must do something to scare away the demons, and asking what noise he might make. In a few days Genji would see the child no more; and sadly he recited the verse: "Whilst I in heedless grief have let the days go by, together now the year and my own life are ebbing to their close." He gave orders that the New Year ceremonies should be performed with more than usual splendor, and saw to it that the princes and Court officers who came to the Palace should receive such presents and bounties as never before.

---

[*] On the 21st, 22nd, and 23rd of the twelfth month.

[†] The long, priest's begging-staff, with metal rings attached to the top.

[‡] Genji's father.

PART FIVE
THE LADY OF THE BOAT

LIST OF MOST IMPORTANT PERSONS (alphabetical)

Agemaki . . . . The elder daughter of Hachi no Miya. Loved by Kaoru.

Akashi, Princess . . . . (The Empress). Daughter of Genji and the lady whom he brought back from exile. Married to the Crown Prince—the Emperor of Part V. Aged thirty when this part begins.

Akikonomu. . . . . Consort of the ex-Emperor Ryozen.

Ben no Kimi. . . . . An old woman, servant in the house of Hachi no Miya.

Chujo, Lady . . . . Daughter of Genji's great friend To no Chujo. Concubine of the ex-Emperor Ryozen.

Emperor, The. . . . . Son of the ex-Emperor Suzaku. Aged thirty-three when this part begins.

Empress, The . . . . See *Akashi*.

Hachi no Miya. . . . . (Prince Hachi). A much younger half-brother of Genji. Father of Agemaki and Kozeri.

Higekuro. . . . . Husband of Makibashira, whose madness is described in Part IV. Already dead when Part V begins.

Himegimi . . . . Daughter of Tamakatsura. Loved by Kurodo no Shosho.

Kaoru . . . . Son of Nyosan and To no Chujo's eldest son, Kashiwagi.

Kashiwagi . . . . The real father of Kaoru. Dead before Part IV begins.

Kobai . . . . Kashiwagi's brother.

Koremitsu. . . . . Genji's favorite retainer, now dead.

Kozeri . . . . Younger sister of Agemaki. Becomes Niou's concubine.

Kumoi. . . . . To no Chujo's daughter; Yugiri's wife.

Kurodo no Shosho . . . . . Yugiri's son; in love with Himegimi.

Murasaki. . . . . Genji's second wife. Already dead.

Naka no Kimi. . . . . Kobai's second daughter.

Niou . . . . Genji's grandson. Child of the Emperor and of the Akashi Princess. Aged fourteen when this part begins.

Nyosan . . . . Kaoru's mother. Now turned nun.

Oigimi . . . . Kobai's elder daughter.

Ryozen . . . . The ex-Emperor. Thought by the world to be the son of the old Emperor (Genji's father), but really Genji's son by the old Emperor's concubine, Fujitsubo. Aged forty-one when Part V begins.
Sochi . . . . Prince Genji's half-brother.
Tamakatsura . . . . Daughter of To no Chujo and Yugao (the lady who dies in the deserted mansion in Part I). Adopted by Genji. Aged forty-five when Part V begins.
To no Chujo . . . . Genji's great friend. Already dead when Part V opens.
Wakagimi . . . . Tamakatsura's younger daughter
Yugiri . . . . Genji's son by his first wife, Aoi. Aged thirty-eight when Part V begins.

Niou

Genji was dead, and there was no one to take his place. True, he left behind him a considerable number of descendants. But in one way or another many of these were disqualified. The ex-Emperor Ryozen, for example, could not for obvious reasons be publicly regarded as his heir.[*] Among his grandchildren Niou, the Akashi Princess's third son, was a good deal talked of as a possible successor; while another candidate was Nyosan's little boy Kaoru,[†] who had been brought up under Genji's care. Both of them were thought to promise well, and had indeed more than a common share of good looks and charm. There was however nothing dazzling about them either in mind or appearance. They were merely two very agreeable and presentable young men who, if they were fêted and sought after far more than, at a like age, Genji himself had been, owed it not to any superiority of their own but simply to the fact that they were so closely connected with him.

Niou had been Murasaki's special favorite and after her death he continued to live in her old quarters in the Nijo-in. The Emperor and Empress were however also extremely attached to him and, apart from the Crown Prince, there was no one about whom they took more trouble. They were anxious indeed that he should occupy rooms in the Imperial Palace. But this idea did not appeal to him, and he remained in the Nijo-in where he had lived since he was a child. As soon as his Initiation[‡] was over he was given an honorary position in the Board of War. His sister, the First Princess, occupied the eastern wing in the southern block of Genji's New Palace. These rooms too had been occupied by Murasaki, and the young Princess, in devotion to her memory, was at pains to keep the arrangement of them exactly as it had been in old days. Niou's brother[§] too, in addition to his official suite at the Imperial Palace, also had rooms at Genji's New Palace. He was married to Yugiri's second daughter, and as he stood only at two removes from accession to the Throne he was regarded as a person of considerable importance, an impression which was increased by the uncommon vigor and independence of his character.

---

[*] He was in reality Genji's son, but was supposed to be the child of the old Emperor, Genji's father.

[†] Supposed to be Genji's son, but in reality Kashiwagi's.

[‡] Into manhood.

[§] Who, in age, came between him and the Crown Prince.

Yugiri's daughters were indeed very numerous. The eldest was married to the Crown Prince, and had managed to maintain her position very well.* The Emperor and Empress seemed to assume that, as things had started like this, nothing remained but in due course to marry off the rest of their sons to Yugiri's successive daughters; and the same assumption was made by society at large. But Niou made it clear that if he married it would be to please himself and not with the object of rounding off some neat family scheme. Yugiri himself was inclined to sympathize with this view, but at the same time if a definite proposal had come from the Palace he would have been prepared to consider it, and with such a possibility in view he devoted to the education of his remaining daughters an unusual degree of care. The most popular was his sixth daughter,† with whom at the time of which I write every self-respecting young prince or nobleman imagined himself to be passionately in love.

Prince Genji had collected under his roof, at one time and another, a considerable number of gentlewomen whom after his death it was no longer practicable to harbor; and there was a succession of tearful departures. An exception was the Lady from the Village of Falling Flowers, to whom quarters in the eastern court of the Nijo-in had been specially bequeathed. Nyosan‡ lived in her father's palace in the Third Ward; the Empress was always at Court. Genji's New Palace began indeed to have a depressingly deserted air. "One knows," said Yugiri, "so many cases of houses which it has cost infinite trouble to plan and build, being allowed to go to rack and ruin the moment the owner died. The spectacle of such ruins may provide an edifying lesson on the uncertainty of human projects; but so long as I am here I am determined that not only shall this palace be kept in repair, but that the avenues which lead to it shall be as thronged as in my father's lifetime."

He therefore moved Lady Ochiba into the quarters which the Lady from the Village of Falling Flowers had vacated, sleeping half of each month with her, and half with Kumoi who was living in the Third Ward.

It seemed as though the Nijo-in with all its improvements and repairs and a great part of the New Palace—residences that were a byword for their spaciousness and magnificence—now existed chiefly for the benefit of the Akashi Lady and her descendants, and indeed it was to her that (as part of her duty towards the numerous princes and princesses under her care) fell the task of administering these two great households—a business in which Yugiri did not interfere.

---

* I.e. not to be supplanted by some subordinate consort.

† His child, not by his wife Kumoi, but by Koremitsu's daughter. For Yugiri's wooing of Koremitsu's daughter, see Part III, p. 422.

‡ Kaoru's mother.

But he was obliged to confess to himself that if, instead of the Lady of Akashi, it had been Murasaki* who had been left in this position, he would not have bean content to stand aside. With what pleasure and alacrity would he have hastened to her assistance! With what ingenuity would he have contrived, in her case at least, to carry out Genji's wish that those he left behind him should be deprived of none of the comforts that they enjoyed before! And a thousand times he regretted that he had never during all those years once had the courage to give her some inkling of the feelings she aroused in him.

In the country at large Genji's loss was felt and lamented at every turn. The spectacle of life lost all its glamor; it seemed as though a sudden darkness had spread over the whole world. Of the depression which reigned at his two palaces it is needless to speak; and here another loss—that of Murasaki—weighed constantly on the minds of those who were left behind, and of the two bereavements was indeed perhaps felt the more keenly. For she had died very young, and her memory, like the flowers whose blossoming is shortest, was the more highly prized.

It had been Genji's wish that Nyosan's boy Kaoru should be put under the ex-Emperor Ryozen's care. It so happened that his consort, the Lady Akikonomu, had no children of her own, and she was delighted to have Kaoru under her care. His Initiation took place at Ryozen's palace. In the second month of his fourteenth year he received the rank of lieutenant, which in the autumn was changed to that of Captain of the Bodyguard of the Right. These promotions were of course secured for him through Ryozen's influence, and in consequence of them he found himself, though only just arrived at man's estate, already ranked as a public officer of the Fourth Class. A wing near to the rooms occupied by Ryozen himself was fitted out as Kaoru's official quarters, where the ex-Emperor saw to it that the pages, ladies-in-waiting and under-servants should be the very best that could be procured, taking quite as much trouble over the matter as he had done in the case of his own daughter.

He handed over to the boy a number of his own handsomest and most agreeable ladies-in-waiting, and Akikonomu did the same. They seemed indeed both of them determined to make his life in their house as easy and agreeable as they could. By his consort Lady Chujo† Ryozen had one daughter, and the fact that Kaoru, who ranked as Akikonomu's adopted child, figured quite as prominently in the household as did this only princess was regarded as further proof of the surprising ascendancy that Akikonomu, at Lady Chujo's expense, had gained over the ex-Emperor's affections.

---

* It will be renumbered that Yugiri was in love with Murasaki. See particularly Part III, p. 531.

† To no Chujo's daughter.

Nyosan* appeared to be entirely absorbed in her devotions. Every month priests were summoned to her apartments to hold a great prayer-meeting, and twice a year she held the Eight Recitals of the *Hokkekyo*.† But at times when she was not thus occupied she looked to Kaoru for protection and advice, and his visits were more like those of a parent than of a child. He was extremely fond of her, but Ryozen and the Emperor, not to mention the Crown Prince and other princes who were constantly requiring his presence at banquets and musical parties, made such frequent calls upon his time that it often seemed impossible, short of, as the phrase goes, "cutting himself in two," to make any engagement without offending somebody, and he saw his mother less often than he would have wished.

Ever since his childhood he had been vaguely aware that some mystery attached to the circumstances of his birth, but could think of no one who would be likely to enlighten him. The obvious person was Nyosan herself. But it was impossible to embark on the subject without revealing to her that certain suspicions existed; and this might be a painful shock. The longing to discover the real facts about his origin continually haunted him. Was he fated to spend his whole life with this uneasy thought perpetually like a shadow at his side? If only he were possessed of the art that enabled the Resourceful Prince‡ to dispose so easily of a similar doubt! And he recited to himself the poem: "Who, who will rid me of my doubts? For groping now I know not whither I am carried nor whence into this world I came."

But there was none to answer him.

He was constantly oppressed by a feeling of insecurity. He would turn the matter over and over in his mind, and just when he was half-convinced that his suspicions were in reality ungrounded, it would occur to him, for example, that his mother's sudden retreat from the world§ just when she was looking her best was not likely to have been dictated solely by an access of religious feeling. Such actions were far more often the sequel to some scandal or disastrous entanglement. If anything of this kind had occurred there must be someone besides Nyosan who knew about it, and the fact that he had, no doubt quite deliberately, been left in such complete ignorance, only showed how unpalatable to him the real facts were judged to be.

Nor had he much confidence in the efficacy of his mother's devotions. For constant though were her observances he could not feel that

---

* Kaoru's mother.

† The work was read in eight portions, at eight sittings.

‡ Buddha's son Rahula was born when his parents had been separated for six years. Other members of the family threw doubts upon his claim to be Buddha's heir; but Rahula, by means differently described in various scriptures, skillfully allayed their suspicions.

§ Nyosan became a nun after Kaoru's birth. See Part IV, p. 691.

her gentle and rather helpless character was at all consonant with such a strength of conviction as would "turn the dewdrops on her lotus into heavenly jewels." Vaguely too there came into his mind something about "the five drawbacks,"* and he felt that, if only he had been the person to give it, she needed help far more urgently in regard to her future life† than over the small affairs of her everyday existence.

Then there was the other person in the case.‡ Constantly he figured in Kaoru's thoughts, a restless and distracted ghost. To meet him face to face—that was the boy's one desire, even though to do so he must himself become an inhabitant of that darker realm. It was accordingly with no very eager anticipation that he approached the ceremonies which would formally admit him to manhood. But spontaneously, and in such a way that he could not in any case have avoided them, favors, distinctions, and decorations were thrust upon him. In the eyes of the world he was uniquely fortunate; but sunk in perpetual broodings and speculations Kaoru himself barely noticed the grandeurs that made many shy of approaching him.

Yet his position was an extraordinary one. For the Emperor was Nyosan's brother, and was therefore bound to take an especial interest in him. The Empress§ still continued to treat him with the same affection as when he had run about and played with her children in the New Palace. She remembered indeed how in his last days Genji had constantly regretted that he had not lived to see the child¶ grow to manhood, and this made her all the more determined to do for him whatever Genji might under happier circumstances have done. And as if this was not enough, the Minister of the Right** treated him with extraordinary kindness, often taking more trouble about him than about his own sons.

In the old days Genji had indeed enjoyed an extraordinary popularity and prominence. But almost immediately a hostile faction had arisen, and this, combined with the early loss of his mother, had given his character a serious side, which to some extent counterbalanced the dazzling impression made by his gifts and beauty. Then came real disaster,†† leaving however no permanent trace behind it; and in the years that followed his patience and good-temper had enabled him time after time to pass quietly through each portending crisis.

---

* The five drawbacks of being a woman. She cannot, in a future incarnation, become Brahma, Indra, Yama, a Wheel-turning Monarch, or a Buddha.

† I.e. her next incarnation.

‡ His father.

§ The Akashi Princess, Genji's daughter.

¶ Kaoru must have been about six when Genji died.

** Yugiri.

†† Genji's banishment to Suma.

Kaoru's career was shaping very differently. Prominence had come to him far earlier in life, and nothing had outwardly happened to shake his self-esteem. His life indeed seemed to the eye of the spectator more like that of a fortunate spirit casually frequenting the earth than of the world of men.

In his appearance there was nothing that could be singled out as in any way pre-eminent or remarkable. He was merely a very pleasant-looking, rather shy young man with, one would say, a sensibility far beyond the average. The one remarkable thing about him was his personal fragrance. This, of an exquisite and even entrancing quality, was perceptible wherever he went, and at such a distance that it was indeed a "hundred-step scent." But it was entirely natural; for unlike most young men in his position, who are convinced that they can only survive competition by scrupulously concealing their natural advantages and substituting for them attractions of a wholly factitious kind, Kaoru, who above all disliked anything that tended to make his private goings and comings difficult to conceal, never used scent of any kind. But his precautions were useless; for so strong was this natural smell that it eclipsed each and every of the countless perfumes buried away in his Chinese scent-boxes. The very plum-blossom in the garden, if he but chanced to brush the tree with his sleeve, took on an altered fragrance; and the "orchids that we love to gather though we be drenched in the dripping of the spring rain"—the blue-skirted orchids that "lie ownerless in the autumn-fields"—suddenly took on an altered and bolder fragrance from the fact that he had touched them. And this surprising scent of Kaoru's own body—a thing which naturally aroused comment wherever he went—was, among many other points of rivalry, one of the principal things that stirred his friend Niou to emulation. The young prince was for ever rummaging among his stores for fresh forms of incense and perfume, devoting indeed a substantial part of the day to the blending of new and striking scents. All the springtime his eye was upon the flowering orchards, which he laid freely under contribution; while in the autumn it wandered from the petal of "the flower the world loves"* to the dew "upon the leaf which is the young deer's bride."† No perfumed plant or tree escaped him. From the plant of immortality‡ he tore a fragrance, from the fading orchid and even from the inconspicuous *waremoko*.§ So that at Court it was as an expert in the blending of perfumes that in those days he was best known, and it was thought a pity a young man should become immersed in an art that made so little call upon his robuster side. And indeed the fact that he allowed himself

---

* The *ominabeshi*.

† The lespedeza.

‡ The chrysanthemum.

§ The burnet.

to be thus identified with a particular distraction showed how different was his nature from that of Genji, who would never have suffered one enthusiasm to eclipse the rest.

At musical parties in Niou's rooms it often fell to Kaoru in some way or another to compete with his host, and there was, as I have said, a keen rivalry, though only such as commonly exists between young persons in such circumstances. Their names—people called them the Fragrant Captain and the Perfumed Prince—were on everyone's lips, and there was not a good family with marriageable daughters that was not immediately aflutter at the sound of these names.

Nor did Niou for his part wholly disregard the numerous hints that reached him, but made a point, in quarters where the prospects were at all favorable, of conducting his own investigations. But so far he had come across no one that really appealed to him. If only he had been offered Ryozen's daughter, Ichi no Miya! There was a wife obviously worth having! The mother[*] was a woman of extraordinary taste and refinement, and it was generally said at Court that the Princess herself was all that one would expect.

But Niou had more particular information. Chance had brought him into contact with some of her nearest personal attendants, and what they told him made Niou extremely anxious to know her.

Kaoru, on the other hand, feeling that he might at any moment find, life at Court utterly unendurable,[†] kept clear of any relationship that could be regarded as involving a permanent responsibility. So at any rate he explained to himself his own circumspection, which may in reality have been due merely to the fact that he had never yet chanced to fall seriously in love. Still less did he feel drawn towards affairs of an irregular or illicit kind.

In his nineteenth year he was promoted to the Third Rank while still retaining his rank as Captain of the Guard. To the world he seemed the most enviable man at Court. The Emperor and Empress showered kindnesses upon him; an outside person[‡] had rarely occupied such a position. But all the while he was haunted by the feeling that he was not what he was supposed to be. He grew melancholy, losing all capacity for throwing himself into the pleasures of the moment, and his manner became so restrained and subdued that those who met him felt he had grown old before his time.

Ichi no Miya, Niou's admiration for whom seemed to increase every day, Kaoru naturally knew very well, for they had been brought up together

---

[*] Lady Chujo.

[†] The alternative was to take Buddhist vows.

[‡] As Genji's son (or equally if regarded as Kashiwagi's son) Kaoru was not a member of the Imperial clan. Genji had been alliliated to the Minamotos, and Kashiwagi was a Fujiwara.

in Ryozen's palace. From what he heard of her and what he himself knew he felt sure that the extraordinary care taken in her upbringing had been duly rewarded, and he sometimes felt that if he was ever to be married at all this girl was probably the sort of person that it would be least unendurable to have about one for the rest of one's life. But though in every other respect the ex-Emperor Ryozen showed the greatest confidence in him, as regards Ichi no Miya he was not in the least accommodating. The two young people were never allowed to meet, and to evade this restriction would have led to more trouble than the meeting was worth. Should such an encounter prove a success, should he find that she really attracted him, the consequences would be disastrous to both of them.

Meanwhile Kaoru's popularity was proving embarrassing. He had only to write a trivial poem or a few conventional words, and at once a host of confidences would pour in upon him. His admirers, with startling alacrity, would cast themselves at his feet, and he would find himself involved in countless visits and correspondences which did not in the least interest him. He was careful never to respond to these solicitations in such a way as to arouse excessive expectations. But if he was not actually rude he would often find that his admirer, greatly flattered by this unlooked-for encouragement, had procured herself a post among the waiting-women in his mother's palace.

To Yugiri, who would otherwise, as he rightly suspected, have pressed upon him each of his many daughters in turn, he explained that most of his time was taken up in looking after his mother. So long as she was alive marriage was out of the question. Yugiri accordingly refrained from discussing the matter. And indeed so close was the relationship[*] that such a match would in some ways have been a rather uninteresting one. But one might certainly search the world in vain for a husband so eligible in all other ways as this young man.

As a matter of fact Roku no Kimi, Yugiri's child by Koremitsu's daughter, was far prettier than any of her half-sisters[†] and seemed likely to prove very intelligent. At Court however she was, owing to her mother's low rank, likely to be somewhat condescendingly treated, and knowing how women feel anything of that kind, he took her from her mother and had her brought up as the daughter of Princess Ochiba, who had no children of her own. Quietly, without calling attention to what he was doing, he began, whenever he had the chance of doing so, to introduce her to such young men of his acquaintance as seemed likely to appreciate her merits, certain that if he left things to themselves she would not fail to make an impression. He allowed her indeed a good deal more freedom than was

---

[*] Yugiri was Genji's son, and Kaoru was supposed to be.

[†] His children by Kumoi.

customary, and at the same time took pains to initiate her in all the lighter arts and graces of modern life, so that if one accomplishment failed to attract she should always have another to fall back upon.

The banquet in honor of the mounted archers* took place this year in Yugiri's palace. He was at great pains to arrange it in such a manner as would appeal to the royal princes, and the invitation was indeed accepted by all of them that were old enough to appear on such an occasion. Among the Akashi Princess's handsome and high-spirited sons Niou attracted by far the most attention. His younger brother, Prince Hitachi, was the Emperor's child by a waiting-woman, and though this may have been mere prejudice, he did certainly seem very lumpish compared with the rest. As usual it was the Bodyguard of the Left that had won, and so easily that the whole thing was over much earlier than usual. On leaving the Palace Yugiri invited Niou, Hitachi and the Empress's youngest son Nakatsukasa to join him in his carriage. Kaoru had been on the losing side and was creeping silently away when Yugiri called to him: "The princes are all coming home with me. Are you not going to help me entertain them?" Kaoru halted. A crowd of young men were there— Yugiri's sons Emon no Kami, Gon Chunagon, Udaiben, and many more. Yugiri extended his invitation to them all, packed them into one carriage or another, and the whole party drove off towards the New Palace. The road, and they had a good way to go, was covered with a thin layer of snow that sparkled in the evening light. It was the moment for music, and in every carriage the noise of flutes was still sounding as they entered the palace gates. And what Paradise, what abode of Gods, they wondered, could be more enchanting than the snow-covered gardens through which they were now being drawn?

As usual the party assembled in the southern verandah of the Main Hall. Kaoru was at once placed among the guests of honor with his face to the garden, while many of the princes and gentlemen had to content themselves with being "under the hedge."† After the great tankard had been passed round and things had warmed up a little the *Motomeko*‡ was danced. Close to the verandah the plum-trees were in bloom, and the waving of the dancers' sleeves shook and scattered the delicate flowers, which cast a shower of perfume as they fell. But mingled with this fragrance was another,§ equally agreeable. "It is too dark to see; but judging

---

* At the beginning of the year a competition of mounted archers took place in the Emperor's presence, and afterwards the competitors were entertained by the Minister of the Right or the Minister of the Left.

† *Ega*, i.e. facing the house; the position of those who are invited to assist in entertaining the guests of honor.

‡ One of the *Azuma Asobi,* "Eastern Dances"; the meaning of its name is unknown.

§ Kaoru's own.

by the smell it can surely be no one else," murmured one of the ladies-in-waiting, peeping from inside the house. Yugiri also both noticed and envied it. He had never seen the boy look more charming than he did tonight. But why did he remain so cold, so aloof? "Come," he said to Kaoru, "join in the singing. One would have thought that by now you must feel pretty well at home in this house." "A god dwells..."* Kaoru sang without hesitation...†

---

* From the folk-song *Ya Otome,* the refrain of which is "The many virgins! Oh, my many virgins." It was sometimes used to accompany the *Motomeko* dance, so that Kaoru had an excuse for singing it now. But he was of course alluding mischievously to Yugiri's many unmarried daughters.

† The sentence is not meant to break off in this way. A word or two is missing at the end of the chapter (Kaneko).

Kobai

Kashiwagi's younger brother Kobai, who as a child[*] had already shown signs of unusual capacity, rose as the years went by to a position of great importance. His first wife died young; and he was now married to Makibashira's daughter, the little girl who had clung to the pillar of her home.[†] She too had been married before—to Prince Sochi.[‡] Her relationship with Kobai began soon after Sochi's death and continued for some years to be a secret one. But there came a time when there was no further object to concealment and she moved into Kobai's house bringing with her an only daughter. Kobai already had two daughters by his first wife. He was now extremely anxious for a son and in answer to his prayers the Gods and Buddhas vouchsafed him a boy. For his part he treated Prince Sochi's girl exactly as though she had been his own child; but there was a good deal of jealousy and mischief-making between her waiting-maids and those of the other daughters. Fortunately the new wife was, in the modern manner, very sensible and straightforward in her ways of dealing with people, and generally managed to smooth out these squabbles. Even where the intrigues were aimed at her self she showed a very easy and forgiving disposition, paying to such petty outbursts no more attention than they deserved.

The three daughters grew up to womanhood and in turn assumed the Skirt.[§] Oigimi, Kobai's elder daughter, was given apartments in the south wing; the second girl, Naka no Kimi, in the west; while Prince Sochi's daughter lived on the east side. It was of course a disadvantage for this girl that her father, who could have done much for her, was no longer alive. But from one quarter and another she had brought with her a substantial inheritance, and she was able to live in an extremely handsome style. It was known that Kobai had spared himself no pains in directing the three girls' upbringing and education, and they were naturally regarded as excellent matches. Both the Emperor and the Crown Prince had hinted to Kobai that they would not be unwilling to receive one of these girls into their household. But it was generally known that the Emperor was entirely absorbed in the Akashi Princess, and the career of a girl in his entourage did not promise to be a very interesting one. Almost the same situation

---

[*] For a description of Kobai at the age of eight, see Part II, p. 218.
[†] See Part II, p. 579.
[‡] Genji's half-brother.
[§] Went through their Initiation into womanhood.

prevailed in the Crown Prince's household, where Yugiri's eldest daughter held a position which it would certainly be hard to invalidate. But none of these considerations seemed to justify keeping from service at Court a girl who obviously had as good a chance as anyone of holding her own, and in the end it was agreed that Oigimi should be installed in the Crown Prince's palace. She was a handsome girl, about seventeen years old, and from all points of view a very desirable addition to his household.

After this event it seemed a pity to give Naka no Kimi, who had perhaps even more charm than her sister, to a member of one of the ordinary dans, and Kobai sometimes wondered whether Prince Niou might not be willing to consider her. His son Tayu[*] was now a page at Court, and Niou when he chanced to catch sight of him there would often carry the boy off to take part with him in some sport or game. He was a promising boy, with particularly intelligent eyes and expression. "Tell your father," Niou said to him one day, "that I am a little hurt at his only allowing me to know one member of his family."[†] Kobai smiled complacently when the boy delivered this message. "Well, well," he said, "for an ordinary girl, who would not have a chance of coming to the fore in the Imperial household, Niou would not make a bad match. He is quite unattached, and if he set his mind to it, he could certainly provide anyone whom he really fancied with an extremely agreeable existence." But before anything further could be done in this direction Oigimi must be settled in her new position. If only the God of Kasuga,[‡] who was supposed to have taken such things into his hands before, would again intervene! And in his prayers Kobai pointed out to the clan-god that here was an opportunity to re-establish his credit, and show that the women of the clan could not always be set aside[§] so lightly as Lady Chujo had been. Thus praying, he took Oigimi to Court, and it was generally agreed that the Crown Prince was exceedingly pleased with her. As she was quite inexperienced, and it was doubted whether she would at first be capable of looking after herself, her mother came with her and indeed helped and directed her at every turn.

At home Naka no Kimi, who had never been separated from her sister before, was very disconsolate. So too was Sochi's daughter, who had been exceedingly intimate with the elder girl, sleeping beside her and relying on Oigimi to instruct her in all the small accomplishments and distractions that were current at the moment. She was a very unusual girl, shy beyond all reason. It was only by the greatest effort that she could bring herself to

---

[*] Kobai's son by his new wife.

[†] A hint that he would like to know Kobai's daughters.

[‡] The clan-god of the Fujiwaras. In ancient days he was supposed to have appeared on earth and commanded that the Imperial consorts should be chosen from no other clan.

[§] By Ryozen, in favor of Akikonomu, who was not a Fujiwara.

let even her mother really see her, and in general she carried the dislike of being looked at to the verge of insanity. Yet she had no defect either of person or intelligence which could have prompted her to behave in this fashion. On the contrary she had in looks and in every other way more to recommend her than most of her contemporaries could boast of.

Kobai, with whom it was a point of honor to take as much trouble over a stepchild as about his own children, soon began to feel that Sochi's daughter was being neglected. "We must do something for her," he said to his wife. "Think it over and tell me what you have decided. I should be very sorry not to do as well for her as for the others." "I assure you," she answered, "that no thoughts of marriage or anything of the kind ever enter the girl's head, and indeed any allusion to that sort of thing upsets her so much that I see nothing for it but, so long as I am here, to leave her as she is. When I am dead, dismal though the prospect sounds, I really think the best thing to do with her would be to send her into a convent, where at any rate she would be left to herself and be free from the ridicule into which her peculiarities are otherwise bound to bring her." Though at the same time, with tears in her eyes, she thanked Kobai for his kind intentions towards a child that was not his own.

Kobai, though he had so scrupulously avoided making any difference in his treatment of Sochi's daughter, had strangely enough, owing to her extraordinary bashfulness, never yet seen her.[*] He could not in the least understand all this secrecy and thought it a poor return for his kindness. He often crept softly to her apartment hoping to catch a glimpse of her without her knowledge; but she invariably disappeared. He sent a message one day to say that, in her mother's absence at Court, it was clearly his duty to look after her. "It makes me unhappy," he said, "that you should seem so determined to have nothing to do with me." Seated in front of her screen-of-state, he managed this time to obtain a few murmured words from her and in a dim way to discern the outlines of the figure crouching within. She had an agreeable voice and so far as he could make out a distinguished and even captivating presence. He had made up his mind that one might search the wide world around without finding handsomer girls than his own two daughters, and the thought that perhaps here in his own house was one who might prove to be more than their equal rather piqued him.

"I have been so busy lately," he said, "that it is months since I heard you play. I believe Naka no Kimi has been taking a lot of trouble over her lute-playing, and is getting on very well. It is an instrument which, if unskillfully handled, can easily be very disagreeable to listen to. When you have nothing better to do, please help her with it a little. I have only

---

[*] She had always been hidden by the curtains of her couch, been behind a screen, or the like.

heard you trying pieces over occasionally, but I could see at once that yours is the true, old-fashioned style. I have never been able to make a special study of music. But in the old days I played a great deal, and as far as knowing what things ought to sound like, I think you can trust me pretty well. Yugiri, nowadays, is the only one whose playing is at all like what Genji's used to be. Kaoru and Niou are both, by what I can hear, young men of remarkable attainments and they have taken a lot of trouble about their playing. Perhaps in other respects they may be on the same level as their forerunners. But as regards their lute-playing I can tell you it is certainly not so. There is something weak and indecisive in their touch. Yugiri's playing is entirely lacking in that defect, and yours reminds me of his. With the lute a great deal of tone is not required. What matters is an accurate use of the frets and a wide range of different strokes with the quill. These you have, and particularly in a woman that is all one should require. Come, let us have some music. Bring the lady her instrument."

Unlike their mistress the maids to whom this order was addressed showed no disposition to shrink from the display of their charms; all save one very young girl, obviously of better birth than the rest. She, out of laziness or timidity, simply remained where she was. "You are beginning to teach even your maids to be shy of me," Kobai said testily.

The boy Tayu was just about to start out to the Palace. He was in the informal costume used for night attendance, and looked even more charming than in his usual Court dress. "Here is a message for your sister at Court," Kobai said to the boy, looking at him admiringly. "Tell her that I am feeling tired and hope she will forgive me if I do not come up to the Palace this evening."

"But let me hear how you are getting on with your flute," he added. "It would be awkward, you know, if you were commanded to play at the Palace. You have still so much to learn." "Let us have the notes of the Sojo tuning,"* he said smiling, and Tayu blew them very creditably. "That is not too bad," said Kobai. "Now you will be able to accompany the lute." "Play something for him," he urged his step-daughter, and after a while, with an air of great reluctance, she obeyed, doing no more than softly finger† the strings, but following the boy's flute very skillfully.

Close to the verandah of the eastern wing, almost touching the eaves, there grew a red plum-tree, the scent of which was unusually fine. "What a splendid show of blossom you have outside your rooms!" said Kobai. "I happen to know that Prince Niou is at the Palace. You might pluck a spray of the blossom and give it to him. 'Who better than he...?'"‡

---

* Roughly, the scale of G major, but with F natural.

† Not using the plectrum.

‡ "To whom but to my lord can I send it—this plum-tree spray? Who better than he can prize its gift of color and smell?" Poem by Ki no Tomonori, 9th and 10th centuries.

"When I was your age," he went on, "I used to meet Prince Genji at Court just as you are meeting Niou now. I shall never forget those days; it was just when he was at the height of his career. These young princes of yours are certainly somewhat out of the ordinary—though their circumstances are such that they were bound in any case to be flattered and admired—but when people compare them with *him,* I cannot imagine what they mean. Ah well, perhaps this is mere prejudice. Often one cannot recognize qualities simply because one does not expect them to be there. Not that I ever knew Genji very well; enough however to realize what must be the feelings of those to whom his death was a real and intimate loss." He stood silent for a while, and then, as though glad to busy himself with something that would help him to shake off a train of melancholy reflections, he helped the boy to pluck a spray of blossom and get ready to go off to Court.

"Perhaps after all," Kobai added, "Niou will one day surprise us as Ananda surprised the Assembly.* I do not want to bore him, but for the sake of old remembrances I will write a word or two for you to take with the flowers..." "Since purposeful the wind comes laden with the perfume of Spring flowers, soon surely you will visit, O nightingale, the garden where they grow." Such was the poem that he now wrote on scarlet paper in a hand that strove not to appear old-fashioned, and folding it in Tayu's handkerchief, he sent the boy to Court. Tayu was delighted at any excuse for talking to the grown-up person whom he most admired, and hurrying as fast as he could he arrived just when Niou, accompanied by a large troupe of attendants and admirers, was leaving the Empress's apartments. The boy joined this throng, but was immediately noticed by Niou, who said to him, "You disappeared very early yesterday. How long have you been back?" "I came back this evening," he said, "to make up for going away so early yesterday; besides, I heard that you were here." He spoke boyishly, but without any trace of shyness. "You must come home with me one day to the Nijo-in," said Niou; "one can't do anything here. You would have great fun. There are always crowds of young people there." He beckoned Tayu to wait. His followers withdrew to a respectful distance or disappeared, and when he and the boy were alone Niou said: "Does the Crown Prince never send for you now? I remember a time when you and he were inseparable. I am afraid you have been completely cut out by your sister."† "It was a nuisance having to go there so often," said the boy. "I would much rather be with you." "He does not take much interest in me," said Niou, "and indeed there is no particular reason why he should. But it

---

* After Buddha's death, at the first Assembly, his disciple Ananda, who had seemed an insignificant person by Buddha's side, made so imposing an impression that for a moment it was believed that Buddha had returned to life.

† Oigimi, who had become the Crown Prince's concubine.

does rather annoy me when he behaves as though people who are not heirs to a Throne were scarcely human beings at all. You might remind him, if you get the chance, that we are after all both members of the same musty old family." It was at this moment that Tayu produced the plum-blossom. Niou laughed. "In another minute," he said, "I should have been saying something disagreeable about your father too." He held the flower in front of him for a long time. It was a magnificent spray, unsurpassable not only in color and scent, but also in the formation of the blossoms and the way they were set on the bough. "People are struck by the color of the red flowers," said Niou, "and pretend that it is to the white ones one must go for smell. But I challenge anyone to say about these that the scent is less amazing than the color." They were indeed his favorite flower and he was genuinely delighted at receiving them. "I am on duty tonight," he said presently, "and I have to sleep in the Palace. Will you not stay with me?"

Forgetting all about his message for the Crown Princess the boy followed him and lay happily enough beside this prince, the scent of whose garments put even the perfume of Kobai's blossom to shame. "Why was it," Niou asked him presently, "that your father chose Oigimi for the Crown Prince instead of giving him this other sister, from whose garden the flowers came?" "I don't know," said the boy. "They said something about having to wait till they could find someone who would understand her." Niou imagined this to be merely an excuse of Kobai's for preferring his own daughter. But for some reason he himself felt more interest in the stepchild, and in his answer was careful to avoid making any definite response to Kobai's hint. With the letter which the boy brought home next day, scribbled rather carelessly, was the poem: "Were my heart such that by the scent of any flower it could be thus enticed, think you that I would pass unheeded the perfumed message of the wind?" "Give this to your father," he said. "But be sure to put in a word for me with the other-one* when your elders are out of the way."

Tayu had always taken a particular interest in his unapproachable stepsister. The fact that she surrounded herself with such an atmosphere of mystery made her seem to him far more important that his whole-sisters, who allowed him to consort with them on perfectly natural and friendly terms. He had been indignant when Oigimi was chosen as participant in the splendors of the Crown Prince's palace, and was now delighted that, as a sequel to the plum-blossom incident, there was a chance of her wrongs being righted.

Kobai was evidently not best pleased by Niou's answer. "It is ridiculous," he said, "for him to speak of himself in such terms.† It is well

---

* Sochi's daughter.

† "Were my heart such that by the scent of any flower..."

known he has numerous affairs on hand, and if his disposition leads him in that direction there would be no sense in his forcing himself to behave unnaturally. But he has got it into his head that Yugiri and I disapprove of his life, and whenever we are there he makes this absurd parade of austerity."

Not long afterwards his wife came back from Court. "The other morning," she said, "Tayu came from the Emperor's Palace smelling deliciously. We thought at first that it was natural. But the Crown Prince noticed it as soon as he came in and said at once that he must have been with Prince Niou. "That's the way things are," he said. "Tayu has quite deserted me lately." He was chaffing the boy, of course, but he pretended to be really angry. I assure you it was very amusing. I heard something too about your writing to Niou..."

"That is true," said Kobai. "He is fond of plum-blossom, and as the red plum-tree on the other side of the house was in full flower I felt I must pluck some for him. You know that he is an expert in perfume-making. I am sure that none of the ladies at Court understand the business half so well. Prince Kaoru, on the other hand, does not go in for perfumes at all, and has no need to, for his natural smell is unsurpassed. No doubt this is due to something that happened in a previous incarnation. I should like to know more about it. But it is no odder that some human beings should smell nice than that some flowers should. Certainly the plum-flower, which grows on such a common-looking little tree, is a perpetual wonder to me." So he rambled on about scents and flowers, but was all the time thinking in reality about Niou and his second daughter.

Sochi's girl was neither childish nor ignorant. She knew quite well what was going on in the world around her and had merely made up her mind that she preferred to remain as she was. Nor did anyone make much effort to break in on her seclusion, for suitors are in general more attracted to girls with fathers who can back their interests than to a fatherless creature immured in dull seclusion. It was however just the accounts of her strange and depressing existence that had excited Niou's interest, and he was determined to get into contact with her. Tayu was made the bearer of continual secret letters and messages. Of these the girl's mother was not unaware and it was with distress that she saw Kobai still obstinately striving to obtain from Niou some hint that his project had not failed. "I am afraid," his wife said to him one day, "that Niou's interest is all in a direction where it is entirely wasted. He has begun sending notes. It is a hopeless business."

The notes were not answered; but this only increased Niou's determination. Sometimes it seemed to the girl's mother that she must be forced at all costs to accept a match which would not only provide her with an excellent position at the moment but also held out such glowing prospects for the future. But, apart from everything else, the mother heard very disquieting accounts of Niou's character. It appeared that he was conducting an inordinate number of secret affairs, and had also become deeply involved in an entanglement with one or the other of Prince Hachi no Miya's daughters and spent a great deal of his time at Uji. In short, she was obliged to conclude that he was thoroughly dissipated and untrustworthy, and finally dismissed from her mind all thought of encouraging him. But occasionally, for the sake of politeness, she would write a brief and formal acknowledgement of the notes that he continued to shower upon her daughter.

"Bamboo River"

What here follows was told me by some of the still surviving gentlewomen of Tamakatsura's household. I myself was inclined to regard much of it as mere gossip, particularly where it concerned Genji's descendants, with whom they can have had very little contact. My informants however were indignant at the idea that Genji's or Murasaki's women must necessarily know better than they. "If anyone gets things wrong," they said, "it is far more likely to be Genji's people, who are all so old that their memories are beginning to fail."

For my part I have made no effort to decide the question, but simply put things down as I was told.[*]

Tamakatsura[†] and Higekuro had three sons and two daughters, for each of whose careers their father had made elaborate plans. But while he was still impatiently counting the months and days that must elapse before his schemes could be fulfilled, death suddenly carried him off, and the dream of his life, which was that one at least of his daughters should be accepted at the Palace, had now no prospect of being fulfilled. So time-serving a creature is man that no one could hold a public position[‡] such as Higekuro's without accumulating a vast quantity of gifts and lands. Thus in one way his family cannot be said to have been left badly off. But the magnificence of their home and possessions only served to accentuate their loneliness and isolation. True, Tamakatsura was related through her father to some of the best families in the land. Unfortunately however it is precisely such families that take least trouble about their relations. Moreover Higekuro's peculiarities—his unreliable temper and curious lack of sensibility—had prevented him from making any close friends. Genji had of course continued to treat her exactly as before, and in his written testament her name figured next to that of the Akashi Princess as a residuary heir. Moreover Yugiri, in obedience to his father's wishes, occasionally visited her.

Her boys were growing up. But though the death of their father very much injured their prospects, Tamakatsura felt little doubt that they

---

[*] It is clear from this preamble that "Bamboo River" was written at a time when Murasaki was separated from her manuscript and feared that her memory might play her false.

[†] Yugao's child by To no Chujo. Discovered by Genji and treated for a while as his child; afterwards married to Higekuro. The ex-Emperor Ryozen had been in love with her.

[‡] Minister of the Right.

would make their own way. The future of the daughters presented a far more disturbing problem. During his lifetime Higekuro had informed the Emperor of his great desire to see one of his girls at the Palace. They were at that time mere children; but the Emperor had not forgotten Higekuro's request, and as soon as sufficient time had elapsed to allow of the girls having reached a suitable age, he reminded Tamakatsura of her husband's promise. He repeated this invitation several times. But Tamakatsura avoided any definite reply. It was clear that the Empress* was for the present occupying the Emperor's whole attention, and Tamakatsura could not reconcile herself to the idea of seeing a daughter of hers relegated to an inferior position among a host of superfluous nonentities. The ex-Emperor Ryozen also wrote in an encouraging way, reminding her of the disappointment she had caused him in old days. "I am getting old," he said, "and have in my own person nothing to offer that a young girl could possibly find attractive. She would have to regard me in the light of a friend and father, ready to shoulder for her all the burdens and anxieties of existence."

Her own marriage had turned out very badly, and she was certain that Ryozen must at the time have thought her mad to make so extraordinary a choice. To give him one of her children seemed a way of admitting her mistake and (so far as at this late day such a thing could be) making amends for the injury she had done to his pride.

The two girls were said to be very good-looking, and a great many young men were already anxious for their favors. Kurodo no Shosho, one of Yugiri's sons by Kumoi, was continually sending poems. He was the favorite among all the sons, and had been brought up with immense care.

In more than one way† the two houses were connected by close ties, and it was natural that Tamakatsura should allow Yugiri's sons to run in and out of her house as they pleased. But Tamakatsura's women began to complain that Kurodo was becoming a nuisance. Day and night he pestered them with messages to Himegimi, the elder girl, till they were tired of the sight of him. Tamakatsura herself thought that things were going too far, and she was not best pleased that both the boy's mother and Yugiri were continually pressing Kurodo's claims upon her. "He has still to make his way in the world," Yugiri said. "But we should both be very grateful if you would consider the matter." But she was determined the elder girl at any rate should not be the wife of a commoner. The second girl perhaps—if and when Kurodo reached a position of rather more stability and importance.

---

* The Akashi Princess.

† As Genji's adopted daughter Tamakatsura ranked as Yugiri's half-sister; moreover Kumoi, Yugiri's wife, was (like Tamakatsura in reality) a daughter of To no Chujo.

But little as she liked the prospect of Kurodo as a husband for her elder daughter, it would be a far worse calamity if he were allowed to force himself upon her as a clandestine lover, and Tamakatsura kept on imploring the ladies who were acting as his go-betweens not to allow the affair to get out of hand. Thus, pestered on both sides, these ladies had no very enviable time of it.

At the moment of which I am speaking Kaoru was still only about fourteen, but his character seemed to be already formed, and in general he promised so well for the future that Tamakatsura would not have been at all averse—and, indeed, why should she have been considering that the boy was Genji's son, the Emperor Suzaku's grandson, the adopted son of the ex-Emperor Ryozen, and already an officer of the Fourth Rank—to accepting him as her daughter's suitor.

Her palace and that of Kaoru's mother were both in the Third Ward, and it often happened that Tamakatsura's boys would bring Kaoru home with them. The house happened at the time to be full of particularly lively young waiting-girls, who were a source of great interest to the visitors. Among those visitors one of the handsomest and by far the most frequent was Kurodo. But the most elegant and, in a reserved way, the most attractive, was undoubtedly the boy in the Fourth Rank.* Everywhere, partly because something extraordinary was expected of Genji's son, he was treated as someone different and apart. The young girls in Tamakatsura's service were lost in admiration of him, while she herself declared that he was "extraordinarily good to look at," and had long, intimate conversations with him whenever he came to the house, maintaining that he was the only person left whom she could even expect to remind her of Prince Genji. "For Yugiri," she said, "is now a public character of such importance that except on special occasions I can no longer hope to see him." She regarded Kaoru in the light of a brother, and he too accepted the house as one which he could treat almost as his own. It surprised Tamakatsura that he was so singularly lacking in any taste for the frivolous pursuits of the day. Indeed his quietness was lamented by the young girls both in her house and his own, and they declared that, in the last resort, it made him very disappointing to deal with.

On New Year's Day Tamakatsura's brother Kobai, Higekuro's son To no Chunagon, and Yugiri with his six sons all came to see her. Yugiri himself was looking extraordinarily handsome and imposing. The boys were, each in his own way, quite presentable. All of them had received very encouraging promotions at the New Year, and it was, Tamakatsura thought, a family that must on the whole cause very little anxiety. But it was strange that the youngest son, Kurodo no Shosho, despite the fact

---

* Kaoru.

that such a fuss was made about him at home, looked every time she saw him more preoccupied and depressed.

Yugiri stationed himself in front of her screen-of-state and discoursed on affairs in general much as he had been used to do in old days. "It is a long while since I have managed to get here," he said. "As the years go on I seem to go about less and less. I assure you a visit, except to the Palace, is quite an experience for me. Yet I am constantly thinking how agreeable it would be to come and chat with you about old times. My sons however have more leisure than I. Do make them useful sometimes. They are always saying they wish they knew of anything they could do for you." "People take so little notice of my existence nowadays," she answered, "that I sometimes wonder whether I do really exist at all. But to be visited by someone like you makes me almost feel that the old days have come again..." and her mind went back to Genji's marvelous visits.

They fell presently to talking of the offers that had come from the ex-Emperor Ryozen. "I am puzzled what to do about it," she said. "It is a great risk to let a girl go to Court unless she has really powerful backing." "I hear," said Yugiri, "that you have also had a request from the present Emperor; so that there is a further question for you to decide. Ryozen's glories are of course a thing of the past, and there is always a certain atmosphere of depression in a household of that kind. But he himself has a charm that time does very little to diminish. I can only say that if I myself had a girl of a fairly suitable kind, I would not hesitate. But unfortunately I have not one whose circumstances are such that she could move comfortably in such surroundings.* Your daughter would certainly have the advantage of Lady Chujo's† support; whereas it has been precisely a fear of opposition from that quarter which has held several people back from offering their girls."

"Lady Chujo," she replied, "has very little on her hands nowadays, and if she set her mind to it she could certainly give the girl a very good time. Yes, I think if Lady Chujo were to suggest it, that would decide me."

The visitors then went on in a body to Lady Nyosan's, bringing with them Tamakatsura's sons. For Nyosan was still visited both by such of her father's‡ relations as continued to feel obligation towards him, and by those of Genji's friends whom he had begged not to neglect her, and it was now quite a troupe that flocked through her doors—Tamakatsura's sons Sakon no Chujo, Uchuben and Jiju; Yugiri and all his sons, with a great crowd more. Towards evening Kaoru came in. All day long the place had been full of young men, none of whom could

---

* He is thinking of Roku no Kimi, his illegitimate child by Koremitsu's daughter.

† Lady Chujo, daughter of To no Chujo, was Tamakatsura's half-sister.

‡ The ex-Emperor Suzaku.

have been called commonplace or ugly. But no sooner did Kaoru enter the house than every eye was turned upon him. "What a difference!" one of the young waiting-girls whispered. "*There's* the bridegroom that Lady Tamakatsura ought to be thinking about for her elder girl!" And indeed there was a singular charm in his boyish air and in the fragrance that wafted from him wherever he went. Inexperienced though Lady Tamakatsura's daughter was supposed to be, it was hard to believe that, if she were in her senses at all, she could be in any doubt on which side her choice should lie.

Tamakatsura at once summoned Kaoru to her private chapel, and mounting the eastern step he conversed with her through the curtain that screened the chapel-door. Near by on a plum-tree that was just timorously struggling into bloom a nightingale was singing its first fragmentary song. Even at such a moment as this, was it impossible to make this strange young man unbend? So the ladies of the household asked themselves, and made more than one attempt to engage the boy in conversation. But he answered sedately in the fewest possible words, and at last a girl called Saisho no Kimi became so provoked that she recited the verse: "Would that your color[*] like your scent, O first flower of the plum, grew sweeter close at hand!" It was only an improvisation, and he contented himself with the reply: "Fair and sweet-scented are the buds it hides—the tree that from afar seemed black and bare." "If you doubt it..." he added, and laughing held out his sleeve. They were still trying one after another to elicit some sign of interest from him, when Tamakatsura, coming across to them, whisperingly interceded: "You tiresome creatures, can you never leave anyone alone? Don't you see that you are only making him uncomfortable? He is a serious young man."

"A serious young man." He overheard this depressing description, and did not feel flattered.

Tamakatsura's third son, Jiju, now came back, for business had not yet recommenced at Court and he had no desire for the usual round of New Year visits. He brought in fruit and wine on two trays of aloe-wood. "Yugiri," said Tamakatsura, "grows more like Prince Genji every day. But in you, Kaoru, I can see no likeness at all. Of course when he was quite young[†] he may have had your sort of quietness and gentleness of manner. Yes, I dare say that was just what he *was* like at your age."

Later in the month, when the plum-blossom had come into full bloom, Kaoru set out to call on Jiju, Tamakatsura's son. He was determined on this occasion to efface the impression that he was "serious" or difficult

---

[*] A play on *iro* "color" and *iro* "love," "gaiety."

[†] Tamakatsura, having been brought up by Yugao's woman Ukon in the country, did not see Genji when he was quite young.

to get on with. As he was going through the big door that led into the courtyard of the women's apartments he became aware that someone, dressed like himself in ordinary clothes,* was standing in the shadow, apparently hoping not to be observed.

Kaoru caught hold of the intruder's sleeve and found, not greatly to his surprise, that it was Kurodo no Shosho. Somewhere inside a zithern and lute were being played, and it was no doubt this sound that had drawn Kurodo no Shosho to his hiding-place behind the door. Kaoru was pained. Kurodo, it was clear, had set his heart on a prize that he could never, by fair means, hope to win. There would be trouble, dire trouble. The music had stopped, and Kaoru said quickly, "show me the way. You know the house better than I do." They crossed together to the western corridor and halted at the foot of a red plum-tree that grew outside, Kaoru whistling as he approached it the air *Bough of the Plum-tree.*† Someone inside set the double-doors ajar, and several zitherns began at once to accompany Kaoru's tune. That the players were women he could at first hardly believe, for the song is in one of the ryo‡ modes; but when he repeated it someone inside, this time on a lute, followed the melody with faultless skill.

This was evidently a quarter worth cultivating! Kaoru's interest was aroused; for once, he began almost to be carried away by what was going on around him.

Presently someone handed out a Japanese zithern from behind the curtains. Kaoru motioned to Kurodo to take it, and he in turn tried to make Kaoru play; so that the zithern remained where it was. This seemed a pity, and Tamakatsura§ sent her son Jiju to Kaoru with a message saying that she had been told his touch on the zithern resembled that of his late Excellency To no Chujo, and she was curious to hear whether this was so. Though at the moment Kaoru was feeling like doing anything in the world rather than exhibit his touch, he picked up the instrument and carelessly played a few notes. She saw however at once that he had a great command over the instrument. "You know, it is not so much To no Chujo as his son Kashiwagi that your playing reminds me of," she said. "You are really extraordinarily like him in many ways." And though she had not known Kashiwagi very well, the mere thought that someone was no longer in the world was enough—as is the case with most people who are themselves growing old—to bring tears into her eyes.

---

* I.e. not in Court dress.

† "Look, to a bough of the plum-tree the nightingale has come...." See Part IV, p. 598.

‡ The modes were divided into two classes, *ryo* and *ritsu*, only the latter of which were generally mastered by women, being considered more appropriate to their sex.

§ Who was behind the curtains.

Kurodo, who had a very agreeable voice, now sang *The Trefoil*,* and as there were no tiresome elderly people there to interrupt with instructive suggestions the two of them went on from one old song to another. But Tamakatsura's boy Jiju being, like his father, a poor hand at music had nothing to do but sit and make headway with the wine. "Come," they said to him at last, "you must have a try, if only for luck!" and timidly he joined in when they were singing *Bamboo River*.† His voice was still quite unformed but not at all disagreeable.

After a while the great earthenware tankard was brought out from the inner rooms. Kaoru had already drunk a good deal, and he remembered having heard that after a certain point one begins to talk without wanting to about things one meant to keep secret. He pushed the tankard away. "Do you like this better?" said Tamakatsura, sending him a *hosonaga*‡ with a *ko-uchigi*§ inside it, both agreeably scented and arranged just as she had worn them. Kaoru pretended not to know what they were, and after much scuffling and laughing succeeded in passing them on to Jiju. He then tried to get away, but Jiju prevented his leaving the house, and again decked him with Tamakatsura's dress. "Let me go," said Kaoru; "I cannot spend all night in the water-stables!"¶ and he dashed away.

Kurodo no Shosho was convinced that if Kaoru began frequenting this part of the house, he himself would have no chance at all. He became very depressed, and told everyone that the life of anyone so unattractive as himself was not worth living.

Next morning Jiju had a letter from Kaoru. It was written chiefly in *kana*,** so that it was evidently meant to be shown to Jiju's mother. It was clear that he regarded himself as having behaved very wildly the evening before. "What can you all have thought of me?" he said. On the margin of his letter was written the poem: "On Bamboo River, standing at the bridge, 'twas but a shallow trickle that I showed of my deep heart's full tide."

In Tamakatsura's room she and Jiju examined the letter. "It is a delightful piece of handwriting," she said. "I cannot think where he has picked up all his accomplishments. He was only a few years old when his father died, and his mother has given very little attention to him." She hoped the sight of this letter was making Jiju feel a little uncomfort-

---

* "Rich is my house that has three roof-beams, like the trefoil that grows three leaves upon one stem..."

† See Part III, p. 478.

‡ A garment used by women and young boys.

§ An undergarment used exclusively by women.

¶ When half their round of visits was over the New Year mummers stopped for refreshments at a building called the Water Stables. One of the songs they sang was *Bamboo River*, which Kaoru and the rest had now been singing. Kaoru means that he has other calls to pay.

** The syllabic writing used by women.

able about his own uncouth handwriting. "It was only the water-stables* that we minded," Jiju wrote in reply. "No one noticed anything else to complain of." With the letter was the poem: "Small wonder that you fled; for in the garden of flowers by Bamboo River is no perch on which your thoughts could rest."

But this was evidently not quite true, for Kaoru began coming to Jiju's rooms with a frequency which needed some explanation, and which filled Kurodo no Shosho, who could not imagine that anyone would not instantly prefer Kaoru to himself, with utter despair. And Kurodo's assumption did indeed appear not to be far wide of the mark. Jiju, to name one member of the household only, was content that any circumstance should have given him a companion so intimate and so delightful.

It was the third month, which is the real season of cherry-blossom, for not only are the boughs laden with it but the very air quavers with a storm of falling flowers. At Tamakatsura's palace a profound stillness reigned. No visitor had set foot there all day, and it seemed so unlikely that anyone would come that Himegimi and her sister were sitting at the window, both of them handsome, lively girls of about seventeen to eighteen.

Himegimi herself was certainly the more striking of the two, and her beauty was so thoroughly in the style fashionable at the moment that it seemed inconceivable she would not do better for herself than marry into an ordinary clan. She wore a white dress lined with dark purple, and a skirt of a tint that recalled the globe-flower, as fold on fold it spilled its yellow shimmer on the floor. There was about her a singular air of competence and self-possession.

Her sister was dressed in a light reddish-brown, a color which suited† the long, rippling tresses of her hair. She was very tall, but graceful and adroit in her movements. Her expression was more serious than that of her sister, and she looked as though she were capable of far deeper feelings.

Himegimi, the elder girl, was generally considered the more attractive of the two. On this particular occasion they were sitting opposite one another playing draughts, an occupation that can show a woman's charms to great advantage, with its dangling tresses and raising and sinking of the head. Their younger brother Jiju was with them, "to see that they did not cheat," he said. Presently the two elder brothers, Sakon no Chujo and Uchuben, looked into the room. "Jiju *has* stolen a march upon us," they said. "Look, their ladyships have taken him on as referee in a game of draughts." And with a rather patronizing air, complete men of the world, they advanced towards the draughts-board, leaving it to the ladies-in-waiting to make room for them.

---

* I.e. your treating us as a temporary halting-place.
† A brownish tinge is not unknown in Japanese women's hair.

"It is too bad," said Sakon no Chujo, "that while I am slaving at the Palace Jiju should step in and supplant me here." "And what about me?" said Uchuben. "My work in the Council of State takes up far more time, and I might easily be forgiven for neglecting my courtly duties in this house, were I so faithless as to do so."

The girls had stopped their game and were sitting looking in front of them with an air of slight bewilderment that was very engaging. Sakon no Chujo knew how much, both at the Palace and wherever he went, he missed the late Minister's support. And as he looked at his sisters tears filled his eyes at the thought that their case was worse than his own. But he was now twenty-seven. He was beginning to have some influence, and he must use the whole of it to do for these girls some part, at least of what his father would have done.

Out in the garden there was, among the many flowering trees, one particular cherry-tree with a scent that far exceeded that of all the rest. Sakon sent someone to pluck a branch and set it in his sister's hands.

"What blossom!" Himegimi said. "There is no flower like it!" "That is the tree," said Sakon no Chujo, "about which we had a quarrel when we were small. Each of you said that it was yours, and I said it belonged to me. Father said it was Himegimi's, and mother said it was Wakagimi's* tree. But no one said it was mine, and I remember that though I did not cry or make a fuss, I was very unhappy about it. It is growing old itself— this cherry-tree," he went on, "and makes one feel old along with it. So many people that once shared it with us are gone now." He spoke sadly, yet half-smiling. The sisters had seldom seen him in so serious a mood. He was married now, and lived with his wife's people, so that he could seldom spend a quiet hour like this at his mother's house. But today he had been determined to come, simply for the sake of this tree.

It was strange to think that this full-grown man was Tamakatsura's son, for she looked far younger than her age, and had indeed retained much of her beauty; and if the ex-Emperor Ryozen continually asked about her intentions with regard to Himegimi, it was not so much the daughter as the mother who was in his thoughts. For turning the matter over in his mind he saw no other prospect of his ever meeting Tamakatsura again.

About his sister's future Sakon no Chujo had decided views. "Everything has its time," he said, "and Ryozen's is long past. He is, I grant, still a fine-looking man; but even if he were the handsomest and most attractive person in the world, his present situation would make his life a depressing one to share. It is the same with everything. The zithern and the flute with their tunes, the trees with their blossom, the birds with their song—each

---

* The younger sister.

keeps to its own season and then only can please the eye or ear. But the Crown Prince, now..."

"Oh come," broke in Tamakatsura, "she is not wanted there. His attention is already fully occupied. If Higekuro were alive, we could take the risk; but now we must arrange something that will make her future, if not brilliant, at any rate secure."

When Sakon no Chujo went away his sisters resumed their game of draughts. It was to be the best out of three, and the winner, they laughingly decided, should have the cherry-tree for her own. As it was getting dark they moved the board as close as possible to the window, and their respective waiting-women, raising the blinds, gathered round, each bent on the victory of her own side.

Presently, as usual, Kurodo no Shosho arrived and went straight to Jiju's room; but Jiju had gone out with his brothers. There seemed indeed to be no one about, and as the door of the corridor leading to the women's apartments was ajar, Kurodo stepped lightly towards it and looked in. He was dumbfounded at his own good fortune. His heart stood still as it might have done if Buddha himself had suddenly risen up in front of him. It was misty as well as late, but soon among the mass of dark figures he distinguished the sharp contrasts of a "cherry"* dress. Yes, that surely was she. He gazed and gazed, that he might at least have something to remember "when the flowers were fallen."† He saw her clearly now; but her beauty filled him only with a greater sadness. Better now than ever before he knew how much it was that he was doomed to lose.

The young girls in attendance, who were for the most part very lightly and negligently clad, presented a charming spectacle in the evening light. The elder sister lost the match. "Where is the Korean‡ fanfare?" someone wittily asked. "The trouble has always been," said one of Wakagimi's ladies, "that although you have a tree of your own, for it is nearest to your lady's room, you people would insist year after year that this other one was your tree. Well, that's over anyway!" The "junior side," elated by its victory, was becoming quite truculent.

Kurodo had not the least idea what all this was about. But the conversation amused him, and he longed to join in it. This however was for the moment out of the question, for to break in upon a party of ladies whose costumes and attitudes showed so clearly that they were counting on not being disturbed, would be the height of ill-breeding. He slipped away and, hoping that before long a better opportunity would occur, hung about somewhere in the dark.

---

* The robe that Himegimi wore was called a "cherry dress."

† In allusion to the old poem: "I will dye my dress to the deepest cherry hue, that when the flowers are fallen I may have something to remember them by."

‡ After the horse races when the "junior side" won a Korean fanfare was played.

It was a windy evening, and now the cherry-blossom, for the possession of which the two sisters had contended, was tumbling in great showers to the ground.

"Though you would not be mine, uneasy, faithless blossoms, grows my heart, to see the night-wind rise." Such was Himegimi's poem, and her maid Saisho: "A brittle victory, that at the wind's first breath casts all its guerdon shivering to the ground." And Wakagimi: "Though flower from branch be this world's windy law, because the tree is mine, my heart can have no rest."* And her maid, Taiu: "Wise flowers that fall towards the margin† of the lake, and lapping surf-like drift to your own side."

At this, one of Wakagimi's page-boys went to the foot of the tree and collected an armful of petals which he brought back, reciting: "Though the great winds of heaven scatter them, mine are they, mine to gather as I will—these blossoms of the cherry-tree." To which Nareki, a little girl in Himegimi's service answered: "Were your sleeve wide enough, even the perfume, O selfish folk, you would enfold, I think, and keep it for your own."‡

As time went on the ex-Emperor became more and more insistent. Lady Chujo, his Consort, also wrote, pointing out that Tamakatsura's delay§ was awkward for her also; for Ryozen had got it into his head that it was owing to her protestations that Tamakatsura still hesitated. "Up till now," she wrote, "he has only suggested this jokingly. But I am in a very difficult position. Unless you have any special reason against doing so, I implore you to carry the matter through without further delay."

Tamakatsura saw that she could not allow the royal pair to plead any longer. This was evidently to be Himegimi's fate, and there was nothing left but to get together as quickly as possible such things as she and her gentlewomen would need in the ex-Emperor's palace. The news of these preparations soon reached Kurodo no Shosho's ear. Beside himself, he rushed to his mother, Lady Kumoi, imploring her to take some step in the matter. His life, he wildly said, depended on it. She accordingly wrote to Tamakatsura, saying: "I know it is very foolish and impertinent on my part to write to you about such a thing; but there is some excuse for me if I am astray, for the darkness¶ in which perhaps I have lost my way is the blackest that life holds. You indeed, who are in my own position, should be the last to misunderstand me. I am sure you will find some way to set my misgivings at rest."

---

* Play of words on *utsurou* = (1) change ownership, (2) wilt.

† Play of words on *migi* = (1) the junior side, the right, (2) the margin of a pool or lake.

‡ The little girl has in mind the old poem: "Oh that my sleeve were wide as the great heavens above! Then would the storms of spring no longer at their will destroy the budding flowers."

§ In sending Himegimi to the ex-Emperor.

¶ The love of parents for children is called *Kukoro no yami,* "darkness of the heart."

It was a distressing letter to receive, all the more so because Tamakatsura was by no means certain that she had acted for the best. "I assure you," she answered, "that I myself am extremely uneasy about it all, though I feel that Ryozen's insistence left me with no choice. I can only ask you to wait patiently for a while. Later on I hope I may be able to suggest a way out of the difficulty that will prove creditable and satisfactory to everybody." What she had in mind was that, when it was all over, Kurodo no Shosho might be persuaded to take the younger girl, Wakagimi, instead. Ryozen, she was sure, would have consented to take both girls into his household. But she felt that to suggest such an arrangement would be rather an imposition. Kurodo no Shosho, on the other hand, was at a stage in his career when his prospects were wholly uncertain... She need not however have troubled to debate the matter, for Kurodo himself, so far from being prepared to shift his affections at a word of command, was more than ever obsessed by his unattainable desire. The memory of that spring evening perpetually haunted him, and even now, though all his hopes had vanished, his only thought was how that momentary vision might be repeated.

One evening when, as so often before, knowing that his errand would be fruitless, yet unable to keep away, he came to Jiju's room, he found him reading a letter from Kaoru. Jiju at once put the letter away. This was sufficient to convince Kurodo no Shosho of the subject* with which the letter must deal, and he snatched at it unceremoniously. To keep it from him would merely be to admit that his suspicion was well-founded, and as in reality it was not at all in the nature of a love-letter, containing indeed only the vaguest expression of a general discontent, Jiju made no attempt to recover it.

The note of gentle and restrained melancholy which pervaded Kaoru's letter irritated Kurodo profoundly. For it seemed by contrast to make his own wild outbursts, to which as he was aware his friends were so well accustomed that they no longer paid the slightest attention to them, appear merely ill-bred and ridiculous. He handed back the letter without a word, and for a moment thought of going to see Omoto, a gentlewoman of Himegimi's, to whom he was in the habit of unburdening himself. But what was the use of saying all over again what he had said so often before?

"I must answer this letter," Jiju said presently, and went off towards Tamakatsura's room, evidently meaning to show her the letter before he answered it. A moment later Kurodo, despite himself, was again in Omoto's room, describing his sufferings in a manner more harrowing than ever before. To take him seriously was impossible; to laugh at him would have been brutal. She simply let him talk.

---

* Kaoru's love for Himegimi,

Presently he revealed the fact that on the evening when Himegimi lost her draughts-match he had watched the game unseen, and he told Omoto that if she could only, before Himegimi departed for ever, promise him another such fleeting glimpse, it would give him for the moment at least something to live for. "For soon I shall lose everything," he said, "even these talks of ours which, painful though you have made them for me, will one day seem precious, for they will be all that I shall have to look back on."

She knew him too well to dream of cajoling him by Tamakatsura's too simple method,* and irritated at her own inability to say anything that could comfort him, she began to scold him instead. Really, he was more trying tonight than ever before. It was no doubt the unfortunate incident of the other evening that had brought on the change. "If I were to tell Lady Tamakatsura of your insufferable conduct the other night," she said, "she would certainly never let you into the house again. And as far as I am concerned I have lost all sympathy with you. I feel that you are no longer to be trusted at all."

"I don't care what you feel," he said. And Lady Tamakatsura may do as she pleases. Do you think that anyone suffering as I suffer is likely to be frightened of her, or of anything? And as for your sympathy—you could easily have helped me if you had wanted to. The other night, for example, you could have sent for me to watch the game. As a matter of fact, I saw all the time what moves your side ought to have made, and I could have helped you to win."

But in an altered voice he suddenly recited the verse: "Why, unaccountable partner of my days, has it pursued me thus—the thought that I could win?"

The next day was the first of the fourth month.† But Kurodo instead of going with his brothers to pay the compliments of the season at Court, sat moping at home.

"I wish now," said Yugiri to his wife, who, worn out by Kurodo's ceaseless lamentations, was herself almost in tears, "I wish now that I had put in a word for Kurodo when I saw Tamakatsura on New Year's Day. But the first thing she told me was that the girl was being courted by the ex-Emperor Ryozen, which made me think it was useless for me to say anything. Since then, however I have sometimes thought that if I had pressed Kurodo's claims very strongly, I might have made some impression."

In Tamakatsura's quarters a discussion arose among some of the higher gentlewomen concerning the manner in which Himegimi's various suitors were bearing the prospect of her departure.

---

* Offering him the second daughter.
† The beginning of summer.

Outwardly of course Kurodo's case seemed to be by far the most desperate. But many of the ladies insisted that all this talk about dying for love and so on meant nothing at all. "I wish it were so," said Omoto, with feeling. And Tamakatsura, who overheard the conversation, felt very uneasy, not merely on the boy's behalf, but also because she foresaw a complete breach between herself and his parents. For a moment she thought of suggesting to Ryozen that he should accept the younger daughter instead. But the idea of allowing a person in Kurodo's position to stand between Himegimi and the ex-Emperor was, when one came to look into it, preposterous. Moreover it was concerning Himegimi and not the younger girl that Higekuro had left particular instructions which debarred her from marrying a commoner. It was doubtful even if in accepting Ryozen's offer she was aiming as high as Higekuro would have wished.

The Presentation took place on the ninth day of the fourth month. Yugiri provided a coach and a great number of outriders. Kumoi felt very little disposed to make any sign. But after years of estrangement this affair had brought her once more into communication with her sister,[*] and it seemed a pity to let their relationship lapse once more, as it certainly would if she did nothing now, and in the end she made a very handsome present of stuffs and dresses. "I have had poor Kurodo," she wrote, " so much on my hands and have felt so alarmed by his condition that I am afraid I have quite neglected your affairs. I am however disappointed to have heard no more from you with regard to a suggestion that you once made..." The tone of the letter, Tamakatsura was ready to admit, could scarcely have been more conciliatory, nor the hint[†] which it contained more delicately suppressed. Yugiri excused himself from coming on the ground that it was a bad[‡] day for him; but he sent his elder sons, begging Tamakatsura to make use of them in any way she could. The coaches for the ladies-in-waiting were provided by Kobai. Being closely related both to Tamakatsura and to her late husband[§] he would, but for Higekuro's curious disposition, probably have been a constant visitor. But as it was, they had not seen him for years.

To Chunagon, Higekuro's son by his first wife,[¶] was in charge of the proceedings, assisted by Sakon no Chujo, Uchuben, and the rest. Tamakatsura surveyed the preparations sadly. It was Higekuro's plan that they were carrying out that day, and he alone was not there to witness it!

---

[*] Tamakatsura.

[†] That Tamakatsura should give the younger daughter to Kurodo, as she had vaguely suggested.

[‡] Astrologically speaking.

[§] Higekuro.

[¶] The mad wife, see Part IV, p. 577.

Kurodo was making the darkest threats. In a letter which Omoto received that day he spoke of having only a very short while to live. "Surely, no woman, however great her general indifference, could hear this without feeling some sort of sympathy with the doomed man? And who knows but that she might not vouchsafe to him the one word of pity that even now would rally him to a brief prolongation of his days?"

Omoto went with the letter to her mistress's rooms. She found the two sisters in very low spirits. Himegimi's Presentation robes, though more beautiful than anything she had ever worn before, were a constant reminder to her not only of the separation that was about to ensue, but also of her father and the joy it would have been to him to see her thus attired. She was already in a state of considerable emotion when she took the letter from Omoto's hand.

She felt completely mystified. The young man could scarcely have been in a more enviable position. At home his parents were devoted to him, a prosperous career lay open before him; and yet, as the result of one small disappointment, he imagined himself to be dying of melancholy. But what if he should indeed be dying? She hesitated for a while and then wrote in the margin of Omoto's letter: "Not to one mortal only but to all that in this dark world dwell, that word* I must accord." "Understand," she added, "that this is written only in view of the terrible news which your letter contains."

Kurodo was at first overjoyed; but his pleasure soon gave place to the reflection that, had she not known that in a few hours she would be safely in another's possession, even these few cold words would never have been written, and once more he gave way to an uncontrollable paroxysm of despair.

Presently he folded the letter back and on the outside, after various descants on the theme of "When I die of love,"† he wrote the poem: "That word, save to the dead refused, I shall not hear; for living speech to dead men's ears is mute." "Were I but certain," he added, "that you would lay your pity on my tomb, how swiftly would I go!" She saw at once that it had been a great mistake to reply at all. This time she would return the letter to him just as it was. But when Omoto offered to take it, she said neither yes nor no.

Soon it was time to start. Received with elaborate pomp and ceremony, waited upon and attended by a magnificent bevy of gentlewomen and pages, she could scarcely have begun her new life with more splendor even had Ryozen still been on the Throne.

---

* "Pity."

† "When I die of love, though death walks daily in the world and is no marvelous thing, what name but yours upon men's lips will rise?" Poem by Fukayabu, 10th century.

On her arrival she was taken by her mother straight to Lady Chujo's rooms. It was not till late at night that she was brought to Ryozen. His other consorts—Lady Chujo and Akikonomu—were no longer young and had lost much of their good looks; the newcomer was at the height of her youth and beauty. Ryozen could not fail to be charmed, and it was indeed at once apparent that she had made an excellent impression. Great personage though he was, she did not find him in the least alarming. His manner towards her was easy and natural. In every way her new life seemed to have started as well as could be wished. He had indeed secretly hoped that Tamakatsura, who had accompanied her daughter, would remain with her for some time, and it was a great disappointment to hear that she had slipped away at the earliest opportunity.

Kaoru's position in this household was one such as no commoner had occupied in an Imperial palace since Genji's early days. Not only was he constantly in the ex-Emperor's company, but both with Akikonomu and Lady Chujo he was on terms of the utmost familiarity. It was natural therefore that he should cultivate the friendship of this newcomer[*] to the palace. His behavior was indeed such as to suggest that he felt a considerable partiality towards her; but in reality he was chiefly curious to discover whether she felt any interest in him.

Most of Himegimi's suitors had by now transferred their attentions to her sister. Remembering her promise to Kumoi, Tamakatsura wrote to Kurodo, hinting that his suit would be particularly acceptable. But she received no answer. Yugiri's sons had always been constant visitors to Ryozen's palace; but after Himegimi's arrival there, Kurodo completely absented himself. He indeed appeared at Court at all only on the rarest occasions and spent most of his time buried away at home, interested in nothing that went on and flying from all who approached him.

The Emperor was surprised that Higekuro's wishes[†] had not been respected, and sent for Tamakatsura's son Sakon no Chujo to ask for an explanation. "I am afraid the interview is going to be a very difficult one," he said to his mother. "I told you from the start that we were certain to be adversely criticized. But you thought otherwise. I have already been finding it difficult to defend our action, and now comes this Imperial message. You have put yourself as well as me into a very awkward position."

"Oh come," she answered, "you cannot pretend that the matter was settled with any undue haste. It was only when Ryozen, after months of patience, began to press urgently for a decision that I was forced once and for all to balance up the advantages and disadvantages of the two offers. I came to the conclusion that the Emperor's household, where there was no

---

[*] Himegimi.

[†] That Himegimi should be sent to the Emperor.

one in particular to look after her, had from the point of view of her real happiness hardly anything to recommend it; whereas Ryozen—But you have seen for yourself how happily she is settled. It is a pity if you were so much against it that you none of you made this clearer while there was still time. Yugiri is just the same. He has been telling me that he entirely disapproves of what I have done. I'm sorry; but the thing had to be."*

She spoke with quiet confidence. It was evident that she was not in the least shaken by all these criticisms. "Unfortunately," replied Sakon no Chujo, "it is my sister's present life with which we are dealing and not what may have happened to her in some previous existence. No doubt His Majesty's annoyance was also decreed by *karma,* but that does not make it any the easier for me to pacify him. Nor is it any use my saying that we were afraid of offending the Empress; for he will immediately ask why we are not equally afraid of offending Ryozen's consorts.† And as a matter of fact, though at present Lady Chujo seems disposed to be friendly and helpful, this cannot possibly go on. Consider the question dispassionately and you will see at once the absurdity of your attitude. What, pray, would become of the Court if the existence of an Empress prevented any other lady setting foot there? The mere fact of being called on to serve the Emperor has in the past always been considered a sufficient honor in itself, irrespective of how many other people were similarly honored. The situation at Ryozen's is quite different. There her whole comfort depends on the good nature of others. A single slight misunderstanding, and there may spring up such a wrangle between aunt and niece‡ as will provide the world with a very unedifying spectacle."

She found that her second son, Uchuben was of exactly the same opinion, and began to feel very uneasy.

Meanwhile Ryozen seemed to become more engrossed in his new favorite every day. In the seventh month it became clear that she was going to have a child. Her indisposition however seemed only to enhance her beauty, and those in charge of her could well understand why she had been so eagerly courted and why news of Tamakatsura's decision had been greeted in so many quarters with such extraordinary outbursts of rage and disappointment.

Her principal recreation was music, and the ex-Emperor spent hour after hour listening to her. On these occasions he often brought Kaoru with him. He was interested not so much in her playing as in that of her maid Omoto. She it was, he ascertained, who had accompanied so skillfully the day he whistled the Plum-tree tune. Ryozen would now often

---

* Was determined by something that happened in a previous incarnation.

† Akikonomu and Lady Chujo.

‡ Lady Chujo was Tamakatsura's sister, and therefore Himegimi's aunt.

send for her to play on the Japanese zithern, which she did in so delightful a manner that Kaoru found himself thinking a good deal about her.

Next year the Palace mumming was held. There happened at the time, among the young men at Court, to be a great many who danced and sang well, so that the Emperor had a wide choice in making up the two teams. The right side was captained by Kaoru, and Kurodo was also chosen to dance. An almost full moon was shining from a cloudless sky when they made their way from the Emperor's Palace to that of Ryozen. Both Lady Chujo and Himegimi were with the ex-Emperor on this occasion. A great crowd of princes and courtiers who had followed the mummers from the Palace were also among the audience; but it was noticed that every single visitor of any importance belonged either to Yugiri's or To no Chujo's* family. The world seemed at the moment able to produce good looks and real elegance in no other quarter.

It was known that in matters of this kind Ryozen was far more fastidious than the present Emperor, and the performers were all particularly on their mettle. None indeed more so than Kurodo no Shosho, who being aware that Himegimi was present could scarcely conceal his agitation. The costume, with its head-dress of cotton plumes, is an uncouth one, but Kurodo had the right figure for it and looked unusually well; his singing too was very good. *Bamboo River* was one of the mummers' songs, and as he approached the royal dais singing this tune a rush of recollection assailed him, and the tears so filled his eyes that he could scarcely stumble through his part.

Another performance was given in Akikonomu's apartments, and Ryozen was again present. It was now very late, but the moon was high in the sky and shone down upon the dancers with so searching a light that they showed up even better than in the daytime. "Was she looking at him? What was passing through her mind?" Kurodo no Shosho, obsessed by these thoughts, might have been treading on air, so little was he conscious of the movements of his feet; and when, after the dance, wine was handed along, he surprised everyone by absent-mindedly clinging to the cup as though it had been meant for him alone.

Kaoru was tired out when he got back to his mother's palace in the Third Ward, for he had spent the whole night dancing and singing in place after place. No sooner, however, had he lain down than a message came summoning him back to Ryozen's apartments. "How irritating!" he said. "I did think that this time I was really going to get a little rest." And grumbling as he went, he set off to obey the summons. Ryozen merely wanted to hear some details about the performance at the reigning Emperor's Palace. "It has always been the custom," he said presently,

---

* Genji's great friend. Father of Kobai, Tamakatsura, Lady Chujo, etc.

"to choose one of the older men as captain. So you may consider the Emperor paid you a great compliment," and he eyed the young man admiringly. Presently he led Kaoru off to Himegimi's rooms, humming the Bansuraku* as he went. Her apartments were still crowded with friends whom she had invited to see the performance, and the scene was one of great elegance and animation. At the door of the cross-gallery Kaoru heard a voice that he knew—it was no doubt one of the gentlewomen from Tamakatsura's palace—and got into conversation. "I can't imagine what we looked like," he said. "Moonlight, when it is as strong as that, is terribly unbecoming. Poor Kurodo no Shosho seemed to be completely dazzled by it; though oddly enough at the Emperor's, where the moonlight was almost as strong, he did not seem to be in the least put out.†

Some of the gentlewomen who heard this remark thought it rather spiteful. But one of his flatterers, thinking to please Kaoru by bringing the conversation back to the subject of his own appearance, assured him that he need not worry. "Everyone," she said, "was remarking how particularly well the strong contrasts of the moonlight suited features such as yours." And she pushed out a scrap of paper with the poem: "Do you remember that night in the garden, and *Bamboo River?* Or in your memory for things unmemorable is there no room at all?"

"Ceaseless since that hour the waters of the River have flowed and carried with them all fond hopes to the deep." So he answered, and the words seemed to contain a suggestion of such infinite melancholy that everyone within hearing was deeply touched. Yet in point of fact, compared with those of a person really in love, Kaoru's feelings towards Himegimi were of a quite negligible order. But there was something about his appearance and character which tended to arouse sympathy even when he was least in need of it, and he was constantly being credited with emotions that he did not in the least feel. "This positively mustn't be repeated," he said rising to go. "Indeed, it was wrong of me to talk in that way at all." At this moment a message came from Ryozen asking what had become of him, and though he was in no mood for further exertion he was obliged to go.

"Genji," said Ryozen, "on the morning of the men's mumming had women's dancing as well. Apparently it was a great success. Yugiri told me about it. I don't think we could manage that now; we lack the talent. It is extraordinary to think what a number of unusually accomplished and gifted women there were at the New Palace in those days. They made it

---

* The tune that the mummers sing when they are about to depart. See Part III, p. 479.

† Kaoru is ironically suggesting that it was not the moonlight, but the presence of Himegimi which confused Kurodo.

possible to do all sorts of delightful and entertaining things." The instruments were then tuned, Himegimi playing the thirteen-stringed zithern, Kaoru the lute, and Ryozen himself the Japanese zithern. They played *The Trefoil*[*] and other tunes. It was extraordinary what progress the girl had made under Ryozen's tuition. Her touch was in the latest style, and neither song-accompaniments nor the most difficult zithern-pieces gave her any trouble. It was impossible, Kaoru was sure, that someone so unusually gifted in every other way should not also have great beauty.[†]

Occasions of this kind were frequent at Ryozen's palace, and in course of time Kaoru naturally got to know the girl very well. When, as sometimes happened, he expressed his great admiration for her, it was always in the most guarded and respectful terms, though he would sometimes go so far as to hint that her mother's decision had been a great disappointment to him.

The disappointment indeed may not have been only on his side. Who knows?

In the fourth month Himegimi bore a daughter. The event was not of course of the same importance as it would have been in the case of a boy, or if Ryozen had still been on the Throne. But it was evident that the ex-Emperor was delighted and everyone at Court, from Yugiri downwards, thought it permissible to mark the occasion by sending toys and birth-presents. The child was born at home. Tamakatsura instantly took a great fancy to it, and was never tired of dandling it in her arms. But Ryozen kept on insisting that Himegimi should return at the earliest possible moment, and on the fiftieth day after her delivery she came back to his palace. Apart from Ichi no Miya,[‡] who was now grown up, he had no other daughter. Himegimi's baby, who was indeed an exceptionally fine and promising child, at once became a great favorite, and Ryozen tended more than ever to spend all his time in Himegimi's quarters.

This state of affairs was resented more by Lady Chujo's gentlewomen than by herself. Between her people and Himegimi's feeling began to run high; and a number of unpleasant incidents occurred. Tamakatsura heard of what was going on, and remembered her conversations with Sakon no Chujo. He was young, and at the time she had not been inclined to pay much attention to his warnings. But he was the girl's brother. He had been right to speak out, and certainly everything seemed to be happening just as he had foretold. Ryozen, it could not be doubted, was deeply attached to the girl. But if Lady Chujo's women, who had been in her service for years, made up their minds to cause trouble between her and

---

[*] See above, p. 780.

[†] He had of course only seen her behind her curtains or screen-of-state.

[‡] Lady Chujo's daughter.

the girl, nothing Ryozen could do would save Himegimi from finding herself in a very painful position.

The Emperor, it seemed, was still constantly hinting that he would like to have the second girl, Wakagimi, at the Palace. Determined not to expose her to the same vexations as Himegimi was enduring, Tamakatsura made up her mind to offer Wakagimi not as a concubine but in a public capacity. The easiest way to effect this was to hand on to Wakagimi her own office of Lady-of-the-Bedchamber. The position was one for which suitable occupants were difficult to discover, and though Tamakatsura had sent in her resignation many years ago, it had never been accepted. It was however discovered on looking into the matter, that there were ancient precedents for the office descending from one generation to another, and in consideration for the services which Higekuro had rendered to the Government the Emperor gave his consent. It seemed indeed providential* that Tamakatsura's resignation should have remained unaccepted for, so many years.

There really did seem to be some chance that Wakagimi was now disposed of in a way that would ensure her happiness. But Tamakatsura's own troubles were not at an end. She was conscious that she had more or less promised the younger girl to Kurodo no Shosho, whose mother would now no doubt consider that she had behaved very badly. With the hope of putting this right she sent her second son Uchuben to Yugiri,† asking him to explain that had she been free to act as she chose she would not, quite apart from her obligations to Yugiri's family, ever have dreamt of putting both her daughters into Court service. Such a course, she knew, must savor of ambition. But the Emperor's decree had left her no choice... "The Emperor," replied Yugiri, "was very much annoyed by what had already occurred; and he had good reason to be. As for the office of Lady-of-the-Bedchamber—personally I think your mother should have been allowed to resign years ago, when she stopped appearing at Court. The sooner Wakagimi takes it over, the better."

It was thought advisable to obtain formal permission from the Empress, a somewhat humiliating step which, Tamakatsura sadly reflected, would have been quite unnecessary had Higekuro been still alive and in power. The Emperor had heard a great deal about Himegimi's extraordinary charm, and very little about Wakagimi. He was however agreeably surprised by her. She had great elegance, and set about her work at Court very competently.

It seemed to Tamakatsura that her task in the world was finished and she decided to take the Vows.‡ But her sons persuaded her that her

---

* Literally, *karma*-determined.
† Kurodo's father.
‡ To become a nun.

thoughts were in reality still far too much occupied with the welfare of her two daughters. "Wait," they said, "till you can apply yourself calmly and wholeheartedly to your devotions." She let the matter drop, and even took to paying an occasional secret visit to Court, where she saw Wakagimi, but never the older girl, for she did not feel capable of responding to Ryozen's gallantries.[*] She felt indeed that she had more than made up for the pain she caused him in old days by the concession[†] she had now made in defiance of everyone's advice. As for herself, she had reached an age when anything of that kind, or even the suspicion of it, merely served to make one ridiculous. She had however of course not explained this to Himegimi, and the girl was hurt that Tamakatsura never visited her. But her sister, Himegimi reflected, had always been Tamakatsura's favorite. Even in the trivial matter of the cherry tree this preference had been evident. Only Higekuro had ever really been fond of her! She felt very unhappy about it. Ryozen himself, who had looked forward to constant visits from Tamakatsura, was naturally very much disappointed... "Though I can see that there is every reason why she should prefer the other Palace," he said. "Here we are all growing very dull and out-of-date."

Several years later Himegimi bore a son. In all these years his three consorts had between them only produced two children, and both were girls. The event therefore caused a considerable stir, and Ryozen himself was delighted. For his son's sake, indeed, he now regretted that he was no longer on the Throne, for he seemed by his abdication to have wantonly deprived the child of what would have been a magnificent position.[‡] Ichi no Miya,[§] to whom he had formerly been devotedly attached, ceased after the arrival of Himegimi's two children to interest him at all, and even Lady Chujo, long-suffering though she was, felt that things had gone too far. Incidents were constantly occurring which it was very difficult to smooth over, and whereas the ill-feeling had previously been confined to their rival gentlewomen, relations between the two mistresses themselves now became more and more difficult.

In situations of this kind, in whatever class of society they occur, opinion from that of the most insignificant menial upwards is always loudly voiced on the side of old-established rights as opposed to the claims of a new-comer. And at Ryozen's palace everyone from top to bottom, irrespective of how little their duties brought them into contact with either side, would hear nothing said against the two great ladies'[¶]

---

[*] Ryozen, it will be remembered, had always been in love with her.
[†] Giving Himegimi to Ryozen.
[‡] That of Heir Apparent.
[§] Lady Chujo's daughter.
[¶] Akikonomu and Lady Chujo.

who had for so many years had things all their own way, but invariably attributed whatever Himegimi did or said to the basest possible motives. The worst that Tamakatsura's sons had foreseen was being fulfilled, as they themselves were not slow to point out to her. She saw all about her girls for whom no such ambitious plans had been made settling down to a quiet and comfortable existence, and she felt a sudden conviction that except for people with every possible circumstance in their favor, Court service was a complete mistake.

Meanwhile, as the years went by, Himegimi's former suitors rose from rank to rank, and many of them were now, as Tamakatsura was bound to confess, in such high positions that there no longer seemed to be any incongruity in the idea of their marrying a Grand Minister's daughter. Kaoru, for example, whom in the old days she had regarded as a mere schoolboy, was now a Counselor with the rank of Colonel in the Bodyguard, and he and Niou were the most talked-of figures at Court. That two such desirable young men should remain unmarried struck Tamakatsura as quite unaccountable. She knew indeed for a fact that they had rejected offers from one great prince and statesman after another. "They were certainly both interested in Himegimi," she said. "But in those days they were mere boys and it was impossible to tell how they would turn out. If they had been as they are now..."

Kurodo no Shosho was also a Colonel, and a counselor of the Third Rank. The more malicious among Tamakatsura's gentlewomen lost no opportunity of mentioning his success in her presence. "And as far as good looks go," they would add, "there was never much amiss with him." "It would have been better than all this unpleasantness,"* they whispered behind her back, wondering how a woman of her experience could have behaved with so little discretion.

The new Colonel† was apparently still in exactly the same love-sick condition as years before. He had accepted as his wife a daughter of the Minister of the Left, but did not take the slightest interest in her. He seemed still to cling to the idea that somehow, in the end, Himegimi would be his, and the Oracle of Hitachi‡ figured continually both in his conversation and in his copybooks.§

Meanwhile Himegimi, worn out by the constant bickerings at Ryozen's palace, spent more and more time at her mother's, which only served to make Tamakatsura feel how completely her plans had failed. Wakagimi,

---

* Better if she had married Kurodo.

† "Kurodo.

‡ "Surely as if the oracle of Hitachi had spoken it, the oracle that is at the end of the Eastern Road, I know that in the end we shall meet." The oracle at Kashima in Hitachi Province specialized in advice on love-affairs.

§ In which he practiced handwriting.

on the other hand, caused no anxiety. She delighted in her new life, and had indeed become one of the most conspicuous figures at Court.

Kurodo's father-in-law, the Minister of the Left, died about this time, and there was a general adjustment of offices. Yugiri became Minister of the Left, and Kobai Minister of the Right, with the rank of Major-General. In the general shuffling Kaoru was promoted to the position of Middle Counselor, while Kurodo filled Kaoru's old place.

In his round of visits* Kaoru began with Tamakatsura, and did formal obeisance to her in the courtyard in front of her rooms. Subsequently she received him in private. "Nowadays," she said, "'the grass grows so deep at my doors' that you might easily have passed me by. But I am glad you did not forget me, for your visits never fail to remind me of certain occasions in days long ago."† Her voice always pleased him. There was something in it gracious, distinguished—a youthful buoyancy, even, that always astonished him. No wonder that after all these years Ryozen still hankered after her. Perhaps even now, Kaoru thought as he listened to that fresh, animated voice, something might come of it.

"I don't particularly want to be congratulated," he said. "There is indeed nothing very exciting about this promotion. But it gave me an excuse for coming to see you—which I have been meaning to do for a long time. I am afraid your remark about my not passing you by was a hint that I sometimes seem to do so..." "What I really want to do," she said, "is to talk to you about this trouble at Ryozen's palace. Today, I know, is hardly the time to worry you with an elderly woman's perplexities. But I could hardly ask you to come on purpose, and it is all far too complicated to write about. Lady Chujo, as you know, promised to take a special interest in the girl, and Akikonomu went out of her way to assure me that she had no objection. But now they both seem to treat her as though she were some drab who has been clandestinely smuggled into the Palace. The two children must remain where they are. But Himegimi herself was becoming so worn out by all this that I decided to bring her home, where at any rate she can get a little rest and quiet. But Ryozen has already said that it looks bad for her to stay here so long, and I do not know what is going to happen. Do speak to Ryozen about it the next time you get a chance. I see now that under the circumstances it was madness on my part to have any confidence in either of her sponsors. But both of them were so friendly and made such definite promises that I was completely taken in. I cannot think how I can have been so childishly incompetent." "You make far too much of all this," said Kaoru. "A certain amount of friction is and always has been inevitable in such situations, and it is bound to be worse in a

---

* Paid in order to receive congratulations on his promotion.

† Genji's visits on similar occasions.

household like Ryozen's where, compared with what it used to be before his retirement, life is rather tame and monotonous. So far as I can see both of the ladies in public maintain a perfectly friendly attitude.* But it would be strange indeed if they were not inwardly a little bit jealous. As a matter of fact both of them have always been rather inclined to take offence where it was not meant and to brood over small trifles. But you must have realized that there would occasionally be misunderstandings of this sort when you sent her there. All Himegimi needs is a little patience and the capacity sometimes to shut her eyes to what is going on around her."

"My poor grievances!" she said laughing. "It was hardly worth storing them up for you so long if you were going to dispose of them so easily." It was as though she had suddenly thrown off all weight of parental responsibility, and could for the moment take the thing as lightly as he did. He had an impression that Himegimi was capable of just such transitions, and it was certain that what most attracted him in the Princess of Uji† was something very much of this kind.

Soon after this Wakagimi also paid a visit to her home, and with both wings of the house occupied and the quiet, happy life of the sisters going on just as in old days it seemed as though nothing had ever happened to interrupt it. Kaoru was indeed almost the only visitor. He was always acutely conscious, when he came to the house, that two pairs of eyes, used lately to far more animated scenes, were giving him their undivided attention. This put him on his best behavior, and Tamakatsura regretted more than ever that she had not given a young man so well-balanced and sensible the chance of entering her family.

The new Minister of the Right‡ lived in a palace inherited by his wife from Prince Sochi. It was the next house to Tamakatsura's. At the Great Banquet§ a vast number of princes and nobles were present, and Kobai had hoped to get Prince Niou, who had recently consented to appear both at the Archers' Banquet given by Yugiri and at the Wrestlers' Feast. But though Kobai had assured him that the whole success of the occasion depended on his being there, Niou failed to appear. It was known to be Kobai's great ambition to secure him for Oigimi or Naka no Kimi, the two daughters to whom he was so devotedly attached. But for some reason Niou showed no signs of interest in the plan.

Failing him, there was much to be said (as both Kobai and his wife agreed) for the Middle Counsellor,¶ who seemed to be turning out uncommonly well.

---

* Towards Himegimi.
† See the next chapter.
‡ Kobai.
§ Given by Kobai to his new colleagues.
¶ Kaoru.

The rattle of coaches and the shouting of the outriders were plainly audible in the house next door. Such sounds, Tamakatsura remembered, had once enlivened her own courtyard, and they started a train of absorbing recollections. "Some people," she said at last, "have criticized Sochi's widow for allowing Kobai to frequent her house so soon after the Prince's death. But there is after all perhaps something to be said for keeping the flame of love burning. One cannot make rules about such things. Sometimes I feel that she was right."

On the evening after the Banquet Kurodo no Shosho called. He had no doubt discovered that Himegimi was in residence again, and this had thrown his feelings into a fresh access of commotion. "It is of course gratifying in a way," he said, "that the Government has recognized my services. But inwardly I remain in such a state of continual torment that I am barely conscious of my promotion. This has been going on, as you know, for years now, without a moment's respite." He passed his sleeve across his eyes, as though to brush away a tear. But she felt that this was done chiefly for effect. He was now about twenty-seven, a strong, handsome man, with a fresh healthy complexion which it was difficult to associate with an incurable despair. "These young men," thought Tamakatsura, "are really becoming insufferable. They are so used to having everything their own way that honors and promotions no longer mean anything to them." Her own sons, who had no father to get fair play for them, were far indeed from having time to mope about in this way, fretting over trifles. Sakon no Chujo had by his own efforts become Major in the Bodyguard of the Right, and Uchuben was a Senior Adviser in the Executive Department; but neither of them was on the Grand Council, which was miserable. To no Jiju, the youngest, was a senior in the Chamberlain's Department, which was not bad for his age, but wretched compared with most other people.

So Tamakatsura impatiently reflected, while Kurodo, still in the same strain...

The Bridge Maiden

There still lived at that time a certain old Prince Hachi no Miya, one of Suzaku's many brothers, whose very existence was almost forgotten at Court. His mother was of good birth, and it was at one time generally supposed that he was destined for very great things.* But times changed; the conspiracy in which he was intended to play the leading part became impossible of execution, and he found himself not merely deprived of his former brilliant prospects, but cut off from all hope of public credit or advancement. His supporters and guardians,† unable to face the ignominy into which the exposure of their schemes had brought them, had in one way or another soon all completely vanished, at least from secular life, and in the end the young Prince found himself, both privately and politically, in a state of unparalleled isolation.

His only consolation was his wife. She was the child of a former Grand Minister who had fondly imagined that in securing for his favorite daughter this prince's hand he had made the most brilliant provision for her future. What, the Princess often wondered, would her father have thought, had he lived to see her in her present inglorious situation? And she herself, naturally enough, suffered not infrequently from fits of depression. But husband and wife were bound together by so unusual a degree of affection that to both of them their mutual attachment seemed an ample compensation for all their losses and disappointments.

Another sorrow however was soon to cloud their lot. The birth of a child would more than anything else have helped to relieve the emptiness and monotony of their present existence. But years passed, and no child came. At last, however, to the Prince's intense delight, a girl was born—a fine and handsome child on whom the parents lavished every care. In due time it was apparent that the Princess was again to become a mother. A boy was of course ardently hoped for, but this wish was not fulfilled. The delivery was easy, and the mother seemed at first to be recovering very well. But an unexpected relapse set in, her condition became more and more alarming, and not long afterwards she died.

---

* After Suzaku's accession Kokiden (Genji's wicked stepmother) attempted to make Hachi no Miya Heir Apparent instead of Ryozen.

† His father, the Old Emperor, was dead, and we must suppose that his mother was dead too.

The Prince was beside himself with grief and bewilderment. Even with her love to console him he had often found the ignominy of his situation difficult to endure, and but for his unwillingness to desert her he would long ago have taken the Vows. And now he was left to face his troubles in what was worse than solitude; for upon him fell the sole care of two young children. He at once determined that it would be ludicrous and unbecoming (for after all, despite his misfortunes, he was still a prince) for him to attempt to take charge of them himself, and he looked about for someone to whom he could entrust them, intending as soon as they were safely disposed of to fulfill his great desire.[*] But no suitable person could be found, and so things went on from month to month and year to year, the Prince half-thinking of simply deserting the children, but never able to bring himself to do so.

Meanwhile the girls grew up, and as time went on so far from being a burden to him they became his great comfort and distraction.

The waiting-women, as is commonly the case, could never forget the circumstances of the second child's birth,[†] and it was with difficulty that they overcame their feeling of repugnance sufficiently even to look after her properly. The Prince, too, could not help to some extent sharing in this prejudice. But his wife had almost with her last breath besought him not to neglect the child; moreover, though its birth was the immediate cause of the present disaster, the child itself, he knew well enough, could only be regarded as the innocent instrument of Fate. His first unreasoning sentiment soon gave way to feelings of compassion, and as the child grew up she began to assume in his affections no less important a place than that already occupied by Agemaki, her sister. In beauty indeed Kozeri, the younger girl, as the years went by became more than Agemaki's equal. In disposition however the elder had perhaps the advantage, showing from the first signs of a deeper and tenderer nature, while there was in her manners a grave restraint and dignity which made her, despite Kozeri's great beauty, undoubtedly the more distinguished figure of the two.

The Prince did all that lay in his power to procure for them the usual advantages. But a series of further misfortunes overtook him, and it became every year more difficult to maintain in his palace any sort of life or stir at all.

His servants could hardly be expected to put up indefinitely with such an existence, and one by one they found other and more hopeful employment. In the general confusion which followed upon the wife's illness sufficient attention had not been paid to securing a really good nurse.

---

[*] To become a monk.

[†] The fact that the child's birth had caused the mother's death. In primitive communities such children are often done away with.

The woman they had hurriedly found left, as was to be expected, long before they could get on without her, and the child's upbringing fell almost entirely upon the Prince himself.

The Palace was large and its grounds very pleasantly laid out with knolls and pools, the charm of which no neglect could impair. But gradually the house itself was falling into hopeless decay, and there was no one left to repair it, or indeed to do any of the work that was needed. Weeds were sprouting in the courtyards, and *shinobu*-grass doing as it pleased with the roofing of the eaves. The Prince himself made no effort to save his spacious garden from becoming a mere wilderness. In his wife's lifetime he had taken a great interest in it; but such an interest needs to be shared, and now the scent of blossom and the scarlet of autumn leaves meant nothing to him, and such resources as he could still dispose of he expended solely on the adornment of the private chapel where in prayer and meditation he now spent the greater part of the day.

Though to his great regret circumstances made it impossible for him actually to escape from secular life, he regarded himself as in effect no longer a participant in the ordinary carnal world, and he became, as the years went by, so completely detached from mundane affairs that in spirit, if not in actuality, he finally ranked as an ecclesiastic rather than a mere layman. Since his wife's death he had not shown the slightest interest in any of life's ordinary pleasures or amusements. Still less had he shown any sign of intending to marry again. The general view was that he had carried things too far. "No doubt," the world said, "he was unusually devoted to his wife, and it was natural enough that at first he should feel her loss very deeply. But it is now high time that he began to behave like other people... One thing however is certain; no newcomer to the house would tolerate for a single day the disgusting state of dilapidation into which he has allowed that handsome palace of his to fall."

These and many other observations of the same nature reached the Prince's ear, some of his critics even going so far as to hint how their advice might most appropriately be carried out. But he paid not the slightest attention. What little leisure his religious observances left him he devoted to the education of his daughters. Music came first; then draughts, the word-game,* and other lighter accomplishments, which though unimportant in themselves gave him an opportunity of seeing in what way their characters were forming. It was apparent that Agemaki, the elder girl, was the more painstaking and serious-minded of the two, while Kozeri had the sweeter and easier disposition, though she was not without a certain shyness about the things that deeply affected her.

---

* Guessing characters of which one half is covered.

One fine spring day he happened to notice two water-birds sporting wing to wing on the sunny waters of the pond. There was something about their happy darting and chirruping that reminded him with a sudden bitterness of his own widowed and desolate state, and to distract his thoughts he decided to give the girls their music-lesson. Considering their tender age they handled their zithers with remarkable skill, and the tears welled to his eyes.*

"How long thus comfortless, like a bird that has lost its mate, on the waters of life shall I float?"

Such was his poem. He was a handsome old man, and though constant watching and fasting had made him somewhat frail, there was in his bearing a great dignity and charm, enhanced at the moment by the tattered old court-dress that he had just sent for in honor of the music-lesson. The elder girl, gently drawing the ink-stone towards her, began tracing letters upon it for practice. "Write on this," the Prince said, handing her a piece of paper. "Ink-stones are not meant for writing on."† Rather timidly, she wrote the poem: "How should I learn to spread my wings, O water-bird, and leave the nest, had you not lingered on the lake?" It was not at all a good poem, but it pleased him at the moment. In the handwriting there was considerable promise, though she still did not join up her letters properly.

Kozeri, being called upon in her turn, took a much longer time and her production, though creditable, was quite childish: "Had not the water-bird, despite its sorrow, wrapped me in its wings, ne'er should I have been hatched!"

Everything that he possessed was going to ruin. There had for years past been no one in the house capable even of mending his clothes, much less of distracting him by their conversation. And now he discovered to his delight that in the midst of all this desolation were two creatures who could acquit themselves with so much credit in an interchange of poems!

Still holding a sacred book in one hand he would sometimes break off from his regular intoning and sing the words of the tune that the girls were playing. He had taught Agemaki the lute and Kozeri the thirteen-stringed zithern. Young though they were they had spent a great deal of time practicing, and they now really played unusually well together, so that it was quite a pleasure to hear them.

Prince Hachi no Miya himself had, as we have seen, been left an orphan at an early age. His guardians took very little trouble about his education and he grew up with only a scanty knowledge of books and

---

* As regards music "sad" and "beautiful" are interchangeable terms in the Far East.

† In medieval Japan there was a superstition that it was unlucky to write on ink stones. It is not certain however that this belief existed so early as Murasaki's time.

an ignorance of worldly affairs which was quite extraordinary. Compared indeed with other noblemen of his age he seemed, in his complete lack of practical training, far more like some grand lady, who has never had to trouble her head about what she would consider sordid details. He had inherited from the late Grand Minister, his mother's father, what should by rights have been a very considerable property, but somehow or other, without his having any notion as to what had become of it, the whole of this fortune disappeared, and he was left with nothing even to remind him of it, save some handsome and imposing pieces of furniture. For political reasons hardly anyone came to the house, and to occupy himself he took lessons from some of the best music-masters of the day, and worked with them so hard that in time he acquired, in this art at any rate, a most unusual proficiency.

The great disaster of his life had been that, at the time when Ryozen was Heir Apparent, Kokiden, as part of a general scheme to combat Genji's growing influence, had attempted to make Prince Hachi no Miya heir to the Throne. The plot ended in total failure, but Prince Hachi's connection with it at once estranged from him all those whose sympathies were on Genji's side. Kokiden's faction meanwhile rapidly sank into complete impotence and obscurity, and soon there was no longer any quarter where the unfortunate Prince was not looked at askance. But for years past his mind had become more and more centered on spiritual things, and now in his old age he never gave the whole unhappy business a thought.

Meanwhile a fresh disaster befell him. His palace caught fire and was totally destroyed. No other suitable house could be found at the Capital, and he was obliged to move to Uji,[*] where fortunately he still possessed a small estate. It cannot be said that his life at the Capital had been such as to make him suppose he should leave with regret. But when it came to the point, the move cost him many a pang. His new house had what at first seemed great disadvantages. It was near to the fish-weirs, which rather spoilt the view; moreover, he found the continual noise of the rapids very disturbing. However there was nothing to do but make the best of it, and after a time he began once more to take an interest in flowers and autumn woods, and would even spend hour after hour simply watching the river flow. How happily, he often thought, would his wife have shared with him this wild and sequestered life.

Of visits or company of any kind there was of course less question than ever, now that he was buried away in the depths of the country. No one indeed came near the house save the few gnarled peasants and rough country people who did the work on his estate; and loneliness lay fast upon him as a mist upon the morning hills. But soon a welcome

---

[*] About eleven miles south of Kyoto.

relief came, for in a neighboring country temple there lived a certain holy Teacher. Though a man of great erudition and deeply respected at Court, he took no part in public ceremonies, and indeed could seldom be prevailed upon to leave his mountain retreat.

Hearing however that Prince Hachi had settled so near by and was sadly in need of distraction, he would sometimes go and assist the Prince in his observances, or study some passage of the Scriptures with him, and finding in Hachi a real devotion to the faith, he took to coming more and more frequently.

For the first time Prince Hachi began to understand the inward meaning of the doctrines with which he had been familiar for so long. More than ever before he felt the life of the senses to be meaningless and unsatisfying. "My thoughts," he explained to the Teacher, "dwell wholly in another world. But I have young children with me, and so long as they need my care I must be content to have altered only my spiritual guise; the greater change must wait."

The Teacher was also on intimate terms with the ex-Emperor Ryozen, who had studied the Scriptures with him. Happening one day at about this time to have gone down to the City, the Teacher presented himself at Ryozen's palace, and after giving his assistance with regard to a number of difficult passages he led the conversation on to the subject of Prince Hachi. "Of sacred literature," the Teacher said," he has a very wide knowledge, and shows a profound understanding of it. I cannot help feeling that the priesthood is his true vocation. In his utter detachment from worldly things he is indeed already the equal of many a professed saint." "I wonder," said Ryozen, "that he has not entered the Church. 'The priest in disguise'—that is what the young people call him. It is a pity."

Kaoru happened to be present on this occasion. He too, like this prince of whom the Teacher spoke with such respect, had set his heart on what lay beyond the shifting fabric of the visible world. But his devotions, he was obliged to confess to himself with shame, had not hitherto been of a kind that could possibly have excited anyone's admiration. The notion that it might be possible to rank as a holy man without actually abandoning the life of the world was new to him, and he pricked up his ears.

"Prince Hachi's one great desire," the Teacher continued, "has indeed always been to join the priesthood. But obstacles of one kind or another stood in the way. And now I am sorry to say that this desire is less likely than ever to be fulfilled; for he has two growing daughters whom it is impossible for him to leave."

The Teacher had a great love for music. "These two girls," he added, "play together remarkably well on their zitherns.* Could you hear their

---

* The word *koto* is used of all stringed instruments, including the lute.

music blend with the splash of the neighboring river, you would imagine yourself in Paradise." Ryozen smiled. The old-fashioned style in which the Teacher expressed himself always amused him. "That is indeed unexpected," he said. "One would not have thought that the circumstances of their upbringing would have favored the learning of such accomplishments. But if the Prince is indeed so perplexed as to how to dispose of them, why does not he entrust them to me? So long as I am spared I would do whatever I could..."

Ryozen was considerably younger than Prince Hachi. The proposal, he thought, was quite a reasonable one. Had not Suzaku entrusted his daughter Nyosan to the late Prince Genji under very similar circumstances? And he began to imagine how agreeably a leisured person like himself might while away the hours with two such accomplished musicians at his beck and call. Kaoru, on the other hand, had hardly noticed the mention of the daughters. It was the account of the father that interested him. In what did his piety consist? What were his thoughts and strivings? How, in any case, he longed to meet such a man! "Would you mind telling Prince Hachi," he said, slipping up to the Teacher just as he reached the door, "that I should very much like to do some reading with him? Don't arrange anything definite, but simply find out whether he is willing."

Ryozen, after this conversation, sent a message to Prince Hachi. "Someone," he said," has given me a most moving account of your present situation." With this letter was the poem: "How comes it that the sullen, high-packed clouds have rolled between us who in our scorn for worldly things are one?"* The Teacher arrived at Uji sooner than Ryozen's messenger, and went straight to Prince Hachi's house. It was seldom indeed that a messenger of any kind found his way to this remote spot. The Prince was overjoyed, and taking advantage of the Teacher's warning he hastily got ready such entertainment as the produce of stream and garden could afford. "Wholly to scorn the world I cannot claim, though the world's scorn alas drove me to these sad hills." Such was the poem with which he replied, and it was meant merely to disclaim the compliments which Ryozen had paid to his eminence as a spiritual authority. But Ryozen took the Prince's words as a rebuke to those who had worked against him, and regretted that Hachi should be so unwilling to forget the past.

"He seems to be seriously interested in these things," said the Teacher, in mentioning Kaoru's request. "It appears he is most anxious to get a thorough understanding of the Scriptures, and has been studying them since he was a mere boy. But I am told he lives in such a whirl of engagements both at Court and at home that other work is impossible;

---

* Ryozen compares his abdication of the Throne to Prince Hachi's retirement from Court. Their estrangement was of course due to the plot to put Hachi in Ryozen's place.

and his position in the State is not such as to allow of his retiring for any length of time to a monastery or other suitable place. He could do so of course occasionally, so long as he did not create the impression that he was abandoning public life. But he has so much to get through and is (it appears) often so worn out that such periods of tuition would be very difficult to arrange. He was therefore particularly interested by my account of your studies, and begged me to find out whether there was any chance of your accepting him as a pupil."

"His case is very unusual," said Prince Hachi. "A realization of the vanity of life is almost always the result of some personal sorrow or particular disappointment. For a young man at the height of his career, with every advantage that fortune can bestow, to show such an interest in the life to come is indeed remarkable. In my own case you would think that enough had happened to weary me of my present existence and turn my thoughts wholly towards spiritual things. Catastrophe has indeed followed so fast on catastrophe that it has almost seemed as though the Lord Buddha, knowing the stubbornness of my heart, had been determined that I should not have one excuse left for feeling any attachment to the outward world. Yet here I am, on the brink of the grave, with half my thoughts still tied to this life, unmindful of the future, deaf to the warnings of the past—that such a one should set up as an instructor is unthinkable. Tell him that if he comes it must be not as a pupil, but as a friend and equal in the Law."

An exchange of letters followed, with the result that a visit was arranged. It was a strange life that he stepped into at Uji—far stranger than he had been led to suppose. The house, to begin with, which he had not expected to be large or elaborately furnished, turned out to be a mere cottage, furnished with only the barest necessities. Again, one of the great advantages of the country is its quiet. But here the perpetual roar of the stream gave such a feeling of unrest that one could settle one's thoughts on nothing else. Was it possible, Kaoru wondered, what with this noise of rushing waters and the icy blasts that rising from the river shook the little house—was it possible that anyone here ever managed to get a moment's sleep? Such a place might be suitable enough as a scene for the Prince's vigils and penances. But how did two young girls manage to exist here? They must, he felt sure, long ago have divested themselves of all ordinary feminine tastes and characteristics. Only a paper partition divided him, as he sat working with Prince Hachi, from the room where the young princesses seemed always to sit. The thoughts of anyone less serious-minded would have been almost bound under these circumstances to wander occasionally to the other side of the partition; and indeed a certain curiosity as to what girls brought up in these strange conditions could look like or say for themselves was inevitable. But it was not to waste time in casual flirtations that he had come to this remote and unfrequented spot. Only indeed the determination to have done forever with such trifling could have brought him to this place at all, and he resolutely drove out of his head all thoughts as to what was going on behind the paper door. To Prince Hachi he at once took a great fancy, and his visits to Uji soon became frequent.

From his lessons with the Prince he got exactly what he wanted. Though only an *ufasaka** Prince Hachi was thoroughly competent to explain both the sacred texts and the observances of his religion, and he did so in the simplest manner, without any display of irrelevant erudition. There are of course always plenty of pious scholars and learned priests who if one had the courage to trouble them with one's questions could no doubt be of great assistance. Kaoru indeed had come across many such, but they were men in high positions, with the affairs of their monasteries and congregations to look after—far too busy and too important to be easily approachable. Then on the other hand there were common priests, the sort who prided themselves on being plain "disciples of Buddha" and had nothing to their credit but the harsh austerity of their lives.

Unfortunately he found that their shabbiness, vulgar accents and clumsy familiarities jarred on him so much that it was impossible to have any dealing with them. In the daytime they might perhaps have been tolerable. But it was only at a very late hour that his engagements left him any leisure for these interviews, and to have such people brought to one's pillow-head seemed, when they arrived, to be merely a willful outrage upon the tranquility of the night.

How different was his present experience! Prince Hachi was distinguished in appearance, subdued in manner, and used a language so different from that of the ordinary expounder that it was at first hard to believe he was dealing with the same texts and doctrines. There was nothing complicated or mysterious in what he taught; indeed, he tended towards parables and illustrations of a very simple and easy kind. But the fact that he was a man of breeding and sensibility seemed to make all the difference. Kaoru became more and more devoted to him, and was miserable if his duties at Court caused him to miss a single lesson. Indeed, he would have liked them to have gone on continuously.

Kaoru's constant visits to Uji brought about a renewal of relations between Prince Hachi and his brother, the ex-Emperor Ryozen, whose messengers now began to give quite an air of animation to this lonely place. At New Year and other such times Ryozen sent very handsome presents, while Kaoru, whenever a chance presented itself, showed his gratitude to the Prince by gifts both of an ornamental and of a solidly useful kind.

---

* Corresponds to the lay reader of the Anglican Church.

So three years passed. It was the end of autumn and the time had come for the Prince's seasonal Prayers. He was finding the noise of the stream, as it beat against the fish-weirs—a noise which at this time of year becomes positively deafening—very unrestful, and he decided to spend a week at the temple where the Teacher lived, though he knew that his daughters would have a very dull and depressing time while he was away.

It happened that Kaoru had been unable to leave Court for some while. But one night, enticed by a moon that rose late, he determined to set out there and then. He went secretly, with only a single groom to escort him and inconspicuously dressed. Fortunately the house was on the near side of the river. There was no need to worry about ordering a boat. He could go on horseback all the way. As he entered the village, a heavy mist came down. He lost the path and was obliged to push his way through dense woods, where he was soon drenched to the skin with the dew that shook upon him from the leaves that were pattering down on every side. It was indeed a chilly adventure that he had let himself in for, and it was of a kind that was wholly new to him, and gave him an agreeable thrill.

He had no desire to wake the villagers, and forbade his groom to announce his approach.[*] As he passed through the brushwood hedge that surrounded the estate, he had to cross a number of minute rivulets, and even here he walked his horse very carefully, so as to avoid making any noise. But to many a cottage there floated, as he stole past, a sweet smell unlike the fragrance of "any flower they knew."[†]

As he approached the house he heard a vague sound of music. He knew of the Prince's fondness for it, and had for a long while been wanting to hear him play. But he had never had the chance. This seemed to be an excellent opportunity. It was, he soon discovered, a lute that was being played. It was tuned to the Ojiki mode[‡] and at the moment only an ordinary accompaniment was being tried over. But the place and hour gave the familiar notes a new sound, and the back-strokes of the plectrum were delightfully firm and clear. Every now and then a thirteen-stringed zithern would join in very sweetly and delicately. He decided to wait for a while and listen; but despite all his precautions his arrival had been heard, and a rough fellow, who seemed to be a sort of night-watchman, came out and accosted him. "The Prince isn't here," he said. "He's staying at the Temple. Do you want us to send for him?" "Certainly not," said Kaoru. "He is probably only there for a few days, and I should not dream of interrupting his devotions. It will be enough, I think, if I ask

---

[*] By shouting "Clear the way!" or the like.

[†] Allusion to a poem by the priest Sosei, end of the 9th century.

[‡] Approximately G sharp, B, D, G sharp.

the princesses to tell him how sorry I was to go back without seeing him, after getting wet all through like this..." "I'll see that they hear about it," said the man, with a broad and rather unpleasant grin. "Wait a moment," said Kaoru, calling him back. "I am very anxious to hear your young mistresses play. I am always being told that their talent for music is remarkable, and this seems too good an opportunity to lose. Is there not some corner where I could listen properly without being seen? I know that if I announce myself in the ordinary way they will at once stop playing, which is the last thing I desire." The watchman, common villager though he was, had by now begun to realize that he was dealing with someone of distinction and importance. Speaking this time in a more respectful tone he said: "When no one is about, they often play from morning till night. But if there are strangers here, particularly anyone from the city, no matter who it is they will not play a note. The fact is, I don't think His Highness likes it to be known that they are here at all—not generally known, that is to say." "If that is so," said Kaoru laughing, "his efforts to conceal their existence have certainly been very unsuccessful. I constantly hear them spoken of as the two most talented girls of the day. But come now, show me the way! Whatever they may be like, they must certainly—when one thinks of the way they have been brought up—be something quite out of the ordinary."* "I don't much care about this," said the man. "There's going to be trouble for me afterwards..." But yielding to Kaoru's importunity he led him to a bamboo fence that screened the whole of the side on which the Princesses lived. There he left him, himself taking charge of Kaoru's groom, whom he entertained in the western verandah. There was a gate in the fence, and pushing it ajar Kaoru peeped in. Heavy wreaths of autumn mist were trailing across the moon and it was no doubt in order to enjoy the beauty of this effect that the people within had left one of the blinds slightly raised. On the *sunoko*,† looking rather cramped and miserable in the cold, crouched a young waiting-maid, and near her was what seemed like an older woman. Inside the room, partly hidden by a pillar, was someone with a lute in front of her and the plectrum still in her hand. She made a casual movement with the plectrum, and it so happened that just at that moment the moon, which had been hidden behind a bank of mist, suddenly came out in all its brightness. "How strange!" said the lute-player. "One can beckon to the moon with one's plectrum just as one summons people with a fan," Her face was raised towards the window while she spoke, and Kaoru could see enough of it to reach the conclusion that the speaker was decidedly good-looking.

---

* For *tamawanu* read *tamayenu*.

† A narrow platform running round the outside of a house.

"It was to turn back the setting sun that the plectrum was used.* Yours is quite a new idea." The person who said this was propped against a cushion, and her head was bowed over a zithern that lay on the floor in front of her. She laughed as she spoke, but there was at the same time a certain seriousness in her manner of making the correction, as though facts were of great importance to her. "Well, whether I invented the idea or no," replied the elder girl, "you cannot deny that lutes and moons have a great deal to do with one another."†

The conversation continued in this strain. It showed a readiness of wit and neatness of phrase which were far indeed removed from what he had expected to find in girls brought up under these strange circumstances.

He had thought hitherto that the finding of marvelously handsome and cultivated young ladies locked away in remote country mansions was a thing that belonged not to real life, but exclusively to the type of romances read by young waiting-women. It now appeared that these stories were much more like life than he had supposed. He wished that the mist were not so thick. He could see hardly anything now. But when at last the moon came out again, down went the blind! No doubt the people inside had been warned that someone was about. Indeed, before the blind was drawn they had, without any display of panic, gently and gracefully withdrawn to the back of the room. He noted many things in their favor. They moved well, and silently, not with a great rustle of skirts like country girls. He was becoming very much interested.

Retiring from his post of observation Kaoru now gave orders for his carriage to be fetched from the city. "I was unfortunate," he said to the watchman, "in not finding His Highness here. But thanks to you I have not altogether wasted my time. I should be glad if you would now tell their ladyships that I wish to wait upon them. I imagine they would not like me to go without giving them a chance of apologizing for the wetting I got in coming here."

That Kaoru had actually been watching them did not of course occur to the ladies. But even the thought that he had perhaps heard them practicing on their instruments annoyed and embarrassed them extremely. "Did you not notice that strange perfume?" said Agemaki.‡ "How slow of us not to guess that he was here!"

---

* Kao Ch'ang-kung, Prince of Lan-ling in Shantung, who was obliged to go into battle masked because his womanish beauty would have heartened rather than dismayed his enemies, is shown in one form of the *Raryo* dance turning back the sun to noon, that the Chinese armies might have more time to defeat the Turks. See Takano's *Nihon Kayo Shi,* p. 103, 1. 2. The Prince flourished in the third quarter of the 6th century A.D.

† The two sound-holes on the face of the lute are called the "half-moons."

‡ The elder girl.

The girl to whom the watchman had given Kaoru's message seemed to be very incompetent, and feeling that the circumstances justified him in taking matters into his own hands, he felt his way back through the heavy mist to the window through which he had been looking before. The country girls who did service in the house had no notion how to address him, and when he attempted to converse with them, made no reply. But one of them, very awkwardly and clumsily, pushed out a cushion for him to sit on. "I cannot say that it is very comfortable out here," he protested. "The journey from the city to this place is something of an undertaking. The road is steep and in places none too good. I think I am entitled to rather better treatment. I hoped at any rate that before I repeated my damp journey you would at least show some appreciation of my endurance." None of the young maids felt capable of replying in this rather elaborate strain, and to rescue themselves from their embarrassment they sent someone to fetch another gentlewoman who was apparently asleep somewhere at the far end of the house. But the woman took a long time coming, and feeling that all this fuss was ridiculously artificial, Agemaki herself presently intervened. "I am afraid we none of us have any idea what you are talking about," she said in a low voice, at the same time retiring to the back of the room. "Airs of innocence are common enough at Court," said Kaoru, "but I should be sorry indeed if I were to force you, Madam, to assume them. For I cannot believe that it is possible to live under one roof with anyone so widely informed as the Prince your father and to remain ignorant of the commonest deserts and obligations. No, Madam! Your powers of judgment are I am sure excellent, and I entreat you to use them—if indeed you can bring yourself to regard the state of my feelings (which I make no effort to conceal from you) as an object worthy of your consideration.* Needless to say, it is not in any spirit of gallantry that I approach you. Towards such levities I have no inclination of my own, nor have the persuasions of others ever in the faintest degree prevailed upon me, as indeed you are no doubt already aware. All that I ask is that you should permit me to relieve the tedium of my existence by an occasional talk or correspondence; and I cannot believe that you on your side, when you get to know me better—living as you do in this lonely place—will find such a distraction wholly unwelcome."

What was one supposed to say in answer to such a discourse as this? Fortunately Agemaki's embarrassment was relieved by the arrival of an elderly lady—the gentlewoman who had just been dragged from her bed. She at any rate was not afflicted with shyness.

"Shame on you now! Where are your manners?" she cried briskly, turning to the maids. "What a place to leave a gentleman waiting in!

---

* Kaoru speaks in the elaborate style used by the courtiers of the period.

Bring him inside at once! These young girls, sir," she exclaimed, "don't seem to understand their duties at all..." Old though she was she spoke with a firm authoritative voice which (the princesses felt) put their own incompetence to shame.

"Your visit, sir," she went on, "is all the more welcome because so many of those whose duty it is to come here seem to have put it out of their heads that there is such a person as His Highness my master in the world at all. I confess that even I, little though it is my place to say so, feel touched by your visit, and I am sure that the young ladies would say the same and more; were they not too shy to speak."

She took a good deal upon herself, Kaoru thought, and he was at first inclined to dislike her. But she seemed to have a great deal of character, and her voice was distinctly agreeable.

"I was just beginning to feel desperate," he said. "But I see that you really understand things, and it is a great relief to me that you have come." So saying he stepped into the room and seated himself with his back against a stool.* The maids, peeping at him from behind their screen, saw by the growing light of dawn, which now made colors distinguishable, that his hunting-cloak—a very plain and common one at that—was completely soaked with mist and dew. Yet it exhaled a perfume so entrancing that it seemed to come from another world.

Suddenly the old lady burst into tears. "O Sir," she said, "I know I am going beyond my duty, and I have tried to restrain myself, but there is something I feel you should know... For years past I have been hoping for a chance—not to tell you the whole story, for that would take too long, but just to get a word with you. Why, I have mentioned it, Sir, in all my prayers, and now that they have been answered and you are here in front of me, just when I am beginning to tell you what I wanted, I am taken like this. I am afraid it is no good," she said sobbing. "I shall have to stop."

He knew that old people are often prone to tears. But it seemed that in this case something more definite could alone account for such an outburst. He was curious to know what it could be. "I wish they had told me about you before," he said. "This is not the first time that I have got wet through coming here, but hitherto I have always set out again through those drenching thickets without getting so much as a word of sympathy. However, as regards what you were going to tell me—had you not better try to finish the story? We are not likely often to get so good an opportunity."

"That is true enough," she answered through her sobs, "and even should such an opportunity come, who knows whether I shall be here to take advantage of it? For we none of us, as they say, know whether we

---

* Stools were for leaning against, not for sitting on.

shall wake up alive in the morning. Well, I will try at least to tell you how an old woman like me comes to be mixed up in it. You must know that what I want to tell you concerns Princess Nyosan, your mother. My name is Ben no Kimi, and my Cousin Kojiju* was this Princess's favorite gentlewoman. Kojiju died long ago; and indeed all those with whom I was brought up are dead now, though I did not learn of it till afterwards, for I was a long way off, almost (it seemed) in another world.† But five or six years ago I came back, and took service where I now am. I do not know whether you have ever heard of Kashiwagi, the elder brother of our present Grand Counsellor?‡ I imagine you must have heard his name mentioned in one connection or another. He died—oh dear, how well I remember it all, though it must be a great many years ago now since that terrible day, for you were only a baby then, and here you stand before me a full-grown man! Well, this dear Lord Kashiwagi's nurse was my mother, and in those last days it was I who looked after him all the time. So he grew used to me, and though I was not at all of his station in life he got into the habit of telling me whatever was on his mind. There were things that he did not care to mention to anyone else. But to me he would often speak pretty freely, and when at the end of his illness he knew that his time had come, he sent for me and told me a great many things he wanted me to do when he died. Above all, there was something I was to tell you. But if you want me to go on, you must come close and let me whisper in your ear. The maids over there are already nudging one another. They are wondering, and small blame to them, how I can have the presumption to detain you so long."

He felt as though he had been listening to the rigmarole of some witch or fortune-teller. The old lady, he could not help thinking, was unnecessarily mysterious. But one thing was certain; whatever this secret was that she was trying to reveal, it must surely have some connection with the great uncertainty which had for so long oppressed him. The moment, however, was singularly unfavorable. Many eyes were, as the old lady had already observed, turned questioningly upon them, and to be seen thus precipitately plunging into an intimate colloquy which bid fair to last for the rest of the night was so embarrassing that he rose to his feet, saying: "I am afraid I still have very little idea what it is you wish to tell me. But it always interests me deeply to hear about those old days, and if the moment were not so unsuitable I would gladly go on listening. But as it is, I have already stayed much longer than I intended. Besides, as you must already have noticed, I am not dressed in a manner

---

* See Part IV, p. 661 *seq.*
† In, the Province of Chikushi. See below, p. 822.
‡ Kobai.

at all suited to broad daylight. In a moment the mist will have cleared, and I dread to think what a spectacle I shall present! You must tell me the rest another time."

As he spoke the bell of the temple where Prince Hachi was staying began to toll dimly and at the same time the mist once more descended, wrapping the house in a dense pall. What a depressing thing it would be to live in such a place! No wonder the young princesses, condemned to these dispiriting surroundings, should have become somewhat morose and unapproachable.

"Him whom I sought the mountain mists withheld,* and now at daybreak bar my homeward way."

Such was the poem that he sent, while waiting for his carriage to arrive. The people of the house were beginning to stir and it may be imagined with what curiosity they stared at this young man whose appearance, even in the Capital where it is so hard to attract notice, never failed to create a sensation. Agemaki could not persuade her maids to answer on her behalf, and at last with a faint sigh she recited the verse: "Who over cloud-girt hills on perilous tracks at autumn's mistiest hour would choose to seek his way?" Her answer was brought to him just as he was setting out.

It was strange how reluctant he was to leave a place that had, if one considered it dispassionately, so little to recommend it. However he was anxious to get back to the city unobserved.

"The slender acquaintanceship that we have made tonight," he wrote to Agemaki, "only makes me feel how much there is that I should like to tell you, if you would only take me a little more into your confidence. That you should persist in treating me like some ordinary visitor from the outside world pains me, and shows indeed a lack of discrimination such as I should not have expected of you." And so saying he went off to the western wing where a room had been got ready for him.

"Have you seen the people down by the fish-weir?" his groom asked. "I should think by the look on their faces that it's a poor catch." He it seemed knew all about these things, which to Kaoru were so unfamiliar and mysterious.

Down the stream strange rafts were now passing loaded with timber. All along the river were people busy in one way or another with the humble tasks that kept them alive. How strange an existence it must be, day in and day out, to live thus frailly supported above the peril of those tossing waters! And yet how often had he, amid his terraces of jade, felt that he too was perilously afloat—was drifting from uncertainty to uncertainty, with no solid ground beneath his feet!"†

---

* Prince Hachi was away at the Temple.

† Botankwa Shohaku (1443-1527), commenting on this passage, admires the skill with which

He sent for an ink stone.

"Sad must her life be truly—the Lady of the Bridge,* if even my sleeve be dripping with the spray of ships that pass."

"You too must often watch them," he added, and sent it to her by the night-watchman who, he noticed, looked a poor, pinched, shivering creature in the morning light. It was humiliating to answer such a note on ordinary, unscented paper; but it would have taken a long search to find anything better, and as an immediate reply seemed to be the essential thing, she wrote at once: "No life more of the waves than mine, whose lot at dawn and dusk the Guardian of the Stream† with dripping oar bedews."

Anyone whose handwriting was so full of distinction must, Kaoru felt sure, be interesting in other ways, and he felt very disinclined to hurry away. But it had already been announced more than once that his carriage was at the door, and promising to come again as soon as Prince Hachi returned, he got the night-watchman to help him out of his wet clothes and put on a day-dress that had been sent from the Capital.

Naturally, what was uppermost in his mind all the way home was the old lady's unfinished story. But at the same time there floated before him the images of Agemaki and her sister. Yes, they were certainly both of them far more attractive than one could possibly have expected. The world, after all, he began to feel, despite all his resolutions, was rather an enjoyable place to live in. At any rate, for the moment he felt in no particular hurry to leave it.

He was careful not to give his letter of thanks in any way the appearance of a love-letter. It was written on rather thick, plain paper. But he chose and prepared his writing-brush with great care, and the gradations of tone were contrived with considerable delicacy and skill. "I find myself," he said, "regretting now that, in my great fear of seeming impertinent, I left so many things unsaid. But, as I have already to some extent confessed, I am counting on you to allow me on future occasions a far freer access. So soon as I hear that His Highness's retreat is ended, I shall make haste to wait upon you, confident that you will this time clear away the perplexities of our late groping and misty conversation."

The tone was certainly sober enough. He gave it to one of his retainers, a certain Sakon no Jo, with instructions that it was to be delivered by Ben no Kimi, the elderly woman with whom he had previously conversed.

Murasaki depicts the egotism of Kaoru, "He brings everything, however trifling, into connection with his own thoughts and feelings."

* The Hashihime, "Bridge Maiden," was the guardian-spirit of Uji Bridge. Here Kaoru compares Agemaki to the Bridge Maiden.

† Agemaki compares her father to the Kawa-osa, or river-headman, whose duty it was to go morning and evening up and down the river inspecting the banks, bridges, etc.

Remembering the starved appearance of the night-watchman he sent him a great hamper full of good things to eat. The day after he sent presents to the Uji temple. It was in an exposed position, and he imagined that the priests must at this time of year suffer terribly from cold. No doubt Prince Hachi would desire to recompense them in some way for his stay there, and in order to enable him to do this on a handsome scale, Kaoru sent him a large quantity of silk and cotton-quilting, which arrived just on the morning of the Prince's departure, so that he had the satisfaction of being able to reward every resident in the temple with either a new cassock and under robe, or enough stuff to make them out of. He had already told the night-watchman to keep the wet hunting-cloak that he had discarded at the time of his last visit. It was a magnificent garment, made of a priceless white damask. The man who under all this splendor remained the same poor skinny creature as before, cut an extraordinary figure in it. Moreover, wherever he went, there hung about him a strange fragrance which, though it procured for him several gratifying successes, in the end proved so embarrassing that he did everything he could think of to get rid of it. "These Court gentlemen do know how to make themselves smell!" he said. "It's beyond me how they get hold of such scents."

Soon came Agemaki's reply. It was artless and almost childlike in its simplicity. Prince Hachi on his return was shown this correspondence, and noted the sobriety of Kaoru's tone. "It is not, I grant," he said, "at all in the style* that most young men would adopt under the circumstances. But that is easy to explain. His interest in you is due to a hint I once let fall—we were talking about what would become of you both in the event of my death, and he was kind enough to say that he would keep an eye on you. Under these, circumstances a tone of gallantry would have been quite out of place."

In his own letter of thanks Prince Hachi qualified Kaoru's presents as so far "exceeding the capacity of his solitary hill-cave" that it was impossible to express his gratitude in writing. This of course constituted an invitation to an immediate visit. But Kaoru suddenly remembered that to make such a discovery as he himself had just made—to unearth in some improbable and secluded spot a girl whose beauty and talents were entirely unsuspected by the rest of the world—had long been Prince Niou's dream, and he could not resist the temptation to give his friend a somewhat highly colored account of his recent experience. So soon therefore as he had a free evening he called on Niou and presently managed to bring round the conversation to the subject of Prince Hachi and his daughters. It was obvious from the start that his description of this

---

* The commentators wrongly interpret these remarks as referring, not to Kaoru's letter, but to Agemaki's reply.

romantic daybreak adventure was interesting Niou extremely, and Kaoru as he went on found himself embellishing the story with every such detail as was most calculated to inflame his friend's excited imagination.

"And then," said Niou, when Kaoru came to a pause, "She presumably wrote a reply, which if you were a decent fellow you would show to me. You know quite well that if I got such a letter..."

"Oh, do I though?" said Kaoru, indignantly. "How many, of the hundreds that you must obviously have received, have I ever so much as set eyes on? But I have not the least desire to keep these girls to myself. They would indeed be sadly wasted! My first thought, I assure you, was that you must certainly get to know them. I quite forgot for the moment that you are not free to go about as you please.* My position is, of course, quite different. If I wanted to carry on secret affairs, there would be nothing to prevent it. And it certainly seems as though anyone who had a taste for such adventures could find abundant material for them, even in what one would have regarded as the most unlikely places. Out in the country, scattered about in all sorts of queer holes and corners, there must be any number of girls, just of the kind you have always dreamed of, buried away in lonely farms and country houses, with nothing to do but brood on their own misfortune. At this place I have been telling you of one would never have expected to find any but the most raw-boned, awkward creatures, with no knowledge of anything outside their father's prayer book. For years past I have known that they existed, but never bothered even to ask whether they were the sort of girls who were worth cultivating. Yet judging by the fleeting glimpse I caught of them the other night, they are perfect. Such grace of movement, such profiles... So far as I could see if one were imagining the ideal woman, one would not make her different."

Niou took all this quite seriously and he was by now feeling dreadfully jealous. Coming from Kaoru, who in general showed little interest in such matters, the story made all the deeper an impression. "You will of course try to see her again?" he said, as though he were afraid Kaoru would let the matter drop, but in reality (as Kaoru saw much to his amusement) burning with rage at the thought that the restrictions of his position debarred him even from initiating, let alone pursuing such adventures.

"Come," said Kaoru, "you must surely have seen that I was only teasing you. I am not like other people. There is something which I cannot speak about that has always prevented me from taking any part in the ordinary pleasures of the world. It has had the effect of making me very bad even at the usual sort of banter that men exchange with women, and when it comes to a question of real love, of the kind when one's whole

---

* Members of the Imperial family could not leave Kyoto without permission.

being becomes changed—that for me is out of the question, for it would mean giving up what in my heart of hearts I know to be my only real purpose and conviction."

"Tremendous!" said Niou, laughing. "I have of course heard you speak in this elevated way many times before, but I did hope that after what you were telling me about this evening we should be spared this sort of thing at any rate for a while."

But during all this visit and indeed at every moment since his return from Uji, Kaoru's inmost thoughts had been solely occupied with the aged woman's revelation, and it was all one to him how beautiful, interesting, or accomplished these or any other females might be.

It was early in the tenth month before he got a chance to go to Uji. "You will be going to the Fishers' Fête,* of course?" everyone said to him. "No," said Kaoru, "I think I shall manage to keep clear of the *ajiro*,† as indeed most of the fish do."

He went practically unattended, not on horseback but in a light, basket-work carriage, dressed in a shot-silk robe and baggy trousers, which he had ordered to be specially made for the occasion.‡

Prince Hachi was delighted to welcome him back and prepared in his honor what was, considering the slender resources of the place, a magnificent banquet. When it grew dark they sat together near the lamp and went back over the texts they had studied before. There were still certain points that the Prince did not feel competent to explain, and he presently sent up to the temple for the Teacher to help him with some of the more obscure and difficult passages. It was a wild night. A high wind, blowing up from the river, crashed through the trees outside the house, whirling leaves and branches in every direction, and the roar of the stream was so loud as to be terrifying. Sleep was out of the question, and towards dawn, or at any rate when he felt that the night would surely soon be over, Kaoru started a conversation about music, in the course of which he mentioned that on the occasion of his recent early-morning call he had heard a few notes played on an instrument which struck him as unusually fine. He was very anxious to know all about it. The Prince sent someone for his zithern. "I doubt though," he said, "whether I shall be able to play anything on it. My mind has been too much occupied with quite other things. I believe however if anyone else were to play, I could still manage to accompany..." and he sent for a lute, which he placed in Kaoru's hands. "There is no question," Kaoru said, when he had tuned it, "but that this is the instrument the tone of which I admired so much

---

* When the people from all round come to see the trapping of the fish in the fish-weirs. In Kaoru's reply there is a pun which I have not attempted to translate.

† Fish-weir.

‡ So that he might be less easily recognized.

the other day, little as you would think it from the sounds that I have just been producing. I see now that the qualities I was so much struck by depended chiefly on the way it was played." "Come," said the Prince when Kaoru, after playing a few notes, put the lute aside, "you are being absurd. It can only have been my daughters whom you heard playing, and who is there here who can possibly have taught them to play in a way that could excite your admiration?" So saying the old Prince took up his zithern and began to play a very strange and moving tune, which owed perhaps some of its beauty to the fact that its notes were mingled with the noise of wind rushing through the steep woods above the house. But he still insisted that he had forgotten everything he ever knew; and this was the only proper piece that he played right through. "I confess," he said, putting the instrument aside, "that I have myself sometimes been surprised at the progress my daughters seem to have made. Occasionally I have caught sound of a passage or two on the thirteen-stringed zithern[*] that really seemed to me masterly. But it is some time since I have been able to give any real attention to their music. If they have got on at all, it must be in a style entirely of their own invention. For the noise of the river is the only music but their own that they have ever heard, and if it came to playing in time and tune with outside people, I imagine they would find that they had got nowhere at all." However he sent a message asking his daughters to play something. But they thought it quite enough that Kaoru should have taken the liberty of listening on that previous occasion, when he must have known that they were playing only for their own amusement, and nothing would now induce them to repeat their performance. Kaoru was naturally very disappointed, and the old Prince himself was in despair. That they should be shy was, considering the circumstances of their upbringing, inevitable; but to find them so utterly incapable of taking their part in the most ordinary acts of social intercourse was a sad surprise. "I have of course brought them up very quietly," he said to Kaoru, and they have met scarcely anyone. But I confess I hardly realized to what a pitch things had come. It is indeed very perturbing, for I am not likely to be here much longer, and what will become of two young girls so wholly unfitted for general society I tremble to think."

"I can of course quite understand," said Kaoru, "that you should not consider me suitable as an actual guardian. But I have already undertaken, as you know, to do what I can for them in a general way, in the event of my surviving you, and you may count on me not to forget my promise."

"Yes, yes," said the Prince, "that is of course a great comfort," and as it was already close on daybreak, went off to say his prayers.

---

[*] "The instrument played by Kozeri, the younger daughter.

When he was gone Kaoru sent for the old gentlewoman Ben no Kimi, who immediately resumed her story. She must, he thought, have been almost sixty, but there was nothing in her speech to suggest decrepitude nor any influence of the remote province in which she had lived so long. In telling the tale of Kashiwagi's desperate love, the illness that ensued upon it and his miserable end, she wept profusely. The story was of a kind that would certainly have moved Kaoru profoundly even if it had in no way specially concerned him. But now as he heard the great uncertainty that had weighed upon him ever since he could remember, being step by step removed, he too could hardly refrain from tears. For years he had never uttered a prayer to Buddha without imploring that these torturing doubts might be resolved, and now suddenly, when he had given up hope, the whole of that pitiful past flowed by him as in a dream.

"Tell me at once," he said, "how many other people know about this. It is not very easy to believe that I am the first person to whom you have told a story of so sensational a description—though it is strange, I must say, that no inkling of it has ever yet got round to me." "My cousin Kojiju," said the old lady, "is the only person besides myself who ever knew anything about it. Despite our humble position in life your father had singled us out for constant attendance upon him, and we could hardly be at his beck and call at all hours of the day and night without having some notion of what was going on. Moreover it was through our hand—and ours only that all communications passed—for even after he had ceased to see the Princess your mother there were times when his feelings got the better of him and he could not refrain from writing. But he naturally never discussed the matter with us. It was only on his deathbed that he referred to it openly, at the same time entrusting me with a commission such as was bound to prove most embarrassing to a person in my humble position. For years I prayed and prayed that some chance might enable me to carry out his desire. And now I know that there is indeed a Buddha in the world, for my prayers have been answered and here I find you standing in front of me. And it is as well that this has happened now, for I had quite decided to burn the things. "Who knows," I said to myself, "how suddenly I may be taken away?" I did not like the idea, you see, that if I risked leaving them behind they might fall into wrong hands. But from the moment I heard that you were visiting here from time to time I was thankful that I had waited. For I felt certain that sooner or later I should get a chance to carry out my commission. However, as things are, it has all turned out providentially." And between her tears she now told him the whole story of his birth.

"Close upon all these upsets," she went on, "came my own mother's illness and death, and I was so shaken by all this trouble and bereavement that when a man far below me in social position, who had been paying me attentions for years, offered once more to take me away with him I could not resist the temptation to get clear from all this, and went off with him far away to the West, where I lost all touch with the people I had known in the Capital. But presently my lover too fell ill and died, and after an absence of nearly ten years I came back to what seemed like an unknown world. My first thought was to seek service with Lady Chujo, the ex-Emperor Ryozen's consort; for she, as you know, is my late master's sister, and I used to hear a great deal about her in old days. But when it came to the point I did not feel equal to plunging all at once into the life that is led at a place of that kind. I am, as a matter of fact, related to the young ladies here. My father was a connection of their late mother's. I have known Prince Hachi since my earliest days, and so it came about that in the end I did not stay in the Capital, but have got fixed like an old tree-stump in the mountainside. Kojiju, my cousin, is dead, as indeed are almost all of the people I knew in those old days. No, there is not much pleasure in lingering like this, when all one's friends have gone on before..." She was evidently prepared to go on talking for a long while. But it was now broad daylight, and Kaoru was obliged to check her. "I fear," he said, "there is not time for you to finish your story now. You must continue it the next time we can arrange to be together quietly like this. Jiju I vaguely remember, but I can only have been about five years old when she died suddenly—of consumption, I think it was. As for what you have told me, I need say no more than that, but for our meeting, I might have gone on forever living with the weight of a terrible sin upon me."*

Ben no Kimi now brought out a bag containing a number of scraps of paper, all neatly folded and tied together, but already moldering with age. "Do not let this out of your hands," she said as she handed it over. "His Excellency put these papers together and gave them to me when he knew that his time was come. He thought that it would be easy enough for me to convey them to you through Kojiju, whom he imagined I must constantly meet. But as a matter of fact I was never able to see her again, though it worried me far more to be swept off leaving His Excellency's commission undone than it did to leave my own affairs all topsy-turvy."

He took the little bag and without a word stuffed it into the folds of his dress. That the old woman should really have been capable of keeping so exciting a story to herself seemed to him very improbable. But she had sworn by everything holy that it was so, and he supposed that he had better try to believe her. His mind was in a turmoil; but at this moment a servant arrived with his soup and steamed rice. There was no time to be lost, for though yesterday had been a public holiday today the taboo was

---

* Unable to make the offerings that a son ought to make to his father's spirit.

at an end and he had a great deal to get through at the Palace. Moreover, Princess Ichi no Miya* was unwell and it was his duty to pay a visit of enquiry. He sent a message to Prince Hachi, promising to return before the autumn leaves fell. "Your visits," said the Prince, "make us, under the shadow of our secluded hill, feel as though we were not quite cut off from what is going on in the world."

His first act on his return was to take out the little bag. It was of damask with a raised pattern, and near the top the one word *Jo*† had been written. It was gathered together at the mouth by a delicate cord to which was attached a slip with his‡ name on it. His hands trembled while he untied the knot. There were a number of papers, containing notes and messages of all kinds. Among them were five or six in Nyosan's hand. Of those that were evidently from Kashiwagi to her, some were written quite at the end of his illness, when circumstances had no doubt made it impossible for them to be delivered. One of these referred to Nyosan's having become a nun. It covered five sheets of Michinoku paper, and was written in a shaky, sprawling hand, as though a bird had hopped over the paper. "My soul a longer sadder journey goes than you who, while I linger, haste to leave the world." Such was his poem, and beside it a reference to Kaoru himself, concerning whom Kashiwagi professed to feel no anxiety, "for it will never be known," he wrote, "that he is not Genji's child." Here the letter broke off, and in a hand even more shaky and confused was written on the outside, "To be given to Kojiju." The paper had been attacked by bookworms and was in a moldering condition, but the characters were as clear as if they had been written yesterday, and seeing them staring at him there, as plain as day, Kaoru was thankful indeed that the documents had passed safely into his hands. So full was his mind of this story of his birth—the strangest tale, incidentally, that he had ever heard told—that he found it impossible to face going to the Palace, and presently went to his mother's chapel. She was sitting placidly reading the Scriptures. She looked very inexperienced and young. She hid her book§ when she saw him enter. What point could there be in telling her that he knew? He sat for a long while wrapped in his own thoughts, which sorely needed time to recover from their confusion.

---

* Ryozen's eldest daughter.
† "Upper," meaning that it concerned the "upper people," i.e. Ben'i masters.
‡ Kashiwagi's.
§ It was unbecoming for a woman to be seen reading the Scriptures.

At the Foot of the Oak-Tree

On the twentieth day of the second month Niou made a pilgrimage to Hasedera.[*] He did so in pursuance of a vow made many years ago, and the fact that now, after letting the matter drop for so long, he suddenly put this project into execution was perhaps chiefly due to his curiosity about Uji, where a halt is generally made on the way back to the Capital. The name of this place, thanks to a certain well-known verse,[†] has indeed an unenviable notoriety; but Niou had more particular reasons for looking forward with interest to a journey that would take him in that direction. He was accompanied by so vast a throng of friends and retainers that the Court seemed strangely derelict. Arrangements were made for his reception at an estate on the far side of Uji river. The house, a large and very agreeable one, had been inherited by Yugiri from Genji. Yugiri himself at first intended to meet the returning pilgrims at Uji, but the astrologers had suddenly discovered this to be very unadvisable, which of course was in a way a disappointment. But on the other hand Kaoru promised to come, which was very fortunate, for his presence imposed no restraint on the company, and he would be useful owing to his acquaintance with Prince Hachi; whereas with Yugiri there one had to be on one's best behavior—no, it was on the whole a great relief that he could not come.

But his sons, Udaiben and the rest, were all there. Indeed owing to the great preference for him which was shown by both the Emperor and the Empress Niou was immensely sought after even by those who nominally adhered to other factions; while among those, of whatever rank, who had the slightest connection with the New Palace[‡] he was looked upon as a kind of private sovereign and master.

Everything possible had been done to make his halt in this rustic place agreeable. What with draughts, backgammon, and *tagi*[§] the time passed quickly enough. Early in the afternoon Niou, tired out by the journey (it was the longest he had ever made) and being anxious for other reasons not to hurry away from the place too quickly, went and lay down. But towards evening he sent for his zithern and the whole party made music.

---

[*] The great shrine of Kwannori southeast of Nara.
[†] The poem in which Kisen (9th Century) puns on "Uji" and *ushi* "dismal."
[‡] Built by Genji and inhabited by his descendants.
[§] Played with six counters a side. They are flipped across a raised "hill" in the center of the board.

In quiet places such as this, particularly where there is water, sound carries with remarkable clearness. Prince Hachi's house, though on the far side of the river, was only a short distance away, and every now and then a gust of wind would carry to him tunes and cadences that awakened deep-buried memories. "I wonder who that is playing the flute?" he said to himself. "Whoever he is, he knows how to blow. Genji was our great flute-player in old days, and certainly he got charming effects out of the instrument. But this fellow has a clearer tone, and gets more expression into it too. I should think it must be someone connected with To no Chujo's family."*

What a long time it was, the old man thought, since he had himself taken part in such festivities! Yes, it was appalling to think how many years this dead-alive existence had been going on at Uji. But for *them*—for his unhappy daughters—it must stop. They must not go on forever living thus tucked away in the hills. Of course Kaoru was the one person who would have been perfect as a son-in-law. But Kaoru showed no sign of desiring any such thing—though this was in a way an additional advantage, for had he shown a disposition to flirt with the girls in the way most modern young men would have done, one would have ceased to feel the same confidence in him. It was all very perplexing. The old man gazed across the river. It seemed as though this spring night would never end. But to Niou, for whom a night away from home was a great event, it seemed as if this visit to Uji, to which he so much looked forward, had lasted no time at all. But he had drunk a good deal, and had rather a confused impression of what had actually occurred.

Great wreaths of mist stretched across the sky. The air was full of cherry-blossom, yet every tree seemed laden with buds that were only just opening. What lovely things there were to look at! Those willows on the river bank, for example, swaying gently up and down, their every movement reflected in the water. Niou had never seen such things before and was filled with delight and astonishment.

Kaoru naturally did not wish to lose this opportunity of visiting the house on the other side. But he had no desire to bring a whole crowd of people with him, and to go off in a boat all alone would be to treat the rest of the party in too offhand a manner. He was hesitating what to do when a messenger came from Prince Hachi. "Though through the morning mist the hill-wind carries the music of your flute, yet to my sorrow lie unbraved between us the white waves of the stream."† It was penned in a very delicate cursive hand. Niou, who was near by, guessed at once

---

* Presumably Kaoru was the flute-player. Being in reality not Genji's, but Kashiwagi's son, he was To no Chujo's grandson.

† A hint that a visit would be welcome.

from what quarter this graceful reminder came. "Give it to me," he said. "I will write the answer."

"Though, set between, the torrents of Uji roll yet, gladly would I think, on either bank the self-same gentle wind its music blows."

So Kaoru and Niou set out, taking with them those among the company who were most interested in music.* While crossing the stream they played the *Kansuiraku*.† Their landing was effected with no difficulty, for there was a very convenient gangway leading straight into a portico which overlooked the river. It had been specially contrived by the old Prince, who had once been an expert in such matters. The place had been simply but very tastefully prepared for their reception, the screens being of wattled bamboo with lacquered wooden frames—in fact, just such as ordinary country people use. He had looked out a number of very fine ancient instruments, which he left lying about casually in one place and another, so that they might not give the impression of having been routed out purposely for the occasion. The guests formed themselves into an orchestra and played the *Cherry Man*,‡ transposing it into the Ichikotsu mode.§ Prince Hachi's skill as a musician was well-known, and everyone was anxious to hear him. But though he sat with the thirteen-stringed zithern in front of him, he only joined occasionally in the accompaniment. To these young people however his manner of playing was quite unfamiliar, and they found it a welcome change from the superficial style to which they were accustomed. The whole manner of the entertainment was indeed an agreeable surprise. The Prince was assisted by a number of quite distinguished-looking elderly persons, all apparently members of the Imperial Clan, and some of them officers of the Fourth Rank without official employment,¶ who having heard of Niou's visit to Uji were upset at the idea of their kinsman having to entertain him single-handed, and had at the last moment offered their services. The royal visitors thus found themselves waited upon by persons of their own standing, and it was generally voted a very well-arranged if rather old-fashioned country entertainment. But was nothing going to be heard of the two princesses who were supposed to live here? Naturally all the guests were exceedingly curious about them, and not least so Niou himself, who at this moment felt more than ever the disadvantages of a position in society which made his every gesture a matter of comment. He could not however resist getting someone to pick a fine spray of cherry-blossom which he gave to the

---

* Prince Hachi being celebrated as a musician.

† Some texts read *Kasuiraku,* i.e. River Water Music.

‡ See Part III, p. 368.

§ D major, with C natural. This was a more convenient mode for the flute-players.

¶ The Prince's relations—members of that section of the Imperial family which had fallen into disrepute owing to their plot against Genji.

prettiest among the Imperial pages who were in attendance upon him, with orders that it was to be taken to the mistress of the house. With it he sent the poem: "Led hither by the scent of flowering woods, this garland—flower to fair flower—I send." Agemaki was at a sad loss how to reply to this effusion, but the elderly gentlewomen about her insisted that a lady seems at once to attach an undue importance to such trifles if she fails to deal with them promptly, and when Agemaki could not be prevailed on to reply, they pressed her sister Kozeri into the service. "What save the search of flowers to wreath his head could in this desolate spot a traveler's feet detain?" Such was the poem that the gentlewomen dictated, and Kozeri wrote it out very skillfully and daintily.

More music followed, and presently Kobai arrived in an official capacity to conduct the young Prince* back to the city. It was with a great clatter and bustle that this notable concourse of visitors now made ready to depart, the younger among them casting back many longing glances at a quarter the amenities of which they would gladly have further explored.[†] Niou, for his part, was fully determined that this should not be his last visit.

All around them, as they made their homeward way, were misty hills, covered with trees in fullest bloom. Naturally many Chinese and Japanese poems were made; but with these it is unnecessary for me to trouble you. Niou was not at all certain that amid the interruptions and distractions of the moment he had managed to convey exactly the meaning he intended, and on his own account[‡] he followed up his cherry-poem with a series of messages and letters. "You had better answer," said Prince Hachi, "though only in a natural, friendly way. Anything of the other sort would suggest that you are taking him far too seriously. He has the reputation of being very susceptible, and I imagine he never visits a house where there are young people such as you without beginning a correspondence of this kind. He really does not mean anything." The task of framing these replies fell to Kozeri; for Agemaki had an invincible dislike for these gallant exchanges of fashionable insincerity.

During the ensuing spring months Prince Hachi was more than ever perturbed concerning the future of the two princesses. He would sometimes find himself going so far as to wish that there were discoverable in either of them some such fault or deformity as would serve, if not as an excuse for his failure, at least as a mitigation of his responsibility. But no; every day their beauty grew more radiant and complete. And he had indeed reason to feel that the matter was an urgent one, for Agemaki was already twenty-five and Kozeri twenty-three.

---

* Niou.

† They would like to have been introduced to the princesses.

‡ Without waiting for Kaoru's assistance.

It happened that this was for Prince Hachi a dangerous year,* and he took the precaution of redoubling his daily penances and devotions. As far as his own life and convictions went, it would have been hard to imagine a case where Salvation seemed more thoroughly assured— provided only that at the moment of departure his serenity was not clouded by this one ineradicable affection.† Whether however, as matters stood, he had any chance of leaving the world with a heart set solely on the things of the spirit not only he himself but all those about him were inclined gravely to doubt.

It could not be said that he was unduly ambitious. If even a tolerable son-in-law, not necessarily of good birth but merely with a position that would make the match not too great a scandal, had come to him with a genuine desire to offer either of his daughters proper support and protection, the Prince would have been willing to overlook a great deal. Indeed, even with only one of the girls properly established, he would die quite happily; for the married one would naturally be in a position to make a home for the other. But so far no serious suitor of any kind had presented himself. Occasionally on one feeble pretext or another irresponsible young men had tried to enter into gallant correspondence; but it was clear that they meant nothing by it—were merely looking for something to serve as a distraction on their way to or from places of pilgrimage, and imagined that, despite the Prince's royal birth, girls brought up in such a wilderness would welcome any escapade, however discreditable, provided it made a break in the monotony of their existence—to such suitors as these Prince Hachi would give no countenance, and he saw to it that their communications remained unacknowledged and unanswered. Of course, there was Prince Niou. Hachi profoundly hoped that before long he would repeat his visit. Yes; something might come of it.‡

It was this autumn that Kaoru became Middle Chancellor. This promotion brought with it many new responsibilities at a time when his own private troubles, made it difficult for him to turn his mind to anything else. For years he had been continually tormented by uncertainty. But the truth, once he had heard it, was of a kind indeed that removed all further doubt or speculation, but was far from calculated to set a troubled conscience at rest. The circumstances§ of Kashiwagi's death were such that the

---

* See Part IV, p. 655.

† Only those who have divested themselves of all human affections can go to Paradise.

‡ Literally "some *karma* may have determined it." When *karma* determines a thing, "something comes of it." For example, when *karma* determines a marriage (when the parties have been united in a previous incarnation) "something happens," i.e. children are born; but otherwise the marriage is childless. Such idioms had become part of current speech, and are not to be interpreted in their strict theological sense.

§ He had died in love, which meant that he was certainly in Hell.

filial offices* which Kaoru's ignorance had forced him to leave unperformed could not have been more imperatively required. Here was a task to which he longed to set himself in earnest, and he was deeply grateful to the old woman, whose revelation had at least set him on the right track; and though he was for a long time unable to go to Uji in person, he managed in an unconspicuous way to show the old lady many small kindnesses.

It was the seventh month when he was at last free to pay another visit. In the City there was as yet no sign of autumn. But as he approached Mount Otoha† there was a cold touch in the wind, and on the slopes of the Maki Hills‡ the leaves had already begun to change color. Kaoru was delighted to find himself—and fortunately just at the loveliest moment—once more amid such scenes as this, and Hachi was particularly glad to see him, for there was much that lay heavily on the old man's mind. "I hope you will sometimes come and look after these girls for me a little when I am gone," he said, not content till he had heard Kaoru repeat his previous assurances. "Why, of course," Kaoru answered quickly. "I thought that was already understood. As far as I am concerned, I shall be only too happy to do what I can for them. A word from you was all that was needed... But you must not count on me too much. I am determined as soon as I can manage it to retire from the world,§ and it would therefore be wrong for me to undertake any great commitments. So long however as I am available, I will continue to do my best. That I promise absolutely."

The Prince appeared to be much comforted.

Late at night the moon came out from behind the clouds, seeming almost to touch the shoulder of the hill, and sitting in the moonlight Prince Hachi recited his prayers. Afterwards he fell to talking of old times. "I do not know how it is now," he said, "but when I was at Court they used always to have a grand concert at the Palace on such nights as this. All the best performers on every instrument were summoned and there was a long succession of very elaborate orchestral pieces. I confess it was all too formal for my tastes. There is only one place in the Palace where one hears music worthy of the name, and that is in the private quarters of some of the more important ladies-in-waiting. That is where you will hear a music that vibrates with real passion; for it is the only means by which the bitter jealousies and rivalries that all the time exist under the surface can find their outward expression. And what tragic intensity there was in those throbbing notes that used suddenly to break the stillness of the autumn night!

---

* Masses for the Dead.
† Near Kyoto.
‡ Near Uji.
§ Become a monk.

"Indeed, in all sports and pastimes woman is the fittest companion. For though she is in herself in every way inferior to man, her mere presence keys him up to a great capacity for pleasure and excitement; which is of course the reason why she is regarded as the principal cause of human sin. And when one thinks of the anxiety that children cause their parents, the sons really do not come much into account. It is chiefly the daughters one thinks of—though really I believe a parent does best, after a certain point, simply to let a girl take her chance, however difficult it may be to make up his mind to it..." He spoke as though he were merely referring to parents in general. But it was obvious enough that it was his own case that he had in mind. Kaoru thought it better to change the subject. "Music," he said, "is a thing to which I have never given serious attention, at any rate so far as my own playing was concerned. I suppose I have felt about it as about so many other things that for anyone in my position[*] it was hardly worthwhile. But this does not prevent me from taking a great interest in other people's performances, which is surely quite permissible, for did not even Kasyapa, the sternest of the Sages, rise up and dance at the sound of Drama's lyre?"[†]

What he was hoping for was that the Prince might tonight succeed in persuading Agemaki to play properly, for he was intensely curious to hear her, and hitherto had really never heard more than a few stray notes. Hachi at once went off to the women's quarters. "Perhaps Agemaki would give us a tune," he said, delighted to find that there was at any rate this one link between Kaoru and his daughter. But it was the thirteen-stringed zithern[‡] that after a while sounded out of the stillness, only to relapse into sudden silence after one short tune.

The remoteness of the spot, the singular beauty of the night, the utter silence of the house—all conspired to make him find in these few, simple notes an otherwise unaccountable charm. He was on the point of proposing that the two sisters should play together properly. But no, that would certainly be useless.

"Well, now that I have set things going," said Hachi, "I must leave you to deal with these two young people as best you can," and he disappeared into his small chapel, reciting the poem: "Though, when I am gone, of this grass hut no stick or straw remain, yet shall one word of yours a shelter be from every storm and fray. Forgive me," he added, "if I have been rather tiresome tonight. I felt it was probably our last meeting, and that made it difficult for me to control myself."

---

[*] Anyone about to become a monk. The playing of musical instruments, except the zithern (*koto*), was forbidden to monks.

[†] See *Druma Kinnara-raja Sutra.* Taisho Tripitaka XV, p. 371.

[‡] Kozeri's instrament.

As now it sits, firm shall it be forever—the thatch that promise binds upon your grassy roof."

Such was Kaoru's poem. "I shall be very busy for the present with the Wrestling Competition[*] and other things of that kind," he said. "But as soon as they are over I will call again."

When the Prince was safely in his chapel, Kaoru sent for the old lady, Ben no Kimi, and questioned her about various points which her previous story had not made clear.

He went then to the Princesses' quarters. The moon, now close to the horizon again, was shining straight into the room and through the curtains-of-state, setting off the forms of the two sisters in delicate outline. He began to talk to them quietly and seriously about a number of topics, in a manner wholly devoid of any touch of sentiment or gallantry; and this time both of them occasionally replied.

What would not Niou give (he could not help thinking) for such an opportunity as this? And indeed he wondered whether there was anyone else in the world who, having been given the encouragement[†] that he had just received, would have been so slow to benefit by it. Yet this did not in the least mean that he found the sisters unattractive. On the contrary, in the course of the present conversation he was more than ever struck by their unusual intelligence and sensibility, and he realized that he would not at all like it if anyone else took a fancy to them and carried them away—which seemed to show, he reflected, that he already to some extent regarded them as his own property.

He was obliged to leave before dawn. He thought continually about the old Prince's appearance and conversation that night. Never had he seen him in such low spirits, and he made up his mind to go back to Uji the moment that things at Court had quieted down a little. Niou too was very anxious to get out to Uji sometime before the autumn leaves were gone, and was trying to find an excuse for absenting himself. He still continued to write to Agemaki who, though she was convinced that he was merely amusing himself, since his letters did no one any harm occasionally sent a reply.

As the autumn drew on Prince Hachi became more and more depressed. He determined at last that the time had come for him to retire once more to his usual place of retreat, where he had at any rate the advantage of being able to apply himself to his religious exercises without fear of interruption. "I feel," he said, when giving his daughters various final instructions prior to his departure, "that the time is soon coming when I

---

[*] At the end of the present month. Strong men from all over Japan took part in it. Needless to say Kaoru's activity was only as an organizer.

[†] The permission to make friends with the princesses.

shall have to bid you a final farewell. You know as well as I do that such a moment is bound to come, and could you look to the natural quarter* for support and consolation, I should not be so concerned. But as it is, I confess I am very worried about you; for so far as I can see there is no one on whom you will really be able to rely. I must however make an effort to put all this out of my head; otherwise it is clear enough that I shall myself suffer countless eons of darkness and perdition without any corresponding advantage to you. It would be absurd if after managing to abstract my thoughts fairly successfully from worldly things even while you were at my side I could not now stop worrying about what is going to happen when I am no longer there to see. But it is not only of myself I am thinking. Do, I beg of you, if only for your dead mother's sake, avoid doing anything rash or unseemly. Above all, on no account let yourselves be persuaded to stray a single step from your present home, unless in exchange for it you are offered some position of the most definite and absolute security. It may be that, if the worst comes to the worst, you will have to end your days here where they began. In that case, be patient, bear with the hours as they come, and you will find that even in idleness and solitude time passes far more quickly than you would ever have supposed. And indeed for women, to whom a single false step is often of such fatal consequence that they are rightly thought to have achieved no small success in life if they have merely managed to pass through it without incurring unpleasant notoriety—for women such an existence as yours has its own advantages."

So far were Agemaki and her sister from worrying about who would look after them after their father's death that they had hitherto hardly managed to conceive the possibility of their surviving such an event by a single hour, and all these over-anxious instructions and premonitions merely bewildered them. What pained them most was the discovery that all the while when he had looked after them day by day and seemed to take such pleasure in being with them, he had only been pretending to be fond of them and had in his heart of hearts all the time been wanting to get away. They could not understand why, unless one was tired of people, one should want to separate oneself from them. On the day before his departure for the temple he was unusually restless, wandering continually from room to room of this house that he had never till now regarded as more than, a mere temporary refuge after the destruction of his city palace. But today he could see it only as the scene where would be enacted the events that his mind now brooded on with perpetual apprehension—the place where, after he was gone, Agemaki and Kozeri would cope unaided with all the difficulties of life.

---

* Their mother, who was dead.

With tears in his eyes and tremulous voice he recited his prayers, and then sent for the older members of the household. "I entrust Their Highnesses to your safekeeping," he said. "Remember that they are not of that walk of life in which the downfall of a family from one generation to another is so common a thing as to pass almost unperceived. Their position is very different. Quite apart from any regard for the good opinion of others they owe a solemn duty to the august line from which they spring. Remember then that what I commit to your charge is not merely the credit of your mistresses but also the fair name of a mighty house that has maintained its honor from generation to generation.

"I know well that your life here is not a gay one. It is however no worse than that of countless other people in your position, and you must content yourselves with the reflection that to carry out faithfully the duties that belong to one's station in life is the only way not merely to gain the good opinion of others, but also to keep one's own self-respect. Above all, do not in the hope of securing for yourselves and them a life less cut off from the common excitements and pleasures of the world, ever dream, I entreat you, of embarking on ambitious schemes which, if they end as they are only too likely to do, can bring nothing but dishonor upon those whose good name it is your duty to defend." It was arranged that he should start before dawn, and he now went once more to the sisters' room.

"When I am dead," he said, "you must try to keep up your spirits. There is no sense in giving way to sorrow. Devote yourselves to music, and things of that kind. Do not worry your heads about worldly affairs[*] which, life being what it is, one must take as they come and not expect them to happen as we ourselves should choose."

It was with an aching heart that he left them, and again and again he looked back longingly. In many long conversations that stretched far into the night the sisters tried to dispel the dismal forebodings that weighed upon them after the old Prince's departure. On one thing they were agreed: whatever happened, they must stick together. But the ways of the world are uncertain, and each at once imagined herself left solitary at Uji. The idea was hideous and they burst into tears. But a moment afterwards they were laughing at the absurdity of their own fancies. For not only did they share the same feelings about the deeper things of life, but they were also amused by the same trifling jokes, and so long as they were together time never seemed to hang heavy upon their hands.

On the evening when the Prince's course of devotions was supposed to end and the Princesses were expecting him back at any moment, a messenger arrived saying that His Highness was unwell, and that his

---

[*] I.e. love.

return had had to be postponed. "It began this morning," the man said. "We think it must be a cold and are treating it accordingly. But the worst thing about it is that he is worrying so at not being able to see Their Highnesses."

How serious was it? There was no means of telling; and in consternation the sisters at once dispatched piles of warm clothing and other comforts to the temple.

Days passed, and the Prince still did not arrive. Agemaki sent letter after letter to her father begging him to give more particulars about his disorder, but when at last an answer came it was only a verbal message to the effect that there was really not much wrong with him. It was a general feeling of discomfort, impossible to define. As soon as it passed off he would make an effort to get home. The Teacher was with him all the time. "Your illness," this holy man told him, "is not in itself of any great importance. But I think all the same that you are drawing near your end. You must now make an effort to put family matters entirely out of your head. It is time you realized that misery or good fortune will come to your daughters according to their *karma,* and that it is useless for you to worry about them."

He kept on constantly putting before the sick man the necessity of detaching his thoughts from material things and finally urged him to put out of his mind all idea of return to Uji.

It was the twentieth day of the eighth month, a time when the weather is always very depressing, and this year at Uji there was a thick mist which never cleared for a moment night or day. Suddenly however towards dawn the moon shone out brightly, darting its rays on the stream, and the Princesses were looking out over the river at a window on that side of the house when through the raised shutters came the faint tolling of a bell. "Can it be so late?"* they were wondering, when a messenger came running from the temple. "He died just before midnight," the man said, brushing the tears from his eyes. They had lived in constant expectation of this news for weeks past, and yet it came in the end with the shock of a complete surprise. Such sorrow as theirs seems in some strange way to dry up tears at their source. The sisters did not weep, but sat for a long while motionless, their faces buried in their hands.

They felt, naturally enough, that terrible though their loss was in any case, it would have been easier to bear if they could have been with him to the last. In their first bewilderment of grief it seemed to them indeed

---

* The morning bell was sounded at 3 A.M. What they heard was of course the "parting bell," tolled because it helped the dead man's spirit to cohere and solidify in the nebulous regions of the Intermediate State.

impossible that their existence could go on without him. But death, they began to realize when the first stupefying shock was over and tears came at last, would join them to him at its own good time. There might not be long to wait.

The Teacher, in fulfillment of a promise made many years before, undertook all the arrangements for the funeral. To the Princesses' request that they be allowed to look for a last time at their father's body, the holy man gave a discouraging reply. "I succeeded," he said, "in persuading him that it was for his good to cut himself off from you entirely in those last days, and you on your side must now lose no time in learning to do without him." They longed to hear more about their father's life at the temple and all that had happened during those last days. But the Teacher's accounts, full of moralizing and theology, seemed to them painfully inhuman, and certainly told them nothing of what they really wanted to know. It had indeed greatly distressed the pious man that Prince Hachi, having allowed his affection for his daughters to stand in the way of religion till the very end, should even on his death-bed have been so visibly preoccupied with this unsuitable worldly attachment.

It was with deep regret that Kaoru heard the news. He felt that with one more quiet long talk he could have come to an understanding about so many things that needed settling in a clearer way. The uncertainty of life appalled him, and he wept bitterly. Not that he had not been warned. Hachi himself had said that they would probably not meet again. But then he was always saying things of that kind, and Kaoru had paid no particular attention. It was a terrible blow. He at once wrote letters of condolence to the temple and to Uji. It was the only letter of the kind that the sisters had up to the present received, and distraught though they were they could not but be touched by this fresh sign of solicitude in one who had, they were bound to confess, been kindness itself for years past.

It is the way of the world for bereaved persons to regard their own loss as unique and to feel that they are entitled to give way to their grief to an extent that in others they would consider exaggerated. But here if ever (Kaoru thought) was a loss which it would require the very summit of fortitude to endure. There was little he could do. But he sent to the Teacher an ample supply of incense and other such things as he imagined would be needed for the funeral ceremonies and subsequent ritual, while to the old gentlewomen of the household he gave such presents as would enable them to pay for special prayers to be said.

Would the long night of their sorrow never end? Every day, now that the ninth month was come, the weather grew gloomier and wilder. Fallen leaves raced over the sodden ground, the stream roared, and all the while, as though the sisters too were possessed with the tempestuous spirit that swept the dripping countryside, their tears fell and fell.

"This," said the gentlewomen who were in charge of them, "will never do. If we cannot find some way to stop them they will, poor souls, have cried themselves into their own graves before the year is out."

But nothing availed. Services were held at Uji as well as at the temple, and one or two friends of the Prince who had occasionally come out to see him during his lifetime, now went into retreat in his chapel during the seven weeks of mourning, so that both here and on the mountain[*] prayer for the dead man's soul was going on without intermission.

From Niou messages of condolence and enquiry now kept continually arriving. But the princesses felt utterly incapable of answering them. He was certain that Kaoru was not treated in this way, and felt hurt that despite all his attentions to the household he himself should still be regarded as so very distant an acquaintance. He had meant to visit Uji at the season of red leaves, hoping to get material for a few Chinese poems that he had planned to write. But Prince Hachi's death, coming just at this moment, put a stop to all thoughts of such a visit, and the plan was reluctantly abandoned.

But the forty-nine days of prayer were now over, and imagining that the sisters must surely by now have somewhat recovered from the shock of their bereavement, he wrote a long and circumstantial letter.

"On such a night as this when tears trickle from the flowers and the young deer cry in the cold, how fares it with you, tell me—at autumn, in your mountain home?" Such was his poem (for it was a rainy night) and in the letter that accompanied it: "Surely on such an evening it would be harsh indeed once more to deny me all recognition of my solitude! Must I gaze across these sodden fields with no hope of a word to rouse me from my despondence?"

"It does indeed seem very rude to let him go on writing like this," said Agemaki to her sister. "I think you had better make an effort to reply."

How strange it was to be sitting down once more to write! Kozeri began to count the days, and this brought back the tears into her eyes. She pushed the ink-stone away. "It's no use," she said. "I thought I was beginning to be able to do things again. But when it comes to this, I simply haven't the heart..." and she burst into such pitiful weeping that Agemaki felt she could not pursue the matter.

Niou's messenger had started from the city late in the evening and it was already night when he arrived. "He had better wait here till tomorrow morning," Agemaki said. But it appeared that the man had instructions to bring back an answer immediately. Under these circumstances Agemaki—not that she herself felt any more in the mood for such an effort than did Kozeri, but something had to be done—took the task

---

[*] At the temple.

upon herself: "Behind a screen of tears that cuts the mountain village from their sight, as with one voice the mournful deer lament."

The poem was written on dark paper* by a dim light. There could be no question of producing anything in the way of fine calligraphy, and she dashed off these few lines, folded the paper and conveyed it immediately to the messenger.

The path over Mount Kohata, particularly during a storm, at dead of night, is not without its terrors. But this was a stout fellow who had been chosen because it was known that he would ride full tilt in the dark through any thicket or tangle, and soaked to the skin he was back at the city in no time. Niou gave him a handsome reward, and hastened to scan the paper he had brought. He saw at once that the handwriting was not that of the notes he had previously received. He thought it was a more formed hand and probably that of an older person. But as he had imagined the previous notes to be penned by Agemaki, he was inclined, despite appearances, to regard the present poem as the work of her sister. He puzzled over the question so long, just when the waiting-women who looked after him were hoping he would at last go to bed, that they began to lose patience. "First he said he must sit up because he was waiting for an answer," they grumbled, "and now that it has come, he seems as if he were going to sit staring at it for the rest of the night. It's something serious this time, that's quite clear." And no wonder they were in a bad temper, for they were all longing for bed.

He rose early next morning. "Can I with common pity hear its cry— the deer whose friend the baleful mists enfold?"

In his letter too he described himself as prostrate with grief. Agemaki felt that the correspondence had reached a point at which great caution was required, if tiresome consequences were not to ensue. Hitherto she had always been able in the last resort to appeal to her father for advice when things were threatening to take an undesirable turn. But now she felt that it was dangerous to let matters go even so far as to require delicate handling. Moreover it was concerning the risk of just such entanglements as this that her father had particularly warned her, and if anything were to go wrong, it would seem in a way like an insult to his memory. These considerations embarrassed her so much that she did not succeed in answering at all. But it must not be thought that she put Niou on a par with the common ruck of young courtiers, with their stock of insincere compliments. Both the calligraphy and the diction of the notes that he hurriedly tossed off made a deep impression upon her, partly because her experience in this direction was very small. This however only increased her difficulties; for she felt that the particular tone

---

* Grey paper used for mourning.

of well-bred gallantry and concern in which his letters were couched was one she was totally incapable of imitating. No, it was no use. A hermit* she had been brought up and a hermit she would remain. With Kaoru however it was fortunately not so difficult to deal. He really seemed to mean what he said, and she no longer found any difficulty in writing to him. As soon as the forty-nine days were over, he hastened to Uji. He found the sisters in the deepest mourning and seated not on the dais but on the lower level of the room.†

His presence, like a sudden light flashing upon the darkness of their bereavement, at first bewildered and blinded them. "I am afraid," he said, finding them completely tongue-tied, "that if our conversations are to be so very one-sided it will be difficult for me to help you in the way your father intended. I am quite unused to the sort of situations in which everything has to go round by way of a third party. Indeed if I am not directly addressing the person for whom my remarks are intended I become completely incoherent."

"I think you do not realize, seeing us sitting here," said Agemaki, "how little we have yet managed to shake off the first terrible impressions of our loss. One surely cannot be expected to converse sensibly and freely with people from outside when one is in this dazed condition?" "I know," said Kaoru, "how deeply you feel things and did not for a moment suppose that I should find you going about and doing things as though nothing had happened. That clearly would be wrong. But I am very sorry your feelings compel you to cut yourself off so completely from me, for I came hoping that some at any rate of your difficulties were of a kind which it would be really worth while confiding to me. But if you are certain that I can be of no use..." "However bad you may be feeling, Madam," Agemaki's gentlewomen said, "you must try to be more open with him, for it is clear he really wants to be of use." So they coaxed her; and gradually, as she became less agitated and was able to reflect a little on the situation in general, she saw that quite apart from any interest Kaoru might feel in herself and her sister, it was after all in obedience to their father's wishes that he was paying this visit. It was a long way to come! And feeling that she had been rather ungracious, she moved a little nearer, while Kaoru discussed with the utmost delicacy and consideration both the difficulties of her present situation and the best means of performing the friendly offices with which her father had entrusted him. There was in his manner a gentleness that was almost feminine, and she found that she slipped easily enough into confiding in him without any of the embarrassment that she would at present have felt in the case of an

---
* A *yamabushi*, a particularly *farouche* type of mountain ascetic.
† As a sign of mourning.

ordinary visitor. But he saw that the effort to speak to anyone from outside and to appear interested and hopeful were costing her dear. Painful recollections, it was only too evident, were crowding upon her at every turn of the conversation, and it was clear that she was still in far too distracted a condition to give him more than a very small part of her attention. He could not help contrasting the figure that he now dimly descried disconsolately huddled behind the black mourning-curtains with that first moonlit vision years ago, at dawn. "Sad when at autumn's close the woods and fields their darkened dress put on!" He murmured the verse to himself, not meaning her to hear.

"Happier the autumn fields, on which the dew of Heaven still falls, than we who for our tears no resting-place can ever hope to know."* "The frayed threads..." she began, but her voice died away, and if she now stole back to the far side of the room, it was not in unfriendliness, but merely that she could control herself no longer. He saw that for the moment it would be cruel to detain her, and reluctantly he allowed the ever-willing Ben no Kimi to take her place. The old woman certainly had a wonderful collection of strange and moving tales, both old and new. Moreover he could not forget that but for her he would never have discovered the one thing that it concerned him most to know, and old though she was he had become extraordinarily attached to her.

"Genji's death," he said to her presently, "happening when I was a mere child made—I now think in looking back upon it—a disastrous impression upon me. I grew up feeling that nothing was stable, nothing worth while, and though in course of time I have risen to a fairly high position in the State and have even managed to win for myself a certain degree of celebrity, these things mean nothing to me. I would much rather have spent my time in some such quiet place as this. And now Prince Hachi's death has made it less possible for me than ever to seek satisfaction in the ordinary pleasures of the world. To say that it is on the Princesses' account that I still put off taking my Vows might give a wrong impression. But the delay really is connected with them, for as you know I am bound by promises to their father which at present make it impossible for me to follow my own inclinations. But above all of course the terrible thing you told me now makes it imperative that I should sever myself from the world at the very earliest moment I get the chance." He wept as he spoke, and she too was in no condition to reply; for Kaoru's extraordinary resemblance to her late master brought back at every turn some forgotten incident of those terrible days, and she was completely overcome.

This old woman, Ben no Kimi, was, as has been said of, a better class than ordinary waiting-women, her father Sachuben having been the uncle

---

* There is a play of words on various senses of *oku*, "to settle."

of the Princesses' mother. It was indeed because of her unusual capability and good sense that Prince Hachi had taken pains to secure her. Though she had lived for years in the closest possible contact with the Princesses—Prince Hachi had got her there principally that the two girls might have an older person to appeal to—and was on very intimate terms with them, concerning her previous place she was scrupulously careful never to utter a word. But Kaoru, knowing that old people often chatter more than they should, could not help feeling rather apprehensive. He was sure she would not have gossiped about the secret to all and sundry. But it seemed almost inconceivable that she had not said something to the Princesses, on whose discretion she would no doubt feel that she could completely rely. And, though he was not aware of it, probably the fear that with the departure of either of the Princesses from Uji his secret too would go beyond his control made him additionally reluctant to take any definite steps about their future.

There seemed no longer any particular point in staying for the night,* and he now started back towards the city. But all the way home there ran in his head the sound of Prince Hachi's voice, telling him that this might be their last meeting. Why had he not heeded the warning? He should have kept in touch, visited the Prince more regularly. There was so much that they had both left unsaid. And when one came to think of it, though it seemed now an interminable time since he heard that Hachi was dead, it was only a matter of days. Around him, as he rode, was autumn—the same autumn. It seemed unbelievable that Hachi should now be none knew where, while in his quarters—which though they had always been very scantily furnished and utterly devoid of the ornaments and knick-knacks with which ordinary people surround themselves were always scrupulously clean and well kept—priests were tramping in and out, and even knocking up temporary partitions,† so that the whole place was in a state of litter and disorder. His rosaries, books and so on, were being left as they were. But Agemaki had heard that all the sacred images were to be transferred to the temple. For the moment the presence of all these holy men gave a kind of spurious air of animation to the house. But once they were gone it would be, thought Kaoru, a terrible place to go on living in.

One of his men now came and reminded him that it was getting very late. He roused himself from his reverie and turned to go. Just as he was starting a wild goose flew crying overhead.

"So desolate the place that even in the high country of the autumn clouds the wild goose passes with a cry."

---

* He used to pass the night reading texts with the old Prince.
† To use as cells while they were in residence performing masses for the dead.

Whenever Kaoru was with Niou their conversation turned upon the household at Uji. Niou had mistakenly assumed that Prince Hachi's death would make the sisters much easier of access, and he had again begun to write constantly to Uji. But the sisters found it more than ever difficult to frame even the barest acknowledgment; for Niou was at this time continually being quoted as the great connoisseur of elegant and tender correspondences. How he had got it into his head that, buried away as they had been, either their poetical conceits or their handwriting could possibly come up to the standard they did not know. But in any case the mere sight of his notes made them at once feel stupid and behind-the-times.

So the days at Uji passed sadly but uneventfully by. The uncertainty of life and the need to be prepared against it had indeed been a constant topic in their father's conversation. But familiar though his maxims had become, the sisters accepted them as general laws of the world, merely implying that nothing can go on indefinitely; and the actual situation in which they now found themselves was one which during his lifetime they had never really contemplated.

When they looked back on the past it seemed to them that, comfortless though it had in many ways been, their life had about it at least an agreeable quietness and sense of security. But now they seemed to live in a constant state of panic and humiliation. "It is ridiculous," Agemaki said, "a sudden gust of wind, or the sound of someone arriving at the door, if the attendants' voices are unfamiliar to me, is enough to put me into a state of the most appalling agitation." And both of them agreed that these sudden fits of terror were at the slightest provocation constantly overcoming them. The loneliness of their life was indeed becoming almost intolerable.

And so, with tears seldom far away, they saw the year draw to its close. There were heavy storms of hail and snow. The weather was indeed no worse at Uji than elsewhere. But the sisters, for the first time since they had lived there, felt that it was a terrible affliction to be in the depth of the country at this stormy season. Their waiting-women had great hopes that the coming of the New Year would make things better. "The Spring," they said, "always helps people in trouble to make a fresh start." But the Princesses could not feel that a turn of the calendar was going to improve matters.

In old days there had been a good deal of going and coming between Hachi's house and the temple, for during his Retreats he had made the acquaintance of a good many priests. But now even the Teacher no longer came in person, but contented himself with a brief occasional letter of enquiry.

That these old acquaintances of their father's should not continue their visits was natural and inevitable, as the Princesses realized. But it meant a complete absence of company or news from outside such as was very difficult to endure. Since their father's death indeed even the occasional appearance at the house of uncouth country people, whose presence they would in old days scarcely have noticed, became an exciting event. Now and again some peasant would come with firewood or such wild fruits as happened to be in season, or someone would come from the Teacher with a present of charcoal or the like, for the holy man feared that the Princesses would feel hurt if he discontinued these small offerings that he had been in the habit of making for many years past; and they on their side remembered the wadded clothing and other comforts that the Prince always sent at this time of year, to help the Teacher through the rigors of his winter retreat.

They stood at the window watching the little band from the temple—some priests and an acolyte or two—struggling through the deep snow with their cumbrous burden, now vanishing, now reappearing at some turn in the path that wound up the hill. "Of course, even if father had lived," said Agemaki, with tears in her eyes, "he would sooner or later have become a priest. But even then he would not have been far off. Messengers would have been going between here and the temple all the time, and perhaps—though indeed it would have been a sad sort of meeting—we should sometimes have been allowed to see him."

Kaoru knew that once the New Year set in he would be too busy to get away, and despite the bad condition of the roads he determined to visit Uji before the end of the month. The snow had indeed been so heavy as to put a stop to traffic of every kind, and that anyone in Kaoru's position should so lightly have embarked on it was really—the Princesses were bound to admit—extremely flattering, and they took great trouble to receive him in a way that would show their gratitude, even going so far as to rout out from the store-cupboards a brazier that had not been painted black.* There was indeed such a polishing and sweeping as had not, everyone said, attended Kaoru's arrival since the old Prince's days.

The preparations then left nothing to be desired. For the interview itself Agemaki felt very little inclination. "But when people are so extravagantly kind, what can one do?" she said, and though still far from being at ease with him, she was certainly much more communicative than she had ever been before. So attractive indeed, once she began to talk more freely, did he find her great range and delicacy of feeling that he began to wonder whether it was after all going to be so easy a matter to carry out the task of renunciation that he had so lightly set himself to perform. Strange that one's whole attitude towards life could change so radically from one moment to another; yet that such might be the case, experience had taught him on more than one occasion before.

---

* In sign of mourning.

"Niou is very cross with me," he said. "Somehow or other—possibly owing to some hint that I inadvertently let drop or merely by a lucky guess of his own, for he has such a quick mind that it is never much use trying to keep things from him—he has managed to find out about my promise to your father.[*] He assumes that under the circumstances I must certainly have a great influence over you and that your present discouraging attitude towards him is entirely due to me. You must surely admit that I was far indeed from forcing his society upon you. Circumstances arose in which I was obliged to bring him here; but now that it has happened, it is most unfair on me that you should treat him as you do. People, I am told, make out that he is dissipated. But underneath all that he has an unusually solid character; indeed I know of few people capable of such deep and lasting emotion. There may of course be cases—I have heard of some myself—where he may seem to have behaved badly. But this has only happened where it was clearly understood that both sides were merely amusing themselves, and the conduct of the women involved has always from the outset been of a kind so utterly frivolous and irresponsible as to deprive them of any claim to be treated with a delicate or scrupulous consideration. He is however the sort of man who if a woman took things as they came, did not set herself and her reputation on a pinnacle, was broad-minded and willing to take the world as she found it, overlooking casual short-comings here and there and accepting a certain number of unpleasantnesses as inevitable in any relationship—to such a woman I believe Niou might show a most uncommon degree of fidelity. Too often however a woman will allow one crumble in the cliffs of Tatsuta River to mar love's whole stream.[†] But to a sensible woman, capable of the sort of tolerance I have described, Niou would, I am certain, if he had once evinced a strong affection for her, remain devoted to the end. I believe, as a matter of fact, that there is no one who understands his character better than I do, and if what I have told you makes you feel that you would like to know him better, my services are completely at your disposal. Try me in this new capacity of a go-between, and you will find that the energy with which I throw myself into the task will surprise you."

The offer seemed to be made in all seriousness. Agemaki's only difficulty was to frame her reply in such a way as to make clear that the proposal concerned her only in her capacity of elder sister and adviser. "Up till now we had been getting on much better, hadn't we?" she said. "But at this point the conversation seems to be taking a turn which makes it more difficult for me than ever to think out a reply..."

---

[*] To look after the sisters.

[†] The ferruginous soil of the cliffs reddens the whole stream when there it anything in the nature of a landslide.

She spoke quietly but with a faint suggestion of mockery that he found very attractive.

"Nothing in the least difficult is expected of you," Kaoru said. "All I hope for is a word or two of gratitude, to which I think I can justly lay claim after coming all this way through the snow. It is in your sister Kozeri that Niou is interested, as indeed he has always hinted in his poems and letters; though under the circumstances it was not very easy for him to make this clear. I do not know, by the way, which of you has been in the habit of writing the replies?" Fortunately for Agemaki she had as a matter of fact never herself written more than a word or two. But the thought of how easily she might have chanced to do so and might, without the least intending it, have given Niou the impression that she took his advances as addressed to herself, now covered her with such confusion that she could not bring herself to reply. On a piece of paper however she wrote the poem: "Look on the snow-clad hills and you will find no track that leads to other gate save yours,"* and handed it out to him from behind her screen.

"That is a poor excuse," he said. "Indeed, your treatment of Niou is a sign of unfriendliness to me rather than the reverse. "Over the ice-bound river that splinters under my horse's hoofs how dare I send others, till I myself have crossed?"† That much encouragement I can at least lay claim to, if I am to throw myself with full energy into my task."

She had not expected this sort of thing from him, nor was it at all to her taste, and she did not reply. This however did not surprise him. It would have been strange indeed, considering her upbringing, if she could have thrown herself at once into the business of pretty speeches and poetical rejoinders so aptly cultivated by the young people of the day. It was enough for the moment that she was not definitely hostile or discouraging. He had formed his conception of her character and would have been disappointed if, even to his advantage, she had behaved at variance with it. After several further attempts to bring the conversation round to the subject of his own feelings towards her—attempts which Agemaki was careful completely to ignore—he suddenly began to feel rather ashamed of himself, and in the end fell back upon harmless anecdotes and reminiscences. "It is snowing so hard," one of his men presently announced, "that if we wait till dark we shall certainly lose our way."

"I cannot bear to think of Their Highnesses living out here under such conditions as this," Kaoru said, as he went out. "There are parts of my mother's palace that are just as quiet and unfrequented as it is here, and

---

* I write to no one but you.

† Kaoru hints that it would be only fair if Agemaki encouraged him by a little kindness on her part, before expecting him to interest himself on Kozen's behalf.

if Their Highnesses ever cared to honor us with a visit..." The offer was overheard by some of the waiting-women, who were naturally enchanted at the idea of getting their noses into so resplendent a place as Nyosan's palace. Agemaki was out of earshot. But Kozeri, who was sitting with these gentlewomen, caught the remark, and remembering her father's warning* instantly made up her mind on no account to let herself be lured by any such proposal.

Orders were given that Kaoru's fruit was to be served as daintily as possible in the men's quarters, and a special supply of dried fish was sent for his followers, along with the great earthenware wine-flagon. The watchman to whom Kaoru had given his cloak was standing about, with a peculiarly helpless expression on his rustic, heavily whiskered† face. It was disquieting to think that the safety of the Princesses depended on so wretched a creature. Kaoru called the man to him and asked how he was getting on now that he was left to his own devices. "Why, sir," he said, "I spent thirty years of my life in his service and had not another friend in all the world. Believe me, if I was to go out beyond these gates today there isn't, as the saying goes, so much as a tree that would hold its branches over me." While he spoke his face underwent the strangest contortions and the tears streamed down. He did indeed present a most distressing spectacle.

Before leaving, Kaoru sent for the key of the late Prince's apartments. The Buddha's splendor was still untarnished, but dust lay deep on the floors. The main piece of furniture was a low couch, of the kind used for the practice of religious exercises. He had this shifted, and got his men to give the whole place a good sweeping. As he stood by, superintending this work, there came into his mind the occasion when he had told the Prince of his desire to become a priest and promised that, when he did so, Hachi should be his Master.

"Alas that of the oak-tree under whose spreading boughs I thought to take my rest nothing should be left now save a bare and empty bed!"‡

He stood leaning against a pillar as he recited this verse, in an attitude which filled the younger maids, who could just see him from their room, with deep admiration.

---

* Not to leave Uji.

† *Kazura-hige,* "Wig-whiskers" an expression that has puzzled all the commentators, is surely an abbreviation of *Takazura-hige,* "hair on the upper part of the face" as opposed to the chin (cf. *Uji Shui Monogatari. Bungaku Taikei* X, 239). The upper classes wore only slight "imperials" on the point of the chin.

‡ Prince Hachi was an *upasaka* or lay-brother, and an old folk-song says, "Alas for the *upasakas* who do penance in the hills; for under the oak they lie and the hard earth is their bed." For the correct text of this folk-song, see *Utsubo Monogatari,* chapters "Kiku no En" and "Saga no In." It does not, as the commentators state, occur in the "Kokin Rokujo" (at any rate as we possess the work), and the last word should be *araneba,* not *aranedo.*

It was so late that Kaoru's men, not at all certain that he did not intend to stay the night, had on their own initiative sent for fresh supplies of horse-fodder, which were easy to procure, for he happened to have several properties in the neighborhood. The news that Kaoru was at Uji had thus spread over the countryside, and to his embarrassment on leaving the house he found himself gaped at by a curious crowd of laborers and peasants.

He preferred it to be thought that his business at Uji was with the older gentlewomen of the household, and in order to give this impression he now sent for one of them and engaged her in conversation. He then addressed the country people, begging them to serve the Princesses and their household with the same alacrity that they had shown in coming to welcome him today.

After the New Year milder weather set in, the ice disappeared from the garden lakes, and the sisters began to realize that despite all their misery they had struggled through to another spring. From the Teacher's cell came a present of wild parsley, rock-fern, and other green things that were springing up from the wintry earth. He hoped they would be a welcome addition to the Princesses' meager* diet, and the gentlewomen of the household remarked that, if one lived in such a place, it was pleasant from time to time to set eyes on things like this, which at least helped one to keep count of the days and months as they passed.

To the Princesses, however, such reminders seemed merely painful.

"Were he still dwelling on the hilltop whence these fern shoots came, I could believe that spring was here." Such was Agemaki's poem. And Kozeri's: "The young parsley that on the snowy margins of the pool wakes to fresh life, for whom now shall we cull?" Often they would compose verses of this sort, which trivial though they were, at least helped the long hours to pass.

New Year letters came punctually both from Kaoru and Niou, but they contained nothing of consequence and it is not necessary to trouble you with them. Niou remembered, when the cherry-trees came into bloom, how last year he had sent the sisters a wreath to wear, and all the lords and gentlemen who were with him on that occasion recalled with pleasure their reception at Prince Hachi's hands and regretted that they had not been to Uji again. Niou indeed was extremely anxious to make further progress in this direction, and sent the poem: "This year my garland shall it be, the cherry-blossom that in days gone by through veil of spring I spied." While not wishing to seem actually to encourage him Kozeri was anxious to keep up at any rate a reasonable-semblance of good manners. Moreover the poem came at a moment when time was hanging particu-

---

* Fasting went hand in hand with mourning.

larly heavy on her hands, and it was evident that he had taken great pains with the handwriting. "Where, since a cloud of mourning hangs dark upon our house, would you pluck gay cherry for your wreath?"

Niou had expected something a great deal more forthcoming than this, and was very disappointed. His disappointment was indeed more than he could keep to himself, and the only possible confidant was Kaoru, whom he still upbraided as the person really responsible for his difficulties. This under the circumstances was rather comic. But Kaoru did not reveal the fact that he had been interesting himself on his friend's behalf. On the contrary, he played to perfection the part of a crusty guardian, rebuking Niou whenever his imagination seemed to be running ahead too fast with regard to his chances at Uji, so that Niou found it necessary to protest: "I know you think I am not to be trusted," he said. "And it is true that I have had rather a large number of affairs. But that, I assure you, was only because I had never found anyone that really attracted me." He was in trouble at the moment with Yugiri because he refused to be interested in Roku no Kimi, Yugiri's sixth daughter. "It is not only that the match itself has no particular attraction for me," Niou privately explained to his friends. "But the prospect of having His Excellency* always fussing round to see whether I am behaving myself is really more than I can face."

Early that summer there was a fire at Nyosan's palace in the Third Ward. Kaoru was obliged to move his mother into the New Palace† in the Sixth Ward, which involved making a great many arrangements, and what with one thing and another he found himself for weeks on end unable to get away from the City. This however did not worry him. He had made up his mind to let things at Uji take their course. It was not in his nature to force his attentions on anyone who seemed to hold back. Agemaki was virtually his; of this he felt sure. But at present she was not in the mood for that kind of thing, and undoubtedly the best way to win her confidence was to convince her that he was bent on serving the household at Uji in the spirit of her father's dying behest. As the summer went on the heat became almost unendurable. The thought of the cool breeze that always blew up from the river suddenly decided him to put all business aside. He started for Uji very early in the morning. But even at this hour he found the sun overpowering by the time he arrived, and was glad to rest for a while in the western side-room, where Hachi used to have his quarters. He had one or two matters to discuss with the night-watchman, and asked someone to send the man to him. The sisters had been at prayer in the chapel. But on being told of Kaoru's arrival they moved to their own rooms at the back of the house. They tried to make as little noise

---

* Yugiri.
† Built by Genji.

as possible, but the chapel opened out of the room where Kaoru was sitting, and he was bound to hear them leave. He remembered noticing that there was a small chink in the sliding-door that led from the main hall into the women's apartments—the hole through which the latch went had split a little at the sides. He tiptoed to the spot, but though there was as yet no noise of footsteps and he knew that he was in good time, he found that a screen had been put against the door on the outer side. He lifted it away, only to discover that a curtained couch was standing right against the door on the inside. He was just turning away in disappointment, when a voice from inside said: "Just look at those window-blinds! People can see right in. Push that couch over here. It's no good where it is, and it will help to keep the blinds in place." Evidently a gust of wind had blown back the blinds of the windows that looked onto the garden. "Thank you!" said Kaoru to himself, and returning to his post found that two curtained couches, a large and a smaller one, had been moved from the door and set up against the blinds of the two windows at the side of the room. Opposite to Kaoru's door was another, through which as he knew the sisters must presently emerge. And indeed at that instant a figure appeared, but turned instantly towards one of the couches by the window, and reclining there began to watch Kaoru's men, who were walking up and down enjoying the cool of the garden. This, he knew, must be Kozeri. She was in an unlined dress of dark grey-brown, that was pleasantly set off by her wide sedge-colored trousers. Some people are born to wear mourning—so far from being disfigured by it they look more radiant than ever, and it seemed that Kozeri was one of these. Her long sash was hitched up and in its folds her rosary lay tucked. She was unusually tall but had, he saw, an extremely well-proportioned figure. Her hair, which must, he thought, reach well below her knees, was smooth and glossy, and though rather thick seemed to be of a lovely quality and texture. Her profile was good, and her movements singularly graceful and deliberate. Niou's sister, the First Princess, to whom he had been rather attracted when they were both children, must, he thought, have grown up to be very like this. Another figure, evidently that of Agemaki, was now visible in the room. "That door ought not to be left uncovered," she said, looking nervously in Kaoru's direction. "Oh, that's all right," one of the maids replied. "There is a screen on the other side. Anyone would have to take that away first before he could see in." "Are you sure?" Agemaki asked, only half-reassured. "There is nothing so disagreeable as the feeling that one may be being watched"; and as she retreated to the screened couch, casting watchful glances as she went, he thought he had never seen a bearing that indicated such sensibility, such passionate pride.

Though she wore a dark, lined cloak, the general color-scheme of her costume was the same as that of her sister's. But in her he found it infinitely more attractive, and his sympathies* were moved to a point that was positively disquieting.

Her hair, which she had evidently plucked in sign of mourning, looked a little thin at the ends, but it was of a marvelous quality, having in it that slight kingfisher tint which he always found so enchanting, and it hung straight and rather stiff on her back, like the threads in a loom. In one hand she held a Buddhist book, the characters of which were written on purple paper. He was able to study this hand and was struck by its extreme fragility. She was certainly much thinner than Kozeri, in fact rather alarmingly emaciated. At this moment something happened in the room which made the younger sister look straight towards him. And it was evidently something amusing, for there was a smile on her face. Yes, certainly she too was in her way very attractive.

---

* *Aware* implies both sympathy and admiration.

Agemaki

Never in all their many autumns at Uji had the wailing of the river wind struck such a chill into the hearts of the sisters as this year while they hurried forward the preparations for the Anniversary.* The general form that the ceremonies were to take was decided by Kaoru and the Teacher. But for their help the Princesses would have been entirely at a loss, there were so many questions concerning the setting out of the sacred books, the correct use of sacerdotal robes and innumerable other points of ritual that had to be settled. It was indeed a fortunate accident that such excellent advisers were at hand. Kaoru called from time to time, and on the day when their full mourning came to a close he wrote in the kindest and most solicitous manner; while the Teacher called in person.

On one occasion during the preparations for the Anniversary, Kaoru arrived when the sisters were plaiting scented tassels,† and murmuring the words of the old poem "Could life's thread..."‡ Part of the wooden frame on which they were doing their plaiting was visible through a tear in their screen-of-state. He guessed at once what they were making and in his turn murmured the verse: "Would that my tears were pearls that I could thread..."§ Lady Ise herself could not have put more feeling when she first recited them—so everyone else thought. But the Princesses, faced with the necessity of finding a quotation which fitted in with the circumstances of the moment and at the same time showed that they had recognized Kaoru's allusion, were sorely perplexed. Tsurayuki's "Were you like a thing on a thread..." occurred to them, and it was appropriate in that it carried on the same conjunction of sorrow with weaving. But it referred to a living person and was therefore wholly unsuitable on the present occasion. Unsuccessful though they were in finding a verse that would do, they realized now, as never before, how helpful this business of *furukoto*¶ might be as a means of giving vent to one's feelings.

Kaoru had been writing the drafts of some Buddhist inscriptions that were needed in connection with an offering of Scriptures and sacred

---

* Of their father's death.

† For the four corners of the altar.

‡ "Could life's thread by sorrowful thoughts be snapped, I had not woven this trailing strip of years upon its loom."

§ From a poem written in 907 by Lady Ise, on the death of her mistress, the Empress Atsuko.

¶ "Old words," allusions to ancient poems.

images that he was making in the late Prince's memory. His inkstand still lay by him, and taking up his brush he now wrote: "Would that like the threads of the tassel, that once lay apart but now forever are joined, we too might be united in the bond of steadfast love!" and handed the poem through the curtains.

"Why should he find it necessary to affect sentiments of this kind?" Agemaki wondered. "Too bitter and too many are my tears to string on love's short thread..." Such was her answering poem. "On what thread am I to string my days?" he thought dejectedly, recalling another ancient poem.[*] But he was determined not to importune her with unwelcome advances, and seeing that she still gave him no encouragement, he turned the conversation to the topic of Niou. "You may think it strange," he said, "that on the strength of a single visit Niou should have fallen so deeply in love. But whether this is due to the exceptional impressionability of his character or to the strong emotions that are often aroused by opposition to one's desires, I cannot say. Certain however it is that the attachment he has formed for your sister is of the deepest kind and you may forward his suit without the slightest misgiving. You are not, I can see, so ignorant of the usages of the world but that you could find ways of encouraging him, if you wished to do so. And you must surely realize that your failure to do this is not merely impolite to him but shows a rather ungrateful attitude towards me, considering all the trouble I have taken to be of use to you. In any case, I think you might make some attempt to give me a clearer idea of what your real views are in the matter."

"There can be no question of ingratitude," she said. "Indeed, it is only in recognition of all you having done that we have allowed you what is, I would have you remember, an unparalleled degree of liberty in this house. The fact that you take these privileges as a matter of course seems to me to show on your side a rather curious lack of perception.

"You will say that living here with nothing to do all day my sister and I have at least had time to consider the question of our future. But we ourselves are, as you know, completely incompetent to decide about such matters, and our father, though before his death he left us instructions how to deal with all sorts of contingencies, and was in a general way clearly much preoccupied with the question of what was to become of us, gave no indication whatever as to how we were to deal with such an offer as you have just transmitted. Indeed, we both have the impression that he meant us simply to go on living in the old way. But I realize that particularly for my sister, who still has all her youth before her, it is a thousand pities to remain buried away in this desolate corner of the hills,

---

[*] "If like the side-threads of the loom we are to be forever apart, on what thread am I to string my days?"

and though I have not hitherto said much about it, I feel as strongly as you do the necessity of getting her away. But how it ought to be done, I have not the least idea." And she sighed with an air so troubled and perplexed that he longed to comfort her. But clear-headed and sensible though she evidently was, it was hardly to be expected that at her age she should feel capable of taking the responsibility in such a matter, and going to the outer rooms he sent for the old lady, Ben no Kimi.

"As you know," he said, "I came here originally as Prince Hachi's pupil, and for years I knew nothing about the rest of his family. But when he began to feel that his health was failing, he became anxious that I should be on friendly terms with the Princesses and made me promise to do all I could to help them, leaving it entirely to me to decide what form this help should take. Unfortunately they seem to have made up their minds to do everything in their power to prevent me from carrying out their father's request, and I am even beginning seriously to wonder whether they have not, without consulting me, committed themselves in some quite unsuspected direction. As you probably know, I am so constituted that my feelings do not easily run away with me—which under the circumstances is providential, for most people would have found the situation as it has existed up to the present a quite impossible one. Gossip has of course already begun to link my name with theirs, and if I am ever to marry at all, there would surely be something to be said for such a match. It would certainly be the simplest way of carrying out Prince Hachi's desires, and though I am not of course their equal in birth, even taking me for what I am, there would be nothing unprecedented in such a marriage."

Had Ben no Kimi been of the class from which waiting-women are ordinarily drawn, he would have got nothing from her but a mixture of cringing compliments with impertinent and meddlesome advice. But Ben was a woman of a very different kind, and though she longed for nothing so much as to see one or other of the Princesses wedded to Kaoru, she merely said: "I suppose it comes of their living such a strange life here—but however that may be I can truthfully say that I have never known them once betray the slightest interest of a sentimental kind in any outside person; so that on that score you need not have the slightest anxiety. But as to their going on living as they do now—even we servants began years ago to feel that we were stranded here without any prospects at all, and those of us that had any ambition drifted off to find better places elsewhere. Many of those that went had been connected with the family for generations, and if even consideration for Prince Hachi did not hold them back, it is not likely that in the future we shall be able to keep anything of a household together. The waiting-maids can understand that Prince Hachi had old-fashioned ideas and that while he was alive it was impossible for our mistresses to consider a match with anyone of a different rank in society; but in the present circumstances they are free to marry anyone in the world that takes their fancy, and no one in his senses will think the worse of them. They cannot, whatever happens, go on living in their present way, nor ought they to expect anyone else to. Why, even among the holy hermits of the mountain dispensations prevail, and something more than the dew of a pine-leaf is permitted when one of them is in danger of actual collapse. And what is more, those for whom a discipline is too strict may, while remaining good Buddhists, go off and found a sect of their own. Such threats and criticisms are constantly reaching the Princesses' ears, and I can see that they are very much upset. Agemaki herself seems to have no intention of giving way, but I feel certain that she is now very anxious to find an escape for Kozeri. She is, I know, deeply grateful to you for your constant visits and all the kindness that you have shown them in years past, and would be very sorry to lose the benefit of your help and advice; so that what she would really like is that *you* should marry Kozeri. Despite all his poems and letters she does not think that Niou can be taken very seriously."

"There is no question," answered Kaoru, "of my interest in Their Highnesses ever ceasing, come what may. My promise to their father alone suffices to make such a thing impossible. That Agemaki should have sufficient confidence in me to desire me as a husband for her sister is of course very gratifying; but it implies that it is a matter of complete indifference to me which of them I marry, and that is far indeed from being the case. It is Agemaki alone who attracts me, and it is the hope of one day winning her affection that has for the moment reconciled me to a world which, as you know, I was on the very point of abandoning. Convenient though this might be, I fear I cannot adjust my feelings so easily as she supposes.

"It is not however love in the ordinary sense of the word for which I ask. What I long so passionately for and have never been able to find is someone to whom I could speak freely and openly about whatever came into my head, however trivial or however secret and intimate the thing might be—it comes perhaps of never having had brothers and sisters or anyone with whom I stood on that sort of footing. I have been terribly lonely—all my sorrows, joys, enthusiasms have been locked up inside me, and if at the present moment my greatest craving is simply for someone to share my life with, to talk to, and to be near—is that so very unnatural? There is of course the Empress,[*] who is supposed to be my sister. But with a person in that position it is impossible ever to be really at ease. One sees her only for a few minutes at a time and in so ceremonious and

---

[*] The Akashi Princess, who was Genji's daughter, and therefore theoretically Kaoru's sister.

formal a way that it would be out of place to trouble her with anything so trivial as one's own feelings and affairs. My mother indeed seems so extraordinarily young that one is inclined to regard her as belonging to one's own generation. But she leads a life apart,* and I do not feel that I can ever have any real intimacy with her. As for the other women with whom I have come in contact—one and all they have inspired a sort of horror in me, and though I just now complained of being lonely, I realize quite well that it is I who am chiefly to blame; for at the slightest sign of advance on the part of others, I instantly run away. Even at the ordinary jokes and repartees of casual intercourse I am excessively awkward and incompetent, directly they take at all an amatory turn; and when it comes to really deep feelings, such as mine towards Agemaki, I find it absolutely impossible to express myself. It is very stupid, I know; but a sudden wave of shame overcomes me and I drop the subject. The result is that she has not the least conception of all that I am suffering.

"But as to my plan about Niou—she must surely see that I have no motive but her sister's good, and I hope she will not go so far as actually to impede it."

As far as the old lady was concerned, on every ground—it might even bring a little brightness into her own life—nothing would have pleased her better than to see Agemaki married to Kaoru. But it seemed to her that when two people were both so outrageously sensitive and difficult, it was better to interfere as little as possible.

He hung about all day, doing nothing in particular. In the evening, he hoped, there would be a chance for a quiet conversation with Agemaki. But when the time came she found the attitude of vague reproachfullness that had been growing on him for some time very difficult to deal with. If only he would make up his mind to explain in so many words exactly what it was that he expected of her! But apart from this she found him so entertaining and in every way so extraordinarily sympathetic that she could not bring herself to refuse him a hearing.

Tonight Agemaki was in the chapel. She had left the door open, and the lamps at the altar were burning brightly, while screens had been set against the edges of the blinds through which Kaoru, seated on the verandah, was expected to converse with her. Outside, too, the great lamp had been lit. "I was feeling tired this morning," Kaoru said, "and dressed rather carelessly. I would far rather not be so conspicuous," and pushing the lamp to a distance, he laid full length on the ground. Here he was brought his evening fruit, which was served in the simplest manner, while his servants had their wine and fish in a sort of verandah on the other side of the house. Everyone indeed had tonight collected on that

---

* Nyosan had become a nun.

side, and the chapel-wing was absolutely silent and deserted. Though it seemed that she still felt this strange shyness in his company, Agemaki, he thought, spoke tonight in a tone which certainly expressed good will—perhaps even something bordering on affection. And while with apparent unconcern he continued to discuss the topics of the day, there flamed up within him such a yearning for her as he had never felt before. What separated them at this minute? A strip of paper, a few sticks—ludicrous obstacles indeed to a man that felt as he did, if it was they alone that kept him from her side.

But he knew that this was not so. The real barrier—and one, it seemed to him, far more ridiculous—consisted in his own miserable timidities and compunctions. Always there was this dread of striking too soon, of inflicting upon her against her will caresses that, if he had waited, she would in the end have come to desire.

Agemaki had arranged with several of her maids that they should remain within call. But the girls had no desire to stand in Kaoru's way, and had very soon withdrawn to a safe distance. Most of them indeed were now fast asleep, so that there was not even anyone to see after the lamps.

Agemaki felt uneasy and tried to attract someone's attention. But no one came. "I feel rather worn out," she said at last. "Perhaps I had better rest a little now. I will see you as soon as it is light tomorrow morning" and it seemed that she was making ready to return to the women's quarters. "I imagine I am quite as tired as you," he said, "considering the distance I have traveled. But your conversation has charmed me so much that I have not till this minute realized how fatigued I really am. You really cannot be so unkind as to go off and leave me."

As he said these words he pushed the screen back a little and squeezing between it and the blind stepped into the room. She was already halfway towards the door and now stood rooted to the spot in terror that was mingled with indignation. "Now at any rate I know what you mean by asking that I should allow you more freedom," she said contemptuously; "and I confess I had thought better of you," and she turned upon him a look of scorn that so far from bringing him to his senses served only further to fan the flame of his excitement. "Yes, indeed," he answered quickly, "your failure to understand in what sense I use this word 'freedom' has for some time past been exasperating me, and if I have now taken steps to show you what I mean, I see no reason why you should think the worse of me. I swear by the Buddha whose image stands before us that you have no cause whatever to be afraid. A strange, a mad compunction—I call it so because I see no sign that the rest of the world is handicapped in any such inconvenient way—makes it absolutely impossible for me, however strong my feelings, to force upon other people demonstrations of affection that they have shown they do not desire."

As he spoke one of the dying lamps suddenly flamed up for a moment, casting its flickering light full on her upturned face from which, with an impatient gesture of the hand, she was brushing back the long strands of her silky hair.

She stood before him lonely, unprotected. It was wrong, he felt, that she should be living in such a place; and it occurred to him that had he not been for long past their only visitor—had any ill-disposed person arrived at such an hour—things would not have remained as they were. "And why should they?" he asked himself, astounded once more at the folly of his own hesitation when she was so completely in his power. But at that moment he suddenly saw that she was trembling and weeping. Whatever feelings there might be on his side, on hers it was evident were only those of utter misery and fear. A wave of contrary feeling overcame him—of tenderest pity for her helplessness and isolation. No, it could not be done, anything rather than this. He must wait—and surely the time would not be very long—till her feelings had come to match his own. For the moment his only desire was to comfort her in her distress.

"You know quite well," she said at last, "that if I had for a moment supposed you to be capable of behaving as you have done tonight, I would never have allowed you to slip into the habit of meeting me on the intimate terms that you have now grown accustomed to. Nor does it make matters well that this has happened at a time when I am in deep mourning, and have, I should have thought, a particular claim on your consideration. But leaving all that aside, what bitterly distresses me is my own imprudence, and for that you cannot even pretend to console me."

She was no longer afraid; but it still annoyed her exceedingly that he should have seen her like this, with the lamplight full upon her, dressed in mourning, which she felt did not at all become her and at a moment when she was far indeed from having prepared herself for public inspection.

"I am sorry," Kaoru said, "that the thought of ever having admitted me to your friendship should so much depress you, and there is no more to say. As for your being still in mourning—that is of course true enough. But considering how often I have been here since your father's death I could hardly expect that you would wish me to treat you exactly as if your loss were still in its first days. I think to bring up the question of your mourning at all is really rather pedantic"

He revealed to her then how he had first seen her playing her lute by moonlight on that morning years ago, and how since that day stage by stage his love had continually grown, till it was beyond his power any longer to hide it. She listened with mingled feelings of shame, as he told of the various occasions when he had contrived to catch a glimpse of her, and astonishment at the success with which he had for so long concealed his true feelings.

She was once more seated on her couch, which was protected by a low screen on one side. Pushing this away towards the altar where the Buddha stood, he came and lay down by her side.

A strong smell of anise and other holy perfumes floated down from the altar, pervading the whole room, and Kaoru, deeply religious as he was, found that this familiar smell of incense seemed to set a sudden barrier between him and his desire. An instant before, mourning or no mourning, he was ready to act on the spur of the moment, by force if need be; but now all his old resolutions came back to his mind. He was appalled at his own levity. Afterwards, perhaps, when the period of mourning was over, if Agemaki herself seemed to desire it... A sudden and extraordinary fit of sobriety had overtaken him.

From time to time a gust of wind blew down from the hills; there was a low buzzing of insects in the hedge: It was indeed an autumn night such as even in the City would have been poignant in its beauty, and here was of an inconceivable loveliness. He began to talk of one thing and another, giving her news of what was going on in the world. Her occasional comments and replies struck him as singularly sensible and intelligent.

The sleepy maids, convinced that by now everything had happened as they hoped and intended, had one and all withdrawn to their own rooms. As for Agemaki, she realized now only too well what her father had meant when he warned her of the embarrassments and false positions into which a girl in her position might so easily be led. Such an indescribable depression filled her soul that she felt, should she now begin to cry, her tears would flow on forever, like the waters of the swirling stream outside.

Faint signs of dawn were appearing. Some of his followers were already awake, and their voices, as they gave signal for the mustering of his retinue, and the neighing of the horses somehow reminded him of scenes of travel that he had read about or heard described. He suddenly had the feeling that he was on a journey, and a strange excitement came over him. He pushed open the paper-window at which light was beginning to come and both of them sat silently watching the dawn. Presently she moved a little nearer the window. Quite close to her the dew was lying thick on the grasses of the eaves. Now the sunlight, moving slowly across the house, began to sparkle in the dew. Now it shone full into the room, lending a golden loveliness, Kaoru thought, to him and her. "This is what I ask for, this and nothing more," he said. "For you and I have the same feelings about such things—moonlight, flowers, the sky, all the subtle changes that go on in the world about us—and should never be unhappy so long as we could watch them together."

He spoke so kindly, so tenderly, that it was impossible for her to be any longer afraid. "You must not think," she said, "that even when we cannot be together like this—when there are curtains or lattices between—my feelings are quite shut off from you." It was now day indeed. There was a rustling of many wings as bird after bird fluttered past the window. In the distance, floating hazily on the morning air was the sound of a temple-bell. She wished that he would go. Surely he could see what impression it would make if he were found here when the household began to stir. Kaoru however showed no sign of moving. "I had better stay quietly where I am," he said presently. "Nothing could look worse than to be seen plunging out into the morning dew. But in any case it is useless to expect anyone else to understand the nature of our friendship. Let them draw what conclusions they please, so long as we may meet again in the same way. All that matters is that you yourself should feel safe with me. Surely after what has happened tonight, you cannot doubt that I am capable of showing self-control?"

A sudden fit of resolution seized her. She was *not* going to have him found idling in her room. "As for what you will or will not be capable of on subsequent occasions," she said, "I can express no opinion. That is your affair. But at this moment you will do as I tell you."

Evidently there was nothing for it but to obey. "I think you are rather severe," he said. "It is not as though I had any experience of these morning partings...I do indeed feel like 'losing my way.'"* Somewhere a long way off a cock crowed, reminding him of the City,† and he recited the verse: "As though the countryside had not already its multitude of sights and sounds, the cock must needs disturbing us, in this mountain village at dawn!" "Safe from life's fret and stir these hills and woods I thought, yet even here the worldly crowing of the cock has tracked me down"; such was the answer she gave him as she followed him to the door. Back in the men's quarters, he lay down, but could not sleep. Why had this uncontrollable agitation suddenly descended upon him, when for months past he had found no difficulty in behaving coolly and sensibly? He longed passionately to be back in her room and it was only by a great effort of will that he dragged himself from the house and prepared to set off for the Capital.

Agemaki too lay awake on her bed. She knew only too well what everyone in the house must be thinking. It was misery to have no disinterested person to turn to. Never before had she felt herself so utterly in the power of those who were supposed to serve her. Hardly a day passed but odious messages of one kind and another reached herself or Kozeri by way of some unscrupulous member of the household. Sooner or later, it seemed to her, if they went on living in this way, both she and her sister were bound to get involved in some sort of unpleasantness. Kaoru alone

---

* Reference to a poem which says, "so unfamiliar to me is this whole sensation of parting at dawn, that in the strange world which lies before me I fear I shall lose my way."
† The cock was an urban bird.

offered them a respectable way of escape. But though she far from actually disliked him, and her father, she remembered, had sometimes spoken of him in such a way as to suggest that he would not altogether have disapproved, Agemaki herself did not feel the slightest inclination to change her lot. Kozeri was different. That her youth and charm should continue to be wasted in this deserted place was deplorable, and Agemaki felt there was nothing she would not do to secure for her a reasonable share of life's ordinary pleasures and distractions. "If only there were in the entire world anyone to look after me as I look after Kozeri!" she thought. As for Kaoru, if he had been some humble, insignificant person, she would have felt it to be almost impossible, considering all the kindness she had consented to receive at his hands for many years past, not to soften her heart towards him and give him what he asked. But his beauty, his talents, his intelligence—all the qualities that had given him, as she knew, so conspicuous a place in society—so far from recommending him to her served merely to fill her with an exasperating sense of her own dullness and insufficiency. No, marriage, she felt sure, was not for her; and thinking again about the whole unhappy course that their lives seemed lately to have taken, she lay weeping till, overcome at last by the need to have someone near her, she went and lay down in Kozeri's room. Waking several times during the night Kozeri had heard the sound of a whispered conversation going on in her sister's room. She hoped this meant that Agemaki's relations with Kaoru had at last come to a head. And now, spreading the coverlet that Agemaki had brought with her from the other room, this hope was completely confirmed; for she recognized the moment she handled this coverlet the scent that had made Kaoru's cloak so embarrassing a gift for that wretched night-watchman. Perhaps indeed this had been going on for some time. Some of the maids had hinted as much. And feeling hurt that Agemaki should not have taken her into her confidence, Kozeri pretended to fall asleep.

Kaoru, before his departure, had his usual conversation with Ben no Kimi and gave her a long message for Agemaki. Reading it she suddenly remembered his poem, "Would that like the threads of the tassel..." which now took on a new significance.* Had he meant it in that way at the time? In any case it could scarcely have occurred to Kozeri that like the boy in the song he had been content to lie "with a hand-stretch between." She felt too utterly wretched and humiliated to face the world, and saying she did not feel well remained all day in bed. "This is the last day before the mourning expires," everyone said. With so much to

---

* I.e. seemed as if it must be an allusion to the old folk-song *The Tassel.* "Boy with the tasseled looks, a hand-stretch away, a hand-stretch from me you tried to sleep. But I rolled towards you; rolled over till I touched you."

be arranged and no one to manage things but her, she could not have chosen a worse time to fall ill.

Kozeri set to work on the braiding for the altar* and managed to finish them single-handed. But she had no idea how to make the rosettes and Agemaki was at last prevailed upon to creep out under cover of the growing darkness and show her how it was done. While they were at work, a letter came from Kaoru. She did not write an answer, but simply sent word that she had been ill all day and hoped he would excuse her from replying—behavior which greatly shocked the waiting-maids. "She ought to have manners enough at her age," they said indignantly, "not to answer a next-morning letter† by word of mouth."

It was not with any feeling of pleasure or relief that next day, their period of full mourning being over, the sisters put away their black clothes. Could it be a whole year? And there was a time when it seemed impossible to live without him for a single hour! But sadly though they put on their light grey,‡ Agemaki could not help noticing that the color was very becoming, particularly to her sister, who seemed to her to grow lovelier every day. Indeed while helping Kozeri to wash her hair she became so lost in admiration of her sister's beauty that for a while she forgot all her troubles. One thing was certain: if she could only carry out her secret plan for bringing those two§ together, Kozeri could not fail to carry all before her. Such scheming might indeed be thought unwomanly. But someone must plan for the girl as a father would, and there was no one else to do so.

Believing that Agemaki's mourning was indeed the main reason for her coolness towards him, Kaoru waited impatiently for the Anniversary. At last the day arrived, and he set out at full speed. Assuming that he would at any rate not be received less favorably than before, he sent in a note to announce his arrival. A message came back that Agemaki was unwell. He sent note after note imploring her to see him, but all to no purpose. "This comes as a complete surprise to me," he wrote. "I will not ask you to consider my feelings. But do at least reflect a little upon the impression that your treatment of me must be making in this house." To all his entreaties however he got no reply save a message that she was completely overcome by the emotions of the day and could not think of receiving anyone. In consternation at this rebuff Kaoru sent for Ben no Kimi and told her what was happening. Like all the servants in the house this old lady was far indeed from wishing that Kaoru should have any difficulty in obtaining access to her mistress; for on the success of his suit depended their

---
* In connection with the anniversary of her father's death.
† A letter sent after a love-meeting.
‡ Half-mourning.
§ Kaoru and Kozeri.

one chance of getting back to a reasonable and civilized existence. And Agemaki herself had some inkling of their attitude; which was confirmed by the fact that she had lately seen Kaoru in earnest conference with Ben no Kimi, stroking her hand and treating her with a familiarity which she was sure Kaoru would never have shown unless the two of them were hatching some dangerous scheme. In novels this was always how trouble came. Some old and trusted servant, the last person of whom such a thing would have been expected, flatly disobeys her mistress's instructions. It was best to count on no one; and if her own household betrayed her, then she must turn their treachery to Kozeri's good. She felt certain that even if her sister had been far less attractive than she was Kaoru's objections would not survive the first real and unhampered meeting; and as it was, he was bound to succumb completely as soon as he found himself face to face with her. "After all," she thought, "when I made the suggestion* he could not very well jump at it straight away, as though that was what he had wanted all the while. But in reality I do not think that he is held back by any real preference for me. What worries him is the impression that such a change might make on others. He has a horror of appearing to be the sort of person that does not know his own mind." If however she embarked on any scheme for getting Kaoru painlessly started on his new path her sister must certainly be informed of it. To act without her knowledge and approval would be exceedingly wrong. And going to Kozeri she began to put the whole situation before her.

"Father," she said, "made us promise him that, if the worst came to the worst, we would make up our minds to go on just as we are sooner than put ourselves into the power of unscrupulous people. Anything, he said, was better for a girl—even the dull and empty existence that we are leading here, than the risk of losing her good name. I always felt it to be a dreadful thing while he was alive that we stood between him and his religion, and I think the least we can do now is to follow his advice—but then for me that is not very difficult, for really I have grown so used to living like this that it scarcely troubles me at all. The only thing I cannot bear is having everyone in the house against me. They think I am simply being obstinate, which is not the case at all. But as far as you are concerned there is a good deal of truth in what they say. It certainly does depress me beyond measure to think of you going on year after year making no use of your youth and looks, and I confess it would take a great load off my mind if we could discover some way of giving you a more reasonable sort of existence."

Kozeri however would not let her continue. "I am sure," she said indignantly, "that whatever father may have said, he never intended one

---

* That he should marry Kozeri instead.

of us to get married and the other to go on as before. If he had thought there was any chance of that happening, he would have been even more worried about us than he was. I don't see why you should have a load to be taken off your mind at all, so long as we are here to keep each other happy." I have only succeeded in hurting her feelings, thought Agemaki, without doing any good. "I didn't mean to hurt you," she said. "It is all the fault of these wretched people. Really, they are driving me distracted by all the horrible things they are saying about me..." and she did not return to the subject.

The day drew on and Kaoru showed no signs of leaving the house. From time to time Ben no Kimi brought a note or message from him, but despite the old woman's entreaties—and really, Ben felt, he had this time good cause to complain—Agemaki absolutely refused to make any reply.

Was she acting rightly? She hardly knew. Certain it was that if either of her parents had been alive and had found a husband for her she would have accepted him with resignation whether he attracted her or not, for she knew well enough that these are matters in which one cannot expect to follow one's own inclinations; nor would anyone dream of regarding such a disinclination on her side as a drawback to the project. But she saw no reason to submit with the same meekness to the dictates of a parcel of old women who, while making a great display of advising her only for her own good, were obviously thinking of nothing but their own interests. They might go on forever pointing out the marvelous convenience and suitability of the match. Agemaki knew perfectly well that not one of them had breeding and good sense enough to make her advice of the slightest value. All they were thinking about in reality was how to get away from Uji. The sooner they stopped all this browbeating and arguing the better. For nothing they said could have the slightest effect on her at all. Kozeri, with whom she had hitherto shared all her troubles, was evidently, as their recent conversation showed, too young to understand or sympathize with her present difficulties. Wishing that she were anyone but herself, Agemaki lay with her face turned to the wall.

"Madam, how would it be if you were to wear colored clothes just for tonight?"

Why must they all keep on coaxing and worrying her? One thing was certain; they had all set their hearts on it! There would be no protection in that quarter. And as for hiding in a house built like this—the pear-tree on the naked hillside might as soon think of concealing itself.

Nor was it in the least to Kaoru's taste that his affairs should be managed for him with all this whispering and fuss. A relationship of this kind should, he felt, be allowed to pass secretly and insensibly from one stage to another, and if at any point Agemaki felt for the moment disinclined to continue it, he had no desire that she should be hustled. It exasperated him beyond measure to see Ben no Kimi, of whom he had thought better than this, holding open conclave with her cronies. What must Agemaki's feelings be, with this going on all around her? All this was not in the least like Ben when he first knew her. Had age played some strange trick with her character?

Agemaki, meanwhile, the next time that Ben came to her room, called the old woman to her. "Listen," she said. "This friend of ours succeeded in persuading my father that he was some kind of paragon, devoid of any human weaknesses. I was foolish enough to accept this notion of him and allowed him, I am afraid, to take unheard-of liberties. It now turns out, as I might have foreseen, that he is in no way different from other human beings. No doubt, regarded simply as a means of escape into less dismal surroundings, his offer has much to recommend it. But for my own part, I made up my mind long ago to remain where I am and these continual reproaches and remonstrance only serve to exasperate me. But that is no reason why Kozeri should be condemned to waste the best years of her life shut away in this desolate spot, and if Kaoru is really bent on carrying out my father's wishes, he ought to regard himself as responsible for her happiness no less than mine. My father—if one can look at the matter in that way—bequeathed to us an equal share in his affections. Very well then; you may tell him, putting it in any way you please so long as he understands, that I renounce my half in Kozeri's favor." She intensely disliked having to discuss the matter; but it was high time, she felt, that Ben should understand her point of view.

"There is nothing new to me in all this," the old lady declared; "I saw for myself long ago that you felt like this, and have told him so time and again. But he says that quite apart from his own feelings in the matter, Niou has really taken a great fancy to your sister and would be deeply offended if for no apparent reason Kaoru suddenly stood in his way. "And I think," he says, "that if I get her Prince Niou as a husband, Kozeri can hardly complain that I have neglected my duties towards her." And really I do not see how if both your dear parents were here to lavish on you all their scheming and care they could possibly have done any better for you both than this.

"I don't know whether I ought to mention such things—but I am afraid we are running very near to the end of our resources up here, and however your marriages might turn out in other ways, you would at any rate, as regards the ways and means of life, be magnificently provided for.

"It is natural enough, I am sure, that you should want to do as your father would wish. But all his warnings were against people of a very different kind from these two gentlemen. What he was afraid of was that you might get mixed up with people not of your own class. 'If His

Excellency* were to take a fancy to either of them,' he said to me more than once, 'nothing of course would please me better.'

"Orphans, as you know—and it is the same in all classes of society—are bound to be at a great disadvantage and are often obliged to content themselves with alliances far below what under happier circumstances they would have every right to expect. This is understood by everybody, and no girl situated as you are was ever thought the worse of for taking such chances as came her way. You ought then, if I may say so, to think yourselves uncommonly fortunate each to have the prospects of such a match as you could surely not improve upon in your wildest dreams.

For even if, like the Prince your father, you shut yourself up and say your prayers from morning to night, you cannot live on air..."†

All this seemed to Agemaki quite beside the point. She buried her face in her hands and made no reply.

Kozeri, without knowing exactly what was wrong, saw that her sister was unusually depressed and determined, as under such circumstances she had often done before, to spend the night in her room.

That something unpleasant was going to happen Agemaki was convinced, but though she thought of one place after another where it might be possible to hide, she soon realized that none of them would really be of any use, and tucking her own soft, lovely blanket over Kozeri, she herself lay down at a little distance, for she found the night oppressively hot.

Kaoru, when the old lady told him what Agemaki had said, took the news with far more resignation than she had expected. "I cannot really be angry with her," he said, "because I am convinced that all this is due to a state of mind that I myself know only too well. I can see that she has been got hold of—and considering how long she lived shut up with a man like her father, it is hardly to be wondered at—by the feeling that life is too short and uncertain for anything to be worth while. But whether this explanation is right or not, I can hardly be expected to go back now to the old business of conversation through curtains and screens. It is of the utmost importance that I should discuss matters with her, and I must ask you to arrange secretly for me to get into the place where she is spending the night."

Ben no Kimi and one or two of her older associates accordingly contrived to pack off all the maids to their rooms at an unusually early hour.

It was a windy night, and soon every door and shutter in the house was rattling. Ben could not have wished for a better opportunity. Amid so much banging and clattering neither footsteps nor the opening of

---

* Kaoru.

† Literally "on clouds and mist." Ben had already hinted that the material resources of the establishment were dangerously depleted.

doors could possibly be heard, nor had she already slipped Kaoru safely into the room before Agemaki became aware that anything was wrong. It was a pity; Ben thought that they should have chosen this particular night to sleep in the same room. But with that arrangement it was now obviously too late to interfere, and no doubt in a minute or two Kozeri would have the sense to retire. There was light enough in the room, Ben was certain, for him at any rate to see which was which.

Agemaki was lying wide awake on her curtained couch. Suddenly she became aware that there was someone standing in the room. She got up, and quietly slipped into the passage. But no sooner was she there than she repented of her flight. Kozeri was asleep. Surely it would be a terrifying experience for her suddenly to wake up and find a stranger by her bedside and though Agemaki's flight was part of a scheme that she had thought out carefully beforehand, her first instinct now was to go back and wreck all her own plans by waking Kozeri and taking her with her. But it was too late to turn back, for casting a trembling glance over her shoulder into the dimly lit room she caught sight of a coatless figure that, advancing towards the couch, calmly drew back the curtains and slipped in. "Poor little thing, how frightened she'll be!" thought Agemaki, aghast at the situation she had created, and none too comfortable herself at the moment, for the only refuge she had been able to find was the space between some screens and a very knobbly wall. She remembered how horrified Kozeri had been at the mere suggestion that she could ever think of Kaoru as a future husband. "She will never, never forgive me," Agemaki kept on saying to herself. She thought of all the miseries and affronts that they had endured together since Prince Hachi's death. Oh! How at this moment she longed for him, her dear father—picturing him as she remembered him best, going up the hill to the temple on that last evening.

For a moment Kaoru, who had been warned by Ben that Agemaki would not be alone, finding only one figure on the bed, imagined that Agemaki had sent her sister away; but his excitement and delight were soon rudely dispelled by the discovery that the girl asleep on the bed was not Agemaki at all.

It was indeed someone, he was obliged to confess to himself as he gazed down at her, a good deal handsomer and better made than Agemaki. She opened her eyes, and it was immediately apparent by the look of utter bewilderment which came into her face that whatever plot there might have been, Kozeri herself knew nothing of the part she had been made to play. He felt very sorry for her and at the same time indignant at the way in which Agemaki had treated both himself and her. He did indeed feel strongly drawn towards Kozeri. But he had not yet given up all hope of success in the only quarter where it could really mean anything to him, and were he now to yield to the impulse of the moment one thing was certain—all chance of succeeding with Agemaki was gone forever. But to some small extent it cheered him to feel that if fate proved to be utterly against him, he had at any rate something to fall back upon. In any case, Kozeri was no stranger, and having intruded upon her in this way it behaved him at least to be civil. He pulled himself together, and successfully concealing every trace either of disappointment or excitement he began to talk to her in just the same tender and reassuring manner that he had adopted towards Agemaki so often before.

"Things are not going as they ought to," said one of the old ladies whom Ben had taken into her confidence, "or we should have heard Kozeri go back to her room long ago." "It sounds as though something were happening all the same," said another, straining her ears. "It beats me how anyone can have the heart to treat him like this," whispered another—a fearsome-looking old hag—'such a dear young gentleman as he is. Why, simply to see him about the house the way we do is enough, I don't mind telling you, to make me feel as I haven't felt for many a long year. It's not right or natural to go on the way Madam is doing, and if you ask me I believe the Evil One* has got at her!" And as she hissed these last words through a gap in her teeth she herself looked the very essence of all that is old and evil. "Now then, old sorceress, leave the Bad Spirits alone, will you, and not talk nonsense about people being bewitched, when it's easy enough to see why she is still so scared? Who wouldn't be, brought up like this, with not a soul ever coming near the place, and no one to tell her about things in the proper way? Just give her time to get used to him, and you see if she doesn't come round." "Well, let's hope she won't be too long about it," said another, "for a better match she'll certainly never find." So they chattered together, while at intervals a violent sound of snoring would announce that one or another of them had fallen asleep.

The autumn night, which would have ended all too quickly had he spent it as he had hoped to do, dragged on and on. At last a little light began to filter in from the world outside. Yes, she was certainly as beautiful as Agemaki; that could not be denied. Yet here he was, about to leave this room as irritated and unsatisfied as ever, despite the fact that this time the fault was entirely his own. "Think kindly of me," he said. "Never let your sister teach you how to make me as unhappy as she has done." And promising to visit her again as soon as he could, he slipped out of the room. Had it all been a fantastic dream? Surely now that it was over, the longed for meeting with Agemaki would begin? He must calm himself, he must rest.

---

* The evil spirit who is supposed to possess girls who remain virgins too long.

He was already lying down in his usual quarters when Ben no Kimi put her head in at the door of Agemaki's room. "What has become of Kozeri?" she said, imagining the figure on the bed to be that of the elder sister. Kozeri did not stir. What had it all meant? The events of the night left behind them at first nothing save a vague feeling of shame and bewilderment. But presently she remembered yesterday's conversation. If that had anything to do with it, then Agemaki had played a cruel and hateful trick upon her...

At that moment Agemaki, like a cricket that the full light of day has driven out of its chink in the wall, crept dazed into the room. What must Kozeri be thinking of her? As for Kaoru, perhaps now that he had tormented each of them in turn he would be content to leave them alone. As far as she was concerned, he had forfeited for good and all whatever regard she had once had for him.

Meanwhile Ben no Kimi was hearing from Kaoru's own lips the whole story of her mistress's outrageous obstinacy.

"Up till now," he said, "she has always shown some kind of consideration for my feelings, and I have come away from our meetings discouraged perhaps, but not altogether in despair. But after what happened last night I really feel as though I had better go straight into a monastery, which I should have done long ago, had not Hachi's pitiable concern about the future of these Princesses involved me inextricably in all this wretched business. Henceforward, if I come here at all, it can only be as a matter of courtesy. Such downright rudeness is a thing I can hardly be expected ever to forget. I realize now that I am the last person in the world to deal with a temperament such as that of your mistress. What she needs is someone not too sensitive—someone like Niou, in fact— who would go straight for what he wanted, without stopping at every turn to consider what impression he was making. Well, I do not blame her; his, no doubt, is by far the better way. I unfortunately am not so constituted, and being what I am should feel more comfortable if these good friends of yours* were not kept so well posted in all my movements. Please remember that next time; and above all tell no one of the absurd position in which I found myself last night."

"One can't help feeling sorry for both of them," the maids whispered, seeing him hurry away from the house far earlier than usual and evidently very much out of humor.

Even Agemaki, now that it was all over, felt that she had perhaps gone too far. What if Kaoru should really have taken offence and abandon them both altogether? If only the people round her would stop interfering with things they did not in the least understand! However, perhaps

---

* Ben's confidantes. The honorific *tatematsuramu* is ironic.

things were not as black as she feared, for his next-morning letter came as usual, and she found herself for once in the odd position of being positively glad to receive it. The letter was attached to a branch, half of which the autumn seemed to have strangely neglected, for the leaves were still green, though the leaves on the other half were tawny red. "Thought you of autumn, O Lady of the Hills, or spring, when this one branch with opposite tinge you hued?" Such was his poem, and though the letter that accompanied it was brief and simple, there was nothing in it to suggest that he bore her any ill-will. It seemed indeed as though he were ready to pass over the whole incident as of no importance. But she was still too agitated easily to concentrate her thoughts upon composing an answer, and when her women clamored round her, urging her to lose no time, her first instinct was to bid them go to Kozeri for a reply. But on second thoughts, little though she felt inclined for such an effort, it seemed better to do what she could.

"In what intent I know not, but on the autumn side she lays her deeper hue—this Lady Goddess of the Hills." So she answered, and though the poem was written hastily there was such beauty in the brush-strokes that he knew he should never be angry with her for long.

But reviewing all that had happened he realized now that this idea of handing him over to Kozeri had started far earlier than he had supposed. Irritated (as he saw it now) by his persistent refusal to fall in with her plan, she had devised last night's unfortunate stratagem, and the fact that he had failed to succumb to it would, he was sure, serve only to aggravate her sense of grievance. In short, his prospects of success were nil, and his suit was at present serving no other purpose but to provide gossip for the old women whom Ben had so kindly enlisted. His great mistake consisted in ever beginning this sort of thing at all. It was already bad enough that he had made himself ridiculous by going about everywhere saying he was on the point of becoming a monk, and then being seen year after year taking no steps in that direction at all. But what must people be thinking now? Here he was—he who had renounced the world—drifting "like a rudderless boat"* always to the same spot, helpless as the most fatuous rake to resist the current of his own desires. He lay tossing wretchedly all night, and while the beauty of dawn was still in the sky went to visit Niou.

Since the fire at Nyosan's, he had been staying in the Sixth Ward† and was constantly in Niou's company—a state of affairs which Niou felt sure he would before long be able to turn to good account.‡ For the visitor it was an ideal place of retreat. All the arrangements of the house

---

* Allusion to an anonymous love-poem in the *Kokinshu*.

† At the New Palace, where Niou lived.

‡ Niou hoped to persuade Kaoru to bring him to Uji

worked with perfect smoothness, the gardens were the finest in existence, and indeed it was strange how here even the commonest plants and trees took on an unfamiliar air, bending, it seemed, more delicately to the winds that passed; while at night when the moon was on the moat the scene was one of such surpassing beauty that it was impossible to believe Niou would be in bed.

Nor indeed was he. The familiar perfume, floating through the night, told him at once who this visitor was, and hastily adjusting his dress he went to meet his friend. Half-way up the steps Kaoru sat down, and Niou, without urging him to come any further, leant against the wooden railings and plunged at once into conversation. The subject of Uji was not long in cropping up. It was one concerning which Niou expressed him with considerable bitterness. And Kaoru, who after much thought about the matter had decided that, his own suit having gone so badly, the one chance of ultimate success lay in first disposing of Kozeri, showed himself much more ready than before to further Niou's cause.

At daybreak a cold mist rose, through which the moonlight straggled brokenly, leaving grey spaces under the overhanging branches of the trees. The scene, in its solemn beauty, reminded Kaoru of many that he had witnessed in the garden at Uji, and some such thought had evidently crossed Niou's mind. "You won't put it off too long?" he said. And when Kaoru began once more to make difficulties, he laughingly recited the verse: "Who so churlish that he would set up a fence round the meadow where sweet-maidens* bloom?"

"Thick lies the mist upon the fields at dawn, and shrewdly must he search that would those flowers descry." He could not resist the temptation to tease his friend. "Surely this joke has gone on long enough," he said at last, beginning to feel really annoyed.

In old days when this subject cropped up, he had discouraged Niou partly because he himself still knew very little about Kozeri, and was afraid that, at close quarters, she might prove hopelessly to belie the glowing descriptions by which he had so recklessly kindled his friend's imagination. On this score, at any rate, he no longer had any misgivings. The awkward thing was that Agemaki seemed to have set her heart on his marrying Kozeri himself. But really it was too much to expect that he should be able to transfer his affections at a moment's notice to suit other people's convenience, and though he would have done anything else in the world to win her approval, this she ought to realize was out of the question. It would indeed be preposterous if by bringing such a bridegroom as Prince Niou into the family he forfeited either Agemaki's or Kozeri's affection.

---

* The name of a flower.

Meanwhile Niou, he could see, had not the least idea what was going on in his head, and evidently attributed his hesitation to mere selfishness.

"Listen," he said at last. "I have not the least objection to your coming with me if you really want to, but it must be clearly understood that I am not bringing you there to amuse yourself in your usual way. I am responsible for what happens there, and should like to feel rather more certain that you are not simply going to make her unhappy."

"Your imagination," said Niou, "is running on a great deal too fast. It still remains to be seen whether I shall like her at all."

"Judging by my own experience," Kaoru confessed, "I should say they were both of them pretty well able to look after themselves. Let us fix a day."

The Higan* ceremonies closed on the twenty-sixth, and this seemed a good moment to choose. Rumors about Niou's way of life had lately been reaching the Empress's ears, and she had strictly forbidden him to leave the City. But he had set his heart on this excursion, and though all the lying and pretences involved was a great nuisance, he succeeded at last in persuading his parents that the expedition was of a perfectly harmless character.

This time he did not make use of Yugiri's mansion which, besides being on the wrong side of the river, was far too much under observation to be suitable to his present purpose. Instead, Kaoru took him to a house on an estate of his own which was on the near side of the river and ensconcing him there very secretly—for though the place was uninhabited there was a watchman who was apt to come there on his rounds—he went on to Uji and announced himself in the usual way.

It was with far less trepidation than usual that Agemaki heard he was there. One thing seemed certain: it could hardly be for her sake that he had come—considering all that had occurred. She could only suppose then that he had come to see Kozeri, and it was a comfort that he was capable of showing so much good sense. Kozeri, meanwhile, was not in the least agitated by the news of his arrival, for it was in Agemaki—Kaoru himself had made this sufficiently clear—and Agemaki alone that he was interested. "This time, however," Kozeri said to herself, "I will take good care to keep out of their way." It was terrible to have to be on one's guard against Agemaki, of all people in the world! But since that fatal night Kozeri had lost all confidence in her sister.

There were various matters of business to arrange with the mistress of the house. Kaoru made no attempt to see her, but dealt with these by an exchange of notes. Evidently, thought all the waiting-women, matters

---

* Celebrated for a week in spring and autumn, at the time of the equinox. Though a Buddhist festival, it is apparently unknown in India and China.

were going from bad to worse. Niou arrived on horseback and Kaoru slipped him into the house unperceived in the darkness. "I must have one word with Agemaki," Kaoru said to Ben no Kimi. I feel very reluctant to face her, after the way she treated me the other night, but I have something to tell her which it is really essential I should get off my mind immediately. Later on I should like you to let me into the room you took me to before."

This seemed clear enough.[*] "Well, it's all one to me which of them he wants," thought Ben, "provided he goes through with it," and she went off to deliver her message. "What a relief!" thought Agemaki. "He has really behaved sensibly and taken my advice." She made sure that the door which led into Kozeri's quarters was not bolted, and having securely bolted her own, she talked to him through the latticed window. "There is something private I want to tell you," he said. "I dare not speak any louder. Can't you open the door a little? One feels so cut off." "There's no need to," she answered. "I hear you perfectly well." However probably all he wanted was to obtain her formal assent to the new arrangement—which was only civil, considering that Kozeri was her younger sister. There was really no reason to treat him more distantly on this occasion than she had done before. "I had better make an effort to be nice to him for a few moments," she thought. "As he is on his way to Kozeri he certainly won't stay here very long." And leaving her couch, she came close up to the grill through which he was speaking. Stretching his hand through the opening he caught at her sleeve and began to pour out a flood of lamentations and reproaches. She cursed herself, while she listened to him, for having been so foolish as to believe for a moment that he was to be trusted. But as he had evidently arranged to go to Kozeri, the sooner she could get him there the better. She did everything she could think of to quiet him. "We are almost the same person," she said gently, "and if you are fond of me you cannot help liking her in just the same way."

Meanwhile Niou arrived at the door of the women's apartments and rustled his fan, as Kaoru had told him to. Someone—it was Ben no Kimi[†] of course—drew the bolt on the inside and let him in. He was amused to see the smooth way in which these clandestine arrangements worked. Evidently they were not being put in practice for the first time. Of all this however Agemaki was quite unaware, and she continued to do everything in her power to start Kaoru on his way.

He was able, despite his unhappiness, to see that there was a comic side to the whole situation. It would however be putting himself in an

---

[*] She thought Kaoru had transferred his suit to Kozeri.

[†] Ben is not in the secret, and imagines that she is admitting Kaoru.

impossible position if he let her go on in ignorance of what was happening in Kozeri's room. "Niou," he said, "kept on bothering me to bring him here, and in the end I could not refuse. In fact, he is now with Kozeri. The officious Ben smuggled him quietly in. So if you drive me from here, there is nowhere for me to go."

She gasped. What was it he was saying? It was incredible. Strange as his ideas were, she would never for a moment have expected that he would be capable of such a baseness as this. What a simpleton he must think her, to have fallen so easy a prey to his crude deception!

"Well, the thing is done now," he said, "and I am afraid it is quite useless for you to protest. But if it is any relief to your feelings, pray tear me and my character to pieces as savagely as you please. Niou has of course much more to offer in every way than I have, and I can quite understand that you should be disappointed at losing him.* But you must admit that the person who comes out of it worst is myself; for here I am, left in midair, with nothing to hope for now either from you or her. And yet—what have you to gain from all this obstinacy? The mere fact that this door remains locked and barred is not going to convince anyone that nothing happened. Do you suppose, for example, that Niou imagines I am spending the night in this depressing way?"

For a moment it looked as though he meant to force the door. She was at her wits' end how to deal with him, but knew that it would be fatal to show her agitation. "As for the explanation that you have chosen to give of what you call my 'disappointment,'" she said quietly, "I shall pass that over in silence. I have real troubles enough both now and in prospect without your inventing imaginary ones for me. But I think, all the same, I have a right to ask what induced you to behave in this extraordinary way. I am still so appalled that I can hardly grasp what has happened. The whole thing seems too grotesque to have any connection with real life—if people ever hear about it all, I am sure they will think it comes out of some novel. And what, I should like to know incidentally, does Prince Niou make of this ingenious arrangement? That is a subject I should very much like to have a little light on. For my own part, I can only beg you to spare us for the present any more of these surprises. Some day, when I have had time to recover a little from the shock of the present one, we will continue our conversation. At the moment I am afraid I do not feel equal to any further discussion, and should like to go and rest. So please let go of my dress."

He could not help seeing that the request was a very reasonable one. Her patience and gentleness put him to shame. "Go, then," he said. "It

---

* Kaoru, in his anger, pretends to believe that Agemaki's consternation was due to his having sent Niou to Kozeri and not to her.

is clear that you recognize me for what I am—a prodigy of meekness and obedience. But, if you really dislike me as much as you seem to, I have nothing more to say. My last hold on life is gone." "If I do this," he said, letting go of her sleeve, "you will still speak to me through the lattice—you will not go away altogether?" She retreated a short way, but showed no signs of leaving the room. "We will stay each of us where we are," he said, as she sank wearily down. I see enough of you to be a little consolation to me. Sleep quietly. No harm shall come to you." He too lay down, but could not sleep. There was the usual night-wind and the deafening noise of the river.

So, like a pair of mountain-pheasants, they spent the night each in a separate nest.* At last came the usual tokens of dawn. Footsteps stirred; the temple-bell chimed. But of Niou there was still no sign, No doubt he was sleeping heavily. Kaoru went to the door and called softly. There was no reply.

"Not he whose steps I led, but I—distracted guide—in night's dark avenues have lost my way." Such was the poem he recited. And she, hearing him: "Willing you lost your way; more hapless we by blundering tracks decoyed into the maze of night." The low voice in which she murmured these words enchanted him, and he began once more the worn-out reproaches of last night, simply in the hope of hearing her speak again.

Suddenly the door of Kozeri's room opened and in the uncertain morning light appeared the figure of a young man. Never had the old women who were already astir about the house been so surprised in all their lives. For the figure, whose languid and sensuous movements were accompanied by a heavy smell of burnt-incense, was certainly not that of Kaoru. However, presumably Kaoru knew all about it, and they were sure he would not have brought anyone to Uji whom it was not suitable that the Princesses should know.

Anxious to arrive at the City before people were about, they set out at once. To Niou, who had so seldom left the Capital, the distance seemed enormous. He saw that it was going to be difficult enough for him to get there even occasionally, and as for "not a night will I miss..."† that was out of the question. Noticing how long the journey was taking, he became very depressed. It was not however really so very late in the morning when they arrived, and scarcely anyone was about. On entering the grounds of the New Palace they left their horses and were smuggled into a litter meant for women. Here they cut such odd figures that looking at one another they suddenly burst out laughing.

---

* Such is the popular belief about the *yamadori*, copper pheasant.

† "Now that my new bride, fresh as the young grass, has pillowed her head on my arm, not a night will I miss..." *Manyoshu* 2542. Anon. Attributed in the *Kokin Rokujo* to Tsurayuki.

"Well," Kaoru said when they arrived, "that's over. You've done your duty by your cousins at Uji." He gave no hint of the disastrous way in which, from his point of view, last night's arrangement had worked out.

Niou lost no time in dispatching his next-morning letter. The household at Uji was this morning in a general state of turmoil and bewilderment. Kozeri had a fresh grievance against her sister, for she felt sure that what had happened last night was the result of a plot between her and Kaoru, and she thought it infamous that she had not been consulted. Agemaki quite realized that this must be her impression, but felt utterly incapable of explaining the whole distasteful business. Meanwhile the ladies of the household made desperate efforts to discover what it all meant. Why, for example, with Kozeri sitting there looking still so scared and bewildered, did their mistress make no attempt to enlighten or comfort her? And who on earth, in any case, was this mysterious visitor?

The letter was handed to Agemaki. She read it and passed it on. Kozeri was still lying on her couch, staring in front of her. For a long time she held it unread in her hand. The messenger began to grow impatient. At last Agemaki saw that she must take the matter into her own hands.

"Were this a common dalliance, would I through the dew-deep grass have cut my toilsome way?"

The meticulous spacing and management of the ink proclaimed it for what it was,[*] and though if she could have brought herself to look at it simply as a piece of beautiful writing, the poem would certainly have delighted her, she was for the moment far too much occupied with the question of Niou's ultimate intentions.

It was easy enough to compose a suitable answer. The difficulty was to get Kozeri to write it, and Agemaki felt shy of doing so herself. At last she succeeded in making Kozeri sit up and write to her dictation. The messenger, when the reply was handed to him, was rather embarrassed to receive at the same time a pale-green dress[†] and a pair of doubly lined trousers. Considering the secret nature of his mission the gift was an inconvenient one. He had the clothes wrapped up in a cloth and gave them to his servant to carry. You are perhaps already picturing this messenger as some great lord or valued retainer. He was however merely the little page boy who generally waited upon Niou in the Palace. This present to his messenger did not, Niou was sure, come from Kozeri herself; for he had made it clear to her that he wished the affair to be kept secret. More probably it was an effort on the part of one of the waiting-women—the old lady who had unlocked the door to him—to show her familiarity with Court usage. In any case it was very tiresome.

---

[*] A next-morning letter.

[†] A *shion,* brown-red with pale-green lining. The giving of such a present to the messenger who brought the morning letter was part of the traditional Court betrothal ceremonies.

That night he tried to persuade Kaoru to go with him again. But he said he had accepted an engagement at Ryozen's palace, and could not now get out of it. Niou felt that his friend was shocked by his eagerness to rush back to Uji. Well, that was just the difference between them. He could never hope to emulate Kaoru's cold and detached attitude towards things of that kind.

Agemaki meanwhile felt that there was nothing for it but to make the best of a bad business. The limited resources of the house made it far from easy to receive such a visitor as Niou in a suitable way. But it would not do to be taken unawares, and she managed in the end to provide for his entertainment in a way which she hoped was not too inadequate. His prompt arrival on the following day was both gratifying and wholly unexpected; for she knew that for anyone in his position it was regarded as a long journey. Kozeri herself was in an agitated and nervous condition, and many a tear fell upon the sleeve of the dark-red bridal-dress in which her maids were robing her. Nor was her agitation lessened when she saw that her sister too was weeping.

"You are the only thing in life that is precious to me," Agemaki said between her tears, "and if I have ever brought myself to consider plans that would take you from me, it was only because the people here kept on dinning into my ears day and night that it was my duty to arrange a marriage* for you. As they are older than me and have far more experience of the world, I did not feel capable of pitting my own vague instincts against their solid arguments and assurances, and in the end I faced the fact that sooner or later I must lose you. But that the thing should begin in this sudden and irregular way I never for a moment contemplated or intended. However Fate seems to have decided the matter for us, and I can think of nothing that it is of any use to say, except that until this had happened I knew nothing whatever about it. So it is wrong of you to feel cross with me. You have no reason to at all."

She stroked Kozeri's head while she spoke, trying to coax her back into a better humor. The girl made no reply. But in reality her silence did not mean resentment; she was certain that whatever part Agemaki had played in the matter her sister had, not meant to harm or distress her. Indeed what filled Kozeri's thoughts at the moment was the dread not so much of what she herself would suffer if Niou proved fickle, as of the effect that such a dereliction would have upon Agemaki.

Niou arrived with no misgivings. Even last night, when it was obvious that, owing to the unexpected nature of his visit, she was bound to be rather shy, she had completely captivated him. Tonight, of course,

---

* "Marriage with Niou," say the commentators; wrongly, I think, for the household had not previously any reason to regard Niou as a suitor.

everything would be different. She was no longer faced with the terror of the unknown.

But when he began to tell her about the journey that seemed to him so tremendous and eventful an undertaking—he was still aching in every limb, he said—she showed no signs of being particularly impressed. He was used to girls who, however carefully they might have been brought up, had at any rate some notion how to deal with men; for there were generally brothers or other male relations in the house, and a girl had opportunities of noticing how more experienced women handled them. But he was quite prepared to find that Kozeri, though he did not suppose she had been nearly so strictly watched and guarded as most of the girls he knew, would be extremely awkward, shy, and countrified in her ways. Very few visitors, he imagined, ever came near the house, so that she must be quite unused to receiving company of any kind, and to find herself suddenly closeted with someone of whom she still knew so little must, he was sure, be somewhat intimidating. But when, though he patiently tried one topic after another, he could not succeed in getting two connected words out of her, he began to feel very puzzled. "And this," he said to himself ruefully, "is according to all accounts the cleverer and livelier of the two sisters!"

"We must have the cakes ready for tonight," the old women said; and Agemaki vaguely realized that the cakes in question must be in some way connected with her sister's betrothal. "You had better make them in my room," she said, not prepared for the fact that the maids would appeal to her for directions. She felt the absurdity of having so grandly taken charge of the proceedings, and being now discovered by her women not to have the least idea of what was needed. The others saw that she was blushing, and thought how well a little extra color became her. Presently however she threw herself into the work with a will, and no one seeing her light-hearted and eager movements as she helped her maids would have recognized the severe and discouraging Agemaki of the encounters with Kaoru. But in the capacity of elder sister one is a different person.

Presently a letter came from Kaoru. "I thought of coming tonight," he wrote, "but there seems to be very little I can do for you at present, and I dislike obtruding myself where I am evidently not wanted. I might perhaps have been of some assistance to you in arranging the betrothal ceremonies. But I have not yet by any means recovered from the effect of last night's very distressing and uncomfortable experiences, and on the whole I feel more inclined to stay quietly here and rest."

It was written straight ahead* on coarse Michinoku paper. With the letter came a large parcel of flat dress-boxes. They contained, however,

---

* Without decorative spacing.

not stuffs made up into dresses, but simply a number of rolls of various kinds of material. The parcel was addressed to Ben no Kimi, who assumed that these must be his betrothal gifts to Kozeri's ladies. No doubt he had simply taken what lay to hand in Lady Nyosan's limited* wardrobe. It was a wonder indeed that he had found as much. But hidden away under some rolls of silk and damask she found two exquisitely made undershifts of the costliest material. These evidently were intended for Agemaki and her sister. Upon the sleeve of one of them—a custom that is fast disappearing—he had written the dedication: "On these that are love's trappings, though love's self be scorned, must kindness look askance?"

The implication was true enough; there were few indeed of their secrets that he had not explored. So ambiguous indeed had their relations with him become that neither of them could find a suitable answer. The messengers grew tired of waiting and disappeared. It was found, however, that one under-servant, who had helped to carry the parcel, was still hanging round, and though he was a person of the lowest possible class, they were obliged in the end to entrust him with their answer: "Though kindness like a garment next the heart from day to day be worn, must it needs claim the glamor of love's garb?" They felt this to be very commonplace, but hoped he would realize that it had been written at a moment of hurry and distraction. To Kaoru, however, who had prepared himself for something even more discouraging in tone, it gave considerable pleasure.

That day Niou felt obliged to appear at the Palace, and as evening came on it did not seem as though he were going to get a chance of slipping away. He was already fuming inwardly when his mother the Empress said to him, "It is high time, you know, that you settled down and got married. People are beginning to talk in a way that is doing you a great deal of harm. You must really pull yourself together. The Emperor is getting very worried."

He knew that what made the worst impression were his frequent disappearances at night. It was very tiresome, but this evening there seemed nothing for it but to write. He went off to his own room and was in the middle of a letter to Uji when Kaoru was announced. "You are just the person I wanted," Niou said. "I am in a terrible fix. I have been hoping to get away all the evening, but it has been absolutely impossible, and now it is horribly late. I don't know what to do about it..." "You've been in the Palace very little lately," said Kaoru, curious to test the strength of Niou's devotion, "and if you disappear again tonight, I have an impression that Their Majesties will not be best pleased. I have just been in the ladies' common-room and heard things that made me turn blue at the thought of what is going to happen to me if my responsibility in this

---

* Because she was a nun.

matter ever becomes known." "You always read such a sinister meaning into everything you hear said," Niou retorted. "In any case, if they are saying anything that appears to be at all to my discredit, the facts must have been grossly distorted. What have I ever done, I should like to know, and that any reasonable person could object to. It's no fun, I can assure you, and being hedged round with warnings and restrictions, as one is in my position." Kaoru relented. "There'll be worse trouble at Uji, if you don't go," he said. I shall be in the Palace tonight and am ready to take all the blame, if there is any unpleasantness. That Kohata hill is nothing with a good horse. Of course, you're more likely to be recognized than in a coach. But time is short—and really, does it matter so very much what people think or say?"

It was indeed very late, and if he was going at all he must do so in the quickest way. "You understand why I do not offer to come with you?" Kaoru said. "It is only because I can be more use to you on the spot." He went off to the Emperor's rooms, and Niou went to order a horse.

"Where is Niou, pray?" asked the Empress. "You don't mean to say he has gone out again! This is intolerable. What will everyone think? If the Emperor finds out he will think I did not scold him properly when I spoke about it today. It is really most inconsiderate of him."

Though she now had several grown-up sons, the Akashi Princess[*] was as lovely as ever. People said that her daughter, the First Princess, was going to be very like her. But the girl was being very strictly brought up, and Kaoru, though he spent so much time in the house, had never yet managed to even hear her voice.

What a strange feature, in great families such as this, were these shadowy presences—beings always at hand and in a way familiar as the rest of the household, yet utterly unapproachable! Anyone else, frequenting this part of the New Palace as much as he did (Kaoru thought) would find such a situation exceedingly tantalizing, and more probably than not would end by losing control over him and getting into an appalling scrape. Naturally he himself had always taken a certain interest in the First Princess; but he was not so constituted that curiosity of this kind could ever seriously disturb him. So fixed was this habit of regarding himself as quite different from other people that even his recent experiences at Uji had not uprooted it, and only as an afterthought did it occur to him that this view of his character was rather out of date.

Still it remained a fact that though the Empress had not one lady in her service who was not in one way or another unusually clever and good-looking, and though there were several among them who definitely attracted him, he could say confidently that here in the New Palace at any

---
[*] The Empress, Niou's mother.

rate his record was absolutely clear. This perhaps was due in part to Her Majesty's own high sense of decorum which she succeeded in imposing to a large extent upon those about her. But among so large a number there were bound to be some who were less amenable than others to this repressive discipline, and though outwardly a very severe standard of reticence and modesty were preserved, one or two of them had found means of indicating clearly enough that their virtue was not so unassailable as appearances might lead him to suppose. But though he was never insensible either to cleverness or good looks, here in the New Palace nothing that happened ever for a moment banished the sense of life's futility and insecurity which had haunted him since he came into the world.

At Uji it had been a bad day. First came Kaoru's tiresome letter; then one from Niou, the tone of which made it doubtful whether they were to expect him. Now it was getting very late, and there seemed no chance whatever that he would appear. When therefore close upon midnight, flushed with his long ride through the cold wind, he burst upon them in all his eager youth and freshness, it was small wonder that they found him irresistible. Kozeri indeed was completely carried off her feet. She was very lovely, he thought—radiant, in fact, decked out as she was in all the splendor of her crimson dress. His experience of women was fairly large, but among all the professed beauties of the Capital he could really think of none to compare with her. And he was beginning tonight to find that she was far indeed from being so dull and slow-witted as he had thought.

"There now," muttered one of the waiting-women, with a wicked, toothless old grin, "wouldn't it have been a thousand pities if Madam had married her the way she wanted to?* This really is a wonderful bit of luck!" And they whispered that Agemaki herself had better be quick and make up her mind, for it would be a miracle indeed if she ever got another such chance as the one she was now being so foolish over.

To celebrate the occasion the old ladies had all made themselves costumes out of the most garish and striking material they could lay hands on.

"Such patterns at their age! Really, it's unforgivable," Agemaki said to herself, glancing at the old women severely. Suddenly it occurred to her that she was too now no longer so very young. She looked in the mirror. She had become much thinner lately, that was true. Still she could not honestly call herself ugly. But that proved nothing, for it was clear enough that these old women by no means regarded their own looks as past repair. Did one not see them scraping forward their poor thin locks over their foreheads (regardless of the terrible effect from behind), powdering, rouging, and in general getting themselves up in a way that

---

* To Kaoru, a commoner (i.e. not a member of the Imperial Clan).

showed they had no notion of what they really looked like? "Obviously," Agemaki said to her, "I am not an absolute monster, my eyes and nose are in the right place..." And yet after all, how could one tell? Where one was concerned, there were evidently no limits to one's blindness. In any case she felt more than ever determined to hide herself from everyone that mattered. Whatever she might be now, in a few years she would certainly have lost every vestige of good looks; and she gave way to an access of self-pity which anyone seeing the extreme emaciation of her hands would have known to be due chiefly to mere bodily weakness.

In the midst of his happiness Niou remembered that though on this occasion he had succeeded in playing truant, the experiment was not one which it was going to be easy to repeat. He began to tell Kozeri about his difficulties with the Empress. "Promise," he begged, "that if despite all I do I cannot manage to come again for some little while, you will not be cross with me. If every time they prevent me from coming, you take it into your head that I am making excuses and have really found something better to do, it's going to be absolute torture. But all this is only for the moment. As soon as it can be arranged I will move you to somewhere more at hand."

But Kozeri, who knew nothing of the Court and its rules, but had heard a great deal about Niou's supposed frivolity, the moment she heard him talk of intervals and difficulties began to wonder whether her lot was indeed as beatific as those around her seemed to suppose.

At daybreak he opened the double-doors and they stood together watching the river. Now and again, half hidden by the heavy autumn mist that trailed across the stream, a boat would pass laden with timber, leaving behind it a long white track. "How wonderful it would be to live in such a place!" thought Niou, sensitive as he was to every kind of beauty and utterly unfamiliar with any sights save those of the town. There was sunlight now on the tops of the hills. He turned to gaze tenderly at the girl by his side. There were certain qualities, a fineness of skin, and a delicacy of feature that he had thought belonged only to the pampered children of great houses such as the one where he himself had been reared. But among all the Court beauties of his own class and standing he could think of few who in these respects came up to this neglected country girl; and he began to think that much of the supposed superiority of such women as Ryozen's daughters or his own sister, the First Princess, was the outcome of mere snobbery. More than ever he wished that she lived somewhere he could get to without all these difficulties. If only she were in the Capital!

The place began, as the morning wore on, to lose its charm for him. A menacing note came into the noise of the stream; the country on the far side stood out of the mist in all its solitary wildness. The bridge looked gaunt and forbidding. How, he wondered, could anyone manage to endure such an outlook year after year? And Kozeri herself felt ashamed* that he should see the surroundings amid which her life had been spent.

He began now to whisper in her ear the tenderest vows and promises. How strange it was, she thought, while she listened to him, that she should find herself here, hand in hand with a handsome young man whom she had known only for three days, and yet feel not the slightest trace of embarrassment! Whereas if it had been Kaoru, whom she had known all these years... With Niou, although of course when he was still a mere name to her, she had found it embarrassing to be constantly receiving letters from him, once she got to know him she did not feel in the least shy; indeed, so fast had things gone that the thought of being parted from him for what might not after all be more than a few days was making her feel thoroughly miserable. It was strange about Kaoru. She was never at her ease with him; indeed, incredible though this might seem, she had really been more embarrassed by his harmless visit the other night than by Niou's startling incursion!

Niou's men were calling to him. If he meant to arrive in the city at a respectable hour there was no time to be lost.

"Did absence mean forgetfulness then might you well, O Lady of the Bridge, spread out your sleeve and weep."

Such was his parting poem. But it was hard to go, and many times he turned to leave her, and then came back.

"Though absence and forgetfulness prove one, patient in her far home she needs must wait—the Lady of the Bridge."

So she answered; but looking into her face he read all too clearly the misgivings that her words did not express. No wonder if her young heart fluttered as she watched him go; for it was a figure of rare and entrancing grace that vanished into the dawn. Nor was it she alone who was moved, for the ladies of the house, seeing him now by daylight for the first time, were lost in admiration. "His Excellency,"† one of them said, "is very taking, but rather on the quiet side. This Niou—though perhaps one would not think so if one did not know he was a prince—has just an extra touch of something that makes all the difference."

All the way back to the city he kept on recalling her trusting yet troubled expression. He could hardly restrain himself from flinging prudence to the winds and turning back to give her one last assurance; but there was his reputation to think of, and he managed to restrain himself.

Once back in the city he found to his chagrin that he was virtually a prisoner. So closely, at any rate, was he watched that a secret evasion was impossible. He managed however to convey letters to Uji several times a

---

* It was considered a disgrace to live in the country.

† Kaoru.

day and there seemed at first no reason to doubt that he was really very much in love. But as time went on and still he failed to appear Agemaki began to harbor misgivings which were none the less painful for the fact that the situation was precisely the one which she had always foreseen. She was careful not to make matters worse by letting Kozeri see how worried she was. But as far as she herself was concerned, this experience made her feel less inclined than ever to embark upon a similar hazard.

Kaoru, too, was watching the situation with great concern. He felt that if things went wrong he would, not unnaturally, be held responsible, and he made a practice of dropping in on Niou at unexpected moments to see what impression he would make when taken unawares. Invariably he found him in a state of listless melancholy which seemed to show that, from Kaoru's point of view, there was no cause for alarm.

As things were turning out, the only solution—Niou began to think—was to bring Kozeri to the city. But where could he put her? The obvious place was the New Palace. But there she would be under the same roof as Yugiri, "which would be very awkward," Niou thought, "after the way he has continually pressed his own daughter* upon me." It was indeed, he felt convinced, largely owing to complaints from Yugiri concerning his loose life that his reputation with Their Majesties had suffered. Of course the remedy suggested by Yugiri was that Niou should be subjected to the steadying influence of marriage, and he had persuaded Their Majesties that for this purpose a woman of the highest rank and consequence was essential—someone, in fact, like his own daughter. This made it in the highest degree unlikely that a girl such as Kozeri, without family influence and utterly unknown at Court, would be accepted by his parents as a possible match. If he had simply taken a fancy to her he might, in order to have her close at hand, have procured for her some post in the Empress's household. But his feelings towards her were of a very different kind. Niou knew it had been arranged that if his father died and his brother succeeded to the Throne, he himself should become Heir Apparent. Then he would be in a position to do something really splendid for her. This made it all the more irritating that for the present he was obliged to treat her so shabbily.

Kaoru, who was not hampered by the same difficulties, was fully determined to bring Agemaki to his palace as soon as the rebuilding of it was finished. It was really distressing, he felt, that Niou's position should make a simple matter such as his affair with Kozeri so difficult and distressing for both of them. He felt strongly tempted to explain the whole business to the Empress and try to obtain her support. Niou might resent his interference; but from Kozeri's point of view it could certainly do no

---

* His sixth daughter, Roku no Kimi.

harm. Nothing indeed could be worse than the present state of affairs, and if attention were called to the Princesses' condition, it might lead to something being done towards restoring them to their proper position in the world. Meanwhile, thinking that they might be in difficulties over their winter decorations, he sent the bed-curtains and wall-hangings which he had really intended for Agemaki's use later on, if he were able to persuade her to come to the palace he was rebuilding. "There is no reason you should not have the use of them at once," he said, sending them very secretly. He also sent a number of costumes for the maids, which he chose in consultation with his own old nurse.

At last, on the first day of the eleventh month, an opportunity for getting Niou to Uji seemed to present itself. It was the time when the fish-traps are at work, which gave him some excuse for suggesting Uji as a suitable place for Niou's maple-leaf excursion.* Permission was duly accorded, and it was arranged that the expedition should be of a quite private character, only one or two of his closest friends being asked to join the party. But, as in the case of all Niou's plans, the news soon leaked out, and much to his annoyance he suddenly found that Yugiri's son Kurodo no Shosho had been added to the party. However, the only officer of high rank was Kaoru, though there were of course a good many ordinary courtiers in attendance.

Kaoru thought it as well to warn the people at Uji. "They are certain to make this their headquarters," he said, "so you had better be prepared. Several of the gentlemen who came with Niou to see the spring flowers a year or two ago are to be with him again, and are most anxious to improve their acquaintance with you both."

Hasty preparations were at once set afoot. The curtains were changed, the house vigorously swept, the river bank cleared of dead leaves and the moat of encumbering water-weeds. Kaoru sent a handsome supply of fruit and fish, and lent a number of his own servants. It was painful to her to be so completely dependent on him; but it was really impossible to refuse, and considering how diminished their own resources were at the moment, it was certainly providential that he was there to step into the breach.

Pleasant strains of music, growing louder then dying on the breeze as the boat paddled idly up- and down-stream, were the first intimation that the visitors were at hand. Immediately the young maids crowded to the windows on that side of the house, hoping to catch a glimpse of these wonderful gentlemen from the Capital. But so laden was the boat with great boughs of maple that it was impossible to distinguish anybody— even Niou himself—and all they got to satisfy their curiosity was the

---

* The "viewing of the autumn-leaves"; in the case of a Prince of the Blood it had a semi-official character.

music that poured out in tempestuous gusts from under this leafy arcade. Niou, these ladies felt, must be an immensely important person, if even on a small and private excursion such as this he was attended by a bevy of followers so magnificent as those whom they could dimly descry between the red leaves, and they felt that, even though like the Spinning Maiden and the Herd Boy[*] he and Kozeri met but once a year, she might still consider herself fortunately matched.

As he meant to write some Chinese poems Niou brought professors with him. When twilight began the boat was moored on the far shore, and while the music still continued, he began attempting to compose. How pleased with themselves they all looked with their garlands of light and dark leaves, playing the Sea Fairies' Music on their flutes! Niou could think only of the girl across the stream. Nothing could have been more tantalizing than to be so near and yet so far away. Would she understand his difficulties?...

But now the professors gave out a series of themes suitable to the season and occasion, and everyone began droning snatches of verse. He had just arranged that the moment this was over Kaoru should help him to slip away,[†] when one of Kurodo no Shosho's elder brothers suddenly arrived with a whole company of retainers and attendants, saying the Empress had given orders that he was to join the party. It appeared that on the records being looked into no case could be found of a Prince of the Blood setting off like this on his Maple Leaf Excursion with only one officer of high rank in attendance, and it was thought most undesirable to create a precedent. Both Kaoru and Niou were naturally aghast at this fresh intrusion, and as far as Niou was concerned it meant that the proceedings lost all further interest for him. Everyone drank a good deal, there was a lot of rather inconsequent music and dancing, and in the general excitement no one noticed that both Kaoru and Niou were standing aloof. As though enough had not already been done to keep Niou under observation, the Controller of the Empress's household now arrived with a crowd of lesser courtiers saying that he hoped for the pleasure of seeing His Highness safely home, and Niou now saw to his dismay that he was going to be hustled back to the City without the chance of so much as a word with Kozeri. He sent her a note in which he explained exactly what had happened that day and professed the keenest disappointment. But it contained none of the usual pretty and tender touches and might quite as well have been written to a complete stranger. She imagined him entirely preoccupied by his noisy companions. A letter reaching him at such a moment would be passed round. She made up her mind not to reply.

---

[*] Two stars that are said to meet once a year.
[†] To Kozeri.

The sight of Kaoru and Niou among their friends only made Agemaki feel all the more acutely how hopelessly unfitted she was for that kind of society. As for Kozeri, during the long period of his absence she had managed to persuade herself that painful though the separation was, she had no cause for alarm. He had explained that it was not his fault, and certainly he seemed as much upset by the situation as she was. But to have him disporting himself like this at her very door, and then see him go away without making any real effort to see her was more than she could bear; though had she known it, Niou's agitation was fully as great as hers.

Even the *hio* fish seemed to be on their mettle today, and there had been a splendid catch at the traps. These were now served on a bedding of various autumn leaves, amid a general acclamation in which Niou did his best to participate. But he could hardly have felt less inclined than at that moment for the company in which he found himself, and it was all he could do to be civil.

He gazed across the river. Prince Hachi had taken particular trouble with his trees. But now these great cedars, overgrown with a tangle of ivy, seemed, even from a distance, to give the place a gloomy air.

It made Kaoru very unhappy to think of all the wasted preparations that, solely on the strength of his own assurances, had been made in the house on the other side.

Some of the visitors, who had accompanied Niou to Uji while Prince Hachi was still alive, spoke of his kindness to them on that occasion, and of the terrible loss his death must have been for the two daughters. It was evident from the remarks of one or two of them that they knew something of Niou's relations with Kozeri; and even among those who were quite ignorant in this respect there were many who displayed a knowledge concerning the general affairs of the household that was remarkable considering its remoteness and obscurity.

"The younger one is exceedingly good-looking," someone informed the company, "and plays the thirteen-stringed zithern. Music was the old Prince's specialty, and he devoted all his time to teaching her."

"Sad is it now, for those that once in gay and lusty bloom this garden saw, beneath the desolate shade of wilting boughs to stand."

Such was Kurodo no Shosho's poem, addressed to Kaoru, whom he regarded as protector of the family.

"Beauty was lost, but in red leafage came again, and once again was lost. Of thee, best mirror of the World's incertitude, O cherry-tree, I speak."* Such was Kaoru's reply; and Kurodo's brother: "Go we less loath

---

* The poem refers partly to Kozeri's ups and downs.

today from the bright shadow of the maple-trees than he[*] whom once another autumn drove from this his mountain home?"

"Can he be gone, when still upon the rocks' hard face the steadfast arrow-root precarious clings?" Such was the Controller's poem. Alone among those present he was the late Prince's contemporary, and recalling Hachi as he had known him when they were both young men he was deeply moved.

"On these sad gardens, desolate enough at autumn's close, blow not too harshly, wind from the mountain-woods!"[†] This was Niou's poem. There were tears in his eyes while he recited it, and those who knew something of his relations with Kozeri began to think that the affair was more serious than they had imagined. They realized how painful it must be for him to be thus spirited away without a chance to see her, and would have done anything for him that they could. But in the face of this constantly growing supervision his well-wishers were helpless.

During the course of the visit a great many Chinese poems had been made, and passages from these were now recited, together with numerous Japanese poems. But parties of this kind, where a great deal of drink goes round and everyone is rather over-excited, do not produce poetical masterpieces, and on going through these pieces I cannot find one that is really worth preserving.

The sisters, when first they realized that the party was on its way back and then heard the voices of the outriders growing dimmer and dimmer in the distance, were grievously disappointed, as were naturally all those who had taken part in the wasted preparations.

To Agemaki it seemed clear enough that Niou's reputation was thoroughly well-founded. She had of course often heard her women say that lying was "the only thing men were any use at," and that they thought nothing of addressing the most passionate speeches to women about whom they hardly cared at all. But she had always supposed that this applied only to men of the same class as these women themselves—people among whom it was natural that a low standard should prevail; whereas men of decent breeding, quite apart from any question of higher principles, knew that the eyes of the world were upon them and simply did not dare to treat people too badly. Evidently she had been mistaken. Her father knew better; he had always spoken doubtfully of Niou's character, and taken the view that it would be a bad thing to have too much to do with him. Certainly to admit him into the family as they had done was to court disaster. What, Agemaki wondered, did Kaoru think of the situation that his officiousness had produced? The only consolation she could think of

---

[*] Prince Hachi. I follow Moto-ori's interpretation.
[†] The poem expresses a hope that Kozeri is not too unhappy.

was that here in Uji there was no one who mattered sufficiently for one to mind him witnessing one's discomfort. All the same, it was not very pleasant, however little respect one might have for the people about one, to meet mocking glances wherever one went... She fretted so much about the whole affair that she became positively ill; whereas Kozeri, though bitterly disappointed at not seeing Niou, still refused to admit that all his tender vows and promises had been mere hypocrisy. He maintained that he was being prevented from seeing her, and for the present she must believe him. But she could not manage to appear very cheerful, and Agemaki, watching her sister continually and brooding over her misfortunes, mistook for a tragic sorrow what was no more than a momentary fit of disappointment and depression. Never would he have dared treat Kozeri in this way, Agemaki said to herself, had she lived in the ordinary way and occupied the place in society to which her birth entitled her; and this reflection made her all the more apprehensive concerning her own future, for it was obvious that she was herself exposed to exactly the same dangers. Kaoru's promises that their friendship should remain on whatever footing she chose to give it meant nothing at all. He said this merely to humor her, and presently it would begin all over again. However determined she might be to make him keep his distance, it was at the best a wearing business, and in the end she felt certain that all her efforts would be frustrated by the machinations of one or the other of these incorrigible old busybodies, who seemed to have no other thought in their heads.

She knew now why her father had always spoken of an unmarried girl's dealings with the World as if they demanded a quite extraordinary degree of circumspection and care.

The truth was that both of them were evidently born to misfortune. Losing their parents was only the beginning of it. Kozeri's present situation was all part of the same thing, and as every fresh disaster that overtook them was also a fresh torment for their parents in the world beyond, Agemaki was determined for her part to escape from life before this tragic destiny was fulfilled, and partly for this reason, partly because she was really feeling very unwell, she began to refuse all food.

Niou kept on thinking that he would presently find a chance to escape from the Palace. But the difficulties were greater than ever, for on returning from Uji Yugiri's eldest son* had gone straight to the Emperor, telling him that Niou's sudden determination to view the maple leaves at Uji was now fully explained; it was clear that this was one of the places where he carried on a secret and scandalous intrigue. Niou's conduct in turning the autumn excursion to account in this impudent way had, he said, excited much unfavorable Comment.

---

* Who had been sent to keep an eye on the maple-leaf party.

The Empress sighed, and the Emperor looked very cross. "The whole thing is entirely wrong," he said. "This comes of letting him go and live at home* whenever he feels inclined." Stern measures were taken, and Niou placed on perpetual duty at the Palace. He still told Their Majesties flatly that he was not interested in Yugiri's daughter, Roku no Kimi, but despite this the arrangements for the marriage were already being made. Kaoru heard of this and was extremely upset. A fine end to all the efforts he had made on Kozeri's behalf! And it had all, from the very beginning, been due to the odd disposition with which an unkind fate had endowed him. For it was on account of his supposed immunity from the common foibles of mankind that Hachi had selected him as guardian to his beloved daughters. No one could say that Kaoru had taken his obligations lightly. The idea that two girls so richly endowed with every sort of charm should waste their lives in solitude and obscurity was as painful to him as it could have been to anybody, and it would have been perverse indeed if he had resisted Niou's continual demands for an introduction, coming as they did at a time when Kaoru himself was racking his brains to find some scheme which would set their lives on a reasonable footing. He had been piqued of course at Agemaki's attempt to get him off her hands by passing him on to her sister, and this had led to his bringing Kozeri and Niou together far too precipitately. As things were before this ghastly blunder it would have been perfectly possible for him to bring both girls to the City. But the mischief he had done was irretrievable, and he could only curse his own miserable stupidity.

For Niou meanwhile nothing could have been more painful than this gilded captivity. What could he do or say that would make Kozeri believe in him? He chafed and fretted continually, and it became so obvious there was something on his mind that his mother said to him at last: "If there is anyone you really care for, you had better bring her here and put the thing on a respectable footing. When your father dies you will be heir to the Throne, and it is of the utmost importance that people should begin to feel you are someone whom they can take seriously."

One very rainy day, when nothing was going on at the Palace, Niou paid a visit to his sister, the First Princess. No one else was there, and she was occupying herself quietly with her books and pictures. He sat outside her screened couch and began to talk to her. For years she had been his ideal. Where else could one ever hope to find this extraordinary combination of haughtiness and yielding charm, of proud reserve and gaiety? If anyone could possibly be compared to her it must, he imagined, be the ex-Emperor Ryozen's daughter, about whom he had heard things that interested him very much, though he had never man-

---

* In the New Palace, where the Empress had her private residence.

aged to get into touch with her. But now... However this was not the moment to begin thinking again about Uji, and to distract himself he began looking at the picture-rolls that were lying scattered on the floor. There were some sets of famous women and their lovers, with views of gardens and country houses that kept on reminding him of various incidents at Uji. He thought for a moment of telling his sister something about it all and asking if he might have some of these pictures to send to Kozeri. One of the rolls was *The Tales of Ise,* and going through it he came to the episode of the brother and sister.* The picture showed him teaching her to play the zithern. "What would the First Princess think of this picture?" Niou wondered. He drew a little nearer. "I should like to have lived then," he said mysteriously; "nowadays sisters do not treat one half as well." "What picture can it be that he has got hold of?" she was wondering, when he held up the roll in front of her. She bent her head over it, and her hair fell forward, the ends protruding beneath the fringes of the curtain. Yes, she was very attractive; it was tantalizing that a mere accident of birth should suffice to set so rigid a barrier between them. "How loath am I that alien hands should tear from fresh and tender roots the plant I may not touch!"

Such was his poem. It meant either nothing at all or else something too horrifying to think of. She knew that several of her women, shy of meeting Niou when they had not had time to prepare themselves, were hiding behind a screen. This added to her embarrassment, and she made no attempt to reply—which was perhaps the best plan, thought Niou, for even he would have been shocked if her reply had in any way resembled that of the lady in the story.†

Niou and the First Princess had been Lady Murasaki's favorites and in childhood had spent much time together in her rooms; indeed among all his brothers and sisters she was still the one he saw most of. The Empress doted on her, and gave her everything her heart could desire. In particular she would have thought it a crime that a single one of the Princess's women should not reach the very highest standard both in looks and upbringing, and many among them were daughters of the greatest dignitaries in the land.

It would have been surprising if anyone as susceptible as Niou, who since his confinement in the City met these wonderful creatures more constantly than ever, had not, indulged in a good deal of flirtation. This did not mean that his feelings towards Kozeri had in any way changed, but it seemed to take up a lot of time, and for days on end the usual letter to Kozeri failed to get written.

---

* Episode 49 of the *Ise Monogatari.*

† The reply of the lady in the *Tales of Ise* was not by any means discouraging.

Just when the suspense at Uji was at its height and everyone was saying that unless news came immediately it would be clear that the whole thing was over, Kaoru arrived, saying that he had come to enquire after Agemaki, having heard that she was indisposed. Weak though she felt, she was not feverish or delirious and was quite capable of carrying on a conversation. But she was glad to be able to use her illness as an excuse, and sent word that she could not see anyone. "If I am only to hear other people's reports about her condition," he said, "I might as well have stayed in the City. It was to see her for myself and form my own opinion that I came all this way, and nothing else will allay my anxiety." She consented finally to let her people bring him to her sick-room and put his seat at the side of her curtained bed. She did not at all like receiving a visitor under such circumstances. But she did not, now that he was here, wish to seem bad-tempered, and pushing her hair back from her face, she exchanged the usual greetings with him. He told her how unhappy Niou had been the other day at being carried back to the City without seeing Kozeri. "There is nothing to worry about," he said. "In any case, it is not Niou who is to blame." "He has stopped writing," she said. "I can see I have let Kozeri spoil her life in much the way my father warned us against. It is a terrible thing to have done." "A woman's life is a difficult business at the best of times," Kaoru answered, feeling all the same none too happy about the part that he had played in this matter. "If you had as much experience of the world as I have you would realize that difficult though Kozeri's position may be, there is really nothing very unusual about it. As to Niou's ultimate intentions I have not in my own mind the slightest doubt. A little patience on your side is all that is required." But was he, Kaoru asked himself, in any way authorized to make such undertakings on Niou's behalf? In reality the whole affair was making him feel very uneasy.

Her worst time was generally at night, and Kozeri, thinking that, in case another of these attacks came on, she would rather not have a stranger in the room, suggested to Kaoru that he should now retire to his usual quarters. In this she was backed by several of the old ladies, and he was obliged to consent. "I think it is rather unfair to send me away now," he said to Ben no Kimi; "it was on purpose to be present at one of these attacks that I came here, for what I had heard of them was causing me great anxiety. You might easily, at such moments, be glad to have someone at hand on whom you could rely." He thought it would be a good thing that services of intercession should be held, and spoke to Ben about it.

It irritated her that all these efforts should be made to prolong her life, when she herself, who surely had a right to be consulted, asked for nothing but to be allowed to die in peace. But to protest in any way would have seemed very ungracious, and she was touched by Kaoru's evident anxiety to keep her alive.

"I hope you feel more yourself today," he wrote next morning. "In any case I will come presently and sit with you as I did last night." She sent back a message saying that she had for some time past been growing weaker every day, and had not expected any improvement this morning. But of course, if he liked to come, she would do her best to receive him.

He expected to find some terrible change and it was with relief and delight that he saw, from the moment he approached the bed that she looked, if anything, better than yesterday. He sat as close as he could and began telling her about everything that had been happening. Presently however she interrupted him, saying in a very faint voice that he was tiring her. Perhaps sometime later on in the day when she was feeling a little better...

However he could not hang about here all day with nothing to do, and though he still felt very anxious, he made up his mind to go back to the City. "Her living out here makes everything much more difficult," he said to Ben no Kimi. "As soon as she can be moved we must get her to somewhere more convenient. Her illness in itself provides an excuse for such a move,* and having sent word to the Teacher that Agemaki needed his prayers, he set out for home.

It happened that a retainer of Kaoru's was courting one of Agemaki's younger maids. "You've heard the news, I suppose?" this man said to the girl one day. "They've put a stop to Prince Niou's excursions. He has to report at the Palace every night. The Minister of the Left is bent on the Prince marrying his sixth daughter. The lady herself has been in love with him for a long time past, and they have made all arrangements for the wedding to take place before the end of the year. But Prince Niou has no mind to lose his liberty. They say that even at the Palace he thinks about nothing else but carrying on with the ladies-in-waiting. The Emperor and Empress are always calling him to order, but he takes not the slightest notice. My own master is as different from him as possible. He gets no fun out of life at all; I Sometimes thinks it bothers him to get too much mixed up with other people. That makes it the entire stranger that he should come here so often. But people say that this is his one exception." All this was repeated by the girl to her friends and bandied from mouth to mouth in Agemaki's hearing.

This was the end. Hitherto, though she had believed Niou's affair with Kozeri merely to be one of many frivolous attachments, she had

---

* Illness was thought to be due to "possession," and it was believed that the possessing spirit could be got rid of by moving the patient about. We call the same form of treatment a "change of air."

at least believed him not to be committed in any influential quarter. Of this not a word had been breathed, and she suddenly felt a conviction that the whole of Niou's courtship had simply been undertaken to suit Kaoru's convenience. In any case Niou had behaved in the most callous way imaginable. Agemaki, weak enough already, felt the last atom of any desire to live slipping away from her while she listened to the recital of this incredible piece of news. It did not much matter what these people thought; but all the same she closed her eyes and pretended not to be listening. By her side lay Kozeri, who was not merely pretending to be asleep. Lately indeed, the night being Agemaki's worst time, Kozeri had got into the habit of dozing a good deal during the day. "This dozing against which my dear parents warn me..."* Agemaki remembered the old poem, and seeing her sister lie there, her head propped on her bent arm, her lovely hair flooding the pillow, again and again she reproached herself for having so wantonly neglected her own dear father's warning.

Was he in some sphere of being where he knew of their predicament? Though he had died a layman, still the weight of his sins was not such as to have borne him down into the remoter depths of retribution. "Send for me," she said passionately. "I will come to you wherever you are. Do not abandon us in our misery. If our waking eyes may not see you, visit us at least in our dreams."

It was growing late. Outside, from a gloomy, sodden sky the rain swept across the woods, and the wind howled. A sudden gust shook everything in the house and Kozeri woke with a start. In her yellow dress faced with light blue, her cheeks flushed with sleep, she looked particularly gay, and it would have been a clever person indeed who could have recognized in this handsome, lively girl the victim of a heartrending tragedy!† "I have just been dreaming of father," she said. "He kept on glancing anxiously in my direction, as though he were afraid something dreadful was going to happen to me."

"I have longed to dream of him ever since he died; but he has never come to me." Agemaki burst into tears, and seeing her weep, Kozeri wept too.

Long after it was quite dark, a messenger arrived from Prince Niou. For the moment things began to seem a little brighter. "Answer nicely just as though nothing had happened," Agemaki advised, seeing Kozeri hesitate before opening the letter. "When I am dead you will have to defend yourself against people even less scrupulous than he, and you will certainly have less trouble with them if it is thought that a person in

---

* "This habit of dozing by day, against which my dear mother warns me, comes (if she only knew) of being too unhappy to sleep at night." Anonymous poem from the *Shuishu*

† Murasaki implies, of course, that Agemaki takes her sister's situation too tragically.

Niou's position has you to some extent under his protection. I think in that way he may be of some assistance."

"You must not speak of one going before the other," Kozeri said. "I cannot bear it" and she hid her face in her sleeve. "That is what I felt before father died," Agemaki said. "But somehow or other one lives on from day to day, simply because one must. But then, I had you to think of…"

The lamp was brought in and she read Niou's letter. It was certainly very affectionate, but seemed only to repeat the old phrases. "Since over both our heads the self-same tempest hangs, why should this rainy night beyond all bounds my restlessness increase?"

Such was his poem. "Not all the rains of the Godless Month…"* with this and other well-worn allusions he had attempted to give the appropriate tone. But Agemaki thought the whole affair very perfunctory, and her spirits sank once more. But Niou, she reflected, was not only very good-looking but also knew very well how to lay himself out to please. That Kozeri should be taken in was only natural. Indeed, no young girl in her place could be expected to realize that all his fine speeches and attentions meant as little as they actually did.

Kozeri herself, though the long suspense was becoming rather a strain, never for a moment believed that Niou meant to let things stay as they were. His promises had been so definite, the strength of his affection (it seemed to her) so obvious—but in any case, even if he was merely trifling with her affections, what point could there have been in his committing himself in all these unnecessary ways? The messenger sent word that he could wait no longer, as he had orders to be back before dawn. With the help of her women Kozeri produced the verse: "Day in, day out upon our lonely hills the hailstone falls, while dark above and ever darker grows the country of the sky." She sent it by itself, with no covering letter.

This happened on the last day of the tenth month. A whole month had gone by without his getting to Uji. Niou was horrified to find how the time had passed, and every night he made plans for slipping away, but something always prevented it. Halfway through the eleventh month his prospects of escape grew more remote than ever, for the Gosechi Dancing fell early this year, and he was soon immersed in Palace festivities which entirely occupied his time and attention. Thus quite against his will the period of his absence from Uji was still further protracted. Needless to say he did not pass these two months in complete seclusion from the female society. Nevertheless, he was thinking about Kozeri all the time, and was very unhappy. "We are both very anxious to see you settle down properly," the Empress said to him one day, speaking of the arrangements for his

---

* "Not all the rains of the Godless Month [tenth month] have wetted my sleeve so much as this hour of weeping."

marriage to Roku no Kimi. "But once you are married, if there is anyone else you have a particular fancy for, there is nothing to prevent you're bringing her here as well and putting the thing on a proper footing."

"There is no hurry about that, is there?" he said. "I should like time to think it over."

Kozeri knew nothing of the plans he was making on her behalf, and after all these weeks of waiting she was indeed beginning to feel rather in despair. Kaoru too decided that Niou was after all a hopelessly untrustworthy character; the way he had treated Kozeri was really unforgivable. And for a time the two friends seldom met. But with Uji Kaoru remained in constant communication.

Early in the eleventh month he heard that Agemaki was rather better, and as he had a great deal of business on hand for nearly a week on end he did not send anyone to enquire. Then he suddenly became nervous and canceling all his engagements he rushed to Uji. Here he found that, although he had given instructions for the ritual of intercession to be carried on until Agemaki was completely recovered, the Teacher had already allowed her to send him away, on the plea that she was going on as well as could be expected. Indeed the place seemed almost entirely deserted. The account that Ben no Kimi gave was not reassuring. "She has no very alarming symptoms," the old woman said, "and does not seem to be exactly in pain. But she eats nothing at all. She was never really strong, and since this disappointment about Prince Niou, which she seems to have taken terribly to heart, she won't as much as look at her food. Naturally she is losing strength every day, and it does not look to me as though she will last much longer. There is nothing we can any of us do, and I wish I had not lived to see this day, indeed I do..." and she burst into tears.

"If things are really as bad as that, I wish you had let me know before. I have been so busy the last few days that it has been absolutely impossible for me to send anyone. But I have been very anxious..." He hurried to her bedside, but when he spoke to her she did not seem to have the strength to reply. He was furious that they had not let him know of the grave turn that things had taken, but it was no use grumbling, and he began at once to make arrangements for the Teacher and all the most celebrated wonder-workers he could lay hands on to begin a great service and recitation of Scriptures at the break of day.

A number of his retainers had joined him at Uji, there was a rumble and stir in the courtyards; and the presence of so many men about the place gave to the waiting-women a sense of security such as they had not known for many a long day.

At dusk they told him that his supper had been served in the usual place. But he wanted to go again and see for himself how she was. The place where he sat before was now occupied by the recitant priests; but the maids screened a space for him on the other side of the bed, and he stationed himself there without bothering about his food. Kozeri was afraid that Agemaki might be upset by this intrusion, but the general view seemed to be that Kaoru was on terms with her that entitled him to do as he chose, and no effort was made to restrain him.

In the last watch before midnight the Continuous Reading of the *Hokkekyo* began. The twelve priests chosen for the purpose all had marvelous voices, and the effect was very impressive. There was a lamp in the adjoining room, but where the sick woman lay it was almost dark. He raised the corner of one of the bed-curtains and, pushing his head and shoulders through the gap, peered in. Two or three old women were watching by the bedside. Kozeri, who had been lying beside her sister, slipped away, and he found Agemaki lying on the bed alone. He took her hand and begged her to try and speak. "My mind is quite clear," she said, in a voice so low that it was hardly audible, "but I have not the strength to speak. Why have you not been here for so long? I was afraid I should not see you again..." Did she then really attach some importance to his visits?

He touched her forehead. It seemed rather hot. "I think you are feverish," he said. "I wonder why you should be. Very often, they say, it is the result of having made someone else unhappy." And he began to whisper once more in her ear the tale of his own sufferings.

She could not bear it. Why, why could he not spare her this agony? She covered her face with her sleeve. How still she lay! For a moment he thought that all was over.

"You must be tired out with so many nights watching," he said presently to Kozeri, who had appeared again. "Go and rest. I will take duty tonight." She would not under ordinary circumstances have dreamed of leaving him with Agemaki like this. But perhaps in such an emergency... She resigned her place to him, but was careful to keep within call.

Agemaki's face was still buried in her sleeve. But she was conscious that he had crept closer and was looking down at her. Providence seemed to have sent him to look after her: it was useless to resist the decree. And after all he was extraordinarily sympathetic and gentle. She could not imagine herself having such confidence in any other man as sick-nurse— in Niou, for example, who whatever might be his superiority in other respects would not, she felt sure, for a moment compare with Kaoru at such a time as this. She hated to think of him looking back upon her after she was dead as hard-hearted and ungrateful. She determined not to let him feel that she was repulsing his kindness. But though at intervals throughout the night he got her people to bring her broth and one thing and another in the hope of persuading her to take nourishment, these efforts were quite in vain. His failure both mortified and alarmed him, for he was convinced that in getting her to take food immediately lay the only chance of saving her.

The chanting of the Scriptures was going on all the time. The sudden breaking in of a new voice* at dawn was particularly impressive.

The Teacher was also spending the night in the house, it being hoped that his sanctity would repel evil influences. He had dozed for a while, but now woke up and began to recite a *darani*.† His voice was thin and cracked, but gave the impression that he knew his business thoroughly, and somehow inspired one with confidence. Having enquired how Agemaki was, he began with trembling voice to speak of his friendship with the old Prince. "I had made sure," the Teacher said, "that by now his soul had safely won its way to Paradise. But a night or two ago he appeared to me in a vision, just as we knew him on earth, saying that though he had successfully rid himself of all other earthly attachments and desires, there was still one ill-ordered thought that persistently barred the road to Salvation; and he begged me to do something to assist him. I could not at the moment make up my mind what would be the most suitable rite, but as five or six of the priests at our temple happened to be at my disposal I set them to work upon the Recitation of Amitabha's name. Since then however it has occurred to me that the Sadaparibhuta‡ would probably be the most helpful and I have arranged for its performance."

Unfortunately he said all this in Agemaki's hearing and it had a deplorable effect upon her. It was bad enough that already during her father's lifetime she and her sister had impeded his devotions; but that his affection for them should bar his progress even in the world beyond was a terrible thought. Of one thing however she was more than ever determined. She must join him now, while his soul still hovered between incarnation and incarnation, so that they might be born together in the Land of Happiness.

The Teacher relapsed into silence and presently left the room. The priest whom he had sent out to perform the Sadaparibhuta visited all the surrounding villages and even got so far as the outskirts of the Capital. But at dawn a heavy storm drove him back to shelter,§ and he was presently seen doing his final homage, this time to the Teacher, who was waiting near the main gate. Kaoru, sensitive as he was to such impres-

---

* The *Hokkekyo* was being read by twelve priests in rotation.

† Sanskrit spell.

‡ Consisting in going round from place to place doing homage to whomever one met. In reverence for the Buddha-nature that is in all of us. The rite is based on Chapter XX of the *Hokkekjyo;* but in China it was associated with the heretical Sankai Sect, and was suppressed.

§ Unlike the abbot Shonyo (9th century), whose sanctity was such that when he was performing this rite (he held the record, having abased himself before 167,800 people) the heaviest rain failed to wet his coat.

sions, found the whole scene and in particular the closing words of the valediction* inexpressibly moving.

Presently however he heard Kozeri steal up to the far side of the screened couch to see how Agemaki was getting on. "Wasn't the chanting wonderful?" he said, sitting up and arranging himself more tidily. "It is a ritual that is never used on public occasions, but I know none that is more impressive: 'Sad as the haunting cry of birds at dawn that shake the glittering hoar-frost from their wings.'" Had it been Niou that now suddenly stood before her and recited these words, she would, despite the heartlessness with which he had treated her, have answered readily enough. But with Kaoru—though the two were in some ways strangely alike—do what she would she could never overcome her shyness. Happily Ben no Kimi was standing close by, and it was to her that Kozeri whispered the answer: "Know they how great a sorrow fills this house—the birds whose woe pervades the frozen shore?" A more unlikely substitute† could hardly have been imagined; but she acquitted herself of the task with Great Spirit.

Though in other ways she closed her heart to him, for interchanges of this kind Agemaki had before her illness already begun to show a marked inclination, and Kozeri's unwillingness made him feel all the more how irreparable her loss would be.

The description of Hachi as he had appeared to the Teacher in a vision—still distracted by the same pitiable anxiety as had hampered his spiritual progress on earth—suspended, as it were, between this world and the next, harrowed Kaoru so much that though his messengers were already flying from shrine to shrine on Agemaki's behalf, he also found time to arrange that special services should be said for the old Prince's soul at the temple where he died. Indeed his whole time seemed now to be occupied in arranging for innumerable intercessions and purifications, and his own affairs both public and private had to be put entirely aside.

Had Agemaki's illness indeed been the work of some offended deity, all these efforts might have produced some effect; and still more might this have been the case if she had herself been willing to pray for her own recovery. On the contrary, she felt that her release could not have come at a better hour. Unwillingly she had been drawn on by Kaoru into habits of intimacy from which she saw no means of extracting herself, and though it was obvious that at present he felt a considerable affection for her, Agemaki was certain that once they had lived together for a little while he would find, just as Niou had done in Kozeri's case, that she did not come up to his expectations—a discovery which would, she knew, lead

---

* *Ekomon.* Numerous forms are used, the commonest ending with the words "May we and every creature that has life in all the worlds attain Buddha's Way."

† Ben recited the poem on Kozeri's behalf.

to a situation as painful to him as to her. If by any chance she recovered, she was determined to become a nun; for this, she was certain, was the only way to ensure that their friendship should really be lasting. The plan however was by no means an easy one to carry out. It would obviously be a mistake to mention it to Kaoru. She did indeed ask Kozeri to speak about it to the Teacher, saying she had heard that in cases such as hers the taking of religious Vows often had a beneficial effect. But the idea met with a clamor of protestation on every side: His Excellency[*] was worried enough already. He would go into frenzy if it were so much as suggested. How could such an idea have entered her head? She saw that even if she persisted no message of hers to the Teacher or any other person capable of helping her[†] would ever get delivered.

The news of Kaoru's retirement at Uji was beginning to spread, and a large number of visitors now waited upon him daily. It was apparent to everyone that his deepest feelings were involved, and several of his followers and intimate retainers initiated services of intercession at their own expense.

One day he suddenly realized that Carnival[‡] had begun in the City. Here the weather was atrocious; nothing day after day but blizzards and howling winds. At the Capital, people said, it was not anything like as bad. What good, he sometimes asked himself, was he doing by hanging on here? Why give himself the pain of seeing with his own eyes what he would in any case be able to guess so easily—that she had died without relenting towards him. But just as he was thinking of what a relief it would be to give the whole thing up, to escape from all this stress and strain, he remembered the supreme happiness that a word or look of hers, though he knew all the time they meant so little, had often given him, and the faint hope that she might even if it were only for a few moments recover strength enough to talk with him as she used to do, held him rooted where he stood.

The day ended cheerless as it had begun.

"Dawn follows dawn, but still no daytime comes to these wild uplands where in sorrow's cloud the garland of light[§] is hid."

Such was his poem. He felt himself simply to be wasting time. As a matter of fact however his presence at Uji was a great help and comfort to everyone.

He was sitting by the couch as usual when a violent blast of wind blew up the curtains, and Kozeri prudently retreated into the inner room. The two or three maids who were watching at the sick-bed happened to be particularly unpresentable old creatures, and they too beat a hasty retreat.

---

[*] Kaoru.
[†] The commentators were certainly wrong in taking *tanomoshibito* as referring to Kaoru.
[‡] *Toyo-akari,* the merry-making that marks the close of the solemn harvest rituals.
[§] A reference to the sunflower worn by the feasters in their hair on Carnival Day.

"How do you feel?" he said, bending over the couch. "Surely you might find one word to say to me, after all the trouble I have been taking to make you better. You must really try hard to get well, mustn't you? I don't know how I should get on without you." For hours past she had seemed to be unconscious; yet she had strength and wit enough, the moment he approached, to draw her sleeve over her face. "Sometime," she said, "when I am feeling a little better, I want to talk to you. Just at the moment it is impossible. I am feeling much too faint..." There was a note of great tenderness in her voice. He could control himself no longer, and though there was nothing he more disliked than violent displays of emotion, he began to sob loudly and bitterly. Sometimes after long illnesses people, he knew, lost all their attractiveness, and he felt that in a way this must make their death easier to bear. He gazed at Agemaki, almost hoping to find in her some such sinister change. Certainly her arms and hands were very thin; she was indeed a mere shadow. But her skin, in its delicate pallor, was lovelier than ever. She had thrust back the coverlet and lay among the billowing folds of her white dress like a doll in its box. Indeed as it was she who had been grievously ill for so long that looked dainty and unruffled; while the women about her, half of whose time seemed to be spent in peering anxiously into the mirror, already showed signs of the stress through which they were passing.

Kaoru began to speak of Kozeri. Surely the sound of her sister's name would draw some spark of animation from that dumb, motionless form.

"You must not count on me to look after her," he said. "Something tells me that if you leave me now I shall not very long survive you; and even if I do live on for a little while, it will not be here or at Court—that is quite certain. I shall be in a hermit's cell, far off among the loneliest hills." The mention of Kozeri was not without effect. Agemaki half-uncovered her face.

"It was partly," she said, "because I felt I would not live long that I wanted you to take Kozeri instead of me. In this way I was giving, I felt, not less but more than you asked. If you had listened to me then, with what happy tranquility might I now be going to my death! For there is no other reason that could make me loath to die." "You asked what was impossible," he protested. "I had never cared for anyone but you, and indeed could never have brought to you this store of garnered feeling had not fate locked my heart for so long. What I did for Kozeri cannot be undone; but I still believe that you have not the slightest grounds for anxiety on her account."

So he sought to reassure her. But it was evident that she was in great pain. Once more he summoned the miracle-workers to her bedside. The most potent spells were recited, the darkest powers invoked, while he himself called passionately on Buddha's name. But, as though the gods had determined this time once and for all to wrest his thoughts from the shackles of earthly desire, at each prayer that he uttered he saw her shrink and fade.

At the last moment the old women, in their superstitious terror of the dead, dragged Kozeri, who was but half conscious of what was happening, from her sister's side.

At first Kaoru was as though in a dream. What was all this clamor and confusion? She was unconscious—had fainted perhaps. But she could not be dead. He held up the lamp close to the bed. Her face, uncovered now, was lovelier than he had ever known it. She lay as though asleep. Her spirit had flown. But could she, as an insect leaves its husk, have left behind her this sleeping form, he felt that to gaze upon it would have been happiness enough. Someone brushed the hair back from her forehead. Why, if Buddha wished us to turn with frightened hearts from life and love, did he make death so tranquil, so beautiful?

For a while he prayed desperately for consolation. But whence could it come? He threw himself almost with a feeling of relief into making the various arrangements that were necessary in connection with the death-services and interment; though when the day came it was with trembling and uncertain steps that he followed the bier. A constant stream of condolences came from Niou during the course of the day. But the belief that a single gesture from him, made at the right time, might have saved her sister's life deprived these belated attentions of any merit in Kozeri's eyes. With Kaoru, despite his assurances that Agemaki wished her to confide all her difficulties to him, she would at first have no dealings at all; and even when he had persuaded her to let him visit her, she hardly spoke a word. But there were various matters that they had to decide between them, and he felt that he was getting to understand her better than before. Her judgment in practical matters was excellent, and though still subject to childish lapses her taste was on the whole excellent. But in range of feeling and power of imagination it seemed to him that she was far from equaling her sister.

Once when all day long he had sat watching the snow whirling through the dark sky, at dusk the clouds suddenly cleared, and raising the blinds he looked out on such moonlight as only the glittering nights of late winter can show. Far off the faint chiming of the temple-bell whispered that another day had passed.

"Beyond the reach of gathering darkness, with the moon that drops through the clear spaces of the western sky,[*] would that my soul might walk!" Such was his poem.

---

[*] Reference to Amida's Paradise, where he imagines Agemaki's soul to be. Pun on *sumu* "to dwell," and *sumu* "to be clear, cloudless."

The wind was very strong. He went to let down the shutters, and looking out saw hilltop after hilltop white with snow and glittering in the moonlight; while on the moat there was bare ice that shone like a polished mirror. Lovely as the sights of winter might be in the Capital, what was there ever to compare with this? If only there were someone here at the window with him who felt about such things as he did! He thought of those magical Snow Mountains famous in story: "Because without you I am lonely, would that like a track in the snow of desolate mountains my life might magically cease!" Once, he remembered, on those far-off mountains a boy* had yielded up his life to the hungry spirits of the place... But the comparison was blasphemous; for it was a craving higher than earthly love that had made this Himalayan boy so ready to die.

Presently he gathered the people of the house about him, and encouraged them to talk. Among the younger maids his graceful bearing and delicate sensibility caused many an admiring sigh; while the old women shook their grey heads once more at the thought that death had denied them the spectacle of so lovely a match. "If you ask me," one of them said, discussing the cause of Agemaki's illness, "I believe it was disappointment about Prince Niou and nothing else that did it. She made up her mind not to let her sister see what she was suffering, and it was all that trouble, shut up in her own heart, that did the mischief. She was not one to show her feelings; but underneath, from the time Prince Niou began to cool off, she felt she had betrayed her dear father's trust; and as the days went by and still Niou did not come, she worried over her sister day and night, ate nothing at all, and finally, poor soul, fretted herself into the grave."

The old woman quoted things that Agemaki had said to her during the illness, and soon everyone was in tears.

And all this, despite his excellent intentions, was Kaoru's doing. A thousand times he cursed the facile self-deception that had persuaded him Niou could be trusted. In violent discontent with himself and the world in general he began to tell his beads, and spent the whole night in fervent prayer. Suddenly, just before dawn, voices came floating to him through the dark, snowy air; then a noise of horses. Was it conceivable that anyone could have come at this hour and on such a night? But he had not dreamt it; the priests too had woken with a start. A moment later a figure heavily muffled and disguised hurried dripping into the house. At the first rap on the door Kaoru had recognized Niou's knock, and hidden himself away.

Niou knew that the Forty-nine Days were not over. He should have kept away. But a chance of escape had presented itself; his anxiety was

---

* He gave his life in order to hear the second half of the Hymn of Impermanence. See *Nirvana Sutra,* Southern Version, Takakusu, vol. xii, p. 692.

becoming unendurable, and here he was, after spending the whole night losing his way in the trackless snow. Surely this was enough to wipe out the memory of all his delinquencies! To his surprise however he received a message that Kozeri was unable to see him. The truth was that his arrival was painful to her in several unexpected ways. It made Agemaki's tragic attitude towards the whole matter seem forced and superfluous in a way that, at the moment, was more than Kozeri could bear. Then again, the feeling that a visit of this kind a few weeks ago would certainly have saved Agemaki's life made his present belated arrival definitely painful to her. But when everyone in the house had one after another taken up Niou's cause, she at last relented so far as to speak to him from behind a screen. He began to pour out the whole tale of his repeated efforts to escape from the City, and their continual frustration. She seemed to be very little interested, and replied to his questions in so weak and listless a voice that he became seriously alarmed. Was she too about to fade away like that unfortunate sister? So great was his anxiety that he determined to throw prudence to the winds and spend the rest of the day at Uji. Again and again he begged her to dispense with the screen; but she replied that at present she did not feel that she had self-possession enough to do so.

Kaoru heard of these difficulties and hoped to improve the situation by remonstrating with Kozeri. "He must, I know," he said to her in a note, "seem to you to have behaved very neglectfully and I can quite understand your feeling that he stands in need of a rebuke. But I must remind you that he is not used to so severe a discipline and may take it to heart more than you desire or suppose." The well-meant advice only strengthened her determination to do as she felt inclined. "This is terrible!" Niou bewailed. "I might as well be a complete stranger. You seem to have entirely forgotten all that has passed between us."

As night came on, the wind grew very noisy. No one who was not used to the place (Kozeri knew) would have a chance of getting to sleep. In Niou's case the obvious remedy was for him to go back to the Capital. But as he showed no signs of doing so, she sent for him and let him again talk to her through the screen. He vowed by every god and shrine that come what might he would never desert her; but these passionate protestations came so glibly from his tongue that he must, she felt, have had considerable practice at them. But it was one thing to disapprove of him when he was not there and quite another to resist, at such close quarters as this, his singularly endearing and engaging ways.

"Of what has gone before, short was my memory indeed if in the things to come I dared to put my trust." She murmured the random verse half audibly. It wounded him; he felt even further away from her than he had been during all those weeks in the City.

"Since yesterday is past, and promises you deem too short to trust, this day alone for tenderness is left."

"Life is not long enough for us to enjoy each other's good points," he said, "let alone to reprove each other's shortcomings." "I am feeling so tired," she said, and disappeared into the inner room. Apart from all else, his vanity was wounded. He was not used to being seen left out in the cold. It was not her refusing that he minded, but the way she did it. She was of course still in mourning, and he ought not to have come so soon. But there was no need to treat him as though their relationship had never existed at all. He wept tears of anger and mortification; yet this very indignation served only to make him realize what she herself must have suffered during the long days of his absence, and soon they were tears not of anger but of tenderness.

On going later on to Kaoru's quarters he could not help being touched and at the same time amused by the air of complete proprietorship with which he ordered everyone about and had his meals served by a whole bevy of gentlewomen. Niou was however shocked to observe how haggard and pale Kaoru was looking. It was evident that he was very much upset by his loss. They had a long and serious conversation. For a moment Kaoru thought of revealing the fact that his relations with Agemaki had never been such as Niou evidently supposed. But what object could there be in gratuitously exposing his own inadequacy? It was true, as Niou had noticed when they first met, that the events of the last days had left their mark on Kaoru, not however in any unbecoming way. Indeed he felt a little nervous of leaving Kozeri so long in Kaoru's hands, for he could not see how any young girl could fail to find him extremely attractive, and once more he began to devise plans for bringing her to the Capital in some way that would not cause too disagreeable a conflict. But Kozeri herself would be extremely annoyed if she found that he had broached the matter to his mother the Empress just now, when there was a rift between them.

Before returning perplexed to the Capital he tried by every conceivable plea and endearment to get a few affectionate words from her. But it was no use; she seemed determined to let Niou know for once in his life what it felt like to be harshly treated.

The year closed with blizzards that even down on the plains below were the worst that anyone could remember, and at Uji the drifts were so deep that it was impossible to move. Kaoru spent the days in a kind of stupor, his only occupation being the arrangement of the Masses that were to be said for Agemaki's soul. Niou too sent lavish provision for the reciting of Scriptures. From every side however Kaoru was receiving appeals not to shut himself up at Uji any longer. Surely, his friends wrote, he would come back for the celebration of the New Year? He saw that they were right; but he could hardly have been more loath to go, not only on his own account but on that of his friends here, who he now realized had grown used to having him about the house and would, now that all their visitors both lay and clergy were deserting them, begin to feel their mistress's death more acutely than during the stir and bustle of those first days. They had indeed got to know him far better during this sad time than during all the years of his hurried comings and goings; they had learnt to appreciate his extraordinary kindness and consideration for the feelings of others even in matters of the most trivial kind, and they were exceedingly depressed at the prospect of losing him.

Niou wrote that, unable to face the prospect of being again cut off for an indefinite time from all chance of getting to Uji, he had managed to arrange for Kozeri to live "somewhere much closer." What had actually happened was this: the Empress had heard of Kaoru's devotion to Agemaki and his great unhappiness at her death. This seemed somehow to have suggested to her that, since everyone said the two sisters were so much alike, Niou's feeling for Kozeri might be of much the same kind. In any case she suddenly relented, took a great interest in the affair and privately suggested to him that Kozeri should have rooms in the western wing of the Nijo-in, where he could visit her from time to time. Though Her Majesty did not actually say so, it was clear that she intended Kozeri to act as lady-in-waiting to Niou's sister, the First Princess. He regarded such an arrangement as very unsuitable, but was pleased all the same, for anything was better than having her buried away at Uji.

Kaoru, when he heard of the plan, could not help betraying a certain disappointment. The rebuilding of his palace in the Third Ward was almost finished. To see the rooms he had intended for Agemaki wholly untenanted would be melancholy indeed, and for a time he had derived a certain consolation from the thought that they might at least be useful to Kozeri. But Niou was quite wrong in assuming, as he seemed to do, that there was any particular understanding between them. Kaoru had long ago been entrusted with the direction of her practical affairs, and at present it did not seem as though anyone else intended to take over the serious side of his responsibility.

Fern-Shoots

"Spring shines on ruined walls..." To Uji, as to the rest of the world, the sun came back; the nightingale sang again. But Kozeri sat dreaming. The beauty of the changing seasons seemed wasted now. All their lives she and Agemaki had shared these things—the flowers, the trees, the music of the birds. One would begin a poem, the other would end it; and as the year went on there were so many thoughts and fancies to be expressed that there was no time to remember the miseries and vexations of their derelict existence. But now she had no one with whom to share either her amusements or her sorrows; and this second loss, far more than her father's death, which Agemaki had helped her to bear, for the time utterly crushed Kozeri's spirit. A letter came from the Teacher. "How does the New Year find you?" he wrote. "I pray constantly for your welfare, and at this glad season have redoubled my prayers." He also sent a very pretty basket full of fern-shoots and mullein, saying that a boy had brought them to him as an offering "Since, Lady, for you too* were meant my oft-repeated offerings spring by spring, shall they forget their custom now the fields are green—these first shoots of the year?" The poem and letter were marked "to be read aloud to Her Highness," which was no wonder, for the writing was extremely bad, the poem in particular being written in clumsy sprawling letters which he had made no attempt to join.† "But she felt sure that the composition of the poem, simple though it was, must have cost the old priest a great deal of time and effort, and it was certain at any rate that the sentiment it expressed was entirely sincere, and not simply used as an excuse for the introduction of pretty conceits and phrases, as too often seemed to be the case with more expert and elaborate epistles.‡

"Since with the dead I cannot share them, in the trough of remembrance shall they be left—these young shoots of the hill?"

She was deeply touched by the letter, read it again and again with tears in her eyes, and gave the messenger a reward.

Kozeri had always been much less slim and fragile-looking than her sister. But since her recent troubles she had grown much thinner in the face,

---

* As well as Prince Hachi.
† He was more used to writing Chinese characters, in the square detached form used in Buddhist texts.
‡ In particular, those of Niou.

which not only gave her a more distinguished appearance, but increased her resemblance to Agemaki. To their women indeed, who constantly saw them side by side, they had never seemed alike at all.

But often now they would for an instant forget all that had happened and take Kozeri for her sister. They wondered whether Kaoru had been struck by this increasing resemblance. It did indeed seem a thousand pities that Kozeri was otherwise disposed of; for they could see how strongly Kaoru felt about anything that in the least reminded him of Agemaki, and they were certain that but for Kozeri's unfortunate entanglement with Niou he would now inevitably be turning to her, the very image and counterpart of Agemaki, for companionship and consolation.

Several of Kaoru's retainers were courting girls at Uji, and thus through her maids Kozeri heard almost daily accounts of him. It seemed that he was finding great difficulty in settling down to his occupations in the Capital, and had after all taken very little part in the New Year festivities which were the chief reason for his return. It touched Kozeri to find how deep had been his affection for her sister, and her feeling of antipathy towards him began to disappear.

Niou meanwhile was chafing more than ever at the restraints that his position involved, and was determined to lose no time in getting Kozeri to the Capital. After the busy period of the Palace Banquet and other New Year celebrations was over, he was visited one still and lovely evening by Kaoru, who was longing to talk about Agemaki to someone who had known her.

Niou was sitting near the window, enjoying the fragrance of the plum-blossom—his favorite flower—and playing the thirteen-stringed zithern. Kaoru as he passed plucked a spray from the lower boughs of the tree, and came towards Niou holding it out in his hand. The scent was indeed astonishing.

"Small show they make, like the heart of him that plucked them, these close-folded buds, yet inward hide a fragrance unforeseen." Such was Niou's poem; and Kaoru's: "Warily in the garden must we walk if they who watch would read so deep a moral into the plucking of a scented spray!" It was a very successful meeting. Niou was naturally very anxious to hear recent news of Uji, and to Kaoru it was a great relief to tell the whole story of Agemaki's illness and death, and his own unhappiness ever since. But it must not be supposed that Kaoru's tale was one of unbroken gloom. There were always things that, even under the blackest circumstances, struck his imagination and amused him. Indeed, during this long conversation they laughed quite as much as they wept. It was in fact one of the advantages of Niou as a companion that his extreme impressionability was not by any means confined to his own experiences. Never could there have existed in the world anyone whose tears flowed more readily at the misfortunes of others. Moreover there was, when they first began to talk, even in the misty sky above them, a strange look of softness and gentleness that made the winter seem far away indeed. Suddenly however an icy wind sprang up, the lamp blew out, and they were left in cold and darkness. But barely conscious of what was going on about them they talked far into the night, and at the end of it all still had the feeling that they had said but half of what they wanted to.

"You surely don't mean to say nothing more ever happened?" Niou asked in astonishment after listening to a long description of Kaoru's dealings with Agemaki. Either Kaoru (he thought) must be the oddest person in the world or else the account, judging from all his own experiences of women, must certainly be very incomplete. But Niou was always singularly quick to understand other people's emotions even when they were of a kind he would himself have been the last to feel, and by a word of commiseration here or encouragement there he could often succeed in clearing away the darkest clouds of depression. Here was an excellent opportunity to employ this talent, and he did indeed use it to such good effect that Kaoru found himself gradually led on to talk about things of a sort he had never imagined he could bring himself to speak of to anyone.

Niou, in turn, spoke of his plans for bringing Kozeri to the city. "I am very thankful you are going to," said Kaoru. "I was beginning to be afraid that in introducing you to her I had made a terrible mistake. Not that I have any such interest in her as you seem constantly to assume but she is the only person in the world who in the least reminds me of Agemaki, and it is only natural that I should like to keep in touch with her and help her in any way I can." He went on to tell Niou how Agemaki had wanted him to marry her sister; he did not however say anything about the night when she had fled from the room leaving him and Kozeri "in the forest of Iwase"* together.

But inwardly he was beginning to feel that, like though she was to Agemaki, he was not going to get much comfort out of the fact with things on their present footing. He ought really to be in Niou's place. But it was too late to go back on that now. Things must of course remain as they were; the slightest suspicion of anything else would give rise to a most awkward and unpleasant situation, and was surely the one thing to be avoided. He would indeed have been glad if there had been someone to whom he could hand over the business of helping her to arrange her move to the city. But unfortunately no such person existed, and he applied himself to the task with the best grace he could. At Uji the younger maids and serving-girls who had been chosen to follow Kozeri to the Capital were naturally counting the days in a state of wild excitement.

---

* The allusion has not been explained.

But Kozeri herself felt no such elation. She had known no other home, and the thought of leaving the place—dear to her despite all its disadvantages—to fall into neglect and decay, filled her with unspeakable sadness. But if she felt that she could well enough have put up with the loneliness and monotony of her present existence for a long time to come, Niou viewed the matter in another light. "I could not be fonder of you than I am," he wrote, "but I am afraid that even my affection is likely in the end to be damped by the difficulty of getting to you in your present preposterous place of residence. You have never made the journey, and do not realize what a business it is."

No doubt, she admitted, it was a great nuisance for him to come so far; but on the other hand the last thing that she felt inclined for was to leave this place that she loved and knew.

The move was arranged for the beginning of the second month, and as the time drew near Kozeri wandered from tree to tree, lingering anxiously over the buds that this year she might never see unfold. To leave these hills just when the mists were beginning to rise, to go among strange people, into a world she had never known—filled her with dread. The Court with its censuring eyes and thousand unfamiliar usages could never become her home. She spoke of her fear to no one, but thought now of nothing else all day. The end of her three months' mourning was also at hand. There seemed something callous in this perfunctory lustration that was supposed to mark the limit of her grief. As she had never known her mother and Agemaki had played almost a mother's part it seemed to Kozeri as if she owed something more than the scanty period of mourning that convention assigned. But this seemed to be regarded as out of the question, and henceforth she must mourn in secret.

Kaoru supplied Doctors of Ceremony to superintend the lustration, as well as coaches and outriders for the move.

"Scarce winter's garb is cut; when shimmering mist athwart the hills proclaims it time to wear the flowery robe of spring."

Such was his poem, and it was indeed a delightful choice of colored dresses that he sent. Nor did his forethought end here. It would be necessary for her to give suitable presents to the gentlemen who formed her escort on the journey, and although for this purpose he provided nothing showy or of great value, he thought out carefully what would be suitable to every person concerned, and made quite certain that her store would not run short.

Could anyone in the world ever have shown such unfailing thoughtfulness on all possible occasions? "Your own brother could not do more for you," someone said.

It was indeed the practical and solid aspect of his devotion that most impressed the more staid and elderly among the gentlewomen. But the younger ones were agreed that there were other things besides Kaoru's actual assistance that Kozeri would badly miss. "She has been used to seeing him here so frequently," they said. "Of course everything is bound to be quite different now, and her's sure to feel it at first; he has always been so good to her."

Kaoru himself arrived at Uji early on the day before the move, and was at once shown to his old quarters. He was convinced that if Agemaki had lived she would by now have grown used to the idea of his approaching her as a lover. It was strange to think that long before Niou figured in the business at all he had himself planned for Agemaki just such a move as they were preparing for today. He kept on calling to mind with strange vividness things that Agemaki had done or said in this house that he was perhaps visiting for the last time. It did not seem to him now that she had really ever behaved as though she actually disliked him. More than anything else it was his own diffidence—his inability in such matters ever to press home an advantage—that had kept them apart. He remembered the hole in the door. There it still was. He put his eye to it; but something solid had been placed in the way, and he could see nothing at all. He could however hear a great deal of weeping going on inside. The preparations for the move kept on recalling to Agemaki's maids memory after memory of their dead mistress; while Kozeri herself lay so stupefied by continual weeping that she could give no attention to the arrangements for tomorrow's move. Presently came a note from Kaoru saying that he had often been rather worried about her during his long absence from Uji and should be very glad of a quiet conversation. "If possible," he wrote, "I should much prefer to see you today in a friendly, informal way. You can imagine how strange it feels to come back here under these circumstances." She had no desire to be "unfriendly" but really this was a very unfortunate moment for him to have chosen. Everything was in confusion, and she hardly knew what she was doing or saying. She felt quite incapable of replying to his questions in a reasonable and connected way; but her maids one after another pleaded with her not to be unkind to him, and in the end she let him come and talk to her through the half-opened door. She was astonished by his beauty. Had she forgotten how handsome he was, or could he really have changed in so few weeks' space? Of course his taste in dress was wonderful, and that helped. In any case she was amazed. And Kaoru on his side was drawn towards her by the fact that she immediately began to talk about Agemaki. "We must not talk about sad things today," he said presently—"I shall be moving back into my own palace in a few days. It is quite close to the Nijo-in where you will be, and when one is as near as that it is always possible to find a stray moment—'neighbors call at odd hours,' you know the proverb. But though as far as I am concerned I should always be glad to go on helping and advising you just as I have done in the past, I don't know whether you would want me to. People feel very differently about such things, and it is not a question about which I myself hold very decided views." "I am far too much upset about leaving my real home," she said distractedly, her voice often fading away in the middle of a word, "to be able to think about the advantages of our living in the same part of the Capital." There was a note of weariness in her voice that reminded him instantly of Agemaki; but so far from allowing himself for this reason to slip into a tone of greater intimacy, he kept up an attitude so courtly and correct as to contrast strangely even with his behavior on that night of wasted opportunities.*

Close by her window stood a red plum-tree, singularly lovely both in color and scent. Even the nightingales seemed to be irresistibly drawn towards it, and if for a moment they perched elsewhere would always come back again to sing. For such a conversation as theirs, stricken as they both were with the consciousness that "spring was not the spring of old,"† it was as moving a place and hour as they could well have chosen. How many times had she sat with Agemaki at this tree! How often had its beauty driven from both their hearts all thought of their own weariness or misery: "Far hence the soul of her that gazed the winds of fate have carried, but still there lingers as of old the fragrance of the mountain tree." Such was the poem that she murmured faintly to herself in broken cadences. Kaoru repeated the words tenderly. "Touched by a vanished sleeve, with such familiar scent the tree is charged that scarce can I believe the garden which awaits it is not mine."

Such was his poem. He managed hastily to brush away the tears that he felt coming, but could not trust himself to speak further. "You must often let me come and talk with you like this," he said presently, and after settling some points connected with tomorrow's journey, left the room. There were still various arrangements to make about the move, and the upkeep of the estate after Kozeri's departure. The house itself was to be left in charge of the bearded watchman; but the grounds were to be looked after by the people on his own property which lay near at hand. He went into all the practical details with the utmost care, and then sent for Ben no Kimi. He was deeply affected to learn that she had taken her Vows. It had been suggested that she should accompany Kozeri to the city. But she dreaded meeting fresh people who had not known her in her less decrepit days and would make her feel more than ever that she had outlived her time. "If death does not choose to take me," she said, "I can't help lingering; but there is no reason why anyone should know

---

* When he found himself with Kozeri instead of Agemaki.
† From the *Tales of Ise*.

I am still in the world." She made difficulties at first about meeting him; but he insisted on her coming and for a long while she sat telling him stories of the old days.

"Of course I shall have to come here occasionally to see that everything is in order," Kaoru said presently, "and it would be very melancholy to find no one at all living here; so that I am particularly glad you have made this decision."

"It sometimes seems," she said, "as though the more one longs to escape the tighter life clings. I felt when my mistress left me as though she had done so on purpose to take away my last excuse, and lingering day after day I began not only to hate myself, as we all of us have the right to, but also the world and everything in it, so that from morning to night I do nothing but grumble and complain, which is I know a grievous sin."

She was very difficult to deal with; but in the end he managed to coax her into a rather less lugubrious frame of mind. Despite her great age she had still kept a fine head of hair, and the loss of it changed her appearance and expression in a way that was at first rather startling. But Kaoru came to the conclusion that she really looked younger and more distinguished in her present guise. He wondered whether it might not perhaps have been worth while to make Agemaki take this step. It did sometimes seem to give people a new lease of life. She would certainly have grown to have a deep understanding of her religion, and he would have loved to talk about such things with her. He envied Ben no Kimi. She alone had succeeded in doing what he and so many others still only talked about. He pushed the screen behind which she was sitting slightly to one side and talked earnestly to her for a long time. Her powers of mind were by no means decayed, and she expressed herself in a way that clearly showed she had once been something better than her present appearance would suggest.

"Better were it for the aged could they be drowned in the river of their own quick tears, rather than that their dear ones should go before them to the grave." Such was her poem. "To drown oneself," Kaoru protested, "is a worse sin than grumbling! If you talk in that way you will never get to the Far Shore, but on the contrary sink to the lowest depths of Damnation. What one should try to do is to look upon the world as real only from our own particular point of view, and therefore incapable of producing in us affections that have any finality."

He had stayed talking so long that it was now getting very late; but though he had no desire to return he felt that it would make a bad impression on Niou if he spent the night, and he set out in darkness for the city.

Ben repeated to Kozeri the whole of her conversation with Kaoru and had of course to be caressed and comforted all over again. It irritated the old woman particularly to see Kozeri's gentlewomen, many of whom were not much younger than herself, plying their needles on what she considered the most inappropriate finery, and evidently counting the minutes till they should make their entry at Court—an event that it seemed inconceivable they should look forward to without some misgivings.

"I am not made for that sort of life," Kozeri consoled her. "You will in all probability see me back again before long. But I wish you were coming with me, for as you know I shall find it hard to get on without you even for the short time that I am likely to be at Court. However, happily you have not joined an Order that insists on strict seclusion, and there is no reason why, even as you are, you should not occasionally come and see me in the city, just as you would if you were an ordinary person." She then went with Ben through Agemaki's things, setting many of them aside to be left in Ben's care. "I know," Kozeri said, "that you felt her death more than any of the others did. No doubt you were brought together in some previous incarnation. It draws my heart toward you when I think of it..." At which the old woman once again broke into a wailing as dismal as that of a newborn child.

The early part of the next day was spent in a tremendous clearing out and tidying. Presently the carriages arrived. The escort was of an imposing kind, consisting entirely of high Court officials, mostly of the Fourth and Fifth Ranks. Niou was extremely anxious to come in person, but it was thought that this would be making more of the affair than was at the moment advisable, and he was obliged to remain hanging about at Court, concealing his agitation as best he could. A large number of Kaoru's retainers also joined the escort, and it was he indeed who made all the detailed plans for the removal and journey, providing with extraordinary foresight and care for every possible contingency, while Niou gave only the vaguest and most general directions.

"The sun will soon be down," people were calling inside the house and out. To what fate would this journey lead her, Kozeri asked herself with darkest forebodings as she set foot in her carriage. "Well, I'm glad that I for one didn't cast myself into this river or any other!" exclaimed one of the gentlewomen who came with her, in mocking reference to Ben no Kimi's tearful poem. Her satisfaction at getting clear of Uji and all its memories plainly jarred on Kozeri's distracted nerves. "Well, surely," said another, "we may all be glad of what's happening today without forgetting what is done with and gone." They were both women who had been in the house a long time and had been devoted to Agemaki. But they were now so full of this new adventure that they seemed positively anxious not to spoil the pleasant anticipations of the moment by allowing her name to be mentioned. "How little people really care!" Kozeri thought, and took no part in the ensuing conversation.

The distance was far greater than she had imagined, and as they toiled along the steep and dangerous mountain paths she began to feel that Niou, so far from making (as she had often thought) an unnecessary fuss about the journey, had shown extraordinary devotion in coming at all. The autumn moon shone from a sky that was cloudless but veiled with a faint mist. But Kozeri, utterly unused to the fatigues of travel, was already too worn out to enjoy the beauty of the scenes through which they were passing.

"Because I dread the world and its ways, would that I too, like the moon that from the hillside rose, to the hills might turn again!"

Such was the poem that she murmured. It seemed to her now that all the miseries and discomforts of the last few years had been as nothing compared with the torturing hazards and uncertainties of the unknown life upon which she was embarking. It was already well into the night when they arrived. The oxen were unyoked and the carriages drawn in past building after building of a splendor such as she had never pictured in any dream. In a moment Niou, who had been waiting in a fever of impatience, was at her carriage-side; he took her hand and led her in.

The apartments designed for her own use could not have been more magnificent, and even those intended for her various gentlewomen had been arranged with the utmost taste and care. Indeed the reception was in every way perfect, and from the first moment left no doubt in the minds of those about her that all apprehensions could be set aside; it was to the supreme place in this household and to nothing less that their fortunate mistress had been assigned—an assumption that was at once confirmed by the deferential attitude of everyone both here and in the world at large.

Kaoru was now hoping to get into his palace in the Third Ward on about the twentieth of the month. He went there every day to see how work was getting on, and as it was almost next door to the Nijo-in[*] he stayed there till late in the night in order to get early news of Kozeri's safe arrival.

The retainers whom he had lent as part of the escort found him waiting amid the litter of his unfinished house and at once told him about Kozeri's move and extremely gratifying reception. Kaoru would certainly have been upset had he been told that she had been badly received. And yet, he found himself much less pleased than he would have expected to hear about her welcome. No one could have been more conscious than he was of the absurdity involved in feeling, under the circumstances, anything akin to jealousy—no, it was not that; but one thing at any rate was certain: could it have been granted to him to live this part of his life over again, he would have handled matters very differently!

---

[*] Genji's old palace, where Niou had installed Kozeri.

Unfortunately it was in this same month that Yugiri had fully intended to send his daughter Roku no Kimi to the New Palace, and the arrival of Kozeri at the Nijo-in, happening just at this moment, was bound to be looked upon by him as an attempt to forestall this plan. The last thing Niou desired was to incur this powerful personage's hostility, and he was careful not to suspend his usual correspondence with Roku no Kimi. Her Initiation* was an event that, had been so much talked about beforehand and was awaited at Court with such interest that though under the circumstances Yugiri would rather have delayed it, he felt that to do so would seem too much like an admission of defeat, and she was duly robed on the twenty-first, the date originally fixed. For a time Yugiri's thoughts began to turn towards an alternative plan. Kaoru was of course only a commoner, and a match with him had none of the attractions of marriage into the Imperial clan; moreover he was so near a relation that as a son-in-law he would bring no fresh element into the family. But in every other way he was a desirable match, and if it was true that, as some people said, he had recently suffered a secret bereavement, he was probably rather at a loose end, and would be glad of something that would distract his attention. He got someone to sound him on this subject; but Kaoru seemed hurt at the suggestion. "It is true," he said, "that I have recently suffered a severe loss. But I do not know why people should take for granted that an experience of this kind will incline one towards marriage. Personally, I feel far more like turning my back on the world altogether."

"These young men," said Yugiri, when Kaoru's attitude was reported to him, "might at least be civil. No one, I think, can say that I am the sort of person to pester anyone with a proposal, if I see it is not welcome." But there was something in Kaoru's character that intimidated Yugiri and prevented him from using his family authority in the way that their close relationship made natural. The matter was never referred to again.

The trees were now in full bloom and Kaoru, looking across towards the gardens of the Nijo-in, thought at once of the "deserted house"† and its exquisite cherry-blossom, the petals of which must now be "fluttering unmourned." Longing to talk of Uji he went to look for Niou, who in these days was almost invariably to be found in the Nijo-in, a fact which could only be regarded as extremely satisfactory. And yet somewhere at the back of his mind lurked, a secret desire—as surprising to Kaoru himself as it could have been to anyone—that things should not go quite so idyllically. But it was of no importance, he decided—this strange side-

---

* Into womanhood.

† "The cherry-blossom of the deserted house far off among the reeds—in the light wind it flutters to the earth unmourned." Ekei Hoshi, end of 10th century. Kaoru refers, of course, to the house at Uji.

current of feeling. What else could he really desire? What else could bring him any satisfaction or peace of mind save that Niou should be as devoted to Kozeri as possible?

They talked together for a long time about one thing and another till towards evening Niou was obliged to get ready for a visit to the Emperor's Palace. A number of retainers, who were to form his escort, began to assemble, and Kaoru slipping away from this crowd went off to Kozeri's rooms. How different a life it was already that went on behind those screens! He could see the forms of gaily dressed page-girls moving to and fro. No sooner had he given in his note than a cushion was handed out for him to sit on—an attention that he owed no doubt to one of the maids who had known him in Uji days.

"I am of course so near," he said, " that it is no trouble to me to come round, and I would gladly spend much more time with you, did I not feel that perhaps, as things are, Niou dislikes my coming here, except to discuss some particular arrangement. I realize that henceforward things are bound to be quite different. I have come now because your cherry-blossom (that I can see all shimmering in the mist, from my own garden) reminded me so much of Uji. But I am afraid that is a very insufficient reason..."

She was very sorry for him. It was clear that he needed a companion. If only he had been able to marry Agemaki! And Kozeri began picturing to herself how delightful it would have been if they had come to the City together, and her sister were now in the Third Ward. They would run in and out of each other's palaces all the year round, enjoying together the coming of each new songster or flower... For the moment she felt lonelier in the midst of her new gaieties and splendors than she had ever felt in the desolation of her mountain village.

"O Madam," her maids were clamoring round her, "now is the time to show him how grateful you are for all he has done for us. You must not treat him like an ordinary visitor." She was just debating in her mind whether she should come and meet him face to face when Niou arrived to say good-bye to her before going to Court. She loved to see him all dressed up like this, on grand occasions. "Don't be too hard on him," Niou whispered, seeing Kaoru seated outside the curtains. "Of course I have always been rather uncomfortable about his doing so much for you; indeed it has probably been very foolish of me to allow it. But as things are, you owe him a great debt of gratitude, and you must not let him feel that you are unaware of it. There is no harm in your receiving him in a less formal way, just to talk about old times and so on. All the same," he added a moment later, "I think you ought to be rather careful. I am really not at all certain what his feelings towards you are. I sometimes have the feeling that underneath..."

Well, what line *did* he want her to take? These contradictory admonitions made it very hard to know. As far as she herself was concerned she was glad to be given the chance to show Kaoru her gratitude for all he had done. In particular she wanted him to feel that she was touched by his desire to play in her life to some extent the same part that Agemaki had played. But if there was any truth in Niou's suspicions, such a relationship was going to be far from easy to maintain.

The Mistletoe

Besides the Empress, the present Emperor had another Consort, the daughter of a former Minister of the Left, who had come to him in very early days, a considerable time before he ascended the Throne. He was extremely attached to her and it seemed at first certain that he would reserve for her the supreme position. But later came his marriage to the Akashi Princess, who was soon proclaimed Empress, and as time went on less and less was heard of this earlier Consort who to her additional disadvantage had only one child, whereas the Empress's numerous sons and daughters were now beginning to exercise a predominant influence at Court.

This one child was a daughter, known as the Second Princess, and the mother's one desire was to secure for this girl a future exempt from the humiliations and discomfitures of her own career. The Second Princess was exceedingly pretty and a great favorite with her father the Emperor, and if she had not in the world at large anything like the celebrity of the First Princess,[*] her position in the Palace was exactly the same as that of the Empress's children. Nor was she on the material side at all at a disadvantage, for her grandfather, who had been very well off, left his affairs in good order; it was possible to secure for her waiting-women of distinguished family and appearance, and she was dressed on every occasion in excellent taste and in the height of fashion.

Her Initiation was to take place when she was fourteen, and from the beginning of the year the Emperor devoted himself almost exclusively to the preparations for this event, determined that it should eclipse every ceremony of the kind that the Court had hitherto known. The Palace treasuries were ransacked for heirlooms that he would not on any other consideration have dreamt of touching, and everyone was working frantically to make the thing a success when the Princess's mother, who had picked up a demoniacal possession of some kind during the hot weather, suddenly died. The Emperor was heartbroken. She was a woman of singularly lovable and engaging disposition. Those whom she met as equals were agreed that no other loss could have cast such a gloom over the Court, and there was not a serving-girl at the Palace who did not feel she had lost a true friend.

---

[*] Niou's whole-sister.

For the Princess, who was after all still a mere child, this sudden bereavement was a terrible experience. The Emperor was extremely sorry for the young thing and as soon as the Forty-nine Days* were over he had her brought secretly back to the Palace, where he visited her every day. He thought she looked very distinguished in black and found her mind already singularly well formed. It even seemed to him that though less lively than her mother she perhaps had a better judgment, and it was obvious that as far as her personal qualities went she would make a most desirable match. What she lacked was family support on her mother's side. There were two uncles; but they were only half-brothers to the late Consort, and unfortunately neither their rank nor general influence and standing were sufficient to be much help to a young girl just embarking on what was, without substantial backing of this sort, always apt (as the Emperor well knew) to be so painful and difficult a course. He saw that despite her superficial advantages it was not going to be easy to do so well for her as he would have liked, and he worried about it a good deal.

One autumn day when the chrysanthemums in front of the Palace had wilted to the loveliest hue† and the rainy sky had a melancholy beauty of its own, the Emperor thought at once of the young Princess and went to see her in her room. He talked for a while about her mother, and was very favorably impressed by her answers, which were sensible and reasonable without being unfeeling. Both in character and appearance she had everything in her favor, and it was certain that as soon as she became known at Court she would have plenty of admirers. Her position naturally reminded him of Princess Nyosan's, whose father on the eve of his complete retirement had handed her over to be looked after by Genji. It was indeed possible that something of this kind would prove the best solution in the present case. "But such arrangements are not always very satisfactory," he said to her, "and I hope we shall be able to do better than that." But if Nyosan, despite her retreat from worldly life, had managed to retain a distinguished place in society and was still universally regarded as a person of great importance, this was entirely due to the devotion of Kaoru, who had always watched over her interests and directed her affairs in a way no other son would ever have done. But for his efforts it was certain that she would not merely have drifted into obscurity, but would probably have been taken advantage of and imposed upon in a very disagreeable manner.

Kaoru's record on this head alone sufficed to make him worth taking into consideration, and on looking further into the matter the Emperor found that there was really no one else at all who had the requisite qualifications.

---

* During which the soul is in the Intermediate State between one incarnation and the next.

† The color to which white chrysanthemums faded was much admired.

That Kaoru's birth entitled him to marry a princess of the blood could not be questioned. The only unfavorable circumstance was that, according to some reports, his affections were already engaged.* But he was not the kind of person who, if he got as far as accepting the Second Princess as his legitimate wife, would treat her with any open or scandalous disregard, and as he was certain, like everyone else, to get married in the end, it might be a good thing to sound him on the subject at once, though the Princess's mourning had still many months to run.

Today he was keeping her amused by playing draughts and other such games. As evening came on the garden became more and more lovely, sharp showers alternating with moments when the setting sun flashed among the dripping flowers. "What courtiers are there in the Palace?" the Emperor asked. "Prince Nakatsukasa,† Prince Kanzuke,‡ and His Excellency the Middle Counselor,§ may it please Your Majesty," the gentleman-in-waiting replied. "Send His Excellency to me," the Emperor commanded.

"It is difficult to know how to amuse oneself on a rainy day like this," he said when Kaoru arrived. "Music of course would be out of place just now. What do you feel about a game of draughts? The Princess and I find it a very pleasant way of passing the time."

There was nothing unusual in his sending for Kaoru like this. Presently however His Majesty added mysteriously: "You shall have a present if you win, and a handsome one too—something I am not at all anxious to part with; but you know how fond I am of you..." Kaoru began to suspect what was afoot; but he made no remark and continued to wait attentively upon his sovereign. In the match that followed Kaoru won two games out of three. "You wretch!" said the Emperor. "You shall be paid presently. Meanwhile you may take one of those flowers as a pledge." Without answering Kaoru went straight to the garden and brought back a handsome spray of white chrysanthemum. "Were this a flower that in the hedgerow of a common garden grew, then would I gaze my fill." The words could not have been chosen more diplomatically.

Other hints of the same kind followed from time to time, and coming direct from His Majesty they were certainly very gratifying. Later on perhaps (Kaoru thought, with his usual tendency to put off all such decisions) he might feel more inclined to consider the question. But to embark on such a marriage would be quite against the principles that he had laid down for himself, and if after successfully avoiding anything of the kind for all these years he were suddenly to involve himself in so great a responsibility he would feel, he knew, very much like an ecclesiastic when

---

* An allusion to his relations with Agemaki.
† Niou's brother.
‡ Otherwise unknown.
§ Kaoru.

he dresses up as a layman and has for the time being to take his part as an ordinary being in the common affairs of the world. Certainly however he ought to feel flattered. There were any number of young men at Court who were burning to receive from His Majesty such a hint as those that Kaoru was now getting almost every day. But as a matter of fact if there were any question at all of his marrying one of the Emperor's daughters, he would far rather it had been the First Princess, in whom he had always taken a great interest. But that, no doubt, was asking too much.*

Yugiri had continued to hope that, if his plans with regard to Roku no Kimi† and Niou ultimately fell through, it might still be possible to persuade Kaoru to reconsider his decision. It seemed to him indeed difficult to believe that Kaoru would under the circumstances be so disobliging as to persist in his refusal. He was therefore not best pleased to hear that Kaoru had been offered the Second Princess. It looked as though Roku no Kimi would have no choice but to make the best of Niou, who, though his courtship could hardly be described as enthusiastic, still continued to send her the most charming and amusing letters. And even supposing his serious affections were engaged elsewhere—he could not be blamed if it were so, for such matters do not lie within our own control—surely it would be far better for the girl that she should play the part even of a mere distraction in Niou's life rather than marry some humdrum person who, however devoted he might be and however much fuss he might make about her, was simply not in a position to give her such surroundings as she had been brought up among and had every right to expect. "This business of finding husbands for one's daughters is really becoming very formidable. I gather that even His Majesty is not finding matters any too easy," Yugiri said to his friends rather spitefully, "and you can imagine how difficult things are for a mere commoner like myself, especially in the case of a girl like this who has been talked about for some time..." As usual he carried his grievances to the Empress. "I really didn't know what to say to him," she told Niou afterwards. "Considering how you have tried his patience during the last two years, I can't help thinking we should be behaving very badly if we tried to get out of it. I must say he has always been very reasonable. You probably do not realize to what an extent the influence of people in your position ultimately depends on a good marriage. Your father has quite made up his mind to retire shortly, and you will have to look elsewhere for support. Even commoners do not find that the plan of having one woman in the household and one only can really be made to work satisfactorily. Look at Yugiri himself. He is generally supposed to be an unusually serious-minded character, but for

---

* The First Princess (Niou's sister) was the child of the Empress, not of a subordinate consort.

† Yugiri's daughter.

years past he has divided his attentions between Kumoi and Ochiba, and so far as one can judge the arrangement has always been very successful. And why you, who if all goes well will shortly find yourself in a position of the greatest eminence, should not in addition to your lawful wife have one or indeed several consorts of your own choosing, I find it hard to see."

This was all perfectly reasonable, and to Roku no Kimi herself Niou had never had any objection. What he dreaded was living under the constant observation of Yugiri. This he felt sure would mean the end of such scanty remnants of liberty as still remained to him, and the prospect was one which he had dreaded for years. But disagreeable though such a situation might be, he had sense enough to see that a complete breach with the Grand Minister,[*] would entail even greater disadvantages. Probably it would be better to see the thing through. Meanwhile Roku no Kimi was by no means the only recipient of his lighter attentions. Among others there was Kobai's daughter, with whom he still carried oh an animated correspondence. He was sorry, indeed, that he saw so little of her. With the New Year came the termination of the Second Princess's mourning, and it was now time to get to business. Kaoru was several times told that the Emperor was waiting for a sign on his side. Completely to ignore the situation would clearly be ungracious. He made more than one guarded allusion to the project and it was obvious from the Emperor's replies that he was far from wishing to discourage the topic. Indeed from private sources of information he learnt that His Majesty had actually settled on a date for the wedding, and from his own observations Kaoru could well believe it. But he was still completely obsessed by the memory of Agemaki. The thought that he had allowed this great love—the only deep and lasting passion of his life, of that he felt sure—to end as it had done, barren and unconsummated, destroyed all his happiness. He felt that could there be any question now of his feelings ever again being stirred it would not be by some pampered creature such as the Second Princess, but rather by anyone of however low a rank in society who in mind or feature in the least resembled the lady he had lost.

The marriage of Niou and Roku no Kimi was now announced for a date in the middle of the eighth month. Kozeri heard the news with consternation. She was convinced that all was now lost. Soon she was certain would come those first signs of coldness that Niou's reputation had long ago taught her to expect. But nothing of the kind occurred. So far from reassuring her, this merely made her dread all the more the sudden change which at a given moment must inevitably occur. But perhaps there would be no sudden change. Ordinary people, she knew, were capable of simply breaking off a relationship. To Niou, she realized, there would seem to be

---

[*] Yugiri.

a certain crudity in any such downright behavior. That however would not alter the facts of the situation. In effect she had lost him, and there was no further object in her remaining at Court. But it would be an ignominious return, and the prospect of facing the village rabble, who at the best of times were not much given to sparing one's feelings, was by no means an, attractive one.

With Niou however she tried to behave as usual, and made no reference to what she had heard; while he on his side, without openly alluding to the matter, tried to show her by every possible mark of tenderness and affection that nothing could ever change his feelings towards her.

In the fifth month she began to show signs of indisposition. It was evidently nothing very serious; but her appetite was not so good as usual and she tired easily. Niou, who had very little experience of these matters, attributed her condition to the weather, which was unusually hot. At the same time there were symptoms which rather puzzled him. When he suggested the obvious explanation she blushed but said she had no reason to think so, and henceforward tried to behave as though nothing were the matter. Her women of course had formed their own conclusions; but none of them took it upon themselves to inform Niou, who remained uncertain.

The eighth month came, and Kozeri began to pick up details about the arrangements for the wedding. Niou had no desire to keep her in ignorance of what was afoot, but the subject was a painful one to embark on, and though the time was now so close at hand he had still never once referred to the matter. This she attributed to a stupid secrecy, which made her very indignant. Surely he must realize that it was a public event, openly discussed in every quarter? It was ridiculous and insulting to imagine that she alone ought to be kept in ignorance of it.

Since her arrival at the Nijo-in, except on very special occasions, even during his periods of duty at the Palace he had always come back to her in the evening and had entirely given up all his other places of night resort. But he would soon be obliged* to absent himself occasionally and in order to make this less of a shock he purposely remained on duty at the Palace all night on one or two occasions just before his marriage. This too was of course interpreted by Kozeri as a sign that his affection was already cooling.

Kaoru was very much upset by the news. A person so susceptible as Niou, fond though he obviously was of Kozeri, would certainly be captivated by Yugiri's handsome and fashionable daughter, who belonged so much more to his own world. Roku no Kimi herself he knew to be singularly capable of looking after her own interests. She would certainly

---

* By his marriage with Roku no Kimi.

see to it that no one else occupied any considerable share of Niou's time and attention, and even if Niou managed occasionally to escape from the New Palace, it was certain that Kozeri, who for months past had hardly been separated from him for a single hour, would be completely heartbroken by this new situation. What struck him now as absolutely unbelievable was that he himself should ever have been so insensate as to arrange the affair. Viewed by itself his conduct on that fatal night when he had first brought Kozeri and Niou together seemed sheer insanity. He let his mind travel back over the whole history of the business. He had always been used to think of himself as vowed to an existence which was at any rate much simpler than that of other people; there was a whole side of life which did not concern him, the stream of his thoughts ran on unruffled by any wave. But suddenly all this had been upset by his love for Agemaki, and the disturbing preoccupations which seemed to convulse the rest of humanity, so far from being kept out of his life, in an instant filled the whole of it, to the exclusion of everything else. And yet there remained in him from the past a settled habit of restraint which made it impossible for him to lead the way—to force upon her high-handedly a love that did not spring from her own heart. So he had gone on year after year, building on the future, waiting for signs of a change that did not come; while she on her side, liking him a great deal (though in a quite different way) and looking about for some way of keeping him as a friend and at the same time making him happy, hit upon the unfortunate suggestion that he should marry Kozeri instead. At the moment this proposal of Agemaki's had stung him to the quick. In a fit of senseless petulance he had determined to show her that he was not so easily to be fobbed off. If Kozeri were disposed of—that must have been his motive, but now the whole thing seemed so childish as to be scarcely believable—Agemaki's last avenue of escape would be cut off.

"Surely," he thought, "even Niou, unless, as is likely enough, he has completely forgotten the part I played in bringing him and Kozeri together, must feel slightly uncomfortable about the way he has treated me in the matter. And come to think of it, he certainly has forgotten; at any rate he never now makes the slightest allusion to that period. But after all, it is not only women that people of Niou's sort treat badly. Such total irresponsibility as he has shown comes from a radical defect of character, and is bound to be just as evident in his treatment of his own sex." For he was apt to judge others with a severity which took no account of the fact that his own standards of conduct were, as he had long ago recognized, highly irrational and peculiar.

Night after night alone on his bed (when there was no reason why he should be alone) Kaoru would go back time after time over all that had happened, waking at the least noise of wind or rain to begin all over again. As far at any rate as his relations with other people were concerned, his life, he decided, had been a complete failure in the past and seemed likely to remain so. He had plenty of acquaintances, people with whom it was agreeable to talk, dependants whom he was used to having about him and to some of whom he was, in a way, rather attached. But among them all there was not a soul with whom he was in any real sense intimate. He remembered Niou's suggestion that hidden away in remote country houses there must be many girls whose families had seen better days, and that one ought to get hold of them. He had listened without the slightest interest while Niou unfolded these dreams. How could they concern someone who, like himself, was on the very brink of retiring for ever from the world? Indeed his one thought in those days had been to keep his life clear of all responsibilities and encumbrances. Then came his visits to Uji and the discovery of the two Princesses, who strangely enough were the very incarnation of the girls imagined in Niou's daydream. What followed was utter ruin—the abandonment of his resolutions, the betrayal of his convictions, the defeat of all his plans...

It was growing light. One by one the flowers in the garden, seen before only as grey objects, began to stand out against the misty hedge. Among them, showing dimly here and there, were some pale blossoms of the morning-glory "that in the self-same hour both blooms and fades"— flowers that in his fancies had always played a special part, imbued as he was with a constant sense of life's uncertainty. He opened all the wooden shutters and lying down again dozed a little. When he awoke it was quite light. Already the morning-glory had crumpled and faded. He was the only person who had seen it bloom!

"I am going round to the Nijo-in," he said to one of his servants. "Tell them to get ready—any carriage will do." "Prince Niou," the man said, "has been at His Majesty's Palace since yesterday. I saw his carriage come back empty to the Nijo-in last night." "In that case," said Kaoru, "I will go to Princess Kozeri's apartments. I hear she has been unwell. I am on duty at the Palace today and must get this visit over before the Court is astir." He dressed and on his way out turned aside for a moment to walk among the flowers. Lovely gestures and attitudes came naturally to him, and it would have been a mistake to suppose that at this moment his exceedingly alluring movements as he stooped to peer at blossom after blossom were designed to attract attention. He caught hold of a morning-glory by the stem and pulled the flowers towards him. A shower of dew fell on his sleeve.

"Why to my heart must things be ever dearest, that vanish swifter than the morning dew?" Such was his poem. He went off with the flowers in his hand. With the coming of full day the mist had risen and was circling in beautiful patterns through the sky. To knock at the shutters or double-door at an hour when the ladies of the household were presumably still in bed seemed rather inconsiderate; nor did he care to shout for admittance. Perhaps it was an absurdly early hour to have called at all. But a man whom he sent to look at Kozeri's side of the house through the middle gate reported that her shutters were all open and her women evidently dressed and astir. Leaving his carriage he stole through the mist and crept softly into the house. The ladies within could not see who it was and thought at first that Niou had suddenly returned from some secret excursion. But in a moment Kaoru's scent betrayed him. "Handsomer he could not be," whispered the younger waiting-women. "The only pity is that he takes everything so seriously." They showed no sign of surprise, but promptly handed out a cushion and seemed in every way disposed to welcome this early visit. "No doubt it is by your mistress's orders that you have put me here, and I do not wish to seem ungrateful. But I find it so painful to be treated in this formal way that I have not the courage to come here nearly so often as I would do if she showed more confidence." "Well, then, where do you want us to put you?" someone asked. "I should have thought," he said, "that for an old friend like me somewhere in the shelter of the alcove would be a more natural place. But no doubt you are, as I have said, only acting on your mistress's instructions, and I have no choice but to accept her ruling." Her curtained couch was near the door and he really was very uncomfortably poised on the threshold. "Let him come round the other side," the gentlewomen pleaded with Kozeri. His appearance was always, she was bound to confess, far indeed from being in any conceivable sense aggressive or alarming. It was odd that she always had in his presence this uncomfortable feeling of embarrassment and restraint. But at the present moment he looked so singularly gentle and subdued that Kozeri found herself gradually overcoming her usual distrust and talking to him quite naturally and easily, as though he were an ordinary person. It was only when he began to ask about her health that she relapsed into silence. He could see for himself that she was in very low spirits and took great trouble to distract and amuse her, discussing the events of the day and trying to arouse her interest in what was happening around her in his best fraternal manner. At every meeting now he found in her some point of resemblance with Agemaki that he had never noticed before. Scarcely able to believe that it was not Agemaki herself who was seated behind the curtain he put out his hand meaning to pull it away; but the eyes of her gentlewomen were upon him, and his hand fell to his side. There were things in life, he was coming to the conclusion, that were impossible to evade. And continuing his thoughts aloud he said: "Of course I never had any prospect of a very brilliant career from the worldly point of view. But I always had the idea that it was possible to get through life without the violent stresses and upheavals by which most people seem to destroy their health and happiness. It is rather strange to look back on that ambition now! For what with Agemaki's death on the one hand and my own cursed folly about you* on the other I could hardly be further removed from the tranquility that was my ideal. And yet all around me I see people in real trouble—losing their employment and so on—and cannot help feeling that they have a far better right to be miserable."

He had laid the morning-glory on a fan, and looking at them now he saw that they were already turning a rusty brown. But they were, he thought, if anything more lovely than when he plucked them, and taking them up very gently he handed them to her through the curtains: "Still shines it lovely as at dawn, though all its whiteness to the dewdrops now the morning-glory has bequeathed."†

She was charmed by the dexterity with which, without any apparent precautions, he had contrived to lay the flowers before her with the dewdrops still upon them: "Happier the flower that in dawn's freshness died than I that dew-like lingering meet the blaze of day." "Yes, even these dewdrops have their resting-place, but I..." she murmured the words under her breath and broke off as though afraid he might hear her. Again it was as if Agemaki herself were behind the curtain.

"Lately," he said, "I have been more depressed than ever—as tends to happen in autumn—and to pass the time I paid a visit to Uji; but it was almost more than I could bear to see how things there are going to ruin. People have told me how two or three years after Genji's death when they visited the New Palace or the monastery at Saga, where he spent so much of his time in those last days, they had much the same impression. The stream, the flowers, the trees—everything reminded them of him, and their one thought was to get away as quickly as possible. It was of course extraordinary what an attraction he had for everyone, high and low, that was brought into the slightest contact with him. The ladies of his household lost all interest in life and most of them drifted away into various nunneries and retreats. Pitiable stories are told of waiting-women who, though their relations with him had been of the most superficial kind, were so overwhelmed by his loss that they wandered away among the woods and hills, and have never again been seen in the Capital. But just when it seemed that the "herb of forgetfulness" was about to possess for ever the halls of the New Palace, Yugiri went to live there, and presently various of the Royal Princes put the place in order, so that in a short time it looked much as it used to in old days. And it was felt that if an event so tragic as Genji's death could thus fade from everyone's

---

* His precipitate handing over of Kozeri to Niou.

† It is hinted that Kozeri has inherited all Agemaki's beauty.

memory, there must, happily for the world, be no grief that time could not efface. Of course I am telling you all this from hearsay. I myself was far too young at the time of Genji's death to feel it as others did. I tell myself that there is no reason why, as the years pass, we too should not recover from our own recent loss. But I feel, all the same, that as far as I am concerned I shall carry my sorrow with me beyond the grave."

He wept bitterly. Even had she not shared his grief, the sight of such affliction must have moved her heart towards him. For a moment she too could not speak and while she wrestled with her tears they sat in silent sympathy.

"I would give anything to be back at Uji," she said at last. "'Loneliness cannot wound...'* I knew the poem, but till now I had no chance to compare. This much I know, that however dull life might be there, if I could only go back I would never leave the place again. You cannot imagine how I envy Ben no Kimi.† In a few days it will be the Anniversary of my father's death. I long to hear the tolling of the temple-bell and have been trying to bring myself to ask whether it would not be possible for you to take me there.

"I am afraid that is out of the question," he said. "At this time of year the road is difficult even for a man. I meant to go again myself and get things into better order; but it has been quite impossible. It is more than a month since I was there. I have made all the necessary arrangements with the Teacher for the celebration of your Father's Anniversary. If I were you I should let him turn the place into a temple. Going there occasionally, as I have been doing, only serves to awaken painful memories and does no good to anybody, whereas to turn the place into a temple would certainly bring great comfort to the souls of the dead. I would not of course dream of doing anything in this direction without your consent. Tell me what you feel about it. You may be sure I shall do exactly as you think best."

"I should like to dedicate some scriptures and statues beyond those that you have arranged for with the Teacher," she said. "Could not that be made an excuse for my spending a short time there in retreat?"

"No, that is impossible," he said. "For the present you must try and make the best of things as they are."

The morning was already far advanced and visitors were beginning to arrive. It would look bad if he stayed too long. "I could never feel reconciled, either here or anywhere else," he said as he rose, "to remaining outside your curtain. But all the same, I promise you that shall not prevent me from coming again."

---

* "Desolate indeed is the village; yet its loneliness cannot wound like the stabs of the busy world." *Kokinshu,* Anon.
† Who was still living at Uji.

It occurred to him that unless he gave some explanation Niou might be annoyed at his having called when he was away, and sending for one of Niou's servants he explained to him that he had imagined Niou to be back from Court. "I heard that he came back last night," he said. I came early hoping to catch him, as I myself am on duty at the Palace this morning." "His Highness will be returning from Court later in the day," the man said. "I will come back in the evening," said Kaoru.

It was with the same reflections that he always returned from a visit to Kozeri. Why, when Agemaki proved obdurate, had he not listened to her advice instead of plunging both himself and Kozeri into all this gratuitous unhappiness?

He still continued to be as deeply immersed as ever in prayers and penances for the good of Agemaki's soul. His mother, Lady Nyosan, who in general was little given to asserting her authority and rarely, if ever, interfered with Kaoru's affairs, began to be seriously alarmed by this preoccupation. "When I am gone," she said, "of course you may do as you please. But don't now deprive me of my only pride and comfort. It is strange, I know, that having taken the Vows myself I should put any obstacle in your way. But you must consider that if you were to take such a course it would upset me terribly, and so prove a fatal hindrance to my salvation." Poor soul! That was the last thing he desired. Henceforward he was careful to avoid in her presence any allusion either to his general unhappiness or to his penances and devotions.

It was on the sixteenth night of the eighth month that Niou was expected in the eastern wing of the New Palace,* where under Yugiri's orders a tremendous polishing and sweeping had been taking place. When the moon rose higher and higher and still Niou did not appear Yugiri began to grow seriously alarmed, all the more so because he knew well enough Niou had for years past been doing his best to avoid this match. A messenger whom he had sent to enquire what was happening came back with the news that His Highness had left the Emperor's Palace early in the evening and gone straight to the Nijo-in.† That did not sound very promising, for Yugiri knew he had installed a mistress there; but everyone was expecting the betrothal to be consummated that night and he would look very foolish if Niou failed to appear. He sent his son Kurodo no Shosho with the poem: "High stands the moon above the expectant house. Night's hours creep on, and still no footstep comes."

It had been Niou's original intention to go straight from the Emperor's to the New Palace without calling on Kozeri, for he thought that such

---

* To consummate his betrothal to Roku no Kimi. The wedding ceremonies did not take place till the third night after the consummation of the marriage.
† To Kozeri's rooms.

an arrangement would really give her less pain. But while he was at the Emperor's Palace he wrote her a note and received a reply that determined him to go back for a little while to the Nijo-in, and once there he found it extraordinarily difficult to get away. Never had he found her more attractive. It cut him to the quick that he was forced to grieve her, and sitting with her in the moonlight he poured out a thousand tender vows and promises; while Kozeri, who for days past had been living in perpetual terror of this hour, was determined that he should not see what she was suffering, and succeeded so well in hiding her feelings that even when Kurodo was announced it would have been impossible to tell from her demeanor that she knew the significance of his arrival. Touched though he was by her bravery, Kurodo's note reminded him that there were, after all, other people to be considered. "I shan't be long," he said.

"Don't look at the moon[*] while I am away. It is a bad thing to do unless one's thoughts are occupied elsewhere," and to make a better impression[†] he went back first to the main building before going out to join Kurodo. For a moment she watched him go. He did not turn round. She sank back on her pillow, knowing that something terrible had happened but hardly conscious of what it was. Then came a flood of tears, and her mind began to work more clearly: this was jealousy, the thing she had heard so much of and vowed it should never come her way; jealousy, the greatest torment that the soul of man can be called upon to bear!

Her childhood had been melancholy enough, with no one to care for herself and Agemaki but a father who had long ago transferred his thoughts from this world to the next. Yes, those years at Uji had been uneventful and even depressing, but they were at least immune from the agitations and torments that had been her lot since she entered into the larger world.

True, when her father died and again when his death was followed by a loss even more terrible, she had felt that the end of everything had come. But so far from stopping her life had presently taken a new turn. Her match with Niou had astonished everyone. It was more than, in her position, she had any right to hope for or expect. But she herself had never lost her head. From the first she knew that the thing could not last, and though his apparent devotion had in the end somewhat allayed her suspicions, she was now under no delusion; the end had come.

And yet—this could not be said in the sense that it was true of those whom death had taken from her. Despite what was happening tonight she believed in her heart of hearts that he had loved her and might love her again.

---

[*] A woman who looks at the moon when alone loses her good looks and dies young.

[†] "A better impression upon Kurodo," is, I think, the meaning. The commentators may however be right in saying that it means "a better impression on Kozeri."

It was a hushed and gentle wind that, as she sat gazing at the comfortless moon, whispered through the pine-trees of the palace garden—a pleasant contrast, her ladies thought, to the deafening tempests that shook the solitary house at Uji. But Kozeri at that moment would gladly have exchanged the sighing of those gentle breezes for the roar of the wind in the oak-trees: "Never did the wind of the mountains in that solitary village at autumn's wildest strike such a chill to my heart!"

So easily can the suffering of the moment efface the sorrows of the past!

"Come away from the window," an old dame called to her. "Don't you know it is dangerous to look at the moon? Mercy on us, look at her supper! She has not touched a thing. Madam, what has come over you? Do you want to go the way of your poor sister? Come now, you must try to be reasonable." The younger maids were inclined merely to wring their hands and say that it was a bad business. "Not at all!" said one of them however. "I know someone who is really in love when I see him. Mark my words, he will come back. This other affair counts for nothing at all."

Why could they not be quiet and let things take their course? It was her business, not theirs, to criticize or condone. "He's not the only person in the world. There's His Excellency[*] who's as fond of you as can be and would be glad enough to take His Highness's[†] place." On one thing they were all agreed: something very strange must have happened to Kozeri in a previous existence.

Painful though he found it to leave Kozeri, Niou approached the New Palace in a state of considerable curiosity and excitement. He was anxious to appear at his best and had perfumed himself with his choicest incenses; while Roku no Kimi's rooms had been marvelously decorated and arranged. He could not expect to find in her the fragile charms of extreme youth; but on the other hand she would in many ways be more interesting than a mere child. What he dreaded was the pretentiousness, the hard, self-satisfied brilliance that made so many girls of her sort utterly distasteful to him. But he saw at once that she was of quite a different type. It was clear that they were going to get on together very well.

The long autumn night was soon over. It was indeed far spent before he arrived. As soon as it was light he hurried back to the Nijo-in, not however straight to Kozeri's rooms, but to the men's quarters, where he slept for a while and then composed his next-morning letter. "He does not look at all as though it had been a disappointment," whispered the ladies who were in attendance upon him. "It's a poor lookout for our mistress.

---

[*] Kaoru.
[†] Niou.

The Prince's heart may be as high as heaven and as wide as earth, but with things as they are she is bound to suffer in the end." Their attitude towards the situation was indeed not wholly dispassionate, for most of them had in some degree enjoyed his favors and had no desire to see his allegiance transferred to the New Palace.

Niou would rather have stayed where he was till Roku no Kimi's answer arrived. But he knew that the hours which had elapsed must necessarily have been painful ones for Kozeri, and as soon as his own letter was dispatched he hastened to her side, just as he was, without waiting to tidy his hair or dress. She had given up trying to sleep and was half-sitting, half-lying on her couch looking, he thought, lovelier than he had ever known her as she crouched there, turning towards him a face flushed with weeping. For a moment tears of tenderness and pity started to his own eyes. He gazed at her without speaking, and loath to meet his eyes she buried her face in the pillows, her lovely hair trailing across the couch. He felt rather uncomfortable. It seemed impossible to get back immediately to the endearments of the evening before and to hide his embarrassment he began to talk about her indisposition. "I wonder why it is," he said, "that you are still so poorly. We thought, you remember, that it was due to the heat; but that cannot really be so, for the hot weather stopped long ago. I have been having all sorts of liturgies recited on your behalf. But they seem to produce extraordinarily little effect. However the only thing to do is to go on with these rituals. I wish we could find a priest who was any good. I have an abbot in mind whom I think I will ask to take duty here at night."

She knew well enough that he was saying all this simply in order to gain time, and his glibness irritated her. It seemed silly to continue a conversation in which neither of them was interested, but at the moment nothing was more painful than silence. "It really isn't anything new," she said. "I have always tended to be different from other people in this way. The best thing is to let it alone. It always comes right in the end." She spoke so naturally and sensibly, it was as though the cloud had suddenly blown over. How enchanting she was! But even this thought no longer stood by itself. His admiration of her was linked at once in his mind with a new point of comparison, and though she survived the contrast, the mere fact that it was made showed Roku no Kimi to have taken an uncommon hold upon his thoughts. All the same so long as he was with Kozeri nothing, he assured himself, had changed a jot. Once more he vowed to cherish her in this life and all lives to come; but while she listened to him she could not help reflecting that, short as this present life is, he had already found time in it to break her heart once, and it was asking a good deal to expect that she should look forward to their union in a succession of future existences with any great sense of comfort or security. The efforts of yesterday and of the many unhappy days that had preceded it, during which she had struggled so bravely to hide from him all that she was suffering, had worn her out, and now quite suddenly she lost all power to restrain herself. Tears began to come, and once they had started could not be stopped. Humiliated by her own weakness she tried to turn her face away from him; but he would not let her. "I have been believing all this while that you really trusted me," he said. "But now I see that I was completely deceived—unless indeed you have changed since yesterday," and he began to wipe away her tears with his own sleeve. "Changed since yesterday! Thank you for supplying me with those words," she said, smiling through her tears. "You do not know how childish you are being," he protested. "However my conscience is quite easy. I have promised a great deal; but by no means, more than I can perform. Your ignorance of the world and its ways is no doubt part of your charm, but it has its inconvenient side. You must try to put yourself in my place. At present I am not my own master. But unless something unforeseen occurs I shall before long be in a position to do all I want to for my friends.[*] I know this sounds like mere boasting, but it is all perfectly true, as you will live to discover...

The messenger now arrived from the New Palace. He had been given so much to drink that, entirely forgetting the delicate nature of Niou's situation, he staggered straight towards the southern windows of Kozeri's wing, under a load of priceless damasks and brocades, that made the nature of his errand only too obvious.[†] "When and where had Niou written the letter to which this messenger had brought the answer?" Kozeri wondered uneasily.

Niou indeed would far rather have kept his dealings with Roku no Kimi quite separate and apart, and he wished that the messenger had shown more tact. But as things were there was no sense in making a mystery of the business, and he at once sent a lady-in-waiting to bring in the letter. Since it had to be delivered in Kozeri's presence it was better, he felt, to take her entirely in to his confidence, and there was certainly—he was relieved to see as soon as he opened it—no particular need for secrecy; it was not in Roku no Kimi's handwriting, but in that of her stepmother, Lady Ochiba.[‡] But even so it was, as he soon found, far from being intended for general circulation. "I hope you will not think me very interfering," she wrote. "I did my best to make her write a proper reply. But she seems very upset this morning, and there was no way out but for me to answer: 'How comes it that since I walked there

---

[*] When he became Crown Prince.

[†] The bearer of a first "next-morning letter" was rewarded with costly presents.

[‡] Yugiri's second consort. She had adopted Roku no Kimi, who was Yugiri's child by a concubine of low rank.

the flower of my garden should so suddenly have faded? Can it be that the dewdrop of the morning, unkind, has passed her over?'"

The handwriting was very graceful and distinguished. "These people are determined to keep me up to the mark," Niou said. "It is really rather bad luck, when all I want from life at the moment is to be left in peace to enjoy myself in my own way."

Actually however he knew well enough that even had he desired to do so his position made it impossible for him to set up permanently, as common people do, with one wife and devote the whole of his attention to her alone. Indeed, even had he been an ordinary member, of the Imperial Clan, no outside person would have expected this of him or dreamt of regarding Kozeri, for example, as an injured party merely because circumstances had forced upon him another obligation. Still less in the case of anyone with his expectations was there any possible reason why he should not enlarge his household to any point he chose. He knew that as a matter of fact, in the world at large, Kozeri was regarded as singularly fortunate to have had him to herself all this time. The trouble came from his having spoilt her; he had let her get accustomed to a position which could not in any case be more than temporary. Naturally the inevitable change had been a shock to her and she was bound to feel it very much at first.

Of situations such as that in which she now found herself Kozeri already knew a good deal both from novels and also from stories of real life. She had often wondered why people in such circumstances could not manage to behave more sensibly. But now nothing she had read or heard any longer in the least surprised her.

Meanwhile Niou's manner towards her was even more tender and affectionate than usual. "You seem nowadays to be eating nothing at all," he said. "That is very bad" and sending for dainties from his palace he made his own cook prepare them specially for her. But she could not be persuaded to touch a single thing and at last, in despair, he retired to the men's quarters. It was a windy evening with lovely cloud-effects which Niou, who like most modern young men had a great feeling for that sort of thing, was able to appreciate to the full. But Kozeri was in far too agitated a condition to get any pleasure from the beauty of this autumn evening. Each sight and sound reminded her of the mountain home that she had lost. Even the chirping of the crickets, that at Uji used to charm her, seemed now a note of bitter woe. Tonight Niou set out quite early for the New Palace. As the voices of his outriders died away in the distance she burst once more into a fit of uncontrollable weeping. She lay listening and listening, while there swept through her a storm of feelings such as she herself hated and condemned. Every unkind thing that he had ever said or done rushed to her mind, and for the moment it seemed to her that she detested him. She was ill too. How was that going to end? Her family seemed to be very short-lived. Perhaps after all it would be a good thing if she did die—if only she had been in a better frame of mind* to meet her end. Daylight came, and she had not closed her eyes.

It was announced next morning that the Empress was unwell and everyone hurried to Court. But it turned out to be nothing worse than a cold, and Yugiri was back at the New Palace† before noon, bringing Kaoru in the same carriage.

It was evident that, though it was after all only a domestic affair, Yugiri was determined to celebrate the occasion in the most formal and elaborate way. He had at first felt disinclined to invite Kaoru, who might possibly feel that his own refusal to receive the girl into his household had been too lightly accepted. But it was usual for an uncle to play a prominent part in such affairs and Kaoru was his only brother; moreover there was no one else whose presence was better calculated, in a general way, to enhance the importance of the gathering. However it would have flattered his paternal feeling if Kaoru had accepted rather less promptly. It was evident that the passing of Roku no Kimi into other hands did not arouse in him the slightest feeling of regret; indeed during the rest of the day Kaoru threw himself into the task of arranging this evening's celebrations with an enthusiasm which Yugiri found rather irritating.

Niou arrived rather late. The entertainment was given in the side-rooms on the south side of the main hall. There were eight tables, all splendidly laid out with the customary silver vessels, and on one side two diminutive tables upon which the wedding-wafers were daintily arranged in goblets with floral stands; but I will not weary you with tedious descriptions. Presently Yugiri complained that it was getting very late and sent a lady-in-waiting to summon Niou from the bridal-chamber. Apparently however the moment was not a favorable one, and another long wait ensued. At last Lady Kumoi's brothers, Sayemon no Kami and To no Saisho, managed to produce him. Yugiri's son Kurodo no Shosho bore the Cup and waited on Niou at table. The great earthen tankard went round again and again. In all the ceremonies of toasting and congratulation no one was more punctilious than Kaoru. Indeed Niou was almost inclined to suspect that his friend was making fun of him; for he remembered confessing to Kaoru that the one thing which made him doubtful about the match was Yugiri's fussiness about all sorts of dreary rites and ceremonies. But it was impossible to detect in Kaoru's countenance the slightest sign of mockery.

---

* If she died when her mind was not a rest she would not get to Paradise.

† To prepare for the wedding-ceremonies, which took place on the third day after the consummation of marriage.

Niou's followers were entertained in the eastern wing. Most of them were Court officers of high standing. There were six of the Fourth Rank, each of whom received as his guerdon a *bosonaga** as well as an ordinary woman's dress. The ten members of the Fifth Rank received Chinese robes, doubly lined, the waist-bands of each being differently ornamented. The four officers of the Sixth Rank received each some such garment as a damask *bosonaga* or a pair of trousers, and though it was of course not possible to reward the various minor officials on the same scale, no one among the whole band received a present that was not either in pattern or cut a thing of unusual beauty. Even among the messengers and so on there were many who received such presents as people of that sort had never set eyes on before. At the risk of disappointing my reader,† who I fear may have turned to this story chiefly in the hope of finding minute particulars of weddings and other festive ceremonies, I shall confine myself to the above meager description.

Back in his palace Kaoru overheard one of his men giving a description of the proceedings. "And the worst of it is," the fellow said, "that it ought by rights to have been our master who was married tonight. Think of the presents we should have got! It's a bad business to be in service with a bachelor!" Kaoru was particularly amused because the man had no business to have been there at all. No doubt, being a person of little consequence, he had slipped into the New Palace unrecognized and passed himself off as one of Niou's followers. How the other servants, listening sleepily to this man's story, must be envying Niou's men, who no doubt were still having a magnificent time at Yugiri's expense!

Yes, it was all very well for the guest, thought Kaoru, lying in his own room, but for the bridegroom himself what a trying experience the whole thing must be! Tonight, for example. Of course Niou knew Yugiri very well, and was indeed related to him; but the Minister of the Left remained none the less a formidable personage. And then the bridal-chamber with its blaze of torches, the interminable ceremonies of the banquet. However looking back on it he could not remember that Niou had once shown the slightest sign of discomposure. It was extraordinary how well he figured on such occasions. "If I had a daughter myself," Kaoru reflected, "I believe I would give her to Niou, rather than let her go into the Emperor's Palace." However for some time past it had been on Kaoru that numerous parents, disappointed by the news of Niou's betrothal, had set their hopes. Already he had begun to be pestered in innumerable quarters, so that evidently for some reason or another he too was considered a great

---

* A "narrow-long" woman's dress.

† Earlier novels (for example, *The Hollow Tree,* Utsubo Monogatari) had consisted largely of minute descriptions of banquets, weddings, concerts, etc.

catch; which particularly for anyone who was accustomed to regard himself as a failure in society was really rather gratifying.

Then there was always this offer* of the Emperor's. If it still held good, a difficult situation was going to arise, for Kaoru's own feelings about the matter had not in any way altered since he first affected to ignore the proposal. Of course such a match would add enormously to his prestige, if only he could bring himself to it. The First Princess did indeed remind him rather of Agemaki, and he felt that if she had been offered he might perhaps have considered it. And even as things were, the offer was clearly not one that he ought to dismiss from his mind altogether. As usual he could not get to sleep, and bored with lying there he went to the room of Azechi no Kimi, a young maid of his mother's whom he liked rather better than the rest. Much to her disappointment however he left her soon after daybreak, rather hurriedly, for he wanted to be back in his own room before the household was astir. "If in this land where you have brought me no eye must see that I dwell, what shall it profit me to have forded the shallows that lie between?" Such was her poem. "Though shallow to the eye it may seem—the river that divides these lands—yet far down beneath the troubled waves runs a current that will never cease." So he said to comfort her. But it was the visible "shallowness" that wounded her, and it was not likely that she should get much comfort from the improbable things that were alleged to be going on underneath. On his way out he opened the double-doors and begged her to come and look at the sky. "You really mustn't go on lying there when there are such lovely things to look at," he said. "You will see that it is worthwhile to be up early on such a morning. I know something about sunrises—not that I have much experience of stealing home at dawn. But I have been sleeping very badly of late—tormented by all sorts of doubts and worried about this life and the next—and my one consolation has been that I have not, like so many people, missed the beauty of these early hours."

There was something in his appearance and manner that, even when nothing he actually said in any way justified such a conclusion, made people feel that he was deeply interested in them. And it happened again and again that ladies with whom he had perhaps only exchanged a few trivial words would—as everyone else thought—ruin their careers by seeking employment in Lady Nyosan's cloistral establishment,† simply in order to have a further chance of getting into touch with him; an expectation in which they were for the most part grievously disappointed.

Niou was better pleased than ever with Roku no Kimi when, next day, he saw her by daylight for the first time. She was just a good height and

---

* Of his daughter, the Second Princess.
† Nyosan, Kaoru's mother, had taken her vows.

very well-proportioned. The poise of her head and the way her hair hung were admirable. Her complexion was excellent—the only thing that could possibly be said against it was that there was perhaps a trifle too much color in her cheeks—her features were exceedingly delicate and refined, her eyes lively and intelligent though not in the least pert. In short she was a beauty of the rarest order. She was of course well over twenty; she had thus had far more time than most girls when they marry to correct whatever natural defects she may have possessed; hers indeed was the beauty not of the bud, but of the flower in full bloom. It was easy for Niou to understand why Yugiri had expended such extraordinary care on this girl's upbringing. Her gentleness reminded him at times of Kozeri. But in conversation, although not tiresomely glib, she was far readier than Kozeri and showed indeed extraordinary talent in a variety of directions. Her father had given her thirty maids and six young girls to wait on her, all of good birth and appearance. Niou, Yugiri was certain, must be sick to death of the ordinary costumes, however costly might be the stuff they were made of, and a completely new style was designed, of a daintiness that was calculated to allure the most jaded eye. Yugiri had indeed always taken even more trouble over this girl than over his eldest daughter, the Crown Princess; partly because Niou was credited with being more fastidious than any other member of his family.

For some time afterwards Niou was of course unable to spend a night at the Nijo-in, and as his days were to a great extent taken up by public duties, he found it very difficult to see Kozeri at all. Roku no Kimi's rooms were those that Murasaki had once lived in and Niou had spent so much of his childhood on this south side of the eastern wing that he felt quite at home. It was only on the rarest occasions that he got as far as the Nijo-in, and though Kozeri had for long past been preparing herself for a time when his visits would be less frequent, she had never envisaged so complete a dereliction as this. The Court—as she had always guessed, but now knew to her bitter cost—was no place for stray intruders such as herself. Looking back at her life since she left Uji it seemed to her utterly unreal. She was determined to get back there, even if it was only for a short time. Above all things she needed repose—an interval in which to gain strength to meet her troubles. Surely this could be managed without giving offence to Niou or anyone else. It was however impossible for her to carry out such a plan without assistance, and though loath to do so she determined to approach Kaoru. "The Teacher," she wrote, "let me know of all your kindness at the time of the Anniversary.* It is sad, but true, that of all my father's friends you alone retain any remnant of feeling for the past. I am touched by

---

* Of Prince Hachi's death.

what you have done and should be glad of an opportunity to express my gratitude in person."

The letter was written on stout Michinoku paper and was a businesslike document, not in any way tricked out or ornamented; but it was beautifully written. He had indeed arranged for the usual services of Intercession on the Anniversary of Hachi's death, and there was nothing surprising either in Kozeri's writing to thank him or in her manner of doing so. But there was something about the letter which made him feel that she was really grateful. True, it was exceedingly short and restrained, but that had always been the case, even when she was not, as on this occasion, initiating the correspondence, and the desire to express her gratitude "in person" was quite unprecedented.

He knew Niou well enough to be sure that at the moment he was not finding much time to spare for visits to the Nijo-in. He could well imagine what Kozeri must be suffering, and was touched at her having made the effort to write at such a time. It could hardly be said that the letter showed anything more than ordinary politeness; but it gave him extraordinary pleasure, and he read it again and again.

"It is true," he wrote in reply, "that I was at Uji the other day, and took part in the religious ceremonies. I had, as you know, good reason for concealing this project.* I am only sorry that you should speak of my feeling for the past as a thing that time could ever dim. I have much to tell you when we meet. With deep respect." This was written in a restrained and sober hand, on a plain white slip.

It was not till the evening of the next day that he made his appearance. It may have been that he set certain secret hopes on this encounter, for he dressed with the utmost care, choosing garments of the softest material and scented himself so heavily that even his clove-dyed fan, after he had carried it about for a little while, would by itself have filled any room with its fragrance.

Kozeri, remembering as she often did his behavior on the night when Agemaki had left him with her and his extraordinary consideration and kindness ever since, sometimes went so far as to feel that, so long as things stopped at the same point, she would not be at all sorry to find herself in the same position again.† Looking back on her dealings with him now that she was older and had some experience of life, she felt that she had often treated him with an unnecessary coldness—in a way indeed which he must often have thought ill-bred. Today, for the first time, she admitted him behind the curtains of the side-gallery, herself withdrawing behind a screen set up against the curtains of the main room.

---

* If Kozeri had known she would have wanted to come too.
† Left alone with Kaoru.

"Your invitation did not," he said, "name any particular hour or day. But I was delighted that, for once, you should send for me, and would have come yesterday had I not heard that Niou was here. I am touched indeed that at last you are beginning to feel some confidence in me. Inside the screens! That is indeed an encouraging sign, though not unmerited, I think, after so many years of devotion."

Now that she had him in front of her all her desire to express her gratitude to him completely vanished. But having summoned him, how could she remain silent? "I have let you do so much for me without attempting to thank you," she said, "that when I heard of your recent visit to Uji I felt I must really make an effort this time to show some small part of the gratitude which indeed I have always felt and shall continue to feel." She had retreated so far towards the back of the room and spoke so low, particularly at the end of her sentences, that he really found it difficult to hear her. "Won't you come a little nearer?" he said. "I am most anxious to hear how you have been getting on, and at this distance conversation of a connected kind is almost impossible." This was true, and she drew up a little nearer to the screen. He heard the swish of her skirt as she moved, and the sound thrilled him. But he kept himself under control, and began in a calm and dispassionate way to discuss Niou's remissness, admitting that his friend was behaving in a manner hard to forgive, but saying everything he could think of to console her. She herself contributed little; for not only did she feel that she could not without disloyalty complain to him of Niou's conduct, but more than that—she had really ceased to feel that she had anything to complain of. The fault, if there was any, was hers in having intruded into a world to which she did not belong. But she was still very anxious to escape at any rate for a short time to Uji,

"I should like to help you," he said. "But I am afraid I can do nothing about it on my own responsibility. If you ask Niou nicely, I dare say he will raise no objection. In that case I will do all I can. Otherwise, if anything went wrong, he would think I had encouraged you in a gross imprudence and the situation would be very unpleasant. But if you can secure his permission I will guarantee to take you there and fetch you back. There would surely be nothing compromising in that; Niou knows better than anyone how admirably I am qualified for such a task."

Presently however he began to hint how bitterly, ever since the fatal night when he handed her over to Niou, he had regretted his folly and wished that the past could be undone. He went on in this strain till it was growing quite dark. She began to think he would never stop. "I am feeling very unwell," she said at last. "I shall be better presently, and then you shall finish what you are saying." She made as though to retire to the inner room. "When do you think of going to Uji?" he asked, as a pretext to detain her. "The road is in very bad condition and I should like to know beforehand, so that I may send some of my people to improve it." She paused. "I don't think this month would be possible," she said. "We had better make it the first of the ninth month; and I would rather that no one knew. I do not want all the fuss of explaining to everybody and getting permission.

And something in her voice and manner of speaking reminded him so strangely of Agemaki that he could not restrain himself, and supporting himself against a pillar he stretched out as far as he could under the screen with his other hand and caught hold of her sleeve. "So that was what he was after!" Sharp words came to her tongue, but she was too much taken aback to utter them and contented herself with retreating at full speed towards the inner room. Kaoru, however, still clutched her sleeve and diving under the screen calmly seated himself against the pillar, this time with his head and shoulders entirely inside the screen. "I thought," he explained when she looked at him in consternation, "you said you would rather no one knew. Naturally I took this to mean that you wanted to discuss the matter in private. If I misunderstood you, please enlighten me. If I was mistaken, I apologize. But there is really no need in any case to look so horrified." She was seeing a side of him that she was not at all prepared for and was quite at a loss what line to take. She managed however to say at last with some show of calm: "This is the last thing I should have expected of you. What will my women think?, You might show me some consideration!" Despite her efforts to remain calm the tears were welling to her eyes. If she felt like this, of course he must humor her. But what had he done that anyone could possibly be shocked by? "We have been together like this even in old days at Uji," he protested. "Indeed your sister expressly permitted and even desired it. I cannot think you would show such horror if you realized that I am doing nothing which would not have her complete approval. And I promise most absolutely that I will not in any way take unfair advantage of such latitude as you allow me."

He did indeed behave with the utmost gentleness and restraint. But he continued to tell her how in the last few months his regret over the manner in which he had disposed of her had gradually grown into being a perpetual torment—on and on the story went, so that she began to wonder whether he would ever let go of her sleeve. But it was hard to see what she could do, except resign herself to what was at any rate a harmless experience compared with many that she had lately been called upon to endure. If only these confessions had come from someone whom she did not know or care for! She began to find the recital unendurably painful, and burst into tears.

"Come," he said, "what is this? You are behaving childishly." But seeing her, despite her present distress, even more lovely in her grave womanhood than on that night of their first encounter, he himself, at the thought of what he had lost, was none too far from tears.

Two gentlewomen were supposed to be in attendance, and had it been a stranger who thus suddenly intruded on the wrong side of the curtains, they would have come to the rescue. But Kaoru was so old a friend that they imagined Kozeri must wish to discuss some private matter of business with him, and they thought it discreet to retire to another part of the house.

She was thus left entirely in his hands. It cannot be said he succeeded entirely in fulfilling his promises of good behavior. But, just as on that first night, when he saw that she was in real distress, he could nor bear to force her, and he did not do all that he would have wished to do. It is not necessary that I should go into further details. Suffice it to say that in the end he saw that it was useless to insist. The house was already astir, which seemed strange, as it was surely not much beyond midnight. To his surprise he found it was almost light. He would certainly be seen leaving the house, which was very annoying for Kozeri.

He put it to himself that he could not have behaved otherwise than he had done. Consideration for the state she was in alone sufficed to make a high-handed policy out of the question. Yet he knew quite well that at the bottom of his failure lay the same defect of character as had proved his undoing so often before. But after all what he wanted was a return of his affections. Supposing that, carried away by the excitement of the moment, he had forced himself upon her—once that had happened he would never have been able to think of her in any other way. A secret intrigue would have followed under circumstances which would necessarily make it of the most harassing description for himself as well as Kozeri. So he wisely reflected. Yet even while he did so, by a strange perversity, he continued to imagine to himself scenes in which he possessed her. It made no difference that she had driven him away. Her presence—the delicate features, rather thinner than in old days, the grace and dignity of her movements—seemed still to attend him, to the exclusion of all besides. It seemed clear that she was anxious to go to Uji and willing to let him take her there. But would Niou consent? It hardly seemed likely, and to effect the visit without his knowledge would be to treat him in a way that was really unpardonable. How, Kaoru asked himself, agitatedly tossing on his bed, how could he effect his purpose without involving them both in disgrace?

His next-morning letter arrived very early. It was in the form of a twisted note and had, outwardly at any rate, the usual business-like air. In his poem he reminded her of that other autumn night when he had come away empty-handed. "It is useless for me to attempt any comment on our meeting last night. Your attitude has left me utterly dumbfounded."

To leave the letter unanswered would merely excite the curiosity of her people. She had the excuse that at the moment she was actually feeling very unwell and she merely wrote: "I have received your letter, but am too unwell to answer it."

It was terribly brief and discouraging. To comfort himself he was obliged to call up before him once again the gracious image that at once belied these brief, cold words. Looking back on it he was surprised by the calm self-assurance with which she had resisted him. But of course she was no longer a mere inexperienced girl. She had indeed been obviously shocked and distressed; but there was nothing panic-stricken about her resistance. She had simply talked him into reason in the gentlest and most considerate way. He went back over the whole scene again and again, each time more bitterly provoked at the hopeless position in which his own incompetence had landed him. In every way she seemed to him to have improved since the old days at Uji. If, as seemed probable, Niou abandoned her altogether, she would be forced—Kaoru reflected—to look to him for assistance. But even so an open alliance would be out of the question. But it would be easy enough to have access to her secretly. Yes, she should be the great love of his life, the first and the last—so his thoughts ran on, perpetually moving towards more and more dangerous channels. "Prince Niou is at the Nijo-in."* For the first time he heard this announcement not with the satisfaction of one responsible for Kozeri's happiness, but with the jealousy of a lover.

Niou himself, after an absence of several days, had seized with alacrity on the first opportunity of absence from the New Palace. Kozeri on her side was determined to show no resentment. What was left for her now in life but to put the best face on things that she could? All her hope of a retreat to Uji had been dashed to the ground by Kaoru's behavior the other night. She contrived indeed to meet Niou with such gentleness and good humor that he was both touched and delighted, and with every conceivable endearment begged her to forgive him for his repeated absences. He saw that she had let out her belt a little even since he was last with her. He had never before been at close quarters with a woman in her condition and felt the greatest concern. But it was with little conviction that she listened to his endearments. Had not Kaoru with equal eloquence been assuring her for years past that her interests were his only care? Yet now he had shown not only that his motives were of a very different kind, but that he was capable of pursuing them without the least regard for her feelings and reputation. It was hard indeed, after what had happened, to believe in his assertion that his relations with Agemaki had been innocent. "Most likely the whole

---

* I.e. with Kozeri.

story was invented simply to put me off my guard," Kozeri thought bitterly. In any case sufficient had happened to show that she could never trust him again. He would of course be indignant at such precautions as had now become necessary, and would eventually suspend his visits. But she felt quite incapable of conducting her affairs without his assistance and in her feeling of helplessness she threw her arms about Niou and clung to him in a way she had never done before. His delight at this exhibition of confidence and affection was suddenly arrested. He became conscious of a strange yet familiar perfume. Expert as he was in this art he knew at once that it was not any of the usual burnt-incenses. At once a suspicion rushed to his mind which was amply confirmed when, upon his questioning Kozeri, she merely shrank away from him with a look of agonized entreaty. But the matter could not be allowed to rest there. Not that the discovery was any surprise to him. For from the first he had suspected that their relation was of a very different kind from what Kaoru had always pretended.

She had indeed changed every particle of clothing that she was wearing the night before. But all to no purpose, for the perfume seemed to have sunk into her very flesh. In vain too did she now protest that, though Kaoru had been with her, nothing had occurred. He would not believe her. No scent, he persisted, could transfer itself in this way merely through two people sitting in the same room. She heard him storming and raging at her, and longed only to escape, to hide. "You ought by this time to know something about my feelings towards you," he went on. "But even if you thought that I was going to desert you, this business of 'getting in first'* is a mean trick. And after all, have I really left you to yourself long enough to give you any cause for disquiet?"

He continued to pour out rebukes and reproaches too numerous to recount. But Kozeri made no reply.

By next morning however he had completely recovered his serenity. He had his washing-water and breakfast brought to her room. After Roku no Kimi's apartments, resplendent with damasks and brocades from Korea and China, these rooms looked almost dingy; and among Kozeri's people there were some whose dresses had seen their best days. She herself wore a mantle of soft, light brown stuff, with a robe of nadeshiko† style, the contrasts of facing and lining very negligently arranged. But she looked, he thought, quite as smart as Roku no Kimi in her faultlessly correct and fashionable attire. For his affection was strong enough to cause that strange partiality which makes merits out of defects.

---

* If our love is going to end, I may as well get in first; for so little do I trust you that not even in your unkindness can I any longer trust." *Kokin Rokujo* (Zoku Kokka Daikwan 32974).

† Yellow outside; green-blue inside.

She had grown, he noticed, not only thinner in the face since her pregnancy, but a trifle paler, which made her look more than ever distinguished. Even before this incident of the perfume it had seemed to him utterly inconceivable that anyone, other than a parent or brother, could be constantly at close quarters with a girl so unusually attractive without entertaining other feelings than those to which Kaoru had always professed. Such a relationship as he conceived must certainly have betrayed itself in their correspondence. At moments when he found himself alone in her rooms he made a hasty search for such documents in likely boxes and drawers; but he found nothing but the briefest and most matter-of-fact communications left lying about or stuck into things in a way that showed them not to have been regarded as of the slightest consequence. But even this was not enough to allay his suspicions. It was obvious, after the perfume incident, that love-letters must exist, even if a superficial search had failed to reveal them. That Kaoru should fall in love with her he had already decided to be inevitable. And why should she reject his advances? They were very well suited to one another...

Niou was working himself up into a frenzy of jealousy. He spent all day at the Nijo-in, but wrote no less than three times to the New Palace,* a fact which the old women in Kozeri's service, noting that the length of these communications was out of all proportion to the short period of time that he and Roku no Kimi had been separated, interpreted as an ill sign for Kozeri's permanent happiness.

Kaoru, when he heard that Niou was still at the Nijo-in, was at first plunged in despair. Presently however he succeeded in reminding himself that he was, after all, responsible for the success of the match and ought by rights to be glad or at any rate to make some effort to be glad that, Niou was still conscious of his obligations. In his letters to Kozeri there was, despite all his efforts to recapture the sensible and business-like tone of their previous correspondence, henceforward a constant under note of passion, which made their arrival a fresh burden upon her already harassed existence. If he had been a stranger, it would have been easy enough to send him about his business. But everyone knew of her dependence on him in the past and any open breach between two such old friends would at once arouse just the suspicions that she most wished to avoid. Moreover she was, she could not help confessing, extremely fond of him, and it was singularly unfortunate that he had reduced things to a pass in which the slightest indication of her feelings was bound to prove disastrous. Among her waiting-women there was not one whom she cared to take into her confidence. Several of the younger ones seemed quite decent, sensible

---

* I.e. to Roku no Kimi.

creatures; but they had been with her only a few months and she hardly felt that she knew them at all. The old women, who had come with her from Uji, were mere peasants, with whom she felt no inclination to discuss her private affairs. Never had she so longed for her elder sister's comfort and advice. But if Agemaki had been alive, the situation could indeed never have arisen. Kaoru's behavior now weighed upon her mind even more than the prospect of Niou's dereliction.

Kaoru had made up his mind to keep at a distance, but one rather gloomy evening, unable to support his loneliness, he called once more at the Nijo-in.

After some delay a cushion was handed out to him from inside the screens; but he was told that Kozeri was indisposed and could not possibly see him. This was a terrible blow, but the presence of her gentlewomen forced him to conceal his disappointment and he sent in the message: "I have come hoping to be of service to you. But if we are merely to exchange messages in this way, I fear my visit will be in vain. You think nothing, however ill you may be feeling, of admitting completely unknown priests and even mere apothecaries and so on behind your screens..."

He spoke in as light a tone as possible; but his great disappointment was obvious to Kozeri's people, who having seen him admitted behind the curtains a few nights before could not understand why he should now be treated so inhospitably. They therefore took it upon themselves to let down the blinds between the alcove and the main room and lead him to the seat[*] where the night-priest was usually accommodated.

Kozeri was indeed actually feeling very unwell. But to raise objections to what her maids had done would merely have excited their suspicion; and in the end, reluctantly enough, she even moved a little towards the alcove side of the room and allowed him to converse with her. Her languid posture and occasional murmured replies reminded him painfully of Agemaki during her last illness—an impression which became so intense that he found it difficult to continue the conversation. Moreover, she seemed to be so far away from him that talking was a strain. He reached under the blind and pulled her curtained couch a little further to his side. Kozeri however felt in no mood for a performance such as that of the other evening, and immediately called out to her maid Shosho: "I've got such a pain in my heart. Do come and massage[†] me for a little." "Ah, pains at the heart! I know what it costs to repress them," he sighed, making room for Shosho to pass, though it scarcely pleased him that a third person had been added to the party.

---

[*] In the alcove.

[†] Literally "press down." There is, in Kaoru's exclamation, a play on *osau*, "to press down with the hand," and *osau*, "to repress feelings."

"You ought not to be suffering so continuously," he said presently. "People tell me that as a rule the bad periods are quite short and between times you should be feeling perfectly well. You must try not to think so much about it. It seems to me that you are worrying about yourself far more than is really necessary."

"The pain I spoke of," she answered, "is nothing to do with this. I have had it constantly all my life. Agemaki was just the same. They say it is a sign that one will not live long."

Were all his friends going to be swept off like this one after another? Kaoru was deeply moved, and despite the presence of Shosho, he began to pour into Kozeri's ear a fresh recital of his passion. This time however he showed a discretion for which, she was duly thankful—carefully omitting references to anything of an embarrassing character, and indeed so framing and directing his remarks that Shosho could make out very little of what was said. Moreover he soon left the subject of Kozeri herself, to turn to that of her sister.

"You know," he said, "that from my childhood I had made up my mind to become a monk and for years on end framed all my life and habits to that end. Never till I met Agemaki had anything shaken this resolution. But when I had lost her, it was impossible to resume the habits of the past. Not that my nature was changed; but it was imperative that I should find some way of distracting my thoughts. I went aimlessly hither and thither hoping always to chance upon some diversion. But it seemed as though no other wind could blow me. You will think all that has happened since very strange, considering that at the time when Agemaki permitted and even encouraged it, I made so little effort to pursue your acquaintance. You must remember that I was sunk in despair and hardly capable of attending to what was going on around me. Above all things I should hate you to regard me as unfaithful to her memory. I know that it is not borne out by what happened the other night—it was horrible, and shall never occur again. But there is no reason why we should not often meet like this and talk things over. Surely there is no harm in it? It would not perhaps do if anyone else came in this way; but everyone knows I am different. You need not be afraid."

"If I had any tendency to be afraid," she answered, "I should hardly be receiving you as I am doing at this minute, in a way that any outside person would be astounded at. Indeed, if I do so, it is only because I always remember that you have done innumerable kindnesses to me both here and at Uji for years past. You know how precious your help is. Did I not send for you specially, not so long ago?"

"Did you?" he said. "I am not sure that I remember. I feel flattered, anyhow, that you should have thought of using me. Oh yes, of course. It was when you were so anxious to get back to Uji, and could think of no one but me to arrange it for you! Well, I suppose I ought to feel it to have been a great privilege..." He was about to launch out on a further, embittered harangue, when he fortunately noticed that Kozeri's people were well within earshot, and managed to hold himself in check.

It was growing dark outside. From the garden came no sound but the continual chirping of insects. The "mountain"* cast heavy shadows; everything was enveloped in gloom. Kaoru sat staring out of the window with a depressed air, and it seemed certain that, despite his assurances, more trouble was brewing.

"If only I had something that would recall her to my mind," he said at last. "Some place where I could go and weep my fill. I should like to put up a statue or picture of her[†] somewhere at Uji—not necessarily in a special building—and go there sometimes to burn incense and so on in front of it. Do you think that could be done?"

"It is a beautiful idea," she said. "But I cannot help associating the making of images with the desire to forget[‡] rather than with the wish to perpetuate someone's memory. And one dreads to think what sort of picture of her a painter would produce! No doubt he would make her hideous unless we paid him tremendous sums."

"You are right," he said. "What an ordinary painter or sculptor could produce would never satisfy us. Nothing short of a magician would be any good—someone like that man—and after all the thing happened not very long ago—whose statue was so beautiful that the sky rained flower-petals upon it."[§]

She was touched by his devotion to Agemaki's memory. Despite his curious behavior, this did seem to be perfectly genuine. She came a little closer. "Your talking about images and portraits," she said, "reminds me of a most surprising thing that happened lately."

There was this time something singularly friendly and encouraging in the way he spoke. "Tell me about it," he said, at the same time stretching out under the curtains and feeling for her hand, which he took in his. It did not seem, thought Kozeri at her wits' end, that all her efforts to calm and distract him were having much success. But to draw away her hand would only have called her people's attention to the liberties he was taking, and it seemed better to behave as though nothing were amiss. "This summer," she said, I suddenly got a letter from someone I had not heard of for years and indeed scarcely imagined to be still alive. She said that she had just returned from a distant province, and wished to see me.

---

* An artificial mound in the garden.

† Agemaki

‡ People desiring to escape from the toils of love cast images of the loved person into a sacred stream. If the god "received" the image, the lover was able to "forget."

§ This reference has not been explained.

It is someone with whom I am in a way connected. But there seemed no reason why she should suddenly descend on me in this way, and I was not very encouraging about the visit. However, she insisted on coming, and to my surprise I discovered that she bore the most astonishing resemblance to Agemaki. We were friends immediately. You have often told me that I remind you of her; but no one else sees it. Whereas this girl, who is far less closely related to me, is almost indistinguishable from Agemaki. Really, it is such a likeness as you would hardly think conceivable."

It all sounded like a dream. "She must have had some particular reason for suddenly claiming kinship with you like this," Kaoru said. "The whole thing puzzles me. Why did you not tell me about it at the time?" "Until quite recently," she said, "I knew no better than you do what reason these people had for getting into communication with me. Besides, it is not a thing that I want people to know about. It is bad enough that I have fulfilled my father's worst anticipations as to what would become of us both when he was dead, without reminding people of this other failure of his..."

From what she said it was clear to Kaoru that it must be some illegitimate child of Prince Hachi's who had now suddenly turned up. He would not have been much interested, save for the mention of her extraordinary likeness to Agemaki. "If she is indeed as closely related to you as what you say seems to suggest, I think that having told me so much you might just as well tell me the rest," he said. She felt she had told him quite as much as he could reasonably expect. "That is all I know," she said. "If you want to make her acquaintance there is no difficulty about it; I can give you her address. I don't intend to tell you any more about the impression she made upon me, for fear you should be disappointed when you see her."

"You know well enough," he said, "that if it were indeed a question of one moment's meeting with Agemaki herself I would go down to the bottom of the deepest sea to find her. What you have told me is of course a very different matter. But all the same, I admit that my curiosity is aroused. I would, you may well imagine, far rather have a living person to remind me of her at Uji than set up the statue we spoke of! I wish you would tell me the rest of the story." "I am not at all sure," she said, yielding at last to his insistence, "that I ought to have told you about her at all. It is clear that my father did not wish her to be regarded as his child. But it really did seem a pity that you should begin looking round for magicians to construct her likeness, when all the while there was this living image of her so near at hand. Exactly what happened was this. Ukifune—for that is her name—was brought up in a very remote place. Her mother longed to do better for her and wrote, rather impertinently I thought at the time, trying to get into touch with me. I could not refuse point-blank; and the next thing was that the girl, who had travelled up from the country on purpose, presented herself at my doors. It is true that I saw her in the evening, by a rather dim light; but I was certainly astonished by her appearance, considering the circumstances under which she has been brought up. Her mother evidently has great ambitions for her; but I think that even she might regard your proposal to set the girl up like a god on an altar as a little excessive!"

If she laughed at him it was not out of unkindness, but merely because she was ready to clutch at any means of diverting his attention and avoiding unpleasant happenings of the sort that had marked his previous visit. He saw this clearly enough, and was piqued, but at the same time grateful. It was something that, though determined to keep within bounds, she should see the necessity for a certain amount of subterfuge. It at any rate showed that she realized his feelings about her to be deep, and wished to spare them. It was getting very late. Kozeri felt that the eyes of her gentlewomen were turned questioningly upon her, and catching Kaoru unawares she slipped from his grasp, and retired to the far side of the room.

In a way he was glad that the interview had ended thus. Yet at the same time he was disappointed and aggrieved, and torn by a medley of conflicting emotions he was on the verge of tears. But other eyes than hers were upon him—after all there could be no such thing as a happy issue to any of their meetings. For the more successful he was, the greater the miseries and complications that he was bound in the end to bring both to himself and her.

Somehow or other, he reflected when he reached home, he must contrive to escape out of the present dilemma, which was so rapidly making his life insupportable. Surely there must be some way of getting at her without endangering anyone's reputation. So small was his experience in these matters, he had not learnt of the risks that in such cases must inevitably be taken, and all night long he lay inventing schemes for the protection now of his good name, now of Kozeri's.

As for this Ukifune, who was said to bear so strong a resemblance to Agemaki, he was curious to see for himself how far the likeness went; and as the girl's mother was apparently of quite low rank there would be no difficulty in getting access to her. It would be awkward however if he found he did not take to her. Perhaps it would be better to do nothing about it.

PART SIX
THE BRIDGE OF DREAMS

LIST OF MOST IMPORTANT PERSONS (alphabetical)

Agemaki	The elder daughter of Prince Hachi. Dead before this part begins.
Ben no Kimi	An old nun at Uji.
Colonel, The	Engaged to Imoto's daughter, who dies young. Makes love to Ukifune at Ono.
Emperor, The	Son of the ex-Emperor Suzaku.
Empress, The	Daughter of Genji and the lady he brought back from Akashi.
Hachi, Prince	Father of Agemaki, Kozeri and Ukifune. Dead before this part begins.
Hitachi, The Governor of	Ukifune's stepfather.
Imoto	A nun, sister of Sozu.
Jiju	Gentlewoman to Ukifune at Uji.
Kaoru	Passes in the world as Genji's son. but is in reality the son of Kashiwagi, who deceives Genji with Kaoru's mother, Nyosan. Aged about twenty-five when this part begins.
Kosaisho	Lady-in-waiting to the First Princess. Has a long-standing friendship with Kaoru.
Michisada	Niou's retainer.
Miya no Kimi	Daughter of Genji's half-brother. Is reduced to taking service as a lady-in-waiting.
Nakanoru	Kaoru's retainer.
Niou	Third son of the Emperor and Empress. Aged about twenty-four when this part begins.
Princess, The First	Niou's elder sister.
Princess, The Second	Born to the Emperor by a concubine. Becomes Kaoru's wife.
Roku no Kimi	Sixth daughter of Yugiri; becomes Niou's secondary wife.
Sakon	Engaged to Ukifune, but breaks it off on the discovery that she is not the Governor's daughter.
Shosho	A nun at Ono.
Sozu	An important clerical dignitary at Yogawa on the Hieizan.

Tokikata	Niou's retainer.
Ukifune	Illegitimate daughter of Prince Hachi.
Ukifune's Mother	Badly treated by Prince Hachi. Afterwards marries the Governor of Hitachi.
Ukon	Gentlewoman to Ukifune; daughter of her old nurse.
Yugiri	Genji's son by his first wife, Aoi. Aged about fifty when Part VI begins.

The Mistletoe

It was a long while since Kaoru had been to Uji. He felt he was getting out of touch with the past, and towards the end of the ninth month, in a heavy gale, he set out once again on the familiar road. The aspect of the place could not have been more depressing than on this stormy, grey afternoon. In the wind-swept gardens there was not a sign of life. The menacing roar of the flooded river pervaded the whole house, and seemed indeed to have become its only occupant. At last, however, the old nun,[*] Ben no Kimi, appeared behind the grey[†] curtains of a couch that had been pushed towards the open door. "Forgive me!" she said. "I haven't the heart to let you see me as I am. I wasn't much to look at before; but now, in this strange garb..." "I've often wondered how you were getting on," Kaoru said. "You're the only person in the world who can really enter into my feelings about what happened last year[‡]—yes, a whole year ago it is now. How the days have flown!" Tears dimmed his eyes and the old woman was already weeping bitterly. "It's just the same wild sort of weather, too," she said," as when my dear lady was worrying so terribly about my Lady Kozeri. How this hateful autumn wind brings it all back to me! Never have my eyes been dry since it began to blow. And it seems my poor lady was not so far wrong either, judging from what I hear..." "Oh, things aren't going so badly,"[§] Kaoru said. "I don't doubt that it will all come right in time. What mattered was that she convinced herself it[¶] would be a disaster. Undoubtedly it was this conviction that brought about her death; and I, who arranged the match, shall never—that is what is so terrible—escape from the feeling that it was I who killed her. But as a matter of fact even now[**] there is really nothing to worry about. Such situations are the commonest thing in the world. So, too, you will say, is death. And indeed it is not hard to face the fact that we ourselves and those we love must turn to ashes in the end. What haunts one is the thought of being left behind, as has happened to me now..." Again his tears began to flow.

---

[*] For Ben no Kimi's decision to become a nun, see Part V, p. 910.
[†] In sign of mourning for Agemaki.
[‡] Agemaki's death.
[§] Between Kozeri and Niou.
[¶] Kozeri's marriage with Niou.
[**] Even now that Kozeri has a rival in the shape of Roku no Kimi.

Presently he sent for the Teacher. "I have thoughts of making some changes here," he said, when he had given directions for the celebration of the Anniversary.* "I shall be obliged to come here from time to time; and to find the place just as it was in the old days save for the absence of those who made it dear to me is an experience which I do not wish to repeat. What I should like to do would be to pull down the main wing and rebuild it in the form of a chapel, close to your temple on the hill. And if you are in favor of this, the sooner the work begins the better." He made a sketch showing what he wanted to be done, how the cloisters were to lie, where the priests' cells were to be, and so on. The Teacher signified his entire approval. "I hope you don't think it heartless of me," Kaoru said, "to undo the work that Prince Hachi planned with so much taste and care. What I feel is that he would certainly have done something of this kind himself, had he not been deterred by consideration for those† whom he was leaving here. On Agemaki's death the place of course went to Kozeri, and through her it has now passed into the control of Prince Niou. That being so, I cannot simply hand it over to you to use as a temple. In any case, the situation is unsuitable. There is a good deal of traffic on the river, and you would not here have the quiet necessary for monastic life. It would certainly be much better to pull down the main hall and rebuild it elsewhere; though naturally I cannot do anything of the kind without obtaining His Highness's permission." "Whatever the upshot of this may be," the Teacher replied, your determination to obliterate useless reminders of the past is thoroughly in accordance with the precepts of our Faith. I wonder if you know the story‡ of the man who for years on end carried the remains of his dear one in a sack tied to his neck. At last he met the Buddha, who by a pious ruse persuaded him to drop the sack and enter on the True Path. These buildings would be a continual reminder of what it is better to forget, and you would be upset every time you came here. Whereas the dedication you propose would certainly be of great avail to you in the life to come. I hope you will allow me to carry it out at once. Let me know what date your astrologers consider suitable, provide me with a few competent overseers, and I will see to it that all is done in accordance with the dictates of the Blessed One." By the time he had discussed the details of the plan, and given the necessary instructions to the people from his estates, whose services he put entirely at the Teacher's disposal, Kaoru found that it was too late to return to the City, and decided to stay the night. He felt he must go and have a last look round. The Buddha-images had all gone to the

---

* Of Agemaki's death.

† Agemaki and Kozeri.

‡ Said to occur in the Great Commentary on the *Vairocana Sutra* (Takakusu, vol. xxxix, p. 579). It is not to be found in the versions accessible to me; but the work exists in several different forms.

temple on the hill, and save for Ben no Kimi's few things the place was entirely denuded. He hated to think of her dragging out her existence in the midst of such desolation. "I have a plan," he said, "for rebuilding these quarters, and while the work is going on you had better move into the side wing. If you come across anything that belongs to my lady in the Capital* you can get one of the men who work on my estate to take it to her."

A strange pair they made, Kaoru and this old creature, as far into the night they lay side by side whispering together, almost like lovers, anyone at a first glance might have thought. The opportunity was indeed an excellent one and he was able, without fear of their being overheard or disturbed, to hear much that was new to him in his father's unhappy story. "When I remember," she concluded, "how constantly in those last days he questioned me about you and how full his thoughts were of your future, I cannot cease to marvel and be thankful that at last this strange chance has brought us together and that after all these years I can reckon myself a servant of my dear master's child! But what with our great sorrow† and then these troubles‡ that followed so soon, I don't nowadays feel fit for much, and though our dear lady in the Capital has begged me time and again to visit her and told me she would take it as very unkind to her if I shut myself up here till the end, I have not felt, since I became as I am,§ that I wished to look on any face save that of Amida the Blessed One."

They talked for a long while about Agemaki, Ben repeating to him things that her mistress had said, on this occasion and that, in the years gone by, and recalling in her tremulous yet by no means displeasing voice the stray verses that Agemaki had made when moved by the beauty of spring blossom or autumn leaves. In language many of these poems were crude and inadequate, but they showed a point of view that was intensely sympathetic to him, and he listened eagerly. Compared with Agemaki as she then was, Kozeri as he knew her today seemed an easygoing woman of the world. But then he only knew her on one side. To someone like himself, in whom she had confidence, she might appear quite lacking in timidity or reserve. But he could imagine that to any stranger who attempted to get onto terms of intimacy, she would give very short shrift. And so from the two sisters he had known his thoughts passed to that other, about whom he was still curious—that Ukifune¶ who was said to be the living image of the lady he had lost.

---

* Kozeri.
† The death of Agemaki.
‡ Kozeri's troubles with Niou.
§ Became a nun.
¶ The name means Floating Boat.

"I don't know whether she is in the Capital now or not," said Ben no Kimi. "I only hear about her indirectly. While Prince Hachi was still at the Capital, shortly before his wife's death, he took a fancy to one of the upper serving-women. The affair was of no importance and no one knew of it, but they met once or twice in secret, and a child was born. He knew that the little girl was his, but coming as it did when his thoughts were absorbed in his great sorrow, he could not bring himself to see the mother again. She saw that he had quite lost interest in the world and was leading to all intents and purposes the life of a monk. In this life there could be no place for her, and quitting his service she married the Governor of Michinoku and went with him to his province. After a year she wrote to Prince Hachi reminding him of the little girl's existence. But his only reply was to beg her never to allude to the subject again. Later on her husband was moved to Hitachi, and for years I heard nothing more about her. This spring, however, someone told me that she had come back to the Capital and been to see Lady Kozeri. The girl must by now I suppose be about nineteen. I know that in a long letter she wrote some time ago to Lady Kozeri her mother spoke of her as being very good-looking, which made it, she said, all the sadder that she could not come into her own." Kaoru drank in every word. All this exactly confirmed what Kozeri had told him. He felt an intense desire to make Ukifune's acquaintance. "I would travel the world over," he said eagerly, "to get so much as a glimpse of anyone who might turn out to bear the faintest resemblance to Agemaki. The fact that Hachi did not acknowledge her cannot from that point of view make any difference to me. I don't want you to go out of your way to do it, but if you should by any chance come across her, tell her about what I have just said." "The mother," Ben no Kimi replied, "is related to the family of Prince Hachi's wife, and so am I. But she has been away so much that I can scarcely say I know her at all. I did indeed have a message not long ago from one of Lady Kozeri's women saying that it was thought the girl ought to visit her father's grave, and begging me to do what I could about it. But she has never been here. Certainly, however, if she does come, I will tell her what you have said."

Meaning to return to the Capital at break of day, Kaoru had, after his arrival at Uji, sent for silk, wadding, and so on, and he now dispatched a supply to the Teacher. For Ben no Kimi too he had a present, as also for the priests and the women who waited on Ben, to all of whom he sent parcels of stuffs. Certainly life was not particularly gay at Uji; but so long as Kaoru's visits continued it could not be said that for a person in her position, anxious to lead a life of quiet devotion, Ben no Kimi did so badly.

The autumn storms had been particularly violent and not a leaf remained on any bough. The great untrodden carpets of red leaf that stretched before him were of a beauty that kept him lingering long after he had meant to start. But bare though were the forests one tree stood out, mantled in a blaze of red. It was some kind of mistletoe or creeper growing upon an old withered tree. He sent someone to pluck a cluster of it, to bring back to Kozeri.

"Had not remembrance found, like mistletoe upon the bough, its host and harbor, desolate indeed were this night's sojourning. Such was the verse that Ben no Kimi heard him murmuring; and she in reply: "How dire the case, when even upon this tree-stump, scared and tottering, the mistletoe can deign to rest." Her poem could scarcely have been, in its cadences, more stiff and out-of-date. But the allusion[*] touched him and he was thankful for her sympathy.

On arriving at his palace he at once sent round the mistletoe to the Nijo-in. Niou was present when it arrived, and rather to Kozeri's embarrassment it was brought to her with the message "From the palace to the south."[†] Any attempt at concealment would only have made matters worse. Kaoru's notes (and one was attached to the spray) were not always very discreet. She could only hope for the best. "Those are very pretty leaves!" Niou said meaningly, and asked if he might look at the present. He glanced at the note. "What have you been doing lately?... I have just come back from Uji. But of that and the 'morning mist on the hilltops'[‡] I will tell you when we meet. I have spoken to the Teacher about rebuilding the main hall. Nothing shall be moved without your express permission. You can give your instructions to Ben no Kimi, who has promised me to see to everything." "Well, that's harmless enough, anyway," exclaimed Niou, "which, however, is easy to account for: he knew I should be here when it arrived." This was meant more or less as a joke, but was in fact not entirely untrue. She was in any case relieved that the letter he had chanced to light on happened to be so harmless. Yet oddly enough she at the same time felt injured that Niou should have regarded it with any suspicion at all. But as she sat there her expression, half of relief, half of indignation, entranced Niou to such an extent that he would have forgiven her ten thousand faults or indiscretions.

"Now you must write your answer," he said. "Say what you please. I won't look." And he turned his back. To make any difficulty about replying in his presence would again arouse his suspicions, and she at once wrote: "So you have been at Uji? I can't tell you how jealous that makes me. I approve entirely of your plan for turning the hall into a sanctuary. Sooner or later I shall need somewhere of that sort to retire to,

---

[*] Ben's poem is an allusion to the fact that she and Kaoru were drawn together by their common sorrow at the death of Agemaki.

[†] I.e. from Kaoru's palace.

[‡] Symbol of unending sorrow, in reference to a poem in the *Kokinshu* about morning mists on the hilltops that "never clear up."

and I had far rather go back there than have to wander round searching for a refuge. I hoped that some way might be found of keeping the hall intact, and if you can manage something of the kind you suggest I shall be deeply grateful."

She showed her answer to Niou. It was certainly a model of correctness. But as such a relationship between man and woman as this letter suggested was a thing that he had never himself experienced, he was not in the least reassured, but on the contrary more and more convinced that behind all this show of innocent helpfulness something sinister must be concealed.

Amid the desolation of the autumn garden only the pampas-flowers stood out, their long stems beckoning from the borders like waving arms. Even on those that had run to seed pearl-chains of dew still hung quavering. These were not flowers of great beauty, yet now, in the evening air, the scene was not altogether devoid of charm. "O pampas-grass, though innocent your flower, those beckoning sleeves betray you,[*] drenched in sorrowful dew!" So Niou murmured. He was informally dressed, wearing only a simple cloak, and had sent for his lute. He began to play an accompaniment in the *ojiki*[†] mode, and Kozeri cared far too deeply for the instrument to remember, once he started playing, any of her anxieties or grievances. Leaning on a stool behind a screen-of-state so small that it only in part concealed her, lost in the rapture of the music, she looked lovely enough to charm the heart of any prince. "That desolate autumn hurries through the fields apace, to nodding flowers the wind's cold breath betrays."[‡] So she recited. "Though not for me alone..."[§] she added, shedding a tear that she hastily hid with her fan. Niou watched her critically. She seemed at that moment the embodiment of goodness and gentleness. And yet—it was just this sweetness, this look of having no harm in her, which he was convinced must prove irresistible to Kaoru. The chrysanthemums[¶] were only beginning to turn, and indeed here where they were so well tended they kept their whiteness very late. Scanning the borders, Niou had some difficulty in finding one that was really at its best. At last, however, he chose his flower, humming as he did so those lines of the Chinese poet: "It is not that of all flowers..."[**] "One evening when a certain prince[††] was admiring such flowers as these,"

---

[*] Pun on *ho ni izu,* "run to seed" and "show in the face."
[†] See Part V, p. 809.
[‡] Pun on *aki,* "autumn," and *aki,* "satiety," suggesting that he had transferred his affections to Roku no Kimi.
[§] "...is autumn sad." Reference to a poem in the *Kokinshu.*
[¶] White chrysanthemums were particularly admired when their petals had turned gold-brown.
[**] "It is not that of all flowers I like this one best, but only that when this has gone, there are no more flowers." By Yuan Chen, died A.D. 832.
[††] Various stories are told of how the spirit of the Chinese lute-player Lien Ch'eng-wu appeared

Niou reminded her, "a spirit came flying through the air and taught him a lute song. If only we had lived then! Nothing of that sort ever happens to people nowadays," and with a despondent gesture he pushed the instrument away from him. "Such things do not happen to us," Kozeri reasoned with him, disappointed, "because we no longer deserve it. But even if we have changed for the worse, the old tunes have not," and she begged him to show her the right way to take several passages about which she was uncertain. "Why not?" he said. "But it would be far better if you accompanied me. It is much more amusing!" He sent for his thirteen-stringed zithern and set it before her. "I had some lessons once with my father," she said, "but I never really got very far." "Oh come," he exclaimed indignantly, "it is too much if my being here makes you shy even over such a trifle as this. That other friend of mine, though I have known her such a short time, is not in the least ashamed to let me help her with things that she is only just learning. I don't think that Kaoru, whom you are so fond of quoting, would at all approve of such mock modesty. I have often heard him say that in women an easy, obliging disposition is the first essential. I am sure that you make no difficulty about playing when he is with you. But then obviously you are made for one another."

She sighed, and taking up the instrument began rather half-heartedly to tune it. The strings had stretched a good deal, and it was simplest to tune it to the *banjiki*[*] mode, in which she now accompanied him. He thought she followed very creditably, and her touch was good. The waiting-women, gathered behind screens, and curtains, heard his clear fine voice singing the "Sea of Ise"[†] and beamed with satisfaction. "What matter," someone said, "if he has more establishments than one, and why shouldn't he? Our lady has much to be thankful for; there's no denying it. And to think that, after all those years cooped up at Uji, she should now be talking of going back there!" "What? Back there?" the younger women cried. "Don't speak of such a thing!"

So what with lute lessons, zithern lessons, and the like several days went by without Niou leaving the Nijo-in. The plea of a ritual defilement that he sent to the New Palace was far from satisfying Yugiri, who now, on his way back from the Emperor's Palace, came bustling round to find out what was happening. "It is such a bore," Niou said, "to have him always coming round like this." However, he pulled himself together and duly appeared in the reception-hall. "It always feels strange to be back here," Yugiri said. "Of course in my father's time I was here a great deal, but

---

in Japan.

  * B, C sharp, D, E, F sharp, G sharp, A.
  † "By the sea of Ise, on the clean sea-beach, I will gather shells..."

now it is different." After a few anecdotes and reminiscences he took Niou by the arm and dragged him off to the New Palace: They were accompanied by many of Yugiri's sons, as well as by a host of noblemen and courtiers, forming a procession which gave to Kozeri's peeping ladies an imposing notion of the rival family's importance. "Just look at His Excellency the Minister," they cried. "What a fine gentleman! For all the youth and strength they've got on their side, there's none of his sons can touch him." "And yet," said another, "he can't get the Prince to his house without coming all the way to fetch him. Well, I suppose if the truth were known everyone has his troubles!"

But Kozeri, contrasting her own quiet upbringing with the brilliance of Roku no Kimi's surroundings, felt utterly unable to satisfy anyone to whom this life, with all its glitter and glibness, was a matter of course. More than ever she felt that the one sensible thing to do was to return once more to the solitary life that she understood.

So the year passed. From the end of the first month onwards she was very unwell. Niou, in his complete inexperience of such matters, became very anxious and had all manner of rites and supplications added, in temple after temple, to those that he had already commanded. Hearing that Kozeri's condition really gave cause for alarm, the Empress herself sent to enquire; and Niou's friends, despite the fact that the relationship had remained nominally a secret one, being pretty generally aware that his affections had been engaged in this quarter for the uncommonly long period of three years, felt themselves able without indiscretion to convey to him their sympathy and good wishes. Kaoru was naturally no less perturbed than Niou. But he felt that at such a moment it was more tactful to keep in the background, and though he sometimes sent to enquire, he did not call in person. He too, however, secretly arranged for services to be held on her behalf.

This was the time that had been fixed for the Second Princess's Putting on of the Skirt, which event was the great topic of conversation at Court. Such minute personal attention did the Emperor give to all the preparations for the coming ceremony that the Princess's bereaved* condition hardly made itself felt. Much of what was necessary had been set aside for her by her mother, and offerings also poured in both from the Office of Works and from the treasuries of numerous provincial governments. It was assumed that so soon as this event was over the Princess's marriage to Kaoru would follow as a matter of course, and there was much that he ought to have been arranging. But as a matter of fact he hardly gave these coming responsibilities a thought, so occupied was his mind with Kozeri's condition.

---

* She had lost her mother.

In the second month came the announcement of what I believe are called the Supplementary Appointments. Kaoru became Acting Chief Counselor, with the military rank of General of the Right, a vacancy having been created by the retirement of Kobai from the post of General of the Left. Among numerous other visits which Kaoru paid in connection with this new appointment was one to the Nijo-in. Niou was at the moment in particular anxiety about Kozeri and was in her apartments when Kaoru arrived. "It is too bad," Niou said, "to bring you here at such a time. As you see, we are overrun by priests." The upheavals in the household were not at all reflected in Niou's appearance. He came down the steps to go through the formal act of congratulation in a new and faultlessly adjusted dress, and was indeed perfectly turned out from top to toe. "You won't fail me, will you," Kaoru said when the formalities were over, "at my banquet tonight—the entertainment, you know, that I have to give to my future colleagues?" But Niou seemed very uncertain whether, with things as they were, he would be able to get away. It was decided that the banquet should be modeled on that given when Yugiri became Minister, and it was to be held in the New Palace. The number of princes and noblemen who came to help Kaoru entertain his guests was so great that the whole affair had more the air of an Imperial Banquet than of a private entertainment. Niou put in an appearance, but hurried back to the Nijo-in long before the proceedings were over, to the chagrin of Yugiri and his friends, who regarded so perfunctory an attendance almost as an affront. As a matter of fact in actual rank Kozeri was more than the equal of her rival, and the general assumption that Roku no Kimi must necessarily be treated with infinitely more deference and consideration was due merely to Yugiri's immense public prestige.

Early next morning, to Niou's delight, Kozeri was safely delivered of a boy. It was too a great weight off Kaoru's mind, and as soon as he heard the news he went round to the Nijo-in, where indeed he would have been going anyhow to thank Niou for his attendance at last night's festivity. The place was crowded with visitors, people knowing that for the next few days they would be certain to find him at home. Following the usual custom the birth-presents on the third day came only from Niou himself. But on the night of the fifth day there came from Kaoru a present of fifty rice-balls, counters for gambling at draughts, and other customary trifles, and for the mother a nest of thirty boxes containing a nursing robe of five thicknesses, with swaddling-clothes for the child. He had chosen simple things, but all of them bore witness on closer examination to his taste and powers of invention. To Niou he sent flour-cakes on sandal-wood trays and high one-legged stands. To the ladies-in-waiting he sent, in addition to the usual nests of boxes, thirty picnic hampers full of all sorts of supplies. But he took care, in making these gifts, to attract as little attention as possible.

On the night of the seventh day presents arrived from the Empress, the messengers being accompanied by a host of influential visitors, including the Intendant of the Empress's Household.

"After all," the Emperor said when he heard of the event, "it's a thing that happens only once in life—having a first child. I feel rather inclined to do something about it..." and he sent the child a sword.* On the ninth day a deputation came from Yugiri. He was naturally far from enthusiastic about what had happened, but he saw that it was for many reasons inadvisable for him to be on bad terms with Niou, and he instructed all his sons to go and pay their respects. Kozeri indeed had no cause of any kind to complain of the way in which the event had been received, and now, after a long period of illness and worry had reduced her to a state of permanent despondence, the marks of friendliness and even deference with which the birth of her child had been greeted did much to restore her spirits and self-confidence. Kaoru felt that the event must inevitably set a fresh distance between them. It seemed certain in any case that the birth of the child would serve to cement her relationship with Niou, which in a way was a relief to him, since he was responsible for bringing them together.

Towards the end of the second month the long-expected Initiation of the Second Princess took place, and on the following day Kaoru visited her at the Palace. The actual ceremonies of union that night were of a private character. The Second Princess had for long been so much in the public eye owing to the Emperor's marked partiality for her that her marriage to a commoner† came rather as a disappointment. Many people thought that, whatever the Emperor's personal feelings towards Kaoru might be, he would have done better to look round a little first. But his Majesty, once he had decided on a plan, liked to carry it out immediately, and could never be persuaded to waste time in the usual search for precedents. As a matter of fact such a marriage as this was by no means unprecedented, though it had perhaps seldom happened that the daughter of a reigning monarch had been disposed of after her Initiation with a haste usually witnessed only in the matrimonial affairs of ordinary families. "I cannot help regarding the young man," Yugiri said, "as singularly fortunate. It was only after Suzaku's abdication and indeed on the eve of his complete retirement from the world that he offered Genji his daughter.‡ And as for me, if I was fortunate enough to secure you"—

---

* As a sign that he acknowledged the child as his grandson.
† I.e. not a member of the Imperial family.
‡ Nyosan, the mother of Kaoru.

he was speaking to Princess Ochiba*—"it was certainly not owing to any encouragement from your parents." This was true indeed, and Princess Ochiba, looking slightly embarrassed, made no reply.

On the evening of the third day, at the Emperor's request, the Second Princess's guardian† and all her retainers and supporters secretly distributed presents among Kaoru's outriders, attendants, runners, and house servants. All the ceremonies, however, were of a completely private character. In the days that followed Kaoru continued to visit the Princess. He found it, however, impossible to banish from his mind the memory of the lady he had lost. It was a strange life—hurrying home in the morning, only to pack off again reluctantly to the Palace when night came. It involved altogether too great a change in his habits, and he made up his mind to bring the Princess to his mother's house. Nyosan was delighted and even offered to move out of her own apartments.

To this he would not at first consent, but eventually planned a new wing close to the chapel, on the west side of which he erected new quarters for his mother. The east wing of the palace had suffered severely in the fire, and though it had been rebuilt and was quite comfortable, he now had it completely refurnished. The Emperor heard that he was planning to install the Princess at home and, with a parent's natural anxiety, could not help wondering whether such a step were not somewhat premature. In his letters to Nyosan his Majesty continually referred to the marriage, begging her to let him know if it seemed to be going well. The ex-Emperor Suzaku had on his death-bed given special instructions to the Emperor concerning the treatment of Nyosan, and though she was now a nun she held a position of considerable influence at Court, her every request to the Emperor being invariably granted and all her interests forwarded with the utmost dispatch.

That two such exalted personages should be conspiring together on behalf of his domestic happiness ought, Kaoru knew, to have been very gratifying. But actually the thought inspired him with considerable uneasiness. He found himself indeed, since his marriage, more restless than before, and could interest himself in nothing save the building operations that were in progress at Uji. He kept count of the days and was ready, when the fiftieth day came,‡ with his offering of cakes, himself supervising the making of the boxes and cases in which they were to be presented. He went indeed so far as to assemble for the purpose all the best workers in sandal-wood, cedar, gold, and silver, who vied with one another to achieve such craftsmanship as the world had never seen before. Waiting as

---
* Also a daughter of the ex-Emperor Suzaku.
† Her maternal uncle.
‡ Since the child's birth.

usual till he knew Niou to be absent from the Nijo-in, he went to pay his respects. Was it, Kozeri asked herself, only her fancy, or had he indeed changed somewhat since his promotion? Certainly it seemed to her that there was something more authoritative and self-assured in his manner. It was a comfort at any rate that he was now a married man, and there could be no more difficulties of the kind that had till now tended to spoil their friendship. But the moment that they embarked upon a conversation it became evident that such an assumption was premature. He began at once to tell her that his marriage meant nothing whatever to him, his life was a complete failure, he saw no gleam of happiness anywhere. "It's very unwise of you to talk of your marriage like that," she protested. "You may easily have been overheard." But though she did not say so, she was in reality rather pleased to find that the highest favor a monarch can bestow was powerless to console him. His nature, it could not be denied, was extraordinarily faithful, and that was a quality which one ought to appreciate. He was anxious to see the baby, and although she felt rather shy about it she told herself that it would be churlish to deny him such pleasure as it was in her power to give when there was so much that she was forced to withhold, and she at once ordered the nurse to show him the child. Coming of such parents he was sure it would not be ugly. But now he was amazed by the delicate whiteness of its skin; and while the child lay before him roisterously laughing and crowing he felt that, if it were his, life would assume a very different aspect. Or indeed what a difference it would have made if Agemaki had left him such a child! Strangely enough, not once did it occur to him that he might presumably expect soon to become a father in another quarter. I am afraid that his whole attitude towards his marriage gives a rather unpleasant impression of his character. I can only say that if he had really been so ineffectual a character as he must necessarily appear to be in the story which I have to tell, it is obvious that he would never have been singled out by the Throne and heaped with honors, as in fact he was.

He appreciated her having shown him the child long before it was likely to be seen by any other outsider. They talked for a long while, getting on together far better than usual; but his obligations at the Palace made it impossible for him to stay nearly as late into the night as he could have wished. The young waiting-maids crowded to peep at him as he went out. "We shall be having the nightingales looking us up," they said; so sweet was the fragrance that drifted to them as they watched him go.

Kaoru would have liked to bring the Princess home in the summer. But the astrologers said that the conjunction of the stars would be unfavorable, and it was therefore necessary to make the move before the first of the fourth month. On the day before her departure the Emperor visited her and held the Wisteria Festival in her apartments. The curtains of the southern side-wing were raised, and the Imperial party accommodated there. The occasion was regarded as a public one and the whole burden was not allowed to fall on the princess, the entertainment of the various courtiers and officers who were present being undertaken by the Treasury. The Administration was represented by Yugiri, Kobai and Higekuro's two sons; the Imperial clan by Niou and several of his brothers. At the foot of the tree in the courtyard facing the Imperial Seat the courtiers and lesser guests were accommodated. In a neighboring portico the musicians had been assembled, and when evening came the flutes played an overture in the *sojo* mode.[*] The instruments for the Emperor's own use were offered by the Princess herself, and were placed before him by Yugiri, who was also charged to put at His Majesty's disposal two volumes of zithern-airs to which a spray of five-needled pine was daintily attached. Various zitherns, native and Chinese, and a lute came from the collection of the ex-Emperor Suzaku. The flute was the one of which Kashiwagi had spoken to Yugiri when he appeared to him in a dream.[†] The Emperor had on a previous occasion expressed amazement at the beauty of its tone, and it seemed that there could be no better moment than the present for producing it again.

Kaoru, everyone agreed, had never played[‡] so well as today, and as the other guests had been chosen chiefly for their skill in accompanying instruments with the voice the concert was a very agreeable one. The refreshments were provided by the Princess. They were served on four aloes-wood trays, laid out on a high sandal-wood stand. The mats were dyed to different tints of wisteria color and embroidered with a pattern of blossom-blossom. The dishes were of silver, the cups of crystal, the bowls of lapis lazuli. Higekuro's son Hyoye no Suke was in charge of the general arrangements. The presentation of the Imperial tankard had fallen so often to Yugiri's lot that everyone felt a change was needed. Among the princes, however, there was none who seemed particularly well suited for the task. Finally Kaoru was asked if he would not undertake it, and as this choice was evidently approved of by the Emperor, he was at last prevailed upon to accept. The call for silence—a familiar sound on public occasions—fell on the ears of the feasters with an unusual impressiveness, coming as it did from one so closely concerned with the occasion of the present gathering. He carried through the Emptying of the Cup[§] and the final genuflections in a masterly manner, and these ceremonies, interesting enough when carried out by a Prince of the Blood or First Minister, were made even more impressive by the fact that they heralded

---

[*] Part V, p. 779.
[†] See Part IV, p. 704.
[‡] The flute.
[§] The emptying of what the Emperor had not drunk into an earthen receptacle.

the coming to Kaoru's house of an Imperial bride. It seemed indeed a strange contrast when, after all was over, he once more took his place among the ordinary guests.

For Kobai the occasion was a somewhat painful one; he had been very much in love with the Princess's mother and even after her installation at the Palace had remained on terms of considerable intimacy with her. It seemed to him natural that he should be entrusted with the Princess's upbringing, and he had indicated his readiness to accept this responsibility. But his claim had been ignored. "I should be the last person," he said, "to deny Kaoru's exceptional merits. But to permit a commoner access to a reigning monarch's daughter seems to me, to say the least of it, excessive. However, one could let that pass. But really, what has happened today is positively scandalous!" He had indeed been in two minds about accepting the invitation at all; but curiosity got the better of him, and inwardly raging he sat out the whole feast.

Paper lanterns were lit and a number of poems made. The faces of those who had handed in their compositions at the desk expressed complete self-satisfaction. But this, one knows from long experience, is not incompatible with the compositions in question being the dreariest possible collection of outworn tags. So I am afraid I was lazy about getting copies of them all. Judging, however, from the specimens before me, which include several by dignitaries of the most exalted class, the standard was not very high.

The following must I suppose have been made by Kaoru when he went into the courtyard to pluck a spray for the garlanding of the Imperial brow: "Too high for common reach* the world had thought it—the bough to which I stretched my hand to pluck that garland for the royal brow," he seems to have written, almost in a triumphant strain.

"Great must its claims have been beyond all human thought—the tree that license found in these high realms to grow!" This must surely be by the outraged Kobai. It may be said that I have spoiled these poems by reporting them inaccurately; which is possible, but I cannot think that they were ever very noteworthy. As night wore on the proceedings became more lively. Kaoru's rendering of the *Ana toto*† was a great success, and Kobai, whose voice still retained something of the charm that had won him such applause on that night long ago,‡ joined in with excellent effect. Yugiri's seventh son, who was still a mere child, blew the reed-organ, and his performance pleased the Emperor so much that he rewarded him with the present of a cloak.

---

* In allusion to his marriage.
† An old folk-song.
‡ See Part II, p. 218.

The Princess's removal to Kaoru's palace had all the character of a State ceremony. She was escorted by all the ladies of the Emperor's household. She herself rode in a silken palanquin with projecting roof; there were three ordinary palanquins, twenty-six rush-roofed coaches of which six were gilded, and two coaches of wattled cypress-wood. There were thirty ladies-in-waiting, each with eight little girls or maids to wait on her. In the escort sent by Kaoru there were twenty carriages full of his own people; and finally there came a vast concourse of courtiers, gentlemen and officials, making in all a procession of the utmost magnificence.

Only now that she was in his house and part of his daily life did he become conscious of how exceedingly pretty she was. Indeed nowhere in her small and elegant person could the most critical eye have detected the slightest flaw. It was evident to him that he ought to be extremely proud of her—ought indeed to be the happiest person on earth. But always the memory of Agemaki and his longing for her stood between. He would die—now he knew it for certain—still bound by the strange, compelling devotion that from its first day had brought him nothing but despair. Only if in some future life he could reach such enlightenment as would enable him to understand the cause of his own fate—only then would he at last be able to escape. And still, despite all the outward changes in his life, it was only in the work at Uji* that he found any real satisfaction. Towards the end of the fourth month, when the bustle of the Kamo Festival had subsided, he was once more able to leave the City. After visiting the workmen and giving a number of necessary directions he was on his way to exchange a word or two with Ben no Kimi, who he knew would be disappointed if she did not see him, when he saw a carriage coming from the direction of Uji bridge. It was a woman's carriage, not a very grand one, escorted by a number of rather rough-looking men with swords at their hips—apparently natives of one of the eastern provinces. They in turn were accompanied by a crowd of humbler followers, and it was evident that the traveler, though not a woman of the Capital, was someone of a certain consequence. Kaoru's own equipage had just entered the gates when the other carriage again came into view, making straight for the house. Silencing his attendants, who were making a great clatter, Kaoru sent someone to find out who the traveler was. The man who answered spoke with a strong provincial accent. It appeared that the occupant of the carriage was the daughter of his Honor the ex-Governor of Hitachi. She was on her way back from a pilgrimage to Hatsuse and was breaking the journey at Uji as she had done on her way out. This then beyond all doubt must be the step-sister of whom he had heard. And bidding his men draw to one side, he sent word begging the strangers to

---

* The transformation of Prince Hachi's apartments into a temple.

bring the carriage straight in. The presence of another guest would not incommode them, for the north wing was entirely at their disposal.

Kaoru's attendants were not in Court dress and there was nothing to show that their master was anyone out of the ordinary; yet something in their bearing at once intimidated the provincials, who began hastily to back their horses to a respectful distance. The lady's carriage drew up at the western corner of the portico. The main wing was in course of redecoration. The antechamber had no blinds and the shutters were all up and barred. There was, however, a chink in the sliding door that led into the back part of the house, and with his eye to it Kaoru obtained a perfect view of the arriving carriage. But his clothes rustled tiresomely, and throwing them off he stood watching in his undergarments. There was a pause after the carriage drew up, and a message was sent in. Apparently the lady, before entering the house, was bent on discovering who it was with whom she was expected to share it. Kaoru had, however, already given instructions that his identity was on no account to be disclosed, and his servants now begged the travelers to make themselves at home at once. "The other visitor will not be in your way," they said. "He is in quite a different part of the house." At this moment a young waiting-woman jumped out of the carriage with alacrity and began to fasten up the blinds. She at any rate showed no sign of sharing her mistress's compunctions. A second lady, rather older, now got out and called to her mistress to make haste. "I don't feel as though we were at all protected here,"* said a voice from inside the carriage—a voice that, though he could barely make out the words, struck him at once as very distinguished. "Now, Madam, are we going to start that sort of thing all over again? It does surely seem a little unnecessary. The whole of that part of the house is completely shut up. Can't you see that the windows are all bolted and barred?" said the other, in a tone of superior wisdom. At last the lady herself appeared cautiously at the doorway of the carriage, and at once—first in the poise of her head, then in the delicate proportions of her whole frame, there was something that strangely reminded him of Agemaki. Just, however, at the moment when he was craning to catch a glimpse of her face, she hastily hid it with her fan. There was rather a long step down from the carriage to the ground. It seemed to present no difficulty to the maids, but Ukifune looked down at it for some time in dismay before she at last descended and slipped into the house.

Her overmantle was dark red. Her close-fitting dress, of "carnation"† pattern; her kirtle the color of young rice. A four-foot screen had been set against the door at which he stood, but by an effort he could just see over

---

* From being peeped at.
† Pink outside, lined with blue.

it and had a perfect view of all that was going on within. Ukifune still seemed suspicious of that side of the house, and to his disappointment sat with her back to him. "She looks tired, doesn't she?" one waiting-woman said to another. "I don't wonder. It really was quite frightening today getting across that Izumi River. It was not nearly so bad in the second month; but that time the water was much lower. But my goodness, when one thinks what travelling is like in the east country, there's nothing anywhere in these parts bad enough to make a fuss about." The women chattered on evidently quite at their ease, while Ukifune lay silent and motionless. He was able to see her arms, and noted that they were molded with a delicacy that would have alone sufficed to disprove any kinship between her and a Provincial ex-Governor.

Kaoru's position was none too comfortable, but he determined to hold out a little longer. "What a lovely smell!" one of the women said. "Someone must be burning incense. I suppose it must be the old lady who lives here." "Ah, yes," said an older woman. "That's a very special blend of some kind. You may depend on it that even now Ben no Kimi isn't satisfied with anything short of the best. That's the way with these town people. Even our master, for all that he was the biggest man in the East, never set eyes on such perfumes as this. You can see the same in everything. Ben lives very quietly, no doubt, but everything she wears is of the best. All grays and browns, of course, but good stuff... At this point a little girl came in announcing that the water was hot, and presently a number of trays were brought in. The women began helping themselves, "but Ukifune did not stir. "Madam is served," they called, and brought her one dainty or another. But still she slept on, undisturbed even by the crunching of two girls who were eating some very noisy kind of nut a few inches away from her. Kaoru, utterly unused to the sight of ladies thus occupied, felt slightly embarrassed, but he was still hoping for something more, and could not bring himself to leave his post. And so this young man, used to the society of all the most beautiful and distinguished women at Court, from the Empress downwards—laughed at and even scolded by his friends for being so absurdly hard to please, stood for hours on tiptoe hoping to catch a glimpse of one who, judged by his ordinary standards, had no doubt little to boast of in person, upbringing or attainments. Ben no Kimi could not make out what had become of him and sent a note; but his men refused to deliver it, explaining tactfully that Kaoru was unwell and was trying to get a little sleep. But Ben knew how anxious Kaoru was to see Ukifune, and the present opportunity seemed too good to be wasted. It did not enter her head that he had already taken matters into his own hands. Presently the men from Kaoru's farms arrived with hampers of good things, and having arranged for the travelers to receive their share, Ben put on her best clothes and went to Ukifune's room, looking indeed if not as fashionable as the waiting-woman had declared, at any rate quite presentable. "We were expecting you yesterday morning," she said. "How is it that you did not get here till this afternoon?" "Our mistress was very tired," an old woman said, "so after crossing the Izumi we made a halt, and this morning we did not start out again till she seemed ready to face the journey." They called once more to Ukifune, who this time woke with a start. As she turned rather apologetically to greet the visitor, Kaoru was able for the first time really to study her face. The remarkably fine setting of her eyes, the way her hair parted—all sorts of details reminded him, though it was seldom that he had had the chance to study Agemaki's face so closely, of the elder sister, and suddenly the old tears flowed. So soon, however, as she began talking to Ben no Kimi her voice—though from where he was he could not hear very well—sounded more like Kozeri's. In any case she delighted him, and his only regret was that he had not taken steps to become acquainted with her long ago. Anyone, even in the very lowest rank of society, who bore so strong a resemblance to Agemaki could not have failed to interest him; and this lady, apart from all else, being (despite the old Prince's refusal to acknowledge her) a member of the Imperial family, was in reality far from ranking as his social inferior. It was indeed a marvelous find, and his impulse was to rush out that moment from his hiding-place and tell her what the discovery of her existence had meant to him. After all, the wizard in the story,* though his wanderings brought him at last to the Islands of the Blest, could bring back no more than a hairpin as token from the lady whom he sought; while Kaoru had for himself discovered one who, though indeed she was not Agemaki, would he felt certain do something to make up for Agemaki's loss. Yes, undoubtedly this meeting was providential.

After a little further talk with Ukifune, Ben withdrew. It is not improbable that the familiar perfume had revealed to her Kaoru's near presence and thus put a check upon the conversation.

It was now getting dark, and Kaoru slipped quietly from his hiding-place, put on his clothes and summoned Ben no Kimi to the hatch through which they usually conversed. "How did it happen," Kaoru asked, "that we arrived exactly at the same moment? If it was your doing you certainly arranged it marvelously." "No," said Ben. "Ever since you spoke about it, I tried hard to find an opportunity. Last year I could manage nothing; but this year in the second month I saw them when they were doing their spring pilgrimage to Hatsuse. I told the mother of your long attachment to Agemaki and consequent interest in the sister, and she was evidently quite flattered that you should notice a child of hers

---

* Told by the ninth-century Chinese poet Po Chü-i in *The Everlasting Wrong*.

in this way. But I heard that you were otherwise occupied at the time, and thought it would be better for the moment not to trouble you. This month they made the pilgrimage again, and she is stopping here on her way back to the City. She stops at Uji like this simply in order to visit her father's tomb. This time the mother was delayed at Hatsuse and the young lady has come alone. She has not of course the least idea that you are here." "Possibly not," said Kaoru. "I gave strict orders to my people not to let it be known. But some under-servant or groom is pretty certain to have given me away. In any case, the sooner she is told, the better. The fact that she should on this one occasion have come alone makes the coincidence even more extraordinary. Such a meeting cannot be a mere accident. It must have been ordained by Fate. Tell her I said so." "Won't it seem a little sudden?" asked Ben with a smile. "Well, if you wish it I'll tell her," she continued, and as she turned to go she heard him murmur to himself the poem: "Because the magic of your voice strangely recalled the past I could not rest, O far-off woodland bird, till I had found the pathway to your home." This and all that he had said to her the old woman reported to the visitor.

The Eastern House

It was, as may well be imagined, Kaoru's one desire now that he had reached the "foothills of Mount Chikuba" not to turn back till he had "forced his way through thicket after thicket to the crest."* But the circumstances of the case made secrecy well-nigh impossible, and openly to run after a girl of the class to which she appeared† to belong was, for anyone of his standing, utterly out of the question. He therefore made no attempt even to send messages or write, but contented himself with letting the mother know, through Ben no Kimi, how favorable an impression Ukifune had made upon him. These hints were repeated time after time, and he hoped that they would in the end lead to an offer on her side.‡ The mother quite failed to realize that anything more than a casual compliment was implied. But she was naturally always pleased when Ukifune's appearance attracted notice, and had it not been for the hopeless disparity in social position, she would have been glad enough that something further should follow. The Governor of Hitachi had a considerable family by his first wife, and Ukifune's mother had also borne him a number of children, including a daughter who was now almost grown up, and half a dozen youngsters who were still in the nursery. He naturally took more interest in his own children, and the mother had hard work to prevent the child§ she had brought with her from being pushed completely into the background. What made the situation particularly difficult was that the Governor's own children were all heavy and plain, whereas Ukifune was from her earliest days remarkably pretty and attractive. To see treats and fineries lavished on *them* while Ukifune was forgotten was more than the mother could bear, and she did all in her power to secure on her own account for Ukifune every advantage which the other children enjoyed.

It was known that there were several daughters in the house, and a number of fairly eligible young men frequented it. The Governor himself came of quite a good family and many of his near relations held posts of considerable importance. He had inherited a very large fortune and

---

* In allusion to a poem in the *Kokinshu*. Mount Chikuba was in Hitachi, where Ukifune had been brought up.

† Though in reality Prince Hachi's child, she had been brought up as the daughter of the Governor of Hitachi.

‡ In which case he could without impropriety have taken Ukifune as his concubine.

§ Ukifune.

made great efforts to live in a style commensurate with his position. But a complete lack of natural discrimination made him utterly incapable of reaching the standard of elegance after which he strove. Everything in his house was* in the worst possible taste, and he himself, owing to long residence in remote provinces, had not only acquired an accent of the most uncouth description, but could no longer even express himself in a correct way. He had, however, an exaggerated, almost cringing respect for those in authority, and had always performed his official duties in the most punctilious and methodical way. For such things as music, poetry and so on he had no comprehension at all. But in practical ways he was competent enough, being a remarkably good shot with his bow.

The lavish scale on which his establishment was run had, despite its disadvantages, drawn into his service quite a number of fairly presentable ladies, whom dressed in the most impossible fashion he would compel to organize poetry competitions, write novels, sit up on Monkey-nights,† and in general attempt to convince the world that the house belonged to a man of taste and culture.

Among the suitors whom the report of Ukifune's beauty had drawn to the place was a certain Sakon, an officer in the Emperor's Bodyguard, who, though he was already twenty-two, was supposed hitherto to have had no love-affair of any importance, which may have been due to the fact that though very sound in judgment and well educated, he was rather awkward and heavy in manner. On the whole Ukifune's mother was inclined to encourage him. He seemed a sensible kind of young fellow who meant what he said. His prospects were good, and though at present he had not got far, it seemed unlikely that anybody better placed would show interest in one who ranked as a Governor's daughter. She therefore saw to it that Ukifune answered his letters in an encouraging way. Whatever view the Governor might take of the matter she was perfectly confident that one glance at Ukifune herself would suffice to make any suitor set his heart on carrying the thing through. She made up her mind that the marriage should take place in the eighth month, and so as to be independent of her husband began to collect things for the girl's trousseau. Anything that had really good lacquering or inlay—in the way of furniture, musical instruments, or the like—she decried to the Governor, persuading him that something else totally valueless was infinitely superior. Nor was he likely in any case to notice the loss of a few stray articles, possessed as he was with a mania for collecting objects of every conceivable kind without any sort of understanding or discrimi-

---

* At the Capital, after his return from Hitachi.

† On the night of the fifty-seventh day in the cycle of sixty days; a Taoist practice that had crept into Buddhism. It was in connection with this observance that the familiar figures of the three monkeys—the Unseeing, the Silent and the Unhearing—were used.

nation, till the house was so full of them that there was barely room to sit down. Incidentally, another of his ambitions was that his daughters should shine as musicians. A person purporting to be a member of the Imperial College of Music came constantly to the house, and when at last the young ladies were able to stumble through their first tune, the Governor was so overcome with delight that he flung himself at the professor's feet and heaped so many gifts upon him that he was almost buried alive. When finally the girls had mastered several quite lively tunes and were able on fine evenings to give a little concert with their teacher, the Governor was so deeply stirred that he broke into tears. It was difficult for the mother who had some knowledge of music to express any great enthusiasm for these proceedings. "You'd be pleased enough if your own child showed half such talent," he said crossly.

Meanwhile Ukifune's suitor, Sakon, pressed for an earlier date. If they were to be married at all, he said, why wait for the eighth month? The mother became nervous. Sakon, she felt sure, would be certain to detect that the preparations for the marriage were being undertaken single-handed, and she felt that it was better to tell him at once that Ukifune was not the Governor's child. She sent for the friend who had acted as intermediary in the first place and begged him to explain this to Sakon. The fact that Ukifune had no father, she said, placed her entirely at her future husband's mercy, and if he for any reason failed to discharge his responsibilities, the girl would find herself in the most wretched position. She therefore begged him to think very carefully before he finally committed himself. "There has never been a hint of all this before," said Sakon, much taken aback. "Naturally it makes no difference to me whose daughter she is. But I have to think of the impression it will make if I accept an illegitimate daughter. Allow me to say I consider it most wrong of you not to have told me from the start." The friend explained that he too had been under a complete misapprehension. Never had it occurred to him that all the children were not the Governor's. Sakon then became extremely disagreeable. For him to marry into that class at all, even with a legitimate child, was a great condescension; and when it came to a girl in Ukifune's position—there could be no further question of such a thing. No one would understand his motives, and in view of the Governor's great wealth the conclusion would quite certainly be drawn that he had been bribed to take the girl off the stepfather's hands. Two of the legitimate children were already married, and he would find himself not merely patronized by their husbands but barely recognized as a member of the family by the Governor himself. It would be altogether too unpleasant. For the matchmaker, a man whose one desire was to keep on good terms with everybody, the situation was very distressing. The best he could do was to suggest that if Sakon felt like that he had better make an offer for one of the legitimate daughters. "I should be delighted to act once more on your behalf," he said. "There is a middle daughter of whom the Governor is particularly proud." After some demur Sakon accepted the suggestion, explaining his readiness to fall in with what might seem so heartless a plan by saying it was from the beginning chiefly his admiration for the sterling qualities of the Governor's character that had attracted him to the family. To be connected with such a man would in itself be an immense advantage. He had no desire, he said, to secure a great beauty. There were plenty of handsome women of the highest rank who were his for the asking. But he had seen, he said, too many cases of people who, hoping to advance themselves by a fashionable marriage, had ended in the most sordid misery. "I am not at all an ambitious man," he said. "My only desire is to lead my own life in a quiet way, and people can think or say as they please. Yes, it might be worth while your mentioning this to the Governor, and if he accepts, well—we shall see what we shall see." As a matter of fact the matchmaker's sole connection with the house was the women's quarters, his sister being in service there, and he had no acquaintance with the Governor at all. This however did not deter him from going straight to the Governor's rooms and asking for an interview. The Governor was indeed vaguely aware that someone of that name occasionally came to the house, but he sent back a curt message saying that he only saw people whom he had sent for. When however the man declared that he had come on behalf of His Honor the Captain of the Bodyguard of the Left, the Governor's manner at once changed. The visitor was admitted and after a certain amount of beating about the bush told the Governor exactly what had happened, laying particular emphasis on the fact that Sakon's motive was rather the desire to have so admirable a man as the Governor for his father-in-law than to secure a particular daughter as his bride.

The Governor was extremely gratified. "You must forgive my rudeness," he said. "I had of course no idea that you came from the Captain. I can assure you I have always made a point of treating the girl Ukifune as though she were my own. But I have a number of other children and have to do what I can for them too. This has sometimes led to misunderstandings with my wife, who imagines that I am prejudiced against her child, and now tells me very little about what is happening in that quarter. I did hear something about Sakon making an offer, but I had no idea that it was due to his admiration for my poor qualities." He went on to suggest that Sakon should take his middle daughter, concerning whose future his mind was particularly exercised. He presently recollected that in his youth he had for a time been in the service of Sakon's father and would, but for his long absence in distant parts, no doubt be now continuing his connection with the family into the second generation.

Nothing, he said, could more have delighted him than this proposal, and he saw only one difficulty—his wife might wonder what Sakon would think of her if she failed to carry out a plan that had been decided upon so many months ago. The matchmaker assured him that there need be no scruples on this head. Sakon had from the start been perfectly willing to accept any daughter the parents chose to give. He only made one stipulation, and that was that he should be on a proper footing in the family. He detested the idea of giving people an impression that he had, so to speak, crept in at the back door.

The man then went on to describe Sakon's character and prospects in the most glowing terms. His rank and salary were not of course for the moment very high. But it was an absolute certainty that next year he would be raised to the Fourth Rank, and, what was more, he had been promised the next vacancy among the Assistants of the Treasury—the Emperor himself had mentioned it. His Majesty, it appeared, had a particular regard for Sakon and was most anxious to see him happily married. "Just choose your lady and let me know," he said, "and I will undertake that within a few days you shall have a seat in the Cabinet."

"I think it would be as well if you made up your mind fairly soon," the matchmaker continued. "Naturally offers are coming to him thick and fast, and if you hesitate, you may find that the opportunity is gone. I can assure you I know what I am talking about." The story would not have deceived anyone with the slightest knowledge of Court life. But the Governor believed it all. He assured the man that it did not matter at all if Sakon's position was not at the moment a very lucrative one. "As long as I am alive I will see to it that they have enough to get on with," he said. "And afterwards there will be no trouble about anything of that kind, for all my lands and possessions are settled on the girl that I am offering him. If he makes a success of the marriage, there's nothing his wife won't be able to do for him. If for example he were standing for the post of Grand Minister, which I believe can't be got without spending a good deal, it would mean nothing to a woman as well off as she is going to be to pay all his expenses." Without even letting his sister know what was going on, much less going near Ukifune's mother, the matchmaker went straight to Sakon with what he imagined could not fail to be exceedingly welcome tidings. Sakon listened at first with an indulgent smile, merely thinking the Governor's point of view a little crude and unsophisticated. But the offer to purchase him the place of Grand Minister was really rather more than he could swallow! When he asked whether the mother had been told of this plan and expressed a fear that he might seem to have behaved rather badly towards her, the matchmaker had the effrontery to say that she would not raise the slightest objection, being quite as fond of her daughters by the Governor as of Ukifune. Indeed she had only offered

Ukifune in the first place because the girl was getting rather old* and she was anxious to settle her as soon as possible. This was at such complete variance with everything the man had said before that Sakon hardly knew what to believe. But being a very sensible young man he saw that it was well worth his while to quarrel with the mother, and even to lose the good opinion of various other people concerned, in order to secure the permanent advantages of the new arrangement. Nor did there seem to be any point in altering the date of his wedding, and he presented himself on the night that had already been fixed.

Meanwhile the mother had been busily preparing for Ukifune's wedding. Her maids all had new dresses and everything in the place had been scrubbed and furbished. Finally she washed the girl's hair, and while dressing it she could not help feeling that her child would be wasted on a man like Sakon. If only Prince Hachi had acknowledged her, even though he had died immediately, Kaoru's admiration—though of course this was aiming rather high—might really have led to something. But as it was she must keep all such thoughts to herself. In the eyes of the world at large Ukifune ranked as a mere Governor's child, and even those who knew she was illegitimate had no conception who the father really was. But what could be done? Ukifune was no longer very young; Sakon came of quite a respectable family and his prospects were fairly good, moreover he seemed very keen on the match—she believed indeed all that the matchmaker had told her, which in an inexperienced woman was hardly to be wondered at. A day or two before the appointed day, when everyone in Ukifune's rooms was in a fever of activity and the mother was completely absorbed in putting the last touches to Ukifune's headdress and attire, in walked the Governor and in the most offhand way told her of his conversation with the matchmaker and Sakon's consequent change of plan. He even went so far as to accuse her of cutting in between his own child and a desirable suitor. "You have lived long enough in the world by now," he told her, "to know that an officer of the Guard is not a man to be trifled with. Oh I beg your pardon! The young lady's father was a Prince. Fancy my forgetting that! So no one is too good for her, to be sure. But strangely enough, humble person though I am, Sakon's idea was to marry one of my girls, and despite your clever plan, that is still his intention, and I have told him he can have her." It was his way, when he was out of temper, to fling about the wildest accusations without the slightest regard for anyone's feelings. The mother was too much taken aback to make any reply. In utter despair at the heartlessness of everyone with whom she was fated to deal she left the room and hurried to Ukifune's side. If beauty alone could bring happiness, she thought, looking fondly

---

* She was about twenty.

at the girl, this child of hers would have little indeed to fear. "No one can say, I am sure, that I would not do my duty towards the husband of any child of mine," she said, discussing the matter with Ukifune's old nurse, "but for this Sakon, while I was foolish enough to think that he was going to bring happiness to my dear girl, I would have given my life. And now he turns round and says she has no father, and he means to take the other one instead—a child that is barely more than half his age. Most people would take good care not to have anything more to do with a man who could behave so disgracefully. But my husband, so far from seeing anything amiss, has no words too good for him and is ready to do whatever he suggests. In fact one's as bad as the other. But they must not expect me to countenance such proceedings; I shall go away somewhere till it is all over."

The nurse was of course no less indignant at the way in which Ukifune had been treated. "All I can say is, she's lucky to be rid of him," she said, "such a miserable lowdown wretch! We must find our young lady someone with a little decency and proper feeling about him. And what could be easier? Why, they say even His Excellency* has taken rather a fancy to her, and you couldn't want a nicer, handsomer gentleman than that. That's the sort of thing she's meant for, if you'd only give her a chance."

But the mother had heard that Kaoru was extremely hard to please. He had, she was told, for years consistently refused offers from Yugiri, Kobai, all the greatest families in the land, and now had secured the Emperor's favorite daughter. That such a person could take any serious interest in a girl like Ukifune she could not for a moment believe. Sometimes, indeed, she had thought of sending her as a lady-in-waiting to Princess Nyosan; but she was not at all sure how Ukifune would get on in surroundings so very different from those she had been used to. Then there was her half-sister, Kozeri. But here again it was the same story. For a while it had seemed as though everything were going well; but now her troubles† had begun. Was there nowhere in the world a man who for two moments knew his own mind? "Look at my own experience," she said to the nurse. "Up till the last moment Prince Hachi treated me like a queen; nothing was too good for me. And then at the end he would not even acknowledge the child! However I must say this for my husband, despite his commonness and rough ways there are some things he has spared me. He has never brought another woman to the house. Not but what I haven't had a good deal to put up with, for he has often been very inconsiderate and unkind. But I have always told him frankly what I felt, and though this has sometimes led to hot words, we have got on pretty well. The truth

---

* Kaoru.

† Niou's numerous infidelities.

of the matter is that great officers and princes are all very well for those whom they are pleased to regard as their equals; but to us plain folk they are no use at all. Yes, in this life rank is everything, it's no use pretending the contrary, and this poor girl is feeling the loss of it at every turn. How I wish I could settle her respectably..." At this moment the Governor rushed in saying that as Ukifune seemed to have more maids than she knew what to do with, would she mind lending some of them? "I see you have got new screens-of-state," he added, looking round. "As things have happened rather suddenly I am afraid we shan't have time to recover ours, so you can send round yours." "Here's a better idea still," he said suddenly. "We'll have the marriage over here. That will save no end of trouble," and he began rummaging round among Ukifune's things and dragging about the furniture. It went to the mother's heart to see him undo all the arrangements she had made with such infinite care. He bustled about setting up dozens of screens where none were wanted, pushing cupboards, shelves and chests into overcrowded corners—it was agony to witness, but she made up her mind from the start that it was useless to interfere.

"I think you might have the decency to come and help me," the Governor said. "After all, she's your child quite as much as the other one is. It's a surprise to me, I confess, to find that you take so little interest in her as this. But it can't be helped. Disown her if you like. There are other motherless children in the world..."

Meanwhile the Governor's favorite was vigorously tidied up by two nurses. She was about fifteen, a plump little thing, still quite babyish. Though happy enough himself in regard to the wedding, he was afraid people would think it strange that he should accept a suitor whose affections were supposed so recently to have been engaged in another quarter; and he went round explaining to everyone that Sakon was a man of such exceptionally high character and so certain to be one of the leading men of the future that, unusual though the circumstances might be, he was thankful to have secured him. "I was only just in time," he said, "half the Court was after him." Though for this he only had the matchmaker's authority.

Sakon on his side had nothing to complain of. The Governor continued to treat him with the highest respect, and as there seemed to be no point in choosing a fresh date, he began coming to the house on the day already fixed.

For Ukifune's mother and nurse the situation was painful and humiliating beyond endurance. To leave the house might seem undignified, but to stay and give countenance to such proceedings was impossible, and the mother made up her mind to write to Kozeri and ask if she might bring the girl for a change of air. "A person like myself can do very little for her," she said in her letter, "and lately she has been suffering very much from lack of proper support. I could think of no one better qualified..." and so on. The letter put Kozeri in an awkward position. It was not, she felt, for her to accept as a sister one whom the Prince her father had never acknowledged as his child. Yet it seemed cruel to let the girl go on living under these wretched conditions when it was in her power to prevent it. One thing was certain, to establish Ukifune in the house on exactly the same footing as herself would be disrespectful to her father's memory, and was out of the question. She decided to talk the matter over with her maid Tayu. "I am sure she would never have ventured to write," the woman said, "unless something very unpleasant were happening. You must not be hard on them. It is not at all unusual for girls born under such circumstances to he received by their betters. I shouldn't, if I were you, refuse before thinking the matter over very carefully." Finally she prevailed upon Kozeri to let her answer the letter. "We can give you very quiet rooms in the western wing," she wrote. "I am afraid they are rather small and inconvenient, but I dare say you would get on all right there for a little while." The mother was delighted and in great secrecy set out at once. Ukifune had heard a great deal about Kozeri and was longing to see her. She was indeed far more interested in the prospect of making her sister's acquaintance than she had been in that of getting married, and was not in the least sorry that things had turned out as they had. They brought with them only the nurse and two or three young maids. Their rooms were at the back of the western side-wing, in a very secluded part of the house.

Though the circumstances of their upbringing had been so different, they were after all very closely related, and from the moment that the mother* appeared Kozeri felt thoroughly at home with her. She had the baby in her arms when the visitors were admitted; and seeing her there surrounded by every comfort and attention, Ukifune's mother, while delighted by Kozeri's manners and appearance, could not help feeling a certain bitterness. It was not as though Kozeri's mother, whom Prince Hachi had treated so very differently, belonged to a different level of society. On the contrary, they came of the same family. It was harsh indeed that she herself should have always been regarded as a mere servingwoman and her child relegated to a class which was universally despised, while her cousin's children lolled in palaces, leaving to her the embarrassing task of claiming a relationship. It had been put about that Ukifune's move was due to a ritual defilement, and they received no visitors. The mother herself stayed only two or three days, but by the time she left she felt quite familiar with the ways of the Palace. She was of course longing to see Niou. Before long it was announced that he had just arrived, and

---

* She was a niece of Kozeri's mother.

peeping between the screens she was able to get a very good view of him. He was wearing a wreath of cherry-blossom and round him knelt several officers of the Fourth and Fifth Ranks, reporting the progress of various negotiations and commissions which had been entrusted to their charge. They were merely his ordinary household retainers; yet how insignificant her own husband, whom despite all their differences she was still in the habit of regarding as a person of considerable authority and importance, would look beside the least of these gentlemen! A number of young courtiers were also there, most of whom she did not know. Presently however the husband of one of her stepdaughters arrived with a message from the Palace. She noticed that though he held, as she knew, a post in the Treasury as well as the rank of clerk to the Board of Rites, he did not venture to do more than hover in the distance. She had often felt indignant at the latitude that was allowed to Niou and his sort. Why should a mere accident of birth entitle them to behave in a way that in ordinary people would be considered heartlessly cruel? But now, dazzled by Niou's beauty and by the magnificence of the whole setting in which the lives of such people moved, she no longer felt that the women who were taken up and cast aside had anything to complain of. A moment's contact with such splendors as these was worth a lifetime of commonplace affection.

Niou now took the baby in his arms and for a while sat playing with it. Kozeri was behind a low screen, which he presently pushed aside; and sitting there together, talking and playing with the child, they did indeed make a remarkable pair. Ukifune's mother could not help contrasting the life here with that which she had known in the old days at Prince Hachi's moldering palace. And yet he too, strange to remember, was an Emperor's son! Presently the child was handed to its nurses, and Kozeri vanished into an inner room. Visitor after visitor still arrived; but they were told that Niou was resting. He reappeared in the evening and supped with Kozeri in her rooms. How squalid, compared with the stately and ordered life of this palace, they seemed to her now despite their continual striving towards elegance and harmony—the houses of petty officers and officials!

The one thing that now seemed worth doing was to secure for Ukifune a place, of whatever kind, in some such establishment as this. After all, there was no reason why she should not be at least as ambitious on her behalf as her husband was on behalf of his girls. He, no doubt, had wealth on his side; but in looks it was Ukifune who had the advantage.

Next day Niou rose late, and saying that he must go to the Palace and enquire after the Empress, who had not been well, he went off to be robed in his State dress. Ukifune's mother was able to catch a glimpse of him as he returned from the robing-room, and a magnificent sight he was; and not merely magnificent but a gracious and lovable figure as coming back to Kozeri's room he played with the infant, off whom it seemed he could hardly bear to take his eyes. After breakfast he went out into the hall and a number of gentlemen who had been waiting in the antechambers came forward to salute him. Among them was one with a hard, unpleasing expression of face, but an air of being thoroughly well satisfied with his own appearance. He wore a loose cloak and a big sword at his belt. She did not know his face, but the part that he played was evidently not one of importance. "That's the one who has married the Governor of Hitachi's daughter," a waiting-woman whispered. "He was to have had this girl who has come here, but he thought himself too good for anyone that wasn't the Governor's own daughter, and took a little fat baby of a thing instead. Needless to say that's not the story that they tell here, but I heard it through one of the Governor's people."

The women did not of course know that the girl's mother was within earshot, but it was in any case far from agreeable to hear such talk going on. Of one thing the mother was now convinced: Sakon was far indeed from occupying at Court the position that the matchmaker had attributed to him. It was obvious from the way he was treated and spoken of that he was a mere nonentity, and certainly Ukifune was well rid of him. Niou now saw that the baby had crawled out of Kozeri's room and was peeping at him round a curtain. He turned back to wave to it, and called to Kozeri that if the Empress was better he would come straight back, but that if she was really bad he would have to spend the night at the Palace. "It's terrible nowadays how I miss you both if I have to be away even for a single night," he said, and having fondled the child once more he left the house, upon which a sudden desolation seemed to fall at the withdrawal of so lovely and radiant a presence.

She could not forbear from going straight to Kozeri and telling her—in terms the artlessness of which made Kozeri smile— just how Niou had struck her. They talked of Kozeri's childhood and the lonely life at Uji, of Agemaki's death... "For me too life has not always been very easy," said Kozeri; "but things are better now. The loss of my parents was of course a terrible blow—of my father, I should say, for my mother I never knew. But it was Agemaki's death that was the real calamity, not for me only but also for Kaoru, who I am afraid will never get over it. It is terrible to see anyone in such a condition, and it still goes on; it seems as though he would never be able to take an interest in anyone else." "Surely," the mother said, "he must be gratified by the confidence that His Majesty the Emperor has shown in him. They say such a thing has never happened before. And in a way it is a comfort that Agemaki is not here; for he would have been bound to accept this marriage..." "In which case,"

Kozeri interposed, "her position would have been no worse than mine.* No, Kaoru is different in this way from anyone I have ever known. Think how long it is since my father died, and yet he is always doing one thing and another about masses for his salvation, about the upkeep of the graves and so on." "Ben no Kimi has told me," the mother ventured, "that he takes an interest in my poor girl and was even anxious to meet her—though that is a thing I should never dare to suggest—because of her connection with Agemaki. I don't know how much truth there is in it, but you may be sure I was deeply touched." Bit by bit she began to tell Kozeri about Ukifune's troubles, though when it came to the episode of Sakon's callous behavior she kept a good deal back, for she did not know who might be listening. "As far as I am concerned," she went on, "I ask for nothing better than to have her at my side. But I must think of the future; I am getting on in years, and I tremble to think what will become of her when I am gone. Sometimes I think it would be better to give up all idea of marriage or anything of that kind, and settle her as a nun in some convent far away from everywhere. But that is only in my darkest moods." "I am terribly sorry about it all," Kozeri said. "I know only too well from my own experience that girls without a father or brothers to protect them cannot expect to be treated with much consideration. But that hardly seems a reason for giving up the world altogether, unless one feels a very strong call towards the life of the cloister. And even then—it is a grave step to take. My own inclinations have always been entirely in that direction, yet here I am! No, I cannot bear to think of your making a nun of her."

The mother was delighted by Kozeri's interest and sympathy; and Kozeri thought her an agreeable woman, quite good-looking considering her age and betraying the humble surroundings in which her life had been spent in nothing but a certain rotundity of figure. "After the way her father disowned her and everyone in consequence has treated her as though she were no one at all, I cannot tell you," the mother continued, "what a comfort it is to my poor girl that you should receive us and let us tell you about all we have been through." She went back over her life, telling Kozeri about her husband's first Governorship in Michinoku, and giving her an account of many strange things she had seen in that remote province. Then there was Mount Chikuba. How terribly lonely she had been in Hitachi! There was not a soul to whom she could really open her mind.

"I could go on telling you about it forever," she said. "But my children at home must be wondering what has become of me. I expect there is a fine rumpus going on by now. I wish I felt less worried about this girl

---

* Niou had been forced to take Roku no Kimi as his consort.

I am leaving here. I know only too well what a handicap it is to belong to the class that her father's attitude towards her has forced her into. However, as long as she is with you, I shan't worry..."

The mother was trying, Kozeri could see, to make her feel that it was her duty to make up for the harm that Prince Hachi had done. In any case, she was determined to do everything for Ukifune that she could. The girl was certainly both agreeable and good-looking. She did not seem to be inordinately shy, and though she was rather backward for her age, she was evidently far from stupid, and when she was with Kozeri's ladies no one would have picked her out as a girl who had not had the same advantages. It was extraordinary how much her way of speaking and so on reminded one of Agemaki. Kozeri remembered her conversation with Kaoru about Ukifune. It would certainly be worthwhile bringing them together. The matter crossed her mind more than once. But she did nothing in particular about it. Quite by chance however, while Kozeri and the mother were sitting together, Kaoru was suddenly announced. Kozeri quickly adjusted the curtains and began putting herself to rights. "Now at last I shall see him!" the mother said. "Everyone tells me he is wonderful, but I shall be very much surprised if he is anything compared with Niou." "It's really not so easy to decide," one of the gentlewomen declared. "When they are together I sometimes think that Niou comes out of it none too well. But when they are apart one does not think there is much to choose between them. However, it is obvious that they are both really very good-looking, and there is not much sense in these comparisons." "All the same," another woman said smiling, "there's small doubt on which side Madam's private prejudice lies. And it would be a marvel indeed if anyone could be found to match our dear Prince!"[*] The word was passed round that Kaoru was just getting down from his coach. Ukifune's mother heard a great clattering and shouting, but for what seemed a very long while no one appeared. At last a young man walked quietly into the room. It would never have occurred to the mother to call him strikingly handsome; but charm he certainly had, coupled with a look of extreme refinement and distinction. Instinctively, though she knew she was hidden from him, she put up a hand to tidy her hair. The scrupulous formality of his dress and the great size of the escort whose clamor she could hear outside gave her a somewhat misleading notion of his habits and personality. So soon, however, as he spoke she realized that all this was due to his having come straight on from an official Visit of Enquiry at the Palace. "As none of the Royal Princes could be found I was obliged to take duty at the Palace last night," he explained. "It was rather unfortunate that Niou did not put in an appearance, for Her

---

[*] Niou.

Majesty is far from well. However, I think I made things all right for him. Even this morning he arrived inordinately late—for which I suppose we must hold you responsible." "It was exceedingly kind of you to take his place," said Kozeri, ignoring the accusation. She knew well enough that Kaoru had chosen today for his visit because he counted on Niou having to stay late at the Palace. However, he seemed to be in a good mood, and said nothing that one could possibly object to, though even today there was perceptible in all his conversation a vague background of the usual tragic description. It was difficult to believe that, as he constantly asserted, time had done nothing to reconcile him to his loss. Human beings, Kozeri felt, are not so constituted, and she sometimes felt that his melancholy was becoming a mere matter of habit—was due simply to an inability ever to relinquish, in her presence, the attitude that he had taken up at the start. But soon some look or word would come that would have convinced a heart far harder than hers of his absolute sincerity. What distressed her most were the hints—bound sooner or later to come into every conversation—that, great though his sufferings were, it lay in her power to relieve them; and now, hoping no doubt to distract him from this unwelcome vein, she reminded him of his vow to set up a statue of Agemaki at Uji* and of her suggestion that a "living image"† might well take its place.

"The girl of whom I spoke," Kozeri said, "is here on a secret visit." The news interested him a good deal more than he cared to show. "Come," he said, "unless you can assure me that this new deity of yours can be relied on to vouchsafe my prayers, I had better keep away. Mere pilgrimages to the shrine will serve only to disturb my meditations." "Your notions about religion seem after all to be very hazy," Ukifune's mother heard Kozeri laughingly reply. "That's as may be," he said. "But please tell the mother quite definitely that I am counting on a meeting... By the way, there is something terribly familiar about this situation."‡ And with tears in his eyes, yet half in jest, he recited a poem in which he wondered whether, just as the touch of the *nademono*§ cleanses the worshipper of his sin, so the mere presence of Ukifune at his side might not relieve him of his pain. But in her answer Kozeri reminded him that, after its use, the *nademono* is thrown into the stream—"when hands enough have soiled it." "You will I am sure forgive my pointing out that the allusion was not very happily chosen." "What can I," he answered, "who am myself but foam on that same stream—what can I offer but a moment's dalliance?

---

* See Part V, p. 947.

† I.e. Ukifune.

‡ Kozeri is trying to pass him on to Ukifune, just as Agemaki had tried to pass him on to Kozeri. See Part V, p. 865.

§ Images against which the Shinto worshipper rubs himself in order to transfer his sins to them.

The bourne* of my hopes—none knows better than yourself—was fixed long ago. Indeed if there is any *nademono* in the case, it is surely I, and she the stream into which I am cast aside."

"You are staying very late," she complained. "I must remind you that there are strangers in the house. I think tonight you must really try to get away in decent time." "If you mean the people we have been talking about," he said, "I can't think that it much matters... However, be sure to tell them about all this, and make it quite clear that it is not a sudden whim. Obviously it isn't; you know that I have been longing to meet her for years. Anyway, try to put it so that the whole thing does not seem too odd. I am sorry to give you the trouble; but you know what a hash I should make of it...

Peeping after him as he left the house, Ukifune's mother could not help wondering whether she would not after all do better to accept the nurse's advice. If there was a chance of the girl standing in any kind of relationship whatever to such a man as this, was it not a pity to waste her on some ordinary, humdrum official—someone like Sakon, who she now realized would never have imposed on her had she not become inured to the society of mere louts and savages during her long exile in Hitachi and Michinoku?

There clung to the pillar against which Kaoru had been leaning and to the cushion upon which he had sat so strange and indescribable a perfume that even the gentlewomen of the house could not help remarking upon it. "No wonder," someone said, "that in the Scriptures one reads so much about perfumes. It seems indeed that among the marvels of Paradise its smells are praised beyond all the rest. Certainly our Lord Buddha looked upon a sweet fragrance as the highest gift he could bestow. Don't you remember his promise in the *Yaku-o Bon*?† I don't know about sandalwood of the Bull's Head Mountain, whatever that may be, but certain it is that when Lord Kaoru is at hand one knows that the Buddha did not make such promises in vain. He may well have studied this chapter, for from his childhood he has been deeply pious." "It's more likely to be due to something that happened to him in a previous existence," another gentlewoman said. All this was overheard by the mother, who smiled to herself while she listened.

"Well, that is his message," Kozeri said to her later. "You must think it over. Of this much I can assure you, he always means what he says. Indeed, once he has got an idea into his head, he clings to it with extraor-

---

* The whole passage is a network of poetical allusions which it would be tedious to explain.

† The twenty-third chapter of the Saddharmapundarika: "From the mouth of any that accepts, rejoices in, and praises this chapter shall issue the smell of blue lotus flowers, and from every pore of his skin the perfume of Sandalwood of the Bull's Head Mountain."

dinary tenacity. I admit that he has responsibilities* which must from your point of view seem a great disadvantage. But as you have even gone so far as to talk of putting her in a convent, it would surely be worth while at any rate to give this a trial first." "I am sure I have no desire to make a nun of her," the mother replied. "But this I do say: even the 'wilderness where no bird sings' is heaven for such a girl, compared with a house where she had to put up with insults and humiliations at every turn. True enough, when one sees Kaoru one feels that any post would be worth taking—I'd be glad enough myself to clean the pots or scrub the floor—for the mere pleasure of being near such a gentleman; and a young girl must feel that way even more than I. But one asks oneself, is it wise to plant the seeds of love where they'll get so little chance to grow? It seems to me like going out of one's way to look for trouble. However, perhaps her worst misfortune, poor soul, is to have been born a woman at all; for we none of us, high or low, seem to be given much of a chance either in this world or the next!† I can only ask you to do what you think best and afterwards, however things may turn out, stand by her and help her in every way you can."

It was a terrible responsibility. "I can only say that I have never known him to behave heartlessly," Kozeri said. "As to what may happen in the future..." and she broke off with a sigh. A long silence followed.

Soon after daybreak a carriage arrived, and one of the Governor of Hitachi's servants brought in a very cross letter demanding the mother's instant return.

"Well, I leave everything in your hands," she said to Kozeri. "I can't tell you how grateful I am. Keep her here a little longer while I am turning things over in my mind. I dare say the cloister will turn out to be the best we can do in the end. But meanwhile treat her, as far as you can, as though she were one of yourselves and help her to do whatever you think best." There were tears in her eyes, and naturally Ukifune was upset by the parting. But she would have been sorry indeed to be torn away just yet from surroundings so uncommonly gay and agreeable.

The carriage was just being drawn‡ to the gates and it was beginning to get light when Niou arrived from the Palace. He had suddenly become anxious about the baby, which had not been very well. He left the Palace secretly in a modest vehicle borrowed from one of his men and now, finding a strange carriage blocking his way, he called to his driver to stop, and entered by a side-door. "Whose carriage is that?" he asked. "It seems rather an odd hour for anyone to be here." He assumed

---

* His wife, the Second Princess.

† Women were not admitted to Amida's Paradise.

‡ By hand. The oxen were left outside.

at once that someone was trying to escape, before the house was astir, from a clandestine love-meeting. Were his worst suspicions going to be confirmed? "I have made enquiries," a retainer announced, "and am told it belongs to His Excellency the Lord Governor of Hitachi." "A fine sort of Excellency!" one of the young outriders commented in an aside which was audible to the occupant of the carriage and brought home to her only too vividly the contempt that even people of this sort felt for officials of her husband's class. Not that she minded for herself. But it was heartrending indeed that owing to a father's neglect Ukifune must take her share of the contempt that attached to a class to which she did not in reality belong.

"Someone calling himself 'the Governor of Hitachi' seems to be in the habit of coming here to see you and hurrying away before daylight, accompanied by a whole band of grooms and attendants." Kozeri was with her women when Niou burst in with this announcement, and she thought that, whatever his suspicions were, he might have had the decency to keep them to himself till they were alone together. "There is no reason to excite yourself," she said. "Tayu or one of my women has known the Governor's wife since they were children. I am surprised you should be so interested in their affairs. But you seem to go out of your way to make remarks that, whatever you may mean by them yourself, are bound to give people a most unfortunate impression. I see that if there is to be anything left of my reputation..." and she turned her back upon him. He was in no hurry to make it up, for he found her outbreaks very attractive.

He did not leave her apartments till very late in the morning. On appearing at last in the outer rooms he found a great concourse of visitors waiting. To his relief he heard that things at the Palace were going better. It did not seem as though the Empress's illness was anything very serious, and she was already on the mend. He spent the rest of the morning playing draughts and rhyme-covering* with Yugiri's sons. Late in the afternoon he went back to Kozeri's rooms. He found, however, that she was washing her hair. Her women were all resting in their rooms and he could find no one to talk to. Presently a small girl came along. "Can you take a message?" he said. "Say I cannot imagine why Madam must needs choose this moment to embark upon her toilet. It's not very amusing for me to hang about here all alone." "We always try to get that kind of thing done when you are not here," said Tayu, in the message she sent in reply. "But Madam has been wanting to have it washed for days, and this month there is not a single other possible† day. That means waiting another two months...‡

---

* A game in which the rhyme-words of a Chinese poem were covered and had to be guessed.
† Lucky.
‡ The ninth month was taboo for Buddhist, the tenth month for Shinto reasons.

The baby was asleep and his nurses could not leave him. Niou wandered listlessly from room to room. On reaching the western wing he met a young waiting-girl whose face he did not know. She must, he supposed, belong to some gentlewoman who had recently entered Kozeri's service, and he peeped in.* One sliding-panel in the middle of the partition near which he stood was not quite closed and a foot or so behind it he could see a large folding-screen, apparently put there to protect a curtained couch that stood close up against the window. Beyond the couch-curtains protruded on one side what could only be part of a woman's sleeve—a glimpse of gay aster-pattern, faced with *ominabeshi* brocade. Had not some careless person forgotten to unfold one panel of the screen even this much would not have been visible. "This must be looked into," he said to himself and tiptoeing to the door of the room he gently pushed it open. The flower-tubs in the courtyard on this side of the house were ablaze with every imaginable color, and the moat at this point ran between very high stone walls, so that Ukifune loved to have her couch as near as possible to the windows, and she was now gazing in front of her, entranced by the beauty of her new home. Niou opened the door a little wider and peeped round the corner of the big folding-screen. This time she became aware that someone had entered the room. She naturally supposed, however, that it was one of her own people, who were always going in and out, and she did not look round. Her pose as she lay there, half-raising herself on one hand to get a better view of the garden, delighted him, and it seemed to him the most natural thing in the world at once to seek her acquaintance. Closing the sliding-panel that he had found ajar and seating himself between it and the big screen, he plucked at the skirt of her dress. She started and looked swiftly over her shoulder, at the same time covering her face with her fan. He was struck by the graceful movement of her shoulders and head, and seizing the hand that held the fan, "Who are you?" he said. "Don't be frightened. I only want to know your name." A wild suspicion rushed to her head that this must be Kaoru of whose strange interest in her she had been told—Niou was sitting with his face hid—and the strong perfume that had filled the room since this intrusion made her almost certain that it must be he. This idea, however, did not diminish her feeling of utter helplessness and bewilderment. But a partial deliverance was close at hand. The old nurse, passing that way, had heard a strange voice in the room and now came bustling in to discover what was going on. Her arrival, whatever else it may have averted, did nothing to check the flow of Niou's conversation, and he continued in the most easy and natural way to talk to her about this and that, for all the world as if he had known her for years. The old woman, apart from

---

* At the door which shut off the western wing.

an occasional "What next, I wonder?" and "Well, I am surprised," made no attempt to interfere.

It was now getting late. "You have only to tell me your name," Niou said, "and I will let you go." By this time he was lying stretched full length beside her, to the consternation of the old nurse, who had of course long ago recognized who it was.

The great lamp, though not yet lighted, had already been put on its stand. "He'll have to be going along there in a minute,"* everyone said. The Palace was being shut up for the night. Everywhere except in Kozeri's apartments the shutters were being fastened. The noise came nearer and nearer; finally Ukon, the daughter of Kozeri's maid Tayu, ran bustling in to deal with the shutters on the western side. At last even Niou became somewhat uneasy, and the nurse entirely lost her head. "Mind where you step!" she blurted out. "Things aren't what they might be in here. That's to say—I know as well as anybody that it ought never to have happened. But I ask you, what was I to do?" For the moment Ukon was completely mystified; but presently, groping her way through the darkness, she became aware that stretched at Ukifune's side was the coatless figure of a young man. It was not difficult to guess who the visitor was, and at the same time highly improbable that he was there by invitation. "No, I don't like this at all," she said, shaking her head. "But the less I say about it now, the better. I am going back to Madam, and of course I shall have to tell her about it." She marched off with her head in the air. Her threat produced a look of consternation on the face of the old nurse and some other servants who heard it, but had no such effect on Niou. Who, he kept on asking himself, could this beautiful and distinguished creature be? From Ukon's way of speaking of her he felt more than ever convinced that she was not simply a new lady-in-waiting. Unperturbed he continued to question and coax her. She simply sat and listened, without any sign of hostility or even impatience. But he could see nevertheless that his presence was still causing her a veritable agony of embarrassment, and he was very gentle with her, doing everything he could think of to put her at her ease.

Ukon went to Kozeri and reported what she had witnessed. "I dread to think what the poor soul must be going through," she said indignantly. "It's the tiresome sort of thing he's always doing," said Kozeri. "I am afraid the mother will be very much upset if she hears of it. She begged me again and again to look after her, and said this was the only place she would have felt it safe to leave her." It would after all have been very unlike him, Kozeri reflected, not to have discovered the arrival of a young good-looking girl. But all the same, in this particular case she

---

* I.e. Niou will be having to go to Kozeri's rooms.

really thought that every precaution had been taken. It was certainly very tiresome that such a thing should have happened. She motioned to Ukon to withdraw, and the girl was reduced to discussing the matter in an indignant whisper with her colleague Shosho! "Generally," she said, "on days when a lot of gentlemen call he stays amusing himself with them till late in the afternoon. That's why everyone today was resting when it happened. Not that we could have done anything to prevent it. But that nurse is a silly old fool. She ought to have sat right down at my lady's side, ready to pull my lord away the moment anything happened." At this moment a messenger came from the Palace saying that since this evening Her Majesty had been very unwell and was now in an extremely grave condition. "Very inconsiderate of her, I'm sure he'll think, to have chosen this moment to get worse," Ukon said sarcastically. "I shall go and tell him at once." "I shouldn't, if I were you," whispered Shosho. "The harm must be done by now. You'd do far better not to pester him." "It wasn't my impression that things were going so fast as that," said Ukon, and returning to Ukifune's room she reported to Niou what the messenger had said, adding several alarming touches of her own. Kozeri overheard some of this whispering. Niou's habits were really very inconvenient, she thought. Soon no self-respecting parent would allow a good-looking girl into his house at all.

Niou seemed rather skeptical about the message from the Palace and showed no signs of moving. "Who brought the message?" he asked. "They're always trying to frighten me with stories like this, and when I arrive I find there is nothing wrong." "It was one of the Empress's own officers," said Ukon. "Taira no Shigetsune I think they said his name was." He did not, however, seem at all inclined to move, and shocked by his indifference to the opinion of the Court, Ukon was about to have the Imperial messenger himself sent round to the western wing when the servant who had brought the first message into the house reappeared saying that Niou's brother, Prince Nakatsukasa, had already hurried to the Palace and the Intendant of Her Majesty's Household was on his way there. "They met his carriage in the road," the man said. It sounded as though this were indeed one of the sudden attacks from which the Empress suffered from time to time. Niou supposed he had better go: he would certainly get into great trouble if he did not, and after many final protestations and caresses, he at last left the house. Ukifune found her nurse standing over her fanning her vigorously. It was as though she had suddenly woken from some terrifying dream, and she was drenched with sweat. Poor thing," the nurse was saying, "this is a terrible place to have brought you to, and no mistake! If it's like this at the start I tremble to think what will be happening before long. Prince he may be and I don't know what else besides, but it's not in this part of the house that he belongs,* and if you're to be friends with a gentleman, good or bad, he'd better at least be someone outside the family. I thought for a moment he was going to do something really bad and I gave him such a look! Would you believe it, when he saw I was making a face at him, he gave me a great pinch in the arm. I suppose he thought I was just a common waiting-woman. Common indeed! I don't mind telling you the way he carried on seemed to me for all the world like any ordinary fellow making up to a girl. *I* couldn't see the difference, anyway!"

"By the way," she added, hoping to distract Ukifune's thoughts from what had occurred, "when I was round at your father's today there were words again between him and your mother—the same old story, he said your mother cared only about you and did not do her duty by the other children. The new son-in-law thought it very strange, he said, that your mother must needs go away on a visit the moment he set foot in the house. And didn't they half go for one another, with all the under-servants listening too! I can tell you, for my part I hate that young Sakon. You were getting on all right till he came along. True, your father and mother had a bit of a row about you now and then, which wasn't any too pleasant. But if only things had been left as they were, you wouldn't have had much to complain of." But Ukifune for the moment was not greatly concerned with what was going on at home, nor with what might or should have been done for her. She could think of nothing but the odious experience through which she had just passed, bad enough in itself but likely to be even more unpleasant in its consequences if the thing should come to Kozeri's ears. She lay weeping, her face buried in the cushions. "Never mind then," said the nurse. "You mustn't take on like that. Things might be worse. You're not an orphan altogether, and though it's terrible, I'm sure, to have no father, that's not half so bad as if your father were there and had given you over to a wicked stepmother. We'll put things right for you in the end, so don't fret yourself so. Look how often you've done the pilgrimage to Hatsuse! It's a very long way for anyone not used to travelling, and I'm sure that if I pray to Kwannon, she will soon bring you into your own again and make all these wicked people sorry they ever dared take advantage of you. Yes, you shall have the laugh of them one day, I'll warrant."

Presently Ukifune, from where she lay, heard Niou's voice. He was leaving by the western gate, no doubt because he was in a hurry and it was the nearest to the Palace. He was reciting, with great taste and feeling she was bound to admit, some lines from a beautiful old poem, but she was far from being in the mood to appreciate his performance. Relay horses awaited him, and he galloped away with only ten courtiers in attendance.

---

* He has no business except in Kozeri's apartments.

Kozeri could well imagine what her sister's feelings must be, and without any reference to what had occurred sent a message begging Ukifune to come round to her rooms: "Niou's mother," she said, "is unwell and he has been obliged to go to the Palace. I am feeling tired after having my hair washed, and am lying down. So do come if you have nothing better to do." "My mistress says that you must excuse her for the moment as she is feeling very much upset, but she will look in later," the nurse replied. "Upset?" said Kozeri. "I am very sorry to hear it. Ask her what she is upset about." "Nothing in particular," the reply came again, "just out of sorts and depressed." "I wonder whether something really did happen," whispered Shasho, nudging Ukon. "Madam will be in a terrible taking if she thinks it did." Kozeri was indeed very worried. Here was Kaoru just beginning to take an interest in the girl, and at once this unfortunate incident had happened which, if he heard of it, would certainly prejudice him against her and perhaps put him off entirely. He took things so seriously—quite unlike Niou, who though he was ready to twist the most harmless incidents into evidences of double-dealing and intrigue, when it came to any real and serious infidelity would probably be very indulgent. What had happened, however, was just the sort of thing that Kaoru would take very much to heart, and it looked as though, as far as he was concerned, Ukifune's chances were ruined forever.

Kozeri was rapidly becoming very much attached to this sister, of whose very existence she had known nothing for so many years. She herself had been through trying experiences, but she had at any rate never been turned adrift like this unhappy girl. "Indeed," Kozeri thought to herself, "if only Kaoru would stop behaving so tiresomely towards me, I should not nowadays have much left to complain of."

She had a great deal of hair and was tired of sitting up so long waiting for it to dry. She was wearing a single white wrap, in which she looked very fragile and pretty. It was quite true that Ukifune was feeling definitely ill; but the nurse urged her to pull herself together. "Go and see her for a little while," she said, "and try to behave as usual, or she will think something bad really happened. I will go first and explain to Ukon or one of them, and then come back for you." "She's had a shock, the poor thing," the nurse said to Ukon, "that's all it is. But I think she is a little feverish, and she certainly feels very poorly. However, I hope if I bring her round here you and Madam may be able to cheer her up a bit. You may say there is no need for her to take on so when nothing happened and she hasn't really anything to worry about. But you mustn't forget that she is an innocent thing and doesn't even know, as anyone else would, that no harm was done. I think myself that it's small wonder she's feeling upset. Yes, I'm very sorry for her indeed." Ukifune was still in tears. But the nurse managed at last to drag her to her feet and bring her round to Kozeri's rooms. She was still, after what had happened, in a state of absolute terror at the prospect of facing the rest of the world. Her nurse and other servants were indeed obliged almost to carry her; but being of a singularly gentle disposition, much though she longed to be left in peace, she offered no resistance. Conscious that her hair was still moist with perspiration, she seated herself with her back to the lamp. Much as they had always admired their mistress, Kozeri's maids Ukon and Shosho were obliged to confess that this newcomer was more than able to stand comparison with her, and they feared that if Niou, whom they had more than once known to lose his head over far less interesting rivals, really took a fancy to her, the result might be very serious. Kozeri, apart from these two maids, had no one with her, and before long the visitor began to feel a little bit more at ease. "I should hate it," Kozeri said, "if you thought of my rooms as the sort of place that it was alarming to be brought to. I have been very lonely ever since my father and then, so soon afterwards, poor Agemaki died, and I cannot tell you what a comfort it is to me to have someone here who so much reminds me of her. Perhaps as time goes on you will begin to feel towards me rather in the way that she did. How happy that would make me!" The invitation, though obviously sincere, made Ukifune feel shyer than ever. She sought for some polite phrase with which to acknowledge it, but could find none. "It's very nice really to meet you," she said, rather with the manner of a small child speaking to a grown-up person, "after hearing so much about you for years past." Presently Kozeri sent for some picture-rolls, which they looked at together, while Ukon read out the texts. Before long Ukifune had quite got over her shyness, and looking at her as she sat there in the lamplight, her head bent over the picture that was being unrolled, Kozeri was astonished by her beauty. Certainly there was something in the shape of her brow, in the setting of her eyes—a fineness and distinction such as she had seen in no other face than Agemaki's. And Kozeri found herself no longer looking at the pictures, but gazing all the while at her sister's face, and wondering how the likeness came to be so complete. Had Agemaki taken much after her mother, such a resemblance would of course be impossible. But servants who had been in the family a long time often said that while Kozeri certainly took after her mother, in Agemaki one could see no resemblance at all. And indeed Agemaki's likeness to her father was all the easier to trace because, despite his extremely dignified and aristocratic bearing, there was about him a strange sort of gentleness and softness—carried indeed to a point most unusual in a man.* Of course Ukifune was still very inexperienced

---

* This sentence has been understood in various ways. I follow the interpretation which seems to make the best sense, though it is doubtful whether the text as it stands can yield this meaning.

and shy, and this made her at present appear rather dull and ordinary compared to Agemaki. But there seemed to be no reason why, given a little time to get used to Court life, the girl should not suit a man like Kaoru very well. They talked for a little while longer and then, as dawn was already appearing, went to bed, Kozeri making Ukifune lie beside her on her own couch and, before they went to sleep, telling her a little about the old Prince and their home at Uji while he was still alive. The girl was naturally intensely curious about this father whom she had never known, and listened eagerly to all that Kozeri could tell.

"I wonder what will happen to that young lady," Shosho whispered to Ukon. "Madam seems to have taken quite a fancy to her for the moment; but if my lord does not manage to keep his hands off her, she won't be a favorite here for long. I must say, I'm sorry for her." "Well, I don't believe things have gone very far yet," said Ukon. "You heard the nurse talking about his pinching her when she made a face at him and all that... It didn't sound to me at all as though anything much were happening. And I'll tell you another thing—all the verses I heard him humming as he went out were about 'meetings that are no meetings.' Of course, that may only have been to put us off the scent. But I had a good look at her myself just now when she was sitting full in the lamplight, and something in her face seemed to tell me that he hadn't done anything to her at all."

The first thing the nurse did next day was to borrow a carriage and go round to the Governor's house. The mother heard her story with the greatest consternation. From every point of view the episode was disastrous; but, above all, in the effect it must evidently have on the girl's relations with Kozeri. "When it comes to that sort of thing[*] there isn't much difference between a great lady and her scullery-maid," she said. "At any rate I know well enough what I should feel myself." And in a panic she rushed off to the Nijo-in. Fortunately Niou was still at the Palace and she was able to see Kozeri by herself. "Of course I am quite happy about the girl," she said. "I know she could not be in better hands. But she is still such a child... I try to do my best by them all, but those wretched children at home are always complaining of me, and now, as you see, I've come scuttling round here. First this way, then that, for all the world like a squirrel!" "Really, she isn't so childish as that," Kozeri protested laughing. "There is no need, I am sure, for you to go running after her with your hand screening your eyes."[†] The mother, however, thought that she detected a look of embarrassment in Kozeri's face and suspected that though outwardly adopting so friendly a tone she no doubt felt very differently. It was, after all, impossible to know what was going on in Kozeri's mind, and

---

[*] Jealousy.
[†] As squirrels are supposed to do.

the mother decided to make no definite allusion to what had happened. "It's been my dream for years," she said, "to put her in your care, and it's a great advantage for her, I'm sure, not only in itself, but because it will be a great help to her if people hear that you have taken her up like this. All the same, I've thought it over, and am not quite sure—I think I had better go back to my first plan and send her to some convent in the hills. It might be safer," and she burst into tears. "But why have you suddenly become afraid for her to be here?" Kozeri protested. "Of course if you had any reason to suppose I was tired of having her, it would be different. Of course, too, all kinds of people come to a house like this, and I can think of someone in particular who is certainly not always so scrupulous as he might be. But then everyone knows about him, and it is quite easy to take precautions. You cannot imagine that there is the slightest real danger in that quarter. What then is it that is worrying you?" "I am sure," the mother said, "that from you she will get nothing but kindness. After all, if her father had behaved as he ought to have done—we needn't go into all that again—you would have been brought up together; and quite apart from that, I have some right on my account to approach you, for I too am pretty near of kin." But suddenly changing her manner she added, "In a day or two I have to enter upon a period of strict retreat, and I think I shall take Ukifune with me. She looks to me as though a rest would do her no harm. I will bring her back later on." And with that she left the house, the girl on her arm. It was evident that she was very much flurried and distracted, for she rushed out of the room without so much as a thank you or good-bye. It was a terrible disappointment for Kozeri; but it seemed no use trying to stop her. The place that the mother had chosen for her "retreat" was a cottage very prettily situated in the Third Ward. Unfortunately part of it had been left unfinished, and it had never been properly fitted and furnished. "Poor child," she said. "At present your life seems merely to consist of one misfortune after another. The truth is, without influence it's impossible to have any existence that can be called a life at all. But we can't leave you in a place where you are treated in a way no one would dare to if you were really counted by your sister as an equal. For myself I no longer mind about company or position or any such things, and could get along very nicely all alone in a place such as this. But I am afraid you won't know what to do with yourself. However, though it isn't the life one would choose for you, you must try and put up with it. No one, of course, must know that you are here; but it won't in any case be for very long. I shall soon have arranged something better for you." The mother herself was obliged to go home at once. Never had Ukifune felt so forlorn. It seemed as though, one after another, every avenue of existence was closed against her. No stranger but would have been touched to see her lie there weeping, abandoned in this cheerless unfamiliar place; and for the mother this outcome to all her tender hopes and ambitions was heart-rending indeed. But anything was better than exposing her to incidents such as that of the previous evening, and here, wretched though she might be, she could at least be certain of preserving her good name. The mother was at ordinary times quite a sensible woman; but when angry or frightened she was apt to lose her head and fly to extreme courses without stopping to take anyone's advice. Granted that Ukifune must be kept in seclusion, this might equally have been effected in the Governor's house. But with Sakon coming and going she made up her mind that the girl would feel her position more acutely if she remained at home. Hence the present plan. But for both of them the separation was extremely painful. "I wish things here were in better order," she said before leaving the girl. "The place looks, I know, so very unfinished, and of course you will have to make sure that you are properly guarded. However, I have arranged all that with the watchmen. I don't think you will find it really uncomfortable. I have put servants into all the spare rooms, and you have only to send for them if you want anything. I wonder how you will get on? You may be sure I shouldn't leave you like this if I could help it. But I should get into terrible trouble at home..." and weeping bitterly she returned to the Governor's house.

He was still making a great fuss of his new son-in-law and complained continually that his wife made things very difficult for him by holding aloof. But she could not forget that Sakon's appearance on the scene had been responsible, directly or indirectly, for all her daughter's troubles, and it was with difficulty that she could bring herself to have anything to do with him. Moreover, ever since she had seen what a poor figure he cut in surroundings like those of the Nijo-in, he appeared quite differently in her eyes, and she was amazed at her own lack of judgment in ever for a moment considering that so wretched a creature could be a desirable acquisition. She made up her mind, however, that she must try to shake, off this unflattering impression. The circumstances under which it had been formed were after all very exceptional. Perhaps seen at his case, in surroundings to which he really belonged, he would appear less ridiculous. One morning when he was sitting quietly with his young wife in her room, the mother went and peeped at them. Sakon was wearing a smart mantle of thin white silk over a quite stylish shot-silk dress of the fashionable light-pink shade. Seated there by the window, scanning with evident appreciation the Governor's well-ordered garden, he cut by no means so contemptible a figure. His wife, still looking a mere baby, nestled contentedly at his side. It was strange indeed to contrast this pair with that other couple[*] whom she had recently seen together under not

---

[*] Niou and Kozeri.

dissimilar circumstances. From time to time Sakon would turn to make some remark to one or other of the waiting-women, and really—the mother was obliged to confess—his conversation was by no means ill-bred or unamusing. So different an impression, indeed, did he now make that she could hardly believe this was the same Sakon she had seen at the Nijo-in. "There is no *hagi** anywhere to match Prince Niou's," he said presently. "I can't imagine where he got the seeds from. It is certainly not a different species of plant, but the flowers are of a beauty… Unfortunately he was in the garden when I was there the other day or I would have picked some. I wish you could have heard him humming those lines of Lady Ise's† as he passed."

He made one or two very pretty poems of his own, and it seemed to the mother strange indeed that this was the man who from the most sordid motives had behaved so abominably to her daughter, and who, seen in the company of his betters, had hardly seemed to exist as a human being at all. She could not resist the temptation to remind him that there were people to whom he did not figure in so amiable and innocent a light, and she sent in the poem: "How comes it that on under-leaf instead the dewdrop rests, when to the unfolding flower alone its gift of love was pledged?" "Had it but known from what Royal Fields‡ the flower sprang, never would the dew have wavered from its first intent." "I should very much like an opportunity of talking the whole thing over with you," he added. It was evident that he had discovered the facts about Ukifune's birth and was now repenting of his treachery. Surely now that people were beginning to regard her in this light, something might be done to retrieve her position? The image of Kaoru, as she had seen him at the Nijo-in, floated before the mother's mind. Of course if he were in the least like that odious Niou—except that they were both equally handsome nothing could be more unlike what she knew of Kaoru than the insulting way Niou, merely for the sake of a little idle amusement, had forced himself upon the unfortunate girl—there would be no use in thinking any more about him. But Kaoru, though it was clear that he took a real interest in Ukifune, had hitherto taken no steps to pursue the acquaintance; indeed, his discretion was carried to a point that was positively embarrassing. The fact that Ukifune had now seen Kaoru and knew him to be interested in her made it all the more impossible ever again to suggest her putting up with any such creature as this miserable Sakon. But the more she turned the whole matter over in her mind, the less

---

* Bush-clover, lespedeza.

† "Fearful lest in my hand they should fade, even upon the *hagi* I have plucked the dew remembers to fall."

‡ I.e. had I known that Ukifune was Prince Hachi's daughter. *Miyagi-no* (literally, Palace Wall Fields) was a place famous for its *hagi*.

she felt convinced that a union with Kaoru was really to be desired. His high public position, the circumstances of his upbringing, his existing obligations—all made it most improbable that he would really" devote himself even to a girl with claims far greater than Ukifune's. The more she saw of the world, the more certain she became that no good could come from mixing people of different birth and position. She could see for herself how much her other children suffered by comparison with Ukifune; and Sakon, who here cut quite a respectable figure, no sooner set foot in the Nijo-in than he became—what she had seen for herself. No, to become the favorite of someone who was already married to an Emperor's daughter could lead to nothing but continual embarrassment and mortification. It was a dreadful predicament.

Meanwhile life passed very dully at the cottage in the Third Ward. The garden contained nothing but weeds, and no one came near the place save a few uncouth serving-men with barbarous eastern accents. If only there had been some flowers! But the garden had been left quite unmade, and Ukifune spent one melancholy day after another, thinking often of Kozeri and longing to be back with her, thinking too even of Niou—he had said some beautiful things to her, or they seemed so at the time, for she was not at all sure what they meant. Sometimes she fancied that her clothes still smelt of the strange perfume he was wearing, and at once the terror she had felt on the night of their encounter would again take possession of her.

A letter full of the tenderest anxiety and affection arrived from her mother, but it only served to make Ukifune feel more depressed than ever, for it seemed to her that her case must be hopeless indeed if even such devotion as this were powerless to assist her. "What do you do all day long?" the mother wrote. "I am afraid you must feel very homesick. But try to put up with it for a little longer." "I am managing to fill in the time," Ukifune answered, "and am not really at all unhappy." To her answer was attached the poem: "Happy I am, yet happier far would be did I not know that even in this desolate place the world is with me still.[*] That such sentiments should come from a girl of Ukifune's tender age was terrible indeed, and weeping bitterly the mother wrote: "In the world's midst or far from ways of men—what matters it, could I but find a place where you at last might thrive?" There was indeed nothing admirable about these compositions, but they served to give vent to the tense feelings of the moment.

Towards the end of autumn[†] Kaoru as usual found himself growing very restless and, unable to fix his mind on anything else, set out for Uji

---

[*] She wants to leave the world, i.e. go to a convent.
[†] The anniversary of Agemaki's death.

where the rebuilding of the old Prince's quarters was now complete. It was so long since he had been in the hills that the beauty of the autumn woods came to him almost as a surprise. This time every trace of the former building had vanished. Kaoru conjured up before his mind the old Prince's rooms as he had known them, almost monastic in their bare simplicity. He thought indeed of them and their occupant with such affection that for the moment he almost wished that he had left things as they were. The fittings of the old place were too definitely ecclesiastical in style for general use. Some of them he had altered so as to be suitable for a lady's use, and others—such as some wattled screens and plain, solid pieces of furniture—he turned to account in fitting out the priests' quarters in the new temple. Where, however, new things were required he had them made in a style suitable to a country residence, but at the same time neither makeshift nor commonplace. After his tour of inspection was over he sat for a long while on a rock near the moat. "O waters, changelessly flowing, almost had I thought to find in you the image of him that is no more!" Such was his poem, and tears were still in his eyes when he came, as usual, to Ben no Kimi's room. Seeing that he was in low spirits she too began to pucker a little at the brow. He approached the room from the courtyard and sat for a time on the ledge outside her window, pulling up one side of the blind and talking to her through the curtains of the couch where she lay concealed. "I believe," he said presently, "that the 'image'* of whom we have sometimes spoken was at the Nijo-in the other day when I was there. But I am afraid I was too shy to communicate with her. I am waiting, as a matter of fact, for you to break the ground a little more thoroughly." "I have just had a letter from her mother," said Ben. "She says that an awkward conjunction of planets has obliged her to move Ukifune from place to place. Here is the letter. Yes... 'At present my daughter has retired to a very odd little house—not at all the sort of place for her, and if only Uji were not so far off I should certainly ask you to take her in for a while.'" "The journey here has long ago become such a habit with me," Kaoru sighed, "that I often forget what a fuss most people would make about it. It is indeed a strange fate that has kept me all my life toiling up and down that mountain road... However, this seems a good opportunity to get into touch with her. Perhaps you could send a message, or better still go and see her there?" "I can send any message you like," said Ben. "But you must not ask me to go myself to the City. Why, I do not even go to see Niou's lady at the Nijo-in!" "I can understand your not wanting to appear in public," Kaoru said. "But in this case not a soul need know about it; and even the hermits of Mount Atago sometimes go down to

---

* Ukifune. See Part V, p. 947.

the valley if occasion demands it. They say that even the strictest vows not only may but should be broken, if it be a help to a friend." "My staying up here or going down to the City has nothing to do with vows or salvation or anything of that kind. I just think it looks bad for anyone in my position to go gadding about town, that's all." "I may never get such a chance again," pleaded Kaoru. "Listen, I shall send a carriage to fetch you sometime within the next few days. Meanwhile please find out where this cottage is. You know me well enough to be sure that I shall do nothing rash or indiscreet." "What then *did* he intend to do?" the old lady wondered, and despite his protestations she would indeed have felt very uneasy had she been dealing with anyone less scrupulous than Kaoru. And indeed, quite apart from any consideration for Ukifune's feelings, a man in Kaoru's position had his own reputation to consider. "Very well then," Ben said at last, "write a letter, and I am ready to take it there whenever you please. But I am not going without one, for I don't at all want them to think that I have taken it upon myself to arrange a match for her. I'd far rather leave that sort of thing to the witch-women of Iga."* "It's easy enough to write a letter," Kaoru said. "But one never knows into whose hands it may fall. You object to being thought of as an old sorceress of Iga; but on the other hand it won't be very pleasant for me if people go round saying "His Excellency the Minister of the Right is courting the daughter of a provincial Governor"—and not a very refined specimen of his class either, judging by what I have heard of him." Ben laughed; it did indeed sound very bad.

It was now getting dark, and remembering that he ought to bring back something for the Second Princess, Kaoru went off to look among the grass for an autumn flower or two and find a handsome spray of maple-leaf. He did what he could to prevent her feeling that she was thrown away upon him, and was careful always to treat her with the utmost deference and consideration; but it had long ago become apparent that there could never be any real intimacy between them. Even had his own conscience not dictated it he would indeed have been obliged in any case to pay her a great deal of attention, for the Emperor despite his many preoccupations continued to show on her behalf a full degree of common, parental solicitude and was in constant communication with Kaoru's mother. A marriage perpetually subjected to such august superintendence was no light responsibility, and he knew quite well that he was the last person in the world who ought to go out of the way to involve himself in a fresh commitment.

Early on the morning of the appointed day he sent a carriage to Uji. It was in charge of a single well-trusted groom and the driver was a man

---

* The old ladies of Iga were famous as go-betweens.

whom no one would be likely to recognize. "On the way back you can get some country lads from one of my estates to accompany you," he said. Ben no Kimi was far from pleased with the mission he had imposed upon her, but there seemed to be no getting out of it, and after dressing herself up in her best clothes she climbed reluctantly into the carriage. The journey however did not seem very long, for the hills were at their loveliest and at each fresh turn of the road she remembered some long-forgotten line of verse. Much to her relief the entrance, when they arrived, turned out to be a very inconspicuous one. The oxen were unyoked and the carriage drawn up to the house without attracting the slightest attention. She sent in her name and presently a young girl whom she recognized as having been with Ukifune on the Hatsuse pilgrimage appeared at the door and begged her to come in. Time indeed hung so heavily on Ukifune's hands in this dismal place that any distraction was welcome; and Ben no Kimi was not merely a friend from old days but also particularly interesting to her owing to the old lady's long connection with her father.

"Ever since you were at Uji," Ben said, "I have been thinking about you and wondering to myself how you were getting on. But since I became a nun I have quite given up going about at all—I do not even go to, see Kozeri at the Nijo-in. But Kaoru talks so much about you that in the end I felt I really must come." It seemed rather an odd reason; but Ukifune could hardly fail to be gratified that anyone like Kaoru—both she and the nurse had admired him immensely when they saw him at the Nijo-in—should remember her. That he could possibly have any intention of pursuing the matter further did not for a moment enter her head. Late in the evening, however, there was a knock at the door. "It is someone from Uji," said a voice outside. Ben guessed that it was someone with a message from Kaoru, and sent Ukifune's nurse to the door. "It's someone for you," the women said, mentioning a name which Ben knew to be that of one of Kaoru's bailiffs. She could hear, however, that a carriage was being drawn in at the gates, which struck her as rather odd. It was a wet, windy night, and as Ben approached the door there blew in upon her a damp, chilly blast. Suddenly she and those who stood behind her noticed that this dank night-wind was becoming laden with an indescribable fragrance. Consternation prevailed. To receive such a visitor suitably would have required whole days of forethought and preparation, and here they were, caught utterly unawares. What was to be done? They were hurriedly debating the question when Kaoru sent in a message saying that the matter he had come to discuss with Ukifune was one that had been in his mind for months. "This seems to be a quiet place," he said, "where we are not likely to be interrupted." She was wondering what this mysterious topic could be and in what terms his note ought to be answered when the nurse came to her side. "You may depend upon it," she said, "that he would not have come specially like this, so late at night, just for the sake of a little conversation. You can't answer a note of that sort offhand. I had better go round to your mother and tell her about it. I shan't be long." "No, I shouldn't do that," Ben no Kimi said, "it would seem very fussy. Surely a girl can have a little conversation with a young man without her whole future being at stake. Things don't move so fast as that—and in any case Kaoru is the last person in the world to let his feelings run away with him. I can answer for it that if she allows him in he won't take any liberties."

Rain was still falling and it was very dark. Out in the garden the watchmen were on their rounds, making strange cries as they went. "That's a dangerous-looking bit of wall at the corner of the house there. It will be coming down on someone's head before long," one of them said to another. "I wish they'd pulled in that carriage properly so that one could lock the gate. You'd think they'd have more sense, but those people's servants are always like that." It was not a conversation calculated to make Kaoru, perched on the edge of the rickety *sunoko*,* feel very much at home. "No roof to shelter me,"† Kaoru hummed, and presently he recited the poem: "What massy weed-clump blocks your door, O Eastern House,‡ that I so long must shiver in the rain?" and as he shook the raindrops from his coat there floated into the house a waft of perfume for which the lower servants, simple villagers from the East, were unable to account. It was impossible simply to send him away, and at last Ukifune gave orders for him to be shown into the southern side-room. It was with some difficulty, however, that her nurse and the rest succeeded in dragging her out to welcome him. The place into which he had been shown was separated from the front room, where Ukifune was now seated, by a makeshift door which, though it was bolted, fitted so badly that there was quite a gap between it and its frame. "A wonderful piece of carpentry!" Kaoru exclaimed. "The Craftsman of Hida could pick up a hint or two from the man who made that! But I am afraid I am not used to carrying on a conversation in the face of such obstacles," and the next moment—she had no idea how he had managed to squeeze through—Ukifune found him at her side. Avoiding any mention of her resemblance to Agemaki he began telling her how ever since he had caught sight of her for a moment at Uji he had been longing to know her. Since then so continually indeed had his thoughts been turned towards her that it was certain they were

---

* A narrow ledge running round the outside of the house.

† Allusion to a poem about waiting in the rain at the ford of Sano, by Okumaro (*Manyoshu* 265).

‡ "Eastern House," in allusion to Ukifune's sojourn in Hitachi and the eastern patois spoken by her servants; but also to the folk-song *Eastern House* (*Azumaya*), which is about a lover locked out in the rain.

destined to be friends. And looking at her while he talked he saw that the opinion he had formed of her at Uji was not in the least exaggerated; she was a girl of quite exceptional grace and charm. It was beginning to grow light, but it seemed that in this part of the town the dawn was heralded, not by the crowing of cocks, but by the raucous voices of peddlers crying their wares—if indeed that was what they were doing, for the noises they made were entirely unintelligible. There seemed to be whole tribes of them. He looked out. There was something ghostly about them as, seen against the grey morning sky, they struggled along with strange packages piled high upon their heads. Apart from everything else the unfamiliarity of the whole experience fascinated him. Presently he heard the watchman unlock the gates and go off. Everyone in the house was asleep. He routed out one of his men, had his carriage brought quietly round to the double-doors of the main room, and taking Ukifune in his arms, put her inside. The alarm was soon given and the maid Jiju came rushing out. "Come back, come back, what are you thinking of?" she screamed. "It's the ninth month."* Ben no Kimi, who also appeared on the scene, was completely taken aback at finding Kaoru behaving with such precipitation, and wished that the whole thing had been handled in quite another way. But she nevertheless came to the rescue, pointing out that the actual festival did not begin till the fourteenth of the ninth month. "Today is only the thirteenth," she said. "There's no need for you to worry. He's thought of all that." "But I'm afraid I can't go back to Uji with you," she said to Kaoru. "Kozeri would never forgive me if she heard that I had been so close without ever coming to see her." Was the old lady going straight round to the Nijo-in with an account of tonight's proceedings? Kaoru, though he had no intention of concealing the matter from Kozeri indefinitely, thought that this would be rather premature. "I'll put that right for you afterwards," he said to Ben. "It's essential that you should be there to help us find our way about at Uji; and we had better bring one of the maids." Jiju at once jumped into the carriage. The nurse and a girl who had come with Ben found themselves left behind.

It soon became clear that they were going not, as Ukifune at first supposed, to Kaoru's town house, but to Uji. A change of oxen awaited them, showing the journey was not unpremeditated. By the time they reached the Hosoji† it was quite light.

Jiju for her part had no misgivings whatever about this sudden flight. She had been day-dreaming about Kaoru ever since she saw him at the Nijo-in. People might think what they pleased; she was ready to follow him to the ends of the earth. Her mistress, however, seemed to take the

---

* It was unlucky to begin a love-affair during the Buddhist ceremonies of the ninth month.
† In the Ninth (southernmost) Ward of the Capital.

matter very differently. Speechless with fear and astonishment she lay huddled in the corner where Kaoru had put her. For a while he left her to herself, but presently he took her in his arms. "We are coming to a place where the road is very stony," he said. "You must let me hold you so that you don't feel the jolting." A garment hung across the middle of the carriage had at first given Ben no Kimi some slight sense of privacy; but now bright sunshine poured in upon her through the thin, flapping silk and she felt terribly unprotected. She could not help thinking all the while that it ought to be Agemaki there in the corner of the carriage. Never, never had she dreamed that she would live to see such a day as this! And though it was the last thing she wanted to be heard doing at such a moment, she burst out sobbing. Jiju was profoundly shocked. It was bad enough to have a nun with one at all on such an occasion as this; she might at least have the decency to behave cheerfully. For knowing none of the circumstances the girl imagined Ben merely to be indulging in one of those fits of senseless weeping to which old people are often prone. And even Kaoru, happy though he was, could not, as past one familiar corner after another they drove on into the autumn hills, wholly banish from his mind those autumn journeys of long ago; and a mist rose before his eyes. His arms resting on the carriage window, he gazed before him. Soon his long sleeves, hanging at the carriage side, were so wet—for coils of dank morning mist were rising from the stream—that the bright scarlet of his under robe showed through the flowery pattern of his mantle. Presently there came so sharp a drop in the road that the sleeves dangled into his view, and he hastened to retrieve them, murmuring to himself as he did so the verse: "Short was my happiness, for soon the mists of unforgotten autumns rose between, and swelled my sleeves with dew."[*]

"Well, these are funny people," Jiju thought. "There's that old lady crying again"—for Ben had overheard Kaoru's poem and was now weeping copiously—"for all the world as though she were going to a funeral. You'd think on a journey like this they would all be merry-making." "I am afraid I must seem to you rather a dismal companion," Kaoru explained. "But you will understand, I am sure, that to find myself once more on a journey that years ago I used to make so frequently, moves me deeply. Sit up a little and look at the color on those hills. I am sure you can see nothing from down there where you have buried yourself." She made no effort to stir, and he was obliged to hold her up to the window. But the gesture with which, glancing timidly out onto the road, she covered her face with her fan, reminded him once more of Agemaki. Yet he feared that after all the resemblance was perhaps merely superficial. For Agemaki,

---

[*] "*Tokoro-seki made nururu*" means "terribly wet," but also "so wet that there was no room for them," i.e. he had to lean out of the window to conceal his tears from Ukifune.

despite her lack of experience, thought about things for herself and was always interesting to talk to, whereas this girl seemed almost too spiritless and docile. No, he had a long way to travel yet before he came to the end of his troubles!

When at last they arrived at Uji he had all the while the feeling that Agemaki was there watching him, and it was strange to find himself inwardly arguing with the invisible presence—protesting that this was not the mere light-hearted adventure that it seemed. "It is for you, you only, that I have come," he whispered to himself again and again.

With his usual consideration he left her to herself for a little after they arrived. She was still worrying a good deal about what her mother would think; but Kaoru had treated her since the first moment with such kindness and spoken to her so tenderly that it seemed as though he must really be fond of her, and she began to feel much less scared and miserable.

Ben no Kimi had remained in the carriage and driven round to a side entrance, seeming to indicate—rather too pointedly Kaoru thought—that henceforward Ukifune was mistress of the household. He had said nothing to suggest that he intended to keep her there permanently.

The bailiffs from his various estates in the district, having heard of his arrival, now came one after another to pay their respects, and Kaoru was kept busy till late in the day. Ukifune's dinner was sent round from Ben's quarters. The road to Uji had passed through thick forests, and it was a great relief to get out into the open, with this wide view of the river and the mountains beyond. The grounds too, so spaciously laid out, were a great contrast to the untidy plot of land to which she had lately been confined, and she would have been happy to stay here as long as he would keep her—if only she knew why he had brought her and what it was he really did intend!

When he had dealt with his visitors Kaoru wrote to his mother, to the Second Princess and others saying that he had been meaning for some time to inspect the decorations of the new temple, and suddenly discovering today that it was possible for him to get away, he had come post-haste to Uji. As he was feeling rather tired and had also remembered a taboo that necessitated his remaining in retirement for a few days, he thought the simplest thing would be for him to stay where he was.

Ukifune thought that the informal dress Kaoru had now changed into suited him infinitely better than his Court clothes; indeed, she found him so charming that, although when he joined her in her room she at first felt rather shy, she made no attempt to keep him at a distance.

He thought her clothes surprisingly well made and the colors chosen with extremely good taste, though naturally there were unfashionable touches here and there. Agemaki indeed owed nothing to her clothes, which had always seen a good deal of wear; but how graceful, how distinguished she always looked in them! In one point Ukifune could certainly stand comparison with anyone at Court, and that was her hair. It fell from her shoulders in faultless line; not even the Second Princess, whose hair was said to be the loveliest in the land, could in this respect claim any superiority.

Meanwhile he was faced with the none-too-easy problem of what to do with her.

To establish her at the Capital as mistress of his house was out of the question in view of the conflicts[*] to which such a step would lead. To give her an ordinary post in his household was easy enough; but he did not like the idea of setting her down as an equal among a promiscuous horde of gentlewomen. For the present the best thing to do seemed on the whole to leave her where she was. But that—considering how difficult he found it nowadays to get to places as far out as Uji—was a depressing prospect for both of them. He sat with her for the rest of the day, trying hard to make her feel completely at her ease. But though he talked much of her father, concerning whom she was evidently so curious, and told her all sorts of interesting and amusing things about life at Uji in the old days, he felt he was not really making any progress; she still remained exasperatingly tongue-tied and shy. However, it was a fault on the right side, and one which a little tact and encouragement would quickly overcome; whereas if her upbringing had produced in her the sort of ill-bred pertness and forwardness that one often came across in country girls, there would be small hope indeed of her ever turning out to be a second Agemaki!

Presently he sent for the old Prince's zitherns. It occurred to him, however, much to his disappointment, that Ukifune must have had very little opportunity to study music, and he tuned the instruments himself. It was strange to think that very likely this was the first time they had been touched since Hachi's death, and lost in thought he sat for a long while running his fingers absent-mindedly over the strings. Suddenly the moon came out. Prince Hachi, of course, was far from being a notable performer; but his playing, Kaoru remembered, always showed great taste and feeling. "How I wish you had known Uji when they were all here!" he said, turning to Ukifune. "You would understand better then how deeply it moves me to hear the sound of this instrument once more. You must, I am sure, realize that there was something singularly lovable about him, when you see how fondly his memory is cherished even by outsiders[†] like myself. It is indeed a thousand pities that you wasted all those years in a place like Hitachi!" She colored slightly and looked down, clutching and unclutching her white fan. Seen in profile, her rising color enhancing the

---

[*] With the Emperor.
[†] I.e. people not related to him.

dazzling whiteness of her brow, she was so strangely like Agemaki that he could not help feeling it would be the easiest thing in the world to teach her anything that Agemaki had known. "Do you play at all?" he asked, not very hopefully. "They ought at any rate to know something about this one where you come from," and he pointed to an eastern-zither. "We called it a Japanese zithern," she said, "and to us in Hitachi the music of real Japan was as strange as its songs."[*] The reply, which this time came readily to her lips, showed that she had a good deal more to say for herself than he had supposed. More than ever he wondered whether he would be able to endure keeping her at a place like this, where he could so seldom come. He pushed the instrument away from him, humming as he did so the line[†] "Down from the Prince of Ch'u's terrace came the sound of a zithern at night." The girl Jiju, who, having been brought up in the Governor's house, was a good deal better versed in terms of archery than in Chinese poetry, was lost in admiration at the ease with which gentlemen from Court could fling off an appropriate quotation. She would have been less impressed had she ever read the poem in question, or even known the other line[‡] of the couplet, which could indeed hardly have been of more unfortunate omen. No sooner had the words escaped from Kaoru's lips than he was aghast at his blunder. It seemed almost inconceivable that anyone having the whole realm of poetry to choose from should hit on such a line. A box of fruit now arrived from Ben no Kimi. On the lid were laid some sprays of maple-leaf and creeper, and deftly hidden among them was a strip of paper with a message of some kind roughly scribbled upon it. The full moon was shining straight onto the box, and Kaoru noticed Ben's note at once. He was feeling very hungry, and while spreading out the paper with one hand, he stretched with the other towards the contents of the box.

"Changed, as an autumn wood when on its trees the mistletoe hangs golden, is this house; yet comes the moonlight as of old."[§] The message, scrawled in Ben no Kimi's old-fashioned hand, stung him to the quick. "Upon a face that is, yet is not hers, O moon of Uji, to your sorrowful[¶] name still true, you bend your pitiless light." He murmured the lines to himself, not meaning them as an answer; but Jiju took upon herself to report them.

---

[*] The eastern-zither (*azuma-koto*) was also known as *Yamato-koto* (i.e. zithern of central Japan); and Japanese poetry (as opposed to Chinese) was called *Yamato-kotoba*.

[†] By Aritsura, tenth century.

[‡] "A lady sits unwanted in her bower, like a fan when autumn comes," i.e. she has been cast aside like a fan when the heat of summer is over.

[§] The house was doubly changed—by the death of Agemaki and by the fact that it had been rebuilt. "The moonlight that comes as of old" is Kaoru. The poem reproaches him with accepting Ukifune in place of Agemaki.

[¶] "*Uji*" means "sorrowful."

Ukifune

Meanwhile Niou thought constantly of his brief meeting with the mysterious occupant of the western wing. Probably she came from some quite ordinary family; but she was certainly a delightful creature, and nothing could have been more irritating than that she should disappear after a single encounter of so tantalizing a description. As for Kozeri, he could not imagine what had come over her. It was ridiculous in any case that she should allow herself to be put out at all by such a trifle; but that she should lose her head to the extent of sending the girl away... No, it was not in the least like her. Kozeri, however, saw nothing for it but to put up with his continual scoldings and reproaches, leaving him to draw whatever conclusions he pleased. To tell him the real facts was impossible without at the same time giving him a clue as to her present whereabouts—a clue which, if she knew him, he would certainly use to the full! She would, moreover, be behaving badly towards Kaoru, who, though circumstances made it difficult for him to put the relationship on a formal footing, was evidently very much in love with the girl.

However, Niou being what he was, she could not count on her own discretion being of much avail. Again and again she had seen him succeed in tracking down girls with whom he had decided to have a brief flirtation to the most unbelievable places, and it was very unlikely that in a case of this sort where evidently something more than a passing fancy was concerned—for it was now several months since it began—it was indeed unlikely that he would fail to get hold of her. The most Kozeri could do was to keep silent. If he managed to get information elsewhere, it would not be her fault; and though if anything happened she would be very sorry on Kaoru's behalf and Ukifune's too, there was nothing further she could do. Where such matters were concerned Niou was completely intractable. It would have been bad enough whoever the girl was; but the fact that a sister was concerned would certainly be regarded as additionally scandalous. In any case, even if in one way or another the disaster was inevitable, Kozeri was determined that no imprudence of hers should contribute towards producing it; and despite all questions and reproaches she obstinately refused to tell him either who the girl was or what had become of her. Most people of course would have got out of the difficulty by inventing a plausible story; but to Kozeri the idea of such a course never for a moment occurred, with the result that Niou was at a loss to attribute her silence to anything save a common petty jealousy to which he would never have thought her capable of descending.

Kaoru, who found it hard to realize that other people might be less patient and reasonable than himself, had his business to attend to and was in other ways so tied that (as indeed he was sure Ukifune understood) a visit to Uji, unless some excuse happened to turn up, was more difficult for him than if "the gods themselves had prevented it."[*] However, he thought constantly about her, and hoped that she was not wondering what had become of him. For the present he did not think it would be wise to move her. The best arrangement seemed to be to make her as comfortable as possible at Uji. He was sure to be going there from time to time, and it would be delightful always to find her there. Or, better still, if he could sometimes find an excuse for staying there several days, so that they could spend a little time quietly together. It was better at first to keep her secretly at Uji and let their relationship develop unobserved. For one thing it gave her a chance to overcome her shyness; and he for his part would far rather get to know her quietly, without having the feeling that everyone was asking: "Who is it that he has got hold of?" "How long has it been going on?" and so on. Moreover, by the world at large his visits to Uji had always been supposed to be of a religious[†] nature, and the discovery that he had other reasons for going there would place him in a rather undignified position. What Kozeri would feel about the whole affair he did not quite know. Certainly if he brought Ukifune to the Capital and severed his connection with Uji entirely she would feel that he had forgotten Agemaki, which was not true. In fact, as was usual with him, he took far too many things into account, when on the whole it would have been better to act as the impulse of the moment prompted him to do. However, he looked forward to a time when he would be able to bring Ukifune to the Capital and even went so far as to begin making alterations in the arrangement of his palace with a view to eventually installing her. Meanwhile his new preoccupations in no way diminished his devotion to Kozeri. People to whom the history of this strange friendship was unknown were apt to regard it as something of a mystery. But as Kozeri's knowledge of life increased she realized how extremely rare a thing such fidelity as Kaoru's was; and regarding his attitude towards herself merely as a reflection of his feelings towards Agemaki, she was deeply touched. Sometimes—particularly when Niou's vagaries had been unusually trying—she would even go so far as to wish that she had taken Agemaki's advice,[‡] particularly when she saw how highly everyone spoke

---

[*] In allusion to the poem: "If it were true that you loved me you would come, unless the gods themselves prevented it," i.e. you would not let yourself be stopped by men.
[†] He had first gone there to study Buddhism with Prince Hachi.
[‡] To marry Kaoru.

of Kaoru, who seemed to her indeed to have improved a great deal since she first knew him. But she was very shy of spending too much time with him. To people who did not know the whole story it must seem simply the case of a married woman continuing to receive a former suitor—a thing which she believed was sometimes tolerated in ordinary families, but which was looked upon very severely by the people among whom she had been used to move. It must indeed seem to people that she—the wife of a Royal Prince—ought to be the last to ignore such a convention. Niou still persisted in regarding their relationship with suspicion and was so tiresome about it that Kozeri found herself gradually drifting into a coldness towards Kaoru which did not at all correspond with her real feelings. Yet though his jealousy estranged her from Kaoru, Niou's own behavior was of a kind that often made things extremely difficult for her. However, she was the mother of his only child—the boy grew lustier and handsomer every day. This gave Kozeri a great advantage over all her rivals. His relations with her were indeed on a far tenderer and more intimate footing, and as time went on her situation seemed on the whole to improve. As soon as the New Year ceremonies at Court were over, Niou hurried to the Nijo-in to celebrate the child's safe entry into its second calendar year. He was playing with it one morning when a very young waiting-girl came tripping into the room with a tiny model of a fir-tree in a " hairy"* basket. To the tree was attached a folded note on a large sheet of light-green tissue-paper, while she carried an ordinary, formal letter. Without a moment's hesitation she ran straight to Kozeri and laid the things at her feet. "Hallo, where do those come from?" asked Niou. "The man who brought them said they came from Uji," the girl replied, "and were to be given to Tayu; but as things from Uji are always for Madam I brought them straight here. Isn't it a pretty basket? It's made of wire really, but they've painted it over. And isn't the tree cleverly made? Just look at its dear little branches..." and she chattered on, dancing up and down with excitement. "Come on now, bring it over here. It's my turn to look at it now," said Niou, laughing. "No, not the letters," Kozeri called hastily. "You must take them to Tayu." She blushed as she spoke, and it at once occurred to Niou that this was Kaoru's secret method of communication. The present was said to come from Uji, and what more likely than that Kaoru should use the old lady there as his intermediary? He took up both the letters; but felt as soon as they were in his hands so certain they were from Kaoru that he had not the courage to open them. "There's no harm in my opening these and having a look at them, is there?" he said, glancing up at Kozeri. "Well, I must say I think it's going rather far," she answered indignantly. "Private letters from one waiting-woman

---

* With loose ends left sticking out.

to another... But do as you please." Kozeri's expression, he decided, was not at all what it would have been if the letters were really from Kaoru. "I think I'll have a look at them, all the same," he said. "I've often wondered what sort of thing women of that kind say when they write to one another." He opened the green note and saw at once that it was not in a man's hand. The writing was that of a girl,* and a young one too. It was an ordinary New Year's letter, not phrased with any particular skill. "The tree," said a postscript, "is for the little Prince. I only wish it were something nicer." The only interesting thing about the note was that he could not imagine who there was living at Uji nowadays that was likely to have written it. He turned with some interest to the second letter.† This too was obviously in a woman's hand. "I suppose you've all been having a gay time of it, seeing the old year out and the new year in. Just now too you're sure to be having a fine lot of people coming to the house.‡ Here, I must say, they do everything they can to make us comfortable; but I don't consider it the right sort of place for my lady. I say to her sometimes that instead of sitting here all day staring in front of her, she'd far better go up to the City from time to time and stay for a little with you. But owing to what happened to her there before she can't bear to hear the name of the place, and I'm afraid there's not a chance of ever getting her to set foot in it again. She asks me to send these hare-sticks§ for the little Prince, but says will you please give them to him sometime when his father and mother are not there."

The writer did not seem to have been able to decide whether it was to be a New Year's letter or not. If it was intended for one, the part about something disagreeable happening ought not to be there. It struck him as a curious letter, though certainly an incompetent and clumsy one. "I think it's about time you gave up this mystification and told me who wrote these letters," he said. "It's quite simple," Kozeri replied. "She's the daughter of a woman who used to be in service with us at Uji. She is spending a little time there with her family, that's all." But it was evident that the first letter was not from anyone in that sort of position at all. Then again—that passage in the other letter about someone having "a disagreeable experience," apparently at the Nijo-in. Suddenly an idea dawned on him.¶ Yes, of course; how well it all fitted together! Those hare-sticks too were obviously the work not of a common waiting-woman but of a person of taste with plenty of time on her hands. Attached to a forked branch of the toy pine-tree he found some little balls painted

---

* The letter was, of course, from Ukifune.
† From Ukon to Tayu.
‡ To convey the good wishes of the season.
§ Sticks used on the first Day of the Hare in the year, in the ritual of expelling demons.
¶ That it was the girl he had found in the western wing.

to look like oranges. To the forked bough was pinned the poem: "This little tree, though newly made,* denotes the self-same wish, in timider wise, that immemorial forest pines convey." The verse was commonplace enough, and would not have interested him in the least had he not now made up his mind that the writer of it must be no other than the girl for whom he had so long been searching. "It's kind of her to have sent these things," Niou said, "whoever she is. You must answer, of course. As there is obviously nothing in the least private about the letters, I cannot imagine why you were so upset at my opening them. Good-bye," and he went off. "This ought not to have happened," Kozeri said afterwards to one of her maids. "A little girl like that ought never to be allowed to bring things in without someone having a look first." "I can only say that if I had seen her," the woman answered, "I should never have let her go in. But these children are all the same. No matter what you tell them they always think they know better. When they've shown they're wiser than the rest of us... till then they'd better do as they're told." "Poor little thing. Don't be hard on her," Kozeri said. The child in question had only been at the Nijo-in since the winter. She was extremely pretty, and a great favorite with Niou.

"It's all a very queer business," thought Niou, back in his own room. He knew of course that Kaoru had been going regularly to Uji for years past, and people said that he sometimes spent the night there. Fond though Kaoru had undoubtedly been of Agemaki, it had always been difficult to believe that he went all the way to Uji and, as it appeared, spent whole nights there, merely out of regard for her memory. Now the mystery was solved! It occurred to him that a certain Michisada, an officer in the Imperial Secretariat, whom Niou also employed to look after his books and papers, had married the daughter of one of Kaoru's household retainers. Probably he could throw light on the subject. Niou sent for the man and asked him to look out some volumes of poetry suitable for the rhyme-covering game and put them on one of the shelves in the room where he was sitting. "I hear Kaoru is still going regularly to Uji," he said casually. "They say the temple he has been building there is very fine. I wish I could see it." "Yes, my father-in-law tells me it is a magnificent place," said Michisada; "there's a chapel of Perpetual Meditation† and I don't know what else besides. He planned the whole thing himself. He has been going there much more frequently in the last few months. I heard about it through one of the under-servants only the other day. The man told someone in confidence that His Excellency is keeping a woman at Uji now. It's certainly someone he thinks a great deal of, for the people on his

---

* Pun on *mata,* "fork," and *mada,* "not yet."
† A place of retreat for those who wished to enter into long periods of religious trance.

estates near by have orders to provide everything she needs, supply watchmen for the house, and even go secretly to the City if she fancies anything that isn't to be had on the spot. 'She's lucky, of course,' the man[*] said, 'but between times she can't find life at a place like that very amusing. It was just before New Year that he was telling someone about it.'"

"That is very interesting," said Niou. "I suspected something of the kind, but have never heard anything definite before. I was always told that the old nun Ben no Kimi was the only person still living there." "The nun," said Michisada, "has retired to a side-wing. It is this lady I spoke of who occupies the part of the house he has just rebuilt. They say she has any number of gentlewomen to wait upon her—all very well dressed and so on; the whole place, it appears, is being run on the most lavish scale." "What a queer business!" said Niou, "I wonder who she is and—for that matter—what he keeps her there for? Of course, if he were anyone else, the whole thing would be natural enough. But, as I dare say you know, he has always had the most extraordinary ideas about women. The Minister of the Left[†] is becoming quite worried about it. He is certain the way Kaoru lives is doing his reputation a great deal of harm. The fact is, he says, the people don't like a man in Kaoru's responsible position to be too religious. No one would mind his spending an occasional night at a mountain temple; but he oughtn't to make a habit of it. I have always been certain myself that there must be some other explanation for these constant visits to Uji. Many people believe that he went out of devotion to the memory of that elder daughter of Prince Hachi, the one that died years ago; and all the time this other affair was going on! He certainly is the most baffling creature. How can he have the face to go about pretending to be superior to all this sort of thing? Just think of the amount of time and trouble it must have cost him to arrange this business! It's unbelievable that anyone can be such a humbug." But there seemed no reason to disbelieve Michisada's story, for his father-in-law Nakanobu was one of Kaoru's most trusted retainers, and was certain to be well informed about such a matter.

Niou's one thought was how to discover whether this girl at Uji was indeed the same as the one who had vanished from the Nijo-in. The way the establishment at Uji was being run made it certain that she was not of the ordinary waiting-woman class. If the identification were correct, it would seem as though she had some connection with Kozeri and almost as though Kozeri and Kaoru had hatched the plot between them.

The thing obsessed him. All through the great Archery Meeting and the Imperial Literary Banquet he could think of nothing else, and during the quieter period that followed, the numerous visitors who hoped to

---

[*] The under-servant.
[†] Yugiri.

secure his support in connection with the forthcoming New Year appointments received only the most casual attention, Niou's thoughts being almost entirely occupied with plans for a secret visit to Uji. It happened that Michisada was hoping for a new appointment and was therefore particularly anxious at the moment to ingratiate himself with his master. He noticed one day that Niou was treating him with unusual affability. "There's something I want you to manage for me. I am afraid it may not prove to be very easy," Niou suddenly said to him. The man made a low bow. "It's a thing I hardly like to trouble you about," Niou continued. "You remember our conversation the other day about that girl at Uji? I strongly suspect she is someone I know. Everything seems to fit in. My friend suddenly disappeared, and I am almost certain it was Kaoru who made off with her. There seems to be only one way of settling the question: I must go to Uji and have a look at her for myself. I am afraid it won't be very easy; but of course there's no need for me actually to meet her. A single glance would be enough. Naturally no one must know that I have been there. Do you think you could possibly arrange it for me?" "To begin with," said Michisada, to whom such a commission did not at all appeal, "there's the question of how you're to get there. It's right across the mountains, and there's only a very rough road. Of course the actual distance is not very great. Suppose, for example, you left here in the afternoon; you would probably be there by midnight and could be back in the City before people were about. No one need know about it except the servants you took with you, and they of course need not be told why you were going." "Oh, it's not the idea of the journey that's worrying me," said Niou. "As a matter of fact I've been there several times before. The difficulty is that Their Majesties don't like my going about on my own. They're always thinking I shall get into a scrape of some kind and disgrace the Imperial family." Time after time Niou decided that such an expedition would be mere folly, considering how little was to be gained by it and how exceedingly unpleasant the consequences if anything went wrong. However, he had definitely asked Michisada to arrange it and did not like to back out. He was to be attended by two or three men who had been with him to Uji before, and by a few trusted retainers, including Michisada and a young son of Niou's old nurse, who had just been promoted to the Fifth Rank.

Michisada had previously ascertained that there was no chance of Kaoru's being at Uji either that day or the next. Niou went in his carriage as far as the Hosoji, and there changed to horseback. It all seemed strangely familiar. Who was he with that second time? Why, of course, with Kaoru; and he became slightly uncomfortable when he remembered all the trouble his friend had taken to bring him and Kozeri together. "I am afraid he would think this rather an odd way of repaying his kindness," Niou said to himself. Even in the Capital his position made it extremely difficult for him to amuse himself as he chose, and he was used to going about at night with the utmost secrecy. But the present occasion demanded even greater precautions. He was heavily disguised, in clothes of a most awkward and unsightly kind, and was compelled to sit for hours in the saddle—a thing he particularly disliked. But he had a vast fund of curiosity, and as they drew nearer and nearer to Uji his excitement became so intense that he hardly noticed the tedious windings of the mountain-road. How was it going to turn out? Was it so certain after all that it was his girl? However, that did not really matter. He only wanted to know. But was that all? Certainly if she proved to be someone different he would feel extremely flat on the way home.

They kept up a good pace, and it was only just after midnight when they arrived at Uji. Michisada, owing to his connections with the house, had been able to find out something about the habits of the night-watchmen. It appeared that his best chance of evading them would be to approach the house on the western side, and now, leaving Niou behind, he crept up to the hedge that surrounded that part of the house and, gently breaking it down a little at a convenient place, managed to squeeze through. It was only after a good deal of stumbling and groping that he at last found his way to the house, for though he had undertaken to act as guide he had not, as a matter of fact, ever been there before. He felt his way round to the front of the building. Even here there did not seem to be a soul astir. But at one of the windows he presently noticed a very dim light and could hear a faint hum of whispered conversation. "They don't seem to have gone to bed yet," he reported to Niou. "You'd better get through the hedge where I did," and he led Niou to the lighted window. The shutters were fastened, and the light that Michisada had observed came through a fault in the wood. Niou raised himself gently onto a ledge and got as close as possible to the hole. A bamboo blind rustled as he did so, and startled him so much that he nearly lost his hold.

This part of the house had of course only just been rebuilt and everything ought to have been in perfect order. But somehow or other the overseers had passed a faulty piece of wood, and though it would have been easy enough to stop up the hole, that is the sort of thing that at quiet places like Uji no one ever bothers to do. There was a curtained couch inside; but the flaps were pinned back. Three or four women sat sewing, holding their work close to the lamp. A very pretty little girl was twisting thread into a ball. He could have sworn she was the child he met to start with that night, coming from the direction of the mysterious lady's rooms. However, children sometimes look very much alike and he was not absolutely sure, when he heard one of the women addressed as "Ukon." He recognized her at once as the girl who had come to close the shutters and had almost fallen over him in the dark. Last of all his eye lit upon the lady herself. There she was, her head pillowed on her arm, gazing towards the lamp. He should have known her at once, if only by the way those thick locks fell across her forehead. Surely she must be in some way connected with Prince Hachi's family. She certainly had something of Kozeri's distinction and charm.

"It isn't as though you could be there today and back tomorrow," Ukon was saying, while she plied her needle. "I wouldn't risk it if I were in your place. The messenger who came yesterday said that he[*] would certainly be coming here the moment all the new appointments were published. Not later than the first[†] in any case. But didn't he say anything about it in his letter?"

The lady made no reply. She looked very depressed. "Well, I don't know what he'll think if he comes and finds you've run off like this just when he was expected," Ukon continued. "If you're really going you'd better write at once and let him know," another of the women said. "You can't be so rude as just to slip off without a word. And when the pilgrimage is over don't let your mother take you home. I'm sure that's what she'll try to do. Come straight back here and try to get used to the place. I'm sure I don't know why you should have taken against it. You must admit we could hardly be more comfortable; everyone for miles round seems to be at our beck and call. I don't think you'd be very happy at home now you've got so used to having everything your own way." "I wouldn't go at all if I were you," another said. "I should just stay here quietly and make the best of it. You'll have time enough to see your mother later on, when he brings you to live in the City. I know who put this idea into your head. It's Nurse; she's always in such a hurry. Don't you listen to her. They say patience brings its reward; and certainly without it no one ever yet did any good in the world." "Nanny is getting old," said Ukon. "It's a pity we ever let her suggest it. She's really becoming very tiresome." With this judgment Niou could cordially agree. He remembered what a nuisance some old woman—no doubt the nurse they were talking of—had made of herself that night. It was all like a strange dream. Before long Ukon's remarks became so personal as to be embarrassing. "Niou's lady," she said, "is getting on very nicely nowadays. Of course it seemed a great disadvantage at first that she had the Minister of the Left always fussing round and doing everything in his power to make things unpleasant for her. But it seems that now she's got the child His Highness[‡] is treating her a lot better. That's a lesson for you, my lady!

---

[*] Kaoru.
[†] Of the second month.
[‡] Niou.

Where do you suppose she would be now if she'd listened to the advice of old busybodies like your nanny?" "There's no reason you shouldn't be quite as well off before long," another chimed in, "if you stay here quietly and don't do anything to make your gentleman change his mind." "How often have I asked you not to talk about me in that way?" the lady said at last, sitting up a little—"always pitting me against other people. I dislike it intensely. And please never discuss Princess Kozeri's affairs in that way. She would have every right to be very annoyed if it got round to her." Something in the way she spoke of Kozeri suggested that they were related. But in what way? Very closely, Niou thought, judging from the extraordinary resemblance. Of course Kozeri bore herself in a much more distinguished manner and her expression denoted a good deal more character and originality. But in actual beauty of feature this girl was quite her equal; he found her in fact extraordinarily attractive.

Even had she somewhat disappointed him, the mere fact that she had occupied his thoughts for so many weeks—and there was no longer any doubt of the identity—would have been sufficient to make him feel very disappointed if the matter went no farther. Small wonder then if, confronted at last with a creature in whom even his experienced eye could detect no flaw, he was in a torment of impatience to make her his.

He had gathered that she was starting next day on a pilgrimage, and was to be fetched by her mother. Once she had left Uji he would not have the least idea where to look for her. It was in all probability a case of tonight or never. A thousand wild schemes rushed through his head, but as though rooted to the spot he continued to stare through his hole. "I'm feeling very sleepy," Ukon said presently. "I don't know why I should sit up all night like this. There'll be plenty of time to finish these things tomorrow; however early they start, the carriage* can't be here till late in the morning." She folded the things she had been sewing and hung them carefully across the top of the couch; then, apparently unable to keep her eyes open any longer, she sank onto a cushion and began at once to doze. The lady went and lay down on a couch in a recess at the far side of the room, and presently Ukon, waking with a start, went into the back room for a minute or two, and when she returned, settled herself for the night close behind her mistress's bed. A moment later it was obvious that she was sound asleep. There was no point in staying where he was. In fact only two courses were open to him: either he must give the whole thing up and go home, or else get someone to open the shutter, for it was firmly barred on the inside. He knocked, gently at first and then louder. Ukon heard. "Who is it?" she asked. He coughed, not with a vulgar noise but in the discreet manner that belongs to persons of refinement. Not doubting

---

* The carriage in which Ukifune's mother was coming to fetch her.

for an instant that Kaoru had suddenly arrived, she sprang up and came to the window. "I'm locked out," he whispered. "I'm very sorry," she said. "But we understood you would not be coming today. And in any case it's surely rather an odd hour to arrive?" "Nakanobu came to me tonight," he whispered, "with some story about a pilgrimage. He said you were starting tomorrow morning, so naturally I rushed off at once—though of course it was terribly inconvenient. I'm still locked out," he reminded her. He spoke in so low a whisper and imitated Kaoru's tricks of speech so well that Ukon was completely taken in, and hastened to undo the catch. "I had a rather unpleasant and alarming experience* on my way here," he explained, "and have arrived in the most extraordinary get-up. I'm not really fit to be seen, so please take away that light." The shutters were now open, but he was still crouching outside. Ukon was deeply concerned. It must have been a terrible adventure indeed that could reduce anyone to such a plight as he described. She hastened to remove the light. "That's right," he said. "I would much rather no one saw me. Please don't wake people and tell them I am here." He was so plausible, and now he had got into the swing of it was managing to imitate Kaoru's voice and manner so successfully that, though he was standing only a few yards away from her in the darkened room, Ukon had no suspicion that anything was amiss. From the way he had spoken of the condition he was in she was afraid he must have suffered some appalling disfigurement, and was frightened to look his way at all. But at last she plucked up courage to peep from behind a screen and was in time to see a slim figure in a soft closely fitting robe steal lithely across the room, undress and install himself at her mistress's side. She did indeed notice a very strong perfume as he passed. This, however, was entirely consistent with supposing that the visitor was Kaoru. "Are you going to stay there?" she asked, surprised that they did not retire to their usual couch. Receiving no answer, she pushed some bed-clothes towards them and waking some gentle-women who were asleep near by, she sent them into an adjoining room. Kaoru of course always brought with him a certain number of retainers and attendants; but it occurred to no one to ask what had now become of them, for they always spent the night in the part of the house occupied by the old nun. "Just fancy his travelling all through the night like this," said one of the gentlewomen while they were settling down, "and then she talks as though he didn't do his duty by her! Some people are never satisfied." "You hussy, you ought to be ashamed of yourself, talking in that way about your mistress," Ukon protested. "And you'd better be careful what you say," she added. "One can hear every whisper in this house at night."

---

* Such as meeting bandits or the like.

Ukifune saw at once that it was not Kaoru; but Niou was holding her fast in his arms before she could so much as utter a cry. The preliminaries, he considered, had already been got over at the Nijo-in; here he could let himself go. Had he allowed a single instant to elapse between his onslaught and the moment when she first discovered that he was not Kaoru, she might have done something to save herself. But now that the worst had happened, what use was it to cry for help? "...ever since we met in the autumn..." fragments of what he was saying drifted through her stupor. "Why were you so unkind to me that night?" she heard him ask. It was Niou! The truth had dawned upon her at last, and she was appalled. As for herself, she had ceased to care what became of her; but Kozeri... that was too horrible to think of. She burst into tears. For a very different reason Niou too was weeping; she had proved even more desirable than he expected, and he was profoundly depressed at the thought that he might never have such an opportunity again.

It was now growing light, and his attendants were calling to him. Ukon heard them, and came into the room. Niou, needless to say, would much rather have stayed where he was. It was difficult enough to escape, and having done so he would gain nothing by returning before nightfall. No doubt at the Palace a hue and cry had been raised long ago. But presumably they wished to get him back alive, and at the moment he definitely felt it would kill him to tear himself away. He sent for Ukon, no longer making any attempt to conceal his identity. "People may think what they please," he said, "but I intend to stay here all day. You must find somewhere close at hand to hide my attendants; if anyone came they might be recognized. Tokikata* had better go to the City and say I am in retreat at a mountain temple. If he is asked any questions he can tell whatever story he pleases, so long as it hangs together."

Ukon stared at him dumbfounded. It was an inexplicable, an appalling mistake that she had made last night, and she almost fainted at the thought of the dreadful consequences that her carelessness had entailed. But to denounce the intruder at this late stage, or indeed to make a fuss of any kind, could do no possible good; moreover, it was not for her to keep Royal Princes in order, much as they might need it. The fact that all these months after the incident at the Nijo-in he should have taken so much pains to track her down showed at any rate that Ukifune had made a deep impression on him. She consoled herself, finally, with the thought that so wild a scheme could hardly have been successful unless Fate† had decided that they should meet, in which case human interference would have been of no avail.

---

* One of Niou's attendants.

† Literally the *karma* of their previous incarnations.

"I suppose you've heard," she said, "that my lady is starting on a pilgrimage today. Her mother is sending to fetch her and the carriage may be here at any moment. I am not going to say anything myself about the way you have seen fit to treat my lady. Maybe you were bound to come together anyway, and it's no use people struggling against what's decreed by Fate. But I am afraid that is not the view her mother will take. In fact, you've chosen the one morning that's no good. Surely you had better go home now; you can come and see her quietly some other time—that's to say, if you are still feeling inclined to. As a matter of fact, it's the rarest thing in the world for her to be absent or engaged."

Niou was not to be cajoled so easily. "Listen," he said, "I've been thinking about her for months, day and night, the whole time—I've been almost out of my senses. And do you suppose that now I have found her at last I care what her mother or anyone else may think? I am in love with her, madly in love. You don't seem to know what that means. It's no use talking to me about what people will think or say. If I cared the least bit about that, I should never have come here at all. Besides, it's quite easy to deal with her mother. Tell her that your mistress is under a *mono-imi*,[*] or anything else you choose—except the truth; unless indeed you are bent on making trouble for both of us." It astounded her to hear anyone in Niou's position talk so recklessly; she could only put it down to his being, as he himself insisted, wildly, frantically in love.

Michisada now came to her and asked if she knew when Niou would be ready. Ukon explained the situation. "I wish you'd make him see how awkward it is for us," she said. "I think all you gentlemen are very much to blame. You know quite well that he couldn't do any of these wild things unless you backed him up. I am sure I don't know how you managed to get him into the grounds at all—scrambling into people's gardens like a pack of naughty urchins! You ought to be ashamed of yourselves. Nice things the workmen and gardeners will say of him!"

Looking back upon it Michisada was obliged to confess to himself that the escapade had indeed been rather disgraceful. He stood looking a trifle embarrassed. "Which of you is Tokikata?" Ukon asked. He came forward, and she gave him Niou's instructions.[†] "I don't think I should have had the courage to stay here much longer in any case," he said laughing. "There's nothing I dislike so much as being scolded. But, seriously—he's got a way when he is really excited about anything of making one feel that nothing else in the world matters at all. One would give one's life to help him... But I must make haste or the watchmen will see me go," and he hurried off to the City.

---

[*] A taboo.
[†] To go to the City and say that Niou was at a mountain temple.

To Ukon fell the task of concealing Niou's presence from the rest of the household. The other gentlewomen were now getting up. "The moment I saw him," Ukon said to them, "I noticed that he wasn't quite as usual. He seemed not to want to show himself. No wonder, poor gentleman! He had a terrible experience on the way. He has had to send to town for fresh clothes." There were murmurs of horror and commiseration. "Of course it's a dreadful thing," one lady said. "But I've been expecting it for a long time. That Mount Kohata has a very bad reputation. Ben no Kimi's people tell me he didn't bring any of his usual servants with him. I suppose he thought it would make things worse if he were recognized. Fancy his having been through all that. It's really terrible." "Now mind, all of you," Ukon said, "not a word about this to any of the under-servants, or we shall have them all too scared to do their work."

So far all seemed to be going well, but Ukon felt none too comfortable. For one thing, at any moment a messenger might arrive from Kaoru, which would be very awkward; and feeling that nothing short of a miracle could enable the imposture to be kept up safely all day, she prayed passionately to the Blessed Kwannon of Hatsuse.

The pilgrimage was to have been to Ishiyama. Her maids were to go with her and all of them had prepared themselves by fasting and prayer. It was a great disappointment to hear that the whole thing was postponed. Late in the morning Ukon went again to Ukifune's quarters and opened the shutters, but lowered all the blinds and pasted notices upon them with the word *mono-imi* written in large characters. But this would not keep out Ukifune's mother, who, though she had only premised to send a carriage, would most probably come in person, and Ukon put it about that Ukifune had had a disquieting dream.* As it was getting very late she thought she had better bring Ukifune her hot water and so on. The things were quite ordinary, but they struck Niou as exceedingly primitive. "Let me see you do it first," he said, when Ukifune offered them to him. Kaoru always retired discreetly at such moments. It was a new and rather flattering experience to be with someone who seemed unable to tear himself away for a single second. She felt indeed that till that night she had never really known what love meant. It was a terrible position to find oneself in. Even if Kaoru never found out, there were other people—her mother, and worst of all Kozeri. What a tangle things were in!

"And all this time," Niou said, "I have not the least idea who you are. I think it is ridiculous of you not to tell me. You know quite well I shan't think the worse of you even if you tell me you are the lowest of the low. In fact, quite the contrary..." He asked her again and again, but to these questions she would give no reply. So soon, however, as this

---

* A dream warning her against seeing her near relations.

subject was dropped they got on famously together. She seemed to be completely at her ease with him, made some very amusing remarks, and proved indeed to be in every way the most delightful companion he had ever encountered.

The people sent to fetch her arrived towards midday. The mother was to be picked up later. There were two carriages, accompanied by the usual rough-looking horsemen. Their arrival was as embarrassing to the other ladies* as it was to Ukon. There were seven or eight of them and a wild-looking mob they seemed as they rode in, jabbering to one another all the while in their clipped, eastern jargon, and someone ran out immediately and begged them to retire to a corner where they could not be seen from the house. Ukon's first impulse was to tell them that Kaoru was there, but she saw on reflection that this would be a very unsafe thing to do, for the goings and comings of anyone in Kaoru's high position were sure to be pretty generally known at the Capital, and without consulting the other ladies she wrote a note for Ukifune's mother: "Yesterday evening I am sorry to say my lady's period came on unexpectedly,† and during the night she had a dream of such a disquieting sort that I felt she ought to be very careful today, and have arranged for a *mono-imi*. Of course it's a great pity, but I am sure it is wiser to take this precaution." She handed the men this note, and having seen to it that they were given some food, sent them away. To Ben no Kimi she told the same story. The whole of this perfect spring day was theirs, but to Niou it seemed to be going by in a flash; and it was a strange experience for Ukifune, to whom evening after evening at this place it had seemed as though the sun would never set behind the misty hills, to find herself, with him at her side, aghast at the speed with which the shadows grew. He for his part would have been content to sit gazing at her forever. What was it about her, he wondered, that so much attracted him? She was not really as good-looking as Kozeri, and no doubt in the fashionable world to which Roku no Kimi‡ belonged she would be entirely eclipsed; but for the moment he lost all sense of proportion, and despite his extremely varied experience it was as though he had never seen a beautiful girl before. As for Ukifune, it was beginning to occur to her that, much as she admired Kaoru, the world might after all contain other people equally handsome and charming.

Presently Niou drew the ink-slab towards him and began tracing characters with a dexterity that could not fail to fascinate a young girl. Then he drew pictures for her, a thing he was very good at. "You must look at this one sometimes when I am prevented from being here with you,"

---

* Who still thought that the visitor was Kaoru and that he had been kept in ignorance of the intended pilgrimage.

† Which on ritual grounds rendered the pilgrimage impossible.

‡ Daughter of Yugiri. She was Niou's other consort.

he said, showing her a pretty drawing of two lovers lying together. "If only we could always be together like this!" he sighed. "'Always,' I say! Yet in a world so frail even 'tomorrow' were a pledge that mocked the sanctity of love!" "I know it is terrible to speak of such things now; but I really do feel that if I can't see you whenever I want to—if I can only be smuggled into the house once in a way when no one happens to be here, it will kill me. It would have been better if I had left things as they were after that first meeting and never tracked you down." She took up the writing-brush, which was still wet, and wrote: "Were there no other thing but life itself uncertain in this world, how happy then were this our mortal state!"* Looking over her shoulder as she wrote these words he felt that she really needed his love and would mind very much indeed if he gave her up.

"How much experience have you, I should like to know, of people's affections changing?" he asked, laughing. He was very curious to discover how her relationship with Kaoru had begun, but she refused to tell him anything about it. "You've done that before," she said, rather pettishly. "Directly you see I don't wish to talk about something, you start pestering me about it." There were plenty of other ways he could find out, but somehow he felt that there would be a curious sort of satisfaction in hearing the story from her own lips. At nightfall Tokikata returned from the Capital. "I found a deputation from the Empress asking what had become of him," he reported to Ukon, "and a very stiff message from the Minister of the Left:† 'His Highness has no business to go off like this without telling anyone. He's too casual altogether, and inconsiderate towards me too, for when Their Majesties hear about this kind of thing it is always I who get into trouble,' and more to the same effect. I told them that Prince Niou had gone to visit the Hermit of the Eastern Hills." "There," Tokikata continued, "you see now that it's you women who are at the bottom of all the wickedness that goes on in the world. And it isn't only their lovers they send to perdition; here am I, who don't know the lady at all, telling lies to save her reputation." "It was a good lie anyway," said Ukon. "Fancy you even finding the hermit a name! So much the better for him. They say it's no sin to be the cause of a pious lie. But tell me, has he always been like this? I was never so taken aback in my life. Not that I could have done much under the circumstances, even if I had known he was coming. One daren't be rough with people like that, and it certainly wouldn't have been any use trying to argue with him." Having dealt with Tokikata, Ukon went to Niou and reported what the man had said. Niou saw that things were going to be made very unpleas-

---

* I.e. love is even more uncertain.
† Yugiri.

ant for him on his return. "How I wish I could turn into an ordinary person for a little while!" he said afterwards to Ukifune. "I am sick to death of all this fuss. You see for yourself what these people* are like; it's absolutely impossible to hide anything from them. I'm worried about Kaoru too. Circumstances, of course, have always brought us together a great deal; but quite apart from that I am in fact very fond of him and should hate him to feel that I had treated him badly. Not that I really have—for it's obvious that if he really cared for you he wouldn't leave you moping here for weeks on end. But the last thing likely to occur to him is that it's he who's to blame. The only thing to do will be to take you to some absolutely secret place where no one will dream of looking for you. We can't go on meeting here." The night was almost over, and though he knew that to leave now would be like wrenching body from soul, to spend a second day in the same delightful manner was out of the question. His attendants were impatient to get him started before daybreak, and at last he rose to go. Ukifune went with him as far as the big double-doors. "How can I hope through tortuous hills to trace the unbeaten way, when even at your door so dark a veil of tears blots out the road?" Such was his poem; and she: "Would that my sleeve were wide enough† to check my own poor tears; then might I hope to stay the parting that you dread."

It was a dismal business, this farewell in the dim morning light, with an icy wind howling and everything soaked with dew. Even after he had mounted his horse, Tokikata and the rest had the greatest difficulty in getting him started. But things were getting beyond a joke. It was absolutely essential that he should be back in the Capital well before midday, and there was no time to lose. He was in no condition to look after himself, and until they got safely into the plain Michisada and Tokikata, who were the two officers of highest rank in the party, led his horse by the bridle, walking one on each side. At one point their path lay along a frozen river-bed, and he thought he had never heard a more melancholy sound than the ringing of the ice under his horse's hoofs. It was this same mountain-road—the only one in fact that he knew—which in days gone by had carried him to Kozeri. It seemed as if some strange tie linked him to that obscure village.

On arriving at the Nijo-in he went and lay down in his own room. He did not feel inclined to see Kozeri, whom he felt more than ever had behaved very badly in hiding this girl‡ away. But he could not get to sleep, and feeling badly in need of company, he was reduced at last to

---

* The Empress, Yugiri, etc.
† I.e. that I were a person of sufficient importance for you to accept openly.
‡ Ukifune.

going to Kozeri's rooms. She did not seem to have been at all upset at his sudden disappearance. He had indeed seldom seen her looking so well and handsome, and his first thought was that, whatever he might have felt during the infatuation of the moment, Kozeri was really a thousand times better-looking than that other girl. But the resemblance between them was so strong that being with the one only made him all the unhappier at losing the other, and, flinging himself onto Kozeri's couch, he lay there silently brooding. Presently she came and lay by his side. "I am not at all well," he said. "It's worrying; I feel it may turn out to be something serious. What shall you do if I die? Of course it would really be rather convenient for you. You'd be able to do what you've always been wanting to."* There was nothing in his manner to suggest that he was not speaking perfectly seriously. "You realize, don't you," she said, "that it would be most unpleasant for me if it got round to Kaoru that you say things like that. He would only be able to account for it by supposing that I had given you a quite untrue idea of the sort of terms we are on. And if you are joking, I can only say that I have had too many troubles in life much to appreciate jokes of that kind." She turned over and lay with her back to him.

"If you can't bear me to mention the subject even when you see that I am joking," Niou said, "what would happen, I wonder, if you thought I was in earnest? After all, I have done a good deal for you—far too much, some people think.† I have never hidden from myself the fact that you much prefer him.‡ I can quite understand that; you seem to be made for one another.§ All I mind is your trying to hide it from me." "Made for one another...." When, Niou asked himself, had he last used just that phrase? Why, of course, to the girl at Uji only a few hours ago; and remembering their parting he burst into tears.

Evidently he had just heard something that had very much upset him—something apparently about herself and Kaoru. She did not attempt to reply. It was grossly unfair that, because their own relationship had begun in rather an informal way, he should regard her as completely immoral. Nor indeed was the match so very informal. Kaoru had introduced them, and the only irregularity of the proceeding consisted in the fact that he was not a parent or guardian but only a friend.¶ It would be monstrous indeed if Niou allowed such a thing as that to lower her in his estimation.

---

* Go off with Kaoru.

† Roku no Kimi's supporters.

‡ Kaoru.

§ Literally: "Your relationship is decreed by previous *karma*"; but the phrase, like the English equivalent I have used, had outworn its theological implications.

¶ I take the whole emphasis of the sentence to be on *suzuro-naru hito*, but this is not the common interpretation.

He saw that she was looking very disheartened, and felt sorry for her. He did not want, at any rate for the present, to tell her about his adventure at Uji; but she was bound to notice that something was wrong, and he had merely dragged up the subject of Kaoru in order to put her off the scent. However, he seemed so much more serious about it than usual that Kozeri was certain something definite must have happened; someone must be spreading completely untrue stories about her. It was clear that Niou believed them, and until she had got to the bottom of the matter, she felt she would rather not see him.

Presently it was announced that a letter had arrived from Her Majesty the Empress. He got up and, without any of his usual tender words to Kozeri, went off to his own rooms. "What became of you yesterday?" his mother wrote. "The Emperor was expecting you all day. He kept on asking where you were. I can see he is quite upset about it. Unless for some reason it is absolutely impossible, I should strongly advise you to come round to the Palace immediately. As for myself—I hardly dare to think how long it is since I set eyes on you..." and so on. He was sorry to have agitated them; but it was really perfectly true that he was not feeling up to appearing in society. Another day passed, and still he played truant from Court. Numerous visitors called to enquire; but he would see nobody and spent the day lying listlessly on his curtained bed. Towards nightfall, however, Kaoru was announced, and Niou asked for him to be shown in. "You'll excuse my not getting up?" he said. "I heard you weren't well," Kaoru said. "That is why I came. Your mother's rather worried about you.* You didn't give her any idea what sort of illness it is." But it was very difficult to get anything out of him. The truth was that at the moment he found Kaoru's presence very agitating. But though his conscience sorely pricked him, he could not help feeling rather indignant. This, if you please, was the fellow who had managed to persuade the world that he was some sort of mountain-yogi, whose whole life was spent in prayer and fasting! And then, having purloined a charming girl, simply to deposit her miles away from anywhere and leave her to her own devices for months on end... Kaoru's pretensions to complete indifference about women had never convinced him, and in the past he had often tried to expose them. He naturally felt strongly tempted to let Kaoru know that the time had come for him to drop once and for all this irritating veil of hypocrisy. But when it came to the point he could not bring himself to do so.

He certainly did not look at all himself, Kaoru thought. "I'm awfully sorry about this," he said. "Of course, I'm sure it's not really anything much; but it seems to be rather difficult to shake off. You must take great

---

* Evidently Niou had written to the Empress giving the excuse that he was ill.

care of yourself." "I wish I were as handsome as that," Niou thought, as he watched the visitor depart. "I don't see how she can help preferring him." For he now related everything to his chances of success at Uji.

Meanwhile life, for Ukifune and her ladies, had resumed its usual monotony now that even the Ishiyama project had fallen through. Desperate letters from Niou arrived with extreme frequency. It was arranged that, as a precaution, they should be brought by a servant of Tokikata's, who had no idea either for whom they were really intended or from whom they came. They were directed to Ukon. "It's an old lover of mine," she explained. "He has suddenly turned up among Kaoru's attendants and seems anxious for us to get back onto our old terms." She was growing so used to inventing stories of this kind that it had ceased to give her any trouble. The month drew to a close, and still Niou had not revisited Uji. Again and again he planned a secret escape; but each time, just when his arrangements were complete, he found himself prevented from leaving the City. He was not at all well. In fact, he felt that the continual worry was slowly killing him, so that to his other woes was added a constant anxiety about his own condition.

At last the pressure of public business relaxed a little, and Kaoru was able to find time for a short visit to Uji. He went first to the temple, and after performing his prostrations before the Buddha-images and other objects of veneration, listening to a recitation of the Scriptures, and distributing presents among the priests, towards evening he made his way to Ukifune's rooms. He too, no doubt, had been obliged to come secretly, but not in disguise. On the contrary he was dressed rather smartly in *eboshi** and flowing gown. And how different the manner of his entry! A feeling of constraint came over her. For some reason she felt frightened of him—frightened to submit herself to his cool, deliberate inspection, she who had fallen so easy a prey to Niou's boisterous love-making! "Since meeting you I have lost all interest in other women and have broken with them completely, though some of them I had been seeing constantly for years." So Niou said in one of his letters; and apparently it was no exaggeration, for she had heard from other sources that he had put it about he was unwell and could see nobody. He seemed to be constantly fussing about all sorts of rituals and ceremonies,† which people said was very unlike him. What would he think if he knew that Kaoru was with her at this moment? Kaoru took great trouble in explaining all the reasons that had obliged him to leave her to herself for so long, and though unlike Niou he used no violent expressions about "unbearable torments," "dying of love," and so on, she felt that it really did very much distress him to see

---

* A black bonnet, the crown of which folded back over the side.
† On behalf of his own health.

so little of her. It was indeed in this habit of restraint that lay the secret of his extraordinary persuasiveness, a few quiet words of his carrying far more conviction than other people's most emphatic oaths and assurances. Viewed simply as a lover he was not, she now realized, very satisfactory; but there could be no question which of the two would in the long run make the better friend and supporter. The thought that Kaoru might at any moment discover what was happening appalled her. It was exciting, of course, to find oneself the object of love so stormy and passionate as Niou's. But for both of them it was an escapade, no more; they would soon learn to do without one another. But to hurt Kaoru, to let him feel that she did not need him any more—no, it was unthinkable, those feelings went far too deep. Come what might, if he were to forsake her she would feel utterly alone.

She seemed, Kaoru thought, to be in rather a nervous, agitated condition. In fact she had changed a good deal since his last visit. She struck him, somehow, as far less childish and immature. But it would not do to leave her too long in this lonely place where she had nothing to do but sit and brood. It was not to be wondered at that she had fallen into rather a morbid condition; he must try to cheer her up. "I have good news for you," he said. "The place I am finishing for you in the Capital is nearly ready. I was there only the other day. I am sure you will like it. There is a river; but it won't frighten you as this one does—it runs quietly through flowery meadows. My mother's palace is only a few steps away. I am longing to have you somewhere close at hand, where I can come to see you every day, and I hope if all goes well to move you in before the end of next month."

By a strange coincidence Niou, in a letter received only yesterday, had informed her that he had succeeded in finding "a quiet little house, just the place he was looking for..." Now, quite unwittingly, Kaoru had outbidden him. Well, this meant that to all intents and purposes her relation with Niou was at an end. That perhaps was a good thing. But suddenly his image rose up before her, she felt again his touch, the pressure of his limbs... "I am terribly unhappy," she said, and burst into tears. Kaoru looked at her with astonishment. "I can't understand what has come over you," he said. "You used always to be so sensible and patient; it was a great comfort. I can only suppose someone has been telling you lies about me. All I can say is this: considering how bad the roads are and how difficult it is for anyone in a ministerial position to get away for more than a few hours, do you suppose I should ever come at all if I were not extremely fond of you?" He took her to the window to watch the new moon rise. How many times had he stood there with Agemaki! And while his thoughts wandered back to old days, hers dwelt with desperation on this new entanglement: she had seen chequered days, but other troubles had come and gone, from this there could be no imaginable escape. A mist lay over the hills and outlined against it was the figure of a heron stiffly poised on a bare ledge of rock. The bridge lay shimmering in the mist, looking a long way off. Now and again a boat would pass under it, laden with timber. "A strange, a haunting place—this Uji," Kaoru thought. One seemed to hear and see at the very door so many things that one came across nowhere else; which made it all the harder coming back like this, to shake off the past. So many associations indeed had every bend of the river, every tree, that even had Ukifune not been who she was, it would have moved him intensely to find himself here at such an hour. Small wonder then if the company of one who resembled so strangely the lady he had loved and who, to his delight, was now fast losing the backwardness and rusticity that had at first disguised this resemblance, Kaoru lost himself in memories of the past. But do what she would, Ukifune could not check her tears, and trying in vain to console her he recited the verse: "Step lightly past the gaps. Be not afraid that Uji Bridge will fall, for long as time itself shall those stout planks endure." "You will soon see," he added. "Since gaps it is, naught else, that in the world of love are perilous, how can I trust the Bridge of Uji to hold fast?" Such was her answer to his verse.

He had never felt so loath to leave her, but today there were urgent reasons for his return—as indeed was likely to be the case each time he came. Fortunately, however, there seemed to be every hope of moving her from here before very long. He left at dawn, meditating as he rode. She seemed suddenly to have left childhood behind, which made her a far more interesting companion. In a way, however, he found it painful; for she was beginning now to remind him almost too much of Agemaki.

A Chinese-poetry competition was held in the Palace on the tenth day of the second month. Kaoru and Niou were both present. The proceedings opened with a concert of appropriate music. Niou sang the "Plum Tree"[*] so admirably that people felt there was no line in which he could not have excelled if he chose; it was a thousand pities that so much of his time was frittered away in pointless philandering. A sudden snowstorm brought the concert to an abrupt end. Niou retired to his own official apartments,[†] where he was presently joined by Kaoru and other friends. After refreshments had been served they all lay down and rested. At nightfall someone went out for a moment, apparently to give a message, and remained standing by the window, his figure outlined against a sky in which the stars shone faintly through the falling snow. Niou too had woken, and even "in the darkness of the spring night" he could not fail

---

[*] See Part V, p. 779.

[†] Allotted to him in the Emperor's Palace.

instantly to recognize whose the figure was. What lines were those that Kaoru was murmuring to himself, there by the window, apparently with the deepest emotion? "Tonight too on half-spread cloak..."* Those were the few words he caught; but there could be no mistaking the allusion, and though Niou instantly lay back and pretended to be asleep, his mind was in reality a ferment of activity. Kaoru then did after all feel strongly about her! "I have judged him unfairly," Niou said to himself. "I took for granted that it was only I to whom the thought of her waiting there night after night was painful." In a way he was touched at the discovery that someone else felt exactly as he did. Yet at the same time he was in despair. For if Kaoru really cared for her seriously, what chances had he of ousting such a lover?

Next morning the snow lay so deep that it was quite difficult to get to Court. Everyone thought that when he appeared before the Throne to hand in his poem Niou was looking particularly well and handsome. Kaoru, though there was only a year or two's difference between them, had an air of circumspection and responsibility that on these occasions always made him appear considerably Niou's senior. It was agreed that he was the perfect pattern of aristocratic dignity and refinement; the Emperor certainly could not have made a better choice.† It was seldom one found such erudition‡ combined with a high degree of practical capacity.

When the poems had been read out and commented upon, the company dispersed. People crowded round Niou assuring him that his was by far the best. He had no idea what he had said, nor indeed how he had managed to produce anything at all, for his thoughts had all the time been far away. So disquieted was he by his new discovery that a few days later, throwing prudence to the winds, he set out once more for Uji.

At the Capital only a few patches of snow lingered half-heartedly, but in the mountains it was still very deep. This made the narrow path more difficult than ever to find, and his attendants, often up to their waists in snow and forced continually to retrace their steps, would have been glad indeed to be back in their beds. Michisada, besides the post he held at the Palace, was also under-secretary at the Board of Rites, and it was hardly in keeping with his dignity that he should be forced to tuck up his skirts and struggle through the snow like an ordinary coolie.

Niou had previously sent word that he was coming. But it was evident on his arrival that, owing no doubt to the very heavy snow, they were not expecting him. Moreover, the hour was extremely late. He sent in a message to Ukon who was astonished that he should even have attempted

---

* A reference to the old poem: "Tonight too, her cloak half-spread upon her mat, will she be waiting for me, the Maiden of Uji Bridge?"
† In selecting a husband for the Second Princess.
‡ A reference to Kaoru's Buddhist studies, etc.

the journey under such conditions, as was also her mistress. Ukon was becoming extremely worried at the situation that had arisen and realized more than ever how fatal it would be if the secret were to get out. But she was feeling the strain of managing the whole thing alone, and tonight, though if she had had the heart to she would much rather simply have sent Niou away, she took into her confidence a girl called Jiju, a sensible creature whom she knew Ukifune liked and trusted. Jiju promised faithfully not to say a word to anybody, and between the two of them they managed to smuggle Niou into the house without attracting attention. His clothes were wringing wet, and this, when he entered the warm house, brought out their perfume more strongly than ever, which under other circumstances would have been embarrassing, but in the present case rendered deception all the easier.

He had no mind to be driven out of the house as soon as it was light, and as Ukon could not guarantee to keep him successfully hidden during the day, when secrecy was obviously much more difficult, he arranged with Tokikata that a little house on the other side of the river should be put at his disposal. Shortly before dawn Tokikata came and announced that all was ready. "I think you'll be pleased with the place," he said. "What new folly was this?" Ukon wondered, as blinking and yawning she was once more dragged from her bed, and while she hastily put together Ukifune's things she found her teeth chattering like those of a tattered urchin driven out to play in the snow. "You'd better stay and look after things here. We'll take this girl with us," Niou said, pointing to Jiju, and without a word of explanation as to where they were going he picked up Ukifune in his arms and carried her out of the house. They seemed to be making straight for the river. Here lay the little boat that she had so often noticed from her window, wondering whether it was ever used; for it looked, she thought, very unsafe. Now they were pushing off. It seemed a terribly long way to the other shore; Niou felt her clutch at him in her alarm. It was a cloudless dawn; the; moon burnished the rippling waters that spread round them far and wide. "We will stop for a moment at the Island," Niou said, and presently they came to a great ledge of rock that had been converted into a kind of river-garden. "They call it the Orange-Tree Island," he said. "Isn't it amazing that they can get them to grow even on such a perch as that? Yet once give them their shovelful of soil and they will fill the place with green, summer and winter, for a thousand years." "Sooner shall you, O orange-tree who crown the little, island, shed your faithful leaves than this our love grow cold." Such was his poem; but she, still counting the hazards of the voyage on which they were embarked: "Faithful from spring to spring the orange-tree may keep its vow; but whither will have drifted the Lady of the Boat?" He did not resent her distrust, still less rebuke it; such indeed was the spell of the place and moment that nothing she said or did could do otherwise than enchant him.

When at last they disembarked on the far shore, though they had some way to go, he would not let anyone else carry her; but seeing that he walked rather unsteadily under the burden Tokikata followed close behind, and sometimes gave him a helping hand. Who was this woman, the man wondered, and how came she to be at Uji—a personage apparently of such exalted rank that no one but a Royal Prince might handle her? The place they were going to was on an estate belonging to Tokikata's uncle, the Governor of Inaba. It was simply a farm-building without fittings or furniture of any kind, save for a few rough wattled screens and other strange objects such as Niou had never seen before. It was very ill-protected against the wind. Great piles of half-melted snow blocked the courtyard, and more was falling.

The storm, however, was a short one. Soon a brilliant sun was shining, and Ukifune, sitting in the light that glinted from the icicles under the eaves, looked lovelier than he had ever seen her. Both of them were very simply dressed, for he was in the hunting-cloak that he had used on the journey as a disguise, and she, when the sun came out, had slipped off her mantle and was looking particularly slim and pretty in her plain white under dress. She was feeling, however, very disheveled and untidy, and longed to put herself to rights. But there seemed to be nowhere she could retire to, and she had to make up her mind to face him just as she was. As a matter of fact he saw nothing to criticize. He found her simple costume far more pleasing than those elaborate confections in which, down sleeve and skirt, fold chimes with fold in every imaginable harmony of texture and hue. Never would Roku no Kimi have dared to show herself to him in this guise. No, nor Kozeri either. But this girl certainly stood the test. Jiju too, he thought, was by no means bad-looking. "They haven't told me who you are," he said, turning to her, "which does not matter so much, as long as you don't say who I am. She was delighted at his condescending to address her. Ukifune, however, very much wished the girl was not there. How many more people, she wondered, was Ukon going to let into the secret?

A housekeeper was on the premises. He was allowed to think that Tokikata was the master, and Niou and the rest his servants. He therefore installed Tokikata in great state in the main room, shutting it off from the place where Niou was, and it so much tickled Tokikata to hear the deferential manner in which the fellow insisted upon addressing him that he could hardly keep a straight face. "You had better know why I have come here," he managed to say at last. "A soothsayer whom I consulted has unfortunately discovered that it would be extremely dangerous for me to remain anywhere inside the boundaries of the Capital. He said that for the present the safest thing I could do was to shut myself up and see nobody. So I must ask you to let me have the place to myself."

The housekeeper carried out his task to perfection. Not a soul was allowed to enter, and the lovers had a wonderful day. But these caresses, these tender speeches and pretty ways—supposing it had been Kaoru who had brought her here today—would she not as gladly have lavished them on him instead? Assuredly she would, Niou told himself bitterly, and in jealous spite began telling her about Kaoru's deferential attitude towards the Second Princess and his extreme fear of doing anything that might wound her pride. Complete candor would have obliged him also to mention the lines that he had heard Kaoru murmuring to himself that night at the Palace window. But to this episode Niou made no allusion. Tokikata had procured some fruit which he now served to them with his own hands, also bringing them some water to wash in. "You mustn't let our friend the housekeeper see you doing this sort of thing," said Niou, "or he will soon begin to discard some of the honorifics* I heard him heaping upon you this morning."

Jiju too had a very happy day, for she was not the sort of girl to let time hang on her hands when there was a man about, and an officer of the Fifth Rank!† She thought herself in luck's way indeed.

Looking out across the river, Ukifune saw that the air was again thick with snow; only a few treetops standing out above the mist marked the spot where the Uji mansion stood. But there was sun on the peaks that seemed to hang like mirrors in the glittering sky. Niou began to tell her more of the adventurous journey that had brought him to Uji last night. "Where snow-drifts were deepest, where the ice gave under my feet, unerringly I found my way; it was only about you that I was lost."‡ There was a rough sort of ink-slab in the house, and sending for it he did some hand-practice,§ choosing such lines as, "Though in the village of Kohata I could have got a horse."¶

"As a flake that the wind whirls skywards from the snow-drift on the frozen shore hangs in the air and vanishes, so shall I end my days," she wrote in characters that grew fainter and fainter, so that the words "in the air"** stood out from the rest, and at once caught Niou's eye. He colored slightly and picking up the distasteful poem tore it to shreds. But the

---

* Deferential verb-endings, etc.

† Tokikata.

‡ An untranslatable poem, depending for its point on the two senses of *madou* (1) to lose one's way, (2) to be madly in love.

§ Calligraphy.

¶ "....so impatient was I to see you that I came across the mountains on foot." Cf. *Manyoshu* 2425 (Book XI). But there are several versions of the poem.

** To be "in the air" means to "fall between two stools."

thought that she was still wavering so far from chilling his ardor only spurred him on. Already he had wooed her, he would have thought, to some purpose; tonight he would show her what love really was.

The pretext upon which he had obtained leave of absence from Court made it unnecessary for him to be back till late next day, so they had quite a long while together and felt that this time they had really got to know one another. Certainly he had found her more delightful than ever; and he felt that she too was becoming very fond of him. Today Ukon managed to smuggle in a parcel of clothes and so on. Ukifune was able to put her hair a little to rights, and her red plum-blossom mantle, worn over a dark-purple dress, made an agreeable effect. Jiju too appeared today quite smartly dressed. She had come in an odd sort of over-wrap—the first thing that lay to hand, and Niou now put this discarded garment over Ukifune's knees, lest her dress should be splashed while she was being washed.

What an excitement there would be even in the First Princess's[*] apartments—and among her gentlewomen there were many who belonged to the greatest families in the land—if such a creature as this were suddenly to arrive. All day they played the most absurd and childish games together; sometimes Jiju hardly knew which way to look. Again and again at more serious moments he would speak of his plans for bringing her secretly to the Capital. He tried to make her swear that meanwhile she would not see Kaoru again. Her only answer was to bury her face in her hands and weep. If even when he was with her she felt like that, what hope was there—Niou asked himself—of her remaining faithful to him in the intervals? He stormed at her and even wept. But his time had run out. Already it was almost midnight, and they hastened to the boat. Again he carried her in his arms. "I am doing something for you now that he, I feel pretty sure, has never done. I hope you give me credit for that," he said. It was true enough. She nodded, and some-how he felt reassured. Ukon met them at the double-doors and let her mistress in.

It was all over. He was back leading his usual life in the Nijo-in. He felt very ill and had no appetite at all. Day after day it was the same. Everyone noticed how thin he was getting; it was most alarming. At the Palace there was consternation; a gloom began to spread over the whole Court. At Uji a fresh complication had arisen owing to the return of the old nurse who had been away for some time attending the confinement of her married daughter. The officious old woman was devotedly attached to her mistress and never for a moment left her side, so that Ukifune had the greatest difficulty in getting a chance to read even the brief and occasional notes that Niou managed to send. Ukifune's mother

---

[*] Niou's unmarried sister.

saw with satisfaction the lavish scale upon which Kaoru was enabling the establishment at Uji to be run. But she counted on the arrangement, so unsatisfactory in many ways from her daughter's point of view, being merely a temporary one. The sooner he moved her, secretly if need be, to some place much closer at hand, the better for both of them, and she was already preparing to make herself useful in such an emergency by choosing for Ukifune a number of gentlewomen and girls of a kind suitable for a town establishment. As for Ukifune, she had loved to conjure up the vision of this quiet house in the Capital, where Kaoru was going to visit her every day; but now no sooner did she turn her thoughts towards the event which she had once so eagerly anticipated than Niou's image—his laughter, his tears, his passionate caresses and reproaches—rose up before her. No, she could never suffer herself to be shut up in a place where he could not come to her... It was terrible; she could not now close her eyes for an instant without dreaming of him.

It had rained without stopping for days on end and the mountain-road would for the present, Niou knew, be impracticable even were he free to come and go as he chose, were not " shut in like the silkworm in the cocoon"* by the august solicitude of the Imperial pair. He wrote to Ukifune at much greater length than for a long while. "As through the dark I peer, the clouds that hide your village soon themselves invisible will grow, so thick the air with rain." Such was his poem. In the writing, loose and negligent though his style was, there were passages of real genius, astonishing in their freedom and audacity. She would have been strangely constituted indeed if, at her impressionable age, she had not found it a thrilling experience to receive such letters. Yet all the while she felt that Kaoru's less impulsive character was in reality much more admirable; moreover, his was the first love that she had known. Her friendship with him had been her whole life; without it she could not imagine herself existing at all. How terrible, too, it would be for her mother, who kept on asking when Kaoru was going to bring her back. "How little parents know their own children. Certainly Mother would never have believed it of me," Ukifune thought. Of course everyone said that Niou was utterly unreliable; but supposing in this case he really did what he had promised—set her up in the Capital and devoted all his time to her, what about Kozeri? It was unthinkable. However, it was no use supposing that in this world anything could remain secret for long, and it was certain that, even if things went on as they were, Kozeri would soon know. Had not Niou, with much less to go upon, succeeded (despite all Kaoru's precautions) in finding out about Kaoru's relations with her? "I

---

* "When I cannot see you I feel like one of the silkworms that my mother breeds—shut up in their cocoons." By Hitomaro. *Shuishu* 895.

could bear to lose him," she was saying to herself, her mind returning to Kaoru, "if he wanted to be free. What I cannot bear is that my own wickedness and folly should turn him against me..." Another letter. This time from Kaoru. But Niou's was very long and there were large parts that she still had not read. It seemed somehow better to get it done with first, and, picking it up once more, she left the second letter unopened. Ukon and Jiju exchanged significant glances. "I don't blame her," Jiju said afterwards, "handsome though His Excellency is. There are other things, quite apart from looks, that count; and I know what I am talking about, for I've seen Prince Niou when he was really letting himself go. If I were she, sooner than stay moping here, I'd take whatever job I could get in the Empress's household. They could manage to see something of one another there, anyway." "Well, there's no doubt whose side you're on," said Ukon, "but I don't know, I'm sure. For my part, I don't think he's a patch on His Excellency. Just as regards looks and so on, he may be. But when it comes to mind and character... No, I'm very sorry indeed that things have gone this way. I can't see that any good can come of it." But though she could not take the whole matter so lightly as Jiju, it was a comfort to her now to have someone with whom she could discuss the matter—'someone to help her with her lies," she called it. "I am very sorry I have not been able to come. I wish you would write more often. You know that it is not my fault..." Kaoru's was a short letter. In the margin was the poem: "Here ceaseless rains block out the darkened world. In far-off Uji to what new mark has bounded the menace of the flood?" "I think of you more constantly than ever," he said. It was written on a white poetry-slip and folded in formal style. There were no points of particular beauty in the writing, but it always seemed to her a distinguished and interesting hand. There was a curious contrast between the two letters; his looking so large and containing so little, Niou's of inordinate length but folded into the minutest of love-knots. "You'd better answer the Prince's first while no one's about," said Ukon. "I don't feel like answering it today," she said, but in her copybook she wrote: "Well do you earn your name*—what life could prove it better than mine—O village by the ford of Uji River that through Yamashiro runs." Now and again she took out the picture that Niou had made for her. Would she ever see him again? The thing must not, could not go on, she saw that clearly enough; yet the idea of being shut away where he could not get at her was terrible. "Weary of wandering like a homeless cloud from crest to crest, would that I too might vanish in the welter of the rainy sky." "No speck of foam would mark..."† That was all she wrote to him. The tears

---

* The usual play on Uji and *ushi*, "wretched."

† "So smooth the boat glides that should it be merged with the waves no speck of foam would

started to Niou's eyes. It touched him deeply that their parting should weigh so heavily upon her, and the picture of her sitting disconsolate in that lonely place rose vividly before him.

In answer to Kaoru's rain-poem she wrote: "If other floods be out I know not, but the flood-mark of my tears shows that to me the world is dark indeed." Studying it and restudying it in his leisurely way, he felt that she was going just now through a very trying time, and was sorry for her. He still had it in mind when he was with the Second Princess that night, and presently he said to her: "There is something I have been meaning to tell you about, but I was not sure how you would feel about it. However, it all happened a long while ago... Someone I used to know is now living at a remote place in the country under very unhappy circumstances, and I feel I ought to bring her to town. When I was young the life I found myself in the midst of had no attraction for me and I intended at the earliest possible moment to escape from it all—to end my days peacefully in some far-off cloister. She was fully aware of this and knew that she could not count on me. However, my marriage to you has obviously quite changed the situation. She sees that I am no longer in a position to quit the world even if I wished to do so and would, I am afraid, think it very unfeeling of me if I did not step in and do something for her." "I cannot imagine why you supposed that I should raise any objection," the Princess replied. "No, obviously there is no reason why you should mind," Kaoru said. "What I am really afraid of is that the Emperor may hear some entirely misleading account of the whole affair. You know how recklessly people exaggerate. However, I don't know that it much matters; His Majesty will soon see for himself that there is nothing to worry about."

He was very anxious, too, that the work he was doing in the house in which he intended to settle Ukifune should attract as little attention as possible, and instead of calling in anyone from outside he put the whole business in charge of his own retainer, Nakanobu. He could not have made a more unfortunate choice, for Nakanobu's daughter, it will be remembered, was married to Niou's librarian, Michisada. The wife naturally heard all about the work that her father was doing, and it was not long before the whole story got round to Niou. "I understand that no professional painters are being employed," Michisada said; "the decorations are being carried out entirely by his own people. But several of them have a taste for that kind of thing, and with His Excellency to keep an eye on them I think they are going to make a very nice job of it." Niou instantly rushed round to a house on the outskirts of the City which he had reason to believe might soon be vacant, for it belonged to his old

---

mark the spot where we rowed," *Shinchokushu* 941.

nurse, whose husband had secured a provincial post and would presumably soon be taking up his duties. "It is not for myself," he explained, "but for a friend whom I am helping to hide. It is most important for me to find somewhere immediately." Nurse's husband did not much like the idea of handing over the house for a purpose of this kind to someone he knew nothing about. But it was obvious that Niou was desperately anxious to secure it, and considering who the request came from he could not very well refuse.

So that was settled! It was a great weight off his mind. He was promised possession on the thirtieth of the month and saw no reason why he should not move her in that very day. He wrote and told her of the plan, cautioning her not to breathe a word about it to anyone. It was useless at present to think of going to Uji. His own engagements at Court made it particularly hard for him to get away, and Ukifune wrote that her old nurse, who had now installed herself there, insisted on knowing everything that was going on and would in any case have been so extremely difficult to evade that a visit was hardly worthwhile.

Kaoru told her that he had now definitely decided on the tenth of the fourth month. So far from feeling "should a wave entice, I would go..."* Ukifune was appalled at the growing urgency of the decision that awaited her. She felt that in order to think the thing over she must get away; it was impossible here at Uji, where it had all happened, to settle anything at all. She asked if she might come to her mother for a little while. Unfortunately, however, Sakon's wife was going to have a baby, and the place was full of priests and magic-workers. The same reason made a visit to Ishiyama impossible.† It ended by the mother coming to Uji. She was met at the door by the old nurse, who was in raptures over the stuffs that Kaoru had sent for the gentlewomen's new dresses. "You'd think they would want to make something pretty, wouldn't you, after all the trouble His Excellency has taken. Of course it was not for nanny‡ to say anything, but between you and me I thought when I looked at what they were doing that I'd never seen such a hash made of good stuff in all my life!" Little they suspected—either Nurse or her mother—that at any moment a word, a look might suddenly reveal her to Kaoru as she was. There would soon be an end then to all these cheerful preparations! But only today there had come a letter from Niou asking her whether she could promise definitely to accept the place of retreat he had offered her. "Do not think that I shall let you be lonely," he said. "It will be quite easy for me to come to you; but were the place ten times as far away,

---

* In allusion to Komachi's famous poem. See my *Noh Plays of Japan,* p. 85.
† Contact with a pregnant woman made it impossible for her to enter a temple.
‡ She refers to herself thus in the third person as *mamma* ("nanny").

I swear that no power on earth could prevent my getting there, even if it meant that we must live as outcasts for the rest of our lives." Did he really mean it? If only she could make up her mind!

"I don't think you are looking at all well," her mother said. "I have never seen you so thin and pale." "She's been like this for days," Nurse said. "There's certainly something the matter with her. I can't get her to eat so much as a scrap." "You don't think she's picked up an evil influence of some kind, do you?" said the mother; "I am afraid it looks rather like that." "Well, I've had my ideas about what it might be," said Nurse, "but her not being able to go to Ishiyama the other day doesn't look much like that."* The girl colored and buried her face in her hands. It was the hour when she had crossed the river with Niou. The moon was shining brightly. It had been just such a night as this. Somehow or other she must prevent herself from crying. That was the last thing that could do any good.

The mother, wishing to hear about old times, sent for Ben no Kimi, who fell to talking about Agemaki's last days—how terribly she took things to heart, worrying long after there was nothing more that could be done, and how agonizing it had been to stand by helpless while she fretted herself step by step into the grave. "If only she had lived," Ben went on, "she might be in just the same sort of position today as her sister Kozeri—yes, all their sorrow might have turned to joy." "And what about my poor girl?" the mother could not help thinking. If things went as she now had every reason to believe they would, Ukifune was well on the way to a position quite as desirable as that of Kozeri. "I have of course been very worried about this girl," she said. "But it looks as if things would go better now. I am afraid, however, that will mean the end of these quiet talks of ours, for when my daughter has moved into the City I am not likely to be coming here again. Though it would be a great pleasure to hear a little more about those old days." "Being what I now am,"† said Ben, "I do not feel fit company for the rest of the world and have seen very little of Ukifune since she has been here. But I am sure that we shall all miss her. However, I am very glad for her sake that she is leaving. One is cut off from everything out here; it's not at all the place for a young girl. I am sure Kaoru would soon make some better arrangement; he never goes back on his word. Didn't I tell you to start with that he would never have taken her up as he did if he had not formed a very deep attachment to her? You see now that I knew what I was talking about." "I must say that so far he has always been kindness itself," the mother admitted.

---

* It has occurred to the nurse that Ukifune may be with child; but the fact that the onset of her period prevented her from going to Ishiyama seems to dispose of this theory.

† A nun.

"Of course one can't say how things will turn out later on; but I am certainly very grateful to you for bringing them together. Kozeri was very kind to her at one time, too; but there was trouble while she was staying at the Nijo-in and I had to take her away. She has had a very difficult time of it, poor girl." "I can easily imagine what kind of trouble it was," said Ben, smiling. "It's a scandalous state of affairs. They're finding it difficult to get any decent girl to stay in service there. One of Tayu's daughters was telling me about it only the other day. 'He's a nice enough gentleman," she said, "in every other way. But this sort of thing is very trying; we find it makes our relations with Madam so difficult.'" "Quite," said Ukifune to herself, listening from her bed. Who, alas, knew the truth of this better than she? "You don't say so," exclaimed the mother. "What a dreadful thing! Kaoru of course is married already. But I do not see why that should make things difficult. It is not as if they were going to be in the same house. Well, we must hope for the best. I turned the matter over in my mind a great many times before venturing to make this decision. I don't see that I could have done any better for her, and I hope she is grateful. This much I can say, that if after all the trouble I've taken things were to go wrong through any fault on her side—I am thinking of what happened at the Nijo-in—though it would break my heart to lose her, I don't think I could ever bear to see the girl again."

Ukifune heard every word and her blood ran cold. This decided it. She must do away with herself before the thing got out. But how? The roar of the flooded river was deafening. "Generally speaking I rather like the sound of running water," the mother remarked, "but a noise like this is a very different matter. I think it's terribly depressing, and this poor child never able to get away from it for months on end! I can quite understand his not wanting to leave her here a moment longer than is necessary." Everyone began telling stories about the terrible swiftness of Uji River and the accidents that had happened when it was in flood: "Only the other day the bridge-keeper's little grandson slipped when he was punting the boat and fell in. They've never found the body. You'd be surprised how many people that river makes away with every year." That was the very thing. Why had she not thought of it before? No one would know what had become of her. Of course her mother and the rest would be terribly upset for a time; but they would soon get over it. Whereas if she let things drift on till he found out—no, she could not face it; that meant unending misery and shame. Whereas this way was so easy; all would be over in a moment. At last the agony of doubt and indecision was over. Her mind worked clearly now; she planned down to the last detail exactly how she would manage it all. It would be over before anyone began to look for her; nothing could possibly go wrong. Yet, it was sad to die...

Her mother continued with maddening persistence to fuss about the arrangements for the move. Presently she returned to the subject of Ukifune's health. "I think you ought to arrange for a service on her behalf," she said to Nurse, "and a purification* would not be a bad thing..." Little they knew that the gods had already rejected her offering!† "I am afraid you won't have any too many women to take with you," the mother continued, "for I would rather you did not take any of these new girls unless you are certain that they are thoroughly suitable. I don't doubt that the Princess herself will take a reasonable view of the matter. But if things turn out to be at all difficult, a few tactless inexperienced girls might cause no end of trouble. So without their knowing it keep an eye on them and notice how they are shaping." "Well, I must be going," she said at last. "I don't like to be away from home too long just now.‡ Would she then never see her mother again? She longed intensely to spend a few quiet hours with her before they parted and, making her health the excuse, suggested that she should go back with her now. "I feel that it would do me good," she said, "to be at home for a little while." "I am afraid it is out of the question at present," her mother said. "Not only because of your sister. We've got all these sewing-women in the house, making things for you to wear in town. It's all we can do to find room for them. Once you are settled in we shall see plenty of one another. And indeed if you were going to live in "Take-u which is at the land's end"§ I should manage somehow to come and see you, as you know very well. I only wish I were in a position to do more for you!" she said sadly as she turned to go. Another letter from Kaoru came today. He heard that Ukifune was unwell and was anxious for further news. "I was hoping to come myself," he said, "but a lot of unexpected business has turned up at the last moment and I cannot get away. I am afraid you are passing through a very difficult, unsettling sort of time." There was also a very long and agitated letter from Niou, to whose last note she still had not replied. He told her that she must make up her mind immediately. "This waiting to see which way the wind will blow is becoming impossible to endure." The same two messengers who had met here the day when it rained so, found themselves once more face to face. Kaoru's man recognized the other as a fellow he had often seen at Michisada's house. "What brings *you* here so often, Liegeman?" he asked. "I have friends of my own

---

* In a sacred river.

† Cf. Part V, p. 947. Ukifune means that she has struggled in vain to free herself from the toils of love.

‡ Just before her younger daughter's confinement.

§ Reference to an old song: "Blow wind, kind wind and tell my mother that to Take-u they have carried me, to the Governor's house in Take-u which is at the land's end." Take-u was in the province of Echizen.

here," the man said. "That's a very dainty letter you are carrying to these 'friends of your own.' But our liegeman* starts and hides his letter! Pray, friend, why such secrecy?" The man saw that he had betrayed himself. "The truth of the matter is," he said, "this letter is not mine. It is from my lord Tokikata† to one of the gentlewomen here." Kaoru's messenger saw no reason to believe that this story was any truer than its predecessor; but people were listening, and he did not think it wise to pursue the matter any further for the moment. However he was a capable fellow, and when both the messages had been delivered he took aside a page-boy who had accompanied him and told him to follow Niou's man back to the City. "Keep well out of his sight," he said. "What I want to know is whether he goes to my lord Tokikata's house." "It was not to Tokikata's that he went," the boy said when he came afterwards to report. "He went straight to Prince Niou's and handed a letter to my lord Michisada." Niou's messenger had of course behaved with extraordinary indiscretion; but he was only an under-servant who knew nothing about the intrigue at Uji and had not the slightest reason to suppose that he was being watched. On going to deliver the letter that he had brought from Uji, Kaoru's messenger found his master just leaving the house. The Empress was staying for a while at the New Palace,‡ and he was going there to pay an informal visit. There were one or two gentlemen with him, but not the usual throng of outriders and attendants. Handing the letter to one of these gentlemen the messenger said, "I noticed something peculiar when I was out there today. I thought it was worthwhile looking into, and it seems I was not far wrong." Kaoru overheard some of this. "What was worth while looking into?" he asked casually, as he left the house. The gentleman to whom the letter had been handed was standing close by. The man looked at him, and hesitated. "Very well, then," said Kaoru; "some other time." He saw that the matter was confidential.

He found the Empress very unwell. All her children were there, and the place was packed with people who had come to condole and enquire. It seemed, however, to be simply one of her usual attacks. As a member of the Imperial Secretariat Michisada had the right to be admitted to the Presence, though his turn did not come till late. Knowing that he should find Niou there, he brought the letter from Uji with him. He was told that his master was in the gentlewomen's common-room. Niou came to the door to receive it and was standing there hastily breaking the seal when Kaoru passed by on his way back from the Empress's room. It amused him to see the eagerness with which Niou snatched at the

---

* He uses, ironically, a rather antiquated expression.
† Niou's retainer.
‡ The Empress's *sato* (private residence) as opposed to the Emperor's Palace, which was her official residence. She inherited it from Genji. Part of it was occupied by Yugiri.

letter, and he halted for a moment in the corridor. Who did it come from? he wondered. Niou had so many charming friends. He could only see that it was written on thin pink paper in a very close hand. From the way Niou's eyes were glued to the letter it was evident that this was a very serious affair indeed. "I wonder how long it will be before he notices that I am standing here," Kaoru was thinking, when he saw Yugiri coming down the passage. He coughed, and Niou at last looked up. "The Grand Minister!" Kaoru warned him. But Yugiri was already upon them, arriving just in time to see Niou hastily stuffing the letter into the folds of his dress. He was still fastening his belt when Yugiri came up. "I am going back," he said, "I don't think it's anything fresh; but it is a long time since she had an attack of this kind, and I confess I feel rather alarmed. I think a service ought to be read at the Hieizan. I must get into touch with the abbot," and he bustled off, taking Niou with him. It was late, the visitors were all leaving. A throng of princes and courtiers followed Niou to Yugiri's rooms. Kaoru went somewhat later. It occurred to him on the way home that the messenger who had taken his letter to Uji had apparently wanted to say something to him in private. He had better hear what it was. His attendants had stopped to light their torches. Kaoru beckoned to the messenger. "What was it?" he said. "You can tell me safely now." The man repeated his story. "Tell me quickly," said Kaoru aghast, "what sort of letter was it, what did it look like?" "Of course I didn't see it myself," the messenger said, "it was the page who saw it. But I asked him what sort of letter it was and he said it was on pink paper. 'Reddish-colored fancy paper, and very good quality'—those were his exact words." That settled it. The man seemed to have acted very smartly; it was, however, impossible to question him further at the moment, for the other attendants were again within earshot. But what he had heard was enough! How had Niou got into touch with her? How, for that matter, did he know of her existence? It was appalling. He had thought that at any rate out there at Uji, miles from anywhere, a girl would be safe from this sort of thing. "Though, knowing Niou as I do, it was childish of me to suppose so," he reflected. "But if he is going to roam the country in this way, he might at least have the decency to find somewhere new. After all, it was I who introduced him there to start with. No one could have taken more trouble than I did to make things easy for him then, and this is how he repays me! I think he has behaved abominably." How different was his own behavior with regard to Kozeri, about whom he had felt so deeply during all these years! And even if he had shown less restraint, his conduct would still have borne no resemblance whatever to that of Niou. He had known Kozeri intimately years before Niou set eyes on her, and if he chose to keep their relationship on its present footing, this was because for certain reasons it would be painful to him that it should assume any other character. Most people would think him a fool to have wasted such an opportunity.

It was difficult to see how Niou managed to conduct such a correspondence at the present moment, with his mother at home[*] and the whole place packed with visitors from morning to night. It was hardly conceivable that he had actually been there; Niou was not free like other people to come and go as he pleased. True, he managed to conduct an unconscionable quantity of amours—but at places it was possible to slip round to for a few hours and be back before one was missed, which was far from being the case with Uji, as Kaoru had every reason to know! However, come to think of it, Niou did sometimes disappear mysteriously. He had been missing for a whole day only a short while ago. Then there was this fuss about his health. It was not the first time that Kaoru had seen him in such a condition; he had fretted himself into just the same state years ago, when circumstances were making it difficult for him to see Kozeri. Kaoru had wondered too why Ukifune, who knew that she had only a few more weeks to get through at Uji, should be in such particularly low spirits. This of course went a long way towards explaining it. "Naturally the prospect of living at a place where I may turn up at any moment does not much appeal to her," he thought ruefully.

How little one ever really knew about what was going on in the minds of other people! He had always thought her a singularly gentle and affectionate character, inclined perhaps to lean on him almost too much. And all the while these unpleasant cravings were going on. It was disgusting. She was obviously the sort of woman who could not exist without a lover for a single day. She had in fact the same disagreeable tendencies that were ruining Niou, and they would make an excellent pair. He felt inclined simply to break off all communications and let Niou provide for her, if he wished to. Perhaps he had better think things over before doing anything of that sort. Obviously if she had been the formal mistress of his household he could not possibly have condoned such a fault; but under the circumstances it might be wiser to give her another chance. He would certainly miss her very much if he never saw her; though of course his opinion of her had completely changed.

One thing was certain, if she had really ceased to care for him and decided definitely to throw in her lot with Niou, a terrible disillusionment awaited her. Niou had his way of dealing with such situations. There was nothing he would not do for a woman so long as she continued to attract him. What became of her after she ceased to do so he seldom troubled to enquire. At the most—and Kaoru could recall two or three instances

---

[*] I.e. at the New Palace.

of this kind—he got her taken on in his sister's household as an ordinary waiting-woman. To watch this process being repeated in Ukifune's case would be a painful experience. Whatever steps he might ultimately have to take, the first thing to do was to get into touch with her, and find out how things actually stood. He sent for his usual messenger and taking him aside asked whether my lord Michisada was still seeing Nakanobu's daughter. The man said that so far as he knew he was.

"And you say that he is constantly sending this messenger to Uji? It looks to me," Kaoru asserted disingenuously, "as though he had heard something from Nakanobu's daughter about the establishment there, and were trying to get into touch with my lady, not of course knowing her to be in any way connected with me." "And take care not to be followed," he added. "I don't choose to have the whole world know where my letters go to." The man bowed. That Michisada was receiving constant information about Kaoru's private affairs and in particular about the situation at Uji was true enough. The messenger, had he thought it his place to do so, could on the subject of this leakage have made some interesting revelations. His expression, indeed, implied as much; but Kaoru, feeling disinclined to take a mere under-servant into his confidence, refrained from questioning him further.

Another letter! Under happier circumstances Ukifune would have felt flattered by this constant stream of correspondence. Now it only served to harass and bewilder her. This one, however, was at any rate very short. It consisted simply of the verse: "Sooner, I had thought, would the sea rise up and cover the tree-tops of the hill." In the margin were the words: "At all costs avoid scandal!" The shock staggered her. She fought for breath. To answer was impossible. Who had told him? How much did he know? To show that she understood the allusion* would seem an admission of her guilt; to avoid referring to it would seem equally suspicious. "I return this," she wrote, "as it was apparently brought to me by mistake. I do not feel well enough to write more..." Kaoru, when the letter came back to him, could not help admiring the clever way in which she had extricated herself. He would never have credited her with such adroitness. It was irritating, of course, to be scored off in this pert manner; but somehow he found himself more amused than angry. She meanwhile was not feeling by any means so elated as he supposed. All this was no use. What purpose could such an answer serve? It would only force him to state more crudely what he had already hinted at with sufficient plainness. It was enough that he knew; life under such circumstances was inconceivable... Ukon came bustling in: "Why couldn't you use fresh paper?

---

* Kaoru's poem which is in reality even vaguer than in my version, would be unintelligible to anyone who did not recognize it as an allusion to *Kokinshu*, No. 1093.

Don't you know that it's very unlucky to send people's letters back to them?" she asked indignantly. "I could not make head or tail of it," Ukifune murmured, "I think it must have been brought here by mistake." As a matter of fact Ukon, though she knew she ought not to have done so, had opened the letter before returning it to the messenger, for it struck her as very odd that it should be sent back. "I think things are going to be rather difficult for you and your Prince," she said, "now that His Excellency is on your tracks." The blood rushed to Ukifune's cheeks. "Who told you?" she was on the verge of asking, for she did not know that Ukon had seen the letter and supposed that the girl was repeating some rumor that was already afoot. But she could not bring herself to discuss the matter. It was intolerable that all these people should be busying themselves with her affairs. They of course would never understand, would judge her as though the thing were of her own doing, which was not so. It happened of itself, happened because it must. All through her life it had been the same... She sank back wearily and was falling asleep, when Jiju came in. "Do you know," Ukon said to her, "this all reminds me terribly of something that happened in Hitachi—to people of a very different rank, of course; but otherwise it was just the same. My own sister—the elder one—was going with two men. They were both madly in love with her, and she did not know which to choose. But she found that on the whole she cared more for the new one and the other, seeing this, murdered him out of jealousy. As far as my sister was concerned, she had lost both of them at a stroke; for the one that was left never came near her again. It meant a serious loss to the province. The dead man was a strong young fellow—just the sort to make a good soldier, and the other was one of the Governor's best men. But after what had happened it was impossible to go on employing him. And, to crown all, my sister too was turned adrift; for the Governor said that in the long run it was always the woman's fault when such things happened, and would not have her in his service. The result was that when they all came back to the City[*] she was left behind. I don't suppose we shall ever see her again. Your nanny,[†] Madam, still cries whenever my sister's name is mentioned. It's a terrible judgment on us all. You'll think it's a bad moment to talk of such a thing. But it's as well to remember that when it comes to tangles of this sort it makes no difference whether it's peasants in Hitachi or grand folk here—the risk is the same. Not that anyone's life is in danger now. That kind of thing does not happen to people in this rank of society. But there's their pride to be reckoned with, and things can happen which ordinary folk soon get over, but which to them are

---

[*] When the Governor had completed his term of office.
[†] Ukon's mother.

worse than death. So be quick, my lady, and make up your mind. If after all you like the Prince better than His Excellency and think he is really in earnest, tell them so. There's nothing terrible in that. You'll do no good anyhow by lying there fretting yourself into a decline. I can't help thinking it's a great mistake for your mother to make all this fuss and Nanny to rush things on the way she's doing, when everything is still so uncertain. Who knows where you'll be by the time His Excellency is ready? Other plans, I understand, are being made for you,* and are going along faster too." "How can you talk like that in front of her?" said Jiju. "You'll only frighten her. Listen, Madam. Don't worry about other people. Just look into your own heart. You'll know soon enough then which way to decide. If it's to be the Prince, no one will think the worse of you. We all know it's no use trying to force oneself, when it comes to things like that. 'It's as Fate wills,' that's what I always say. With the Prince—I hope you don't mind my speaking of it—caring for you so deeply as I can see he does, you would be making a great mistake if you let them bustle you over this move. If I were you, I wouldn't see His Excellency at all till you have thought the whole thing out quietly and made up your mind." The advice was not unbiased; for Jiju herself had a great partiality for Niou.

"Well, I'm sure I hope it will all turn out for the best," said Ukon, "I'm having prayers said for you at both Hatsuse and Ishiyama. I don't see what more I can do. I'm afraid, though, there may be trouble very soon. The men on His Excellency's farms round here have a way of picking quarrels, and Uji nowadays is packed with them. This man they call Udoneri, who has been put in charge here, has a lot of power. Most of the tenants on His Excellency's estates in Yamashiro and Yamato are connected with him in one way or another. That Tayu, for example—the officer who is in charge of this house—is Udoneri's son-in-law. Of course, as I said before, one knows that as between gentlemen like the Prince and Lord Kaoru, whatever else may happen, there's no fear of it coming to blows. But with these men it's different. After all, they're only rough country fellows. They take turns to go on duty here, and each band is responsible for what happens during its watch. If the least thing goes wrong it's they who get into trouble, and it's not to be wondered at that they sometimes go too far. I don't mind telling you now what a fright I was in the whole time that night he took her on the river. He hadn't a soul with him. That of course was so as not to attract attention. But then if they'd caught him—alone like that and dressed as he was—what would they have taken him for? No, it doesn't bear thinking about."

---

* The house hired by Niou would be at their disposal on the 28th of the third month. Kaoru's on the tenth of the fourth month.

These people, Ukifune thought, for some reason all took it for granted that she had in reality made up her mind long ago in favor of Niou. It was not true. Indeed, looking back on the hours she had spent with him she could not feel that they belonged to her real waking life at all. His excitement, his passionate embraces—why should someone like Niou have such feelings about her? No, it all seemed utterly unreal. It was not the thought of him that was worrying her, let her women suppose what they pleased. It was the knowledge that she had lost her helper, her one true friend, who had stood by her all this while. Well, they were right. Death was going to close the story, though not as it had closed the one Ukon told. "Ukon, dear Ukon," she said, "I want so much to die. I am terribly unhappy; indeed I cannot think that even among the poorest and most down-trodden in the land there can often have been so wretched a life as mine." "Come, you mustn't say such things as that. I see I ought not to have talked as I did; I hoped it would help you to make up your mind. But I don't know what has come over you in these days. You always used to take everything so quietly, one could hardly tell whether you minded or not; and often it would have been natural enough that you should mind. But since this business started you seem to take every little thing to heart."

So much for those who were in the secret. To the old nurse it still seemed that everything was going splendidly and she was in high spirits. She had gathered round her the more likely-looking of the new girls and they were helping her dye stuffs. "They're such dear little things. Won't you have some of them in to play with you?" she said to Ukifune. "I don't like to see you lying there like that all day. It won't do for you to get an illness just when we're due to start for the City." Days passed; from Kaoru himself nothing more was heard, but one morning Udoneri, the head bailiff of whose importance Ukon had spoken with bated breath, suddenly presented himself, saying that he wished to see one of the ladies. He was an old man with a husky voice and manners that made no pretension to refinement, but with an air of authority that contrasted strangely with his coarse, undistinguished appearance. Ukon was fetched. "I have come straight here after being with His Excellency," Udoneri said. "I got a message saying he wished to see me and went there this morning. Among other things, he talked about the arrangements for looking after this house at night. He said he thought that my people were attending to that; otherwise he would have sent special night-watchmen from the City. Someone, it appears, has told him that strangers have been getting into the house at night and carrying on with the women here. 'If that's so,' he said, 'your people must have let them through. They're supposed to challenge everyone that comes. How do you explain it?' I knew nothing about it whatever. 'My health has been very bad for some time past,'

I said,* 'and I have not been able to go on duty at night. But I chose reliable men and gave them very strict orders. If anything out of the way had happened, they would certainly have reported it.' He said I must have the place guarded much more strictly and made it clear that if such a thing happened again the watchmen concerned would get into very serious trouble. I don't know what it's all about, I'm sure. But those are his orders, and they must be obeyed."

Ukon made no reply. This was sinister† news indeed. "What do you make of that?" she said to Ukifune. "I wasn't far wrong, was I, when I told you that His Excellency was on your tracks. And then your not having heard from him all this while... It's a bad business." Nurse had overheard something about Udoneri's visit. "I'm very glad of it indeed," she said. "There have been a lot of burglaries round here lately. These watchmen were all right to start with. But now they have taken to going to bed themselves and sending other people to do it for them—mere riff-raff who don't know how to manage night-rounds at all." "Ukon is quite right," Ukifune thought; "something terrible‡ may happen here at any minute. I must not delay." To her consternation there arrived at this very moment a letter from Niou expressing the most passionate desire to see her. There was only one way to save the situation. Many lives,§ she felt, were now at stake, and if she sacrificed her own she would only be doing what other women under such circumstances had done before her, and by the same means that she proposed to use.¶ If she lived, inevitable disaster awaited her; if she died who, in the long run, would care? Her mother of course would be upset for a time; but she had her other children to look after and would soon manage to console herself. "It would be far worse for her," Ukifune thought, "after all that she has hoped and planned, to see me drag out a pitiable existence, homeless, ruined, and despised."

No one seeing this gentle, frail-looking creature would have supposed her capable of framing, still less of carrying out such a plan. But in her early days she had not led the quiet and sheltered life that falls to the lot of most girls. Hitachi is a wild place; she had seen and heard much, and her childhood there had given her a degree of courage and independence that would otherwise have been surprising.

She went through her papers and tore up everything that was incriminating, burning the fragments at the lamp piece by piece, or throwing

---

* Literally, "caused to be said," which indicates that Udoneri was not actually admitted to Kaoru's presence.

† Literally, "worse than an owl-hoot," the owl being the bird of evil omen.

‡ To Niou, if he tries to visit her.

§ In particular, those of Niou's and Kaoru's attendants.

¶ Had drowned themselves. There are many such stories in early Japanese literature. See *Manyoshu*, xvi. I.

them into the river. This did not strike most of her women as in any way remarkable. She was soon going to move house, and it seemed quite natural that she should want to get rid of all the odd scraps—writing-exercises, rough drafts, and the like—that had accumulated since she was there. But Jiju recognized some of the papers she was destroying and protested violently: "I don't like to see you doing that," she said. "Of course one doesn't want everyone to see letters of that sort, full of all one's innermost feelings. The thing to do with them is to put them at the bottom of a box and have a look at them when you're feeling inclined. It will give you a lot of pleasure in days to come. Look what handsome paper they're written on—let alone all the lovely things he says. I can't think how you have the heart to destroy them, I can't indeed." "Why must you be so tiresome? Surely I can do as I please? Supposing anything were to happen to me—and I have a feeling that I shall not live very long—it would be very unpleasant for him[*] if these letters were found... And in any case, whether I am alive or not, Kaoru might hear that they existed, and I should not like him to think that I had gone out of my way to keep them."

She looked forward calmly to her fate. Only one circumstance troubled her. She had sometimes been told—though apparently on no very good authority—that to have left a parent behind was a great handicap in the world-to-come.[†]

The proprietor of the house that Niou had taken was to leave for his province on the twenty-eighth of the third month. Already the twentieth had passed. He wrote to Ukifune telling her that he would fetch her on the night of the twenty-eighth: "No one but Ukon and Jiju must know; I of course shall not dream of breathing a word to anybody. Do not mistrust me." Probably he would be turned back before he reached the house at all, driven away—by her, he would think—without so much as a word of explanation or farewell. And even if by any chance he managed to elude the guard, what point was there in his coming to the house? There was not the slightest chance, as things were now,[‡] of getting him safely to her rooms. She could not bear to think of him protesting, entreating, and at last turning sadly away... It had begun again! His image, that she had tried so hard to banish, once more rose up before her and would not go away. She loved him, loved him passionately. What use was there in denying it? And taking his letter she pressed it against her cheek, struggling in vain to check her tears. "Now, now, my own dear lady, there are people about; you mustn't do things like that. Already they're beginning

---

[*] Niou.
[†] The idea being that earthly ties impede the upward progress of the soul.
[‡] With Nurse always on the spot, and so on.

to wonder what's making you carry on as you do. If you sat up and answered it properly, it's my opinion you'd be better employed. I know what it is; you're worrying about how he's to get you away. Don't you think about it any more. I'll see to all that. It would be strange indeed if we couldn't smuggle you out somehow—a little slip of a thing like you!" "Stop, stop! I can't bear it," Ukifune managed to say through her tears. "I've never for a single moment had any intention of letting him take me away. The whole thing is mere madness. If only he would stop writing about it—always as though I had consented, when I have never done anything of the kind! I'm terrified about it. One feels one simply does not know what wild thing he may not be meaning to do."

Niou was very much disappointed. He had felt from the start that she was not really in favor of the plan, and now that he put it before her in a definite form, she did not even reply. Probably Kaoru was on the spot again and it was not surprising that, faced with the necessity of deciding one way or the other, she should have gone over to his side, which he saw was from her point of view much the easier and safer thing to do. That she was, or at any rate had been, very much attached to him he felt sure, but no doubt during the long intervals between his visits to Uji such of her people as were in the secret did everything in their power to prejudice her against him. There was nothing to be done. He tried indeed to dismiss the whole thing from his mind. But this was impossible. He must at least know what was happening. He could not drift on in this distracted, unsettled state, unable to fix his thoughts on anything he was doing. Somehow or other, risky though it always was, he must manage to get away.

He was just about to climb through the hedge at the usual place when a chorus of rough voices challenged him. He hastily retired, and scribbling a note gave it to a servant who had constantly delivered his messages at Uji. The watchmen knew the man quite well, but to his surprise absolutely refused to let him pass. He was explaining that it was an urgent message from my lady's mother in the City when he caught sight of a woman who worked for Ukon, and knowing her name he was able to call her to the hedge. "Dear, dear, this will never do," Ukon said to herself when she read Niou's note. "Forgive me for sending you away," she wrote, "but what can I do? Tonight is absolutely out of the question." What was the meaning of all this? Why were they keeping her from him? Niou asked himself in desperation. As a last resort there still remained Jiju. "Can't you get at her somehow," he said to Tokikata, "and see if *she* can do anything?" Tokikata was not the man to be baffled by circumstances such as these. By a cunning ruse he got past the guard and managed to get Jiju sent out to where he was waiting. "I don't see that there's anything I can do," she said. "The watchmen say they have orders at present to challenge everyone who comes—apparently it's His Excellency himself who has given these instructions—and there isn't a chance of his getting in.* I am sure that's what my poor lady is worrying about so. She can't bear to think of his coming all the way out here and then being sent away. She's making herself quite ill, she frets so about it. But tonight the guard are on the alert; they've turned him back once, and if they catch him trying to get in again, I'm afraid they may use violence on him. The night he comes to fetch her away, Ukon and I will arrange between us to get her out to him somehow. We'll let him know about that later on." She also explained to him the difficulties they had with Nurse and other busybodies in the household. "I've never seen him so worked up about anything as he was about coming here today. It seems dreadful just to go back and say it's no good. Look here! It would be a great help if you'd come and help me to explain." "I don't like to," she said, "it's not me he wants to see." But he succeeded in persuading her. It was now getting very late. Niou, who was again on horseback, had retired to some distance from the house. His attendants were not much enjoying their task. The party was approached time after time by packs of village dogs, who to judge by their barking were anything but well disposed. Moreover, they were very few in number and knew that if robbers or other undesirable characters were suddenly to appear on the scene they would have great difficulty in defending themselves.

"Faster, faster!" cried Tokikata, hurrying Jiju on. She had very long hair and finding that it hampered her had twisted it across her arms. A nice-looking girl, he thought. He had tried to put her on his horse, but to this she would not consent, so there was nothing for it but to catch hold of her by the skirt and drag her along. Finding that she was barefoot he gave her his shoes and borrowed others for himself—the oddest he had ever worn—from a country fellow who was with him. "I think Your Highness will have to dismount," Tokikata said. They were close to a farmhouse that was surrounded by a hedge. He noticed a place that was protected by a tall clump of goose-grass, and spreading a splash-cloth there he invited Niou to sit down. "You'll be able to talk more comfortably like that," Tokikata told him. But there was not much to say. It was a terrible blow. Must he return empty-handed? Already the reputation that he had gained owing to adventures of this kind was such as to mar his prospects in every other direction. He felt as though the ground had been taken from under his feet. For Jiju, admiring him as she did, it was terrible to witness the tears of humiliation and disappointment which, as the result

---

* Niou was masked and disguised, so that they would at once have suspected him; if he had thrown off his disguise, they would at once have seen that he was someone out of the ordinary, and perhaps even recognized him.

of her tidings, were now coursing down his cheeks. She felt indeed that had he been, as the saying goes, "the ghost of her worst enemy" instead of the sweet prince he was, her one desire would have been to help him. "Mayn't I then even exchange one word with her?" he said, managing to control himself at last. "Why has all this business about the watchmen suddenly started? It never used to be so. But I know well enough what it is. One or the other of you has been telling tales." "No, indeed," she said, and told him about Udoneri's visit and the fresh instructions to the guard. "When you come to fetch my lady," she said, "be sure to let me know in good time. We'll manage to get her to you somehow. I'm sure for my part I'd rather die than let you go home like this again."

That was all very well; but how about today? He felt outraged, but though there was a great deal more he would have liked to say he saw that the night was nearly over; he must start instantly if he was to escape unseen. The dogs were still howling despite all the efforts of his people to drive them away. This commotion, heard from afar, had evidently alarmed the watchmen and the twangings of their bows, accompanied by raucous cries of "*Danger, danger!*" added to the general feeling of strain and suspense that pervaded the night. The noise, the continual flurries and agitations were intolerable; his one longing now was to escape from it all. Yet as he rose to his feet, a terrible sense of foreboding suddenly came upon him, rooting him to the spot where he stood. Why ever return, why leave these cloud-capped hills? Nothing in his life down there in the City was worth going back for. "My hour of shame has come," he wrote. "What dwelling need I now but what the fold of yonder hill supplies to those that shun the world?" "You'd better get back as fast as you can," he said to Jiju, handing her the poem. The damp night air had brought out the perfume of the strange scent that he always wore. Her sweet, her handsome prince! She could not bear to leave him, and wept bitterly all the way to the house.

Ukifune had already received from Ukon the agitating news that they had been obliged to send Niou away, and now came Jiju with her melancholy story. She heard it in silence, not trusting herself to speak, lest her tears should again begin to flow. Already her pillow was soaked, and she knew that both Jiju and Ukon would interpret these tears in the way she least desired. Moreover her eyes were growing red with weeping, and this when the time for action came might attract inconvenient attention. She lay with her eyes shut as long as she could, and then, slipping on her belt and putting herself a little to rights, sat up and read the Scriptures, praying that if it was indeed a sin to die before her mother, the Lord Buddha might have mercy upon her.

She remembered that she had not thrown away his drawings. The one of himself and her was extraordinarily good. It made her almost feel as though that wonderful day had come back and they were still sitting together. It was terrible to think of his going back tonight without a word from her. Her memories of Kaoru were of a very different nature, just as his love for her was of quite another sort. It was strange indeed to contrast his calm, steady affection with Niou's passionate outbursts and exaltations. But again and again Kaoru had told her that she could count on him implicitly till her dying day; and she believed that it was true. He would miss her, she was sure of that; and, what was worse, it was by no means certain that even after her death some malicious person would not tell him of her infidelity. But better that than live with the knowledge that her name had become to him a byword for fickleness and treachery. "All these my miseries one act can end. Would that I thought the waves of death could cover the slur that blots my name!" She folded the poem and slipped it under her ink-slab.

There were so many people whom she would like to have seen just once again. Her mother, of course; but everyone at home, even the ugly little brothers and sisters in whom she took, as a rule, no interest at all.

And Kozeri!

Here everyone was busy; not a corner of the house but someone was sewing, cutting out, or dyeing stuffs. She tried to shut herself off from the bustle and noise. When night came she soon gave up trying to sleep and instead occupied herself by once more rehearsing her plan. She had it all by heart, just how she would get clear of the house without being seen, which way she would take down to the water. It was indeed so long since she had slept at all that she felt sick and giddy. At dawn she rose and looked out towards the river. It was a matter of moments now; she felt "like a sheep dragged to the slaughter."*

A letter from Niou was brought in, written after his return. It was full of the bitterest upbraidings and reproaches. To answer them was impossible. "Chide me no more, for from the world I vanish, body and soul together, lest you should say that to another was given what is yours." That was all she wrote. She felt that it was wrong not to let Kaoru know of her resolution—would like at least to have wished him good-bye. But she knew that he saw Niou constantly. If she wrote such a letter to Kaoru he would think that Niou ought to see it. They would discuss it together. She could not bear the idea. It was better simply to disappear without telling anyone what had become of her.

Another messenger arrived, this time with a letter from her mother. "I had a terrifying dream about you last night," she said, "and at once had prayers for your safety read at several temples. I had a very disturbed

---

* A stock phrase drawn from Buddhism, not from the daily life of Japan, in which sheep have played a very small part.

night in consequence and was obliged to rest during the morning. Again I had a dream about you in which I saw you—but it is too terrible to mention. I sat down to write this letter the moment I woke. I entreat you to be on your guard. There is a certain person,* a connection of someone whom I need not name, whose thoughts I know are harming you. There is nothing else that these dreams could mean, coming as they do at a time when you are suffering from an illness which no one can explain. I would come myself; but Sakon's wife is still causing us all great anxiety, and if I were to leave her for so long, the Governor would never forgive me. I want you to have prayers read at the temple near by." She enclosed a letter of instruction to the priests, and suitable offerings.

Little they mattered to her now, could her mother but know—these baleful visions and forewarnings! While the messenger was going to the temple, she sat down to answer the letter. There was much that she would have liked to say. But no, silence was best.

"Not here, but in a place by the world's dreams and omens undefiled, doubt not that we shall meet!"

The service had begun. Listening intently she could hear where she lay, now soft, now loud, as the wind rose and died, the tolling of the temple-bell. Presently the man came back, bringing with him the *kwanju*,† upon the margin of which she wrote: "Be this your message, that with the last dim echoes of the tolling bell my sorrow reached its close." "It's too late for me to go back now," the man said, and keeping the *kwanju* she tied it to a spray of green leaves. "Something is going to happen, I know that," said Nurse, coming in. "You should hear the way my heart's beating! And then these bad dreams your mother has had..." And she bustled off to see to it that the night-watchmen were all at their posts.‡

"Aren't you going to have any supper at all?" she asked presently. "Here's some nice broth, or if you don't fancy it... she went on suggesting one thing after another, till it was hard indeed to keep patience with her. Yet fussy and tactless though Nurse was, Ukifune could not help feeling sorry for her. "How will she exist when I am gone?" she asked herself. For it was hard to suppose that anyone would give employment to this hideous, toothless old creature. "Would it not," she wondered, "be kinder to prepare her—give her at least some sort of hint that I am not likely to live very long?" But she felt herself beginning to cry again before she had time to speak. Ukon now came in to sit with her for a little. "When a person goes on tormenting herself as you are doing, we all know what

---

* Kaoru's wife, the Second Princess. It was a fixed idea of the mother's that this lady's hostility constituted the one menace to Ukifune's happiness.

† A statement rendered by a temple showing the exact "number of chapters" (*kwanju*) that had been recited.

‡ The nurse is still worrying about burglars.

happens: the soul gets loose from the body and goes wandering about by itself. That's why your mother has been having these bad dreams. There's nothing to worry about. Just make up your mind one way or the other, and it will be all right. At least I hope so," she said with a sigh.

Ukifune lay with the soft bed-clothes pressed tight against her face.

The Gossamer-Fly

Of the hue and cry at Uji next morning, when it was discovered that Ukifune had disappeared, I need not speak. Who has not read countless descriptions of such scenes, the abduction of high-born ladies being the stock theme of old-fashioned tales? Suffice it to say that the mother, who had counted on the messenger returning the same day, sent another to find out what had become of him. "It's evidently very urgent," the man said; "it was before cock-crow that I got my orders to start." It was in vain that he addressed himself to one member of the household after another. From Nurse it was impossible to get any information at all. She was of course completely stupefied by the shock of Ukifune's disappearance, which she was at a loss to account for in any way at all. Ukon was in a very different position. Knowing as she did something of what had been going on in her mistress's mind, she thought it more than probable (though she kept the suspicion to herself) that Ukifune had taken her own life. With tears in her eyes she now opened the mother's letter: "I have not been seeing you in my dreams again—more than just a glimpse or two—for the simple reason that I have been feeling so worried and anxious about you since I last wrote that I have had no real sleep at all. I do not know why it is, but I cannot shake off the feeling that something terrible is going to happen. I suppose it is only that I am nervous about this move of yours. It would certainly be a great comfort if you could come here for a little while first, and I hope to arrange it. But I am afraid that we must wait till this rain stops." Ukon thought it would be as well to see what was in the letter Ukifune had written to her mother last night. The poem,* which was all that it contained, made it only too clear that Ukon's suspicion was well-founded. Never since the days when they were children together had there been, so far as Ukon knew, the smallest thing that Ukifune had kept from her. Yet now, as though they had been strangers all their lives, she set out on this terrible last journey without a hint, without a word. She had been calmer than the others before, but at the thought of what her mistress must have suffered all alone in those last hours she broke down altogether and, flinging herself to and fro, wept with the reckless abandonment of a little child. Jiju too, knowing in how desperate a state of mind Ukifune had been, would at

---

* "Not here, but in a place..." See above, p. 1057.

once have concluded that she had done violence to herself, had she not thought her mistress, whose character she fancied she knew pretty well, utterly incapable of carrying out so grim a resolution. One possibility after another occurred to her, only to be rejected. She was at a complete loss; as much so indeed as Nurse, who could do nothing but sit there like one demented, helplessly repeating over and over again the same words: "What are we to do, what are we to do?"

"Chide me no more, for from the world I vanish..."* What did it all mean, Niou wondered when her last poem was brought to him. Presumably it was her way of telling him that she was playing him false and had accepted Kaoru's offer of a house in town. He was not surprised. She had at one time certainly taken a great fancy to him, but her feelings towards Kaoru had never changed. He sent a messenger who, arriving when the confusion was at its height and finding no one among all this throng of weeping ladies to whom it seemed possible to commit Niou's letter, was forced at last to address himself to a rough country maid who seemed alone to retain possession of her senses. "It seems," the girl told him, "that my lady died† suddenly in the night; that's why they're all in such a state. There isn't a soul in the house to whom they can turn for help, and they don't know what to do." The man knew no more than that he had been told to take a letter to Ukon. He knew nothing about Niou's relations with the household at Uji, and without troubling to ask any further questions he returned to the City. "The mistress of the house died in the night," he mentioned when reporting that he had delivered Niou's letter.

It was incredible. She had apparently been rather unwell for some time; but surely Ukon would have let him know if it had been anything serious. He looked again at the poem she had sent. The writing was very good—better in fact than usual; certainly not the hand of someone who was lying on a death-bed. "Tokikata," he said, "you must go at once to Uji and find out what has happened. Don't be afraid of asking questions. I want to have the fullest account possible." "I think it would be much better if I kept away at present," Tokikata said. "His Excellency must certainly know what has happened, and with the guard tightened up as it is now and everyone being cross-questioned who tries to get in, he's very likely to hear of my being there, apparently for no particular reason. He'll think it very odd, and knowing that I often act on your behalf, I am afraid he may draw conclusions... Surely it would be very unwise. At a moment like this, with the whole house in disorder, it would be more

---

* See above, p. 1056.

† This is the account that Ukon, wishing to avert the suspicion of abduction or suicide, has given to the under-servants.

difficult than ever to get a quiet word with the people one can speak to freely." "I dare say you are right," said Niou. "But I feel I must know. Can't you manage to get hold of Jiju as you did the other day and find out for me what it all means? So far all that I have heard comes from a kitchen-maid or some such person. It may be a complete misunderstanding." It was obvious that Niou was in a terrible state of anxiety and, risky though he thought it, Tokikata set out for Uji that afternoon. Without Niou the journey was a very different matter, and he was surprised how little time it took him to get there, despite the fact that though the rain was beginning to clear, the road was in a very bad condition. Arriving disguised as a peasant among the villagers of Uji he found them discussing the matter in excited groups. "I hear the funeral is going to be tonight," he was rather surprised to hear someone say. He tried first to communicate with Ukon. She sent back word that at the moment she felt quite incapable of doing anything. Later in the day perhaps... But probably Tokikata was in a hurry to get back. "I certainly don't want to be here longer than I can help," he said. "But I can't possibly go back till I have some information to bring. Surely one or the other of you..." Finally Jiju appeared. "Yes, it was very sudden," she said. "I don't think she herself had time to realize that it was anything serious. Of course it has been a terrible shock for all of us. I am sure the Prince will understand our not having taken any steps to let him know. There is really very little to tell, except that she had been in low spirits for several days, and was certainly very much upset at not being able to see him when he came the other night. However, if you will come back when the funeral is over and things have settled down a little, I will try to tell you as much as I can. Of course I should like the Prince to know exactly how it all happened, and perhaps I shall feel more capable of talking about it by then." She was weeping bitterly. From the inner room, too, came a noise of perpetual wailing and lamentation: "Where are you, my lady, my sweet one?"—it could only be the old nurse who was speaking— "Come back to us, come back! But if she is dead, where is her body? Of course I want to look at you, my lovely one. Haven't you been the joy of my eyes, noon and night? Why, all I have lived for was to see the day when you would come into your own. And now, just when everything was beginning to come right, you go away and leave us. We've looked high and low for you. We don't know where you are. But they'll bring her back, they won't keep my lady. There's no god or devil that would have the heart to do it. Don't we know that the great god Indra* himself takes pity on poor mortals and gives back those whom he has snatched? But whether

---

* In her "distracted condition," Nurse confuses Indra, the sky-god, with Yama, the god of the underworld, about whom many stories of the Proserpine type are told.

it's a man or demon that's hiding her, and whether she's alive or dead, let him send her back to us, send her back!"

The nurse of course was in a distracted condition, and it would be a mistake to pay too much attention to her wild ramblings. But how had she got it into her head that the body was not there? Tokikata began to wonder whether Jiju's story was not a pure invention. "Look here," he said, "I have a strong suspicion that she is not dead at all but has been hidden by somebody. Prince Niou sent me here as his deputy for no other purpose but to find out the truth. You may succeed in putting him off with this story for a time. But he'll find out in the end, and I shall get into trouble for having been so foolish as to believe what you have just told me. He has evidently got the same suspicions as I have. But he was absolutely confident that if I could see either of you privately, he would be certain to hear the whole truth. I hope you will show him that his confidence was not misplaced. You must remember that this was no mere casual affair. He was madly, desperately in love with her—I have never seen anyone in such a condition before." Thus appealed to, Jiju saw nothing for it but to tell him at any rate some part of the truth. That Ukifune had not died of illness, Niou was almost certain to discover. "If I knew that she was merely in hiding, can you suppose," she said, "that I should be in such a condition as this? As you are aware, she had been out of sorts for some time. But what really upset her was a letter she got from His Excellency, containing (or so I gather) some reference or other which made her think he had got wind of what was going on. It distressed her very much, too, not to be able to tell her mother and the old nurse who were still fussing over the preparations for her move, that she had made other arrangements with you, and would be gone by the time His Excellency came for her. This all preyed on her mind, and at the end she was in such a state of desperation that I think she was glad to go. That's all Nurse meant by the stream of queer talk she poured out just now. She's half out of her mind with it all, poor thing." "Very well then," he said, more certain than ever that she was not telling the truth, "I won't trouble you any further just now. I think I have found out enough to go on with. But there's a good deal more that His Highness will want to know, and I expect that before long he'll be coming to enquire for himself." "I'm sure I hope, with due respect to His Highness, that he'll do no such thing," Jiju exclaimed. "Of course it has been a great thing for her—seeing him in this way; but I think that under the circumstances she would still much prefer that people didn't get to know about it. The secret has been well kept till now, and he'll surely have the kindness..." She had managed to satisfy the household in general that their mistress had died an ordinary death. But Tokikata was not to be put off so easily. She saw that if she let him stay there questioning her, the truth might at any moment slip out, and she answered as she did merely in order to try his patience and get him out of the way. Despite the torrents of rain that were still pouring, Ukifune's mother presently arrived. To have seen her daughter die by illness or accident in the ordinary way would have been terrible indeed. But that she should have vanished—should have done away with herself, as it now seemed—was unbelievable. What motive had she? A question natural enough to one who knew nothing of the terrible dilemma in which she had become involved. That Ukifune had taken her own life the mother could not believe; sooner indeed than think that, she was ready to accept the most fanciful explanations. In old-fashioned romances one constantly read of people being devoured by demons or lured away by lovely maidens who turned out to be foxes in disguise, and it could not be proved that such monsters did not still exist. There was, however, no need to indulge in remote suppositions. Was there not only too near at hand a quarter from which she had all along expected that danger would come? Yes, that was it. Some old nurse or other menial in the household,* hearing that Kaoru was about to set up a rival establishment and regarding this as a deadly affront to her mistress, had hatched some wicked plot to get Ukifune out of the way. Such a plot, however, could hardly have been effected without connivance on this side, and it occurred to her that one of the new maids had probably been suborned. She suggested this, but was told that it was impossible, for the simple reason that none of them were any longer in the house. "They told me," Ukon explained, "that they were not used to living so far away from everything and didn't know what to do with themselves. They said they knew there was a lot of work to be got through and not much time, but they were sure they could get on with it just as well at home; so we let them pack up all the stuff and take it with them to town. They were to rejoin us there, of course, as soon as we arrived."

As a matter of fact, not only the newcomers but a good many of the other gentlewomen as well had gone on ahead to the City, leaving Jiju and Ukon very short-handed. Jiju, in the course of tidying up the room, moved the ink-slab and found underneath it the poem† Ukifune had left there. It showed clearly enough, if indeed there was need of further proof, that her act had not been unpremeditated. Ukon too now remembered that quite a long time before the end her mistress had said something— to which she had paid little attention at the time—about wishing that she were dead.‡ The two women stood together at the window. It was

---

* Of the Second Princess, Kaoru's wife.
† "All these my miseries one stroke shall end..." See above, p. 1056.
‡ See above, p. 1050.

terrible, knowing what they did, to listen to the thunder of those waters, to see the pitiless waves go swirling by.

"It's dreadful to let her mother go on suspecting this person and that, and hunting high and low in the hope that she has been spirited away somewhere and may still be alive." Jiju agreed. "And while we are about it," she added, "wouldn't it be much better to tell her the whole story? I don't think she would mind her mother knowing now. It isn't as though it was through any fault of hers that it all began. She didn't like to be talked about, of course. But that was for his sake and not because she, poor thing, had anything to be ashamed of. There are other people,* too, who will think it very strange they were not given a chance to see the body, and though there's no need to tell them everything, I don't think we can let them remain entirely in the dark. In order to satisfy the people here there will have, of course, to be some pretence of a funeral, and the sooner the better. Already they are beginning to wonder why no one has seen the corpse. I don't, as I say, mind telling her mother; but that's no reason why all the world should know."

She took the mother aside and succeeded in telling the story. To do so, however, proved to be no such easy matter as she had supposed; for when it came to describing in so many words the terrible thing that they believed Ukifune to have done, Jiju found herself turning faint, and was several times obliged to break off in the middle of what she was trying to say. No wonder, the mother thought, when at last she grasped what Jiju was attempting to tell, no wonder this wild river had from the first moment inspired her with such a feeling of horror! "Surely you have looked for the body," she said, when she had recovered from the first shock—and there was a moment when in her anguish she came near following Ukifune's example and flinging herself into those dread waters—"You must know more or less where she did it. It's terrible not to be able even to have a funeral." "It would not have been any use," Jiju said. "Just look at the pace of the stream. The body won't have stayed where she went in. Indeed, I should think it must have reached the sea by now. Besides, if we're seen searching the river, people will begin to talk." Was it really no use to make any kind of search? Perhaps they were right; the mother was by no means sure. But at the moment she felt too dazed and shattered to begin doing anything.

Ukon and Jiju sent for a cart and put onto it their mistress's cushions, fans and other personal belongings, as well as her bed-clothes, which had remained just as they were since she threw them aside and slipped away. They then got hold of some priests—a son of Nurse's who was in Orders and an uncle who was a Teacher of Doctrine, together with some of his

---

* Nurse, for example.

disciples and some elderly bonzes whom Jiju had known since she was a child—and arranged that they should go into Retreat together during the Forty-nine Days* and read Masses for the Dead. The sight of the cart, got up so as to look as much like a hearse as possible, affected the mother and old nurse no less deeply for the fact that they knew it to be the mockery it was, and they swayed to and fro, covering their faces with their hands, as it drove towards the gate. At this moment Udoneri, with his son-in-law and some of the redoubtable night-watchmen, suddenly appeared. "As regards this funeral," Udoneri said, "you'll have of course to tell His Excellency what you have arranged. He'll very likely want to fix the date himself, and he'll certainly insist on everything being done in the correct way." "I am afraid it is too late to consult him now," said Ukon. "It's going to take place after dark tonight. We decided that it was better to do it as quietly as possible."

The cart was taken to the foot of a neighboring mountain and the contents-set on fire, no one being allowed to approach save the priests who were already in the secret. A sickly grey wreath trailed over the plain; nothing could have been more unlike the smoke of a real pyre. So far from being indifferent about such matters, country people regard funerals and the like as occasions of the greatest importance; indeed they hold death and everything connected with it in such awe that nothing will induce them to mention such things by their real names. "I can't make it out at all," one of the peasants said. "That's not what I call a proper funeral. They've certainly made very quick work of it. She was mistress of the house, after all." "That's just the reason," said another. "Those people from the Capital are all alike. If it's a husband or father that's managing it, he'll take some trouble. But when it's only brothers, as I dare say it was today, they don't seem to care." This, together with other disparaging remarks, was overheard by Ukon. It was not very agreeable to have even people of this sort criticizing the proceedings, though in a way it did not matter what they thought or said. But rumor flies fast, and if it should happen to reach Kaoru's ear that there had not been a proper funeral, he would at once suspect that the whole thing had been a ruse designed by Niou in order to get Ukifune safely away. This, however, could not last long. They were closely connected, and even if Kaoru decided that under the circumstances it was better to ask no questions and simply leave things as they were, it was bound to become apparent to him in time that his suspicions had been ill-founded. But more probably he would make enquiries, and having ascertained that she was not in Niou's hands, he would be forced to conclude that someone else was harboring her—that it was in fact merely a case of vulgar elopement. That such a thing should be believed about her

---

* During which the soul is in the Intermediate State between one incarnation and the next.

now that she was dead was a cruel injustice indeed to one the sole intimacies of whose life had been, as Ukon well knew, of a kind so different from the sordid entanglement with which she would now be credited—not by Kaoru only, but by some of her own people at Uji as well; for in the general confusion it had been impossible to manage everything as they intended, and there were, even among the lower servants, several whose suspicions had been aroused. There was nothing for it but to go to them one by one, reassure them as best she could or at any rate persuade them to keep their suspicions to themselves. "Later on," Ukon said to Jiju, "I am going to tell both of them.* But I think it's fairer to her to let them go on thinking that it happened in a natural way. I am afraid they will feel rather differently towards her when they know the truth. I believe I could make them understand about it if I got the chance of a quiet talk, but it's not the sort of thing one can send messages about."

In reality, however, the chief reason for all this secrecy was that they felt they were themselves very much to blame for what had occurred.

Kaoru meanwhile was at the temple of Ishiyama, where he had gone into Retreat in order to pray for his mother Princess Nyosan, who had gone there to recover from an illness. The news of Ukifune's death and hasty burial reached him through his bailiffs at Uji. But they were unable to give him a word of information as to how or why a young girl apparently in enjoyment of perfect health should suddenly have expired. He wished he had known sooner; the people at Uji would certainly have expected to hear from him and would indeed feel it to be very strange that he had not at once rushed to their assistance. So soon, therefore, as this terrible news reached him he dispatched an urgent letter which did not, however, arrive at Uji till early next day. "I would have come immediately," he wrote, "but I am pledged to remain here in Retreat for a fixed number of days in order to pray for my mother's recovery. I cannot understand why you were in such a hurry about the funeral, which I hear was carried out in a very inadequate way. You should have written to me and given me time to arrange for things to be done properly. It could surely have been put off for a couple of days. Of course you and I know well enough that all that sort of thing makes no difference. But I hear that the way the body was disposed of made a very bad impression on the villagers, and I am afraid they will think I am to blame." The letter was brought by Nakanobu. He found the household in a state of complete prostration. Lady after lady burst into tears when addressed, and having failed to get any sort of coherent answer even out of Ukon, who professed to be still too much overcome to speak, he was obliged to return to Ishiyama no wiser than he came. Kaoru was naturally very

---

* I.e. Kaoru and Niou.

much disappointed, but the scene at Uji was one which, from his own experience,* he could, alas, only too well imagine. What had possessed him to leave her in this lonely place, haunted with dismal memories of the past? If she had indeed taken steps to console herself the fault was not hers, but his own for having taken so little trouble about her, as no doubt Niou had pointed out. It was just what had always happened; he knew well enough that there was some strange defect in him that made him handle affairs of this sort in an incompetent, half-hearted way. It was clear that the state of agitation he was in was having, indirectly, a bad effect on his mother, and he hurried back to town. He did not feel he could face seeing the Second Princess: "Nothing alarming has happened to me myself," he said in his message, " but I have been brought into contact with an occurrence of very horrifying kind and am feeling so much upset that I fear I should be bad company..."†

A feeling of utter hopelessness and despondency had indeed descended upon him. It was futile to recall now, as he did at every moment, her face, her movements, her gentle ways; whereas while she was alive long periods would go by during which he scarcely thought about her at all. But he could form, it seemed, no human attachment that was not fated to end in misery. At the beginning of his life he had, it was true, intended to devote himself to quite other ends, and it seemed as though Buddha were angry with him for not fulfilling those early promises, and had sent calamity after calamity in the hope of turning him back to the true path. If that were so, the Blessed One had been successful indeed in concealing, for the purpose of the occasion, his merciful and compassionate nature! But the more he thought about it the more he felt that what had happened was in some way a retribution, and he had many services read.

For a time Niou was in an even worse condition. He fainted, wept, raved like one possessed. But at the end of two or three days he began to calm down, his tears dried and, though this terrible loss still weighed heavily on his spirits, to outward appearance he was completely himself again. He did his best during those first days to conceal from the world at large the pitiable condition that he was in and it was given out that this strange breakdown was due solely to the strain of his prolonged illness. But there were many who when they heard his state described felt certain that so violent and alarming an attack could not suddenly have descended upon him without some definite reason. Kaoru on his return to the Capital naturally heard rumors of his friend's sudden and inexplicable collapse. The first reflection which occurred to him was that it had certainly not stopped short—this affair between Niou and Ukifune—

---

* At the time of Agemaki's death.
† In the ritual, not in the social sense.

at a mere exchange of letters. They must have known one another, and very intimately. She was indeed the sort of woman who was bound from the first moment to attract Niou immensely. And in a way it mitigated Kaoru's grief to feel that, had she lived, the rift between himself and her could only have grown wider and wider.

At Court Niou's illness was the one topic of conversation, and everyone made a point of calling to enquire. Kaoru felt that if he shut himself up completely, above all if he failed to put in an appearance at Niou's, where everyone would naturally expect to see him, he would seem to be laying too much stress upon what to the world must seem a comparatively mild bereavement. The question whether he should wear mourning did not present itself, for his uncle Prince Shikibu had recently died, and he would have been obliged in any case to avoid bright colors, as indeed he naturally felt inclined to do at the present moment.

Kaoru, everyone thought, was looking handsomer than ever, though it was noticed that he was rather thin and pale. Niou was up and about again, and though he was not mixing in general company, all his more intimate friends had been admitted to his room. A meeting with Kaoru was at the moment the last thing he desired; but to turn him away when he had seen everyone else would have been very marked, all the more so because it was evident that Kaoru had outstayed the other guests on purpose to see him alone. "I don't myself regard it as anything very serious," Niou said, still struggling with the painful train of emotion that Kaoru's entry had aroused. "But it is hard not to become frightened about oneself when everyone else persists in taking such a black view. I am afraid they have succeeded in thoroughly scaring the people at the Palace,* which was quite unnecessary." It must, he felt, seem to Kaoru very absurd that while talking in this light-hearted strain he should have to pause at every other minute to wipe away his tears. "I am sure that he is thinking I am much more worried about myself than I choose to admit, and will set me down as a terrible coward," Niou said to himself, trying in vain to recover his composure.

But in point of fact Kaoru's reflections were of a very different order. He had been told that Niou had practically recovered, and had deduced from this that even if he and Ukifune had met, the affair could not have been of very long standing. But the scene that he was now witnessing obliged him to take another view. He felt convinced now that the thing had been going on for months—in fact, all the time. How they must both have laughed at him behind his back! It was infuriating to think of. Obviously she had not cared for him in the least, and it was absurd of him to mind what had become of her.

---

* The Emperor and the Empress.

"It's very odd that he seems to feel it so little," Niou thought, "when one thinks how extremely sensitive he is. I have seen him—over things that were a mere trifle compared to this—work himself up into such a state of emotion that the cry of a passing bird was enough to draw his tears. It must be obvious to him, whether he guesses the true cause or no, that I am very unhappy, and it is extraordinary that he should not attempt to show the slightest sign of sympathy. Well, I admire the fortitude with which he bears his loss, though he is the last person I should have expected to take such a thing lightly, considering he has always pretended that the thought of death perpetually haunted him, casting a gloom over his whole existence." Niou felt aggrieved; but the fact that Kaoru, however lightly he might take her death, was "a pillar she had leaned on" touched him. Yes, it was strange to think, he said to himself, gazing at Kaoru, how often she must have seen him sitting beside her couch in just such an attitude as he is sitting in by mine now. Kaoru was in a sense the only memorial of her that would remain to him. They talked for a while about indifferent things, but it was uphill work. It seemed better to embark, after all, on the topic that was in fact occupying both their minds. "In old days," Kaoru said, "when we had time to meet more frequently, my first thought, if anything interesting happened to me, was to come to your rooms and talk about it. But my present position gives me so much business to attend to, and you have so many engagements, that except on public occasions we seem to have ceased ever to meet at all. I wish I had time to come here more often. I feel that we are getting out of touch. I don't think, for example, that I have ever had the chance to tell you about a relation of Agemaki's whom I came across quite unexpectedly some time ago. I should like to have had her somewhere close at hand and been able to see her fairly frequently; but it happened at a time* when I had to be very careful about things of that kind and I thought it better that she should live out at Uji. I knew of course that I should never be able to get there for more than a day or two at a time, and I already had suspicions that I was by no means her only admirer. If I had ever regarded the relationship as anything more than a pleasant distraction from the cares of my official life, such an arrangement would of course have been very unsatisfactory. But all that I intended was to pass a few hours with her there occasionally. She was a charming companion and the plan seemed to work quite successfully, when suddenly she fell ill and died. You know that at the best of times I am apt to take rather a gloomy view of life, and naturally at the present moment, with this on my mind, I am feeling more than usually depressed. She was quite well only a few days before—but I dare say you have heard about it."

---

* At the time of his state marriage to the Second Princess.

It was Kaoru's turn to weep now. He tried, just as Niou had done a few moments before, to keep himself under control. But once they had started to flow the tears would not stop, and much to his own embarrassment he now broke down altogether. Niou was both touched and surprised. This showed, he thought, how easy it was to misjudge people. "Yes, it's a sad story," he said, affecting not to notice Kaoru's condition. "I heard something about it yesterday. I thought of writing to you, but I was not sure whether one was intended to know..." His voice died away. He too was still none too sure of himself. "Oh, I do not in the least mind your having known," Kaoru said. "Indeed I often thought of introducing you to her. Come to that, I dare say you knew her. You would have been quite likely to come across her at the Nijo-in." He paused significantly on these words. "However, it's very inconsiderate of me," he continued, "at a time when you are so unwell yourself, to come here harrowing you with sad stories about things that don't in any way concern you. Take care of yourself," he said, and after some further enquiries about Niou's health he hurried away.

It had not, Kaoru now saw clearly enough, merely been one of Niou's habitual escapades; he had been passionately fond of her. No destiny could ever have presented such strange contrasts as hers. Her brief existence had, to outward appearances, been of the most obscure and uneventful kind; yet strange to reflect, there was hardly a person throughout the length and breadth of the country who had not in some way or other been affected by it. Because[*] of her the walls of every holy place in the land had for weeks on end resounded with continual prayers and incantations; not an altar, not a holy stream, but had been turned to account by Prince Niou in his extremity—by Niou, darling of his Royal Parents, the foremost personage—at any rate the most sought after and admired—in the fashionable life of his time. Yes, to be singled out by Niou was a compliment indeed, for his experience was wide; yet it was clear that in those last months this country girl had held her own against all the most beautiful and intelligent women of the day. And as if that were not enough, she had at the same time been loved by a person of considerable public importance,[†] whose attentions had in a way been even more flattering, since they involved the risk of giving fatal offence in the highest quarters.[‡] But violent though the manifestations of Niou's grief were, Kaoru did not believe either that his own feelings for her had been less strong than Niou's or that his present sufferings were in reality less than those of his friend. It was only that he had a greater fear of making himself

---

[*] At the time of Niou's illness.

[†] I.e. Kaoru himself.

[‡] The Emperor would be offended and Kaoru's career ruined if it was thought that he had treated his wife (the Second Princess) with lack of consideration.

ridiculous. But though Kaoru was determined to banish the whole thing from his mind and go about his affairs as usual, there were moments when his composure deserted him, and flinging himself upon his bed he murmured "flesh and blood, not stocks or stones..."* There were many lesser aspects of the business that still very much worried him. It was certainly most unfortunate that the funeral had been such a perfunctory affair. Kozeri, for example, would be horrified if she heard about it. He could see that his own tenants were shocked at the hasty and irreverent manner in which the whole thing had been performed, and could only attribute it to the ignorance or inattention of Ukifune's own relations, who were known to be people of no great refinement. He felt indeed that he still knew singularly little about what had been occurring at Uji. It seemed hard to procure reliable information, and he felt tempted to go and make enquiries in person. But it was impossible at the moment for him to get away for more than a few hours. He knew that he should find a visit of that sort extremely harrowing and upsetting. Indeed, all things considered, it hardly seemed worthwhile. The fourth month came. It was a particularly trying period for Kaoru, for the tenth day of that month was the date he had fixed for bringing Ukifune to town. On the evening of that day he was sitting alone at the window in very low spirits when a cuckoo, attracted no doubt by the ravishing smell of the orange-blossom, passed over the garden, crying twice as it flew. "O Headman of the Fields of Death..."† He knew that Niou was spending the day with Kozeri at the Nijo-in, and plucking a spray of orange-blossom he sent it with the poem: "What means the message of the bird that haunts Death's mountain save that, bitter as my own, your tears in secret flow?"

Niou, when the letter was brought, was sitting alone with Kozeri, looking out into the night. In many ways she was, he thought, extraordinarily like Ukifune, and it was a consolation to be with her. "Heartless the Bird of Death, that silent should have passed a house where this sad fragrance‡ fills the night." Such was his answer. Kozeri saw the poems and knew quite well what they referred to. For her the news of Ukifune's sudden death at so early an age had been particularly disquieting. Of the three sisters she alone survived—perhaps because she had really had on the whole a singularly happy life. But it was clear that some sort of weakness ran in the family, and she feared that her turn would soon come.

---

  * "After all we are flesh and blood, not stocks or stones; if we do not like our feelings to bestirred, we must keep out of beauty's way." Po-Chü-i.
  † A name by which the cuckoo was popularly known. It was supposed to fly to and fro between this world and the land of the dead. Kaoru has in mind *Kokinshu*. 855, an anonymous poem the sense of which is: "O cuckoo, if it be true that you frequent the Realms of the Dead, seek out my lady and tell her that since the day she died I have never ceased to weep."
  ‡ The fragrance of the orange-blossom is the scent of remembrance.

It was impossible for Niou to conceal from her the fact that Ukifune's death had very much upset him; under the circumstances it seemed kinder to take her into his confidence, and he began now to give her an account—not quite accurate in all its particulars—of the whole business from start to finish. She showed plainly that she resented his not having told her all this long before. But the fact that she knew the whole story had the effect of drawing them together more than ever. Reports about the alarming state of his health had lately drawn such a quantity of visitors to the New Palace*—his father-in-law and that endless succession of Roku no Kimi's brothers were becoming a perfect nuisance—that he was particularly thankful to have this quiet place to escape to.

Like Kaoru he was not at all satisfied by the accounts he had received of Ukifune's illness and death. It struck him as very strange that a healthy girl should die so suddenly. The best thing to do seemed to be to send for Ukon. The place, when Tokikata† arrived, seemed completely deserted. Ukifune's mother, unable to endure the noise of the river, had not stayed out the full period of mourning. One or two priests were about, but he knew there was no harm in their seeing him as they were already in the secret. As for the watchmen—it was strange indeed to remember how on that last unhappy occasion, which had cost Niou such bitter disappointment, they had leapt out upon him. Today they let him pass without a word. Being one of Niou's most confidential servants, he had witnessed some of his wildest outbursts of grief in those first days and had deplored them as exaggerated and undignified. After all, Ukifune was not a person of any consequence, and Niou had only known her for an extremely short time. But now that Tokikata was here again, those few but memorable excursions—above all the night when he had taken them in the boat—rose vividly before him. He remembered how handsome, how delightful he had thought her, and it moved him deeply to know that he should never see her again. He noticed that several of the men he had brought with him were in tears and it did not surprise him to find Ukon still weeping bitterly. He hastened to explain his mission, but she seemed very unwilling to comply. "It would set everyone talking," she said, "if I were to go away just now.‡ And in any case I feel quite unable to talk about it at present. When the Forty-nine Days are over I might be able to get away for a few days—I could say I was going to a temple or something of that sort. By then it would seem quite natural. I hope too that by that time I shall be more myself again. There's no need for him to send for me. Tell him that as soon as I can manage it, I should like very much

---

* Where he lived with his official consort Roku no Kimi, the sixth of Yugiri's many daughters.

† Niou's retainer.

‡ I.e. until the Forty-nine Days were over. During this period the soul, being suspended, as we have seen, between one incarnation and the next, is in need of constant prayers.

to come and tell him quietly just how it all happened." He pointed out that it would be much more convenient if she came there and then; but she would not stir. "Of course, I know much less than you do about their friendship," Tokikata said, with tears still in his eyes, "but it is clear enough that to the Prince it meant a great deal. There is no doubt that he would have brought her up to the Capital. You ladies, of course, would in that case have accompanied her. I may say that we were all of us looking forward to the pleasure of getting to know you better, and it is a great disappointment to us that under the circumstances we are not likely to meet again. You have our deepest sympathy, ladies!" Then looking round for Jiju: "You'll surely not let me take back an empty carriage, when His Highness selected it with special care and sent it here on purpose to fetch one of you?" Ukon called her into the room. "I think you'd better go," she said. "I don't know why you should think that I'm any better able to tell him about it than you are," Jiju objected. "Moreover, as you say, the period of mourning is not over and His Highness won't want me there while I am still unclean."* "During his illness," Tokikata said, "he went in for all kinds of avoidances and purifications; but I can assure you he is not in the mood now to worry about whether anyone coming from here is unclean or not. On the contrary, nothing I am certain would please him better than to join the mourners† in the death-chamber itself. He cared a great deal more deeply for her than you seem to suppose. In any case, the Forty-nine Days are nearly over.‡ Surely one of you will come." Jiju was indeed longing to see Niou again. This might be her last chance, and she felt she had better not refuse. She looked very well in black. She could not find a black apron, and remembered with a pang that, thinking she would have no further need for such a garment§ now, she had not had one dyed. She was obliged in the end to take a light-brown one, such as she usually wore. She felt very lonely in the carriage. It was a different journey indeed from the one to which she had been looking forward—the breathless escape, the perilous moonlight flitting that would have given her a chance at last to show the lovers what staunch devotion meant.

Niou was touched at her having come. He felt, however, that it would be better if Kozeri did not hear of it, and he had Jiju's carriage brought round to a side door. "Now tell me all about it," he said. "She had been in very low spirits for several days," Jiju said, "and on the night it happened I could see she had been crying. I did my best to find out what was the matter, but it was very difficult to get anything out of her. She just said she was unhappy and so on; it was all quite vague. But I had the

---

* Through contact with the dead.
† The room where anyone died was unclean for forty-nine days.
‡ This was perhaps a slight exaggeration.
§ The apron, *mo*, was only worn in the presence of superiors.

impression that there was something she was keeping from us—something terrible that no living soul must ever know. Never for a single instant did it occur to me that the very idea of doing such a thing could possibly enter her head." She then told him of the desperate act by which Ukifune had met her end. "I'm afraid there's not the slightest doubt of it," she said. This was far, far worse than anything he had supposed. Only the most agonizing despair could, he felt, have given her the courage to plunge into those seething waters. Why had he not been there to rush out to her, to drag her away? It was torture to think how easily he or anyone might have prevented it. But it was no use talking about that now. "You'll think, I know," Jiju said, "that we ought to have suspected something when she burnt those letters..." Far on into the night she stayed there telling him about the last days—their vain efforts to find out what was going on in her mind and the discoveries[*] they had made when it was too late. Niou had till tonight taken no particular interest in Jiju; but now their common loss drew him to her. "I should think you had better stay here,"[†] he said, "I am sure you would be welcome." "Perhaps when I am out of mourning..." she said. "It is very good of you to suggest it; but I am afraid I don't at the moment feel much like taking up a fresh post." "Well, in any case come and see me again," he said. It would be a comfort to him, he felt, sometimes to have a talk with her. It was dawn indeed before he let her go. He insisted on her accepting a box of combs and a chest packed with dresses. There were all sorts of other things that he had intended for Ukifune, and having no further use for them he would gladly have seen Jiju take them all away. But he knew that such a gift would be embarrassing and only picked out a few things that were suitable for Jiju's personal use. Even so, she would far rather have not accepted them; for people would think it very strange that, having set out empty-handed, ostensibly to visit a temple, she should return with so much luggage. But it seemed churlish to refuse. "The trouble is," she said afterwards, when she was beguiling an idle moment by going through the things with Ukon, "I don't know where to put all these dresses till we are out of mourning." They were in faultless taste and style. It was clear that Niou had taken infinite pains over every detail, and it was heart-rending that Ukifune should never even have seen them.

Kaoru had, it is true, made-up his mind that no good purpose could be served by his going in person to Uji. But he still regarded the accounts he had received as extremely unsatisfactory, and he finally decided that it would be better to go. As scene after scene of the familiar journey unfolded before him, his mind went back over the past, to those far-off

---

[*] Such as the poem attached to the temple account.
[†] Go into service with Kozeri.

days when he first heard Prince Hachi's name. A fatality seemed to hang over all his dealings with that house. It was as though Buddha, having guided him there solely for his spiritual advantage, were determined to teach him by one terrible lesson after another that such a place could not with impunity be profaned.

"There is still a great deal more that I should like to know," he said to Ukon when she came out to him. "I did not mean to come till the mourning was over; but the accounts I have heard are so very confused and unsatisfactory that I felt I could not wait. Tell me first of all what sort of illness it was that carried her off with such terrible rapidity." Ukon had a whole glib story on the tip of her tongue—the experience of the last few weeks had made her pretty well at home in inventions of that kind—and if instead she changed her mind and for once in a way told the truth, it was because Ben no Kimi had now found out that it was not a case of illness, so that he was bound to hear about it in the end. It was better, she thought, that he should get the facts from someone like herself who knew them accurately than pick up mere gossip. Moreover, it was one thing to concoct a story for use in case of his arrival, but quite another to bring it out, with Kaoru himself sitting there in front of her looking so terribly in earnest.

For a moment Kaoru was too much taken aback to make any comment. But what possible reason was there to believe this story, he almost instantly reflected? Ukon had on her own showing lied once already, and the story she was now telling was on the face of it ridiculous. So far from being the sort of person to fly off into a sudden fit of rage or despondency, Ukifune was extraordinarily sensible, even-tempered, dependable. No, it was obviously a clumsy invention, designed by Ukon and Jiju to hide their mistress's tracks. And yet—it was hard indeed to believe that Niou's grief was merely simulated. Moreover, his own arrival here today had been quite unexpected; but he had found not the gentlewomen only, but the whole household from top to bottom in a state that could not conceivably have been assumed merely for his benefit. "I have still some questions to ask," he said. "For example, did anyone else disappear more or less at the same time? That's a thing I should like to be quite certain about. I am afraid, you see, that I don't find your account of the affair at all convincing. People do things like this when they are suddenly confronted with some appalling situation from which, at the moment, death seems the only possible escape. Yet all you can tell me is that she was depressed at my coming here so seldom. There is something that you are keeping back..." She had expected as much; but it put her in a very awkward position. "You must consider all the circumstances," she said. "As I dare say you've heard, my mistress had the misfortune to be brought up amid rather undesirable surroundings.* She had only been at the Capital a very short while when she came here. Uji is a different matter from Hitachi, to be sure; but one could hardly be more cut off from the world, and I think she was often very unhappy. Of course the one thing she looked forward to was your visits. Little though the time was that you and she actually spent together, she felt, I know, that her friendship with you made amends for all the misfortunes of her earlier days. Then came the news that you wanted to have her close at hand, somewhere where you could see her every day. You can imagine how excited she was. She didn't say much, but I could see that she was thinking of nothing else from noon till night. Everyone here, of course, regarded it as settled, and all around her she saw her people, who were naturally delighted at the prospect of such a move, hurrying on with the preparations; and her mother too, who felt that, after that dreadful start in the wilds of Hitachi and all the other troubles and humiliations that the poor child had endured, things were at last beginning to come right. Then suddenly came an extraordinary letter from you and all that fuss about the watchmen, which was due, we understood, to your having complained that people from outside were carrying on with the maids. These guards are rough country people, and I dare say they went far beyond their instructions; but if it was merely trouble in the servants' quarters that they were supposed to stop, they certainly set about it in an extraordinary way. She generally heard from you every few days. But after that one strange letter, you gave up writing altogether. You can surely imagine the impression that made on someone as easily cast down as she was, after all that she had been through since her earliest days. It wasn't only that she was hurt at your treating her like this. She knew what a terrible blow it would be to her mother, whose one desire in life had been to secure for her a proper footing in the world, to see her disgraced and cast aside. I think it was that more than anything else that weighed upon her mind. That's all I can tell you. As for your idea—you have not said it in so many words, but I can see it's one of the things that are at the back of your mind—as for this idea of yours that someone or other has spirited her away, all I can say is I only wish there were the slightest evidence that you are right."

Ukon wept so bitterly as she said these last words that once more all Kaoru's suspicions† disappeared. "You realize, I am sure," he said, "that if I had been anyone in a less conspicuous position—if I had been free to come and go as I chose, I should never have been content to leave her even for so short a while in a place where I could so seldom see her. The

---

* In the remote province of Hitachi. It was considered a great social disadvantage to be brought up in the country.
† That Niou had carried Ukifune away.

arrangement was of course very unsatisfactory, but I consoled myself with the thought that before long I should be able to carry out plans which would not only have ensured our meeting much more frequently, but would also have given her for the rest of her life the sort of surroundings to which her rank entitled her. Up to a certain point I think she understood all this and made allowances for me; but I feel that other influences were at work. There is something I rather hesitate to mention now that this is all a thing of the past. However, since we are alone together... Tell me, this affair with Niou—when did it begin? I know how attractive he is, and I can quite well imagine her falling madly in love with him, as indeed innumerable women have done. Then when it suddenly became impossible for her to see him, she would have fallen into a state of terrible despair. Hasn't it occurred to you that this may be the explanation? I see from your face that it has. Very well, then, hadn't you better drop all this secrecy and tell me the whole story from beginning to end?"

This was no mere conjecture on his part, of that Ukon felt certain. Someone had told him. But how much? It was most inconvenient not to know. "I am very sorry you've been told about that unfortunate business," she said. "If I had thought for a moment that such a thing could happen there, I would never have left her side." She paused to reflect. "I don't know how much you have been told," she went on. "It was one evening when my lady was staying with her sister at the Nijo-in. How His Highness ever discovered that there was such a person in the house we can none of us imagine, but somehow or other he found his way to her rooms. We had to speak pretty sharply before we could get rid of him; but fortunately we managed it just in time—I mean, before any real harm was done. However, her mother wouldn't hear of her remaining in the Palace after a thing like that had happened, and removed her at once to that queer little place in the Third Ward, where she was living when you made her acquaintance. The Prince did not so much as know my lady's name, and she naturally imagined that she had heard the last of him. But not at all; early this year—no one knows how—he discovered that she was here at Uji and began writing to her. For some time she paid no attention to his letters; but her people pointed out that to treat a Royal Highness in that rude way was a far worse thing than any harm which could possibly come of answering the letters politely; and in the end she did occasionally reply. That's all it amounted to, so far as any of us are aware."

The tone in which she said these last words seemed to imply that, having gone so far, she would go no farther. No doubt that was all she was at liberty to say, and to insist would be unkind. However, he felt that he saw the whole thing pretty clearly now. She had of course fallen very much in love with Niou, and it was agonizing for her suddenly to be cut off from him. But there was more in it than that. "The trouble was,

I am certain," he said to himself, "that she still remained deeply attached to me too." It was the difficulty of making up her mind one way or the other that had eventually unsettled her reason. But even so, if this terrible river had not been so close at hand, the idea of taking her own life would probably never have entered her head. If only he had not chosen this, of all places, for her to live in! Here she had hardly a step to go. A sudden desperate impulse and the thing was over. If she had been somewhere on the hills, for example, however desperate her state of mind had been, she would never have set out to trudge the countryside, vaguely hoping to find a river. How he hated this place and everything connected with it! There had been times, more than once in his life, when the very stones of that wild mountain-road had been dear to him because it led here. But now his one desire was never to set foot on it again, never so long as he lived to hear the fatal village so much as named.

Suddenly he remembered the evening when Kozeri had first revealed to him the fact of Ukifune's existence. How sinister seemed to him now the name* that, since that conversation, he and Kozeri had given her! Yes, it was by his doing that she had died, as surely as though he had cast her with his own hands into that hated stream. Then there was the mother. Up till now he had been thinking rather unkindly of her, because he imagined that it was she who had made the very inadequate arrangements for the disposal of the body. But now, of course, all this was explained.† It was terrible to think of what she must be suffering. She knew, he supposed, nothing about the affair with Niou; and indeed, though she claimed‡ more for her child than usually fell to the lot of a Governor's daughter, the possibility of so exalted a connection could not have occurred to her in her wildest dreams. Consequently she must regard Ukifune's troubles as solely due to some complication§ that had developed on Kaoru's side.

He knew now of course that there was no question of pollution. But his attendants were naturally still under the impression that someone had died in the house, and he thought it better not to go in. He got someone to fetch the shaft-rest of his carriage and tried sitting on that, just outside the main door. But this was very uncomfortable, and finally he moved to a mossy bank under a wide-spreading shady tree. He looked about him. "When to this house, whence those I loved are fled, my steps no longer turn, who will remain to tend its crumbling walls or garner in the secrets of this ancient tree?"

---

* "The Image." The same word is used for the images that those desiring to escape from the toils of love cast into sacred streams. See Part V, p. 947 *seq.*

† It was only a mock funeral.

‡ On the ground that Ukifune was in reality Prince Hachi's child.

§ For example, opposition on the part of Kaoru's wife, the Second Princess.

Such was his poem. The place was too full of memories. He felt more than ever that he would never come there again. He sent for the Teacher, who had now risen to the rank of Professor of Monastic Discipline, and put him in charge of the measures that were being taken for the good of Ukifune's soul. The number of priests who were in occupation of the death-chamber was considerably increased, and in view of the manner of her death[*] it seemed that special rites of propitiation were necessary, and it was arranged that on every seventh day[†] there should be a dedication of holy books and images.

It was now quite dark, but he could not face the prospect of spending a night here alone. He had already made efforts to see Ben no Kimi, but she sent back word that she now felt herself to be too broken in body and spirit to have any dealings with the outside world. He had no desire to force himself upon her. Why had he not arranged for the move[‡] to take place a little earlier? There was nothing really to prevent it. The noise of those swirling waters echoed in his ears long after he had left the river far behind him. It was terrible to know that she was still there, on some rocky floor, amid the weeds and shells. Ukifune's mother, fearing that she would get into trouble if it was thought that she had come straight from a place of defilement to her younger daughter's[§] bedside, had not ventured to go home, but was drifting aimlessly from one hired lodging to another. It was a great anxiety to be away from home at such a time; but fortunately everything went well. However, the period of mourning was still not over, and she felt it would be wrong[¶] to go to the house. She had lain for days on end entirely wrapped up in her own sorrow, without even a thought of her other children and stepchildren, when something happened which, despite the condition she was in, gave her real pleasure. A messenger arrived with a letter from Kaoru. "I should have written long ago," he said, "had I not been entirely overcome by this terrible and unexpected loss. Moreover, judging by my own state, I could well imagine that you were in no condition to deal with correspondence, and it seemed better to let a little time go by. I am of course completely shattered by what has happened; but if I have the misfortune to survive this bereavement[**] I very much hope that you will find time to call on me. It would be a comfort to talk to someone who cared for her as you did." "He also asked me to tell you," said Nakanobu, who brought the

---

[*] Suicide was regarded by Buddhists as a crime. It was only at a later period that it came to be regarded as meritorious.
[†] The seventh, fourteenth, twenty-first, etc., are the critical days in the soul's journey.
[‡] Of Ukifune to the Capital.
[§] Sakon's wife, who was having a baby.
[¶] Unlucky for the child.
[**] A formula obligatory in the mouths of mourners.

letter, "that he feels you must think it very remiss of him not to have got into touch with you long ago. He wants you to know that he has been on the point of doing so time after time, ever since he made your daughter's acquaintance, and trusts you will understand that his silence has been due to dilatoriness, not to ill will. If there is anything, now or in the future, that he can do for you he hopes you will not hesitate to let him know. He believes, for example, that you have young sons who will shortly be making their appearance at Court, and if a word from him in any quarter would make things easier for them..."

Explaining that her defilement was of a very slight nature—as she was in reality not defiled at all, there seemed no harm in this—she insisted upon Nakanobu's entering the house,* while with tears in her eyes she set about answering Kaoru's letter. "I neither expected nor desired to survive this terrible loss," she wrote; "but I cannot now feel sorry to have been spared. It seems indeed as though a kindly fate was unwilling to release me till I had received at your hands the undreamt-of honor and privilege that you have conferred upon me today. As you know, the difficulties of my daughter's early life were all the more painful for me to witness because I believed them to be entirely due to my own shortcomings. But having failed miserably myself to secure any sort of footing in the world, I was determined that Ukifune should have every possible chance to do better, and the rumor which reached me of your extraordinarily flattering intentions† on her behalf made me feel that my prayers had been answered, and that I could at last face the future with little or no anxiety. Well, it has all come to nothing. Once more that dreadful place—for does not "Uji" means sorrow?—has well deserved its ominous name. As for your touching offer to forward the interests of my younger children—it alone suffices to make me hope that I shall be spared a little longer, and if I am, you may be certain I shall avail myself of your kindness. For the moment, however, I must not try to write any more..."

She felt she ought to give something to Nakanobu. But it was obviously impossible to give him the sort of present that would have been suitable for an ordinary messenger. She remembered that she had set aside a belt with panels of carved rhinoceros-horn and a very handsome sword, meaning to offer them to Kaoru on the occasion of Ukifune's removal to town. She put them in a bag and sent them out to Nakanobu, who was already entering his carriage, with a note to the effect that Ukifune had intended them for him. "I am afraid it was only that the mother felt she had to give you something," Kaoru said when Nakanobu showed

---

* Nakanobu thought Ukifune had died of illness, and knowing that the mother had been to Uji would regard her as taboo. The defilement would only have been regarded as "of a slight nature" if, for example, she had not entered the death-chamber, had not touched the body, or the like.
† Of giving her a house in town.

him this present. "It never occurred to me that she would think that." "I saw her personally," Nakanobu said, "and told her of your offer to do something for the other children. I could see that she was delighted that you should have thought of it. She said she hoped you wouldn't expect much of her boys. They are young and have not had time to get very far. But if you are sure you will not be ashamed to have such graceless youngsters under your roof, she would be delighted, she said, to send all or any of them round at once, to serve you in whatever capacity." This was really rather more than Kaoru had intended. These boys were not of a class with which he usually associated. It would be impossible, if he had them in the house, not to treat them more or less as friends, and to do so would be in effect to make the first open acknowledgment of his relationship with Ukifune. For apart from that relationship there could be no possible reason for his consorting with youths of such humble origin. He was reluctant that what the world would regard as an affair with a Governor's daughter should become generally known. But the prejudice against such unions was certainly a very unreasonable one. Girls of that class had often been received into the Emperor's household and had sometimes become notorious favorites; and countless persons in much the same position as Kaoru himself had kept girls of the peasant class—and not girls only, but even women who were by no means novices in the world of love. If he had ever for a moment contemplated giving her a position that would compete with that of the Second Princess, he would indeed have been gravely guilty. What mattered most, though, was that this was the one way open to him of showing his sympathy with the mother in her bereavement and making her feel that his connection with the family had not been wholly and exclusively disastrous.

It was not long before the mother received a visit from her husband, who upbraided her bitterly for absenting herself at such a moment.* He had not, during all these months, ever troubled to enquire where Ukifune was living or what had become of her, assuming when he gave the matter a thought at all that she was eking out her existence in some very obscure and humble way. The mother had thought it better to say nothing about the subject till Ukifune came up to town. She could well imagine how astonished he would be to learn that so far from having gone down in the world the girl was living under Kaoru's protection in a splendid mansion of her own. But there was no point now in further concealment, and she told him the whole story. Like most men of his kind he stood in exaggerated awe of his betters, and when his wife showed him Kaoru's letter he handled it as though it were something almost too sacred to be touched by common hands. "Just imagine," he murmured, "what a

---

* When the younger girl was having a baby.

stroke of luck! And with His Excellency too— it's hard to believe. And then with a future like that in front of her, to die and lose it all! I can't imagine anything more terrible. Of course I know His Excellency quite well. I don't mean I have ever been really intimate with him; I should say that very few people had. And he has promised to help my boys—to bring them on a little? Well, that's excellent news, to be sure. It will make a lot of difference to them."

The mother fondly imagined that if Kaoru were disposed, even now that Ukifune was dead, to do something for her family, he would have helped them all a thousand times more if she had still been alive; and though she was glad they were not going to be wholly forgotten, it distressed her bitterly to think of all they had lost. She little knew that had not Kaoru considered him responsible for Ukifune's death and longed, inadequate though such compensation might be, to do anything for the mother that he could, these rough, ungainly youths were the last people in the world he would ever have dreamt of patronizing.

He knew that strictly speaking it was not permissible to solemnize the full rites of the Forty-nine Days in the case of a death that was merely presumed. He felt, nevertheless, that the circumstances justified him in disregarding this objection, and arranged with the Teacher that the ceremony should be performed in the privacy of his mountain temple. He gave instructions, however, that the full complement of sixty priests was to be employed, and saw to it that they were rewarded by an ample distribution of alms. The mother was also there, and arranged for a number of additional Masses. From Niou came a silver bowl containing several bars of gold.[*] It was of course impossible for him under the circumstances to make an offering of this kind in his own name, and he presented it through Ukon. Jiju and one or two others at once realized whence it came, but the rest were sorely puzzled to know how such things could have come into Ukon's possession. All Kaoru's more intimate retainers were there, and many to whom they described the proceedings of the day were at a loss to understand why such a stir should have been caused by the death of this obscure country girl. It was rumored that she was not the Governor's daughter at all, but a child of one of the greatest houses in the land. This, however, seemed to be contradicted by the fact that the Governor himself had turned up at Uji and behaved in such a way as to suggest that, though he preferred to keep in the background, it was really he who had organized the whole affair. In point of fact he was annoyed that even a private occasion of this kind should so far exceed anything that he himself could have attempted. At the time of his daughter's confinement he had not merely ransacked his own considerable collections,

---

[*] Not for use as currency, but for the gildings of images.

but had sent for things both to China and Shi-ragi.* Yet what a poor show he had made compared with such a ceremony as he was witnessing today! It was perhaps just as well that Ukifune had died, for with backing of this sort she was certainly destined to throw his other daughters into the shade. Kozeri too had special services read, and sent supplies for the entertainment of the officiating priests, choir, and ministrants and so on, at the conclusion of the ceremony.

The whole business made so much stir that it reached the Emperor's ears. It was the first intimation he had had of Kaoru's infidelity. He was however, far from feeling any resentment. On the contrary, it harrowed him to think that respect for the Second Princess should have obliged Kaoru to do violence to his own feelings by according such inadequate treatment to someone of whom he had obviously been very fond.

The loss was one that affected Niou and Kaoru in very different ways. This sudden shock to his feelings just when passion was at its full tide had completely prostrated Niou at the time. He felt that he must at all costs find some means of distracting himself, and his experiments in this direction multiplied so rapidly that he was soon leading much the same life as before. Kaoru meanwhile hoped that by immersing himself in the affairs of the strange brood he had taken under his wing he would escape from, or at any rate soften the pangs of sorrow and remorse. The expectations, however, proved to be ill-founded.

The Empress, who was in half-mourning owing to the death of her uncle, was still at the New Palace. The vacancy at the Board of Rites which had been caused by Prince Shikibu's death was filled by Niou's elder brother, the Second Prince, who seemed to be taking his duties very seriously, for he hardly ever joined in the gaieties of the New Palace. It was, however, chiefly here, and above all in the apartments of his sister the First Princess, that Niou came to seek distraction. It piqued him that among his own sister's gentlewomen there should be any good-looking girl who had not allowed him to cultivate her acquaintance. There was, however, a certain Kosaisho, with whom Kaoru had once been rather intimate. She was certainly good-looking, but it was chiefly for her accomplishments that he valued her. He knew no one whose touch pleased him more, whether on the lute or other stringed instruments. She wrote a very good letter and her powers of conversation were far above those of most of the girls he knew. Naturally Niou too was attracted by her and had taken for granted that he would as usual have no difficulty in cutting Kaoru out. To his surprise, however, she refused to have anything to do with him. "Someone had to," she said, "if only to break the monotony." "At last," Kaoru thought, "I have found someone who is different from

---

* Part of Korea.

the rest." Nothing could have been better calculated to send her up in his estimation.

Hearing of his bereavement Kosaisho, though it was a long time since she had seen him, felt that she must write. "Not least, in comprehension of your loss—last though it be in time—judge this belated word from one whose lot the world holds too obscure to proffer sympathy." Such was her poem. "Could I but have died in her place—"* It was written on carefully selected paper, and reaching him in the hush of the summer evening, was well attuned to the melancholy thoughts that were passing through his mind. "Strange that you read thus well the thoughts of one so sternly schooled to loss that not a sigh betrays his sorrow to the world."

He felt he must go and see her at once. "Your note gave me such pleasure," he explained, "that, as you see, I have come round immediately to thank you for it." Her room, or so it was called, but it was barely more than a cubicle boarded off from the passage, was hardly (she felt) the place to receive a personage so important as Kaoru had now become; moreover, it was extremely unlike him to pay such a visit at all. To see someone of such importance squeezed in an undignified attitude into the narrow space between the lintels of her rickety door was rather embarrassing. But she made no attempt to apologize. Her manner of receiving him could not, indeed, have been more judicious. She talked freely and very much to the point about every topic that he raised; but without the slightest trace of presumption or over-familiarity. She was of course far more intelligent than Ukifune. It was a thousand pities that she had been obliged to go into service. He for one would not be at all sorry to have her in his keeping. He was on the verge of telling her about Niou's part in the unhappy business at Uji, but at the last moment refrained from doing so.

The lotuses were now in bloom, and the Empress decided to hold a solemn Recital of the Hokkekyo.† A number of holy books and images were dedicated in memory of Genji, Murasaki and other deceased members of her family. The ceremonies‡ on the day of the Fifth Roll were particularly magnificent, and as the ladies of the Court were given permission to ask their friends the attendance was enormous. On the morning of the fifth day, when the last service was over, came the very considerable business of putting things straight again. Endless hangings and decorations had to be removed, furniture put back in its place, gangways closed. So vast had been the crowds that it was difficult to give everyone a view, and in the end the whole Palace had been laid completely open, back and front alike. The First Princess,§ whose own apartments had become involved in the

---

* There is no doubt an allusion, but it has not been satisfactorily traced.
† The Lotus Scripture.
‡ The ritual drama of Shakyamuni's servitude to the Rishis. See Part IV, p. 737.
§ Niou's elder sister, for whom Kaoru had always felt a great admiration. See below, p. 1086,

general disorder, was accommodated for the moment in the cross-wing that connected her usual quarters with the main building. Most of her ladies were worn out with so much listening, and in the afternoon were allowed to go and rest in their own rooms. The Princess, indeed, found herself left practically alone. Kaoru, after changing his clothes, went and waited near the fishing-bower, hoping to catch the priests on their way out; for there was something important he wanted to say to one of them. It seemed, however, that they had already gone, but he stayed for a while to enjoy the cool air that rose from the moat.

The few ladies who remained in attendance on the First Princess—among them was Kaoru's friend Kosaisho—had done what they could to make the place comfortable for her, setting up screens and turning it into a sort of ante-chamber.

Kaoru, who was standing in the garden just outside, heard a rustle of skirts. One of the sliding-doors at the back of the building was not properly shut. Wondering whether by any chance Kosaisho was among the ladies within, he peeped through the gap. The place was not in the usual disorderly condition in which things are left when such ladies are alone together. Indeed so thoroughly had everything been tidied up and put away that he was able to obtain an unusually clear and unimpeded view of what was happening within. He expected to see the Princess; but she was certainly not one of those three women whom he saw chipping an ice-block, and for the rest there was only a little girl. The women had discarded their long cloaks and the child was jacketless. They all seemed very much at their ease, and he was just beginning to wonder whether the Princess was there after all, when he caught sight of her, dressed in flimsy white, watching with an air of much amusement the scramble that was going on to get hold of the best bits of ice. It was an enchanting smile, and altogether an exquisite face. She was sitting with her head bent slightly towards him, letting her splendid hair fall in one straight line to the ground. The weather was extremely hot, and no doubt it bothered her to have her neck and shoulders encumbered. There was not a shadow of doubt about it; she was far and away the handsomest woman he had ever seen. The three ladies in attendance, who would all generally have been considered very good-looking, suddenly seemed to him by contrast quite heavy and plain. One of them, wearing a gown of unstiffened yellow silk and a light-brown apron, was however obviously a person of considerable refinement. She was partly hidden from him; but he could tell it merely by the way she handled her fan. "And this is supposed to be the way to get cool!" she exclaimed, laughing. "Your Highness is lucky only to be looking on." The moment he heard the voice he knew that this was Kosaisho.

---

note.

The other three continued to hammer valiantly at the ice-block, melting the chips in their hands, on their foreheads, against their chests, and going through all sorts of absurd antics. Kosaisho wrapped up a piece of ice in paper and held it in front of the Princess, who passed her delicate hands over the cool block. "No, I won't hold it myself," the Princess said. "I hate to have things dripping on me." He could only just catch her words. But after all these years of waiting* to have at last heard her voice was an unspeakable joy. She was a mere child when he had last seen her, and he himself had only been capable of admiring her in a boyish way. What offence had he committed that the gods should have given him this chance today? For one thing was clear, unless he speedily subdued this new and least forgivable folly, misery and frustration, of a sort only too familiar, were what he must look forward to. Yet he still gazed as before.

Suddenly he heard a rapid footstep behind him. An under-servant who had been in attendance, overcome by the heat, had gone to the back of the house to get a little fresh air. Suddenly, however, she remembered that in her hurry she had forgotten to close the catch of the door, and frightened that if this were noticed she would get into trouble, the woman now came rushing back. She saw that there was a man standing at the door and wondered who it could be. She did not, however, make any attempt to hide from him; the only thing she was thinking about was how to get the door shut as soon as possible. Kaoru was obliged to retreat rapidly. The woman might easily recognize him, and the situation in which he had been found was somewhat compromising.

The woman on reaching the door discovered to her consternation that the screens, though neatly arranged, did not quite touch, and the greater part of the room was all too plainly visible from the spot where the intruder had been standing. It couldn't have been, she was sure, a complete stranger. Probably it was one of Yugiri's sons. If there was trouble about it people would at once ask who left the door open. But she had noticed that the eavesdropper was wearing a suit of unstiffened silk, which hardly rustled at all, so that it was quite possible no one had heard him.

The fatal thing, Kaoru said to himself as he hastened away, was ever to have deviated from the course he had set for himself in those early days of study and prayer. From that moment a succession of entanglements, each more disastrous than the last, had darkened his life. If only he had turned his back on the world before all this began! He would now be installed in some far-off mountain temple, there to end his days, beyond the reach of anything that could agitate or unsettle him. For years he had

---

* For Kaoru's feelings towards the First Princess, with whom he had played as a child (Part IV, p. 705), see Part V, pp. 878, 920, 936.

been longing to see her; he could not now imagine why. He should have known that, if he valued his peace of mind, he ought on the contrary to have done everything in his power to keep out of her way.

He rose early next morning. It could not be denied that the Second Princess was looking extremely pretty. But that was all one could say. There was no question of comparing her with her sister; she had not a trace of the indescribable brilliance and distinction that, in the First Princess, had yesterday amazed him. Of course accidents of circumstance—lighting, dress, or what not—might yesterday have played their part. "You have got on much too thick a dress," he said, "for such a day as this. One gets tired of seeing a woman always wearing the same sort of clothes, and the weather we are having gives a chance to break the monotony..." "Go to my mother's rooms and ask Daini to look up some thin silk and make an unlined dress," Kaoru said to one of the Second Princess's people, who were delighted to find him at last taking an interest in their mistress's appearance. He then went off to say his prayers, and after spending some time attending to various matters in his own rooms, he came back to the Princess's quarters. The dress he had ordered was hanging across the back of her couch. "Why haven't you put it on?" he asked. "I agree that it is bad form to wear very thin silks when there are a lot of people about. But at such a moment as this, what possible harm can there be?" and he dressed her in it with his own hands. The knickerbockers she had on happened to be just the same color as the reddish ones that the First Princess had worn under her white dress. Her hair both in thickness and quality seemed to be every bit as good as her sister's. And yet for reasons hard indeed to define, it made quite a different impression. However, having got so far, he might as well complete the picture; and sending for some ice he made her people split the block, just as the First Princess's maids had done yesterday, and taking a piece he laid it in the Second Princess's hands. His task ought, surely, to be far easier than that of painters who were often called in to produce portraits of the beloved; for after all these two were sisters, which gave him the advantage of having a great natural resemblance to work on. But the sole result of his artistry was to make him long to have been able to take the same part in yesterday's scene as he was taking here today, instead of merely viewing it hurriedly and furtively from the outside.

"Do you ever write to the First Princess?" he asked. "I used to in old days," she said, "when I was living at the Palace.† But only when the Emperor told me to. It must be a very long time now since I last wrote."

---

* It will be remembered, that the First Princess was wearing a very thin "flimsy" dress.

† It would seem to us that when two people were living in one house there would be no need for letters. But in Japan a great deal of social intercourse was carried on in writing.

"I quite understand that," Kaoru said. "In coming to me here you have lost your rank, and it is true that etiquette forbids a subject to initiate a correspondence with a member of the Royal family. I will mention it to the Empress and explain to her that you are feeling hurt." "But I am not feeling hurt," she protested. "I should be very sorry indeed if you said anything of the kind." "All I meant," he assured her, "was that I think the Empress ought to be told why it is you don't write. I shall simply say that you feel you are regarded at the Palace as a subject and therefore don't venture to address a member of the Royal family unless commanded to do so."

He went to see the Empress next day. On his way to her rooms he encountered Niou, looking particularly handsome in a summer dress of very dark clove-dyed silk. He had in the extraordinary clearness of his skin and liveliness of his expression some at any rate of the qualities that made his sister's* beauty so dazzling. He was somewhat thinner than in old days, but seemed to be in excellent trim. But now that Kaoru had seen the First Princess, Niou's startling resemblance to her at once set in train the agitating emotions that he knew he must at all costs suppress, and he hastened on. Niou had brought with him a large number of picture-rolls which he entrusted to some ladies-in-waiting to take to the First Princess and he presently joined her in her rooms.

After congratulating Her Majesty on the success of the Lotus Ceremony and talking for a while of people whom they had both known when they were young, Kaoru glanced at some of the pictures Niou had left lying about after choosing those he had sent across to his sister. "I am afraid that the Second Princess feels terribly out of it, living where she does now,"† he said. "It is of course a sad come-down, after the life she was used to here. I think it would make a lot of difference if she heard from her sister occasionally. As it is, she feels that you all regard her as having definitely ceased to be one of yourselves, and I can see that this distresses her. If, for example, the First Princess sometimes sent her some pictures—one of these perhaps—or a book to look at... It would not be at all the same thing if I were to bring it, as I am sure you will understand." "What nonsense!" exclaimed the Empress? "Naturally when they both lived here they were always sending notes to one another; and now that they are separated, they have got out of the habit of writing. But I'll remind her; and you must tell the Second Princess not to get such absurd ideas into her head." "I need hardly say," Kaoru replied, "that there could never be any question of coldness on her‡ side. And as for *your* feelings towards

---

* The First Princess.
† With Kaoru in Nyosan's (Kaoru's mother's) palace.
‡ The Second Princess's.

her—I am happy to think that even if you had no other reason to admit her to your friendship, the fact that she is now allied to me would alone suffice to recommend her; for you and I are, after all, very closely related.* But as it is, there are better reasons still; for years on end she lived on intimate terms with you all, and it would be cruel indeed if you were now to turn your backs upon her." That there was any ulterior motive in Kaoru's desire to bring the two Princesses together was an idea that did not for an instant enter the Empress's head.

When the interview was over he went towards the western crossing, vaguely hoping that Kosaisho might again be where he had seen her the other day. He went into the garden, and skirting the house strode past the First Princess's quarters. Her ladies, peeping through the window-blinds, drew back when they saw who it was, for he figured in their minds as a great public personage, in whose presence one had to be on one's best behavior. On reaching the cross-wing he found that there were already visitors—Yugiri's sons and some other young men. He paused at the door. "I feel quite out of touch with you all," he said. "Of course I am frequently at the Palace, but it is very difficult for me to find time for visits such as this. Things change so fast. There is hardly one of you here now whom I know. It makes me feel quite an old man. I must certainly get into the habit of coming here more often. You young people mustn't think I shall spoil your fun." He glanced at Yugiri's sons. "His Excellency need not worry," one of the gentlewomen said. "The fact that he has altered his habits shows that he has regained his youth." A string of further remarks followed in the same light vein. He was astonished to find how smart everyone was. As for himself, after calling attention so elaborately to his visit, he found he had nothing whatever to say. He attempted to start a conversation on matters of general interest, but without success. Soon he relapsed into silence, feeling even more out of it than usual.

The First Princess was visiting her mother the Empress. "What happened to Kaoru after he left me?" Her Majesty asked. "I have an impression that he went your way." "That's very likely," said Dainagon, the woman who had brought the Princess across. " He was probably looking for Kosaisho." "The awkward thing about serious-minded men like Kaoru," the Empress said, "is that when they do fall in love they expect so much of a girl beyond mere good looks. It's a severe test for a woman's intelligence; but I should think Kosaisho has as good a chance of surviving it as anyone." Though Kaoru was her half-brother the Empress had never herself felt quite at ease with him. He struck her as extremely critical, and she imagined that her gentlewomen must all feel somewhat afraid of him. "He is certainly very fond of her," Dainagon said. "It seems that he went

---

* The Empress was Genji's daughter, and Kaoru his reputed son.

to her private room the other day and stayed there talking till late into the night. People say that he often spends the evening there; but I doubt if it is a love-affair in the ordinary sense of the word. Prince Niou took a fancy to her at one time. But she thought he had too many other affairs on hand already, and refused to have anything to do with him. I think His Highness was rather taken aback," she said, smiling. The Empress laughed too. "I think it's a scandal that he should go on leading the life he does," she said, "and I am delighted that someone should have had the courage to let him see what she thought of him. It's high time he took himself in hand. It's disgraceful. And the people he gets hold of, too!"

"I've just heard a very strange story," Dainagon said. "It seems that this friend of Kaoru's who died the other day was a sister of my lady Kozeri—or a half-sister, anyway. They say her mother was the wife of some provincial Governor—from Hitachi, I think—but other people make out that she was this woman's niece, not her daughter. Anyhow, whoever she was, Prince Niou started a secret affair with her. Kaoru apparently found this out and made up his mind to bring her to town as soon as possible. Meanwhile he had the whole place picketed with special watchmen, and Niou, coming as usual, was unable to get in. It's an extraordinary story. It seems that he was treated abominably—had to wait there on horseback for hours, and was then obliged to go back without a word. The lady was so much upset when she heard of it that she suddenly collapsed and died—or took her own life, which seems a terrible thing, but that's what her old nurse and one or two others believe." "It sounds most improbable," the Empress said. "Who told you about it? It's a dreadful thing that such a story should be going about. If anything as startling as that had happened I should quite certainly have been told about it. Kaoru himself never gave the slightest hint of any such thing. He evidently regarded it as a perfectly natural death. Indeed, he said how sad it was that all Prince Hachi's family seemed to have such poor constitutions." "I wondered myself," said Dainagon, "whether it was not mere gossip; but the other day a girl who was in service at Uji told Kosaisho the whole story, and was so positive about it that there really seems no doubt as to the way she died. It was when Kosaisho was on leave and went to stay with her people. But the girl said they were determined it should not get out that it was suicide, and they hushed the whole thing up so cleverly that it's not surprising you should not have heard about it." "I should be obliged if you would see to it that this girl is told she must not spread such a story any farther," the Empress said. "It's just the kind of thing that does most harm to Niou's reputation. People are beginning to doubt whether someone who gets into scrapes of that kind will ever be fit to occupy a responsible position."

Not long afterwards the Second Princess at last received a. letter from her sister. The handwriting was of extreme beauty. It gave Kaoru intense pleasure to study it, and he only wished he had put this correspondence in motion long ago. The Empress sent a large number of picture-rolls, from which Kaoru selected a few that he thought, would particularly interest his wife. One of these was a set of illustrations to the *Serigawa no Daisbo*.* The scene where Togimi, one autumn evening, falls suddenly in love with the Emperor's eldest daughter and goes away disconsolate was admirably painted, and strangely appropriate to Kaoru's own case. He remembered, however, that the Princess in the story had soon relented. If only he had the slightest reason to suppose that his own First Princess would do the same!

"Chill strikes it at my heart when evening comes—the wind that once in Serigawa's woods raveled the autumn dew." Such was his poem; and he was on the point of attaching it to the picture when he sent the rolls back to the Empress. But that would be risky; he must at all costs avoid doing anything that could by the remotest possibility arouse suspicion. If it occurred for a moment to any living being that he was attracted by the First Princess the consequences would be disastrous. He seemed now—he of all people—to have got into a state in which his life consisted solely in rushing from one senseless agitation to another. Such a condition, he felt all the time, was quite unnatural to him. If Agemaki had lived, his whole existence would have been devoted to her. He would not then of course have dreamt of allowing himself to be forced by public considerations into a marriage of convenience; nor indeed would the Emperor, knowing him to be otherwise preoccupied, ever have thought of him as a suitable recipient for such an honor.

"O Bridge Maiden, my Bridge Maiden,"† he cried, "why did you close your heart to me?" Yes, it was his failure to overcome her strange mistrust that had lain at the root of all this train of miseries. It was to heal that wound that he turned—but too late, for his own folly had already cut her off from him—to the mistress‡ of the Nijo-in. Here he was doomed to utter failure from the start, and it was Kozeri herself who, harassed by his persistence, had involved him in the affair which had just ended so tragically.

As for Ukifune's death, he could not hold himself altogether responsible for it. It was not, he felt certain, a thing deliberately decided upon and planned. She had simply yielded, as a child will sometimes do, to a sudden unreasoning impulse. Probably she hardly realized what she was doing. All the same it was no doubt his own sharp reminder, coming just at a time when the affair with Niou was at its height that threw her

---

* A romance that no longer exists.
† Agemaki.
‡ Kozeri.

into the desperate state of agitation which her people had described. Of course what had happened showed only too clearly, that she was far too flighty and impressionable ever to have made a good wife. But he had never intended the relationship to be open and formal, and even if her affections had continued sometimes to wander, that would not have made him any the less fond of her. Whatever he might have felt in the heat of the moment, he now no longer had the slightest feeling of resentment against Niou, still less of bitterness towards Ukifune. For the more he thought about it the more clearly he saw that the whole thing was due to the half-heartedness that was the fatal defect of his own character.

In a way, however, the loss was an even greater one for Niou, for whereas Kaoru's thoughts and time were necessarily devoted during the greater part of the day to matters of public importance, to Niou adventures such as the affair at Uji represented the main business of life. The gap was one which he found it hard to fill, and there were still moments of depression when he longed for someone to confide in. Unfortunately it was obvious that Kozeri was growing rather tired of the subject. This was not surprising considering that she had only known Ukifune a few days, their acquaintance having been abruptly terminated under circumstances which made Kozeri hardly the right person to come to for sympathy now; so he tried once more to persuade Jiju to take service at the Nijo-in. She, Ukon, and the old nurse were the only servants who had stayed on at Uji after the mourning was over. Jiju of course had not been connected with Ukifune so intimately as the other two, and if she stayed for a while, it was chiefly to keep them company. But the noise of the river, which she had managed to put up with so long as she regarded her mistress's residence there merely as a dull prelude to stirring days that were to come, soon depressed her to such an extent that she was glad to exchange her quarters at Uji for a very humble lodging at the Capital, where Niou had some difficulty in finding her. If it had been a matter of taking service with him she would gladly have consented. But considering Kozeri's relation to the affair, Jiju did not feel by any means sure that her presence at the Nijo-in would really be welcome, and she said she would greatly prefer it if he would allow her to go to Her Majesty the Empress. "That's an excellent idea," he said. "I should be able to keep an eye on you without attracting undesirable attention." This, she thought, would at any rate be better than remaining completely at a loose end; and having acquaintances in the Household, she easily procured herself an appointment. "Quite a nice girl," the gentlewomen at the Palace rather grudgingly admitted. "She ought to do very well as an under-servant."[*] Kaoru of course was frequently in the Empress's rooms; and Jiju at first

---

[*] At Uji of course Jiju had been far from an under-servant; but here the standards were different.

looked forward to seeing him, but she soon found that to do so arouse too many painful memories. She had always heard that the Empress's household consisted of a flock of fairy princesses, each more fabulously beautiful than the last. But as she gradually got to know them better she came to the conclusion that there was not a single one that could for a moment be compared to her late mistress.

Prince Shikibu,* who died in the spring, left behind him a quite young daughter. There was a stepmother, but she and the girl did not get on well together. This woman's brother, a person of no consequence or standing, had taken a fancy to the young Princess. Such a match would, for an Emperor's granddaughter, indeed have been a piteous come-down, but this did not deter the stepmother from encouraging it. Fortunately the Empress happened to hear what was afoot and expressed such strong views on the subject that the idea was given up. However, the girl was obviously very unhappy at home, and people suggested that as the Empress took such an interest in her, she had better try her fortunes at the Palace. She was fetched in a coach sent by the Empress herself. Virtually the girl's rank was hardly inferior to that of the First Princess, and it was clear that she could not be treated as an ordinary lady-in-waiting. However, that was the capacity in which she had come; she was known simply as Miya no Kimi,† and though she was excused from wearing the Chinese cloak, she wore the apron—a bitter experience for anyone whose up-bringing and prospects had been such as hers.

Niou naturally took an interest in her arrival. It was quite possible, he thought, that she might somewhat resemble Ukifune, seeing that her father and Prince Hachi were brothers.‡ But in any case, the loss of Ukifune had in no wise abated his habitual curiosity about anyone new, and he determined to lose no time in making her acquaintance.

Kaoru disapproved strongly of the way her case had been handled. It seemed to him scandalous that the daughter of one who had only a few years ago narrowly escaped being Heir-Apparent should be relegated to so unpromising a position. The extent of the decline was brought home to him by the fact that the girl had at one time been talked of as a suitable bride for Kaoru himself. From this to her present position was indeed a terrible fall. If *she,* now, had thrown herself into a river, he could very well have understood it. He had seldom felt so sorry for anyone.

The Empress and her people were far better off at the Palace in the Sixth Ward§ than in the Imperial Palace, where space was very limited. Here there were endless wings, galleries, outbuildings that seemed capable

---

* Genji's half-brother.
† "Miss Princess" or, strictly speaking, "Miss Prince."
‡ Evidently Niou had by now discovered Ukifune's identity.
§ Genji's "New Palace," which now belonged to Yugiri.

of holding an infinite number of people, and the numerous temporary hands whom the Empress took on during such visits could all be accommodated without the slightest difficulty. The place was kept up by Yugiri in a style certainly not less lavish than had prevailed in Genji's days. But the life that went on there was in a way even more dazzling; for whereas there had in the background always been a certain opposition to Genji's party, Yugiri and his supporters were now in unchallenged supremacy. Niou should indeed, during these last months, have been having the time of his life. But he seemed to have become very much quieter lately, and it was even suggested that he had outgrown his dissipated habits. The affair with Miya no Kimi, which began in the very first days after her arrival at the Palace, showed however that he could scarcely be regarded as having completely settled down. It was known that as soon as cooler weather set in the Empress would return to the Imperial Palace, where the autumn leaves were not to be seen at nearly so good advantage and the young men were all hastening to call at the New Palace while the gardens were at their loveliest and Her Majesty's presence still gave unwonted glamor to the life that went on within. There were continual boating-parties, concerts by moonlight and so forth, in all of which Niou played a leading part. Kaoru, it appeared, thought it beneath his dignity to join in such frivolities; in any case, he was seldom seen, which people said was perhaps as well, for his presence always seemed to put a restraint on the proceedings. One day, peeping from behind the screens, Jiju saw that both he and Niou were waiting upon Her Majesty the Empress. They were certainly the two handsomest visitors who frequented those apartments, and with whichever of them Ukifune had decided to throw in her lot, the world would have considered her fortunate indeed. But there was no one among Jiju's present companions to whom she could unburden herself, and it was with a bitter heart and a feeling of great loneliness that she sat brooding upon all that her mistress had lost. Niou had a number of family matters to discuss, and presently Kaoru slipped away. Jiju felt that he would think it callous of her not to have waited till the anniversary before taking fresh service, and hid her face as he passed. Today, for a change, he went to the eastern cross-wing. Through an open door came the sound of hushed voices. A number of ladies were evidently discussing their private affairs. "Please go on with what you were saying," he entreated the company. "It is really very distressing that you should always find it necessary to stand on ceremony with me. I assure you I am the most harmless person in the world. Perhaps you think I do not care for the sort of things you are most interested in," he continued. "That is a great mistake. I know far more about your tastes and employments than you suppose; indeed, I am sure there is much that I could teach you better than any woman could. As it is, I do not feel that you in the least understand me..." An embarrassed silence on the part of the ladies followed this appeal. "Haven't you ever noticed that we women are never really at our ease except with men whom we have every reason *not* to regard as harmless? It ought, I know, to be the other way round. But one must take the world as one finds it. There, you see that I at any rate am not frightened of you! But that doesn't in this case mean that I have discovered you to have loose designs on me; but only that it would go hard with a woman who has knocked about the Court as long as I have if she couldn't help you out of your difficulties." The speaker was a lady called Ben no Omoto,[*] a rather older woman than the rest, and the reverse of shy.

"I am sure I don't know what you set me down for if you are not frightened of me, even though I give you every cause to be," Kaoru said. Most of the ladies, he saw, had discarded their Chinese cloaks so as to have more freedom in wielding the brush, for there were signs that they had been practicing handwriting. In the cover of the ink-stand were stuck some flowers, which they had evidently been using as their theme. Some of them had, on his approach, retreated behind the curtains, others were partly concealed by the flap of the open door, everywhere heads bobbed up and disappeared. Drawing the ink-stand towards him Kaoru wrote the verse: "Though in a field where wanton-ladies[†] grow I wend my way, such am I that no breath of ill-repute will cling to my fair fame." "You have no cause to hide from me," he pleaded, as he handed his poem to a lady who was behind the open door. Instantly, without any of the whisperings and nudging that under such circumstances usually precede a reply, came the answer: "A name is but a name. Think not because the flower is frail in reputation it will bend a wanton head to any wind that blows." The hand, so far as he could judge from these few lines, had many good points. Who she was, he wondered. She must certainly be a gifted creature in more ways than one. He had the impression that she was on her way to the Empress's apartments and had been obliged by his sudden appearance at the doorway to take refuge as best she could.

"I don't like your poem," Ben no Omoto said to Kaoru. "Why do you take up such an elderly tone?" And she handed in her own poem. "Say not that youth is past or passion spent, till you have lain a night on those green banks where wanton-ladies grow." "We'll tell you afterwards how your reputation stands," she said. His answer was: "Though seldom in those flaunting fields I walk, yet bidden as a guest for one short night, what harm to dally with a flower?" "Now you are trying to put me out of countenance," Ben no Omoto protested. "You know quite well there was

---

[*] Surely Ben no Omoto is a "take-off" of Sei Shonagon, authoress of *The Pillow Book*. The tone and diction are exactly hers.

[†] *Ominabeshi*, the name of a flower, written with Chinese characters meaning "wanton," "courtesan," etc.

nothing personal about the invitation. I was of course only referring to the attractiveness of green hillsides in general." It was seldom indeed that Kaoru had been known to take part in banter of this kind, and everyone was hoping that there was more to come when he disappointed them by saying: "I am so sorry; I am afraid I have been standing in this lady's way. In any case, I can see that I have come at a bad moment; I am sure you are expecting someone," and he disappeared. The other ladies could only hope he had not gone off with the impression that they were all as impudent as Ben any Omoto.

He went to the eastern portico, and leaning on the railings looked out across the Empress's gardens, where border after border of bright autumn flowers shimmered in the failing light. "Of the four seasons each in its turn has a sadness of its own; but no time so rends the heart as these autumn days."* He was humming the lines softly to himself when he heard the swish of a skirt. No doubt it was the lady in whose way he had stood, now hurrying to the Empress's rooms. Suddenly Niou appeared upon the scene. Who was it that just went out?" he asked. "The Princess's maid, Chujo no Kimi," someone at once replied. It astonished Kaoru that they were ready to disclose the girl's name in this casual way to anyone whose curiosity she might chance to arouse. It was not, he would have thought, very pleasant for Chujo. Niou seemed to be on extraordinarily intimate terms with them all. It was very provoking. He treated them in the most offhand way, apparently with no regard at all for their feelings. But he was certainly very successful. Kaoru could not help envying him, and at the same time longing for a further opportunity to turn the tables upon him as he had managed to do in Kosaisho's case. Nothing, he felt, would give him greater satisfaction than to make off with one of these ladies just when Niou was laying hands on her with his usual calm effrontery. "It would do him a great deal of good to know for once what it feels like," Kaoru said to himself," and surely among so many there must be one with sense enough to see that in the long run she would get far more out of a friendship with me?" But people were very odd. There was Kozeri, for example. Niou treated her abominably, as she was perfectly well aware. Yet this did not seem to spoil their relationship. Of course she disliked everyone knowing about it; that was all. To her feelings towards Niou it did not seem, in all these years, to have made any difference whatsoever. The whole thing was most extraordinary.

But if he had hitherto found so few sensible women, it was perhaps because he had made so little effort to get into touch with these ladies at all. Now was the time. He had no special engagement, and was not feeling at all tired—But no, it was too late in life to begin that sort of

---

* Po Chü-i.

thing. To his own surprise, however, he found himself making straight towards the scene of last night's encounter.

The First Princess was spending the evening with her mother, and her ladies-in-waiting had installed themselves in the secluded western cross-wing, where they could enjoy the moonlight and chatter to their hearts' content. Someone was playing the thirteen-stringed zithern with a touch of remarkable delicacy. "It is not fair to 'play so provocatively,'" said Kaoru suddenly, creeping up to the windows unperceived. They were taken completely by surprise, and for a moment no one had the least idea what he meant. But presently through the space under a half-lowered blind came the reply: "It is not I who has such a brother" and he knew that his allusion* had been understood. The speaker, he thought, was the girl Niou had asked about—the one they called Chujo. "I at any rate am myself the uncle,"† Kaoru promptly said, continuing the quotation. "I suppose the Princess is with Her Majesty as usual?" he asked, after a little further banter of the same kind. "What does Her Highness do all day when she is away from home‡ like this?" "What a question!" exclaimed one of the ladies? "How does she occupy herself? As though it could make the slightest difference to Her Highness whether she is in one place or another!" Yes, it was true enough. The Princess moved in a sphere of her own, high above the changes and chances of ordinary human existence. A deep sigh escaped him, to cover which he drew towards him a Japanese zithern that happened to lie within reach and without stopping to tune it began to run his fingers over the strings. But though he found it was tuned to one of the *ritsu*§ modes and the intervals accorded well enough with the occasion, after playing a chord or two he laid the instrument aside, much to the disappointment of those who were eagerly listening within.

Why was it, he asked himself, that everyone insisted upon, regarding the First Princess as a being sacred and apart? She was the daughter of an Emperor. But so was his own mother, Princess Nyosan. Nyosan's mother, it was true, had never been invested with the title of Empress. But that was a small difference, and certainly Nyosan had been as great a favorite with the Emperor Suzaku¶ as this princess was with his pres-

---

* To a passage in the Chinese story (the first quarter of the eighth century), *The Cave of the Amorous Fairies,* in which it is said of the heroine: "Now and again her slender fingers toy provocatively with the strings. Small wonder she is lovely; for she is the sister of P'an Yo (the Chinese Adonis); how could she fail to be clever, seeing that Ts'ui Yen (the paragon of intelligence) is her uncle?" Chujo implies that the allusion would be more appropriate if applied to her mistress, the Princess.

† As Genji's reputed son, Kaoru passed as half-brother to the Empress, and therefore as uncle to the First Princess.

‡ I.e. from the Imperial Palace.

§ See Part V, p. 779.

¶ Nyosan's father.

ent Majesty. And what about the Empress's own origins? No one could pretend that Akashi* was a very distinguished place to hail from. People however appeared to think that he was very fortunate to have secured even the Second Princess, who was only a stepdaughter, and they would certainly be astounded to learn that he was presumptuous enough to want the First Princess as well!

Miya no Kimi's† rooms were not far off. A bevy of quite young girls was visible at her windows, enjoying the moonlight. He was very sorry for Miya no Kimi. By birth she too belonged almost to the same rank as these other princesses of whom he had been thinking. She must surely be feeling her present position very much. There could obviously be no harm in his calling upon her. Indeed, it was only civil that he should do so, considering that her father had at one time intended her for him. Two or three little girls, very prettily dressed as pages, were wandering about outside her rooms; but the moment they heard him coming they scampered into shelter. He was on the verge of once more taking offence. But he must not, he told himself, read meanings into everything. It was perfectly natural that the children should run away. A rather older girl eventually came to receive him. "I have come," he explained, "because I particularly want Her Highness to know how much I have been thinking about her since these troubles came. No doubt she has received a great many messages of condolence, all couched in pretty much the same terms. Everything one can say under such circumstances has been said so often that it has grown stale, and must necessarily seem insincere. But the feelings I wish to express be perfectly genuine, and I only wish I could find words that had a truer ring." The maid, instead of carrying this message to the Princess, had the impertinence to answer on her own account. "Her Highness has certainly had a very trying time," she said, "and I know she will be very much touched to hear that you have not forgotten her father talking to you about her. I am sure she would be glad that you should sometimes come round in this kind way and get news of her." "Who did this woman take him for?" Kaoru wondered indignantly. He certainly had no intention of allowing her to put him in his place like this. "My relationship‡ to Her Highness," he said, " is one which in any case renders it unnecessary that she should stand on ceremony with me; and her present situation makes it all the more inappropriate that she should do so. My only desire is to be of service to her in any way I can; but if it is to be merely a matter of polite messages, I have no intention of repeating my visit." He had evidently succeeded in making some

---

* Genji had become acquainted with the Empress's mother during his exile at Akashi.

† Prince Shikibu's daughter, who had become a lady-in-waiting: "Miss Princess."

‡ They were cousins.

impression on the woman. She retired. A whispered consultation took place, and there were sounds within as of someone being bustled towards the window. "It is very nice to be reminded that we are cousins," said a young agreeable voice in which there was an accent of real friendliness, "particularly just now when I am feeling the loss or disappearance of so many old friends." Had Miya no Kimi belonged by birth to the position in which she now found herself, it would have been with feelings of unmixed pleasure that he heard this charming voice. But as it was, he could not help remembering the painful efforts it must have cost her to acquire the habit of speaking* to outside people. He felt certain that she was very pretty, and would have given a good deal to see her. But what was the use? It was fairly certain that Niou had as usual forestalled him. People said that beauty and talent were rare; but he was surprised, on the contrary, to find how often one came across them, and sometimes in the most unexpected quarters. This did not of course apply to Miya no Kimi. She was of the highest possible birth and had been brought up by a father who doted on her and had given her every advantage. It would have been surprising indeed if she did not possess rare distinction and charm. What astonished him was that, with a father entirely absorbed in his prayers and meditations and with a home tucked away in an inaccessible corner of the hills, both Agemaki and Kozeri should have turned out as they did. And even in Ukifune, on whom one would have expected the extremely unfortunate circumstances of her upbringing to leave some trace, he had never been able to detect the faintest sign of roughness or ill-breeding.

One evening when as usual he was pondering on the strange fate that time after time, with so fatal an issue, had bound his fortunes to those of this one family, that intangible thing they call a gossamer-fly flitted across his path. "'Now you are caught!' I cried, and thought I held it safe. But when I looked the gossamer-fly had vanished—vanished, or never been in my hand!"

Such was the poem that he recited, sitting alone.

---

* Exalted ladies communicated with the outside world through intermediaries, or in writing.

Writing-Practice

There lived at Yogawa* in those days a very pious Vicar-general named Sozu. His mother, who was well over eighty, and his sister Imoto, a woman of about fifty, had both become nuns, and were living at Ono;† so that he had them within easy reach. Hearing that in fulfillment of a long-standing vow the two women were about to undertake the pilgrimage to Hatsuse, Sozu sent his favorite disciple to accompany them, entrusting him at the same time with the dedication of a number of scriptures and holy images. All went well till on the way home while they were crossing the Nara Hills, the old nun fell ill, and it soon became apparent that she was unfit to travel. The nearest place where they knew people who would take her in and look after her was at Uji. They had a very anxious time getting her there, but still hoped that after a day's complete rest she might be able to continue the journey. Next day, however, she was so bad that Imoto felt obliged to send for her brother. Sozu was very loath to come; for he had set his heart on remaining a whole year in the mountains, completely shut off from every human distraction. But the account of his mother's condition greatly alarmed him, particularly as she was still so far from home, and he set out for Uji immediately.

There seemed, in view of her great age, very little hope of saving her; but he had brought with him a disciple who had a great reputation as a healer, and the two of them at once set in motion all the most powerful spells they knew. The noise of their chanting and incantations soon reached the ears of the man to whom the house belonged. It so happened that he was undertaking the thousand days' preparation for the Great Ascent.‡ The nature of the ceremonies that were now being performed seemed to suggest that the old woman's case was much more serious than he had supposed; and if anything were to happen to her, it would be very awkward. He explained this to Sozu, who saw at once that under the circumstances it would be very inconsiderate to let his mother remain there. In any case, the quarters were cramped and uncomfortable. The best thing to do seemed to be to move homewards by easy stages. Unfortunately it was not possible for them at the moment to go on to

---

* On the Hieizan, two and a half miles from the main temple, northeast of Kyoto.
† On the western foothills of the Hieizan.
‡ Of the Golden Peak, near Yoshino.

their next halting-place, owing to an unfavorable conjunction of the stars, and it was necessary to find somewhere close at hand where they could remain for another two or three days. It suddenly occurred to Sozu that the place known as the Old Uji Palace could not be far off. It was where the ex-Emperor Suzaku had spent his latter days. Fortunately he knew the Intendant of the Palace quite well, and sent a note explaining his predicament. The messenger came back, announcing that the Intendant and his family had left for Hatsuse only the day before. The only person there was a queer old housekeeper, whom the messenger had persuaded to come back with him. "You can come any time you please," the old man said to Sozu. "There's plenty of room. The family doesn't use the main building nowadays, and we often let pilgrims sleep there." Sozu would not under ordinary circumstances have cared to make use of an Imperial Residence in this way; but as no one at all was there, he thought he had better at any rate send someone to have a look at the place. The old man was evidently used to looking after guests, and though the arrangements were very simple, it seemed as though it would be quite possible to stay there for a few days. Sozu and his disciples moved in immediately. The old nun was to follow later on. They found themselves the only inhabitants of a vast, dilapidated building. It was rather an alarming experience. "You had better read something,"* he said to the priests he had brought with him. Meanwhile he sent his favorite disciple and another priest of similar standing on a tour of inspection, accompanied by a younger priest carrying a torch.† "Just make sure that we've got the place to ourselves," he said. Behind the building was a piece of waste ground, on which stood a clump of trees forming a sort of grove, in the dark recesses of which they felt that anything might lurk. They advanced towards it and immediately saw that something white lay stretched under the trees. Holding a torch to the entrance of the grove they saw that it was no mere object, but a figure of some sort lying or crouching on the ground.

"It's a fox that has changed itself into a woman," said one of the priests. "You filthy thing, we'll soon put a stop to that!" He was advancing towards the figure when another priest held him back. "Leave the horrible creature alone," he said. "What's the use of looking at it? We know already that it's an unclean thing of some kind, and that's enough." So saying he began twisting his fingers into all the magic gestures that are supposed most to discomfort ghosts and demons, staring fixedly at the thing on the ground. Suddenly to his horror—indeed if he had had any hair on his head it would certainly have stood on end—he saw the young priest who was carrying the torch step up to the recumbent figure and begin calmly

---

* I.e. read a passage from the scriptures outloud.
† The time is evidently just before dawn on the night of Ukifune's disappearance.

examining it. What he saw was a young girl with long and very lovely hair sitting propped up against a huge gnarled tree-trunk, weeping bitterly. "I don't know what to make of it, I'm sure," one of the priests said. "Hadn't somebody better fetch the master?" It was agreed that things could not be left as they were, and someone went in search of Sozu. "People are always telling these stories about foxes changing themselves into human beings," Sozu said, "but so far as I know no one has ever seen it happen."

The younger and more active of the priests were busy helping in the kitchen and elsewhere to get things ready for the arrival of the old nun and her daughter, who were now expected at any minute. However, Sozu succeeded in finding four or five of them who seemed to have nothing in particular to do and took them with him to investigate this wonder. The priests gazed awe-stricken at the prostrate figure, but nothing happened. It was rapidly growing light. In a moment there would no longer be any doubt as to what the thing was. The good men were hard at work running over in their heads all the spells and magic gestures they knew when Sozu, thinking that if they looked for themselves they would surely now realize that there was nothing to be frightened of, said to them: "Come now, this is no monster, but a perfectly ordinary human being. If you doubt it, go up to her and question her. Nor is she dead; though it may very well be that she was left here for dead, and afterwards came to herself." "Who would think of leaving a corpse in a place like this?" one of the priests said. "If she is a human being at all, it was certainly not a man that brought her here, but a fox or tree-spirit that bewitched her and carried her away. It's certainly a great pity that we are bringing your good mother to a place that's haunted in this way." Someone suggested fetching the old housekeeper. They shouted to him, and their voices echoed* through the deserted precincts in a truly alarming way. He came running out of the house, his hand clapped to his forehead with an air of vexation and bewilderment. "Is there a young woman living anywhere near here?" they asked, and showed him the figure under the tree. "Oh yes, it's a fox that has done that," he said. "They're always doing odd things just here. It's their favorite tree. Only last autumn one of them carried off a child or two and brought it to this very spot. And when I came running up, do you suppose that fox took any notice of me? Not at all." "What a dreadful thing!" said one of the priests. "The child, I suppose, was dead?" "No, it wasn't," said the old man rather testily, "it was alive. Fox isn't a fellow to do any real harm. He just likes to give people a bit of a fright sometimes; that are all." He seemed to regard their discovery as a matter of very little interest. The truth was that his mind was otherwise occupied; for he had come straight from the kitchen

---

* The tree-spirit was supposed to be responsible for echoes.

where it was proving far from easy to supply all these suppers at short notice in the middle of the night.

"Come along now," said Sozu to the boldest of the holy men. "Even if it is a fox that dragged her here, it won't do you any harm to have a look at her." Thus exhorted the priest bent over the crouching figure and performed the solemn conjuration: "Spirit of earth, spirit of air, fox-spirit, tree-spirit, or whatever thing you be that have bewitched this human creature, I charge you instantly to declare yourself, lest to your own great hurt and detriment our master should have no choice but to use upon you the powers that have spread his fame throughout the world." So saying he caught hold of her sleeve; but she shook herself free and burying her face deep in the folds of her dress began to weep more bitterly than ever. "Oho," said the priest, "so you are a tiresome spirit, are you, and mean to give all the trouble you can? We'll soon put a stop to that!" And quaking with fright—for he fully expected to see some such eyeless or nose less monster as old stories tell of—but bent on showing the others what a brave fellow he was, he took a firm hold of her dress and pulled. Too quick for him, she rolled over, and lying face downwards on the ground she now not merely wept but groaned most piteously. "Of course she may only be a woman after all. But if so, how did she get here? It's all most unaccountable." He was on the point of seizing her and twisting her round so that he could see her face when it came on to rain very heavily. "One thing is certain," said the priest, "if we leave her where she is, with the tree dripping right onto her, she'll soon be dead for good and all. Let's at least carry her to that dry place under the wall."

"She does not look much like an ogress, does she?" said Sozu. "It's a terrible thing to think of people abandoning her like that while there was still life in her limbs. It is bad enough that people should treat dumb things as they do—dragging fish out of the pond and letting them die in agony on the shore, or chasing the frightened deer and leaving them to die of their wounds. It's a thing one prevents if one possibly can; and when it comes to human beings, even if at the best it can only be a question of prolonging life for a few hours, it's our sacred duty, laid down for us in the scriptures, to do the utmost that lies in our power. I don't profess to know how this woman comes to be here. But whether she is possessed by demons, as you say, or was, as I myself think, lured here by a foul trick, or fled here to escape from the clutches of some wicked man—it makes no difference. From death by any of such causes we know that, if we invoke the Blessed One's name,[*] she can surely be saved. How would it be to see if she won't take a little broth? Not that she looks as though that would save her. But it can't do any harm to try."

---

[*] For the nine forms of violent death see Waley, *Paintings from Tunhuang*, p. 69.

He tried to get the priests to carry her into the house, but found them very unwilling to do so. We don't know what dreadful creature she mayn't really be," one of them said, "and it's not right at all to bring her into a house where someone will presently be lying ill. Besides she may die, and a nice mess* we shall all be in then!" There were others, however, who felt rather uncomfortable at the thought of leaving a dying woman outside in the rain. But knowing that if the peasant-girls whom the old nun had brought with her were to see this derelict creature they would be thoroughly upset and go round spreading all sorts of ridiculous stories, Sozu had her carried by such of his disciples as were willing to touch her into a remote corner of the building where it was very unlikely that she would be discovered. The arrival of the two nuns was attended by a great deal of commotion, for the old woman had an acute attack of pain just as the carriage drew up, and everyone rushed to her assistance. When they had got her safely into the house and things had quieted down a little, Sozu sent one of the priests to see how the girl was getting on. "None too well," he reported. "She seems too weak to say anything, and I don't think she really knows what's going on around her. There is not much doubt that she's bewitched." Sozu's sister, Imoto, happened to overhear this conversation. She asked what they were talking about, and was told the whole story, to which she listened with great intentness. "Well, I have lived in the world for over sixty years," Sozu said, "and seen some strange sights. But nothing such as this has ever come my way before." "What is she like?" asked Imoto eagerly. "I had a dream when I was at Hatsuse... I must see her at once." There were tears in her eyes. "Well, you haven't got far to go," said Sozu. "She's lying just inside the doorway round at the side there." Imoto hastened to the spot. There lying on the floor all alone she found a girl of extraordinary beauty, clothed in a richly perfumed dress of the finest white damask, and trousers of red silk. Convinced, in consequence of the dream she had at Hatsuse, that this was her long-lost daughter† come back to life again, Imoto sent for her maids and told them to carry the lady into the main room. These girls, unlike the people who had first discovered the ghostly white figure in the dark grove, were not as it turned out in the least mystified or scared, but quietly picked her up and carried her to Imoto's own bed. Here she lay, giving no sign of life at all, save that her eyes sometimes moved. "Speak," entreated the nun. "Tell me who it was that brought you to this place." Imoto managed to get a little broth past the girl's lips, but it seemed to have no effect. "I am afraid she is dying," Imoto said to a priest who was passing by. "Can't you say some spell?" He was the

---

* In the ritual sense, of course.

† As we shall see later, it was on the death of this daughter that Imoto became a nun.

disciple who had taken them to Hatsuse, and had a great reputation as a healer. "I will to oblige you," he said, "though I am surprised you should let her take up your time at a moment such as this."* He began reciting at random a number of passages suitable for the subdual of various spirits† and demons, and praying Buddha to defeat their wiles. "That's not the right way," said Sozu, coming along to see what was afoot. "You should pray for power to subdue the evil influence whatever it may be." He took his master's advice; but the girl seemed all the while to be fading under their very eyes. I am afraid I can't do anything," the priest said at last. "It's going to be very awkward. We shall all have to stay shut up here owing to a death that doesn't really concern us at all. Despite the end she has come to, one can see now that she must have belonged to a very good class of society. It won't be simply a question of disposing of the body. We shall have to give her a proper funeral." It was, as everyone agreed, a very tiresome responsibility to be landed with. "You'll make things much more difficult if you go round chattering to everyone about it," Imoto protested. Her thoughts were now far more occupied by this unknown girl's condition than by the old nun's illness, and she seldom left her side. She was indeed, despite her muteness, so attractive merely to look at that Imoto's only difficulty was how to keep people away and soon the strange spectacle was presented of a whole household vying with one another to fetch and carry for a complete stranger.

For the most part she paid no heed at all to the bustle that was going on around her. Once or twice, however, she suddenly raised her head, a different expression came into her eyes, and she burst into a fit of violent weeping. "Hush, hush, my dear one, I can't bear to see you do that," Imoto would say. "You must be quick and get well. It's your plain duty; for it can't be by chance that you came under my care. Once, long ago, I had a child of my own who fell sick and died, and it was to take her place that the Lord Buddha sent you here. Try to stop crying just for one little minute and tell me what's the matter." Words came at last: "You don't understand. I'm not worth keeping alive," she said in a low whisper. "Tonight as soon as it is dark carry me down to the river..." Terrible though her words were, it was something at any rate (Imoto thought) that she had recovered the power of speech. But what had happened to make her say such a thing, and how came she to be where they found her? Imoto began to pour out a stream of questions. But all in vain. Not a word did the girl say. It occurred to Imoto that it was perhaps some blemish or disfigurement that made her speak of herself in this way. But it

---

* When the old nun's condition was so critical.

† *Kami* throughout the whole passage has referred to the evil spirit which the priests supposed had possessed Ukifune. The commentators see here a reference to a mixed Shinto-Buddhist ceremony called Jinbun; but I very much doubt whether Murasaki had this in mind at all.

soon became apparent that on the contrary she was singularly well shaped and comely from tip to toe. It would be terrible indeed should it turn out that she was after all no creature of flesh and blood, but a semblance assumed by some demon of iniquity to snare the hearts of men. During the days that followed, in the prayers and incantations of the holy men, which had before been directed only towards the aged nun's recovery, the words "on behalf of these two persons," " may they both..." and so on were constantly heard to recur. That Imoto should allow a complete stranger to be thus named in one breath with her mother was hardly credible, and there was much speculation as to who the girl really was, and in what way she was connected with Sozu and his family.

Several laborers now living near Uji happened previously to have been in Sozu's employ, and hearing that he was in the neighborhood they came to pay their respects. "I suppose you have heard of the dreadful thing that has happened at Uji?" one of them said. "A young girl at the Palace—a daughter of old Prince Hachi, so they say—suddenly died in the night. They can't account for it. She'd been perfectly well the day before. There's been no end of excitement about it, because His Excellency Lord Kaoru was interested in the girl and used to come all the way from town to visit her. That's why we didn't come to see you yesterday. They hurried on the funeral and we were needed to give a hand."

It at once occurred to Imoto, when she heard this report, that some demon had filched the dead girl's astral semblance* and discarded it in this deserted grove. She gazed steadfastly at the motionless figure before her, and felt that there was indeed a strange dimness and unreality about it. It was terrible to think that this being, which had become so dear to her, might at any moment vanish as mysteriously as she had arrived. "Yes, we saw some smoke," the people of the house said, "but it looked more like a bonfire or something of that sort." "I dare say it did," said one of the laborers. "It wasn't a proper pyre at all, and the whole thing was done in what we thought a very offhand, irreverent sort of way." As they had taken part in the funeral Sozu did not ask them into the house, and in fact rather hustled them away. "I don't understand that story at all," someone said. "It's quite true that Kaoru was in love with one of Prince Hachi's daughters. But she died years ago. He's got one of the Imperial Princesses now, and couldn't very well start another affair, even if he wanted to."

As the old nun was now much better and the position of the stars was no longer unfavorable they made up their minds to get her home as soon as possible; for it was very difficult to look after her properly in makeshift quarters such as these. "If they take this poor girl with them she'll never

---

* The *tamashii*.

get to Ono alive," someone said. "She's got no strength at all." But they managed to get hold of a second carriage and putting her mother in the first under the charge of two nuns, Imoto made a sort of bed in the other, upon which the girl was laid. She allowed no one else into the carriage and tended her patient with minute care every step of the way. Indeed, so often did she call for a halt that she might heat broth, rearrange the bed and so on that the driver said he doubted if they would reach Ono by nightfall and wished they had made arrangements to halt halfway. However, though it was past midnight when they arrived, they got there in the end. Sozu took charge of his mother, Imoto got the stranger carried safely into the house, and soon everyone was sound asleep.

Old age is a disease from which there is no recovery, but the old nun's recent attack had certainly been brought on chiefly by the fatigue of so much traveling. When she had been at home for a day or two, she was pretty much her usual self again, and Sozu felt that he could safely go up to his temple. That a reverend gentleman like himself should have picked up a good-looking girl, traveled in her company all the way from Uji, and finally deposited her in his sister's charge would, he knew, by anyone who had not actually witnessed the extraordinary circumstances of the case, be regarded as a gross scandal,* and he was careful to prevent the story from going any farther. Imoto, too, for quite other reasons, extracted promises of absolute secrecy from everyone concerned, her one dread being lest the girl's friends should get to hear what had become of her and fetch her away. Her appearance, her clothes, everything about her made it in the highest degree unlikely that she belonged to the remote country district where she was found. Casting about in her mind for some explanation of how a City girl could have strayed to such a place, Imoto came to the conclusion that she had probably come from the Capital on a pilgrimage to Hatsuse or some other temple, and falling ill on the way had been abandoned at Uji owing to the machinations of someone, such as a stepmother, who had motives for wishing to be rid of her. Except on that one occasion she had not been heard to utter a single word, nor had she walked about or taken the slightest part in what was going on around her. Imoto was at her wits' end. She did not any longer, in her heart of hearts, believe that there was any real chance of saving her; but as a last resort she sent for the disciple who had accompanied them to Hatsuse, and telling him about her dream there she got him to perform in secret the Ceremony of Burnt Offerings.† But neither this nor anything else seemed to have the slightest effect. More than two months had now

---

* The traveling of priests in the company of women other than nuns is specially forbidden in the *Vinaya*.

† A ceremony of the Esoteric (Shingon) Sect, based on Hindu sacrifices, but of course not involving the sacrifice of living creatures.

elapsed since the girl came into her hands, but despite all the care that Imoto had lavished upon her, there was not the slightest change in her condition. It seemed very unlikely that Sozu would be willing to break his vow by coming down to Ono; but in the present extremity Imoto made up her mind to appeal to him. "I am now convinced that it is a case of possession by an invading spirit of someone who is otherwise perfectly sound. Think it over, my Blessed Man! I am not asking you to go to the City, but only as far as here, which surely does not count as leaving the mountains at all." He had not in the least expected the girl to survive. It was indeed an extraordinary feat on Imoto's part to have kept her going all this time, and it would be a thousand pities if the loving labor of so many nights and days were not rewarded. It could not, Sozu felt, be by mere chance[*] that he too had become involved in this strange business. He felt that it was his duty to go back and make a final attempt to achieve a cure. Should he fail, one might reasonably assume that her Karma was exhausted and that there was nothing more that could be done.

Imoto was overjoyed to see him, and prostrating herself at his feet began to tell him at once exactly how matters had stood since he saw the girl two months ago. "The strange thing is," Imoto said, "she does not look in the least like anyone who has been ill for a long time. Her color is good, her face is not drawn... and yet she lies there day after day, always seeming as though she were on the point of death, but still somehow managing to survive." Imoto was weeping bitterly. "It is indeed the strangest case from beginning to end," said Sozu. "Well, well, I suppose I had better go and have a look at her." "You're perfectly right," he said, when Imoto had led him to the girl's side, "one would hardly know there was anything the matter. Indeed, I don't know when I've seen a lovelier face. A lot of virtue[†] must have gone into the making of such beauty as that. I do indeed wonder what mischance can have brought her to such a pass as this. Hasn't she said anything whatever about where she came from?" "She hasn't uttered a single word, apart from the one time that I told you of," Imoto replied. "But what does it matter where she comes from? The Blessed Kwannon of Hatsuse sent her to me for my own; that's all I need to know." "Of course one can put it in that way," said Sozu, "though in reality if the chain of Cause and Effect had not already determined it, she could never have been led to you. 'Where there is an effect, there was a cause'—you know what they say."

The fact that Sozu, who for years past had time after time refused to leave his mountain retreat even at the request of the highest dignitaries in the land, had immediately responded to this appeal on behalf

---

[*] I.e. it was owing to Karma.
[†] Patience is the virtue that leads to beauty in the next incarnation.

of a completely insignificant and unknown person might, if it became known, not only cause great offence but also give rise to rumors of the most unpleasant description. "You'll be very careful not to tell anyone about this, won't you?" he said to his disciples. "I've done in my time all sorts of things that I am ashamed of, and have no doubt broken a considerable number of Rules.* But as regards women I have a perfectly clear conscience, and it is strange indeed at the age of over sixty to find myself in circumstances which, as I know well enough, are only too likely to lay my conduct open to suspicion on that score." I think myself it's better if possible to avoid doing things that may be got hold of and misrepresented by people hostile to our religion," one of the priests said. "Unfortunately stories circulated under such circumstances do quite as much harm as if they were true."

    Feeling that if he failed now all would indeed be lost, Sozu prayed all that night as he had never prayed before. When dawn came he determined to make a final effort at any rate to discover the nature of the evil influence that was producing the girl's affliction. He sent for a medium and set his disciples to experiment patiently with one conjuration after another. Transference† was at last affected, and the possession which had successfully escaped detection for months on end was compelled to declare itself: "I am the last whom you would think to find here"—so spoke the Voice which announced the ultimate surrender—"and the last who I myself would ever have thought could be subdued by these familiar spells. For me, too, in my day was a master of magic such as yours. But I died with something on my mind. Not much—a trivial resentment; but it was enough to hold me back, to keep me drifting hither and thither, back and forth between this world and the next. I walked into a house. It was full of beautiful women. One‡ of them I destroyed. Then I bided my time, and presently this girl here gave me the chance I sought. Day after day, night after night, she lay moaning and weeping, and calling for death to come. At last, one evening when it was very dark, I saw her get up and leave the house. I followed her, and when she was alone, I did my work. But do not think that your spells could have ever sufficed to subdue me. It is at the bidding of Kwannon, who all the while has protected her, that I let go my hold." Sozu immediately tried to get further particulars. But the medium was tired and his answers were no longer intelligible.

---

  * A thing that could easily happen as there were thousands of Rules, extending to the minutest and most trivial details of daily life; such, for example, as the exact way in which it was permissible to clean one's teeth.
  † Of the "possession" to the medium.
  ‡ Agemaki. This is not inconsistent with the idea that her death was caused by worrying about Kozeri's marriage, for the Japanese believe that one "catches" evil influences (we should say germs) when one is "run down."

Ukifune felt an extraordinary change come over her. Before, everything had been confused and blurred; but gradually now she was beginning to understand the things she saw. She looked about her. The room she was in was thronged with people. But who were they? There was not one among them whom she could remember ever to have seen before. Why had they all such gnarled, wrinkled faces? And, stranger still, why were they all either priests or nuns? Life here would, she felt, be a gloomy business if such people as this were the sole inhabitants of the strange land into which she had come. As for the past—certain scenes and incidents gradually came back to her, but she still had not the vaguest notion where she came from or who she was. She knew, however, that a moment had come in her life when everything seemed to be at an end. Then she had drowned herself; about that at any rate she was quite clear. But no, that could not possibly be so; for in that case how came she to be here? She made a determined effort to remember exactly what had happened. First she saw herself lying on her bed, terribly unhappy, waiting till everyone in the house was asleep. Then she had managed to unfasten the double-doors. Outside a fierce wind howled, the swollen river crashed and roared. Hardly knowing what she was doing—for the din of wind and wave was so stupefying that it was impossible to think or feel at all—but too frightened nevertheless to go on standing there all alone, she stepped down on to the narrow boarding that ran round the base of the house. Here she came to a standstill. It was pitch dark, and she could not see how to go on. To return to the house, to be pointed at in scorn as one whose courage had at the last moment ignominiously failed, was unthinkable. Far better that some roving denizen of space, some hungry ghost should devour her where she stood. Suddenly, as though in answer to her thought, a figure appeared at her side. Not that, however, of a demon or ghost, but of a beautiful young man. "Come, I will take care of you," he said, gently lifting her. And lying in his arms she had the feeling that it was not a stranger who was carrying her but someone called Niou. From that moment onwards, however, her memories became very confused. In the end she had found herself propped up against a tree in a place where she had never been before. The young man was nowhere to be seen.

She was alive. She had not done what she meant to; all her plans had gone astray. She could remember well enough the shock of suddenly realizing the terrible fact of her failure, and how lying in that strange place she had wept and wept. But after that everything stopped. These people told her that she had been with them for several months. It was hateful to think of having been tended day and night by complete strangers during all that time—without having the faintest idea what terrible things she might not unwittingly have said or done. In a way her condition now gave Imoto more anxiety than ever. For whereas when she was unconscious it was possible to give her a certain amount of nourishment, her return to waking life and to the realization of her shameful failure induced a depression from which it seemed impossible to rouse her, and for days on end she could not be persuaded to eat anything at all. "I'm terribly disappointed about you," Imoto said to her. "I quite thought that, when you came round from that fever or whatever it was and began to know what was going on around you, we should soon see you on the mend." She went on, however, though often with tears in her eyes, patiently tending the girl as before; and indeed the other members of the household were hardly less anxious than she was to coax so lovely a creature back to health and happiness. Ukifune's one longing was still to die; but the mere fact that she had survived her recent illness showed that her powers of resistance were unusually great. At last, to Imoto's intense relief, she began to sit up and soon to eat a little; though she still remained alarmingly thin. Imoto was just beginning to flatter herself that her efforts were at last to be rewarded, when to her disappointment Ukifune told her that she was resolved to take her Vows. "I feel it is only as a nun," she said, "that I can possibly go on living." "A beautiful girl like you!" Imoto exclaimed. "It would be a thousand pities. How can you suppose we should ever allow such a thing?" But to humor her she cut off her fringe and let her take the Five Vows.* This was far indeed from satisfying her; but she saw that Imoto was rather slowwitted.† An argument with her was likely to prove a difficult business, and for the moment she did not feel strong enough to insist. "There!" said Sozu, when he had performed this small rite. "That ought to be a great help to her. All that remains is that you should make her stop regarding herself as an invalid." So saying he left them and went back to his temple at Yogawa. Imoto set to work with alacrity. The task that Sozu had set for her proved to be a hard one; but where this girl was concerned Imoto was willing to take endless trouble, and presently she got her into the habit of sitting up and even moving about a little. At last it was possible to comb her hair, which Imoto did with her own hands. Although during the whole time of her illness it had been left loosely held together by a single ribbon, it did not prove, when it was let down over her shoulders and combed out, to be in any great disorder and Imoto was amazed by its fineness and luster. Indeed, in this place where everyone else was old and grey, her beauty was dazzling. It was as though an angel had descended in their midst. But such visitants, Imoto well knew, are apt at any moment to float back to the airy regions whence they came; and often she wondered uneasily whether this girl, whose real station in

---

* Not to kill, steal, fornicate, lie, drink wine.
† Such was the judgment of Ukifune, used to quite different surroundings. But Murasaki is at pains to show us afterwards that Imoto was in reality far from stupid.

life was obviously so very different from her own, was not bound, sooner or later, to be snatched away by those to whom she rightfully belonged. "You must surely see," Imoto said to her one day, "that it is very painful for someone as fond of you as I am still to be treated as a complete stranger. I should have thought we knew one another well enough by now for you to tell me something about yourself—where you came from, who you are, and how you came to be where we first found you." A troubled look came into Ukifune's face. "When I came to," she said, "from the strange state that I was in, I could not at first remember anything about me at all. Even now it is only a few vague scenes and impressions that have come back. I can remember being very unhappy, and lying evening after evening by the window, longing to escape into some other world. It seems to me that one night someone stepped out from the shadow of a big tree that stood close to the house and took me away with him. That is all I can tell you." "But don't, don't ask me any more questions," she begged, suddenly bursting into tears. "They must none of them ever know that I am still alive. It might get round. No, it must not. That would be too terrible." It became apparent that any effort to recapture the past had an extremely bad effect on her, and in the end Imoto saw that she must be content to accept her as a sort of Kaguyahime,* bound ultimately to vanish as mysteriously as she had first appeared.

But though Imoto regarded Ukifune as belonging to an utterly different sphere, she herself came of quite good family. Her husband had been a member of the Imperial Council, but he had died young, leaving her with an only daughter, to whom she was devotedly attached. The marriage of this girl to an officer of high standing had already been arranged, when she too suddenly fell ill and died. It was then that Imoto, completely shattered by this loss, took her Vows and retired to the mountain village where she and her mother had lived ever since. Here there were no distractions of any kind whatever, and she felt her loss more bitterly every day. If only she could succeed in discovering some girl of about the same age and appearance whom circumstances made it possible to adopt! That such a wish would ever be gratified was, as she knew, most unlikely and years passed without her hearing of anyone in the least suitable. Now, in a fashion totally unexpected and inexplicable, her longing had at last been more than fulfilled. It seemed too good to be true, and often she found it hard to convince herself that the whole thing was not merely a dream.

The nun was no longer young. But she was not, Ukifune thought, by any means ugly; nor was her ways in the least common or unrefined. As for the place—it had at least this advantage over Uji that the stream

---

* The heroine of the *Taketori Monogaiari* ("The Woodcutter's Story"), who was found in a bamboo-stem, and subsequently ascended to the sky.

flowed gently and silently. The grounds had been laid out with considerable taste, the plantations cleverly planned, and the gardens immediately round the house could scarcely have been more beautiful than they were. In autumn the place was enchanting. The harvesters came to "cut the rice at the door," and went through their rustic mimicry, while a troupe of young girls sang and shouted to egg them on. The noise of the bird-rattles too, like so many things here at Ono, reminded her of her childhood in the East. The place was somewhat farther from the Capital than Lady Ochiba's[*] mansion, and was built right upon the face of the hill. Dense pine-woods stretched away on every side, through which the wind murmured softly and sadly. It was indeed an ideal place for meditation and prayer, and it was to these and other religious exercises that Ukifune now devoted the greater part of the day. On moonlit nights Imoto sometimes played the zithern, and there was a young nun who played the lute and other instruments as well. "Don't you play at all?" Imoto said to Ukifune. "It's a great help in a place like this, where there is so little to do."

Imoto played at any rate sufficiently well to get a great deal of pleasure out of it; and seeing what a resource music could be even to an elderly woman like this, Ukifune felt more than ever what a terrible disadvantage it was to have been brought up amid such barbarous conditions. The little she knew of music, indeed of all the arts and graces of life, she had been obliged to pick up for herself, under circumstances that made real proficiency impossible. What a series of disasters her whole life had been! For a time she had at any rate been able to promise herself an ultimate escape; but now the future, whose menace she no longer felt any power to evade, once more loomed up before her, filling her with dread. In a sudden burst of self-pity, as a theme for hand-practice[†] she wrote the verse: "When like a leaf that falls in the stream my sorrow should have engulfed me, life trapped me on its weir and would not let me go."

Music was not the only entertainment on these moonlit nights. The old nuns went so far as to exchange quite spirited poems. They were fond, too, of listening to stories, and each would manage to produce some interesting reminiscence of bygone days. "It's your turn now," they said to Ukifune, but it seemed that she alone had nothing to tell. She sat for a while silently staring in front of her. "To those who thought my troublous course was run tell it not in your Palace,[‡] sovereign moon that thus I loiter in the world."

At the time when she made up her mind to die she had thought a great deal about the people she was leaving, even about all sorts of rela-

---

[*] Yugiri's consort.
[†] *Te-narai*, "handwriting-practice." Hence the title of this chapter.
[‡] The Court at Kyoto was often spoken of as *Tsuki no Miyako*, "The Palace of the Moon."

tives and stray acquaintances that she hardly ever saw. Now it was quite different. The whole of that world seemed utterly remote. At the most, she sometimes thought with certain remorse of her mother, who must, she knew, have been very much upset. Nurse, too, who was so bent on seeing her handsomely set up in life, must have been terribly disappointed. What could have become of her? And had it, Ukifune wondered, ever occurred to her or any of them that she was still alive? There was no one else that she now minded about at all; though she naturally thought from time to time of Ukon and Jiju with whom, owing to the fact that they alone shared her secret, she had become, in a way, very intimate during those last days.

At a place like this, where so few amusements were to be had, young people could hardly be expected to live for long on end. Indeed, during the greater part of the time the household consisted solely of seven or eight nuns, all of them well beyond middle age. But one had a daughter, another a granddaughter in service at Court, and these girls occasionally came for short visits, sometimes bringing their friends. It was likely enough, Ukifune feared, that among these visitors one or another might turn out to be connected in some way with her former existence. Should she become friendly with them, even if they themselves did not know who or what she was, they might easily say something on their return that would give her away. She profoundly hoped, of course, that no one belonging to her past would ever find out what had become of her; but naturally what she dreaded beyond all else was that something might get round. If either of them heard, he would be bound at once to rush to completely false conclusions* as to how she came to be where she was. No! The mere thought of such a possibility filled her with unendurable humiliation; and when visitors came she was careful to keep out of their way. Apart from the nuns, the only people with whom she came into contact were Jiju and Komoki,† two maids of Imoto's who had been told off to wait upon her—a pair whose ideas and behavior were fortunately not such as to suggest that they had ever had connections of any kind with the Capital.

It must, Imoto felt, be for some very good reason that Ukifune shut herself off so resolutely from contact with the world, and she was careful not to tell anyone else even the little about her that she knew.

The man who was to have married Imoto's daughter had risen to the rank of Colonel. He had a younger brother who was studying with Sozu and seldom came to the City. From time to time the Colonel went up to Yogawa to see this brother, and as he was bound in any case to pass

---

* Kaoru would think that Niou had carried her off, and *vice versa*.
† No connection with the Jiju of the last chapter. "Komoki" is a child's name.

through Ono, he often arranged to visit Imoto on the way. His arrival, preceded by a host of outriders, could not fail to remind Ukifune, as she watched it from her window, of the similar scenes* that she had so often witnessed in old days. In some ways, indeed, the place itself was not unlike Uji. It was certainly just as much cut off from the bustle of the world. But the house and gardens wore a much more cheerful air. Imoto and her mother had lived here a long time and taken great trouble to make the place attractive. At present the border along the hedge was a mass of carnations; and the wanton-ladies and Chinese bell-flowers were just coming into bloom. The Colonel's followers—a numerous band, mostly quite young men—were clad in gay hunting-cloaks, that made the space in front of the house a blaze of color. The Colonel, clad in the same informal dress, seated himself beneath Imoto's window, and sat gazing rather sadly at the scene before him, while he waited for her to appear. He was a man of about twenty-seven, but looked somewhat older and had the air of possessing considerable abilities. Imoto's couch was pushed towards the window, and she conversed with him through the curtains. "What a long time ago it all seems!" she said. "I am sure that we have no right to expect you to go on remembering us. But as you know, for us in this mountain village a visit from you is a very great privilege and honor. Indeed, I feel quite overwhelmed." She wept bitterly. "It is out of the question," he said, "that I should ever forget the bond that joins us, and if I see you so seldom the fault is surely yours rather than mine; for it is natural to suppose that you would scarcely have established yourself in a place so remote as this if you had wished to keep in touch with your old friends. However, no one could feel more strongly than I do the attraction of such a life as you lead here. I assure you I envy my brother at Yogawa and spend as much time with him there as I can; but hitherto tiresome people have always insisted on attaching themselves to my party. You would not have liked my bringing them here, and it was impossible to shake them off. This is really the first chance I have had..." "As to your envying your brother's existence at Yogawa," Imoto said, "I am afraid I cannot take statements of that kind very seriously. So far from persuading me that you have any real desire for seclusion such a remark merely convinces me that you are thoroughly worldly; for nothing is more fashionable nowadays than such professions as you have just made. What I value in you is your loyalty to the past. Such an attitude is, I am afraid, far indeed from being fashionable in these frivolous times, and I admire you for it more than I can say." A meal was served in the garden for the Colonel's men, while he himself partook in Imoto's presence of some lotus-seeds and other light refreshments. To find himself

---

* The arrival of Kaoru at Uji.

thus eating without the least embarrassment* in the presence of a woman whom he so seldom saw reminded him, with a sudden pang, of the intimate footing upon which they had once stood. Owing to heavy rain having set in he stayed much later than he had intended. They talked for a long time, and Imoto felt that she had lost at one stroke not merely a beloved daughter but also, save for brief and occasional meetings, one whose sound judgment and trustworthy character would have made him her most valued friend. If only she had died leaving a child! That would have made everything very different. So touched and delighted was she at this long visit that she became very communicative, and in the end said a good deal more than was wise.†

Ukifune could now remember everything in its entirety, which gave her, as may be imagined, a great deal to think about. She was sitting now gazing out into the garden clad in a dress of pure, unbroken white, such as is generally thought to be too startling in effect unless relieved by- trousers of a dull, grayish tinge. Ukifune instead had chosen an absolutely lusterless heavy black, her object being to guard against recognition by dressing in a manner as different as possible from that to which her friends were accustomed. The material, too, was of an unusual stiffness and coarseness of texture. It was indeed a somewhat original costume, but one which became her singularly well. "Doesn't she often remind you very much of our own poor lady?"‡ one of Imoto's people whispered to another. "I wish the Colonel could see her. I am sure he could not fail to be struck by the likeness. And come to that, if he means to marry again, I don't see how he could do better. They'd make a lovely pair." Ukifune overheard the suggestion. But the thought of ever again being seen by a man filled her with horror and repulsion. No, no! Henceforward, till her dying day, she must banish that whole side of life from her thoughts utterly and entirely; therein lay the only hope of escaping from the agonizing memories that the mere mention of such a thing conjured up with terrifying vividness before her.

Imoto had now withdrawn to her room. Presently the Colonel, who was growing tired of hanging about waiting for the sky to clear, heard a voice within that he recognized as that of Shosho, a woman who used to wait upon Imoto's daughter, and had now become a nun. He called to her to come to the window and talk to him. "Yes, we are all still here," she said. "But I think some of them are rather hurt that you so seldom come to see us, and are keeping out of your way." Shosho had been a great favorite of the daughter who died, and naturally she and the Colonel

---

* Men only eat in the presence of a mother, mother-in-law, wife, etc., but not in that of women with whom they were merely acquainted.

† About the finding of Ukifune; or so we may suppose.

‡ Imoto's daughter.

had plenty to talk about. "You'll be able to tell me," he said, after a long conversation about the old days, "who it was that I caught sight of as I came along. A sudden puff of wind blew up the corner of the blind and I saw someone with hair down her back. I thought you were all nuns here nowadays. It was at one of those windows in the cross-wing. She certainly wasn't a servant or anything of that kind." There was no doubt that he had caught a momentary back view of the stranger as she hurried away from the window on hearing that a visitor had arrived. If this sufficed to arouse his interest and curiosity, what would he not feel if he were to see her properly? For she had much the same sort of beauty as the Colonel's betrothed; though unquestionably this girl was far the handsomer of the two. These reflections, however, Shosho was careful to keep to herself. "It's a girl that Imoto happened to come across," she said. "She is, as you know, still terribly unhappy, and she felt it would be a help to her to have someone to look after. It's certainly being a great success; Imoto is devoted to her and never lets her out of her sight. I am rather surprised that you should have seen her. You must have happened just to catch her at an unguarded moment."

The Colonel was very much interested by this information. Where, he wondered, had Imoto managed to pick her up? She was certainly, so far as he could judge from the little he had been able to see, quite unusually handsome. He questioned Shosho; but she affected to know no more about the matter than she had told him; and feeling that it would create a false impression if he showed too much interest in the subject, he did not persist. "I think we had better be starting," one of his men said. "The rain has stopped and it is getting very late." The Colonel at once turned to go, stooping as he did so to pluck a wanton-lady that grew in the border by the window. "Why waste your fragrance here..." he murmured, pausing for a moment with the flower in his hand. "Well, *he* minds what people say, there's no denying it," said one of the old nuns, capping the quotation. They were all delighted at taking part once more in a diversion of this kind. "He has turned out very well, hasn't he?" Imoto said afterwards. "One couldn't wish for a handsomer, more agreeable young man. I must say he is still the one person I should look to if I had a daughter to get married. They say that he is supposed to be engaged to one of To Chunagon's[†] girls. But I don't think he really cares for her. He seems to spend more time at his parents' house than anywhere else." "You know it's really time you took yourself in hand and stopped moping like this," Imoto continued, turning to Ukifune. "You don't tell me what

---

[*] In reference to a poem (*Shu-i-shu* 1098) by the priest Sojo Henjo, the sense of which is: "Why, wanton-ladies, waste your fragrance where none dares enjoy it for fear of the harsh things people may say?"

[†] Eldest son of Higekuro. See Part V, p. 787.

it's all about, and it hurts me terribly to sit by, unable to do anything. What happened had to happen. That's the way you must look at it. In any case, you must try not to be so gloomy. It makes all the difference in the world if one has got something fresh to occupy one's thoughts. Look at me. For six years after my girl died I was miserable every moment of the time; but since I've had you to look after, I've really become almost myself again. That's what makes me so anxious for you to make a fresh start. There can't be anything that you can regard as a real tie. No one you knew before has any idea that you are alive. And in any case time is passing, and there's nothing in this world, pleasure or pain, that goes on being just what it was when it began." "You mustn't say that I am unkind to you," Ukifune answered, weeping. "I tell you as much as I can. You don't know what it felt like to wake up in a new world and have to grope one's way about, still in a sort of dream. Whether anyone knows what has become of me I have not the least idea. But in any case I have put all that out of my head, and you are the only person that I care about now." She said this so charmingly that a smile of pleasure appeared on Imoto's face as she sat gazing at the girl admiringly.

Sozu was almost as delighted by the Colonel's visit as his sister had been. They had a long talk about public affairs, the Colonel consented to stay for the night, and the time passed very agreeably, for till the early hours of the next day Sozu made one recitant after another intone the scriptures, and without exception they had magnificent voices. I looked in at Ono on the way here," the Colonel said to his brother.[*] "It was of course rather a depressing visit. But I must say that I quite enjoyed having a talk with Imoto. There are very few women who, after becoming nuns, still go on taking such an interest in everything." "A blind blew up as I came along the side of the house," he continued, "and I was rather surprised to catch a glimpse of a girl with long and particularly beautiful hair. She was just turning away from the window. I imagine she had heard of my arrival and was retiring to the inner room. Judging from her carriage and so on, I should say she was someone rather out of the ordinary. I don't think its right to expect a girl of her class to live in a place like that, where she sees no one but nuns and priests from morning till night. No doubt she has got used to it; but I confess I really felt rather shocked." "It's an odd story," the brother said. "I'm told they picked her up while they were on a pilgrimage to Hatsuse." He had only heard about it at second hand, and could give the Colonel no further details. "Poor creature," he said, "I wonder who she is. She must certainly have been very unhappy or she would never have consented to burying herself in a place like that. It all sounds like something out of an old romance."

---

[*] Sozu's pupil.

Next day the Colonel appeared again at Ono. "I felt I must just look in on my way through," he explained. They had half expected this, and the nuns who had known him when the daughter was alive had taken care to make themselves as smart as they could. The Colonel, though he missed the slashed sleeves and gay facings of old days, thought some of them still quite personable. It was once more with a somewhat tearful face that Imoto met him. "Who is this friend of yours whom you keep in the background?" he asked in the course of conversation. It was tiresome that he had caught sight of the stranger; but under the circumstances to refuse information would merely arouse his curiosity the further. "She's a girl who came to live with me two or three months ago," Imoto said. "It seemed a sin to waste the rest of my life pining and grieving, and to have someone new to look after was the only remedy I could think of. She has been in great trouble of some kind, and does not want any of her friends to know that she is still alive, and I thought that Ono would be just the place for her. Apparently, however, she's not quite so well hidden here as I supposed!" "I think it's rather unfriendly of you not to have introduced me to her," the Colonel said. "However, even if I had no other connection with this house and had been drawn here solely by the desire to see her, the mere fact that I had travelled so far would give me the right at least to tender my respects. And considering that she is, as I gather from what you tell me, taking the place here of the woman I was to marry, I may reasonably be excused for being interested in her. It must, indeed, have been a terrible injustice or calamity that made her sever herself in this way from all the pleasures of the world! I only wish there were anything I could do..."

Before leaving he gave Shosho a folded note, asking her to take it to the lady in the inner room. "Hold out, fair flower, against the passing winds, till from afar I come to build a fence about the storm-swept meadow where you grow." "You need not have any hesitation about answering it," Imoto said. "The Colonel is a man of unimpeachable character—indeed, scrupulous to a fault." "I am ashamed of my handwriting," Ukifune protested, and as nothing would induce her to write, Imoto herself undertook to reply. "Should I in this chaste hermitage have set a flower that to the follies of the world could ever turn a thought?" Such was her poem. "As you may perhaps have gathered from what I told you," Imoto added, "her circumstances have been most unusual, and you must not expect her to respond to your civilities as an ordinary person would." The Colonel thought it quite natural that on a first occasion of this kind she should show a certain embarrassment, and he went home feeling that he had not made a bad start. It was one thing, however, to write a note when he was at Ono for other reasons, but a very different matter to begin sending special messengers from the City. But he was haunted by the memory of that one unsatisfying glimpse. And though he still had not the least idea what kind of disaster had overtaken her, the thought of anyone being so unhappy as this girl apparently was weighed upon him continually, and towards the middle of the eighth month, the Lesser Falconry Meeting having brought him in this direction, he called once more at Ono. "Since that brief vision I have known no peace."* Such was the message that he sent by the hand of the nun Shosho. On this occasion there could be no question of its being Ukifune's duty to reply, and Imoto sent back the message: "I am beginning to think that it is a case of 'Matsuchi no Yama.'"†

"I can't bear to think of anyone being so unhappy," he said to Imoto, when she came out to him later on. "What was it that happened to her? I long to know the whole story. I am particularly interested because I, too, find no satisfaction whatever in my present existence and am continually thinking of giving everything up and retiring to some place of this sort. Unfortunately I have ties which make it hard for me to get away. People who have never had any troubles find me difficult to get on with. They think me gloomy and discontented. What I need is someone equally unfortunate who would understand it if my conversation were sometimes a little bit dismal..." "If all you want is someone in low spirits to talk to," Imoto assured him, "I can answer for it that you're not likely to find her too cheerful. But if you have thoughts of going any farther, I can't hold out much hope that you will be successful. It's clear enough that she has set her face once and for all against everything of that kind; indeed, she is constantly asking us to let her take her Vows. However, I devoutly hope that we shall be able to persuade her not to. It was all very well for me—I was old when I did it, and had nothing to look forward to. All the same, I own it was a great wrench. But for a girl like this, just in her prime, to shut herself off forever from all the enjoyments of life is a very different matter. I confess I very much doubt whether she'll really bring herself to do it."

"Try just to write a word or two," she said, going in to Ukifune. "Finding you living here like this he could not very well do otherwise than show you some small sign of respect and sympathy. Common politeness demanded it." "What sense is there in my writing to him?" she asked. "I have nothing whatever to say." "I sent a message," the Colonel complained, "and am waiting for the answer." But nothing would induce her to stir from where she lay. "I don't believe for one moment that it's because she is pledged to someone else," the Colonel said reproachfully to

---

* Probably an allusion.

† In reference to a famous poem (*Shinkokinshu* 336) in which the poetess Komachi puns on *matsu*, "waiting," and "Matsuchi," the name of a mountain. The meaning is that Ukifune is "waiting for someone," i.e. is in love with someone else.

Imoto. "You invented that as an excuse." And he sent in a poem* in which he said that he had been drawn thither by the chirping of the *matsumushi*, but had got nothing for his pains save a wetting from the dewy reeds of the plain. "Come now," said Imoto to Ukifune. "Don't be hard on him. It will surely do you no harm to write an answer to that." But she had no inclination whatever to embark upon an elegant interchange of this kind; moreover, once she had given way on the point there would be no end to it. The nuns would pester her for poems every time he came. To everyone's disappointment she absolutely refused to reply. Imoto, however, had in her younger days been rather an adept at this sort of thing, and she was not at all loath to try her hand again. "Hawking and hunting, through the autumn fields you trailed your cloak; and if it now be wet, why blame the goose-grass at my cottage door?" "We had the greatest difficulty in getting it out of her," said Imoto, pretending that Ukifune had composed the poem. The other nuns, who knew nothing of Ukifune's determination to conceal from the world in general the fact that she was alive, were at a loss to account for her obstinacy. They saw that if things went on like this, she would soon succeed in driving the Colonel away; which they would very much have regretted, for they had all taken a great interest in him in old days, and had been longing for a chance to meet him again. "You view these things much too seriously," one of them said to Ukifune. "He's not at all the sort of man to take advantage of you just because you have consented to write a few words to him. I can quite understand that you may not want it to turn into a courtship in the ordinary sense of the word. But that's no reason for treating him with absolute rudeness." They did everything in their power to incite her, even going so far as to string together a number of would-be gallant, but in fact most lame and comical, verses—a pastime singularly ill-suited to their age and present condition. It was precisely to such pursuits and all they stood for that she was resolutely determined never to return. She had failed to escape from them in the way that would have been best; but even if her life was fated to be prolonged—if she must drag out some kind of existence in this remote place, elsewhere at any rate it must continue to be thought that her courage had not failed.

The Colonel meanwhile sat apart, abandoning himself to a despondency which, though it was in part caused by his present failure, had nowadays become habitual with him. From time to time he took up his flute and played a snatch or two; then, laying it down, murmured to himself lines of such import as: "Woken by the cry of the deer..."†

---

* The Colonel's poem, besides containing several plays on words *(matsu*, "waiting," and *matsumushi* "pine-tree insect," and possibly *mata*, "again," and *mata*, "not waiting"), depends on an allusion that has not been explained, and is therefore impossible to translate.

† "Sad indeed are the nights in this mountain village in autumn, when time after time one is

His behavior was indeed such as to suggest that he was very badly hit. "I think I had better go back," he said at last. "This place arouses too many painful recollections. I was foolish enough to suppose that things would now be different. But I see that from the quarter from which I looked for it not the smallest sympathy is likely to be forthcoming," and he rose as though to go. "What!" cried Imoto, "so early on a night such as this?" She came and looked out of the window. "Yours is not the only garden upon which the moon shines," he said. He did not at all want to give the impression that he was seriously in love. The glimpse that he had caught of her had certainly aroused his curiosity, and living by himself as he did, it was natural that he should in moments of idleness have indulged in occasional fancies about her. But it was clear that she was impossible to get into touch with. Indeed, she gave herself standoffish airs which, could she but know it, were ludicrously out of keeping with the situation in which she found herself. Hoping at least to induce him to play another tune, Imoto handed out the poem: "Dead to the beauty of the sinking moon must his soul be who ere the night is spent forsakes a home so near the mountain crest." It was an indifferent performance. But Imoto passed it off as coming from Ukifune, and the Colonel, somewhat recovering his spirits, seemed disposed to prolong his stay. "Should I stay on until behind those hills the moon has sunk, through crevices of woe who knows but that some cheering ray may leak?"* Such was his answer. Imoto's old mother, who despite her hardness of hearing had become vaguely aware that music was going on, now tottered into the front room. Her voice was very tremulous and her cough troubled her a good deal; but she had her wits about her sufficiently not to begin at once harping on bygone days in the presence of one whom she naturally regarded as a complete stranger. For she had never met the Colonel, and no one had explained to her who he was. "I wish someone would play the Chinese zithern," she said. "Though of course the flute is very pleasant in its way, particularly when the moon is shining. Won't one of you go and fetch a zithern?" The Colonel at once guessed who she was. What, he wondered, was her story? How came it that she had shut herself up for the greater part of her life in this remote place? Strange indeed were the ways of death, that let her drag out a useless existence, while others were carried off in their prime.

He took up his flute and sounded the notes of the *banjiki*† mode. "There you are," he said, "that's your tuning. Who is going to take the zithern and accompany me?" "You play so well," Imoto said, "that I

---

woken by the cry of the deer." By Tadamine, *Kokinshu 214.*

* Puns made this poem too impossible to translate satisfactorily, *Ita*, "pain"; *ilama*, "chink in a plank." *Mune*, "breast"; but also "the ridge of a roof."

† See above, p. 960.

haven't the courage to join in. But perhaps I give you too much credit. I am certainly a poor judge, for I can't remember when it last was that I heard any other flute-playing save that of the wind among the hills. However, I don't mind trying, though I am afraid I shall make a terrible mess of it." In the circles in which the Colonel moved the Chinese zithern was quite out of favor, and so far from regarding Imoto's performance critically, he was delighted to get a chance of accompanying the instrument again. The conditions could not have been more favorable, for there was not a cloud in the sky, and a gentle breeze, rustling through the pine-woods, mingled with the sound of the flute. The old lady was enchanted, and nothing would induce her to go back to bed. "The Japanese zithern was my instrument in the old days," she said, "and I played it very well. But I am told the style of playing is quite different now. I gave it up a long time ago. My son Sozu didn't like me to play. He said it was a worldly amusement, and I had far better spend the time in prayer. But I've still got my zithern somewhere here. It's a very good one too..." It was obvious that she was longing to try her hand once more. "I think Sozu would be hard put to it to justify such an attitude," said the Colonel, smiling discreetly. "We know that in Paradise all the Bodhisattvas make music, while angels and other divine beings dance and sing. To my mind it is far indeed from being right to regard music simply as a profane interruption, taking up time that should be given to spiritual exercises. I shall be very much disappointed if I go away tonight without hearing you." The old lady needed no further encouragement. "Just run in, one of you, and fetch..." she began, but was interrupted by a violent fit of coughing. Everyone felt rather embarrassed; but after her plaintive reference to Sozu's harsh treatment they had not the heart to refuse. She made no attempt to discover even what mode the Colonel was playing in on his flute, but simply tuned to the native scale, and striking up a lively measure, proceeded to go her own way. Everyone else, including the Colonel, was of course obliged to stop playing. This, however, did not upset her, for she thought they had paused the better to enjoy her own performance. *Taritanna chiri-chiri tari-tanna...* her fingers ran with incredible rapidity over the strings. "Splendid!" exclaimed the Colonel; for her tunes, though antiquated, really had an astonishing swing about them. "I wish more people played tunes like that nowadays." "I'm told no one cares for that sort of thing any longer," she said when someone had repeated the Colonel's remark to her, for she was rather hard of hearing. "I don't know what has come over these modern young people. Take that girl we've had here all the summer. She's very good-looking; but she shuts herself up all day and, as far as I can make out, does nothing whatever. As for music and games and so on, I am sure the mere mention of them would shock her..." The old woman rattled on, chuckling loudly at her own sallies. Imoto and the other nuns felt rather uncomfortable, wondering what the Colonel would make of her. But as a matter of fact her tunes had cheered him up immensely, as was plainly audible from the lively manner in which he played his flute while he descended the hillside. The delighted nuns sat listening till he was out of earshot, and dawn had come by the time they got to bed. Early next morning the Colonel's letter of thanks arrived. "I would have stayed with you longer," he said, "had I been in a better frame of mind. The visit of course was bound in any case to have an agitating effect on me. But there are now additional reasons... Do what you can to make her understand. I would not trouble you with such a request had I not struggled in vain to overcome my feelings." Imoto's reply gave him little ground for encouragement. "You have heard for yourself," she wrote, "the impression that she makes on my mother. I fear it is only too true that in such matters she is entirely devoid of ordinary human feelings." He tossed the letter aside. But before long he wrote once more to Ukifune, and in the days that followed his notes and letters continued to fall upon her thick as forest leaves. Why, when she made it so clear that his attentions were entirely unwelcome, must he continue thus to torment her? The situation, however, so far from being, as those about her imagined, unfamiliar to her, recalled with painful vividness just those experiences that she was most anxious to banish from her thoughts forever. It was now clear that one step alone could save her from such persecutions, and constantly praying that the time when she could take it might not be further delayed, she prepared herself by earnest study of the scriptures. As time passed and still the girl showed no interest in the distractions suitable to her looks and age, Imoto began at last to think that she was not merely suffering from the depression caused by her unfortunate experiences, but was by nature singularly low-spirited and lacking in any taste for ordinary recreations and amusements. There were times indeed when had it not been for her great beauty, which even in her most unresponsive moods made it a pleasure to be with her, Imoto felt tempted to give her up in despair. But things were not always as bad as this. There were even occasions, few and far between, when Imoto's efforts were rewarded by a smile, the memory of which the nun treasured for many a day to come.

  In the ninth month Imoto decided to make another pilgrimage to Hatsuse. After years of great unhappiness, during which she had found herself utterly unable to shake off the depression caused by her bereavement, the unaccountable discovery of this strange girl had completely changed her life. So mysteriously had the thing happened that she felt sure Kwannon the Compassionate had sent this consolation in answer to her prayers, and it was to give thanks for this miracle that she was now going on pilgrimage. "You'll come with us, of course?" she said to Ukifune.

"You need not be afraid. It is most unlikely that you'll meet anyone who knows you. Of course Buddha is the same wherever one goes; but I must say devotions performed there seem to be particularly efficacious. Hardly a day passes but one hears of some example..."

That was what her mother and nurses had never tired of telling her, and she had been with them to Hatsuse time after time. But so far from any good having come of it, the one thing[*] she prayed for had been ruthlessly snatched away from her just when it seemed within her grasp. Under no circumstances would she have felt inclined to repeat an undertaking that had stood her in such ill stead; but least of all had she any desire to embark on such a journey in the company of strangers. "I am still feeling very unwell," she said, not wishing to give offence, "and I am afraid the journey would be too much for me." It was natural enough, Imoto thought, that after an illness like that she should be nervous about herself; and she did not insist.

"Never again, O fir-tree of the double stem by the Old River, shall I search you out, since you to life condemned me when I longed to die." So she wrote in her copybook. "Either you've forgotten how the poem[†] ends, or are secretly longing to meet someone there," Imoto said teasingly, catching sight of what she had written. The sally was rewarded; for Ukifune blushed deeply, looking extremely pretty as she did so. "Fir-tree of Hatsuse,[‡] I am content to have you for my child, and will not ask from what twin-stock you grow." Such was the nun's answering poem—no masterpiece, it is true, but improvised with extreme fluency. Imoto's idea had been to go to Hatsuse very quietly with only one or two companions. But it turned out that everyone wanted to join her. Not liking to leave Ukifune completely alone, Imoto persuaded the nun Shosho and another named Sayemon, who was also a trustworthy, sensible creature, to stay behind and keep her company. Otherwise there was no one in the house save the old mother and a few young servants. Going to the window to watch them start, Ukifune was surprised to find that, though there was not one among them for whom she had any real attachment, she suddenly felt very lonely. Once more the agonizing memory of her disaster completely possessed her thoughts, and she was seeking in vain for some means to distract herself when a messenger from the Colonel was announced. "You'll surely read his letter?" Shosho protested; but she would not open it. Hour after hour she lay in the silence of the empty house, brooding over the miseries of the past and the fresh ordeals that might at any moment confront her. "You'll only make yourself worse,"

---

[*] Death.

[†] *Kokinshu* 1009: "O twin-stemmed fir-tree growing on the banks of the old River at Hatsuse, would that after all these years I might see you again."

[‡] I.e. Ukifune.

Shosho said, "if you sit there all day doing nothing. You'd far better occupy yourself in some way. We'll have a game of draughts." "I'm no good at it," she demurred, but consented to try a game. Shosho ran to fetch the board and, taking Ukifune at her word, gave her the first move. To her surprise, however, Shosho found herself badly beaten, and in the end had to accept a handicap. "How I long for Imoto to come back and see you play!" she said to Ukifune. "Wouldn't she be excited! You know, you're really very good. Sozu has always been very fond of draughts, and thought himself pretty good—indeed he had reason to, for he was champion up at Yogawa. 'Oh, I'm not really anything remarkable,' he said to Imoto when she was wondering whether she dared to play with him, 'but I think I can tackle you.' Would you believe it, she beat him twice running. She must be a wonderful player, mustn't she, to beat a champion?" Ukifune thought all this childish excitement about a trivial pastime very unbecoming to an elderly woman of Shosho's holy calling. It was clear, moreover, that henceforward the nuns would always be pestering her to play, and she was sorry she had given herself away. "I am tired," she said, and retired to her couch again. "You ought sometimes to try and be a little more cheerful, you know," Shosho protested. "It wouldn't matter so much if you were stupid and plain; but apart from this you have every possible advantage, and I can't help feeling that it's a great pity. It really spoils you, in a way, or so it seems to me."

Suddenly, who should be announced but the Colonel! Such a visit, following hard upon his letter and persisted in despite Imoto's absence, could bode no good. She fled in consternation to the inner room, pursued by the nun Shosho. "Come now, that's too much," she said. "It's all very well to hide when Imoto is here to receive him. But it's clear that today he has come on purpose to see you, and you are bound in common charity at least to let him tell you what's on his mind. You can't treat him as though he were the plague." It was evident that this woman was not going to be of much assistance to her. She thought of sending word that she was not in the house; but probably the messenger who had brought the letter earlier on had ascertained that she had not gone with the others to Hatsuse. The Colonel was loud in his lamentations. "She might at any rate give me a chance to speak to her," he said. "If she docs not like what I say, there's no need for her to reply. It would be bad enough to meet with such treatment under any circumstances. But at such a place and such an hour…"

"Who better knows than one bereaved as I the autumn sadness of this desolate house, when darkness falls upon the hills?" Such was his poem. "I had hoped that your own troubles would incline you to sympathy," he added. "If Imoto were here, she would write something for you and pass it off as yours," Shosho said. "But you really mustn't get to depend on that.

Come now, write something yourself. It's too ill-mannered simply to leave him without a reply." "Strange that there should be one who knows no more of all there is to know, save one trite thing—that I am sometimes sad." Such was the answer that Shosho brought by word of mouth. It was far indeed from being in any strict sense a reply to his own poem, but the Colonel was touched at her acknowledging it in any way at all. "That's better," he said to the nuns. "Now, if you set yourselves to it, I think you could probably get her to come out for a moment to the window." "She's not so easy to deal with as you think," said Shosho. And sure enough when she got back to the inner room Ukifune was nowhere to be seen. It presently transpired that she had slipped into the old nun's room, a place where she had hardly ever set foot before. "I'm really very sorry for her," the Colonel said, when he heard where she had ensconced herself. "I'm certain she doesn't content herself with this sort of life merely because she lacks ordinary tastes or affections. In fact mere coldness or want of perception could never have led her to treat me with actual rudeness such as this. I feel quite certain she has had some unfortunate experience that has influenced her whole outlook. I am sure you know all about it. Tell me why she is so unhappy and how long she is going to stay here—in fact, everything." Shosho did not feel at liberty to gratify his curiosity, even to the small extent that she was able to do so. "Imoto has known the family for years," she said, "but had not seen much of them lately. Quite by accident we ran across this girl during a pilgrimage to Hatsuse, and Imoto asked her to come and stay here."

The old nun's quarters, which had always struck Ukifune as singularly uninviting, turned out to be the worst place imaginable in which to spend a night. Sleep was out of the question. Not only did the old mother herself snore in a manner that was positively terrifying, but the two equally decrepit old nuns who slept with her, as though determined not to be outdone, snorted and grunted in their sleep in a way so indescribably ferocious that Ukifune felt she was in a den of wild beasts who might at any moment leap up and devour her. It was contemptible, she knew, to feel afraid. To begin with, there was nothing to be frightened of; and even if they had indeed been savage monsters and not the harmless old women that they were, was not death the one thing for which she had prayed? But the fact remained that she was quivering with fear—for all the world like the man who came back because he had not the courage to cross the one-plank bridge.* Komoki had brought her here, but was not the sort of girl to keep in the background when a visitor such as the Colonel was

---

* The story is unknown. Presumably the person in question intended to kill himself, but was deterred by the fact that in order to do so (perhaps in order to hang himself on a particular tree or the like) he had to cross a rickety bridge.

at hand, and saying that she would be back in a minute she had slipped away to the front of the house. Hours passed, and still she did not return. But what could one expect of a flighty creature like that?

Tired of pleading and arguing, the Colonel at last took his departure. "Did you ever hear of anyone behaving in such a way—with her looks and figure too!" one of the nuns exclaimed; and leaving the fugitive to her own devices they all trooped off to bed. It must, Ukifune supposed, have been about midnight when the old nun, seized with a violent fit of coughing, woke with a start and sat up in bed. A lamp was burning, and by its light she saw to her astonishment a face that glimmered strangely white against a black coverlet. Shading her eyes with her hand the nun peered squirrel-wise* at the intruder. "I don't know you. Who is it?" she asked, in a voice that to Ukifune's ears sounded so menacing that she once more felt as though the old woman were some fabulous monster who might at any moment stretch out its claws and devour her. Well, worse things had happened to her. But no, in a way not worse. For when, that night at Uji, the evil spirit had entered into her, she had at least lost consciousness. But it had been terrible to wake in the end to the perplexities that she thought to have escaped for ever. And now, on top of all the terrors and miseries of the past, fresh trials and annoyances crowded upon her. However, it was as well to remember that if she had died, she might at this moment have been in company far more alarming than that of these three old women! Lying awake all night she could not prevent her thoughts from retracing the whole history of her unhappy past. The father whom she had never known, the long years wasted in repeated† exile, her pleasure at the reunion with her sister suddenly dashed to the ground. Then had come a time when things seemed to be going better. Kaoru's solid affection had at last set her on firmer ground. But at the critical moment she had thrown her one chance of happiness away, and when she looked back now on all that had happened she could not understand how she had ever come to forgive Niou for the cruel injury that he had inflicted upon her. Everything down to this night of sordid terror was his doing, and his alone. The memory of his swift wooing— the little boat, the island, every detail of the whole adventure—filled her now with nothing but distaste and remorse; whereas the thought of Kaoru's calm, steady affection—the innumerable acts of kindness that she found herself recollecting at every turn—still made him infinitely dear. It mattered in reality very little whether other people knew or did not know of the depths to which she had fallen; he at any rate must never know. He must always think of her as dead; and yet before she died, just

---

* See above, p. 996.
† Her stepfather had been Governor first of Michinoku, then of Hitachi.

once, if only from afar—but she knew that it could never be. What use was it to go over all this again, when she had done so to no purpose a thousand times before? At last the cock crowed. The relief was almost as great as though it had been her own mother's voice.* She felt utterly worn out, and was longing to get back to her room. But no one came to take her back, and she was lying there hoping at every moment that Komoki would appear, when the snoring suddenly ceased and the old nuns began making gruel or some such horrible stuff, which they were most anxious that she should share. "Drink it up quickly," said the old mother, advancing towards her with the mixture. Ukifune had no notion what the stuff was; but it filled her with repulsion, and she shuddered, in any case, at the mere thought of taking anything at the old woman's hands. She protested that she had no appetite; but the nuns continued to pester her in the most irritating way.

Next day a number of common priests arrived from Yogawa announcing that Sozu would shortly be passing through Ono on his way to the Capital. "That's very sudden," someone said. But it appeared that the First Princess had fallen ill, and as all efforts on her behalf, even those of the Abbot of Hieizan, had hitherto been unsuccessful, it was thought that the one chance of a cure lay in persuading Sozu to come down to the Palace. Yesterday morning the Empress had sent a special messenger to fetch him, and another in the afternoon; but each time he refused. Finally very late in the night one of Yugiri's sons had arrived bearing an urgent appeal written in the Empress's own hand. Ukifune had hardly realized before how important a personage Sozu was. She felt shy of approaching him, but made up her mind all the same to see whether he was willing to receive her forthwith as a nun. The absence of Imoto, who would certainly raise objections, made the opportunity too good to be lost. "When Sozu comes," she said to the mother, "would you ask him to accept my Vows? I feel terribly ill† and am afraid to leave it any longer..." The old woman nodded, without seeming fully to have taken in what she said. Back in her room Ukifune began struggling to do her own hair. Hitherto Imoto had always dressed it, and she could not bear the thought of being touched by anyone else. But it was so long that it was not really possible for her to deal with it herself. Standing at the mirror with her hair hanging loose down her back, she could not help wishing that her mother could see it once more before it was shorn away.

Sozu arrived at dusk. The place was soon swarming with bald-pates rushing this way and that in their hurry to prepare quarters in which

---

* A rather forced allusion to the poem (*Gyokuyoshu* 2614), "Hearing the sad cry of the bird, I wonder whether it is for its father or its mother that it calls."

† It was customary, in cases of dangerous illness, to administer the Vows, the rite corresponding in a general way to the Supreme Unction of the Catholic Church.

their master might take a few hours' rest. While this was going on he went to see his mother. "How have you been getting on all this long while?" he said. "I hear Imoto is away on a pilgrimage. I suppose she took the stranger with her?" "She's still living with us; but she did not go to Hatsuse. She's here in the house now, very ill, and wants you to administer the Vows." He went at once to Ukifune's room. "Are you in there?" he said, seating himself at the foot of her curtained couch. She edged shyly towards him. "Our first meeting," he said, "was of so extraordinary a kind that I feel sure it must have been due to some relation between us in a previous life. Don't think that I have forgotten you all this while. I have constantly mentioned you in my prayers, and I would have written asking you to give me news of yourself; but we priests have to be very careful about that sort of thing, and I thought it better to wait till circumstances brought us together. Tell me now, how do you get on here? Don't you find it very dull living with people who have given up the world?" "Imoto has been very kind to me," she said. "I can't be grateful enough for all she has done. But I wanted to die, and despite everyone here being so good to me, I still bitterly regret that I survived. Not that it will be for long. I do not feel that I have any hold on life, and before it is too late, I want you to receive me as a nun. I know that even if I remain alive, I shall never again lead an ordinary life."* "You're too young," Sozu said, "to make a decision of that kind. You may feel very differently later on. So far from being a merit, the step you wish to take becomes a sin unless the vocation is sure. I don't doubt the sincerity of your desire at the present moment. But months, years hence, will you still be in the same mood? Women, as you know, are particularly subject to sudden resolutions and repentances." "It isn't sudden at all," she said. "Even when I was a small child I was so serious that everyone said I ought to become a nun. And having been like that when I was a child, it was only natural that afterwards, when real troubles came, my thoughts should turn more and more away from the passing pleasure of this world and be set upon the world to come. I feel very weak and cannot believe that I shall last much longer. That is why I am so anxious to take my Vows at once." It was indeed a most extraordinary thing that a handsome girl like this should hold such melancholy views. How, he wondered, had it all begun? He remembered that the "possession" had spoken of being able to enter her owing to the profound state of dejection in which she was. It was a miracle that the same thing had not happened again. She was certainly right in regarding her present state as in the highest degree precarious. "Your request," he said, "in any case implies a proper attitude towards our Faith and its holy institutions, and is one with which, let me say at once, I am bound

---

* Have lovers and so on.

to comply. The administration of the Vows is a short and simple matter. But the Princess's need is urgent and I have promised to be at the Palace tonight. The rites which I am to perform will begin early tomorrow morning and are to be continued for seven days. After that I shall be glad to do as you ask." But by that time Imoto would have returned and would certainly prevent the thing being done. She suspected that in reality he was reluctant to take such a step without his sister's leave. It would make it easier for him perhaps if he could represent that the state of her health had compelled him to act immediately. "I feel that my strength is ebbing fast," she said. "In a few days it may no longer be possible to do what I ask. I should be very grateful if you could find time before you go…" She wept so bitterly that he had not the heart to refuse, nor did he feel that, as a priest, he had any right to insist on such a step being deferred. "It must, I imagine, be getting very late," he said. "I used in old days to think nothing of the walk down from Yogawa, but I confess that nowadays it takes a good deal out of me, and I meant to get an hour or two's rest here before going on to the City. But since you tell me that the matter is so urgent, I have no choice but to deal with it at once." It seemed too good to be true. Hastily she looked for her scissors, put them on the lid of her comb-box and handed them out to him through the curtains. Sozu called to two of his disciples who had been present at the scene of Ukifune's discovery and happened to have accompanied him here today. So parlous had been her condition when they last saw her that so far from being surprised when Sozu bade them cut off her hair they were astonished that such a step had not been taken long ago. But when she bent down and through a tear in the flaps of her couch* her lovely hair rippled at their feet, for a moment their hearts misgave them, and the young priest who held the scissors could not bring himself to begin his task.

It happened that one of the priests who had come was a brother of the nun Shosho, and she was entertaining him in another part of the house. Sayemon, too, was busy looking after the other priests, several of whom she knew, and at the moment when the thing was done only the girl Komoki was anywhere at hand. She of course rushed off and told Shosho, who arrived just as Sozu, putting his own priestly mantle on Ukifune's shoulders, was bidding her make obeisance to her parents for the last time. "Bow in the direction where you suppose them to be," he said, seeing her hesitate. She looked helplessly about her; then burst into tears. "Stop, stop!" Shosho screamed. "She doesn't know what she is doing. And Imoto away on a journey too! Oh, what will she say, what will she say?" But Sozu, now that he had consented to take the task in hand, had no intention of allowing it to be interrupted by such an outburst. He sternly

---

* The rules of their order forbad them to see a woman, even under such circumstances as this.

called the nun to order and she was obliged to stand in reverent silence at Ukifune's side while Sozu continued the service of Ordination. "Caught in the Wheels of Life..."[*] The words struck a chill to her heart. She had indeed "cut herself off." The actual shaving of the head was a work that the priests could not undertake. "You can get that done afterwards by one of the nuns," Sozu said. "It is of no consequence for the moment." But he shaved her temples with his own hand, pronouncing as he did so the solemn words: "In the sad guise that today I put upon you, you must remain for ever. I charge you never to repent." Under the circumstances he might have been expected to hurry through the proceedings as rapidly as possible. But so far from doing so he stayed for some while after the actual rites were over, explaining to her the duties and privileges of her new existence. It was long since she had felt so happy. At last, it seemed to her, she had something to live for.

Sozu and his companions were gone. Once more there was no sound in the house save the sighing of the night wind. "It *is* a depressing place," one of the nuns said as they lay listening to the wind. "But there was no reason why she should go on living here for ever. With her good looks she could not have failed to do well for herself in the end. It's a terrible thing for a girl to do when she still has all her life before her. I wonder how she will get on." But she herself had no misgivings. At last she could face the future without dread. She felt as though a great weight had been lifted from her breast and was profoundly thankful to Sozu for what he had done. But she knew that everyone in the house regarded it as a calamity, and next morning, rather than let them see her thus, she kept the shutters fastened and hid herself away in the darkened room. Her hair, roughly shorn as it was, felt very uncomfortable, and if there had been anyone in the house whom she could have trusted to put it to rights without a continual stream of lamentations and reproaches, she would gladly have had it attended to. It was long since there had been anyone to whom she could confide her innermost thoughts, and now it was less use than ever to expect other people to understand what she was feeling. Once again, as so often before, her only resource was to draw the ink-slab towards her and industriously practice her hand, "Long since, both to myself and all who held me dear, have I been dead; strange that a second time I bid the world farewell!" "It is all over now!" So she wrote, and could not help feeling moved at her own words. And again: "Is this indeed the end? Long since I thought that life was over. Strange that once again the world and I should part!" And thus, to distract herself, in verse after verse she handled

---

[*] The purport of this hymn is that for those who are still in secular life it is unlawful to cut themselves off from their parents' love; but nevertheless the surest way to repay such love is to forsake the home and enter on the True Path. For the ceremony of Admission and the use of this hymn see the *Takakusu Tripitaka,* Vol. LIV, p. 29 *b.*

and rehandled the same thought. Suddenly a messenger was announced. It seemed that even in the midst of last night's commotion someone had found time to inform the Colonel of what had taken place. He was, of course, very much upset. But as far as his own chances were concerned, he had already given up all hope. For he felt certain that she knew her own mind, and her persistent refusal to enter into correspondence could only mean that she was determined never to have anything to do with him. All the same, it was a great pity. Only the other night he had asked Shosho if it would not be possible to procure for him a nearer view of her lovely hair which he had seen for one tantalizing moment on the occasion of his first visit, and Shosho had promised to do her best. He had written, then, by return. "I have just heard news," he said, "of which I dare not trust myself to speak." "Down to the shore I hasten, lest I be too late to catch the fisher's* craft that with swift oar makes for the open sea." Such was his poem. For once in a way she opened the letter. She did not feel at the moment like judging anyone hardly, and if the news that there could now be no further question of meeting her had come as a shock to him, she was sorry. But she on her side had certainly done nothing to raise his expectations. "Though from the shores of this calamitous world it draws away, I know not whither it sails—the fisher's fragile craft." Such was her poem, scribbled in the margin of one of the sheets upon which she had been practicing. Shosho happened to see it, and folding the sheet up was about to hand it to the Colonel's messenger. "If you're going to send it, you might at least copy it out on a clean piece of paper," Ukifune protested. But Shosho said that if she did that she would only spoil it. "The Colonel," she insisted, "would far rather have it just as it is." He had not expected an answer of any sort, and this scrap, which was at any rate written in her own hand, both touched and delighted him.

Imoto on her return was of course horrified to hear of what had happened. "I know you must think that being a nun myself," she said, "I have no right to disapprove. But I certainly do; and you'll understand why as time goes on. If you were my age it would be different; but you have far too long a life before you. In any case you must surely understand that for me it is a terrible blow. My one prayer for months past has been that I might live long enough to see you safely settled in the world among people whom I could trust to make you happy when I am gone. It is more than I can bear..." She wept bitterly, and seeing the distress that her retreat from the world was causing to one who after all was no more than a stranger, Ukifune realized as never before what the feelings of her mother must have been on learning not that she had become a nun or even merely that she had died, but that—as no doubt

---

* *ama* means "fisherman," but also "nun."

they had all supposed—she had taken her own life. She sat in silence, her face half-turned away, and seen thus she still looked young and lovely as ever. "No, it was a wicked thing to do," Imoto said. "I feel I shall never be able to forgive you." Nevertheless, with tears in her eyes, she began to busy herself with the question of Ukifune's clothes. She herself generally wore dove-grey, and she set her people to making a skirt and habit of that color. "She was like a light in the darkness, moving among us here," said someone, needle in hand. "It's a shame to be putting her into this drab gown"; and everyone agreed that Sozu was greatly to blame.

As all his disciples had predicted, Sozu's ministrations to the First Princess were astonishingly successful. She was already well on the way to recovery, and his reputation at Court stood higher than ever. He warned Their Majesties that unless the treatment was continued there might be a recurrence, and they persuaded him to stay at the Palace a little longer. One wild, rainy night the Empress sent for him and asked him to take night-duty* in the Princess's rooms. Her people were worn out by many nights of watching and most of them were fast asleep. The Empress herself was resting on the Princess's bed. "The Emperor," she said to Sozu, "has for long past had a very high opinion of your powers. But on this occasion what you were able to do when everyone else had failed has amazed him. "With a man like that to pray for one's Salvation," he said, "one can really feel some confidence about the world to come." "The Blessed One," Sozu replied, "has lately vouchsafed me signs that I have not many months in which to prepare myself for my end, and it was my hope to devote such time as is left me to uninterrupted fasting and prayer. No other command but yours would have brought me from my cell." He went on to speak of the Princess's illness and the extremely stubborn nature of the evil influence that he had finally expelled. "I have seldom heard a spirit give so many conflicting accounts of itself,"† he said, "though I have had some very strange experiences in dealing with cases of this kind. Only last spring, for example, my old mother, on her way back from a pilgrimage to Hatsuse, stopped at the Old Palace at Uji. A house like that, now almost uninhabited and full of rambling passages and vast empty rooms, is the last place I should have chosen; for my mother's health was in a very precarious condition, and one could be sure that there if anywhere evil spirits must certainly have made their lair. Events showed that I was not far wrong...," and he proceeded to tell the story of Ukifune's rescue and mysterious derangement. So vividly indeed did he tell it and with such a wealth of horrifying detail that the Empress lost her nerve completely

---

* Priests sat up all night in the Palace reciting spells to keep away evil spirits.

† Not till a "possession" had been persuaded to reveal its true identity could it be subjugated and expelled.

and insisted on all the sleeping gentlewomen being roused and coming to keep her company. The only one among them who had been awake during Sozu's recital was Kosaisho, the lady in whom Kaoru sometimes confided. Sozu saw that he must hurry on to a less painful part of the story, and giving no further particulars about Ukifune's illness and cure he went on to describe how passing through Ono on his way to the City he had found Ukifune alone there, and yielding to her entreaties had administered the rites of Ordination. "My sister," he said, "who after losing her husband also lost an only daughter to whom she was devotedly attached, took a great fancy to this girl and is naturally very disappointed that she has taken her Vows. I myself felt it to be a great pity, for I have seldom seen a better-looking girl. I wonder who she really is." "It does not seem very likely," Kosaisho interposed, "that a girl of the better sort could have got stranded in such a place as that. But surely by now your sister must have got into touch with her family?" "I dare say," said Sozu. "I haven't enquired. It is true that if she were anyone of importance, a hue and cry would have been raised. Probably she is only a peasant's daughter. Birth is not everything; we all know the story of the dragon's daughter.* But if she comes of an ordinary family, only a prodigious accumulation of merit† can account for such beauty." The Empress remembered now that there had been a great to-do, just at the time Sozu mentioned, about the disappearance from Uji of the girl in whom Kaoru took such an interest; and Kosaisho at once recollected that Princess Kozeri, to whom the girl was apparently related, had spoken to her earlier in the year about this mysterious disappearance. But neither she nor the Empress felt absolutely certain that it was the same person. "I know you will not let this go any further," Sozu said. "The girl is evidently most anxious that her present whereabouts should not be discovered; indeed it almost looks as though she has incurred the hostility of some violent gang, and believes her life to be in danger. I only told you about it because I felt certain you would be interested." The other gentlewomen naturally asked Kosaisho what it was that had given the Empress such a fright; but she would not tell them. However, she saw no harm in discussing the matter afterwards with the Empress herself. "I am inclined to agree with you," Her Majesty said. "Don't you think Kaoru ought to be told?" And she tried to persuade Kosaisho to mention the matter to him. But it was a delicate subject to embark upon, particularly while it was still so doubtful whether it actually was the same person; moreover Kosaisho never felt entirely at her ease with Kaoru, and in the end she decided not to say anything.

---

* Who achieved Buddhahood, despite the serious disadvantage of being born on the animal-plane. The story is told in the *Hokkekyo*.

† In previous existences. As mentioned above, patience is the particular merit that gives rise to beauty.

As soon as the First Princess had completely recovered Sozu set out for Yogawa, halting at Ono on the way. "I consider it a most dangerous thing to administer Vows to a girl of her age," Imoto said, "and I think you might at least have consulted me." But Sozu took no notice, and turning to Ukifune he said: "For you there remains nothing now but to pursue your devotions quietly and earnestly. To the young, as to the old, the world of desire can bring no peace or security. Let no one persuade you that you are wrong to put your trust in surer things." She hung her head. "Should you need a fresh habit..." he said, and he presented her with a parcel of damasks and thin silks of the better sort. "So long as I am alive," he said, "I will see to it that you have all you require. About such things as that you need not worry. The world is hard to leave. Ambitions, affections—both our own and those of others for us—seem so long as we are involved in them to form an invincible barrier. But it is not so. You yourself were brought up amid the uncertainties of common life and knew its trials. Now, in the heart of the forest, free alike from resentment and remorse, you pass your days in meditation and prayer, life weighing upon you 'no heavier than a dry leaf.'[*] Yes, you will see, on many a dawn, 'the moon lingering at the pine-wood gate...'"

She had never met with a priest who spoke so well.[†] She felt he was a man whom one could respect; certainly no one had ever spoken to her on such subjects in a way more entirely to her mind. After he had left she went to the window and presently saw appearing round a distant fold of the hill a throng of riders in hunting-cloaks of every hue. It seemed that they must be going up to the Hieizan. But the way through Ono, which lay aside from the road, was very seldom taken except by priests going up from Kurodani,[‡] and the arrival of this party of laymen remained a mystery, till someone suddenly recognized the familiar figure of the dejected Colonel. He had come partly to express his regret at the step which Ukifune had taken, partly because the autumn colors were finer here than in any other place he knew. From the first moment of his arrival in the hills the beauty of the scene had completely overcome him. What a comfort it would have been if in such a place as this he had discovered someone in an ordinary, sociable frame of mind! "I hadn't much to do," he explained to Imoto, "so I thought I would take the opportunity of coming to enjoy your woods now that they are at their best. Can you give me shelter once again?" "Down from the hills so fierce a storm has blown through these our woods that not a sheltering leaf is left on any tree." Such was Imoto's poem; and his: "No welcome had I hoped ever again

---

[*] From a poem by Po Chü-i.
[†] I.e. introduced quotations from Chinese poetry into his conversation.
[‡] At the foot of the Hieizan, farther south than Ono.

to find in this sad village; yet I thought the clustering tree-tops beckoned as I passed." Sending for Shosho he talked with her for some time about the irrevocable step that they both so much deplored. "Wouldn't it, as things are, be possible to let me see her for a moment?" he asked. "I am very curious to know how she looks as a nun. I think my deep interest in her at any rate deserves that much reward." Shosho went to Ukifune's rooms to see what could be done. In a habit of grey damask worn over a dark brown kirtle she looked, Shosho thought, more lovely than ever, her fragile figure being set off by these somber garments with an effect that was positively elegant and stylish. Her cropped hair spread fan-wise over her forehead and clustered behind her ears in a most attractive manner. There was a faint flush in her pale cheeks that could not have been rivaled by the most dexterous use of rouge or powder. She had evidently been saying her prayers; a rosary still dangled over the end of the bed. Now, with rapt attention, she was poring over a volume of the scriptures. It was a scene such as would have gladdened a painter's heart. Shosho for her part could never look upon her now without tears coming to her eyes, and she could well imagine what the Colonel's feelings would be. It happened that the wood under the bolt of her door had cracked slightly, as though on purpose to serve as an eye-hole on the present occasion, and leading the Colonel to the spot, Shosho went back into the room and rearranged the screens so that he might have an uninterrupted view. In a moment he saw that her appearance was such as to exceed his wildest dreams. She was not merely handsome but a beauty of the rarest order, and the thought that he had himself presumably been to a large extent responsible for the desperate measure she had taken filled him with shame and remorse. At the same time a wild desire to fling all restraint aside and rush into the room suddenly possessed him, and fearing that he might not be able to control it he beat a hasty retreat.

That the people to whom she belonged had simply allowed such a creature as this to vanish without making any attempt to discover what had happened to her was incredible. She must have parents or guardians of some kind who would surely have made every effort to trace her, and even if as the result of some distressing experience she had deliberately cut herself off from the world, her disappearance must have created a considerable sensation and some rumor of her identity would surely have reached those into whose hands she had come. Beauty such as hers could apparently survive even the sad transformation to which she had been subjected. The strange garb seemed indeed positively to enhance her beauty, and so far from this glimpse of her setting his heart at rest, he began now to turn over in his mind plans for secretly getting her into his power. "I can understand that before this change she may well have been nervous about my intentions," he said to Imoto. "But it is obvious that there can now be no harm whatever in allowing me to address her. Will you try to convince her of this? For my associations with the house are bound in the future to bring me here from time to time, and it would be a great comfort to me if I could use these occasions to better our acquaintance." "I am naturally very anxious about what is going to become of her later on," Imoto said, "and it would be a great comfort if I thought that you could be relied on to help her in practical ways. I am afraid she may have a very difficult time when I am gone." From the solicitude that Imoto showed concerning this girl and the tone in which she spoke of her, the Colonel was inclined to think that they must in reality be closely related. It seemed important to discover the truth of the matter. "Life is full of uncertainties," he said, "and of course I do not know how long I myself shall be spared. However, you may count on me to give her the sort of assistance that you have mentioned so long as I am here. But I confess I am rather worried at not knowing where she comes from. At any moment people with far more right to do so than I may turn up and provide for her. Not that it would really place me in an awkward position if they did. But I feel it would make my relations with her less unsatisfactory if I knew." "If I had been able to get her back into ordinary society, where she would have mixed with people in the usual way, no doubt she would sooner or later have been recognized," Imoto said. "But as it is, there is small hope of any such thing ever happening. Here as you see she is entirely cut off from the world, which is indeed what she herself seems most to desire." "Hateful should I be to myself indeed, were I to think that not from the World's snare, but from my love you fled." Such was the poem that he sent in to her, accompanied by many pleadings and entreaties. "Let me be a brother to you," he wrote. "You will surely be glad sometimes to hear what is going on in the world," and so forth. "I fear that your information, interesting though it would no doubt be to anyone who understood such matters, would be wasted on me." That was all; there was no answering poem. In reality it was not ignorance but rather a knowledge bred of much unhappy experience that made her reject this offer of brotherly conversation. She was resolved henceforth to live unseen, like an old tree-stump in the ground. But her success in achieving the first step towards establishing the right to such an existence, so far from making her more serious and unresponsive, caused a change which Imoto noted with delight. She was often willing now to join in sports and light distractions, and seemed to be ready for a game of draughts or chess at any time of the day or night. She did not, however, forget her devotions. In the study of the *Hokkekyo* she was of course* assiduous;

---

* As a disciple of Sozu, who belonged to the Tendai sect, which made the *Hokkekyo* its principle scripture.

but she found time for other scriptures as well. As winter came on and the snow piled up thick on the roads, visitors became rarer than ever, and the time hung heavy on everyone's hands. At last, however, late in the spring, a grandson of the old nun, called Ki no Kami, arrived at Ono. He was a man of about thirty, good-looking and vivacious. "Well, Grandmother," he said, "how have things been this long while? Two years, isn't it?" But the old lady's mind had been failing rapidly of late, and she scarcely seemed to know him. "It's very sad," he said, coming back to Imoto. "She seems to be breaking up altogether. I wish I had been able to see more of her in her last years; but the distance made it impossible. I owe a great deal to her, for after my parents died she took sole charge of me. And the Governor of Hitachi's wife—do you ever get news of her?" The person referred to was apparently Imoto's sister. "As the years go on," Imoto said, "I seem to hear less and less about what goes on in the world. In as far as I have had anything to occupy me, it has been my own troubles and difficulties, and of these I have had my full share. I have had no news of the Governor's wife for a long while. I am afraid that unless she comes soon she is not very likely to find your grandmother still alive."

Ukifune started at the sound of this name, which was identical with her mother's; but in a moment she realized that the Governor in question must obviously be a quite different person from her stepfather. "I have been back at the Capital* for a long time now," Ki no Kami said, "but business of one kind and another has always prevented my coming here. Only yesterday I had fully intended to come; but at the last moment His Excellency Lord Kaoru sent for me to go with him to Uji. He was interested at one time, it appears, in a daughter of the late Prince Hachi. She died, and sometime afterwards he brought a girl there who according to some accounts was likewise a daughter of the old Prince. A year ago, however, this lady also died, and it was to arrange for the Anniversary that His Excellency went out to Uji yesterday. The abbot of the temple there is in charge of the ceremony. I shall have to make an offering† myself. Do you think you could have a dress made for me to give as alms? I should have liked, of course, to have something woven on purpose, but I am afraid there is hardly time." Her own Anniversary! Afraid of betraying her emotion Ukifune turned her face to the wall. "I always understood that Prince Hachi had only two daughters," Imoto said. "Which of them was it that Prince Niou married?" "The second one that His Excellency used to visit was by a different mother—someone of no importance, I believe,"

---

* A woman's robe may seem a strange offering to make to priests; but currency was very little used at this time, its place being taken by articles of common use, such as clothes, musical instruments, etc.

† On his return from the province of which he had been Governor.

Ki no Kami explained. "The relationship was never openly acknowledged, but he was certainly very much attached to her. They tell me that when the first one died, he was completely prostrated, and was on the point of taking his Vows." It was evident that this visitor was extremely well posted up in all Kaoru's affairs. What would come next? Ukifune's heart beat faster and faster. "It was a terrible thing," he went on, "the two sisters dying one after another like that, in the same house. His Excellency's distress when we went there yesterday was pitiable to see. He stood for a long while on the river bank, gazing steadfastly into the water; then going into the house: 'Can I have thought that in these plunging waves her face as in a mirror I should find, that gazing thus I swell the swollen flood?' So he wrote, and nailed the poem to a pillar. He said nothing to any of us; but we could see that he was in a state of deep emotion. How handsome he is! One sometimes almost wishes he were a woman. Beauty of that kind is, in a way, wasted on a man. I have known him since I was a boy and always had so great an admiration for his extraordinary gentleness and refinement that a word from him has meant more to me than the notice of the Regent or Prime Minister. I don't know what would have become of me without his help and encouragement." Such, thought Ukifune, deeply moved, was the impression that he made even on a man like this, who did not seem to be a person of any great discernment. "I can't believe that any of them can for a moment be compared with Genji," Imoto said. " Indeed the young men whom people point to with admiration nowadays are all Genji's descendants, and no doubt owe their success to having inherited some part of his charm and attainments. What about Yugiri?" "He is certainly a fine- looking man," he said," and no other public character is so much respected today. Prince Niou too is very much to the fore, though for different reasons. It is his success with women that makes him so conspicuous." Despite her emotion at these echoes from a far-off world that now seemed like a dream, Ukifune could not help being amused at the way in which, unconscious of her identity, he enlightened the company on one subject after another, about which she was far better qualified to speak. After a great deal of information of the same kind he at last took his leave.

So Kaoru had not forgotten her; still less, no doubt, had her mother. For a moment she had been tempted to reveal herself. But what was the use? It would give them more pain than pleasure to see her as she was now. It gave her a curious sensation to see the good nuns industriously dyeing silks for the costume which Ki no Kami had bespoken. But she said nothing. "I wish you would give me a hand with this," Imoto said, holding out an undergarment at which she was working. "You hem much more neatly than I do." Ukifune started back as though in horror and, to excuse herself, pretended that she was not feeling well. Imoto, despite the urgency of the work, dropped it immediately and hurried to her side. "It's just the sort of thing you ought to be wearing yourself," someone said, picking up the kirtle—a cherry-weaving lined with scarlet. "It's a shame to dress you in grey." Her answer was a poem in which she asked whether they thought she held the world of billowing skirts and gay sleeves so dear that at the mere sight of a patterned dress she must regret her holy garb. But sooner or later, even if it were only after she was dead, Imoto and the rest were bound to discover who she was, and would feel hurt, nay outraged, that she should have let this farce go on. She hesitated; then at last brought herself to say: "I remember very little about my past; but for some reason the sight of this work that you are busy upon has upset me. It recalls some sort of vague memory—I can't quite say what." "I shouldn't be at all surprised," rejoined Imoto, "to find that you remembered a good deal more than you choose to admit. I really think it is time you should confide in me. It is not only to you that the sight of these gay stuffs brings back sad memories. Look how badly I've cut this out. That comes of being out of practice. If my girl had lived, I should be doing it every day. There must surely have been someone who was fond of you. I know that even though my daughter died under my eyes, I went on feeling for a long time that she was not really gone and that I should find her, if only I knew where to look. And even if your people had reason to give you up for dead, they cannot have been sure, and must certainly be taking steps to discover what became of you." "One of my parents was alive," Ukifune said. "But whether she is still so after all this time..." she broke off; then mastering her tears: "No, it is not really that I do not remember, but that things happened which are too terrible to speak about. You must not think that I want to keep a distance between us; that is not it at all."

Kaoru returned from the ceremony at Uji feeling that the whole pitiful business was now indeed over; for Ukifune herself he could do nothing more. But he did not forget his promise about the brothers. For one of them, who had just celebrated his coming-of-age, he secured a post in the Treasury; for another, a commission in his own regiment of the Guard. One of the younger boys, who was much more presentable than the rest, and was indeed quite an agreeable lad to have at hand, he used as a page. One rather dismal, rainy night when the Empress's rooms were almost deserted he mentioned in the course of general conversation that he had recently been out to Uji. "I used to go there a great deal at one time." he said, "and was criticized for doing so; rightly perhaps, but some curious bond of fate seemed for years on end, in one fashion or another, to link me to the place. However, all around me I saw people considering themselves perfectly free to follow their inclinations in matters such as that, and I did not see why I should be the sole exception. But a curse seemed to be upon the house; it became connected in my mind with death and disaster; moreover my own circumstances made it more and more difficult for me to undertake such a journey, and for many months I never set foot there. The other day, however, I was obliged to go there again, on business of a very melancholy nature, and looking back on all that had gone on there I got so gloomy and forbidding an impression of the place that I could not help feeling Prince Hachi chose it for his residence with the deliberate intention of turning the hearts of all who came there towards the consolations of the life to come." The Empress at once remembered Sozu's story. No wonder Kaoru should feel as he did about the scene of such a disaster. "It certainly seems as if some evil spirit haunted the place," she said. "But how, exactly, did the person you mention meet her end?" It was not clear whether she realized that there had been two disasters, or was only referring to Agemaki. "A lonely place like that," he said, "is of course very apt to become the haunt of evil spirits. But even so, what happened is hard to explain." At this point, however, he dropped the subject, and the Empress, feeling that he was embarrassed at her already knowing so much more about his secret than he imagined, did not wish to press him. Her interest in the question was indeed chiefly due to the fact that Niou too was involved. No doubt it was this same disaster, at which Kaoru had hinted so ominously, that was responsible for Niou's extraordinary collapse last year. For her as well as for Kaoru the subject was an embarrassing one. But though at the time she said no more, she still felt that he ought to be told. "I was very much touched by what His Excellency told me tonight about a recent visit to Uji," she said to Kosaisho afterwards, "and was on the point of telling him about Sozu's story; but after all, one cannot be certain that it is the same person. You know as much about it as I do. Couldn't you manage to say something to him? There's no need, of course, to repeat the whole story. But you might manage in the course of conversation just to let him know that you have heard something of the kind that Sozu told us about." "If even Your Majesty feels unable to tell him," Kosaisho said, "I don't quite see why you should think it any easier for me. I have no connection with the matter in any way at all." I think the position you are in makes it a great deal easier for you than for me," the Empress said. "But quite apart from that, there are personal reasons..." Kosaisho smiled to herself, knowing quite well what these personal reasons[*] were. She could not very well continue to refuse, and on the next occasion when Kaoru visited her she led the conversation on to the subject of Sozu, and repeated all that she had heard. He realized, when he had recovered from the first overwhelming sensations of surprise and bewilderment, that the Empress's questions,

---

[*] I.e. the connection of Niou with the affair.

which had puzzled him at the time, were due to her having heard the same story. Why then had she broken off in that strange way? No doubt because she felt embarrassed at showing how much she knew of an affair that he had scrupulously avoided mentioning to her. The odd thing was that even now, though it was evident that others knew even more about the whole thing than he did, this did not make it any easier to discuss the matter. No doubt it had always been absurd to make such a mystery of it. For even where the living are concerned secrets are seldom kept, and this was a case of someone who was supposed to be dead. Yet even to Kosaisho, whom he had known so long, he could not bring himself to admit in so many words what his own connection with the affair had really been. "I heard of someone disappearing in much the same way," he said guardedly. "What happened in the end to the girl in Sozu's story?" "He stopped at Ono on his way down to the City," Kosaisho said, "and made her a nun. The people who found her would not let this be done even when she was so ill. Apparently she is very good-looking and they thought it would be too great a pity. But she had set her heart on it, and when everyone was out of the way, she managed to persuade him." The place, the time—everything fitted exactly. He had no real doubt that it was she. But it was impossible to ask further questions without giving himself away. By some means or other, however, he must find out the truth. Why not go to Ono and discover for himself? He felt very much inclined to set out immediately. But his intentions would certainly be misinterpreted; moreover, Niou might hear of his visit and it was only too likely that the moment he heard Ukifune was alive he would try to renew the old relationship. For he could well imagine that Niou would think nothing of compelling a nun to profane her Vows. But it was not at all improbable that Niou knew already; indeed, the whole story about Ukifune having become a nun might well be a trick on his part to prevent Kaoru getting into touch with her. Come to think of it, this was almost certain. It was no doubt because Niou had pledged her to secrecy that the Empress had been unwilling to discuss the matter. It was very unnatural that, had she in reality heard so remarkable a story, she should not have repeated it to him. If Ukifune was indeed still in Niou's clutches,[*] passionately though he longed to see her, it was better for him to pretend to himself that she was dead. It might be that from time to time rumors would still reach him which spoke of her as alive. But they would only seem such tidings as in dreams and visions drift back from the world beyond the grave. On his part he would make no further effort to get news of her, still less to wrest her from Niou's hands. As for the

---

[*] A colony of nuns may seem an odd place at which to conduct such an intrigue; but the distinction between the world and the cloister was not at that time a very rigid one.

Empress—of course he would never mention the subject again. But here he wavered. It would certainly be interesting to discover what the position really was, and finding himself alone with her a few days later he could not resist the temptation to introduce the topic once again. "Someone told me the other day," he said, "that extraordinary story about the girl who was supposed to have died at Uji turning out merely to have wandered away and to be still living with strange people in a remote and unfrequented place. I confess I am not surprised. That she should have shown sufficient resolution to take her own life in the way that was alleged at the time always seemed to me most improbable. It now appears to be thought that she was suffering from a possession, which seems much more likely." He went on to confess in a guarded way, carefully veiling the part that Niou had played and showing no trace of rancor, his own connection with the girl's history. "I am very anxious Niou should not have the impression that I have been taking steps to get into touch with her," he said. "He would certainly misunderstand my motives, and I do not intend to let him see that I have heard she is alive." "I know nothing about the matter," the Empress said, "beyond what Sozu told us the other day. I had been passing through a trying time, and really gave very little attention to what he said. As for Niou—I am convinced that he has heard nothing about the matter, and the last thing I should do would be to tell him; I know only too well what that would lead to. As a matter of fact, I am still very worried about the life he leads. Everyone knows about it and people have quite ceased to look up to him as they should." The Empress, Kaoru knew, was not at all the sort of person to repeat things that had been told to her in confidence, and he felt sure his admissions would go no farther. It was annoying that he still did not know where this out-of-the-way place was at which Ukifune was said to be living. The easiest way to discover, without it being known at Court that he was making enquiries, would be to get into touch with Sozu himself. Kaoru was in the habit of performing special devotions to the Buddha of Healing on the eighth day of each month. For this purpose he very often went to the main temple at Hieizan. Nothing could be simpler than to go on from there to Yogawa. This he determined to do, and took with him the young brother* who was now acting as his page. He felt that to have the boy with him would in a way lessen the shock of the meeting or at any rate make her more disposed to open her heart to him. It was in a state of great excitement that he set out. But at the same time terrible misgivings beset him. What if he should find out that she had hidden herself away among these mysterious, hooded figures merely in order to conceal the fact that she had surrendered to some new lover?

---

* Of Ukifune.

The Bridge of Dreams

At the Hieizan, after performing his usual devotions, he made a special offering of holy images and books. Next day he went on to Yogawa, where Sozu, despite the complete unexpectedness of the visit, received him with every mark of consideration. Kaoru had on many occasions in the past availed himself of Sozu's assistance when carrying out rites and services of various kinds, but had not till recently been on terms of intimacy with him. However, his astonishing success in dealing with the First Princess's malady had convinced Kaoru that the old priest must possess extraordinary spiritual powers, and while Sozu was in the Palace, he had more than once sought his guidance on points of faith and doctrine. Little as he liked to be disturbed, Sozu could not help feeling gratified that a person of such public importance should have come so far to visit him. After they had chatted for a while refreshments were served, and when the other priests had withdrawn: "I think you know those people who live at Ono," Kaoru suddenly said. "Yes," said Sozu, "they are relations of mine. You no doubt wonder what induced them to settle in such a place. The fact is, I have no residence of my own at the Capital, and when my mother became a nun, the best thing to do with her seemed to be to settle her somewhere within reach of my own hermitage. I can start from here in the evening and be back before daybreak. It is really very convenient." "It is of course only in recent years that Ono has become so deserted," Kaoru said. "I believe in Princess Ochiba's time it was quite a popular resort..." Breaking off, he came across and seated himself close by Sozu's side. "There is something I want to ask you about," he said, in a lower voice. "I feel rather shy of mentioning the subject because I am sure you will think it very strange that the matter should interest me at all. I heard not long ago that someone I once knew is now living with your relatives at Ono. I took no steps to find out if this were so; but later on a rumor reached me that she was indeed there, and, further, that she had become your disciple and had received the Vows of Abstinence at your hands. She is quite a young woman and her mother is still alive. I am interested in the matter because I have reason to believe that certain people have accused me of hiding her where she now is." So the girl was, after all, someone of rank and importance. Sozu had always, he told himself, found it difficult to believe anything to the contrary. It was evident, moreover, from the way in which Kaoru spoke of her, that they had once been on very intimate terms. Priest though he was, worldly considerations still influenced him sufficiently to make him very uneasy about what he had done, and he paused for some while before making his reply. It seemed as though Kaoru had very definite information on the subject, and. without knowing exactly how far this information extended, it was difficult to gloze over what had happened in such a way as to escape responsibility. "I am not sure," the priest said after a long pause, "that I know what you are referring to. But it is true that a girl who is a complete stranger to us all has been living with my relations at Ono for some months past. My mother and sister had been at Hatsuse in pursuance of a vow, and on the way back they stopped at the ruined Palace of Uji. While they were there I received a message asking me to join them immediately. My mother had found the journey too much for her and was in a state of acute exhaustion. When I arrived they told me an extraordinary story about someone having been found near by in the most deplorable condition, and I was obliged for the moment to defer dealing with my mother's case in order to do what I could for this girl whom they had rescued. At first sight one would have taken her for dead. But closer examination showed that there was still breath in her body, and I came to the conclusion that she had been left for dead, such a mistake being by no means impossible, for one has heard of people waking from a trance to find themselves laid out in a mortuary. I sent for such of my disciples as have most gift of healing and set them to work on one spell after another. I was then able to devote myself to praying for my mother, whose recovery, owing to her great age, was hardly to be expected—but I hoped at least to spare her the misery of dying amid unfamiliar surroundings, so far away from home. My efforts on her behalf completely engrossed me, and during the rest of the time that I was there I hardly saw the stranger at all. But from what people told me I concluded that she had been bewitched by a *tengu*,[*] tree-spirit, or some such malign power. They managed to get her back to Ono, but for three months she remained in practically the same condition, showing little or no signs of life. It happens that my sister some years ago lost an only daughter of just about this girl's age. She felt the loss very deeply, and had indeed for a long time past dragged out her existence in a state of profound depression. The arrival of this beautiful girl completely changed her. She was from the first moment convinced that the stranger had been sent by Kwannon in answer to her prayers, to take her own child's place, and, the fear that all the care she

---

[*] In China the *tengu* were spirits of comets and shooting-stars. In Japan, where they play a much more important part in popular belief, they were winged figures with long beaks or snouts. They often disguised themselves as monks or mountain-ascetics.

lavished upon her might turn out to be in vain so preyed upon my sister's mind that after a time I felt obliged to go down once more to Ono and see what I could do. Fortunately, as the result of further spells and rituals, I was able at last to bring her back at any rate to some semblance of life. But she felt that the spirit which had possessed her had not altogether lost its hold, and that she could not wholly escape from its influence and devote herself calmly to preparation for the life to come so long as she was in her present worldly guise. Not only was I deeply touched by her entreaties, but as a priest it is clearly my duty to promote rather than to discourage such changes of heart, and it is true that I administered the Vows. You must admit that under the circumstances I could not possibly have guessed that Your Excellency ought to have been consulted. However, though the story, so singular from start to finish, would if it had been allowed to go any farther soon have become the talk of the town, my sister was evidently determined to prevent its becoming known. She enjoined strict secrecy upon everyone concerned and during all these months not a word about the whole business has reached the outside world." Sozu had, in fact, done no more than repeat what Kaoru had already heard. But the previous reports had been mere hearsay and left him only half-convinced. Now, hearing the story from Sozu's own lips, he accepted it unhesitatingly, and the sudden realization that one whom he had thought to be dead was not merely alive but close at hand completely overwhelmed him. He was on the verge of breaking down; but the presence of Sozu compelled him to master his feelings, and he was under the impression that he had managed to appear quite unconcerned. The old priest, however, saw clearly enough the effect that his words had produced, and felt extremely uncomfortable. It was evident that he had robbed Kaoru of a mistress to whom he was passionately attached, and though he had acted unwittingly, he feared His Excellency would find it hard to forgive him. "Possessions of the kind from which she suffered," he said, making no further effort to defend himself, "cannot be avoided; they are always due to some happening in a previous existence. But what surprises me is that, having been afflicted in this way, she should have been left to her fate. My impression was that she came of a very good family." "I believe she is connected in some way or other with the Imperial family," Kaoru said. "I got to know her quite accidentally, and saw her only at long intervals. But considering her circumstances it surprises me as much as you that she should have been found wandering homeless. I understand at the time of her disappearance that it was feared she had drowned herself; however, this was only one of many theories that were put forward, and I was quite at a loss to know what had really happened. As for your having made her a nun—I am delighted to hear of it. If it is indeed true that she attempted to make away with herself she has a grievous load of sin to bear, and it is well that you have done what you could to lighten it. But I am not the only person concerned. She has a mother who was passionately devoted to her, and whom I should very much like to inform of what I have heard. But I hesitate to take any step of that sort without consulting your sister, who might, I fear, resent my interference; for she must have good reasons of her own for keeping the whole thing secret for so many months. However, I cannot bear to think of the mother's grief being protracted now that she and the girl might so easily be brought together." "I am afraid this is asking too much of you," Kaoru added after a pause, "but do you think you could find time to go down to Ono and arrange matters for me? I feel that, knowing what I do now, I cannot simply leave things as they are. The case is one which, in a way, interests me very deeply, and though my relationship with the girl is now no more to me than a dream, I shall not feel content till I have had one final meeting with her and heard from her own lips what really happened." Sozu found the appeal hard to resist. After all, not much harm could come of it, now that she had finally turned her back upon the world. But even priests of long standing and ardent piety sometimes, he reflected, found to their consternation that feelings which they thought long ago to have eradicated still had power over them. How could he be certain that this girl, confronted with a former lover so soon after her retirement from the world, would not be led astray? He felt that in arranging such a meeting he would be taking a very heavy responsibility. The situation was one which, to say the least of it, he did not at all relish. "At the present moment," he replied at last, "it is absolutely impossible for me to get away. But next month, if you still wish it, I will take a message." "In that case," Kaoru said, "I think I will send this boy"—indicating Ukifune's young brother, who was standing at his side—"to get into touch with her at once. They are closely related, and if you could give him just a line or two saying that someone—there is no need to mention any name—asked you for news of her, that will be quite enough." "Frankly," Sozu said, "I would rather have nothing to do with it. I have told you all I can, and I do not see what there is to prevent you from doing the rest for yourself." Kaoru smiled. "Your hesitation only shows how little you know me," he said. "It is a mere accident that I am not myself dressed in cassock and gown. From the time when I was a mere child I set my heart on leaving the world. But my mother strongly opposed such a step, and as my very inadequate support was all she had to lean on, I felt it would be unkind to insist. In consequence of this tie I found myself gradually becoming involved in public business which, as my rank advanced, sufficed apart from private considerations to make it impossible for me to live in accordance with my own desires. I felt this very much; but there was no escape, and as time went on I became, despite myself, so deeply involved in growing obligations both at home and at Court that I fear there is now little prospect of this longing ever being fulfilled. At the same time no priest could be more concerned than I am faithfully to carry out the Buddha's commandments in so far as my scant opportunities of study have made them known to me. An indiscretion of any sort in the present case would, I am perfectly well aware, constitute an offence of the most heinous kind, and on that score you may set your mind at rest once and for all. But I am extremely sorry for the girl's mother, and I shall not be at ease till I have looked into this matter and obtained permission to enlighten her." He went on to tell Sozu more about his religious studies and aspirations. The old man nodded approvingly, and a conversation followed in which he enlightened Kaoru on many obscure points of religion. It was now growing late; but he felt too restless and unsettled to spend the night where he was, and had already risen to take his leave when Sozu, who had not before taken any notice of the boy at Kaoru's side, suddenly became aware that he was extremely good-looking and complimented Kaoru on having secured so attractive a page. "That reminds me," Kaoru said, "you were going to give this boy a note." Sozu wrote a few lines and handed them to him. "You must come and amuse yourself here sometimes, he said to the handsome child. "I have more reasons[*] than you think for taking an interest in you." The boy looked puzzled; but took the letter and set out in Kaoru's company. At the foot of the hill Kaoru spaced out his escort and told them to attract as little attention as possible.

Ono at evening was indeed a strangely different place from Uji. Instead of the noisy torrent, green wooded hills stretched far into the distance, and only the fireflies on the moat, which sometimes dimly recalled the fishermen's torches at the weir, reminded Ukifune of days gone by. She was gazing in front of her, as she had done evening after evening for long past, at all this wealth of green, when horsemen, evidently clearing the way for some great personage, appeared at a fold of the hill. They had lit their torches and the string of dancing lights, appearing and disappearing down the leafy path, soon attracted the attention of the nuns, who came crowding to the front of the house. "Who can it be?" they said. "Someone of consequence, you may be sure. Just count those lights!" "As likely as not it's the General of the Right. Imoto sent some dried seaweed[†] up to Yogawa this morning and in his answer Sozu said it had come in very handy because His Excellency the General had just arrived unexpectedly, and they had been at their wits' end what to offer him." "That's the one who married the Second Princess, isn't it?" someone asked. They were all

---

[*] He refers to the fact that Ukifune was his disciple.
[†] A favorite delicacy.

very vague about what was going on in that far-off world. Ukifune was in no such uncertainty. Among the voices that sounded through the dusk she had already recognized several that in days gone by she had many times heard echoing down from the mountain-road that led to Uji. To what purpose had every accent and turn of these men's speech lain all this while buried in her memory? To distract herself she sank into prayer.

Kaoru had fully intended to stop at Ono and send the boy straight to the nuns' hermitage. But the road by which he had come went only to Yogawa; the nuns would probably have heard of his visit to Sozu, and if he halted here now it would be impossible to conceal his identity. He decided, therefore, to go straight home, and send the boy early next day, with a few trusted followers and attendants whom he had often sent to Uji in old days. "Child," he said, taking the boy apart, "do you remember your sister that died? Should you know her if you saw her? I have good reason to suppose that the whole story about her death was a complete mistake. But it is better at present that outside people should not be told. That is why I am sending you to make sure whether what I have heard is true. Don't say anything to your mother about it. I don't want to risk upsetting her for nothing; and unless we are careful the wrong people may easily get to hear about it. But of course we will tell her when the time comes; indeed, it is for your mother's sake that I am making these enquiries." Though he had many brothers and sisters he had never cared for any of them as he did for this handsome half-sister whom, young though he was, he always felt to be quite different from the rest. He had been terribly upset at the news of her death, and was delighted by what Kaoru now told him. Tears of joy started to this eyes at the thought of seeing her again, but he quickly brushed them away and in a voice that the emotion with which he contended made sound strangely loud and gruff he managed to bring out the one word "Yes."

Before he reached Ono a letter from Yogawa had already arrived. "Yesterday, Sozu wrote, "a young lad came with a message from His Excellency the General, who, it appears, has heard of your friend's Ordination and wishes her to know that he views the step she has taken with dismay and alarm. There is much that I should like to say to her in person; but I see no chance of getting to Ono for some time to come." Imoto had not the least idea what all this was about. "Can you throw any light on this letter from Sozu?" she asked. Ukifune flushed. On the one hand she was horrified to discover that her secret was well on the way towards becoming public property; on the other, she saw that Imoto was terribly hurt at her never having given a hint of any such connection during all these months. She hung her head and did not attempt to reply. "Tell me about it, do!" Imoto besought her. "It makes me so unhappy that you keep everything from me." In the midst of her agitated appeals someone came in saying that a boy had arrived with another letter from Sozu. It was strange that a second letter should come so soon; but hoping that it would throw light on the first, Imoto asked that the messenger should be sent to her immediately. To her surprise a handsome page-boy, attired with extreme elegance, tripped up to her window. A cushion was handed out to him and he was invited to sit outside while the letter was brought into the house. "His Reverence said I was on no account to deliver it to anyone but his sister," the boy protested. Whereupon Imoto came close to the blind, exchanged a few words with him, and took the letter in her own hand. "This is for you," she said to Ukifune, who could not deny the fact, for it was addressed to "The Lady Novice," a designation which applied to no one at Ono but herself. But so far from taking the letter, she fled to the back room, where she lay quivering on her couch, and would let no one come near her. After protesting in vain against this strange behavior Imoto, who was under ordinary circumstances the last person in the world to take liberties, felt bound to open the letter and see what it contained. "While he was with me today," Sozu wrote, "His Excellency the General asked about you, and I told him the whole story from the beginning. I need hardly say that when I accepted your Vows and encouraged you to continue in your present remote and obscure surroundings I did not for a moment suspect the existence of an attachment such as that between yourself and His Excellency. Had I done so, I should have pointed out that the course you proposed was, under the circumstances, highly reprehensible. While human attachments still hold you to the world, the mode of life you have adopted, so far from speeding Salvation, can only lead you to disaster.* It is written,† as you know, that to have been a nun for a single day or night is in itself accounted as a merit of incalculable potency, and my advice to you is to make the best of the advantages you have already secured. As for the steps necessary for your return to secular life, do not think that they represent any insurmountable difficulty. We will discuss all that when I come to Ono later on. Meanwhile, I have sent this young lad to see you, and I am sure you will find that his view upon the matter is the same as mine." The letter, though clear enough to Ukifune herself, contained much that Imoto still failed to understand. "Who then is this boy?" she asked. "Surely the time has come when you might put an end once and for all to these mystifications and explain to me what is going on." She consented at last to come with Imoto to a point from which the messenger was visible. She recognized the boy at once. She remembered how on that

---

* For the doctrine that it is better to renounce vows than to risk breaking them see the *Maharatna Kuta*, chap. lxxxviii. Takakusu, Vol. XI, p. 507 *a*.
† In the "Sutra on the Merit of leaving the House," Takakusu, Vol. XVI, p. 814.

last night at Uji he had been one of those to whom her thoughts had turned most fondly, despite the fact that at home he had always been terribly wild and unmanageable. But shocking little nuisance though he was, his mother could not bear to be parted from him for a single day, and had often brought him with her to Uji. As time went on, however, he had very much improved and she had become extremely fond of him, as he of her. Already a certain amount of information about Kaoru and the others had leaked through to her. But about her mother she had still heard nothing, and longed at once to ask for news. Here indeed was her opportunity; but, instead of doing so, she turned away and burst into tears. The lad had something of his sister's beauty. "Why, he's your brother, I'm sure he is," Imoto exclaimed. "There must be lots of things you want to talk about together. You had better let him come to you behind the curtains." How could she? The boy thought she was dead, and suddenly to show her to him not as he had known her, but cowled and shorn, was more than she could bear. What plea could she use? She hesitated for a moment. "I wouldn't for worlds have him think that I have forgotten him," she said at last. "But it is useless for me to try to talk to him. I know well enough that I should break down, and not be able to say a word. You saw for yourself the strange condition I was in on the night when you rescued me. Well, I am sure that even after I came round, my senses—I can find no better way to explain what I mean—never really fitted back into their proper places. Unless something happens, like the visit of Ki no Kami the other day, to recall particular incidents belonging to the past, my mind is still a blank. I cannot of myself bring back anything at all. Something that he said when he was talking of people at Court did in a vague way remind me of places and things that I knew. But afterwards, when I tried to get clearer about what these memories were, the whole thing faded from my mind entirely. But there is one person about whom I have thought constantly since I woke from my trance—someone very dear to me. It was terrible not even to know whether she was still alive. But I am determined that the world at large must never know I failed to die; and though the sight of this boy, whom I knew when he was a little child, tempts me to reveal myself, I must not be weak; One day perhaps, if the person* I speak of is still in the world, I will ask her to visit me. But the man Sozu mentioned, and all the rest must somehow be made to go on thinking that I died. Say it is a mistake—that it is not I. Say what you will, so long as it sends them away." "I'm sure I don't know what you propose I should say," Imoto protested. "It's not as easy as you think. Holy hermit though he is, Sozu has his wits about him, and is not going to be put off with talk of that

---

* Her mother.

kind. His Excellency knows quite well that you are here, and a man in his position can't be sent about his business as though he were a mere nobody." All the nuns, had now gathered round, and added a chorus of scoldings and cajolings. The double-doors were opened and a curtained couch set just inside. The young messenger was then brought into the house. He knew from what he had overheard that Ukifune was within, but now that the moment had come when he was actually on the point of hearing the voice of this long-vanished sister, the lad felt awkward and shy. "I've got another letter," he said, "besides the one from Sozu. And when he gave me his he said I should be able to have a talk with her..." "That's quite right, my dear, pretty boy," Imoto said, caressing him. "She's just in there. But we don't understand what all this is about. Tell us now. They wouldn't, I am sure, have chosen a little fellow like you as messenger, unless you knew all about it." "I don't want to talk to you," he said, "or to stay here any longer. She isn't fond of me anymore or she wouldn't hide herself away like this. Please let me hand in the letter and go away. I was told I must not give it to anyone else." "Of course you mustn't," Imoto said. "Come now," she continued, addressing Ukifune. "You're not behaving nicely at all. Other people manage to take their Vows and so on, without being so disagreeable..." She pushed the boy close up to the curtains. Disguised* though Ukifune was in cassock and hood, he would yet have known her anywhere. He stretched his hand through the curtains and slid the letter towards her. "An answer is required at once," he said, deeply wounded by her treatment of him and anxious to escape immediately. Seeing that she paid no attention to the letter Imoto went and opened it and spread it out in front of Ukifune. It was the familiar handwriting, and the paper was scented with the same strange fragrance as of old. The nuns watched from a distance, and little though they could see of the writing, the more irrepressible among them could not refrain from cries of admiration and astonishment as the letter was unfolded. "I regard the step you have taken as utterly unjustifiable from every point of view," the letter ran. "But respect for Sozu prevents my saying any more on that subject. Naturally I long to hear from your own lips the whole story of those last terrible days. But I know in my own heart that it would be wrong for us to meet now. And if I blame myself for desiring it, how much the more would others blame me." Here the letter broke off. "By what false path through hills I had not thought again to tread have your Truths led me on, O Master of the Law!" Such was the poem that followed. "I wonder whether you have quite forgotten the bearer of this letter," he continued. "I keep him about me in remembrance

---

* The costume might indeed have been merely a disguise. That is why what the boy has seen does not convince Kaoru that she has indeed become a nun.

of our love." Had the letter contained merely a few colorless lines of conventional greetings or enquiries it would have been possible to pretend that it was meant for someone else. As it was, she could not disown it. But the thought that the boy had no doubt already seen her—that the barrier between the past and her new life had already broken down—completely overcame her, and making no attempt to deal with the letter she sat with her face buried in her hands. Imoto, afraid that she was ill again, stood over her, trying to discover what was wrong. "I must give the boy an answer of some sort, mustn't I?" she said. "Yes, but not now," Ukifune pleaded. "My mind is quite confused. It all happened a long while ago. It will come back to me in time—like a dream; but it means nothing to me now. Later on, when I am calmer, I shall understand this letter and know what to say. But no, he had better take it back with him. It is a mistake, perhaps. I don't feel that it was meant for me." Without folding it up, she handed the letter back to Imoto. "Oh, come, that's too bad," the nun protested. "I should be sorry to see you behave as rudely as that. Even if you don't mind yourself what people think of you, you might at least consider our feelings. You'll get us all into terrible trouble." "Leave me alone!" she cried, and buried her face in the cushions.

"It's all due to her long illness," Imoto explained to the boy. "She has never really been herself since; and particularly now that she has taken her Vows, she worries all the time lest someone should track her down and see her in her cowl. We all felt very sorry for her, but of course did not know what exactly it was that she feared. It's dreadful to think that all the while we were looking after her here His Excellency was wondering what had become of her. I very humbly beg His Excellency's pardon, I'm sure. You must tell him that in the last few days she has been very poorly. I think all this has upset her. Certainly she seems more distracted than usual. Indeed, she does not really take in what one says to her... Someone came in and asked the boy if he would not take some refreshments. It was difficult in a place like that to provide anything very elaborate; but they had really prepared quite a dainty and appetizing meal. The lad did not, however, feel like settling down to enjoy the good things they had prepared. "I don't know what I'm to say when I get back," he murmured. "Can't you get her to write just a line or two?" "You're quite right, she certainly ought to," Imoto said, and tried once more to prevail upon the girl to send some sort of reply. But it was hopeless; this time she could not get a word out of her. "If I were you," she said to the boy, "I should just go home and tell your master of the condition she's in. I am sure he will understand. After all it's not as though we lived at the other end of the world. The mountain winds may blow; but one day or another you'll surely come again." It was not his fault. Kaoru, he was certain, would not expect him to wait about here indefinitely. There was nothing for it but to go home. He felt injured. They all seemed worried about what Kaoru would think; but no one seemed to realize that for him too it was a terrible blow not to have been able to get so much as a word out of the sister whom he had loved so dearly.

For Kaoru the suspense had been torturing, and the complete failure of the boy's mission was a heavy disappointment. He did not know what to think. The story that she had become a nun and shut herself off entirely from the world, he was not so simple as to believe. If she was indeed living at Ono, no doubt some lover had secretly installed her there and was looking her up from time to time, just as he himself, all too infrequently, had visited her at Uji.